The Mysteries of Londo

Volume 2

George W. M. Reynolds

Alpha Editions

This edition published in 2024

ISBN : 9789361472756

Design and Setting By
Alpha Editions
www.alphaedis.com
Email - info@alphaedis.com

As per information held with us this book is in Public Domain.
This book is a reproduction of an important historical work. Alpha Editions uses the best technology to reproduce historical work in the same manner it was first published to preserve its original nature. Any marks or number seen are left intentionally to preserve its true form.

Contents

CHAPTER CXXXVII. RATS' CASTLE.	- 2 -
CHAPTER CXXXVIII. A PUBLIC FUNCTIONARY.	- 7 -
CHAPTER CXXXIX. THE CONFIDENCE.	- 12 -
CHAPTER CXL. INCIDENTS IN THE GIPSY PALACE.	- 18 -
CHAPTER CXLI. THE SUBTERRANEAN.	- 24 -
CHAPTER CXLII. GIBBET.	- 28 -
CHAPTER CXLIII. MORBID FEELINGS.—KATHERINE.	- 33 -
CHAPTER CXLIV. THE UNFINISHED LETTER.	- 38 -
CHAPTER CXLV. HYPOCRISY.	- 43 -
CHAPTER CXLVI. THE BATH.—THE HOUSEKEEPER.	- 47 -
CHAPTER CXLVII. THE RECTOR'S NEW PASSION.	- 53 -
CHAPTER CXLVIII. THE OLD HAG'S INTRIGUE.	- 58 -
CHAPTER CXLIX. THE MASQUERADE.	- 63 -
CHAPTER CL. MRS. KENRICK.	- 67 -
CHAPTER CLI. A MYSTERIOUS DEED.	- 72 -
CHAPTER CLII. THE DEATH BED.	- 78 -
CHAPTER CLIII. PROCEEDINGS IN CASTELCICALA.	- 83 -
CHAPTER CLIV. REFLECTIONS.—THE NEW PRISON.	- 87 -
CHAPTER CLV. PATRIOTISM.	- 93 -
CHAPTER CLVI. THE DECISION.	- 97 -
CHAPTER CLVII. THE TRIAL OF KATHERINE WILMOT.	- 100 -
CHAPTER CLVIII. A HAPPY PARTY.	- 107 -
CHAPTER CLIX. THE INTERVIEW.	- 111 -
CHAPTER CLX. THE RECTOR IN NEWGATE.	- 116 -
CHAPTER CLXI. LADY CECILIA HARBOROUGH.	- 121 -
CHAPTER CLXII. THE BEQUEST.	- 128 -
CHAPTER CLXIII. THE ZINGAREES.	- 132 -
CHAPTER CLXIV. THE EXECUTIONER'S HISTORY.	- 138 -
CHAPTER CLXV. THE TRACE.	- 145 -
CHAPTER CLXVI. THE THAMES PIRATES.	- 149 -
CHAPTER CLXVII. AN ARRIVAL AT THE WHARF.	- 154 -
CHAPTER CLXVIII. THE PLAGUE SHIP.	- 158 -

Chapter	Title	Page
CHAPTER CLXIX.	THE PURSUIT.	- 165 -
CHAPTER CLXX.	THE BLACK VEIL.	- 171 -
CHAPTER CLXXI.	MR. GREENWOOD'S DINNER-PARTY.	- 175 -
CHAPTER CLXXII.	THE MYSTERIES OF HOLMESFORD HOUSE.	- 179 -
CHAPTER CLXXIII.	THE ADIEUX.	- 185 -
CHAPTER CLXXIV.	CASTELCICALA.	- 190 -
CHAPTER CLXXV.	MONTONI.	- 197 -
CHAPTER CLXXVI.	THE CLUB-HOUSE.	- 203 -
CHAPTER CLXXVII.	THE HISTORY OF AN UNFORTUNATE WOMAN.	- 210 -
CHAPTER CLXXVIII.	THE TAVERN AT FRIULI.	- 233 -
CHAPTER CLXXIX.	THE JOURNEY.	- 238 -
CHAPTER CLXXX.	THE "BOOZING-KEN" ONCE MORE.	- 242 -
CHAPTER CLXXXI.	THE RESURRECTION MAN AGAIN.	- 250 -
CHAPTER CLXXXII.	MR. GREENWOOD'S JOURNEY.	- 254 -
CHAPTER CLXXXIII.	KIND FRIENDS.	- 259 -
CHAPTER CLXXXIV.	ESTELLA.	- 264 -
CHAPTER CLXXXV.	ANOTHER NEW YEAR'S DAY.	- 272 -
CHAPTER CLXXXVI.	THE NEW CUT.	- 277 -
CHAPTER CLXXXVII.	THE FORGED BILLS.	- 284 -
CHAPTER CLXXXVIII.	THE BATTLES OF PIACERE AND ABRANTANI.	- 291 -
CHAPTER CLXXXIX.	THE BATTLE OF MONTONI.	- 301 -
CHAPTER CXC.	TWO OF OUR OLD ACQUAINTANCES.	- 305 -
CHAPTER CXCI.	CRANKEY JEM'S HISTORY.	- 310 -
CHAPTER CXCII.	THE MINT.—THE FORTY THIEVES.	- 325 -
CHAPTER CXCIII.	ANOTHER VISIT TO BUCKINGHAM PALACE.	- 334 -
CHAPTER CXCIV.	THE ROYAL BREAKFAST.	- 342 -
CHAPTER CXCV.	THE ARISTOCRATIC VILLAIN AND THE LOW MISCREANT.	- 347 -
CHAPTER CXCVI.	THE OLD HAG AND THE RESURRECTION MAN.	- 352 -
CHAPTER CXCVII.	ELLEN AND KATHERINE.	- 357 -
CHAPTER CXCVIII.	A GLOOMY VISITOR.	- 361 -
CHAPTER CXCIX.	THE ORPHAN'S FILIAL LOVE.	- 366 -
CHAPTER CC.	A MAIDEN'S LOVE.	- 372 -
CHAPTER CCI.	THE HANDSOME STRANGER.—DISAPPOINTMENT.	- 378 -
CHAPTER CCII.	THE PRINCESS ISABELLA.	- 382 -

Chapter	Title	Page
CHAPTER CCIII.	RAVENSWORTH HALL.	- 387 -
CHAPTER CCIV	THE BRIDE AND BRIDEGROOM.	- 392 -
CHAPTER CCV.	THE BREAKFAST.	- 396 -
CHAPTER CCVI.	THE PATRICIAN LADY AND THE UNFORTUNATE WOMAN.	- 401 -
CHAPTER CCVII.	THE HUSBAND, THE WIFE, AND THE UNFORTUNATE WOMAN.	- 406 -
CHAPTER CCVIII.	THE RESURRECTION MAN'S HOUSE IN GLOBE TOWN.	- 411 -
CHAPTER CCIX.	ALDERMAN SNIFF.—TOMLINSON AND GREENWOOD.	- 416 -
CHAPTER CCX.	HOLFORD'S STUDIES.	- 423 -
CHAPTER CCXI.	THE DEED.	- 428 -
CHAPTER CCXII.	THE EXAMINATION AT THE HOME OFFICE.	- 433 -
CHAPTER CCXIII.	THE TORTURES OF LADY RAVENSWORTH.	- 436 -
CHAPTER CCXIV.	THE DUELLISTS.	- 441 -
CHAPTER CCXV.	THE VOICES IN THE RUINS.	- 447 -
CHAPTER CCXVI.	THE PROGRESS OF LYDIA HUTCHINSON'S VENGEANCE.	- 452 -
CHAPTER CCXVII.	THE PRISONER IN THE SUBTERRANEAN.	- 461 -
CHAPTER CCXVIII.	THE VEILED VISITOR.	- 466 -
CHAPTER CCXIX.	THE MURDER.	- 471 -
CHAPTER CCXX.	THE EFFECT OF THE ORIENTAL TOBACCO.—THE OLD HAG'S PAPERS.	- 476 -
CHAPTER CCXXI.	THE RETURN TO ENGLAND.	- 481 -
CHAPTER CCXXII.	THE ARRIVAL AT HOME.	- 487 -
CHAPTER CCXXIII.	THE MARRIAGE.	- 493 -
CHAPTER CCXXIV.	MR. BANKS'S HOUSE IN GLOBE LANE.	- 498 -
CHAPTER CCXXV.	THE OLD HAG'S HISTORY.	- 505 -
CHAPTER CCXXVI.	THE MARQUIS OF HOLMESFORD.	- 514 -
CHAPTER CCXXVII.	COLDBATH FIELD'S PRISON.	- 521 -
CHAPTER CCXXVIII.	A DESPERATE ACHIEVEMENT.	- 526 -
CHAPTER CCXXIX.	THE WIDOW.	- 533 -
CHAPTER CCXXX.	BETHLEM HOSPITAL.	- 540 -
CHAPTER CCXXXI.	MR. GREENWOOD AND MR. VERNON.	- 546 -
CHAPTER CCXXXII.	SCENES AT RAVENSWORTH HALL.	- 550 -
CHAPTER CCXXXIII.	A WELCOME FRIEND.	- 555 -
CHAPTER CCXXXIV.	A MIDNIGHT SCENE OF MYSTERY.	- 559 -
CHAPTER CCXXXV.	PLOTS AND COUNTERPLOTS.	- 565 -

CHAPTER CCXXXVI.	WOMAN AS SHE OUGHT TO BE.	- 573 -
CHAPTER CCXXXVII.	THE JUGGLERS.	- 579 -
CHAPTER CCXXXVIII.	THE PERFORMANCE.	- 586 -
CHAPTER CCXXXIX.	THE RESURRECTION MAN'S RETURN HOME.	- 596 -
CHAPTER CCXL.	A NEW EPOCH.	- 599 -
CHAPTER CCXLI.	CROCKFORD'S.	- 605 -
CHAPTER CCXLII.	THE AUNT.	- 613 -
CHAPTER CCXLIII.	THE FIGHT.—THE RUINED GAMESTER.	- 618 -
CHAPTER CCXLIV.	THE HISTORY OF A GAMESTER.	- 623 -
CHAPTER CCXLV.	THE EXCURSION.	- 638 -
CHAPTER CCXLVI.	THE PARTY AT RAVENSWORTH HALL.	- 648 -
CHAPTER CCXLVII.	THE STRANGER WHO DISCOVERED THE CORPSE.	- 655 -
CHAPTER CCXLVIII.	AN UNPLEASANT EXPOSURE.	- 659 -
CHAPTER CCXLIX.	THE RESURRECTION MAN'S LAST FEAT AT RAVENSWORTH HALL.	- 666 -
CHAPTER CCL.	EGERTON'S LAST DINNER PARTY.	- 671 -
CHAPTER CCLI.	THE OBSTINATE PATIENT.	- 682 -
CHAPTER CCLII.	DEATH OF THE MARQUIS OF HOLMESFORD.	- 687 -
CHAPTER CCLIII.	THE EX-MEMBER FOR ROTTENBOROUGH.	- 692 -
CHAPTER CCLIV.	FURTHER MISFORTUNES.	- 699 -
CHAPTER CCLV.	GIBBET AT MARKHAM PLACE.	- 704 -
CHAPTER CCLVI.	ELIZA SYDNEY AND ELLEN.—THE HOSPITAL.	- 707 -
CHAPTER CCLVII.	THE REVENGE.	- 713 -
CHAPTER CCLVIII.	THE APPOINTMENT KEPT.	- 719 -
CHAPTER CCLIX.	CONCLUSION.	- 727 -
EPILOGUE.		- 729 -

CHAPTER CXXXVII.

RATS' CASTLE.

Richard Markham, though perfectly unpretending in manner and somewhat reserved or even sedate in disposition, possessed the most undaunted courage. Thus was it that, almost immediately recovering himself from the sudden check which he had experienced at the hands of the Resurrection Man, he hurried in pursuit of the miscreant, followed by the policeman and the people whom the alarm which he had given had called to his aid.

The people were, however, soon tired of running gratuitously for an object which they could scarcely comprehend; but the police-officer kept close to Markham; and they were speedily reinforced by two other constables, who, seeing that something was the matter, and with characteristic officiousness, immediately joined them.

From an inquiry put to the waterman of the adjacent cab-stand, who had seen a person running furiously along a moment or two before, Markham felt convinced that the object of his pursuit had plunged into the maze of Saint Giles's; and, though well aware of the desperate character of that individual, and conscious that should he encounter him alone in some dark alley or gloomy court, a fearful struggle must ensue between them, he did not hesitate, unarmed as he was, to dash into that thicket of dangerous habitations.

Soon outstripping the officers, who vainly begged him to keep with them, as they were unacquainted with the person of whom he was in pursuit,—forgetting every measure of precaution in the ardour of the chase, Richard rushed headlong through the dark and ill-paved streets, following the echo of every retreating footstep which he heard, and stopping only to scrutinise the countenances of those who, in the obscurity of the hour and place, seemed at first sight to resemble the exterior of the Resurrection Man.

Vain was his search. At length, exhausted, he sate down on the steps of a door-way to recover his breath, after having expended an hour in his fruitless search up one street, down another, and in every nook and corner of that district which we have before described as the Holy Land.

Accident shortly led the officers, who had originally entered upon the chase with him, to the spot where he was seated.

"Here is the gentleman himself," said one, turning the glare of his bull's-eye full upon our hero.

"No luck, I suppose, sir?" observed another. "You had much better have remained with us and given us some idea of the person that you want."

"Fool that I was!" exclaimed Markham, now perceiving his imprudence in that respect: "I have left you to pursue a shadow, instead of depicting to you the substance. But surely the name of Anthony Tidkins———"

"The Resurrection Man, as they call him," hastily remarked one of the constables.

"The same," answered Markham.

"Why—he blew himself up, along with some others and a number of our men, last year, down in Bethnal Green," said the constable who had last spoken.

"No—he lives, he lives," exclaimed Richard, impatiently. "My God! I know him but too well."

"And it was after him that you gave the alarm just now in Tottenham Court Road?"

"It was. I knew him at once—I could not be mistaken: his voice, laden with a curse, still rings in my ears."

"Well, since the gentleman's so positive, I 'spose it must be so," said the constable: "we musn't sleep upon it, mates. Ten to one that Tidkins has taken to burrow in one of the low cribs about here; and he means to lie quiet for two or three days till the alarm's blown over. I know the dodges of these fellers. You two go the round of Plumptre Street; and me and this gentleman will just take a promiscuous look into the kens about here."

The two constables to whom these words were addressed, immediately departed upon the mission proposed to them, and Richard signified his readiness to accompany the officer who had thus settled the plan of proceedings.

"We'll go first to Rats' Castle, sir, if you please," said the policeman: "that is the most likely place for a run-away to take refuge in at random."

"What is Rats' Castle?" asked Markham, as he walked by the officer's side down a wretched alley, almost as dark as pitch, and over the broken pavement of which he stumbled at every step.

"The night-house where all kind of low people meet to sup and lodge," was the reply. "But here we are—and you'll see all about it in an instant."

They had stopped at the door of a house with an area protected by thick wooden palings. All the upper part of the dwelling appeared to be involved in total darkness: but lights streamed through the chinks of the rude shutters of the area-windows; and from the same direction emanated boisterous merriment, coarse laughter, and wild hurrahs.

"You knock at the door, sir, if you please," said the policeman, "while I stand aside. I'll slip in after you; for if they twig my coat, and Tidkins really happens to be there, they'd give him the office to bolt before we could get in."

"Well thought of," returned Markham. "But upon what plea am I to claim admittance?"

"As a stranger, impelled by curiosity. You carry the silver key in your pocket."

The policeman withdrew a few paces; and our hero knocked boldly at the door.

A gruff voice challenged the visitor from the area.

"Who's here?"

"No one that will do you any harm," replied Richard. "I am anxious to witness the interior of this establishment; and here is half-a-crown for you if you can gratify my curiosity."

"That's English, any how," said the voice, softening in its tone. "Stop a minute."

Markham heard a door close in the area below; and in a few moments the bolts were drawn back inside the one at which he was standing.

"Now then, my ben-cull—in with you," said a man, as he opened the front door, and held a candle high up above his head at the same time.

Markham stepped into a narrow passage, and placed his foot against the door in such a way as to keep it open. But the precaution was unnecessary, for the policeman had glided in almost simultaneously with himself.

"Now, no noise, old feller," said the constable, in a hasty whisper to the man who had opened the door: "our business isn't with any of your set."

"Wery good," returned the porter of Rats' Castle: "you know best—it isn't for me to say nothink."

"Go first, sir," whispered the officer to Markham. "You seem to know *him* better than me, for I never saw him but once—and then only for a minute or two."

"Which way?" demanded Richard.

"Straight on—and then down stairs. You keep behind us, old feller," added the policeman, turning to the porter.

Markham descended a flight of narrow and precipitate steps, and at the bottom found himself in a large room formed of two kitchens thrown into one.

Two long tables running parallel to each other the entire length of the place, were laid out for supper,—the preparations consisting of a number of greasy napkins spread upon either board, and decorated with knives and forks all chained to the tables. Iron plates to eat off, galley-pots and chipped tea-cups filled with salt, three or four pepper-boxes, and two small stone jars containing mustard, completed the preparations for the evening meal.

The room was lighted by means of a number of candles disposed in tin shades around the walls; and as no one gave himself the trouble to snuff them, the wicks were long, and infested with what housewives denominate "thieves," while the tallow streamed down in large flakes, dripping on the floor, the seats, or the backs of the guests.

Crowded together at the two tables, and anxiously watching the proceedings of an old blear-eyed woman, who was occupied at an immense fire at the farther end of the room, were about thirty or forty persons, male and female. And never did Markham's eyes glance upon a more extraordinary—a more loathsome—a more revolting spectacle than that assemblage of rags, filth, disease, deformity, and ugliness.

Mendicants, vagabonds, impostors, and rogues of all kinds were gathered in that room, the fetid heat of which was stifling. The horrible language of which they made use,—their frightful curses,—their obscene jests,—their blasphemous jokes, were calculated to shock the mind of the least fastidious:—it was indeed a scene from which Markham would have fled as from a nest of vipers, had not a stern duty to society and to himself urged him to penetrate farther into that den.

The appearance of himself and the policeman did not produce any remarkable degree of sensation amongst the persons assembled: they were accustomed to the occasional visits of well-dressed strangers, who repaired thither to gratify curiosity; and the presence of the officers of justice was a matter of frequent occurrence when any great robbery had been perpetrated in the metropolis, and while the culprits remained undiscovered.

"He is not here," whispered Markham to his companion, after casting a hasty but penetrating glance around.

"He may come: this is the most likely place in Saint Giles's for him to visit," returned the policeman. "We will wait half-an-hour."

Richard would gladly have retired; but he was ashamed to exhibit a disgust which the officer might mistake for fear. He accordingly seated himself at a small side-table, in compliance with a sign from his companion.

A waiter, wearing an apron which, by its colour, seemed also to do the duty of dish-cloth, now accosted them, and said, "Please to order anythink, gen'lemen?"

"Two glasses of brandy-and-water," replied the constable.

This command was speedily complied with; and, a few minutes afterwards, supper was served up on the two long tables before described. The old woman who presided over the culinary department of the establishment had amply catered for those present. Legs of mutton, both roasted and boiled,—rounds of beef, flanked with carrots,—huge pies,—boiled legs of pork,—immense quantities of sausages,—and sheep's heads, constituted the staple of the banquet. These viands, accompanied by piles of smoking potatoes "in their jackets" and heaps of cabbages, were all served up on iron dishes, from which no thrifty hand ever removed the rust.

Then commenced the clattering of the knives and forks, the din of which upon the iron platters was strangely blended with the rattling of the chains that held them to the tables. The boisterous merriment and coarse conversation were for a time absorbed in the interest occasioned by the presence of the repast.

"What a strange assembly," whispered Markham to the constable.

"Strange to *you*, sir—no doubt," was the answer, also delivered in a tone audible only to him to whom the words were addressed. "That sturdy feller sitting at the head of the nearest table, with the great cudgel between his legs, is one of the class that don't take the trouble to clothe themselves in rags, but trust to their insolence to extort alms from females walking alone in retired parts. That feller next to him, all in tatters, but who laughs louder than any one else, is one of them whining, shivering, snivelling wretches that crouch up in doorways on rainy days, and on fine ones sit down on the pavement with '*Starving, but dare not beg,*' chalked on the stone before them. The man over there in sailor's clothes tumbled down an area when he was drunk, and broke his leg: he was obliged to have it cut off; and so he now passes himself off as one of Nelson's own tars, though he never saw the sea in his life. That chap almost naked who's just come in, is going to put on his coat and shoes before he sits down to supper; he always goes out begging in that state on rainy days, and is a gentleman on fine ones."

"I do not understand you," said Markham, astonished at this last observation.

"Why, sir," replied the policeman, "there's certain beggars that always turn out half-naked, on rainy days, or when the snow's on the ground; and people pity them so much on those occasions that the rogues get enough to keep them all through the fine weather. If they have wives and children to go out with them, so much the better: but that feller there isn't married; and so he goes with a woman who frequents this place, and they hire three or four children from the poor people in this neighbourhood, at the rate of two-pence a day each child, and its grub. To see them go shivering and whining through the streets, with no shoes or stockings, you'd think they were the most miserable devils on the face of the earth; and then, to make the scene complete, the man and woman always pinch the little children that they carry in their arms, to make them cry, whenever they pass a window when several ladies are looking out."

"Is this possible?" whispered Markham, his face flushing with indignation.

"Possible, sir! Don't I see it all every day of my life? Look at them men and women blowing their hides out with all that good meat; and now look at the pots of porter that's coming in. Every soul there has sworn a hundred times during the day that he hasn't tasted food for forty-eight hours, and will repeat the same story to-morrow. But they all had good suppers here last night, and good breakfasts here this morning; and you see how they are faring this evening."

"But there are real cases deserving of charity?" said Markham, interrogatively,—for he almost felt disposed to doubt the fact.

"Certainly there are, sir," was the reply; "but it's very difficult for such as you to decide between the true and the false. Look at that man who carves at the second table: he can see well enough to cut himself the tit-bits; but to-morrow he will be totally blind in one of the fashionable squares."

"Totally blind!" said Richard, more and more astonished at what he heard.

"Yes, sir—totally blind; led by a dog, and with a placard upon his chest. He keeps his eyes fast shut, and colours the lids with carmine and vermilion. But that is nothing. That feller next to him, who uses his knife and fork so well, will to-morrow have lost his right arm at the battle of Salamanca."

"But how can that imposture be effected?"

"His right arm is concealed under his clothes, and the coat-sleeve hangs down loose," replied the constable. "That tall stout man who has just jumped so nimbly over the form in his way back to his place, has walked on crutches in the streets for the last twenty years; and when you see him so, you would think he could hardly drag himself along. The feller over there is a frozen-out gardener in winter, and a poor Spitalfields' weaver in summer. The one next to him will have a black patch over his left eye to-morrow; and yet you may see that it is as good as his right. The short man opposite to him bends his left leg back, and has a wooden one to support the knee, when he is in the street. That woman there has been dressed in widows' weeds for the last fifteen years, and always has a troop of six children with her; but the children never grow any bigger, for she hires fresh ones every year or so."

"This is the most extraordinarily combined mass of contradictions and deceptions I ever gazed upon," whispered Markham.

"You may well say that, sir," said the policeman. "The ragged feller down at the bottom of the second table sits as upright as you or me: well, in the streets he crawls along the ground with two iron supporters in his hands. He is the most insolent feller in London. The man next to him goes about on a sort of van, or chaise, and the world believes that he has no legs at all; but they are all the time concealed in the body of the vehicle, and the stumps of the thighs which are seen are false. Those three hulking chaps over there, sitting with the three women that laugh so much, are begging-letter impostors. The eldest of the three men has been seventeen years at the business, and has been in prison twenty-eight times. One day he is a bricklayer who has fallen from a scaffold, and broken his leg, and has a wife and eleven young children dependent on him; another day he is a licensed clergyman of the Church of England, but unemployed for two years—wife and six children totally dependent on him. Then he changes into a stanch Tory, ruined by his attachment to the cause, and proscribed by all his friends on account of his principles: in this shape he addresses himself to the old Tory noblemen, and makes a good harvest. The very next day he becomes a determined and stanch Reformer, who lost his employment through giving his vote for the Tower Hamlets to the liberal candidate at the last election, and has since met with an uninterrupted series of misfortunes—sold up by a Tory landlord,—his wife been dead only a fortnight, and seven motherless children left dependent on him. This kind of letter always draws well. Then he becomes a paralytic with an execution in his house; or a Spitalfields' weaver, with nine children, two of which are cripples, and one blind; or else a poor Scotch schoolmaster, come to London on business, and robbed by designing knaves of the means of returning to his own country. The women are just as bad. They are either wives with husbands in hospitals and bed-ridden mothers; or daughters with helpless parents and sick brothers and sisters dependent on them;—and so on."

"But if you be aware of all these monstrous impositions, why do you not interfere to protect the public?" inquired Markham.

"Lord, sir!" said the constable, "if we took up all persons that we know to be impostors, we should have half London in custody. We only interfere when specially called upon, or when we see cases so very flagrant that we can't help taking notice of them. Some of these chaps that are eating here so hearty now, will seem to be dying in the streets to-morrow."

"Merciful heavens, what a city of deceit and imposture is this!" observed Richard, painfully excited by the strange details which he had just heard. "Were the interior of this den but once exposed to general view, charity would be at an end, and the deserving poor would suffer for the unprincipled impostor."

"True enough, sir. And now look—the cloth is removed, and every one is ordering in something strong to wash down the supper. There goes a crown-bowl of punch—that's for the begging-letter impostors: and there's glasses of punch, and cold spirits and water, and shrub, and negus. That's the way they do it, you see, sir."

Markham did indeed see, and wondered more and more at what he so saw—until his feelings of surprise changed into sentiments of ineffable abhorrence and disgust; and he longed to leave that odious den.

"The person whom we seek does not appear to come," he said, after a long interval of silence. "Two hours have elapsed—and we are only wasting time here."

"He must have taken refuge in some other crib, sir," returned the constable. "Let us leave this one, and make the round of the other lodging-houses in this street."

Markham was glad to hurry away from Rats' Castle, the mysteries of which had so painfully shocked his generous feelings.

CHAPTER CXXXVIII.

A PUBLIC FUNCTIONARY.

Urged by that sense of duty to which we have before alluded, and which prompted him to neglect no step that might lead to the discovery of a great criminal's lurking-place, Richard accompanied the police-officer to various houses where the dregs of the population herded together.

The inspection of a plague-hospital could not have been more appalling: the scrutiny of a lazar-house could not have produced deeper disgust.

In some the inmates were engaged in drunken broils, the women enacting the part of furies: in others the females sang obscene songs, the men joining in the chorus.

Here a mother waited until her daughter should return with the wages of prostitution, to purchase the evening meal: there a husband boasted that his wife was enabled, by the liberality of a paramour, to supply him with ample means for his night's debauchery.

In one house which our hero and the constable visited, three sisters of the respective ages of eleven, thirteen, and fourteen, were comparing the produce of their evening's avocations,—the avocations of the daughters of crime!

And then those three children, having portioned out the necessary amount for their suppers and their lodging that night, and their breakfast next morning, laughed joyously as they perceived how much they had left to purchase gin!

For GIN is the deity, and INTEMPERANCE is the hand-maiden, of both sexes and nearly all ages in that district of London.

What crimes, what follies have been perpetrated for Gin! A river of alcohol rolls through the land, sweeping away health, honour, and happiness with its remorseless tide. The creaking gibbet, and the prison ward—the gloomy hulk, and the far-off penal isle—the debtors' gaol, and the silent penitentiary—the tomb-like workhouse, and the loathsome hospital—the galling chain, and the spirit-breaking tread-wheel—the frightful mad-cell, and the public dissecting-room—the death-bed of despair, and the grave of the suicide, are indebted for many, many victims to thee, most potent GIN!

O GIN! the Genius of Accidents and the Bad Angel of Offences worship thee! Thou art the Juggernaut beneath whose wheels millions throw themselves in blind adoration.

The pawnbroker points to thee and says, "Whilst thy dominion lasts, I am sure to thrive."

The medical man smiles as he marks thy progress, for he knows that thou leadest a ghastly train,—apoplexy, palsy, dropsy, delirium tremens, consumption, madness.

The undertaker chuckles when he remembers thine influence, for he says within himself, "Thou art the Angel of Death."

And Satan rejoices in his kingdom, well-knowing how thickly it can be populated by thee!

Yes—great is thy power, O GIN: thou keepest pace with the progress of civilisation, and thou art made the companion of the Bible. For when the missionary takes the Word of God to the savage in some far distant clime, he bears the fire-water with him at the same time. While his right hand points to the paths of peace and salvation, his left scatters the seeds of misery, disease, death, and damnation!

Yes—great is thy power, O Gin: a terrible instrument of evil art thou. Thou sweepest over the world with the wing of the pestilence: thy breath that of a plague:—like the poisonous garment of Dejanira on the burning limbs of the Centaur, dost thou cling around thy victims.

And where the grave-yard is heaped up with mouldering bones—and where disease and death prevail in all their most hideous shapes—and where misery is most keenly felt, and poverty is most pinching—and where the wails of hapless children ascend to heaven in vain appeal against the cruelty of inhuman parents—and where crime is most diabolical,—there are thy triumphs—there are thy victories!

But to continue.

The clock of St. Giles's Church proclaimed the hour of midnight; and though our hero and the constable had visited many of the low dens and lodging-houses in the Holy Land, still their search was without success.

"Unless my mates have been more lucky than us," observed the policeman, halting at the corner of a street, "we must conclude that the bird is flown."

"And even if they should chance to enter a house where the miscreant has taken refuge, how would they be enabled to recognise him?" asked Richard.

"One of them knows him well," replied the constable.

At that moment a violent scream issued from the upper part of the house close to which Markham and the constable were standing.

The dwelling was high, narrow, and, if possible, more gloomy, when viewed by the feeble rays of a watery moon, than the neighbouring houses.

From the uppermost window streamed a strong light, which danced upon the black wall of the building opposite, making the sombre appearance of the locality the more sinister as it was the more visible.

That scream, which expressed both horror and agony, caused Markham to start with momentary consternation.

The constable did not, however, appear surprised; but merely observed with a strange coolness, "Ah! there's Smithers at his old tricks again."

"And who is Smithers?" inquired Richard.

But before the constable could reply to the question, the window, whence the light emanated, was thrown up with crashing violence, and a female voice shrieked for assistance.

"Had we not bettor ascertain what is the matter here?" exclaimed Markham, hastily.

"I dare not force an entry, unless there's a cry of '*Murder*,'" answered the officer.

Scarcely were these words uttered when the sound of a heavy blow, like that of a thong or leathern strap upon a person's back, echoed along the street; and then terrific shrieks, mingled with cries of "*Murder!*" issued from the open window.

In another instant the female was dragged away from the casement by some one in the room where this scene occurred; then the blows were resumed with frightful severity, and the screams and cries continued in a more appalling manner than at first.

Immediately afterwards, and just as the constable was preparing to force an entry, some one was heard to rush precipitately down the stairs inside the house: the door opened, and a strange-looking being darted madly into the street.

"Now, Gibbet," cried the policeman, catching the hump-backed lad—for such Markham perceived him to be—by the collar, "what's all this about?"

"Oh! you are an officer!" exclaimed the hump-back, in a tone of surprise and delight: "for God's sake come up—father's murdering Kate!"

The screams and the sounds of the blows still continuing up stairs, the constable did not hesitate to comply with the request of the deformed lad whom he had saluted by the singular name of Gibbet; and Markham hastened after him, anxious to render any assistance that might be required at his hands.

The policeman and our hero hurried up the narrow stairs, lighted by the officer's bull's-eye; and speedily reached the room whence the screams had emanated.

But we must pause for a moment to describe that apartment, and to give the reader some idea of the inmates of the house to which we have introduced him.

The room was situated at the top of the house, and bore the appearance of a loft, there being no ceiling to conceal the massive beams and spars which supported the angular roof.

From one of the horizontal beams hung a stuffed figure, resembling a human being, and as large as life. It was dressed in a complete suit of male attire; and a white mask gave it the real but ghastly appearance of a dead body. It was suspended by a thick cord, or halter, the knot of which being fastened beneath the left ear, made the head incline somewhat over the right shoulder; and it was waving gently backwards and forwards, as if it had been recently disturbed. The arms were pinioned behind; and the hands, which were made more or less life-like by means of dingy white kid gloves, were curled up as it were in a last convulsion. In a word, it presented the exact appearance of a man hanging.

Markham started back when his eyes first fell on this sinister object; but a second glance convinced him that the figure was only a puppet.

This second survey brought to his view other features, calculated to excite his wonder and curiosity, in that strange apartment.

The figure already described was suspended in such a way that its lower extremity was about a foot from the ground; but it was concealed nearly up to the knees by a small scaffold, or large black box, it having been suffered to fall that much through a trap-door made like a drop in the platform of that diminutive stage.

From this strange spectacle,—which, in all respects, was a perfect representation of an execution—Markham's eyes wandered round the loft.

The walls—the rough brick-work of which was smeared over with white-wash,—were covered with rude pictures, glaringly coloured and set in common black wooden frames. These pictures were such as are sold in low neighbourhoods for a few pence each, and representing scenes in the lives of remarkable highwaymen, murderers, and other criminals who had ended their days upon the scaffold. The progress of Jack Sheppard to the gibbet at Tyburn,—the execution of Jonathan Wild,—Turpin's ride to York,—Sawney Bean and his family feasting off human flesh in their cave,—Hunt and Thurtell throwing the body of Mr. Weare into the pond,—Corder murdering Maria Martin at the Red Barn,—James Greenacre cutting up the corpse of Hannah Brown,—such were the principal subjects of that Gallery of Human Enormity.

But as if these pictorial mementos of crime and violent death were not sufficient to gratify the strange taste of the occupants of that apartment, some hand, which was doubtless the agent of an imagination that loved to "sup full of horrors," had scrawled with a burnt stick upon the wall various designs of an equally terrific nature. Gibbets of all forms, and criminals in all the different stages of their last minutes in this life, were there represented. The ingenuity of the draughtsman had even suggested improvements in the usual modes of execution, and had delineated drops, halters, and methods of pinioning on new principles!

Every thing in that spacious loft savoured of the scaffold!

Oh! had the advocates of capital punishment but been enabled to glance upon that scene of horrors, they would have experienced a feeling of dire regret that any system which they had supported could have led to such an exhibition!

But to proceed.

On a rude board which served as a mantel over the grate, was a miniature gibbet, about eight inches high, and suspended to the horizontal beam of which was a mouse—most scientifically hung with a strong piece of pack-thread.

The large silver watch belonging to the principal inmate of the house was suspended to a horizontal piece of wood, with an oblique supporter, projecting from the wall above the fire-place.

In one corner of the room was a bed, over which flowed curtains of a coarse yellow material; and even these were suspended to a spar arranged and propped up like the arm of a gibbet.

A table, on which the supper things still remained, and half a dozen chairs, completed the contents of this strange room.

And now a few words relative to the inmates of that house.

The hump-backed lad who had rushed down the stairs in the manner already described, was about seventeen or eighteen years of age, and so hideously ugly that he scarcely seemed to belong to the human species. His hair was fiery red, and covered with coarse and matted curls a huge head that would not have been unsuitable for the most colossal form. His face was one mass of freckles; his eyes were of a pinkish hue; his eyebrows and lashes were white; and his large teeth glittered like dominoes between his thick and blueish lips. His arms were long like those of a baboon; but his legs were short; and he was not more than four feet and a half high. In spite of his hideous deformity and almost monstrous ugliness, there was an air of good-nature about him, combined with an evident consciousness of his own repulsive appearance, which could not do otherwise than inspire compassion—if not interest.

The moment the policeman, who entered the room first, made his appearance upon the threshold, a young female precipitated herself towards him, exclaiming, "For God's sake protect me—but do not, do not hurt my uncle!"

This girl was about sixteen years of age, and, though not beautiful, possessed a countenance whose plaintive expression was calculated to inspire deep interest in her behalf. She was tall, and of a graceful figure: her hair was light chesnut; her eyes dark blue, and with a deep melancholy characterising their bashful glances; her teeth were small, white, and even. Though clad in humble attire, there was something genteel in her appearance,—something superior to the place and society in which we now find her.

The man from whose cruel blows she implored protection, was of middle height, rather stoutly built, with a pale countenance, and an expression of stern hard-heartedness in his large grey eyes and compressed lips. He was dressed in a suit which evidently had never been made for him,—the blue frock coat being too long in the sleeves, the waistcoat too wide round the waist, and the trousers scarcely reaching below the knees.

"For God's sake protect me!" exclaimed the young girl, as above stated; "but do not—do not hurt my uncle," she added in a tone which proved the sincerity of the prayer.

"Come, come, Master Smithers," said the constable, "this won't do: you musn't alarm the neighbourhood in this manner."

"Why, then, does she interfere between me and Gibbet?" cried the man brutally, at the same time flourishing a thick leathern thong in his right hand.

"She does it out of good-nature, I suppose," observed the constable. "Every one knows how shameful you treat your son Gibbet; and this poor gal takes her cousin's part."

At these words the hump-back cast a timid but affectionate glance towards Katherine, who, on her part, threw a look of profound compassion upon the unfortunate lad.

"She does it out of good-nature, does she?" repeated the man: "then why won't he learn my business? He never can be fit for any other. But, no—the moment I leave him, he is off to the side of Miss there; and she makes him read in her outlandish books, so that he despises his father and the business that he must take to, sooner or later."

"But you ought not to beat Miss Katherine, Smithers," reiterated the policeman. "The next time I hear the cry of '*Murder*' in your house I'll walk you off to the station—and that's all about it."

"I suppose that I may leather my own son if I choose?" said the man, savagely.

"You ought to remember that he is deformed through your cruelty," cried the constable, "and that his mother died of fright and grief——"

"Hold your tongue, blue-bottle!" interrupted Smithers, his lips quivering with rage. "It isn't for you to come and make mischief in a family. Get out with you!"

"But if we leave this poor girl to the rage of her uncle," said Markham to the constable, whom he drew aside and thus addressed in a whisper, "he will do her some injury."

"What is to be done with her, sir?" demanded the officer. "Smithers says she is his niece——"

"Is it not certain that she stands in such a degree of relationship towards him?" inquired our hero, whose humane heart was moved in favour of the suffering girl.

"Now, then, what are you chattering about there?" ejaculated Smithers. "I want to go to bed: Gibbet, you be off to your room—and, Kate, you go to yours. This is mine—and I should advise the blue-bottle with his spy in plain clothes to make themselves scarce."

"Remember, I shall report you to our serjeant," said the policeman; "and he will tell the Division to keep an eye on you."

"Tell him whatever you like," returned the man doggedly.

The hump-back and Katherine had already left the room in obedience to the command of Smithers.

The constable repeated a caution to the ruffian who had ill-used them, and then took his departure, followed by Richard Markham.

When they were once more in the street, our hero said to his companion, "Who is that man?"

"The PUBLIC EXECUTIONER," was the reply.

CHAPTER CXXXIX.

THE CONFIDENCE.

So astounded was Markham by this information, that for some moments he was unable to utter a word.

"I see that you are surprised, sir," said the policeman; "but couldn't you guess where you was when you saw the room filled with gibbets, real or in pictures?"

"It never struck me who the owner of those terrific symbols might be," answered Richard. "I concluded that some man of morbid taste dwelt there; but not for one moment did I imagine that I was in the presence of the public executioner."

"Did you ever see such a horrible-looking object as his son is?" asked the policeman.

"Poor creature—he is greatly to be pitied! Surely his father cannot in reality have conferred upon him the name by which you called him?"

"I don't suppose that Gibbet is his real name, sir, but it is the only one I ever heard him called by. You see, sir, Smithers wishes to bring the lad up to the same line: he wants an assistant, and he thinks that Gibbet is old enough to help him. Besides, there's plenty of work always after Assizes in the country; and the London hangman may get the jobs if he likes. He's considered more skilful than any one else; and, after all, practice makes perfect. As it is, he is forced to refuse a good many offers, because he can't be here, there, and everywhere. Now if Gibbet would only take to the business kindly, he might help his father to earn a fortune!"

"But if the poor lad have a loathing for the horrible avocation—as well he may," observed Markham, with a shudder, "why should he be forced to embrace it?"

"Because he can never do himself good elsewhere," answered the constable. "Who will employ the son of Jack Ketch? Why, will you believe it, sir, that not a soul visits Smithers' family? Although he lives in this neighbourhood, where, God knows, people ain't over nice and partickler, not a human being would cross his threshold."

"Does that aversion arise from disgust or superstition?" demanded Markham.

"From both, sir," was the reply. "The people that live in this district are of two kinds—the poor and ignorant, and the rogues and vagabonds. The poor and ignorant are afraid of the public executioner; and the rogues and vagabonds hate him, although he's merely an instrument. Miss Kate goes to market for him; and the shop-keepers that know who she is, are scarcely civil to her. They seem as if they'd rather she'd keep away."

"And you say that she is the executioner's niece?" observed Markham.

"Smithers says so himself," was the reply; "and of course I know nothing to the contrary; but it does seem strange that so amiable, genteel, and clever, a young gal should belong to such a family!"

"Her own parents are dead, I presume?"

"Yes, sir,—she is an orphan. When Smithers is very dull and miserable with his lonely situation, he sometimes comes down to the station and has a chat with us constables; and then he's pretty communicative. He told me one day that Katherine's parents had died when she was very young, and so he was compelled to take care of her. All the while she was a child Smithers let her do pretty well as she liked; and it is a wonder that she has turned out a good gal. But she regularly frequented the School established in the parish of Saint David's by the Rev. Mr. Tracy; and in that way she picked up a tolerable smattering of knowledge. Since then she's instructed herself as much as she could, and has bought books with the little money that her needle has produced her."

"But who employs her as a sempstress, if, as you say, so terrible a stigma affixes itself to each member of the hangman's family?" inquired Richard.

"The old housekeeper at Mr. Tracy's is very friendly disposed towards the poor creature, and gives her work," answered the policeman. "Katherine does all she can to console that poor hump-back Gibbet; and she has taught him to read and write—aye, and what's more, sir, to pray."

"Policeman," said Richard, after a pause, "the manner in which you have spoken relative to that poor girl, shows me that you have a good heart. Is there any mode of ameliorating her wretched situation? I feel the deepest compassion for her miserable lot; and all you have told me of her excellent character makes me anxious to see her removed from the vile society of that ruffian under whose roof she lives."

"I believe she is anxious to go out to service, sir, or open a little school," answered the constable; "but her family connection is against her. Or else I don't think that Smithers would care about parting with her."

"What induces you to suppose that such are her wishes?" asked Markham.

"Because she told me so, sir," was the reply. "One evening I went to Smithers' house, with a certain message from the Sheriff of London—you can guess what, I dare say——"

"To acquaint him with the day fixed for some wretch's execution, no doubt?"

"Precisely, sir; but Smithers wasn't at home, and so I sate down and waited for him. It wasn't in Jack Ketch's own room up stairs where we went just now, and where he teaches his son how to hang by means of that puppet; but it was in a little parlour they have got down stairs, and which Miss Kate keeps as clean and comfortable as if they saw no end of company. Well, I got talking to the young gal; and though she never said a single word against her uncle, but spoke of him in a grateful and kind manner, she let out that if he *could* spare her, she should like to earn her own bread by her own exertions. And then the poor creature burst out crying, and said, that no one would take her as a servant, and that she should get no scholars even if she was to open a school."

Markham made no answer; but he reflected profoundly on all that he had just heard.

"Poor gal!" continued the policeman, after a few moments' silence; "she don't deserve to suffer as she does. My beat is about this quarter: and I know pretty well all that's going on. I see more than other people about here, because I've opportunity and leisure. Besides, it's my business. Well, sir, I can assure you that there isn't a more charitable or generous-hearted gal in all London than Miss Katherine. If a poor neighbour's ill, it's ten to one but some female muffled up in her shawl knocks at the door of the sick person's house, leaves a parcel, and runs away; and then there's tea, and sugar, and gruel, for the invalid—and no one knows who brought it, or where it comes from. Or if a family's in want, the baker calls with bread that's paid for, but won't say who sent it. Or may be it's the butcher with a small joint—but always sent in the same quiet manner. Then, while the poor creatures whose hearts are made glad by this unlooked-for charity, are wondering whether it was the parson, or the parson's wife, or this benevolent gentleman, or that good lady, who sent the things, Kate buries herself in her room, and doesn't even think that she has done any thing out of the way."

"Is this possible?" cried Markham.

"I know it, sir—for I've seen her do it all," answered the policeman, "when she couldn't see me and little thought that any body noticed her."

"And she the niece of the public executioner!" exclaimed Richard: "a pearl concealed in this horrible swamp!"

The conversation between Markham and the good-hearted constable was cut short by the sudden appearance of the other two policemen, who had undertaken to visit the low houses in Plumptre Street.

"Well, what news?" asked Richard's companion.

"None," was the reply. "We have been in every flash crib down yonder, and can't hear or see any thing of the Resurrection Man."

"Then we must abandon the search for to-night, I presume," said Richard. "The clock has struck one, and I begin to be wearied of this fruitless ramble."

"We will exert ourselves to discover the miscreant that blew up our comrades in Bethnal Green," observed the constable who had been our hero's companion that night. "Should we succeed in capturing him, sir, where can I wait upon you to communicate the tidings?"

"My name is Markham," was the reply, "and I live at Holloway. If you discover the villain Anthony Tidkins, lose not a moment in making me acquainted with the circumstance."

Richard then rewarded the three constables liberally for the trouble they had taken; and ere he departed from them, he drew aside the one who had been his companion.

"My good fellow," he said, slipping an additional sovereign into his hand, "you have too kind a heart for the situation which you fill. Should you ever require a friend, hesitate not to come to me."

"And should you, sir, ever need the humble aid of Morris Benstead, you know the Division I belong to, and a note to the chief station will always command my attention."

Markham thanked the officer for his civility, and then struck into the nearest street leading from the Holy Land to Tottenham Court Road, where he hoped to find a vehicle to take him home.

But scarcely had he proceeded twenty paces, when he heard hasty footsteps behind him; and, turning round, was accosted by a man whose slouched hat almost entirely shaded his countenance.

"I beg your pardon, sir," said the man; "but I heard you mention two names a few moments ago that are familiar to me."

"Indeed!" cried our hero, surprised at this strange mode of address.

"Yes:—I was lurking in a court, and I heard you say that you were Mr. Richard Markham," resumed the man: "and you mentioned a certain Anthony Tidkins."

"I did. Do you know him?" demanded Richard.

"But too well," answered the man bitterly.

"Who are you?" inquired Markham.

"No matter who I am: I know *you*—and I know *him*. I was in a certain place at the same time that you were there; though we were not in the same ward. But I heard all about you *then*; and when you mentioned your name just now, I felt sure you was the same person. Has Tidkins ever injured you?"

"Cruelly," replied Richard. "But I am not influenced by petty motives of revenge: I am anxious to deliver a monster into the grasp of justice."

"And what should you say if you heard that Tidkins was beyond your reach in this world?"

"I should rejoice that society was relieved from such a fiend."

"Then I think that I can make your mind easy on that score," said the man.

"What do you mean?" cried Richard, eagerly.

"I mean that this hand has done the law's work," responded the stranger.

"You mean—you mean that you yourself have acted the part of an avenger?" said Markham.

"Precisely what I *do* mean: in plain terms, I've killed him."

"My God! and you tell me this so coolly!" exclaimed Richard. "Whatever that man's crimes may be, you are not the less a murderer!"

"Pooh—pooh! I should have thought you'd more pluck than to talk in this way. What does it matter whether Jack Ketch or a private enemy did the job?"

"Where did this happen? when?—how long ago?" inquired Markham, not knowing whether to believe the statement thus strangely made to him, or not.

"If you really wish to know all about it," said the man, "step up this court, where we can talk in peace, and I will tell you. What! you think I am going to hurt you too? Well, be it so. Goodnight—or rather good morning."

At that moment Saint Giles's Church struck two.

"Stay," cried Richard, catching the man by the arm: "I will accompany you."

They walked together into a dark court, our hero keeping himself in readiness to resist any sudden hostility, were such a proceeding intended.

But the man appeared to have no such aim in view, for, leaning himself tranquilly against the wall, he said, "Can you keep a secret?"

"If I promise to do so," answered Richard.

"Then promise not to betray what I am going to tell you."

"I promise," said Markham, after some hesitation.

"You must know," continued the man, satisfied with this assurance, "that I have lately partaken of the hospitality of a race of persons, at whose head-quarters—not a hundred miles from where we are now standing—I met Anthony Tidkins———"

"When?" demanded Richard impatiently.

"About two hours ago."

"Ah! then it may be true———"

"True! what interest have I to tell you a lie? I have been some time in search of that villain; and accident threw us together to-night. This dagger———" here he took Markham's hand, and made him feel the point of the elastic poniard,—"this dagger drank his life's best blood!"

Richard could not suppress an ejaculation of horror.

The assassin laughed.

"Unhappy man," said our hero, "are you not aware that your life may be forfeited on account of this deed?"

"And this good blade should reach the heart of any one that attempted to take me," was the resolute and indeed significant reply.

"I promised to betray nothing that you might communicate to me, and I shall keep my word," rejoined Markham, in a firm tone, and without retreating a single step. "Did I wish to forfeit my pledge, your dagger would not intimidate me."

"You are a brave fellow," cried the stranger; "and all brave men may be trusted. Would you like to satisfy yourself, with your own eyes, that Anthony Tidkins has received his death wound?"

"I should," answered Markham; "both on my own account and on that of society."

"And you will not betray the place that I shall take you to, or the people that you may see there?"

"Most solemnly will I keep your secret."

"Come with me, then. I will leave you at the door; and your own ingenuity must obtain you admittance. But, one word more: you will not state to any one there that you have met me?"

"I will not even allow my motive for visiting the place you speak of to transpire."

"I believe all you say. Come!"

The man led the way out of the court, accompanied by our hero.

They threaded several narrow streets and alleys, and at length stopped at the door of a large house.

"Knock, and demand shelter: admittance will not, I fancy, be refused."

"Is there any danger to be encountered?" asked Markham: "not that I fear it—but I am unarmed."

"There is no danger. This is the head-quarters of the Gipsies, or Zingarees: they never use the dagger or the pistol. And, once more, remember your promise."

"I shall not forget it," said Richard. "But, before we separate, answer me one question."

"Speak—and be speedy," returned the man.

"In one word, then, why, when you overheard my conversation with the policeman, did you resolve upon making me the confidant of a deed which might send you to the scaffold?"

"Because I am proud of that deed," replied the man, grasping Richard forcibly by the wrist, and grinding his teeth in horrible triumph;—"because it is the result of four years of pent-up yearning after vengeance;—because, in avenging myself, I have avenged all who have suffered through that miscreant;—because I am anxious that those who have been injured by him should know the fate that has overtaken him at last."

With these words, Crankey Jem (whom the reader has doubtless already recognised) disappeared precipitately from the spot.

CHAPTER CXL.

INCIDENTS IN THE GIPSY PALACE.

For a few moments Richard remained rooted to the spot where the returned convict had left him. He was uncertain how to proceed.

Warned by the desperate adventure which had nearly cost him his life at Twig Folly, he feared lest the present occurrence might be another scheme of the Resurrection Man to ensnare him.

Then he reflected that the individual who had just left him, had met him accidentally, and had narrated to him circumstances which had every appearance of truth.

We have before said that Markham was not a coward—far from it; and he moreover experienced a lively curiosity to satisfy himself concerning the fate of an individual whose inveterate malignity had so frequently menaced not only his dearest interests, but his life.

This reflection decided him; and, without farther hesitation, he knocked boldly at the front door of the Gipsies' Palace.

Some minutes elapsed ere his summons appeared to have created any attention within; and he was about to repeat it, when the door slowly moved on its hinges.

But to Markham's surprise no person appeared in the obscure lobby into which the pale moon threw a fitful light; in fact, the front door was opened by means of a simple mechanism which the porter worked in his lodge overhead.

While Markham was lost in wonder at this strange circumstance, the trap was suddenly raised above, and a strong light was thrown through it into the lobby.

"Who are you?" demanded the gruff voice of the porter.

"I seek a few hours' repose and rest," answered Markham.

"Who sent you here?"

"A person who is a friend to you."

"Do you know what place this is?"

"Yes—it is the head-quarters of the Zingarees."

"So far, so good," said the porter. "Well—wait a few moments—I must see."

The trap closed—the lobby was again involved in total darkness; and for the next ten minutes the silence of death appeared to reign within the house.

At the expiration of that time the inner door was opened:; and the porter, bearing a light, appeared.

"You may enter," he said. "The Zingarees never refuse hospitality when it can be safely granted."

Markham crossed the threshold without hesitation.

The porter closed both doors with great care.

"Follow me," said the man.

He then led the way up stairs to the first floor, and conducted our hero into a room where there were several beds, all of which were unoccupied.

"You have your choice of the downies," observed the porter, with a half smile; "and I shall leave you this light. Do you require any food?"

"None, I thank you."

"So I should think," said the man drily, as he surveyed Markham's appearance in a manner which seemed to express a wonder why a person in his situation of life had come thither at all.

We have, however, before observed that curiosity formed but a faint feature of the gipsy character; and, even when it existed, it was not expressed in verbal queries. Moreover, individuals in a respectable sphere not unfrequently sought in the Holy Land a refuge against the officers of the laws which they violated; and hence the appearance of a person had nothing to do with the fact of admission into the gipsies' establishment.

Nevertheless, the porter did survey Markham in a dubious way for a moment; but whether the preceding incidents of the night, or the calm tranquillity of our hero's manner,—so inconsistent with the idea that he was anxious to conceal himself from the eyes of justice,—excited the suspicions of the porter, it is impossible to say.

But that glance of curiosity was only momentary.

Averting his eyes from our hero, the porter placed the light upon the floor, wished him a good night's rest, and retired.

But to the surprise and annoyance of Markham, the gipsy locked the door of the apartment.

As the key turned with a grating sound, a tremor crept over Richard's frame; and he almost repented having sought the interior of an abode the character and inmates of which were almost entirely unknown to him. Indeed, all that he knew of either was derived from the meagre information of the man (and that man an acknowledged assassin!) who had induced him to visit the place where he now found himself.

"How weak I am to yield to this sentiment of fear!" he exclaimed. "Rather let me determine how to act."

He proceeded to examine the room in which he appeared to be a prisoner. The numerous beds seemed to indicate that he really was in a species of barrack, or lodging-house of some kind; and this circumstance, coupled with the fact that the porter who had admitted him was evidently a member of the Egyptian or Bohemian race, reassured him—for he felt convinced that he was actually in the abode of gipsies.

So far the stranger, who had been the means of his visit to that strange tenement, had not deceived him.

But how was he to satisfy himself in regard to the Resurrection Man? He tried the door—it was indeed fastened; he examined the windows—they were not barred, but were of a dangerous height from the back-yard on which they looked.

Markham paced the room uncertain how to act.

Suddenly his reverie was interrupted by the tread of many steps upon the stairs; and then a species of subdued bustle took place throughout the house.

The whispering of voices—the removal of heavy objects overhead—the running of persons hither and thither—and the opening and shutting of doors, announced that some extraordinary movement was taking place.

Richard listened with breathless anxiety.

At length the sounds of several heavy steps, in the landing outside his door, met his ears; and this noise was at short intervals varied by deep groans.

The groans seemed to accompany the tread of the heavy steps just mentioned.

These steps and those expressions of human suffering grew fainter and fainter, as they descended the stairs, until at length they were no longer audible.

Nevertheless Markham kept his ear fixed to the key-hole of his chamber-door.

Silence now once more reigned throughout the house; but in a few minutes the noise and bustle seemed to have been transferred to the yard.

Richard hurried to the window; but the moon had gone down and the darkness without was intense.

He concealed the light in a corner of the room, and then gently raised one of the windows.

But he could distinguish nothing with his eyes; and the sounds that met his ears were those of footsteps bustling to and fro. At length these ceased; a door was closed at the end of the yard; and almost immediately afterwards Richard heard, in the same direction, the rumbling noise of a vehicle moving heavily away.

When that din had ceased, the most profound tranquillity prevailed not only in the home but also in its neighbourhood.

That silence was interrupted only for a few moments by the sonorous bell of St. Giles's Church, proclaiming the hour of three.

"Time wears on," said Markham impatiently; "and no opportunity of satisfying myself upon the one point seems to present itself. To attempt to seek repose is impossible; to pass the dull hours in suspense like this is intolerable!"

Then he seated himself on one of the beds, and considered what course he should pursue.

Slowly—slowly passed the time; and though he revolved in his mind many plans, he could fix upon none.

At length the clock struck four.

"The hour for departure will come, and I shall leave this house as full of doubt and uncertainty as when I entered it!" he ejaculated, starting up.

His eye chanced to fall upon a long nail in the wall opposite to the bed from which he had just risen.

A scheme which had already suggested itself to his mind, now assumed a feasible aspect:—he knew that the door was only locked, and not bolted; and that nail seemed to promise the means of egress.

He, however, first examined the candle which had been left him, and which still burned in the corner where he had concealed it:—to his joy he found that there was an inch remaining.

"With the assurance of light for another half hour, and good courage," he said to himself, "I may yet accomplish my purpose."

Having extracted the nail from the wall, he proceeded to pick the lock of the room-door—an operation which he successfully achieved in a few minutes.

Without a moment's hesitation, he issued from the room, bearing the candle in his hand.

As he crossed the landing towards the staircase, which he resolved to ascend, his foot came in contact with some object.

He picked it up: it was an old greasy pocket-book, tied loosely round with a coarse string, and as Markham raised it, a letter dropped out.

Richard was in the act of replacing the document in the pocket-book, which he intended to leave upon the stairs, so as to attract the notice of the inmates of the house, when the address on the outside of the letter caught his eyes.

The candle nearly fell from his hand, so great was the astonishment which immediately seized upon him.

That address consisted simply of the words "ANTHONY TIDKINS!"—but the handwriting—Oh! there was no possibility of mistaking *that*! Markham knew it so well; and though years had elapsed since he had last seen it, still it was familiar to him as his own—the more so, as it remained unchanged in style;—for it was the writing of his brother Eugene!

With a hasty but trembling hand he opened the letter, the wafer of which had already been broken;—he did not hesitate to read the contents;—judging by his own frank and generous heart, he conceived that such a licence was permitted between brothers. Moreover, he experienced a profound and painful anxiety to ascertain what link could connect his brother with the terrible individual to whom the letter was addressed.

But all that the letter contained was this:—

"Come to me to-night without fail, between eleven and twelve. Knock in the usual manner."

Richard examined the handwriting with the most minute attention; and the longer he scrutinized it, the more he became confirmed in his belief that it was Eugene's.

But Eugene a patron or colleague of the greatest miscreant that had ever disgraced human nature! Was such a thing possible?

The letter bore no date—no signature—and was addressed from no place. It had no post-mark upon it, and had, therefore, evidently been delivered by a private hand.

"Oh!" thought Richard within himself, "if my unhappy brother have really been the victim, the associate, or the employer of that incarnate demon, may God grant that the wretch is indeed no more—for the sake of Eugene!"

And then his curiosity to ascertain the truth relative to the alleged assassination of Tidkins, became more poignant.

"It must be so!" reasoned Markham within himself; "that stranger has not deceived me:—the presence of this pocket-book here is an undeniable trace of the miscreant. Oh, how much it now behoves me to convince myself that he is indeed removed from the theatre of his crimes!"

Subduing as much as possible the painful emotions which that letter had suddenly excited within him, Markham secured the pocket-book about his person; for now that accident had revealed to him to whom it belonged, he did not consider himself called upon to part with an object which, in case the statement of Tidkins' death should prove untrue, might contain some paper calculated to afford a clue to his haunts or proceedings.

Scarcely decided in what manner to pursue his investigation in that house, and trusting more to accident than to any settled plan to aid him in testing the truth of the self-accused stranger's statement relative to Tidkins,—Markham stole softly up the staircase.

Arrived on the first landing to which it led, he listened attentively at the various doors which opened from it.

All was silent as death within the rooms to which those doors belonged.

Not even the sound of human respiration met his ears. Could it be possible that the house was deserted? Perhaps the bustle which he had heard ere now was caused by the departure of its occupants?

As this idea grew upon him, he was emboldened to try the latch of one of the doors at which he had already listened. It yielded to his hand; he pushed the door open with great caution, and entered the chamber.

Not a human soul was there.

He visited the other rooms upon that landing, the doors of which were all unlocked; and they were alike untenanted.

There was another storey above; and thither he proceeded.

The first three rooms which he entered were empty, like the preceding ones; but in the fourth there were three men. They were, however, fast asleep in their beds; and Richard's visit was so noiseless that they were not in the least disturbed.

Hastily retreating, and closing the door carefully behind him, Markham descended to the landing on which his own room opened, and where he had found the pocket-book.

On that floor were four apartments, as on each of the upper flats, in addition to the porter's lodge, which, it will be remembered, was precisely over the lobby below.

To avoid elaborate detail, we may state that Markham found the doors of the other three rooms (besides his own) on the first floor unlocked, and the chambers themselves untenanted.

He was about to leave the last room, when the appearance of one of the beds attracted his attention; and on a closer examination, he perceived that it was saturated with blood. Moreover, on a chair close by, there were pieces of linen rag, on which large stains of gore were scarcely dry, together with lint and bandages—unquestionable proofs that a wound had very recently been dressed in that apartment.

"No—that self-accuser has not deceived me!" thought Markham, as he contemplated these objects. "All circumstances combine to bear evidence to the truth of his assertion! Doubtless the gipsies have departed, carrying away the corpse with them!"

He stood gazing on the blood-dyed bed at his feet musing in this manner; and then he thought how fearful was the fate of the miscreant, the evidences of whose death he believed to be beneath his eyes, cut off in the midst of his crimes without a moment's preparation or repentance!

But suddenly he asked himself—"Am I certain that he is no more? That lint to stanch the blood—those bandages to bind the wound,—do they not rather bear testimony to a blow which was not fatal, but left life behind it? And yet, for what purpose could the body be removed—save for secret interment? Oh! if that man be yet alive—and if Eugene be indeed his accomplice or his patron——"

And Markham experienced emotions of the most intense anguish! He loved his brother with the most ardent affection; and the idea that the individual so loved could be a criminal, or the friend of criminals, was harrowing to his soul.

"But, after all," thought Richard, his naturally upright and almost severe principles asserting their empire in his mind,—"after all, ought I not to rejoice, if this man be indeed still alive, that he has survived the assassin's blow—that he is allowed leisure for repentance! My Maker, who can read all hearts, knows that I am not selfish; and yet it is a principle of our frail human nature to rejoice at the fall of a deadly enemy! Oh! when I think of all the wrongs and injuries I have experienced at the hands of that man,—exposures—persecutions—attempts upon my life,—I cannot pray that he may live to be the scourge of others—and perhaps of my brother—as he has been of me!"

Unwilling to contend longer with the varied emotions which agitated his breast, Markham hurried from the room.

The lower part of the house yet remained to be explored:—perhaps the body—if the Resurrection Man were indeed dead—had been removed to a room on the ground floor?

Determined to leave no stone unturned to satisfy his doubts, Markham cautiously descended the stairs, and visited the refectory-rooms, one after the other.

They were all empty.

His candle was now waxing dim; but he saw that his search was nearly over. A flight of steps, apparently leading to offices in the basement of the building, alone remained for him to visit.

To that part of the house he descended, and found himself in a small place which had the appearance of a scullery.

On one side was a massive door, secured with huge bolts, and evidently leading into a vault or cellar. But scarcely had Markham time to cast one glance around him in the subterranean, when the candle flickered and expired.

At the same moment a hollow groan echoed through the basement.

Richard started: he was in total darkness—and a momentary tremor came over him.

The groan was repeated.

His fears vanished; and he immediately concluded that the Resurrection Man, wounded and suffering, must be somewhere near.

At that idea, all sentiments of aversion, hatred, and abhorrence,—all reminiscence of injury and wrong, fled from the mind of that generous-hearted young man: he thought only that a fellow-creature was in anguish and in pain—perhaps neglected, and left to die without a soul to administer consolation!

Reckless of the danger which he might incur by alarming the inmates of the house, he determined upon rousing the porter in order to obtain a light.

He turned from the scullery, and was rushing up the stone steps in pursuance of his humane intention, when he suddenly came in violent contact with a person who was descending the same stairs.

CHAPTER CXLI.

THE SUBTERRANEAN.

The violence of the concussion threw Richard backwards; and in a moment he felt the rough hand of a man grasp him by the throat.

"Who is it?" was the demand simultaneously put to him.

"I will answer you when we are on equal terms," replied Markham; and, hurling the man away from him, he sprang upon his feet. "Now—stand off," he cried; "for I am not to be injured with impunity."

"I don't want to injure you," said the man. "But who are you? I know by your voice that you're not one of us."

"You then are an inmate of this house?" observed Markham, fencing with the other's question.

At that instant another hollow groan echoed through the subterranean.

"She lives!" cried the man; and in another moment Markham heard him drawing back the bolts of the massive door which he had observed in the scullery.

Richard groped his way towards him, and said, "*She lives?* whom do you allude to? Surely there cannot be a female imprisoned———"

"Be silent, in the name of heaven!" interrupted the man, in a whisper. "The life of an unhappy woman depends upon your secrecy—whoever you may be."

"Then would I rather aid than harm you and her, both," answered Markham.

Another groan was heard; and Richard could now distinguish the direction from which it came.

But still the massive door remained unopened.

"This bolt,—this bolt!" muttered the man in a tone expressive of commingled rage and despair. "Oh! for a light!"

"Can you not procure one?" demanded Richard.

"Stay," said the man—"a good thought! There should be candles somewhere here—and matches. By Jove! here is a candle—and, on this shelf—yes—here are matches also!"

The man struck a light.

By a natural impulse he and Markham immediately cast scrutinising glances at each other.

"Ah! I thought so by your voice—you are a gentleman," said the man: "then you will not betray me?"

"Betray you!" repeated Markham, surprised at this observation.

"I will tell you what I mean presently: there is no time to be lost! Hark—another groan: she is dying!"

The man, who was tall and good-looking, and evidently not a scion of the Bohemian race—gave Markham the candle, and proceeded to open the massive door, the presence of the light enabling him to remove the fastenings with ease.

He then beckoned Richard to follow him into the cellar, where he instantly set to work to draw the bolts of a second door.

This task was speedily accomplished; and as the door grated upon its hinges, another heart-wrung moan emanated from the interior of the second vault.

The man rushed in; Markham followed with the light, and beheld a woman stretched almost lifeless upon the mattress.

The groans had all along emanated from her lips:—then where was the Resurrection Man?

"Margaret—cheer up—it's me—it's Skilligalee—I'm come to save you," said the protector of the Rattlesnake as he bent over her.

"How long has she been immured here?" inquired Markham.

"Only three or four hours," answered Skilligalee; "and so it must be fright that has half killed her. Pray get some water, sir—there's plenty in the scullery."

Markham hastened to comply with this request; and Skilligalee bathed the woman's face with the refreshing element.

She opened her eyes, and a smile came over her faded countenance as she caught sight of the friendly face that greeted her fearful glance.

"How long have I been here?" asked the Rattlesnake in a faint tone, while her whole frame was convulsed with terror as recent events rushed to her mind.

"Not many hours, Meg," answered Skilligalee.

"And you will not leave me here any longer?" she said. "Oh! do not let me die in this horrible place!"

"I am come to save you," returned Skilligalee. "Are you able to get up and walk?"

"Yes—for the sake of freedom," cried the Rattlesnake, rising from the mattress. "But who is that?" she added, as her eyes now fell upon Markham for the first time.

"That's exactly what I don't know myself," said Skilligalee. "The gentleman has, however, behaved himself as such; and that's enough for us. Hark! there's the clock on the staircase striking five? We haven't much time to lose: come on."

Markham led the way with the light: Skilligalee followed, supporting the Rattlesnake, who was weak and exhausted with the effects of extreme terror.

"Which way shall we go?" she inquired, as they paused for a moment in the scullery, to listen if all were quiet.

"By the back gate," answered Skilligalee. "I have secured the key. The porter keeps the keys of the front door."

"And what has become of *him*—that dreadful man who was the cause of all this misery?" asked the Rattlesnake. "Was he killed by the blow that the Traveller dealt him with his long dagger?"

These words struck a chord which vibrated to Markham's heart.

"Was any one wounded in this house during the night?" he demanded hastily.

Skilligalee hesitated: he knew not who Markham was, nor what might be the consequences of a reply consistent with the truth.

"Answer me, I conjure you," continued Richard, perceiving this unwillingness to satisfy his curiosity. "I have every reason to believe that a person whose name is Anthony Tidkins——"

"Oh! yes—yes," murmured the Rattlesnake, with a convulsive shudder.

"Then I have not been deceived!" cried Markham. "That individual, who is better known as the Resurrection Man, was dangerously wounded—if not killed—in this house a few hours since. "You," he continued, addressing himself to Skilligalee, "are evidently acquainted with the particulars of the occurrence: as I have assisted you to liberate this woman who seems dear to you, reward me by telling me all you know of that event."

"First tell me who you are," said Skilligalee. "And be quick—I have no time for conversation."

"Suffice it for you to know that I am one whom the Resurrection Man has cruelly injured. Twice has he attempted my life: once at his den in Bethnal Green, and again on the banks of the canal at Twig Folly——"

"Then you, sir, are Mr. Markham?" interrupted be Rattlesnake. "Oh! I know how you have been treated by that fearful man; and there is no necessity to conceal the truth from you! Yes—sir, it is true that the wretch who has persecuted you was stabbed in this house; and—if I did not believe that the wound was mortal——"

Here the Rattlesnake stopped, and leant heavily upon Skilligalee for support—so profoundly was she terrified at the mere possibility of Anthony Tidkins being still in existence.

Her companion perceived her emotion, and fathoming its cause, hastened to exclaim, "But he is no more! You need dread him no longer."

"Are you sure? are you well convinced of this?" demanded Markham.

"I saw him breathe his last," was the answer.

"Where? Not in this house?" cried Richard.

"No," returned Skilligalee. "Between two and three this morning the King, his family, and all the Zingarees, except those who stay to take care of this establishment, took their departure; and I was compelled to go along with them. In consequence of some communication between the person you call the Resurrection Man and Aischa, the Queen of the Zingarees, after he was badly wounded by the Traveller——"

"How do you call the individual who attacked him?" demanded Richard.

"The Traveller," answered the Skilligalee. "But, it appears, that he had another name—Crankey Jem: at least, he said so after he had stabbed the man."

"I should know that name," said Richard, musing. "Oh! I remember! Proceed."

"Well—in consequence of something that the Resurrection Man told Aischa, when she was attending to his wound, it was determined to take him along with us; and four of our men carried him down to the van which was waiting at the back gate. He groaned very much while he was being removed."

"I heard him," said Richard, instantaneously recalling to mind the groans which had met his ears when he was listening at his chamber door to the bustle of the gipsies' departure.

"You heard him?" repeated Skilligalee.

"Yes—I was in the house at the time. Proceed."

"We conveyed him down to the van, where we laid him on a mattress, and he seemed to fall asleep. Then we all divided into twos and threes, and got safe out of London, into a field near the Pentonville Penitentiary. But when the van, with Aischa, Eva, and Morcar,—those are some of our people, sir,—came to the place of appointment, we found," added Skilligalee, his voice assuming a peculiar tone, "that the Resurrection Man was dead."

"God be thanked!" ejaculated the Rattlesnake, with a fervour which made Markham's blood run cold.

"And now that I have told you all I know, sir," said Skilligalee, "you will have no objection if me and my companion here go about our business; for it is dangerous to both our interests to remain here any longer."

Skilligalee uttered these words in his usually jocular manner; for he was anxious to reassure his female companion, who still laboured under an excess of terror that seemed ready to prostrate all her energies.

"Yes—let us leave this fearful den," said Markham: "to me it appears replete with horrors of all kinds."

Skilligalee now took the candle and led the way, still supporting Margaret Flathers on his arm.

They all three effected their egress from the palace without any obstacle.

When they were safe in the alley with which the back gate communicated, Markham said to Skilligalee, "From what I can understand, you have fled from the gipsies in order to return and liberate your companion from the dungeon where we found her."

"That is precisely what I did," answered Skilligalee. "I gave them the slip when they had set up their tents in the field near the Penitentiary."

"It is probable that you are not too well provided with pecuniary resources," said Richard: "the contents of my purse are at your service."

"Thank you kindly, sir—very kindly," returned Skilligalee. "I am not in want of such assistance."

Markham vainly pressed his offer: it was declined with many expressions of gratitude. The truth was that Skilligalee had the greater portion of his share of Margaret's gold still remaining; and there was something so generous and so noble in the manner of Richard Markham, that he could not find it in his heart to impose upon him by taking a sum of which he did not stand in immediate need.

"At all events, let me advise you to avoid such companions as those with whom you appear to have been allied," observed Richard, "and who are cruel enough to immure a female in a subterranean dungeon."

"I shall not neglect your advice, sir," returned Skilligalee; "and may God bless you for it."

"And you," continued Richard, addressing himself to Margaret Flathers, "second your companion in his good intentions. I know not what deed on your part could have led to your incarceration in that cell—neither do I seek to know;—but to you I would give similar advice—avoid those whose ways are criminal, and whose vengeance is as terrific as it is lawless. Farewell."

"May God bless you, sir, for your good counsel!" said Margaret Flathers, weeping.

She had not merely repeated, with parrot-like callousness, the words uttered by her companion: that benediction emanated with fervid sincerity from a heart deeply penetrated by anxiety to renew a long-forgotten acquaintance with rectitude.

"Farewell, sir," said Skilligalee.

He and the Rattlesnake then struck into one of the streets with which the alley at the back of the gipsies' palace communicated.

Richard took another direction on his way homewards.

CHAPTER CXLII.

GIBBET.

A fortnight had passed since the incidents just related.

It was a Monday morning.

The clock of St. Giles's had just struck six, when the faint, flickering gleam of a candle struggled through the uppermost windows of the hangman's house.

The few persons who were passing along at that hour, and on that dark winter's morning, shuddered as they caught a glimpse of the sickly glare through the obscurity and the mist—for they thought within themselves, "The executioner is up early on account of the man that's to be hanged at eight o'clock."

And such was indeed the case.

Smithers rose shortly before six; and, having lighted the solitary candle that stood upon the mantel, proceeded to the floor below to call his son.

"Gibbet, you lazy hound!" he cried, thundering with his fist at the door of the hump-back's room; "get up."

"I'm getting up, father," replied the lad, from the interior of the chamber.

"Well, make haste about it," said the executioner in a savage tone.

He then returned to the loft.

There was something horribly fantastic in the appearance of that place. The dim and sickly light of the candle did but little more than redeem from complete obscurity the various strange objects which we have already described. But as the penetrating eye of the executioner plunged into the visible darkness of the loft, and beheld the ominous figure balancing beneath the beam, while its mask of a livid white hue wore a ghastly appearance in contrast with the black body and limbs which it surmounted,—no sentiment of horror nor of alarm agitated his heart.

The avocations of the man had brutalized him, and blunted every humane feeling which he had once possessed.

He walked up and down the room impatiently for several minutes, until the door opened and his son entered.

The hideous countenance of the lad was ghastly pale, and distorted with horror. His eyes glared fearfully, as if terrific apparitions flitted before them.

"Gibbet," said his father, "you shall try your hand this morning on a living being instead of a puppet."

"This morning!" repeated the lad, his teeth chattering, and his knees knocking together.

"To be sure. Didn't I tell you so last night?" cried the executioner. "Why, you hump-backed scoundrel, you—you ought to have prayed that no reprieve might be sent for the chap that's to be tucked up this morning, instead of working yourself up to this state of cowardly nervousness. But I'll take it out of you, I will."

With these words, Smithers seized his leathern thong, and was advancing towards the hump-back, when the wretched lad threw himself on his knees, clasped his hands together, and cried, "No,—don't, father—don't! I can't bear that lash! You don't know how it hurts.—I'll do all you tell me."

"Well, that's speaking proper—that is," said the executioner, dropping the already uplifted thong.

"It's all for your good that I use it now and then, Gibbet. Don't I want to make a man of you? Look at the money you can earn if you'll only make yourself a name like me. D'ye think the sheriffs throughout England would all apply to me to do their work for them, if I wasn't celebrated for my skill? Why—even the criminals themselves must look upon it as a regular blessing to have such a knowing hand as me to tie their last cravat for them. I'd bet a pound that the man who's to be turned off presently, isn't half as miserable as people think—'cos why, he's well aware that I shan't put him to no pain."

"I know you've got a great name in your business, father———"

"We'll call it *profession* in future, Gibbet; it's more genteel. And, after all, it's as good as a barrister's; for the barrister gets the man hanged—and I hang him. That's all the difference."

"I know it's very respectable, father," resumed the lad, submissively; "but—still—I———"

"Still what?" cried Smithers, savagely, and taking up the thong again.

"Nothing—nothing, father," faltered Gibbet.

"So much the better. Now come to the model, and take and pinion the figure—'cos that's what I mean you to do presently down at Newgate. Begin by degrees, as the saying is; you shall pinion this man to day; you shall let the drop fall for the next—and you shall put the halter on the one that comes arter him, whoever he may be."

"Must I—pin—in—ion the man this morning, father?" inquired the lad, the workings of whose countenance were now absolutely terrific.

"Must you? Of course you must," answered Smithers. "Why, what the devil are you snivelling at now? I'd wager a crown to a brass farthin' that there's many a young nobleman who'd give fifty pounds to be able to do it. Look how they hire the winders opposite Newgate! Lord bless their souls, it does me good to think that the aristocracy and gentry patronises hanging as well as the other fine arts. What would become of the executioners if they didn't? Why—the legislature would abolish capital punishment at once."

Gibbet clasped his hands together, and raised his eyes in an imploring manner, as much as to say, "Oh! how I wish they would!"

Fortunately for him, his father did not perceive this expression of emotion, for the executioner had approached the candle to the model-gallows, and was now busily occupied in arranging the figure for his son's practice.

"I'll tell you who are the patrons of my business—profession, I mean," continued the executioner; "and if you had a grain of feeling for your father, you'd go down on your knees night and morning and pray for them. The old Tories and the Clergy are my friends; and, thank God! I'm a stanch Tory, too. I hate changes. What have changes done? Why swept away the good old laws that used to hang a man for stealing anything above forty shillings. Ah! George the Third was the best king we ever had! He used to tuck 'em up—three, four, five, six—aye, seven at once! Folks may well talk of the good old times—when an executioner could make his twenty or thirty guineas of a morning! I'd sooner take two guineas for each man under such an excellent system, than have the ten pounds as I do now."

While Smithers was thus talking, he had lowered the figure until it stood upon the drop. He then took off the halter; but the puppet still retained its upright position, because it was well stiffened and had heavy plates of lead fastened to the soles of its feet.

"Now what a cry the rascally radical Sunday papers make against the people they call the *saints*," continued Smithers, as he unfastened the cord which pinioned the arms of the puppet; "and yet those very *saints* are the ones that are most in favour of punishment of death. For my part, I adore the *saints*—I do. When Fitzmorris Shelley brought forward his measure to do away with capital penalty, didn't Dinglis and Cherrytree and all those pious men make a stand against him? And don't they know what's right and proper? Of course they do! Ah! I never read so much of House of Commons' business before, as I did then:—but I was in a precious fright, it's true. I thought of calling a public meeting of all the executioners in the kingdom to petition Parliament against the measure; but I didn't do it—because the House of Commons might have thought that we was interested."

Smithers paused for a moment, and contemplated the puppet and the model-gallows with great admiration. He had fashioned the one and built the latter himself; and he was not a little proud of his handiwork.

"Now, come, Gibbet," he at length exclaimed; "it's all ready. Do you hear me, you infernal hump-back?"

"And if I am a hump-back, father," returned the lad, bursting into tears, "you know———"

"What?" cried the executioner his countenance assuming an expression truly ferocious.

"You know that it isn't my fault," added the unfortunate youth, shrinking from the glance of his savage parent.

"None of this nonsense, Gibbet," said the man, a little softened by the reminiscence that he himself had made his son the object of the very reproach levelled against his personal deformity. "Come and try your hand at this work for a few minutes before breakfast; and then we'll go down yonder together."

Gibbet approached the model-gallows; but his countenance still denoted the most profoundly-rooted disgust and abhorrence.

"Let's suppose that the culprit is as yet in his own cell, Gibbet," continued the executioner. "Well, it's time to pinion him, we'll say; there's the sheriffs standing there—and here's the chaplain. Now, you go for'ard and begin."

Gibbet took the whip-cord which his father handed to him.

"That's right. Now you won't bounce up to the poor devil just like a wild elephant: remember that he's more or less in an interesting situation—as the ladies say. You'll rather glide behind him, and insinuate the cord between his arms, whispering at the same time, '*Beg pardon*.' Mind and don't forget that; because we're under an obligation to him to some extent, as he's the means of putting money in our pocket, and we get the reversion of his clothes."

Here Gibbet cast a hasty but terrified glance towards his father's attire.

"Ah! I know what you're looking at, youngster," said Smithers, with a coarse laugh; "you want to see if I've got on my usual toggery? To be sure I have. I wear it as a compliment to the gentleman that we're to operate on this morning. This coat was the one that Pegsworth cut his last fling in: this waistcoat was Greenacre's; and these breeches was William Lees's. But go on—we mustn't waste time in this way."

Gibbet approached the puppet, and endeavoured to manipulate the string as his father instructed him; but his hand trembled so convulsively that he could not even pass it between the arms of the figure.

While he was still fumbling with the cord, and vainly endeavouring to master his emotions, the leathern thong descended with tremendous violence upon his back.

An appalling cry burst from the poor lad; but the executioner only showered down curses on his head.

At length Gibbet contrived, through fear of another blow, to pinion the figure in a manner satisfactory to his brutal parent.

"There!" exclaimed Smithers; "I shall make something of you at last. What virtue there must be in an old bit of leather: it seems to put the right spirit into *you*, at all events. Well, that's all you shall do this morning down at Newgate; and mind and do it as if the thong was hanging over your head—or it will be all the worse for you when we get home. Try and keep up the credit of your father's name, and show the Sheriffs and the Chaplain how you can truss their pigeon for them. They always take great notice—they do. Last time there was an execution, the Chaplain says to me, says he, '*Smithers, I don't think you had your hand nicely in this morning?*'—'*Don't you, sir?*' says I.—'*No,*' says he; '*I've seen you do it more genteel than that.*'—'*Well, sir,*' says I, '*I'll do my best to please you next time.*'—'*Ah! do, there's a good fellow, Smithers,*' says the Chaplain; and off he goes to breakfast with the Sheriffs and governor, a-smacking his lips at the idea of the cold fowl and ham that he meant to pitch into. But I only mention that anecdote, to show you how close the authorities take notice—that's all. So mind and do your best, boy."

"Yes, father," returned Gibbet.

"So now we've done the pinioning," continued Smithers, once more busying himself with the puppet, which he surveyed with an admiration almost amounting to a kind of love. "Well, we can suppose that our chap has marched from the cell, and has just got on the scaffold. So far, so good. We can't do better than polish him off decently now that he *is* here," proceeded Smithers, alluding to the figure, and rather musing aloud than addressing himself to his son. "Now all we've got to do is to imagine that the bell's a-ringing:—there stands the parson, reading the funeral service. Here I am. I take the halter that's already tied nicely round the poor devil's neck—I fix the loop on this hook that hangs down from the beam of the gibbet—then I leave the scaffold—I go underneath—I pull the bolt—and down he falls so!"

"O God!" cried Gibbet, literally writhing with mental agony, as the drop fell with a crashing sound, and the jerking noise of the halter met his ear a moment afterwards.

"Now, then, coward!" exclaimed the executioner; and again the leathern thong elicited horrible screams from the hump-back.

The lad was still crying, and his father was in the midst of sundry fearful anathemas, levelled against what he called his son's cowardice, when a knock was heard at the door of the loft.

"Come in!" shouted the executioner.

The invitation was obeyed; and an elderly man, dressed in a shabby suit of black, entered the room with an affected solemnity of gait.

CHAPTER CXLIII.

MORBID FEELINGS.—KATHERINE.

"Holloa, Banks!" exclaimed the executioner. "Got scent of the morning's work—eh, old feller?"

"Alas! my dear Mr. Smithers," returned the undertaker, shaking his head in a lachrymose manner, "if men will perpetrate such enormities, they must expect to go to their last home by means of a dance upon nothing."

And, according to a custom which years had rendered a part of Mr. Banks's nature, he wiped his eyes with a dingy white pocket-handkerchief.

"There he is again, the old fool!" ejaculated Smithers, with a coarse guffaw; "always a-whimpering! Why, you don't mean to say, Banks, that you care two straws about the feller that's going to be tucked up this morning?"

"Ah! Smithers, you don't know my heart: I weeps for frail human natur', and not only for the unhappy being that's so soon to be a blessed defunct carkiss. But, Smithers—my boy——"

"Well?" cried the executioner.

"How much is it to be this time for the rope?" asked Mr. Banks, in a tremulous tone and with another solemn shake of the head.

"Five shillings—not a mag under," was the prompt reply.

"That's too much, Mr. Smithers—too much," observed the undertaker of Globe Lane. "The last one I bought I lost by: times is changed, Mr. Smithers—sadly changed."

"Ain't the *morbid feelings*, as the press calls 'em, as powerful as ever?" demanded the executioner savagely.

"The morbid feelings, thank God, is right as a trivet," answered Banks; "but it's the blunt that falls off, Smithers—the blunt! And what's the use of the morbid feelings if there's no blunt to gratify 'em?"

"Do you mean to tell me, Mr. Banks," cried the executioner, "that you can't get as ready a sale for the halters as you used to do?"

"I'm afraid that such is the actiwal case, my dear friend," responded Mr. Banks, turning up his eyes in a melancholy manner. "The last blessed wictim that you operated on, Mr. Smithers, you remember, I gived you five shillings for the rope; and I will say, in justice to him as spun it and them as bought it, that a nicer, stronger, or compacter bit of cord never supported carkiss to cross-beam. But wain was it that I coiled it neat up in my winder;—wain was it that I wrote on a half sheet of foolscap, '*This is the halter that hung poor William Lees*;'—the morbid feelings was strong, 'cos the crowd collected opposite my house; but the filthy lucre, Smithers, was wanting. Well—there the damned—I beg its pardon—the blessed cord stayed for a matter of three weeks; and I do believe it never would have gone at all, if some swell that was passing quite promiscuously one day didn't take a fancy to it——"

"Well, and what did he give you?" demanded the executioner impatiently.

"Only twelve shillings, as true as I'm a woful sinner that hopes to be saved!" answered the undertaker.

"Twelve shillings—eh? And how much would you have had for the rope?"

"When the blunt doesn't fall short of the morbid feelings, I calkilates upon a guinea," answered Mr. Banks.

"Why, you old rogue," shouted the executioner, "you know that you sold William Lees's rope a dozen times over. The moment the real one was disposed of, you shoved a counterfeit into your winder; and that went off so well, that you kept on till you'd sold a dozen."

"No, Smithers—never no such luck as that since Greenacre's business," said the undertaker, with a solemn shake of his head; "and then I believe I really did sell nineteen ropes in less than a week."

"I only wonder people is such fools as to be gulled so," observed Smithers.

"What can they say, when they see your certifikit that the rope's the true one?" demanded Banks. "There was one old gen'leman that dealt with me for a many—many years; and he bought the rope of every blessed defunct that had danced on nothing at Newgate for upwards of twenty year! I quite entered into his feeling, I did—I admired that man; and so I always sold him the real ropes. But time's passing, while I'm chattering here. Come, my dear Smithers—shall we say three shillings for the rope and certifikit this morning?"

"Not a mag less than five," was the dogged answer.

"Four, my dear friend Smithers?" said the undertaker, with a whining, coaxing tone and manner.

"No—five, I tell you."

"Well—five then," said Banks. "I'll be there at a few minits 'afore nine: I s'pose you'll cut the carkiss down at the usual hour?"

"Yes—yes," answered Smithers. "I'm always punctiwal with the dead as well as the living."

The undertaker muttered something about "blessed defuncts," smoothed down the limp ends of his dirty cravat, and slowly withdrew, shaking his head more solemnly than ever.

"See what it is to be a Public Executioner!" cried Smithers, turning with an air of triumph towards his son: "look at the perk-visits—look at the priweleges! And yet you go snivelling about like a young gal, 'cos I want to make you fit to succeed me in my honourable profession."

"O father!" cried the lad, unable to restrain his feelings any longer: "instead of being respected, we are abhorred—instead of being honoured, our very touch is contamination! You yourself know, dear father, that you scarcely or never go abroad; if you enter the public-house tap-room, even in a neighbourhood so low as this, the people get up and walk away on different excuses. When I step out for an errand, the boys in the streets point at me; and those who are well-behaved, pass me with stealthy looks of horror and dread. Even that canting hypocrite who has just left us—even *he* never crosses your threshold except when his interest is concerned;—and yet he, they say, is connected with body-snatchers, and does not bear an over-excellent character in his neighbourhood. Yet such a sneaking old wretch as that approaches our door with loathing—Oh! I know that he does! You see, father—dear father, that it is a horrible employment; then pray don't make me embrace it—Oh! don't—pray don't, father—dear father: say you won't—and I'll do any thing else you tell me! I'll pick up rags and bones from the gutters—I'll sweep chimneys—I'll break stones from dawn to darkness;—but do not—do not make me an executioner!"

Smithers was so astounded at this appeal that he had allowed it to proceed without interruption. He was accustomed to be addressed on the subject, but never to such a length, nor with such arguments; so that the manner and matter of that prayer produced a strange impression on the man who constantly sought, by means of rude sophistries, to veil from himself and his family the true estimation in which his calling was held.

Gibbet, mistaking his father's astonishment for a more favourable impression, threw himself at his feet, clasped his hands, and exclaimed, "Oh! do not turn a deaf ear to my prayer! And think not, dear father, that I confound *you* with that pursuit which I abhor;—think not that I see other in you than my parent—a parent whom———"

"Whom you shall obey!" cried the executioner, now recovering the use of his tongue: "or, by God!" he added, pointing with terrible ferocity towards the model-gallows, "I'll serve you as I did that puppet just now—and as I shall do the man down in the Old Bailey presently."

Gibbet rose—disappointed, dispirited, and with a heart agitated by the most painful emotions.

But why had not Smithers recourse to the leathern weapon as usual? why had he spared the poor hump-back on this occasion?

Gibbet himself marvelled that such forbearance should have been shown towards him, since he now comprehended but too well that his father was inexorable in his determination with regard to him.

The truth was that Smithers was so far struck by his son's appeal as to deem it of more serious import than any previously manifested aversion to his horrible calling; and he accordingly met it with a menace which he deemed to be more efficacious than the old discipline of the thong.

"Now, mind me," said the executioner, after a few moments' pause, "you needn't try any more of these snivelling antics: they won't succeed with me, I tell you before-hand. If you don't do as I order you, I'll hang you up to that beam as soon as yonder mouse in the noose on the mantel. So let one word be enough. Hark! there's seven o'clock: we've only just time to get a mouthful before we must be off."

Smithers proceeded down stairs, followed by Gibbet.

They entered a little parlour, where Katherine was preparing breakfast.

It being still dark, a candle stood on the table; and its light was reflected in the polished metal tea-pot, milk-jug, and sugar-basin. The table napkin was of dazzling whiteness: the knives and forks were bright as steel could be;—in a word, an air of exquisite neatness and cleanliness pervaded the board on which the morning's repast was spread.

Nor was this appearance confined to the table. The little room itself was a model of domestic propriety. Not a speck of dust was to be seen on the simple furniture, which was also disposed with taste: the windows were set off with a clean muslin curtain; and the mantel was covered with fancy ornaments all indicative of female industry.

Then Kate herself!—her appearance was in perfect keeping with that of the room which owed its cleanliness and air of simple comfort to her. A neat cap set off her chesnut hair, which was arranged in plain bands: her dark stuff gown was made high in the body and long in the skirt, but did not conceal the gracefulness of her slender form, nor altogether prevent a little foot in a neat shoe and a well-turned ankle in a lily-white cotton stocking from occasionally revealing themselves. Then her hands were so slightly brown, her fingers so taper, and her nails so carefully kept, that no one, to look at them, would conceive how much hard work Katherine was compelled to do.

Though so rigidly neat and clean, Kate had nothing of the coquette about her. She was as bashful and artless as a child; and, besides—whom had she, the executioner's acknowledged niece, to captivate?

Although she endeavoured to greet Smithers and the hump-back with a smile, a profound melancholy in reality oppressed her.

It was one of those mornings when her uncle was to exercise his horrible calling:—this circumstance would alone have deeply affected her spirits, which were never too light nor buoyant. But on the present occasion, another cause of sorrow weighed on her soul—and that was the knowledge that her wretched cousin was that morning to enter on his fearful noviciate!

She entertained a boundless compassion for that unfortunate being. His physical deformities, and the treatment which he experienced from his father, called forth the kindest sympathies of her naturally tender heart. Moreover, he had received instruction and was in the habit of seeking consolation from her: she was the only friend of that suffering creature who was persecuted alike by nature and by man; and she perhaps felt the more acutely on his account, because she was so utterly powerless in protecting him from the parental ferocity which drove him to her for comfort.

She knew that a good—a generous—a kind—and a deeply sensitive soul was enclosed within that revolting form; and she experienced acute anguish when a brutal hand could wantonly torture so susceptible a spirit.

And to that wounded, smarting spirit she herself was all kindness—all softness—all conciliation—all encouragement.

No wonder, then, if the miserable son of the public executioner was devoted to her: no wonder if she were a goddess of light, and hope, and consolation, and bliss to him! To do her the slightest service was a source of the purest joy which that poor being could know: to be able to convince her by a deed,—even so slight as picking up her thread when it fell, or placing her chair for her in its wonted situation,—this, this was sublime happiness to the hump-back!

He could sit for hours near her, without uttering a word—but watching her like a faithful dog. And when her musical voice, fraught with some expression of kindness, fell upon his ear, how that hideous countenance would brighten up—how those coarse lips would form a smile—how those large dull orbs would glow with ineffable bliss!

But when his father was unkind to her,—unkind to Katherine, his only friend,—unkind to the sole being that ever had looked not only without abhorrence, but with unadulterated gentleness on him,—then a new spirit seemed to animate him; and the faithful creature, who received his own stripes with spaniel-like irresistance, burst forth in indignant remonstrance when a blow was levelled at her. Then his rage grew terrible; and the resigned, docile, retiring hump-back became transformed into a perfect demon.

How offensive to the delicate admirer of a maudlin romance, in which only handsome boys and pretty girls are supposed to be capable of playing at the game of Love, must be the statement which we are now about to make. But the reader who truly knows the world,—not the world of the sentimental novel, but the world as it really is,—will not start when we inform him that this being whom nature had formed in her most uncouth mould,—this creature whose deformities seemed to render him a connecting link between man and monkey,—this living thing that appeared to be but one remove above a monster, cherished a profound love for that young girl whom he esteemed as his guardian angel.

But this passion was unsuspected by her, as its nature was unknown to himself. Of course it was not reciprocated:—how could it be? Nevertheless, every proof of friendship—every testimonial of kind feeling—every evidence of compassion on her part, only tended to augment that attachment which the hump-back experienced for Katherine.

"Well, Kate," said the executioner, as he took his seat at the breakfast-table, "I've drilled Gibbet into the art of pinioning at last."

The girl made no answer; but she cast a rapid glance at the hump-back, and two tears trickled down her cheeks.

"Come, Gibbet," added Smithers; "we've no time to lose. Don't be afraid of your bread-and-butter: you'll get nothing to eat till you come home again to dinner."

"Is John going with you this morning, uncle?" inquired Katherine timidly.

"Why, you know he is. You only ask the question to get up a discussion once more about it, as you did last night."

This was more or less true: the generous-hearted girl hoped yet to be able to avert her uncle from his intention in respect to the hump-back.

"But I won't hear any more about it," continued the executioner, as he ate his breakfast. "And, then, why do you call him John?"

"Did you not give him that name at his baptism?" said Kate.

"And if I did, I've also the right to change it," returned the executioner; "and I choose him to be called *Gibbet*. It's more professional."

"I think the grocer in High Street wants an errand boy, uncle," observed Katherine, with her eyes fixed upon her cup—she dared not raise them to Smithers' face as she spoke: "perhaps he would take John—I mean my cousin—and that would be better than making him follow a calling which he does not fancy."

"Mind your own business, Miss Imperence!" ejaculated the executioner; "and let me mind mine. Now, then—who knocks at the front door?"

Gibbet rose and hastened from the room.

In a few moments he returned, holding in his hand a paper, which he gave to his father.

"Ah! I thought so," said Smithers, as he glanced his eye over the paper: "my friend Dognatch is always in time. Here's the *last dying speech, confession, and a true account of the execution* of the man that I'm to tuck up presently—all cut and dry, you see. Well—it's very kind of Dognatch always to send me a copy: but I suppose he thinks it's a compliment due to my sitiwation."

With these words Smithers tossed off his tea, rose, and exclaimed, "Now, Gibbet, my boy, we must be off."

"Father, I don't feel equal to it," murmured the hump-back, who seemed fixed to his chair.

"Come—without another word!" cried the executioner, in so terrible a tone that Gibbet started from his seat as if suddenly moved by electricity.

"Uncle—uncle, you will not—you cannot force this poor lad—" began Katherine, venturing upon a last appeal in favour of the hump-back.

"Kate," said the executioner, turning abruptly upon her, while his countenance wore so ferocious an expression of mingled determination and rage, that the young girl uttered an ejaculation of alarm,—"Kate, do not provoke me; or——"

He said no more, but darted on her a look of such dark, diabolical menace, that she sank back, annihilated as it were, into her seat.

She covered her face with her hands, and burst into an agony of tears.

For some moments she remained absorbed in profound grief: the fate of the wretched hump-back, and the idea that she herself was doomed to exist beneath the same roof with the horrible man whom she called her uncle, were causes of bitter anguish to her tender and sensitive soul.

When she raised her head, and glanced timidly around, she found herself alone.

CHAPTER CXLIV.

THE UNFINISHED LETTER.

The dawn was now breaking; and Katherine extinguished the candle.

How gloomily does the young day announce itself to the dwellers in the narrow streets and obscure alleys of the poor districts of the metropolis! The struggling gleam appears to contend with difficulty against the dense atmosphere and noxious vapours which prevail in those regions even in the midst of winter; and as each fitful ray steals through the dingy panes, its light seems leaden and dull, not golden and roseate as that of the orb of day.

Kate wiped away her tears, and set to work to clear the table of the breakfast-things.

Having performed this duty, she slipped on her neat straw bonnet and warm shawl,—purchased by the produce of her own industry,—and repaired to market.

But, alas! poor girl—as she passed rapidly through the streets, she could not help noticing the people, that were lounging at their doors, nudge each other, as much as to say, "There goes the executioner's niece."

And no friendly voice welcomed her with a kind "Good morning:" no human being had a passing compliment,—not even one of those civil phrases which cost nothing to utter, mean perhaps as little, but still are pleasing to hear,—to waste upon the executioner's niece.

Some old women, more hard-hearted than the rest, exclaimed, as she hurried timidly by the spot where they were gossiping, "Ah! her uncle has got business on his hands this morning!"

And when the poor girl reached the shop whither she was going, her eyes were bathed in tears.

The shopkeeper was cool and indifferent in his manner towards her—not obsequious and ready as towards his other customers. He even examined with suspicion the coin which she tendered him in payment for her purchases—as if it were impossible that honesty could dwell in the heart of an executioner's niece!

The ill-conditioned fellow! He saw not the mild blue eyes, with a tear glittering in each like twin-drops of the diamond-dew;—he marked not the pretty lips, apart, and expressive of such profound melancholy;—he observed not the thick folds of the shawl across the gently-budding bosom rise and sink rapidly:—no,—he beheld not that interesting young creature's grief; but he treated her rudely and harshly, because she was the executioner's niece!

Kate retraced her steps homewards. She saw other girls of her own age nod familiarly to their acquaintances at the windows, as they passed;—but she had no friend to receive or return her smile of recognition!

Shrinking within herself, as it were, from the slightest contact with the world which despised her, the poor young creature felt herself an interloper upon the very pavement, and even stepped into the muddy street to make way for those who passed.

With a broken spirit she returned home, her fate weighing upon her soul like a crime!

And so it was with her always on those mornings when her uncle was called upon to exercise his fearful functions.

She was glad to bury herself once more in that dwelling the threshold of which a friendly step so seldom crossed: her little parlour, embellished with her own hands, appeared a paradise of peace after the contumely which she experienced in the bustling streets.

She had returned home in so depressed a state of mind that she had forgotten to close the front door behind her.

She opened her work-box, seated herself at the table, and commenced her toil of pleasure—for that young girl loved her needle, and abhorred idleness.

She then fell into a reverie as she worked.

"To be a hangman is something horrible indeed," she mused aloud; "but to be a member of a hangman's family is far worse. *He* knows that he merits what reproach is levelled against him, if indeed his office deserve reproach at all; but *I*, who abhor the bare idea, and never so much as witnessed an execution—why should shame and obloquy redound upon *me*? It is like suffering for a crime of which one is innocent! O God, is this human justice? What have I done that the vilest and lowest should despise me? Am I not flesh and blood like them? do my clothes carry pollution, that the ragged beggar draws her tatters close to her as she passes me? Oh! give me strength, heaven, to support my wretched fate; for there are moments when I despair!"

"You are wrong to mistrust the goodness of the Almighty," said a mild voice close behind her chair.

Kate started, and looked round.

It was the rector of St. David's who had entered he room, unperceived by the young maiden.

"Pardon me, reverend sir," answered Kate; "I know that I am often forgetful of the wholesome lessons which I have received from your lips; but——"

"Well, well, poor child," interrupted Reginald Tracy, to whose cheeks the phrase "*wholesome lessons*" brought a flush of crimson—for he remembered how he himself had deviated from the doctrines which he had long successfully and sincerely taught: "be consoled! I know how sad must be our lot; and I have called this morning to see if I cannot ameliorate it."

"What? better my condition, sir?" exclaimed Katherine. "Oh! how is that possible?"

"We will see," answered the rector, taking a chair near the young maiden. "You are not altogether so friendless as you imagine."

"I am aware, sir, that through your goodness I received an education at the school which your bounty founded; and your excellent housekeeper, Mrs. Kenrick, has furnished me with needle-work. Oh! sir, I am not ignorant how much I owe to you both!"

Kate raised her mild blue eyes towards the rector's countenance; but her glance drooped again instantaneously, for his looks were fixed upon her in a manner which she had never noticed in him before, and which excited a momentary feeling of embarrassment—almost of alarm—in her mind.

But that feeling passed away as rapidly as it had arisen; and she blushed to think that she should have experienced such a sentiment in the presence of so holy a man and so great a benefactor.

"I did not wish to remind you of any trifling services which myself or my housekeeper may have rendered you, Katherine," said Reginald. "I alluded to another friend who interests himself in you."

"Another friend!" ejaculated the young girl. "Is it possible that I have *another friend* in the whole world?"

"You have," replied Mr. Tracy. "Did not a gentleman, accompanied by a police-officer, visit this house about a fortnight ago?"

"Yes—I remember—late one night——"

And she stopped short, being unwilling to allude to that instance of her uncle's cruelty which had led to the visit mentioned by the rector.

"Well, that gentleman feels interested in you," continued Reginald. "He saw how you were treated—he knows that you are unhappy."

"And do strangers thus interest themselves in the wretched?" asked Katherine, her eyes swimming in tears.

"Not often," replied the rector. "But this gentleman is one of the few noble exceptions to the general rule."

"He must be indeed!" exclaimed Katherine, with an enthusiasm which was almost pious.

"That gentleman learnt from the policeman enough to give him a favourable impression of your character, and to render him desirous of serving you. He pondered upon the matter for some days, but could come to no determination on the subject. He heard that you were anxious to leave this house and earn your own bread."

"Oh! yes—how willingly would I do so!" exclaimed Katherine fervently. "But———"

"But what?" demanded Reginald, in whose eyes the young maiden had never been an object of peculiar interest until at present;—and *now* he observed, for the first time, that her personal appearance was far—very far from disagreeable.

The truth was, that, since his fall, he had viewed every woman with different eyes from those through which he had before surveyed the female sex. When he himself was chaste and pure, he observed only the feminine mind and manner:—now his glances studied and discriminated between external attractions. His moral survey had become a sensual one.

"But what?" he said, when Katherine hesitated. "Do you object to leave your uncle?"

"I should be a hypocrite were I to say that I object to leave him," was the immediate answer. "Nevertheless, if he demanded my services, I would remain with him, through gratitude for the bread which he gave me, and the asylum which he afforded me, when I was a child and unable to earn either. But he would not seek to retain me, I know; for he does not—he cannot love me! Still, there is one poor creature in this house———"

"My housekeeper has told me of him. You mean your uncle's son?" said Reginald.

"I do, sir. He has no friend in the world but me; and, though my intercessions do not save him from much bad treatment, still I have studied to console him."

"If he be grateful, he will feel pleased to think that you may be removed to a happier situation," said the rector.

"True!" exclaimed Kate. "And if I only earned more money than I do here, I should be able to provide him with a great many little comforts."

"Assuredly," replied the fashionable preacher, who during this colloquy had gradually drawn his chair closer to that of the young maiden. "The gentleman, to whom I have before alluded, called upon me yesterday. It appears he learnt from the policeman that you had been educated at the school in my district, and that my housekeeper was well acquainted with you. He nobly offered to contribute a sum of money towards settling you in some comfortable manner."

"The generous stranger!" exclaimed Kate. "What is his name, sir—that I may pray for him?"

"Mr. Markham———"

"Markham!" cried the young girl, strangely excited by the mention of that name.

"Yes. Have you ever heard of him before?" asked the rector, surprised at the impression thus produced.

Katherine appeared to reflect profoundly for some moments; then, opening a secret drawer of her work-box, she drew forth a small satin bag, carefully sewed all round.

She took her scissors and unpicked the thread from one end of the bag.

The rector watched her attentively, and with as much surprise as interest.

Having thus opened one extremity of the bag, she inserted her delicate fingers, and produced a sheet of letter-paper, folded, and dingy with age.

Handing it to the rector, she observed, with tears streaming down her cheeks, "These were the last words my mother ever wrote; and she had lost the use of her speech ere she penned them."

Reginald Tracy unfolded the letter, and read as follows:———

"Should my own gloomy presages prove true, and the warning of my medical attendant be well founded,—if, in a word, the hand of Death be already extended to snatch me away thus in the prime of life, while my darling child is * * * * and inform Mr. Markham, whose abode is———"

The words that originally stood in the place which we have marked with asterisks, had evidently been blotted out by the tears of the writer.

Reginald folded the letter as he had received it, and returned it to Katherine.

The young girl immediately replaced it in the little bag, which she sewed up with scrupulous care.

It was the poor creature's sole treasure; and she prized it as the last and only memento that she possessed of her mother.

"And you know not to whom that unfinished letter alluded?" said the rector, after a long pause, during which the bag, with its precious contents, had been consigned once more to the secret drawer in the work-box.

"I have not the least idea," answered Kate, drying her tears. "I was only four years old when my mother died, and of course could take no steps to inquire after the Mr. Markham mentioned in the letter. My uncle has often assured me that he took some trouble in the matter, but without success. Markham, you know, sir, is by no means an uncommon name."

"And your father, Katherine—do you remember him?"

"Oh! no, sir—he died before my mother. When I was old enough to comprehend how dreadful it is to be an orphan, Mr. Tracy, I made that little satin bag to preserve the letter which Death would not allow my poor mother to finish."

And again the young maiden wept bitterly.

The rector was deeply affected; and for some minutes his sensual ideas concerning the damsel were absorbed in a more generous sympathy.

"But did not the medical man who attended your mother in her last moments, and who is also alluded to in the letter," asked Reginald,—"did he not afford some clue to unravel the mystery?"

"That question I have asked my uncle more than once," answered Kate; "and he has assured me that the medical man was a perfect stranger who was casually summoned to attend upon my poor mother only the very day before she breathed her last. Since then the medical man has also died."

"Your mother was your uncle's own sister, was she not?" asked the rector.

"She was, sir."

"And she married a person named Wilmot?"

"Yes—for my name is Katherine Wilmot."

"I remember that you were so entered upon the school-books," said the rector. "Your mother must have been a superior woman, for the language of that fragment of a letter is accurate, and the handwriting is good."

"The same thought has often struck me, sir," observed Katherine. "And now how strange it is that a person bearing the name of Markham should interest himself in my behalf!"

"Strange indeed!" exclaimed Reginald, whose eyes were once more fixed upon the interesting girl near him,—fixed, too, with an ardent glance, and not one of tender sympathy. "Mr. Richard Markham—the gentleman of whom I speak—called upon me, as I ere now stated, and besought me to exert myself in your behalf. He seems to think that my position and character enable me to do for you that which, coming from him, might awaken the tongue of scandal. The cause of my visit this morning is now at length explained."

"I am very grateful, sir, for Mr. Markham's good intentions and your kindness," said Katherine. "The coincidence in names, which led me to show you that letter, seems a providential suggestion to me to follow the counsel of such generous—such disinterested friends."

"I thought as I came along," resumed the clergyman, "that I would procure you a situation with some friends of mine in the country. But—" and he cast upon her a burning look brimful of licentiousness—"I have my doubts whether it would not be better for you to come to my house and assist Mrs. Kenrick in her domestic duties—especially as she is getting very old—and——"

He paused for a moment:—he hesitated, because at the back of the offer there was an unworthy motive at which his guilty soul quaked, lest it should betray itself.

But that pure-minded and artless girl only saw in that offer a noble act of kindness; and she frankly accepted it—upon the condition that her uncle approved of her conduct in doing so.

The rector rose—he had no farther excuse for protracting his visit.

The young girl thanked him for his goodness with the most heart-felt sincerity.

He then took his leave.

CHAPTER CXLV.

HYPOCRISY.

Reginald Tracy proceeded from the dwelling of the hangman to the corner of Tottenham Court Road, where his carriage was waiting for him.

He stepped into the vehicle, and ordered the coachman to drive him to Markham Place near Lower Holloway.

Richard was not at home: he had gone for a short walk with Mr. Monroe, who was yet too feeble to move far without the support of a companion's arm. They were, however, expected to return in a short time;—besides, Miss Monroe was in the drawing-room; and the rector therefore decided upon walking in and waiting for Mr. Markham.

The name of Miss Monroe produced a powerful sensation in the breast of that man whose passions until lately dormant from his birth, now raged so furiously. He had seen her in a voluptuous *negligee*, attending by the sick-bed of her father;—he had heard her utter words of strange self-accusing import, in connection with that parent's illness;—and his curiosity, as well as his desires, was kindled.

He had been fascinated by that charming girl; and our readers will remember *that he had felt himself capable of making any sacrifice to obtain her love*!

His mind, too, entertained a distant suspicion—a very distant one, but still a suspicion—that she had strayed from the path of virtue;—for of what else could a daughter, whom he had seen hanging like a ministering angel over her father's couch, accuse herself?

This suspicion—and, at all events, that mystery which hung around the accusation alluded to, served to inflame the imagination of a man who now sought to place no bridle upon his passions. The idea suggested itself to him, that if another had revelled in her charms, why should not he? In a word, his heart glowed with secret delight when he learnt from Whittingham that Miss Monroe was alone in the drawing-room.

On his entrance, Ellen rose from the sofa, and welcomed him with a cordiality which originated in a sense of gratitude for the spiritual comfort he had rendered her father during his illness.

At a glance his eyes scanned the fair form of Ellen from head to foot; and his imagination was instantly fired with the thoughts of her soft and swelling charms—those graceful undulations which were all her own, and needed no artificial aids to improve the originals of nature!

"I am pleased to learn from the servant that your father, Miss Monroe, is able to take a little exercise once more," said the rector.

"Oh! all danger is now past," exclaimed Ellen cheerfully. "But at one time, Mr. Tracy, I had made up my mind to lose him."

"I saw how much you were afflicted," observed the rector; "and I was grieved to hear you reproach yourself to some extent——"

"Reproach myself!" interrupted Ellen, blushing deeply. "You heard me reproach myself?"

"I did," answered the rector. "And now, forgive me, if—by virtue of my sacred calling—I make bold to remind you that Providence frequently tries us, through the medium of afflictions visited upon those whom we love, in order to punish us for our neglectfulness, our unkindness, or our errors, towards those so afflicted. Pardon me, Miss Monroe, for thus addressing you; but I should be unfaithful towards Him whom I serve, did I not avail myself of every opportunity to explain the lessons which his wise and just dispensations convey."

"Mr. Tracy," exclaimed Ellen, cruelly embarrassed by this language, "do you really believe that Providence punished my father for some misconduct on my part?"

"Judging by the reproach—the accusation which your lips uttered against yourself—perhaps in an unguarded moment—when you ministered with angelic tenderness at your father's sick-bed———"

"Sir—Mr. Tracy, this is too much!" cried Ellen, tears starting from her eyes, while her cheeks were suffused with blushes: "it is unmanly—it is ungenerous to take advantage of any expressions which might have been wrung from me in a moment of acute anguish."

"Pardon me, young lady," said the rector with apparent meekness: "heaven knows the purity of my intentions in thus addressing you. It is not always that my spiritual aid is thus rejected—that my motives are thus cruelly suspected."

"Forgive me, sir,—I was wrong to excite myself at words which were meant in kindness," said Ellen, completely deceived by this consummate hypocrisy.

"Miss Monroe," continued Reginald, "believe me when I assure you that I feel deep compassion—deep interest, wherever I perceive grief—especially when that sorrow is secret. And, if my eyes have not deceived me, methinks I have read in your young heart the existence of some such secret sorrow. My aim is to console you; for the consolation which I can offer is not human—it is divine! I am but the humble *instrument* of the supernal Goodness; but God imparts solace through even the least worthy of his ministers."

"I thank you sincerely for your friendly intentions towards me," said Ellen, now recovering her presence of mind; "but, since my father is restored to health, I have little to vex me."

"And yet that self-reproach, Miss Monroe," persisted the rector, determined not to abandon the point to which he had so dexterously conducted the conversation,—"that self-accusation which escaped your lips———"

"Is a family secret, Mr. Tracy, which may not be revealed," interrupted Ellen firmly.

"I ask you not for your confidence, Miss Monroe: think not that I seek to pry into your affairs with an impertinent curiosity———"

"Once more, sir, I thank you for the kindness which prompts you thus to address me; but—pray, let us change the conversation."

These words were uttered in so decided a tone, that Reginald dared not persist in his attempt to thrust himself into the young lady's confidence.

An awkward silence ensued; and the rector was thinking how he should break it, when the door opened.

Almost at the same moment, a female voice was heard outside the room, saying, in tender playfulness, "Come to mamma! come to mamma!"

Then, immediately afterwards, Marian entered the apartment, bearing an infant in her arms.

Whittingham had neglected to tell her that there was a visitor in the drawing-room.

Poor Marian, astounded at the presence of the rector, could neither advance nor retreat for some moments.

At length she turned abruptly away.

Ellen sank back upon the sofa, overcome with shame and grief.

The rector threw upon her a glance full of meaning; but she saw it not—for her own eyes were cast down.

This depression, however, lasted only for a moment. Suddenly raising her head, she exclaimed with that boldness and firm frankness which had been taught her by the various circumstances of the last few years of her life, "You now know my secret, sir: but you are a man of honour. I need say no more."

"Who has been base enough to leave this grievous wrong unrepaired?" asked Reginald, taking her hand—that soft, warm, delicate hand.

"Nay—seek to know no more," returned Ellen, withdrawing her hand hastily from what she however conceived to be only the pressure of a friendly or fraternal interest; "you have learnt too much already. For God's sake, let not my father know that you have discovered his daughter's shame!"

"Not for worlds would I do aught to cause you pain!" cried the rector, enthusiastically.

"Thank you—thank you," murmured Ellen, completely deceived in respect to the cause of Tracy's warmth, and mistaking for friendly interest an ebullition of feeling which was in reality gross and sensual.

With these words Ellen hurried from the room.

"I have discovered her secret!" said the rector triumphantly to himself, as he rose and paced the apartment, mad passions raging in his breast; "and that discovery shall make her mine. Oh! no sacrifice were too great to obtain possession of that charming creature! I would give the ten best years of my life to clasp her in my arms, in the revels of love! Happy—thrice happy should I be to feel that lovely form become supple and yielding in my embrace! But my brain burns—my heart beats—my eyes throb—my blood seems liquid fire!"

Reginald threw himself, exhausted by the indomitable violence of his passions, upon the sofa.

Scarcely had he time to compose himself, when Markham entered the room.

The rector communicated to him the particulars of his interview with Katherine Wilmot, and concluded by saying that, as the girl was known to his housekeeper, he had determined upon taking her into his service.

"With regard to the fragment of the letter," observed Richard, "allusion must have been made to some person of the name of Markham who is totally unconnected with our family. We have no relations of that name. I feel convinced that the mention of the name could not in any way refer to my father; and my brother and myself were children at the time when that letter must have been written."

"It is a coincidence—and that is all," observed the rector. "But as you have to some extent constituted yourself the benefactor of this young person, do you approve of the arrangement which I have made for her to enter my household?"

"My dear sir, how can I object?" exclaimed Richard, who, in the natural generosity of his heart, gave the rector credit for the most worthy motives. "I consider myself your debtor for your noble conduct in this instance. Under your roof, Mr. Tracy, the breath of calumny cannot reach that poor creature; and *there* no one will dare to make her family connexions a subject of reproach."

Some farther conversation took place between Reginald Tracy and Richard Markham upon this subject, and when the former rose to depart, they both observed, for the first time during their interview, that a violent shower of rain was pouring down.

Richard pressed the rector to remain to dinner—an invitation which he, whose head was filled with Ellen, did not hesitate to accept.

The rector's carriage and horses were accordingly housed in the stables attached to Markham Place; and Whittingham was desired to make Mr. Tracy's coachman and livery-servant as comfortable as possible—instructions with which the hospitable old butler did not fail to comply.

Dinner was served up at five o'clock; and Reginald had the felicity of sitting next to Miss Monroe.

The more he saw of this young lady, the more did he become enraptured with her,—not, however, experiencing a pure and chaste affection, but one whose ingredients were completely sensual.

The evening passed rapidly away;—the rain continued to pour in torrents.

As a matter of courtesy—indeed, of hospitality, for Richard's nature was generosity itself—the rector was pressed to stay the night at the Place; and, although he had a good close carriage to convey him home (and persons who have such equipages are seldom over careful of their servants), he accepted the invitation.

There was something so pleasing—so intoxicating in the idea of passing the night under the same roof with Ellen!

CHAPTER CXLVI.

THE BATH.—THE HOUSEKEEPER.

It was scarcely light when the rector of Saint David's rose from a couch where visions of a most voluptuous nature had filled his sleep.

Having hastily dressed himself, he descended from his room with the intention of seeking the fine frosty air of the garden to cool his heated brain.

But as he proceeded along a passage leading to the landing of the first flight of stairs, he heard a light step slowly descending the upper flight; and the next moment, the voice of Ellen speaking fondly to her child, fell upon his ear.

For nurses and mothers will talk to babes of even a few months old—although the innocents comprehend them not!

Reginald stepped into the recess formed by the door of one of the bed-chambers in that spacious mansion; and scarcely had he concealed himself there when he saw Ellen, with the child in her arms, pass across the landing at the end of the passage, and enter a room on the other side.

She wore a loose dressing-gown of snowy whiteness, which was confined by a band round her delicate waist, and was fastened up to the throat: her little feet had been hastily thrust into a pair of buff morocco slippers; and her long shining hair flowed over her shoulders and down her back.

The licentious eyes of the clergyman followed her from the foot of the stairs to the room which she entered; and even plunged with eager curiosity into that chamber during the moment that the door was open as she went in.

That glance enabled him to perceive that there was a bath in the apartment to which Ellen had proceeded with her child.

Indeed, the young lady, ever since her residence at Markham Place, had availed herself of the luxury of the bathing-room which that mansion possessed: and every morning she immersed her beautiful person in the refreshing element, which she enjoyed in its natural state in summer, but which was rendered slightly tepid for her in winter.

When the rector beheld her descend in that bewitching *negligee*,—her hair unconfined, and floating at will—her small, round, polished ankles glancing between the white drapery and the little slippers,—and the child, with merely a thick shawl thrown about it, in her arms,—and when he observed the bath in that chamber which she entered, he immediately comprehended her intention.

Without a moment's hesitation he stole softly from the recess where he had concealed himself, and approached the door of the bath-room.

His greedy eyes were applied to the key-hole; and his licentious glance plunged into the depths of that sacred privacy.

The unsuspecting Ellen was warbling cheerfully to her child.

She dipped her hand into the water, which Marian had prepared for her, and found the degree of heat agreeable to her wishes.

Then she placed the towels near the fire to warm.

Reginald watched her proceedings with the most ardent curiosity: the very luxury of the unhallowed enjoyment which he experienced caused an oppression at his chest; his heart beat quickly; his brain seemed to throb with violence.

The fires of gross sensuality raged madly in his breast.

Ellen's preparations were now completed.

With her charming white hand she put back her hair from her forehead.

Then, as she still retained the child on her left arm, with her right hand she loosened the strings which closed her dressing-gown round the neck and the band which confined it at the waist.

While thus occupied, she was partly turned towards the door; and all the treasures of her bosom were revealed to the ardent gaze of the rector.

His desires were now inflamed to that pitch when they almost become ungovernable. He felt that could he possess that charming creature, he would care not for the result—even though he forced her to compliance with his wishes, and murder and suicide followed,—the murder of her, and the suicide of himself!

He was about to grasp the handle of the door, when he remembered that he had heard the key turn in the lock immediately after she had entered the room.

He gnashed his teeth with rage.

And now the drapery had fallen from her shoulders, and the whole of her voluptuous form, naked to the waist, was exposed to his view.

He could have broken down the door, had he not feared to alarm the other inmates of the house.

He literally trembled under the influence of his fierce desires.

How he envied—Oh! how he envied the innocent babe which the fond mother pressed to that bosom—swelling, warm, and glowing!

And now she prepared to step into the bath: but, while he was waiting with fervent avidity for the moment when the whole of the drapery should fall from her form, a step suddenly resounded upon the stairs.

He started like a guilty wretch away from the door: and, perceiving that the footsteps descended the upper flight, he precipitated himself down the stairs.

Rushing across the hall, he sought the garden, where he wandered up and down, a thousand wild feelings agitating his breast.

He determined that Ellen should be his; but he was not collected enough to deliberate upon the means of accomplishing his resolution,—so busy was his imagination in conjuring up the most voluptuous idealities, which were all prompted by the real scene the contemplation whereof had been interrupted.

He fancied that he beheld the lovely young mother immersed in the bath—the water agitated by her polished limbs—each ripple kissing some charm, even as she herself kissed her babe!

Then he imagined he saw her step forth like a Venus from the ocean—her cheeks flushed with animation—her long glossy hair floating in rich undulations over her ivory shoulders.

"My God!" he exclaimed, at length, "I shall grow mad under the influence of this fascination! One kiss from her lips were worth ten thousand of the meretricious embraces which Cecilia yields so willingly. Oh! Ellen would not surrender herself without many prayers—much entreaty—and, perhaps, force;—but Cecilia falls into my arms without a struggle! Enjoyment with her is not increased by previous bashfulness;—she does not fire the soul by one moment of resistance. But Ellen—so coy, so difficult to win,—so full of confidence in herself, in spite of that one fault which accident betrayed to me,—Ellen, so young and inexperienced in the ways of passion,—Oh! she were a conquest worth every sacrifice that man could make!"

The rector's reverie was suddenly interrupted by the voice of Whittingham summoning him to the breakfast-room.

Thither he proceeded; and there Ellen, now attired in a simple but captivating morning-dress, presided.

Little did she imagine that the privacy of her bath had been invaded—violated by the glance of that man who now seated himself next to her, and whose sanctity was deemed to be above all question.

Little, either, did her father and friend suppose that there was one present who had vowed that she should be his, and who, in connection with that determination, had entertained no thought of marriage.

The ramble in the garden had so far cooled the rector's brain, that nothing in his behaviour towards Ellen was calculated to excite observation; but, from time to time, when unperceived, he cast upon her a glance of fervent admiration—a long, fixed, devouring glance, which denoted profound passion.

At length the hour for departure arrived; and his carriage drove round to the front door.

The rain of the preceding evening had changed to frost during the night;—the morning was fine, fresh, and healthy, though intensely cold; there was hence no shadow of an excuse for a longer stay.

The rector expressed his thanks for the hospitality which he had experienced, with that politeness which so eminently characterised his manners; and when he shook hands with Ellen, he pressed hers gently.

She thought that he intended to convey a sort of assurance that the secret which he had detected on the previous day, was sacred with him; and she cast upon him a rapid glance, expressive of gratitude.

Reginald then stepped into the carriage, which immediately rolled rapidly away towards London.

Upon his arrival at home, he proceeded straight to his study, whither he was immediately followed by the old housekeeper.

"Leave me—leave me, Mrs. Kenrick," said the rector; "I wish to be alone."

"I thought something had happened, sir," observed the old woman, fidgetting about the room, for with senile pertinacity she was resolved to say what she had upon her mind: "I thought so," she continued, "because this is the first time you ever stayed out all night without sending me word what kept you."

"I am not aware that I owe you an account of my actions, Mrs. Kenrick," said the rector, who, like all guilty persons, was half afraid that his conduct was suspected by the old woman.

"Certainly not, sir; and I never asked it. But after all the years I have been with you, and the confidence you have always reposed in me—until within the last week or two," added the old housekeeper, "I was afraid lest I had done something to offend you."

"No such thing," said the rector, somewhat softened. "But as the cares of my ministry multiply upon me——"

"Ah! sir, they must have multiplied of late," interrupted the old woman; "for you're not the same man you were."

"How do you mean?" demanded Reginald, now once more irritated.

"You have seemed restless, unsettled, and unhappy, for some two or three weeks past, sir," answered the housekeeper, wiping away a tear from her eye. "And then you are not so regular in your habits as you were: you go out and come in oftener;—sometimes you stay out till very late; at others you come home, send me up to bed, and say that you yourself are going to rest;—nevertheless, I hear you about the house——"

"Nonsense!" ejaculated Reginald, struck by the imprudence of which he had been guilty in admitting Lady Cecilia into his abode. "Do not make yourself unhappy, Mrs. Kenrick: nothing ails me, I can assure you. But—tell me," he added, half afraid to ask the question; "have you heard any one else remark—I mean, make any observation—that is, speak as you do about me——"

"Well, sir, if you wish for the truth," returned the housekeeper, "I must say that the clerk questioned me yesterday morning about you."

"The clerk!" ejaculated Reginald; "and what did he say?"

"Oh? he merely thought that you had something on your mind—some annoyance which worried you———"

"He is an impertinent fellow!" cried the rector, thrown off his guard by the alarming announcement that a change in his behaviour had been observed.

"He only speaks out of kindness, sir—as I do," observed the housekeeper, with a deep sigh.

"Well, well, Mrs. Kenrick," said the rector, vexed at his own impatience: "I was wrong to mistrust the excellence of his motives. To tell the truth, I have had some little cause of vexation—the loss of a large sum—through the perfidy of a pretended friend—and———"

The rector floundered in the midst of his falsehood; but the old housekeeper readily believed him, and was rejoiced to think that he had at length honoured her with his confidence in respect to the cause of that restlessness which she had mistaken for a secret grief.

"But no one else has made any remark, my dear Mrs. Kenrick?" said the rector, in a tone of conciliation "I mean—no one has questioned you—or———"

"Only Lady Cecilia Harborough sent yesterday afternoon to request you to call upon her, sir."

"Ah!—well?"

"And of course I said to her servant-maid that you were not at home. She came back in the evening, and seemed much disappointed that you were still absent. Then she returned again, saying that her mistress was ill and wished to consult you upon business."

"And what did you tell her, Mrs. Kenrick?"

"That you had not returned, sir," answered the housekeeper, surprised at the question, as if there were any thing else to tell save the truth. "The servant-maid seemed more and more disappointed, and called again as early as eight o'clock this morning."

"This morning!" echoed Reginald, seriously annoyed at this repetition of visits from Lady Cecilia's confidential servant.

"Yes, sir; and when I said that you had not been home all night, she appeared quite surprised," continued the housekeeper.

"And you told her that I had not been home all night?" mused Reginald. "What must Lady Cecilia think?"

"Think, sir?" cried the housekeeper, more surprised still at her master's observations. "You can owe no account of your actions, sir, to Lady Cecilia Harborough."

"Oh! no—certainly not," stammered the rector, cruelly embarrassed: "I only thought that evil tongues———"

"The Reverend Reginald Tracy is above calumny," said the housekeeper, who was as proud of her master as she was attached to him.

"True—true, Mrs. Kenrick," exclaimed the rector. "And yet—but, after all no matter. I will go and call in Tavistock Square at once; and then I can explain———"

Up to this moment the housekeeper had spoken in the full conviction that annoyance alone was the cause of her master's recent change of behaviour and present singularity of manners; but his increasing embarrassment—the strangeness of his observations relative to Lady Cecilia—his anxiety lest she should entertain an evil idea concerning his absence from home,—added to a certain vague rumour which had reached her ears relative to the lightness of that lady's character,—all these circumstances, united with the fact of Cecilia having sent so often to request Mr. Tracy to call upon her, suddenly engendered a suspicion of the truth in the housekeeper's mind.

"Before you go out again, sir," said the housekeeper, wishing to discard that suspicion, and therefore hastening to change the conversation to another topic, "I should mention to you that yesterday afternoon—between one and two o'clock—Katherine Wilmot arrived here———"

"Indeed! What, so soon?" exclaimed the rector.

"And as she assured me that you had only a few hours before offered her a situation in your household," continued Mrs. Kenrick, "I did not hesitate to take her in. Besides, she is a good girl, and I am not sorry that she should leave her uncle's roof."

"Then you approve of my arrangement, Mrs. Kenrick?" said Reginald.

"Certainly, sir—if I have the right to approve or disapprove," answered the old lady, who, in spite of the natural excellence of her heart, was somewhat piqued at not having been previously consulted upon the subject: then, ashamed of this littleness of feeling, she hastily added, "But the poor girl has a sad story to tell, sir, about the way in which she left her uncle; and, with your permission, I will send her up to you."

"Do so," said the rector, not sorry to be relieved of the presence of his housekeeper, in whose manner his guilty conscience made him see a peculiarity which filled his mind with apprehension.

In a few minutes Katherine Wilmot entered the rector's study.

Her story was brief but painful.

"After you left, sir, I sate thinking upon your very great kindness and that of Mr. Markham, and how happy I should be to have an opportunity of convincing you both that I was anxious to deserve all you proposed to do for me. The hours slipped away; and for the first time I forgot to prepare my uncle's dinner punctually to the minute. I know that I was wrong, sir—but I had so much to think about, both past and future! Well, sir, one o'clock struck; and nothing was ready. I started up, and did my best. But in a few minutes my uncle and cousin came in. My uncle, sir, was rather cross—indeed, if I must speak the truth, very cross; because his son had absolutely refused to assist him in his morning's work. I need not say, sir," continued the girl, with a shudder, "what that work was. The first thing my uncle did was to ask if his dinner was ready? I told him the whole truth, but assured him that not many minutes would elapse before it would be ready. You do not want to know, sir, all he said to me; it is quite sufficient to say that he turned me out of doors. I cried, and begged very hard to part from him in friendship—for, after all, sir, he is my nearest relation on the face of the earth—and, then, he brought me up! But he closed the door, and would not listen to me."

Katherine ceased, and wiped her eyes.

The poor girl had said nothing of the terrific beating which the executioner inflicted upon Gibbet the moment they returned home, and then upon Katherine herself before he thrust her out of the house.

"Have you brought away your mother's letter with you, Katherine?" inquired the rector, who during the maiden's simple narrative, had never taken his eyes off her.

"My uncle sent round all my things in the evening, by my unfortunate cousin," replied Katherine; "and amongst the rest, my work-box where I keep the letter. It is safe in my possession, sir."

"Take care of it, Kate," observed the rector; "who knows but that it may some day be of service?"

"Oh! sir, and even if it should not," ejaculated the girl, "it is at all events the only memento I possess of my poor mother."

"True—you told me so," said Reginald, prolonging the conversation only because the presence of an interesting female had become his sole enjoyment. "And now, my dear," continued the rector, rising from his seat, and approaching her, "be steady—conduct yourself well—and you will find me a good master."

"I will not be ungrateful, sir," returned Katherine.

"And you must endeavour to relieve Mrs. Kenrick of all onerous duties as much as possible," said the rector. "Thus, you had better always answer my bell yourself, when the footman is not in the way."

"I will make a point of doing so, sir," was the artless reply.

The rector gave some more trivial directions, and dismissed his new domestic to her duties.

He then hastened to Tavistock Square, to appease Lady Harborough, whose jealousy, he suspected, had been aroused by his absence from home.

CHAPTER CXLVII.

THE RECTOR'S NEW PASSION.

To make his peace with Lady Cecilia was by no means a difficult matter; and it was accomplished rather by the aid of the rector's purse than his caresses.

He remained to dinner with the syren who had first seduced him from the paths of virtue, which he had pursued so brilliantly and triumphantly—too brilliantly and triumphantly to ensure stability!

In the evening, when they were seated together upon the sofa, Reginald implored her to be more cautious in her proceedings in future.

"Such indiscretion as that of which you have been guilty," he said, "would ruin me. Why send so often to request my presence? The most unsuspicious would be excited; and my housekeeper has spoken to me in a manner that has seriously alarmed me."

"Forgive me, Reginald," murmured Cecilia, casting her arms around him; "but I was afraid you were unfaithful to me."

"And to set at rest your own selfish jealousies, you would compromise me," said the rector. "Do you know that my housekeeper has overheard me moving about at night when I have admitted you, or descended the stairs to let you out before day-light? and, although she attributes that fact to restlessness on my part, it would require but little to excite her suspicions."

"Again I say forgive me, Reginald," whispered Cecilia, accompanying her words with voluptuous kisses, so that in a short time the rector's ill-humour was completely subdued. "Tell me," she added, "may I not visit you again? say—shall I come to you to-night?"

"No, Cecilia," answered the clergyman; "we must exercise some caution. Let a week or a fortnight pass, so that my housekeeper may cease to think upon the subject which has attracted her notice and alarmed me; and then—then, dearest Cecilia, we will set no bounds to our enjoyment."

Reginald Tracy now rose, embraced his mistress, and took his leave.

But it was not to return home immediately.

His mind was filled with Ellen's image; and, even while in the society of Lady Cecilia, he had been pondering upon the means of gratifying his new passion—of possessing that lovely creature of whose charms he had caught glimpses that had inflamed him to madness.

Amongst a thousand vague plans, one had struck him. He remembered the horrible old woman of Golden Lane, who had enticed him to her house under a pretence of seeing a beautiful statue, and had thereby led him back to the arms of Lady Cecilia Harborough.

To her he was determined to proceed; for he thought that he might be aided in his designs by that ingenuity of which he had received so signal a proof.

Accordingly, wrapping himself up in his cloak, he repaired directly from Lady Cecilia's house to the vile court in Golden Lane.

It was past seven o'clock in the evening when he reached the old hag's abode.

She was dozing over a comfortable fire; and her huge cat slept upon her lap. Even in the midst of her nap, the harridan mechanically stretched forth her bony hand from time to time, and stroked the animal down the back; and then it purred in acknowledgment of that caress which to a human being would have been hideous.

Suddenly a knock at the door awoke the hag.

"Business—business," murmured the old woman, as she rose, placed the cat upon the rug, and hastened to answer the door: "no idle visitor comes to me at this time."

The moment she opened the door the rector rushed in.

"Gently, gently," said the old hag: "there is nothing to alarm you in this neighbourhood. Ah!" she cried, as Reginald Tracy laid aside his hat and cloak; "is it you, sir? I am not surprised to see you again."

"And why not?" demanded the rector, as he threw himself into a chair.

"Because all those who wander in the mazes of love, sooner or later require my services," answered the hag; "be they men or women."

"You have divined my object in seeking you," said the rector. "I love a charming creature, and know not how to obtain possession of her."

"You could not have come to a better place for aid and assistance, sir," observed the harridan, with one of her most significant and, therefore, most wicked leers.

"But can I trust you? will you be faithful? what guarantee have I that you will not betray me to Lady Harborough, whose jealousy is so soon excited?" cried Reginald.

"If you pay me well I am not likely to lose a good patron by my misconduct," answered the old woman boldly. "In a word, my left hand knows not what my right hand does."

"Well spoken," said the rector; and, taking gold from his purse, he flung it upon the table, adding, "Be this your retaining fee; but it is as nothing compared to what I will give you if you succeed in a matter on which I have set my heart."

"You must be candid with me, and tell me every particular, sir," said the hag, as she gathered up the gold with avidity.

"I have seen the young lady to whom I allude, but on three or four occasions," continued the rector; "and yet I have discovered much concerning her. She has been weak already, and has a child of some six or seven months old. That child was not born in wedlock; nor, indeed, has its mother ever borne the name of wife."

"Then the conquest cannot be so difficult," murmured the hag.

"I am not sure of that," said Reginald Tracy. "Without knowing any thing of her history, I am inclined to believe that some deep treachery—some foul wrong must have entrapped that young lady into error. She lives in the most respectable way; and neither by her manner nor her looks could her secret be divined. Accident alone revealed it to me."

"It may serve our purpose—it may serve our purpose," cried the harridan, musing.

"She dwells with her father, at the house of a friend—a very young man——"

"Ah!" cried the hag, struck by this information. "What is her name?"

"Ellen Monroe," replied the rector.

"I thought so," exclaimed the old woman.

"You know her, then?" cried Reginald Tracy in astonishment. "Are you sure she is the same whom you imagine her to be?"

"She resides at the house of Mr. Markham in Holloway—does she not?"

"She does. But how came you to be acquainted with her? what cause of intimacy could exist between you and her?" demanded the rector.

"My left hand never knows what my right hand does," said the hag. "If I reveal to you the affairs of another, how could you put confidence in me when I declare that your own secrets shall not be communicated to Lady Harborough or any one else who might question me?"

"True!" said the rector: "I cannot blame your discretion. "But tell me—have you any hope that I may succeed?"

"The business is a difficult one," answered the hag. "And yet greater obstacles than I can here see have been overcome—aye, and by me, too. Did I not tell Lady Harborough that I would bring you back to her arms? and did I not succeed? Am I then to be foiled now. Show me the weakness of a human being, and I direct all my energies against that failing. Ellen Monroe has two vulnerable points——"

"Which are they?" asked the rector eagerly.

"Her vanity and her love for her father," replied the harridan. "Leave her to me: when I am ready for you I will call upon you."

"And you will lose no time, good woman?" said the rector, overjoyed at the hopes held out to him.

"I will not let the grass grow under my feet," returned the hag. "But you must have patience; for the girl is stubborn—sadly stubborn. Art, and not entreaties, will prevail with her."

"In any case, manage your matters in such a way that I cannot be compromised," said the rector; "and your reward shall be most liberal."

"Trust to me," murmured the hag.

Reginald Tracy once more enveloped himself in his cloak, and took his departure.

"And so I have made a discovery this evening!" mused the hag, when she was once more alone. "Miss Ellen is a mother—she has a child of six or seven months old! She never told me that when she came to seek my aid, and I gave her the card of the Mesmerist;—she never told me that when she sought me after that, and I sent her to the Manager;—she never told me that when I met her at Greenwood's house in the country, and from which she escaped by the window. The cunning puss! She does not even think that I know where she lives;—but Lafleur told me that—Lafleur told me that! He is the prince of French valets—worth a thousand such moody, reserved Italians as Filippo! So now the rector must possess Miss Ellen? Well—and he shall, too, if I have any skill left—if I have any ingenuity to aid him!"

Then the hag concealed the five pieces of glittering gold which the rector had given her, in her Dutch clock; and having thus secured the wages of her iniquity, she proceeded to mix herself a steaming glass of gin-and-water to assist her meditations concerning the business entrusted to her.

"Yes," she said, continuing her musings aloud, "I must not fail in this instance. The rector is a patron who will not spare his gold; and Ellen may not be the only one he may covet. I warrant he will not keep me unemployed! These parsons are terrible fellows when once they give way; and I should think the rector has not been long at this game, or he could scarcely have contrived to maintain his reputation as he has. How the world would be astonished did it know all! But I am astonished at nothing—not I! No—no—I have seen too much in my time. And if I repent of any thing—but no I do not repent:—still, if I *did* sometimes think of *one* more than *another*, 'tis of that poor Harriet Wilmot! I should like to know what became of her. It must be sixteen or seventeen years since *that* occurred;—but the mention of the name of Markham just now, brought it all fresh back again to my mind. Well—it cannot be helped: it was in the way of business like any thing else!"

Let us leave the horrible old hag at her musings, and relate a little incident which occurred elsewhere, and which, however trivial the reader may deem it now, is not without importance in respect to a future portion of our narrative.

The rector had reached the door of his own house, after his interview with the old hag, and was about to knock when he perceived, by the light of the gas lamp, a strange-looking being standing on the step.

"What do you want, my good lad?" asked Reginald.

"Please, sir, I want to speak to Kate Wilmot, my cousin," answered Gibbet—for it was he.

"Indeed! I suppose, then, that you are the son of—of——" and Reginald stopped; for he did not like to wound the hump-back's feelings by saying "of the hangman," and at that moment he had forgotten the name of Katherine's uncle.

"My name is Smithers, sir," said the lad.

"Ah! Smithers—so it is," cried the rector. "Well, my good lad, I cannot think of preventing Katherine's relations from coming to see her if they choose; but, as she is now in a good place and respectably settled, it would perhaps be prudent that those visits should occur as seldom as possible—I mean, not too often."

"I'm sure, sir, I'm very sorry if I have offended you, by coming," sobbed the poor hump-back; "and I would not for all the world injure Kate in the opinion of those friends who have been so kind as to provide for her."

"Yon have done no harm—I am not angry with you," said the rector. "Only Mrs. Kenrick, my housekeeper, is very particular, and does not like the servants to have many visitors."

"Then I won't come any more, sir," murmured Gibbet, whose heart was ready to break at this cruel announcement.

"Yes—you may come and see your cousin every Sunday evening."

"Oh! thank you, sir—thank you kindly, sir!" ejaculated the hump-back, in a tone of touching sincerity.

"Every Sunday evening, then, let it be," continued the rector. "And now go round by the back way, and see her to-night, since you wish to do so."

The hump-back literally bounded with joy off the steps, and hurried to the stable-yard, whence there was a means of communication with the servants' offices attached to the rector's house.

As he drew near the back-door, he observed lights through the kitchen-windows; and he stopped for a moment to observe if Katherine were within.

In order to see into the kitchen, which, with its offices, formed a sort of out-house joining the main dwelling, the hump-back was compelled to climb upon a covered dust-hole standing in an obscure nook on the opposite side of the yard, and so shrouded in darkness that no one passing through the yard could observe a person concealed there.

The idea of ascertaining if Kate were in the kitchen at that moment, was not a mere whim on the part of the hump-back: he was afraid that, if she were not, he might not be allowed to return, and was therefore apprehensive of not seeing her that evening at all.

Accordingly, he clambered upon the dust-bin, which stood in a nook formed by the irregularity of the high wall that separated the yard of the rector's house from that of the stables; and from this point of observation, which his quick eye had thus detected, he commanded a full view of the interior of the kitchen.

Yes—Kate was there, seated at the table, and occupied with her needle.

She was alone too.

Gibbet remained in his hiding-place for some minutes, contemplating, with melancholy pleasure, the interesting countenance of the young girl.

At length it struck him that it was growing late, and that his visit must not last long.

He let himself gently down from the eminence to which he had clambered; and as he was about to turn away, to cross the yard to the kitchen door, he stopped short, as if an idea had suddenly entered his mind.

Casting a look back upon the obscure place from which he had just emerged, he muttered between his teeth, "No Kate—they shall not prevent me from seeing you of an evening when I will—and when, too, you will little suspect that I am so near."

He then walked over to the kitchen door, and knocked gently.

Kate herself rose to open it, and with unfeigned pleasure admitted the hump-back.

"Mr. Tracy says that I may come and see you every Sunday evening, Kate," were Gibbet's first words: "you won't say no—will you, Kate?"

"Certainly not, John," answered the maiden. "I shall always be glad to see you, my poor cousin," she added compassionately.

"Oh! I know you will, Kate," exclaimed the hump-back. "I have missed you so all yesterday afternoon, and all to-day; and father is more unkind to me than ever," he added, the tears trickling down his cheeks.

"We must hope that better times await you, John," said Katherine, in a soothing tone.

"Never for me," observed Gibbet, with a profound sigh. "Father does not cease to upbraid me for my conduct yesterday morning. But I could not help it. I went down to Newgate with the intention to do my best; but when I got there, and found myself face to face with the miserable wretch who was about to suffer,—when I saw his awful pale face, his wild glaring eyes, his distorted features, his quivering limbs,—and when I heard him murmur every other moment, '*O Lord! O Lord!*' in a tone scarcely audible and yet expressive of such intense anguish,—I could not lay a finger upon him! When my father gave me the twine to pinion him, it fell from my hands; and I believe I felt as much as the unfortunate man himself. Oh! heavens—his face will haunt me in my dreams as long as I live. I never shall forget it—it was so ghastly, so dreadful! I would not have had any thing to do with taking that man's life away—no, not for all the world. I did not see a criminal before me—I only saw a fellow-creature from whom *his* fellow-creatures were about to take away something which God alone gave, and which God alone should have the right to recall. I thought of all this; and I was paralysed. And it was because my nature would not let me touch so much as the hem of that man's garment to do him harm, that my father upbraids and beats me. Oh! it is too cruel, Kate—it is too cruel to bear!"

"It is, my poor cousin," answered the girl; "but let me entreat you to submit patiently—as patiently as you can. Times must change for you—as they have for me."

These last words she uttered in a half-tone of self-reproach, as if she upbraided herself with having left her unfortunate cousin to the mercy of his brutal father.

But how could she have done otherwise, poor girl?

The conversation between that interesting young creature and the hump-back continued in pretty much the same strain for about half-an-hour, when Gibbet took leave of his cousin.

"You will come and see me next Sunday, John," said Katharine, as she shook him warmly by the hand.

"Next Sunday evening, dear Kate," he replied, and then departed.

CHAPTER CXLVIII.

THE OLD HAG'S INTRIGUE.

On the morning after she had received the visit from the Reverend Reginald Tracy, the old hag rose early, muttering to herself, "I must lose no time—I must lose no time."

She then proceeded to dress herself in her holiday attire, each article of which was purchased with the wages of her infamous trade.

Female frailty—female shame had clothed the hag: female dishonour had produced her a warm gown, a fine shawl, and a new bonnet.

When she was young she had lived by the sale of herself: now that she was old she lived by the sale of others.

And she gloried in all the intrigues which she successfully worked out for those who employed her, as much as a sharp diplomatist triumphs in outwitting an astute antagonist.

It is said that when Perseus carried the hideous head of the Gorgon Medusa through the air, the gore which dripped from it as he passed over the desert of Libya turned into frightful serpents: so does the moral filth which the corruption of great cities distils, engender grovelling and venomous wretches like that old hag.

Well—she dressed herself in her best attire, and contemplated herself with satisfaction in a little mirror cracked all across.

Then, having partaken of a hearty breakfast, she sallied forth.

By means of a public conveyance she soon reached the vicinity of Markham Place.

She had never been in that neighbourhood before; and when she beheld the spacious mansion, with its heavy but imposing architecture, she muttered to herself, "She is well lodged—she is well lodged!"

The hag then strolled leisurely round Richard's miniature domain, debating within herself whether she should knock boldly at the front door and inquire for Miss Monroe, or wait in the neighbourhood to see if that young lady might chance to walk out alone.

The day was fine, though cold; and the hag accordingly resolved to abide by the latter alternative.

Perceiving a seat upon the summit of the hill, whereon stood the two trees, she opened the gate at the foot of the path which led to the top.

Then she toiled up the hill, and seated herself between the two ash trees—now denuded of their foliage.

Presently, as her eyes wandered hither and thither, they fell upon the inscriptions engraved on the stem of one of the trees. Thus they stood:—

Eugene.

Dec. 25, 1836.

Eugene.

May 17th, 1838.

The old woman marvelled what that name, twice inscribed, and those dates could mean.

But she did not trouble herself much with conjecture on that point: she had other business on hand, and was growing impatient because Ellen did not appear.

At length her penetrating eyes caught a glimpse of a female form approaching from the direction of the garden at the back of the mansion.

The hag watched that form attentively, and in a few moments exclaimed joyfully, "It is she!"

Ellen was indeed advancing up the hill. She had come forth for a short ramble; and the clearness of the day had prompted her to ascend the eminence which afforded so fine a view of the mighty metropolis at a little distance.

When she was near the top, she caught sight of a female seated upon the bench between the trees, and was about to retreat—fearful that her presence might be deemed a reproach for what was in fact an intrusion upon private property.

But, to her surprise, she observed the female beckoning familiarly to her; and she continued her way to the summit.

Then, with profound astonishment and no little annoyance, she recognised the old hag.

"What are you doing here?" demanded Ellen, hastily.

"Resting myself, as you see, miss," answered the harridan. "But how charming you look this morning! That black velvet bonnet sets off your beautiful complexion; and the fresh air has given a lovely glow to your cheeks."

"You have not uttered that compliment without a motive," said Ellen, vainly endeavouring to suppress a half-smile of satisfaction. "But you must not suppose that your flattery will make me forget the part which you played when Mr. Greenwood had me conveyed to his house somewhere in the country."

"My dear child, do not be angry with me on that account," said the old hag. "Mr. Greenwood thought that you would prefer me as your servant instead of a stranger."

"Or rather, he hired you to talk me over to his wishes—or, perhaps, because he knew that you would wink at any violence which he might use. But I outwitted you both," added Ellen, laughing.

"Ah! now I see that you have forgiven me, my child," cried the hag. "And when I behold your sweet lips, red as cherries—your lovely blue eyes, so soft and languishing—and that small round chin, with its charming dimple, I feel convinced——"

"Nay—you are determined to flatter me," interrupted Ellen; "but I shall not forgive you the more readily on that account."

"How well this pelisse becomes your beautiful figure, my child," said the hag, affecting not to notice Ellen's last observation.

"Cease this nonsense," cried Miss Monroe; "and tell me what brings you hither."

"To see you once more, my child."

"How did you discover my abode?"

"A pleasant question, forsooth!" ejaculated the hag. "Do you think that I am not well acquainted with all—yes, *all* that concerns you?" she added significantly.

"Alas! I am well aware that you know much—too much," said Ellen, with a profound sigh.

"Much!" repeated the hag. "I know *all*, I say,—even to the existence of the little one that will some day call you mother."

"Who told you that? Speak—who told you *that*?" demanded Ellen, greatly excited.

"It cannot matter—since I know it," returned the hag: "it cannot matter."

"One question," said Ellen,—"and I will ask you no more. Was Mr. Greenwood your informant?"

"He was not," answered the hag.

"And now tell me, without circumlocution, what business has brought you hither—for that you came to meet with me I have no doubt."

"Sit down by me, my child," said the hag, "and listen while I speak to you."

"Nay—I can attend to you as well here," returned Ellen, laughing, as she leant against one of the trees—an attitude which revealed her tiny feet and delicate ankles.

"You seem to have no confidence in me," observed the hag; "and yet I have ever been your friend."

"Yes—you have helped me to my ruin," said Ellen, mournfully. "And yet I scarcely blame you for all that, because you only aided me to discover what I sought at the time—and that was *bread at any sacrifice*. Well—go on, and delay not: I will listen to you, if only through motives of curiosity."

"My sweet child," said the harridan, endeavouring to twist her wrinkled face into as pleasing an expression as possible, "a strange thing has come to my knowledge. What would you think if I told you that a man of pure and stainless life, who is virgin of all sin,—a man who to a handsome exterior unites a brilliant intellect,—a man whose eloquence can excite the aristocracy as well as produce a profound impression upon the middle classes,—a man possessed of a fine fortune and a high position,—what would you think, I say, if I told you that such a man has become enamoured of you?"

"I should first wonder how such a phœnix of perfection came to select you as his intermediate," answered Ellen, with a smile, which displayed her brilliant teeth.

"A mere accident made me acquainted with his passion," said the hag. "But surely you would not scorn the advances of a man who would sacrifice every thing for you—who would consent to fall from his high place for one single hour of your love—who would lay his whole fortune at your feet as a proof of his sincerity."

"To cut short this conversation, I will answer you with sincerity," returned Ellen. "Mr. Greenwood is the only man who can boast of a favour which involves my shame: he is the father of my child. I do not love him—I have no reason to love him: nevertheless, he is—I repeat—the father of my child! That expresses every thing. Who knows but that, sooner or later, he may do me justice? And should such an idea ever enter his mind, must I not retain myself worthy of that repentant sentiment on his part?"

"You cherish a miserable delusion, my child," said the hag; "and I am surprised at your confidence in the good feelings of a man of whom you have already seen so much."

"Ah! there is a higher power that often sways the human heart," observed Ellen; and, as she spoke, her eyes were fixed upon the inscriptions on the tree, while her heart beat with emotions unintelligible to the old hag.

"You will then allow this man of whom I have spoken, and who has formed so enthusiastic an attachment towards you, to languish without a hope?" demanded the woman.

"Men do not die of love," said Ellen, with a smile.

"But he is rich—and he would enrich you," continued the old harridan: "he would place your father in so happy a position that the old man should not even experience a regret for the prosperity which he has lost."

"My father dwells with a friend, and is happy," observed Ellen.

"But he is dependant," exclaimed the old hag: "for you yourself once said to me, '*We are dependant upon one who cannot afford to maintain us in idleness.*' How happy would you be—for I know your heart—to be enabled to place your father in a state of independence!"

"Would he be happy did he know that he owed the revival of his prosperity to his daughter's infamy?"

"Did he divine whence came the bread that was purchased by your services to the statuary, the artist, the sculptor, and the photographer? You yourself assured me that you kept your avocations a profound secret."

"Were I inclined to sell myself for gold, Greenwood would become a liberal purchaser," said Ellen. "All your sophistry is vain. You cannot seduce me from that state of tranquil seclusion in which I now dwell."

"At least grant your unknown lover an interview, and let him plead his own cause," exclaimed the hag, who did not calculate upon so much firmness on the part of the young lady.

"Ah! think not that he is unknown," cried Ellen, a light breaking in upon her mind: "a man of pure and stainless life, virgin of all sin,—a man endowed with a handsome person, and a brilliant intellect,—a man whose eloquence acts as a spell upon all classes,—a man possessed of a large fortune and enjoying a high position,—such is your description! And this man must have seen me to love me! Now think you I cannot divine the name of your phœnix?"

"You suspect then, my child——"

"Nay—I have something more than mere suspicion in my mind," interrupted Ellen. "Oh! now I comprehend the motive of that apparent earnestness with which he implored me to reveal the secret sorrow that oppressed me! In a word, old woman," added the young lady, in a tone of superb contempt, "your phœnix is the immaculate rector of St. David's!"

"And do you not triumph in your conquest, Miss?" demanded the hag, irritated by Ellen's manner.

"Oh! yes," exclaimed the young lady, with a sort of good-humoured irony; "so much so, that I will meet him when and where you will."

"Are you serious?" inquired the hag, doubtfully.

"Did I ever jest when I agreed to accept the fine offers which you made me on past occasions?" asked Ellen.

"No: and you cannot have an object in jesting now," observed the old woman. "But when and where will you meet him who is enamoured of you?"

"You say that he will make any sacrifice to please me?"

"He will—he will."

"Then he cannot refuse the appointment which I am about to propose to you. On Monday evening next there is to be a masked ball at Drury Lane Theatre. At ten o'clock precisely I will be there, dressed as a Circassian slave, with a thick veil over my face. Let him be attired as a monk, so that he may be enabled to shroud his features with his cowl. We shall not fail to recognise each other."

"Again I ask if you are in earnest?" demanded the old woman, surprised at this singular arrangement.

"I was never more so," answered Ellen.

"But why cannot the appointment take place at my abode?" said the hag.

"Oh! fie—the immaculate rector in your dirty court in Golden Lane!" ejaculated Ellen.

"That court was once good enough for you, my child," muttered the old woman.

"We will not dispute upon that point," said the young lady. "If I am worth having, I am worth humouring; and I must test the sincerity of the attachment which your phœnix experiences for me, by making him seek me at a masked ball."

"Oh! the caprices of you fair ones!" ejaculated the hag. "Well, my child, I will undertake that it shall be as you desire."

"Next Monday evening at ten o'clock," cried Ellen; and with these words she tripped lightly down the hill in the direction of the mansion.

The old hag then took her departure by the path on the opposite side; and, as she went along, she chuckled at the success of her intrigue.

CHAPTER CXLIX.

THE MASQUERADE.

The evening of the masquerade arrived.

It is not our intention to enter into a long description of a scene the nature of which must be so well known to our readers.

Suffice it to say that at an early hour Old Drury was, within, a blaze of light. The pit had been boarded over so as to form a floor level with the stage, at the extremity of which the orchestra was placed. The spacious arena thus opened, soon wore a busy and interesting appearance, when the masques began to arrive; and the boxes were speedily filled with ladies and gentlemen who, wearing no fancy costumes, had thronged thither for the purpose of beholding, but not commingling with, the diversions of the masquerade.

To contemplate that blaze of female loveliness which adorned the boxes, one would imagine that all the most charming women of the metropolis had assembled there by common consent that night; and the traveller, who had visited foreign climes, must have been constrained to admit that no other city in the universe could produce such a brilliant congress.

For the fastidious elegancies of fashion, sprightliness of manners, sparkling discourse, and all the refinements of a consummate civilization, which are splendid substitutes for mere animal beauty, the ladies of Paris are unequalled;—but for female loveliness in all its glowing perfection—in all its most voluptuous expansion, London is the sovereign city that knows in this respect no rival.

In sooth, the scene was ravishing and gorgeous within Old Drury on the night of which we are writing.

The spacious floor was crowded with masques in the most varied and fanciful garbs.

There were Turks who had never uttered a "Bismillah," and Shepherdesses who had seen more of mutton upon their tables than ever they had in the fields;—Highlanders who had never been twenty miles north of London, and Princesses whose fathers were excellent aldermen or most conscientious tradesmen;—Generals without armies, and Flower-Girls whose gardens consisted of a pot of mignonette on the ledge of their bed-room windows;—Admirals whose nautical knowledge had been gleaned on board Gravesend steamers, and Heathen Goddesses who were devoted Christians;—Ancient Knights who had not even seen so much as the Eglintoun Tournament, and Witches whose only charms lay in their eyes;—and numbers, of both sexes, attired in fancy-dresses which were very fanciful indeed.

Then there was all the usual fun and frolic of a masquerade;—friends availing themselves of their masks and disguises to mystify each other,—witticism and repartee, which if not sharp nor pointed, still served the purpose of eliciting laughter,—and strange mistakes in respect to personal identity, which were more diverting than all.

There was also plenty of subdued whispering between youthful couples; for Love is as busy at masquerades as elsewhere.

The brilliancy of the dresses in the boxes, and the variety of those upon the floor, combined with the blaze of light and the sounds of the music, formed a scene at once gay, exhilarating, and ravishing.

At about a quarter before ten o'clock, a masque, attired in the sombre garb of a Carmelite Friar, with his cowl drawn completely over his face, and a long rosary hanging from the rude cord which girt his waist, entered the theatre.

He cast a wistful glance, through the slight opening in his cowl, all around; and, not perceiving the person whom he sought, retired into the most obscure nook which he could find, but whence he could observe all that passed.

At five minutes to ten, a lady, habited as a Circassian slave, and wearing an ample white veil, so thick that it was impossible to obtain a glimpse of her countenance, alighted from a cab at the principal entrance of the theatre.

Lightly she tripped up the steps; but as she was about to enter the vestibule, her veil caught the buttons of a lounger's coat, and was drawn partly off her face.

She immediately re-adjusted it—but not before a gentleman, masked, and in the habit of a Greek Brigand, who was entering at the time, obtained a glimpse of her features.

"What? Ellen *here*!" murmured the Greek Brigand to himself: "I must not lose sight of her!"

Ellen did not however notice that she had been particularly observed; much less did she suspect that she was recognised.

But as she hastened up the great staircase, the Greek Brigand followed her closely.

Although her countenance was so completely concealed, her charming figure was nevertheless set off to infinite advantage by the dualma which she wore, and which, fitting close to her shape, reached down to her knees. Her ample trousers were tied just above the ankle where the graceful swell of the leg commenced; and her little feet were protected by red slippers.

The Brigand who had recognised her, and now watched her attentively, was tall, slender, well made, and of elegant deportment.

Ellen soon found herself in the midst of the busy scene, where her graceful form and becoming attire immediately attracted attention.

"Fair eastern lady," said an Ancient Knight in a buff jerkin and plumed tocque, "if thou hast lost the swain that should attend upon thee, accept of my protection until thou shalt find him."

"Thanks for thy courtesy, Sir Knight," answered Ellen, gaily: "I am come to confess to a holy father whom I see yonder."

"Wilt thou then abjure thine own creed, and embrace ours?" asked the Knight.

"Such is indeed my intention, Sir Knight," replied Ellen; and she darted away towards the Carmelite Friar whom she had espied in his nook.

The Ancient Knight mingled with a group of Generals and Heathen Goddesses, and did not offer to pester Ellen with any more of his attentions.

"Sweet girl," said Reginald Tracy (whom the reader has of course recognised in the Carmelite Friar), when Ellen joined him, "how can I sufficiently thank you for this condescension on your part?"

"I am fully recompensed by the attention you have shown to the little caprice which prompted me to choose this scene for the interview that you desired," answered Ellen.

Both spoke in a subdued tone—but not so low as to prevent the Greek Brigand, who was standing near, from overhearing every word they uttered.

"Mr. Tracy," continued Ellen, "why did you entrust your message of love to another? why could you not impart with your own lips that which you were anxious to communicate to me?"

"Dearest Ellen," answered the rector, "I dared not open my heart to you in person—I was compelled to do so by means of another."

"If your passion be an honourable one," said Ellen, "there was no need to feel shame in revealing it."

"My passion is most sincere, Ellen. I would die for you! Oh! from the first moment that I beheld you by your father's sick-bed, I felt myself drawn towards you by an irresistible influence; and each time that I have since seen you has only tended to rivet more firmly the chain which makes me your slave. Have I not given you an unquestionable proof of my sincerity by meeting you *here*?"

"A proof of your desire to please me, no doubt," said Ellen. "But what proof have I that your passion is an honourable one? You speak of its sincerity—you avoid all allusion to the terms on which you would desire me to return it."

"What terms do you demand?" asked the rector. "Shall I lay my whole fortune at your feet? Shall I purchase a splendid house, with costly appointments, for you? In a word, what proof of my love do you require?"

"Are you speaking as a man who would make a settlement upon a wife, or as one who is endeavouring to arrange terms with a mistress?" demanded Ellen.

"My sweet girl," replied Reginald, "know you not that, throughout my career, I have from the pulpit denounced the practice of a man in holy orders marrying, and that I have more than once declared—solemnly declared—my intention of remaining single upon principle? You would not wish me to commit an inconsistency which might throw a suspicion upon my whole life?"

"Then, sir, by what right do you presume that I will compromise my fair fame for your sake, if you tremble to sacrifice your reputation for mine?" asked Ellen. "Is every compromise to be effected by poor woman, and shall man make no sacrifice for her? Are you vile, or base, or cowardly enough to ask me to desert home and friends to gratify your selfish passion, while you carefully shroud your weakness beneath the hypocritical cloak of a reputed sanctity? Was it to hear such language as this that I agreed to meet you? But know, sir, that you have greatly—oh! greatly mistaken *me*! By the most unmanly—the most disgraceful means you endeavoured to wring from me, a few days ago, a secret which certain expressions of mine, incautiously uttered over what I conceived to be my father's death-bed, had perhaps made you more than half suspect. Those words, which escaped me in a moment of bitter anguish, you treasured up, and converted them into the text for a sermon which you preached me."

"Ellen," murmured the rector; "why these reproaches?"

"Oh! why these reproaches?—I will tell you," continued the young lady, whose bosom palpitated violently beneath the dualma. "Do you think that you did well to press me to reveal the secret of my shame? Do you think that you adopted an honourable means to discover it? When you addressed me in that saintly manner—a manner which I now know to have been that of a vile hypocrisy—I actually believed you to be sincere; for the time I fancied that a man of God was offering me consolation. Nevertheless, think you that my feelings were not wounded? But an accident made you acquainted with that truth which you vainly endeavoured to extort from me! And now you perhaps believe that I cannot read your heart. Oh! I can fathom its depths but too well. You cherish the idea that because I have been frail once, I am fair game for a licentious sportsman like you. You are wrong, sir—you are wrong. I never erred but once—but once, mark you;—and then not through passion—nor through love—nor in a moment of surprise. I erred deliberately—no matter why. The result was the child whom you have seen. But never, never will I err more—no, not even though tempted, *as I have been*, by the father of my child! You sent to me a messenger—the same filthy hag who pandered to my first, my only disgrace,—you sent her as your herald of love. Ah! sir, you must have already plunged into ways at variance with the sanctity of your character—or you could not have known *her*! I told her—as I now assure you—that I do not affect a virtue which I possess not;—but if I henceforth remain pure and chaste, it is because I am a mother—because I love my child—because I will keep myself worthy of the respect of *him* who is the father of that child, should God ever move his heart towards me. Say then that I am virtuous upon calculation—I care not: still I am virtuous!"

The individual in the garb of the Greek Bandit drew a pace or two nearer as these words met his ears.

Neither the rector nor Ellen observed that he was paying any attention to them: on the contrary, he appeared to be entirely occupied in contemplating the dancers from beneath his impervious mask.

"Ellen, what means all this?" asked Reginald: "are you angry with me? You alarm me!"

"Suffer me to proceed, that you may understand me fully," said Ellen. "You mercilessly sought to cover me with humiliation, when you rudely probed that wound in my heart, the existence of which an unguarded expression of mine had revealed to you. Your conduct was base—was cowardly; and, as a woman, I eagerly embraced the opportunity to avenge myself."

"To avenge yourself!" faltered Reginald, nearly sinking with terror as these words fell upon his ears.

"Yes—to avenge myself," repeated Ellen hastily. "When your messenger—that vile agent of crime—proposed to me that I should grant you an interview, I bethought myself of this ball which I had seen announced in the newspapers. It struck me that if I could induce you—you, the man of sanctity—to clothe yourself in the mummery of a mask and meet me at a scene which you and your fellow-ecclesiastics denounce as one worthy of Satan, I should hurl back with tenfold effect that deep, deep humiliation which you visited upon me. It was for this that I made the appointment here to-night—for this that I retired early to my chamber, and thence stole forth unknown to my father and my benefactor—for this that I now form one at an assembly which has no charms for me! My intention was to seize an opportunity to tear your disguise from you, and allow all present to behold amongst them the immaculate rector of Saint David's. But I will be more merciful to you than you were to me: I will not inflict upon you that last and most poignant humiliation!"

"My God! Miss Monroe, are you serious?" said the rector, deeply humbled; "or is this merely a portion of the pastime?"

"Does it seem sport to you?" asked Ellen: "if so, I will continue it, and wind it up with the scene which I had abandoned."

"For heaven's sake, do not expose me, Miss Monroe!" murmured Reginald, now writhing in agony at the turn which the matter had taken. "Let me depart—and forget that I ever dared to address you rudely."

"Yes—go," said Ellen: "you are punished sufficiently. You possess the secret of my frailty—I possess the secret of your hypocrisy: beware of the use you make of your knowledge of me, lest I retaliate by exposing you."

There was something very terrible in the lesson which that young woman gave the libidinous priest on this occasion; and he felt it in its full force.

Cowering within himself, he uttered not another word, but stole away, completely subdued—cruelly humiliated.

Ellen lingered for a few moments on the spot where she had so effectually chastised the insolent hypocrite; and then hastily retired.

The Greek Brigand made a movement as if he were about to follow her; but, yielding to a second thought, he stopped, murmuring, "By heavens! she is a noble creature!"

CHAPTER CL.

MRS. KENRICK.

The rector of Saint David's returned home a prey to the most unenviable feelings.

Rage—disappointment—humiliation conspired to make him mad.

The old hag had raised his hopes to the highest pitch; and at the moment when the cup of bliss seemed to approach his lips, it was rudely dashed away.

A woman had triumphed over him—mocked his passion—spurned his offers—read him a lesson of morality—taught him that proud man must not always domineer over feminine weakness.

Oh! it was too much for that haughty—that vain—that self-sufficient ecclesiastic to endure!

As he returned home in a hired cab, he threw from the window of the vehicle the Carmelite gown and cowl which he had worn; and bitterly did he reproach himself for his folly in having been seduced into the degradation of that masqued mummery.

Arrived at his own house, he rushed past the housekeeper who opened the door, and was hurrying up-stairs to the solitude of his chamber, when the voice of the old lady compelled him to pause.

"Mr. Tracy—Mr. Tracy," she exclaimed; "here is a note from Lady Harborough."

"Tell Lady Harborough to go to the devil, Mrs. Kenrick!" cried the rector, goaded almost to madness by this new proof of Cecilia's indiscretion.

The old housekeeper dropped the candle and the note, as if she were thunderstruck.

Was it possible that she had heard aright? could such an expression have emanated from the lips of her master—of that man whom the world idolized?

"What is the matter now, Mrs. Kenrick?" asked the rector, suddenly recovering his presence of mind, and perceiving the immense error into which his excited feelings had betrayed him.

"Nothing, sir—nothing," answered the housekeeper, as she re-lighted her candle by means of a lamp which was standing on the hall-table; "only I thought that something very terrible had occurred to annoy you."

"Yes—yes—I have indeed been grievously annoyed," said Reginald; "and you must forgive my hasty conduct. I was wrong—very wrong. Do not think anything more of it, Mrs. Kenrick. But did you not observe that Lady Harborough had sent a message——"

"A note, sir. Here it is."

And as the housekeeper handed her master the perfumed *billet*, she cast a scrutinizing glance upon his countenance.

He was as pale as death—his lips quivered—and his eyes had a wild expression.

"I am afraid, sir, that something very dreadful has happened to you," she observed timidly. "Shall I send for the physician?"

"No—no, Mrs. Kenrick: I shall be quite well in the morning. I have received a violent shock—the sudden communication of ill news—the death of a dear friend——"

"Ah! sir, I was convinced that all was not right," observed the housekeeper. "If you would follow my advice you would take something to compose you—to make you sleep well——"

"An excellent thought, Mrs. Kenrick! If it be not too late, I wish you would send and procure me a little laudanum: I will take a few drops to ensure a sound slumber."

"I will do so, sir," answered the housekeeper.

She then repaired to the kitchen, while Reginald hurried up to his own chamber to read Lady Cecilia's letter, the contents of which ran as follow:—

"Nearly a week has elapsed, dearest Reginald, and I have not seen you! neither have I heard from you. What is the meaning of this? Is it neglect, or extreme caution? At all events the interval which you enjoined for the cessation of my visits to you, has nearly expired; and my impatience will brook no longer delay. I must see you to-night! Precisely as the clock strikes twelve, I will be at your front-door, when you must admit me as on previous occasions—or I shall imagine that you are already wearied of your

"CECILIA."

"After all," said the rector, "the presence of Cecilia will in some degree console me for my disappointment of this evening! I cannot remain alone with my reflections—it drives me mad to think of what I am, and what I have been! And laudanum is a miserable resource for one who dreads a sleepless night: it peoples slumber with hideous phantoms. Yes—I will admit Cecilia at the appointed hour:—my housekeeper does not suspect me—my guilty conscience alone makes me think at times that she reads the secrets of my soul?"

The rector seated himself before the cheerful fire which burnt in the grate, and fell into a long train of voluptuous meditation.

He had become in so short a time a confirmed sensualist; and now that his long pent-up passions had broken loose, they never left him a moment of repose.

His reverie was interrupted by a knock at the door; and Mrs. Kenrick entered.

"Kate was fortunate enough to find a druggist's shop open, sir," she said, "and procured some laudanum. But pray be cautious how you use it."

"Never fear," returned the rector: "I may not avail myself of it at all—for I feel more composed now."

The housekeeper wished her master a good night's rest, and withdrew.

The rector then took a decanter of wine from a cupboard, and tossed off two glasses full, one immediately after the other.

The idea that Cecilia would shortly be there and the effects of the wine inflamed his blood, and brought back the colour to his cheeks.

Midnight soon sounded: the rector threw off his shoes, took a candle in his hand, and hastened down stairs.

He opened the front-door with the utmost caution; and a female, muffled in an ample cloak, darted into the hall.

"Cecilia?" whispered the rector.

"Dearest Reginald," answered the lady, in the same under tone.

They then stole noiselessly up stairs, and reached the rector's chamber without having scarcely awakened the faintest echo in the house.

The remainder of the night was passed by them in the intoxicating joys of illicit love. Locked in Cecilia's arms, the rector forgot the humiliation he had received at the hands of Ellen, and abandoned himself to those pleasures for which he risked so much!

It was still dark—though at a later hour in the morning than Cecilia had been previously in the habit of quitting the rector's house—when the guilty pair stole softly down stairs, without a light.

"Hasten, Cecilia," murmured the rector: "it is later than you imagine."

"My God!" whispered the lady: "I hear a step ascending!"

The rector listened for a moment, and then said in a faint tone, "Yes: we are lost!"

A light flashed on the wall a few steps beneath those on which they were standing: it was too late to retreat; and in another moment Mrs. Kenrick made her appearance on the stairs.

"What! Mr. Tracy?" ejaculated the housekeeper, her eyes glancing from the rector in his dressing-gown to the lady in her cloak.

Then the good woman stood motionless and silent—her tongue tied, and her feet rooted to the spot, with astonishment.

Lady Cecilia drew her veil hastily over her countenance; but not before Mrs. Kenrick had recognised her.

A thousand ideas passed rapidly through the rector's brain during the two or three moments that succeeded this encounter.

At first he thought of inventing some excuse for his awkward situation;—next he felt inclined to spring upon his old housekeeper and strangle her;—then he conceived the desperate idea of rushing back to his room and blowing his brains out.

"Mrs. Kenrick," at length he exclaimed, "I hope you will say nothing of this."

The housekeeper made no reply to her master; but, turning a contemptuous glance upon the lady, said, "Madam, allow me to conduct you to the front door."

Cecilia followed her mechanically; and Reginald rushed up the stairs to his room, a prey to emotions more readily conceived than described.

The housekeeper preceded Lady Cecilia in silence, and opened the front door.

"My dear Mrs. Kenrick," said the frail patrician, who had now nearly recovered her presence of mind, "I hope you will take no notice of this unpleasant discovery."

"I shall remain silent, madam," answered the housekeeper; "but through no respect for you. I however value the reputation of a master whom I have served for many years, too much to be the means of ruining him."

She then closed the door unceremoniously, and, seating herself on one of the mahogany benches in the hall, burst into tears.

That good woman loved her master with a maternal affection; and she was shocked at this dread confirmation of the faint suspicions which she had already entertained, and which had so sorely afflicted her.

"It is then true!" she thought within herself. "He has fallen! He is a living, breathing falsehood. His eloquence is a mere talent, and not the spontaneous outpouring of holy conviction! The world adores an idle delusion—worships a vain phantom. Oh! what a discovery is this! How can I ever respect him more? how can I ever talk with others of his virtues again? And yet he may repent—oh! God grant that he may! Yes—he must repent: he must again become the great, the good man he once was! It behoves me, then, to shield his guilt:—at the same time all temptation should be removed from his presence. Ah! now I bethink me that he has cast wistful eyes upon that poor girl whom he has taken into the establishment. I must remove her: yes—I will remove her, upon my own authority. He will thank me hereafter for my prudence."

Thus did the good woman reason within herself.

When she had somewhat recovered from the first shock which the unpleasant discovery of her master's criminality had produced upon her, she repaired to her domestic avocations.

Kate was already in the kitchen, occupied with her usual duties.

"Katherine, my dear child," said Mrs. Kenrick, "I am going to give you my advice—or rather to propose to you a plan which I have formed—relative to you——"

"To me, ma'am?" exclaimed the young maiden, desisting from her employment, and preparing to listen with attention.

"Yes, my dear girl," continued the housekeeper; "and when I tell you that it is for your good—entirely for your good—you would thank me———"

"Oh! I do, ma'am—I thank you in advance," said Kate; "for I have already experienced too much kindness at your hands not to feel convinced that all you propose is for my good."

"Well, then, my dear—without giving you any reasons for my present conduct—I am anxious that you should leave this house———"

"Leave, ma'am?" cried Kate, astonished at this unexpected announcement.

"Yes, Katherine: you must leave this house," proceeded Mrs. Kenrick. "But think not that you will be unprovided for. I have a sister who resides a few miles from London; and to her care I shall recommend you. She will be a mother to you."

"But why would you remove me from the roof of my benefactor?" asked Kate: "why would you send me away from London, where my only relations on the face of the earth reside?" she added, bursting into tears; for she thought of her poor persecuted cousin the hump-back.

"Do not ask me, my good child," returned Mrs. Kenrick: "my reasons are of a nature which cannot be communicated to you. And yet—if you knew them, and could rightly understand them—you would not object———"

"Alas! ma'am, I am afraid that I understand them but too well," interrupted the girl: "the executioner's niece brings discredit upon the house of her benefactor."

"Oh! no—no," exclaimed the good-natured housekeeper; "do not entertain such an idea! Not for worlds would I have you labour under such an error. You know I would not tell a falsehood; and I declare most solemnly that you have totally misunderstood me and my motives."

There was an earnestness in the way in which Mrs. Kenrick spoke that immediately removed from Katherine's mind the suspicion she had entertained.

"Why should you send the poor girl away, Mrs. Kenrick?" said the footman, now suddenly emerging from the pantry, which joined the kitchen.

"Have you overheard our conversation, then, Thomas?" exclaimed Mrs. Kenrick, angrily.

"I couldn't very well avoid it," answered the footman, "since I was in there all the time."

"It would have been more discreet on your part to have let us know that you were there, when you heard a private conversation begin," remarked the housekeeper.

"How should I know the conversation was private?" exclaimed Thomas. "I suppose you're jealous of the girl, and want to get rid of her."

"You must value your place very little by speaking to me in this way," said Mrs. Kenrick. "However, I scorn your base allusions. And you, my dear," she continued, now addressing herself to Katherine, "look upon me as your friend—your very sincere friend. What I am doing is for your good: to-day I will write to my sister—and to-morrow you shall, proceed to her abode."

The housekeeper then resumed her avocations with the complacency of one conscious of having performed a duty.

"Thomas," she said, after a pause, "go up and inquire if your master will have breakfast served in his own chamber, or in the parlour."

The footman hastened to obey this order.

"Master says he is very unwell, and desires no breakfast at all," was the information which the man gave on his return to the kitchen.

The housekeeper made no reply: she was however pleased when she reflected that the rector felt his situation—a state of mind which she hoped would lead to complete repentance and reform.

The morning passed: the afternoon arrived: and still Reginald Tracy kept his room.

The housekeeper sent the footman up to ask if he required any thing.

Thomas returned with a negative answer, adding "Master spoke to me without opening the door, and seemed by his tone of voice to be very unwell."

Again the housekeeper remained silent, more convinced than before that contrition was working its good effects with her master.

Hour after hour passed; the sun went down; and darkness once more drew its veil over the mighty city.

Mrs. Kenrick again sent up Thomas with the same inquiry as before.

The servant returned to the kitchen with a letter in his hand.

"This time master opened the door," he said; "and gave me this letter to take up to Mr. Markham at Holloway. But I shall take the omnibus there and back."

Thomas then departed to execute his commission.

Shortly after he was gone, the bell of the rector's room rang.

Mrs. Kenrick hastened to answer it.

She found Mr. Tracy sitting in a musing attitude before the fire in his bed-room.

"My dear Mrs. Kenrick," he said, "I wish to have some conversation with you—I need scarcely now explain upon what subject. I have sent Thomas out of the way with an excuse: do you get rid of Katherine for an hour; I am faint—and require refreshment; and I will take my tea with you in the kitchen."

"In the kitchen, sir!" exclaimed the housekeeper, in surprise.

"Yes—if you will permit me," answered the rector: "I can then converse with you at the same time."

Mrs. Kenrick left the room to execute her master's wishes; and, as she descended the stairs, she thought within herself, "I am right! he has repented: he will become the virtuous and upright man he once was!"

And the good woman experienced a pleasure as sincere as if any one had announced to her that she was entitled to a princely fortune.

To send Katherine out of the way for an hour was no difficult matter. The old housekeeper gave her leave to repair to Saint Giles's to visit her relatives; and the young girl, thinking that her uncle might repent of his recent harshness towards her, now that she was no longer dependant upon him, gladly availed herself of this permission.

Katherine accordingly proceeded to Saint Giles's; and the moment she had left the house Mrs. Kenrick spread the kitchen table with the tea-things.

CHAPTER CLI.

A MYSTERIOUS DEED.

Katherine tripped lightly along towards Saint Giles's; but as she drew near her uncle's door, she relaxed her speed, and her heart grew somewhat heavy.

She was afraid of experiencing an unkind reception.

It was, therefore, with a pleasure the more lively as it was unexpected, that the poor girl found herself welcomed by a smile on the part of her dreaded relative.

"Come in, Kate," said he, when he perceived his niece; "I felt myself dull and lonely, and was just thinking of you as you knocked at the door. I'm almost sorry that I ever parted with you; but as you're now in a place that may do you good I shall not interfere with you."

"I am very much obliged to you for thinking so kindly of me, uncle," said Kate, wiping away a tear, as she followed Smithers into the little parlour, which, somehow or another, did not look so neat as it had been wont to do in her time.

"I can't help thinking of you now and then, Kate," continued Smithers. "But, I say," he added abruptly, "I hope you've forgotten all about the manner in which we parted t'other day?"

"Oh! indeed I have, uncle," answered the girl, more and more astonished at this unusual urbanity of manner.

"I am not happy—I'm not comfortable in my mind, somehow," said Smithers, after a short pause. "Since the night before last I haven't been myself."

"What ails you?" asked Kate, kindly.

"I think my last hour's drawing nigh, Kate," returned the public executioner, sinking his voice to a low and mysterious whisper; but, at the same time, his countenance grew deadly pale, and he cast a shuddering look around him.

"You are low-spirited, uncle—that's all," said Kate, surveying him attentively—for his peculiarity of manner alarmed her.

"No—that's not it, Kate," continued the executioner; then, drawing his chair closer towards that on which his niece was seated, he added, "I have had my warning."

"Your warning, uncle! What mean you?"

"I mean what I say, Kate," proceeded Smithers, in a tone of deep dejection: "I have had my warning; and I s'pose it will come three times."

"Uncle—dear uncle, I cannot understand you. You must be unwell. Will you have medical advice? Say—shall I fetch a physician?"

"Don't be silly, Kate: there's nothink the matter with my body;—it's the mind. But I'll tell you what it is," continued Smithers, after a few moments of profound reflection. "It was the night before last. I had been practising—you know how——"

"Yes—yes, uncle," said Katherine, hastily.

"And it was close upon midnight, when I thought I would go to bed. Well—I undressed myself, and as there was only a little bit of candle left, I didn't blow the light out, but put the candlestick into the fire-place. I then got into bed. In a very few minutes I fell into a sort of doze—more asleep than awake though, because I dreamt of the man that I hanged yesterday week. I didn't, however, sleep very long; for I woke with a start just as Saint Giles's was a striking twelve. The light was flickering in the candlestick, for it was just dying away. You know how a candle burnt down to the socket flares at one moment, and then seems quite dead the next, but revives again immediately afterwards?"

"Yes, uncle," answered Katherine; "and I have often thought that in the silent and solemn midnight it is an awful thing to see."

"So it struck me at that moment," continued the executioner. "I felt a strange sensation creeping all over me; the candle flared and flickered; and I thought it had gone out. Then it revived once more, and threw a strong but only a momentary light around the room. At that instant my eyes were fixed in the direction of the puppet; and, as sure as you are sitting there, Kate, *another face* looked at me over its shoulder!"

"Oh! my dear uncle, it was the imagination," said the young girl, casting an involuntary glance of timidity around.

"Is a man like me one of the sort to be deluded by the imagination?" asked Smithers, somewhat contemptuously. "Haven't I been too long in a certain way to have any foolish fears of that sort?"

"But when we are unwell, uncle, the bravest of us may perceive strange visions, which are nothing more than the sport of the imagination," urged Kate.

"I tell you this had nothing to do with the imagination," persisted the executioner. "I saw *another face* as plain as I see yours now; and—more than that—its glassy eyes were fixed upon me in a manner which I shall never forget. It was a warning—I know it was."

Kate made no reply: she saw the inutility of arguing with her uncle upon the subject; and she was afraid of provoking his irritable temper by contending against his obstinacy.

"But we won't talk any more about it, Kate," said the executioner, after a pause. "I know how to take it; and it doesn't frighten me; it only makes me dull. It hasn't prevented me from sleeping in my old quarters; nor will it, if I can help it. But you want to be off—I see you are getting fidgetty."

"I only received permission to remain out one hour," answered Kate. "Is my cousin at home?"

"The young vagabond!" ejaculated the executioner, whose irritability this question had aroused in spite of the depression of spirits under which he laboured; for he could not forget the unwearied repugnance which Gibbet manifested towards the paternal avocations:—"the young vagabond! he is never at home now of an evening."

"Never at home of an evening!" exclaimed Kate, surprised at this information.

"No," continued the executioner; "and at first I thought he went to see you."

"He can only visit me on Sunday evenings," observed the young maiden.

"So he told me yesterday. Howsumever, he goes out regular at dusk, and never comes back till between nine and ten—sometimes later."

"Then I am not likely to see him this evening?" exclaimed Kate, in a tone of disappointment.

"That you are not," replied the executioner. "But I must put a stop to these rovings on his part."

"Oh! pray be kind to him, uncle," said Katherine, rising to depart.

"Kind indeed!" grumbled the man, some of his old surliness returning.

Katherine then took leave of her uncle, and hurried towards Mr. Tracy's residence.

She reached her destination as the clock struck nine, and entered the house as usual, by the back way.

She proceeded to the kitchen, where, to her surprise, she observed Mrs. Kenrick sitting in her arm-chair, but apparently fast asleep. The old housekeeper's arms reposed upon the table, and formed a support for her head which had fallen forwards.

"Strange!" thought Katherine; "this is the first time I have known her sleep thus."

The young maiden moved lightly about the kitchen, while she threw off her bonnet and cloak, for fear of awaking the housekeeper.

Then she sate down near the fire, and fell into a profound reverie concerning the strange tale which her uncle had told her.

Presently it struck her that she did not hear the housekeeper breathe; and an awful suspicion rushed like a torrent into her mind.

For some moments she sate, motionless and almost breathless, in her chair, with her eyes fixed upon the inclined form of the housekeeper.

"My God!" at length Kate exclaimed; "she does not breathe—she does not move;—and her hands—oh! how pale they are!"

Then, overcoming her terror, the young maiden bent down her head so as to obtain a glimpse of Mrs. Kenrick's countenance.

"Oh! heavens—she is dead—she is dead!" cried the horror-struck girl, as her eyes encountered a livid and ghastly face instead of the healthy and good-humoured one which was familiar to her.

And Katherine sank back in her seat, overcome with grief and terror.

Suddenly the thought struck her that, after all, the housekeeper might only be in a fit.

Blaming herself for the delay which her fears had occasioned ere she administered succour, Kate hastened to raise the old lady's head.

But she let it fall again when she had obtained another glance of that ghastly countenance;—for the eyes were fixed and glazed—the under jaw had fallen—and the swollen tongue was lolling, dark and livid, out of the mouth.

Then Kate rushed into the yard, screaming for help.

The rector's groom (who also acted as coachman) was in the stable adjoining; and he immediately hastened to the spot.

"What is the matter?" he demanded, alarmed by the wildness of Katherine's manner and the piercing agony of her cries.

"Mrs. Kenrick is dead!" replied Katherine, sobbing bitterly.

"Dead!" ejaculated the man; and he instantly rushed into the kitchen.

In a few moments afterwards the rector made his appearance, and inquired the cause of the screams which had alarmed him.

"Mrs. Kenrick is dead, sir," said the groom.

Katherine had flung herself into a chair, and was giving full vent to her grief for the loss of her benefactress.

"Dead!" cried the rector. "No—let us hope not. Run for the nearest surgeon—it may only be a fit!"

"I'm afraid it's too late, sir," said the groom, who had now raised the housekeeper from her procumbent posture, and laid her back in the chair.

"Who knows? Run—run," exclaimed the rector impatiently.

The groom instantly departed; and during his short absence the rector was most assiduous in bathing the housekeeper's forehead with vinegar and water, and chafing her hands between his own.

In a few minutes the groom returned, accompanied by a surgeon; and the rector was found in the midst of his vain attentions.

The surgeon's examination was brief; but his words were decisive, as he said, "All human aid is vain, sir; and those appearances are most suspicious."

"What do you mean?" demanded Reginald.

"That your servant is poisoned," replied the surgeon.

"Poisoned!" exclaimed the rector. "Oh! no—you must mistake. She would not take poison herself, and I do not believe she has an enemy on the face of the earth."

"Nevertheless, Mr. Tracy," said the surgeon positively, "she is poisoned."

At these words Kate's sobs became more convulsive.

"But is it too late?" cried the rector: "can nothing be done? Is she past recovery?"

"Past all human succour, I repeat."

"My poor servant—my faithful friend," exclaimed Reginald Tracy, burying his face in his hands: "Oh! what could have induced her to commit suicide?"

"Suicide!" echoed Katherine, starting from her seat, and coming forward: "Oh! no, sir—do not wrong her memory thus! She was too good—too pious—too much bent upon the mercy of her Redeemer, to commit such a crime."

"Alas! suicide it must have been, my poor girl," said the rector; "for who could have administered poison to so harmless, so charitable, so humane a creature? Some secret grief, perhaps———"

At this moment Thomas returned from his mission to Markham Place. The poor fellow was deeply affected when the dreadful spectacle in the kitchen met his eyes, and when the few particulars yet known concerning the death of the housekeeper, or rather the first discovery of her death—were communicated to him.

"I never shall forgive myself as long as I live," exclaimed Thomas, "for having spoken cross to her, poor lady, this morning."

"Spoken cross to her!" cried the rector.

"Yes, sir," answered the man; "I said something to her—but I forget exactly what—because she told Katherine that she should send her away from London."

"Send Katherine away!" said Reginald, in unfeigned surprise.

"Yes, sir; and because I saw the girl didn't like it, I took her part against Mrs. Kenrick; and I'm now heartily sorry for it," rejoined Thomas, wiping away an honest tear.

"Young woman," said the surgeon, who had been attentively examining Katherine for some moments, "did you not visit my shop last evening?"

"I, sir!" exclaimed the young girl, who was too deeply absorbed in grief at the death of her benefactress to have her ideas very clearly distributed in the proper cells of her brain.

"Yes," continued the surgeon: "the more I look at you, the more I am convinced you came last night to my establishment and purchased a small phial of laudanum."

"Oh! yes—I remember, sir," said Katherine: "Mrs. Kenrick sent me for it, and told me that it was for my master."

The surgeon threw an inquiring glance towards Reginald.

"For me!" ejaculated the rector.

"So Mrs. Kenrick said, sir," returned Katherine: "and the moment I brought it in, she went up stairs with it."

"You can in one moment set at rest that point, sir," said the surgeon, with another glance of inquiry towards the rector.

"The laudanum was not for me," answered Mr. Tracy, calmly: "nor did I order my poor housekeeper to obtain any."

"O Katherine!" ejaculated Thomas; "surely—surely, you have not done this dreadful deed!"

"I——a murderess!" almost shrieked the poor girl: "Oh! no—no. God forbid!"

And she clasped her hands together.

The surgeon shook his head mysteriously.

"Merciful heavens!" exclaimed the rector, who was evidently excited to a painful degree, "you do not suspect—you cannot suppose—you do not—cannot imagine that—this young person——"

"I regret to state that the matter is to my mind most suspicious," observed the surgeon, with true professional calmness. "This morning the housekeeper informs that young person she must leave your establishment——"

"But, according to your own admission, the laudanum was purchased last night," interrupted the rector.

"Your humanity in pleading on behalf of that young woman does honour to your heart, Mr. Tracy," said the surgeon; "but was it not likely that she knew *yesterday* of some circumstance which would induce the housekeeper to give her warning *to-day*? and——"

"Oh! my God!" cried the rector, striking his forehead forcibly with the open palm of his right hand.

"To a virtuous mind like yours I know that such a suspicion must be abhorrent," said the surgeon.

He then whispered a few words to the groom.

The groom immediately went out.

"Mr. Tracy—sir—you cannot surely entertain a suspicion against me!" cried Katherine, in a tone of the most piercing anguish. "Oh! that poor creature was my benefactress; and I would sooner have died myself than have done her wrong!"

"I believe you," exclaimed the rector,—"believe you from the bottom of my heart!"

"Thank you, Mr. Tracy," cried the poor girl, falling upon her knees before him, and grasping his hands convulsively in her own.

"You are too good—too generous," muttered the surgeon. "Be not deluded by that tragic acting. At all events I must do my duty."

"What do you mean?" cried the rector. "You cannot say that suspicion attaches itself to this young girl. I would stake my existence upon her innocence!" he added emphatically.

"You know not human nature as I know it," returned the surgeon coolly.

At this moment the groom returned, followed by a police-officer.

"A person has met with her death in a most mysterious manner," said the surgeon; "and strong suspicions point towards that young female."

Then followed one of those heart-rending scenes which defy the powers of the most graphic pen to delineate.

Amidst the wildest screams—and with cries of despair which pierced even to the stoic heart of the surgeon, who had acted in a manner which he had deemed merely consistent with his duty, the unhappy girl was led away in the custody of the officer.

"My God! who would have thought that it would have come to this?" exclaimed Reginald Tracy, as he precipitated himself from the kitchen.

"The surgeon is right," observed Thomas to the groom; "master is too good a man to believe in guilt of so black a nature."

CHAPTER CLII.

THE DEATH BED.

Early on the morning which succeeded the arrest of Katharine Wilmot, Mr. Gregory paid a visit to Markham Place.

The moment he entered the room where Richard received him, our hero observed that some deep affliction weighed upon the mind of his friend.

"Mr. Markham," said the latter, in a tone of profound anguish, "I am come to ask you a favour—and you will not refuse the last request of a dying girl."

"My dear sir—what do you mean?" exclaimed Richard. "Surely your daughter———"

"Mary-Anne will not long remain in this world of trouble," interrupted Mr. Gregory, solemnly. "Hers will soon be the common lot of mortals—perhaps to-day, perhaps to-morrow! She must die soon—God will change her countenance and take her unto himself. Oh! where shall I find consolation?"

"Consolation is to be found in the conviction that the earth is no abiding place," answered Markham; "and that there is a world beyond."

"Yes, truly," said the afflicted father. "We stand upon the border of an ocean *which has but one shore*, and whose heavings beyond are infinite and eternal."

There was a pause, during which Mr. Gregory was wrapped up in painful reflections.

"Come," said he, at length breaking that solemn silence, and taking Richard's hand; "you will not refuse to go with me to the death-chamber of my daughter? You will not offend against the delicacy of that devotion which you owe to *another*; for *she* herself is also there."

Richard gazed at Mr. Gregory in astonishment as he uttered these words.

"Yes, my young friend," continued the wretched father; "within the last four and twenty hours, Mary-Anne and I have had many explanations. By a strange coincidence, it was at the abode of Count Alteroni that Mary-Anne passed a few days at the commencement of last month, and to which visit I alluded the last time I saw you, but without particularising names. I did not then know that you were even acquainted with the Alteroni family—much less could I suspect that your affections were fixed upon the Lady Isabella."

"And your daughter and Isabella are acquainted?" ejaculated Markham, more and more surprised at what he heard.

"They are friends—and at this moment the Lady Isabella is by the bed-side of Mary-Anne. It seems that the young maidens made confidants of each other, during my daughter's visit to the Count's mansion; and they then discovered that they both loved the same individual."

"How strange that they should have thus met!" cried Markham.

"Then was it," continued Mr. Gregory, "that my daughter learnt how hopeless was her own passion! Oh! I need not wonder if she returned home heart-broken and dying! But your Isabella, Richard, is an angel of goodness, virtue, and beauty!"

"She is worthy of the loftiest destinies!" said Markham enthusiastically.

"She was present when my daughter poured forth her soul into my bosom," resumed Mr. Gregory; "and Mary-Anne was guilty of no breach of confidence in revealing to me the love which existed between the Signora and yourself. And Isabella, with the most becoming modesty, confirmed the truth of Mary-Anne's recital. But your secret, Mr. Markham, remains locked up in my breast. You are too honourable and the Lady Isabella is too pure-minded to act in opposition to the will of her father: but God grant that events may prove favourable to you, and that you may be happily united!"

Richard pressed the hand of his respected friend in token of gratitude for this kind wish.

"And now you cannot hesitate to take a last farewell of my daughter," said Mr. Gregory; "for all danger of contagion from her malady has passed."

Markham instantly prepared himself to accompany the unhappy parent.

Few were the words that passed between them as they proceeded to the dwelling which was the abode of sorrow.

On their arrival Markham was shown into the drawing-room for a short time; and then the nurse came to introduce him into the sick-chamber.

The room was nearly dark; the curtains of the bed were close drawn; and thus the dying girl was completely concealed from our hero.

But near the foot of the bed was standing a beauteous form, whose symmetrical shape Markham could not fail to recognise.

Isabella extended her hand towards him: he pressed it in silence to his lips.

Mary-Anne had heard his footsteps; and she also gave him her hand between the folds of the curtains.

"Sit down by the bed-side, Richard," whispered Isabella: "our poor friend is anxious to speak to you."

And Isabella wept—and Richard also wept; for those noble-minded beings could not know, without the liveliest emotion, that one so sweet, so innocent, and so youthful, was stretched upon the bed from which she was destined never to rise again.

Markham seated himself by the side of the bed; and Isabella was about to withdraw.

"Stay with us, my dear friend," said Mary-Anne, in a plaintive but silver tone of voice, which touched a chord of sympathy that vibrated to their very souls.

Alas! that dulcet voice could not move the tuneless ear of Death!

Isabella obeyed her friend's wish in silence.

"This is kind of you—very kind," continued Mary-Anne, after a brief pause, and now evidently addressing herself to Richard. "I longed to speak to you once again before I left this earthly scene for ever; and that angel who loves you, and whom you love, earnestly implored my father to procure for me that last consolation. And now that you are both here together—you and that angel, by my bed-side,—I may be allowed to tell you, Richard, how fondly—how devotedly I have loved you; and I know you to be the noble, the enduring, the patient, the high-minded, and the honourable being I always believed you to be. Oh! how rejoiced I am that you have not loved me in return; for I should not like to die and leave behind me one who had loved me as tenderly as I had loved him."

"You will not die—you will recover!" exclaimed Markham, deeply affected, while Isabella's ill-suppressed sobs fell upon his ears. "Yes—yes—you will recover, to bless your father and brothers, and to make *us*, who are your friends, happy! It is impossible that Death can covet one so young, so innocent, and so beautiful——"

"Beautiful!" cried Mary-Anne, with a bitterness of accent which surprised our hero, and which served to elicit a fresh burst of sorrow from the sympathising bosom of Isabella: "beautiful—no, not now!"

Then there was another solemn pause.

"Yes—I shall die; but you will be happy," resumed Mary-Anne, again breaking silence. "Something assures me that providence will not blight the love which exists between Isabella and yourself—as it has seen fit to blight mine! Such is my presentiment; and the presentiments of the dying are often strangely prophetic of the future truth. Oh!" continued the young maiden, in a tone of excitement, "brilliant destinies await you, Richard! All your enduring patience, your resignation under the oppression of foul wrong, will meet with a glorious reward. Yes—for I know all:—that angel Isabella has kept no secret from me. She is a Princess, Richard; and by your union with her, you yourself will become one of the greatest Princes in Europe! Her father, too, shall succeed to his just rights; and then, Richard, then—" she said, with a sort of holy enthusiasm and sybilline fervour,—"*then* how small will be the distance between yourself and the Castelcicalan throne!"

At that solemn moment, Isabella extended her hand towards Richard, who pressed hers tenderly; and the lovers thus acknowledged the impression which had been wrought and the happy augury which was conveyed by the fervent language of the dying girl.

"Oh! do not think my words are of vain import," continued Mary-Anne, in the same tone of inspiration. "I speak not of my own accord—something within me dictates all I now say! Yes—you shall be happy with each other; all obstacles shall vanish from the paths of your felicity; and when, in your sovereign palace of Montoni, you shall in future years retrospect over all you have seen and all you have passed through, forget not the dying girl who predicted for you all the happiness which you will then enjoy!"

"Forget you!" exclaimed Richard and Isabella in the same breath; "never—never!"

And the tears streamed down their cheeks.

"No—never forget me," said Mary-Anne; "for if it be allowed to the spirits of the departed to hover round the dwellings of those whom they loved and have left in this world, then will I be as a guardian angel unto you—and I shall contemplate your happiness with joy!"

"Oh! speak not thus surely of approaching death," exclaimed Richard. "Who knows that your eyes may not again behold the light!"

"My eyes!" repeated the invalid, with an evident shudder. "But for what could I live?" demanded the young maiden: "what attractions could life now offer to me?"

"You are young," returned Markham: "and hope and youth are inseparable. You can mingle with society,—you can appear in the great world—a world that will be proud of you———"

"Oh! Richard, Richard," murmured the soft tones of Isabella; "you know not what you say!"

At the same time that the Signora thus spoke in a low whisper, deep and convulsive sobs emanated from behind the curtains.

"Pardon me, Mary-Anne," said Richard, not comprehending the meaning of Isabella's words; "I have probably touched a chord———"

"Oh! I do not blame you," said Miss Gregory; "but my father ought to have told you all!"

"All!" echoed Richard. "What fresh misfortune could he have communicated?"

"Did he not tell you that I had been attacked with a grievous malady? that———"

"I remember! He spoke of a dangerous malady which had assailed you; and he remarked that all fear of contagion was now past. But I was so occupied at the time with the afflicting intelligence of your severe illness—so surprised, too, when I learnt that Isabella was here with you,—that I paid but little attention to that observation."

"Alas!" said Mary-Anne, in a faint and deeply-melancholy tone, "I have been assailed by a horrible malady—a malady which leaves its fatal marks behind, as if the countenance had been seared with red-hot iron—which disfigures the lineaments of the human face—eats into the flesh—and—and———"

"The small-pox!" cried Markham with a shudder.

"The small-pox," repeated Mary-Anne. "But you need not be alarmed: all danger of infection or contagion is now past—or I should not have sent to Isabella to come to me yesterday."

"I am not afraid," answered our hero: "I shuddered on your account. And even if there were any danger," he added, "I should not fly from it, if my presence be a consolation to you."

"You now understand," said the dying girl, "the reason why I could not hope for happiness in this world, even if I were to recover from my present illness,—and why death will be preferable to existence in a state of sorrow. How could I grope about in darkness, where I have been accustomed to feast my eyes with the beauties of nature and the wonderful fabrics raised by men? How could I consent to linger on in blindness in a world where there is so much to admire?"

"Blindness!" echoed our hero: "impossible! You cannot mean what you say!"

"Alas! it were a folly to jest upon one's death-bed," returned the young lady, with a deep sigh. "What I said ere now was the truth. The malady made giant strides to hurry me to the tomb: never had the physicians before known its ravages to proceed with such frightful celerity. It has left its traces upon my countenance—and it has deprived me of the blessing of sight. Oh! now I am hideous—a monster,—I know, I feel that I am,—revolting, disgusting," continued Mary-Anne, bitterly; "and not for worlds would I allow you to behold that face which once possessed some attraction."

"The marks left by the scourge that has visited you will gradually become less apparent," said Richard, deeply afflicted by the tone, the manner, and the communications of the invalid; "and probably the eye-lids are but closed for a time, and can be opened again by the skill of a surgeon."

"Never—never!" cried Mary-Anne, convulsively; and, taking Richard's hand, she carried it to her countenance.

She placed his fingers upon her closed eye-lids.

He touched them; they yielded to his pressure.

The sockets of the eyes were empty.

The eye-balls were gone!

"Oh! wherefore art thou thus afflicted—thou who art so guiltless, so pure, so innocent?" exclaimed our hero, unable to contain his emotions.

"Question not the will of the deity," said Mary-Anne. "I am resigned to die; and if, at times, a regret in favour of the world I am leaving enters my mind, or is made apparent in my language, I pray the Almighty to pardon me those transient repinings. Of the past it is useless now to think;—the present is here;—and the future is an awful subject for contemplation. But upon that I must now fix my attention!"

Markham made no answer; and during the long silence which ensued, the dying girl was wrapt up in mental devotion.

At length she said, "Give me your hand, Richard—and yours, Isabella."

Her voice had now lost all its excitement; and her utterance was slow and languid.

The lovers obeyed her desire.

Mary-Anne placed their hands together, and said, "Be faithful to each other—and be happy."

Richard and Isabella both wept plentifully.

"Adieu, my kind—my dear friends," murmured Mary-Anne. "You must now leave me; and let my father come to receive the last wishes of his daughter."

"Adieu, dearest Mary-Anne: we shall meet in heaven!" said Isabella, in a tone expressive of deep emotion.

"We will never—never forget you," added Richard.

He then led the weeping Isabella from the apartment.

As they issued from the chamber of death, they met Mr. Gregory in the passage: he wrung their hands, and said, "Wait in the drawing-room until I come."

The unhappy parent then repaired to the death-bed of his daughter.

Markham and Isabella proceeded in silence to the drawing-room.

CHAPTER CLIII.

PROCEEDINGS IN CASTELCICALA.

The scene, which they had just witnessed, produced a most painful impression upon the minds of the lovely Italian lady and Richard Markham.

For some moments after they were alone in the drawing-room together, they maintained a profound silence.

At length Richard spoke.

"It is a mournful occurrence which has brought us together to-day, Isabella," he said.

"And although this meeting between us be unknown to my father," answered Isabella, "yet the nature of the circumstance which caused it must serve as my apology in your eyes."

"In my eyes!" ejaculated Markham. "Oh! how can an apology be necessary for an interview with one who loves you as I love you?"

"I am not accustomed to act the prude, Richard," returned Isabella; "and therefore I will not say that I regret having met you,—apart from the sad event which led to our meeting."

"Oh! Isabella, if I do not now renew to you all my former protestations of affection, it is because it were impious for us to think of our love, when death is busy in the same house."

"Richard, I admire your feeling in this respect. But you are all our poor dying friend proclaimed you—high-minded, honourable, and generous. O Richard! the prophetic language of Mary-Anne has produced a powerful impression upon my mind!"

"And on mine, also," answered Markham. "Not that I esteem the prospective honours displayed to my view; but because I hope—sincerely hope—that my adored Isabella may one day be mine."

The Princess tendered him her hand, which he kissed in rapture.

"Do you know," said Isabella, after a few moments' silence, "that events are taking a turn in Castelcicala, which may lead to all that poor Mary-Anne has prophesied? There was a strong party in the state opposed to the marriage of the Grand Duke; and the military department was particularly dissatisfied."

"I remember that in the accounts which I read of the celebration of that marriage, it was stated that the ducal procession experienced a chilling reception from the soldiery."

"True," answered Isabella; "and early last month—a few days after the commencement of the new year—that spirit showed itself more unequivocally still. Three regiments surrounded the ducal palace, and demanded a constitution. The Grand Duke succeeded in pacifying them with vague promises; and the regiments retired to their quarters. It then appears that his Serene Highness wished to make an example of those regiments, and drew up a decree ordaining them to be disbanded, the officers to be cashiered, and the men to be distributed amongst other corps."

"That was a severe measure," remarked Richard.

"So severe," continued Isabella, "that General Grachia, the Minister of War, refused to sign the ducal ordinance. He was accordingly compelled to resign, the Duke remaining inflexible. The whole of the Cabinet-Ministers then sent in their resignations, which the Grand Duke accepted. Signor Pisani, the Under Secretary for Foreign Affairs, was charged with the formation of a new ministry—a fact which shows how completely the Duke has alienated from himself all the great statesmen of Castelcicala."

"So that he has been compelled to have recourse to an Under Secretary as his Prime Minister," observed Richard.

"Precisely," answered Isabella. "Signor Pisani formed an administration; and its first act was to carry into force the decree already drawn up against the three discontented regiments. The second proceeding of the new ministry was to banish General Grachia from the country."

"This was madness!" ejaculated Markham. "Does the Grand Duke wish to seal his own ruin?"

"It would appear that he is desperate," continued Isabella, "as I shall show you in a moment. General Grachia left Montoni, accompanied by his family, and followed by immense multitudes, who cheered him as the well-known friend of the Prince my father. The troops also crowded in his way, to show their respect for the veteran chief who had so often led them to conquest. The next morning a ducal ordinance appeared, which showed that the Grand Duke was resolved to throw off the mask, and proclaim a despotism. I have the *Montoni Gazette* in my reticule."

Isabella produced the newspaper, and, opening it, said, "I will translate the ordinance to you."

"Nay—rather allow me to read it for myself," returned Markham.

"How? But it is in Italian," exclaimed the Signora.

"And I will read it in that tongue," said Richard.

"I was not aware—I knew not until now——"

"No, dearest Isabella: until lately the Italian language was as Chinese to me," interrupted Richard: "but I have studied it intensely—without aid, without guidance; and if I cannot speak it fluently nor with the correct pronunciation, I can understand it with ease, and—I flatter myself—speak at least intelligibly."

The lovely Italian girl listened to this announcement with the most tender interest. She received it as a proof of boundless love for her; and sweet—ineffably sweet was the glance of deep gratitude which she threw upon her lover.

Richard took the *Montoni Gazette* from the fair hand which tendered it to him, and then read, with ease and fluency, the following translation of the ducal ordinance alluded to:—

"ANGELO III., BY THE GRACE OF GOD, GRAND

DUKE OF CASTELCICALA,

"To all present and to come, Greeting:

"We have ordered and do order that which follows:—

"I. The censorship of the press is restored from this date: and no newspaper nor periodical work shall be published in our dominions, without the consent of the Minister of the Interior.

"II. Offences against this law, as well as all others connected with the press, shall henceforth be brought before the cognizance of the Captain-General of the province where such offences may occur, instead of before the ordinary tribunals.

"III. No assembly of more than seven persons will henceforth be allowed to take place, without the consent of the local authorities, save for the purposes of religious worship and ceremonial.

"IV. Our Captains-General are hereby authorised to declare martial law in their provinces, or any part of their provinces, should signs of insubordination appear.

"V. Our Minister Secretary of State for the Department of the Interior will see to the execution of this our ordinance.

"*By the Grand Duke*, ANGELO III.

"RAPALLO PISANI,

"Minister of the Interior.

"*January 10th, 1840.*"

"The Grand Duke has thus destroyed the freedom of the press, promulgated a law to suppress political meetings, and menaced the country with martial law," said Richard, when he had terminated the perusal of this ordinance.

"And it would appear, by the newspapers and by private letters which my father has received," added Isabella, "that the Grand Duke would have proceeded to extremes far more dangerous to his throne had not his amiable Duchess softened him. But even her intercessions—and I understand she is a most deserving princess—were ineffectual in a great measure."

"Know you the results of that despotic ordinance?" asked Markham.

"Several riots have taken place at Montoni," answered the Signora; "and the Captain-General of the province of Abrantani has proclaimed martial law throughout the districts which he governs."

"Matters are then becoming serious in Castelcicala," observed Richard. "What has become of General Grachia?"

"No one knows. He left Montoni within twenty-four hours after the receipt of the decree of exile; but my father has received no information of his progress or intentions. Oh! my beloved country," she exclaimed, in a tone of pious fervour, "may God grant that thou wilt not be the scene of anarchy, bloodshed, and civil strife!"

Richard surveyed his beautiful companion with the most enraptured admiration, as she uttered that holy wish,—a wish that spoke so eloquently of the absence of all selfishness from her pure soul.

The above conversation had been carried on in a subdued tone; and its topic had not excluded from the minds of the young lovers the recollection of the sad scene which they had ere now witnessed.

Indeed they only pursued their discourse upon that particular subject, because it was connected with the chain of events which seemed adapted to carry out the prophetic hopes of the dying girl.

Nearly an hour had passed since they had left the chamber of death.

At length the door opened slowly, and Mr. Gregory entered the drawing-room.

His countenance was deadly pale; and yet it wore an expression of pious resignation.

Isabella and Richard knew that all was over.

Mr. Gregory advanced towards them, and taking their hands, said, "She is gone—she died in my arms! Almost her last words were, '*Tell Isabella and Richard sometimes to think of Mary-Anne.*'"

The bereaved parent could subdue his grief no longer: he threw himself upon the sofa and burst into tears.

Nor were the cheeks of Isabella and Richard unmoistened by the holy dew of sweet sympathy.

"Richard," said Mr. Gregory, after a long pause, "you must write to my sons and tell them of this sad affliction. Desire them to return home immediately from college: I was wrong not to have sent for them before; but—my God! I knew not that my sweet child's death was so near!"

Markham instantly complied with Mr. Gregory's request, and despatched the letter to the post.

Scarcely was this duty accomplished, when Count Alteroni's carriage drove up to the door. It was, however, empty, having been merely sent to fetch Isabella home.

The Signora took leave of Mr. Gregory, and bade a tender adieu to Richard, who handed her into the vehicle.

The carriage then drove away.

Richard passed the remainder of the day with Mr. Gregory, and returned home in the evening deeply affected at the misfortune which had overtaken an amiable family.

But Markham, on his arrival at his own house, was doomed to hear tidings of a most unpleasant nature.

"Mr. Tracy's footman has been here with very disagreeable news," said Ellen, the moment Markham entered the sitting-room. "Had I known whither you were gone, I should have directed him on to you."

"Mr. Tracy's footman!" exclaimed Richard. "Why—he was here last evening, with a letter from his master inviting me and Mr. Monroe to dine with him next Monday——"

"I am aware of it," interrupted Ellen. "And you declined the invitation."

"Yes—because I do not seek society," observed Richard. "I wrote a proper answer: what, then, did his servant require to-day?"

"It appears that a young person in whom you felt some interest——"

"Katherine Wilmot?" said Richard.

"That is the name," returned Ellen.

"What about her?" asked our hero.

"She has committed a crime——"

"A crime!"

"A crime of the blackest dye: she has poisoned Mr. Tracy's housekeeper."

"Ellen you are deceived—you are mistaken: it is impossible!" exclaimed Markham, "I never saw her but once, it is true: and still the impression she made upon me was most favourable. I did not mention any thing concerning her to either you or your father, because I sought to do an act of humanity in tearing her away from a wretched home; and I am not one who speaks of such a deed as that."

"I am not deceived—I am not mistaken, Richard," answered Ellen. "The footman came and narrated to me the particulars; and he said that his master was too unwell, through horror and excitement, to write to you upon the subject."

Ellen then related the few particulars yet known in connexion with the case, but the nature of which is already before the reader.

Richard remained silent for a long time, after Ellen had ceased to speak.

"If that innocent-looking girl be a murderess," he exclaimed at length, "I shall never put faith in human appearances again. But, until she be proved guilty, I will not desert her."

"Do you know," said Ellen, "that I do not like your Mr. Tracy at all! Not that I suppose him capable of falsely accusing any one of so heinous a crime as murder; but—I do not like him."

"A female caprice, Ellen," observed Richard. "The world in general adores him."

"Ah! those who stand upon the highest pinnacles often experience the most signal falls," said Ellen.

"The breath of calumny has never tainted his fair fame," cried Richard.

"Alas! we have so many—many instances of profound ecclesiastical hypocrisy," persisted Miss Monroe.

"Ellen, you wrong an excellent man," said Markham, somewhat severely. "I will call upon him to-morrow morning, and learn from his own lips the particulars of this most mysterious deed."

CHAPTER CLIV.

REFLECTIONS.—THE NEW PRISON.

Richard Markham passed an uneasy night.

His thoughts wandered from topic to topic until the variety seemed infinite.

He pondered upon his brother, and again reflected for the thousandth time what connexion could possibly exist between him and the Resurrection Man. The fatal letter, desiring this terrible individual to call upon him, was too decidedly in Eugene's handwriting to be doubted. The other contents of the pocket-book, which Richard had found in the Gipsies' Palace, threw no light upon the subject; indeed, they only consisted of a few papers of no consequence to any one.

Then Richard's thoughts travelled to the Resurrection Man himself. Was this individual really no more? Had the truth been told relative to his death at the Gipsies' encampment near Pentonville prison?

Next our hero's imagination wandered to the death-bed of the innocent girl who had entertained so unfortunate a passion for him. What fervent love was that! what disinterested affection! And then to perish in such a manner,—with the darkness of the tomb upon her eyes, long ere death itself made its dread appearance!

But with what inspiration had she prophesied the most exalted destinies for him she loved! With her sybilline finger she had pointed to a throne!

And then how speedily were those predictions followed by the communication of events which portended grand political changes in Castelcicala,—changes which threatened the reigning sovereign with overthrow, and the inevitable result of which must be the elevation of Prince Alberto to the ducal throne!

And Isabella—how many proofs of her unvaried love for our hero had she not given? She had confessed her attachment to the deceased maiden—she had avowed it to that deceased maiden's father. Then, when Mary-Anne had prophesied the exalted rank which Isabella would be destined to confer, by the fact of marriage, upon Richard, the lovely Italian had ratified the premise by the gentle pressure of her hand!

Next our hero pondered upon the awful deed which had been ascribed to Katherine Wilmot; and here he was lost in a labyrinth of amaze, distrust, and doubt. Could it be possible that the blackest heart was concealed in so fair a shrine? or had circumstantial evidence accumulated with fearful effect to enthral an innocent girl in the meshes of the criminal law? Richard remembered how he himself had suffered through the overwhelming weight of circumstantial evidence; and this thought rendered him slow to put faith in the guilt of others.

Then, amidst other topics, Richard meditated upon the mysterious instructions which were conveyed to him in the document left behind by Armstrong, and which seemed to promise much by the solemn earnestness that characterised the directions relative to the circumstances or the time that would justify him in opening the sealed packet.

Thus, if some of our hero's thoughts were calculated to produce uneasiness, others were associated with secret hopes of successful love and dazzling visions of prosperity.

In three years and a half the appointment with his brother was to be kept. How would they meet? and would Eugene appear on the day named, and upon the hill where the two trees stood? Why had he not written in the meantime? Was he progressing so well that he wished to surprise his brother with his great prosperity? or was he so wretched that his proud heart prevented him from seeking the assistance of one of whom he had taken leave with a species of challenge to a race in the paths which lead to fortune? That Eugene was alive, Richard felt convinced, because the inscriptions on the tree—*Eugene's own tree*—and the letter to the Resurrection Man, proved this fact. The same circumstances also showed that Eugene had been several times in London (even if he did not dwell in the metropolis altogether) since he parted with Richard upon the hill.

Then Richard reflected that if he himself were eventually prosperous, his success would be owing to fair and honourable means; and he sincerely hoped that his brother might be pursuing an equally harmless career. Such an idea, however, seemed to be contradicted by the mysterious note to the Resurrection Man. But our hero remembered that bad men often enjoyed immense success; and then he thought of Mr. Greenwood—the man who had robbed him of his property, but whom, so far as he knew, he had never seen. That Greenwood was rising rapidly, Richard was well aware; the newspapers conveyed that information. So well had he played his cards, that a baronetcy, if not even a junior post in the administration, would be his the moment his party should come to power. All this Richard knew: the Tory journals were strenuous in their praise of Mr. Greenwood, and lauded to the skies his devotion to the statesmen who were aspiring to office. Then the great wealth of Mr. Greenwood had become proverbial: not a grand enterprise of the day could be started without his name. He was a director in no end of Railway Companies; a shareholder in all the principal Life Insurance Offices; a speculator in every kind of stock; chairman of several commercial associations; a ship-owner; a landowner; a subscriber to all charitable institutions which published a list of its supporters; President of a Bible Society which held periodical meetings at Exeter Hall; one of the stanchest friends to the Society for the Suppression of Vice; a great man at the parochial vestry; a patron of Sunday Schools; a part-proprietor of an influential newspaper; an advocate for the suppression of Sunday trading and Sunday travelling; a member of half a dozen clubs; a great favourite at Tattersall's; a regular church-goer; a decided enemy to mendicity; an intimate friend of the Poor Law Commissioners; and an out-and-out foe to all Reform. All this Richard knew; for he took some interest in watching the career of a person who had risen from nothing to be so great a man as Mr. Greenwood was. Then, while he reflected upon these facts, our hero was compelled to admit that his brother Eugene might appear, upon the appointed day, the emblem of infinite prosperity, and yet a being from whom the truly honest would shrink back with dismay.

But we will not follow Richard Markham any further in his reflections during that sleepless night.

He rose at an early hour, and anxiously awaited the arrival of the morning's newspaper.

From that vehicle of information he learnt that Katherine Wilmot had been examined, on the previous day, before the magistrate at the Marylebone Police Court, and had been remanded for one week, in order that the depositions might be made out previous to her committal to Newgate to take her trial for the murder of Matilda Kenrick.

We need not now dwell upon the evidence adduced on the occasion of that preliminary investigation, inasmuch as we shall be hereafter compelled to detail it at some length.

We must, however, observe that when Richard Markham perused all the testimony adduced against the girl before the magistrate, he was staggered; for it seemed crushing, connected, and overwhelming indeed.

Nevertheless, he remembered his own unhappy case; and he determined not to desert her.

He called upon Mr. Tracy, and found that gentleman unwilling to believe that so young and seemingly innocent a girl could be capable of so enormous a crime; yet the reverend gentleman was compelled to admit not only that the evidence weighed strongly against her, but that it was difficult to conceive how the housekeeper had come by her death unless by Katherine's hands.

Richard took his leave of the rector, in whom he saw only a most compassionate man—ready to allow justice to take its course, but very unwilling to utter a word prejudicial to the accused.

From Mr. Tracy's house our hero proceeded to the New Prison, Clerkenwell, to see Katherine.

The New Prison is situate in the midst of the most densely populated part of Clerkenwell. It was originally established in the reign of James I.; but in 1816 it was considerably improved and enlarged, at the enormous cost of £40,000. It is now destined to be levelled with the ground, and a new prison is to be built upon the same site, but upon a plan adapted for the application of the atrocious *solitary system*.

The infamy of the English plan of gaol discipline is nowhere more strikingly illustrated than in the New Prison, Clerkenwell. Between five and six thousand prisoners pass annually through this gaol; and not the slightest attempt at classification, save in respect to sex, is made. The beds are filthy in the extreme, and often full of vermin from the last occupant: thus prisoners who arrive at the prison in a cleanly state, find themselves covered with loathsome animalculæ after one night's rest in that disgusting place. A miserable attempt at cleanliness is made by bathing the prisoners; but the generality of them dislike it, and bribe the wardsmen to allow them to escape the ordeal. And no wonder—for the gaol authorities compel every six individuals to bathe one after the other in the same water, and it frequently happens that a cleanly person is forced into a bath containing the filth and vermin washed from the person of a beggar. The reader must remember, that highly respectable persons—even gentlemen and ladies—may become prisoners in this establishment, for breaches of the peace, assaults, or menaces, until they be released by bail; and yet the gentlemen are compelled to herd with felons, beggars, and misdemeanants—and the ladies with the lowest grade of prostitutes and the filthiest vagrants!

The prisoners pilfer from each other; and the entire establishment is a scene of quarrelling, swearing, fighting, obscenity, and gambling. The male prisoners write notes of the most disgusting description, and throw them over with a coal into the female yard. Riots and disturbances are common in the sleeping wards; and ardent spirits are procured with tolerable facility.

The degradation of mingling with the obscene and filthy inmates of the female Reception Ward was, however, avoided by poor Katherine Wilmot. The Keeper took compassion upon her youth and the deep distress of mind into which she was plunged, and sent her to the Female Infirmary.

When Richard Markham called at the New Prison, he was permitted to have an interview with Katherine in the Keeper's office.

The hapless girl flew towards our hero, as if to a brother, and clasping her hands fervently together, exclaimed, "Mr. Markham, I am innocent—I am innocent!"

"So I choose to believe you—unless a jury should pronounce you to be guilty," replied Richard; "and even then," he added, in a musing tone, "it is possible—I mean that juries are not infallible."

"Oh! Mr. Markham, I am most unfortunate—and very, very unhappy!" said Katherine, the tears rolling down her cheeks. "I have never injured a human being—and yet, see where I am! see how I am treated!"

At that moment Richard recalled to mind all that the policeman had told him relative to the unpretending charity of the poor girl,—her goodness even to the very neighbours who despised her,—her amiability towards her unfortunate cousin,—the pious resignation with which she had supported the ill-treatment of her uncle,—and her constant anxiety to earn her own bread in a respectable manner.

All this Richard remembered; and he felt an invincible belief in the complete innocence of the poor creature with respect to the awful deed now laid to her charge.

"It is not death that I fear, Mr. Markham," said Katherine, after a pause; "but it is hard—very hard to be accused of a crime which I abhor! No—I do not fear death: perhaps it would be better for me to die even at my age—than dwell in a world which has no charms for me. For I have been unhappy from my birth, Mr. Markham: I was left an orphan when I was young—so very young—oh! too young to lose both parents! Since then my existence has not been blest; and at the very moment when a brighter destiny seemed opened to me, through the goodness of yourself and Mr. Tracy, I am suddenly snatched away to a prison, and overwhelmed with this terrible accusation!"

"Katherine," said Richard, deeply affected by the young girl's tone and words, "I believe you to be innocent—as God is my judge, I believe you to be innocent!"

"And may that same Almighty Power bless you for this assurance!" exclaimed Katherine, pressing our hero's hands with the most grateful warmth.

"Although in asserting my conviction of your innocence, Katherine," continued Richard, "I leave the deed itself enveloped in the darkest mystery, still I *do* believe that you are innocent—and I will not desert you."

Richard remembered how grateful to *his* ears had once sounded those words, "I believe that you are innocent,"—when Thomas Armstrong uttered them in the prison of Newgate.

"Yes, Katherine—you *are*, you *must* be innocent," he continued; "and I will labour unceasingly to make your innocence apparent. I will provide the ablest counsel to assist in your defence; and all that human agency can effect in your behalf shall be ensured at any cost."

The poor girl could not find words to express her deep gratitude to this young man who so generously constituted himself her champion, and on whom she had not the slightest claim;—but her looks and her tears conveyed to our hero all she felt.

"Has your uncle been to see you?" he inquired.

"No, sir—nor my cousin," replied Katherine, with melancholy emphasis upon the latter words.

"Perhaps they are unaware of your situation. I will call and communicate to them the sad tidings. As your relatives, it is right that they should know the truth."

He then took leave of the young creature, who now felt less forlorn since she knew that she possessed at least one friend who would not only exert himself in her behalf, but who also believed in her innocence.

From the New Prison Richard proceeded to Saint Giles's, and knocked at the door of the Public Executioner's abode.

But his summons remained unanswered.

He repeated it again: all was silent within.

At length a neighbour,—a man who kept a coal and potato shed,—emerged from his shop, and volunteered some information concerning the hangman and his son.

"It's no use knocking and knocking there, sir," said the man: "Smithers and his lad left London early yesterday morning for some place in the north of Ireland—I don't know the name—but where there's some work in his partickler line. The postman brought Smithers a letter, asking him to start off without delay; and he did so. He took Gibbet with him to give him another chance, he said, of trying his hand. Smithers told me all this before he went away, and asked me to take in any letters that might come for him, or answer any one that called. That's how I came to know all this."

"Do you happen to be aware when he will return?" asked Richard.

"I've no more idea than that there tater," answered the man, indicating with his foot a specimen of the vegetable alluded to.

Richard thanked the man for the information which he had been enabled to give, and then pursued his way towards the chief police station in the neighbourhood.

Arrived at that establishment, he inquired for Morris Benstead.

The officer happened to be on the premises at the moment.

Markham led him to a short distance, and then addressed him as follows:—

"You have doubtless heard of the extraordinary position in which poor Katherine Wilmot is placed. I, for one, firmly believe her to be innocent."

"So do I, sir," exclaimed the officer, emphatically.

"Then you will prove the more useful to my purposes in consequence of that impression," said Richard. "When I saw you on a former occasion, you offered me your services if ever I should require them. Little did I then suppose that I should so soon need your aid. Are you willing to assist me in investigating this most mysterious affair?"

"With pleasure, sir—with the sincerest pleasure," answered Benstead. "You know the respect I entertain for Miss Kate."

"And I know your goodness of heart," said our hero. "You must then aid me in collecting proofs of her innocence. Spare no expense in your task: hesitate not to apply to me for any money that you may need. Here are ten pounds for immediate purposes. To-morrow I will let you know whom I shall decide upon employing to conduct the poor girl's defence; and you can then communicate direct with the solicitor and barrister retained. Are you willing to undertake this task?"

"Need you ask me, sir?" cried the policeman. "I would do any thing to serve Miss Kate."

"Prudence renders it necessary for me to keep myself in the back-ground in this affair," said Richard; "for fear lest scandal should attach an unworthy motive to my exertions in her behalf, and thus prejudice her cause by injuring her character. Upon you, then, I throw the weight of the investigation."

"And I accept it cheerfully," returned Benstead.

Markham then took leave of the officer, and having paid a visit to Mr. Gregory, returned home.

CHAPTER CLV.

PATRIOTISM.

It was late in the evening of the day on which Richard adopted the measures just recorded to ensure the most complete investigation into the case of Katherine Wilmot, that a foreigner called at Markham Place and requested a few moments' private conversation with our hero.

The request was immediately acceded to; and the foreigner was shown into the library.

He was a man of middle age, with a dark complexion, and was dressed with considerable taste. His air was military, and his manners were frank and open.

He addressed Richard in bad English, and tendered an apology for thus intruding upon him.

Markham, believing him, by his accent and appearance, to be an Italian, spoke to him in that language; and the foreigner immediately replied in the same tongue with a fluency which convinced our hero that he was not mistaken relative to the country to which his visitor belonged.

"The object of my visit is of a most important and solemn nature," said the Italian; "and you will excuse me if I open my business by asking you a few questions."

"This is certainly a strange mode of proceeding," observed our hero; "but you are aware that I must reserve to myself the right of replying or not to your queries, as I may think fit."

"Undoubtedly," said the Italian. "But I am a man of honour; and should our interview progress as favourably as I hope, I shall entrust you with secrets which will prove my readiness to look upon you in the same light."

"Proceed," said Richard: "you speak fairly."

"In the first place, am I right in believing that you were once most intimate with a certain Count Alteroni who resides near Richmond?"

"Quite right," answered Richard.

"Do you, or do you not, entertain good feelings towards that nobleman?"

"The best feelings—the most sincere friendship—the most devoted attachment," exclaimed our hero.

"Are you aware of any particulars in his political history?"

"He is a refugee from his native land."

"Does he now bear his true name?"

"If you wish me to place confidence in you," said Richard, "you will yourself answer me one question, before I reply to any farther interrogatory on your part."

"Speak," returned the Italian stranger.

"Do you wish to propose to me any thing whereby I can manifest my attachment to Count Alteroni, without injury to my own character or honour?" demanded Richard.

"I do," said the stranger solemnly. "You can render Count Alteroni great and signal services."

"I will then as frankly admit to you that I am acquainted with *all* which relates to *Count Alteroni*," said Richard, dwelling upon the words marked in italics.

"With *all* which relates to *Prince Alberto of Castelcicala*?" added the stranger, in a significant whisper. "Do we understand each other?"

"So far that we are equally well acquainted with the affairs of his Highness the Prince," answered Richard.

"Right. You have heard of General Grachia?" said the foreigner.

"He is also an exile from Castelcicala," returned Markham.

"He is in England," continued the foreigner. "I had the honour to be his chief aide-de-camp, when he filled the post of Minister of War; and I am Colonel Morosino."

Richard bowed an acknowledgment of this proof of confidence.

"General Grachia," proceeded Morosino, "reached England two days ago. His amiable family is at Geneva. The general visited Prince Alberto yesterday, and had a long conversation with his Highness upon the situation of affairs in Castelcicala. The Grand Duke is endeavouring to establish a complete despotism, and to enslave the country. One province has already been placed under martial law; and several executions have taken place in Montoni itself. The only crime of the victims was a demand for a Constitution. General Grachia represented to his Highness Prince Alberto the necessity of taking up arms in defence of the liberties of the Castelcicalans against the encroachments of despotism. The reply of the Prince was disheartening to his friends and partizans. '*Under no pretence*,' said he, '*would I kindle civil war in my native country.*'"

"He possesses a truly generous soul," said Richard.

"He is so afraid of being deemed selfish," observed the Colonel; "and no one can do otherwise than admire that delicacy and forbearance which shrink from the idea of even appearing to act in accordance with his own personal interests. The Prince has every thing to gain from a successful civil war: hence he will not countenance that extremity."

"And what does General Grachia now propose?" asked Markham.

"You are aware that when Prince Alberto was exiled from Castelcicala for having openly proclaimed his opinions in favour of a Constitution and of the extension of the popular liberties, numbers of his supporters in those views were banished with him. *We know* that there cannot be less than two thousand Castelcicalan refugees in Paris and London. Do you begin to comprehend me?"

"I fear that you meditate proceedings which are opposed to the wishes of his Highness Prince Alberto," said Markham.

"The friends of Castelcicalan freedom can undertake what in them would be recognised as *pure patriotism*, but which in Prince Alberto would be deemed the result of his own *personal interests* or *ambition*."

"True," said Richard: "the distinction is striking."

"The Prince, moreover, in the audience which he accorded to General Grachia yesterday evening, used these memorable words:—'*Were I less than I am, I would consent to take up arms in defence of the liberties of Castelcicala; but, being as I am, I never will take a step which the world would unanimously attribute to selfishness.*'"

"Those were noble sentiments!" ejaculated Markham: "well worthy of him who uttered them."

"And worthy of serving as rules and suggestions for the patriots of Castelcicala!" cried Colonel Morosino. "There are certain times, Mr. Markham," he continued, "when it becomes a duty to take up arms against a sovereign who forgets *his duty* towards his subjects. Men are not born to be slaves; and they are bound to resist those who attempt to enslave them."

"Those words have often been uttered by a deceased friend of mine—Thomas Armstrong," observed Richard.

"Thomas Armstrong was a true philanthropist," said the Colonel; "and were he alive now, he would tell you that subjects who take up arms against a bad prince are as justified in so doing as the prince himself could be in punishing those who violate the laws."

"In plain terms," said Richard, "General Grachia intends to espouse the popular cause against the tyranny of the Grand Duke?"

"Such is his resolution," answered Colonel Morosino. "And now that you have heard all these particulars, you will probably listen with attention to the objects of my present visit."

"Proceed, Colonel Morosino," said Richard. "You must be well aware that, as one well attached to his Highness Prince Alberto, I cannot be otherwise than interested in these communications."

"I shall condense my remarks as much as possible," continued the officer. "General Grachia purports to enter into immediate relations with the Castelcicalans now in London and Paris. Of course the strictest secresy is required. The eventual object will be to purchase two or three small ships which may take on board, at different points, those who choose to embark in the enterprise; and these ships will have a common rendezvous. When united, they will sail for Castelcicala. A descent upon that territory would be welcomed with enthusiasm by nine-tenths of the population; and the result," added Morosino, in a whisper,—"the inevitable result must be the dethronement of the Grand Duke and the elevation of Alberto to the sovereign seat."

"That the project is practicable, I can believe," said Markham; "that it is just, I am also disposed to admit. But do you not think that a bloodless revolution might be effected?"

"We hope that we shall be enabled successfully to assert the popular cause without the loss of life," returned Morosino. "But this can only be done by means of an imposing force, and not by mere negotiation."

"You consider the Grand Duke to be so wedded to his despotic system?" said Markham interrogatively.

"What hope can we experience from so obstinate a sovereign, and so servile an administration as that of which Signor Pisani is the chief?" demanded the Colonel. "And surely you must allow that patriotism must not have too much patience. By allowing despots to run their race too long, they grow hardened and will then resist to the last, at the sacrifice of thousands of lives and millions of treasure."

"Such is, alas! the sad truth," said Richard. "At the same time a fearful responsibility attaches itself to those who kindle a civil war."

"Civil wars are excited by two distinct motives," returned the Colonel. "In one instance they are produced by the ambition of aspirants to power: in the other, they take their origin in the just wrath of a people driven to desperation by odious tyranny and wrong. The latter is a sacred cause."

"Yes—and a most just one," exclaimed Markham. "If then, I admit that your projects ought to be carried forward, in what way can my humble services be rendered available?"

"I will explain this point to you," answered Colonel Morosino. "General Grachia, myself, and several stanch advocates of constitutional freedom, met to deliberate last evening upon the course to be pursued, after the General had returned from his interview with the Prince at Richmond. We sat in deliberation until a very late hour; and we adopted the outline of the plans already explained to you. We then recognised the necessity of having the co-operation of some intelligent, honourable, and enlightened Englishman to aid us in certain departments of our preliminary arrangements. We must raise considerable sums of money upon certain securities which we possess; we must ascertain to what extent the laws of this country will permit our meetings, or be calculated to interfere with the progress of our measures; we must purchase ships ostensibly for commercial purposes; and we must adopt great precautions in procuring from outfitters the arms, clothing, and stores which we shall require. In all these proceedings we require the counsel and aid of an Englishman of honour and integrity."

"Proceed, Colonel Morosino," said Richard, seeing that the Italian officer paused.

"We then found ourselves at a loss where to look for such a confidential auxiliary and adviser; when one of our assembly spoke in this manner:—'I came to this country, as you well know, at the same time as his Highness the Prince. From that period until the present day I have frequently seen his Highness; and I became aware of the acquaintance which subsisted between his Highness and an English gentleman of the name of Richard Markham, who was introduced to his Highness by the late Thomas Armstrong. I am also aware that a misunderstanding arose between the Prince and Mr. Markham: the nature of that misunderstanding I never learnt; but I am aware that, even while it existed, Richard Markham behaved in the most noble manner in a temporary difficulty in which his Highness was involved. I also know that the motives which led to that misunderstanding have been completely cleared away, and that the Prince now speaks in the highest terms of Mr. Richard Markham. Address yourselves, then, to Mr. Markham: he is a man of honour; and with him your secret is safe, even if he should decline to meet your views.'—Thus spoke our friend last night; and now the cause and object of my visit are explained to you."

"You have spoken with a candour and frankness which go far to conquer any scruples that I might entertain in assisting you," said Richard. "At the same time, so important a matter demands mature consideration. Should I consent to accept the office with which you seek to honour me, I should not be a mere lukewarm agent: I should enter heart and soul into your undertaking; nor should I content myself with simply succouring you in an administrative capacity. Oh! no," added Richard, enthusiastically, as he thought of Isabella, "I would accompany you on your expedition when the time came, and I would bear arms in your most righteous cause."

"Generous young man!" cried the Colonel, grasping our hero's hand with true military frankness: "God grant that your answer may be favourable to us. But pray delay not in announcing your decision."

"This time to-morrow evening I will be prepared to give you an answer," returned Markham.

The Colonel then took his leave, saying, "To-morrow evening I will call again."

CHAPTER CLVI.

THE DECISION.

Richard Markham retired to rest, but not to immediate slumber.

The proposal of Colonel Morosino was of a most perplexing nature.

Our hero longed to be enabled to show his devotion to Isabella by exerting himself in what must eventually prove her father's cause; but he was afraid of acting in a manner which might displease the Prince.

Then he reflected that the Prince had uttered those expressive words, "*Were I less than I am, I would consent to take up arms in defence of the liberties of Castelcicala.*"

The more Richard pondered upon these words, the more was he inclined towards the service proposed to him; and when he remembered that he should be associated with some of the most gallant and disinterested of Italian patriots, he felt a generous ardour animate his bosom.

"Oh! if I could but achieve some deed that would render me worthy of Isabella," he thought, "how should I bless the day when I adopted the cause of those brave exiles who now seek my aid! Yes—I will join them, heart and soul; and in me they shall have no lukewarm supporter! The die is cast;—and this resolution must either make or mar me for ever!"

Richard then gradually fell into a profound slumber: but the subjects of his latest thoughts became the materials of which his dreams were woven.

Imagination carried him away from his native land, and whirled him on board a vessel which was within sight of the Castelcicalan coasts. Presently a descent upon the land was effected; and then Richard fancied himself to be involved in the thickest of a deadly fight. Next he saw himself entering Montoni at the head of a victorious army; and it seemed to him as if he were the object of attraction—as if the salutations of countless multitudes were addressed to him—and as if he returned them! Then the scene changed, by one of those rapid transitions so peculiar to dreams; and he found himself standing at the altar, the lovely Isabella by his side. A tiara of diamonds adorned her brow and on his own was a princely coronet. Then the ceremony was completed; and friends with smiling countenances gathered around to congratulate him and his lovely bride; and the swelling words "Your Highness" and "My Lord" echoed upon his ears. He turned to address his thanks to those who thus felicitated him—and awoke!

"A dream—a dream!" he exclaimed, as the gay pageantry of the vision yet dwelt vividly in his mind: "but will the most happy episode therein ever be fulfilled?"

Richard rose with depressed spirits; for a dream of that nature—by raising us to the highest eminence to which our aspirations ever soared, and then dashing us back again to the cold realities of earth—invariably leads to a powerful reaction.

The day passed without any incident of importance; and by the time the evening arrived, Richard had recovered his mental serenity.

Punctual to his appointment, Colonel Morosino made his appearance.

He came in a chaise, accompanied by another individual; but the latter did not alight from the vehicle.

"Mr. Markham," said the Colonel, when he was alone with our hero, in the library, "have you made up your mind?"

"I have," answered Richard, in a decided tone.

"And your decision———"

"Is to join you, heart and soul—to throw myself with enthusiasm into your cause—to co-operate with you as if I were a Castelcicalan subject," said Richard, his handsome countenance glowing with animation, his fine dark eyes flashing fire, and his nostrils dilating with the ardour which filled his soul.

"I am no prophet, if you ever repent this decision," said Colonel Morosino, pressing Richard's hands warmly. "Will you now permit me to introduce a gentleman who has accompanied me?"

"With much pleasure," answered Markham.

The Colonel stepped out, and at the expiration of a few moments returned, accompanied by a tall, thin, military-looking man, whose lofty bearing and eagle eye bespoke him as one who had been accustomed to command.

"Mr. Markham," said the Colonel, "may you soon become better acquainted with General Grachia."

The veteran proffered Richard his hand with true military frankness, and observed, "I rejoice to find that your decision is favourable to our views."

"You will also find that I shall be zealous and unwearied in your service," rejoined Markham.

"Our proceedings," continued General Grachia, "must be conducted with caution, so that no rumour prejudicial to our measures may reach Castelcicala."

"I believe it to be understood," said Markham, "that should the Grand Duke change his policy to such an extent that the Castelcicalans may obtain their just rights and privileges by means of his concessions, before our own projects shall be ripe for execution,—that, in this case, we at once abandon them."

"Assuredly," replied General Grachia. "God knows the purity of my motives, and that I would not plunge my country into civil war without the pressure of a dire necessity. Neither am I adopting extreme measures from vindictive motives because the Grand Duke has banished me not only from office but also from the territory. Had I assented to his despotic decrees I might have retained my high position in the cabinet, and aggrandized my own fortunes at the same time. As a proof of my integrity, Mr. Markham, read this document."

The General produced from his pocket-book a letter which had been sealed with the ducal signet, and was addressed "*To His Excellency General Grachia, Minister Secretary of State for the Department of War.*"

This document he handed to Richard, who found that it was an autograph letter from the Grand Duke to the General, written at the time when the military disturbances occurred at Montoni. It remonstrated with General Grachia for refusing to countersign the ordinance decreeing the disbandment of the three regiments, and promising him the rank of Marquis and the Premiership if he would but consent to aid his Serene Highness in carrying out the proposed rigorous measures.

"To this letter I replied by sending in my resignation," said General Grachia; "and thus I wrecked my own fortunes, and made my wife and children exiles."

"You acted nobly—like a true patriot," cried Markham, contemplating the veteran with admiration. "If for one instant I entertained a scruple in embracing your cause, it is now annihilated; for you have honoured me with the most convincing proofs of your patriotism."

"I served the Grand Duke faithfully," said the General; "and I cannot reproach myself for any measure which I ever recommended to his Serene Highness. Although deeply attached to Prince Alberto, I did not oppose the marriage of the Grand Duke; because I believed that, upon principle, sovereigns are entitled to as much freedom in affairs so nearly touching their domestic happiness, as any of their subjects. I saw in the present Grand Duchess an amiable lady; and I knew that she was a virtuous one from the strong recommendations which she received from his Highness Prince Alberto and the Earl of Warrington to myself and my family. I supported, then, that marriage upon principle—upon a conviction which I entertain. I believe that sovereigns have a right to consult their own happiness in marriage; but I never will admit that they have a right to enslave their subjects. I will maintain the privileges of princes, when I consider them encroached upon by the people: with equal readiness will I protect the people against the tyranny of princes."

Richard listened with admiration to these noble sentiments; and he could not help exclaiming, "How blind sovereigns often seem to the merits and honesty of those who would counsel them wisely!"

"Such is too frequently the case," observed Colonel Morosino.

"The plan upon which I propose to act is simply this," resumed General Grachia:—"one of the most humble, but not the least sincere, of those refugees who support us, will take a house in London in his own name; and there shall our head-quarters be fixed. There shall we hold our meetings; and thence will our correspondence be expedited to those whom we can trust, and on whose support we can rely. In order to avoid all cause of suspicion, I shall take a house for myself and suite at the West End, where I shall, however, lead a comparatively secluded life. Fortunately, the greater portion of my property consisted in money in the public funds of Castelcicala; and for that I obtained securities which may be easily realised in London. My friend Morosino stands in the same position. Between us we can muster some twenty thousand pounds; and other exiles, who are favourable to our views, can throw ten thousand more into the common stock."

"To which I shall also be permitted to contribute my *quota*," interrupted Richard.

"Not if we can manage without it," answered General Grachia; "and I have no doubt that pecuniary resources will not be wanting in this good cause."

The General then proceeded to a more detailed development of his plans; but as we shall have to deal with them fully hereafter, we will take leave of the subject for the present.

Before we conclude this chapter we must record two or three little incidents that maintain the continuous thread of our narrative.

A week after the demise of Miss Gregory, the funeral took place at a suburban cemetery. The bereaved father and afflicted brothers were the chief mourners; but Richard also followed the remains of the departed girl to the tomb. An elegant but chaste and unassuming monument marks the spot where she reposes in her narrow bed.

At the expiration of the seven days during which she had been remanded, Katherine was examined a second time before the magistrate, and was fully committed for trial.

A Coroner's Inquest had in the meantime recorded a verdict of *Wilful Murder* against her.

She was accordingly conveyed to Newgate.

But Richard Markham did not neglect her interests; and Morris Benstead was busy in adopting every possible measure to fathom the deep mystery in which the awful deed was still shrouded.

CHAPTER CLVII.

THE TRIAL OF KATHERINE WILMOT.

The March sessions of the Central Criminal Court commenced upon a Monday morning, as usual.

On the Wednesday Katherine Wilmot was placed in the dock, to take her trial for the murder of Matilda Kenrick.

The particulars of the case had produced a great sensation; and the door-keepers of the gallery of the court reaped a rich harvest by the fees for admission.

Katherine was deadly pale; but she had made up her mind to conduct herself with fortitude; and her demeanour was resigned and tranquil.

Richard Markham was in the gallery of the court; but his manner was uneasy and anxious:—he had heard nothing of Benstead, the policeman, for the preceding forty-eight hours; and not a fact had that individual communicated to the counsel for the prisoner which might tend to prove her innocence or even throw a doubt upon her guilt!

When called upon to answer to the indictment, Katherine pleaded, in a firm tone, "*Not Guilty.*"

The counsel for the prosecution then stated the case, which was supported by the following testimony:—

Henry Massey deposed: "I am a surgeon, and reside in Great Coram Street. One evening, early in February, a young female came to my shop and purchased two ounces of laudanum. She brought no phial with her. I gave it to her in a phial of my own, which I labelled *Poison*. On the following evening I was summoned to the house of the Rev. Mr. Tracy. I was introduced into the kitchen, where I found the deceased lying back in her chair quite dead. A young female was there; and I recognised her to be the one who had purchased the poison at my shop. She is the prisoner at the bar. From this circumstance and others which transpired, I suspected her to have poisoned the deceased; and I had her given into custody. The Rev. Mr. Tracy was in the kitchen when I arrived. He was doing all he could to recover the deceased. He was deeply affected. On the following day I examined the deceased, and found that she had died by poison. That poison was laudanum. I discovered so large a quantity in her, by the usual tests, that she must have experienced a deep lethargy almost immediately after taking the poison, and could not have lived many minutes. I cannot say that she did not take it voluntarily, and with the object of committing suicide. There was nothing upon the table near her—no cup, glass, nor any drinking vessel. The phial produced is the one in which I sold the poison."

Thomas Parker deposed: "I am footman to the Rev. Mr. Tracy. On the morning of the day when the housekeeper was poisoned, I overheard a conversation between her and Katherine Wilmot. The deceased informed Katherine that she must leave the house, but would not assign any reason. The deceased, however, said that she would provide for Katherine at a sister's in the country. Katherine objected to leave London, because her relations live here. I thought Mrs. Kenrick was jealous of Katherine, and wished to get rid of her. I mean that deceased thought that Katherine would perhaps be entrusted to fulfil some of her duties as housekeeper. I came out of the pantry, where I was cleaning the plate, and observed that I supposed Mrs. Kenrick was jealous of Katherine. The housekeeper cut the matter short by saying that Katherine should leave. Katherine was very miserable all day afterwards. In the evening my master sent me with a letter to a gentleman at Holloway. When I came back, I found the housekeeper dead. The first witness was there, in the kitchen. So were my master, Katherine, and the groom. I alluded to the conversation which had taken place between the deceased and the prisoner in the morning. The surgeon mentioned about Katherine having bought the laudanum at his house. Katherine seemed very much confused. She was then given into custody."

James Martin deposed: "I am groom and coachman to the Rev. Mr. Tracy. On the evening in question I heard screams in the yard. I was in the stable adjoining. There is a communication between the yard of the house and the stable yard. I hastened to the yard of the house where the screams came from. I saw Katherine wringing her hands and crying. I asked her what was the matter? She said, '*Mrs. Kenrick is dead.*' I hurried into the kitchen.

Almost immediately afterwards Mr. Tracy came in. He had been alarmed by the screams too, he said. I found the housekeeper lying forward on the table, with her face resting on her arms, as if she had fallen asleep. I raised her, and laid her back in her chair. She seemed quite dead. Mr. Tracy was greatly affected. Katherine did not offer to help, but withdrew to the farther end of the kitchen. She cried very much. Mr. Tracy sent me for a surgeon. When I came back with the first witness, we found Mr. Tracy bathing deceased's head with vinegar, and doing all he could to recover her. Katherine was not assisting him." This witness then confirmed the previous statement relative to the immediate circumstances which led to Katherine's arrest. He concluded his testimony thus: "When I first went into the kitchen, there were no cups, nor glasses, nor any drinking vessels on the table. All the tea-things had been washed and put into their proper place."

The Rev. Reginald Tracy deposed: "I received the prisoner into my service through charity. I had no character with her. I had known her before, because she had attended the St. David's Sunday Schools. I considered her to be a most exemplary young person. I was not aware that Mrs. Kenrick intended to send her away. Mrs. Kenrick had the power, if she chose to do so, as she managed my household for me. I cannot say that Katherine had done any thing to offend Mrs. Kenrick. She had done nothing to offend me. In the evening I was alarmed by screams. I went down into the kitchen, and found the housekeeper in the position described by the last witness. I sent him for a surgeon, and adopted all the remedies within my reach to recover the housekeeper. I think I had observed that something had been preying upon the mind of the deceased. She had lately been melancholy and abstracted."

Cross-examined: "I am not aware that Katherine went out on the evening in question. I do not know that she visited her uncle on that evening. I cannot say that she did not. She would not have asked me for permission to do so. She would have applied to Mrs. Kenrick. I was unwell all day, and did not leave my room until I heard the screams. I was very loath to believe that Katherine could have perpetrated such a deed. I told the surgeon so."

A policeman deposed: "I was summoned to Mr. Tracy's house on the evening in question. I took the prisoner into custody. When I had conveyed her to the station-house, I returned to Mr. Tracy's house. I searched the kitchen. I found the phial, produced in court, upon a shelf. It was empty."

This testimony closed the case for the prosecution.

The general impression which prevailed amongst the auditory was unfavourable to the prisoner.

Richard Markham trembled for her: still his confidence in her innocence was unshaken.

But time wore on: the case was drawing to a close;—and not a sign of Morris Benstead!

Markham knew not what to think.

The manner in which Reginald Tracy gave his evidence was the subject of much comment in the gallery.

"What an amiable man he appears to be!" said one.

"How he endeavoured to create an impression in favour of the prisoner," observed another.

"He said that he was loath to believe her guilty," remarked a third, "and considered her to be an exemplary young person."

"Hush! hush!" said the first speaker: "the case is about to be resumed."

This was the fact. The Judges, having retired for a few minutes, had now returned to the bench.

The counsel for the defence rose.

He began by calling upon the jury to dismiss from their minds any prejudice which the statements in the newspapers in connexion with the case might have created. He then dissected the evidence for the prosecution. He insisted much upon the importance of the fact that the poison had been purchased the evening before the conversation took place between the deceased and the prisoner, relative to the removal of the latter from the house. His instructions were that the prisoner had purchased that poison by order of the deceased, and, as the prisoner understood at the time, for the use of her master who had returned home unwell. There was no proof that Katherine had done any thing wrong, and that she might have anticipated receiving warning from the housekeeper, and thus have actually contemplated murder when she procured the laudanum. It was stated that there was no cup nor glass upon the table—no drinking vessel in which poison could be traced. The inference thence drawn by the counsel for the prosecution was that the prisoner must have administered the poison—most probably in deceased's tea, and had then washed the cup. But might not the deceased have taken the poison with the intention of committing suicide, by drinking it from the phial which was found upon the shelf? Would not the prisoner have concealed or destroyed the phial, had she really administered the poison? The prisoner's account of the case was this. Mrs. Kenrick of her own accord had given her permission to visit her friends for an hour on the fatal evening. The prisoner availed herself of this kindness, and proceeded to her uncle's residence in St. Giles's. He (the counsel) hoped to have been able to prove the important fact of this visit, because it would show that the housekeeper had purposely sent Katherine Wilmot out of the way: but, unfortunately, the prisoner's uncle had not yet returned to town; and although a letter had been sent to the place whither it was supposed that he had proceeded——

At this moment a great bustle was observed in the body of the court; and a man, elbowing his way through the crowd, advanced towards the learned counsel for the defence.

Richard's heart leapt within him: at the first glance he recognised, in that man, his agent, Morris Benstead, dressed in plain clothes.

Benstead whispered to the barrister for some minutes, and then handed him a letter which the learned gentleman perused rapidly.

The most breathless suspense prevailed throughout the court.

"My lords," at length exclaimed the barrister, retaining the letter in his hand, and addressing the Judges, "this case is likely to take a most unexpected turn."

"Heaven be thanked!" murmured Richard to himself: "the poor creature's innocence will be made apparent—I feel that it will!"

Meantime Morris Benstead again forced his way through the crowd, and took his stand close by Reginald Tracy.

Poor Katherine knew not what all this meant; but her heart beat violently with mingled emotions of hope, uncertainty, and apprehension.

"My lords," continued the barrister, "I need not continue my speech in defence of the prisoner. I shall at once proceed to call my witnesses."

The anxiety of the audience grew more and more intense.

"Jacob Smithers!" cried the barrister.

The Public Executioner instantly ascended into the witness-box.

He deposed as follows: "The prisoner is my niece. She called at my house on the evening alluded to. She remained with me at least half an hour. She did not complain of Mrs. Kenrick; nor did she say that she was to leave the Rev. Mr. Tracy's house. I remember that I was very low-spirited myself that evening; and so I suppose she did not choose to annoy me by saying that she was to leave. Or else, perhaps, she thought that I should wish her to return home to me if I knew that she was to leave Mr. Tracy's service. I have been to Belfast where I was detained some days: then I accepted an engagement to go to the Isle of Man. I never received any letter informing me of what had occurred to my niece. The fact is, I do not go by my right name when I travel in that way, because I have to stop at inns, and do not like to be known. That is probably the reason why a letter addressed to me by the name of Smithers did not reach me. I did not see the account of this business in the newspapers until a few days since, when I was in the Isle of Man; and I returned home as quick as possible. I only reached London an hour ago."

"You may stand down," said the barrister: then, after a pause, he exclaimed, "Rachel Bennet!"

An elderly woman, decently attired in mourning, but evidently in a very sickly state of health, slowly ascended into the witness-box.

She deposed: "I am the sister of the deceased, and reside about three miles from Hounslow. I received a letter from my sister early in February. The letter now shown me is the one." (This was the same letter which Benstead had given to the barrister.) "On the following day I received a letter from Mr. Tracy informing me of my sister's death, and stating that it was supposed she had been poisoned by a young person then in custody. I was bed-ridden with illness at the time, and was supposed to be dying. I could not therefore come to London, or take any steps in the matter. Some one came to me yesterday, and induced me to come to town."

The counsel for the defence then passed the letter, which had been placed in his hands by Benstead, to the clerk of the court, by whom it was read.

Its contents were as follow:—

"MY DEAR RACHEL,

"I hope this will find you much improved in health: at the same time I am somewhat anxious at not having heard from you. My present object in writing to you is to request you to receive at your house a young person in whom I am interested, and who is at present in Mr. Tracy's service. Katherine Wilmot is a pretty and interesting girl; and it would be unsafe for her to remain *here*. You know, dear Rachel, that you and I have never had any secrets between us; and I am not now going to break through that rule of mutual confidence which has been the basis of our sincere attachment. The truth is, Mr. Tracy is not what he was. He has fallen from the pinnacle of virtue which he once so proudly occupied; and it was only this morning that I had the most convincing proof of his weakness and folly! O Rachel—I met him and his mistress face to face upon the stairs! But I will not dwell upon this: I sincerely pray to heaven that he may repent, and become the good man he once was. I know that this secret will be sacred with you. But I am determined to remove from him all temptations, as far as lies in my humble power; and you may now comprehend my motives for sending Katherine Wilmot away from this house. In a word, I shall despatch her to you by to-morrow's coach; and will write at greater length by her.

"Your affectionate Sister,

"MATILDA KENRICK."

This letter produced a most extraordinary sensation in the court.

The Judges, the barrister, the prisoner, and the audience were astounded at this revelation of the weakness of that man whom the world almost worshipped as a saint.

"Ellen was right!" murmured Richard Markham to himself: "he is a hypocrite! But I never could have thought it!"

And what of Reginald himself?

The moment the clerk reached that paragraph which proclaimed the astounding fact of his unworthiness, a cold perspiration broke out upon his forehead; and he turned to leave the court.

But Morris Benstead caught him by the arm, and pointing to a seat, said, "You must remain here, if you please, sir: I am an officer."

The rector cast a look of unutterable dismay upon the policeman, and fell upon the bench in a state of mind bordering on distraction.

Meantime the case proceeded.

The counsel for the prosecution said that he should like to ask Rachel Bennet a few questions.

That witness accordingly returned to the box.

"Why did you not empower some one to produce that letter when the prisoner was examined before the magistrate?" inquired the prosecuting counsel.

"Because, sir, I did not conceive that it could be of any use. I never for a moment suspected that any other person besides the one accused could have taken away my poor sister's life. My husband proposed to send the letter to the magistrate; but as my sister had written to me in strict confidence, I would not consent to that step. And now, since you have asked me, sir, I will tell you what I really *did* think; and God forgive me if I have been unjust."

"We do not want to hear what you thought," exclaimed the prosecuting counsel. "You may stand down."

"No," cried the barrister for the defence: "as we are upon the subject, we *will* have the witness's impressions."

"I really thought, sir," continued the woman, "that the Katherine Wilmot alluded to was perhaps no better than she should be, and had become more intimate with Mr. Tracy than my poor sister suspected. That, I thought, was the reason why she had poisoned my sister in order to get her out of the way, and for herself to remain at Mr. Tracy's house. But I did not think that Mr. Tracy himself had any hand in the murder; and so I did not see the good of producing a letter which would only expose Mr. Tracy."

"Now you may stand down," said the counsel for the prisoner: then, in a loud tone, he called, "John Smithers!"

And Gibbet entered the witness-box.

His first glance was towards the dock; and that look, rapid, and imperceptible to others, conveyed a world of hope to the bosom of poor Katherine.

Richard Markham was at a loss to conceive what testimony the hump-back could bring forward in the prisoner's favour.

Every one present felt the deepest interest in the turn given to the proceedings.

The hump-back stood upon a stool that there was in the witness-box; and even then his head was alone visible. His hideous countenance, pale and ghastly through his intense feelings for Katherine's situation, was nevertheless animated with confidence and hope.

Amidst a dead silence of awe-inspiring solemnity, he deposed as follows:—

"I am the prisoner's cousin. She has ever been most kind to me; and I was always happy in her society. When she went to live at Mr. Tracy's house, I thought that I should be able to see her every evening; but on one occasion Mr. Tracy met me, and said that I might only visit her on Sundays. I had, however, discovered an obscure corner in his yard, where I could hide myself and see all that passed in the kitchen of his house. I went to that corner regularly every evening, Sunday excepted; and remained there an hour—sometimes more. I did not want to pry into what was going on in Mr. Tracy's house: all I cared about was to see Katherine."

A murmur, expressive of deep feeling—mingled surprise, sympathy, and admiration—on the part of the audience, followed this ingenuous announcement. Many an eye was moistened with a tear; and even the Judges did not look angrily when that murmur met their ears.

Gibbet continued:—

"One evening when I was concealed in the corner, I saw Mrs. Kenrick address something to Katherine, which I could not hear; but immediately afterwards Katherine put on her bonnet and went out. As I had sometimes seen her do so before, and return very shortly afterwards, I thought she had merely gone to execute some little commission; and I remained where I was. Although Katherine used to pass through the yard, and close by me, when she went out in that manner, I never spoke to her, for fear she should reprove me for what she might think was watching her actions. Immediately after she was gone, Mrs. Kenrick laid the tea things; and in a few minutes Mr. Tracy entered the kitchen. He and the housekeeper sate down to tea. Mrs. Kenrick was pouring out the tea, when Mr. Tracy said something which made her pause. She then put down the tea-pot, fetched a coffee-biggin, and made some coffee. She filled two cups, and then turned towards the shelves to fetch a small jug, which I thought contained milk. But while her back was turned, I saw Mr. Tracy hastily put his hand into his waistcoat pocket, and then as rapidly advance his hand to Mrs. Kenrick's cup. All that was the work of only one moment; and I could not distinctly see why he did so. In fact I did not think much of it, until afterwards. Mrs. Kenrick resumed her seat; and she and Mr. Tracy drank their coffee. I observed that Mrs. Kenrick took no milk, and drank hers very quickly. In a short time I saw her head begin to nod as if she was sleepy: she got up, and walked about. Then she sate down again, and placed her arms on the table as if to support herself. In a short time her head fell forward on her arms. I felt a little alarmed; but still scarcely knew why. Mr. Tracy watched her for some minutes after she had fallen forward in that manner, and then bent down his head to look at her face. In another moment he rose, and to my surprise washed up all the things on the table and placed them upon the shelves. Then I began to fear that something was wrong; and I stole away. When I got home I found my father rather cross with me for staying out; and I was afraid to tell him what I had seen. Early the next morning we left for Ireland; and I never had courage to speak to my father upon this subject until we read the account of the murder and of Katherine's arrest. That was in the Isle of Man."

The reader may imagine the profound sensation which this narrative created.

Richard Markham was literally astounded.

Katherine Wilmot wept abundantly.

Reginald Tracy was crushed, as it were, to the very dust, by this overwhelming exposure of his guilt.

The jury whispered together for a few moments; and the foreman rose and said, "My lords, it is rather as a matter of form than as the result of any deliberation, that we pronounce a verdict of *Not Guilty*."

"The prisoner is discharged," said the senior judge. "It will be the duty of the police to take charge of Reginald Tracy."

"I have him in custody, my lord," exclaimed Morris Benstead in a loud tone.

CHAPTER CLVIII.

A HAPPY PARTY.

In a private room up stairs, at a tavern nearly opposite the Court-house of the Old Bailey, a happy party was assembled.

And yet the group was somewhat motley.

It consisted of Richard Markham, Katherine Wilmot, the Public Executioner, Gibbet, Rachel Bennet, and Morris Benstead.

The best luncheon which the house afforded was spread upon the table.

"And so you really thought I was lost, sir?" said Benstead. "I am not the man to neglect the business that is entrusted to me; neither do I excite hopes unless I know that they'll be realised."

"But you have not yet told me how you came to bring all your witnesses into court at one and the same moment," said Richard Markham.

"Well, sir, I'll soon satisfy your curiosity on that head," returned the policeman. "I made every exertion to sift the entire matter to the bottom; but the farther I went into it, the more mysterious it seemed. At last I was pretty nearly inclined to give it up in despair. One of the principal measures that I adopted was to endeavour to trace, step by step, all that either Mrs. Kenrick or Katherine did on the day when the murder took place. I have seen, in my time, so much important evidence come out of the most trivial—really the most ridiculous things, that I resolved to glean every minute particular I could relative to the motions of both the deceased and the accused on that day. My firm idea was that the housekeeper had committed suicide—saving your presence, ma'am," added Benstead, turning towards Mrs. Bennet. "Well, I found out the principal shops where Mr. Tracy dealt; and I visited them all to ascertain if Mrs. Kenrick had been there on that day; and if so, whether her words or manner had betrayed any thing strange. But I could learn nothing material. Various other schemes I thought of, and put into execution; but as they all failed, there's no use in mentioning them. At length, yesterday evening I happened to call at the post-office near Mr. Tracy's house. I got into conversation with the post-mistress, who seemed to be well acquainted with the late Mrs. Kenrick. In the course of comment and observation upon the mysterious event, the post-mistress said, 'I do really think there's some ground for supposing that the poor dear woman committed suicide; for she came here to pay a letter to her sister only a few hours before she was found dead; and then I saw that she wasn't as she usually was. Something appeared to hang upon her mind.'"

"That was no doubt the sorrow she experienced at having discovered the hypocrisy of her master," observed Richard.

"Most likely, sir," said Benstead. "Well, the moment I heard that Mrs. Kenrick had written to her sister only a few hours before her death, I felt more convinced than ever that it was a case of suicide. It was then nine o'clock; but I was determined to start off at once to investigate the business. The post-mistress knew that Mrs. Bennet lived at Hounslow; and this was fortunate. I thanked her for this information, and hurried away. I was obliged to go to St. Giles's, before I started for the country, to ask my Inspector's leave. As I passed by Mr. Smithers' house, I knocked to see if he had come home. But the green-grocer next door answered me, as on several former occasions when I had called. He told me that Mr. Smithers had not come back. I knew it was important for Miss Kate to prove that she had visited her uncle on the night of the supposed murder; and so I scribbled a note to Mr. Smithers, desiring him, in case he should return home in time to-day, to lose not a minute in coming to this very tavern and sending over into the Old Court to fetch me. This note I left with the green-grocer; and I then hastened to the station. I obtained permission to absent myself, and lost no time in hiring a post-chaise. But it was midnight before I reached Hounslow; and then I learnt that Mrs. Bennet lived three miles away from that town. So I was obliged to wait till the first thing this morning before I could see her. Then a great deal of time was wasted, because Mrs. Bennet and her husband could not rightly understand why I came, or on whose side I was engaged. I do not blame them for their caution:—I only mention the fact to account for our being so late in court. At length I succeeded in persuading Mrs. Bennet to show me her sister's letter to her; and when I read it, the whole affair wore another appearance in my mind. I saw through it in a moment. Then I resolved upon bringing Mrs. Bennet up to London with me; and to her credit, she did not hesitate an instant to accompany me, when I had communicated to her the suspicions which that letter had awakened in my mind, and impressed upon her the necessity of hastening to save an innocent person from the weight of an unjust accusation. To conclude this long and rambling story, we came up in the post-chaise; and, as luck would have it, just as we drove up to this tavern, Mr. Smithers and his son were stepping out of a cab at the door."

"Ah! Mr. Markham," said Katherine, "how can I ever sufficiently express my gratitude towards you; for it was by means of your generosity that Mr. Benstead was enabled to make those exertions which led to this happy result."

"I felt convinced of your innocence from the first," returned our hero; "and it was not probable that I should abandon you when such were my sentiments."

"A life devoted to your service, sir, could not repay the debt which I owe you," said Kate. "And you, my dear cousin," she continued, turning towards Gibbet, who was seated next to her,—"you also have been no unimportant instrument in rescuing me from infamy and death."

"Do not speak of it, Kate," said the hump-back, whimpering like a mere child. "I hope you won't scold me for watching you like a cat every evening as I did."

"Scold you, John! Oh! how can you make use of such words to me—and after the service you have rendered me?" exclaimed Kate, tears also streaming down her own cheeks. "I ought to bless God—and I do—to think that your friendship towards me led you to adopt a step to see me, which has turned so wonderfully—so providentially to my advantage."

"And now, Kate," said the executioner, "tell me one thing: why didn't you mention to me that evening when you called, that you were going to leave the rector's service?"

"Because, my dear uncle," answered the young maiden, "you made one observation to me which showed that you were pleased at the idea of me being in Mr. Tracy's service; and as you were so dull and low-spirited, I did not like to tell you any thing that might occasion you additional vexation. You said—oh! I shall never forget your words—they made me weep as I followed you from the street door into the parlour——"

"Yes—because I so seldom spoke kindly to you, poor Kate," exclaimed the executioner, as if struck by a sudden remorse.

"Do not say that, dear uncle! I owe so much—so very much to you, that even if you have been harsh to me now and then, I never think of it—and then, perhaps I have deserved it," she added slowly; for the amiable girl was anxious to extenuate her uncle's self-accusation in the eyes of those present.

"No—you did *not* deserve it, Kate!" cried the executioner, with resolute emphasis; "you are a good girl—too good ever to have been in such a den as mine!"

Smithers threw himself back in his chair, and compressed his lips together to restrain his emotions.

But nature asserted her empire.

A tear trickled from each eye, and rolled slowly down the cheeks of that man whose heart had been so brutalized by his fearful calling.

Kate rose from her chair, and threw herself into his arms, exclaiming, "Uncle—dear uncle, if you speak kindly to me, I am indeed happy!"

Gibbet cried, and yet laughed—sobbed, and yet smiled, in so strange a manner, as he contemplated that touching scene, that the result of his emotions presented the most ludicrous aspect.

"Sit down, Kate dear," said Smithers: "I am not used to be childish;—and yet, I don't know how it is, but I don't seem ashamed of dropping a tear now. I know I'm a harsh, brutal man: but what has made me so? God, who can read all hearts, has it written down in his book that I was once possessed of the same kind feelings as other people. However—it's no use talking: what I am I must remain until the end."

"Believe me," exclaimed Richard Markham, who was ever sensibly alive to the existence of generous feelings in others,—"believe me," he cried, grasping Smithers' hand, "society lost a good man when you undertook your present avocation."

"What, sir!" ejaculated Smithers, unfeignedly surprised; "do you shake hands with the Public Executioner?"

"Yes—and unblushingly would I do so before the whole world," replied Markham, "when I discover at the bottom of his soul a spark—aye, even the faintest spark of noble and exalted feeling yet unquenched."

The Public Executioner fixed upon the animated and handsome countenance of our hero a glance of the deepest gratitude—a glance of respect, almost of veneration!

He then cast down his eyes, and appeared to plunge into profound rumination.

"You were going to tell us, Miss Katherine," said Benstead, "what observation it was that prevented you from communicating to your uncle the notice Mrs. Kenrick had given you to leave."

"Oh! I remember," exclaimed the young maiden, upon whose heart the noble conduct of Richard Markham towards her despised and degraded relative had made a deep impression: "my uncle said to me, '*I am almost sorry that I ever parted with you; but as you are now in a place that may do you good, I shall not interfere with you.*'"

"Ah! my dear young friend," exclaimed Mrs. Bennet, "how fatal might that place have been to you after all? But where are you going to live now? If you can make yourself happy with me, I will offer you a home and show you the kindness of a mother."

Katherine turned a look of deep gratitude upon the good woman who made her this generous offer; and then she glanced timidly towards her uncle and Richard Markham.

"If I may be allowed to speak my thoughts in this matter," said our hero, "I should counsel Katherine to accept a proposition so kindly, so frankly made; and it shall be my duty to see that she becomes not a burden upon the friend who will provide her with a home."

"I can give no opinion in the matter, sir," observed the executioner: "there is something about you which compels me to say, '*Deal with me and my family as you will.*' Command, sir, and we will obey."

"I never command—but I advise as a friend," said Richard, touched by the strange gentleness of manner which was now evinced by one lately so rude, so brutal, so self-willed. "Katherine, then, has your consent to accompany Mrs. Bennet to Hounslow?"

"And I sincerely thank Mrs. Bennet for her goodness towards that poor girl who has undergone so much," said the executioner.

Mrs. Bennet now suggested that her husband would be uneasy if she remained long absent from home; and Richard immediately summoned the waiter, to whom he gave orders to procure a post-chaise.

This command was speedily executed. Katherine took leave of her relatives, Markham, and Benstead, with streaming eyes.

"God bless you, my girl," said the executioner, in a tone the tremulousness of which he could not altogether subdue.

Gibbet could say nothing: his voice was choked with sobs.

Katherine, however, whispered words of kindness in his ears; and the poor hump-back smiled as he wrung her hand with all the fervour of his affection.

"To you, Mr. Markham," said Kate, "no words can convey the gratitude—the boundless gratitude and respect which I entertain for you."

"Be happy, Katherine," returned Richard, shaking her warmly by the hand; "and remember that in me you have a sincere friend, always ready to aid and advise you."

The young maiden then tendered her thanks to the good-hearted policeman for the interest he had manifested in her favour.

The farewells were all said; good wishes were given and returned; and Mrs. Bennet hurried Katherine from the room. Those who remained behind, watched their departure from the window.

The moment the post-chaise had rolled away from the door of the tavern, Smithers accosted our hero, and said, "I am no great hand at making speeches, sir; but I can't take my leave of you, without saying something to convince you that I'm not ungrateful for what you've done for my niece. Your goodness, sir, has saved her from death; and more than that, has proved her innocence. You are the best man I ever met in my life: you are more like an angel than a human being. I didn't think that such men as you could be in existence. It makes me have a better opinion of the world when I look upon you. How happy would a country be if it had such a person as yourself for its sovereign! I cannot understand my own feelings in your presence: I seem as if I could fall at your feet and worship you. Then I think that I am unworthy even to breathe the same air that you do. But your words have made me happy to some extent: for years I have not felt as I feel to-day. I can say no more, sir: I don't know how I came to say so much!"

And the executioner turned abruptly aside; for he was weeping—he was weeping!

Markham had not interrupted him while he spoke, because our hero knew that it was well for that man to give way to the good feelings which the contemplation of humanity and philanthropy in others had so recently awakened.

But Richard did not perceive that, while the executioner was giving utterance to the invincible promptings of nature, Gibbet had drawn near,—had listened to his father with indescribable interest,—had drunk in with surprise and avidity every word that fell from his lips,—and had gradually sunk upon his knees in the presence of that benefactor whom even a rude, brutalized, and savage disposition was now compelled to believe to be something more than man!

"This, sir," said Benstead, glancing his eyes around, and touching Markham's arm to direct his attention to the scene,—"this, sir, is doubtless a welcome reward for all your goodness."

Richard hastily brushed away a tear, and raising Gibbet from his adoring posture, said, "You, my good lad, possess a heart worthy of a nobleman. Look upon me as your friend!"

Then our hero caught Smithers by the hand, and drawing him into the recess of a window, whispered in a low and rapid tone, "You are not insensible to the charms of being useful to one's fellow-creatures. I implore you to renounce your fearful calling—and I will supply you with the means to enter upon some other pursuit."

Smithers did not answer for a few moments: he appeared to reflect profoundly.

"Yes—I will follow your advice, sir," he at length said: "but not quite yet! I must hang up that rector—and then, *then* I will abandon the calling for ever!"

With these words the executioner turned abruptly away, caught Gibbet by the hand, and hurried from the room.

A few minutes afterwards Richard Markham and Benstead also took their departure, each in a different direction; but the police-officer's pocket contained substantial proofs of our hero's liberality.

CHAPTER CLIX.

THE INTERVIEW.

A week passed away, during which the examination of Reginald Tracy took place before the police-magistrate, and terminated in the committal of the rector to Newgate.

The whole town rang with the extraordinary events which had led to this crisis in the career of a man whose very name had so lately inspired respect.

The clergy were horror-struck at the disgrace brought upon their cloth by this terrific explosion; for people grew inclined to look upon real ecclesiastical sanctity as nothing more nor less than a garb of rank hypocrisy.

Some ministers of the gospel, more daring and enthusiastic than the rest, boldly proclaimed from their pulpits that Reginald Tracy was a saint and a martyr, against whom a horrible conspiracy had been concocted in order to remove the imputation of murder from the young female who had been discharged, and fix it on him.

Other clergymen entered into learned disquisitions to prove that Satan must have obtained especial leave from God, as in the case of Job, to tempt the most holy and pious of men; and that, having failed to seduce him from the right path, the Evil One had accomplished a series of atrocities all so artfully arranged as to fix the stain upon the rector of St. David's.

But there were some reverend gentlemen, who, having always been jealous of Reginald Tracy's popularity, descanted in significant terms upon the shallowness of mere eloquence in the pulpit, and the folly of running after "fashionable preachers." One venerable and holy gentleman, who had been married three times, and had received from his wives an aggregate of seventeen pledges of their affection, bitterly denounced in his sermon the "whitened sepulchre," "tinkling cymbal," and "unclean vessel," who had dared to set his face against the sacred institution of matrimony.

The fashionable world was powerfully excited by the exposure of Reginald Tracy. Some wiseacres shook their heads, and observed that they had always suspected there was something wrong about the rector; others plainly asserted that they had even prophesied what would happen some day. The fair sex all agreed that it was a great pity, as he *was* such a charming preacher and such a handsome man!

The press was not idle in respect to the business. The newspapers teemed with "Latest Particulars;" and all the penny-a-liners in London were on the alert to collate additional facts. Nine out of ten of these facts, however, turned out to be pure fictions. One journal, conducted on more imaginative principles than its contemporaries, promulgated a new discovery which it had made in respect to the rector's history, and coolly fixed upon his back all the murders which had occurred in the metropolis during the previous dozen years, and the perpetrators of which had never yet been detected.

Heaven knows Reginald Tracy was bad enough; but if one believed all which was now said of him in the public journals, no monster that ever disgraced humanity was so vile as he.

Some of the cheap unstamped periodicals treated their readers with portraits of the rector; and as very few of the artists who were employed to draw them had ever seen their subject, and were now unable to obtain access to him, their inventive faculties were put to the most exciting test. And, as a convincing proof that no two persons entertain the same idea of an object which they have never seen, it may be observed that there was a most extraordinary variety in the respective characteristics of these portraits.

In a word, the rector's name engrossed universal attention:—a cheap romance was issued, entitled "The Murdered Housekeeper; or the Corrupt Clergyman;"—one of the minor theatres attracted crowded houses by the embodiment of the particulars of the case in a melodrama;—and Madame Tussaud added the effigy of Reginald Tracy to her collection of wax-works.

But what were the feelings of Lady Cecilia Harborough when the terrible announcement of the rector's arrest met her ears!

We must observe that when she first heard of the death of the housekeeper, she entertained a faint suspicion that Reginald, and not Katherine Wilmot, was the author of the deed. But while the young girl was yet in prison, before the trial, and when Cecilia and the rector met, the latter so eloquently expatiated upon the case, that Cecilia's suspicions were hushed; and she learnt to look upon the housekeeper's death following so shortly on the exposure of the rector's hypocrisy to that female, as a remarkable coincidence only. Moreover, the rector had all along declared his impression that the housekeeper had committed suicide, and that the innocence of Katherine would be made apparent before the judges.

Thus Cecilia's mind had been more or less tranquillised during the interval which occurred between the housekeeper's death and the day of trial.

But when, in the afternoon of the day on which that trial took place, the appalling news of Katherine's acquittal and Reginald's arrest reached her ears, she was thrown into a state of the most painful excitement.

It was true that she could not in the slightest degree be implicated in the enormous crime of which he was accused: but would her guilty connexion with him transpire?

Her conscience entertained the worst forebodings in this respect.

At one moment she thought of hastening to visit him in his prison: then she reflected that such a course would only encourage a suspicion calculated to proclaim that scandal which she was so anxious to avoid.

Fortunately Sir Rupert Harborough was still away from home, with his friend Chichester, and thus Lady Cecilia had no disagreeable spy to witness her distressing emotions and embarrassment.

Day after day passed; Reginald had been committed, as before stated, to Newgate; and Cecilia heard nothing from him.

At length at the expiration of a week from the day of his arrest, a dirty, shabby-looking lad called in Tavistock Square, and requested to see Lady Cecilia Harborough alone.

He was accordingly admitted to her presence.

"Please, ma'am," he said, "I've come with a message from Mr. Tracy, which is in Newgate. He is a wery nice gen'leman, and is certain sure to be hung, they say."

"Who are you?" demanded Cecilia, with ill-concealed disgust.

"Please, ma'am, I belong to an eating-house in the Old Bailey," returned the boy; "and I takes in Mr. Tracy's meals to him."

"And what do you want with me?"

"Please, ma'am, Mr. Tracy says will you go and see him to-morrow morning between ten and eleven?"

"In Newgate!" ejaculated Lady Cecilia, with an unaffected shudder.

"Oh! yes, ma'am: I goes in there three times every day o' my life; and so I'm sure you needn't be afraid to wisit it just for vonce."

"Well—I will think of it. Have you any thing else to say to me?"

"Please, ma'am, Mr. Tracy says that you've no call to give your own name at the gate; but if you pass yourself off as his sister, just come up from the country, you can see him alone in his cell. But if you don't do that you'd on'y be allowed to speak to him through the bars of his yard. He would have wrote to you, but then the letters must be read by the governor before they goes out; and so it would have been known that he sent to you. He never thought of speaking about it to me till this morning; and I promised to do his arrand faithful. That's all, ma'am."

"And enough too," said Lady Cecilia, in a tone of deep disgust, as she threw the lad a few shillings across the table in the room where she received him.

"Is there any message, ma'am, to take back to Mr. Tracy?" asked the boy; "'cos I shall see him the first thing in the morning."

"You may say that I will do as he desires," answered Cecilia: "but beware how you mention to a soul that you have been here. Forget my name as if you had never heard it."

"Yes, ma'am—to be sure," replied the boy; "and thank'ee kindly."

He then pocketed the money, and took his departure.

"Newgate, Newgate!" thought Lady Cecilia, when she was once more alone: "there is something chilling—menacing—awful in that name! And yet I must penetrate into those gloomy cells to see—whom? A murderer! Oh! who would have thought that the rich, the handsome, the renowned, the courted, the flattered rector of St. David's would become an inmate of Newgate? A murderer! Ah—my God, the mere idea is horrible! And that uncouth boy who said coolly that he was certain to be hanged! Reginald—Reginald, to what have you come? Would it not have been better to dare exposure—contumely—infamy—reproach, than to risk such an appalling alternative? But reputation was dearer to this man than aught in the world beside! And he is rich:—what will he do with his wealth? Perhaps it is for *that* he desires my presence? Who knows?"

This idea determined Lady Cecilia upon visiting Newgate on the following day.

She did not reflect that she herself was the first link in that chain which had so rapidly wound itself around the unhappy man, until it paralysed his limbs in a criminal gaol. She often asked herself how he could have been so mad as to commit the deed that menaced him with the most terrible fate; but beyond the abstract event itself she never thought of looking.

The morning dawned; Lady Cecilia rose, and dressed herself in as unpretending a manner as possible.

At half-past nine she went out, took a cab at the nearest stand, and proceeded to Newgate.

She ascertained, by inquiry, which was the prison entrance, and ascended the steps leading to the half-door, the top of which was garnished with long iron spikes.

A stout, red-faced turnkey, with a good-tempered countenance, admitted her into the obscure lobby, behind which was a passage where a gas-light burns all day long.

"Who do you want, ma'am?" said the turnkey.

"Mr. Tracy," was the reply.

"Are you any relation to him?"

"His sister. I have just arrived from the country."

"Please to write your name down in this book."

Lady Cecilia, who seldom lost her presence of mind, instantly took up the pen, and wrote down "ANNE TRACY."

"Excuse me, ma'am," said the turnkey, "but if you have any knife in your pocket you must leave it here."

"I have none," answered Cecilia.

"Take that passage, ma'am, and you will find a turnkey who will admit you to Tracy's cell."

All titular distinctions are dropped in Newgate.

Lady Cecilia proceeded along the passage as she was desired, and at length reached a large stone vestibule, from which several doors opened into the different yards in that part of the building.

She accosted a turnkey, informing him whom she came to visit; and he bade her follow him.

In a few moments he stopped at a massive door, opened it, and said, "Walk in there, ma'am."

She advanced a few steps: the door closed behind her; and she found herself in the presence of Reginald Tracy.

But how changed was he! His cheeks were ghastly pale—his eyes sunken—his hair was in disorder—his person dirty and neglected.

"This is kind of you, Cecilia," he said, without rising from his chair. "Sit down, and lose no time in conversing—we have not much time to be together."

"Oh, Reginald!" exclaimed Cecilia, as she took a seat, "what a place for us to meet in!"

"Now do not give way to ejaculations and laments which will do no good," said Reginald. "If you can maintain your tranquillity it will be advantageous to yourself. You know that I am possessed of some property?"

"The world always believed you to be rich," observed Cecilia.

"I have lately been extravagant," continued Reginald: "still I have a handsome fortune remaining. As I am not *yet* condemned," he added bitterly, "I can leave it to whom I choose. Do you wish to be my heiress?"

"Ah! Reginald—this proof of your affection——"

"No superfluous words, Cecilia," interrupted the rector impatiently. "If you wish to possess my wealth you must render me a service—an important service, to merit it."

"Any thing in the world that I can do to benefit you shall be performed most faithfully," said Lady Cecilia.

"And you will not shrink from the service which I demand? The condition is no light one."

"Name it. Whatever it be, I will accept it—provided that it do not involve my safety," returned Cecilia.

"Selfishness!" exclaimed the rector contemptuously. "Listen attentively. To-morrow my solicitor will attend upon me here. To him I shall make over all my property—in trust for the person to whom I choose to bequeath it. He is an honourable man, and will faithfully perform my wishes. I have not a relation nor a friend in the world who has any particular claim upon me. I can constitute you my heiress: at my death," he added slowly, "all I possess may revert to you,—the world remaining in ignorance of the manner in which I have disposed of my wealth. But if I thus enrich you, I demand from your hands the means of escaping an infamy otherwise inevitable."

"I do not understand you," said Cecilia, somewhat alarmed.

The rector leant forward, fixed a penetrating glance upon his mistress, and said in a hollow and subdued tone, "I require poison—a deadly poison!"

"Poison!" echoed Cecilia, with a shudder.

"Yes: do you comprehend me now? Will you earn wealth by rendering me that service?" he asked eagerly.

"What poison do you require?" demanded Cecilia greatly excited.

"Prussic acid: it is the most certain—and the quickest," answered the rector. "If you are afraid to procure it yourself, the old hag in Golden Lane will assist you in that respect."

"And must it really come to this?" said Cecilia. "Is all hope dead?"

"My doom is certain—if I live to meet it," answered Reginald, who only maintained the composure which he now displayed by the most desperate efforts to subdue his emotions. "The evidence is too damning against me. And yet I imagined that I had adopted such precautions!" he continued, in a musing tone. "I felt so confident that the poor, old woman would appear to have died by her own hand! I sent the footman out of the way, not upon a frivolous cause, but on an errand which would bear scrutiny. I made the housekeeper herself get rid of Katherine. I did all that prudence suggested. But never—never did I anticipate that *another* would be charged with the crime! And yet, when suspicion attached itself so strongly to that poor innocent girl, what could I do? I had but two alternatives—to allow her to suffer, or to immolate myself by proclaiming her guiltlessness. Oh! Cecilia, you know not—you cannot conceive all that I have suffered since that fatal evening! Often and often was I on the point of going forward and confessing all, in order to save that innocent girl. But I had not the courage! When I gave my testimony, I rendered it as favourable towards her as possible. I laboured hard to encourage the suspicion that the deceased had been her own destroyer. But fate had ordained that all should transpire."

He paused, and buried his face in his hands.

A sob escaped his breast.

"This is childish—this is foolish in the extreme," he suddenly cried. "Time is passing—and you have not yet decided whether you will render me the service I require, upon the consideration of inheriting all my wealth."

"I will do what you ask of me," said Cecilia, in a low but decided tone.

"And do not attempt to deceive me," continued Reginald; "for if you bring me a harmless substitute for a deadly poison, you will frustrate my design, it is true—but I shall live to revoke the bequest made in your favour."

"I will not deceive you, Reginald—if you be indeed determined," said his mistress.

"I *am* determined. We now understand each other: to me the poison—to you the wealth."

"Agreed," was the answer.

"The day after to-morrow you will return—provided with what I require?" said Reginald.

"You may rely upon me."

"Then farewell, Cecilia, for the present."

The rector offered the lady his hand: Cecilia pressed it with affected fervour, though in reality she almost recoiled from the touch.

Profligate as she was, she had no sincere sympathy for a murderer.

Nor was she sorry when she once more found herself beyond the terrible walls of Newgate.

CHAPTER CLX.

THE RECTOR IN NEWGATE.

Reginald Tracy awoke early on the morning when Cecilia was to return to him.

He had been dreaming of delicious scenes and voluptuous pleasures; and he opened his eyes to the fearful realities of Newgate.

He clasped his hands together with the convulsiveness of ineffable mental agony; and the smile that had played upon his lips in his elysian dream, was suddenly changed into the contortion of an anguish that could know no earthly mitigation.

"Fool—madman that I have been!" he exclaimed aloud, in a piercing tone of despair. "From what a brilliant position have I fallen! Wealth—pleasure—fame—love—life, all about to pass away! The entire fabric destroyed by my own hands! Oh! wretch—senseless idiot—miserable fool that I have been! But is it really true?—can it be as it seems to me? Have I done the deed? Am I here—*here*, in Newgate? Or is it all a dream? Perhaps I have gone suddenly mad, and my crime and its consequences are only the inventions of my disordered imagination? Yes—it may be so; and this is a mad-house!"

Then the rector sate up in his bed, and glanced wildly around the cell.

"No—no!" he cried with a shriek of despair; "I cannot delude myself thus. I am indeed a *murderer*—and *this* is Newgate!"

He threw himself back on the rude bolster, and covered his face with his hands.

But though he closed his eyes, and pressed his fingers upon the lids until the balls throbbed beneath, he could not shut out from his mind the horrors of his position.

"Oh! this is insupportable!" he cried, and then rolled upon his bed in convulsions of rage: he gnashed his teeth—he beat his brow—he tore his hair—he clenched his fists with the fury of a demon.

His emotions were terrible.

He seemed like a wild beast caught in a net whose meshes were inextricable.

Then a rapid reaction took place in that man of powerful passion; and he grew exhausted—humble—and penitent.

"O God, have mercy upon me!" he said, joining his hands in prayer. "I have grievously offended against thee: oh! have mercy upon me. Why didst thou permit me to fall? Was I not enthusiastic in thy cause? O heaven, have mercy upon me!"

This short prayer, in which reproach and intercession were commingled, was said with profound sincerity.

But the image of Cecilia suddenly sprang up in the rector's imagination; and then his entire form once more became convulsed with rage.

"That wretch—that adulteress was my ruin!" he exclaimed, clenching his fist so violently that the nails of his fingers almost penetrated into his palms. "I was virtuous and untainted until I knew her. She led me astray: she taught me the enjoyment of those pleasures which have proved so fatal to me! The wretch—the adulteress! And to be condemned the day before yesterday to maintain a forced calmness towards her! Oh! I could tear her limb from limb: I could dig my nails into the flesh whose dazzling whiteness and whose charms were wont to plunge my soul in ecstacies. The foul—the vile creature! May she die in a dungeon, as I shall die: no, may she rot upon the straw—may she perish by degrees—of starvation,—a cruel, lingering death of agony! Had I never known her, I should yet be on the pinnacle of pride and fortune,—yet be respected and adored! Ah! these thoughts drive me mad—mad."

And again he beat his forehead and his breast: again he tore his hair, and writhed convulsively on his bed.

"Senseless idiot that I have been!" he continued. "Better—better far were it to have thrown off the mask—to have dared the world! I was rich—and I was independent. I might have lived a life of luxury and ease, pleasure and enjoyment;—but I was too weak to risk exposure. And that poor old woman whom I destroyed—was she not devoted to me! would she have proclaimed my hypocrisy? My conscience made me behold every thing in its worst light. I anticipated complete security in her death. And now I must die myself,—give up this bright and beautiful world in the prime of my existence,—abandon all earth's pleasures and enjoyments in the vigour of my days! Senseless idiot that I was to suppose that murder could be perpetrated so easily—to imagine that the finger of God would not point to me, as much as to say '*That is the man.*' Yes—though millions be assembled together in one vast crowd, the hand of the Almighty will single out the ruthless murderer!"

The rector ceased, and lay for some instants still and motionless.

But his mind was fearfully active.

"Had not all this occurred," he thought within himself, "I should now be awaking, in my comfortable chamber, to a day which would be marked with the same happiness and security that other men are now enjoying. I should be free to go out and come in at will—free to walk hither and thither as I might choose. I should not have death staring me in the face, as at present! I should be able to say with confidence, '*To-morrow I will do this,*' and '*Next day I will do that.*' I should be my own master, possessed of all that can make man happy. But, now—*now* what a wretch I am! Confined to these four walls—a mere automaton that must eat and drink when a gaoler chooses!"

These thoughts were too heart-rending for the miserable man to endure; and, starting from his bed, he threw on his clothes with a rapidity that denoted the feverish state of his mind.

The clock struck eight; and his breakfast was brought to him.

"How many times more shall I hear that sound?" he asked himself. "Once how welcome were the notes of bells to my ears! With what happiness did I obey their summons to that church to which crowds flocked to hear me! Oh! what calm, what peaceful enjoyments were mine *then*—in the days of my innocence! And those days are gone—never to return! No human power can restore me to those enjoyments and to that innocence; and God will not do it!"

Thus passed the time of this truly wretched man.

At length the clock struck nine—next ten.

"Will she come?" he said, as he paced his cell with agitated steps. "Or will she be afraid of compromising herself? And yet she must have confidence in me: I have acted in a manner to inspire it. I suffered her to believe that it was out of regard for her that I did not write to her, and that I recommended her to pass in as my sister. The vile wretch! she little knows that all this was the result of calculation on my part! If I had shown myself indifferent to her reputation—careless of her name,—she would not have so readily consented to do my bidding. Perhaps she would never have come to me at all! Now she believes that I am anxious to avert the breath of scandal from herself; and she will serve me: yes—I feel convinced that she will come!"

Nor was Reginald mistaken.

Scarcely had he arrived at that point in his musings, when the bolts of his cell were drawn back, and Lady Cecilia entered the dungeon.

"You are true to your promise," said the rector.

"Yes—I would not fail you," answered Cecilia, throwing herself into a chair: "but I tremble—oh! I tremble like a leaf."

"Have you brought—*it?*" asked Reginald in a hollow tone.

Cecilia drew from her bosom a small crystal phial, and handed it to the rector.

He greedily withdrew the cork, and placed the bottle to his nostrils.

"Yes—you have not deceived me! Now—now," he exclaimed, as he carefully concealed the phial about his person, "I am the master of my own destinies!"

And, as he spoke, his countenance was animated with an expression of diabolical triumph.

Cecilia was alarmed.

"My God, what have I done?" she cried; "perhaps I have involved myself——"

"Set aside these selfish considerations," said the rector; "you have earned wealth—for I have kept my promise—I have bequeathed all my fortune to you."

"Do not imagine that I shall ever receive enjoyment from its possession, dear Reginald," returned Cecilia, affecting a tenderness of tone and manner which she did not feel.

"Oh! I know your good heart, beloved Cecilia," exclaimed the rector; and as she cast down her eyes beneath his looks, he glared upon her for a moment with the ferocity of a tiger. "But you will be surprised—yes, agreeably surprised," he added composedly, "when you call upon my solicitor—which you must do to-morrow! Here is his address."

"To-morrow!" echoed Cecilia, turning deadly pale. "You cannot mean to——to——"

"To take this poison to day?" said Reginald. "Yes—this evening at seven o'clock you may pray for my soul!"

"Oh! this is, indeed, dreadful!" cried Cecilia. "Give me back that phial—or I will raise an alarm!"

"Foolish woman! Will you not be worth twenty thousand pounds!" ejaculated Reginald. "And fear not that you will be compromised. I shall leave upon this table a letter that will exculpate you from any suspicion of having been the bearer to me of the means of self-destruction—even if it be discovered who it was that visited me here as my alleged sister."

"This consideration on your part is truly generous, Reginald," said Cecilia, in whose breast the mention of the twenty thousand pounds had stifled all compunction.

"We must now part, Cecilia—part for ever," observed the rector. "Go—do not offer to embrace me—I could not bear it!"

"Then farewell, Reginald—farewell!" exclaimed Cecilia, who was not sorry to escape a ceremony which she had anticipated with horror—for the idea that her paramour was a murderer was ever present in her mind.

"Farewell, Cecilia," added the rector; and he turned his back to the door.

In another moment she was gone.

"Thank heaven that I was enabled to master my rage," cried Reginald, when he was once more alone. "Oh! how I longed to fall upon her—to tear her to pieces! The selfish harlot—as if I could not read her soul *now*—as if I were any longer her dupe. But I shall be avenged upon her—I shall be avenged! My death will be the signal of her exposure—my dissolution will be the beginning of her shame! Oh! deeply shall she rue every caress she has lavished upon me—every accursed wile that she practised to ensnare me! Her blandishments will turn to moans and tears—her smiles to the contortions of hell. The fascinating syren shall become the mark for every scornful finger. Fool that she is—to think I would die unavenged! If my existence be cut short suddenly—hers shall be dragged out in sorrow and despair."

Then the rector paced his cell, while from his breast escaped a hoarse sound like the low growling of a wild beast.

But we will not dwell upon the wretched man's thoughts and words throughout that long day.

Evening came.

Six o'clock struck; and Reginald feared no farther interruption from the turnkeys.

He then sate down to write two letters.

Having occupied himself in this manner for a short time, he sealed the letters, and addressed them.

When this task was accomplished, he felt more composed and calm than he had done during the day.

He walked three or four times up and down his cell.

Then he fell upon his knees, and prayed fervently.

Yes—fervently!

Seven o'clock struck.

"Now is the hour!" he exclaimed, rising from his suppliant posture near the bed.

He took the bottle from his pocket: a convulsive shudder passed over him as he handled the fatal phial whose contents were to sever the chain which bound his spirit to the earth.

Then he felt weak and nervous; and he sate down.

"My courage is failing," he said to himself: "I must not delay another moment."

But he still hesitated for a minute!

"No—no!" he exclaimed, as if in answer to an idea which had occupied him during that interval; "there is no hope! My fate would be——the scaffold!"

This thought nerved him with courage to execute his desperate purpose.

He raised the phial to his lips, and swallowed the contents—greedy of every drop.

In a few seconds he fell from his chair—a heavy, lifeless mass—upon the floor of the dungeon.

CHAPTER CLXI.

LADY CECILIA HARBOROUGH.

Cecilia passed a sleepless and agitated night.

Wild hopes and undefined fears had banished repose from her pillow.

She thought the morning would never come.

At length the first gleam of dawn struggled through the windows of her bed-room; and she instantly arose.

She was pale—yet fearfully excited; and there was a wildness in her eyes which denoted the most cruel suspense.

The minutes seemed to be hours; for she was now anxiously awaiting the arrival of the morning paper.

She descended to the breakfast parlour; but the repast remained untouched.

At length the well-known knock of the news-boy at the front door echoed through the house.

The moment the journal was placed on the table by her side, Cecilia took it up with trembling hands, and cast a hasty glance over its contents.

In another instant all suspense relative to the rector's fate ceased.

The following words settled that point beyond a doubt:—

"SUICIDE OF THE REV. REGINALD TRACY.

"Shortly after eight o'clock last evening a rumour was in circulation, to the effect that the above-mentioned individual, whose name has so recently been brought before the public in connection with the murder of Matilda Kenrick, had put a period to his existence by means of poison. It appears that the turnkey, on visiting his cell, according to custom, at eight o'clock, found him stretched upon the floor, to all appearances quite dead. Medical aid was immediately procured; but life was pronounced by the gaol-surgeon to be totally extinct. We have been unable to learn any further particulars."

"It is better so, than to die upon the scaffold," said Cecilia to herself. "Now to the lawyer's: Reginald expressly told me that I was to call upon him this morning."

The heartless woman did not drop a tear nor heave a sigh to the memory of her paramour.

She rang the bell and desired the servant to fetch a cab without delay.

By the time it arrived Cecilia was ready.

During the rapid drive to the City, she arranged a thousand plans for the employment and enjoyment of the wealth which she believed herself to be now entitled to, and the bequest of which she was resolved to conceal from her husband.

When she alighted at the solicitor's door, she assumed a melancholy and solemn air, which she thought decorous under the circumstances.

The solicitor, who was an elderly man, and whose name was Wharton, received her in his private office, and politely inquired the nature of her business.

"Did you not expect a visit from Lady Cecilia Harborough this morning?" asked the frail woman.

"Lady Cecilia Harborough!" exclaimed the lawyer, his countenance assuming a severe tone the moment that name fell upon his ears. "Are you Lady Cecilia Harborough?"

"I am Lady Cecilia Harborough," was the reply.

"So young—and yet so powerful to work evil!" observed Mr. Wharton, in a musing tone, and with a sorrowful air.

"I do not understand you, sir," exclaimed Cecilia somewhat alarmed, yet affecting a haughty and offended manner.

"Do not aggravate your wickedness by means of falsehood," said the lawyer sternly. "Think you that I am a stranger to your connexion with that unhappy man who died by his own hands last night? I have known him for many years—I knew him when he was pure, honourable, and respected: I have seen him the inmate of a dungeon. The day before yesterday I was with him for the last time. He then revealed to me every particular connected with his fall. He told me how you practised your syren arts upon him—how you led him on, until he became an adulterer! He explained to me how he repented of his first weakness, and how you practised a vile—a detestable artifice, by the aid of an old hag in Golden Lane, to bring him back to your arms."

"Spare me this recital, sir, which has been so highly coloured to my prejudice," exclaimed Lady Cecilia. "I confess that I was enamoured of that unhappy man; but——"

"You cannot palliate your wickedness, madam," interrupted Mr. Wharton, sternly. "Mr. Tracy detailed to me every blandishment you used—every art you called into force to subdue him. And as for *your* love for him, Lady Cecilia Harborough—even that excuse cannot be advanced in extenuation of your infamy."

"Sir—that is a harsh word!" cried Cecilia, red with indignation, and starting upon her chair.

"Nay, madam—sit still," continued the solicitor: "you may yet hear harsher terms from my lips. I say that you cannot even plead a profound and sincere attachment to that man as an excuse for the arts which you practised to ensnare and ruin him:—no, madam—it was his gold which you coveted!"

"Sir—I will hear no more—I——"

"Your ladyship must hear me out," interrupted the lawyer, authoritatively motioning her to retain her seat. "When alone in his gloomy cell, your victim pondered upon all that had passed between him and you, until he came to a full and entire comprehension of the utter hollowness of your heart. He then understood how he had been duped and deluded by you! Moreover, madam, it was by your desire that he admitted you into his own house—that fatal indiscretion which, being often repeated, at length led to the terrible catastrophe. Now, then, madam," cried Mr. Wharton, raising his voice, "who was the real cause of my friend's downfall? who was the origin of his ruin? who, in a word, is the murderess of Reginald Tracy?"

"My God!" ejaculated the wretched woman, quivering like an aspen beneath these appalling denunciations; "you are very severe—too, too harsh upon me, sir!"

"No, madam," resumed the lawyer; "I am merely placing your conduct in its true light, and giving your deeds their proper name. You had no mercy upon my unfortunate friend;—you sacrificed him to your base lust after gold;—you hurried him on to his doom. Why should I spare you? You have no claims upon my forbearance as a woman—because, madam, your unmitigated wickedness debars you from the privilege of your sex. To show courtesy to you, would be to encourage crime of the most abhorrent nature."

"Was it to be thus upbraided, sir—thus reviled," demanded Lady Cecilia, endeavouring to recover her self-possession, "that I was desired to call upon you this morning?"

"Desired to call upon me, madam!" exclaimed the solicitor: "who conveyed to you such instructions?"

"Mr. Tracy himself," answered Cecilia in a faint tone—for she now trembled lest Reginald had deceived her.

"Then my poor friend must have been aware of the reception which you would meet at my hands—of the stern truths that you would hear from my lips," said Mr. Wharton; "for to no other purpose could this visit have been designed."

"But—are there no written instructions—with which you may be as yet unacquainted—no papers, the contents of which you have not read——"

"Madam, I am at a loss to comprehend you," said the lawyer. "If you allude to any papers of Mr. Tracy's now in my hands, I can assure you that they bear no reference to any affairs in which you can possibly be interested."

"And you have read *all* those papers—every one—*the last* that was placed in your hands, as well as any others?" inquired Cecilia, in a tone of breathless excitement.

"Merciful heavens, madam!" ejaculated the lawyer, on whose mind a light seemed suddenly to break: "surely—surely *you* cannot be in expectation of a legacy or a boon from that man whom you hurried to his ruin—aye, even to murder and suicide? Surely your presumption is not so boundless as all that?"

Cecilia sank back, almost fainting in her chair: her sole hope was now annihilated; and in its stead there remained to her only the bitter—bitter conviction that she had been deceived by Reginald in that last transaction which took place between them.

"No, madam—no," continued the lawyer, with a smile of the most cutting contempt: "if that unhappy man had bequeathed you any thing, it would have been his curse—his withering, dying curse!"

"Oh! do not say *that*," screamed Cecilia, now really appalled by the energetic language of that man who was so unsparing in his duty to the memory of his friend.

"Ah! I am rejoiced that your ladyship at last feels the full force of that infamy which has accomplished the ruin of a man once so good, so upright, so honourable, so happy! But you are, no doubt, curious to know how your victim has disposed of that wealth of which you would have plundered him had he not been so suddenly stopped in his mad career? I will tell you. He has bequeathed it to that young girl who so nearly suffered for *his* crime—to Katherine Wilmot, who was so unjustly accused of the enormity which *he* perpetrated!"

Lady Cecilia wept with rage, shame, and disappointment.

"Weep, madam, weep," rang the iron voice of that stern denunciator once more in her ears: "weep—for you have good cause! Not for the wealth of the universe would I harbour the feelings which ought to be—*must* be yours at this moment."

A pause ensued, which was interrupted by the entrance of a clerk who whispered something in the lawyer's ear, and then withdrew.

"I request your ladyship to have the goodness to remain here until my return," said Mr. Wharton. "I shall not keep you long."

The lawyer passed into the outer office; and Cecilia was now alone.

The reader can scarcely require to be reminded that this lady was not one who was likely to remain long depressed by a moral lesson, however severe its nature.

Scarcely had the lawyer left her, when she raised her head, and thought within herself, "I have been deceived—cruelly deceived; and if I did Reginald any wrong, he is amply avenged. One thing seems certain—he has retained the secret of the means by which he obtained the poison. He has not compromised me there; or else this harsh man would have been only too glad to throw *that* also in my teeth. Thus, my position might have been worse!"

Such was the substance of Lady Cecilia Harborough's musing during the absence of the lawyer.

This absence lasted nearly a quarter of an hour; and then he returned to the office.

He held an open letter in his hand.

"Lady Cecilia Harborough," he said, in a tone of increased sternness, "the measure of your guilt is now so full, that justice demands an explanation at your hands."

"Justice, sir!" faltered the frail woman, an icy coldness striking to her heart.

"Yes, madam," answered the lawyer; "and even from the grave will the wrongs of Reginald Tracy cry out against you."

"My God! what do you mean?" she exclaimed, her pallor now becoming actually livid.

"Before Reginald Tracy took the poison which hurried him to his last account," continued the solicitor in a low and solemn tone, "he wrote two letters. These were found upon the table in his cell. One was to Katherine Wilmot—the other was to me. The governor of Newgate has just been with me, and has delivered to me this last communication from my poor friend."

"The governor of Newgate!" repeated Cecilia, now overwhelmed with vague terrors.

"Yes, madam: and the contents are to inform me that you—*you*, madam, with an assumed name, and passing yourself off as Mr. Tracy's sister, visited him twice in his cell, and, on the latter occasion, furnished him with the means of self-destruction."

"Heaven protect me! it is but too true!" cried Cecilia; and, throwing herself upon her knees before the lawyer, she almost shrieked the words, "You would not give me up to justice, sir—you will not betray me?"

"No, madam," answered Mr. Wharton; "I had punished you sufficiently when these tidings arrived."

"Thank you, sir—thank you," cried Cecilia, rising from her knees. "But the governor of Newgate——"

"Is gone, madam. I did not tell him that you were here. I must, however, warn you that I communicated to him, as in duty bound, the contents of this letter."

"Then he is aware that I——"

"He is aware that you conveyed the poison to Reginald Tracy; and the officers of justice will be in search of you in another hour," replied the lawyer, coldly.

"My God! what will become of me?" ejaculated Cecilia, now pushed to an extremity which she never had contemplated.

"I would not say that you were here, madam," continued the lawyer, "because Reginald Tracy had contemplated making me the means of handing you over to the grasp of justice; and I am sorry that he should so far have misunderstood me. I now comprehend why he directed you to come hither. He thought that his letter would reach me earlier—before you came, and that I should be the willing instrument of his vengeance. I will not show you the letter, because he has mistaken me—he has misunderstood me; and for this reason alone—and for no merciful feeling towards *you*—have I shielded you thus far. Now go, madam: when once you are away from this house, you must adopt the best measures you can devise to ensure your safety."

"But can you not counsel me, sir—will you not direct me how to act?" cried Cecilia: "I am bewildered—I know not what step to take!"

"I have no counsel to offer, madam," returned the lawyer, briefly.

Cecilia could not mistake the meaning conveyed by this tone.

She rose; and bowing in a constrained manner to the solicitor, left the office.

But when she found herself in the street, she was cruelly embarrassed how to act.

She dared not return home; the paternal door had long been closed against her; she had not a friend—and she had not a resource.

A few sovereigns in her purse were all her available means.

She thought of quitting the country at once, and proceeding to join her husband, whom she knew to be in Paris.

But how would he receive her? The newspapers would soon be busy with her name; and Sir Rupert was not the man to burden himself with a woman penniless in purse and ruined in reputation.

For an instant she thought of Greenwood; but this idea was discarded almost as soon as entertained. She was aware of his utter heartlessness, and felt confident that he would repulse her coldly from his dwelling.

To whom could she apply? whither was she to betake herself?

And yet concealment was necessary—oh! she must hide somewhere!

The feelings of this woman were terrible beyond description.

And now she was walking rapidly along the streets towards London Bridge; for the idea of quitting the country was uppermost in her mind.

Her veil was drawn carefully over her countenance; and yet she trembled at every policeman whom she passed.

She was hurrying down Gracechurch Street, when she heard herself called by name.

She knew the voice, and turned round, saying to herself, "Help may come from this quarter!"

It was the old hag who had spoken to her.

"My good woman," said Lady Cecilia hastily, "all is known—all is discovered!"

"What is known?" asked the old hag, in her usual imperturbable tone.

"It is known that I conveyed the poison, which *you* procured for me, to Reginald Tracy," replied Cecilia, in a hoarse whisper. "You have heard that he is dead?"

"I heard *that* last evening," said the hag. "What are you going to do?"

"To hide myself from the officers of justice," returned Cecilia. "But step into this court, or we shall be observed."

The old woman followed the unhappy lady under an archway.

"I must conceal myself—at least for the present," resumed Cecilia. "Will you grant me an asylum?"

"I! my dear lady!" ejaculated the hag, shaking her head ominously: "I am in danger myself—I am in danger myself! Did I not procure you the poison?"

"True. But I would not betray you."

"No—we must each shift for ourselves—we must each shift for ourselves, as best we can," replied the hag flatly. "Indeed, I may as well remind you, Lady Cecilia, that your day is gone—you are ruined—and, if you had any spirit, you would not survive it!"

"My God! what do you mean?" faltered Cecilia, in a faint tone.

"The river is deep, or the Monument is high," answered the hag, in a significant tone; "and you are near both!"

The wrinkled old harridan then hobbled out of the court as quickly as her rheumatic limbs would carry her.

"Even *she* deserts me!" murmured Cecilia to herself, and with difficulty suppressing an ebullition of feeling which would have attracted notice, and probably led to her detection: "even *she* deserts me! My God—is there nothing left to me but suicide? No—nothing!"

Her countenance wore, beneath her veil, an expression of blank despair, as she arrived at this appalling conviction; and for some moments she stood as if rooted to the spot.

"No—nothing left but *that*," she murmured, awaking from her temporary stupefaction: "nothing—nothing!"

And although these words were uttered in the lowest whisper, still it seemed as if she shrieked them *within herself*.

Then she hurried from the court.

"The river—or the Monument," she said, as she continued her rapid way: "the river is near—but the Monument is nearer. Drowning must be slow and painful—*the other* will be instantaneous. From the river I might be rescued; but no human power can snatch me from death during a fall from that dizzy height."

And she glanced upwards to the colossal pillar whose base she had now reached.

At that moment two men, evidently belonging to the working classes, passed her.

A portion of their conversation met her ears.

"And so she was not his sister, then?" said one.

"No such thing," replied the other. "I heard the governor of Newgate tell all about it to one of the City officers scarcely half an hour ago. The governor was coming out of a lawyer's house—Tracy's lawyer, I believe—and the City officer was waiting for him at the door. He then told him that it was a lady of fashion—with a name something like Cecilia Scarborough, I think——"

The men were now too far for the wretched woman to hear any more of their conversation.

"Merciful heavens!" she said, scarcely able to prevent herself from wringing her hands; "even at this moment I am not safe!"

Then, without farther hesitation, she passed round the base of the Monument, and crossed the threshold.

"Sixpence, if you please, ma'am," said the man who received the fees from visitors.

Lady Cecilia exercised an almost superhuman power over her distracted feelings, so as to appear composed, while she drew forth the coin from her purse.

"It's a fine day to view London, ma'am," said the man, as he took the money.

"Beautiful," answered Cecilia.

She then began the tedious ascent.

And now what awful emotions laboured in her breast as she toiled up that winding staircase.

"My God! my God!" she murmured to herself; "is it indeed come to this?"

Once she was compelled to stop and lean against the wall for support.

Then she wrung her hands in agony—indescribable agony of mind.

"And yet there is no alternative!" she thought; "none—none! But my mother—my poor mother! what will be her feelings? Oh! better to know that I am dead, than an inmate of Newgate!"

And, somewhat encouraged in her dreadful purpose by this idea, she pursued her way.

In a few moments the fresh air blew in her face.

She was near the top!

A dozen more steps—and the brilliant sun-light burst upon her eyes.

It was indeed a lovely morning; and the Thames appeared like a huge serpent of quicksilver, meandering its way amidst the myriads of buildings that stretched on either side, far as the eye could reach.

The din of the huge city reached the ears of the wretched woman who now stood upon that tremendous eminence.

All was life—bustle—business—activity below!

And above was the serene blue sky of an early spring, illuminated by the bright and cloudless sun.

"But yesterday," thought Cecilia, as she surveyed the exciting scene spread beneath her, "had any one said to me, '*Thou wilt seek death to-morrow*,' I should have ridiculed the idea. And yet it has come to this! Oh! it is hard to quit this world of pleasure—to leave that city of enjoyment! Never more to behold that gorgeous sun—never more to hear those busy sounds! But if I hesitate, my heart will turn coward; and then—Newgate—Newgate!"

These last words were uttered aloud in the shrill and piercing tones of despair.

She clasped her hands together, and prayed for a few moments.

Then, as if acting by a sudden impulse,—as if afraid to trust herself with the thoughts that were crowding into her mind,—she placed her hands upon the railing.

One leap—and she stood upon the rail.

For a single instant she seemed as if she would fall backwards upon the platform of the Monument; and her arms were agitated convulsively, like the motions of one who endeavours to gain a lost balance.

Then she sprang forwards.

Terrific screams burst from her lips as she rolled over and over in her precipitate whirl.

Down she fell!

Her head dashed against the pavement, at a distance of three yards from the base of the Monument.

Her brains were scattered upon the stones.

She never moved from the moment she touched the ground:—the once gay, sprightly, beautiful patrician lady was no more!

A crowd instantaneously collected around her; and horror was depicted on every countenance, save one, that gazed upon the sad spectacle.

And that one wretch who showed no feeling, was the old hag of Golden Lane.

"She cannot now betray me for procuring the poison," thought the vile harridan, as she calmly contemplated the mangled corpse at her feet.

CHAPTER CLXII.

THE BEQUEST.

Two days after the suicide of Lady Cecilia Harborough,—an event which created a profound sensation in the fashionable world, and plunged the Tremordyn family into mourning,—Richard Markham was a passenger in a coach that passed through Hounslow.

At this town he alighted, and inquired the way to the residence of Mr. Bennet, a small farmer in the neighbourhood.

A guide was speedily procured at the inn; and after a pleasant walk of about three miles, across a country which already bore signs of the genial influence of an early spring, Richard found himself at the gate of a comfortable-looking farm-house.

He dismissed his guide with a gratuity, and was shortly admitted by a buxom servant-girl into a neat little parlour, where he was presently joined by Katherine.

The young maiden was rejoiced to see her benefactor; and tears started into her eyes, though her lips were wreathed in smiles;—but they were tears of pleasure and gratitude.

"This is kind of you, Mr. Markham," she said, as he shook her hand with friendly warmth.

"I am come to see you upon important business, Katherine," observed Richard. "But first let me inquire after the good people with whom you reside?"

"I am sorry to say," answered Katherine, "that Mrs. Bennet experienced a relapse after her return from London; and she is not able to leave her chamber. She is, however, much better. Her husband is a kind-hearted, good man, and he behaves like a father to me. He is now occupied with the business of his farm, but will be in presently."

"And now, Katherine, listen to the tidings which I have to communicate," said Markham. "Have you received any news from London within the last day or two?"

"No—not a word," returned Katherine, already alarmed lest some new misfortune was about to be announced to her.

"Compose yourself," said Richard; "the news that I have for you are good. But first I must inform you that your late master, Mr. Reginald Tracy, is no more."

"Dead!" exclaimed Katherine.

"He put a period to his own existence," continued Markham; "but not before he made you all the amends in his power for the deep injury which his own guilt entailed upon you."

"Then he confessed his crime, and thus established my innocence beyond all doubt?" said Katherine.

"And he has bequeathed to you his whole fortune, with the exception of a small legacy to Mrs. Bennet, whom his guilt deprived of a sister," added our hero.

"Oh! then he died penitent!" exclaimed Katherine, weeping—for her goodness of heart prompted her to shed tears even for one who had involved her in such a labyrinth of misery as that from which she had only so recently been extricated.

"He died by his own hands," said Richard; "and the world will not generally admit that such an act can be consonant with sincere penitence. That he attempted to make his peace with heaven ere he rushed into the presence of the Almighty, let us hope:—that he did all he could to recompense those whom his crime had injured, is apparent. But this letter will probably tell you more on that head."

Richard handed to Katherine a letter, as he uttered these words.

It was addressed, "*Miss Katherine Wilmot.*"

With a trembling hand the young girl opened it; and with tearful eyes she read the following words:—

"To you, Katherine Wilmot, a man about to appear before his Maker appeals for pardon. That man is deeply imbued with a sense of the injury—the almost irreparable injury which his enormous guilt caused you to sustain. But in confessing that this guilt was all and solely his own,—in proclaiming your complete innocence,—and in offering you the means of henceforth enjoying independence, and fulfilling the dictates of your charitable disposition,—that great criminal entertains a hope that you will accord him your forgiveness, and that you will appreciate his anxiety to do you justice in his last moments. My solicitor is already acquainted with my intentions; and he will faithfully execute my wishes. This letter will be forwarded to him, to be delivered to you, through your benefactor—that noble-hearted young man, Mr. Richard Markham. The bulk of my fortune, amounting to eighteen thousand pounds, I have made over to my solicitor in trust for yourself, and under certain conditions which I have devised exclusively for your benefit. The sum of five hundred pounds I have, in addition, bequeathed to Rachel Bennet, with the hope that she will extend *her* pardon also to the man who deprived her of an affectionate sister. This letter is written in a hurried manner, and under circumstances whose appalling nature you may well conceive. May heaven bless you! Refuse not to pray for the soul of

"REGINALD TRACY."

Katherine perused this letter, and then handed it to Richard Markham.

While he read it, the young maiden prayed inwardly but sincerely for the eternal welfare of him whose course had been dazzling like a meteor, but had terminated in a cloud of appalling blackness.

"Those conditions, to which the unhappy man alluded, I can explain to you," said Richard, after a long interval of silence, during which he allowed Katherine to compose her thoughts. "This letter was placed in the hands of Mr. Tracy's solicitor, by the governor of Newgate, the day before yesterday. The lawyer immediately wrote to me, being unacquainted with your address. I saw him yesterday afternoon; and he gave me the letter to convey to you, entrusting me at the same time with the duty of communicating to you this last act of Reginald Tracy. Mr. Wharton acquainted me with the conditions which Mr. Tracy had named. These are that you shall enjoy the interest of the money until you attain the age of twenty-one, when the capital shall be placed at your whole and sole disposal; but should you marry previous to that period, then the capital may also be transferred to your name. And now I must touch upon a more delicate point—inasmuch as it alludes to myself. Mr. Tracy was pleased to place such confidence in me, as to have stipulated that should you contract any marriage previous to the attainment of the age of twenty-one, without my approval of the individual on whom you may settle your affections, you will then forfeit all right and title to the fortune, which is in that case to be devoted to purposes of charity specified in the instructions given by Mr. Tracy to his solicitor."

"Oh! I should never think of taking any step—however trivial, or however important—without consulting you, as my benefactor—my saviour!" exclaimed Katherine.

"You are a good and a grateful girl, Katherine," said Richard; "and never for a moment did I mistake your excellent heart—never did I lose my confidence in your discretion and virtue."

"No—for when all the world deserted me," said the maiden, "you befriended me!"

"I have yet other matters of business to consult you upon," continued Markham. "Yesterday evening your uncle called upon me. Never—never have I seen such an alteration so speedily wrought in any living being! He said that certain representations which I had made to him at the tavern in the Old Bailey, after you had departed with Mrs. Bennet, had induced him to reflect more seriously upon the course of life which he had been for years pursuing."

"Oh! these news are welcome—welcome indeed!" ejaculated Katherine, clasping her hands together in token of gratitude.

"I communicated to him your good fortune, Katherine," proceeded Markham; "and he wept like a child."

"Poor uncle! His heart was not altogether closed against me!" murmured Katherine.

"I desired him to call upon me to-morrow, and I assured him that in the meantime I would devise some project by which he should be enabled to earn a livelihood whereof he need not be ashamed."

"You are not content with being my benefactor, Mr. Markham: you intend to make my relatives adore your name!" cried Katherine, her heart glowing with gratitude towards our hero.

"I now intend that *you* shall be the means of doing good, Katherine," said Richard, with a smile.

"Oh! tell me how!" exclaimed the amiable girl, joyfully.

"You shall draw upon the first year's interest of your fortune, for a sufficient sum to enable your uncle to retire to some distant town, where, under another name, he may commence a business at whose nature he will not be forced to blush."

"Oh! that proposal is indeed a source of indescribable happiness to me," said Katherine.

"Then I will carry the plan into effect to-morrow," continued Richard. "Your uncle and cousin shall both visit you here, when they leave London."

"Poor John!" said Katherine. "Do you think that his father———"

"Will treat him better in future?" added Markham, seeing that the maiden hesitated. "Yes: I will answer for it! A complete change has taken place in your uncle: he is another man."

"He contemplated your benevolence, and he could not do otherwise than be struck by the example," said Kate.

"I asked him if he desired you to live with him in future; and he replied, '*Not for worlds!*' He then continued to say that dwell where he might, conceal his name how he would, there would be danger of his ancient calling transpiring; and he would not incur the chance of involving you in the disgrace that might ensue. This consideration on his part speaks volumes in favour of that change which has been effected within him."

"The tidings you have brought me concerning my uncle, Mr. Markham," said Katherine, "far outweigh in my estimation the news of my good fortune."

"Your uncle and your cousin will yet be happy—no doubt," observed Richard. "In reference to yourself, what course would you like to adopt? Would you wish me to seek some respectable and worthy family in London, with whom you can take up your abode in entire independence? or———"

"Oh! no—not London!" exclaimed Katherine, recoiling from the name in horror.

"My counsel is that you remain here—in this seclusion,—at least for the present," said Richard. "The tranquillity of this rural dwelling—the charms of the country—the unsophisticated manners of these good people, will restore your mind to its former composure, after all you have passed through."

"This advice I have every inclination to follow," said Katherine; "and even were I otherwise disposed—which I could not be—your counsel would at once decide me."

"Remember, Katherine," resumed Markham, "I do not wish you to pass the best portion of your youth in this retirement. With your fortune and brilliant prospect, such a proceeding were unnatural—absurd. I only feel desirous that for a short time you should remain afar from society—until recent events shall be forgotten, and until your own mind shall become calm and relieved from the excitement which past misfortunes have been so painfully calculated to produce."

"I will remain here until you tell me that it is good for me to go elsewhere," said Katherine.

At this moment an old man, dressed in a rustic garb, but with a good-natured countenance and venerable white hair, entered the room.

This was the farmer himself.

Katherine introduced Richard to him as her benefactor; and the old man shook hands with our hero in a cordial manner, saying at the same time, "By all I have heard Miss Kate tell of you, sir, you must be an honour to any house, whether rich or poor, that you condescend to visit."

Richard thanked the good-natured rustic for the well-meant compliment, and then communicated to him the fact that his wife was entitled to a legacy of five hundred pounds, which would be paid to her order in the course of a few days.

The old man was overjoyed at these tidings, although his countenance partially fell when he heard the source whence the bequest emanated; but Richard convinced him that it would be unwise and absurd to refuse it.

Mr. Bennet hastened up-stairs to communicate the news to his wife.

While he was absent, the farmer's servant-girl entered to spread the table for the afternoon's repast.

On the return of the old man to the room, the dinner was served up; and our hero sat down to table with the farmer and Katherine.

A happy meal was that; and in the pure felicity which Katherine now enjoyed, Richard beheld to a considerable extent the results of his own goodness. How amply did the spectacle of that young creature's happiness reward him for all that he had done in her behalf!

It was four o'clock in the afternoon when our hero took his leave of the old farmer and Miss Wilmot, in order to retrace his steps to Hounslow.

CHAPTER CLXIII.

THE ZINGAREES.

The old farmer had offered to convey Richard to Hounslow in his own spring-cart, or to provide him with a guide to conduct him thither; but our hero felt so confident of being enabled to find his way back to the town, that he declined both offers.

He walked on, across the fields, pondering upon various subjects,—Isabella, his brother, Katherine, Reginald Tracy's crimes, and the frightful suicide of Lady Cecilia Harborough,—and with his mind so intent upon these topics, that some time elapsed ere he perceived that he had fallen into a wrong path.

He looked around; but not an object of which he had taken notice in the morning, when proceeding to the farm, could he now discover.

Thus he had lost the only means which could assist his memory in regaining the road.

As he stood upon a little eminence, gazing around to find some clue towards the proper direction which he should follow, a light blue wreath of smoke, rising from behind a hill at a short distance, met his eyes.

"There must be a dwelling yonder," he said to himself; "I will proceed thither, and ask my way; or, if possible, obtain a guide."

Towards the light blue cloud which curled upwards, Markham directed his steps; but when he reached the brow of the hill, from the opposite side of which the smoke at first met his eye, he perceived, instead of a cottage as he expected, an encampment of gipsies.

A covered van stood near the spot where two men, two women, and a boy were partaking of a meal, the steam of which impregnated the air with a powerful odour of onions.

The caldron, whence the mess was served up in earthenware vessels, was suspended by means of stakes over a cheerful wood-fire.

We need attempt no description of the persons of those who were partaking of the repast: it will be sufficient to inform the reader that they consisted of King Zingary, Queen Aischa, Morcar, Eva, and this latter couple's son.

They were, however, totally unknown to Richard: but the moment he saw they were of the gipsy tribe, he determined to glean from them any thing which they might know and might choose to reveal concerning the Resurrection Man.

He therefore accosted them in a civil manner, and, stating that he had lost his way, inquired which was the nearest path to Hounslow.

"It would be difficult to direct you, young gentleman, by mere explanation," answered Zingary, stroking his long white beard in order to impress Richard with a sense of veneration; "but my grandson here shall show you the way with pleasure."

"That I will, sir," exclaimed the boy, starting from the ground, and preparing to set off.

"But perhaps the gentleman will rest himself, and partake of some refreshment," observed Morcar.

"If you will permit me," said Markham, whose purpose this invitation just suited, "I will warm myself for a short space by your cheerful fire; for the evening is chilly. But you must not consider me rude if I decline your kind hospitality in respect to food."

"The gentleman is cold, Morcar," said Zingary: "produce the rum, and hand a snicker."

The King's son hastened to the van to fetch the bottle of spirits; and Markham could not help observing his fine, tall, well-knit frame, to which his dark Roman countenance gave an additional air of manliness—even of heroism.

Richard partook of the spirits, in order to ingratiate himself with the gipsies; and King Zingary then called for his "broseley."

"You appear to lead a happy life," observed Richard, by way of encouraging a conversation.

"We are our own masters, young gentleman," answered Zingary; "and where there is freedom, there is happiness."

"Is it true that your race is governed by a King?" asked Markham.

"I am the King of the united races of Bohemians and Egyptians," said Zingary, in a stately manner. "This is my beloved Queen, Aischa: that is my son, Morcar; here is my daughter-in-law, Eva; and that lad is my grandson."

Richard started when these names fell upon his ears; for they had been mentioned to him by Skilligalee in the Palace of the Holy Land. He also remembered to have been informed that it was in consequence of something which the Resurrection Man told Aischa, when she was attending to his wound, that the gipsies took him with them when they removed from the Palace to the encampment near the Penitentiary at Pentonville.

"I feel highly honoured by the hospitality which your Majesty has afforded me," said Richard, with a bow—an act of courtesy which greatly pleased King Zingary. "On one occasion I was indebted to some of your subjects for a night's lodging at your establishment in St. Giles's."

"Indeed!" exclaimed the King; and now all the gipsies surveyed Richard with some interest.

"Yes," continued our hero; "and I may as well state to you frankly and candidly under what circumstances I became your guest—for *you* were all inmates of the house at the time I entered it."

"Speak, young gentleman," said Zingary: "we will listen with attention to all you may please to tell us; but we do not seek your confidence of our own accord, as curiosity is forbidden to our race."

"I must inform you," resumed Richard, "that I have sustained great and signal injuries at the hands of a miscreant, whom I one night traced to your dwelling in St. Giles's."

"Call it the Palace, young gentleman," said Zingary, smoking his pipe, and listening with great complacency.

"On that night, the man to whom I allude was desperately wounded——"

"Ah!" ejaculated the gipsies, as it were in a breath.

"And you removed him with you, away from the Palace during the night—or rather very early in the morning."

"Then you, young gentleman," said the King, "were the stranger whom the porter locked in the room to which you were shown, and who escaped from the Palace by some means or other? The matter was duly reported to us by letter."

"It is perfectly true that I liberated myself from the room in which I was imprisoned," said Markham. "But, answer me—I implore you—one question; did that vile man die of the wound which he received?"

"Before I reply to you," observed Zingary, "you will have the goodness to inform me why you left the Palace by stealth on that occasion, and whether you saw or heard any thing remarkable *after* we had taken our departure?"

"I will answer you frankly," returned Markham. "I left my room on that occasion, because I wished to discover whether Anthony Tidkins, to whom I have alluded, was in the house——"

"The Palace," said Zingary.

"I beg your Majesty's pardon—the Palace," continued Richard; "and I thank God that I was more or less instrumental in releasing from a horrible dungeon a poor woman——"

"We know whom you mean," interrupted Zingary, sternly. "Did you see a tall young man———"

"Who called himself by the strange name of Skilligalee?" added Markham, concluding the King's question for him. "I did;—I helped him to release that woman he named Margaret."

"And whom the laws of the Zingarees had condemned to the penalty from which you freed her," said the King. "Was it right, young man, thus to step between the culprit and the decree of justice?"

"I acted in accordance with the dictates of humanity," replied Richard firmly; "and under such circumstances I should act in a similar way again."

"The young gentleman speaks well," said Morcar, who admired the resolution evinced in our hero's tone and manner.

"And he showed a good heart," observed Eva, now speaking for the first time since Richard's arrival, and displaying her brilliant teeth.

"Well—well," exclaimed Zingary: "I will not upbraid the young man more, since even my pretty Eva takes his part. You see," he continued, addressing himself especially to the gipsies, "it is as we thought. Skilligalee deserted us in order to liberate Margaret Flathers. I always believed that such was the case, from the moment we received the account of her escape. But I have one more question to ask our guest. Let him satisfy us how he traced Anthony Tidkins *to* the Palace, and how he learnt that Anthony Tidkins was wounded *in* the Palace."

"On that head I must remain silent," said Richard. "I will not invent a falsehood, and I cannot reveal the truth. Be you, however, well assured that I never betrayed the secrets and mysteries of your establishment in Saint Giles's."

"Our guest is an honourable man," observed Morcar. "We ought to be satisfied with what he says."

"I am satisfied," exclaimed the King. "Aischa, answer you the questions which it is now the young man's turn to put to us."

"I wish to know whether Anthony Tidkins died of the wound which he received?" said Richard.

"It was my lot to attend to his wound," began Aischa. "When he was so far recovered as to be able to speak—which was about half an hour after the blood was stanched—he implored me to have him removed from the Palace. He told me a long and pathetic story of persecutions and sufferings which he had undergone; and he offered to enrich our treasury if we would take him beyond the reach of the person who had wounded him. His anxiety to get away was extreme; and it was in consequence of his representations and promises that I prevailed upon the King to issue orders to those who were to leave London with us, to hurry the departure as much as possible. That accounts for the abrupt manner in which we left at such an hour, and for the removal of the wounded man with us. In answer to your direct question, I must inform you that he did *not* die of the wound which he received."

"He did *not* die!" repeated Markham. "Then he is still alive—and doubtless as active as ever in purposes of evil."

"Is he such a bad man?" asked Aischa.

"He belongs to the atrocious gang called *Burkers*," answered Richard emphatically.

"Merciful heavens!" cried Eva, with a shudder. "To think that we should have harboured such a wretch!"

"And to think that I should have devoted my skill to resuscitate such a demon!" exclaimed Aischa.

"The vengeance of the Zingarees will yet overtake him," said the King calmly.

"Wherever I meet him, there will I punish him with the stoutest cudgel that I can find ready to hand," cried Morcar, with a fierce air.

"Have you then cause to complain against him?" asked Richard.

"The wretch, sir," answered Morcar, "remained nearly a month in our company, until his wound was completely healed by the skill of my mother. We treated him with as much kindness as if he had been our near and dear relative. One morning, when he was totally recovered, he disappeared, carrying away my father's gold with him."

"The ungrateful villain!" ejaculated Richard. "And he was indebted to your kindness for his life?"

"He was," returned Morcar." Fortunately there was but little in the treasury at the time—very little;—nevertheless, it was all we had—and he took our all."

"And you have no trace of him?" said Richard, eagerly.

"Not yet," replied Morcar. "But we have adopted measures to discover him. The King my father has sent a description of his person and the history of his treachery to every chief of our race in the kingdom; and thousands of sharp eyes are on the look-out for him through the length and breadth of the land."

"Heaven be thanked!" exclaimed Markham. "But when you discover him, hand him over to the grasp of justice, and instantly acquaint me with the fact."

"The Zingarees recognise no justice save their own," said the King, in a dignified manner. "But this much I promise you, that the moment we obtain a trace of his whereabouts, we will communicate it to you, and you may act as seemeth good to yourself. We have no sympathy in common with a cowardly murderer."

"None," added Morcar, emphatically.

"I thank you for this promise," said Richard, addressing himself to the King. "Here is my card; and remember that as anxious as I am to bring a miscreant to justice, so ready shall I be to reward those who are instrumental in his capture."

"You may rely upon us, young gentleman," said Zingary. "We will not shield a man who belongs to the miscreant gang of *Burkers*. To-morrow morning I will issue fresh instructions to the various district chiefs, but especially to our friends in London."

"And is it possible that, with no compulsory means to enforce obedience, you can dispose of thousands individuals at will?" exclaimed Markham.

"Listen, young man," said the King, stroking his beard. "When the great Ottoman monarch, the Sultan Selim, invaded Egypt at the beginning of the sixteenth century, and put to death the Mameluke sovereign Toumanbai,—when the chivalry of Egypt was subdued by the overwhelming multitudes of warriors who fought beneath the banner of Selim and his great Vizier Sinan-Pacha,—then did a certain Egyptian chief place himself at the head of a chosen body of Mamelukes, and proclaim death and destruction to the Ottomans. This chief was Zingarai. For some time he successfully resisted the troops of Selim; but at length he was compelled to yield to numbers; and Selim put him to death. His followers were proscribed; and those who did not fall into the hands of the Turkish conquerors escaped into Europe. They settled first in Bohemia, where their wandering mode of life, their simple manners, their happy and contented dispositions, and their handsome persons soon attracted notice. Then was it that the Bohemian maidens were proud to bestow their hands upon the fugitive followers of Zingarai; and many Bohemian men sought admittance into the fraternity. Hence the mixed Egyptian and Bohemian origin of the gipsy race. In a short time various members of this truly patriarchal society migrated to other climes; and in 1534 our ancestors first settled in England. Now the gipsy race may be met with all over the globe: in every part of Asia, in the interior of Africa, and in both the Americas, you may encounter our brethren, as in Europe. The Asiatics call us *Egyptians*, the Germans *Ziguener*, the Italians *Cingani*, the Spaniards *Gitanos*, the French *Bohemians*, the Russians *Saracens*, the Swedes and Danes *Tartars*, and the English *Gipsies*. We most usually denominate ourselves *the united races of Zingarees*. And Time, young gentleman, has left us comparatively unchanged; we preserve the primitive simplicity of our manners; our countenances denote our origin; and, though deeply calumniated—vilely maligned, we endeavour to live in peace and tranquillity to the utmost of our power. We have resisted persecution—we have outlived oppression. All Europe has promulgated laws against us; and no sovereigns aimed more strenuously to extirpate our race in their dominions than Henry the Eighth and Elizabeth of England. But as the world grows more enlightened, the prejudice against us loses its virulence; and we now enjoy our liberties and privileges without molestation, in all civilised states."

"I thank you for this most interesting account of your origin," said Richard.

"Henceforth you will know how to recognise the real truth amongst all the wild, fanciful, and ridiculous tales which you may hear or read concerning our race," proceeded Zingary. "From the two or three hundred souls who fled from Egypt and took refuge in Bohemia, as I have ere now explained to you, has sprung a large family, which has increased with each generation; and at the present moment we estimate our total number, scattered over all parts of the earth, at one million and a half."

"I was not aware that you were so numerous," said Richard, much interested by these details. "Permit me to ask whether the members in every country have one sovereign or chief, as those in England?"

"There is a King of the Zingarees in Spain; another in France; a third in Italy; and a fourth in Bohemia. In the northern provinces of European Turkey, in Hungary, and in Transylvania, there is a prince with the title of a Waiewode: the Zingarees of Northern Europe are governed by a Grand, or Great Lord."

Richard now rose to take leave of the hospitable and entertaining family in whose society he had thus passed an hour; and, as it was growing dark, Morcar himself offered to conduct our hero as far as Hounslow.

This proposal was gladly accepted; and Markham, having taken leave of the King, Aischa, and Eva, set out with Morcar.

In the course of three-quarters of an hour they reached the precincts of the town.

Richard forced a handsome remuneration upon the gipsy, and reminded him of the promise made by his father concerning the Resurrection Man.

"You may rely upon us," said Morcar: "it cannot be very long before you will hear from us, for there are many on the alert to discover the haunt of the villain."

The gipsy then turned to retrace his steps towards the encampment; and Richard proceeded to the inn, where he obtained a conveyance for London.

CHAPTER CLXIV.

THE EXECUTIONER'S HISTORY.

On the following evening Smithers presented himself, according to appointment, at Markham Place.

Richard received him in the library, and treated him altogether with a condescension and a degree of kindness which made a deep impression on the mind of the executioner.

Our hero then proceeded to acquaint him with the good fortune of Katharine, and the arrangement which had been made to supply him with the means to establish him in business.

"But do not imagine that this is all which you are to expect at Katherine's hands," said Richard. "As time progresses, and I find that you are determined not only to persevere in a respectable course of life, but also to make amends, by your altered manner, for the harshness which you have exhibited towards your son on so many occasions,—it will be my pleasing duty to recommend Katherine's trustee, who is disposed to place implicit confidence in me, to grant you such occasional pecuniary succour as may enable you to extend the business, whatever it may be, in which you intend to embark."

"I cannot find words to express my gratitude to you, sir," said Smithers; "and I hope that when you see Kate again, you will ask her forgiveness in my name for all the unkindness I have shown her at different times."

"You shall see her yourself—she wishes you and your son to call upon her," answered Richard; "and Mr. Bennet, to whom I communicated every thing, has sent you both an invitation to pass an entire day at his farm so soon as you can find leisure to avail yourself of the offer."

"Then that shall be to-morrow, sir," exclaimed Smithers; "for now that Katherine has such good prospects, I may as well communicate something to her which she probably will not regret to hear."

And for a few moments Smithers appeared to be absorbed in deep thought.

"And I don't know why I should keep any secret away from you, sir," he continued, suddenly breaking silence; "you have done so much for Kate, and you have produced so great a change in my mind, that I ought to conceal nothing from you. In one word, then, sir—Katherine Wilmot is no more my niece than she is yours."

"Not your niece!" ejaculated Richard.

"No relation whatever in the world to me," replied Smithers. "I never had either brother or sister; neither had my wife: and thus you see, sir, Kate cannot be my niece."

"But she believes herself to be so related to you," said Markham, who was not altogether displeased to learn that the young female for whom he experienced a fraternal interest, was not even a connexion of the Public Executioner.

"The story is somewhat a long one—and to me a melancholy subject," continued Smithers; "but if you will have patience to listen to it, I shall have nerve to relate it."

"Proceed," said Markham. "I feel deeply interested in the topic which now occupies us."

"You will then excuse me, sir, if I begin by telling you something about myself," resumed Smithers; "because it is more or less connected with Kate's early history."

Smithers settled himself in a comfortable position in his chair, and then related the following history:—

"My father was a grocer, in a large way of business, at Southampton. He was a widower; and I was his only son. I was considered to be a steady, exemplary young man; and I can safely say that I attended studiously to my father's business. I never frequented public-houses, but went to church regularly of a Sunday, and was fond of reading good books. Next door to us there lived a corn-dealer of the name of Wilmot;—he also was a widower, and had one child. This was a beautiful girl, about a year or two younger than myself, and whose name was

Harriet. The two families had been acquainted for a long, long time; and Harriet and myself were playmates in our infancy. We were therefore very intimate together; and the friendship of childhood ripened into love as we grew up. And, oh! how I did adore that girl! From amidst all the coarse, worldly, and abominable ideas which have of late years crowded in my brain, I have ever singled out that one bright—pure—and holy sentiment as a star that points to a blissful episode in my life. And she loved me in return! Our parents were pleased when they saw our attachment; and it was understood that our marriage should take place on the day that I attained my one-and-twentieth year. It only wanted seven or eight months to that period, when an event occurred which quite changed the prospect of affairs. The local bank failed, and old Wilmot was ruined."

Smithers paused for a moment, heaved a deep sigh, and then continued thus:—

"Wilmot immediately came to my father and addressed him in these words: '*The failure of the bank will throw me into the Gazette, if I cannot raise twelve or fifteen hundred pounds within a week to sustain my credit. That difficulty being overcome, I have no doubt of retrieving myself altogether.*' My father expressed his great delight at hearing this latter announcement, but instinctively buttoned up his breeches-pockets. Wilmot proceeded to state that he could raise the sum he required if my father would guarantee its repayment. My father was a money-making, close man; and this proposal astounded him. He refused it point blank: Wilmot begged and implored him to save him from ruin;—but all in vain. In the course of ten days the name of Joseph Wilmot, corn-dealer, figured in the list of Bankrupts."

Again Smithers paused for a few moments.

"I must tell you, sir," he continued, "that I did all I could to persuade my father to help Wilmot in this business; but my prayers and entreaties had been poured forth entirely without effect. I, however, took an opportunity of seeing Harriet, and assuring her that my affection was based upon no selfish motive, but that her father's misfortunes endeared *her* more than ever to me. My father viewed matters in quite a different light, and spoke to me openly of the impossibility of my marrying a girl without a penny. I remonstrated with him on the cruelty, injustice, and dishonour of such conduct; but he cut me very short by observing that '*his money was his own—he had made it by his industry—he could leave it to whom he chose—and that if I insisted upon marrying Harriet Wilmot I need not darken his threshold afterwards.*' I replied that I was resolved to consult my own inclinations, and also to do honour to my vows and promises towards Harriet."

"You acted in a generous manner," observed Markham; "although you opposed the wishes of your own father."

"I had no secrets from Harriet," said Smithers; "and I assured her that if she would espouse a man who had nothing but his honest name and exertions to depend upon, I was ready to make her mine. She answered me, with tears in her eyes, that she could never consent to be the cause of marring all my prospects in life, and that, much as she loved me, she would release me from my vows. I wept in concert with her;—for I was not *then* hard-hearted, sir,—nor had my countenance become impressed with that brutal severity which I know—I feel, it has long, long worn."

"As the countenance is more or less the index of the soul," said Markham, "so will yours resume all its former serenity of expression."

"Well—well, sir: let me hope so! I do not wish to die with the word 'EXECUTIONER' traced upon my features. But I will continue my story. Harriet seemed firm in her generous purpose not to be the cause of my ruin: I however implored her to reflect upon the misery into which her decision would plunge me. I then left her. The next morning I heard that Wilmot and his daughter had departed from their house, and had gone—no one knew whither. Malignant people said that the old man was afraid to face his creditors in the local Bankruptcy-court: I thought otherwise. I felt persuaded that Harriet had prevailed upon her father, by some means or another, to leave;—and I now considered her lost to me for ever. My sorrow was great; but I redoubled my attention to business in order to distract my mind from contemplating the misfortune that had befallen me. Weeks and months passed away; and the wound in my heart was closed, but it was still painful. One day, during a temporary indisposition which confined my father to his room, I was turning over some papers in his desk, seeking for an invoice which I required, when I perceived a letter addressed to my father and signed *Joseph Wilmot*. The date especially attracted my attention, because I remembered that this letter must have been written on the very day that I had the last interview with Harriet. I hesitated not a moment to read it; and its contents revealed to me the cause of that precipitate departure which has so distressed me. Indeed, the letter was in answer to one which Wilmot acknowledged to have just before received from my father. It appears that my father had written to offer old Wilmot two hundred pounds if he would quit the town, with his daughters, and that Wilmot should give a note of hand for this amount, which security my father engaged himself not to enforce so long as Wilmot remained away and left me in ignorance of his future place of residence. Wilmot consented to this arrangement: he was a ruined man without a shilling; and he gladly availed himself of the means of embarking in business elsewhere. This stratagem on the part of my father I discovered through Wilmot's letter. I said nothing about the letter to my father: I concluded that he had merely acted under the impression that he was consulting my welfare; and moreover the injury appeared to be irrevocable. Well, sir—six months passed away after the departure of Wilmot and his daughter, and my father, who was usually so cautious and prudent, was induced to embark some money in the purchase of smuggled goods. The excise officers discovered the transaction; and a fine was imposed which swept away every farthing of the sum which my father had been accumulating by the industry and toil of years. It broke his heart: he died, and left me a ruined business, instead of a decent competence. I struggled on for a year, just keeping my head above water, but dreadfully crippled for want of capital. At length I learnt, from a friend, that I had found favour in the sight of a wealthy neighbour's daughter, who was some six or seven years older than myself. I made the best of this circumstance; and, to save myself from total ruin, in a short time married the female alluded to. The fruit of this union was a son—the poor deformed creature whom you have seen. He was not, however, so afflicted at his birth: how he come to be so, I will presently tell you."

Smithers uttered these words in a tone of deep feeling.

"I had married for money, sir," he continued; "and I married unhappily. My wife was of a temper befitting a demon. Then she was addicted to drink; and in her cups she was outrageous. My home grew miserable: and I began to neglect the business; and, to avoid my wife in her drunken humours, I went to the public-house. Then also my temper was so sorely tried that it gave way under the accumulated weight of domestic wretchedness. I grew harsh and uncourteous to my customers; I retaliated against my wife in her own fashion of ill-treatment—by means of stormy words and heavy blows; and, when I was weary of all that, I rushed to the public-house, where I endeavoured to drown my cares in strong drink. In a word, three years after my marriage, I was compelled to abandon my business in Southampton; and, with about a hundred pounds in my pocket—the wrecks of all that my wife had brought me—I removed, with her and the child, to London. On our arrival, I took a small tobacconist's shop in High Street, St. Giles's, and exerted myself to the utmost to obtain an honest livelihood; and for some time my wife seemed inclined to second me. The ruin which our disputes and evil courses had entailed upon us appeared to have made a deep impression upon her mind. She carefully avoided strong drink, and declared her resolution never to take any thing stronger than beer. But one day she was prevailed upon by a female friend to accept a little spirits; and a relapse immediately followed. She came home intoxicated; we had fresh quarrels—renewed disputes; and I myself went in an evil hour to the nearest public-house. From that moment we pursued pretty well the same courses that had ruined us in Southampton; and this conduct led to similar results. I was forced to give up the snuff and cigar shop; and we moved into that identical house in St. Giles's which I now inhabit, and where you first saw me."

Smithers passed his hand over his forehead, as if to alleviate the acuteness of painful recollections.

He then pursued his narrative in the following manner:—

"Our sole hope and only resource now consisted in being able to let the greater portion of the house; and as we had managed to save our little furniture from the wreck of the business in High Street, we had still a decent prospect before us. My wife again promised reformation; and, as I never took to drink except when driven to it by her conduct, I was by no means unwilling to second her in her resolutions of economy. We soon let our lodgings, and I did a little business by selling groceries on commission for a wholesale house to which I managed to obtain an introduction. In this way we got on pretty well for a time; and now I come to the most important part of my story."

Richard drew his chair, by a mechanical movement as it were, closer to that of the executioner, and prepared to listen with redoubled attention, if possible.

"It was twelve years ago last January," continued Smithers, "that I returned home one evening, after a hard day's application to business, when the first thing my wife told me was that our back room on the second floor, which had long been to let, was at length taken. She added that our new lodger was a female of about eight-and-twenty or thirty, and had a little girl of four years old. My wife also stated that she was afraid the poor creature was in a dreadful state of health, and was not very comfortably off, as all her own and her child's things were contained in a small bundle which she brought with her. When my wife asked for a reference she evaded the inquiry by paying a week's rent in advance; and this pittance was taken from a purse containing a very slender stock of money. I inquired if the new lodger had given any name; but my wife replied that she had not asked her for it. The next day I was taken unwell, and was compelled to stay at home; but my wife went out with our boy, who was then six years old, to pass a few hours with a friend. I was sitting in the little parlour all alone, and thinking of the past, when I heard a gentle knock at the door. I opened it, and saw a nice little girl, about four years old, standing in the passage. She asked me to let my wife step up to her mother, who was very ill. I took the child in my arms, and went up to my new lodger's room, to say that my wife was out, but that if I could render any assistance I should be most happy to do so. I knocked at the door; it opened—but the female who appeared uttered a piercing scream, and fell back senseless on the floor. She had recognised me; and I, too, had recognised her,—recognised her in spite of her altered appearance and her faded beauty. It was Harriet Wilmot!"

The executioner paused, averted his head for a moment, and wiped away a tear.

He then continued his narrative.

"I instantly did my best to recover her. I fetched vinegar, and bathed her forehead; and in a few minutes she opened her eyes. I laid her upon the bed; and she motioned me to give her the child. This I did; and she pressed it rapturously to her bosom. I stood gazing upon the affecting scene, with tears in my eyes; but I said nothing. She extended her hand towards me, and murmured in a faint tone, '*Is it then in your home that I am come to breathe my last?*'—I implored her to compose herself, and assured her that she should meet with every attention. She glanced tenderly upon her child, and large tears rolled down her faded cheeks. Oh! she was so altered that it was no wonder if my wife, who had known her years before at Southampton, had not recognized her! I asked her if I should procure medical attendance. She could not answer me: a dreadful faintness seemed to come over her. I told her that I would return immediately; and I hurried for a doctor. The medical man came with me; and we found the poor creature speechless, but still sensible. He shook his head with significant hopelessness at me: I understood him—she was dying! The surgeon hastened back home, and speedily returned with various drugs and medicines. But all was of no avail; the poor creature was on the threshold of the grave. The doctor told me what to do, and then took his leave, promising to return in a couple of hours. I seated myself by the side of the bed, and anxiously watched the patient, who had gradually sunk into a deep slumber. I also amused myself with, and pacified the little girl. In this way hour after hour passed; and at length my wife came home. But in what a state did she return? Her friend—the same, as I afterwards learnt, who had before seduced her away from the paths of temperance—had accomplished this feat a second time. My wife was in a disgusting state of intoxication. Not finding me in our sitting-room, she came up stairs to search for me. The moment I heard her, I stepped out of Harriet's chamber to meet her, and request her assistance in behalf of the dying woman—for as yet I knew not the state in which my wife had returned. But when she saw me come from that room, she rushed upon me like a tigress: her jealousy was suddenly excited to an ungovernable fit of passion. She tore my face with her nails, and dragged out my hair by handfuls. I implored her to hear me; she raved—she stormed—she declared she would have the life of the woman in whose chamber I had been. Then my own anger was fearfully roused: I caught her by the throat, and I do believe that I should have strangled her, had not John—our boy—at that instant caught hold of my legs and begun to kick and pinch me with all his might—for he always took his mother's part. I was now rendered as infuriate as a goaded bull: I hurled my wife away from me, and with one savage blow—may God forgive me!—I knocked the child backwards down the stairs."

Here Smithers covered his face with his hands, and the tears trickled through his fingers.

"The lodgers rushed up to the floor where this horrible scene took place," he continued, after a long pause; "and I, in that moment of my excited and bewildered senses, justified my conduct by declaring that the woman who lay dying in the next room was my own sister. My wife was insensible, and could not contradict me; and thus the tale was believed. The lodgers removed my wife and my child to their bed-room; and the same surgeon who had attended upon Harriet was instantly sent for. Alas! his skill was all in vain. My wife never rallied again, save to give way to dreadful hysterical fits: in a few weeks, during which she lingered in that manner, she breathed her last;—and my son became deformed, as you have seen him!"

Again the miserable man paused, and gave way to his emotions.

Several minutes elapsed ere he continued his narrative; and Markham also remained wrapped in a profound silence.

At length the executioner proceeded thus:—

"The condition into which my rage had thrown my wife and child on that memorable day, did not prevent me from watching by the death-bed of Harriet Wilmot. I even attended to her little girl as if she had been my own. I felt my heart yearn towards that poor woman whom I had once known so beautiful and had loved so tenderly. She slept on,—slept throughout that long and weary night; and there I remained, watching by her bed-side. In the morning the doctor came: Harriet awoke, and smiled when she saw me. Then she made signs that she wished to write. Her powers of speech had deserted her. The medical man addressed her in a kind tone, and said that if she had any thing to communicate she had better do so, as she was very, very ill. She thanked him with a glance for his candour, and for the delicate manner in which he bade her prepare for death. I placed writing materials before her; and she wrote a few lines, which were, however, so blotted by tears——"

"I have already been made acquainted with the contents of the only legible portion which still remains of that letter," interrupted our hero.

"And you are, then, aware, sir, that allusion is made to a certain Mr. Markham?" said Smithers.

"Perfectly," replied Richard. "The late Mr. Reginald Tracy communicated that fact to me."

"The poor creature breathed her last ere she could terminate that letter," continued the executioner. "She suddenly dropped her pen, turned one agonising glance upon her child, fell back, and expired. I buried her as decently as my means would permit; and I determined to take care of Katherine. I repeated my original statement that the little girl was my niece; and, in order not to throw shame upon the memory of her mother, I represented her as having been a widow when she came to my house. I have before said that my wife never sufficiently recovered her senses to contradict this story; and my son John was too young at the time to be aware that it was a fiction."

"And did you never institute any inquiries into the meaning of that allusion to Mr. Markham in the letter?" inquired Richard.

"I obtained various *Directories* and *Guides*, and found that there were thirty or forty persons of that name residing in London, and whose addresses were given in those books. I called upon several; but none knew any thing of the business which took me to them. Then I abandoned the task as hopeless: for I reflected that there might be others of the same name who were *not* to be found in the *Directories*; and I was not even assured that the Mr. Markham alluded to dwelt in London."

"Thus you never obtained any farther clue to Katharine's parentage?"

"Never," answered Smithers. "The little child herself, when questioned by me soon after her mother's death, did not recollect having ever seen any one whom she called *Papa*; and from all I could learn from the orphan girl, her mother must have been living for some time in London before she came to my house. But where this residence was, I could not ascertain. One thing, however, I discovered, which seemed to proclaim the illegitimacy of Katherine's birth: she said that her mamma's name was Wilmot. That was her maiden name!"

"Poor Katherine!" said Richard.

"And now I have told you all, sir, that concerns her early history—at least all that I know. Some time after my wife's death, evil reports got abroad concerning me. It was said that my brutality had produced her death; and my son was a living reproach against me. No one would employ me—no one would lodge in my house. It was then that I accepted the office of Public Executioner,—to save myself from starving, and to give bread to my own son and the little orphan girl. By degrees my temper, already ruined by the conduct of my wife, became confirmed in its ferocity and cruel callousness. I grew brutal—savage—inhuman. I felt the degradation of my calling—I saw that I was shunned by all the world. I was looked upon as a monster who had murdered his wife and made his son deformed;—but the provocation and the circumstances were never mentioned to palliate the enormity of that double crime. At length I heard all the reproaches, and did not take the trouble to state facts in order to justify myself. But all this was enough to brutalize me,—especially when added to the duties of my new calling. In time I even began to ill-treat that poor orphan girl whom I had at first looked upon as my own child. But, bad as I have been towards her when I thought that she encouraged my son to thwart my will,—shamefully as I used her at times, I never would have abandoned her;—for when she thought that I turned her out of my house the day she went to Mr. Tracy's, it was only my brutal way of letting her go to a place which I knew would be creditable to her, and which, by what she told me, I saw she wished to take. Then I thought within myself, '*Yes, even she will now gladly leave me;*'—and, in order to conceal what I felt at that idea—and I *did* feel deeply—I took refuge in my own brutalized temper. But I sent her round all her things in the evening—not forgetting her work-box, which I knew contained the fragment that her poor mother wrote upon her death-bed. Moreover, when she came to see me, I received her with no constrained kindness; for I always liked her—even when I ill-used her;—and I was sorry to have parted with her."

"The world, my good friend, has not altogether read your heart correctly," said Richard.

"Thank you, sir,—thank you for that assurance," exclaimed Smithers; "and when you *good friend* me, sir—you, who are so noble-hearted, so generous, so truly grand in your humanity—I could burst into tears."

"If my example please you," said Markham, kindly, "you will make me happy by profiting by it. Oh! you shall yet live long to convince the world that the human heart never can be so deadened to all good feelings as to be beyond redemption!"

"I do not think I shall live to an old age, sir," observed Smithers, sinking his voice to a mysterious whisper: "I have already had one warning!"

"One warning!" repeated Richard, surprised at this strange announcement.

"Yes, Mr. Markham. One night I was lying in bed;—the candle was flickering in the fire-place;—I happened to turn my eyes towards that puppet which hangs in the loft where I used to sleep until within the last few days,—and I saw *another face* looking over its shoulder at me."

"Another face!" ejaculated Markham: "what do you mean?"

"I mean, sir, *that Harriet Wilmot's countenance appeared above the shoulder of the figure!*" answered Smithers, with a shudder.

"My good friend," said Markham, "your imagination was disordered at the moment. The days of spectres and apparitions are gone by. The Almighty does not address himself to man by means of terrors which nurses use to frighten children. I will show you, by a simple process of reasoning, that it is *impossible* to *see* a ghost—even if such a thing should exist. You do not see with the eye precisely in the way in which you may imagine. Strictly speaking, the eye does not see at all. The effect is this: substantial objects are reflected in the retina of the eye as in a mirror; and the impression is conveyed from the retina into the brain, where it assumes a proper and suitable shape in the imagination or conception. But in order that objects should so strike the retina of the eye, they *must* be *substantial*: they must have length, breadth, and thickness;—they must displace so much air as to leave the void filled up by their own forms. Now, even if the spirits of the departed be allowed to revisit this earth, *no mortal eye can see them*, because they are *unsubstantial*, and they cannot be reflected in the retina of the eye. I have only entered into this explanation to convince you that an unsettled mind or a disordered imagination—arising from either moral or physical causes—can *alone* conjure up phantoms."

"Well, sir, we will not talk any more upon *this* subject, if you please," said Smithers. "I understand what you say; and I thank you for your goodness in explaining the matter to me. I now wish to ask you whether you would rather that I should communicate all I have told you to Katherine; or whether you will yourself?"

"My good friend," said Richard, "you acted so noble a part towards her mother that this duty will better become you. Katherine will thank you for your goodness towards her parent—especially as that goodness arose from no interested motives; and you will rejoice in the grateful outpourings of the heart of that orphan whom you reared, and to whom you gave a home. To-morrow you and your son can visit her: the day after to-morrow, in the evening, I wish both of you—yourself and your son—to call upon me."

Smithers promised to obey our hero's desires in all respects, and then took his leave,—wondering how any human being could possess such influence over the heart, to humanize and reclaim it, as Richard Markham.

CHAPTER CLXV.

THE TRACE.

In order to avoid unnecessary details we shall now concisely state that Smithers and his son paid the visit agreed upon to Katherine Wilmot.

Smithers communicated to her, when they were alone together for half an hour, so much of his own history as involved all the particulars with which he was acquainted concerning her parentage.

The grateful girl expressed a deeper sense of obligation than she had ever yet experienced towards the individual who had supported her for so many years, although she had no claims of relationship upon him.

After one of the most agreeable days which the *late* executioner and his son had ever passed in their lives, they took leave of Katherine and the worthy people of the farm, and returned to London.

Poor Katherine Wilmot! she had that day learnt more concerning her parentage than she had ever known before; but she would have been happier, perhaps, had her original impressions on that subject never been disturbed!

Still Markham had conceived it to be a duty which was owing to the young maiden, to permit Smithers thus to reveal to her those circumstances which seemed to fix her with the stigma of illegitimacy.

That night her pillow was moistened with abundant tears, as she lay and reflected upon her lamented mother!

On the appointed evening Smithers and his son called at Markham Place.

They were conducted by Whittingham to a parlour, where the table was spread with a handsome collation, places being arranged for three persons.

"Sit down, my friends," said Richard Markham, who received them with a warmth far more encouraging than mere courtesy: "after supper we will transact the business for which I have requested your presence here."

"What, sir!" ejaculated Smithers; "can you condescend to have *me* at your table?"

"Not as you lately were," answered Richard: "I receive you as a regenerated man."

John Smithers (for we shall suppress his nickname of *Gibbet*, as his father had already done so) cast a glance of profound gratitude upon our hero, in acknowledgment of a behaviour that could not do otherwise than confirm his father in his anxious endeavours to adopt a course of mental improvement.

Smithers' confidence increased, when he had imbibed a glass or two of generous wine; and he related to Markham the particulars of his interview with Katharine.

Then was it for the first time the hump-back learnt that Katherine was not his cousin.

He said nothing; but, as he drank in all that fell from his father's lips, two large tears rolled down his cheeks.

When the supper was over, Richard addressed Smithers in the following manner:—

"The narrative which you revealed to me the day before yesterday materially alters the position in which Katherine stands with respect to you. When I first proposed that she should advance you at once a small sum, I believed her to be your near relative. But as she is in no way akin to you, it results that you have for years supported one who had no claim upon you. Accident has made her rich; and it is but fair and just that you should be adequately rewarded for your generosity. I have communicated with Katherine's trustee upon the subject; and we have agreed to furnish you with five hundred pounds at once, to enable you to embark in a respectable and substantial line of business. This pocket-book," proceeded Markham, "contains that sum. Take it, my worthy friend—it is your due; and, should you succeed in the career that you are now about to enter upon, you can with satisfaction trace your prosperity to the humanity which you showed to a friendless orphan."

After some hesitation, Smithers received the pocket-book. He and his son then took leave of Richard Markham, with the most sincerely felt expressions of gratitude, and with a promise from the father to write to him soon to state where and how they had settled themselves.

Scarcely had those two individuals, now both made happy, taken their departure, when Whittingham informed his master that a person with a dark complexion, and who gave the name of Morcar, requested to speak to him.

Richard ordered the gipsy to be instantly admitted to his presence.

Morcar was accordingly shown into the parlour.

The moment he found himself alone with Markham, he said in a low and somewhat solemn tone, "We have traced him!"

"I expected as much, the moment your name was announced," said Richard. "Where is he?"

"He has taken refuge in a barge on the river," answered Morcar. "That is all I have been able to learn; but I am confident he is there."

"And do you know where the barge is moored?" asked Richard.

"Close by Rotherhithe. But there are several other barges off the same wharf; and I cannot single out which he is in. I, however, know that he *is* concealed in one of them."

"It is important to discover which," said Markham. "Were we to make our appearance in that vicinity with a body of police, he might escape us altogether."

"And therefore it will be better to take him by means of stratagem," observed Morcar.

"What can have induced him to seek refuge there?" said Richard, in a musing tone. "Some new crime, perhaps?"

"Or else some fresh scheme of villany," returned Morcar. "But perhaps you are not aware, sir, that river piracy still flourishes to some extent?"

"I certainly imagined that with our system of Thames police, that species of depredation was completely ruined."

"No such thing, sir!" exclaimed Morcar. "The man who gave me the information about Tidkins, told me more than ever I knew before on that subject."

"You may as well acquaint me with those particulars, Morcar," said our hero. "They may assist me in devising some scheme to entrap the Resurrection Man, and enable justice to receive its due."

"River piracy, sir," continued Morcar, "is carried on by a set of vagabonds who for the most part have been sailors, or in some shape or another engaged amongst barges and lighters. They are all leagued with the marine-store dealers and people that keep old iron and junk shops on both sides of the river below London bridge. The river pirates usually possess a barge or lighter, which every now and then makes a trip up and down the river between Greenwich and Putney, but with no other freight than bales of sawdust, old rags, or even dung. This they do to keep up appearances and avoid suspicion. But all day long they maintain a good look out in the pool, and take notice of particular ships which they think can be easily robbed. For instance, sometimes a steamer is left with only a boy on board to take care of it; or else a lighter has only one man to look after it. Then these pirates go on board in the night, master the boy or the man, and plunder the steamer or lighter of any thing worth carrying away."

"I begin to understand how these villains may reap a profitable harvest in this manner," observed Richard.

"Oh! you don't know half their pranks, yet," said Morcar. "Sometimes two or three of the gang will go and hire themselves as bargemen or lightermen; and then they easily arrange with their pals how to plunder the vessels thus entrusted to them, while the owners never suspect that their own men are at the bottom of the robbery. When times are bad, and these fellows are driven to desperation, they think nothing of cutting away great pieces of ships' cables, or even weighing the anchors of small craft; and with these heavy materials they will get clean off in their boats to their own barge; and next morning they convey them as coolly as possible to the marine store dealers. Sometimes they cut lighters adrift, when the tide is running out, and follow them in their boat; then, under pretence of helping those on board, they cut away bales of cotton or any other goods that are easily thrown into their boats in dark nights."

"The villain Tidkins has no doubt transferred his operations from the land to the river," observed Markham; "seeing that, by means of a little address and a great deal of courage, such depredations can be effected."

"These river-pirates are of several kinds," continued Morcar. "There's the *light-horsemen*, or men who board the unprotected vessels in the night. Then there's the *heavy-horsemen*, who wear an under-dress, called a *jemmy*, which is covered by their smocks: these fellows obtain employment as *lumpers*,—that is, to load or discharge ships in the pool, during which they contrive to stow away every thing portable in the large pouches or pockets of their under-dress. Afterwards, the *heavy-horsemen*, give information to their pals, and put them on the scent which ships to rob at night. Next there's the *mud-larks*, who get on board stranded lighters at low water, and carry off what they can when the vessels are unprotected, or ask some question to lull suspicion if they find any one on board. This mode of river-piracy is very profitable, because numbers of lighters and barges are often left for hours alongside the banks, without a soul on board. *Game lightermen* are those pirates that are in league with dishonest mates and sailors belonging to vessels that come up the river to discharge: and they receive at night from their pals on board, through the port-holes or over the quarter, any thing that's easy to move away in this manner. Last of all there's the *scuffle-hunters*, who put on smocks, and obtain work as porters on the wharfs where a ship is loading: then, if they can't contrive to steal any thing by those means, they can at all events carry some useful information to their pals—so that the ship is generally robbed in one way or another."

"With so well organised a fraternity and such means of operation," said Markham, who had listened with interest and astonishment to these details, "Tidkins is capable of amassing a fortune in a very short time. But we must stop him in his criminal career. At the same time, let us do nothing without mature consideration. Are you willing to assist? Your reward shall be liberal."

"The Zingaree may not of his own accord deliver up any one to justice," answered Morcar; "but he is allowed to serve an employer who pays him. Moreover," he added, as if ashamed of that sophistical compromise with the rules of his fraternity, "I shall gladly help to punish the miscreant who treated us with such base ingratitude."

"Then you consent to serve me?" said Richard.

"I do, sir," was the reply.

"To-morrow, at mid-day, I will meet you somewhere in the eastern part of London," continued Richard. "I have already a project in my head; but I must consider it more maturely."

"Where shall we meet, sir?" asked Morcar.

Markham reflected for a moment, and then said, "On the Tower wharf."

"I will be punctual, sir," answered the gipsy; and he took his departure.

CHAPTER CLXVI.

THE THAMES PIRATES.

Moored at a wharf at the Rotherhithe side of the river Thames, nearly opposite Execution Dock, were several lighters and barges, all lying together.

Along the upper part of the buildings belonging to the wharf were painted, in rude but gigantic letters, the following words:—"Mossop's Wharf, where Goods are Received, Housed, or Carted."

Mr. Mossop, the sole proprietor of this wharf, was by no means particular what goods he thus received, whence they came when he housed them, or whither they were going when he carted them. He asked no questions, so long as his commission and charges were duly paid.

For the convenience of his numerous customers, he kept his office constantly open; and either himself or his son Ben Mossop was in constant attendance.

Indeed, Mr. Mossop did more business by night than by day. He was, however, a close man: he never put impertinent questions to any one who called to patronise him; and thus his way of doing business was vastly convenient for all those who used his wharf or his store-houses.

If a lighter arrived at that wharf, ostensibly with a freight of hay, but in reality with divers bales of cotton or other goods concealed beneath the dried grass, Mr. Mossop did not seem to think that there was any thing at all strange in this; and if next day he happened to hear that a barge at a neighbouring wharf had been robbed of divers bales of cotton during the night, Mr. Mossop was too much of a gentleman to question the integrity of *his* customers. Even if every wall in Rotherhithe, Horselydown, and Bermondsey, were covered with placards announcing the loss of the bales, describing them to a nicety, and offering a reward for their recovery, Mr. Mossop never stopped to read one of them.

On two or three occasions, when a police-officer called at his wharf and politely requested him just to honour the nearest magistrate with a visit, and enter into an explanation how certain goods happened to be found in his store-rooms, the said goods having been lost by other parties in an unpleasant manner, Mr. Mossop would put an enormous pair of spectacles upon his nose and a good face on the matter at the same time; and it invariably happened that he managed to convince the bench of *his* integrity, but without in any way compromising those persons who might be in custody on account of the said goods.

His son Ben was equally prudent and reserved; and thus father and son were mighty favourites with all the river pirates who patronised them.

Moreover, Mossop's Wharf was most conveniently situate: the front looked, of course, upon the river; the back opened into Rotherhithe Wall; and Mossop's carts were noted for the celerity with which they would convey goods away from the warehouse to the receivers in Blue Anchor Road or in the neighbourhood of Halfpenny Hatch.

The father and son were also famous for the regularity and dispatch with which they executed business on pressing occasions. Thus, while Mossop senior would superintend the landing of goods upon the wharf, Mossop junior was stationed at the back gate, where it was his pleasing duty to see the bales speedily carted as they were brought *through* the warehouses by the lumpers employed.

Mossop senior was also reputed to be a humane man; for if any of his best customers got into trouble (which was sometimes the case) and were short of funds, a five pound note in a blank envelop would reach them in prison to enable them to employ counsel in their defence; and this sum invariably appeared as "*money lent*" in Mossop's next account against them when they were free once more, and enabled to land another cargo at the wharf.

But to continue our narrative.

It was the evening after the one on which Morcar had called at Markham Place; consequently the evening of that day when the gipsy was to meet our hero on the Tower wharf.

Over the particulars of that meeting we, however, pass; as the plans then arranged will presently develop themselves.

It was now about nine o'clock.

The evening was beautiful and moonlight.

Myriads of stars were rocked to and fro in the cradle of the river's restless tide; and the profiles of the banks were marked with thousands of lights, glancing through dense forests of masts belonging to the shipping that were crowded along those shores.

At intervals those subdued murmurs which denoted that the river was as busy and active as the great city itself, were absorbed in the noise of some steamer ploughing its rapid way amidst the mazes of vessels that to the inexperienced eye appear to be inextricably entangled together.

Then would arise those shouts of warning to the smaller craft,—those rapid commands to regulate the movements of the engines,—and those orders to the helmsman, which, emanating from the lips of the captain posted on the paddle-box, proclaim the progress of the steamer winding its way up the pool.

A wondrous and deeply interesting spectacle, though only dimly seen, is that portion of the Thames on a moonlight night.

Then indeed is it that even the most callous mind is compelled to contemplate with mingled astonishment and awe, one of the grandest features of the sovereign city and world's emporium of trade.

The gurgling water, and the countless masts,—the vibration of mighty engines on the stream, and the myriads of twinkling lights along the shores,—the cheering voices of the mariners, and the dense volumes of smoke which moving colossal chimneys vomit forth,—the metallic grating of windlasses, and the glittering of the spray beneath revolving wheels,—the flapping of heavy canvass, and the glare from the oval windows of steamers,—the cries of the rowers in endangered boats, and the flood of silver lustre which the moon pours upon the river's bosom,—these form a wondrous complication of elements of interest for both ear and eye.

The barge that was farthest off from Mossop's wharf, of all the lighters moored there, and that could consequently get into the stream quicker than any other near it, was one to which we must particularly direct our readers' attention.

It was called the *Fairy*, and was large, decently painted, and kept in pretty good order. It had a spacious cabin abaft, and a smaller one, termed a cuddy, forward. The mast, with its large brown sail that seemed as if it had been tanned, was so fitted as to be lowered at pleasure, to enable the vessel to pass under the bridges at high water. The rudder was of enormous size; and the tiller was as thick and long as the pole of a carriage.

The waist, or uncovered part of the lighter in the middle, was now empty; but it was very capacious, and adapted to contain an immense quantity of goods.

On the evening in question two men were sitting on the windlass, smoking their pipes, and pretty frequently applying themselves to a can of grog which stood upon the deck near them.

One was the Resurrection Man: the other was John Wicks, better known as the Buffer.

"Well, Jack," said the Resurrection Man, "this is precious slow work. For the last four days we've done nothing."

"What did I tell you, when you fust come to me and proposed to take to the river?" exclaimed the Buffer. "Didn't I say that one ought to be bred to the business to do much good in it?"

"Oh! that be hanged!" cried the Resurrection Man. "I can soon learn any business that's to make money. Besides, the land was too hot to hold me till certain little things had blown over. There's that fellow Markham who ran against me one night;—then there's Crankey Jem. The first saw that I was still hanging about London; and the other may have learnt, by some means or another, that I didn't die of the wound he gave me. Then again, there's those gipsies whose money I walked off with one fine day. All these things made the land unsafe; and so I thought it best to embark the gold that I took from old King Zingary, in this barge, which was to be had so cheap."

"I suppose we shall do better in time, Tony," said the Buffer, "when we get more acquainted with them light and heavy horsemen that we must employ, and them lumpers that gives the information."

"Of course. When you set up in a new business, you can't expect to succeed directly," returned the Resurrection Man. "The regular pirates won't have confidence in us at first; and as yet we don't know a single captain or mate that will trust us with the job of robbing their ship. How do they know but what we should peach, if we got into trouble, and tell their employers that it was all done with their connivance? But old Mossop begins to grow more friendly; and that, I'm sure, is a good sign that *he* thinks that we shall succeed."

"So it is," said the Buffer. "Besides, this barge is so good a blind, that business *must* come. What should you say to getting into the skiff presently, and taking a look out amongst the shipping for ourselves?"

"Well, I've no objection," answered Tidkins. "But we've already a connexion with several lumpers; and they have put us on to all that we *have* done up to the present time. P'rhaps we should do better to wait for the information that they can give us. They begin to see that we pay well; and so they'll only be too anxious to put things in our way."

"True enough," observed the Buffer.

At this period of the conversation, a woman's head appeared above the cabin hatchway.

"Supper's ready," she said.

"We're coming, Moll," returned the Buffer.

The two villains then descended into the cabin, where a well-spread table awaited them.

Scarcely had the trio concluded their repast, when a man, who had come from the wharf and had walked across the barges until he reached the *Fairy*, called to Tidkins, by the appellation of "Captain," from the hatchway.

"Come below," answered the Resurrection Man.

The person thus invited was the foreman in Mr. Mossop's employment. He was short, stout, and strongly built, with a tremendous rubicundity of visage, small piercing grey eyes, no whiskers, and a very apoplectic neck. His age might be about fifty; and he was dressed in a light garb befitting the nature of his calling.

"Well, Mr. Swot," said the Resurrection Man, as the little fat foreman descended the ladder; "this is really an unusual thing to have the honour of your company. Sit down; and you, Moll, put the lush and the pipes upon the table."

"That's right, Captain," returned Mr. Swot, as he seated himself. "I came on purpose to drink a social glass and have a chat with you. In fact, my present visit is not altogether without an object."

"I'm glad of that," said the Resurrection Man. "We want something to do. It was only just now that I and my mate were complaining how slack business was."

"You know that Mossop never has any thing to do with any schemes in which chaps of your business choose to embark," continued Mr. Swot: "he receives your goods, and either keeps them in warehouse or carts them for you as you like; but he never knows where they come from."

"Perfectly true," observed the Resurrection Man.

"But all that's no reason why I should be equally partickler," proceeded Swot.

"Of course not," said the Resurrection Man.

"Well, then—we are all friends here?" asked Swot, glancing around him.

"All," replied Tidkins. "This is my mate's wife; she answers to the name of Moll, and is stanch to the backbone."

"Well and good," said Swot. "Now I've as pretty a little idea in my head as ever was born there; but it requires two or three daring—I may say *desperate* fellers to carry it out."

"You couldn't come to a better shop for them kind of chaps," remarked the Buffer.

"And if it's necessary, I'll deuced soon dress myself up like a lighterman and help you," added Moll.

"I am very much pleased with your pluck, ma'am," said Mr. Swot; "and I drink to your excellent health—and our better acquaintance."

Mr. Swot emptied his mug at a draught, lighted a pipe, and then continued thus:—

"But now, my fine fellers, s'pose I was to start some scheme which is about as dangerous as walking slap into a house on fire to get the iron safe that's full of gold and silver?"

"Well—we're the men to do it," said Tidkins.

"That is," observed the Buffer, "if so be the inducement is equal to the risk."

"Of course," returned Mr. Swot. "Now one more question:—would you sleep in the same room with a man who had the cholera or the small-pox, for instance—supposing you got a thousand pounds each to do it?"

"I would in a minute," answered the Resurrection Man. "Nothing dare, nothing have."

"So I say," added the Buffer.

"And you wouldn't find me flinch!" cried Moll.

"Now, then, we shall soon understand each other," resumed Swot, helping himself to another supply of grog. "Please to listen to me for a few minutes. A very fine schooner, the *Lady Anne* of London, trades to the Gold and Slave Coasts of Guinea. She takes out woollens, cottons, linen, arms, and gunpowder, which she exchanges for gold dust, ivory, gums, and hides. A few days since, as she was beating up the Channel, homeward bound with a fine cargo, something occurs that makes it necessary for her to run for the Medway, instead of coming direct up to London. But the night before last it blew great guns, as you may recollect; and as she was but indifferently manned, she got out in her reckoning—for it was as dark as pitch—and ran ashore between the mouth of the Medway and Gravesend. Now, there she lies—and there she's likely to lie. She got stranded during spring-tide; and she does not float now even at high water. The gold dust would be very acceptable; the gums, ivory, hides, and such like matters, may stay where they are."

"Then the fact is the owners haven't yet moved out the cargo?" said the Resurrection Man, interrogatively.

"No—nor don't intend to, neither—for the present," answered Swot. "And what's more, there's a police-boat pulling about in that part of the river all day and all night; but I can assure you that it gives the schooner a precious wide berth."

"Well, I can't understand it yet," said the Buffer.

"The fact is," continued Swot, "the *Lady Anne* was on its way to Standgate Creek in the Medway, when it got ashore on the bank of the Thames. Do you begin to take?"

"Can't say I do," answered the Resurrection Man. "Is the crew on board still?"

"The crew consisted this morning, when I heard about it last, of three men and a boy," returned Swot; "and one of them men is a surgeon. But the *Lady Anne* has got the yellow flag flying;—and now do you comprehend me?"

"The plague!" ejaculated the Resurrection Man and the Buffer in the same breath.

"The plague!" repeated Moll Wicks, with a shudder.

"Neither more or less," said Swot, coolly emptying his second mug of grog.

There was a dead silence for some moments.

It seemed as if the spirits of those who had listened with deep attention to the foreman's narrative, were suddenly damped by the explanation that closed it.

"Well—are you afraid?" asked Swot, at length breaking silence.

"No," returned the Resurrection Man, throwing off the depression which had fallen upon him. "But there is something awful in boarding a plague-ship."

"Are you sure the gold dust is on board?" demanded the Buffer.

"Certain. My information is quite correct. Besides, you may get the newspapers and read all about it for yourselves."

"The thing is tempting," said Moll.

"Then, by God, if a woman will dare it, we mustn't show the white feather, Jack," exclaimed the Resurrection Man.

"That's speaking to the point," observed the foreman. "You see there's a guard on land, to prevent any one from going near the vessel on that side; and the police-boat rows about on the river. The plan would be, to get down to Gravesend to-morrow, then to-morrow night, to drop down with the tide close under the bank, and get alongside the vessel."

"All that can be done easy enough," said the Resurrection Man. "But we want more hands. Of course you'll go with us?"

"Yes—I'll risk it," answered Mr. Swot. "It's too good a thing to let slip between one's fingers. If you'll leave it to me I'll get two or three more hands; because we must be prepared to master all that we may meet on the deck of the schooner, the very moment we board it, so as not to give 'em time even to cry out, or they'd alarm the police-boat."

"Well and good," said the Resurrection Man. "But you don't mean to go in the lighter?"

"No—no: we must have a good boat with two sculls," answered Swot. "Leave that also to me. At day-break every thing shall be ready for you; and I shall join you in the evening at Gravesend."

"Agreed!" cried Tidkins.

Mr. Swot then took his departure; and the three persons whom he left behind in the lighter, continued their carouse.

In this way the Resurrection Man, the Buffer, and Moll Wicks amused themselves until nearly eleven o'clock, when, just as they were thinking of retiring for the night,—Tidkins to his bed in the after cabin where they were then seated, and the other two to their berth in the cuddy forward,—the lighter was suddenly shaken from one end to the other by some heavy object which bumped violently against it.

CHAPTER CLXVII.

AN ARRIVAL AT THE WHARF.

The collision was so powerful that the Buffer's wife was thrown from her seat; and every plank in the *Fairy* oscillated with a crashing sound.

The Buffer and the Resurrection Man rushed upon the deck.

A single glance enabled them to ascertain the cause of the sudden alarm.

A lighter, nearly as large as the *Fairy*, and heavily laden, had been so clumsily brought in against the barges moored off the wharf, that it came with the whole weight of its broad-side upon the *Fairy*.

"Now then, stupids!" ejaculated the Buffer, applying this complimentary epithet to the two men who were on the deck of the lighter which was putting in.

"Hope we haven't hurt you, friends," exclaimed one of the individuals thus addressed.

"More harm might have been done," answered the Buffer. "Who are you?"

"The *Blossom*," was the reply.

"Where d'ye come from?" demanded Wicks.

"Oh! up above bridge," cried the man, speaking in a surly and evasive manner. "Here—just catch hold of this rope, will you—and let us lay alongside of you."

"No—no," shouted the Buffer. "You'd better drop astern of us, and moor alongside that chalk barge."

"Well, so we will," said the man.

While the *Blossom* was executing this manœuvre, which it did in a most clumsy manner, as if the two men that worked her had never been entrusted with the care of a lighter before, the Buffer turned towards the Resurrection Man, and said in a whisper, "We must remain outside all the barges, 'cause of having room to run our boat alongside the *Fairy* and get the things on board easy, when we come back from the expedition down to the *Lady Anne*."

"To be sure," answered the Resurrection Man. "You did quite right to make those lubbers get lower down. I'm pleased with you, Jack; and now I see that I can let you be spokesman on all such occasions without any fear that you'll commit yourself."

"Why, if you want to keep in the back-ground as much as possible, Tony," replied the Buffer, "it's much better to trust these little things to me. But, I say—I think there's something queer about them chaps that have just put in here."

"So do I, Jack," said Tidkins. "They certainly know no more about managing a lighter than you and I did when we first took to it."

"Yes—but we had a regular man to help us at the beginning," observed the Buffer.

"So we had. And I precious soon sent him about his business when he had taught us our own."

"Well—p'rhaps them fellows have got a reg'lar man too," said Wicks. "But let 'em be what and who they will, my idea is, that they've taken to the same line as ourselves."

"We must find that out, Jack," observed the Resurrection Man. "If they're what you think, they will of course be respected: if they don't belong to the same class, we must ascertain what they've got on board, and then make up our minds whether any of their cargo will suit us."

"Well said," returned the Buffer.

"But in any case you must be the person to learn all this," continued the Resurrection Man. "You see, I'm so well known to a lot of different people that would show me no mercy if they got hold of me, that I'm compelled to keep myself as quiet as possible. There's Markham—there's Crankey Jem—there's the gipsies—and there's the Rattlesnake: why—if I was only to be twigged by one of them I should have to make myself scarce in a minute."

"I know all this, Tony," cried the Buffer, impatiently; "and therefore the less you're seen about, the better. In the day time always keep below, as you have been doing; but at night, when one can't distinguish particular faces, you can take the air;—or on such occasions as to-morrow will be, for instance,—when we run down the river, and get away from London———"

"Yes, yes," interrupted Tidkins: "don't think that I shall throw away a chance. Those lubbers have managed to make their lighter fast to the chalk barge now: just step across and try and find out what you can about them."

The Buffer immediately proceeded to obey this order. He walked across the barges, which, as we before stated, were so closely moored together that they formed one vast floating pier; and approaching as close as possible to the *Blossom*, without setting foot upon it, he said, "Holloa, friend, there! You mustn't think that we meant any thing by telling you not to lay alongside of us: 'twas only 'cause we expect to be off to-morrow or next day."

"No offence is taken where none's intended," answered the man who had before spoken.

The Buffer now perceived that the other individual on board the *Blossom*, and who had charge of the helm, was a Black, of tall form, and dressed in the rough garb of a sailor.

"You seem well laden," said the Buffer, after a pause.

"Yes—pretty deep," answered the first speaker.

"Do you discharge here, at Mossop's?"

"Don't know yet," was the laconic reply.

"And what may be your freight?"

"Bales of cotton," returned the man.

"Then I suppose you're the master of that lighter?" continued the Buffer.

"Yes," was the brief answer.

"Well, it's a pleasant life," observed Wicks. "Have you been at it long?"

"I've only just begun it," replied the master.

"And that sable gentleman there," said the Buffer, with a laugh,—"I should think he's not a Johnny Raw on the water?"

"Not quite," returned the master. "Poor fellow! he's deaf and dumb!"

"Deaf and dumb, eh?" repeated the Buffer. "Well,—p'rhaps that's convenient in more ways than one."

"I believe you," said the master, significantly.

"Ah! I thought so," cried Wicks, who now felt convinced that the *Blossom* was not a whit better than the *Fairy*. "Ain't there no one on board but you and Blackee?"

"What the devil should we want any more hands for?" said the master, gruffly.

"Oh! I understand," observed the Buffer. "Capital! you're the master—to do as you like; Blackee's deaf and dumb, and can't blab; and you and him are alone on board. I've hit it, you see."

"You're uncommon sharp, my fine feller," said the master. "Step on board and wash your mouth out."

The Buffer did not hesitate to accept this invitation. The Black had lighted his pipe, and was lounging on the deck over the after cabin. The master disappeared down the hatchway of the small cabin, or cuddy, forward; and in a few moments he returned with a bottle and two tin pannikins.

"What's the name of your craft?" he said, as he poured out the liquor, which exhaled the strong and saccharine flavour of rum.

"The *Fairy*," replied the Buffer.

"Then here's a health to the *Fairy*."

"And here's to the *Blossom*."

The master and the Buffer each took draughts of the raw spirit.

"Now let us drink to our better acquaintance," said the master. "You seem an honest, open-hearted kind of a feller———"

"And to be trusted, too," interrupted Wicks.

"Well—I'm inclined to think you are," said the master, speaking deliberately, as if he were meditating upon some particular idea which then occupied his mind; "and it's very probable—it *may* be, I mean—that I shall want a little of your advice; for which, remember, I should be happy to pay you well."

"You couldn't apply to a better man," returned the Buffer.

"And here's to you," said the master. "What sort of a fellow is Mossop, that keeps this wharf?"

"He has no eyes, no ears, and no tongue for things that don't consarn him," answered Wicks.

"Just the kind of agent I want," returned the master. "But I shall also require two or three good fellers in a few days,—chaps that ain't over partickler, you understand, how they earn a ten-pound note, so long as it's sure."

"And you want two or three chaps of that kind?" asked the Buffer.

"Yes. I've a good thing in hand," returned the master. "But I shan't say too much now."

"Well, you may reckon on me at any moment—to-morrow excepted," said Wicks; "and my pal in the *Fairy* will also be glad to row in the same boat."

"What sort of a man is your pal?" demanded the master: "one of the right kind?"

"If he wasn't, him and I shouldn't long hold together," answered the Buffer. "But when do you think you'll want our services?"

"Very soon. You say you're both engaged for to-morrow?"

"Yes—both of us."

"The day after to-morrow, in the evening, you and your friend can come and smoke your pipes with me; and we'll talk the matter over," said the master.

"And if any thing should prevent us coming the day after to-morrow, the evening after that will do p'rhaps?" remarked the Buffer, interrogatively.

"Well—we must make that do, then," answered the master. "Good night."

"Good night," said Wicks; and he then returned to the *Fairy*.

"What can you make of them, Jack?" demanded the Resurrection Man, who was smoking his pipe on the after deck.

"They're of the right sort, Tony," was the reply. "The master seems a good kind of a feller: the only other man on board with him is a Black; and he's deaf and dumb. The master sounded me about Mossop; and that shows that he knows what's what. Besides, he hinted that he'd a good thing in view, but wanted more hands, and so he made an appointment for you and me to smoke a pipe with him in the course of two or three evenings, to talk over the matter."

"You didn't say much about me?" exclaimed the Resurrection Man, hastily.

"Not more than was proper. It's all right—I could tell *that* with half an eye."

"Well, business seems dropping in upon us," observed the Resurrection Man; "but we must be very cautious what we do. And now let's turn in, for we have to get up early, recollect."

CHAPTER CLXVIII.

THE PLAGUE SHIP.

It wanted half-an-hour to day-break, when the splash of oars alongside met their ears; and in a few moments Swot, the foreman, made his appearance.

"I've got all ready for you, my boys," said that individual; "a good boat, and two stout chaps to help."

"Have they got their barkers?" demanded the Resurrection Man, thereby meaning pistols.

"A brace each," replied the foreman. "But they must only be used in case of desperation. There's a false bottom to the boat; and there I've stowed away five cutlasses."

"All right!" cried the Buffer. "Now, Moll, you make yourself comfortable till we get back again."

"You're a fool, Jack, not to let me go along with you," observed the woman.

"Nonsense," answered her husband. "Some one must stay on board to take care of the lighter."

"Well, don't say that I'm a coward—that's all," exclaimed Moll.

"We won't accuse you of that," said the Resurrection Man. "But now let's be off. Where shall we meet you at Gravesend?"

"You know the windmill about a mile below the town," returned Swot, to whom this question was addressed. "Well, close by is the *Lobster Tavern*, and there's a little jetty where the boat can be fastened. Meet me at that tavern at ten o'clock this evening."

"Agreed," answered Tidkins.

The three men then ascended to the deck.

The dawn was at that moment breaking in the east; and every moment mast after mast on the stream, and roof after roof on the shore, appeared more palpably in the increasing light of the young day.

On board of the *Blossom*, the Black was busily employed in washing the deck, and seemed to take no notice of any thing that was passing elsewhere.

"The tide will be with us for nearly three hours," said Tidkins. "Come—we won't lose a moment."

The foreman retraced his steps across the barges to the wharf; while the Resurrection Man and the Buffer, each armed with a pair of pistols, leapt into the boat, that lay alongside the lighter.

Two stout fellows, dressed like watermen, and who were already seated in the boat, instantly plied their sculls.

The skiff shot rapidly away from the vicinity of the barges, and was soon running down the middle of the river with a strong tide.

The morning was beautiful and bright: a gentle breeze swept the bosom of the stream:—and when the sun burst forth in all its effulgent glory, a few fleecy clouds alone appeared on the mighty arch of blue above.

Here and there the mariners on board the outward-bound vessels were busy in heaving up their anchors—a task which they performed with the usual cheering and simultaneous cry,—or in loosening the canvass that immediately became swollen with the breeze.

At distant intervals some steamer, bound to a native or foreign port, walked, as it were, with gigantic strides along the water, raising with its mighty Briarean arms, a swell on either side, which made the smaller craft toss and pitch as if in a miniature whirlpool.

Alas! how many souls have found a resting-place in the depths of those waters; and the spray of the billow seems the tears which old Father Thames sheds as a tribute to their graves! Then, at dark midnight, when the wind moans over the bosom of the river, the plaintive murmurs sound as a lament for those that are gone!

Vain are thy tears, O River! But if they must be shed, let them flow for the living, whose crimes or whose miseries may, with Orphic spell, awaken the sympathy of even inanimate things.

The boat shot rapidly along, the sun gilding its broad pathway.

What evidence of commercial prosperity appears on either side! The clang of mighty hammers denote the progress of new vessels in the various building-yards; and in the numerous docks the shipwright is busy in repairing the effects of past voyages, and rendering the gallant barks fit to dare the perils of the ocean once more!

The river-pirates, whose course we are following, pursued their way: the old *Dreadnought*, stripped of the cannon that once bristled on its lofty sides, and now resembling the worn-out lion that has lost its fangs, was passed;—the domes of Greenwich greeted the eye;—and now the boat merged upon the wide expanse which seems to terminate with Blackwall.

But, no! the stream sweeps to the right; and onward floats the skiff—skirting the Kentish shore.

At length the gloomy and sombre-looking hulks off Woolwich are reached: the boat shoots in between the shipping; and there the pirates landed.

At Woolwich they repaired to a low public-house with which they were acquainted; and, as the fresh air of the river had sharpened their appetites, they called into request every article of food which was to be found in the larder. Liquors in due proportion were ordered; the Resurrection Man paid the score for all; and in this manner the four pirates contrived to while away the time until the tide turned once more in their favour in the afternoon.

At three o'clock they retraced their steps to the boat; and in a few minutes were again gliding rapidly along on the bosom of the river.

"Now," said the Resurrection Man, "as we have drunk a glass and smoked a pipe together, we are better acquainted with each other."

These words were especially addressed to the two men whom the foreman at Mossop's wharf had provided.

"Of course," continued the Resurrection Man, "I needn't ask you if you know the exact nature of the business which we have in hand. I didn't think it prudent to talk about it when we were at the crib in Woolwich just now, because walls have ears; but I took it for granted, from certain words which you two chaps said, that it's all right."

"Yes, yes, master," returned one, who was called Long Bob, in consequence of his height: "Swot put us up to the whole thing."

"We know the risk, and we know what's to be got by it," added the other, who delighted in the name of the *Lully Prig*,[1] from the circumstance of his having formerly exercised the calling with which, in flash language, the name is associated, before he became a river-pirate.

"Then we understand each other," said the Resurrection Man, "without any farther wagging of the tollibon."[2]

"We cut the same lock that you do,[3] old feller," answered the Lully Prig; "and as long as we snack the bit[4] in a reg'lar manner, we're stanch to the back-bone."

"So far, so good," said the Resurrection Man. "But you're also aware that the swag must be taken up the river and put on board the *Fairy*, where it must stay some time till Swot can find a safe customer for it, because it's sure to be chanted on the leer."[5]

"We're fly to all that," said Long Bob. "But Swot promised us ten neds[6] each, if the thing succeeds to-night; so that we shan't object to waiting for the rest of our reg'lars till the swag is dinged."[7]

"Who knows that we shan't find some gobsticks,[8] clinks,[9] or other things of the same kind?" exclaimed the Lully Prig; "and, if so, they can soon be walked off to the melting-pot fence,[10] and the glanthem will be dropped[11] in no time."

"That's understood, my boys," exclaimed the Resurrection Man. "Now, give way with a will, and don't let's delay."

On went the boat with increased rapidity, the Lully Prig and Long Bob plying the oars with strength and skill. Then, when they were wearied, the Resurrection Man and the Buffer took their turns. Occasionally Tidkins handed round his flask, which he had taken good care to have replenished with rum at Woolwich; and at intervals the Buffer or the Lully Prig cheered their labours with a song.

In this manner Erith was reached and passed:—Greenhithe and Ingress Abbey, the front of which splendid mansion is built with the stones of old London Bridge, were in due course left behind;—and soon the antique windmill and the tall tower of Gravesend greeted the eyes of the river-pirates.

At the two piers of the town were numerous steam-packets;—there were large merchant-vessels riding at anchor in the middle of the river;—and, on the opposite side, Tilbury Fort commanded the expanse of water with its cannon.

"Since we're to meet Swot at the *Lobster Tavern*," said the Resurrection Man, "we may as well run down to that place at once."

"So we will," returned the Buffer.

The boat continued its course; and in a short time it was made fast to the little jetty which affords a convenient means of landing at the point mentioned.

The *Lobster Tavern* is a small isolated place of entertainment, upon the bank of the Thames, and is chiefly frequented by those good folks who, in fine weather, indulge in a trip on Sundays from London to Gravesend.

There are sheds, with seats, built in front of the tavern; and on a calm summer's evening, the site and view are pleasant enough.

The four pirates entered the establishment, and called for refreshments.

They thus passed away the time until ten o'clock, when Mossop's foreman joined them.

In another half-hour they were all five seated in the boat; and, in the darkness of the night, they bent their way towards the plague-ship.

They kept close along the Kentish shore; and when Swot imagined that they must be within half-a-mile of the place where the *Lady Anne* was stranded, the oars were muffled.

The sky was covered with dense black clouds: no moon and not a star appeared.

The water seemed as dark as ink.

But the foreman knew every inlet and every jutting point which marked the course of the Thames; and, with the tiller in his hand, he navigated the boat with consummate skill.

Not a word was spoken; and the faint murmurs of the oars were drowned in the whistling of the breeze which now swept over the river.

At length the foreman said in a low whisper, "There is the light of the police-boat."

At a distance of about a quarter of a mile that light appeared, like a solitary star upon the waters.

Sometimes it moved—then stopped, as the quarantine officers rowed, or rested on their oars.

"We must now be within a few yards of the *Lady Anne*," whispered Swot, after another long pause: "take to your arms."

The Buffer cautiously raised a plank at the bottom of the boat, and drew forth, one after another, five cutlasses.

These the pirates silently fastened to their waists.

The boat moved slowly along; and in another minute it was by the side of the plague ship.

The Resurrection Man stretched out his arm, and his hand swept its slimy hull.

There was not a soul upon the deck of the *Lady Anne*; and, as if to serve the purposes of the river-pirates, the wind blew in strong gusts, and the waves splashed against the bank and the vessel itself, with a sound sufficient to drown the noise of their movements.

The bow of the *Lady Anne* lay high upon the bank: the stern was consequently low in the water.

As cautiously as possible the boat was made fast to a rope which hung over the schooner's quarter; and then the five pirates, one after the other, sprang on board.

"Holloa!" cried a boy, suddenly thrusting his head above the hatchway of the after cabin.

Long Bob's right hand instantly grasped the boy's collar, while his left was pressed forcibly upon his mouth; and in another moment the lad was dragged on the deck, where he was immediately gagged and bound hand and foot.

But this process had not been effected without some struggling on the part of the boy, and trampling of feet on that of the pirates.

Some one below was evidently alarmed, for a voice called the boy from the cabin.

Long Bob led the way; and the pirates rushed down into the cabin, with their drawn cutlasses in their hands.

There was a light below; and a man, pale and fearfully emaciated, started from his bed, and advanced to meet the intruders.

"Not a word—or you're a dead man," cried Long Bob, drawing forth a pistol.

"Rascal! what do you mean?" ejaculated the other; "I am the surgeon, and in command of this vessel. Who are you? what do you require? Do you know that the pestilence is here?"

"We know all about it, sir," answered Long Bob.

Then, dropping his weapons, he sprang upon the surgeon, whom he threw upon the floor, and whose mouth he instantly closed with his iron hand.

The pirates then secured the surgeon in the same way as they had the boy above.

"Let's go forward now," cried Swot. "So far, all's well. One of you must stay down here to mind this chap."

The Lully Prig volunteered this service; and the other pirates repaired to the cabin forward.

They well knew that the plague-stricken invalids must be *there*; and when they reached the hatchway, there was a sudden hesitation—a simultaneous pause.

The idea of the pestilence was horrible.

"Well," said the foreman, "are we afraid?"

"No—not I, by God!" ejaculated the Resurrection Man; and he sprang down the ladder.

The others immediately followed him.

But there was no need of cutlass, pistol, or violence there. By the light of the lamp suspended to a beam, the pirates perceived two wretched creatures, each in his hammock,—their cadaverous countenances covered with large sores, their hair matted, their eyes open but glazed and dim, and their wasted hands lying like those of the dead outside the coverlids, as if all the nervous energy were defunct.

Still they were alive; but they were too weak and wretched to experience any emotion at the appearance of armed men in their cabin.

The atmosphere which they breathed was heated and nauseous with the pestilential vapours of their breath and their perspiration.

"These poor devils can do no harm," said the Resurrection Man, with a visible shudder.

The pirates were only too glad to emerge from that narrow abode of the plague; and never did air seem more pure than that which they breathed when they had gained the deck.

"Now then to work," cried Swot. "Wait till we raise this hatch," he continued, stopping at that which covered the compartment of the ship where the freight was stowed away; "and we'll light the darkey when we get down below. You see, that as they hadn't a light hung out before, it would be dangerous to have one above: we might alarm the police-boat or the guard ashore."

The hatch was raised without much difficulty: a rope was then made fast to a spar and lowered into the waist of the schooner; and Long Bob slid down.

In a few moments he lighted his dark lantern; and the other three descended one after the other, the Lully Prig, be it remembered, having remained in the after cabin.

And now to work they went. The goods, with which the schooner was laden, were removed, unpacked, and ransacked.

There were gums, and hides, and various other articles which the western coast of Africa produces; but the object of the pirates' enterprise and avarice was the gold-dust, which was contained in two heavy cases. These were, however, at the bottom of all the other goods; and nearly an hour passed before they were reached.

"Here is the treasure—at last!" cried Swot, when every thing was cleared away from above the cases of precious metal. "Come, Tony—don't waste time with the brandy flask now."

"I've such a precious nasty taste in my mouth," answered the Resurrection Man, as he took a long sup of the spirit. "I suppose it was the horrid air in the fore-cabin."

"Most likely," said the foreman: "come—bear a hand, and let's get these cases ready to raise. Then Long Bob and me will go above and reeve a rope and a pulley to haul 'em up."

The four men bent forward to the task; and as they worked by the dim light of the lantern, in the depths of the vessel, they seemed to be four demons in the profundities of their own infernal abode.

Suddenly the Resurrection Man staggered, and, supporting himself against the side of the vessel, said in a thick tone, "My God! what a sudden headache I've got come on!"

"Oh! it's nothing, my dear feller," cried Swot.

"And now I'm all cold and shivering," said Tidkins, seating himself on a bale of goods; "and my legs seem as if they'd break under me."

The Buffer, the foreman, and Long Bob were suddenly and simultaneously inspired with the same idea; and they cast on their companion looks of mingled apprehension and horror.

"No—it can't be!" ejaculated Swot.

"And yet—how odd that he should turn so," said Bob, with a shudder.

"The plague!" returned the Buffer, in a tone of indescribable terror.

"You're a fool, Jack!" exclaimed the Resurrection Man, glaring wildly upon his comrades, and endeavouring to rise from his seat.

But he fell back, exhausted and powerless.

"Damnation!" he muttered in a low but ferocious tone; and he gnashed his teeth with rage.

"The plague!" repeated the Buffer, now unable to contain his fears.

Then he hastily clambered from the hold of the schooner.

"The coward!" cried Swot: "such a prize as this is worth any risk."

But as he yet spoke, Long Bob, influenced by panic fear, sprang after the Buffer, as if Death itself were at his heels, clad in all the horrors of the plague.

"My God! don't leave me here," cried the Resurrection Man, his voice losing its thickness and assuming the piercing tone of despair.

"Every man for himself, it seems," returned Swot, whom the panic had now robbed of all his courage; and in another moment he also had disappeared.

"The cowards—the villains!" said Tidkins, clenching his fists with rage.

Then, by an extraordinary and almost superhuman effort, he raised himself upon his legs: but they seemed to bend under him.

He, however managed to climb upon the packages of goods; and, aided by the rope, lifted himself up to the hatchway. But the effort was too great for his failing strength: his hands could not retain a firm grasp of the cord; and he fell violently to the bottom of the hold, rolling over the bales of merchandize in his descent.

"It's all over!" he mattered to himself; and then he became rapidly insensible.

Meantime the Lully Prig, who was mounting sentry upon the surgeon in the after cabin, was suddenly alarmed by hearing the trampling of hasty steps over head. He rushed on deck, and demanded the cause of this abrupt movement.

"The plague!" cried the Buffer, as he leapt over the ship's quarter into the boat.

The Lully Prig precipitated himself after his comrade; and the other two pirates immediately followed.

"But we are only four!" said the Lully Prig, as the boat was pushed away from the vessel.

"Tidkins has got the plague," answered the Buffer, his teeth chattering with horror and affright.

Fortunately the police-boat was at a distance; and the pirates succeeded in getting safely away from that dangerous vicinity.

But the Resurrection Man remained behind in the plague-ship!

---

1. A thief who steals damp linen off the hedges in the country.

2. Talking—palaver. "Tollibon" is the tongue.

3. Get our living in the same way.

4. Share the money.

5. Advertised in the newspapers.

6. Sovereigns.

7. Sent to the receiver.

8. Silver spoons.

9. Silver milk jugs or sugar basins.

10. Persons who receive and melt down stolen metal.

11. Money will be obtained.

CHAPTER CLXIX.

THE PURSUIT.

We must now return to the *Blossom*—the lighter which had only arrived at Mossop's wharf the night before the incidents of the last chapter occurred.

When the boat which conveyed the pirates to Gravesend had pushed away from the *Fairy* at day-break, as already described, the Black, who was cleaning the deck of the *Blossom*, cast from beneath his brows a rapid and scrutinising glance at the countenances of the four men who were seated in that skiff.

As soon as the boat was out of sight, the Black hastened down into the after-cabin of the *Blossom*, where a person was lying fast asleep in bed.

The Black shook this person violently by the shoulder, and awoke him.

"I have found him, sir,—I have found him!" cried the Black.

"Indeed!" cried Markham, starting up, and rubbing his eyes. "Where? where?"

"He has just gone with three other men in a boat, down the river," answered Morcar; "and one of these men is him that spoke to Benstead last night."

"Then they both belong to the *Fairy*?" exclaimed Richard.

"Both," replied Morcar; "at least they both came from it just now."

"Go and rouse Benstead," said Markham; "and in the meantime I will get up."

The gipsy, who had so well disguised himself as a man of colour, hastened to the cuddy where Benstead was wrapped in the arms of Morpheus.

The police-officer was delighted, when awakened and made acquainted with Morcar's discovery, to find that the Resurrection Man had been thus recognised; and he lost no time in dressing himself.

The gipsy and Benstead afterwards proceeded to Richard's cabin, where they found our hero just completing his hasty toilet.

"Thus far our aims are accomplished," said Markham, when they were all three assembled. "It has turned out exactly as I anticipated. Morcar, by aid of his disguised appearance, was enabled to keep a sharp look out on all the vessels; while the report which you circulated that he was deaf and dumb prevented him from being questioned. Had Tidkins himself seen Morcar as closely as we are to him now, he would not have known him."

"My suspicions, too, are fully confirmed," observed Benstead. "The moment I saw that feller hanging about us last night, I suspected he was up to no good. But how I managed to pump *him*, when he doubtless thought that *I* was the soft-pated one! By my short, evasive, or mysterious answers, I allowed him to think that the *Blossom* was no better than she should be; and then I saw by his manners and language at once, that he was a pirate. But when I dropped a hint about wanting two or three hands for a good thing which I had in view, how eager the chap was to enlist himself and his pal in the business!"

"And to-morrow night they are coming to talk over the matter with you?" said Richard, half interrogatively.

"To-morrow night, or the night after," returned Benstead. "The pal that the man spoke of is sure to be Tidkins, since our friend Morcar saw the villains leave the *Fairy* together."

"But there were two other men in the boat," observed the gipsy.

"You say that they sculled the boat round to the *Fairy*, from some place higher up the river?" said Richard.

"Yes. But I could not see where they came from, as it was nearly dark when they got alongside the *Fairy*."

"Well," exclaimed Benstead, "it is very clear that those two men who came in the boat, don't belong to the *Fairy*; but that Tidkins and the person who spoke to me last night do. I should think there's no doubt about Tidkins being the pal that the man alluded to."

"Not the slightest," said Markham. "And yet, to make assurance doubly sure, we will not alter the plan which we laid down yesterday afternoon when we first came on board the lighter. You, Benstead, must remain spokesman—the master, in fact, of the *Blossom*; you, Morcar, will continue a deaf and dumb Black," continued Richard, with a smile; "and I must keep close in this cabin until the moment of action arrives. If, to-morrow night or the night after, that man should bring Tidkins with him, our object is accomplished at once: if he bring a stranger, our precautions must be strictly preserved, and we must devise a means of seizing the miscreant on board the *Fairy* or any other lighter to which we can trace him."

This advice was agreed to by Benstead and Morcar; and while Richard remained below, the others took their turns in watching upon the deck.

But all that day passed; and the pirates did not come back to the *Fairy*—they being occupied in the manner related in the last chapter.

Morcar undertook to keep watch during the night; but hour after hour stole away,—another day dawned, and still the *Fairy* was occupied only by the woman whom the pirates had left behind.

That day also passed; and it was not until midnight that Morcar's attention was attracted towards the *Fairy*. Then a boat rowed alongside of the pirate-barge.

The night was pitch dark—so dark that Morcar could not see what was going on in the direction of the *Fairy*: but his ears were all attention.

He was enabled to discover, by means of those organs, that the boat transferred one or more of its living freight (but he could not tell how many) to the *Fairy*: then a brief conversation was carried on in low whispers, but not a distinct word of which reached the gipsy. At length the boat pushed off, and rowed away up the river.

Morcar stood upon the deck of the *Blossom* for a few minutes, attentively listening to catch a sound of any thing that might be passing on board the pirate lighter: but all continued silent in that quarter.

Then Morcar descended to the cabin, where Richard and the policeman were waiting.

To them he communicated the few particulars just narrated.

"It is clear that the pirates have returned from their expedition, whatever it might be," said our hero; "and most probably Tidkins and his friend have just been put on board their lighter. We must contrive to watch their motions; and should they keep their appointment with you, Benstead, to-morrow night, our enterprise will speedily be brought to a conclusion."

"I will keep my watch now on deck till three o'clock," said the policeman; "and Morcar may turn in."

This was done; Richard also retired to rest; and the night passed away without any further adventure.

But at day-break Morcar, who had again resumed the watch, observed some activity on board the *Fairy*. The Buffer and his wife were in fact making evident preparations for departure. They raised the mast by means of the windlass; they shook out the sail; fixed the tiller in the rudder, and performed the various preliminaries in a most business-like manner.

Morcar speedily communicated these circumstances to Benstead and Markham; and these three held a rapid consultation in the after-cabin of the *Blossom*.

"You are certain you saw no one but that man who first spoke to Benstead, and the woman?" asked Markham.

"Not a soul," answered Morcar. "But that is no reason why Tidkins should not be below."

"Certainly not. He has numerous reasons to conceal himself."

"But what is to be done?" said Morcar.

"Benstead must go and speak to the man," observed Richard, after a pause.

The policeman immediately left the cabin.

He crossed the barges and approached the *Fairy*, which was just ready to put off.

"Holloa! my friend," cried Benstead: "you seem busy this morning?"

"Yes—we're going up above bridge a short way," answered the Buffer: "the tide is just turning in our favour now, and we haven't a moment to spare."

"And the appointment with me?"

"Oh! that must stand over for a day or two. How long do you mean to remain here?"

"Till I get a couple of good hands to help me in the matter I alluded to the night before last," answered Benstead.

"Well, I don't like to disappoint a good feller—and *that* you seem to be," said the Buffer, "but I really can't say whether I shall be able to do any thing with you, or not. I've something else on hand now—and I think I shall leave the river altogether."

"You speak openly at all events," said Benstead. "It's very annoying, though; for I relied upon you. Can't your pal—the man that you spoke of, you know—have a hand in this matter with me?"

"No," answered the Buffer shortly. "But I'll tell you who'll put you up to getting the assistance you want:—and that's Mossop's foreman. He's a cautious man, and won't meet you half way in your conversation; but you can make a confidant of him, and if he can't help you, he's sure not to sell you. So now good bye, old feller; and good luck to you."

With these words the Buffer loosened the rope that held the *Fairy* alongside the barge next to it; and then by means of a boat-hook he pushed the lighter off.

"Good bye," exclaimed Benstead; and he hastened back to the *Blossom*.

"Now what must be done?" asked Morcar, when these particulars were communicated to him and Richard.

"It seems clear to me that these men have endangered themselves by something they have just been doing," observed Benstead; "and so they're sheering off as fast as they can."

"And most likely the Resurrection Man is concealed on board the *Fairy*," added Markham. "We must follow them—we must follow them, at any rate!"

"If we take our skiff and pursue them, they will immediately entertain some suspicion," said Benstead; "and if *you* go, sir, the Resurrection Man will recognise you the moment he catches a glimpse of you."

"We have no alternative, my good friends," observed Richard. "Let us all three follow them in our skiff: we will dog them—we will watch them; and if they attempt to land, we will board them."

"Be it so," said Benstead.

This plan was immediately put into operation.

The skiff was lowered: Markham, the policeman, and the gipsy leapt into it; the two latter pulled the oars; and our hero, muffled in a pilot coat, with the collar of which he concealed his countenance as much as possible, sate in the stern.

"Just keep the lighter in view—and that's all," said Richard. "So long as it does not show signs of touching at any place on shore, we had better content ourselves with following it, till we are assured that Tidkins is actually on board."

"Certainly, sir," answered Benstead. "We might only get ourselves into trouble by forcibly entering the *Fairy*, unless we knew that we should catch the game we're in search of."

The rowers had therefore little more to do than just play with their oars, as the tide bore the skiff along with even a greater rapidity than the lighter, although the latter proceeded with tolerable speed, in consequence of being empty, and having a fair breeze with it. Thus, when the boat drew too near the barge, the rowers backed their oars; and by this manœuvring they maintained a convenient distance.

On board the lighter, the Buffer and his wife were too busy with the management of their vessel—a task to which they were not altogether equal—to notice the watch and pursuit instituted by the little boat.

In the manner described, the two parties pursued their way up the narrow space left by the crowds of shipping for the passage of vessels.

The Tower was passed—that gloomy fortalice which has known sighs as full of anguish and hearts as oppressed with bitter woe as ever did the prisons of the Inquisition, or the dungeons of the Bastille.

Then the Custom House was slowly left behind; and Billingsgate, world-renowned for its slang, was passed by the pursued and the pursuer.

To avoid the arch of London Bridge the Buffer lowered his mast; and then midway between that and Southwark Bridge, his intentions became apparent.

He was about to put in at a wharf on the Surrey side, where a large board on the building announced that lighters were bought or sold.

"Pull alongside the *Fairy*," cried Markham: "we must board her before she touches the wharf, or our prey may escape."

Benstead and Morcar plied the oars with a vigour which soon brought the boat within a few yards of the *Fairy*. The Buffer's attention was now attracted to it for the first time; but he did not immediately recognise the two rowers, because they had their backs turned towards the lighter.

"I should know that man!" suddenly exclaimed Richard, as he contemplated the Buffer, who was standing at the tiller, and who had his eyes fixed with some anxiety upon the boat, which was evidently pulling towards him.

"Who?" asked Benstead.

"That man on board the lighter," was the reply.

Benstead cast a glance behind him, and said, "He's the man that spoke to me."

"I remember him—the villain!—I recollect him now!" cried Richard. "Yes—he is a companion in iniquity of Anthony Tidkins: it was he who brought me that false message concerning my brother, which nearly cost me my life at Twig Folly!"

These words Richard spoke aloud; but they were unintelligible to his two companions, who were unacquainted with the incident referred to.

They had no time to question him, nor had he leisure to explain his meaning to them; for at that moment the boat shot alongside of the lighter.

"Markham!" cried the Buffer, in alarm, as he recognised our hero who immediately sprang upon the deck.

"You know me?" said Richard: "and I have ample reason to remember you. But my present business regards *another*; and if you offer no resistance, I will not harm you."

"Who do you want?" asked the Buffer, somewhat reassured by these words.

"Your companion," replied Richard.

"What! my wife?" ejaculated the Buffer, with a hoarse laugh. "Do you know this gen'leman, Moll?"

"Cease this jesting," cried Richard sternly; "and remain where you are. Benstead, take care that he does not move from the deck: Morcar, come you with me."

The Buffer cast looks of surprise and curiosity upon Richard's companions, who, having made the boat fast to the lighter, had leapt upon the deck.

"What! you, my fine feller?" cried Wicks, addressing himself to Benstead. "I suppose, then, this is all a reg'lar plant;—and you're——"

"I am a police officer," answered Benstead coolly. "But, as far as I know, we have no business with either you or your wife—since you say that this woman is your wife."

"Well—so much the better," remarked the Buffer. "And I also suppose your negro is about as deaf and dumb as I am?"

"About," replied Benstead, unable to suppress a smile. "Keep quiet, and no harm will happen to you."

"But who is it that you *do* want?" asked the Buffer.

"Your friend Tidkins—better known as the Resurrection Man."

"Then you won't find him here."

In the meantime, Richard and the gipsy had descended into the after-cabin; and they now re-appeared upon the deck, their search having been fruitless.

"He is not there," said Richard. "Let us look forward."

He and Morcar visited the cuddy; but the Resurrection Man was evidently not in the lighter.

They returned to the after deck; and questioned the Buffer.

"I don't know where Tidkins is," was the reply of that individual, who did not dare reveal the truth relative to the expedition to the plague ship, and its result; "and even if I did, it is not likely that I should blab any thing that would get us both into a scrape, since I see that the whole thing with you is a trap, and that man there," he added, pointing to Benstead, "is a policeman."

"Now, listen," exclaimed Richard. "It is in my power to have you arrested this moment for being concerned in a plot against my life—you know how and when; but I pledge you my honour that if you will satisfy me relative to Anthony Tidkins, we will depart, and leave you unmolested. I scorn treachery, even among men of your description; and I will not offer you a bribe. But I require to know how he came to separate from you—for I am convinced that he was with you a day or two ago."

"Well, sir," said the Buffer, who had found time, while Richard thus spoke, to collect his ideas and invent a tale, "Tidkins, me, and some other pals went on a little excursion the night afore last—you don't want me to get myself into a scrape by saying what the business was; but we fell in with a Thames police boat some way down the river; and Tidkins had a swim for it."

"Did he escape?" demanded Richard.

"Yes," answered the Buffer, boldly. "I saw him get safe on land; and then of course he took to his heels."

"This looks like the truth, sir," said Benstead aside to our hero. "These fellows have been baulked in some scheme—the river-police have got scent of 'em—and that's the reason why this man gets off so quick with his lighter."

"And as I do not wish to punish this man for the injury he has done me," said Richard, glancing towards the Buffer,—"as I can afford to forgive *him*,—our expedition seems to have arrived at its close."

"Without success, too, sir," added Morcar.

"We shall now leave you," continued Richard, turning towards the Buffer; "but rest well assured that, though *we* forbear from molesting you, justice will some day overtake you in your evil and wayward courses."

"That's my look out," cried the Buffer, brutally.

Markham turned away in disgust, and descended to the boat, followed by Morcar and Benstead.

"We will now proceed to the wharf where I hired the *Blossom*," said Richard, when they had pushed off from the *Fairy*; "and, my good friends, there I shall dispense with your further services. The owner of the lighter can send his men to Rotherhithe to bring it up, and thus save us a task which is somewhat beyond our skill."

"It is a great pity we have failed to capture the miscreant," observed Morcar.

"But your reward has not been the less fairly and honestly earned," replied Richard; "as I will prove to you when we land."

CHAPTER CLXX.

THE BLACK VEIL.

Return we now to one whom we have long left, but whom the reader cannot have forgotten.

In a sumptuously furnished room at the house of Mr. Wentworth, the surgeon of Lower Holloway, Diana Arlington was reclining upon a sofa.

She was dressed in an elegant manner; but a large black lace veil, doubled so as to render it more impervious to the eye of a beholder, was thrown over her head. The folds were also so arranged that the elaborately worked border completely concealed her countenance.

She was alone.

An open piano, a harp, and piles of music, together with a choice selection of volumes on the shelves of a book-case, denoted the nature of her amusements during her residence of several weeks at the surgeon's abode.

It was mid-day.

The damask curtains at the windows were drawn in such a manner as to reduce the light of the effulgent sun to a mellow and soft lustre within that apartment.

Beautiful nosegays of flowers imparted a delicious fragrance to the atmosphere.

The bounty of the Earl of Warrington had furnished the room in a style of luxury which could scarcely be surpassed.

But was Diana happy?

Were those sighs which agitated her heaving bosom,—was that restlessness which she now manifested,—was that frequent listening as the sounds of wheels passed along the road,—were all these signs of sorrow or of suspense?

Patience, gentle reader.

The time-piece on the mantel had chimed mid-day.

"He is not punctual," murmured Diana.

Ten minutes elapsed.

"He does not come!" she said aloud.

And her restlessness redoubled.

At length a carriage drove rapidly up to the door; and a long double knock reverberated through the house.

"'Tis he!" cried Diana.

In a few moments the Earl of Warrington entered the room.

"Diana—dearest Diana!" exclaimed the nobleman, starting back when he beheld her countenance covered with that ominous dark veil: "is it indeed thus———"

"Thus that we meet after so long an absence?" added the Enchantress. "Yes, my lord: Mr. Wentworth must have told you as much."

"No, Diana," answered the Earl, seating himself upon the sofa by her side, and taking her hand: "you know not by what a strange idiosyncrasy my conduct has been influenced. I entrusted you to Mr. Wentworth's care: I enjoined him to spare no money that might procure the best advice—the most efficient means of cure. Then I resigned myself to a suspense from which I might at any moment have relieved my mind by an inquiry;—but at the bottom of that suspense was a fond, a burning hope which made the feeling tolerable—nay, even vested the excitement with a peculiar charm of its own. I took it for granted that you would be cured—that your countenance would be restored to that beauty which had originally attracted me towards you;—and now, may I not say—without detriment to my own firm character as a man, and without indelicacy towards your feelings,—may I not say that I am disappointed?"

"And is this my fault?" asked Diana, in a soft plaintive tone. "Does your lordship suppose that I have not also suffered—that I do not at present suffer?"

"Oh! yes—you have—you do," answered the nobleman, pressing her hand with warm affection. "When we were happy in each other's society, Diana," he continued, "I never spoke to you of love: indeed, I experienced for you nothing more than a fervent friendship and profound admiration. But since I have ceased to see you—during the interval of our separation—I found that you were necessary to me,—that I could not be altogether happy without you,—that your conversation had charms which delighted me,—and that your attachment was something on which I could ponder with infinite pleasure. My feelings have warmed towards you; and I—I, the Earl of Warrington—experience for you a feeling which, if not so romantic and enthusiastic as my *first affection*, is not the less honourable and sincere."

"Ah! my lord," said Diana, in a tremulous tone, "why raise the cup of happiness to my lips, when a stern fatality must dash it so cruelly away?"

"No, Diana—it shall not be thus dashed away," answered the Earl, emphatically. "I am rich—I am my own master: not a living soul has a right to control or question my conduct. The joy which I anticipated at this meeting shall not be altogether destroyed. Here, Diana—here I offer you my hand; and on your brow—scarred, blemished by an accident though it be—that hand shall place a coronet!"

"My lord, this honour—this goodness is too much," said Diana, in a tone of deep emotion. "Remember that I am no longer possessed of those charms which once attracted you; and now that they are gone—gone for ever—I may speak of what they were without vanity! Remember, I say, that you will ever have before you a countenance seared as with a red-hot iron,—a countenance on which you will scarcely be able to look without loathing in spite of all the love which your generous heart may entertain for me! Remember that when I deck myself in the garments befitting the rank to which you seek to elevate me, that splendour would be a hideous mockery—like the fairest flowers twining round the revolting countenance of a corpse on which the hand of decay has already placed its mark! Remember, in a word, that you will be ashamed of her whom, in a moment of generous enthusiasm, you offer to reward for so much suffering—suffering which originated in no fault of yours:—remember all this, my lord—and pause—reflect—I implore you to consider well the step you are taking!"

"Diana, I am not a child that I do not know my own mind," answered the Earl: "moreover, I have the character of firmness: and I shall *never* repent the proposal I now make you—provided you yourself do not give me cause by your conduct."

"And on that head——"

"I have every confidence—the deepest conviction, Diana," interrupted the Earl, warmly.

"Your wishes, then, are my commands—and I obey," returned Diana, her voice thrilling with tones expressive of ineffable joy. "But shall we not ratify our engagement with *one* kiss?"

And as she spoke she slowly drew the black veil from her countenance.

The nobleman's heart palpitated, as she did so, with emotions of the most painful suspense—even of alarm: he felt like a man who in another instant must know the worst.

The veil dropped.

"Heavens! Diana," exclaimed the Earl, starting with surprise and indescribable delight.

For instead of a countenance seared and marked, he beheld a pure and spotless face glowing with a beauty which, even in her loveliest moments, had never seemed to invest her before.

Not a scar—not a trace of the accident was visible.

Her pouting lips were like the rose moistened with dew: her high, pale forehead was pure as marble; and her cheeks were suffused in blushes which seemed to be born beneath the clustering ringlets of her dark brown hair.

"Ah! Diana," exclaimed the Earl, as he drew her to his breast, "how can I punish thee for this cheat!"

"You will pardon me," she murmured, as she clasped her warm white arms around his neck, and imprinted a delicious kiss upon his lips, while her eyes were filled with a voluptuous languor,—"you will pardon me when you know my motives. But can you not divine them?"

"You wished to put my affection to the test, Diana," said the Earl. "Yes—I must forgive you—for you are beautiful—you are adorable—and I love you!"

"And if the sincerest and most devoted attachment on my part can reward you for all your past goodness, and for the honours which you now propose to shower upon me, then shall I not fail to testify my gratitude," exclaimed Diana.

These vows were sealed with innumerable kisses.

At length the Earl rose to depart.

"Three days hence," he said, "my carriage will be sent to fetch you to the church where our hands shall be united."

"And our hearts—for ever," returned Diana.

The nobleman embraced her once more, and took his leave.

But he did not immediately quit the house: he had business with Mr. Wentworth to transact.

We know not the precise sum that this generous peer presented to the surgeon: this, however, we can assure our readers, that he kept his word to the very letter—for Mr. Wentworth became rich in one day.

"*If you succeed in restoring her to me,*" had the Earl said, when he first entrusted Diana to the surgeon's care, "*in that perfection of beauty which invested her when I took leave of her yesterday—without a mark, without a scar,—your fortune shall be my care, and you will have no need to entertain anxiety relative to the future, with the Earl of Warrington as your patron.*"

Such were the nobleman's words upon that occasion; and, on the present, he amply fulfilled his promise.

Three days after, Diana became the Countess of Warrington.

The happy news were thus communicated by the bride to her sincerest and best friend:—

"*Grosvenor Square,*

"*March 22nd, 1840.*

TO HER SERENE HIGHNESS THE GRAND DUCHESS OF

CASTELCICALA.

"I steal a few minutes from a busy day, my dearest Eliza,—for by that dear and familiar name you permit me to call you,—to inform you that I have this morning united my destinies with those of the Earl of Warrington. In a former letter I acquainted you with the dreadful accident which menaced me with horrible scars and marks for life:—you will be pleased to know that the skill and unwearied attention of my medical attendant have succeeded in completely restoring me to my former appearance—so that not a trace of the injury remains upon my person. The Earl of Warrington has elevated me to the proud position of his wife: the remainder of my existence shall be devoted to the study of his happiness.

"I regret to perceive by your letters, dearest Eliza, that *you* are not altogether happy. You say that the Grand Duke loves you; but his temper is arbitrary—his disposition despotic. And yet he is amiable and gentle in his bearing towards you. Study to solace yourself with this conviction. He has elevated you to a rank amongst the reigning princesses of Europe; and as you have embraced the honours, so must you endure some few of the political alarms and annoyances which are invariably attached to so proud a position. You tremble lest the conduct of the Grand Duke, in alienating from him those who are considered his best friends, should endanger his crown. Are you convinced that those persons are indeed his friends! Of course I know not—I cannot determine: I would only counsel you, my dearest friend, not to form hasty conclusions relative to the policy of his Serene Highness.

"I perceive by the English newspapers, that there are numerous Castelcicalan refugees in this country. Amongst them are General Grachia and Colonel Morosino, both of whom, I believe, occupied high offices in their native land. They, however, appear, so far as I can learn, to be dwelling tranquilly in London—no doubt awaiting the happy moment when it shall please your illustrious husband to recall them from exile.

"His Highness Alberto of Castelcicala—(for you are aware that the Earl of Warrington communicated to me some time ago the real rank and name of *Count Alteroni*)—continues to reside at his villa near Richmond. This much I glean from the public journals; but doubtless you are well acquainted with all these facts, inasmuch as your government has a representative at the English court.

"Adieu for the present, dearest Eliza:—I knew not, when I sate down, that I should have been enabled to write so long a letter. But I must now change my dress; for the carriage will be here shortly to convey me to Warrington Park, where we are to pass the honeymoon.

"Ever your sincere friend,

"DIANA."

Such are the strange phases which this world presents to our view! That same Fortune, who, in a moment of caprice, had raised an obscure English lady to a ducal throne, placed, when in a similar mood, a coronet upon the brow of another who had long filled a most equivocal position in society.

CHAPTER CLXXI.

MR. GREENWOOD'S DINNER-PARTY.

Some few days after the events just related, Mr. G. M. Greenwood, M.P., entertained several gentlemen at dinner at his residence in Spring Gardens.

The banquet was served up at seven precisely:—Mr. Greenwood had gradually made his dinner hour later as he had risen in the world; and he was determined that if ever he became a baronet, he would never have that repast put on table till half-past eight o'clock.

On the present occasion, as we ere now observed, the guests were conducted to the dining-room at seven.

The thick curtains were drawn over the windows: the apartment was a blaze of light.

The table groaned beneath the massive plate: the banquet was choice and luxurious in the highest degree.

On Mr. Greenwood's right sate the Marquis of Holmesford—a nobleman of sixty-three years of age, of immense wealth, and notorious for the unbounded licentiousness of his mode of life. His conversation, when his heart was somewhat warmed with wine, bore ample testimony to the profligacy of his morals: seductions were his boast; and he frequently indulged in obscene anecdotes or expressions which even called a blush to the cheeks of his least fastidious male acquaintances.

On Mr. Greenwood's left was Sir T. M. B. Muzzlehem, Bart., M.P., and Whipper-in to the Tory party.

Next to the two guests already described, sate Sir Cherry Bounce, Bart., and the Honourable Major Smilax Dapper—the latter of whom had recently acquired a grade in the service *by purchase.*

Mr. James Tomlinson, Mr. Sheriff Popkins, Mr. Alderman Sniff, Mr. Bubble, Mr. Chouse, and Mr. Twitchem (a solicitor) completed the party.

Now this company, the reader will perceive, was somewhat a mixed one: the aristocracy of the West End, the civic authority, and the members of the financial and legal spheres, were assembled on the present occasion.

The fact is, gentle reader, that this was a "business dinner;" and that you may be no longer kept in suspense, we will at once inform you that when the cloth was drawn, Mr. Greenwood, in a brief speech, proposed "Success to the Algiers, Oran, and Morocco Railway."

The toast was drunk with great applause.

"With your permission, my lord and gentlemen," said Mr. Twitchem, the solicitor, "I will read the Prospectus."

"Yeth, wead the pwothpeckthuth, by all meanth," exclaimed Sir Cherry Bounce.

"Strike me—but I'm anxious to hear *that*," cried the Honourable Major Dapper.

The solicitor then drew a bundle of papers from his pocket, and in a business-like manner read the contents of one which he extracted from the parcel:—

"ALGIERS, ORAN, AND MOROCCO GREAT DESERT

RAILWAY.

"(Provisionally Registered Pursuant to Act.)

"Capital £1,600,000, in 80,000 shares, of £20 each.

"Deposit £3 2*s.* per Share.

"COMMITTEE OF DIRECTION.

"THE MOST HONOURABLE THE MARQUIS OF HOLMESFORD,

G. C. B., Chairman.

"GEORGE M. GREENWOOD, Esq., M.P., Deputy Chairman.

- "Sir T. M. B. Muzzlehem, Bart., M.P.
- "James Tomlinson, Esq.
- "Sylvester Popkins, Esq., Sheriff of London.
- "Percival Peter Sniff, Esq., Alderman.
- "Sir Cherry Bounce, Bart.
- "The Honourable Major Smilax Dapper.
- "Charles Cecil Bubble, Esq.
- "Robert James Baring Chouse, Esq.

"This Railway is intended to connect the great cities of Algiers and Morocco, passing close to the populous and flourishing town of Oran. It will thus be the means of transit for passengers and traffic over a most important section of the Great Desert, which, though placed in maps in a more southernly latitude, nevertheless extends to the District through which this Line is to pass.

"The French government has willingly accorded its countenance to the proposed scheme; and the Governor-General of Algeria has expressed his sincere wish that it may be carried into effect.

"The Morocco government (one of the most enlightened in Africa) has also assented to the enterprise; and the Emperor, the better to manifest the favour with which he views the project, ordered his Prime Minister to be soundly bastinadoed for daring to question its practicability. This proof of the imperial wisdom has filled the Committee and friends of the enterprise with the most sanguine hopes.

"The support of the principal tribes, and other influential parties in Algeria and Morocco, has been secured.

"The Emperor of Morocco, on one side, and his Excellency the Governor-General of Algeria, on the other, have signified their readiness to grant a strong armed force to protect the engineers and operatives, when laying down the rails, from being devoured by wild beasts, or molested by predatory tribes.

"The ex-Emir of Mascara, Abd-el-Kadir, has entered into a bond not to interfere with the works while in progress, nor to molest those who may travel by the Line when it shall be opened; and, in order to secure this important concession on the part of the ex-Emir, the Committee have agreed to make that Prince an annual present of clothes, linen, tobacco, and ardent spirit.

"It is with the greatest satisfaction that the Committee of Direction is enabled to announce these brilliant prospects; and the Committee beg to state that application for the allotment of Shares must be made without delay to James Tomlinson, Esq., Stockbroker, Tokenhouse Yard.

"By order of the Board,

"SHARPLY TWITCHEM, Secretary."

"On my thoul, there never wath any thing better—conthith, bwief, ekthplithit, and attwactive!" cried Sir Cherry.

"Sure to take—as certain as I'm in Her Majesty's service—strike me!" exclaimed Major Dapper.

"I think you ought to have thrown in something about African beauties," observed the Marquis: "they are particularly stout, you know, being all fed on a preparation of rice called *couscousou*. I really think I must pay a visit to those parts next spring."

"I will undertake to get one of the members of the government to introduce a favourable mention of the project into his speech to-morrow night, in the House," said Sir T. M. B. Muzzlehem: "but you must send him a hundred shares the first thing in the morning."

"That shall be done," answered Mr. Twitchem.

"Well, my lord and gentlemen," observed Mr. Greenwood, "I think that this little business looks uncommonly well. The project is no doubt feasible—I mean, the shares are certain to go off well. Mr. Bubble and Mr. Chouse will undertake to raise them in public estimation, by the reports they will circulate in Capel Court. Of course, my lord and gentlemen, when they are at a good premium, we shall all sell; and if we do not realise twenty or thirty thousand pounds each—*each*, mark me—then shall you be at liberty to say that the free and independent electors of Rottenborough have chosen as their representative a dolt and an idiot in the person of your humble servant."

"Whatever Mr. Greenwood undertakes is certain to turn to gold," observed Mr. Bubble.

"Can't be otherwise," said Mr. Chouse.

"Mr. Greenwood's name stands so well in the City," added Mr. Sheriff Popkins.

"And his lordship's countenance to the enterprise is a tower of strength," exclaimed Mr. Alderman Sniff.

"I have already had many inquiries concerning the project," said Mr. Tomlinson.

"Yes—Chouse and I took care to circulate reports in the City that such a scheme was in contemplation," observed Bubble.

"Gentlemen, I think that all difficulties have been provided against in this Prospectus," cried Mr. Twitchem:—"the predatory tribes, Abd-el-Kadir, and the wild beasts."

"Nothing could be better," answered Mr. Greenwood. "Take care that the Prospectus be sent as an advertisement to every London journal, and the leading provincial ones. You know that I am a shareholder in one of the London newspapers; and I can promise you that it will not fail to cry up our enterprise. In fact, my lord and gentlemen," added Mr. Greenwood, "I have at this moment in my pocket a copy of a leading article—that will appear in that paper, the day after to-morrow."

"My gwathioth!—do read it, Greenwood," cried Sir Cherry Bounce.

"Yes: I'd give the world to hear it—smite me!" ejaculated Major Dapper.

Mr. Greenwood glanced complacently around, and then drew forth a printed slip, the contents of which were as follow:—

"In our opposition to those multifarious railway projects which are starting up on all sides, as if some Cadmus had been sowing bubbles in our financial soil, we have only been swayed by our fears lest such a number of schemes, which never can obtain the sanction of Parliament, should injure the credit, and impair the monetary prosperity of the country. It must not, however, be supposed that we are inimical to those undertakings which are based upon fair, intelligible, and reasonable grounds. There are many talented, honourable, and wealthy individuals engaged in speculations of this nature; and, their motives being beyond suspicion, no one of common sense can for a moment suppose that we include *their* projects amongst the airy nothings against which we are compelled to put the public on their guard. The extension of railways is internally connected with the progress of civilisation; and when we behold the principle applied to distant and semi-barbarian countries—as in the case, for instance, of that truly grand and promising enterprise, the Algiers, Oran, and Morocco Great Desert Railway—we feel proud that England should have the honour of taking the initiative in thus propagating beyond its own limits the elements of civilisation, and the germs of humanising influences. At the same time we shall continue our strenuous opposition to all railway schemes which we consider to be mere bubbles blown from the pipes of intriguants and adventurers; and we shall never pause until in those pipes we put an effectual stopper."

"Thuper-ekthellent—glowiouth—majethtic—athtounding!" ejaculated Sir Cherry, quite in raptures.

"You perceive how beautifully—how delicately the puff is insinuated," said Mr. Greenwood. "That article will have an astonishing effect."

"No doubt of it," observed the Marquis. "You might have contrived to introduce something relative to the Emperor of Morocco's ladies. Why not state that the Moorish terminus will command a view of the gardens of the imperial harem, where those divine creatures—each of seventeen stone weight—are wont to ramble in a voluptuous undress?"

"No—no, my lord; that would never do!" cried Greenwood, with a smile. "And now, my lord and gentlemen, we perfectly understand each other. Each takes as many shares as he pleases. When they reach a high premium, each may sell as he thinks fit. Then, when we have realized our profits, we will inform the shareholders that insuperable difficulties prevent the carrying out of the project,—that Abd-el-Kadir, for instance, has violated his agreement and declared against the scheme,—that the Committee of Direction will therefore retain a sum sufficient to defray the expenses already incurred, and that the remaining capital paid up shall be returned to the shareholders."

"That is exactly what, I believe, we all understand," observed Mr. Twitchem.

"For my part," said Lord Holmesford, "I only embark in the enterprise to oblige my friend Greenwood; and therefore I am agreeable to any thing that he proposes."

Matters being thus amicably arranged, the company passed the remainder of the evening in the conviviality of the table.

At eleven o'clock the guests all retired, with the exception of the Marquis of Holmesford.

"Now, friend Greenwood," said this nobleman, "you will keep your engagement with me?"

"Yes, my lord: I am prepared to accompany you."

"Let us depart at once, then," added the Marquis, rising from his chair: "my carriage has been waiting some time; and I long to introduce you to the voluptuous mysteries of Holmesford House."

CHAPTER CLXXII.

THE MYSTERIES OF HOLMESFORD HOUSE.

The Marquis and Mr. Greenwood alighted at the door of Holmesford House—one of the most splendid palaces of the aristocracy at the West End.

The Marquis conducted his visitor into a large ante-room at the right hand of the spacious hall.

The table in the middle of the apartment was covered with the most luxurious fruits, nosegays of flowers, preserves, sweetmeats, and delicious wines.

From this room three doors afforded communication elsewhere. One opened into the hall, and had afforded them ingress: the other, on the opposite side, belonged to a corridor, with which were connected the baths; and the third, at the bottom, communicated with a vast saloon, of which we shall have more to say very shortly.

The Marquis said to the servant who conducted him and Mr. Greenwood to the ante-room, "You may retire; and let *them* ring the bell when all is ready."

The domestic withdrew.

The Marquis motioned Greenwood to seat himself at the table; and, filling two coloured glasses with real Johannisberg, he said, "We must endeavour to while away half an hour; and then I can promise you a pleasing entertainment."

The nobleman and the member of Parliament quaffed the delicious wine, and indulged in discourse upon the most voluptuous subjects.

"For my part," said the Marquis, "I study how to enjoy life. I possess an immense fortune, and do not scruple to spend it upon all the pleasures I can fancy, or which suggest themselves to me. I am not such an idiot as to imagine that I possess the vigour or natural warmth which characterised my youth; and therefore I have become an Epicurean in my recreations. I invent and devise the means of inflaming my passions; and then—*then* I am young once more. You will presently behold something truly oriental in the refinements on voluptuousness which I have conceived to produce an artificial effect on the temperament when nature is languid and weak.

"Your lordship is right to fan the flame that burns dimly," observed Greenwood, who, unprincipled as he was, could not, however, avoid a feeling of disgust when he heard that old voluptuary, with one foot in the grave, thus shamelessly express himself.

"Wine and women, my dear Greenwood," continued the Marquis, "are the only earthly enjoyments worth living for. I hope to die, with my head pillowed on the naked—heaving bosom of beauty, and with a glass of sparkling champagne in my hand."

"Your lordship would then even defy the pangs of the grim monster who spares no one," said Greenwood.

"I have lived a joyous life, my dear friend; and when death comes, I can say that no mortal man—not even Solomon, with his thousand wives and concubines—nor any eastern Sultan, who had congregated the fairest flowers of Georgia, Circassia, and Armenia in his harem,—had more deeply drunk than I of the pleasures of love."

Just as the aged voluptuary uttered these words, a silver bell that hung in the apartment was agitated gently by a wire which communicated with the adjoining saloon.

"Now all is in readiness!" exclaimed the Marquis: "follow me."

The nobleman opened the door leading into the saloon, which he entered, accompanied by Greenwood.

He then closed the door behind him.

The saloon was involved in total obscurity; the blackest darkness reigned there, unbroken by a ray.

"Give me your hand," said the Marquis.

Greenwood complied; and the nobleman led him to a sofa at a short distance from the door by which they had entered.

They both seated themselves on the voluptuous cushions.

For some moments a solemn silence prevailed.

At length that almost painful stillness was broken by the soft notes of a delicious melody, which, coming from the farther end of the apartment, stole, with a species of enchanting influence, upon the ear.

Gentle and low was that sweet music when it began; but by degrees it grew louder—though still soft and ravishing in the extreme.

Then a chorus of charming female voices suddenly burst forth; and the union of that vocal and instrumental perfection produced an effect thrilling—intoxicating—joyous, beyond description.

The melody created in the mind of Greenwood an anxious desire to behold those unseen choristers whose voices were so harmonious, so delightful.

The dulcet, metallic sounds agitated the senses with feelings of pleasure, and made the heart beat with vague hopes and expectations.

For nearly twenty minutes did that delicious concert last. Love was the subject of the song,—Love, not considered as an infant boy, nor as a merciless tyrant,—but Love depicted as the personification of every thing voluptuous, blissful, and enchanting,—Love, the representative of all the joys which earth in reality possesses, or which the warmest imagination could possibly conceive,—Love apart from the refinements of sentiment, and contemplated only as the paradise of sensualities.

And never did sweeter voices warble the fervid language of passion through the medium of a more enchanting poesy!

Twenty minutes, we said, passed with wonderful rapidity while that inspiring concert lasted.

But even then the melody did not cease suddenly. It gradually grew fainter and fainter—dying away, as it were, in expiring sounds of silver harmony, as if yielding to the voluptuous enhancement of its own magic influence.

And now, just as the last murmur floated to the ears of the raptured listeners, a bell tinkled at a distance; and in an instant—as if by magic—the spacious saloon was lighted up with a brilliancy which produced a sensation like an electric shock.

At the same time, the music struck up in thrilling sounds once more; and a bevy of lovely creatures, whom the glare suddenly revealed upon a stage at the farther end of the apartment, became all life and activity in a voluptuous dance.

Three chandeliers of transparent crystal had suddenly vomited forth jets of flame; and round the walls the illumination had sprung into existence, with simultaneous suddenness, from innumerable silver sconces.

A glance around showed Greenwood that he was in a vast and lofty apartment, furnished with luxurious ottomans in the oriental style; and with tables groaning beneath immense vases filled with the choicest flowers.

The walls were covered with magnificent pictures, representing the most voluptuous scenes of the heathen mythology and of ancient history.

The figures in those paintings were as large as life; and no prudery had restrained the artist's pencil in the delineation of the luxuriant subjects which he had chosen.

There was Lucretia, struggling—vainly struggling with the ardent Tarquin,—her drapery torn by his rude hands away from her lovely form, which the brutal violence of his mad passion had rendered weak, supple, and yielding.

There was Helen, reclining in more than semi-nudity on the couch to which her languishing and wanton looks invited the enamoured Phrygian youth, who was hastily laying aside his armour after a combat with the Greeks.

There was Messalina—that imperial harlot, whose passions were so insatiable and whose crimes were so enormous,—issuing from a bath to join her lover, who impatiently awaited her beneath a canopy in a recess, and which was surmounted by the Roman diadem.

Then there were pictures representing the various amours of Jupiter,—Leda, Latona, Semele, and Europa—the mistresses of the god—all drawn in the most exciting attitudes, and endowed with the most luscious beauties.

But if those creations of art were sufficient to inflame the passions of even that age when the blood seems frozen in the veins, how powerful must have been the effect produced by those living, breathing, moving houris who were now engaged in a rapid and exciting dance to the most ravishing music.

They wore six in number, and all dressed alike, in a drapery so light and gauzy that it was all but transparent, and so scanty that it afforded no scope for the sweet romancing of fancy, and left but little need for guesses.

But if their attire were thus uniform, their style of beauty was altogether different.

We must, however, permit the Marquis to describe them to Greenwood—which he did in whispers.

"That fair girl on the right," he said, "with the brilliant complexion, auburn hair, and red cherry lips, is from the north—a charming specimen of Scotch beauty. Mark how taper is her waist, and yet how ample her bust! She is only nineteen, and has been in my house for the last three years. Her voice is charming; and she sings some of her native airs with exquisite taste. The one next to her, with the brown hair, and who is somewhat stout in form, though, as you perceive, not the less active on that account, is an English girl—a beauty of Lancashire. She is twenty-two, and appeared four years ago on the stage. From thence she passed into the keeping of a bishop, who took lodgings for her in great Russell Street, Bloomsbury. The Right Reverend Prelate one evening invited me to sup there; and three days afterwards she removed to my house."

"Not with the consent of the bishop, I should imagine?" observed Greenwood, laughing.

"Oh! no—no," returned the Marquis, chuckling and coughing at the same time. "The one who is next to her—the third from the left, I mean—is an Irish girl. Look how beautifully she is made. What vigorous, strong, and yet elegantly formed limbs! And what elasticity—what airy lightness in the dance! Did you observe that pirouette? How the drapery spread out from her waist like a circular fan! Is she not a charming creature?"

"She is, indeed!" exclaimed Greenwood. "Tall, elegant, and graceful."

"And her tongue is just tipped with enough of the Irish accent—I cannot call it *brogue* in so sweet a being—to render her conversation peculiarly interesting. And now mark her smile! Oh! the coquette—what a roguish look! Has she not wickedness in those sparkling black eyes?"

"She seems an especial favourite, methinks," whispered Greenwood.

"Yes—I have a sneaking preference for her, I must admit," answered the Marquis. "But I also like my little French girl, who is dancing next to Kathleen. Mademoiselle Anna is an exquisite creature—and such a wanton! What passion is denoted by her burning glances! How graceful are her movements: survey her now—she beats them all in that soft abandonment of limb which she just displayed. Her mother was a widow, and sold the lovely Anna to a French Field-Marshal, when she was only fifteen. The Field-Marshal, who was also a duke and enormously rich, placed her in a magnificent mansion in the Chausseé d'Antin, and settled a handsome sum upon her. But, at his death, she ran through it all, became involved in debt, and was glad to accept my offers two years ago."

"She is very captivating," said Greenwood. "How gracefully she rounds her dazzling white arms!"

"And how well she throws herself into the most voluptuous attitudes—and all, too, as if unstudied!" returned the Marquis. "The beauty next to her is a Spaniard. The white drapery, in my opinion, sets off her clear, transparent, olive skin, to the utmost advantage. The blood seems to boil in her veins: she is all fire—all passion. How brilliant are her large black eyes! Behold the glossy magnificence of her raven hair! Tall—straight as an arrow—how commanding, and yet how graceful is her form! And when she smiles—now—you can perceive the dazzling whiteness of her teeth. Last of all I must direct your attention to my Georgian—"

"A real Georgian?" exclaimed Greenwood.

"A real Georgian," answered the Marquis; "and, as Byron describes his Katinka, 'white and red.' Her large melting blue eyes are full of voluptuous, lazy, indolent, but not the less impassioned love. Her dark brown hair is braided in a manner to display its luxuriance, and yet leave the entire face clear for you to admire its beauty. Look at that fine oval countenance: how pure is the red—how delicate the white! Nature has no artificial auxiliaries there! And now when she casts down her eyes, mark how the long, silken black lashes, slightly curling, repose upon the white skin beneath the eyes. Is not that a charming creature? The symmetry of her form is perfect. Her limbs are stout and plump; but how slender are her ankles, and how exquisitely turned her wrists! Then look at her hand. What beautiful, long taper fingers! How sweet are her movements—light, yet languishing at the same time!"

"What is the name of that beauty?" asked Greenwood.

"Malkhatoun," replied the Marquis; "which means *The Full Moon*. That was the name of the wife of Osman, the founder of the Ottoman empire."

"And how did you procure such a lovely creature?" inquired Greenwood, enraptured with the beauty of the oriental girl.

"Six months ago I visited Constantinople," answered the Marquis of Holmesford; "and in the Slave-Market I beheld that divinity. Christians are not allowed to purchase slaves; but a convenient native merchant was found, who bought her for me. I brought her to England; and she is well contented to be here. Her own apartment is fitted up in an oriental style; she has her Koran, and worships Alla at her leisure; and when I make love to her, she swears by the Prophet Mahommed that she is happy here. The romance of the thing is quite charming."

"Of course she cannot speak English?" said Greenwood interrogatively.

"I beg your pardon," answered the Marquis. "She has an English master, who is well acquainted with Persian, which she speaks admirably; and I can assure you that she is a most willing pupil. But of that you shall judge for yourself presently."

During this conversion, the dance proceeded.

Nothing could be more voluptuous than that spectacle of six charming creatures, representing the loveliness of as many different countries, engaged in a *pas de six* in which each studied how to set off the graces of her form to the utmost advantage.

The genial warmth of the apartment—the delicious perfume of the flowers—the brilliancy of the light—the exciting nature of the pictures—and the enchantment of that dance in which six beings of the rarest beauty were engaged,—filled the mind of Greenwood with an ecstatic delirium.

Not the rich and luscious loveliness of Diana Arlington, whom circumstances had made his own,—not the matured and exuberant charms of Eliza Sydney, who had escaped his snares,—not the bewitching beauty of Ellen Monroe, from whose brow he had plucked the diadem of purity,—nor the licentious fascinations of Lady Cecilia Harborough, who sold herself to him for his gold,—not all these had so stirred his heart, so inflamed his ardent imagination, as the spectacle which he now beheld.

At length the dance terminated.

The Marquis then advanced towards the stage, accompanied by Greenwood, and said, "Many thanks, young ladies, for this entertainment. Allow me to present an intimate friend of mine—a gentleman whom I am anxious to initiate in the mysteries of Holmesford House."

Greenwood bowed; the six beauties returned his salutation; and the Marquis then proposed to adjourn to the ante-room, where supper was served up.

The ladies descended from the platform by a flight of steps on one side.

"I shall give my arm to Kathleen," said the Marquis. "Do you escort whomever you fancy. There are no jealousies here."

Without hesitation Greenwood advanced towards the charming Malkhatoun, who took the arm which he presented to her, with a sweet smile—as if of gratitude for the preference.

As Greenwood thus stepped forward to meet her, he now for the first time observed the orchestra, which was situated in a large recess on the right of the stage, and had consequently been unseen by him from the place which he had originally occupied at the other end of the saloon.

The party now proceeded to the ante-room before mentioned.

There a magnificent repast was served up.

They all seated themselves at table, Kathleen next to the Marquis, and Malkhatoun by the side of Greenwood.

At first the conversation languished somewhat, the ladies being abashed and reserved in the presence of a stranger; but as they grew warmed by degrees with the generous wine, their tongues were unlocked; and in half an hour they rattled and chatted away as if they had never known restraint.

They laughed and displayed their beautiful teeth: their eyes flashed fire, or became voluptuously melting: and their cheeks were animated with the hues of the rose.

Even the fair Mohammedan did not refuse the sparkling champagne which effervesced so deliciously over the brim of the crystal glass.

The Scotch and Irish girls warbled the sweetest snatches of song which Greenwood had ever heard; and then the French damsel rose and gave admirable imitations of Taglioni's, Ellsler's, and Duvernay's respective styles of dancing—throwing, however, into her movements and attitudes a wantonness which even the most exciting efforts of those *artistes* never displayed.

It was now nearly two in the morning; and Greenwood intimated to the Marquis his wish to retire.

"Just as you please," replied the old voluptuary, who had drawn Kathleen upon his knee, and was toying with her as if they were unobserved: "but if you like to accept of a bed here, there is one at your service—and," he added, in a whisper, "you need not be separated from Malkhatoun."

"Is your lordship in earnest?" asked Greenwood, also in a low tone, while joy flashed from his eyes.

"Certainly I am," replied the Marquis. "Do you think that I brought you hither merely to tantalize you?"

Greenwood smiled, and then redoubled his attentions towards the charming Georgian, who returned his smiles, and seemed to consider herself honoured by his caresses.

On a signal from the Marquis, the Scotch, English, French, and Spanish girls withdrew.

"One glass of wine in honour of those houris who have just left us!" cried the nobleman, who was already heated with frequent potations, and inflamed by the contiguity of his Hibernian mistress.

"With pleasure," responded Greenwood.

The toast was drunk; and then the Marquis whispered something to Greenwood, pointing at the same time to the door which opened into the bathing rooms.

The member of Parliament nodded an enraptured assent.

"There is a constant supply of hot water, kept ready for use," observed the nobleman. "Each room is provided with a marble bath; and vases of eau-de-cologne afford the means of cooling the water and imparting to it a delicious perfume at the same time. You will also find wines, fruits, and all species of delicate refreshments there; and adjoining each bath-room is a bed-chamber. With Malkhatoun as your companion, you may imagine yourself a Sultan in the privacy of his harem; and, remember, that no soul will intrude upon you in that joyous retreat."

Greenwood presented his hand to Malkhatoun, and led her away in obedience to the nobleman's suggestion.

The door by which they left the ante-room admitted them into a passage dimly lighted with a single lamp, and where several doors opened into the bathing apartments.

Into one of those rooms Greenwood and the beautiful Georgian passed.

Shortly afterwards the Marquis and Kathleen entered another.

Here we must pause: we dare not penetrate farther into the mysteries of Holmesford House.

CHAPTER CLXXIII.

THE ADIEUX.

Our narrative must now take a leap of several months.

It was the middle of October.

Once more in the vicinity of Count Alteroni's mansion near Richmond, a handsome young man and a beautiful dark-eyed maiden were walking together.

Need we say that they were Richard and the charming Isabella?

The countenances of both wore an expression of melancholy; but that indication of feeling was commingled with the traces of other emotions.

Richard's eyes beamed with ardour, and his lips denoted stern resolution: Isabella's bewitching features showed that her generous soul entertained warm and profound hope, even though the cloud sate upon her brow.

"Yes, my adored one," said Richard, gazing tenderly upon her, "it is decided! To-morrow I embark on this expedition. But I could not quit England without seeing you once more, dearest Isabella; and for two or three days have I vainly wandered in this neighbourhood with the hope of meeting you—alone."

"Oh! Richard, had I for one moment divined that you were so near, I should have come to you," answered the Princess; "and this you know well! If I have hitherto discouraged clandestine meetings and secret correspondence—save on one or two occasions—it was simply because you should not have reason to think lightly of me;—but you are well aware, Richard, that my heart is thine—unchangeably thine,—and that my happiest moments are those I pass with thee!"

"I cannot chide you, dearest, for that fine feeling which has made you discourage clandestine meetings and secret correspondence," said Richard, gazing with mingled admiration and rapture upon the angelic countenance of Isabella; "but now that circumstances are about to change,—now that I shall be far away from thee, beloved girl,—that restriction must in some degree be removed, and you will permit me to write to you from time to time."

"It would be an absurd affectation and a ridiculous prudery, were I to refuse you," replied Isabella. "Yes, dear Richard—write to me;—and write often," she added, tears starting into her eyes.

"A thousand thanks, Isabella, for this kind permission—this proof of your love. And, oh! to whatever perils I am about to oppose myself face to face,—in whatever dangers I may be involved,—whatever miseries or privations I may be destined to endure,—the thought of you, my own adored Isabella, will make all seem light! But I do not anticipate much difficulty in the attainment of our grand object. General Grachia, Colonel Morosino, and the other chiefs of this enterprise, have so well, so prudently, so cautiously digested all the measures necessary to ensure success, that failure is scarcely possible. The tyranny of the Grand Duke and of his shameless Ministry has reduced the Castelcicalans to despair. We have three fine vessels; and twelve hundred devoted patriots will form the expedition. The moment we land, we shall be welcomed with enthusiasm. And if an opportunity should serve for me to show myself worthy of the confidence that General Grachia and his colleagues have placed in me,—if," continued Richard, his handsome countenance now lighted up with a glow of heroic enthusiasm,—"if the aid of my feeble efforts can in any way demonstrate my zeal in favour of the constitutional cause, be well assured, dearest Isabella, that it is not an idle boaster, nor a braggart coward who now assures thee that he will not dishonour the service in which he has embarked."

"Of that I feel convinced, Richard," exclaimed the Italian lady, whose soul caught the enthusiasm which animated her lover. "But you know not the wild hopes—the exalted visions which have at times filled my imagination, since I heard a few weeks ago that you were one of the chiefs of this enterprise, the preparations for which were communicated to my father. For you are doubtless aware that General Grachia *has* made my father acquainted with his intentions and projects———"

"Which the Prince discountenances," added Richard, with a sigh. "Nevertheless, he is perhaps right: but if we succeed, Isabella—oh! if we succeed, your father becomes the sovereign of a great and enlightened people! Then—what hope will remain for me?"

"Providence will not desert us, Richard," answered Isabella. "Said I not ere now that the wildest hopes—the most exalted visions have dazzled my imagination? I will not describe them to you, Richard; but need I confess that they are connected with yourself? The dying words of our poor friend Mary Anne have made an impression upon me which I can never forget."

"I can well divine all the hopes and aspirations which *her* prophetic language was calculated to excite," returned Markham; "for there have been moments when I was weak enough to yield to the same influence myself. But the future is with the Almighty; and He must ordain our happiness or our misery! I must now leave you, my beloved Isabella:—when I am away thou wilt think of me often?"

"Oh! Richard, will you really depart? will you venture on this expedition, so fraught with danger?" cried Isabella, now giving way to her grief as the moment of separation drew nigh. "I told you to hope—I wished to console you; but it is I who require consolation when about to say farewell to you! Oh! Richard, if you knew what anguish now fills my heart, you would be enabled to estimate all my love for you!"

"I do—I do, adored Isabella!" ejaculated Markham, pressing her to his breast. "How devotedly—how faithfully you have loved me, I never can forget! When spurned from your father's house—overwhelmed with the most cruel suspicions, your love remained unchanged; and in many a bitter, bitter hour, have I derived sweet solace from the conviction that thy heart was mine! Oh! Isabella, God in his mercy grant that I may return from this enterprise with some honour to myself! It is not that I am influenced by motives of selfish ambition;—it is that I may remove at least one of the hundred obstacles which oppose our union. And now adieu, my angel—my dearly-beloved Isabella: adieu—adieu!"

"Farewell, Richard—farewell, dearest one—my first and only love," murmured Isabella, as she wept bitterly upon his breast.

Then they embraced each other with that passionate ardour—with that lingering unwillingness to separate—with that profound dread to tear themselves asunder, which lovers in the moment of parting alone can know.

"Let us be firm, Isabella," said Richard: "who can tell what happiness my share in this enterprise may create for us?"

"Yes—something tells me that it will be so," answered Isabella; "and that hope sustains me!"

Another embrace—and they parted.

Yes—they parted,—that handsome young man and that charming Italian maiden!

And soon they waved their handkerchiefs for the last time;—then, in a few moments, they were lost to each other's view.

Richard returned home to his house at Lower Holloway.

He had visited the farm near Hounslow a few days previously, and had taken leave of Katherine. The young maiden had wept when her benefactor communicated to her his intended absence from England for some time; but, as he did not acquaint her with the nature of the business which took him way from his native country, she was not aware of the perils he was about to encounter.

He had now to say farewell to the inmates of his own dwelling. But towards Mr. Monroe, Ellen, and the faithful Whittingham he was less reserved than he had been to Katherine.

Vainly had the old butler implored "Master Richard not to indemnify himself with other people's business;"—vainly had Mr. Monroe endeavoured to persuade him to refrain from risking his life in the political dissensions of a foreign country; vainly had the beautiful and generous-hearted Ellen, with a sisterly warmth, argued on the same side. Richard was determined:—they deemed him obstinate—foolish—almost mad; but they knew not of his love for Isabella!

"I must now make you acquainted with a certain portion of my affairs," said our hero, addressing Mr. Monroe, "in order that you may manage them for me until my return. I have embarked as much of my capital as I could well spare in the enterprise on which I am about to set out: you will find in my strong-box, of which I leave you the key, a sufficient sum of money to answer the expenses of the establishment until January. Should I not return by that time, you will find papers in the same place, which will instruct you relative to the moneys that will then be due to me from the two respectable individuals who are my tenants. Moreover," added Richard,—and here his voice faltered,—"my will is in the strong-box; and should I perish in this undertaking, you will find, my dear friend,—and you too, my faithful Whittingham,—that I have not left you without resources."

"Richard, this is too generous!" exclaimed Mr. Monroe, tears of gratitude trickling down his cheeks.

Whittingham also wept; and Ellen's sobs were convulsive—for she regarded Richard in the light of a dear brother.

"Render not our parting moments more painful than they naturally are, my dear friends," said Markham. "You cannot understand—but, if I live, you shall some day know—the motives which influence me in joining this expedition. Mr. Monroe—Ellen—Whittingham, I have one last request to make. You are all aware that on the 10th of July, 1843, a solemn appointment exists between my brother and myself. If I should perish in a far-off clime,—or if a prison, or any accident prevent my return,—let one of you represent me on that occasion. Should it be so, tell my brother how much I have loved him—how anxiously I have ever looked forward to that day,—how sincerely I have prayed for his welfare and his success! Tell him," continued Richard, while the tears rolled down his cheeks, large and fast,—"tell him that I have cherished his memory as no brother ever before was known to do; and if he be poor—or unhappy—or suffering—or unfortunate, receive him into this house, which will then be your own—console, comfort him! If he be criminal, do not spurn him:—remember, he is my brother!"

Ellen sobbed as if her heart would break as Richard uttered these words.

There was something fearfully poignant and convulsive in that young lady's grief.

But suddenly rousing herself, she rushed from the room; and, returning in a few moments with her child, she presented it to Markham, saying "Embrace him, Richard, before you depart;—embrace him—for he bears your Christian name!"

Our hero received the innocent infant in his arms, and kissed it tenderly.

No pen can depict the expression of pleasure—of radiant joy,—joy shining out from amidst her tears,—with which Ellen contemplated that proof of affection towards her babe.

"Thank you, Richard—thank you, my brother," she exclaimed, as she received back her child.

The old butler and Mr. Monroe were not callous to the touching nature of that scene.

"I have now no more to say," observed Richard. "I am about to retire to the library for a short time. At five o'clock the post-chaise will be here. Whittingham, my faithful friend, you will see that all my necessaries be carefully packed."

Markham then withdrew to his study.

There he wrote a few letters upon matters of business.

At length Whittingham made his appearance.

"Morcar is arrived, Master Richard," said the old man, "and it is close upon five."

"I shall soon be ready, Whittingham," answered Richard.

The old butler withdrew.

Then Richard took from his strong-box the mysterious packet which had been left to him by Thomas Armstrong; and that sacred trust he secured about his person.

"Now," he said, "I am about to quit the home of my forefathers."

And tears trickled down his cheeks.

"This is foolish!" he exclaimed, after a pause: "I must not yield to my emotions, when on the eve of such a grand and glorious undertaking."

He then returned to the drawing-room.

At that moment the post-chaise arrived at the front door of the mansion.

We will not detail the affecting nature of the farewell scene: suffice it to say that Richard departed with the fervent prayers and the sincerest wishes of those whom he left behind.

Morcar, the gipsy, accompanied him.

"Which road, sir?" asked the postillion.

"Canterbury—Deal," replied Richard.

And the post-chaise whirled him away from the home of his forefathers!

By a special messenger, on the same day when the above-mentioned incidents took place, the following letter was despatched from London:—

"TO HER SERENE HIGHNESS THE GRAND DUCHESS OF CASTELCICALA.

"I have the honour to inform your Serene Highness that the measures which I adopted (and which your Highness condemned in the last letter your Highness deigned to address to me) have enabled me to ascertain the intentions of the conspirators. The three vessels purchased by them are now completely equipped and manned. One has already arrived in the Downs, where the Chiefs of the rebels are to join her. A second sailed from Hull four days ago: and the third left Waterford about the same time. They will all three meet at Cadiz, where they are to take in stores and water. Twelve hundred exiled Castelcicalans are on board these three ships, which are ostensibly fitted out as emigrant vessels for North America. So well have General Grachia, Colonel Morosino, and Mr. Markham planned their schemes, that I question whether even the English government is acquainted with the real destination of those ships, and the object of their crews.

"Beware, then, noble lady! The last meeting of the Chiefs of the expedition was held last evening; and I was present in my presumed capacity of a stanch adherent to the cause of the conspirators. The reasons which I adduced for not proceeding with them on the enterprise, and for remaining in London, were completely satisfactory; and no one for a moment suspected my integrity. Indeed, the confidence which Mr. Markham has placed in me from the beginning, in consequence of the share which I had in saving his life (an incident to which I have alluded in preceding letters to your Highness) on a certain occasion, annihilated all suspicion as to the sincerity of my motives.

"At the meeting of which I have just spoken, it was resolved that the descent upon Castelcicala shall be made in the neighbourhood of Ossore, which, I need scarcely inform your Serene Highness, is a small sea-port about thirty-five miles to the south of Montoni.

"And now I have discharged what I consider to be a faithful duty. If I have fallen in your Highness's good opinion by betraying those with whom I affected to act, I fondly hope that the importance of the information which I have thereby been enabled to give you, will restore me to your Highness's favour.

"But remember, my lady—remember the prayer which I offered up to your Highness when first I wrote concerning this conspiracy,—remember the earnest supplication which I then made and now renew,—that *not a hair of Richard Markham's head must be injured*!

"I have the honour to subscribe myself your Serene Highness's most faithful and devoted servant,

"FILIPPO DORSENNI.

Oct. 16th, 1840."

Thus was it that Mr. Greenwood's Italian valet provided, to the utmost of his power, for the safety of Richard Markham, in case those whom he improperly denominated "conspirators" should fall into the hands of the Castelcicalan authorities.

CHAPTER CLXXIV.

CASTELCICALA.

The Grand-Duchy of Castelcicala is bounded on the north by the Roman States, on the south by the kingdom of Naples, on the east by the Apennine Mountains, and on the west by the Mediterranean Sea.

It is the most beautiful, the best cultivated, and the finest portion of the Italian Peninsula. The inhabitants are brave, enlightened, and industrious.

Castelcicala is divided into seven districts, or provinces, the capitals of which are Montoni (which is also the metropolis of the Grand Duchy), Abrantani, Veronezzi, Pinalla, Estella, Terano, and Montecuculi. Each province is governed by a Captain-General (the chief military authority), and a Political Prefect, (the chief civil authority).

The principal city, Montoni, stands at the mouth of the Ferretti, and contains a hundred thousand inhabitants. It is built on both sides of the river, has a fine harbour, spacious dockyards, and extensive arsenals, and is one of the principal trading-ports of Italy. It is strongly fortified on the system of Vauban.

The entire population of the Grand-Duchy of Castelcicala is two millions. Its revenues are three millions sterling; and the annual income of the sovereign is two hundred thousand pounds.

From these details the reader will perceive that Castelcicala is by no means an unimportant country in the map of Europe.

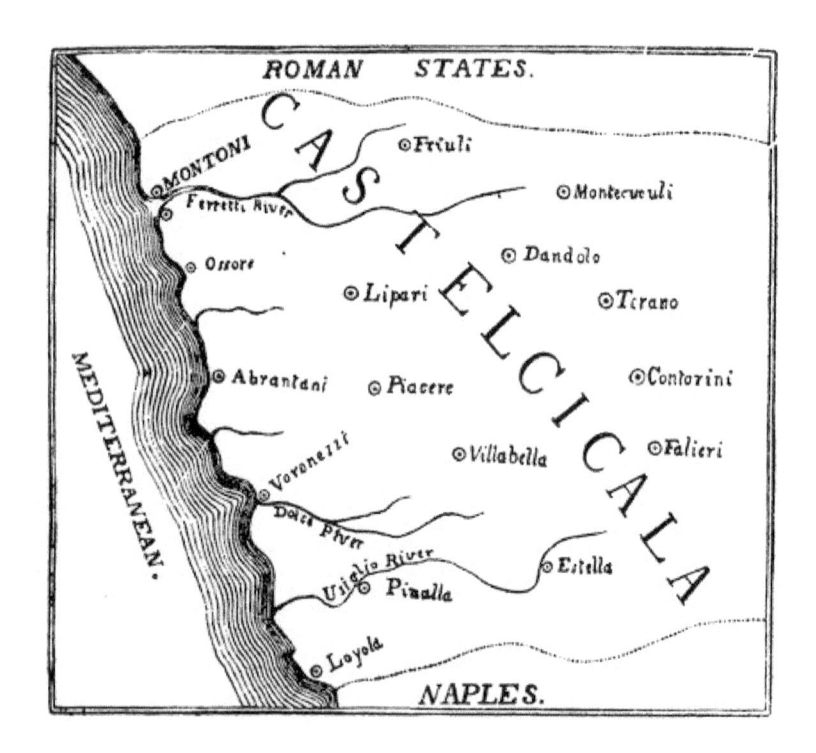

We shall now continue our narrative.

It was the middle of November, 1840, and at an early hour in the morning, before sunrise, when three vessels (two large brigs and a schooner) ran in as close as the depth of water would permit them with safety, on the Castelcicalan coast a few miles below Ossore.

The boats of these vessels were immediately lowered; and by the time the sun dawned on the scene, nearly twelve hundred armed men were landed without molestation.

This force was divided into two columns: one of seven hundred strong was commanded by General Grachia; the other of five hundred was led by Colonel Morosino. Richard Markham, as Secretary-General of the Constitutional Chiefs, and attended by Morcar, accompanied General Grachia. The chiefs and their staff were all provided with horses.

The army presented a somewhat motley aspect, the officers alone appearing in uniforms. The entire force was, however, well provided with weapons; and every heart beat high with hope and patriotism.

The banners were unfurled; an excellent brass band struck up an enlivening national air; and the two columns marched in the direction of Ossore.

It was deemed most important to possess this sea-port without delay; as its harbour would afford a safe refuge for the three ships to which the Constitutionalists (as the invaders termed themselves) could alone look for the means of retreat, in case of the failure of their enterprise.

But of such a result they entertained not the slightest apprehension.

And now the peasants in the farm-houses and hamlets near which they passed, were suddenly alarmed by the sounds of martial music: but the rumour of the real object of the invaders spread like wild-fire; and they had not marched three or four miles, before they were already joined by nearly a hundred volunteer-recruits.

The hearts of the Constitutionalists were enlivened by this success; for while the male inhabitants of the district through which they passed hastened to join them, the women put up audible prayers to heaven to prosper their glorious enterprise.

Ossore was in the province of Abrantani, which had for nearly a year groaned under the tyranny of the Captain-General, who governed his district by martial law, the jurisdiction of the civil tribunals having been superseded by the odious despotism of military courts. The Constitutionalists, therefore, entertained the strongest hopes that Ossore would pronounce in their favour the moment they appeared beneath its walls.

The Constitutionalists were now only three miles from Ossore, which was hidden from their view by a high hill, up the acclivity of which the two columns were marching, when the quick ear of General Grachia suddenly caught the sound of horses' feet on the opposite side of the eminence.

Turning to one of his *aides-de-camp*, he said, "Hasten to Colonel Morosino—tell him to take that road to the left and possess himself of yonder grove. Our landing is known—a body of cavalry is approaching."

These words were delivered in a rapid but firm tone. The *aide-de-camp* galloped away to execute the order; and General Grachia proceeded to address a few brief but impressive words to the patriots of his division, telling them that the moment to strike a blow was now at hand.

"Markham," said the General, when he had concluded his harangue, "we shall have hot work in a few minutes."

Scarcely were these words uttered, when a large body of cavalry made its appearance on the summit of the hill. A general officer, surrounded by a brilliant staff, was at their head.

"That is Count Santa-Croce, the Captain-General of Abrantani!" exclaimed Grachia, drawing his sword. "Parley with him were vain—he is devoted to the Grand Duke. My friends, before us lies death or victory!"

The Constitutionalists gave a deafening cheer in answer to the words of their commander.

Then, like an avalanche bursting from its rest on the Alpine height, and rolling with dread and deafening din in its precipitate path, the ducal cavalry thundered down the hill.

But they were well received; and a terrific contest ensued.

The ear was deafened with the report of musketry and the clang of weapons. Bullets whistled through the air; and as the serried ranks on either side poured forth volumes of smoke,—the Constitutionalists with their muskets, and the cavalry with their carbines,—the shouts of the combatants and the groans of the dying announced the desperate nature of the conflict.

But, alas! the Constitutionalists were doomed to experience a sad blow!

General Grachia,—a patriot whose memory demands our admiration and respect,—was slain at the commencement of the battle. He died, fighting gallantly at the head of his troops; and not before the enemy had felt the weight of his valiant arm.

Almost at the same moment the ensign who bore the Constitutional banner was struck to the earth; and an officer of the ducal cavalry seized the standard.

But scarcely had he grasped it, when Richard Markham, who had vainly endeavoured to protect his chief and friend from the weapons of the enemy, spurred his steed with irresistible fury against the officer, hurled him from his seat, and snatched the banner from his grasp.

Then, waving the flag above his head with his left hand, and wielding his sword in the right, Richard plunged into the thickest of the fight, exclaiming, "Vengeance for the death of our general!"

The moment that Grachia fell, a sudden panic seized upon the Constitutionalists of his division; and they were already retreating, when that gallant exploit on the part of Markham rallied them with galvanic effect.

"Vengeance for the death of our general!" was the cry; and our hero was instantly backed by his faithful Morcar and a whole host of Constitutionalists.

The conflict was desperate—both sides fighting as if all idea of quarter were out of the question, and victory or death were the only alternatives.

Fired by the loss of General Grachia,—conscious of the desperate position in which defeat would place the invaders,—and inspired by the image of Isabella, Richard fought with the fury of the Destroying Angel.

He who had only been looked upon as possessing an able head in administrative matters, now suddenly appeared in a new light,—a gallant warrior, who by his bravery had succeeded in rallying a panic-struck army.

Already were the ducal cavalry retreating;—already had the Captain-General, who surveyed the conflict from the summit of the hill, disappeared with his staff-officers on the opposite side;—already were the Constitutionalists of Richard's division shouting "Victory,"—when Colonel Morosino's corps, which had been engaged by another body of cavalry, was observed to be in full retreat—dispersing in disorder—flying before its triumphant foes.

The rumour that Colonel Morosino himself was slain, and that a strong body of infantry, provided with cannon, was already advancing from the opposite side of the hill, now spread like wild-fire through the ranks of Richard's division.

Vainly did Markham endeavour by his example to inspire the troops with courage. A panic seized upon them: they exclaimed that some villain had betrayed them; and the disorder became general.

The ducal cavalry which were so lately in full retreat, rallied again: their charge was irresistible; they literally swept the slope of the hill down which they rushed.

Backed by a small but gallant band that scorned to retreat, and well seconded by Morcar, Richard fought with a desperation which was truly marvellous in one who had never wielded a hostile brand until that day. But a pistol-bullet disabled his right arm; and he was taken prisoner, together with Morcar and several others.

The Constitutionalists were completely defeated; five hundred fell upon the field of battle; the remainder were dispersed or captured. But scarcely three hundred succeeded in saving themselves by flight.

And almost at the same moment when this unfortunate expedition was thus overwhelmed with ruin, a Castelcicalan frigate, which had put out from Ossore harbour, shortly after the landing of the Constitutionalists, captured the three vessels which were the last hope of those patriots who had escaped from captivity or carnage.

From the summit of the hill, whither he was conducted into the presence of the Captain-General of Abrantani, Richard beheld the three vessels strike their colours to the Castelcicalan man-of-war.

"Treachery has been at work here," he said within himself; "or else how arose these preparations to receive us?"

He was not, however, permitted much time for reflection—either in respect to his own desperate condition, or that of the unfortunate fugitives whose last hope was thus cut off by the seizure of the ships; for the Captain-General—an old man, with white hair, but a stern and forbidding countenance,—addressed him in a haughty and savage tone.

"Know you the penalty that awaits your crime, young man?" he exclaimed; "for in you I doubtless behold one of the chiefs of this monstrous invasion."

"I know how to die," answered Richard, fearlessly.

"Ah!" ejaculated the Captain-General. "What traitor have we here? Some foreign mercenary perhaps. He is not a Castelcicalan, by the accent with which he speaks our native tongue."

"I am an Englishman, my lord," said Markham, returning the proud glance of defiance and scorn which Count Santa-Croce threw upon him.

"An Englishman!" thundered the Captain-General. "Then is a military death too good for you! What brings a wretched foreigner like you amongst us with a hostile sword? You have not even the miserable subterfuge of patriotism as a palliation for your crime. Away with him! Hang him to yonder tree!"

"I have one favour to implore of your lordship," said Markham, his voice faltering not, although his cheek grew somewhat pale: "I am prepared for death—but let me not perish like a dog. Plant your soldiers at a distance of a dozen paces—let them level their muskets at me—and I promise you I shall not die a coward."

"No—you are a foreigner!" returned the Captain-General ferociously. "Away with him!"

Markham was instantly surrounded by soldiers, and dragged to the foot of a tree at a little distance.

An *aide-de-camp* of the Count was ordered to superintend the sad ceremony.

"Have you any thing which you desire to be communicated to your friends in your native country?" asked the officer, who was a generous-minded young man, and who, having beheld Richard's bravery in the conflict, could not help respecting him.

"I thank you sincerely for the kindness which prompts this question," replied our hero; "and all I have now to hope is that those who know me—in my native land—may not think that cowardice or dishonour closed the career of Richard Markham."

"Richard Markham!" ejaculated the officer. "Tell me—is that your name?"

"It is," answered our hero.

"Then there is hope for you *yet*, brave Englishman!" cried the officer; and without uttering another word, he hastened back to the spot where the Captain-General of Abrantani was standing.

Were we to say that Richard was now otherwise than a prey to the most profound suspense, we should be exaggerating the moral strength of human nature.

We have no wish to make of our hero a demigod: we allow him to be nothing more than mortal after all!

It *was*, therefore, with no little anxiety that Markham saw the officer approach the Captain-General of Abrantani, and discourse with him for some moments in a low tone. The *aide-de-camp* appeared to urge some point which he was anxious to carry: Count Santa-Croce shook his head ominously.

"Beloved Isabella," murmured Richard to himself: "shall I never see thee more?"

His eyes were still fixed upon those two men who appeared to be arguing his life or death.

At length the Captain-General took a paper from the breast of his profusely-laced blue uniform coat, and cast his eyes over it.

Richard watched him with breathless anxiety.

This state of suspense did not last long. Count Santa-Croce folded the paper, replaced it where he had taken it from, and then gave a brief command to the officer.

The latter hurried back to the spot where Markham was hovering as it were between life and death.

"You are saved, sir!" cried the Castelcicalan his countenance expressing the most unfeigned joy.

"Generous friend!" exclaimed Richard: "by what strange influence have you worked this miracle?"

"That must remain a secret," answered the *aide-de-camp*. "At the same time I can take but little merit to myself in the transaction—beyond a mere effort of memory. You have powerful friends, sir, in Castelcicala: otherwise his lordship the Captain-General," he added in a whisper, "was not the man to spare you."

"To you I proffer my most heart-felt thanks, generous Italian!" cried Richard; "for to you I am clearly indebted for my life. Let me know the name of my saviour?"

"Mario Bazzano—junior *aide-de-camp* to Count Santa-Croce, the Captain-General of Abrantani," was the answer. "But we have no time to parley," he continued rapidly: "the good news which I have already imparted to you in respect to your life, must be somewhat counterbalanced by the commands which I have received regarding your liberty."

"Speak, Signor Bazzano," said Markham. "You saw that I did not flinch from death: it is scarcely probable that I shall tremble at any less severe sentence which may have been passed upon me."

"My orders are to conduct you to Montoni, where you will be placed at the disposal of a higher authority than even the Captain-General of Abrantani," returned the *aide-de-camp*. "But, in the first place, my lord's surgeon shall look to your wound."

Then once more did the generous-hearted Castelcicalan hasten away; and in a few minutes he returned, accompanied by the Count's own medical attendant.

Richard's arm was examined; and it was discovered that a bullet had passed through the fleshy part between the elbow and the shoulder. The wound was painful, though by no means dangerous; and the surgeon bandaged it with care and skill.

"Now, Signor Markham," said Bazzano, "it is my duty to conduct you to Montoni. I do not wish to drag you thither like a felon—because you are a brave man: at the same time I am answerable to the Count and *to another* who is higher than the Count, for your person. Gallant warriors are usually honourable men: pledge me your honour that you will not attempt to escape; and we will proceed to Montoni alone together."

"I pledge you my honour," answered Richard, "that so long as I am in your custody, I will not attempt to escape. But the moment you are released from your charge of my person, my vow ceases."

"Agreed, signor," said Bazzano.

The *aide-de-camp* then ordered his own and another horse (for Richard's steed had been sorely wounded in the conflict) to be brought to the spot where this conversation took place.

"Signor Bazzano," said Richard, "you have behaved to me in so noble and generous a manner that I am emboldened to ask another favour of you. A young man accompanied me as my attendant in this unfortunate enterprise: he has a wife and child in his native land; his parents are also living. Should aught happen to him, four others would thereby be plunged into the depths of misery."

"Where is this person to whom you allude?" inquired Bazzano.

"He is a prisoner yonder. There—he is seated on the ground, with his face buried in his hands!"

And Richard pointed in the direction where the poor gipsy was plunged into a painful and profound reverie at a little distance.

For the third time the *aide-de-camp*,—who was a tall, active, handsome, dark-eyed young man,—hurried away. Count Santa-Croce had mounted his horse and repaired, with his staff, to view more closely the spot where the conflict had taken place, and to issue orders relative to the interment of the killed and the disposal of the prisoners. Mario Bazzano did not therefore dread the eagle glance of his superior, as he hastened to perform another generous deed and confer another favour on Richard Markham.

"Young man," he said, addressing himself to Morcar, "rise and follow me. You are to accompany your master. My good friend," he added, speaking to the sentinel who stood near, "I will be answerable for my conduct in this instance to his lordship the Captain-General."

The sentinel was satisfied; and Morcar followed the officer to the spot where Richard and the Castelcicalan soldiers who had charge of him, were standing.

A third horse was procured; and in a few minutes the *aide-de-camp*, our hero, and Morcar rode rapidly away from the scene of carnage, towards Ossore.

It were a vain task to attempt to describe the joy which succeeded Morcar's grief and apprehension, when he discovered that his own and his master's lives were beyond danger, and that Mario Bazzano was evidently so well inclined to befriend them.

"As I do not wish to keep you in an unpleasant state of suspense, signor," said the *aide-de-camp* to Richard, "I must inform you that you have little to dread at Montoni. You have powerful friends there. A short imprisonment—or some punishment of a slight nature, will be all the penalty you will both have to pay for your mad freak—or else I am much mistaken. But more I dare not—cannot say."

"Whatever be our fate," exclaimed Richard, "my heart will cherish until death the remembrance—the grateful remembrance of your noble conduct. But tell me, my generous friend—what will become of those unfortunate prisoners?"

"The chiefs of the enterprise have fallen in the conflict," answered Mario; "else the fate of traitors would have been in store for them. As for the mistaken men whom they have led to these shores, imprisonment—a long imprisonment in the citadels of Abrantani, Pinalla, and Estella, will doubtless be the penalty of their treason."

The severe terms in which the young *aide-de-camp*, who was evidently devoted to the Grand Duke's cause, spoke of the Constitutionalists, pierced like a dagger to the heart of our hero; but delicacy and gratitude towards one from whom he had received such signal obligations, prevented him from making any comment.

In a short time the little party reached Ossore, at which town they proceeded to an hotel, where they obtained refreshments. There, also, plain clothes were procured for Markham, in order that his uniform (which was different from that of the Castelcicalan officer) might not create unpleasant notice on his arrival at Montoni. Morcar had no uniform to change.

When the repast was terminated, Lieutenant Bazzano ordered a post-chaise and four; and in a short time the little party was whirling rapidly along the high road to the capital.

During the journey Richard and the *aide-de-camp* rose higher in each other's esteem, the more they conversed together; and by the time they reached their destination, a sort of friendship, which circumstances had tended to invest with unusual interest, already existed between them.

Bazzano assured our hero that the contemplated invasion of the Constitutionalists had been communicated some time previously to the Captain-General of Abrantani; but whence that information had emanated the young officer was unable to state. Preparations had, however, been in existence for at least a fortnight to receive the invaders when they set foot on the Castelcicalan territory. These assurances confirmed Richard in the opinion which he had already formed, that treachery had existed somewhere on the side of the patriots.

CHAPTER CLXXV.

MONTONI.

It was nine o'clock at night when the post-chaise entered the capital of Castelcicala.

In spite of his unfortunate position,—a prisoner, defeated in his grand aims, and with all his hopes apparently blasted,—Richard could not help feeling a glow of pleasure when he thus found himself in the sovereign city which was the birth place of his well-beloved Isabella.

But, oh! in what a state did he now enter its walls!

Instead of accompanying a victorious army to proclaim Alberto Grand Duke of Castelcicala,—instead of the society of the patriotic Grachia and the heroic Morosino,—instead of hearing the welcome voices of a liberated people echoing around,—the young man was in the custody of a subaltern, and, for aught he knew, on his way to a dungeon!

Then—Grachia, Morosino, and the other chiefs of the enterprise—where were they?

Numbered with the dead—or captives in the hands of a savage conqueror!

Oh! how were Markham's fondest hopes blasted! how were his elysian dreams dissipated by the mocking reality of disaster and defeat!

Now, too, how much farther than ever was he removed from the sole object of his toils,—the only hope of his existence,—the hand of Isabella!

Her father, who had all along discountenanced the projects of the Constitutionalists, but who would naturally have pardoned them had they succeeded, could not for a moment be expected to forgive the survivors of that terrible defeat!

All these gloomy ideas annihilated in a moment the temporary glow of pleasure which our hero had experienced on entering Montoni.

The chaise traversed the southern part of the metropolis, crossed the Ferretti by a noble bridge, and entered the most fashionable and imposing quarter of that portion of the city which stands on the northern side of the river.

At length it stopped at an hotel.

"We shall alight here," said Mario Bazzano.

"But this is not a prison!" exclaimed Richard.

"I never told you that you were on your way to such a place," returned the *aide-de-camp*, laughing.

"Did you not hint at imprisonment, signor?" said our hero, surprised at the kind forbearance shown towards him—captured, as he had been, with arms in his hand against the reigning Prince.

"That may, or may not happen," replied Bazzano. "At all events, here we will alight: and, remember, while in my charge, you are on your parole. It is not necessary to let the gossips of this tavern know who you are, or why you are here with me."

"My honour is pledged, and the vow will be punctually fulfilled," said Markham.

They then descended from the vehicle, and were conducted to a private apartment in the hotel.

Bazzano ordered refreshments: then, as soon as he himself had drunk a glass of wine and eaten a mouthful of food, he left the room, simply observing, "I may be absent nearly an hour; but I will thank you not to retire to rest until my return."

Markham bowed an acquiescence with this request; and, as soon as the door had closed behind the *aide-de-camp*, he exclaimed, "If Signor Bazzano be a fair specimen of the Castelcicalans generally, they are a glorious race!"

"Some kind power seems to protect you in this country, Mr. Markham," observed Morcar.

"I candidly confess that I am at a loss to interpret these occurrences," returned our hero. "At the moment when the cord is round my neck, the mention of my name saves my life, and converts an enemy into a stanch friend. Even the ferocious Captain-General of Abrantani relaxes all his natural severity in my behalf. Then, instead of being chained, I am scarcely guarded: instead of being placed between two soldiers with loaded muskets, I am allowed to remain upon parole. He who has charge of me, leaves me for an hour, with a simple request not to retire to rest until his return! Yes—some secret power protects me. It is true that a few years ago I once met her who now occupies a seat on the Grand-ducal throne," he continued, rather musing to himself, than addressing his words to Morcar; "but she can scarcely remember—or, even if she do—could not be supposed to interest herself in one so obscure, so humble as I!"

Then he paced the room—lost in conjecture, and giving way to the immense variety of reflections which his position was calculated to engender.

In an hour the young *aide-de-camp* returned.

"Signor Markham," he said, "you will have the kindness to accompany me whither I shall conduct you. You," he added, addressing himself to Morcar, "must await our return here."

Richard signified his readiness to follow Bazzano; and they left the hotel together.

It was now past eleven o'clock; and, though the shops were all closed, the streets of Montoni were resplendent with the lustre which streamed from the windows of the *cafés*, *restaurants*, and club-houses.

Markham could not help observing to his companion that there appeared to be numerous patrols of military moving about in the capital, and that the sentinels were posted along the streets at very short intervals.

"The news of this morning's invasion reached Montoni several hours ago," answered the *aide-de-camp*; "and I do not disguise from you the fact that until this strong military demonstration was made, the city was in an extraordinary ferment. This I heard just now, previous to my return to the hotel."

"The reigning Grand Duke seems very unpopular," observed Markham.

Bazzano made no reply: it was evident that he could not contradict the assertion; and, being in his sovereign's service, he could not with propriety corroborate it.

A quarter of an hour's rapid walking brought our hero and the young officer to an immense square; and the magnificent buildings on two sides thereof shed a brilliant light from their ample casements.

"This is the ducal palace," said Mario.

Crossing the square, the officer led the way towards a small door in one of the angles of the immense edifice.

Mario knocked gently; and the door was immediately opened by a tall servant in a gorgeous livery.

Markham followed his companion into a small vestibule, brilliantly lighted, and at the end of which was a narrow staircase carpetted all over.

Not a word was spoken: the domestic bowed as the two young men passed him; and Bazzano led the way up the staircase, which was lighted by lamps held in the hands of marble statues placed in recesses.

On the landing which the visitors speedily reached, an usher, dressed in black, and wearing a massive gold chain, advanced to receive them; and, opening a door, conducted them into an ante-room, where he requested them to be seated.

He then opened another door on the opposite side from which they had entered the room, and disappeared for a few minutes.

On his return, he desired Markham to follow him.

Our hero obeyed, and was led through several magnificent apartments, all brilliantly lighted, but unoccupied at the moment.

At length the usher paused in a room smaller, but more elegantly furnished, than any of the preceding ones; and, having requested our hero to take a seat, he retired by the same door by which they had entered that room.

For a few minutes Richard remained alone with his reflections.

He was now in the Castelcicalan palace. But wherefore had he been brought thither? Was it to undergo an examination before the Grand Duke, relative to the invasion of the morning? was it to be overwhelmed with reproaches by that sovereign against whom, and without provocation, he had borne arms? Could treachery be meditated? No—that idea was absurd. He was so completely in the power of the Grand Duke, that there had been no need to exercise treachery towards him, if punishment were intended.

Then our hero thought of the Grand Duchess. Had she learnt that he was engaged in the expedition? had she remembered his name? was it through her he had received that treatment from Mario Bazzano which had so astonished him? could it be possible that she would interest herself in him?

He was in the midst of his reverie, when a door opposite to where he was sitting, suddenly opened; and a lady, elegantly attired, with a tiara of diamonds upon her brow, entered the apartment.

One glance was sufficient for Richard Markham!

He immediately recognised the beautiful woman whom he had seen five years previously, disguised in male attire, at Mrs. Arlington's lodgings, and whose singular history had subsequently reached his ears when he was imprisoned at the same time as herself, though of course not in the same department, in Newgate.

Yes—he recognised *her* who was once Eliza Sidney; and he now bent his head to the grand Duchess of Castelcicala.

Although somewhat pale, and showing a slightly deeper shade of that melancholy expression which her countenance had acquired during her captivity of two years, Eliza was still eminently lovely.

Her form had expanded into those proportions which indicated the maturity of her charms, but which gave to her beauty a voluptuousness that was only attempered by the chaste glances of her melting hazel eyes, and the halo of purity which dwelt on her lofty and spotless brow.

And well fitted was that pure and open forehead to be crowned with the glittering tiara which denoted her sovereign rank, and which set off to such exquisite advantage the large bands of her light, luxuriant, shining, chesnut hair!

Her walk was a dignified and yet harmonious motion;—her gesture expressed no particle of hauteur, but still denoted a consciousness of the respect which she felt to be due to her position as a Princess, and to her character as a woman.

"Resume your seat, Mr. Markham," she said in a sweet tone, and with a manner full of grace: then, placing herself on a sofa at a short distance, she added, "I have had the pleasure of seeing you before; but little did I *then* suppose that the next time we met, it would be under such circumstances as these."

"I comprehend your Serene Highness," answered Markham, firmly, but respectfully. "We meet—your Highness as a sovereign Princess, and I as a prisoner at the disposal of those who have power to command in this State."

"Such is indeed the fact, Mr. Markham," returned the Grand Duchess, with a half smile. "But I did not send for you hither to reproach you. Doubtless you considered yourself justified in the proceedings which you have adopted, and in joining the cause of those mistaken men who this morning set hostile feet upon these shores;—for I have received from an agent of mine in England assurances of your honourable nature and estimable character; and I did not fail some time since to issue those secret instructions to the various authorities, which saved your life this morning, and ensured you good treatment at the hands of those into whose power you were doomed to fall. Moreover, I learn that you behaved most gallantly in the conflict between your party and the ducal troops; and I can respect bravery, Mr. Markham, even in an enemy."

"Your Serene Highness will give me credit for the sincerity with which I express my gratitude for the kindness that I have received at your hands," said Markham; "especially under circumstances, which—whatever opinion I may entertain of them—could not have served me as a very favourable passport to the notice of your Highness."

"Mr. Markham," returned the Grand Duchess, "you are an Englishman—and that is one reason to induce me to exercise some leniency in your case; for however profoundly my interests may be identified with this country, it is impossible that I can forget my own. Secondly, I am better acquainted with your history than you imagine. Do you remember an anonymous letter which your late father received—some years ago,—yes—it was in 1831, I believe,—warning him of a burglarious attempt which was contemplated in respect to his abode?"

"I remember well the letter to which your Highness alludes," answered Markham, surprised at this mention of an incident which had occurred only a short time previously to the separation of himself and his brother on the hill-top.

"That letter was written by myself," said the Grand Duchess, with a smile.

"Written by your Highness!" ejaculated Markham, more and more amazed at what he heard.

"Yes, Mr. Markham," continued Eliza: "it was I who sent that warning. Circumstances enabled me to overhear the discourse of two miscreants in whose den I accidentally took refuge during a storm, and whence I narrowly escaped with my life. But enough of that: I merely mentioned the circumstance to show you that your name has long been familiar to me. Then, about four years after that event, I met you at the abode of a lady from whom I have since received signal kindnesses, and who is now the Countess of Warrington."

"I remember that evening well, your Highness," observed Richard.

"Afterwards," resumed the Grand Duchess, sinking her voice, "you and I were the inmates of a tenement whose severity you deserved perhaps much less than I—though heaven knows the artifice that was used to involve me in that desperate venture!"

"Your Serene Highness has heard, then, that I too was innocent of the crime laid to my charge?" said Markham.

"I imagined so when I first learnt the particulars of your case at the time of its occurrence," answered the Grand Duchess; "and my agent in England has lately confirmed me in that belief. Then, again," she added, with an arch smile, "I am not ignorant of the motives which induced you to embark, like a gallant cavalier, in the enterprise whose results have led to this interview."

"Your Serene Highness will not wrong, by injurious suspicions, an exiled family!" said Markham, well knowing to what Eliza alluded.

"No!" exclaimed the Grand Duchess, solemnly: "I am aware that Prince Alberto did not countenance the expedition; and I can scarcely believe that his charming daughter," she continued, archly smiling again, "could have been very ready to permit you to embark on so mad an enterprise. You see, Mr. Markham, that I am acquainted with more than you would have supposed me to know. And now, perhaps, you will be surprised, when I assure you that I entertain the most profound respect and esteem for Prince Alberto and his family—although I have never seen them. But, oh!" exclaimed Eliza, wiping away a tear, "how great was my grief when I learnt, this afternoon, that my friend General Grachia had fallen in the conflict of the morning!"

"General Grachia invariably spoke to me in the most pleasing terms of your Serene Highness," observed Richard.

"Do not think, Mr. Markham," said the Grand Duchess, after a pause, during which she seemed a prey to deep thought,—"do not think that I have been a party to all the instances of severity and sentences of exile which have lately characterised the political history of Castelcicala. No, Mr. Markham—I would not have you think unworthily of your fellow-countrywoman. But, enough of that! You can well imagine that I am not all-powerful here:—otherwise," she added, with a sigh, "it would be different! Time is, however, pressing; and I have not yet spoken to you on the matter which ought to form the principal topic of our conversation;—I mean your own position. You have heard enough from my lips to show you that you are not unknown to me, and that there are consequently reasons which have induced me to interest myself in your behalf. But, as I ere now observed, my power is not unlimited; and although my secret wishes are commands in the eyes of Count Santa-Croce and his officers, still my influence is not sufficient to protect you from the vengeance of the Grand Duke, did he know that *one* of the invaders was at large and unpunished in his dominions. It is true that I can soften his rigour—as I shall do in respect to those unhappy prisoners———"

"God be thanked that their condition excites the compassion of your Serene Highness!" exclaimed Markham fervently. "A weight is removed from my mind by this assurance!"

"Rest satisfied on that head," said Eliza. "I can promise you that imprisonment is the worst punishment which shall overtake any of them."

When Eliza had first entered the room, Richard had bowed his head low to the Grand Duchess; but now he sank on his bended knee in presence of the humane and tender-hearted woman.

Eliza felt the full force of this expression of feeling:—it rewarded her for her goodness!

She extended her hand towards him; and he respectfully touched it with his lips.

Then he rose, and resumed his seat.

Oh! at that moment, how sweet—how sweet to the amiable and noble-minded woman,—noble in nature, as well as in name,—was the possession of power;—and how amply recompensed was she for its humane use, by that spontaneous tribute of respect which she had just received from her fellow-countryman!

"Mr. Markham," she said, after a pause, "you must escape from Castelcicala: but that is not so easy a matter as you may haply imagine. The Castelcicalan steam-frigates will rigorously guard the coast by sea, and the custom-house officers by land; and not a ship will leave one of our ports without being searched. Orders to that effect have already been issued by the Minister of Marine; and I dare not interfere to prevent their full operation. Are you bold enough to strike far into the country, traverse its length, and obtain refuge in the Neapolitan kingdom?"

"And wherefore not in the Roman States, my lady?" asked Richard. "Their frontier is but a day's distance from Montoni."

"Because the Grand Duke has concluded a league, offensive and defensive, with the Pope; and you would assuredly be detected in the dominions of his Holiness, and sent ignominiously back to Montoni—in which case, Mr. Markham, I could not save you."

"And what chance of safety do I possess by following the plan suggested by your Serene Highness?"

"Every chance," was the decided reply. "In the first place, Signor Mario Bazzano will procure for you a passport: his uncle is Under-Secretary for the Interior. This passport, made out for you in a fictitious name, will be dated from Montoni; and the various authorities will never suspect that one of the invaders could possibly have obtained such a document from the capital itself. Secondly, you can purchase a portfolio with drawing materials, and pass yourself off for an English artist, sent to Castelcicala to design some of the most striking features of Italian scenery. By these means there will be an ostensible reason for avoiding the great cities and towns; and no suspicion will be excited by your keeping as much as possible to the open country. Does my plan please you?"

"How can I ever sufficiently express my gratitude to your Serene Highness for all this kind consideration—this unlooked-for generosity?" cried Markham.

"By abstaining from plans of invasion or insurrection in future," answered Eliza.

"Ah! how can I pledge myself to such a condition?" exclaimed Richard. "Should circumstances induce or compel Prince Alberto to strike a blow———"

"I fully comprehend you," interrupted the Grand Duchess. "In that case, I impose no conditions whatsoever upon you. Go, Mr. Markham—adopt the plan which I have suggested—and you will soon be beyond the reach of danger. And excuse me," she added, after a moment's pause, "if I act as your banker, as well as your adviser. Use this purse; and, on your arrival in England, you can liquidate the debt by affording succour to any needy Castelcicalan whom chance may throw in your way."

"Before I receive this new proof of your goodness—before I take my leave,—your Serene Highness must permit me, on my bended knee,"—and our hero sank to that posture as he spoke,—"to declare that, while I shall henceforth consider myself indebted to your Highness in an obligation which I can never repay,—while I shall ever hold myself ready to serve your Highness by day and night, and to dare every earthly danger in so doing—in order to evince my gratitude for all that your Highness has this day done for me,—still I would rather be delivered up to the hands of justice,—I would rather die on the scaffold to-morrow, or take my stand in front of a platoon,—than renounce—Englishman—foreigner though I be—the cause of Castelcicalan liberty!"

"Rise, headstrong—foolish young man," exclaimed the Grand Duchess, smiling. "I seek to impose no conditions upon you. Go; and when once you are beyond the Castelcicalan territory, use your own free will—let no shackle of any kind curb the ardour of your soul. At the same time, beware! On another occasion, I may seek to protect you in vain!"

"Never—never again, your Highness, will I wantonly aid in provoking civil strife in Castelcicala!" ejaculated Richard. "Two motives shall alone henceforth be powerful enough to induce me to unsheath the hostile weapon in this clime."

"And which are they?" asked Eliza, still half smiling as she spoke.

"In obedience to the command of Prince Alberto—and then only if *his* cause be just; or in order to relieve Castelcicala from some foreign invader."

"And may God grant that neither of those alternatives shall ever occur!" said the Grand Duchess. "But our interview has already lasted a long time; and delay is dangerous to you."

Eliza once more extended her hand towards our hero, who pressed it respectfully, but with fervour, to his lips.

He then withdrew.

In the adjoining apartment he found the usher waiting for him.

They retraced their steps to the ante-room, where Signor Mario Bazzano was seated, expecting their return.

In a few minutes our hero and the young *aide-de-camp* were on their way back to the hotel.

During the walk, Bazzano said, "I presume you have assented to the plan which her Highness has devised for your safe retreat into the Neapolitan territory?"

Markham replied in the affirmative.

"In that case I will procure passports for yourself and attendant, to-morrow morning," observed the young officer. "But, for the present, we all three stand in need of rest."

CHAPTER CLXXVI.

THE CLUB-HOUSE.

We must now transport our readers back to London.

At about the same time when the events of the two preceding chapters occurred in Castelcicala, others of a scarcely less interesting nature took place in the great metropolis of England.

It was about three o'clock in the afternoon of one of those dark, misty, dispiriting November days, when the sun is scarcely visible, and sinks early to rest, that half-a-dozen fashionable gentlemen were lounging in the bay-window of a Club-House in St. James's Street.

They were all dressed in the first style: gold chains festooned over waistcoats of the most recent Parisian fashion; and brilliantly polished boots, without a speck of mud upon them, showed that their owners had not arrived at the Club on foot.

"What news in the political world, Greenwood?" asked the Marquis of Holmesford.

"Nothing particular," answered the gentleman appealed to. "Our party is sure to drive the Whigs out next year; and then I shall show the independent and enlightened freemen of Rottenborough that they will acquire some honour through the medium of their representative."

"I suppose you will do a little good for yourself—eh, Greenwood?" asked the Honourable Augustus Smicksmack—a lieutenant in the Grenadier Guards, and just turned nineteen: "a baronetcy—eh, Greenwood? for that's the rumour, I believe?"

"Well, I *do* hope that Fame for once is not far wrong, my dear fellow," answered Mr. Greenwood.

"And I must beg of you to support my friend the Honourable Gively Starkeley's new Game Bill, which he intends to introduce next session," observed Lord Dunstable—a major in a crack regiment, and whose age was probably one-and-thirty.

"A new Game Bill!" ejaculated Mr. Greenwood, horror depicted on his countenance. "Surely your friend Starkeley cannot mean to relax the penalties which now exist in respect to poaching?"

"Quite the reverse," answered Lord Dunstable. "He thinks—as I think—that the present statute is not stringent enough; and he has drawn up a bill—at least, Rumrigg the barrister did for him—making it transportation for life to shoot game without a license, and transportation for fifteen years for looking at a bird or a hare with an unlawful purpose."

"*That Bill* will receive my most unqualified support, Dunstable," said Mr. Greenwood. "In fact, the laws cannot be too stringent against poachers."

"Certainly not," observed Colonel Cholmondeley, a gentleman of about three-and-thirty who was one of the group in the Club-House window. "For my part, I consider a murderer or a highwayman to be an estimable character in comparison with a poacher."

"Decidedly so," exclaimed Lord Dunstable. "A murderer kills his victim—a highwayman robs a person; and the thing is done. The individuals murdered or plundered alone suffer. But a poacher deprives hundreds of noblemen and gentlemen of their legitimate sport: he preys upon the aristocracy, as it were;—and, by God! I'll defend the privileges of the aristocracy with my life!"

"Oh! certainly—certainly," muttered the Marquis of Holmesford, who, in consequence of swollen gums, had been compelled to lay aside his false teeth for a few days, and was therefore somewhat incomprehensible in his speech. "Always defend the aristocracy! *The millions*, as they call themselves, are ever ready to assail us: they're jealous of us, you see—because we have carriages and horses, and they have not."

"And for many other reasons," observed Mr. Greenwood. "But I always know how to serve the scurvy riff-raff. Why, it was but the other day that some thirty or forty of the independent and intelligent electors of Rottenborough assembled together at the *Blue Lion* in their town, to address a remonstrance to me on my parliamentary conduct, and call upon me to resign."

"And what did you do?" asked Lord Dunstable.

"Oh! I knew my men well enough: it was not the first time they had taken this step," continued Greenwood. "My agent down there wrote me up an account of their intentions; and I sent him instructions how to act. The malcontents met; there was a great deal of speechifying; and the tide flowed strong against my interests. The chairman was about to put to the vote a Resolution condemnatory of my conduct, when the landlord entered, and addressed the meeting in this manner:—'Gentlemen, Mr. Greenwood, having heard that it was your intention to assemble here this evening, has conveyed to me his commands to serve up a little supper—poultry, turtle, venison, and other trifles of the same kind, together with as much port and sherry as you can drink. The supper is now ready, gentlemen: you had better partake of it first, and continue your deliberations afterwards.'"

"Capital—excellent!" exclaimed Lord Dunstable.

"Glowiouth—thuperfine—bwilliant!" cried Sir Cherry Bounce, who was one of the group.

"Strike me—but it was uncommon good!" observed Major Dapper, who was also present.

"Well—what followed?" demanded Colonel Cholmondeley.

"Yes, do tell us," said Mr. Smicksmack.

"Oh! the result was simple enough," continued Greenwood. "The free and independent electors of Rottenborough adjourned to the supper-room, gorged and drank till their senses were completely obfuscated, and then passed a vote of confidence in their Member, one gentleman alone not holding up his hand in its favour."

"What was the reason of that?" inquired the Marquis of Holmesford.

"Simply because he was dead drunk under the table," answered Greenwood. "And then this fellow had the impudence to write a letter next day to all the newspapers to say *that he alone had remained dissentient upon principle*!"

"Pwepotherouth!" loudly exclaimed Sir Cherry Bounce.

"Hold your tongue, Cherry," said Major Smilax Dapper. "You're a——"

"A what, Thmilackth?" asked the youthful baronet.

"A bore—strike me!" replied the major.

There was a general laugh at the expense of Sir Cherry Bounce, who coloured up to the very roots of his hair.

"What's become of Harborough, does any one know?" said Lord Dunstable, when the cachinnation was concluded.

"Gone into the country with his friend Chichester, I believe," replied Greenwood. "Harborough and I have not spoken for a long time; but I heard of him a little while ago."

"A dreadful thing that was about his wife," observed the Honourable Augustus Smicksmack.

"I don't think Harborough cared much about it," returned Greenwood. "They had long led a cat-and-dog kind of a life. The moment Lady Cecilia's suicide reached the ears of Sir Rupert, who was in France at the time, he came over to England, and sold the few things which had belonged to his wife—her trinkets, I mean; for the house in Tavistock Square was a ready-furnished one."

"And *that* he gave up, I believe?" said Dunstable.

"Or rather the landlord took it away from him," answered Greenwood. "That intimacy with Reginald Tracy was a bad business for Lady Cecilia," he continued. "But I had my suspicions of *him* before the exposure took place. The fact is, I saw him at a masquerade ball one night, at Drury Lane theatre."

"At a masquerade?" ejaculated Lord Dunstable.

"Yes. I was dressed as a Greek brigand, and he was attired as a monk."

"The sanctified scoundrel!" said Colonel Cholmondeley, in a tone of deep indignation. "What dishonour he brought upon the cloth! You know my brother the Archdeacon? Well, he's as jovial a fellow as you could wish to meet. Keeps his three mistresses, his horses and hounds, and goes to bed mellow every night of his life. But *he* does things discreetly."

"In a proper manner, to be sure," muttered the Marquis of Holmesford. "But, by the by, Greenwood, you once admired my beautiful Georgian."

"And I often think of her now, my lord," returned the Member of Parliament.

"I'll make you a proposal, if you like," continued the Marquis, grinning like an antiquated goat. "I have taken quite a fancy to your bay mare *Cleopatra*."

"Yes—'tis a beautiful bit of horse-flesh," remarked Greenwood.

"Well—my Georgian for your bay mare?" said the Marquis. "Is it a bargain?"

"A decided bargain," replied Greenwood.

"But how do you know that the lady will submit to the exchange?" asked Smicksmack, with a smile.

"I feel convinced that she will offer no objection," answered Greenwood. "It is true that every slave becomes free when once the foot touches the soil of this country, as I once observed to the independent electors of Rottenborough;—but I am sure that she will wear the gold chain that I shall be delighted to throw around her."

"Well spoken, Greenwood!" cried the Marquis. "Send the bay to my stables in the morning; and fetch away the Georgian when you choose."

"Greenwood's the man for business," observed Lord Dunstable. "By the by, how did the African Railroad scheme turn out?"

"Oh! admirably," replied the capitalist. "I cleared my ten thousand by it: so did the Marquis."

"But I lotht thwee thouthand, though—and a pwethiouth wage I wath in," said Sir Cherry.

"Because you kept your shares too long, my dear fellow," remarked Greenwood coolly. "No, my good woman—I have nothing for you!"

These last words were uttered, in a loud tone, and accompanied by a stern shake of the head, to a poor, ragged, shivering creature, who had paused on the pavement outside to solicit alms from the aristocrats assembled at the window.

The miserable woman cast one glance of ineffable anguish on Mr. Greenwood, and then hurried away, overwhelmed by the savage determination of his refusal.

"That poor wretch has been good-looking in her time," said Mr. Smicksmack. "Although it is nearly dark, I caught sight of her countenance by the light of the lamp."

"And so did I," whispered Lord Dunstable to Colonel Cholmondeley, whom he drew aside. "Do you know who that was?" he asked in a low and somewhat hoarse tone.

"No: how the devil should I?" said the Captain, also sinking his voice—but simply because Dunstable did so.

"If that poor mendicant were not Lydia Hutchinson," returned the young nobleman, "I never was more mistaken in my life. But, my God! how altered!"

And for a few moments his countenance became inexpressibly sad.

"What nonsense to give way to feelings of that kind!" whispered Cholmondeley.

"But she was once so beautiful!" said Dunstable. "Do you remember the first time we ever met her—in Hyde Park———"

"I was thinking a deuced deal too much about Adeline Enfield, at that time, to bother myself about Lydia What-'s-her-name," interrupted the colonel, impatiently. "Come—it's of no use yielding to maudlin feelings of that kind, Dunstable. We are all going to dine together presently: and if you wear that kill-joy countenance, I shall wish you at the devil."

Then the Captain drew the young nobleman back to the group in the window; and in a few minutes the sprightly nature of the conversation banished from Dunstable's mind the unpleasant reminiscences which had been temporarily excited by the sudden appearance of one whom he knew so well!

In the meantime that miserable female pursued her way down St. James's Street.

The weather was cold—dreadfully cold: the streets were damp—and she had neither shoes nor stockings!

An old cotton gown, a wretched rag of a shawl, and a broken straw bonnet, constituted her sole attire.

Not an article of clothing had she more than those enumerated.

She had parted with her under garments to obtain the means of subsistence; not even a petticoat had she beneath that thin cotton gown!

When she stopped for a moment to implore alms at the Club-window, it was the first time she had ever begged. She had not recognised *him* who had recognised her: but the stern countenance of Greenwood, as he refused her a single penny from his immense wealth, had struck her with despair.

If the rich would not assist her, how could she hope for succour from the poor?

She hurried down the street, weak and weary as she was;—but she hurried, with a sort of shuffling pace, because she was cold, and her feet were so benumbed that she could not feel that she had any!

She passed many a brilliantly lighted shop,—many a superb Club,—many a magnificent hotel, from the underground windows of which emanated the savoury steam of delicious viands:—she beheld cheerful fires, roaring up the chimneys of the kitchens whence those odours came;—but she was starving, shivering, dying, all the same!

A carriage, with arms emblazoned on the panels, and with horses whose beauty and appointments attracted the gaze of the passengers, was standing opposite to a splendid shawl-warehouse.

Just as the poor mendicant was passing, a tall footman, carrying a gold-headed cane in his hand, pushed her rudely back, exclaiming, "Don't you see that you're in the way?"

The shivering woman cast a timid look around, and beheld an elderly gentleman handing a lady, much younger than himself, to the carriage above mentioned.

The blaze of light from the shop window illuminated that portion of the street; and as the elegantly-dressed lady turned her countenance towards her companion, to answer some observation which he made to her, the mendicant caught a full view of her beautiful features.

A scream escaped from the beggar's lips: then, in the next moment, she rushed towards the door of the carriage, which the gentleman and lady were just entering.

"Miss Enfield—Adeline!" she exclaimed.

"What do you want, my good woman?" cried the voice of the nobleman—for such indeed he was.

"Miss Enfield—I—I am starving!" answered the beggar, clinging to the door.

"Do you know her, my dear?" asked the nobleman.

"I—I think she was once a teacher at the school, where———" faltered the beautiful lady, evidently by no means pleased at the recognition.

"Oh! a teacher!" cried the nobleman. "Ah! it is easy to see what she has come to:"—and he drew up the carriage window violently.

That was a signal for the coachman to whip his horses: the fiery animals sprang forward—the carriage moved off with a species of jerk—the poor starving, shivering creature was thrown upon the kerb-stone—and there she lay insensible.

In a moment she was surrounded by a crowd, that formed a circle about her, and stood gazing on the prostrate, motionless form as if the spectacle were very interesting, but by no means calculated to awaken compassionate sympathy.

Then a huge policeman elbowed his way through the crowd, crying "Move on here!" in a very savage tone, and crushing divers bonnets, besides upsetting sundry small boys in his endeavours to force a passage.

But at the same moment that he reached the spot where the poor creature was lying, a lady, about six-and-twenty years of age, and well though by no means showily dressed, pressed through the crowd, and immediately bestowed her attention on the mendicant female.

The lady raised the unfortunate being's head; and then, by the light of the lamp, it was discovered that she had received a wound on the temple, from which the blood was flowing freely.

"She must be conveyed to the hospital, if she's got any broken bones," said the policeman; "and to the workus if she hasn't."

"She shall go to neither," observed the lady firmly: "I will take care of her until she is recovered."

"What—do you know her, mum?" demanded the policeman.

"No—I never saw her before in my life, to my knowledge," answered the lady. "But I cannot help feeling for a fellow-creature—especially one of my own sex—in such a position."

A murmur of approbation arose amongst the crowd.

"Will you help me to convey the poor creature to the neighbouring surgeon's?" continued the lady, addressing herself to the officer. "See—she opens her eyes—she moves—but, my God! how wan, how thin, how cold she is!"

The wretched woman was removed to the adjacent establishment of a medical practitioner; and in a short time the benevolent lady had the satisfaction of ascertaining that the wound on the poor creature's forehead was the only injury which she had sustained by the fall.

"She is more in need of sustenance, madam, than medicine," said the surgeon, when he had bandaged the wound. "I will give her a glass of wine and a morsel of light food."

This humane proposal was immediately carried into effect;—the starving creature would have eaten ravenously; but the surgeon prudently checked her;—and in a short time she was considerably revived.

She appeared to be about seven or eight and twenty years of age; and possessed the remains of great personal attractions. But her dark eyes were sunken, and their lustre was dimmed with privation: her cheeks were hollow; and her form was little more than mere skin and bone.

The lady did not ask her if she had any friends, or any home. Such a question would have been a superfluous mockery of one whose appearance was sufficient to convey the sad tale of utter destitution and hopelessness.

"You shall come with me, my poor creature," whispered the lady, in a kind tone. "I know not who nor what you are; but I am touched to the very heart by your sorrowful condition."

"Ah! madam, if you knew all—" began the woman, bursting into tears; "if you knew———"

"I wish to know nothing now," interrupted the lady. "It is sufficient for me that you are in distress."

The surgeon's boy was despatched for a hackney-coach, into which the invalid was conveyed. The lady then entered it, and directed the driver to take them to her residence, which was in Cannon Street, City.

"I have known sorrow myself," said the lady, as they proceeded thither; "and, although, thank God! I have never experienced the stings of poverty, I have nevertheless been forced to endure afflictions almost as poignant."

"Ah! madam," returned the poor woman, "such a heart as yours never ought to be tutored in the ways of unhappiness. But, as you observe, there are other afflictions which may compare with the stings of want!"

And the unhappy creature wept bitterly.

The lady endeavoured to console her to the best of her ability; and even in the short conversation which passed between them during the ride from the West End to the City, the invalid gave proofs of a superior understanding and cultivated mind.

At length they reached Cannon Street, and stopped at a house, the lower portion of which was a stationer's shop. The lady occupied apartments on the first floor.

"Oh! Mrs. Chichester, how long you have been absent!" exclaimed the mistress of the house, who opened the door. "I really began to be alarmed—"

"Thanks for your kind consideration," interrupted Viola, with a smile—for the benevolent lady was none other than the neglected and persecuted wife of Mr. Chichester. "I have brought home a poor creature, whom I found insensible—dying—in the streets; and I request you to provide a room for her."

"Ah! my dear lady, what an excellent disposition you possess!" exclaimed the mistress of the house.

Then she bustled about to help the invalid up stairs; and the poor creature speedily experienced a feeling akin to happiness, when cheered by a comfortable fire and a good meal.

Mrs. Chichester also supplied her with warm clothes; and a night's rest made her an altered being.

On the following day she was enabled to narrate her history, which she did in the ensuing manner.

CHAPTER CLXXVII.

THE HISTORY OF AN UNFORTUNATE WOMAN.

"My name is Lydia Hutchinson. My father was the curate of a small village near Guildford; and fortune had frowned upon him with such continuous rancour from the moment he left the University where he graduated, that it was somewhat late in life ere he ventured to think of matrimony. After filling several different curacies, from which he was invariably removed at the deaths of the old incumbents and the arrival of the new ones, he seemed at length to settle down in the little village to which I have alluded. There he fell in love with the daughter of a half-pay officer as poor as himself; and, with only eighty pounds a year to depend upon, he embarked in the voyage of matrimony. A year after this union, a son was born, and christened by the name of Edgar: an interval of eighteen months elapsed, and I was ushered into the world. But my mother died in giving birth to me.

"To say that my brother and myself were the only consolation which my poor father now possessed, were merely to tell the common tale of parental love in the widowed breast. We were indeed his only consolation! Often and often has he told us this, when we were old enough to comprehend his meaning, and appreciate the full value of his kindness. He was an excellent man. In order to let his children be respectably dressed and maintain a decent appearance—especially at church on Sundays—he stinted himself of almost the common necessaries of life. He undertook my brother's education himself; and from his lips I also learnt the rudiments of the knowledge which I possess. There was resident in the village, a widow lady of great accomplishments, but reduced circumstances; and out of his pittance my father even contrived to spare something to procure her services in giving me lessons in music, drawing, embroidery, and French. Under her tuition I progressed rapidly in those branches; and, when I was sixteen, I was considered to be better educated than if I had been brought up at a boarding-school.

"Since I have mentioned that age, I will not weary you with any farther details concerning the earlier portion of my life. My brother Edgar had already obtained a situation as an usher in a school at Guildford, and my father, though loth to part with us both, was well aware of the necessity of placing us in positions which would, he hoped, enable us to earn our own bread. For of course his small income would cease at his death; and it had been impossible for him to save a single penny. He, however, anticipated that, when we were both provided for, he should be able to lay aside a few pounds during the remaining years of his life, so as not to leave his dearly-beloved children completely dependant on themselves at his decease. Under such circumstances he gladly availed himself of an opportunity of placing me as junior teacher in an extensive ladies' boarding-school at Kensington.

"My father brought me up to London, and left me at Mrs. Lambkin's establishment, which was called Belvidere House. He wept when he took leave of me; but as Mrs. Lambkin (who was a widow, about forty years of age) spoke very kindly, and promised to take great care of me, the sorrow of parting was somewhat mitigated on both sides. I was to receive no salary the first year; but if I suited, my remuneration was fixed at six pounds for the second year, to be increased subsequently.

"When my father took his leave, Mrs. Lambkin said, 'My dear sir, do not be grieved at parting from your daughter. She will find a mother in me. I will be all to her that her own maternal parent would be, were she alive. God bless her! she's a pretty, amiable looking girl; and I already love her!'—Then Mrs. Lambkin put her handkerchief to her eyes; and my poor father was deeply affected. Mrs. Lambkin proceeded to inform him that she had scarcely ever known a moment's happiness since poor dear Mr. Lambkin's death, which took place, she said, five years previously, and in a most distressing manner. 'In fact, Mr. Hutchinson,' she continued, 'Mr. Lambkin lost his valuable life when gallantly attempting to rescue an ill-used and most virtuous young woman from a brutal assault on the part of half-a-dozen intoxicated policemen.'—My father expressed great sorrow at this information. Mrs. Lambkin had wine and cake brought in; and at length my father took his leave, greatly comforted to think that I should have obtained a situation in the establishment of so kind-hearted and excellent a lady.

"Scarcely had my father left the door, when Mrs. Lambkin turned round towards me, and in a tone which I considered somewhat inconsistent with her former manner and language, exclaimed, 'Now, miss, dry those tears, and go up to your room to make yourself decent for afternoon school. The young ladies at Belvidere House all belong to the first families of distinction, and are accustomed to see the teachers well dressed.' Then, ringing the bell, she said to a smart servant who answered the summons, 'Jessica, show Miss Hutchinson to her room.' Jessica took a good long stare at me, then turning sharply round, told me to follow her. We proceeded up two handsome flights of stairs, beautifully, carpetted. On the second floor, the doors of several bed-rooms stood open; and I could not help admiring the comfort—nay, even the luxury, which their interior revealed to the hasty glance that I threw into them. 'These are the young ladies' rooms,' said Jessica abruptly: 'yours is higher up.' On the third floor I also observed the doors of several chambers standing open, and permitting glimpses of great neatness inside. 'These are *our* rooms,' said Jessica—alluding, as I afterwards discovered, to the servants' apartments. Up another flight we went; and now we reached the attics. 'These are the junior teachers' rooms,' cried Jessica, 'and this is yours,' she added, flinging open the door of a garret, wherein I perceived nothing save a mean-looking bed, one chair, a table with a wash-hand basin on it, a brown stone pitcher in a corner, and a glass as large as the palm of my hand hanging to a pin stuck in the wood-work of the window.

"I was about to offer some observation, thinking that Jessica had made a mistake in showing me to this garret; but I checked myself—being unwilling to commence my noviciate at Belvidere House with any thing in the shape of a complaint. 'Will you have the kindness to bring me up my trunk and bonnet-box?' said I, in as polite and meek a manner as possible.—Miss Jessica burst out laughing in my face. 'Well! that is a pretty thing, I don't think!' she exclaimed, tossing her head haughtily: 'an under teacher to ask an upper servant to bring up her trunk! Well—I never!'—'I am very sorry if I have offended you,' I said.—'If you really don't know better,' answered Jessica, looking at me attentively, 'I don't mind forgiving you this time. And I'll do more, too, for I'll tell the scullery girl to help you up with your things; but of course even *she* wouldn't do it alone.'—My heart rose into my mouth; and it was only by means of a desperate effort that I restrained my tears.—'Do the other teachers sleep on this floor?' I asked, more for the sake of concealing my emotions, than gratifying my curiosity.—'Miss Muddle, the head teacher,' replied Jessica, 'sleeps in the room of the first class young ladies: Miss Spinks, the second teacher, sleeps with the second class; Miss Pantile, the third teacher, with the third class; Miss Rhodes, Miss Jessop, and you occupy this part of the house. But I'll go and tell Betsy to help you up with your things.'

"Jessica walked away in the most stately manner, preceding me down stairs, and evidently considering me her inferior. Betsy was summoned; and with no small amount of grumbling, that dirty slattern condescended to hold one end of my trunk, while I carried the other. Scarcely had I dressed myself in my second best gown (I had but three)—when Jessica came up to say that Mrs. Lambkin was excessively angry at the length of time I took to make myself decent. Jessica herself was in a very bad humour at being obliged to mount four flights to convey this message, and told me in an insolent manner not to dawdle so again.

"Trembling, miserable, and unhappy, I went down to the school-room, where Mrs. Lambkin scolded me, before the other teachers and the young ladies, in no measured terms. Then, because I cried, she scolded me the more. At length she set me to teach four little girls, of ages varying from eight to ten. Miss Muddle, Miss Spinks, and Miss Pantile, all surveyed me with the most sovereign contempt: Miss Rhodes and Miss Jessop, who were not much older than myself (whereas the three senior teachers were all past thirty) looked at me in a more friendly manner. The ages of the boarders varied from eight to sixteen. They were all beautifully dressed; and some of the elder ones were very pretty. There were about forty young ladies altogether in the establishment.

"The four little girls whom I had to teach, were as stupid as they well could be, and so pert that I scarcely knew how to manage them. They laughed and giggled at every attempt which I made to instruct them. Sometimes Mrs. Lambkin would exclaim, 'Hutchinson, there's too much noise with your class;'—and when I spoke very low to my pupils, it was, 'Hutchinson, you're literally doing nothing there!' The three senior teachers were alone addressed by Mrs. Lambkin as *Miss*: with the three juniors it was plain *Rhodes*, *Jessop*, and *Hutchinson*.

"At tea-time, the three senior teachers sate near the mistress of the establishment, and had tea and thin bread-and-butter: the three junior teachers sate amongst the little girls, and had milk-and-water, and thick bread-and-butter. The same arrangement existed at breakfast. At dinner, the three junior teachers were expected to eat the cold meat; though none of the little girls were made to partake of it, and, as I once heard Jessica observe, 'such a thing as cold meat was never touched in the kitchen.' I only mention these trifling details to give you an idea of Mrs. Lambkin's fashionable academy. I may add that the junior teachers had to make their own beds, and fetch up their own water in the great stone pitchers.

"I soon found that Mrs. Lambkin was very far from being so amiable as she had appeared in the presence of my father—except of an evening, after about six or seven o'clock; and then she grew more cheerful—nay, jovial, and was very familiar with us all. But she was constantly leaving the room where we all sate, and remaining away for only a few minutes each time; but the oftener she went out in this strange manner, I noticed that the more good-humoured she grew.

"Thus some weeks passed away. One evening I had solicited permission to go out for a few minutes to take a letter to the post for my father (for the servants would do nothing to oblige the junior teachers), when one of the eldest boarders in the establishment (the Honourable Miss Adeline Enfield) accosted me in the passage, and, in a hasty whisper, said, 'Dear Miss Hutchinson, will you put this letter in the post for me?'—'Certainly,' I replied.—'You need not say a word about it, you know,' added Miss Enfield; and she glided away.—I did not think very seriously of the matter, knowing that it was against the rules of the establishment for the young ladies to write to their friends or parents without allowing Mrs. Lambkin to inspect their letters; and as I considered this to be a harsh regulation, I did not hesitate to oblige Miss Enfield—especially as she had addressed me in so kind a tone. I accordingly posted her letter, and thought no more of the subject. But the next time I was going out, Miss Enfield repeated her request, and again ran away ere I could reply. I noticed that this letter was addressed to the same person as the former one—namely, '*Captain Cholmondeley, Barracks, Knightsbridge*;'—but supposing that he might be a relative, I did not hesitate to post the epistle.

"That same night, after I had retired to my garret, the door was opened softly, and the Honourable Miss Enfield entered. She was in her night clothes; and, placing her finger on her lip to enjoin caution, she said, 'My dear Miss Hutchinson, you can do me such a favour, if you will?' '—Certainly I will, if I can,' was my answer.—'Oh! you can very easily,' continued the young lady, who, by-the-by, was a sweet pretty girl, and very interesting: 'a letter will come addressed to you, by the first post to-morrow morning.'—'Indeed!' I said; 'and how do you know that?'—'Because, though the envelope will be addressed to you, the letter inside will be for me,' she answered, laughing.—'And what would Mrs. Lambkin say if she knew it?' I asked.—'She cannot know it unless you tell her; and I am sure you will not do that, dear Miss Hutchinson,' returned the Honourable Miss Enfield.—'I will oblige you this time,' I said, after some consideration; 'but pray do not let this take place again.'—Then she kissed me so affectionately, I was really pleased to have made a friend of her; for I was so forlorn and unhappy in my situation—though I never let my father know how completely we had been deceived in Mrs. Lambkin's disposition.

"On the following morning the letter came: and when I could find an opportunity, I gave the contents (which was a small note carefully sealed) to Miss Enfield. She thanked me with a sweet smile. Three or four days afterwards, another letter came addressed to me, with another enclosure for Miss Enfield. I was determined not to give it to her during the day, because I could find no opportunity to speak to her unobserved. Accordingly, as I anticipated, she came up to my room in the evening, after we had all retired to rest. I then gave her the note, but with a firm and decided assurance that I would not be the intermediate of any further correspondence carried on in so secret a manner. She cried very bitterly at my resolve, and by means of some tale which it is not worth while to repeat, but which seemed to me satisfactory at the time, induced me to convey a letter to the post for her next day, and receive the answer in the usual manner. I foolishly allowed myself to be over-persuaded, and fulfilled her wishes in both respects. I must observe that her letter was addressed to the same person as the two preceding ones.

"She was very grateful to me for my kindness, and treated me with marked attention. Being the daughter of a noble house, her conduct towards me produced a pleasant effect in respect to the three senior teachers, who, seeing that Miss Enfield courted my society, began to treat me more as their equal than they had hitherto done. Mrs. Lambkin also grew less harsh towards me; and my position acquired some degree of comfort.

"One evening, after I had retired to my garret, Miss Enfield paid me another visit. She had another favour to ask me. 'The day after to-morrow,' she said, 'I shall have leave to go out for a little shopping. Will you accompany me?'—I replied that I should do so with much pleasure.—'Very well,' she said; 'leave me to manage it. I will ask Mrs. Lambkin to-morrow night, when she has been out of the room three or four times———.'—'I do not understand why you should choose that moment,' I said.—'Oh!' was the answer, 'when she has had her third or fourth glass, she can refuse me nothing; and she is sure to ask whom I will have of the teachers to accompany me.'—'Her third or fourth glass!' I exclaimed.—'Yes, to be sure,' returned Miss Enfield. 'What! I thought every one knew that she drinks like a fish; although she does do it on the sly. Her husband was a dreadful drunkard.'—'Indeed! I am sorry to hear this,' I observed. 'Moreover, I thought that her husband was a most respectable person.'—'Oh! I dare say Mrs. Lambkin has been telling you that nonsense about her husband's death,' said Miss Enfield, laughing. 'The truth is, he was coming home one night most terribly the worse for liquor, when he became involved in a dispute with a bad woman; and when the police interfered, he made a desperate assault upon them, and was killed by an unlucky blow with one of their bludgeons.'—'She told quite a different tale to my father,' I observed.—'Yes, because your father is a clergyman, and may recommend some boarders to her house,' returned Miss Enfield. 'Did she not also seem mighty civil and polite before him?'—I confessed that she did.—'And the moment his back was turned, did she not turn also?'—This I likewise admitted.—'She cannot keep her temper long, you see. But I must go now, for fear Miss Muddle should awake, and happen to find out that I have left my bed. Good night, dear Miss Hutchinson. The day after to-morrow we will go out shopping together.'

"Then the Honourable Miss Enfield withdrew, leaving me greatly astonished at what I had heard. I lay awake the greater part of the night, reflecting on all that she had told me; and when I thought of this young lady's rank, youth, beauty, and brilliant prospects, I felt sad at the idea that the purity of her soul had been in the least degree interfered with by tales of drunken men, bad women, and police-riots, as well as by the example of an intemperate school-mistress. Miss Enfield's communication had shed a new light upon my mind. The term '*bad woman*' set me thinking what it could mean; and at last I comprehended its signification. Oh! how I shuddered when that first consciousness of the real extent to which female frailty can reach, grew more and more defined in my imagination, until I understood its deep shade of guilt. The first step towards teaching the youthful mind to become infidel, is to suffer it to know that there live men, in Christian countries, who deny the truth of revealed religion:—the first step towards inducing a young girl to harbour impure thoughts, is to show her that female depravity has, in its worst sense, an indubitable existence!

"The Honourable Miss Enfield was as good as her word. She obtained permission to go out shopping, and also for me to accompany her. It was three o'clock, on a beautiful spring afternoon, when Miss Enfield and myself sallied forth together. 'The best shops lie in this direction,' I observed, pointing towards the left.—'Oh! no, my dear Miss Hutchinson,' she said, with a merry laugh: 'the spot that will suit me is in *this* direction;'—and she took the road to London. I made no objection; my duty was to accompany her for the sake of appearances—not precisely to take care of her, because, although eight months younger than I, she was as tall and as matured in form as myself. Indeed she was very precocious, but, as I have before said, very pretty.

"We passed by several linen-drapers' shops; but the Honourable Miss Enfield entered none of them. At length we reached Hyde Park. 'Do let us take a walk here, my dear Miss Hutchinson,' she exclaimed: 'see how beautiful the trees already seem; and what a freshness there is in the air!'—I assented; and we entered the Park. Presently Miss Enfield burst out into a joyous laugh. I inquired the reason; but she only looked archly at me, and renewed her merriment. Scarcely had I time to question her a second time concerning her joyousness, when she pressed my arm significantly; and I beheld two tall, fine-looking military men approaching. I cast my eyes downwards, for I perceived that they were looking attentively at us; but in a few moments I heard one of the officers exclaim, 'It *is* my dearest Adeline! I felt convinced that she would not disappoint me.'—'Not for worlds, Cholmondeley,' she replied;—and, in another moment, she had left me and was hanging on the officer's arm.—'Now, Dunstable, you do the amiable with Miss Hutchinson,' said Captain Cholmondeley to his companion;

and before I could recover from the stupefaction into which these proceedings threw me, I found myself arm-in-arm with a handsome young officer, whom I soon afterwards ascertained to be Lord Dunstable.

"For some time I walked on in profound silence, conscious that I was doing wrong, but unable to muster up the courage sufficient to withdraw from the false position in which Miss Enfield's intrigue had placed me. At length the gentle tones of a kind but manly voice penetrated through the chaos of ideas which agitated in my brain. 'Wherefore so silent, Miss Hutchinson?' said the young officer: 'does my boldness in constituting myself your companion offend you? If so, I will instantly release you from the unpleasant contact of my society.'—I made no answer, but burst into tears.—'By heaven! you are a sweet girl,' he continued; 'and I feel that I can love you sincerely. But dry those lovely eyes: there are persons about who may observe us.'—He was right: I wiped away the tears; and, after hazarding a few brief replies to his remarks, I insensibly fell into conversation with him. By degrees I lost the restraint and embarrassment which had at first possessed me; and ere I had been half an hour in his society, I laughed heartily at his lively sallies and sprightly observations. In the mean time Adeline was walking at a considerable distance in front, with the Honourable Captain Cholmondeley.

"Nearly two hours passed away in this manner; and then I insisted upon returning to Belvidere House. We accordingly overtook Miss Enfield and the Captain; and I signified my desire, observing that Mrs Lambkin would be angry did we remain absent much longer. 'We will not part with you, ladies,' said the Captain, 'unless you promise to lighten our darkness again with your presence ere we are all a week older.'—'This day week we could manage it again,' immediately observed Miss Enfield.—I murmured an objection.—'If you do not come, my dearest Miss Hutchinson,' whispered Lord Dunstable to me, 'I shall either hang or drown myself.'—I smiled; and Adeline, who was watching my countenance, cried, 'Oh! Lydia is such a dear good-natured creature, and we are such friends, I am sure she will not refuse.'—Again I smiled; and this was taken for an assent on my part. Then the two gentlemen looked round, and, perceiving no strangers near at the present, they bade us farewell in a most tender manner:—I mean that Captain Cholmondeley pressed Adeline in his arms, while Lord Dunstable literally glued his lips to mine. And I——Oh! my resistance was but feeble!

"Miss Enfield and myself then retraced our steps towards Belvidere House; but to save appearances, she purchased some articles at the first linen-draper's shop that we came to. 'Ah! Miss Adeline,' I said, as we proceeded homewards, 'what have we both been doing?'—'Enjoying ourselves very much, dear Lydia,' answered the young lady, laughing heartily. 'I am sure you ought not to complain, for you have made the conquest of a lord, handsome, and wealthy.'—'But what will he think of me?' I exclaimed.—'That you are a very pretty, amiable, delightful girl,' rejoined the Honourable Miss Enfield.—'And all this was planned on your part, Miss Adeline?' I said.—'Call me *Adeline* in future,' answered Miss Enfield; 'for now you and I are sworn friends. Yes; the whole matter was pre-arranged so far as my meeting with Cholmondeley was concerned; and as I told him in my last note that *you* would accompany me, he was too gallant not to engage a friend to take charge of you while he and I were conversing together.'—'Are you going to be, married to Captain Cholmondeley?' I inquired.—'He has promised to demand my hand of my parents the moment I leave school,' replied Adeline: then after a pause, she added, 'And if you play your cards well, you may become Lady Dunstable.'—This assurance electrified me: it filled me with new hopes, new visions, new aspirations. In a few moments I saw myself (in imagination) the wife of a Lord, my father a Bishop, through my husband's influence, and my brother a rich gentleman to whose addresses no heiress would turn a deaf ear!

"I could not sleep all that night! I considered my fortune already assured; and I declare most solemnly that I felt more delight, in the visions of prosperity and bliss which I conjured up, on account of my father and brother, than for the sake of myself. The week passed away: I did not oppose Miss Enfield's intimation to me that we should keep our appointment with the two officers; and, permission having been obtained as before, we sallied forth. Hyde Park was soon gained; and we were not kept waiting a moment by our *beaux*—for they were already at the place of meeting. They received us with evident delight; and as Lord Dunstable pressed my hand tenderly, my eyes met his—a deep blush suffused my countenance—and I felt that I already loved him.

"Adeline walked apart with the Captain: and I remained with Lord Dunstable. He spoke to me more freely, but not less respectfully, than on the former occasion. He assured me that he had thought of nothing, since we last met, save the prospect of seeing me again; and he forced from me an avowal that I too had not altogether forgotten him! We had been thus together for half an hour, when it began to rain. The Honourable Captain Cholmondeley and Adeline then turned and joined us. 'This rain is a great nuisance,' said the Captain: 'it is impossible to keep the ladies out in it; and it is equally impossible to part with them so soon.'—'What is to be done?' asked Lord Dunstable.—'My private residence is close by,' said the Captain; 'and if the ladies would take shelter there, until the rain is over, they shall be treated with as much respect as if they were at home.'—'Well, on that condition,' exclaimed Miss Enfield, 'we will assent.'—I was about to offer some remonstrance, when Lord Dunstable whispered a few tender words in my ear; and the objection died upon my lips.

"The Honourable Captain Cholmondeley's private dwelling was in the immediate vicinity of Sloane Street; and thither we repaired. A servant in livery opened the door: we were conducted into an elegantly furnished dining-room, and a cold collation was speedily served up. Champagne was poured out; and, not aware of its strength, I drank two glasses without much hesitation. The Captain told the servant to leave the room; and I remember that we laughed, and chatted, and ate, and drank as happily as if Adeline and myself were in no way tied to time. But presently my senses became obscured; my head swam round; and I was ready to fall from my seat. I have a faint idea of beholding Adeline sitting on the Captain's knee; and then I recollected no more, until I awoke in the morning!

"But, my God! to what did I awake? Oh! even now I shudder as I recall to mind my sentiments on that occasion! I was in bed—in a strange bed; and by my side was Lord Dunstable. Then I comprehended that my dishonour had been effected! I uttered a scream—a wild, terrific, appalling scream! Lord Dunstable caught me in his arms, and said all he could to soothe me. He pleaded the extent of his love, called heaven to witness that he looked upon me as his wife, and swore by all he held sacred to make me so in the eyes of the law as soon as he could complete certain arrangements necessary to such a change in his condition. He spoke with so much apparent sincerity, used so many arguments to convince me of his love, and expatiated so eloquently upon the happiness which we should enjoy when united, that my grief was absorbed in a wild delirium of bliss!

"Then came the sudden thought, '*What was to become of me in the meantime?*'—'You can return to Belvidere House,' answered Lord Dunstable: 'Miss Enfield will make it all right for you.'—'Return to Belvidere House!' I exclaimed: 'impossible!'—'Nay, it is very possible,' rejoined my lover: 'Adeline, who is an uncommonly sharp girl, arranged it all last evening before she left. She said that she should let herself into Belvidere House by the back way, and that she should proceed straight into the parlour, where she should assure Mrs. Lambkin that you, Lydia, had come home with such a dreadful headach, you were obliged to go straight up to bed.'—'That excuse will do for last night,' I said, wringing my hands in despair: 'but this morning?'—'All is arranged equally well,' answered my noble lover. 'It is only now six o'clock: you are to be in the neighbourhood of the school by half-past seven; Adeline will steal out and join you: then you can both walk boldly up to the door, enter, and say that you have been out together for a little stroll, in accordance with a permission to that effect which Adeline declared she would obtain from Mrs. Lambkin last night, when that respectable lady was in her cups.'— These stratagems produced a great relief to my mind, because I saw that they were entirely practicable. But, even in that moment of my agitated soul, I could not help reflecting upon the deep artifice which lurked in the bosom of so young a creature as the Honourable Miss Enfield.

"I rose and hastily dressed myself. Then I took leave of Lord Dunstable. He renewed all his protestations of sincerity, unalterable love, and honourable intentions; and we arranged a plan of correspondence and future meetings. I stole from the house, unperceived by any of the inmates, and proceeded at a rapid pace towards the school. But how changed was my soul—how altered were all my thoughts! I fancied that every one whom I met, read the history of my shame in my countenance! Then I consoled myself with Lord Dunstable's assurance that I was his wife in the sight of heaven, and soon should receive that hallowed name in the eyes of man.

"At a short distance from the school, I met Miss Enfield. I cast down my eyes, and blushed deeply. She laughed merrily. 'Oh! Adeline,' I exclaimed, 'to what has all this intriguing brought me?'—'My dear Lydia,' she returned, 'our positions in that respect are equal; and, as our lovers will keep their words and marry us, where is the harm?'—I stared at the young lady with the most profound astonishment. How were our positions equal in reference to our lovers? She speedily cleared up my doubts. 'If you continue to blush and turn pale alternately, twenty times in a minute, as you are now doing,' she said, 'we shall both be suspected. We must exercise the greatest caution; for if it were discovered that we surrendered ourselves to our lovers———.'—'*We!*' I repeated, contemplating her with increasing astonishment.—'My dear Lydia,' she continued, 'do you suppose that I was more virtuous than you, or the captain less tender than the nobleman? I certainly would not have accepted the invitation to visit Cholmondeley's private abode, if I had foreseen the consequences. But what is done cannot be undone; and we must make the best of it.'—I offered no reply: I saw that we were both completely at the mercy of those who had taken advantage of us,—that our positions were indeed equal in this one respect; and I fervently hoped that we might not live to rue the adventures of the last twelve hours!

"The Honourable Miss Enfield had so well arranged matters, that we entered the house without having excited the least suspicion of my absence throughout the night. And now commenced a new species of existence for me. My whole life suddenly appeared to be wrapped up in the promise which Lord Dunstable had given me to make me his wife. We corresponded often; and his letters to me invariably contained a note from the Honourable Captain Cholmondeley to Miss Enfield. A fortnight after the meeting which was so fatal to my honour, Adeline obtained permission for us to go out again; and we proceeded to Hyde Park, where our lovers joined us. An invitation to the Captain's private residence was again given; the weather was, however, fine—we could walk in the Park—and I positively refused. But Adeline and Cholmondeley disappeared for more than an hour! Dunstable was as kind and tender to me as I could wish: still he did not volunteer a single observation concerning our marriage; and, when I gently alluded to it, he declared that he was hastening his arrangements. Then he changed the conversation. At length the Captain and Adeline returned; and we parted with our lovers, promising to meet them again in a fortnight.

"The two weeks passed away: we met again; and on this occasion the invitation to Cholmondeley's house was renewed—insisted upon—and, alas! accepted. I will not dwell upon this portion of my narrative. Suffice it to say that Cholmondeley's residence was converted into the scene of unlawful pleasure and voluptuousness,—that Adeline with her lover in one room, and myself with Dunstable in another, entered upon a career of wantonness, which grew more insatiable as it progressed!

"Seven months had passed since the first meeting in Hyde Park; and Lord Dunstable never spoke of marriage—never started the subject of his own accord. I often questioned him on the point; and he invariably replied that his arrangements were not yet complete. At length the dream of hope and pleasure in which Adeline and myself had existed for half-a-year, was suddenly dissolved. Hastily-written letters were one morning received by us from our lovers, stating that they were about to proceed on a continental tour; that they had not leisure to meet us for the sake of taking leave; but that, on their return at the expiration of a few months, they should be delighted to renew the intimacy. Not a word of marriage in either letter!

"That night, at eleven o'clock, Adeline came to my garret. I was reduced to despair; and could offer her no consolation, although she needed it even more—oh! far more than I. The moment she found herself alone with me, she gave way to a paroxysm of grief—a convulsion of anguish, which alarmed me. I implored her to restrain her emotions, or we should be overheard. She sank upon my bed; and I soon perceived that she was enduring great bodily pain in addition to deep mental affliction. An idea of the terrible truth flashed through my brain: she was in the agony of premature labour!

"I had not even suspected her condition until that moment. I was bewildered—I knew not what to do. At length I thought it advisable, at all hazards, to alarm the house, and procure medical attendance. But as I was rushing towards the door for that purpose, Adeline caught me by the hand; and, turning towards me her countenance—her ghastly pale countenance, with an expression of indescribable anguish and alarm, she said, 'For God's sake, remain with me! If another be made acquainted with my shame, I will not survive this disgrace.' I locked the door cautiously, and returned to the bed-side. And there—in a miserable garret, and in the depth of a cold winter's night,—with a nipping frost upon the window, and the bright moon high in the heavens,—there, attended only by myself, did the delicately-nurtured Adeline Enfield give birth to a male child. But the little infant's eyes never opened even for a moment upon this world: it was born dead!

"An hour afterwards Adeline dragged herself back to the room in which she slept. That was a fearful night for us both: it was for *me*—it must have been for *her*! I never closed my eyes: this terrible event weighed upon my soul like a crime. I felt as if I had been the accomplice in some awful deed of darkness. The cold and placid moon seemed to reproach me—as if its bright orb were heaven's own all-seeing eye!

"I could not endure that calm—unvarying—steadfast light, which appeared to be a glance immoveably fixed upon *me*. It drove me mad—it pierced my brain. That cloudless moon seemed to shine on none of earth's denizens, save myself. Methought that from its empyrean height it surveyed every nook, every crevice of my lonely garret; and at length so icy became its gaze, that I shuddered from head to foot—my teeth chattered—my limbs grew rigid. There was a deep conviction in my soul that the eye of God was upon me!

"I knelt down at last, and tried to pray. I called upon heaven—I called upon my father—I called upon my brother, to pardon me! Then once more I turned my eyes towards the moon; and its reproachful, chilling glance seemed to penetrate to the depths of my secret soul,—singling me, *me* out for its maddening scrutiny,—marking *me* alone, of all the human race, for its calm, but bitter contemplation.

"At length the orb of night was no longer visible from my window, although its silver flood still inundated the dwellings and the country of which my garret commanded a view. Then I grew more tranquil:—but I could not sleep!

"Never was morning more welcome to the guilty imagination haunted by the fearful apparitions of the night, than it was to me. I composed myself as well as I could; but when I surveyed my countenance in the glass, I was dismayed by its awful pallor—its haggardness—its care-worn look. I did not dare plead illness, as an excuse for keeping my chamber; because I was too anxious to ascertain what course Miss Enfield would pursue to escape those inquiries that her appearance, I felt convinced, must elicit. Besides, there was *something* in my box which—but of that no matter at present.

"I accordingly descended to the breakfast-room. The moment I entered, I cast a hurried glance around, and beheld Adeline seated in her usual place, chatting gaily with Miss Muddle, the senior teacher. We exchanged rapid and significant looks; and I moved in silence to my own chair. But I fully comprehended the indescribable efforts which Adeline was forced to make in order to prevent herself from sinking with exhaustion. Others noticed her extreme pallor, and spoke of the slight indisposition which she declared she experienced: but *I* saw how ill—how very ill, weak, and languid she really was. And I was pale and suffering too; and no one inquired what ailed me. This result of indifference on the part of all save Adeline,—and of prudence on *her* side,—was actually a great source of comfort to me; for had I been questioned, I know not how I should have replied. My confusion was extreme as it was; and yet I had much less to tremble for than Adeline.

"The breakfast was over; and we all repaired to the school-room. As we were proceeding thither, Miss Enfield drew me aside for a moment, and said in a hurried whisper, 'For heaven's sake, keep my secret, dearest Lydia: the honour of a noble family depends upon your prudence!'—I pressed her hand in acquiescence.—'I will ever be your friend, dearest Lydia,' she repeated.—Then we separated to take our respective places in the school.

"The usual routine was progressing in its monotonous and wearisome manner, when Jessica, the upper servant-maid, suddenly burst into the room, and, addressing Mrs. Lambkin, said, 'Ma'am, there's three silver tea-spoons missing; and as we've been quarrelling about it down stairs, I beg that all our boxes may be searched. Of course I don't mean the young ladies; or yet the *senior* teachers, ma'am.'—The loss of three silver spoons was sufficient to rouse Mrs. Lambkin's ire; and she vowed that Jessica's suggestion should be immediately acted upon. The boxes must be searched. I felt as if struck by a thunderbolt.

"Mrs. Lambkin summoned Miss Rhodes, Miss Jessop, and myself to accompany her. Then Adeline rose, and exclaimed, 'Surely, Mrs. Lambkin, you will not subject these three young ladies to the indignity of examining their trunks?'—'Yes, but I will though,' cried Mrs. Lambkin, her anger getting the better of her respect for the scion of aristocracy.—Adeline sank back in her seat: and never—never shall I forget the imploring, despairing, heart-rending glance which she darted upon me, as I followed the school-mistress from the room.

"The servants' boxes were all searched, one after the other; and no spoons were discovered. Then Miss Rhodes was subjected to the same degradation. When the scrutiny in respect to her trunk was concluded,—and, of course, without any success in respect to the lost articles,—she said, 'Madam, I beg to give you one month's warning that I intend to leave your establishment.'—'Oh! very well: just as you like,' returned Mrs. Lambkin.—Miss Jessop's room then passed through the ordeal. No spoons. 'Madam,' said Miss Jessop, 'I beg to give you one month's notice, according to the terms of our agreement. I know that my parents will not blame me, after this insult.'—'Very well, miss,' cried Mrs. Lambkin; 'you'll repent of leaving a good situation before you're six months older.' Then, turning towards me, she said, 'This won't prevent me from searching your boxes, miss; and I shall not die of grief if you give me notice also.'—'Such is not my intention, madam,' I replied, hoping that my submissiveness would plead in my favour, and prevent her from visiting my room.—'No; I should think not,' she retorted; and she walked straight away to the garret which I occupied.

"Miss Rhodes and Miss Jessop had gone down stairs; Jessica, Mrs. Lambkin, and myself were alone together. During the few minutes that intervened between the search in my small boxes and the visit to my large trunk, I revolved in my mind the only alternatives which a certain discovery that I now saw to be inevitable, would leave me: namely, to shield Miss Enfield by accusing myself; or to save myself by exposing her. Then I thought whether I really should save my own honour by this latter course; for, although my frailty had led to none such consequences as those which were connected with Adeline, nevertheless she might proclaim me to have been the paramour of Lord Dunstable. Moreover, I remembered her appealing, despairing look;—I called to mind all the promises of friendship and assistance which she had made me; I knew that she belonged to a noble, wealthy, and influential family; and I had such confidence in the generosity and grateful nature of her disposition, that I felt fully persuaded she would never abandon me.

"But, oh! I did not thus reason so calmly nor so deliberately as I am now speaking. My brain was a whirlwind—my soul was a chaos; and it was only with considerable mental effort, that I could separate and classify my ideas in the slightest degree. And now the school-mistress approached my trunk: she raised the lid—I leant against the wall for support. My clothes were tumbled out on the floor: at the bottom of the box was a small bundle, wrapped round with linen articles. The school-mistress drew it forth—a terrific scream escaped my lips—the corpse of the infant rolled upon the floor!

"Jessica gave vent to an exclamation of horror and alarm, and was rushing towards the door, when Mrs. Lambkin, recovering from the sudden shock which this spectacle had occasioned, held her back, saying, 'In the name of God be cautious; or my establishment will be ruined!' Then turning towards me, her lips quivering and white with rage, she said, in a low hollow tone, 'No wonder you are so pale and ill this morning! But must I look upon you as the murderess———.'—'Oh! no, no, madam,' I exclaimed, falling on my knees, and joining my hands together; 'that child was born dead. Listen to me, and I will tell you all; I will confess every thing!'—'There appears to be but little now to confess,' returned Mrs. Lambkin; 'and I have no time for idle conversation. The honour of my institution is seriously compromised: I will pay you the amount due to you, and you can leave my service this minute. It will be your fault if the real cause ever transpires.'—'Ah! madam,' I exclaimed, 'shall I not then be looked upon as the thief who stole your spoons?'—'No,' answered the school-mistress. 'I will declare in the presence of the entire establishment that my search has proved ineffectual in all quarters; and I will even allow you the merit of having left of your own accord, for the same reason which prompted Miss Rhodes and Miss Jessop to give me notice.' Mrs. Lambkin then turned towards Jessica, to whom she enjoined the strictest secrecy concerning the discovery of the dead child.

"At one moment, when on my knees before Mrs. Lambkin, I was about to confess the whole truth: but, now perceiving the turn which matters had taken, and that she herself was most solicitous to hush up the affair for the credit of her establishment, I saw that no exposure awaited me, and that I might save Adeline from disgrace and ruin without farther compromising myself. I accordingly intimated my readiness to leave on condition that the real motive should never transpire. Then I thrust my things back again into the trunk: but the corpse of the child, wrapped in linen, I left lying on the floor. 'Put every thing into the trunk—*that*, and all!' said Mrs. Lambkin.—'Not for worlds, madam,' I exclaimed, 'would I remove my effects elsewhere, with *that* amongst them!'—"Wretch!" she cried, 'would you have me dispose of your bastard's corpse for you?'—This insulting question brought the blood into my cheeks. Oh! it was too much to be thus reviled for a disgrace which did not really belong to me. Mrs. Lambkin saw how I was agitated, and, dreading a scene, she said in a low tone, 'You can remain here till to-morrow, Miss Hutchinson. If you choose to walk out this evening, *when it is dark*, you have my permission. But, in the meantime, you will have the kindness to keep your box carefully locked.'—I understood the hint, and bowed acquiescence.

"We descended to the school-room once more. The moment I entered I darted a glance towards Adeline which convinced her that *she* was saved. The one she gave in return was replete with gratitude. Oh! how much had I sacrificed, and how deeply had I suffered for her!

"The day passed slowly away. Fortunately the missing spoons were found in the evening: they had merely been mislaid by the cook or scullery-girl. I retired to my chamber at an earlier hour than usual: the presence of the school-mistress was irksome to me in the room below. In a short time Adeline came to me. She had stolen away to have an opportunity of conversing with me. Then I narrated to her all that had occurred in the morning. She threw herself upon my neck, and thanked me with tears in her eyes for having saved her from the depths of disgrace. She called me her 'sister'—her 'friend'—her 'dearest, dearest friend;' and vowed she would never forget the immense service which I had rendered her. Then I felt glad that I had acted as I had done. She even offered to go out, when the other inmates of the house had retired to rest, and dispose of the corpse of the child—her own child; but I knew that it would be death to one in her condition to venture abroad in the night-air. I accordingly undertook to perform that task also. We next conversed on my own prospects. I was averse to return home: I dreaded the numerous questions which my father and brother were certain to put to me. Adeline, who was an uncommonly worldly-minded girl for her age, instantly suggested that I should take a respectable lodging in London, and she would undertake to procure for me a situation as a nursery-governess. The Christmas holidays were at hand: she would be returning in the course of ten days to her parents' house in Belgrave Square; and she assured me that she should then have an opportunity of exercising her influence in my favour. To these proposals I assented; and she withdrew.

"When the house was quiet, I put on my bonnet and cloak, concealing beneath the latter the corpse of Miss Enfield's child. I then slipped out by the back way, and striking into the bye-lanes leading towards Brompton, at length reached a pond, into which a muddy ditch emptied itself. The moon was bright, and thus enabled me to discover a spot fitted for my purpose. I placed two or three large stones in the bundle containing the body of the child: then I threw the whole into the pond. The dark water splashed and gurgled; and in a few moments all was still once more.

"I now breathed more easily; but it was not without some difficulty that I found my way back to Belvidere House.

"On the following morning I took my leave of the inmates of that establishment. I received the money that was due to me; and I requested Mrs. Lambkin to allow me to leave my boxes until I should send for them in the evening. To this she assented; and I repaired by the omnibus to London. Miss Enfield had given me the necessary advice to guide me in searching for a lodging; and I engaged a room in the house of a respectable widow in Bury Street, St. James's. Her husband had been an upper servant in the family of Lord and Lady Rossville (Miss Enfield's parents); and, by using Adeline's name, I was immediately received with civility by the widow.

"I sent a porter for my boxes; and then my first care was to write a letter to my father. This I found to be no easy task. I recoiled from the idea of sending a tissue of falsehoods to that dear, confiding parent. Nevertheless, the duty was imperative. I accordingly concocted a letter, in which I informed him 'that having been grievously insulted by Mrs. Lambkin, I had left her service; but that I had met with a sincere friend in the Honourable Miss Adeline Enfield, one of the young ladies of the establishment, who had taken a great interest in me, and had not only promised to procure me a situation as a nursery-governess in a wealthy family, but had also recommended me, in the interval, to the care of a most respectable widow.' By return of post I received my father's answer. He regretted my precipitation in leaving Mrs. Lambkin until I had written to consult him; but admitted that the provocation in searching my boxes was grave. He expressed his entire confidence in my discretion, and declared his delight at the friendship I had formed with Miss Enfield. But he charged me to return home the moment I experienced the least difficulty in obtaining another situation. He concluded by stating that either he or Edgar would have repaired to London to see me; but that the expense was an almost insuperable barrier to such a step, their limited means being considered.

"Ten days elapsed; and then I knew that Miss Enfield must have returned home for the Christmas holidays. I accordingly expected an early visit from her. Nor was I mistaken. A magnificent equipage one afternoon drove up to the door; and Adeline stepped out. In a few moments she was seated in my little room. 'You see that I have not forgotten you, dear Lydia,' she exclaimed. 'I have told my mother, Lady Rossville, such a fine story about you,—how good and kind you always were to me, and how Mrs. Lambkin persecuted you without any reason,—that she has permitted me to visit you; and, more than *that*, she has recommended you to Lady Penfeather as a nursery-governess. There is Lady Penfeather's address; and you may call on her to-morrow afternoon. I have already said so much to her ladyship concerning you, and assured her of the respectability of yourself and family with such effect, that you will be received immediately.'—I cordially thanked Adeline for this goodness on her part; and she insisted so earnestly upon pressing on me a sum of money to enable me to improve my wardrobe, that I could not refuse her offer. She then embraced me, and took her leave.

"I will not dwell tediously on this portion of my narrative. On the following day I called upon Lady Penfeather, and was received very graciously. After some conversation, she engaged me at a salary of twenty guineas a-year; and I was to remove to her house immediately. She was an easy, affable, good-natured person—about thirty-six years of age, and not very handsome. Her husband, Sir Wentworth Penfeather, was three or four years older than herself, and was a fine, tall, good-looking man. They had three children, whose ages were between six and ten: the two eldest were girls, and the youngest a boy. These were to be my pupils. I hastened back to my lodging, and wrote a letter to my father informing him of my good luck. Then I settled with my kind landlady, and removed to Sir Wentworth Penfeather's residence in Cavendish Square.

"I was very well treated in this family. The servants were all civil and attentive to me; and the children were as ready to learn as children of such an age could possibly be. Sir Wentworth was very frequently in the apartment where I sate with them; and he was particularly kind in his manners toward me. He even laughed and joked, and conversed with me in a very friendly way. But in the presence of his wife, he was reserved, and never addressed a word to me. At length his attentions, when unperceived by Lady Penfeather, grew daily more significant; and he paid me many compliments on my beauty. I discouraged his familiarity as much as possible; but he soon grew more bold, and one day declared in plain terms that he adored me. I rose and left the room.

"Three months had now passed; and I had never seen Adeline since she called upon me at my lodging. I knew that she was not to return to Mrs. Lambkin's establishment, her education being completed (completed indeed!); and I felt hurt that she had not found a leisure moment either to call or write to me. I accordingly wrote a note requesting to see her. I was anxious to obtain another situation, and thus escape from Sir Wentworth Penfeather's importunities. On the following day Adeline called, and desired to see me alone. I was struck by her cold and distant manner. 'Miss Hutchinson,' she said, 'you must not be astonished at my conduct in not visiting you. You did me a great service: I have returned the obligation by procuring you a good situation. There are now no debts on either side. Our ways lie so totally different in the world, that were I to maintain an intimacy with you, my behaviour would be subject to the most annoying comments. We have both of us a deep interest in keeping each other's secrets. Were you, in a moment of anger against me, to state that it was my child that was discovered in *your* trunk, who would believe you? whereas, if you proclaim our respective amours with Captain Cholmondeley and Lord Dunstable, you publish your own shame at the time you denounce me. I am sorry to be compelled to speak thus to you; but I should have thought that your own good sense would have taught you the immeasurable distance which lies between you and me. Henceforth we are mere acquaintances, and nothing more.'

"With these words the honourable Adeline Enfield sailed out of the room, leaving me lost in astonishment—absolutely bewildered—at her behaviour. Then I felt for the first time the bitter ingratitude of the world, and I wept. Oh! I wept abundantly. My head had fallen forward on the table near which I was sitting; and I was giving way to my sorrow, when I heard Lady Penfeather's voice in the passage. She was saying, 'This way, my lord: I am sure you will be delighted to see the dear children. They are all so fond of your lordship! Really it is quite an age since we have seen you!'—'I have been on the continent with my friend Cholmondeley,' was the answer: but the voice in which it was delivered touched the tenderest chord in my heart. In another moment the door opened, and Lady Penfeather entered, followed by Lord Dunstable. 'This is the little school-room, you see, my lord,' she said; 'and this is my governess, Miss Hutchinson. But where are the children?'—'Miss Hutchinson!' exclaimed Lord Dunstable; 'Oh! we are old acquaintances: I have had the honour of meeting Miss Hutchinson before. I used to visit at her father's house, at—at—;' and he hesitated.—'At the Parsonage, near Guilford, my lord,' I instantly added, my courage reviving when I felt my hand tenderly pressed in his.—'Ah! to be sure,' he exclaimed; 'and how is my respectable friend, your father?' he continued, casting a significant look upon me.—I answered the query; and Lady Penfeather was quite satisfied with the manner in which Lord Dunstable's knowledge of me was accounted for. His lordship went on talking to me about Guilford, (which, I really believe, he had never seen in his life); and Lady Penfeather went herself into the next room to fetch the children.

"The moment her back was turned, Lord Dunstable said to me in a hurried whisper, 'Dearest Lydia, you look more beautiful than ever! I have never ceased to think of you since we last met. I have much to say to you: will you meet me to-morrow afternoon, somewhere? Say in the Pantheon, (it is not very far from hence) at three o'clock precisely?'—I murmured an affirmative; and at that moment Lady Penfeather returned, accompanied by the children. Lord Dunstable affected to admire them very highly; and the mother was quite charmed with his amiability. I could not help noticing how much his continental tour had improved him; indeed, I had never seen him looking so handsome before: my heart was once more filled with the fondest hopes;—for I really loved that man.

"When his lordship retired, he shook hands with me again, and we exchanged significant glances. The pleasure I experienced at this unexpected meeting, and the interest he manifested in my behalf, banished from my mind the disagreeable impression created by Adeline's unfeeling conduct towards me. Oh! how slowly passed the hours until the time of our appointment drew nigh! I was so completely my own mistress in Lady Penfeather's family, that I could go out when I chose; and thus I had no difficulty in repairing to the *rendez-vous*. Lord

Dunstable was there; and he advanced to meet me with pleasure depicted on his countenance. I took his arm, and we retired to the picture-gallery, where there happened to be but few loungers at the moment.

"He began by saying 'What must you have thought of my conduct in leaving England so abruptly?'—'It gave me very great pain,' I answered; 'and, after all your promises to me, I considered that I had reason to be both dissatisfied and unhappy.'—'Let me speak candidly to you,' he continued. 'I am so circumstanced, in consequence of being entirely dependent on my father, that marriage is for the present impossible. But I love you very sincerely, and absence has augmented my attachment. Are you happy where you are?'—I then candidly acquainted him with Sir Wentworth Penfeather's conduct towards me, and stated my determination to leave my present situation as soon as I could obtain another.—'Sir Wentworth,' continued Lord Dunstable, 'is the greatest scoundrel in respect to women, in London. If you do not yield to his wishes, he will slander you to his wife in private: and you will be turned away some fine morning without knowing why, and without a character.'—'Can he be so base?' I exclaimed, alarmed at this information.—'He is indeed,' replied Dunstable.

"Then, in a language so plausible—so earnest—so seductive, that I am unable to give you an idea of its speciousness, he proposed that I should at once place myself under his protection. At first I scorned the offer: he implored me to listen to him; he declared that he loved me to distraction, and that the moment his father was dead he would marry me. I wavered—he redoubled his entreaties, prayers; and at length he wrung from me a consent to his proposition! It was agreed that I should invent some excuse to quit Lady Penfeather in the course of the week; and Dunstable promised in the meantime to provide suitable apartments for me. Then we separated.

"But do not imagine that I did all this without a pang, when I thought of my poor father and my brother! Oh! no—I wept bitter, burning tears at my weakness, after I quitted my lover; and I resolved to recall my promise to accept his protection. In this better frame of mind I returned to Cavendish Square. The moment I entered, the servant who opened the door informed me that Lady Penfeather desired to speak to me. I proceeded to the drawing-room, where her ladyship was sitting. Sir Wentworth was also there. I immediately suspected that there was something wrong. Lady Penfeather said, in a cold and freezing tone, 'Miss Hutchinson, I have no farther need of your services. Here is the amount due to you, together with a quarter's salary in addition, as I have not given you a quarter's notice.'—'This is somewhat peremptory, madam,' I observed, when I could recover from this sudden and unexpected announcement.—'I should be even justified in turning you out of the house, without the quarter's salary, Miss,' retorted the lady: 'but I do not wish to behave too harshly to you; I would not, however, advise you to apply to me for a character.'—'My God!' I exclaimed; 'what have I done?'—'The levity of your conduct has been noticed by Sir Wentworth,' returned Lady Penfeather.—'Sir Wentworth!' I repeated, unable to believe my own ears; and then, in a moment, Lord Dunstable's words flashed to my memory.—'Yes, Miss Hutchinson,' continued Lady Penfeather; 'and as I recalled to mind the significant glances which you exchanged with Lord Dunstable yesterday, I deemed it my duty to have you watched this afternoon. Do you desire to know any more?'—'It is perfectly true that I have been with Lord Dunstable ere now,' I exclaimed, my blood boiling with indignation: 'but it is because I would not listen to the infamous proposals of your husband, madam, that I have been maligned, and am treated thus.'—Sir Wentworth started from his seat, livid with rage; and her ladyship ordered me to quit the room. I perceived that all attempts at explanation in respect to her husband's conduct were vain; and I accordingly obeyed this mandate.

"I now resolved to return straight home to my father. I accordingly repaired, with my baggage, in a hackney-coach to the *White Horse Cellar,* for the purpose of taking the first conveyance to Guilford. But my evil star interfered to prevent this prudential arrangement; for it happened that as I alighted at the coach-office in Piccadilly, Lord Dunstable was passing at the moment. I shrank back to avoid him; but he saw me, and was immediately by my side. I then told him all that had occurred at the Penfeathers', and acquainted him with my firm resolution to return home. Need I say how he implored me to abandon this determination? need I describe the earnestness with which he besought me not to make him miserable for life? His language was eloquent—he was handsome—I loved him—I was weak—and I consented to pass a few days with him ere I returned to my father.

"Alas! those few days were prolonged into a few weeks. I did not dare to write home: I fondly hoped that my father imagined me still to be in Lady Penfeather's establishment; and I felt convinced there was no chance of his coming to London so long as he entertained this impression. Lord Dunstable continued very kind to me. He had hired magnificent apartments for me in Jermyn Street, and allowed me a carriage, besides a handsome weekly allowance. He passed with me all the time he could spare from his regimental duties; but he never went abroad with me—except to a private box at the theatre on two or three occasions; and then he was so afraid of being seen by his relations, that I was quite miserable.

"Several times I made up mind to leave him and return home; for the remembrance of my beloved father and brother cut me to the quick. But how could I seek their presence,—I who was now polluted not merely through the treachery of my lover, but also through my own weakness! Nevertheless, day after day I resolved to abandon my present mode of life—retrace my steps to the home of my childhood—throw myself at my father's feet—confess all my errors—implore his blessing—and devote the remainder of my existence to penitence and virtue. Then my lover would make his appearance; and all my prudent designs would flit away as if they had never been.

"But one morning I was aroused from this dream of irresolution—vacillation—weakness—and crime. I was seated alone at breakfast, whiling away an hour with the newspaper. Suddenly my eyes fell upon an advertisement at the head of the second column of the first page. Oh! never shall I forget the agony of my feelings—the deep, deep anguish of my soul, as I read these words:—'*L. H., your father is at the point of death. Your afflicted brother implores you to return home. For God's sake, delay not; or it will be too late! All shall be forgiven and forgotten.*'—And in the corner was the name of my father's village!

"For an instant I felt as if I should go raving mad. My brain seemed actually to whirl. Oh! what a wretch did I conceive myself to be! Another moment, and I became all activity—hurrying the small preparations which were necessary for my departure. The terrible words, '*Delay not, or it will be too late!*' seemed fraught with an electric impulse. A post-chaise and four were immediately ordered: I took with me but a small parcel containing necessaries;—all the trinkets, all the jewels, all the valuables which Dunstable had given to me, I sealed up and left behind me. I moreover penned a hasty note to bid him farewell for ever!

"I lavished gold upon the postillions to induce them to spare not their horses. The chaise rushed along like the wind. God knows what were my feelings during the few hours which that terrible journey lasted. I cannot attempt to describe them. Oh! if indiscretion and crime have their enjoyments, they are also doomed to experience bitter—bitter penalties. And my punishment was now at hand. It was not so long since I had journeyed along that road with my father—when he first conducted me up to London. Then we had travelled by the coach, and not so rapidly as I was now retracing the same path. Then, too, I had marked many of the most prominent features on the road and in the adjacent country,—here a church—there a picturesque farm—a cottage—a mill—or a hamlet! As I was hurried along in the post-chaise, I looked ever and anon from the window; oh! there were the same objects I had before observed;—there they were, apparently unchanged;—but I—my God—was I the same?

"But it was as I drew nearer and nearer to the little village where I was born, that my eyes encountered a thousand objects which aroused feelings of the most acute anguish within me. There was a beautiful hill to the summit of which I had often climbed in my youthful days, accompanied by my brother. There was the stream which turned the huge wheel of the water-mill in the valley, and the path along whose banks was a favourite walk of my father's. The wheel was turning still: my eye could trace the path on the river's margin;—but the days of innocence, in which I had rambled there—a fond, loving, and confiding girl, hanging on my father's arm, or skipping playfully away from him to pluck the wild-flowers in the fields—those days of innocence, where were they? The chaise rolled on; and now the spire of the village church, peeping above the mighty yew-trees which surrounded the sacred temple, met my view. But, ah! what was that sound? The bell was speaking with its iron tongue: its well-known clang boomed over hill and valley. Merciful heavens! it was a knell! 'Oh! no—no,' I exclaimed aloud, clasping my hands together in bitter agony; 'it cannot be! God grant that it is not so!'

"And now the chaise rolled through the village: the humble inhabitants rushed to their doors—Ah! how many faces that I knew, were thrust forth to gaze at the equipage. I can picture to myself that when the condemned malefactor, on the morning of his death, is advancing towards the scaffold, he closes his eyes just at the moment when he feels that he has reached that point whence his glances might embrace all its hideous reality. Urged by a similar impulse, I covered my face with my hands the instant the chaise swept from the main-road towards the home of my childhood. I dared not glance in that direction!

"But in a few moments the vehicle stopped. The knell from the church-tower was still ringing in my ears: by an almost superhuman effort I withdrew my hands from my countenance, and cast a shuddering look towards the house. My terrible apprehensions were confirmed: the shutters were all closed; and I saw in a moment *that there was death in that abode!*

"From that instant all consciousness abandoned me for several hours. Indeed, it was not until the next morning that I awoke as it were from a hideous dream,—and yet awoke to find it all a fearful reality. I was in bed: my poor brother—pale and care-worn—was leaning over me. In a short time I learnt all. My father was indeed no more. He had breathed his last while I was yet on my way to implore his dying blessing. And he *had* left me his blessing—he did not curse me, although I had been the cause of his death! Nor did my brother reproach me: on the contrary, he whispered to me words of consolation, and even of hope! Poor father—beloved brother!

"But I cannot dwell upon this portion of my narrative: it rends my heart—lost, guilty, wretched as I am,—it rends my heart to recall those terrible events to mind! Suffice it to say that Lady Penfeather had written to my father, to state that she had been compelled to discharge me at a moment's notice '*in consequence of the levity of my behaviour,*' and she had added that, '*in spite of the excellent admonitions and example of herself and Sir Wentworth,*' she was afraid I had formed evil acquaintances. This letter was enough to induce a parent even less loving than my poor father, to hasten immediately to London, where he commenced a vigilant search after me. He traced me to the *White Horse Cellar*; and there, by dint of inquiry, he discovered that I had met a gentleman with whom I had gone away. He proceeded to Mrs. Lambkin, with the feeble hope that she might know something about me; and that lady told him sufficient (without, however, mentioning a word about the discovery of the dead infant in my box) to confirm his worst fears that I was indeed a lost and ruined creature! After passing several weeks in London in a vain and ineffectual search after his still dearly-beloved daughter, the poor old man had returned home, heart-broken—to die!

"And I gazed upon his cold clay—and I followed him to the grave which was hollowed for him near the walls of that church wherein for twenty years he had preached the ways of virtue—those ways which he himself had so steadily pursued. Oh! when the minister came to those solemn words '*Earth to earth, and ashes to ashes,*'—and when the cold clay rattled down upon the coffin-lid,—what feelings were mine! You may probably divine them; but the world has no language that can express them!

"Scarcely was my father consigned to his last home, when my brother demanded of me a full account of my late proceedings. He could not believe that one who had been reared with such care, and in whose soul such sublime moral lessons had been inculcated, could have erred willingly. He expressed his conviction that some infernal treachery had been practised towards me. I threw myself upon his breast: I wept—and I told him all,—all, as I have now related these particulars to you. On the following morning he had left home when I descended to the breakfast-table. His absence alarmed me sorely; I was full of vague and undefined apprehensions. Alas! how speedily were they confirmed! Four days afterwards I received a letter from a surgeon in London, breaking to me the fearful news '*that my brother had died of a wound received in a duel with a certain Lord Dunstable.*'—A certain Lord Dunstable;—as if I did not know him too well!

"Was I, then, the murderess of my poor father and my noble-hearted brother? If my hand had not struck a dagger into their hearts, my conduct had nevertheless hurried them to the grave. I hated—I abhorred myself. But the bitterness of my reflections was in some degree mitigated by the hasty preparations which I was compelled to make for an immediate return to London. I had not money enough to enable me to take a post-chaise; and I was therefore obliged to wait for the Portsmouth coach, which passed through the village on its way to the metropolis. I had already made up my mind what course to adopt. Now that my father and brother were no more, I could not bear the idea of remaining in the place where we had all been once so happy together:

I moreover knew that the parsonage-house would soon be required by the new curate who had been appointed as my late father's successor. I accordingly sent for the village lawyer, and gave him instructions to realize in ready money all the little property which had become my sad inheritance. I told him that in a few days I would let him know my address in London; and that he was to forward me the proceeds of the sale. But I retained a few relics to remind me of my departed relatives; and as I wept bitterly over them, I took a solemn vow that my future conduct should prove the sincerity of my repentance for the past!

"The coach made its appearance soon after mid-day: there was not a single person inside; and thus I was enabled to pour forth, without restraint, that grief—that acute anguish which I experienced at being compelled, by my own misconduct, to quit for ever the place of my birth. Oh! then I felt how hard, how bitter it was to arrive at the conviction that I had no longer *a home*! I was now wretched in the extreme: I had lost those who were nearest and dearest to me! Not to me was it given to close the eyes of the author of my being: not to me was it allowed to receive the parting sigh of that brother who had met his death in the cause of his sister's outraged honour! Wretch that I was;—I had no longer a friend—and no longer a home!

"The coach, on its arrival in London, stopped at the *White Horse Cellar*. I took a cab, and immediately proceeded to the house of the surgeon who had written to me. There it was that my brother had breathed his last! The duel had taken place in the neighbourhood of Bayswater: my brother received his adversary's ball in the breast; and although he lived for some hours afterwards, he never spoke again. Lord Dunstable conjured the surgeon to show the unfortunate young man every attention, and then took his immediate departure for the continent. But, from motives of delicacy, neither poor Edgar nor his lordship had communicated to the medical man the cause of the duel. It was only by means of papers found about my brother's person that the surgeon discovered that he had a sister, and ascertained where that sister lived. In the hurry, alarm, and confusion which followed the duel, the surgeon had forgotten to demand, and Lord Dunstable was too bewildered to communicate, any particulars relative to the family or friends of the young man who had fallen in the hostile encounter. Thus, had it not been for certain memoranda which were discovered in my poor brother's pocket-book, the surgeon would not have known to whom to write, and I might have remained for months—or even years—in ignorance of that dear relative's untimely fate. Full well did I comprehend the delicacy of his own conduct: he had not left a written trace which might expose my shame by revealing the motives that had led to the duel!

"There was a coroner's inquest; but, as it was stated that I was not in London at the time when the hostile encounter took place, I was not examined. Thus were my feelings spared a most painful ordeal! The funeral took place;—and the earth closed over the remains of him who was cut off in the flower of his youth—a victim to my misdeeds! The kindness of the surgeon's family had hitherto made me their guest; but on the day after the mournful obsequies, I perceived the necessity of adopting some decided course, so as to intrude no longer on that generous hospitality. But the worthy surgeon questioned me closely; and finding that I had only recently been left an orphan, and was totally friendless, he insisted that I should pass a few weeks longer with his family, until he could obtain for me a situation as governess. I wrote to the lawyer of my native village; and by return of post he forwarded me an order on a London banker for thirty-seven pounds—the poor proceeds of the sale of the furniture in the parsonage house.

"Six months passed away: during that period I was treated with the utmost kindness by the surgeon and his family. But misfortune suddenly overtook that excellent man. The villany of a false friend plunged him from affluence into comparative poverty. This abrupt change preyed so deeply on his mind, that he put a period to his existence. His brother—a man of morose disposition and selfish character—undertook to provide for the widow and her children; and I was then compelled once more to shift for myself. I took an affectionate farewell of those who had behaved so well towards me, and removed to a humble lodging, where I soon experienced all the wretchedness of my lonely and unfriended position. I inserted advertisements in the newspapers, for the purpose of obtaining a situation as teacher in a school or governess in a respectable family; and although I received many replies, I failed to give a satisfactory account of myself. I could not refer to Mrs. Lambkin, nor to Lady Penfeather; and I found that my orphan condition excited but little sympathy in my favour. Thus a year—an entire year—passed; and at the end, I found myself without hope, and without resources. I knew not what would become of me. At length I mustered up all my courage, and proceeded to Rossville House. I inquired for Miss Adeline Enfield. The servant demanded my name, and left me standing in the hall for nearly ten minutes until his return. I was then shown into a small but magnificently furnished parlour; and almost immediately afterwards Adeline made her appearance. She advanced towards me with the most chilling hauteur of manner, and desired to know '*my business.*'—'Oh! Miss Adeline,' I exclaimed, 'have I no claims upon your friendship?'—'You must remember what took place between us the last time we met,' she answered. 'If you require pecuniary assistance, I will succour you *for the last time*; but circumstances compel me to decline seeing you, or even *knowing* you in future.'—'And is this the way you treat me after all I suffered on your account?' I said, bursting into tears. 'Do you not reflect that your reputation is in my hands?'—'If you menace me, Miss Hutchinson,' she said, 'I shall know how to treat you. In a word, who would believe your story were you to proclaim it? You would only draw down upon yourself the vengeance of my family by endeavouring to shift your own disgrace on to my shoulders. The whole world would denounce you as a common impostress.'—An instant's reflection showed me that these assurances were strictly true. But my pride was hurt, and my feelings were poignantly wrung by the blackness of Adeline's ingratitude. Pushing aside her hand which tendered me a purse of gold, I exclaimed, 'From this moment, Miss Enfield, I consider myself absolved from all motives of secrecy on your account;'—and, before she could utter a word of reply, I left the room.

"I hurried back to the house where I lodged. The landlady met me upon the threshold of the door. 'Come, young woman,' she said, 'can you pay the fortnight's rent you owe me?'—'I have been disappointed,' was my reply: 'but in a few days———.'—'People are always being disappointed when they owe money,' she exclaimed. 'I shall keep your things till you settle your rent; and I shall let the room to those who can and will pay.' And she banged the door in my face. This cruel calamity reduced me to despair. I turned away from that inhospitable abode,—not with tears, for there is a grief too profound to find a vent by the eyes—but with an utter hopelessness that was distraction!

"I had eaten nothing since the morning: I was hungry, and I had not a farthing in my pocket. It was moreover cold; and I knew not where to sleep that night. Oh! then how bitterly did I regret the ebullition of pride and feeling which had prevented me from accepting the purse which Adeline had proffered me! It was now too late to conciliate her: I had used menaces; and I felt convinced that it would be impossible to make my peace with that proud and determined spirit. I wandered about the streets in a state of mind which every moment suggested suicide. Then did all the happiness of home and of the days of innocence recur to my memory with a force that nearly crushed me! I thought of my dear departed father and my noble-hearted brother—both hurried to the grave by my wickedness! Evening came—and I was still a wanderer in the streets, without a hope—without a feasible project! Hour after hour passed: midnight was proclaimed by the iron tongues of the thousand towers of this mighty city;—and I sank exhausted on the step of a door in Gerrard Street, Soho. I then became insensible.

"When I awoke, I was in a comfortable bed; and the day-light streamed through the windows of a nicely-furnished room. I started up, and glanced around me. On a small table by the side of the bed stood a decanter with some port wine, and a bowl half-filled with broth. I immediately judged by those appearances, and by my own sensations, that the kind hand of charity had administered sustenance to me, as well as providing me with an asylum. From those objects on the table my eyes wandered round the room; and I was surprised and shocked to observe that the pictures on the walls were of a somewhat indecent description. The unpleasant reflections which this circumstance occasioned were interrupted by the entrance of an elderly woman,—very stout, with small grey eyes, and a red nose. She seemed to have literally flung on the cotton-gown which she wore; and a dirty night-cap was perched on the top of her head. She advanced with a good-natured smile towards the bed, and, surveying me with great apparent satisfaction, exclaimed, 'How do you feel, my poor child? I am delighted to see you looking so much better! Dear me, what a state you were in when I found you, in the middle of the night, on the step of my door.'—'Ah! madam,' I said, extending my hand towards her, 'how can I ever repay you for this goodness?'—She pressed my hand warmly, and declared that she was charmed at being able to serve so sweet a young creature. Then she asked me a great many questions; and I gave her to understand that I was the orphan daughter of a clergyman; that I had failed to obtain the renewal of my engagements as a nursery-governess: that I had been turned into the streets by my landlady, who had detained my boxes; and that I should have perished had it not been for the kindness and benevolence of my present benefactress. When I had concluded this statement of as much of my past life as I chose to reveal, the elderly lady exclaimed, 'And so you are a clergyman's orphan, my dear? How very singular! Poor curates' daughters are always falling into difficulties. But cheer up, my dear: I will be a friend to you. And first tell me the address of your hard-hearted landlady: I will send at once and redeem your things for you.'—I gave her the information which she asked, and once more expressed my profound gratitude for her goodness towards me. She patted my cheek, and then left the room, observing that she would send me up breakfast. In a few minutes a good-looking and smartly-dressed servant entered the chamber, bearing a tray containing coffee, hot rolls, eggs, and the usual concomitants of a good meal. 'What is the name of your excellent mistress?' I inquired.—'Mrs. Harpy,' was the reply, given with a smile the nature of which struck me as being somewhat strange.—'What is she?' I asked.—'She keeps a very respectable boarding-house,' answered the servant.—I did not like to put any farther questions; and the girl withdrew.

"I ate a very hearty breakfast, and then lay down again; for I was not quite recovered from the fatigues of the preceding day. I fell into a doze; and when I awoke, Mrs. Harpy was once more standing by the side of the bed. 'Here are your things, my dear,' she said: 'I paid your landlady fifteen shillings. That was for two weeks' rent owing, and a week she claimed because you had left without giving notice. She gives an excellent character of you, and proves all you have told me to be quite true. I am really as fond of you as if you were my own daughter. You are looking much better; and a nice little boiled fowl, with a glass of Port, will set you to rights. What time do you like to dine, dear?'—'My good lady,' I replied, 'you are heaping favours upon me, and I have not the means of paying you for any one of them.'—'Don't talk of that, my dear girl,' ejaculated Mrs. Harpy. 'I'm sure it is quite a pleasure to do any thing for you. But, by-the-by,' she added, 'you may just as well give me a memorandum for what I am paying for you; and as I shall be able to procure some nice, easy, genteel avocation for you, you can reimburse me at your convenience.'—Of course I was delighted at this opportunity of testifying my honest intentions and good-will; and I instantly affixed my signature to a slip of paper which she produced from her pocket. Mrs. Harpy kissed me very affectionately; and then, casually observing that she kept a very genteel boarding-house, concluded by saying that she would ask some of the young ladies to come up after dinner and keep me company for an hour or two.

"At four o'clock the pretty servant made her appearance with the boiled fowl and a small decanter of wine; and when the things were cleared away, the young ladies were duly ushered in. There were five of them. Their ages varied from seventeen to twenty-three; and they were all remarkably good-looking. It however struck me as somewhat singular that they were every one dressed in extremely low-bodied gowns, so as to exhibit a great deal more of the bust than was consistent with my notions of decorum. But as they were very affable and kind in their manners, and '*dear*'d' me with much apparent sincerity, I ceased to think of that peculiarity. Presently Mrs. Harpy sent up a bottle of wine and some fruit, with her kindest compliments; and then the young ladies laughed and enjoyed themselves in the happiest manner possible. They drank the wine with great freedom and relish; and by degrees their conversation turned upon the topic of love. With this subject they were quite familiar; and the more they drank, the more license they allowed their tongues. They spoke of the kindness of Mrs. Harpy, of the gaiety of the life which they led in her establishment, and of the high acquaintance which they enjoyed. They seemed to know every young lord and wealthy gentleman about town, and compared the various qualifications of those personages. Their discourse became more and more animated in proportion as their imaginations were warmed with the wine; and at length they allowed such observations to escape them which made me blush. I was surprised at their levity, and had already begun to entertain strange suspicions of their virtue, when a bell suddenly rang on the landing. They all started up, and rushed out of the room—leaving me a prey to the reflections which their remarkable conduct had very naturally excited.

"I kept my bed, by Mrs. Harpy's advice, all that day; but I did not feel sleepy in the evening, after the young ladies had left me;—and even if the contrary were the case, I should not have been able to indulge a wish for repose, for after eleven o'clock the whole establishment seemed to be in a constant bustle. People ran up and down stairs; doors were banged; shouts of laughter awoke every echo in the place; glasses rattled on trays that were carried to the different rooms; and the boisterous mirth of men rose at intervals above the other sounds and noises. This confusion, as it appeared to me, continued until about two o'clock; and then the house became quiet. My suspicions were seriously excited relative to the respectability of Mrs. Harpy's establishment; but I endeavoured to quiet them by all the arguments I could conceive in that lady's favour, and which were prompted by my gratitude towards her. At length I fell asleep.

"In the morning the servant brought me up my breakfast. I asked her the meaning of the bustle I had heard during the night. She answered carelessly, 'Oh! Mrs. Harpy is very gay, Miss, and is fond of company.'—After breakfast I got up, and had just dressed myself, when a door was opened violently on the opposite side of the landing, and a male voice exclaimed, 'Well, if the old woman won't give me credit for a miserable bottle of champagne, after all the money I've spent in the place, I'll never set foot in it again. So good bye, 'Tilda. Here's a sovereign for you, my girl. It's the last time I shall ever sleep in this house.'—Thereupon the individual, who had so expressed himself, descended the stairs with a tremendous stamping of his feet, as if he were very indignant at the treatment he had complained of; and Miss Matilda—one of the *young ladies* who had visited in my room on the preceding evening—returned into her apartment, banging the door violently behind her. This incident opened my eyes to the dread truth:—I was in a brothel!

"I threw myself on a chair and burst into a flood of tears. Merciful heavens! for what fate was I reserved? Had I indeed fallen so low that my only home was a loathsome den of iniquity like that? For some minutes after the occurrence of the incident just related, I felt as if my senses were leaving me. Suddenly the door opened, and Mrs. Harpy made her appearance. She seemed astonished at the condition in which she found me, and was about to make some remark, when I threw myself at her feet, exclaiming, 'I conjure you, madam—if you have any pity for a poor friendless orphan—let me leave your house this moment!'—'And where will you go, my dear child?' she said.—'To the workhouse, ma'am: anywhere, rather than remain here!' I answered.—'This is a pretty recompense for my kindness towards you,' she observed. 'If it had not been for me, you would have died in the streets.'—'Far better for me were it, had I so perished!' I exclaimed.—'Now, Miss,' cried Mrs. Harpy, growing angry, 'what is the meaning of all this nonsense?'—'Can you ask me?' I demanded. 'Oh! that the feelings which prompted you to assist me, should have been any other save the disinterested benevolence for which I so sincerely thanked you!'—'Then you know where you are, Miss, I suppose?' she said, with a leer; and, before I had time to give any reply, she added, 'I meant you to find it out in a day or two; and it's as well now as a few hours later. Here you are, and here you will stay. You shall be treated just in proportion as you behave; and this evening, I shall introduce some fine nobleman or gentleman to you.'—'Never!' I cried: then moving towards the door, I said, 'Detain me at your peril!'—'So I shall,' answered Mrs. Harpy, coolly. 'I've got your I. O. U. for twenty pounds; and if you go any where, it will be to Whitecross Street prison, before you're many hours older. Remember, it's for *necessaries*; and so no plea of minority or any other gammon of that kind, will avail you.'—I remembered the slip of paper which I had signed; and my heart sank within me, as I saw how completely I was in the power of that vile woman.—'So now you understand how you are situated,' she continued, softening in her tone and manner. 'This is what all young girls like you must come to, sooner or later; and you'll be very happy here, I can assure you. This evening a nobleman who patronizes my house, will call upon you; and if you have any of your nonsense with him, I'll send you straight to Whitecross Street to-morrow morning.'—With these words she left the room, locking the door behind her.

"I cannot attempt to explain the nature of my feelings during the remainder of that day. A good dinner was sent up to me; but I could not eat a mouthful. The servant asked if I should like to see any of the 'young ladies;' and I answered in a manner which convinced her how I recoiled from the detestable proposal. She smiled—as I thought, significantly,—as much as to say, 'You will talk differently in a very short time.'—At about nine o'clock Mrs. Harpy sent up word that I was to dress myself in my best attire—a command with which I positively refused to comply for I was determined that, happen what might, I would not assist in the sacrifice of myself!

"At ten o'clock the servant brought up waxlights, and a tray containing a bottle of champagne, glasses, and several plates of fruits and cakes. I watched these preparations in a state of dumb despair, bordering on stupefaction. Another half hour passed; and steps once more ascended the stairs. My heart palpitated violently! The door was thrown open;—a man elegantly dressed entered the room;—I cast one glance towards him, and, uttering a faint cry, sank insensible on the carpet. It was Lord Dunstable!

"When I awoke, I found that nobleman hanging over me, bathing my temples. He compelled me to drink a glass of wine; and I soon recovered full consciousness of the miseries of my condition. Starting from the half-embrace in which Lord Dunstable had clasped me, I surveyed him with horror. 'Do I frighten you, Lydia?' he exclaimed. 'I must confess that our meeting is a strange one. The old woman sent to tell me that she had a prize; but I little expected to find you here.'—'My presence in this house of infamy, my lord,' I answered, 'is one of the links in that chain of degradation of which you forged the first link. To you I owe all the disgrace and all the sorrow that I have endured. Not contented with my ruin, you deprived me of my brother.'—'Come, Lydia, this is absurd,' he cried. 'In the first place, a young female who meets a gentleman and walks with him in Parks or elsewhere, must not expect to escape the usual consequences. Secondly, your brother challenged me, like a rash and headstrong young fellow as he was: I sent him due warning by my second that I was certain to shoot him; but he would not take good advice, and I *did* shoot him.'—'And had you no regard for me at that moment?' I asked.—'Egad!' he replied, 'I only thought of myself. I fancied that if I did not shoot him, he might perform that good office for me; and so I was resolved not to give him a second chance.'—'Surely you cannot be in your senses, my lord,' I exclaimed, 'to talk of so serious a matter in such a flippant style?'—'Come, let us understand each other, Lydia,' he said. 'I did not come to such a house as this to receive a lesson in morals. Do you wish me to remain here with you until to-morrow?'—'No: a thousand times *no*,' I replied. 'Your hand is red with the blood of my poor brother.'—'Very well, Lydia,' he answered coolly; 'then I will take myself off as quietly as I came. But for old acquaintance' sake I must do the thing handsomely.'—I heard his observation, the flippant tone of which made me avert my head from him in disgust; and I did not therefore see why he lingered for a few moments. At length he left the room, saying, 'Bye, bye, Liddy;' and when the door closed behind him, he began to hum an opera-tune, as he descended the stairs.

"Scarcely could he have had time to gain the street door, when Mrs. Harpy bounded into my room, exclaiming, 'Well, my dear, you have behaved very well, for his lordship went away in an excellent humour. What did he give you?'—'Give me!' I repeated, surveying that horrible woman with mingled indignation and terror.—'By Jove, he's a lord in name and nature both!' ejaculated Mrs. Harpy, as her eyes caught sight of a bank-note which lay upon the table. 'Twenty pounds, as I'm a living woman!' and she clutched the object of her delighted avarice.—'Hold, madam!' I exclaimed. 'Not one farthing of that money will I retain! The man who gave it killed my brother!'—'I don't care who he's killed, or who he means to kill,' answered the old woman, 'But here's his money; and that I intend to keep.'—'*You* keep it!' I cried.—'Yes; who else? What an ungrateful hussy you must be, after I took you out of the street! This room and your board will cost you a guinea a-day. Then your clothes, washing, and other things are all extra. So I'll keep nineteen pound fifteen shillings on account; and you shall have a crown for pocket money. If that is not generous, I don't know what is; but I like to do the thing what's right.'—With these words she threw five shillings on the table, and walked off with the twenty pound note.

"This unexpected interview with Lord Dunstable and its result stamped my degradation, and made me reckless. He had seen me in a brothel; and in the excitement of our meeting, I had not explained to him how I became an inmate of that house. Then he left behind him a sum of money; and, as I was unable to restore it to him with an indignant refusal of any succour at his hands, he would naturally conceive that I availed myself of his bounty. My pride was wounded to such an irreparable degree, that I felt, if you can understand me, a total unwillingness to endeavour to maintain it any longer. I was spirit-crushed. I fancied that it was no use to contend any more against my fate. I considered myself to be now so lost and degraded in the estimation of that one man whom I had loved, that I had nothing else in the world to induce me to study character, reputation, or pride. I accordingly abandoned myself to what I firmly believed to be my destiny; and, seating myself at the table, I poured out a glass of champagne. For a moment I sighed as I remembered that it was champagne that had led to my ruin in the first instance:—then I laughed at what I called 'my folly,' and emptied the glass. The wine cheered me, but, at the same time, confirmed me in that recklessness which had succeeded the first feeling of utter and irredeemable degradation. I drank another glass: the last spark of virtuous aspiration was then extinguished in my bosom. The other *young ladies* suddenly made their appearance: I received them with open arms;—we sate down to drink and chat;—I was put to bed in a disgusting state of intoxication; and on the following morning I awoke—reconciled to a life of infamy!

"Pardon me, if I dwell for a few minutes upon the characteristics of those houses of abomination, in one of which I was now located. Mrs. Harpy was an admirable type of her profession. She was mean and griping in the extreme when wringing an extra shilling, or even an extra penny, from her *boarders*, as we were called; and yet she was profuse and liberal in supplying us with costly wine. If we complained of having to eat cold meat two days running, she would storm, and declare that we lived too well as it was;—but she would think nothing of giving us a bottle of champagne, which could not have cost her less than eight or ten shillings, after dinner. She took from us every farthing that we received, and invariably made us out her debtors, although she never showed us any accounts. To give you an idea of her way of managing, I will relate a little anecdote. One Saturday afternoon, Matilda (whom I have before mentioned) asked her for a sovereign; adding, 'You know I have given you altogether thirteen guineas this week.'—'Thirteen guineas!' screamed the old woman: 'I'll take my Bible oath it was only twelve.'—'Well, call it even twelve, if you like,' said the young female: 'you can well spare me a sovereign.'—'Lord bless the girl!' cried Mrs. Harpy. 'Why, there's seven guineas for your board and lodging; two guineas for your washing; that's ten; a guinea for pocket money; and a guinea for letters and needles and thread; that makes up the twelve, or else I never went to school to learn compound addition.'—'And multiplication too,' said Matilda. 'Why, I had but one letter all the week, and that was paid.'—'Well, my dear,' answered Mrs. Harpy, 'we will ask the postman. Come! I'll stand another bottle of champagne now, and you shall have an extra sovereign for yourself next Saturday, if you're lucky in the meantime.'

"We were complete slaves to this Mrs. Harpy. She had got a note-of-hand for twenty pounds from each of us; and if any one even so much as hinted at leaving her, she immediately threatened to wreak her vengeance by means of the sheriffs' officer. She seldom allowed us to go out to take any exercise, for fear we should decamp altogether; but every now and then we would all go together to Gravesend or Richmond by the steam-boats, or else to Copenhagen House, in the summer time, and to some minor theatre in the winter. Oh! the misery of that existence! We were slaves to an old wretch who was enriching herself at our expense, whilst we had not an opportunity of hoarding a single guinea against any sudden necessity or misfortune. Then, what atrocious proceedings were frequently enacted in that house! Hard by lived three or four idle fellows, who dressed flashily, spent a great deal of money, and yet had no visible employment or resources. Those ruffians were the *blinks*, or *bullies*, belonging to Mrs. Harpy's establishment. Their tricks were manifold. For instance, they would pick up, at a tavern, coach-office, the theatre, or other public place, some country gentleman, or even a clergyman, whom they would ply with liquor, and then induce to accompany them to '*their aunt's*,' where they would meet '*some delightful girls*.' Of course this was Mrs. Harpy's establishment. The respectable country gentleman, or clergyman, was plied with more liquor; and, if he would not drink fast enough, his wine was drugged for him. When he awoke in the morning, he would find himself in bed with one of the '*delightful girls*.' Presently, one of the bullies would rush into the room, declare that the gentleman had debauched '*his cousin*,' and threaten an exposure. Then the poor victim was glad to compromise the business by paying a considerable sum, in order to hush up the matter at once.

"Sometimes, the bullies would attempt a similar scheme of extortion in reference to individuals who came voluntarily to the house; and if the latter resisted the exorbitant demands made upon them, they were not unfrequently maltreated in a most shameful manner. It often happened that a gentleman would become a regular visitor to the house, if he took a fancy to one particular boarder: in such a case he probably adopted a false name, and took every precaution to avoid discovery as to who he was. The girl whom he visited, was then directed to pump him; and if she failed to elicit the desired particulars, one of the bullies was instructed to watch and dog him when he left the house. By these means, his real name, residence, position, and circumstances, were speedily ascertained. If he were moving in a very respectable sphere, was married, or had any particular motives to induce him to keep his intrigue secret, he was the very kind of person who suited Mrs. Harpy and her bullies. The next time he visited the house, he would be surrounded by those ruffians, menaced with exposure, and forced to pay a considerable sum of money to purchase silence. But the evil did not terminate there. From that time forth, the unfortunate gentleman would be periodically beset by his persecutors; and fresh extortions would be effected to renew the pledge of secrecy on their part. Married men, moving in respectable spheres, have been *driven to suicide* by this atrocious system! Many a time have I read, in the newspapers, instances of self-destruction on the part of gentlemen whose pecuniary, social, or domestic circumstances afforded not the least appearance of any possible motive for such a deed;—and then I have thought within myself that those poor victims had been *hunted to death* by extortioners of the class which I have described! The man who has a *character* to lose, or who has the *peace* of his family to consider, knows not how fearfully both are compromised, both endangered, when he so far forgets himself as to set foot in a house of infamy. He may imagine that his secret never can transpire—that neither his family nor friends can, by any possible means, ever discover that he has thus erred;—but, if he be an individual, who, by his wealth and social position, appears worth the trouble of looking after, he will most assuredly find himself a prey to the vilest of extortioners. His happiness will be undermined and destroyed; he will live in constant dread of exposure: and deeply—deeply will he rue the day that he ever set foot in a brothel!

"The most bare-faced robberies are practised in even what are called '*the respectable dress-houses*.' A gentleman, wearing a handsome watch and chain, is pretty certain to have it stolen from him; and when he remonstrates, he is perhaps met with a counter-accusation of having given a bad sovereign in payment for champagne, on the preceding evening. On one occasion, a young gentleman who was so plundered, and so accused, carried the business to the Marlborough Street Police-Office. Mrs. Harpy attended, denied the robbery in the most indignant manner, and persisted in the accusation relative to the base sovereign. The proceedings took such a turn that the young gentleman was searched; and in his pockets were found *other counterfeit sovereigns*, exactly resembling the *one* produced by Mrs. Harpy. Then Mrs. Harpy sent for her wine-merchant, her butcher, and her baker, who were all her near neighbours: and those tradesmen declared that Mrs. Harpy kept a most respectable boarding-house, and that she was a lady of good connexions and undoubted integrity. The magistrate then appealed to the policeman within whose beat Gerrard Street was included; and as he received five guineas a year from Mrs. Harpy for shutting his eyes, it was not likely that he would open them on that occasion. He fully corroborated the evidence of the wine-merchant, butcher, and baker; and the young gentleman was committed for trial for passing base money. Mrs. Harpy's story was that he had presented himself on the preceding evening at her house, and arranged to become a boarder in her establishment; that he obtained from her the change for the bad sovereign; and that, when accused of the act, he had turned round with a counter-charge relative to his watch. The magistrate declared that there was no doubt of Mrs. Harpy's perfect respectability, and commented severely on the '*infamous behaviour of the prisoner, in trumping up so vile an accusation, as a means of releasing himself from the odium of the charge laid against him.*' This young man belonged to a highly respectable family; and he had given a fictitious name in answer to the magistrate's question, *for he had only been married six months*, and was naturally anxious to conceal his visit to a brothel from the knowledge of his friends. But when he was committed for trial, he was forced to send for them, confess his indiscretion, and implore them to save him from the ignominy of exposure in a court of justice. A compromise with Mrs. Harpy was accordingly effected: she *paid* fifty pounds in forfeit of her recognizances to prosecute: and she *received* two hundred to abstain from farther proceedings! I need scarcely say that the young gentleman really had been plundered of his watch, and that the entire business of the counterfeit money had been arranged to ruin him. Again I declare that no one knows the woeful risks he incurs when he sets foot in a house of ill-fame. That one false step may embitter the remainder of his days!

"Some weeks elapsed ere I was completely aware of the infamies which were perpetrated in Mrs. Harpy's den; and then I resolved to leave the place, whatever might subsequently become of me. At length an opportunity served; and one evening, with only a small parcel of necessaries under my arm, and a few shillings in my purse, I slipped out of that scene of iniquities. I cannot enter into further details; suffice it to say, from that moment commenced an existence of fearful vicissitudes,—starvation one day, luxury the next,—the most abrupt descents into the lowest abyss of destitution, and the most sudden elevations to comfort, though still a career of infamy,—wanderings for many, many nights together, without knowing where to lay my head, and then a lodging and a good bed! Oh! it was horrible, that precariousness of life to which I was doomed!

"How often did I reflect upon the times of my innocence! Now and then I saw well-known names mentioned in the newspapers. The consecutive and rapid promotions of Lord Dunstable and Cholmondeley were not unnoticed by me. The presentation of the Honourable Adeline Enfield to court was an incident which affected me deeply; for it naturally led me to compare her elevated position with my degraded and wretched state. But one event, which was recorded in the newspapers, gave me, I must confess, some satisfaction: this was the bankruptcy of Mrs. Lambkin and her committal to Newgate for having fraudulently disposed of her property. I afterwards learnt that she died miserably in that gaol.

"But my own vicissitudes continued! Oh! let those who are prone to turn away from *the unfortunate woman* with disgust and abhorrence, rather exercise a feeling of sympathy in her behalf. She does not drag her weary frame nightly along the pavement, through *choice*, but from *necessity*. In all weathers must she ply her miserable trade—or starve. Then to what indignities is she subjected! Every drunken ruffian considers himself justified in ill-using her: every brutal fellow jostles against her, and addresses her in terms of insult. Do they think that, because she is compelled to ply her hideous trade, she has no feelings? But it is chiefly from the young men who rove about the streets at night, smoking cigars, wearing pea-coats, and carrying sticks, that the unfortunate woman is doomed to receive the deepest indignity:—yes, from those who ought to have more chivalry in their dispositions! There is one base extortion to which the unfortunate woman is subjected, and which I must mention. I allude to the necessity of feeing the policeman belonging to that beat where the unhappy creature walks. The miserable wretch who deviated from this practice, either through inability or unwillingness, would never have a moment's peace. The moment she was accosted in the street by a gentleman, the officer would come up and order her brutally to move on; and perhaps he would add violence to harsh words. Then, on the slightest pretence—and often without any at all—the miserable woman is dragged off to the station-house, charged with creating a disturbance, and taken next morning before the magistrate. In vain may she protest her innocence of the offence charged against her: in vain may she denounce the vindictive motives of the officer. The word of one policeman is deemed worth the oaths of ten thousand degraded females; and the accused is sentenced to Bridewell accordingly. No one can conceive the amount of the wrongs inflicted by the police upon the most miserable class of women!

"I could enter into details respecting the lives of unfortunate females, which would inspire you with horror—and yet with deep compassion. But I have already dwelt too long on a subject which should never be mentioned without caution to the pure-minded woman. In reference to myself, I need only add that having passed through all the terrible phases of a career of infamy,—each day beholding me more degraded, and sinking lower and lower amongst the low,—I was reduced to a condition when beggary appeared the only resource left From this appalling condition your goodness has relieved me; and God alone must reward you—I never can!"

CHAPTER CLXXVIII.

THE TAVERN AT FRIULI.

Through the broad meadows, the waving woods, and the delicious valleys which lie on the northern side of the Ferretti, in the State of Castelcicala, two foot-travellers pursued their way.

Lovely flowed the river amidst the meads that were clothed in the country's everlasting green.

Busy hamlets, neat farm-houses, and the chateaux of nobles or wealthy gentlemen, varied the appearance of the magnificent landscape.

Although it was the middle of November, the climate was as mild and genial as that of September in the British Islands: the vines had not been entirely stripped of their luscious fruit; and the citrons, so plentiful that they were but little prized by the inhabitants, grew wild by the road-side.

Here groups of mighty chesnut-trees afforded a delicious shade to the way-worn traveller: there the tapering spire of a village church, or the white walls and slated roof of some lordly country-seat, appeared above the verdant mulberry-groves.

Nevertheless, the woodlands of Castelcicala were not characterised by that gloominess of foliage which invests the English and German forests with such awful solemnity; for the leaves were of a brighter green, and the density of their shade was relieved by the luxuriousness of the botany that spread its rich and varied colours over the surface of the land.

The banks of the Ferretti yielded an immense profusion of aromatic herbs, which imparted a delicious perfume and, at the same time, a freshness to the air.

Much as those two travellers had been accustomed to admire the loveliness of their own native England, they could not avoid exclamations of joy and surprise as they pursued their way amidst the fertile plains of Castelcicala.

We need scarcely inform our readers that those travellers were Richard Markham and his faithful Morcar.

Our hero, dressed in a neat but modest garb, and carrying a portfolio of drawing materials under his arm, journeyed along a little in advance of his attendant, who bore a small valise of necessaries.

In his pocket-book Richard had secured the two passports, for himself and follower, which the interest of Mario Bazzano had obtained, and which were made out in fictitious names.

Fastened to a riband round his neck, and carefully concealed beneath his raiment, was a small morocco leather case, containing the sealed letter left him, with such mysterious instructions, by Thomas Armstrong.

The well-filled purse which the generosity of the Grand Duchess had supplied, and a map of the Duchy, completed the stock of materials with which the travellers had deemed it fit to furnish themselves.

Their way now lay, according to the advice which Richard had received from the Grand Duchess, towards Friuli: thence it was his intention to strike off abruptly in a longitudinal direction, and, passing between Dandolo and Lipari, proceed straight toward the Neapolitan frontier.

On the fourth evening the two travellers arrived at Friuli, having walked upon an average thirty miles each day, and slept at night in some cottage or farm-house.

They did not, however, penetrate into the fine and spacious town which they had now reached; but stopped at a small tavern in the suburbs. There they ordered supper, which was served up to them in the public room, as Richard did not think it prudent to excite notice by having a private apartment.

Several other persons were sitting in the public room, busily engaged in imbibing the various liquors suited to their respective palates, and discussing, with great solemnity, the political aspect of the State.

By their conversation Markham judged that they must be the small tradesmen of the suburbs of the town, as they all seemed well acquainted with each other, and spoke as if they were in the habit of meeting at that tavern every evening after the bustle and cares of the day's business.

"Are you certain, neighbour," said one worthy burgher, addressing himself to another, "that the proclamation will be made to-morrow morning?"

"I believe, gentlemen," answered the individual thus appealed to, "you are all aware that my wife's father is Adjunct to the Mayor of Friuli; and the title of Adjunct is pretty nearly synonymous with that of Deputy. Well, then, gentlemen, my father-in-law being, you perceive, as good as Deputy-Mayor," continued the speaker, thinking that his prosiness would add to his importance, "he cannot fail to be in the mayor's secrets. That once granted, gentlemen, you can easily estimate the value of my authority for the tidings I reported to you just now. You may therefore rely on it, that the proclamation placing the entire province of Montecuculi under martial law, will be read in Friuli, as well as in all the other towns, villages, and hamlets of the aforesaid province, to-morrow morning, at nine o'clock."

"Then I suppose the whole Duchy will be placed under martial law?" observed another member of the party.

"No doubt of it," said the second speaker. "The worshipful mayor hinted as much to the not less worshipful adjunct, or deputy, this afternoon."

"The province of Abrantani has been for some time in an exceptional state, you know," said the individual who had first spoken; "and by all accounts, we had much better be under the yoke of the Austrians at once—just like the northern provinces of Italy. I tell you what," added the individual who was now addressing his companions,—"I tell you what," he repeated, sinking his voice almost to a whisper, "there is not a man in Castelcicala who will not be ready to draw his sword against this most odious tyranny."

"Hush! hush!" exclaimed the relative of the civic authority, as he glanced towards Richard Markham and Morcar; "we do not know who may overhear us, as the adjunct often observes to me."

"The gentleman is an artist, and looks like a foreigner, too," said the individual whose freedom of speech had provoked this remonstrance: "he is not likely to meddle with our political business."

"Gentlemen," said Richard, "it is true that I understand your language, although I speak it imperfectly; but if you apprehend that I should make any improper use of the remarks which fall from you, I will at once retire to a private room."

"Well spoken!" ejaculated one of the company. "No, sir—you shall not leave the room on our account. If I mistake not, you must be an Englishman or a Frenchman; and I like both those nations—for they know what true freedom is, while we are slaves,—abject slaves."

"Yes,—and I admire the English, too," cried the person who had before spoken with so little reserve. "Have they not given an asylum to that excellent Prince who is only exiled because he was the people's friend—because he wished to obtain for us a Constitution that would give us Houses of Parliament or Chambers, to be the bulwark of our liberties? Is not our Grand Duchess an Englishwoman? and has she not exerted herself to the utmost to mitigate the severity of Angelo III? *That* is no secret. And, when I think of it, I remember hearing at Ossore (where I was, you know, a few days ago,) that it was a young Englishman who rallied the Constitutionalists when they were flying, after the fall of General Grachia."

"What became of him?" asked one of the company.

"It is known that he was taken prisoner," was the reply; "but as he disappeared almost immediately afterwards, it is supposed that he was hurried off without delay to one of the fortresses in the interior—Pinalla or Estella, for instance. Poor young fellow—I wish he had had better luck! But, as I was saying, you see we have good reason to admire the English—God bless them!"

"Amen!" exclaimed several voices.

The emotions of our hero, while this discourse was progressing, may be more readily imagined than explained: but prudence on his own account, and obedience to the advice of the Grand Duchess, sealed his lips.

Morcar continued to eat and drink without excitement, because the conversation passing around was totally unintelligible to him.

The relative of the mayor's adjunct was dilating pompously on the duties of a sovereign, when a post-chaise drove furiously up to the door of the tavern.

All was immediately bustle and confusion.

"Horses! four horses wanted!" shouted a voice in the passage.

Then commenced the rattling of harness,—the running hither and thither of ostlers,—and the usual calling and bawling which characterise such occasions.

All the inmates of the coffee-room, with the exception of Markham and the gipsy, rushed out to stare at the equipage.

Scarcely was the room thus left comparatively empty, when a tall man, wrapped in an ample travelling cloak, entered hastily, followed by the landlord.

"Here—we have not a moment to lose—give me change for this bank-note," cried the traveller.

"Yes, sir," said the host, and hurried from the room.

"Signor Bazzano," whispered our hero, who had started from his seat at the sound of the traveller's voice.

"What! Signor Markham!" said the young *aide-de-camp*, shaking him kindly by the hand. "This is indeed most fortunate! But I have not a moment to spare. Listen! terrible events have taken place at Montoni: *you* are in danger. You must separate from your attendant, and each gain the Neapolitan frontier by a separate route. Follow my advice, my dear Markham,—*as you value your life*!"

At that moment the host re-appeared with the gold and silver in change for the note; and Bazzano, having hastily consigned the money to his pocket, hurried from the room,—but not before he had darted a significant glance upon our hero.

In a few moments the post-chaise drove rapidly away.

Richard returned to his seat in a cruel state of uncertainty, doubt, and suspense.

What could that precipitate journey mean? was Bazzano the sole occupant of the carriage? what terrible events could have occurred at Montoni? and what was that fearful peril which would oblige him to adopt so painful a precaution as to separate from his companion?

Richard was at a total loss how to solve these queries which naturally suggested themselves to his mind.

While he was yet pondering on the singularity of the incidents which had occurred, all within the space of three or four minutes, the company poured back again to the coffee-room.

"Something mysterious there," said one.

"Yes—a post-chaise with the blinds drawn down," observed another.

"Four horses—and travelling like wild-fire," exclaimed a third. "The tall man in the cloak, who rode outside, came into this room. What did he want, sir?" demanded the speaker, turning abruptly towards Markham; "for I believe you did not leave the room."

"He obtained change from the landlord for a bank-note, sir," answered our hero laconically.

"Oh! that was all—eh? Well—the thing still looks odd—particularly in such troubled times as these. Did anybody hear the orders given to the postilions?"

"The tall man in the cloak said in a loud voice, '*The road towards Dandolo, my boys!*'" observed another of the company.

Richard smiled imperceptibly; for he thought within himself, "Then it is precisely because Bazzano said in a loud tone, '*Towards Dandolo*,' that the travellers are going in another direction."

The company continued to debate, as all gossips will, upon the incident which had just occurred; and Richard determined to lose no more time ere he explained to Morcar, who had of course recognised the young *aide-de-camp*, the nature of the warning he had received from this individual.

He according bade the assembled guests "Good night," and left the room, followed by Morcar.

At his request, the landlord conducted them to a double-bedded room; and the moment the host had retired, Richard communicated to the gipsy all that Bazzano had said to him.

"There is but one course to pursue, sir," exclaimed Morcar.

"Which is that?" asked Richard.

"To follow the Castelcicalan officer's advice," returned Morcar. "He saved your life—he restored me to your service—and he is incapable of deceiving us. He is your friend, sir—and you must obey him."

"But, my poor Morcar," said Richard, "I cannot part with you. I have lured you away from your family and native land, to lead you into these difficulties; and I would sooner die than abandon you in a strange country, with even the language of which you are unacquainted."

"My dear, good master," exclaimed the gipsy, his eyes dimmed with tears, "it will go to my heart to leave you; but if your life is in danger, I shall not hesitate a moment. Besides, the same peril that would overtake one, would crush both, were we together when it came; and it is folly for either of us to run idle risks in such a strait. No—let us follow the advice of your friend."

"Again, I say, Morcar, that I cannot part with you. Were any thing fatal to happen to you, I should never forgive myself. No," continued Richard, "you shall remain with me. If danger come, it is only I who will suffer—for it seems that it is only my life which *is* in danger. And this is probable enough."

"Ah! sir—I am not afraid of myself," exclaimed Morcar: "I would lay down my life to serve you! But I am convinced that you will only attract unpleasant attention to yourself, if you travel with a follower: one person can slip unperceived through so many perilous places, where two together would be suspected. Besides, sir, I shall not be quite so badly off in this strange country, as you suppose."

"How so, Morcar?" demanded Richard, surveying him with astonishment.

"There are Zingarees in this land as well as elsewhere," replied Morcar; "and amongst them I shall be safe."

"On that consideration alone," exclaimed Richard, struck by the truth of the observation, and well-pleased at the idea that his faithful dependant would indeed derive no small benefit, under circumstances, from the aid of that extensive and mysterious freemasonry to which he belonged,—"on that consideration alone I will consent to this separation. At day-break we will rise, and each take a different route. I will give you the map of Castelcicala, as its geography has been so well studied by me that I am fully acquainted with the direction of all the principal towns and cities. But let us fix a place where we can meet again. Our grand object must be to gain the city of Naples. On your arrival there, proceed to the abode of the English Consul, and leave with him the name of the inn where you put up: if I have reached Naples before you, that functionary will be enabled to tell you where I am to be found."

"I will strictly follow your instructions, sir," said Morcar.

"And now, my good friend," continued our hero, "I must speak to you as if I were making my last will and testament; for heaven alone knows whether I shall ever quit this country alive. You remember the secret of my affection for a noble lady, which I communicated to you the night before we landed on the Castelcicalan coast?"

"Not a syllable of what you told me, sir, has been effaced from my memory," replied Morcar. "You enjoined me that, if any thing fatal should occur to yourself, and Providence should enable me to return to England, I was to seek the Princess Isabella, and break to her the tidings and manner of your death, with the assurance that your last thoughts were given to her!"

"Such was my request, Morcar," said Richard. "I need now observe little more than repeat it. Let the one who reaches Naples first wait for the other fifteen days; and, if he come not by the expiration of that period, then let him——"

"Surmise the worst," added Morcar, seeing that our hero hesitated. "Your message to the Princess shall be delivered—if God ordain that so sad a result ensues. And, on your part, sir—if I come not to the place of appointment, and you succeed in reaching it——"

"Say no more, my dear friend," interrupted Markham, pressing the gipsy's hand; "we understand each other!"

And they each dashed away the tears from their eyes.

Richard then divided the contents of his purse into two equal portions, and presented one to Morcar. The gipsy positively refused to accept any thing beyond a few pieces of gold; but Markham was more positive still, and compelled him to assent to the equitable partition of the large sum which Eliza's bounty had supplied.

They then retired to rest.

At day-break Markham started up; but he looked in vain for Morcar.

On the table stood a pile of gold: it was the one which our hero had forced upon the gipsy;—and only two of the pieces had been taken from the heap.

"Generous man;" cried Markham: "God grant that I may one day be enabled to reward him for his fidelity and devotion to me!"

Having hastily dressed himself, our hero concealed about his person the few necessaries that were indispensable, and left the remainder in his valise.

He then descended to the coffee-room, hurried over a slight refreshment, and, having settled the account, took his departure, telling the landlord to keep the valise for him until his return.

But now how lonely, forlorn, and friendless did he feel, as he hurried away from the inn where he had parted with his faithful dependant!

CHAPTER CLXXIX.

THE JOURNEY.

Richard Markham struck into the fields, and pursued his way in a southerly direction.

He avoided even the small hamlets, and kept as much as possible in the open country.

Being unaware of the precise nature of the danger which menaced his life,—although of course connecting it with the part which he had recently played in the invasion,—he feared lest printed descriptions of his person, with rewards for his apprehension, might be circulated; and this source of terror induced him to choose the most secluded paths.

It was long after sunset when he stopped at a small country public-house, where he determined to rest for the night.

To his great joy the coffee-room was unoccupied by other travellers; and the landlord appeared a simple, honest kind of half-farmer, half-publican, who never troubled himself about any one's business save his own.

A good supper and a bottle of very excellent wine tended to raise our hero's spirits: and when the meal was concluded, he fell into a train of meditation on the events of the preceding evening.

A thousand times did he ask himself who could be the occupant of that chaise which was journeying in such haste? for that there *was* some person inside the vehicle, who had urgent reasons for the utmost circumspection, the fact of the drawn blinds would not permit him to doubt. Moreover, the young *aide-de-camp* was evidently riding *outside* for the purpose of answering any questions that might be put, paying the bills, directing the postillions, and in all respects acting with a view to save the person or persons inside from the necessity of giving their own orders.

The words—"*Terrible events have occurred at Montoni*"—were also fraught with a most menacing and mysterious importance. What could they mean? whom had these events endangered? Was it possible that the kindness of the Grand Duchess towards himself had been detected? And if so, what results could such a discovery have produced?

While he was thus lost in the most painful conjectures, a horseman suddenly galloped up to the door of the inn; and in a few moments the traveller himself entered the coffee-room.

He was a slightly-built, middle-aged man, with a good-humoured expression of countenance. He was attired in a kind of undress cavalry uniform, consisting of a foraging-cap with a broad gold band, a laced jacket, trousers with a red stripe down each leg, and a very small black leathern knapsack at his back.

"Now, landlord," he exclaimed, as he entered the room, followed by the individual whom he thus addressed, "some supper at once—not a moment's unnecessary delay—and see that a fresh horse is ready in twenty minutes. That is all the rest I can allow myself here."

The landlord bustled about to serve up the best his house could afford in such haste; and in the meantime the new-comer addressed himself to our hero.

"Rather chilly this evening, sir," he said.

"And yet you can scarcely feel the cold, considering the pace at which you appear to ride," returned Richard with a smile.

"Egad! I do not ride so for pleasure, I can assure you," observed the man. "But I presume that you are travelling in this country for your amusement," he added: "for I perceive by your accent that you are not a Castelcicalan, and I can judge your avocation by that portfolio lying near you."

"You have guessed correctly," answered Richard. "Have you travelled far to-day?"

"A considerable distance. I am, as perhaps you may know by my dress, a government courier: and I am the bearer of dispatches from Montoni to the Captain-General of Montecuculi."

"Any thing new in the capital?" asked Richard, scarcely able to conceal the anxiety with which he waited for a reply.

"Great news," was the answer. "The Grand Duchess has fled."

"Fled!" ejaculated Markham.

"Yes—left the capital—gone no one knows where, and no one knows why," continued the courier. "Montoni is in a dreadful ferment. Martial law was proclaimed there the day before yesterday; and a tremendous crowd collected in the Palace-square in the evening. The military were called out, but refused to fire upon the people. Numerous conflicting reports are in circulation: some say that the Grand Duke has sent to demand the aid of an Austrian force. The people attacked the mansion of the Prime Minister; and the firmness of the Political Prefect alone prevented serious mischief. In fact, sir," added the courier, sinking his voice to a whisper, "we are on the eve of great events; and for my part—although I am in the government employment—I don't think it's treason to say that I would as soon serve Alberto as Angelo."

At that moment the landlord entered with a tray containing the courier's supper; and the conversation ceased. Nor had our hero an opportunity of reviving it; for the courier was too busily engaged with his knife and fork to utter a word during his meal; and the moment it was terminated, he wished Markham good night and took his departure.

Still our hero had gleaned enough to afford him some clue to the mystery of the post-chaise. The Grand Duchess had fled: the reason of her flight was not publicly known. Was it not probable that she was an occupant of the post-chaise which journeyed so swiftly? did not this idea receive confirmation from the fact that Mario Bazzano accompanied the vehicle?

Then again occurred the question, had the Grand Duchess involved herself in difficulty by her generosity towards him? The bare supposition of such an occurrence was the source of the most poignant anguish in the breast of Richard Markham.

He retired to rest; but his sleep was uneasy; and he awoke at an early hour, little refreshed. He was however compelled to pursue his melancholy journey, which he resumed with a heavy heart and with a mind oppressed by a thousand vague apprehensions.

There was one circumstance which especially afflicted him. He had not dared to write a letter to Isabella; and he knew that the tidings of the failure of the invasion would shortly reach her. Then what must be her feelings! She would believe that he had either fallen in the conflict, or was a prisoner in some Castelcicalan fortress; and he entertained so profound a conviction of her love for him,—a love as sincere as that which he experienced for her,—that he dreaded the effects which would be produced upon her by the most painful uncertainty or the worst apprehensions concerning his fate.

Still, how could he write to her with any hope that the letter would reach her? In the existing condition of Castelcicala, he felt persuaded that all correspondence addressed to Prince Alberto or any member of his family, would be intercepted. This conviction had hitherto prevented him from addressing a word to that charming girl whose image was ever present to his mind.

But as he journeyed wearily along, it suddenly struck him that he might write to Whittingham, and enclose a note for Isabella. Besides, he was also anxious to acquaint that faithful servant, as well as Mr. Monroe and Ellen, with the hopes that he entertained of being shortly enabled to return to his native land. He accordingly resolved to put this project into execution.

For that purpose he was compelled to pass the next night at a town where there was a post-office. He wrote his letters in the most guarded manner, and omitted the signature. When they were safely consigned to the letter-box, he felt as if a considerable load had been taken off his mind.

At this town he gleaned a great deal of information concerning the agitated condition of the country. Martial law had been proclaimed in every province; and the worst fears existed as to the Grand Duke's ulterior views. The idea of Austrian intervention appeared to be general; and deep, though not loud, were the curses which were levelled against the policy of that sovereign who could venture to call in a foreign soldiery to rivet the shackles of slavery which he had imposed upon his subjects.

One circumstance peculiarly struck our hero: the Grand Duke seemed to possess no supporters—no apologists. The hatred excited by his tyranny was universal. Castelcicala only required a champion to stand forward—a leader to proclaim the cause of liberty—and Richard felt convinced that the whole nation would rise as one man against the despot.

That the Grand Duchess had fled precipitately from Montoni, was a fact now well known; but the motives and details of her departure were still veiled in the most profound mystery.

There was another circumstance which forced itself on Markham's observation: this was that the deepest sympathy existed in behalf of the prisoners who had been taken in the conflict near Ossore, and who, it seemed, had all been despatched to the fortress of Estella. Richard's prowess in rallying the troops also appeared to be well known; and on more occasions than one, during his wanderings in Castelcicala, did he find himself the object of the most flattering discourse, while those who eulogised him little suspected that the hero of their panegyric was so near.

But it is not our intention to follow him through those wanderings. Suffice it to say that he found his journey more wearisome than he had anticipated; and that he was frequently compelled to avail himself of a carrier's van along the by-roads, or to hire a horse, in order to diminish the fatigues of his wayfaring.

It was on the twelfth evening after he left Friuli, where he had parted with Morcar, that he crossed the river Usiglio at a ferry about four miles to the east of Pinalla.

He was now only forty miles from the Neapolitan frontier; and in twenty-four hours more he fondly hoped to be beyond the reach of danger.

He had partaken of but little refreshment during that day, for the nearer he approached the point where peril would cease and safety begin, the more anxious did he become.

Having crossed the ferry, he inquired of the boatman the way to the nearest inn. A dreary by-lane was pointed out to him, with an intimation that it would lead to a small public-house, at the distance of about a mile.

Richard pursued his way, and had proceeded about three hundred yards down the lane, which was shaded on either side by large chesnut-trees, when several individuals rushed upon him so suddenly that he had no time to offer any effectual resistance.

He, however, struggled desperately, as two of the banditti (for such his assailants were) attempted to bind his arms with cords.

But his endeavours to free himself from their grasp were vain and fruitless, and only provoked a rougher treatment at their hands; for one of the banditti drew a pistol from his belt, and with the butt-end of the weapon aimed a desperate blow at our hero's head.

Richard fell, bleeding and insensible, upon the ground.

When he opened his eyes again, he found himself lying in a comfortable bed.

Putting aside the damask-silk curtains, he glanced anxiously around the room, which was sumptuously furnished.

He fell back on his pillow, and strove to collect his scattered ideas. His head pained him: he raised his hand to his forehead, and found that it was bandaged.

Then the attack of the banditti in the dark lane flashed across his mind; and he mechanically thrust his hand into his bosom.

Alas! Armstrong's letter was gone!

CHAPTER CLXXX.

THE "BOOZING-KEN" ONCE MORE.

We must now direct our readers' attention for a short space to the parlour of the Boozing-Ken on Saffron Hill.

It was nine o'clock in the evening; and, as usual, a motley company was assembled in that place.

A dozen persons, men and women, were drinking the vile compounds which the landlord dispensed as "Fine Cordial Gin," "Treble X Ale," "Real Jamaica Rum," "Best Cognac Brandy," and "Noted Stout."

At one of the tables sate the Buffer, smoking a long clay pipe, and from time to time paying his respects to a pot of porter which stood before him. He occasionally glanced towards the clock as if he were expecting some one; and then an impatient but subdued curse rose to his lips, proving that the individual for whom he waited was behind his time.

"Well, as I was saying," exclaimed an old shabbily-dressed and dissipated looking man, who sate near the fire, "it's a burning shame to make people pay so dear for such liquor as this;"—and he made a quart-pot, which he held in his hand, describe sundry diminutive circles, in order to shake up the liquor whereat he gazed with disgust.

"Why do you drink it, then, friend Swiggs?" demanded the Buffer, in a surly tone. "You was once a licensed witler yourself: and I'll be bound no one ever doctored his lush more than you did."

"Of course I did!" ejaculated the old man. "The publican can't live without it. Look how he's taxed—look how the police preys upon him—look at the restrictions as to hours that he's subject to. I tell you the publican *must* adulterate his liquor—aye, even the most honest. But I don't like to drink it so, none the more for all that. Besides, this beer is so preciously done up, that one does not know whether there's most cocculus indicus or most tobacco-juice in it."

"What's cocculus indicus?" asked the Buffer.

"An Indian berry of so poisonous a nature," was the reply, "that the natives throw it into the ponds to render the fish insensible and make them float on the surface, when of course they are easily caught. That will show you the strength of it—ha! ha!"

And the old man chuckled with a sort of malignant triumph, as he recalled to mind his own practices when he was in business, and ere dissipation ruined him.

"Oh! I have the *Vintners' Guides* all by heart, I can assure you," continued Swiggs; "and now that I'm out of the business, and never likely to be in it again, I don't mind telling you a secret or two. Let us begin with the beer. In the first place the brewer adulterates it, to save his malt and hops; and then the publican adulterates it, to increase its quantity. *His* business is to make one butt of beer into two—aye, and sometimes three. Ha! ha! Now, how do you think he does it? He first deluges it with water: then, of course, it's so weak and flat that no one could possibly drink it. It wants alcohol, or spirit in it; it wants the bitter flavour; it wants pungency; it wants age; and it wants froth. All these are supplied by means of adulteration. Cocculus indicus, henbane, opium, and Bohemian rosemary are used instead of alcohol: these are all poisons; and the Bohemian rosemary is of so deadly a nature, that a small sprig produces a raving intoxication. Ha! ha! that's good so far! Then aloes, quassia, wormwood, and gentian supply the place of hops, and give bitterness to the hell-broth. Ginger, cassia-buds, and capsicum, produce pungency. Treacle, tobacco-juice, and burnt sugar give it colour. Oil of vitriol not only makes it transparent, but also imparts to it the taste of age; so that a butt so doctored immediately seems to be two years old. I needn't tell you what sort of a poison oil of vitriol is: I don't want to suggest the means of suicide—ha! ha! But when the brew has gone so far, it wants the heading—that froth, you know, which you all fancy to be a proof of good beer. Alum, copperas, and salt of tartar will raise you as nice a heading as ever you'd wish to dip your lips in."

"You don't mean to say all that's true, Swiggs?" exclaimed the Buffer; "for though I ain't partickler, I don't think I shall ever like porter again."

"True!" ejaculated the old man, contemptuously: "it's as true as you're sitting there! But there's a dozen other ingredients that go into the stuff you lap up so pleasantly, and pay for as *beer*. What do you think of extract of poppies, coriander, nux vomica, black extract, Leghorn juice, and bitter beans? But all these names are Greek to you. They ain't to the publicans, though—ha! ha! Why half the poor people that go to lunatic asylums, are sent there by the poison called beer."

"What have you got to say agin blue ruin, old feller?" demanded a Knacker, who was regaling himself with a glass of gin-and-water.

"Blue ruin—gin!" cried the old man. "Ah! I can tell you something about that too. Oil of vitriol is the chief ingredient: it has the pungency and smell of gin. When you take the cork out of a bottle of *pure gin*, it will never make your eyes water: but the oil of vitriol *will*. Ha! ha! there's a test for you. Try it! Oil of turpentine, sulphuric æther, and oil of almonds are used to conceal the vitriol in the made-up gin. What is called *Fine Cordial Gin* is the most adulterated of all: it is concocted expressly for dram-drinkers—ha! ha!"

"Rum, I should think, is the best of all the spirits," said the Buffer.

"Because you like it best, perhaps?" exclaimed the old man. "Ha! ha! you don't know that the *Fine Jamaica Rum* is nothing else but the vile low-priced Leeward Island rum, which is in itself a stomach-burning fire-water of the deadliest quality, and which is mixed by the publican with cherry-laurel water and *devil*."

"What's *devil*?" asked the Knacker.

"Aye, what is it, indeed? It's nothing but chili pods infused in oil of vitriol—that's all! But now for *Best Cognac Brandy*," continued the old man. "Do you think the brandy sold under that name ever saw France—ever crossed the sea? Not it! Aqua ammonia, saffron, mace, extract of almond cake, cherry-laurel water, *devil*, terra japonica, and spirits of nitre, make up the brandy when the British spirit has been well deluged with water. That's your brandy! Ha! ha!"

"What a precious old sinner you must be, Swiggs," said one of the company, "if you used to make up such poisons as you're now talking about."

"Dare say I was—dare say I was," observed the old man, composedly. "Nearly every publican does the same, I tell you. Those who don't, go into the *Gazette*—that's all. Ha! ha! But if the poor are cheated and poisoned in that way, how do you think the middle classes and rich ones are served! Shall I tell you any thing about wine—eh?"

"Yes—do," cried several voices. "Let's hear how the swell cove is served out."

"Well, I'll tell you that too," continued the old man. "There's hundreds of *Wine-Guides* that contain instructions for the merchants, and vintners, and publicans. Take a bottle of cheap Port wine, and get a chemist to analyse it: he'll tell you it contains three ounces of spirits of wine, fourteen ounces of cyder, one ounce and a half of sugar, two scruples of alum, one scruple of tartaric acid, and four ounces of strong decoction of logwood. That's the way I used to make *my* Port wine. Not a drop—not a single drop of the juice of the grape. Ha! ha! Families bought it wholesale—three-and-sixpence the bottle—rank poison! Ha! ha! Nearly all fictitious wines possess too high a colour—particularly sherry: the way to make such wine pale is to put a quart of warm sheep's blood in the butt, and, when it's quite fine, to draw it off. I always did that—but I didn't tell the families so, though! Which do you think is the greatest cheat of all the cheap wines?—the Cape. The publicans sell it at eighteen-pence and two shillings. Why—it's nothing more than the drippings from the casks, the filterings of the lees, and all the spoiled white wines that happen to be in the cellar, mixed together with rum-cowe and cyder, and fined with sheep's blood."

"I'm glad to hear the rich is humbugged as well as the poor," observed the Knacker: "that's a consolation, at any rate."

"So it is," said a cat's-meat man, nodding his head approvingly.

"Humbugged!" ejaculated Swiggs, triumphantly: "I b'lieve you! I'll tell you how two-thirds of all the Port wine drunk in the United Kingdom is made:—Take four gallons of cyder, two quarts of the juice of red beet-root, two quarts of brandy, four ounces of logwood, half a pound of bruised rhatany root, and one ounce of alum: first infuse the logwood and rhatany root in the brandy and a gallon of the cyder for ten days; then strain off the liquor and mix all the other ingredients with it; put it into a cask, keep it for a month, and it will be fit to bottle. Not a drop of grape-juice there. Ha! ha! If the colour isn't quite right, an infusion of raspings of red sandars wood in spirits of wine will soon give it a beautiful red complexion. But then the bees'-wing. Ha! the bees'-wing—eh! A saturated solution of cream of tartar, coloured with Brazil-wood or cochineal, will give the best crust and bees'-wing you can imagine. There's for you! Port made in a month or six weeks can be passed off for wine ten or a dozen years old. The corks can easily be stained to indicate age—and who's to discover the cheat? Nobody but the chemist—ha! ha!"

"Well, I've learnt someot to-night," said the Knacker.

"Learnt something! You know nothing about it yet," cried the old man, who was on his favourite topic. "You don't know what poison—rank poison—there is in all these cheap wines;—aye, and in the dear ones too, for that matter. Sugar of lead is a chief ingredient! I needn't tell you that sugar of lead is a deadly poison: any fool knows that. Sal enixum and slaked lime are used to clear muddy wine; and litharge gives a sweet taste to wines that are too acid. Bitter almonds imparts to port a nutty flavour; cherry-laurel water gives it a bouquet; and tincture of raisin seeds endows it with a grapy taste—which it hasn't got and can't have otherwise. But I've told you enough for to-night. And now I dare say you wonder why I drink beer or spirits at all? Because I am old and miserable; because I am poor and wretched; because I must kill care somehow or another; and therefore I take daily doses of those slow poisons."

With these words the old man rose, and shuffled out of the room.

His denunciation of the abominable system of doctoring wines, spirits, and malt liquors produced a gloomy effect upon the company whom he left behind. The Buffer glanced often and often towards the clock: the time was passing rapidly; and yet the person for whom he was waiting came not.

"Who'll tip us a song?" said the Knacker, glancing around.

"There's Jovial Jenkins up in the corner there," exclaimed the cat's-meat man. "He's the chap for a song."

"Well, I don't mind, pals," cried a diminutive specimen of the male sex, dressed in a suit of clothes every way too large for him. "What shall I sing yer? Oh! I s'pose it must be the favourite—eh? Come—here goes, then."

And in another minute the parlour of the boozing-ken reverberated with the intonations of the following strange song:—

THE MAN OF MANY PURSUITS.[12]

Come, lip us a chant, pals! Why thus mum your dubber!

My gropus clinks coppers, and I'll fake the rubber:

Here's a noggin of lightning to slacken your glib;—

Then pass round the lush, and cease napping the bib.

T'other night we'd a precious rum squeeze at the Spell,

And, togg'd as a yokel, I used my forks well;

From a Rum-Tom-Pat's kickseys I knapp'd a green twitch,

And nearly got off the gold glims from his snitch.

But a swell with hock-dockeys and silken gam-cases,

Put the parish prig up to the rig of such places;—
So, finding the nib-cove was chanting the play,
I shov'd my trunk nimbly and got clean away.

As a jolly gay-tyke-boy I sometimes appear,
And chirp for the curs that are spelt in the leer;
Or as a leg-glazier, with fadger and squibs,
I work my way into the nibsomest cribs.

But when on these dodges the blue-bottles blow,
As a flue-flaker togg'd then at day-break I show:
And though from the slavey I get but a flag,
I can fly the blue-pigeon and thus bank the rag.

Sometimes as a mabber I dose the swell fred;—
Or else as a vamper I mill for a ned;
And as soon as my man is tripp'd by the gams,
A pal knaps his ticker, or frisks off his flamms.

But the life that I love is in Swell-street to shine,
With a Mounseer-fak'd calp, and my strummel all fine,
Heater-cases well polish'd, and lully so white,
And an upper ben fitting me jaunty and tight.

Then with nice silk rain-napper, or gold-headed dick,
I plunge neck and heels into sweet river-tick;
And if in a box of the stone-jug I get,
Though hobbled for macing, 'twill prove but a debt.

Then lip us a chant, pals! Why thus mum your dubber?
My gropus clinks coppers, and I'll fake the rubber:
A noggin of lightning will slacken our glib;
So pass round the lush, and let none nap the bib.

"Brayvo, Jovial Jen!" shouted the inmates of the boozing-ken parlour.

"You're the prince of good fellers at a spree," said the Knacker: "and I'll stand a quartern of blue ruin and two outs, in spite o' what old Swiggs said of the lush."

The promised treat was called, paid for, and disposed of.

Scarcely had the applause, which greeted this song, terminated, when the door opened, and Lafleur, Mr. Greenwood's French valet, entered the room.

He was disguised in a large rough coat and slouched hat; but the Buffer immediately recognised his countenance, and hurried to meet him.

"You're late," said the Buffer, in a low tone.

"Yes—I could not come before," answered the valet. "But I knew that you would wait for me, as I told you yesterday that the business was important."

"Well, we can't talk here," observed the Buffer. "There's a snug room up-stairs devoted to them that's got private business: and I'll show you the way."

The Buffer left the parlour, followed by Lafleur, whom he conducted to a private apartment on the first floor. A bottle of wine was ordered; and when the waiter had withdrawn, the Buffer made a sign for his companion to explain the object of the interview.

"You know very well that I am in the service of Mr. Greenwood, the Member of Parliament?" began Lafleur.

"Yes—me and two pals once did a little job for him on the Richmond road," answered the Buffer.

"You mean the affair of the robbery of Count Alteroni?" said Lafleur.

"Well—I do, since you know it. Does your master tell you all his secrets?" demanded the Buffer.

"No—no," was the reply; and the Frenchman gave a sly laugh. "But he can't very well prevent me listening at the door of his room, when he's engaged with people on particular business. I know enough to ruin him for ever."

"So much the better for you. There's nothing like being deep in one's master's secrets: it gives you a hold on him."

"Let us talk of the present business," said Lafleur. "Are you the man to do a small robbery on the Dover road, as skilfully as you helped to do it on the Richmond road?"

"I'm the man to do any thing for fair reglars," answered the Buffer. "Go on."

"I will explain myself in a few words," continued Lafleur. "By dint of listening at doors and looking over my master's papers when he was out, I have made a grand discovery. To-morrow evening Greenwood leaves town in a post-chaise and four for Dover. It seems that he has embarked in some splendid speculation with a house in Paris, and the success of it depends on influencing the rates of exchange between English and French money. He will take with him twenty thousand pounds in gold and Bank of England notes to effect this purpose."

"Never mind the rigmarole of the reasons," said the Buffer; "for I don't understand them no more than the Queen does the papers she signs, they say, by dozens and dozens at a sitting."

"It is sufficient, then, for *you* to know that Mr. Greenwood will leave London to-morrow evening with twenty thousand pounds, in a post-chaise," proceeded Lafleur. "His Italian valet and myself are to accompany him; and we are all to be well armed."

"What sort of a feller is your Italian wally?" demanded the Buffer.

"Not one of our sort," replied Lafleur; "he will do his duty to his master, although I don't think he has any very great love for him."

"Greenwood believes you to be stanch also, s'pose?"

"Of course he does. I shall have to see that his master's pistols are in proper order, and place them in the chaise; but the Italian will take care of his own. There will, consequently, only be *one pair* loaded with ball."

"I understand you," said the Buffer. "Still that one pair of pistols may send two good chaps to Davy Jones."

"Risk nothing, get nothing," observed Lafleur. "The chances are that Filippo and I shall ride together on the dickey: if so, the moment the horses are stopped, I shall have nothing more or less to do than turn suddenly on Filippo and prevent him from doing any mischief."

"So far, so good," said the Buffer. "But I ought to have at least three pals with me. Remember, there's two postillions; Greenwood himself won't part with his tin without a struggle; and Filippo, as you call him, might master you."

"Can you get three men as resolute as yourself to accompany you?" asked Lafleur.

"The notice is so deuced short," returned the Buffer; "but I think I can reckon on two. Long Bob and the Lully Prig," he added, in a musing tone, "are certain to jine in."

"Three of you will scarcely be sufficient," said Lafleur. "Only think of the sum that's at stake: we mustn't risk the loss of it by any want of precaution on our parts."

"Well—I must see," cried the Buffer. "It isn't that I don't know a many chaps in my line; but the thing is to get one that we're sure on—that won't peach either afore or arterwards. Ah! I lost my best pal in Tony Tidkins—poor feller!"

"The Resurrection Man, you mean?" said Lafleur.

"The same. Greenwood was a good patron of his'n," observed the Buffer; "but that wouldn't have perwented him from jining in along with me."

"I remember that Greenwood wanted Tidkins for some business or another nearly a year ago," said the French valet; "and he sent me with a note to him at this very place. He did not, however, come; but I called here a few days afterwards, and heard that he had received the letter."

"That was just about the time poor Tidkins was desperately wounded by Crankey Jem," said the Buffer, rather speaking to himself than to his companion; "and circumstances forced him to keep deuced close arterwards. But that's neither here nor there: let's talk on our own business. Leave me to get a proper number of pals; and now answer me a question or two. At what time does Greenwood intend to start?"

"At seven o'clock. He means to get to Dover so as to have a few hours' sleep before the packet leaves for Calais."

"Then the business mustn't be done this side of Chatham," said the Buffer: "it would be too early. There's a nice lonely part of the road, I remember, between Newington and Sittingbourne, with a chalk pit near, where we can divide the swag, and each toddle off in different directions arterwards. The chaise will reach that place about ten. Now, one more question:—where will the blunt be stowed away?"

"Under the seat inside, no doubt," answered Lafleur. "Then I may consider the business agreed upon between us?"

"As good as done, almost," said the Buffer.

At this moment the conversation was interrupted by a knock at the door.

The waiter entered, and whispered something to the Buffer.

"By God, how fortunate!" ejaculated this individual, his countenance suddenly assuming an expression of the most unfeigned joy. "Show him up—this minute!"

The waiter disappeared.

"Who is it?" demanded Lafleur.

"The very person we are in want of! He has turned up again:—that feller has as many lives as a cat."

"But who is it?" repeated Lafleur impatiently.

Before the Buffer could answer the question, the door was thrown open, and the Resurrection Man entered the room.

<u>12</u>. In order to avoid breaking the sense of this song by a constant repetition of those typographical signs which point a reference to foot-notes, we have deemed it best to give a complete glossary:—

Lip us a chant. Sing us a song.

Mum your dubber. Keep your mouth shut.

My gropus clinks coppers. My pocket has got money in it.

Fake the rubber. Stand treat this time.

Noggin of lightning. Quartern of gin.

Slacken your glib. Loosen your tongue.

Cease napping the bib. Leave off whining.

Precious-rum squeeze at the Spell. Good evening's work at the theatre.

Yokel. Countryman.

Forks. Fingers.

Rum-Tom-Pat. Clergyman.

Kickseys. Breeches.

Twitch. Silk net purse.

Glims. Spectacles.

Snitch. Nose.

Hock-dockeys. Shoes.

Gam-cases. Stockings.

Parish prig. Parson.

Nib-cove. Gentleman.

Chanting the play. Explaining the tricks and manœuvres of thieves.

Shov'd my trunk. Moved off.

Gay-tyke-boy. Dog-fancier.

Chirp. Give information.

Spelt in the leer. Advertised in the newspaper.

Leg-glazier. A thief who carries the apparatus of a glazier, and calls at houses when he knows the master and mistress are out, telling the servant that he has been sent to clean and mend the windows. By these means he obtains admission, and plunders the house of any thing which he can conveniently carry off.

Fadger. Glazier's frame.

Squibs. Paint brushes.

Nibsomest cribs. Best houses.

Blue-bottles. Police.

Flue flaker. Chimney-sweeper.

Slavey. Female servant.

Flag. Fourpenny-piece.

Fly the blue-pigeon. Cut the lead off the roof.

Bank the rag. Make some money.

Mabber. Cab-driver.

Dose the swell fred. Inveigle the fare into a public-house and hocus him.

Vamper. A fellow who frequents public-houses, where he picks a quarrel with any person who has got a ring or a watch about him, his object being to lead the person into a pugilistic encounter, so as to afford the vamper's confederate, or pal, the opportunity of robbing him.

Mill for a ned. Fight for a sovereign.

Gams. Legs.

Ticker. Watch.

Flamms. Rings.

Swell-street. The West End.

Mounseer-fak'd calp. A hat of French manufacture.

Strummel. Hair.

Heater-cases. Wellington boots.

Lully. Shirt.

Upper ben. Coat.

Rain-napper. Umbrella.

Gold-headed dick. Riding-whip.

River-tick. Tradesmen's books.

Box of the stone-jug. Cell in Newgate.

Hobbled. Committed for trial.

Macing. Swindling.

'Twill prove but a debt. Swindlers of this class usually arrange their business in such a manner as to escape a conviction on the plea that the business is a mere matter of debt. In order to induce the jury to come to this decision, recourse is had to the assistance of pals, who depose to conversations which they pretended to overhear between the prosecuting tradesman and the swindling prisoner, but which in reality never took place.

CHAPTER CLXXXI.

THE RESURRECTION MAN AGAIN.

Anthony Tidkins was dressed in a most miserable manner; and his whole appearance denoted poverty and privation. He was thin and emaciated; his eyes were sunken; his cheeks hollow; and his entire countenance more cadaverous and ghastly than ever.

"My dear fellow," cried the Buffer, springing forward to meet him; "how glad I am to see you again. I really thought as how you was completely done for."

"And no thanks to you that I wasn't," returned the Resurrection Man gruffly. "Didn't you leave me to die like a dog in the plague-ship?"

"I've been as sorry about that there business, Tony, ever since it happened, as one can well be," said the Buffer: "but if you remember the hurry and bustle of the sudden panic that came over us, I'm sure you won't harbour no ill-feeling."

"Well, well—the least said, the soonest's mended," growled the Resurrection Man, taking his friend's hand. "Holloa, Lafleur! What are you doing here?"

"Business—business, Mr. Tidkins," answered the valet; "and you're the very man we are in want of."

"The very man," echoed the Buffer. "I give up the command of the expedition to him: he's my old captain."

"In the first place, order me up some grub and a pint of brandy," said the Resurrection Man; "for I've been precious short of every thing at all decent in the eating or drinking way of late;—and while I refresh myself with some supper, you can tell me what new scheme there is in the wind. Of course I'm your man, if there's any good to be done."

The waiter was summoned: Lafleur ordered him to bring up the entire contents of the larder, together with a bottle of brandy; and when these commands were obeyed, the Resurrection Man fell to work with extraordinary voracity, while the French valet briefly explained to him the nature of the business already propounded to the Buffer.

The hopes of obtaining a considerable sum of money animated the eyes of Tidkins with fire and his cadaverous countenance with a glow of fiendish satisfaction. He highly approved of the idea of engaging the Lully Prig and Long Bob in the enterprise; for he entertained a good opinion of their courage, in spite of the affair of the plague-ship. Indeed, he could well understand the invincible nature of the panic-terror which had seized upon them on that occasion; and, as he foresaw that their co-operation would be valuable in other matters, he was disposed to forget the past.

In fine, all the preliminary arrangements were made with Lafleur, who presented the two villains each with a ten pound-note as an earnest of his sincerity, and then took his departure.

When the Resurrection Man and the Buffer were alone together, they brewed themselves strong glasses of brandy and water, lighted their pipes, and naturally began to discourse on what had passed since they last saw each other.

The Buffer related all that had occurred to him after his return to Mossop's wharf,—how he had been pursued by the three men belonging to the *Blossom*,—how one turned out to be Richard Markham, another a policeman in disguise, and the third Morcar,—how they had vainly searched the *Fairy* to discover Anthony Tidkins,—and how he himself eventually sold the lighter.

"Since then," added the Buffer, "I have not been doing much, and was deuced glad when Greenwood's valet came to me last evening and made an appointment with me for to-night to talk upon some business of importance. You know what that business is; and I hope it will turn up a trump—that's all."

"Then the whole affair of the *Blossom* was a damnation plant?" cried the Resurrection Man, gnashing his teeth with rage. "And that hated Markham was at the bottom of it all? By the thunders of heaven, I'll have the most deadly vengeance! But how came you to learn that Morcar was one of the three?"

"Because I heard Markham call him by that name when they all boarded the *Fairy*; and I instantly remembered the gipsy that you had often spoken about. But what do you think? He was the Black—the counterfeit Brummagem scoundrel that could neither speak nor hear. The captain was the blue-bottle; and Markham, I s'pose, had kept down below during the time the *Blossom* was at Mossop's. It was a deuced good scheme of theirs; and if you hadn't been left in the plague-ship, it might have gone precious hard with you."

"Well said, Jack," observed the Resurrection Man. "Out of evil sometimes comes good, as the parsons say. But that shan't prevent me from doing Master Richard Markham a turn yet."

"You must go to Italy, then," said the Buffer laconically.

"What gammon's that?" demanded Tidkins.

"Why, I happened yesterday morning to look at a newspaper in the parlour down stairs, and there I read of a battle which took place in some country with a cursed hard name in Italy, about three weeks ago; and what should I see but a long rigmarole about the bravery of '*our gallant fellow-countryman, Mr. Richard Markham,*' and '*the great delight it would be to all the true friends of freedom to learn that he was not retained amongst the prisoners*'."

"But perhaps he was killed in the battle, the scoundrel?" said the Resurrection Man.

"No, he wasn't," answered the Buffer; "for the moment I saw that all this nonsense was about him, I read the whole article through; and I found that he *had* been taken prisoner, but had either been let go or had made his escape. No one, however, seems to know what's become of him;—so p'r'aps he's on his way back to this country."

"I'd much sooner he'd get hanged or shot in Italy," said the Resurrection Man. "But if he ever does come home again, I'll be square with him—and no mistake."

"Now you know all that has happened to me Tony," exclaimed the Buffer, "have the kindness to tell us how you got out of that cursed scrape in the *Lady Anne.*"

"I will," said the Resurrection Man, refilling his glass. "After you all ran away in that cowardly fashion, I tried to climb after you; but I fell back insensible. When I awoke, the broad day-light was shining overhead; and a boy was looking down at me from the deck. He asked me what I was doing there. I rose with great difficulty; but I was much refreshed with the long sleep I had enjoyed. The boy disappeared; and in a few minutes the surgeon came and hailed me down the hatchway. I begged him to help me up out of the hold, and I would tell him every thing. He ordered me to throw aside my pistols and cutlass, and he would assist me to gain the deck. I did as he commanded me. He and the boy then lowered a rope, with a noose; I put my foot in the noose, grasped the rope tight, and was hauled up. The surgeon instantly presented a pistol, and said, '*If you attempt any violence, I'll shoot you through the head.*' I declared that nothing was farther from my intention, and begged him to give me some refreshment. This request was complied with; and I then felt so much better, that I was able to walk with comparative ease. It, however, seemed as if I had just recovered from a long illness: for I was weak, and my head was giddy. I told the surgeon that I was an honest hard-working man; that I had come down to Gravesend the day before to see a friend; and had fallen in with some persons who offered me a job for which I should be well paid; that I assented, and accompanied them to their boat; that when I understood the nature of their business, I declared I would have nothing more to do with it; that they swore they would blow my brains out if I made any noise; that I was compelled to board the ship with them; that when some sudden sound alarmed them as they were examining the goods in the hold, they knocked me down with the butt-end of a pistol; and that I remembered nothing more until the boy awoke me by calling out to me from the deck. The surgeon believed my story, and said, '*A serious offence has been perpetrated, and you must declare all you know of the matter before a magistrate.*' I of course signified my willingness to do so, because I saw that the only chance of obtaining my liberty was by gaining the good opinion of the surgeon; for he had a loaded pistol in his hand— I was unarmed—and the police-boat was within hail. '*But, according to the quarantine laws,*' continued the surgeon, *'you cannot be permitted to leave the vessel for the present; and what guarantee have I for your good behaviour while you are on board?'"*

"That was a poser," observed the Buffer.

"No such thing," said the Resurrection Man. "I spoke with so much apparent sincerity, and with such humility, that I quite gained the surgeon's good opinion. I said, '*You can lock me in your cabin during the day, sir; or you can bind my hands with cords; and, at night, I can sleep in the hold from which you released me, with the hatches battened down.*'—'*I really do believe you to be an honest man,*' exclaimed the surgeon; '*but I must adopt some precaution. You shall be at large during the day; and I think it right to give you due notice that I carry loaded pistols constantly with me. At night you shall sleep in the hold, with the hatches battened down, as you say.*' I affected to thank him very sincerely for his kindness in leaving me at liberty during the day; and he then repaired to the fore-cabin to attend to his patients."

"Hadn't he got the plague himself?" inquired the Buffer.

"No: but the fœtid atmosphere of the fore-cabin, to which he was compelled so frequently to expose himself, had made him as emaciated and as pale as if he had only just recovered from the malady. I got into conversation with the boy, and found that he had contrived, shortly after you and the others decamped, to free his arms from the cords with which we had bound him; and that his first care was to release the surgeon. They neither of them entertained the remotest suspicion that any of the pirates were left in the ship, until the boy discovered me in the hold shortly after day-break."

"Well—and how did you escape after all?"

"I remained three or four days on board, before I put any scheme into force, although I planned a great many. At night I could do nothing, because I was a prisoner in the hold; and during the day the police-boat was constantly about, besides the sentinels on land. The surgeon always made me go down into the hold while it was still day-light; and never let me out again until after sunrise; so that I was always in confinement during the very time that I might contrive something to effect my escape from that infernal pest-ship. But the surgeon seemed afraid to trust me when it was dark. I never passed such a miserable time in my life. The slight touch that I had experienced of the plague—for it could have been nothing else—kept me in a constant fear lest it should return with increased force. How often did I mutter the most bitter curses against you and the other pals for abandoning me;—but now, in consequence of what you told me of the plant that Markham had set a-going against me, I am not sorry to think that I was left behind in the plague-ship. One evening—I think it was the fifth after my first entrance into the vessel—I observed that it was growing darker and darker; and yet the surgeon did not appear on deck with his loaded pistol to send me below. The boy was walking about eyeing me suspiciously; and at length he went down into the after-cabin. It struck me that the surgeon was probably indulging in a nap, and that the lad would awake him. It was not quite dark; but still I fancied that it was dusk enough to leap from the bow of the ship, which part of the vessel was high and dry, without alarming the sentinels on shore. At all events the chance was worth the trial. Seizing a handspike, I hurried forward, and sprang from the ship. Then, without losing a moment, I ran along the bank towards Gravesend, as rapidly as I could. In a short time I knew that I was safe. I hurled the handspike into the Thames, and walked on to the *Lobster Tavern*. There I obtained a bed—for I had plenty of ready money in my pocket. My only regret was that I had not been able to bring away any of the gold-dust with me."

"Why didn't you knock the surgeon and the boy on the head, and help yourself?" demanded the Buffer.

"So I should if I had seen a chance," replied the Resurrection Man; "but I was so weak and feeble all the time I was on board, that I was no match even for the young lad; and the surgeon always kept at such a distance, with a loaded pistol ready cocked in his hand, when I was ordered into the hold of an evening, or called up of a morning, that there wasn't a shadow of a chance. Well, I slept at the *Lobster Tavern*, and departed very early in the morning—long before it was day-light. I thought that London would be too hot for me, after every thing that had lately occurred; and I resolved to pay a visit to Walmer—my own native place. I was still too weak to walk many miles without resting; and so I took nearly four days to reach Walmer. Besides, I kept to the fields, and avoided the high road as much as possible. I took up my quarters at a small inn on the top of Walmer hill, and then made inquiries concerning all the people I had once known in or about the village. I have often related the former incidents of my life to you; and you will therefore recollect the baronet who was exchequered for smuggling, and was welcomed with open arms by his friends, when he paid the fine. You also remember all that occurred between him and me. I found that he had married his cook-maid, who ruled him with a rod of iron; and that the '*very select society*' of Walmer and Deal had all cut him on account of that connexion, which was much worse in their eyes than all the smuggling in which he had been engaged. In fact, he was a hero when prosecuted for smuggling; but now *no decent persons could associate with him*, since he had married his scullion. In a word, I learnt that he was as miserable as I could have wished him to be."

"And didn't you inquire after your friend the parson?" demanded the Buffer.

"You may be sure I did," returned the Resurrection Man. "He had made himself very conspicuous for refusing the sacrament to a young woman who was seduced by her lover, and had an illegitimate child; and the '*select society*' of Walmer greatly applauded him for his conduct. At length, about a year ago, it appears, this most particular of all clergymen was discovered by a neighbouring farmer in too close a conversation with the said farmer's wife; and his reverence was compelled to decamp, no one knows where. He, however, left his wife and children to the public charity. That charity was so great, that the poor woman and family are now inmates of the very workhouse where his reverence's slightest wish was once a law. I stayed at Walmer for nearly a week; and then departed suddenly for Ramsgate, with the contents of the landlord's till in my pocket. At Ramsgate I put up at a small public-house where I was taken dreadfully ill. For four months I was confined to my bed; and both landlord and landlady were very kind to me. At length I slowly began to recover; and, when I was well enough to walk abroad, I used to go upon the beach to inhale the sea-air. It was then summertime; and bathing was all the rage. I never was more amused in my life than to see the ladies, old as well as young, sitting on the beach, to all appearance deeply buried in the novels which they held in their hands, but in reality watching, with greedy eyes, the men bathing scarcely fifty yards off."

"You don't mean to say that?" cried the Buffer.

"I do indeed, though," returned Tidkins. "It was the commonest thing in the world for elderly dames and young misses to go out walking along the beach, or to sit down on it, close by the very spot where the men bathed, although there were plenty of other places to choose either for rambling or reading. Well, I stayed two more months at Ramsgate; and as the landlord and landlady of the public-house had behaved so kind to me, I took nothing from them when I went away. I merely left my little account unsettled. I walked over to Margate, with the intention of taking the steamer to London Bridge; but just as I was stepping on the jetty, some one tapped me on the shoulder, and, turning round, I beheld my landlord of the little inn on the top of Walmer hill. All my excuses, promises, and entreaties were of no avail: the man collared me—a crowd collected—a constable was sent for, and I was taken before a magistrate. Of course I was committed for trial, and sent across in a cart to Canterbury gaol. There I lay till the day before yesterday, when the sessions came on. By some extraordinary circumstance or another, no prosecutor appeared before the Grand Jury; and I was discharged. I resolved to come back to London;—for, after all, London is the place for business in our way. With all its police, it's the best scene for our labours. So here I am; and the moment I set foot in this ken, I find employment waiting for me."

"Well, I'm sorry to hear you've been lumbered, old feller," cried the respectable Mr. John Wicks; "but it's a blessin' the prosecutor never come for'ard. Let's, however, think of the present; and botheration to the past. I'm heartily glad you've turned up again. I was precious nigh going into mourning for you, Tony. Joking apart, though—this business of the Frenchman's looks well; and we must be about early to look after the Lully Prig and Long Bob. I know their haunts down by Execution Dock, just opposite to Mossop's."

"Where are you hanging out now, Jack?" inquired the Resurrection Man.

"Me and Moll has got a room in Greenhill's Rents—at the bottom of Saint John's Street, you know," was the answer.

"Well, I shall sleep here to-night," said the Resurrection Man; "and by six o'clock to-morrow morning I shall expect you."

CHAPTER CLXXXII.

MR. GREENWOOD'S JOURNEY.

It was six o'clock on the evening following the incidents related in the two preceding chapters.

Mr. Greenwood had just concluded an early dinner (early for him) after having devoted the greater part of the day to business in the City, and a small portion of it to his fair Georgian, for whom he had taken elegantly furnished apartments in Suffolk Street, Pall Mall.

Having disposed of his last glass of champagne, the honourable member for Rottenborough rang the bell.

Lafleur made his appearance.

"Is the chaise ordered for seven precisely?" inquired Mr. Greenwood.

"Yes, sir—seven precisely, sir," answered the valet.

"Did you write to my agent at Rottenborough to tell him that I should pass through that town at half-past eight, and that although I wished to preserve a strict incognito, yet I should not mind being recognised while the horses are changing at the inn?"

"I mentioned all that, sir," replied Lafleur; "and I suggested that he had better get together a hundred or so of persons in the tap-room, to be ready to rush out and cheer you."

"That was well thought of, Lafleur. I have already sent a paragraph to the morning newspaper in which I am a shareholder, stating that I was enthusiastically cheered as I passed through Rottenborough. It will appear to-morrow morning. Have you renewed my positive orders to the policeman on this beat to take all beggars into custody who are found loitering near my door?"

"I have, sir. One woman, with three whimpering children, was dragged off to the station-house half an hour ago, for looking too earnestly down the area windows," said Lafleur. "Her husband has just been to beg you to intercede with the Inspector for her release. He said he was a hard-working man, and that it must be a mistake, as his wife was no beggar."

"And what did you say, Lafleur?" demanded Mr. Greenwood, sternly.

"I said nothing, sir: I merely banged the door in his face."

"That was right and proper. I am determined to put down vagrancy. Nothing is more offensive to the eye than those crawling wretches who are perpetually dinning in one's ears a long tale about their being half-starved."

"Yes, sir—it is very disagreeable, sir," observed Lafleur.

"The free and independent electors of Rottenborough have not sent me to Parliament for nothing, I can assure you," continued Mr. Greenwood.

"No, sir," responded Lafleur.

"And I, from my place in the House, will denounce this odious system of mendicancy," added Mr. Greenwood.

"Yes, sir," observed Lafleur.

"By-the-by, did you send the letter I gave you just now to the post?"

The valet answered in the affirmative.

"I am glad of that. It was to the Reverend Dr. Beganuph—the rector of some place in some county—I am sure I forget where. However—the reverend gentleman is having the parish church enlarged—or made smaller—I really forget which,—but I know it's something of the kind;—and as he has sent a circular to all persons whose names are in the *Court Guide*, soliciting subscriptions, I cannot, of course, refuse to contribute my mite of five pounds to the pious work—especially as the list of subscribers is to be advertised in the principal London and provincial papers. We must support the Church, Lafleur."

"Yes, sir—decidedly, sir," observed the valet.

"What would become of us without the Church?" continued Mr. Greenwood. "It is the source from which flow all the blessings of Christian love, hope, benevolence, and charity. Hark! Lafleur, I do really believe there is a woman singing a ballad in the street! Run out and give her into custody this minute."

"Beg your pardon, sir," said the valet: "it's only the muffin-boy."

"Oh! that's different," observed Mr. Greenwood, rising from his seat. "The chaise will be here at seven, you say?"

"Yes, sir."

"You and Filippo will accompany me. Tell Filippo to see that his fire-arms are in good order; and do you attend to mine as well as your own. Not that I apprehend any danger on such a road as that on which we are about to travel; still it is better to be prepared."

"Decidedly, sir," answered Lafleur, not a muscle of his countenance betraying any extraordinary emotion.

"Take a lamp to my study," said Greenwood; "and then go and see about the fire-arms. Let my case of pistols be put inside the chaise."

"Yes, sir;"—and Lafleur was about to leave the room, when he suddenly recollected himself, and said, "If you please, sir, your boot-maker sent your new slippers this morning, wrapped up in a piece of the *Weekly Dispatch*. I thought I had better mention it, sir."

"By God, you have done well to acquaint me with this infamy, Lafleur!" cried Mr. Greenwood, desperately excited. "The scoundrel! he reads the *Dispatch*, does he?—the journal that possesses more influence over the masses than even pulpits, governments, sovereigns, or religious tracts! The villain! I always thought that man was a democrat at heart; because one day when I told him if he didn't vote for the Tory Churchwarden he would lose my custom, he smiled—yes, smiled! And so he reads the *Dispatch*—the people's journal—the vehicle of all argument against our blessed constitution—the champion to which all who fancy themselves oppressed, fly as naturally as bees to flowers! Lafleur," added Mr. Greenwood, solemnly, "you will send to that boot-maker, and tell him to show his face no more at the house of the Member for Rottenborough."

"Yes, sir."

And Lafleur left the room.

A few minutes afterwards Mr. Greenwood repaired to his study, where the lamp had already been placed upon the table.

He then opened his iron safe, and drew forth a large canvass bag full of sovereigns. This he consigned to a tin box, resembling those in which lawyers keep their clients' papers. Three more bags, of the same size as the first, were taken from the safe and stowed away in this japanned case.

"Four thousand pounds!" murmured Greenwood to himself. "How many a family would be made happy with only the hundredth part of that sum! But those who want the glittering metal should toil for it as I have done."

Mr. Greenwood, having thus complimented himself upon those "toils" whereby he had gained his wealth, proceeded to take a large portfolio from the iron safe.

Partially opening its various compartments, so as to obtain a glance at the contents, he smiled still more complacently than when his eyes lingered on the canvass bags.

"Sixteen thousand pounds in Bank of England notes," he exclaimed aloud, as he consigned the portfolio to the tin case. "And these twenty thousand pounds, judiciously applied in Paris, will produce me twenty-five thousand clear gain—twenty-five thousand at the least!"

His really handsome countenance wore an expression of triumph, as he carefully locked the tin case, and placed the key in his pocket.

"My combinations are admirable! Thirty thousand pounds, already embarked in these Parisian speculations, have prepared the way for enormous gains: and now," continued Greenwood,—"now this sum,"—and he glanced towards the tin box—"will strike the decisive blow! It is a glorious science—that of the financier! And who is more subtle than I? True—I have experienced some losses during the past week—a few thousands: but they are nothing! I was wrong to job as I did in the English funds. The fluctuations in the French securities are the means by which brilliant fortunes can be made! The timid talk of the great risks—Pshaw! Let them combine their projects as I have done!"

He ceased, and surveyed himself complacently in the mirror above the mantel.

He then rang the bell.

Lafleur appeared in about a minute; but so calm, composed, and unruffled was his countenance, that no living soul would have suspected that he had been attentively listening at the door of the study all the while his master was transferring the treasure from the iron safe to the tin box.

"Bring me my upper coat and travelling cap, Lafleur," said Mr. Greenwood, not choosing to lose sight of his tin box.

Lafleur once more disappeared, and speedily returned with his master's travelling attire.

He announced at the same time that the chaise was at the door.

In a few minutes, Mr. Greenwood was ensconced in the vehicle. The tin box was stowed away under the seat: and his case of pistols lay by his side, within convenient reach.

Filippo and Lafleur mounted the dickey: the postillions cracked their whips; and the equipage rolled rapidly away from Spring Gardens.

At half-past eight o'clock precisely the vehicle drove up to the door of the principal inn of which the town of Rottenborough could boast.

The ostlers seemed to bungle in a very unusual manner, as they changed the horses; and full five minutes elapsed ere they could loosen the traces. In a word, they punctually obeyed the directions of Mr. Greenwood's agent in that famous town.

Suddenly the door of the tap-room burst open and vomited forth about eighty of such queer and suspicious-looking fellows, that no prudent man would have walked down a dark lane where he knew any one of them to be lurking.

Out they came—in most admirable disorder—pell-mell—jostling, hustling, pushing, larking with each other.

"Hooray, Greenwood! brayvo, Greenwood!" they shouted, at the tops of voices somewhat disguised in liquor. "Greenwood for ever! Down with the Tories!"

"No—no!" shouted a little man, dressed in deep black, and who suddenly appeared at the head of the mob: "down with the Liberals, you mean!"

"Oh—ah! so it is!" cried the mob; and then they shouted louder than ever, "Hooray for Greenwood! Down with the Liberals! The Tories for ever!"

Then the little man in black, who was none other than the honourable member's agent, rushed up to the carriage window, exclaiming, "Ah! Mr. Greenwood!—you are discovered, you see! Very pretty, indeed, to think of passing through Rottenborough *incog.*,—you who are the hope and the glory of the town! Luckily a party of gentlemen—all independent electors," added the lawyer, glancing round at the ragged and half-drunken mob, "were partaking of some little wholesome refreshment together—quite accidentally—in the tavern; and thus they are blessed with an opportunity of paying their respects to their representative in our glorious Parliament!"

"Brayvo, Greenwood!" ejaculated the crowd of "gentlemen," when the little lawyer had concluded his speech.

"Gentlemen," said Mr. Greenwood, thrusting his head out of the chaise-window, "you cannot conceive the delight which I experience at this most unexpected—most unlooked-for, and entirely spontaneous expression of your good feeling towards me. Gentlemen, when I behold an enlightened—an independent—a respectable—and an intelligent assembly thus coming forward to signify an approval of my parliamentary career, I meet with an ample recompense for all my exertions and toils to maintain the interests of the great constituency of Rottenborough. Gentlemen, the eyes of the world are upon you at this moment——"

"Then the world can see in the dark without spectacles," cried one of the free and independent inhabitants of Rottenborough.

"Yes, gentlemen," continued Greenwood, unabashed by this interruption, which raised a general titter; "the eyes of the world are upon you; for when Rottenborough thus emphatically expresses itself in favour of its member, it is avowing its stanch adherence to the true principles of Conservatism. This is a great fact, gentlemen; and so long as Rottenborough remains faithful to those principles, the democratic disturbers of the public peace must look on and tremble!"

With this splendid finale, Mr. Greenwood sank back in the chaise, which immediately drove rapidly away, amidst the uproarious shouts of the ragamuffins and tatterdemalions whom the lawyer had convoked, according to Lafleur's written instructions, for the occasion.

The ragamuffins and tatterdemalions were, however, well recompensed for their trouble; for they were copiously regaled with beer and tobacco before the arrival of the honourable member; and as soon as the member had departed, a supper of boiled tripe and onion-sauce was served up to them. The entertainment concluded with a quarrel and battle amongst the convivialists, several of whom took home with them broken heads and black eyes as trophies of their prowess.

Meantime the travelling-chaise rolled along the road.

The night was beautiful, clear, and frosty; and the moon rode high in the heavens.

Newington was passed; and Mr. Greenwood was just falling into a delicious sleep, when four men, wearing masks, and enveloped in thick pilot-coats, rushed from a hedge.

The horses were stopped suddenly; and two of the ruffians presented pistols at the heads of the postillions, menacing them with instant death if they offered any resistance.

Greenwood lowered the windows of the chaise, and holding a pistol in each hand, exclaimed, "I'll shoot the first who dares approach me!"

Filippo leapt to the ground on one side, and Lafleur followed him so closely, that he fell over the Italian, one of whose pistols went off by the shock, but without doing any mischief. Before he could make an effort to rise, Lafleur struck him on the head with the butt-end of one of his weapons, and laid him senseless on his back.

Meantime, while the Lully Prig and Long Bob took charge of the postillions, as above stated, the Resurrection Man and the Buffer rushed up to the door of the chaise.

Greenwood fired point-blank at Tidkins's head but without the slightest effect.

The door was opened; and the Resurrection Man sprang into the vehicle.

Greenwood fired his second pistol; but it merely singed his assailant's hair.

Then the Member of Parliament was dragged into the road, and bound hand and foot almost in the twinkling of an eye.

This being done, the Resurrection Man hastened to search the chaise, and speedily secured the tin box.

He gave a long shrill whistle: this was a signal to announce his success; for it had been previously agreed amongst the ruffians that they should not utter a word more than might be absolutely necessary, so that their voices might not be afterwards recognised, in case suspicion fell upon them. Moreover, the Resurrection Man's voice was well known to Greenwood; and thus this precaution was not an useless one.

The four robbers and Lafleur now beat a rapid retreat towards an adjacent chalk-pit, the Buffer leading the way, and the Resurrection Man carrying the box.

CHAPTER CLXXXIII.

KIND FRIENDS.

We left Richard Markham at the moment when, awaking in a strange bed, he perceived that Thomas Armstrong's letter was gone!

It would be impossible to describe his grief at this discovery.

The mysterious document, which he had treasured with so much care, and concerning which such particular instructions had been left by his departed friend,—a document which seemed so intimately to regard his future welfare,—had been wrested from him!

For a few moments he remained a prey to the deepest dejection; and tears stole into his eyes.

But he was not allowed to remain long in that unpleasant reverie.

The door opened slowly; and a light step approached his couch.

He drew aside the curtain, and beheld a middle-aged lady, elegantly dressed, and with a countenance on which the Almighty had written the word "Benevolence" in characters so legible, that a savage might have read and learnt to revere them.

Advancing close up to the bed, the lady said, in a soft tone, and in the Italian language:—"Be not alarmed, Signor Markham; you are with those who will treat you as your dauntless valour and noble mind deserve."

"Where am I, madam?" asked our hero, reassured by the lady's words and manner.

"In the house of my brother, Signor Viviani, the most eminent banker in Pinalla," answered the lady.

"And how did you discover my name, Signora?" inquired Richard.

"By means of a letter which was secured in a morocco-case about your person, and is now safe in my brother's possession," returned Signora Viviani.

"A thousand thanks, lady, for that assurance—a thousand sincere and grateful thanks!" exclaimed Markham, new life as it were animating his soul.

"Hush!" cried the banker's sister, placing her finger upon her lip: "you must not give way to excitement of feelings. You have been ill—very ill."

"How long, Signora, has this illness lasted?"

"Ten days," was the reply. "You have been delirious."

"Ten days!" ejaculated Richard. "Alas! poor Morcar—what will he think? where can he be?"

"Morcar is safe and knows that you are here, Signor," said the lady. "But do not excite yourself. Providence has allowed you to suffer, for its own wise and inscrutable purposes; but it never deserts the good and great."

"Ah! lady, how can I ever thank you sufficiently for the goodness of yourself and your brother towards one who is a perfect stranger to you?" said Markham, pressing the lady's hand respectfully to his lips.

"You are not altogether so much a stranger to us as you imagine," observed the banker's sister, with a mysterious but good-natured smile. "But I will not tantalize, nor excite you by keeping you in suspense. Your deceased countryman Thomas Armstrong was my brother's intimate friend."

"Is this possible?" cried Markham, overjoyed at such welcome intelligence. "Then Providence has not indeed deserted me!"

"I will now hasten and fetch my brother to see you," said the lady. "He is burning with impatience for the moment when he can converse with you."

Signora Viviani left the room, and shortly returned, accompanied by a gentleman of about sixty, and whose countenance was as expressive of excellent qualities as her own.

"Here is our patient, brother," said the lady, with a smile: "a patient, however, only in one sense, for he has been very impatient in his queries; and now you must satisfy his curiosity in all respects."

"I am delighted to find that you are able to devote a thought to such matters, my dear young friend," exclaimed the banker, pressing both Markham's hands cordially in his own; "for as a friend do I indeed regard you," added the excellent man.

"How can I possibly have deserved such kind sympathy at your hands?" asked Richard, overpowered by so much goodness.

"Your deceased and much lamented friend Thomas Armstrong was as a brother to me, during his residence at different times in Castelcicala," answered the banker; "and he constantly corresponded with me when he was in his native country. In the letters which he wrote during the last two years of his life, he mentioned you in terms which, did I know nothing else meritorious on your part, would have induced me to welcome you as a friend—as a son. But your noble conduct in the late attempt to release Castelcicala from the sway of a tyrant, and place that excellent Prince Alberto on the ducal throne, has confirmed my good opinion of you—if any such confirmation were necessary. I learnt from Armstrong that you were generous, intelligent, and virtuous: recent events have shown that you are brave and liberal-minded."

"How rejoiced I am that my conduct in that unhappy affair merits your approval," said Richard. "I have often trembled, since the fatal day when so many brave spirits came to these coasts to meet death or imprisonment, lest the more sensible portion of the Castelcicalan community should look upon the expedition as one concocted only by selfish or insane adventurers."

"Selfish or insane!" ejaculated Viviani. "Was Grachia selfish or insane? was Morosino a mere adventurer? Oh! no—Castelcicala weeps over the bloody graves of her patriots; and thousands of tongues are familiar with the name of Richard Markham."

The countenance of our hero became animated with a glow of generous enthusiasm as these words met his ears.

"How handsome he is!" exclaimed the banker's sister. "An old woman like me may say so without impropriety," she added smiling; "and even the Princess Isabella would not be offended, did she overhear me."

"The Princess!" ejaculated Richard, surprised at this allusion to that beautiful lady.

"You must not be angry with your faithful Morcar," said the banker's sister, smiling, "if he betrayed your secret. But it was with a good motive. When he found that you were with those who were anxious to be considered in the light of your friends, he communicated to us your secret respecting the Princess, in order that we might write to her and relieve her mind of all anxiety by assuring her that you were safe and well. So I took upon myself the duty of addressing a letter to her Highness the Princess Isabella, and I thought that a little falsehood relative to your real condition would be pardonable. I assured her that you were in security and in good health, save a sprain of the right hand which had compelled you to employ a secretary; and in order that the letter might be sure to reach her, my brother enclosed it in one to his agent in London, with special directions that it might be delivered as speedily as possible. Morcar also wrote a note to his father and his wife, and addressed it to the care of some person in a part of the English capital called Saint Giles's. In a word, you need be under no anxiety relative to your friends in England."

"Excellent lady!" cried Markham; "you accumulate kindnesses so rapidly upon me, that I know not how to testify my gratitude. And, Morcar, too—how thoughtful of him! Oh! I have indeed found good friends."

"You are doubtless anxious to learn how you came into this house," said the banker. "I will tell you—for you will not allow your mind to compose itself until you know every thing. I had been to pass the day with a friend whose country seat is at a few miles' distance from Pinalla; and I was returning home in an open chaise, attended by my groom, when, in the middle of a lane which I had taken as a short cut, I was accosted by a man who seemed frantic with grief, and implored me to render assistance to his master. He spoke in English; and fortunately I understand that language tolerably well. In a word, the person who accosted me, was your dependant Morcar. He has since explained to me how you had separated at Friuli, in order to gain the Neapolitan frontier by different routes; and it seems that he was journeying along that lane, when he stumbled over a body in the path. The light of the moon speedily enabled him to recognise his master. At that moment my chaise fortunately came up to the spot. Not knowing who you were, but actuated by that feeling which would prompt me to assist any human being under such circumstances, I immediately proposed to convey you to my own house. Your dependant was overjoyed at the offer; and I desired him to accompany you. He would not tell me your real name, but when I questioned him on that point, gave a fictitious one. The poor fellow did not then know how I might be disposed towards the Constitutionalists who had survived the slaughter near Ossore. You may therefore conceive my astonishment when on my arrival at my house, I discovered a letter in a case fastened to a riband beneath your garments, as I helped to undress you. These words, '*To my dear friend, Richard Markham,*' in a handwriting well known to me, immediately excited a suspicion in my mind; and when I had procured the attendance of my physician and ascertained that there was a hope of your eventual recovery—although your wound was a serious one—I questioned Morcar more closely than before. But he would not confess that you were Richard Markham. I then showed him the letter which I had found about your person. Still he obstinately denied the fact. At length, in order to convince him that I was really sincere in my good feeling towards you, I showed him several letters from the deceased Mr. Armstrong to me, and in which you were favourably mentioned. Then he became all confidence; and I can assure you that he is a most faithful and devoted creature towards you."

While the banker was yet speaking, he drew from his pocket the morocco case containing Armstrong's letter, and laid it upon the bed.

Richard warmly pressed his hand with grateful fervour.

He then in a few words narrated the particulars of the attack made upon him by the banditti in the narrow lane, and concluded by saying, "I consider the fact of the ruffians overlooking that document when they rifled me, as another proof of heaven's especial goodness towards me; for I value this relic of my departed friend as dearly as my life."

"And you are still ignorant of its contents?" said the banker, with a smile.

Richard was about to explain the nature of the mysterious instructions which Armstrong had written on the envelope, when Viviani stopped him, saying, "I know all. Some months before his death Armstrong wrote to me his intentions concerning you; and therefore, I presume that '*when you are destitute of all resources—when adversity or a too generous heart shall have deprived you of all means of subsistence—and when your own exertions fail to supply your wants, you will open the enclosed letter. But should no circumstances of any kind deprive you of the little property which you now possess—and should you not be plunged into a state of need from which your own talents and exertions cannot relieve you,—then will you open that letter on the morning of the 10th of July, 1843, on which day you are to meet your brother.*'"

So astonished was Markham, while the banker recapitulated the *very words* of Armstrong's mysterious instructions, that he could not utter a syllable until the excellent man had finished speaking; and then he cried, in a tone of the most unfeigned surprise, "My dear sir, you know all, then?"

Signora Viviani laughed so heartily at Markham's astonishment, that her good-natured countenance became quite purple.

"Indeed, I do know all," exclaimed the banker, laughing also; "and that is not surprising, either, seeing that every farthing Armstrong has left you is in my hands. But I must not say any more on that head: indeed, I am afraid I have violated my departed friend's instructions to *me* by saying so much already. However, my dear Richard—for so you must allow me to call you, as I am a sort of guardian or trustee towards you—you will not want to open that letter until the 10th of July, 1843; for if you require money, you have only to draw a cheque upon me, and I will honour it—aye, even for ten or fifteen thousand pounds."

"Is it possible that I am awake? am I not dreaming? is this fairy-land, or Castelcicala?" said Richard. "I am overwhelmed with happy tidings and kindnesses."

Again did the good banker and his merry sister—who, though bachelor and spinster, possessed hearts overflowing with the milk of human kindness, and who felt towards Richard almost as a father and mother would feel towards their own child,—again did they laugh heartily; until the lady remembered that their patient might be too much excited.

"And now I dare say you are anxious about your faithful Morcar," said the banker. "In truth, he is a mystery whom I cannot fathom. All I know of him is that he is most devotedly attached to you. He comes to the house every evening, and sits by your bed-side a couple of hours, or perhaps more; and then he takes his departure again. In vain have I pressed him to remain here—to live here so long as you are my guest: no—he declares that he has business on his hands; and he keeps that business a profound secret. He is always absent save during those two or three hours which he spends near you."

"And when he is here," added the banker's sister, laughing, "he will not allow a soul save himself to do any thing for you. No—he must smooth your pillow—he must raise your head, and give you your cooling drink—he must hold your hands when the delirium is on you (but, thank heaven! *that* has passed now);—in a word, no one is permitted to be your nurse save himself."

"The good, faithful creature!" cried Markham, tears standing on his long, dark, and slightly curled lashes. "Heaven grant that he be not involving himself in any difficulty."

"He seems prudent and steady," said the banker; "and those are grand qualities. Moreover, these men of Egyptian origin have strange fancies and whims. In any case, he will be more communicative to you than he is to us."

"You have now gratified my curiosity in many—many ways," said Richard; "but there is one more point——"

"You are interminable with your questions," exclaimed Signora Viviani, laughing. "Now, remember—this is the last we will answer on the present occasion, or we shall really fatigue you."

"Oh! no," returned our hero. "When the mind labours under no suspense, how soon the physical energies revive."

"Speak, then," said the banker.

"What is the present condition of Castelcicala? has it been ameliorated, or rendered more deplorable?"

The banker's countenance fell.

"My dear Richard," he replied, "strange and striking events have occurred during the last few days,—events which it pains me to recount, as it will grieve you to hear them. The Grand Duchess fled from the capital—no one knows wherefore. It is certain that she reached Montecuculi in safety; and her farther progress is a complete mystery. All traces of her cease there. But that is not all. An army of thirty thousand Austrians, Richard,—an army of foreigners has been called into the State by Angelo III. Ten days ago it crossed the Roman frontiers, and encamped beneath the walls of Montoni."

"Merciful heaven!" ejaculated Richard: "an army of occupation in the country!"

"Alas! that I should tell the truth when I say so," continued the banker, in a melancholy tone. "The Grand Duke intends to enforce his despotism by means of foreign bayonets. Four thousand Austrians moved on as far as Abrantani, where they are placed under the command of Captain-General Santa Croce, that province being considered the most unsettled, and the one exhibiting the greatest inclination to raise the standard of liberty. But Montoni, Richard,—Montoni, our capital, has set a glorious example. The same day that the Austrians appeared beneath its walls, its inhabitants rose against the Grand Duke and his infamous Ministers. The Municipal Council, with the Mayor at its head, declared its sittings permanent, and proclaimed itself a Committee of Government. The garrison, consisting of ten thousand brave men, pronounced in favour of the Committee. The Grand Duke and his Ministers fled to the Austrian camp, and took refuge with Marshal Herbertstein, the generalissimo of the foreign army of occupation. And now, Richard—now the Grand Duke and his Austrian allies are besieging the capital of Castelcicala!"

"Alas! these are terrible tidings," said Richard, astounded at all he had just heard, and at the rapidity with which so many important events had occurred.

"Terrible tidings they must be to one who, like you, has fought for Castelcicalan liberty," continued the banker. "Oh! that I should have lived to see my country thus oppressed—thus subject to a foreign yoke! But I have not yet told you all. The Lord High Admiral of Castelcicala has declared in favour of the Grand Duke, and has instituted a blockade, with all his fleet, at the mouth of the Ferretti, so that no provisions may be conveyed into the besieged capital. The garrison of Montoni is, however, behaving nobly; and as yet the Austrians have made no impression upon the city. But a famine must ensue in Montoni;—and then, all hope will be lost!"

"And the other great cities of Castelcicala?" asked Richard: "do they make no demonstration in this terrible crisis?"

"Alas—no! Martial law everywhere prevails; and had we not a humane and merciful Captain-General at the head of the province of Pinalla, our condition here would be desperate indeed. You are doubtless aware that all the Constitutionalists who were taken prisoners at the battle of Ossore, are now prisoners in Estella———"

Signor Viviani was interrupted by the entrance of a servant, who came to announce that Morcar requested admittance to the sick-room.

The kind-hearted banker and his no less excellent sister withdrew, in order to allow the gipsy an opportunity of free and unrestrained intercourse with his master.

CHAPTER CLXXXIV.

ESTELLA.

Nothing could exceed the joy which the faithful Morcar experienced on finding his master restored to consciousness, and evidently in a fair way towards convalescence.

The reader may imagine with what enthusiasm the gipsy dwelt upon the kindness of Signor Viviani and his sister; and when the grateful fellow had exhausted all his powers of speech in depicting the excellent qualities of these good people, he begged Markham to acquaint him with his adventures since they separated at Friuli.

Richard related those particulars which are already known to the reader; and he did not forget to reproach Morcar for having refused to accept his share of the purse at the tavern in the suburbs of the above-mentioned town.

"I knew that I should not require the gold, sir," answered Morcar; "for an individual of my race finds friends and brethren all over the world. Nor was I an exception to that rule. At a short distance from Friuli I fell in with an encampment of *Cingani*—for so the gipsies are called in Italy; and I was immediately welcomed in a way becoming my position as the heir to the sovereign of the Zingarees of Great Britain."

"But how did you render yourself intelligible to your Italian brethren?" asked Richard, with a good-natured smile at the solemn manner in which his follower had uttered the concluding portion of his observations.

"We have a language peculiar to ourselves, sir," replied Morcar; "and although it is not very rich in words, it nevertheless contains sufficient to enable us to converse freely with each other. I travelled with the Cingani belonging to the encampment; and when we arrived in the neighbourhood of Pinalla, I took leave of them with the intention of hastening over the frontier to Naples. God ordained that I should strike into the same path which you were pursuing; and I could not have been many yards behind you, when you were attacked by the banditti in the manner you have just explained to me. You may conceive my grief when I found you lying senseless in that gloomy lane, and when the moonlight, falling on your countenance, showed me who you were. Had it not been for the accidental arrival of Signor Viviani on the spot, and at that particular moment, I cannot say what would have become of us. You know the rest."

"Not entirely, my dear Morcar," said Richard. "I do not wish to penetrate into your secrets; but I am anxious to learn wherefore you refused the hospitality of Signor Viviani's mansion?"

"When I found that you were amongst friends, sir," answered Morcar, "and that there was no longer any necessity for me to proceed to Naples, I returned to my brethren, the Cingani. I have dwelt with them ever since; but have occasionally called to inquire after you."

"Nay, my faithful friend," exclaimed Richard, taking the gipsy's hand, "do not depreciate your own goodness of heart. I have learnt how regularly you came to pass the evening by my side, and how kindly you ministered to me. Heaven grant that the day may arrive when I shall be enabled to reward you adequately."

"You must not talk any more at present, sir," said the gipsy. "If you will only remain quiet for a few days, you will be quite well; and then—"

"And then, what?" asked Richard, seeing that the gipsy checked himself.

"And then we can deliberate on the best course to adopt," replied Morcar.

Our hero saw that his dependant had some plan in his head; but he did not choose to press him on the subject.

A fortnight had elapsed since Richard Markham awoke to consciousness in the house of the generous Castelcicalan banker.

This interval had produced a marvellous change in his physical condition.

A powerful constitution, aided by excellent medical advice, and the unremitting attention of his kind friends, enabled him to triumph over the severity of the treatment which he had experienced at the hands of the banditti.

He was now completely restored to health—with the exception of a partial weakness and pallor which naturally followed a long confinement to his couch.

But by means of gentle exercise in the garden belonging to the banker's house, he was rapidly recovering his strength, and the hues of youth again began to bloom upon his cheeks.

It was on the 26th of December, 1840, that he had a long conversation with the banker and Morcar. A certain project was the topic of this debate,—a project for which Morcar had arranged all the preliminaries during Richard's illness, and which our hero now burned to carry into execution. Signor Viviani raised but one objection; and that was only for the purpose of delaying, not renouncing, the scheme in view. He feared lest Markham's health might not be sufficiently restored to enable him to embark so soon in the enterprise. But this doubt was completely over-ruled by his young friend, whose enthusiastic soul could not brook delay in a matter that was so near and dear to his heart.

The deliberations of the three individuals who formed this solemn council lasted for four hours, and concluded at sunset. Richard then wrote several letters, which he sealed and placed in the hands of Signor Viviani, saying, "You will forward these only in case of my death."

The banker wrung our hero's hand cordially, exclaiming, "No, my generous—my gallant-hearted young friend; something within me seems to say that there will be no need to dispatch those letters to your friends in England; for proud success shall be yours!"

Signora Viviani entered the room at this moment, and in a tone of deep anxiety, inquired the result of the deliberation.

"The expedition is to take place," replied the banker, solemnly.

"Ah! Signor Markham," exclaimed the lady; "have you well weighed the contingencies? Do not imagine that I would attempt to dissuade you from so generous,—so noble an undertaking!—Oh! no,—I should be the last to do so. And yet—"

"My dear madam," interrupted Richard, with a smile, "I appreciate all your kind anxiety in my behalf; but I must fulfil my duty towards those unfortunate creatures who embarked in an enterprise of which I was one of the chiefs."

"It would be improper in me to urge a single argument against so noble a purpose," said the banker's sister. "May God prosper you, Richard."

The old lady wiped the tears from her eyes as she spoke.

It was now quite dusk; and our hero signified his intention of taking his departure. He confided the morocco case containing Armstrong's letter, to his excellent friend, the banker, and at the same time expressed his deep gratitude for all the kindness he had experienced at the hands of that gentleman and his sister.

"Do not talk thus, my noble boy," ejaculated the old man; "it makes me melancholy—as if I were never to see you more; whereas, I feel convinced that there are many, many happy days in store for us all! Here, Richard—take this pocket-book: it contains bank-notes to some amount. But if you require more, hesitate not to draw upon me for any sum that you need. And now, farewell—and may all good angels watch over you!"

Signora Viviani, on her side, felt as acutely in parting with our hero as if she were separating from a near relative—so much had his amiable qualities, generous disposition, and noble character endeared him alike to the banker and his kind-hearted sister.

And now the door of that hospitable mansion closed behind Richard Markham, who was accompanied by his faithful Morcar.

They pursued their way, the gipsy acting as the guide, through the streets of Pinalla, and passing out of the town by the north-eastern gate, followed the course of the river Usiglio for upwards of two miles and a-half.

The night was clear with the pure lustre of the chaste moon; and the air was mild, though fresh enough to be invigorating.

At length they reached the confines of a forest, into which Morcar plunged, closely followed by his master.

They now continued their way amidst an almost total darkness, so thick was the foliage of the evergreens through the mazes of which they pursued their course.

Presently lights glimmered among the trees; and in a few minutes more, Morcar conducted our hero into a wide open area, where a spacious gipsy-encampment was established.

Markham caught his companion by the arm, and held him back for a few moments while he contemplated that scene so strange—so wild—and yet so picturesque.

A space, probably an acre in extent, had been cleared in the midst of the forest; and the tall trees all around constituted a natural barrier, defining the limits of the arena formed for the encampment.

A hundred tents, of the rude gipsy fashion, swarmed with life. Dark countenances bent over the cheerful fires, above which mighty caldrons were simmering; and the lurid light was reflected from dark eyes. The tall athletic forms of men and the graceful figures of women, were thrown out into strong relief by the lambent flames; and the sounds of many voices fell in confused murmurs upon the ears.

"There are four hundred brave men, who will welcome you as their leader, sir!" exclaimed Morcar, stretching forth his arm towards the encampment.

"Oh! my dear friend," cried Markham, all the enthusiasm of his soul aroused by the hopes which those words conveyed: "by what magic were you enabled to collect this band in so short a time?"

"My influence as the son of Zingary was sufficient to induce them to make our cause their own, sir," replied Morcar; "and the extensive organization of the fraternity was already well calculated to gather them thus together. I have moreover informed you that they are all well armed; for their funds have been devoted to the purchase of the weapons and ammunition necessary for the undertaking."

"Which outlay it will be my care immediately to reimburse," said Richard. "But you speak of me as the chief of this band, Morcar? No—that honour is reserved for you, whose energies and influence alone could have brought those four hundred men together."

"That may not be, sir," returned Morcar, seriously. "These men have assembled with the hope that *you* will be their chief: it is *your* name which is enthusiastically spoken of in Castelcicala; and it is *your* presence which will animate this gipsy-band with courage. Come—let me introduce you to the chiefs of the tribe."

"Is the King amongst them?" asked Richard.

"No, sir: the King of the Cingani, or Italian gipsies, is at present in Tuscany; but the chiefs, to whom I will now conduct you, are his relations."

Morcar led our hero through the mazes of the encampment to a tent more conveniently contrived and spacious than the rest; and as they passed along, the groups of Cingani surveyed Richard with curiosity and respect.

They evidently divined who he was.

In the tent to which Morcar conducted his master, three elderly men were seated upon mats, smoking their pipes, and discoursing gravely upon political affairs.

They welcomed Richard with respectful warmth, and instantly assigned to him the place of honour at the upper end of the tent.

A council was then held; but as the results will explain the decision to which the members came, it is not necessary to detail the deliberations on this occasion.

We must, however, observe that Markham accepted the responsible and difficult post of commandant of the entire force; and he immediately handed over to the gipsies an amount in bank-notes equivalent to a thousand pounds, for the purpose of reimbursing the outlay already effected by the Cingani chiefs, and of supplying an advance of pay to all the members of the band.

At about eleven o'clock the fires were all extinguished throughout the encampment; and, sentinels having been posted at short intervals round the open space, those who were not on duty laid down to rest.

At day-break the scene was once more all bustle and life: the morning meal was hastily disposed of; and Richard then issued the necessary orders for breaking up the encampment.

It was arranged that the men who bore arms should proceed by forced marches towards Estella; while the women and children might follow at their own pace.

The farewells between husbands and wives, brothers and sisters, fathers and children, sons and mothers, took place in silence, but in profound sincerity; and the corps, consisting of four hundred men, all well armed with muskets and cutlasses, and some few with axes also, was soon in motion amidst the dense mazes of the forest.

Markham, with a sword by his side and a pair of pistols in the breast of his coat, advanced in front of the column, attended by the three chiefs and Morcar.

It was at day-break on the 29th of December, that the sentinels posted on the southern bastion of the citadel of Estella, observed a small but compact body of men suddenly emerge from the forest which stretches along the Usiglio, from the neighbourhood of Pinalla almost up to the very walls of Estella.

An alarm was given throughout the citadel; for the beams of the rising sun glistened on the weapons of the small force that was approaching; and although no uniform attire characterised the corps, it was easy to perceive that it advanced with a hostile intention.

But ere the garrison could be got under arms, Richard's followers had already cut an opening in the palisades which protected the glacis, and were advancing up the inclined plane towards the rampart. On they went, their youthful leader at their head: the glacis was passed—the covered way was gained—and then the sentinels on the bastion discharged their muskets at the besiegers.

Two of the Cingani fell dead, and one was very slightly wounded.

"Follow me!" cried our hero; and rushing along the covered way, he reached the wooden bridge which communicated with the interior of the citadel.

And now commenced an interval of fearful peril, but for which Markham was not unprepared.

The soldiers of the garrison had by this time flocked to the rampart of the bastion, and commenced a terrific fire upon the besiegers. The latter, however, replied to it with rapidity and effect, while half a dozen of the foremost cut down with their axes a huge beam from the wooden bridge, and, under the superintendence of Markham, used it as a battering-ram at the postern-gate.

The Cingani, however, lost eight or nine of their men while this task was in progress; and their position, exposed as they were to a murderous fire, would soon have become untenable, had not the postern-gate shortly yielded to the engine employed against it.

Then, with his drawn sword in his hand, Markham precipitated himself into the citadel, closely followed, and well supported by the brave and faithful Cingani.

The tunnel beneath the rampart, into which the postern opened, was disputed for some minutes with desperate valour on both sides; but our hero was so ably backed by Morcar, the three chiefs, and the foremost of his corps, that he eventually drove the soldiers before him.

"Constitutional freedom and Prince Alberto!" shouted Richard, as he rushed onward, and entered the court of the citadel.

The cry was taken up by the Cingani; and although the conflict continued in the court for nearly half an hour longer, it was evident that the note of liberty had touched a chord in the hearts of the Castelcicalan soldiers, for they resisted but feebly and, though superior in numbers to the besiegers, rapidly gave way.

On the farther side of the court stood a large but low and straggling building, the windows of which were defended with iron bars.

"Friends," exclaimed Markham, pointing with his blood-stained sword towards that structure, "there is the prison of the patriots!"

These words operated like an electric shock upon our hero's followers; and they rushed onward, driving the soldiers like chaff before them.

The gate of the prison was reached, and speedily forced: Richard entered the gloomy stronghold, and the work of liberation commenced.

Five hundred Castelcicalan patriots were restored to freedom in a short half-hour; and when they recognised in their deliverer him who had been one of the chiefs of the first expedition, and whose valour was so signalised in the battle near Ossore, their enthusiasm knew no bounds.

The name of "MARKHAM" was shouted to the sky: the patriots flocked around him, with heart-felt thanks and the most fervent outpourings of their gratitude; and they hailed him as a deliverer and a chief.

There was not, however, much time for congratulation or explanation. Though the garrison of the citadel was weak, that of the town itself was strong; for the Captain-General had concentrated the greater part of his force in the heart of Estella in order to over-awe the inhabitants. This fact had been previously gleaned by the spies whom Morcar had sent out while Richard was yet an inmate of the banker's house; and hence the attack upon the most exposed part of the citadel in preference to an attempt upon the town.

Richard was now master of the citadel. A portion of the garrison had fled into Estella; but by far the larger part, about three hundred in number, declared its readiness to join the cause of liberty. This offer was joyfully accepted. The armoury was then visited, and arms were distributed to the patriots who had been delivered from their dungeons.

Thus Richard Markham found himself at the head of an effective force of nearly twelve hundred men—a triumphant position, which had fortunately cost no more than about twenty lives on the side of the Cingani.

It was now mid-day; and while his forces were obtaining refreshment, and putting the citadel in a proper state of defence, in case of an attack on the part of the Captain-General of Estella, Richard called a council of the three Cingani chiefs, Morcar, the leading patriots whom he had released, and the officers of the garrison-troops that had declared in favour of "Constitutional liberty and Prince Alberto."

At this council it was resolved that Richard should issue a proclamation to the inhabitants of Estella, declaring the real objects for which the standard of civil liberty had been raised—namely, to release the imprisoned patriots, to expel the Austrians from the land, and to place Prince Alberto upon the ducal throne.

This resolution was carried into effect; and the document was forwarded to the Mayor of Estella. The corporation was immediately assembled; and while the Captain-General prepared to attack the citadel, the municipal body remained in close deliberation.

Three hours elapsed; when a rumour prevailed throughout the town that the troops had refused to leave their barracks at the command of the Captain-General. This proof of sympathy with the successful Constitutionalists decided the opinions of the members of the corporation; and the Mayor, attended by several of the municipal authorities, waited upon Richard Markham and presented him with the keys of the city.

No sooner were these tidings bruited throughout Estella, than the Captain-General, the Political Prefect, and one regiment which remained faithful to the Grand Duke's cause, left the town with extraordinary precipitation: the remainder of the garrison sent a deputation to Markham's head quarters in the citadel to announce their readiness to join his cause; and at seven o'clock in the evening of that eventful day the roar of the artillery on the walls of Estella saluted the tri-coloured flag of liberty which was hoisted on the Town-Hall.

By this grand and decisive blow, Richard possessed himself of one of the principal towns of Castelcicala, and found himself backed by a force of three thousand men.

His first care, when order and tranquillity were restored that evening, was to forward a courier with a letter to Signor Viviani at Pinalla. That letter not only detailed the events of the day, but contained a request that the banker would lose no time in writing an account of the proceedings direct to Prince Alberto (under the name of Count Alteroni) in England. Richard also enclosed a letter to be forwarded to Mr. Monroe, and one from Morcar to Eva.

The corporation had assembled in the Town Hall, immediately after the tri-coloured flag was hoisted, and remained in deliberation until past ten o'clock. The Mayor then published a proclamation in which there were three clauses. The first declared the sittings of the municipal body permanent, under the title of "Committee of Administration for the Province of Estella." The second nominated Richard Markham General-in-chief of the army of that province. The third called upon all good and faithful Castelcicalan patriots to take up arms in the cause of Constitutional liberty and Prince Alberto, and against the Austrian army of occupation.

A copy of this proclamation was forwarded to Richard Markham, who highly approved of the first and last clauses, and accepted the rank conferred upon him by the second.

Early on the following morning uniforms, taken from the store-rooms in the arsenal, were distributed amongst the Cingani and the patriots who had been liberated; and Richard then made his entry into Estella, in compliance with the request of the corporation.

Wearing the uniform of a General-officer, and mounted upon a handsome charger, our hero never appeared to greater advantage.

The garrison of the town lined the streets, and presented arms to the youthful commander whose extraordinary skill and prowess had so materially contributed to the victory of the preceding day, and who was hailed as a champion raised up by Providence to deliver Castelcicala from the tyranny under which it groaned.

He was attended by two officers whom he had appointed his *aides-de-camp*, and by the faithful Morcar, whom nothing could induce to accept any definite rank, but who, in the uniform of a private, was proud to follow his valiant master.

The windows were crowded with faces, anxious to obtain a glimpse of the youthful hero; and while bright eyes shone upon his way, fair hands waved handkerchiefs or threw nosegays of exotics and artificial flowers from the casements.

The bells rang merrily; the artillery saluted the entrance of the General into the town; the crowds in the streets welcomed him with enthusiastic shouts; and the civic authorities, in their official robes, received him as he alighted at the Town-Hall.

There he was complimented on his gallant deeds, and invited to partake of a sumptuous banquet in the evening.

But Richard's answer was firm though respectful.

"Gentlemen," he said, "pardon me if I decline your great kindness. There remains so much to be done, to restore happiness to Castelcicala, that I should deem myself unworthy of your confidence, did I waste valuable time in festivity. A detachment of the Austrian army occupies and overawes the province of Abrantani: in two hours, with your permission, I propose to set out in that direction with all the forces that you will spare me. Should Providence prosper my arms in this new expedition, my course is simple. I shall proceed to Montoni, and either deliver the capital from the besieging force, or perish beneath its walls."

This short but pithy speech was received with enthusiastic cheers by the municipal body.

"Go, sir," said the Mayor, when silence was obtained once more, "and fulfil your grand mission. Take with you the force that you deem necessary for your purposes; and it shall be *our* duty to supply you with a treasury-chest that will not be indifferently furnished. Go, sir: God has sent you to us in the time of our bitter need; and you are destined to deliver Castelcicala from its tyrant."

Markham bowed, and withdrew.

His return to the citadel was a signal for the renewal of that enthusiasm which had greeted his entrance into the town.

But he was not proud! No—he had no room in his heart for pride: hope—delicious, burning, joyous hope,—the hope of accomplishing his mighty aims and earning the hand of Isabella as his reward,—this was the only sentiment which filled his soul!

On his arrival at the citadel once more, he issued immediate orders to prepare for a march. He proposed to leave a garrison of one thousand men in Estella, and take two thousand with him; for he calculated that this number would be considerably increased, by volunteers, on his way to Abrantani.

The evident rapidity with which he intended his movements to be characterised, created a most favourable impression not only amongst the inhabitants of Estella, but also with the troops under his command; and though they all deemed him eminently worthy of the post to which he had been raised, yet few foresaw the future greatness of that hero who was destined to take his place amongst the most brilliant warriors of the age.

It was at two o'clock in the afternoon that the Constitutional army, consisting of two thousand men, defiled through the western gate of the citadel, towards the bridge over the Usiglio. A squadron of four hundred cavalry led the way: next came the corps of Cingani; then the horse-artillery, with twelve field-pieces; next the liberated patriots; and the rear-guard consisted of the regular infantry of the garrison.

As soon as the river was crossed, Richard formed his little army into three columns, and then commenced a rapid march towards Villabella, which he knew to be well affected in favour of the Constitutional cause.

But while he was leading a gallant band over the fertile plains of Castelcicala, incidents deserving notice occurred in his native land far away.

CHAPTER CLXXXV.

ANOTHER NEW YEAR'S DAY.

It was the 1st of January, 1841.

If there be any hour in the life of man when he ought to commune with his own heart, that proper interval of serious reflection is to be found on New Year's Day.

Then, to the rightly constituted mind, the regrets for the past will serve as finger-posts and guides to the hopes of the future.

The heathen mythology depicted Janus with two faces, looking different ways:—so let the human heart, when on the first day of January, it stands between two years, retrospect carefully over the one that has gone, and combine all its solemn warnings for use and example in the new one which has just commenced.

This also is the day that recalls, with additional impressiveness, the memory of those dear relatives and friends whose mortal forms have been swept away by the viewless and voiceless stream of Time.

Nor less do fond parents think, amidst tears and prayers, of their sons who are absent in the far-off places of the earth,—fighting the battles of their country on the burning plains of India, or steering their way across the pathless solitudes of the ocean.

But, alas! little reck the wealthy and great for those whose arms defend them, or whose enterprise procures them all the bounties of the earth.

An oligarchy has cramped the privileges and monopolised the rights of a mighty nation.

Behold the effects of its infamous Poor-Laws;—contemplate the results of the more atrocious Game-Laws;—mark the consequences of the Corn-Laws.

THE POOR-LAWS! Not even did the ingenuity of the Spanish or Italian Inquisitions conceive a more effectual method of deliberate torture and slow death, than the fearful system of mental-abasement and gradient starvation invented by England's legislators. When the labourer can toil for the rich no longer, away with him to the workhouse! When the old man, who has contributed for half a century to the revenue of the country, is overtaken by sudden adversity at an age which paralyses his energies, away with him to the workhouse! When the poor widow, whose sons have fallen in the ranks of battle or in defence of the wooden walls of England, is deprived of her natural supporters, away with her to the workhouse! The workhouse is a social dung-heap on which the wealthy and great fling those members of the community whose services they can no longer render available to their selfish purposes.

THE GAME-LAWS! Never was a more atrocious monopoly than that which reserves the use of certain birds of the air or animals of the earth to a small and exclusive class. The Almighty gave man "dominion over the fish of the sea, and over the fowl of the air, and over every living thing that moveth upon the earth;" and those who dare to monopolise any of these, to the prejudice of their fellow-creatures, fly in the face of the Lord of all! The Game-Laws have fabricated an offence which fills our prisons—as if there were not already crimes enough to separate men from their families and plunge them into loathsome dungeons. That offence is one of human construction, and exists only in certain countries: it is not a crime against God—nor is it deemed such in many enlightened states. The selfish pleasures of a miserably small minority demand the protection of a statute which is a fertilising source of oppression, wretchedness, ruin, and demoralization. The Game-Laws are a rack whereon the aristocracy loves to behold its victims writhing in tortures, and where the sufferers are compelled to acknowledge as a heinous crime a deed which has in reality no moral turpitude associated with it.

THE CORN-LAWS! Were the Russian to boast of his freedom, Common Sense would point to Siberia and to the knout, and laugh in his face. When the Englishman vaunts the glory of his country's institutions, that same Common Sense comes forward and throws the Corn-Laws in his teeth. What! liberty in connexion with the vilest monopoly that ever mortal policy conceived? Impossible! England manufactures articles which all the civilised world requires; and other states yield corn in an abundance that defies the possibility of home consumption. And yet an inhuman selfishness has declared that England shall not exchange her manufactures for that superfluous produce. No—the manufactures may decay in the warehouses here, and the grain abroad may be thrown to the swine, sooner than a miserable oligarchy will consent to abandon one single principle of its shameless monopoly. The Corn-Laws are a broom which sweeps all the grain on the threshing-floor into one corner for the use of the rich, but which leaves the chaff scattered every where about for the millions of poor to use as best they may.

The aristocracy of England regards the patience of the masses as a bow whose powers of tension are unlimited: but the day must come, sooner or later, when those who thus dare to trifle with this generous elasticity will be struck down by the violence of the recoil.

Although our legislators—trembling at what they affect to sneer at under the denomination of "the march of intellect"—obstinately refuse to imitate enlightened France by instituting a system of national education,—nevertheless, the millions of this country are now instructing themselves!

Honour to the English mechanic—honour to the English operative: each alike seeks to taste of the tree of learning, "whose root is bitter, but whose fruits are sweet!"

Thank God, no despotism—no tyranny can arrest the progress of that mighty intellectual movement which is now perceptible amongst the industrious millions of these realms.

And how excellent are the principles of that self-instruction which now tends to elevate the moral condition of the country. It is not confined within the narrow limits which churchmen would impose: it embraces the sciences—the arts—all subjects of practical utility,—its aim being to model the mind on the solid basis of Common Sense.

To the millions thus enlightened, Religion will appear in all its purity, and the objects of Government in all their simplicity. The holy Christian worship will cease to be regarded as an apology for endowing a Church with enormous revenues; and political administration must no longer be considered as a means of rendering a small portion of the community happy and prosperous to the utter prejudice of the vast remainder.

There breathes not a finer specimen of the human race than a really enlightened and liberal-minded Englishman. But if *he* be deserving of admiration and applause, who has received his knowledge from the lips of a paid preceptor—how much more worthy of praise and respect is *the self-instructed mechanic*!

But to resume our narrative.

It was the 1st of January, 1841.

The time-piece on the mantel in Mr. Greenwood's study had just struck two in the afternoon.

That gentleman himself was pacing the apartment in an agitated manner.

His handsome dressing-gown of oriental pattern was not arranged, with the usual contrived air of negligence, to display the beautiful shirt-front, over which hung the gold chain of his Breguet-watch:—on the contrary, it had evidently been hurried on without the least regard to effect.

The writing-table was heaped with a confused pile of letters and accounts—not thrown together for show, but lying in the actual disorder in which they had been tossed aside after a minute investigation.

Though not absolutely slovenly in his present appearance, Mr. Greenwood had certainly neglected his toilet on that day; and the state of his room moreover proved that he was too much absorbed in serious affairs to devote time to the minor considerations of neatness and the strict propriety of order.

There was a cloud upon his brow; and his manner was restless and unsettled.

"Curses—eternal curses upon that Lafleur!" he exclaimed aloud, as he walked up and down with uneven steps. "To think that I should have lost so much at one blow! Oh! it nearly drives me mad—mad! If it had only been the twenty thousand pounds of which the black-hearted French villain and his confederates plundered me, I might have snapped my fingers at Fortune who thus vented her temporary spite upon me! But the enormous amount I lost in addition, by failing to pour that sum of English notes and gold into circulation in the French capital,—the almost immediate fall in the rates of exchange, and the fluctuation of the French funds,—Oh! *there* it was that I was so seriously injured. Fifty thousand pounds snatched from me as it were in a moment,—fifty thousand pounds of hard money—my own money! And the thirty thousand pounds that I had first sent over to Paris were so judiciously laid out! My combinations were admirable: I should have been a clear gainer of five-and-twenty thousand, had not that accursed robbery taken place! May the villain Lafleur die in a charnel-house—may he perish the most miserable of deaths!"

Mr. Greenwood ground his teeth with rage as he uttered these horrible maledictions.

He did not, however, recall to mind that Lafleur was an honest man when he entered his service;—he did not pause to reflect upon all the intrigues, machinations, plots, duplicities, and villanies, in which he had employed his late valet,—thus gradually initiating him in those paths which could scarcely have led to any other result than the point in which they had actually terminated—the robbery of the master by the servant whom he had thus tutored.

"The villain!" continued Greenwood. "And I was so kind to him—constantly increasing his wages and making him presents! Such confidence as I put in him, too! Filippo, whom I did not trust to half the same extent—save in my intrigues with women—is stanch and faithful to me!"

He paused and glanced towards the time-piece.

"Half-past two; and Tomlinson does not come! What *can* detain him? Surely that affair cannot have gone wrong also? If so——"

And Greenwood's countenance became as dark and lowering as the sky ere the explosion of the storm.

In a few moments a double-knock at the door echoed through the house.

"Here's Tomlinson!" ejaculated Greenwood; and with sovereign command over himself, he composed his features and assumed his wonted ease of manner.

The stock-broker now entered the room.

"You are an hour behind your time, Tomlinson," said Greenwood, shaking him by the hand.

"I could not come before," was the answer: "I was detained on your business."

"What news?" asked Greenwood, scarcely able to conceal his profound anxiety.

"Bad," replied Tomlinson. "You have sent sixteen thousand pounds to look after the fifty you have already lost. Fortunately you are a rich man, and can stand reverses of this kind. Besides, one who speculates so enormously as you have done of late, must meet with occasional losses. For my part, I should advise you to leave Spanish alone. It seems that you are doomed to fail in your ventures in the foreign securities:—first, your French scheme was totally ruined by the villany of your servant; and now your Spanish one, so far from enabling you to retrieve your losses, has increased them."

This long speech enabled Greenwood to recover from the shock which the announcement of a new reverse had produced.

"My dear Tomlinson," he said, "I am resolved to follow up my speculations in Spanish. The private information I received from an intimate friend of the Spanish Ambassador is correct—I am convinced it is; and I am sure that Queen Christina, by the advice of Espartero, will appropriate a sum to pay the interest on the passives. The announcement must be made in a few days. Of this I am certain. But all my resources are locked up for the present:—in fact, I do not hesitate to tell *you*, Tomlinson, that I have over-speculated of late. Still—remember—I *have* plenty of means remaining; but they are not instantly available."

"What, then, do you propose to do?" inquired the stock-broker.

"You have raised yourself during the past year to a confidential position in the City, Tomlinson," continued Greenwood: "and people no longer remember your bankruptcy."

"But I do," observed the stock-broker bitterly.

"Oh! that is nothing," exclaimed Greenwood. "I was about to say that you could probably borrow me fifteen or twenty thousand on my bond—say for three months."

"I doubt it," returned Tomlinson. "You have no mercantile establishment—you are known as a great speculator——"

"And as a great capitalist, I flatter myself," added Greenwood, playing with his watch-chain in the easy complacent manner which had so characterised him until lately.

"That you *were* a capitalist, there can be no doubt," said Tomlinson, in his usual quiet way; "but ill news fly fast—and your losses——"

"Are already known in the City, you mean?" exclaimed Greenwood, with difficulty concealing his vexation. "I care not a fig for that, Tomlinson. I have ample resources left; but, as I ere now observed, they are not immediately available."

"I understand you. It is well known that you accommodate the members of the aristocracy and heirs-expectant with loans; I presume that you have a mass of their bills, bonds, and acknowledgments? Now if you were to deposit them as collateral security, I know where I could obtain you an equivalent loan in twelve hours."

"Indeed!" ejaculated Greenwood: then, after a moment's pause, he said, "And you think there can be no difficulty in managing the business in that way?"

"None," answered the stock-broker.

Again Greenwood appeared to reflect.

"And yet," he observed, "all these pecuniary accommodations of which you spoke, are strictly confidential; and I dare not violate——"

"You know best, Greenwood," said Tomlinson, coolly. "At the same time, I can assure you that my friend will not betray you. The whole thing lies in a nut-shell: you deposit, say twenty thousand pounds' worth of securities, for a loan of that amount, to be repaid in three months; you redeem the documents by the day appointed, and none of your aristocratic debtors will be one whit the wiser. The transaction could only become known to them if you failed to refund the money, in which case the holder of the documents would send them into the market."

"I comprehend," said Greenwood. "Well—I have no objection to the arrangement. When will you ascertain whether your friend will advance the money?"

"This afternoon," returned Tomlinson; "and should the reply be in the affirmative—of which I have no doubt—I will make an appointment for four to-morrow."

"Be it so," cried Greenwood. "You will, perhaps, send me word between five and six this evening."

"I will not fail," said the stock-broker.

"Any thing new in the City?"

"Nothing particular."

"And your late cashier—what has become of him?" inquired Greenwood.

"He is still living in an obscure street in Bethnal-Green," was the answer. "The poor old man never stirs abroad; and his health is failing fast."

"Ah! it will be a good thing when he is gone altogether," said Greenwood. "If he had had to do with me, I should have shipped him to New Zealand or Van Diemen's Land long ago."

Tomlinson turned away in disgust, and took his leave.

Greenwood never moved from his seat until he heard the front door close behind the stock-broker.

Then he started from his chair, and all his apparent composure vanished.

"Sixteen thousand pounds more gone!" he exclaimed, in a hoarse, hollow tone, while he clenched his fists with rage. "Loss upon loss! All this is enough to ruin any man! And I—who have been even far more unfortunate of late than I chose to admit to Tomlinson! Nothing short of one bold and successful hit can now retrieve my tottering fortunes. Securities for twenty thousand pounds, indeed! Ha! ha! I have not bills nor bonds in my possession to the amount of three thousand!"—and he laughed wildly. "But I *will* have them, though—aye, and such ones as shall fully serve my purposes."

Then he paced the room in a singularly agitated manner.

"Yes—one more bold stroke, and I shall retrieve myself," he continued. "My good star cannot have altogether deserted me. No—no! These vicissitudes are only temporary. Accursed Lafleur! To think that he should have served me thus! Instead of proceeding to Paris—with the means of following up those schemes which I had combined so well, and in which I had already risked so much—but with such absolute certainties of immense gain,—instead of pursuing my career of success,—to be plundered—robbed at the last moment—and compelled to return to London to raise fresh funds! Then, when in four days I was prepared with the necessary sum once more—with another twenty thousand pounds—to receive letters which convinced me that the delay was fatal, and that all was lost! Yes—Fortune did indeed persecute me then! But I will be even with her yet. My information concerning the Spanish debt is accurate; and on that ground I can build a fortune far more colossal than the one I have lost. Shall I hesitate, then, in obtaining this money through Tomlinson's agency? No—no!"

Having thus buoyed himself up with those hopes which invariably urge on the gambler—whether at the actual gaming-table or in the public funds (for there is little difference in a moral light between the two modes of speculation),—to put down fresh stakes on the chance aimed at, Greenwood recovered his wonted calmness.

He busied himself in arranging his papers, and restoring neatness to his writing-table.

Thus passed the time until six o'clock, when Filippo entered the room with a letter.

It was from Tomlinson.

Greenwood tore it open: the contents were favourable. The stock-broker's friend had agreed to advance any sum up to twenty-five thousand pounds on the terms proposed, and had promised to observe the strictest secrecy in the transaction.

"The rest now depends upon myself!" ejaculated Greenwood. "Fortune has not altogether deserted me."

CHAPTER CLXXXVI.

THE NEW CUT.

At nine o'clock on the same evening, Mr. Greenwood, muffled in a cloak, alighted from a hackney-cab in the Waterloo Road at the corner of the New Cut.

That wide thoroughfare which connects the Waterloo and Blackfriars' Roads, is one of the most busy and bustling, after its own fashion, in all London.

Nowhere are the shops of a more miscellaneous nature: nowhere are the pathways so thronged with the stalls and baskets of itinerant venders.

The ingenuity of those petty provision-dealers adapts the spoilt articles of the regular fishmongers and butchers to serviceable purposes in the free market of the New Cut. The fish is cut in slices and fried in an oil or butter whose rancid taste obviates the putrid flavour and smell of the comestible; and the refuse scraps from the butchers shops are chopped up to form a species of sausage-balls called "faggots." Then the grease, in which the racy slices of fish and savoury compounds of lights and liver have been alike cooked, serves to fry large rounds of bread, which, when thus prepared, are denominated "sop in the pan." Of course these culinary refinements are prepared by the venders in their own cellars or garrets hard by; but when conveyed to the miscellaneous market in the New Cut, the luxuries impart a greasy and sickening odour to the air.

It is perfectly wonderful to behold the various methods in which the poor creatures in that thoroughfare endeavour to obtain an honest livelihood; and although their proceedings elicit a smile—still, God pity them! they had better ply their strange trades thus than rob or beg!

There may be seen, for instance, a ragged urchin holding a bundle of onions in his hand, and shouting at the top of his shrill voice, "Here's a ha'porth!"—and, no matter how finely dressed the passer-by, he is sure to thrust the onions under his or her very nose, still vociferating, "Here's a ha'porth!" Poor boy! he thinks every one *must* want onions!

The immediate vicinity of the Victoria Theatre is infested with women who offer play-bills for sale, and who seem to fancy it impossible that the passers-by can be going elsewhere than to the play.

Here an orange-girl accosts a gentleman with two or three of the fruit in her hand, but with a significant look which gives the assurance that her real trade is of a less innocent nature:—there a poor woman with an array of children before her, offers lucifer matches, but silently appeals for alms.

A little farther on is a long barrow covered with toys; and a tall man without a nose, shouts at intervals, "Only a penny each! only a penny each!" Some of these gimcracks excite astonishment by their extreme cheapness; but they are chiefly made by the convicts in Holland, and are exported in large quantities to England.

In the middle of the road a man with stentorian voice offers "A hundred songs for a penny;" and, enumerating the list, he is sure to announce the "Return of the *H*admiral" amongst the rest.

Nearly opposite the Victoria Theatre there is an extensive cook's-shop; and around the window stands a hungry crowd feasting their eyes on the massive joints which are intended to feast the stomach.

In front of the butchers' shops the serving-men keep up a perpetual vociferation of "Buy! buy!"—a sort of running fire that denotes the earnestness with which competition is carried on amongst rivals in that delectable trade.

Perhaps a new baker's shop is opened in the New Cut; and then a large placard at the window announces that "a glass of gin will be given to every purchaser of a quartern loaf." The buyers do not pause to reflect that the price of the cordial is deducted from the weight of the bread.

The pawnbrokers' shops seem to drive a most bustling trade in the New Cut; and the fronts of their establishments present a more extensive and miscellaneous assortment of second-hand garments, blankets, handkerchiefs, and sheets, than is to be seen elsewhere.

The influx and efflux of people at the public-houses and gin-shops constitute not the least remarkable feature of that neighbourhood, where every thing is dirty and squalid, yet where every one appears able to purchase intoxicating liquor!

On the southern side of the New Cut there are a great many second-hand furniture shops, the sheds wherein the articles are principally exposed being built against the houses in a fashion which gives the whole, when viewed by the glaring of the gas-lights, the appearance of a bazaar or fair.

The New Cut is always crowded; but the multitude is not entirely in motion. Knots of men congregate here, and groups of women there—the posts at the corners of the alleys and courts, or the doors of the gin-shops, being the most favourite points of such assembly.

The edges of the pathways are not completely devoted to provision dealers. Penny peep-shows, emblazoned with a coloured drawing representing the last horrible murder,—itinerant quacks with "certain remedies for the toothache,"—stalls covered with odd numbers of cheap periodical publications,—old women seated on stools, behind little trays containing combs, papers of needles, reels of cotton, pack-thread, stay-laces, bobbin, and such-like articles,—men with cutlery to sell, and who flourish in their hands small knives with innumerable blades sticking out like the quills on a porcupine,—these are also prominent features in that strange market.

In some conspicuous place most likely stands a caravan, surmounted by a picture representing a colossal giant and a giantess to match, with an assurance in large letters that the originals may be seen inside:—then, as the eye wanders from the enormous canvass to the caravan itself, and compares their sizes, the mind is left in a pleasing state of surprise how even *one* of the Brobdingnag marvels—let alone *two*—could possibly stow itself away in that diminutive box.

Branching off from the New Cut, on either side, are numerous narrow streets,—or rather lanes, of a very equivocal reputation; their chief characteristics being houses of ill-fame, gin-shops, beer-shops, marine-store dealers, pawnbrokers, and barbers' establishments.

There are two facts connected with low neighbourhoods which cannot fail to attract the attention of even the most superficial observers in their wanderings amidst the mazes of the modern Babylon. The first is that the corner shops of nearly all the narrow and dirty streets are occupied by general dealers or people in the chandlery-line; and the second is that all the barbers' establishments are ornamented with a blind or placard conveying an assurance that each is "*the original shaving shop*." Here, again, the mind enjoys the excitement of uncertainty, as in the matter of the caravan and the giants; for it is impossible to arrive at any satisfactory decision whether the aforesaid placard means you to infer that the shop to which it belongs was the *first* ever opened in the world for tonsorial purposes, or only the *first* that shed the light of its civilisation upon that especial neighbourhood. We may also observe that some of the proprietors of those establishments are not altogether unacquainted with the mysteries of puffing; inasmuch as we frequently read upon their shop-fronts the truly exhilarating and inspiring words, "*Hair-dresser to the Queen*."

Such are the New Cut and its tributary lanes.

And it was now along the New Cut that Mr. Greenwood, enveloped in his cloak, was pursuing his way.

He scarcely noticed the turmoil, bustle, and business of that strange thoroughfare; for he was too much absorbed in his own meditations.

The truth was, that his affairs—once so gloriously prosperous—were now rendered desperate by various reverses; and he was about to seek a desperate means of retrieving them.

The reader cannot have failed to observe that the characters of George Montague Greenwood and Richard Markham stand out from our picture of London Life in strong contrast with each other; and it is not the less remarkable that while the former was rising rapidly to wealth, rank, and eminence, the latter was undergoing persecutions and sinking into comparative poverty. Now—at the epoch which we are describing—the tables seem to have turned; for while George Montague Greenwood is about to seek a desperate remedy for his desperate affairs, Richard Markham is leading a gallant army over the fertile plains of Castelcicala.

The former, then, may be deemed the personification of vice, the latter the representative of virtue.

They had chosen separate paths:—the sequel will fully demonstrate which of the two characters had selected the right one.

In the meantime we will continue our narrative.

Mr. Greenwood pursued his way, and, having crossed over to the southern side of the New Cut, repaired to a small row of private houses of which this famous thoroughfare can boast at the extremity joining the Blackfriars' Road.

There he stopped for a moment beneath a lamp to consult a memorandum in his pocket-book; and, having thereby refreshed his memory in respect to the address of which he was in search, he proceeded to knock at the door of a house close by.

A dirty servant-girl opened it just as far as a chain inside would permit; and protruding her smutty face, said, with strange abruptness, "Well, what is it?"

"Does Mr. Pennywhiffe live here?" demanded Greenwood.

"No—he don't; and, if he did, you wouldn't come in—'cos I know it's all your gammon," returned that most uninteresting specimen of the female-domestic race.

"Why not?" exclaimed Greenwood, indignantly. "Whom do you take me for?"

"For what you are," replied the girl.

"And what am I, then?"

"Why—a execution, to be sure."

And, with these words, the girl banged the door in Mr. Greenwood's face.

"I must have taken down the wrong number in my memorandum," thought the Member of Parliament, as he turned away from the house, which was evidently in a state of siege. "This is very provoking!"

He then knocked at the door of the next house.

A woman with a child in her arms answered the summons; and, without waiting for any question, said abruptly, "You had better walk in."

Greenwood entered accordingly, supposing that the woman had overheard his inquiry next door, and that he had now found the abode of the person whom he sought.

The woman led the way into a back room, almost completely denuded of furniture, smelling awfully of tobacco-smoke, and very feebly lighted with a single candle that wanted snuffing.

In the midst of a dense cloud of that vapour, a man without a coat was sitting on a trunk; but the moment Greenwood entered, this individual threw down his clay-pipe, and advancing towards the visitor, exclaimed in a ferocious voice, "So you're going your rounds at this hour, are you? Well—I'm as far off from having the tin as I have been all along; and as I am going away to-morrow, I don't mind if I give you a good drubbing to teach you how to pester a gentleman with shabby bits of paper in future."

Thus speaking, the ferocious individual advanced towards Greenwood, squaring away like clock-work.

"Really, sir—you must labour under some mistake," exclaimed the Member of Parliament. "I have never called here before in my life."

"Then who the devil are you?" demanded the pugilistic phenomenon.

"That is quite another question," said Greenwood. "I——"

"Do you mean to tell me, then," exclaimed the man, "that you ain't the Water Rates?"

"No—I am not," answered Greenwood, unable to suppress a smile. "I thought that a Mr. Pennywhiffe lived here."

"Then he don't—that's all," was the rejoinder. "Blowed if I don't believe it's a plant, after all. Come—ain't you a bum? no lies, now!"

Greenwood turned indignantly away from the room, and left the house, muttering to himself, "This is most extraordinary! Every one appears to be in difficulties in this street."

He was not, however, disheartened: it was highly necessary for him to see the person of whom he was in search; and he accordingly knocked at another door.

"Tell him I'll send round the money to-morrow," shouted a masculine voice inside. "I know it's the collector, because he's rapping at every house."

Greenwood did not wait for the door to be opened; he knew very well that Mr. Pennywhiffe could not live there.

The fourth house at which he knocked was the right one.

A decent-looking servant girl replied in the affirmative to his inquiry; and he was forthwith conducted to a well-furnished room on the first floor, where he found Mr. Pennywhiffe seated at a table covered with papers.

This individual was about fifty years of age. In person he was short, thin, and by no means prepossessing in countenance. His eyes were deeply set, grey, and restless; and his forehead was contracted into a thousand wrinkles. He was dressed in a suit of black, and wore a white neckcloth—no doubt to enhance the respectability of his appearance. This was, however, a difficult task; for had he figured in the dock of a criminal tribunal, the jury would have had no trouble in coming to a verdict, a more hang-dog countenance being seldom seen, even in a city where the face is so often the mirror of the mind.

"Ah! Mr. Greenwood," exclaimed Mr. Pennywhiffe, rising to welcome his visitor; "this is an unexpected honour. What can I do for you? Pray be seated; and speak plainly. There's no listeners here."

"I require your aid in a most important business," answered Greenwood, taking a chair, and throwing back his cloak. "To-morrow I must raise twenty or twenty-five thousand pounds, for three or four months—upon bills—*good bills*, Mr. Pennywhiffe."

"To be deposited?" asked that individual.

"To be deposited," replied Greenwood.

"Shall you withdraw them in time?"

"Decidedly. I will convert the money I shall thereby raise into a hundred thousand," exclaimed Greenwood.

"My commission will be heavy for such a business," observed Pennywhiffe; "and *that*, you know is ready money."

"I am aware of it, and am come provided. Name the amount you require."

"Will two hundred hurt you?" said Pennywhiffe. "Remember—the affair is a serious one."

"You shall have two hundred pounds," exclaimed the Member of Parliament, laying his pocket-book upon the table.

"That is what I call coming to the point."

Mr. Pennywhiffe rose from his seat, and opening an iron safe, took thence a memorandum-book and a small tin box.

Returning to his seat, he handed the memorandum-book to Greenwood, saying, "There is my list of noblemen, wealthy gentlemen, and great mercantile firms, *whose names are familiar to me*. Choose which you will have; and make notes of the various sums the bills are to be drawn for. Let them be for the most part uneven ones, with fractions: it looks so much better."

While Greenwood was employed in examining the memorandum-book, which contained upwards of five hundred names of peers, and great landowners, in addition to those of the chief commercial firms of London, Birmingham, Liverpool, Manchester, Leeds, Sheffield, Glasgow, and other places,—besides several belonging to Paris, Lyons, Bordeaux, Havre, and Lille; Brussels, Amsterdam, Rotterdam, and Hamburgh; New York, the West Indian Islands, and Montreal; Calcutta, Bombay, and Madras;—while Mr. Greenwood, we say, was examining this strange register, and copying several of the best names of noblemen, gentlemen, and merchants, upon a slip of paper, Mr Pennywhiffe opened his tin-case.

The contents thereof were numerous paid checks, and bills of exchange, respectively bearing the signatures of the persons or firms whose names were entered in the memorandum-book.

How Mr. Pennywhiffe became possessed of such important documents,—which, seeing that they had all been duly honoured at maturity, ought to have remained in the hands of those who took them up,—was a mystery which he kept to himself. Whether he had collected them by degrees, or had obtained them in a heap by robbery, or any other means, he never condescended to acquaint his clients.

"I have chosen eleven names," said Greenwood; "and have appended to them the various sums for which I require the bills to be drawn. The aggregate is twenty-three thousand two hundred and seventeen pounds, nine shillings, and sevenpence halfpenny."

"A good total, *that*," observed Mr. Pennywhiffe,—"an excellent total—sounds uncommon well. Nothing could be better. Am I to provide the stamps?"

"If you please. I will pay you extra for them."

Mr. Pennywhiffe once more had recourse to his iron safe, and returned to his seat with a small paste-board box, long and narrow, and containing a vast number of bill-stamps adapted to sums of all amounts. As the usual formula of such documents was printed (though in various ways, they having been procured at different stationers' shops) the process of filling them up was by no means a tedious one.

But now the ingenuity of Mr. Pennywhiffe mainly exhibited itself. Each bill was filled up with a different ink and a different pen; and so skilful a caligrapher was he, that the most astute judge of writing could not possibly have perceived that they were all written by the same hand. Then, by the aid of red ink, a few flourishes, and little circles containing initial letters or figures as if each document corresponded with some particular entry in some particular leger or bill-book, the papers speedily assumed a very business-like appearance.

And now the most difficult and delicate part of the entire process was to commence—the signatures. But Mr. Pennywhiffe went to work with the air of one who fully understood what he was about; and with the originals before him as a copy, he perfected acceptance after acceptance in so masterly a manner, that Greenwood, when he compared the fictitious signatures with the genuine, was astounded at the caligraphic proficiency of that man whose dangerous agency he was now rendering available to his purposes.

"So far, all goes well," said Mr. Pennywhiffe.

"The bills are excellent in every point save one," observed Greenwood.

"Which is that?" demanded the caligrapher.

"They look *too new*—the paper is too clean."

"I know it," returned Mr. Pennywhiffe; "but the process is not entirely complete."

He rose and threw a quantity of small coal upon the fire, so as to smother the flame, and create a dense smoke. He then passed each bill several times through the smoke, until the documents acquired a slightly dingy hue. Lastly, he placed them between the leaves of a portfolio scented with musk, so as to take off the odour of the smoke; and the entire process was terminated.

Mr. Greenwood now counted upon the table bank-notes to the aggregate amount of the two hundred pounds promised, and the price of the stamps; and in exchange he received the bills for twenty-three thousand two hundred and seventeen pounds, nine shillings, and sevenpence halfpenny.

"This seems to be a most extraordinary neighbourhood, Mr. Pennywhiffe," said Greenwood, as he placed the bills in his pocket-book. "I knocked by mistake at three houses before I came to yours, and the inmates of each seemed to be in difficulties."

"No doubt of it, my dear sir. This part of London swarms with members of the Swell Mob, broken-down tradesmen, fraudulent bankrupts, insolvents playing at hide-and-seek with the sheriff's-officers, railway projectors, and swindlers of all kinds. I have got a very queer kind of a lodger in my attic: he has no visible means of living, but is out nearly all day long; and he dresses uncommonly well—gold chain—polished boots—figured silk waistcoat—and so forth. He only pays me—or ought to pay me—five shillings a week for his furnished bed-room; and he is six months in arrears. But what is more remarkable still, I don't even know his name; and he never receives any letters, nor has any friends to call. He is about thirty-six or thirty-eight years old, a good-looking fellow enough, and an Irishman."

"Perhaps he also is some railway projector," said Mr. Greenwood, rising to take his departure.

At this moment a double knock at the front-door was heard.

"That must be my lodger," exclaimed Mr. Pennywhiffe.

Urged by curiosity to catch a glimpse of the mysterious gentleman alluded to, Greenwood hurried on his cloak, took leave of the caligrapher, and left the room.

On the stairs he met the lodger, who was ascending to his attic, with a brass candlestick, containing an inch of the commonest candle, in his hand.

The moment he and Greenwood thus encountered each other, an ejaculation of surprise issued from the lips of each.

"Hush! not a word!" said the gentleman, placing his fore-finger upon his lip. "And, of course, Greenwood," he continued, in a whisper, "you will never mention *this* to a soul."

"Never—on my honour!" answered Greenwood.

They then shook hands, and parted—the gentleman continuing his way to the attic, and Greenwood hastening to leave the house.

"Wonders will never cease!" thought the latter, as he proceeded towards the cab-stand near Rowland Hill's chapel in the Blackfriars Road: "who would have thought of one of the Irish Members of Parliament living in an attic in the New Cut?"

CHAPTER CLXXXVII.

THE FORGED BILLS.

At half-past four o'clock on the following afternoon, Ellen Monroe was in the immediate vicinity of the Bank of England.

She had been to receive a small sum of money which an old debtor of her father's, residing in Birchin Lane, had written to state that he was in a condition to pay; and she was now on her return to Markham Place.

The evenings of January are obscure, if not quite dark, at that hour; and the lamps were lighted.

As she was proceeding along Lothbury, Greenwood suddenly passed her. He was walking rapidly, in a pre-occupied manner, and did not perceive her.

But she beheld *him*; and she turned to speak to him; for in spite of all the injuries which her parent, her benefactor Richard, and herself had sustained at his hands, he was still the father of her child!

Scarcely had she thus turned, when he drew his handkerchief from his pocket—still hurrying on towards Tokenhouse Yard.

Ellen quickened her pace; but in a few moments her foot encountered an object on the pavement.

She stooped, and picked it up.

It was a pocket-book.

Conceiving that Greenwood might have dropped it, as she had found it on the very spot where she had seen him take his handkerchief from his pocket, she ran in the direction which she supposed him to have pursued; but as, in the mean time, he had turned into the narrow alley called Tokenhouse Yard, and as she continued her way along Lothbury towards Throgmorton Street, she did not of course overtake him.

Finding that her search after him was unavailing, she determined to examine the contents of the pocket-book, and ascertain if it really did belong to him; in which case, she resolved to proceed straight to Spring Gardens, and restore it to him.

Retracing her steps along Lothbury, she entered Cateaton Street; and turning into the Old Jewry, which was almost deserted, she stopped beneath the light of a lamp to open the pocket-book.

It contained several letters, addressed to "G. M. GREENWOOD, ESQ., M.P.;" and thus her doubts were cleared up at once. But as she was thus investigating the interior of the pocket-book, her eye fell upon a number of bills of exchange, all drawn and endorsed by Mr. Greenwood, and accepted for large sums by noblemen, well-known landowners, and eminent merchants. A rapid glance over these documents convinced Ellen that the aggregate amount which they represented could not fall far short of twenty-five thousand pounds; for, in addition to the fictitious bills obtained from Pennywhiffe, Greenwood had placed in his pocket-book several genuine ones which he legitimately possessed.

Miss Monroe's scrutiny did not altogether occupy a minute; and, carefully securing the pocket-book about her person, she hurried towards Cheapside, where she entered a cab, directing the driver to take her to Spring Gardens.

She did not forget Greenwood's former conduct in having her carried away to his house in the country; but she did not apprehend any ill-usage at his hands in a part of London where succour would be so readily obtained as in Spring Gardens. It was therefore without hesitation that she resolved to proceed direct to his own dwelling in that quarter.

In due time the vehicle stopped at Greenwood's house in Spring Gardens.

With a beating heart Ellen knocked at the door, which was almost immediately opened by Filippo.

"Ah! Miss Monroe!" he exclaimed, as the light of the hall-lamp fell upon her beautiful countenance.

"Yes—it is I at Mr. Greenwood's house," she answered, with a smile: "is he at home?"

"No, Miss—he has gone into the City; but he will be back at six o'clock at the latest."

"Then I will wait for him," said Ellen.

Filippo conducted her up stairs.

In the window of the staircase still stood the beautiful model of the Diana, holding a lamp in its hand,—that model which was the image of her own faultless form.

On the landing-place, communicating with the drawing-room, was also the marble statue, the bust of which was sculptured in precise imitation of her own.

And, when she entered the drawing-room, the first object which met her eyes was the picture of Venus rising from the ocean, surrounded by nereids and nymphs,—that Venus which was a faithful likeness of herself!

Oh! how many phases of her existence did these permanent representations of her matchless beauty bring back to her memory!

When Filippo left her, and she found herself alone, she fell upon a sofa, and gave way to a violent flood of tears.

Then she felt relieved; and she began to ask herself wherefore she had come thither? Was it because she was glad to have found an excuse for calling upon him who was the father of her child? was it because she was anxious to receive his thanks—from his own lips—for restoring to him his pocket-book? She scarcely knew.

Half an hour passed in reflections of this nature—reflections which branched off in so many different ways, and converged to no satisfactory point—when a cab suddenly drove up to the house.

In another minute hasty steps ascended the stairs—they approached the drawing-room—and Greenwood rushed in, banging the door furiously behind him.

"My God! what have I done?" he exclaimed, frantically—for he did not immediately perceive Ellen, whom a screen concealed from his view. "The pocket-book is lost—gone! I am ruined—should those forged bills——"

He said no more, but threw himself upon a chair, and buried his face in his hands.

Ellen instantly comprehended it all:—the bills which she had seen in the pocket-book were forgeries!

Rapid as lightning a train of new reflections passed through her brain:—a project suggested itself;—she hesitated for a moment—but only for a moment:—she thought of her child—and she was resolved.

Assuming all her calmness, and calculating in an instant all the chances of her scheme, she rose from the sofa, and slowly approached the chair on which Greenwood was seated.

He heard a step in the room, and raised his eyes.

"Ellen!" he exclaimed, starting back in surprise.

She murmured a *Christian name*—but it was not *George*.

"Call me not *that*, Ellen!" cried Greenwood, fiercely: "the time is not come! But tell me," he added, speaking thickly, and at the same instant casting upon her a glance which seemed to pierce her inmost soul,—"tell me—were you here—in this room—when I came in?"

"I was," answered Ellen, gazing, in her turn, fixedly upon him.

"And you heard——"

"I heard every word you uttered," continued Miss Monroe, keeping her eyes still bent upon him.

"Ah! then you know———"

"*That you have committed forgery*," added Ellen, in an emphatic tone; "*and that you are ruined*!"

"Damnation!" ejaculated Greenwood. "What did you come for? why are you here? To gloat over my falling fortunes—to make yourself merry at my ruin—to taunt me with the past—to laugh at me in my adversity—to———"

"Then it *is* true," thought Ellen, within herself: "these bills *are* forgeries—and he is in my power.—No," she exclaimed aloud; "such was not my object."

"Then, go—leave me—depart!" cried Greenwood, frantically. "I am in no humour to listen to you now! But, Ellen," he added, suddenly becoming cool—desperately cool:—"tell me—speak—you will not betray me?"

"No—that is, on *one* condition," answered Ellen.

"One condition!" repeated Greenwood: "name it!"

"That you make me your wife," was the steady reply.

"My wife!" exclaimed Greenwood, laughing hysterically. "Do you know whose wife you would become?—the wife of a forger! Have you not learnt that dread secret? But, perhaps, it is to mock me that you offer to become my wife! Oh! I understand you full well, Ellen! When I was rich and beyond the reach of the law, I would not marry you;—and now you mean me to comprehend that since I am ruined, and every moment in danger of being dragged to a station-house, *you* would scorn the alliance! The jest is good:—no—the revenge is just! But it is not the less bitter to me, Ellen!"

"By heavens, you wrong me!" cried Ellen. "Listen with calmness—with composure—if you can!"

"I cannot, Ellen—I cannot! I am mad! A few months—nay, even a few weeks ago, I was happy—wealthy—prosperous:—now I am ruined—miserable—lost! Oh! the grand prospects that were so lately open before me!"

"Again I say, listen. All is not so bad as you imagine," said the young lady, in a hasty tone.

"What do you mean, Ellen? what *can* you mean?" he exclaimed, bewildered. "Do you not understand the nature of a forgery—the consequences which it entails? True—I did not perpetrate the forgery with my own hands;—but the bills are all drawn—all endorsed by me! Oh! it is dreadful—it is terrible!"

"I will not keep you any longer in suspense," said Ellen. "Your pocket-book is found———"

"Found!" repeated Greenwood, electrified by that word, and not knowing whether it imported good or evil to him: "found! Did you say———"

"Yes—found," answered Miss Monroe;—"and by me!"

"By you, Ellen?" cried Greenwood. "No—it is impossible!"

"How, then, should I know that you had lost a pocket-book?" asked the young lady.

"True! And you have found it? Oh! then I am saved—I am saved! Give it to me, Ellen—give it to me!"

And he advanced towards her, with out-stretched hands.

"No—not yet," exclaimed the young lady, in a firm tone. "In this room—yes, in this very room—I went down upon my knees, and implored you to save me from disgrace—to give a father's name to the child who was then as yet unborn. And you refused my supplication—you turned a deaf ear to my agonising entreaties. Oh! I remember that scene but too well. You would not do me justice—and I told you that you might live to repent your cruelty towards me!"

"What! you will now avenge your alleged wrongs!" cried Greenwood, his countenance becoming livid with mingled fear and rage: "you will deliver me up to justice? No—I will tear the pocket-book from you—I will destroy the proofs of my folly—my crime; and then———but why should I waste time in idle words like these; I must act! Give me the book!"

And he rushed towards her, as a tiger springs upon its victim.

But Ellen, light as the fawn, glided away from him, and took such a position that a table was between them, and a bell-pull within her reach.

"Dare to attempt violence towards me," she exclaimed, "and I summon your servants. Then—in their presence—I will proclaim their master a forger! Provoke me not—my spirit is roused—and your fate hangs upon a thread!"

"Damnation!" cried Greenwood, grinding his teeth with rage. "Can nothing move you, Ellen?"

"Yes—the *one condition* that I ere now named," she answered, drawing herself up to her full height, and assuming all the influence of her really queenly beauty.

"Agreed!" ejaculated Greenwood. "Give me the pocket-book—I take God to witness that I will make you my wife within a week from this day."

"You regard an oath no more than a mere promise," replied Ellen, calmly, and with a slightly satirical curl of the lip.

"I will give you the promise in writing, Ellen," persisted Greenwood, urged to desperation.

"Neither will *that* satisfy me," said the young lady. "When our hands are joined at the altar, I will restore you the proofs of your crime; and God grant," she added solemnly, "that this peril which you have incurred may serve as a warning to you against future risks of the same fearful kind."

"You have no faith in my word—you have no confidence in my written promise, Ellen," cried Greenwood: "how, then, can you be anxious to have me as a husband?"

"That my child may not grow up with the stain of illegitimacy upon him—that he may not learn to despise his mother," answered Ellen, emphatically; "for *he* need never know the precise date of our union."

"But you know, Ellen," again remonstrated Greenwood, "that there are circumstances which act as an insuperable barrier to this marriage. Could you tell your father that you have espoused the man who ruined him—ruined Richard,—and also admit, at the same time, that this man was the father of your child! Consider, Ellen—reflect——"

"There is no need of consideration—no need of reflection," interrupted Miss Monroe. "I care not about revealing the fact of my marriage for the present. In a few years—when our child can comprehend his true position,—*then* it would be necessary to declare myself a wife."

"But there is another difficulty, Ellen," persisted Greenwood: "my name——"

"Let us be wedded privately—in some suburban church, where you stand no chance of being recognised as George Montague Greenwood, and where your *right name* may be fearlessly inscribed upon the register."

"A woman who is determined to gain her point, annihilates all difficulties," muttered Greenwood to himself.

"How do *you* decide?" asked Ellen. "Remember that *I* am firm. I have these alternatives before me—either to obtain a father's name for my child, or to avenge the wrongs of my own parent and myself. Consent to make me your wife, and the proofs of your crime shall be returned to you at the altar: refuse, and to-morrow morning I will prepare the way for vengeance."

"Ellen, I consent to your proposal," said Greenwood, in a tone of deep humiliation; "but upon condition that our marriage shall never be proclaimed until that day, when——"

"I understand you; and I cheerfully agree to the proposal," interrupted Miss Monroe. "You can believe *my* word:—besides, you *must* know that I also should have reasons to conceal our union, until you chose to declare your real name."

"Then be it as you propose, Ellen. To-morrow morning, early, I will procure a special license, and we will be united at Hackney. You can meet me at the church precisely at ten o'clock in the morning: I will have every thing in readiness. But whom will you ask to accompany you?"

"Marian—the faithful servant who has been so devoted to my interests," answered Miss Monroe.

"I think that I should prefer the wife of that surgeon—Mrs. Wentworth, I mean—as the witness to our union," said Greenwood. "I dislike the idea of domestics being entrusted with important secrets. Besides, Mrs. Wentworth has never seen me—knows not that I am passing by the name of Greenwood—and, in a word, is a lady."

"Be it as you will in this instance," returned Ellen. "Mrs. Wentworth shall accompany me—I can rely upon her."

She then rang the bell.

"What do you require, Ellen?" asked Greenwood, alarmed by this movement on her part.

"Merely to ensure the presence of one of your servants, as I pass from this spot to the door of the room," replied Ellen. "You can give him some order to avert suspicion."

Filippo made his appearance; and Ellen then took leave of Mr. Greenwood, as if nothing peculiar had occurred between them.

Oh! with what joy—with what fervid, intoxicating joy—did she return to Markham Place! She had subdued *him* whose cold, calculating, selfish heart was hitherto unacquainted with honourable concessions;—she had conquered him—reduced him to submit to her terms—imposed her own conditions!

Never—never before had she embraced her child with such pride—such undiluted happiness as on that evening. And never had she herself appeared more beautiful—more enchantingly lovely! Her lips were wreathed in smiles—her eyes beamed with the transports of hope, triumph, and maternal affection—a glow of ineffable bliss animated her countenance—her swelling bosom heaved with rapture.

"You are very late, my dear child," said Mr. Monroe, when she took her seat at the tea-table: "I began to grow uneasy."

"I was detained a long time at the office of your debtor," answered Ellen. "To-morrow morning I intend to pay a visit to Mrs. Wentworth, and shall invite myself to breakfast with her. So you need not be surprised, dear father," she added, with a sweet smile, "if I do not make my appearance at your table."

"You please me in pleasing yourself, dear Ellen. Moreover, I am delighted that you should cultivate Mrs. Wentworth's acquaintance. Most sincerely do I hope," continued Mr. Monroe, "that we shall have letters from Richard to-morrow. The communications which we have already received are not satisfactory to my mind. God grant that he may be by this time safe in Naples—if not on his way to England."

"Alas! the enterprise has been a most unfortunate one for him!" returned Ellen, a cloud passing over her countenance. "I understand his noble disposition so well, that I am convinced he deeply feels the defeat of Ossore."

We must observe that the news of our hero's success at Estella had not yet reached England.

"It will be a happy day for us all," said Mr. Monroe, after a pause, "when Richard once more sets foot in his own home—for I love him as if he were my son."

"And I as if he were my brother," added Ellen;—"yes—*my brother*," she repeated, with strange emphasis upon these words.

On the following morning, a few minutes before ten o'clock, a post-chaise stopped at the gate of the parish church of Hackney; and Mr. Greenwood alighted.

He was pale; and the quivering of his lip denoted the agitation of his mind.

The clock was striking ten, when a hackney-coach reached the same point.

Greenwood hastened to the door, and assisted Mrs. Wentworth and Ellen Monroe to descend the steps.

As he handed out the latter, he said, in a hurried whisper, "You have the pocket-book with you?"

"I have," answered Ellen.

The party then proceeded to the church, the drivers of the vehicles being directed to await their return at a little distance, so as not to attract the notice of the inhabitants.

The clergyman and the clerk awaited the arrival of the nuptial party.

The ceremony commenced—proceeded—and terminated.

Ellen was now a wife!

Her husband imprinted a kiss upon her pale forehead; and at the same moment she handed him the pocket-book.

In a few minutes the marriage-certificate was in her possession.

Drawing her husband aside, she said, "Let me now implore you—for your own sake—for the sake of your child—if not for *mine*—to abstain from those courses———"

"Ellen," interrupted Greenwood, "do not alarm yourself on that head. My friend the Marquis of Holmesford lent me ten thousand pounds last evening; and with that sum I will retrieve my falling fortunes. Yes—you shall yet bear a great name. Ellen," he added, his countenance lighting up with animation; "*a name that shall go down to posterity!* But, tell me—has your father received any tidings from Richard?"

"None since those of which I wrote to you. We are not yet aware whether he be in safety, or not."

"You will write to me the moment you receive any fresh communication?"

"Rest assured that I shall not forget that duty."

"And now, Ellen, we must pass the day together. We will spend our honeymoon of twenty-four hours at Richmond. Mrs. Wentworth can return home, and send word to your father that she means to keep you with her until to-morrow morning."

"If you command me, it is my duty to obey," replied Ellen.

"I do—I do," answered Greenwood, earnestly. "You are now mine—the circumstances which led to our union shall be forgotten—and I shall think of you only as my beautiful wife."

"Oh! if this be really true!" murmured Ellen, pressing his hand fervently, and regarding him with affection—for he was the father of her child!

"It *is* true," answered Greenwood;—but his bride perceived not how much of sensual passion prompted him on the present occasion. "I know that you have been faithful to me—that the hope of one day becoming my wife has swayed your conduct. Of *that* I have had proofs."

"Proofs!" repeated Ellen, with mingled surprise and joy.

"Yes—proofs. Do you not remember the Greek Brigand at the masquerade, where you met and so justly upbraided that canting hypocrite, Reginald Tracy?"

"I do. But that Greek Brigand———"

"Was myself!" replied Greenwood.

"You!" exclaimed Ellen, with a smile of satisfaction.

"Yes: and I overheard every sentence you uttered. But we may not tarry here longer: speak to Mrs. Wentworth, that she send a proper excuse to your father; and let us depart."

Ellen hastened to the vestry where the surgeon's wife was seated near a cheerful fire; and the arrangement desired by Greenwood was soon made.

The party then proceeded to the vehicles.

Mrs. Wentworth bade the newly-married couple adieu, having faithfully promised to retain their secret inviolate; and Greenwood handed her into the hackney-coach.

He and Ellen entered the post-chaise; and while the surgeon's wife retraced her way to her own abode, the bride and bridegroom hastened to Richmond.

CHAPTER CLXXXVIII.

THE BATTLES OF PIACERE AND ABRANTANI.

We must now request our readers to accompany us once more to Castelcicala.

In an incredibly short time, and by dint of a forced march which put the mettle of his troops to a severe test,—at which, however, they did not repine, for they were animated by the dauntless courage and perseverance of their commander.—Richard Markham arrived beneath the walls of Villabella.

During his progress towards the town, he had been joined by upwards of four hundred volunteers, all belonging to the national militia, and armed and equipped ready for active service.

The daring exploit which had made him master of Estella, had created an enthusiasm in his favour which he himself and all his followers considered to be an augury of the final success of the Constitutional Cause; and in every village—in every hamlet through which his army had passed, was he welcomed with the most lively demonstration of joy.

When, early on the morning of the 1st of January, his advanced guard emerged from the woods which skirted the southern suburb of Villabella, the arrival of the Constitutional Army was saluted by the roar of artillery from the ramparts; and almost at the same moment the tri-coloured flag was hoisted on every pinnacle and every tower of the great manufacturing town.

"We have none but friends there!" exclaimed Richard, as he pointed towards Villabella. "God grant that we may have no blood to shed elsewhere."

The army halted beneath the walls of Villabella, for Richard did not deem it proper to enter those precincts until formally invited to do so by the corporation.

He, however, immediately despatched a messenger to the mayor, with certain credentials which had been supplied him by the Committee of Administration at Estella; and in the course of an hour the municipal authorities of Villabella came forth in procession to welcome him.

The mayor was a venerable man of eighty years of age, but with unimpaired intellects, and a mind still young and vigorous.

Alighting from his horse, Richard hastened forward to meet him.

"Let me embrace you, noble young man!" exclaimed the mayor. "Your fame has preceded you—and within those walls," he added, turning and pointing towards Villabella, "there breathes not a soul opposed to the sacred cause which heaven has sent you to direct."

Then the mayor embraced Richard in presence of the corporation—in presence of the Constitutional Army; and the welkin rang with shouts of enthusiastic joy.

The formal invitation to enter Villabella was now given; and Markham issued the necessary orders.

The corporation led the way: next came the General, attended by his staff; and after him proceeded the long lines of troops, their martial weapons gleaming in the morning sun.

The moment our hero passed the inner drawbridge, the roar of cannon was renewed upon the ramparts; and the bells in all the towers commenced a merry peal.

As at Estella, the windows were thronged with faces—the streets were crowded with spectators—and every testimonial of an enthusiastic welcome awaited the champion of Constitutional Liberty.

Then resounded, too, myriads of voices, exclaiming, "Long live Alberto"—"Long live the General!"—"Down with the Tyrant!"—"Death to the Austrians!"

In this manner the corporation, Markham, and his staff, proceeded to the Town-Hall, while the troops defiled off to the barracks, where the garrison—a thousand in number—welcomed them as brethren-in-arms.

All the officers of the troops in Villabella, moreover—with the exception of the colonel-commandant,—declared in favour of the Constitutionalists; and even that superior functionary manifested no particular hostility to the movement, but simply declared that "although he could never again bear arms in favour of the Grand Duke, he would not fight against him."

When he had transacted business at the Town-Hall, and countersigned a proclamation which the municipality drew up, recognising the Committee of Administration of Estella, and constituting itself a permanent body invested with similar functions,—Markham repaired to the barracks.

Thence he immediately despatched couriers to the excellent banker at Pinalla, to the mayor of Estella, and to the Committee of Government at Montoni.

He then issued an address to his army, complimenting it upon the spirit and resolution with which the forced march to Villabella had been accomplished; reminding it that every thing depended upon the celerity of its movements, so as to prevent a concentration of any great number of adverse troops, before the Constitutional force could be augmented sufficiently to cope with them; and finally ordering it to prepare to resume the march that afternoon at three o'clock.

By means of new volunteers and a portion of the garrison of Villabella, Richard found his army increased to nearly four thousand men.

At the head of this imposing force he set out once more, at the time indicated, and commenced another rapid march in the direction of Piacere.

On the ensuing evening—the 2d of January—the towers of that important city broke upon the view of the van-guard of the Constitutionalists.

The commandant of the garrison of Piacere was an old and famous officer—General Giustiniani,—devoted to the cause of the Grand Duke, and holding in abhorrence every thing savouring of liberal opinions.

Markham was aware of this fact; and he felt convinced that Piacere would not fall into his hands without bloodshed. At the same time, he determined not to pass it by, because it would serve as a point of centralisation for the troops of Veronezzi and Terano (both being seats of the military administration of Captains-General), and moreover afford the enemy a means of cutting off all communication between himself on the one hand, and Villabella and Estella on the other.

Certain of being attacked, Markham lost no time in making the necessary arrangements. He ordered the van-guard to halt, until the troops in the rear could come up, and take their proper places; and he planted his artillery upon a hill which commanded almost the entire interval between his army and the city.

Nor were his precautions vainly taken; for in a short time a large force was seen moving towards him from Piacere, the rays of the setting sun irradiating their glittering bayonets and the steel helmets of a corps of cuirassiers.

In another quarter of an hour the enemy was so near as to induce Richard to order his artillery to open a fire upon them: but General Giustiniani, who commanded in person, led his forces on with such rapidity, that the engagement speedily commenced.

Giustiniani had about three thousand five hundred men under his orders; but although this force was numerically inferior to the Constitutionalists, it was superior in other respects—for it comprised a large body of cuirassiers, a regiment of grenadiers, a corps of rifles, and twenty field-pieces: it was, moreover fresh and unwearied, whereas the Constitutionalists were fatigued with a long march.

For a few minutes a murderous fire was kept up on both sides; but Richard led his troops to close quarters, and charged the cuirassiers at the head of his cavalry.

At the same time the Cingani, in obedience to an order which he had sent their chiefs, turned the right flank of the rifles by a rapid and skilful manœuvre, and so isolated them from their main body as to expose them to the artillery upon the hill.

Excited, as it were to desperation, by the conduct of our hero, the Constitutional cavalry performed prodigies of valour; and after an hour's hard fighting in the grey twilight, succeeded in breaking the hitherto compact body of cuirassiers.

Leaving his cavalry to accomplish the rout of the enemy's horse-guards, Richard flew to the aid of his right wing, which was sorely pressed by the grenadiers, and was breaking into disorder.

"Constitutionalists!" he cried: "your brethren are victorious elsewhere: abandon not the field! Follow me—to conquest or to death!"

These words operated with electrical effect; and the Constitutional infantry immediately rallied under the guidance of their youthful leader.

Then the battle was renewed: darkness fell upon the scene; but still the murderous conflict was prolonged. At length Richard engaged hand to hand with the colonel of the grenadiers, who was well mounted on a steed of enormous size. But this combat was short; the officer's sword was dashed from his hand; and he became our hero's prisoner.

These tidings spread like wild-fire; and the enemy fell into confusion. Their retreat became general: Richard followed up his advantage; and Giustiniani's army was completely routed.

The Constitutionalists pressed close upon them; and Richard, once more putting himself at the head of his cavalry, pursued the fugitives up to the very walls of Piacere—not with the murderous intention of exterminating them, but with a view to secure as many prisoners as possible, and prevent the enemy from taking refuge in the city.

At the very gates of Piacere he overtook General Giustiniani, and, after a short conflict, made him captive.

He then retraced his steps to the scene of his victory, and took the necessary steps for concentrating his forces once more.

That night, the Constitutionalists bivouacked in the plains about a mile from Piacere.

Early in the morning of the 3d of January, the results of the brilliant triumph of the preceding evening were known. Eight hundred of the enemy lay dead upon the field; and fifteen hundred had been taken prisoners. The Constitutionalists had lost three hundred men, and had nearly as many wounded.

Scarcely had the sun risen on the scene of carnage, when messengers arrived from Piacere, stating that the corporation had declared in favour of the Constitutionalists, and bearing letters from the municipal authorities to Markham. Those documents assured our hero that the sympathies of the great majority of the inhabitants were in favour of his cause; and that deep regret was experienced at the waste of life which had been occasioned by the obstinacy and self-will of General Giustiniani. Those letters also contained an invitation for him to enter the city, where the tri-coloured flag was already hoisted.

These welcome tidings were soon made known to the whole army, and were received with shouts of joy and triumph.

Richard returned a suitable answer to the delegates, and then sought General Giustiniani. To this commander he offered immediate liberty, on condition that he would not again bear arms against the Constitutionalists. The offer was spurned with contempt. Markham accordingly despatched him, under a strong escort, to Villabella.

At nine o'clock Markham entered Piacere, amidst the ringing of bells, the thunder of cannon, and the welcome of the inhabitants. The corporation presented him with the keys, which he immediately returned to the mayor, saying, "I am the servant, sir, and not the master of the Castelcicalans."

This reply was speedily circulated through Piacere, and increased the enthusiasm of the inhabitants in his favour.

Richard determined to remain until the following morning in this city. Having seen his troops comfortably lodged in the barracks, he adopted his usual course of despatching couriers, with accounts of his proceedings, to Villabella, Estella, Pinalla, and Montoni. Need we say that every letter which he addressed to the worthy banker contained brief notes—necessarily brief—to be sent by way of Naples, to Mr. Monroe and Isabella?

Having performed these duties, Richard repaired to the Town-Hall, where he countersigned a decree appointing the municipal body a Committee of Administration; and a proclamation to that effect was speedily published.

He next, with the most unwearied diligence, adopted measures to increase his army, for he resolved to march with as little delay as possible towards Abrantani; where a strong Austrian and Castelcicalan force was lying, under the command of the Captain-General of that province. At that point Richard well knew an important struggle must take place—a struggle in comparison with which all that he had hitherto done was as nothing.

But his endeavours in obtaining recruits were attended with great success. Volunteers flocked to the barracks; and the city-arsenal was well provided with all the uniforms, arms, ammunition, and stores that were required.

On the west of Piacere was a vast plain, on which Richard determined to review his troops at day-break, and thence march direct upon Abrantani.

The order was accordingly issued; and half an hour before the sun rose, the army defiled through the western gates. Nearly all the inhabitants repaired to the plain, to witness the martial spectacle; and many were the bright eyes that glanced with admiration—and even a softer feeling—at the handsome countenance of that young man whose name now belonged to history.

Colonel Cossario, the second in command, directed the evolutions. The army was drawn up in divisions four deep, and mustered five thousand strong.

And now, on the 4th of January, a morning golden with sun-beams, the review began. Each regiment had its brass band and its gay colours; and the joyous beams of the orb of day sported on the points of bayonets, flashed on naked swords, and played on the steel helmets of four hundred cuirassiers whom Richard had organised on the preceding evening.

Stationed on an eminence, attended by his staff, and by his faithful Morcar, who had comported himself gallantly in the battle of the 2d, Markham surveyed, with feelings of indescribable enthusiasm, that armament which owned him as its chief.

Cossario gave the word—it was passed on from division to division; and now all these sections are wheeling into line.

The line is formed—the bands are stationed in front of their respective corps: and all is as still as death.

Again the Colonel gives the word of command—"General salute! Present arms!"—and a long din of hands clapping against the muskets echoes around.

The bands strike up the glorious French air of the *Parisienne*; and Markham gracefully raises his plumed hat from his brow, in acknowledgment of the salute of his army.

The music ceases—the word, "Shoulder arms!" is passed from division to division, along that line of half a mile from flank to flank.

Then Markham gallops towards the troops, followed by his staff; the ranks take open order; he passes along, inspecting the different corps,—addressing them—encouraging them.

Again he returns to the eminence: the line is once more broken into divisions; close columns are formed; and the whole army is put in motion, to march past its General, the bands playing a lively air.

From the plain the troops defiled towards the road leading to Abrantani.

But scarcely had Markham taken leave of the mayor and the municipal authorities, in order to rejoin his army, when a courier, covered with dust, galloped up to him. He was the bearer of letters from Signor Viviani. Those documents afforded our hero the welcome intelligence that Pinalla had hoisted the tri-colour, declared in favour of the cause of liberty, recognised Markham as the General-in-Chief of the Constitutional Armies of Castelcicala, and had despatched a reinforcement of two thousand men to fight under his banner.

Richard hastily communicated these tidings to the corporation of Piacere, and then joined his army, throughout the ranks of which the news of the adhesion of so important a city as Pinalla to the great cause diffused the utmost joy.

"Every thing favours me!" thought Richard, his heart leaping within him. "Oh! for success at Abrantani; and such will be its moral effect upon my troops that I shall fear nothing for the result of the grand and final struggle that must take place beneath the walls of Montoni! And, then, Isabella, even your father will acknowledge that I have some claim to your hand as a reward for placing him upon the ducal throne!"

The road that the army now pursued was most favourable for the rapid march which Richard urged. It was wide and even, and afforded an easy passage to the artillery.

Shortly after mid-day the van-guard entered the beautiful province of Abrantani; and there the troops were received by the inhabitants with an enthusiasm of the most grateful description. For it was in this district that the tyranny of the Grand Duke's *régime*, under the auspices of Count Santa-Croce, had been most severely felt.

No wonder, then, that the Constitutional Army was greeted with rapture and delight;—no wonder that blessings were invoked upon the head of its General! The old men went down upon their knees by the road-sides, to implore heaven to accord success to his mission;—mothers held up their children to catch a glimpse of the youthful hero;—and young maidens threw garlands of flowers in his path.

Volunteers poured in from all sides; and the army increased in its progress, like the snowball rolling along the ground.

At sunset the entire force halted in the precincts of a large town, the inhabitants of which hastened to supply the soldiers with provisions and wine.

During that pause, couriers arrived from Veronezzi, with the joyful tidings that it had declared in favour of the Constitutional cause, and was sending reinforcements. Thus the whole of the south of Castelcicala was now devoted to the movement of which Markham was the head and chief.

For two hours was the army permitted to rest: it then continued its march until midnight, when it bivouacked in a wide plain, a wood protecting its right wing, and a hill, whereon the artillery was planted, defending its left.

Richard adopted every precaution to avoid a surprise; for he was well aware that the Count of Santa-Croce was not a man to slumber at such a crisis. But it afterwards appeared that the Captain-General did not dare to quit the neighbourhood of the city of Abrantani, for fear that it should pronounce in favour of the Constitutionalists.

It was, therefore, under the walls of Abrantani itself that the contest was to take place.

There was a flat eminence to the east of the city; and on this had Santa-Croce taken up his position at the head of seven thousand men—three thousand Castelcicalans, and four thousand Austrians.

Against this force was Richard to contend, at the head of six thousand soldiers, the volunteers who had joined him since he left Piacere amounting to a thousand.

But to return to our narrative in the consecutive order of events.

At five o'clock in the morning of the 5th, the Constitutionalists quitted their position where they had bivouacked, and pursued their way towards the city of Abrantani.

The day passed—night came once more—and the troops bivouacked in the immediate vicinity of a large hamlet.

The morning of the 6th saw them again in motion; but Richard allowed them to proceed with diminished celerity, as he had already enough chances against him to warn him not to increase them by over-fatiguing his army.

It was not, therefore, until the evening that he came in sight of the tall spire on the Cathedral of Abrantani.

"By this time to-morrow," exclaimed Richard, pointing in the direction of the city, "the tower on which yon spire stands shall echo with the sounds of its bells to celebrate our triumph!"

"Amen!" ejaculated Morcar, who was close behind him.

The Constitutionalists took up a strong position, with a village on their right and a range of extensive farm-buildings on their left. They were all animated by an enthusiasm worthy of the great cause in which they were embarked; and their ardour was manifested by singing martial songs as they crowded round the fires of the bivouac.

Richard never closed his eyes during the night. Confident that his want of experience in military tactics must be compensated for by unceasing exercise of that intelligence and keenness of perception which had enabled him to direct the movements of his troops so as to achieve the victory of Piacere, he reconnoitred all the positions adjacent to his own—marked those where troops would be advantageously placed, and observed others where they would be endangered—visited the outposts—studied the maps of that part of the country—and held consultations with his most skilful officers. These subordinates were astonished at the soundness of his views, the excellence of his arrangements, and the admirable nature of his combinations.

Markham was resolved to effect two objects, which, he felt convinced, would lessen the chances that were now against him. The first was to throw up a small redoubt, where he might place a portion of his artillery, so as to command the flat eminence on which the Austro-Castelcicalan army was stationed. The second was to send off a small detachment before day-break, to gain a wood about two miles distant, whence it might debouch at the proper time, and fall upon the left flank of the enemy.

The redoubt was commenced, and proceeded rapidly; and an hour before sunrise the corps of Cingani departed on the important service which the General-in-Chief confided to it, with strict orders not to move from the wood until the enemy should have left the eminence and descended to the plain.

Thus, by the time the sun rose on the morning of the 7th, the Cingani were safely concealed in the wood; a redoubt, bristling with artillery, commanded the enemy's position; and the Constitutionalists were formed in order of battle.

Richard commanded the right wing; and Colonel Cossario the left.

The engagement began on the part of the Constitutionalists, with a cannonade from the redoubt; and so well did this battery perform its part, that—as Richard had foreseen—the Captain-General was compelled to descend into the plain, and endeavour to surround the right wing of the Constitutionalists, in order to terminate the carnage occasioned by that dreadful cannonade.

Meantime, Cossario, with his division, advanced to meet three battalions which the Captain-General had detached to attack the range of farm-buildings; and for an hour the combat raged in that point with inconceivable fury. The Austrians precipitated themselves with a desperate ardour upon Cossario's troops, who were at length compelled to retreat and occupy the farm.

On the right, Markham sustained a fearful contest with the force opposed to him. The fire of the musketry was at point-blank distance; and the firmness with which the action was maintained on both sides, rendered the result highly dubious.

But now the Cingani debouched from the wood, and fell upon the left wing of the enemy. The impetuosity of their attack was irresistible: the wing was turned by them; and the Austro-Castelcicalans were thrown into disorder. Then Richard, at the head of his cuirassiers, charged upon the centre of the enemy, and decided the fortune of the day.

In the meantime Cossario had completely rallied his division and had succeeded in repulsing the battalions that were opposed to him.

The Captain-General endeavoured to effect a retreat in an orderly manner towards the eminence which he had originally occupied; but Richard, perceiving his intention, was enabled to out-flank him, and to gain possession of the height. For an hour this important position was disputed with all the vigour and ardour of military combat; but, though the Austro-Castelcicalans manifested a vehemence bordering on rage, and a perseverance approaching to desperation, all their attempts to recover their lost ground were ineffectual.

And equally vain were the endeavours of Santa-Croce to secure an orderly retreat; his columns were shattered—his battalions broken; the flight of his troops became general; but they were closely pursued by their conquerors.

The Cathedral of Abrantani proclaimed the hour of three in the afternoon, when Richard, on the eminence commanding the city, sate down to pen hasty dispatches, announcing this great victory to the Committees of Montoni, Piacere, Villabella, Veronezzi, Pinalla, and Estella. Nor did he forget to enclose, in his letters to Signor Viviani, brief notes addressed to his friend Monroe and the Princess Isabella.

The results of the battle of Abrantani were most glorious to the Constitutional arms. While Richard's loss was small, that of the enemy had been enormous. Two thousand men—chiefly Austrians—lay dead upon the plain; and nearly as many were taken prisoners. Two of the Castelcicalan regiments rallied at a short distance from the scene of the conflict, and placing themselves at the disposal of Colonel Cossario, who had pursued them, joined the Constitutional cause.

The Captain-General, Count Santa-Croce, succeeded in effecting his escape, with several of his superior officers; and, hastening to join the Grand Duke, who was still besieging Montoni, the vanquished chief was the first to communicate to that Prince the fatal result of the battle.

That same evening Richard Markham entered the city of Abrantani, which joyfully opened its gates to receive him; and, as in the other towns which he had occupied, the thunders of artillery, the ringing of bells, and the plaudits of admiring crowds testified the enthusiasm which was inspired by the presence of the youthful General.

Richard determined to remain some days in the city of Abrantani. Montoni was besieged by a force nearly twenty-five thousand strong; and our hero felt the necessity of waiting for the reinforcements promised him, and of raising as many volunteers as possible, ere he could venture to cope with so formidable a force. But in every despatch which he had sent to the Committee of Government at Montoni, he had given the most solemn assurances of his resolution to march to the relief of the capital with as little delay as possible; and it was now, at Abrantani, that he anxiously expected official tidings from the besieged city.

Nor was he kept long in suspense. On the morning of the 10th a courier arrived with despatches from the Committee of Government. These documents are so important, that we do not hesitate to lay them before our readers.

The first was conceived thus:—

"*Montoni, January 9th, 1841.*

"The Committee of Government of the State of Castelcicala have received the various despatches which the General-in-Chief of the Constitutional Army has addressed to them respectively from Villabella, Piacere, and Abrantani. The Committee must reserve for a future occasion the pleasing duty of expressing how deeply they rejoice at the General-in-Chief's various successes, and how anxiously they watch the progress of that cause of which he has become the guide and champion.

"The Committee cannot, however, omit one duty which they now perform by virtue of the full powers of administration and government that have been vested in them by the inhabitants of the capital, and which powers are recognised by all faithful Castelcicalans who have declared in favour of the Constitutional cause.

"This duty is rendered imperious on the Committee by the eminent and unequalled services of the General-in-Chief.

"The Committee of Government have therefore ordained, and do ordain, that the style and title of *Marquis of Estella* be conferred upon the General-in-Chief, the most Excellent Signor Richard Markham.

"And a copy of this decree shall be forwarded to every city or town which has pronounced in favour of the Constitutional cause.

"By order of the Committee of Government—

"GAETANO, *President.*

TERLIZZI, *Vice-President.*"

The second despatch ran thus:—

"To the Marquis of Estella, General-in-Chief of the Constitutional Armies of Castelcicala.

"My Lord,

"We, the members of the Committee of Government of Castelcicala, have the honour to lay before your lordship a few particulars relative to the condition of the capital city of that State. Closely besieged by the foreign force whom the traitor Angelo has invited into the country, and blockaded at sea by the fleet of the Lord High Admiral, Montoni already enters upon the dread phase of *famine*. The garrison performs its duty nobly in defending the capital from the attacks daily directed against it by the insolent Austrian invaders; but it is impossible that we can hold out for any length of time. We are, however, happy to be enabled to assure your lordship that the inhabitants endure their lamentable condition with exemplary fortitude and patience, the brilliant achievements of your lordship and the Constitutional Army having inspired them with the most lively hopes of a speedy deliverance. So sorely are we pressed, that it has been only with the greatest difficulty that your lordship's couriers have been able to pass the lines of the besiegers, and gain entrance into the city.

"We feel convinced that these brief statements will be sufficient to induce your lordship to lose no time in marching to the deliverance of the capital.

"We have the honour to remain, My Lord,

"Your lordship's obedient servants,

"For the Members of } GAETANO, *President.*

the Committee   } TERLIZZI, *Vice-President.*

"Montoni, January 9th, 1841 (Six o'clock in the morning.)"

Most welcome, in one sense, to our hero were these documents. Although he deeply deplored the condition to which Montoni was reduced, he could not do otherwise than experience the most thrilling and rapturous delight at the impression which his conduct had produced upon the Provisional Government of the State, and of the inhabitants of the capital.

Nor shall we depreciate the merits of Richard Markham, if we admit that he received, with the most heart-felt joy, that title of nobility which, he felt convinced, must lead him nearer to the grand aim of all his exertions—the hand of Isabella!

And as he looked back upon the events of the last fortnight,—when he reflected that at the commencement of that short interval he had issued from Pinalla on a desperate undertaking, and that these fourteen days had shed glory on his name, and placed the coronet of a Marquis upon his brow,—he was lost in admiration of the inscrutable ways of that Providence to whom he had never ceased to pray, morning and evening—as well when crowned with success as in the hour of danger!

But as we do not wish to dwell too much upon this grand and remarkable episode in our hero's history, we shall continue our narrative of these events in their proper order.

The Marquis of Estella each day saw his army increasing. The promised reinforcements arrived from Pinalla and Veronezzi: Lipari and Ossore declared for his cause, and furnished their contingents to the Constitutional forces; and each hour brought to Richard's head-quarters at Abrantani tidings of fresh movements in his favour. Troops poured in; and he was compelled to muster his forces in an encampment on the northern side of the town.

Indeed, the battles of Piacere and Abrantani had electrified Castelcicala; and the tri-coloured banner already floated on the walls of the principal cities and towns of the state. Addresses of confidence and congratulation were sent to our hero from all parts; and large sums of money were raised and forwarded to him, to enable him to reward his troops and equip his volunteers.

It was on the 20th of January that Markham put his army in motion. He was now at the head of sixteen thousand men, with a formidable train of artillery. Although the numerical odds were fearfully against him, he reposed the most perfect confidence in the valour of his troops—elated as they were by previous successes, and glorying in a cause which they deemed holy and sacred. Moreover, he knew that the moral strength of his army was incomparably superior to that of the mere drilled Austrian troops, who were trained under a soul-crushing system of discipline, and who regarded their chiefs rather as tyrants and oppressors than as generous superiors exercising a species of paternal influence over them.

On the morning of the 22d, the Constitutional Army reached Ossore, all the inhabitants of which town came out to behold the glorious procession, and testify their admiration of the young General.

It was during a brief halt near this place, that a courier, travel-soiled and sinking with fatigue, arrived from Montoni, with a letter addressed to the Marquis of Estella and containing only this laconic but urgent prayer:—

"Hasten, my lord—delay not! In forty-eight hours it will be too late!

"GAETANO."

Richard instantly despatched a messenger, on whose prudence and daring he could rely, with an answer equally brief and impressive:—

"Fear not, signor! By to-morrow night Montoni shall be delivered, or the army which I am leading to your rescue will be annihilated.

"ESTELLA."

The city was indeed sore pressed. The inhabitants were reduced to the utmost extremities in respect to provision; and the Austrians, headed by the Grand Duke in person and Marshal Herbertstein, were pushing the siege with a vigour that was almost irresistible.

But on the 22d of January those commanders were compelled to concentrate nearly all their troops on the southern side of Montoni: for they were well aware that the Constitutional Army was now approaching.

In the afternoon of the same day, the light cavalry of Richard's force entered upon the broad plain through which the Ferretti rolls its silver way; and at a distance of three miles the tower of Saint Theodosia reared its summit far above the white buildings of Montoni.

By nine o'clock on that night the entire Constitutional Army had taken up a strong position, its left being protected by high sand-banks which overlooked the sea, and its right defended by a large village.

Oh! it was a great cause which was so soon to be justified—and that was a glorious army which was now preparing for the final struggle!

A discharge of cannon from the walls of Montoni announced that the capital awaited its deliverance; and the Committee of Government issued orders that the bells of every church should ring for mass at day-break, in order that the inhabitants might offer up prayers for the success of the Constitutional Army.

As on the eve of the glorious fight of Abrantani, the Marquis of Estella was actively employed during the whole night in making the various dispositions for the great battle which, on the following day, must decide the fate of Castelcicala.

And most solemnly and sublimely interesting was that night! So close were the two armies to each other—only half a cannon shot distant—that every sound on either side could be mutually heard. The very outposts and sentinels were almost within speaking range; and the lights of the two positions were plainly visible. Watchfulness and keen observation characterised both sides.

An hour before sunrise—and by the lurid gleam of the bivouac fire in the grove of Legino—Richard addressed a letter, full of tenderness and hope, to the Princess Isabella; and this he despatched in another epistle to his excellent friend, the banker at Pinalla.

Then, when the first gleam of twilight heralded the advent of the sun, and while the bells were ringing in every tower of Montoni, the hero mounted his horse and prepared for the conflict that was now at hand.

CHAPTER CLXXXIX.

THE BATTLE OF MONTONI.

The morning of the memorable 23d of January dawned, and the bells were ringing in every tower, when three cannon gave the signal for the fight, and the battle of Montoni began.

The light troops of the Constitutionalists opened a smart fire upon the Austrians, and dislodged a strong corps from a position which it occupied on the bank of a small stream. In consequence of this first success, Richard was enabled to stretch out his right wing without restraint; and, remembering the operation effected by the Cingani at Abrantani, he instantly despatched that faithful corps, with a battalion of rifles, to make the circuit of the village, and endeavour to turn the Austrians' left flank.

The left wing of the Constitutionalists soon came to close quarters with the right wing of the enemy; and a desperate struggle ensued to decide the occupancy of the sand-banks, which were quite hard and a desirable position for artillery-pieces. Colonel Cossario, who commanded in that point, succeeded, after a desperate conflict, in repulsing the Austrians; and twenty field-pieces were dragged on the sand-banks. These speedily vomited forth the messengers of destruction; and the dread ordnance scattered death with appalling rapidity.

The Grand Duke, seeing that his cause was hopeless if that dreadful cannonade was not stopped, ordered four battalions of grenadiers to attack the position. Markham, who was riding about the field,—now issuing orders—now taking a part in the conflict,—observed the manœuvre, and instantly placed himself at the head of two regiments of cuirassiers with a view to render it abortive.

Then commenced one of the most deadly spectacles ever performed on the theatre of the world. The Grand Duke sent a strong detachment of Austrian Life-Guards to support the grenadiers; and the two squadrons of cavalry came into fearful collision. The Constitutionalists were giving way, when Markham precipitated himself into the thickest of the fight, cleared every thing before him, and seized the Austrian colours. Morcar was immediately by his side: the sword of a Life-Guard already gleamed above our hero's head—another moment, and he would have been no more. But the faithful gipsy warded off the blow, and with another stroke of his heavy brand nearly severed the sword-arm of the Life-Guard. Richard thanked him with a rapid but profoundly expressive glance, and, retaining his hold on the Austrian banner, struck the ensign-bearer to the ground.

This splendid achievement re-animated the Constitutional cuirassiers; and the Austrian Life-Guards were shattered beyond redemption.

Almost at the same time, the Cingani and rifles effected their movement on the left wing of the enemy, and threw it into confusion. This disorder was however retrieved for about the space of two hours; when the Marquis of Estella, with his cuirassiers, was enabled to take a part in the conflict in that direction. This attack bore down the Austrians. They formed themselves into a square; but vain were their attempts to oppose the impetuosity with which the cuirassiers charged them. By three o'clock in the afternoon, the left wing of the enemy was overwhelmed so completely that all the endeavours of Marshal Herbertstein to rally his troops were fruitless.

Then, resolved to perish rather than surrender, the Austrian commander met an honourable death in the ranks of battle.

In the center the conflict raged with a fury which seemed to leave room for doubt relative to the fortune of the day, notwithstanding the important successes already obtained by the Constitutionalists.

The Grand Duke had flown with a choice body of cavalry to support the compact masses that were now fighting for the victory: he himself rode along the ranks—encouraging them—urging them on—promising rewards.

For nearly four hours more did the battle last in this point; but at length our hero came up with his cuirassiers, all flushed with conquest elsewhere; and his presence gave a decided turn to the struggle.

Rushing precipitately on—bearing down all before them—thundering along with an irresistible impetuosity, the cuirassiers scattered confusion and dismay in the ranks of their enemies. And ever foremost in that last struggle, as in the first, the waving heron's plume which marked his rank, and the death-dealing brand which he wielded with such fatal effect, denoted the presence of Richard Markham.

He saw that the day was his own;—the Austrians were flying in all directions;—confusion, disorder, and dismay prevailed throughout their broken corps and shattered bands;—Marshal Herbertstein was numbered with the slain;—the Grand Duke fled;—and at eight o'clock in the evening Montoni was delivered.

Darkness had now fallen on the scene of carnage; but still the Constitutionalists pursued the Austrian fugitives; and numbers were taken ere they could reach the river. A comparatively small portion of the vanquished succeeded in throwing themselves into the boats that were moored on the southern bank, or in gaining the adjacent bridges; and those only escaped.

Montoni saluted its deliverance with salvoes of artillery and the ringing of bells; and the joyous sounds fell upon the ears of the Grand Duke, as, heart-broken and distracted, he pursued his way, attended only by a few faithful followers, towards the frontiers of that State from which his rashness and despotism had driven him for ever.

Meantime, Richard Markham issued the necessary orders for the safeguard of the prisoners and the care of the wounded; and, having attended to those duties, he repaired to the village before mentioned, where he established his temporary head-quarters at the *château* of a nobleman devoted to the Constitutional cause.

Then, in the solitude of the chamber to which he had retired, and with a soul full of tenderness and hope, as in the morning in the grove of Legino,—he addressed a letter to the Princess—the only joy of his heart, the charming and well-beloved Isabella:—

Head Quarters, near Montoni, Jan. 23.

Eleven at night.

"Long ere this will reach thee, dearest one, thou wilt have heard, by means of telegraphic dispatch through France, of the great victory which has made me master of Castelcicala. If there be any merit due unto myself, in consummating this great aim, and conducting this glorious cause to its final triumph, it was thine image, beloved Isabella, which nerved my arm and which gave me intelligence to make the combinations that have led to so decided an end. In the thickest of the fight—in the midst of danger,—when balls whistled by me like hail, and the messengers of death were circulating in every direction,—thine eyes seemed to be guiding stars of hope, and promise, and love. And now the first moment that I can snatch from the time which so many circumstances compel me to devote to your native land, is given to thee!

"To-morrow I shall write at great length to your honoured father, whom in the morning it will be my pleasing duty to proclaim ALBERTO I. GRAND DUKE OF CASTELCICALA.

"Although men now call me *Marquis of Estella*, to thee, dearest, I am simply

"RICHARD."

Our hero despatched this letter in one to Signor Viviani at Pinalla, by especial courier. He next wrote hasty accounts of the great victory which he had gained, to the chief authorities of the various cities and towns which had first declared in his favour, as before mentioned; and these also were instantly sent off by messengers.

Then soon did rumour tell the glorious tale how Montoni was delivered; and how the mighty flood of Austrian power, which had dashed its billows against the walls of the ducal capital, was rolled back over the confines of Castelcicala into the Roman States, never to return!

We shall not dwell upon the particulars of that night which succeeded the battle. Our readers can imagine the duties that devolve upon a commander after so brilliant and yet so sanguinary a day. Suffice it to observe, that

Richard visited the houses in the village to which the wounded had been conveyed; while Colonel Cossario took possession of the Austrian camp.

That night Montoni was brilliantly illuminated; and the most exuberant joy prevailed throughout the capital.

The Committee of Government assembled in close deliberation, immediately after the receipt of the welcome tidings of the victory; and, although they consulted in secret, still the inhabitants could well divine the subject of their debate—the best means of testifying their own and the nation's gratitude towards that champion who had thus diffused joy into so many hearts.

Early in the morning, the entire Committee, dressed in their robes, and attended by the chief officers of the garrison, repaired on horseback to the village where Richard had established his head-quarters.

Our hero came forth to meet them, at the door of the mansion where he was lodged, and received those high functionaries with his plumed hat in hand.

"My lord," exclaimed Signor Gaëtano, the President of the Committee, "it is for us to bare our heads to you. You have saved us from an odious tyranny—from oppression—from siege—from famine! God alone can adequately reward you: Castelcicala cannot. We have, however, further favours to solicit at your lordship's hand. Until that Prince, who is now our rightful sovereign, can come amongst us, and occupy that throne which your hands have prepared for him, you must be our chief—our Regent. My lord, a hundred councillors, forming the Provisional Committee of Government, debated this point last evening; and not a single voice was raised in objection to that request which I, as their organ, have now proffered to your lordship."

"No," answered Richard: "that cannot be. The world would say that I am ambitious—that I am swayed by interested motives of aggrandizement. Continue, gentlemen, to exercise supreme sway, until the arrival of your sovereign."

"My lord," returned the President, "Castelcicala demands this favour at your hands."

"Then, if Castelcicala command, I accept the trust with which you honour me," exclaimed Markham; "but so soon as I shall have succeeded in restoring peace and order, you will permit me, gentlemen, to repair to England, to present the ducal diadem to your rightful liege. And one word more," continued Markham; "your troops have conducted themselves, throughout this short but brilliant campaign, in a manner which exceeds all praise. To you I commend them—you must reward them."

"Your lordship is now the Regent of Castelcicala," answered the President; "and your decrees become our laws. Order—and we obey."

"I shall not abuse the power which you place in my hands," rejoined Markham.

The President then communicated to the Regent the pleasing fact that the Lord High Admiral had that morning hoisted the tri-coloured flag and sent an officer to signify his adhesion to the victorious cause. In answer to a question from Signor Gaëtano, Richard signified his intention of entering Montoni at three o'clock in the afternoon.

The principal authorities then returned to the capital.

Long before the appointed hour, the sovereign city wore an aspect of rejoicing and happiness. Triumphal arches were erected in the streets through which the conqueror would have to pass: the troops of the garrison were mustered in the great square of the palace; and a guard of honour was despatched to the southern gate. The windows were filled with smiling faces: banners waved from the tops of the houses. The ships in the harbour and roadstead were decked in their gayest colours; and boats were constantly arriving from the fleet with provisions of all kinds for the use of the inhabitants.

The great bell in the tower of Saint Theodosia at length proclaims the hour of three.

And, now—hark! the artillery roars—Montoni salutes her Regent: the guard of honour presents arms; the martial music plays a national air; and the conqueror enters the capital. The men-of-war in the roadstead thunder forth echoes to the cannon on the ramparts; and the yards are manned in token of respect for the representative of the sovereign power.

What were Richard's feelings now? But little more than two months had elapsed since he had first entered that city, a prisoner—vanquished—with shattered hopes—and uncertain as to the fate that might be in store for him. How changed were his circumstances! As a conqueror—a noble—and a ruler did he now make his appearance in a capital where his name was upon every tongue, and where his great deeds excited the enthusiasm, the admiration, and the respect of every heart.

Then his ideas were reflected still farther back; and he thought of the time when he was a prisoner, though innocent, in an English gaol. Far more rapidly than we can record his meditations, did memory whirl him through all past adversities—reproduce before his mental eyes his recent wanderings in Castelcicala—and hurry him on to this glorious consummation, when he finds himself entering the capital as the highest peer in the State.

On his right hand was Colonel Cossario; and close behind him—amidst his brilliant staff—was Morcar,—the faithful gipsy whose devotedness to his master had not a little contributed to this grand result.

On went the procession amidst the enthusiastic applause of the myriads collected to welcome the conquerors,—on through streets crowded to the roof-tops with happy faces,—on to the ducal palace, in whose great square ten thousand troops were assembled to receive the Regent.

Richard alighted from his horse at the gate of the princely abode, on the threshold of which the municipal authorities were gathered to receive him.

Oh! at that moment how deeply—how sincerely did he regret the loss of General Grachia, Colonel Morosino, and the other patriots who had fallen in the fatal conflict of Ossore!

Nor less did memory recall the prophetic words of that departed girl who had loved him so devotedly, but so unhappily;—those words which Mary-Anne, with sybilline inspiration, had uttered upon her death-bed:—*"Brilliant destinies await you, Richard! All your enduring patience, your resignation under the oppression of foul wrong, will meet with a glorious reward. Yes—for I know all:—that angel Isabella has kept no secret from me. She is a Princess, Richard; and by your union with her, you yourself will become one of the greatest Princes in Europe! Her father, too, shall succeed to his just rights; and then, Richard, then—how small will be the distance between yourself and the Castelcicalan throne!"*

CHAPTER CXC.

TWO OF OUR OLD ACQUAINTANCES.

We must again transport our readers to the great metropolis of England.

It was late in the evening of the 24th of January, 1841,—with Byron, we "like to be particular in dates,"—that a man, of herculean form, weather-beaten countenance, and whose age was apparently somewhat past forty, was passing down Drury Lane.

He was dressed like a labourer, with a smock frock and a very broad-brimmed straw hat, which was slouched as much as possible over his face.

Passing into Blackmoor Street, he continued his way towards Clare Market; whence he turned abruptly into Clements' Lane, and entered a public-house on the right hand side of this wretched scene of squalor and poverty.

No one possessing the least feeling of compassion for the suffering portion of the industrious millions—(and how large is that portion!)—can pass along the miserable thoroughfare called Clements' Lane without being shocked at the internal misery which the exterior appearance of many of the dwellings bespeaks. There is ever a vile effluvium in that narrow alley—a miasma as of a crowded churchyard!

Entering the parlour of the public-house, the man with the weather-beaten countenance and slouched hat was immediately recognised by a lad seated apart from the other inmates of the room.

This youth was about eighteen or nineteen years of age, very short in stature, but well made. On a former occasion we have stated that his countenance was effeminate and by no means bad-looking; his eyes were dark and intelligent; his teeth good; and his voice soft and agreeable. His manners were superior to his condition; and his language was singularly correct for one who was almost entirely self-taught, and who had filled menial employments since his boyhood.

He was dressed in a blue jacket and waistcoat, and dark brown trousers; and that attire, together with a boy's cap, contributed towards the extreme youthfulness of his appearance.

A pint of porter stood, untouched, upon a table at which he was sitting.

The man with the weather-beaten countenance proceeded to take his seat next to this lad: he then rang the bell, and having ordered some liquor and a pipe, entered into conversation with his young companion.

"Have you heard any thing more of that villain Tidkins, Harry?" asked the man.

"Nothing more since I saw you yesterday morning, Jem," replied Holford. "I have lost all trace of him."

"But are you sure that it was him you saw the day before yesterday?" demanded Crankey Jem—for *he* was the individual with the weather-beaten countenance and slouched hat.

"Don't you think I know him well enough, after all I have told you concerning him?" said Henry Holford, smiling. "When you and I accidentally met for the first time, the day before yesterday, in this parlour, and when in the course of the conversation that sprang up between us, I happened to mention the name of Tidkins, I saw how you fired—how you coloured—how agitated you became. What injury has he done you, that you are so bitter against him?"

"I will tell you another time, Harry," answered Crankey Jem. "My history is a strange one—and you shall know it all. But I *must* find out the lurking-hole of this miscreant Tidkins. You say he was well dressed?"

"As well as a private person can be," answered Holford. "But did the Resurrection Man put on the robes of the greatest monarch in the world, he could not mitigate the atrocious expression of his cadaverous—hang-dog countenance. I confess that I am afraid of that man:—yes—I am afraid of him!"

"He was well-dressed, and was stepping into a cab at the stand under the Charterhouse wall, you said?" observed Crankey Jem.

"Yes—and he said, '*To the Mint—Borough*,'" replied Holford: "those were his very words—and away the cab went."

"And you have since been to see if you could recognise the cab, and pump the cab-man?" continued Jem.

"By your request I have done so," answered Holford; "and my researches have been altogether unsuccessful. I could not find the particular cab which he took."

"Why didn't you question the waterman and the drivers?" asked Jem.

"So I did; but I could glean nothing. Now if you really want to find the Resurrection Man, I should advise you to go over to the Mint, and hunt him out amongst the low public-houses in that district. Depend upon it," added Holford, "he has business there; for he is not a man to run about in cabs for nothing."

"The fact is, Harry," returned Jem, "that it doesn't suit my schemes to look after Tidkins myself. He would only get out of my way; and—as I have missed my aim *once*—I must take care to *thrust home* the next time I fall in with him."

"You mean to say that you have poniarded him once, and that he escaped death?" whispered Holford.

"Yes: but I will tell you all about it presently, Harry," said Crankey Jem; "and then, perhaps, you will be induced to assist me in hunting out the Resurrection Man."

"I certainly have an old score to settle with him," returned Holford; "for—as I told you—he once laid a plot against my life. To-night you shall tell me how you came to be so bitter against him: to-morrow night I will visit the Mint, and make the inquiries you wish concerning him; and the night afterwards I must devote to particular business of my own."

"And what particular business can such a younker as you have in hand?" asked Crankey Jem, with as much of a smile as his grim countenance could possibly relax itself into.

"I now and then visit a place where I can contemplate, at my ease, a beautiful lady—without even my presence being suspected," answered Holford, in a mysterious tone.

"A beautiful lady! Are you in love with her, then?" demanded Crankey Jem.

"The mere idea is so utterly absurd—so extravagant—so preposterous," replied Holford, "that my lips dare not speak an affirmative. To acknowledge that I love this lady of whom I speak, would be almost a crime—an atrocity—a diabolical insult,—so highly is she placed above me! And yet," he added mournfully, "the human heart *has* strange susceptibilities—*will* indulge in the idlest phantasies! My chief happiness is to gaze upon this lady—and my blood boils when I behold him on whom all her affection is bestowed."

"She is married, then?" said Crankey Jem, interrogatively.

"Yes—married to one who is handsome and young, and who perhaps loves her all the more because he owes so much—so very much to her! But I actually shudder—I feel alarmed—I tremble, while I thus permit my tongue to touch upon such topics,—topics as sacred as a religion—as holy as a worship."

"You have either indulged in some very foolish and most hopeless attachment, Harry," said his companion; "or else your wits are going a-wool-gathering."

"May be both your remarks apply to me," muttered Holford, a cloud passing over his countenance. "But—no—no: I am in the perfect possession of my senses—my intellects are altogether unimpaired. It is a fancy—a whim of my mine to introduce myself into the place I before alluded to, and, from my concealment, contemplate the lady of whom I have spoken. It gives me pleasure to look upon her—I know not why. Then—when I am alone—I brood upon her image, recall to mind all I have heard her say or seen her do, and ponder on her features—her figure—her dress—her whole appearance, until I become astonished at myself—alarmed at my own presumption—terrified at my own thoughts. For weeks and weeks—nay, for months—I remain away from the place where she often dwells;—but at length some imperceptible and unknown impulse urges me thither; I rove about the neighbourhood, gazing longingly upon the building;—I endeavour to tear myself away—I cannot;—then I ascend the wall—I traverse the garden—I enter the dwelling—I conceal myself—I behold *her* again—*him* also,—and my pleasures and my tortures are experienced all over again!"

"You're a singular lad," said Crankey Jem, eyeing the youth with no small degree of astonishment, and some suspicion that he was not altogether right in his upper storey. "But who is this lady that you speak of? and why are you so frightened even to think of her? A cat may look at a king—aye, and *think* of him too, for that matter. Human nature is human nature; and one isn't always answerable for one's feelings."

"There I agree with you, Jem," said Holford. "I have often struggled hard against that impulse which urges me towards the place where the lady dwells—but all in vain!"

"Who is she, once more?" demanded Jem.

"That is a secret—never to be revealed," answered Harry.

Crankey Jem had commenced an observation in reply, when one of the persons who were sitting drinking at another table, suddenly struck up a chant in so loud and boisterous a tone that it completely drowned the voice of Holford's companion:—

FLARE UP.

Flare up, I say, my jolly friends,
And pass the bingo gaily;—
Who cares a rap if all this ends
Some morn at the Old Bailey?
"A short life and a merry one"
Should be our constant maxim;
And he's a fool that gives up fun
Because remorse attacks him.

Here Ned has forks so precious fly,
And Bill can smash the flimsies;[13]
No trap to Tom could e'er come nigh,
For he so fleet of limbs is.
Bob is the best to crack a crib,
And Dick to knap a fogle;[14]
And I can wag my tongue so glib
A beak would wipe his ogle.

Who are so happy then as we—
Each with such useful knowledge?
For Oxford University
Can't beat the Floating College.[15]
To parish prigs one gives degrees,

To lumber-lags[16] the latter:

But I would sooner cross the seas,

Than in a humbox[17] patter.[18]

Each state in life has its mishaps:—

Kings fear a revolution;

The knowing covey dreads the traps—

And *both* an execution.

Death will not long pass any by—

Each chance is duly raffled;

What matters whether we must die

In bed or on the scaffold?

Flare up, I say, then, jolly friends,

And pass the bingo gaily;

Who cares a rap if all this ends

Some morn at the Old Bailey?

"A short life and a merry one"

Should be our constant maxim;

And he's a fool that gives up fun

Because remorse attacks him.

"Now let us be moving, young sprig," said Crankey Jem, when the song was brought to a conclusion. "You shall come with me to my lodging, where we'll have a bit of supper together; and then I'll tell you my story. It is a strange one, I can assure you."

Holford rose, and followed Crankey Jem from the public-house.

The latter led the way to a court in Drury Lane; and introduced the lad into a small back chamber, which was tolerably neat and comfortable.

On a table near the window, were small models of ships, executed with considerable taste; various tools; blocks of wood, not yet shaped; paint-pots, brushes, twine, little brass cannon and anchors,—in a word, all the articles necessary for the miniature vessels which are seen in the superior toy-shops.

"That is the way I get my living, Harry," said Jem, pointing towards the work-table. "I have been a sad fellow in my time: but if any one who has gone through all I have suffered, doesn't change, I don't know who the devil would. Sit down, Harry—the fire will soon blaze up."

Jem stirred the fire, and then busied himself to spread a small round table standing in the middle of the room, with some cold meat, a substantial piece of cheese, and a quartern loaf. He also produced from his cupboard a bottle of spirits, and when there was a good blaze in the grate, he placed the kettle to boil.

"You have got every thing comfortable enough here, Jem," said Holford, when these preparations were concluded.

"Yes; I can earn a good bit of money when I choose," was the answer. "But I waste a great deal of time in making inquiries after Tidkins—yes, and in brooding on my vengeance, as you, Harry, do upon your love."

"Love!" ejaculated Holford. "My God! if you only knew of whom you were speaking!"

"Well—well," cried Jem, laughing; "I see it is a sore point—I won't touch on it any more. So now fall to, and eat, Harry. You're sincerely welcome. Besides, you can and will serve me, I know, in ferretting out this villain Tidkins. If you behave well, I'll teach you how to make those pretty ships; and you can earn six times as much at that work, as ever you will obtain as pot-boy at a public."

"Oh! if you would really instruct me, Jem, in your business," exclaimed Holford, "how much I should be obliged to you! The very name of a pot-boy is odious to my ears. Yes—I will serve you faithfully and truly, Jem," continued the lad: "I will go over to the Mint to-morrow evening; and if Tidkins is *there*, you shall know *where*."

"That's what I call business, Harry," said Jem. "Serve me in this—and you can't guess all I'll do for you."

They ate their supper with a good appetite. Jem—who was somewhat methodical after a fashion—cleared away the things, and placed two clean tumblers and a bowl full of sugar upon the table.

When the grog was duly mixed, and "every thing was comfortable," as the man termed it, he commenced his truly remarkable history, which we have corrected and improved as to language, in the following manner.

---

13. Pass fictitious Bank-Notes.

14. Handkerchief.

15. The Hulks.

16. Transports.

17. Pulpit.

18. Preach.

CHAPTER CXCI.

CRANKEY JEM'S HISTORY.

My father's name was Robert Cuffin. At the death of *his* father he succeeded to a good business as grocer and tea-dealer; but he was very extravagant, and soon became bankrupt. He obtained his certificate, and then embarked as a wine merchant. At the expiration of three years he failed again, and once more appeared in the *Gazette*. This time he was refused his certificate. He, however, set up in business a third time, and became a coal merchant. His extravagances continued: so did his misfortunes. He failed, was thrown into prison, and took the benefit of the Insolvents' Act—but not without a long remand. On his release from gaol, he turned drysalter. This new trade lasted a short time, and ended as all the others had done. Another residence in prison—another application to the Insolvents' Court—and another remand, ensued.

"My father was now about forty years of age, and completely ruined. He had no credit—no resources—no means of commencing business again. He was, however, provided with a wife and seven children—all requiring maintenance, and he having nothing to maintain them on. I was not as yet born. It appears that my father sate down one evening in a very doleful humour, and in a very miserable garret, to meditate upon his circumstances. He revolved a thousand schemes in his head; but all required some little credit or capital wherewith to make a commencement; and he had neither. At length he started up, slapped his hand briskly upon the table, and exclaimed, 'By heavens, I've got it!'—'Got what?' demanded his wife.—'A call!' replied my father.—'A call!' ejaculated his better half, in astonishment.—'Yes; a call,' repeated my father; 'a call from above to preach the blessed Gospel and cleanse the unsavoury vessels of earth from their sinfulness.'—His wife began to cry, for she thought that distress had turned his brain; but he soon convinced her that he was never more in earnest in his life. He desired her to make the room look as neat as possible, and get a neighbour to take care of the children for an hour or two in the evening, when he should return with a few friends. He then went out, and his wife obeyed his instructions. Sure enough, in the evening, back came my father with a huge Bible under one arm and a Prayer-Book under the other, and followed by half-a-dozen demure-looking ladies and gentlemen, who had a curious knack of keeping their eyes incessantly fixed upwards—or heaven-ward, as my father used to express it.

"Well, the visitors sate down; and my father, whose countenance had assumed a most wonderful gravity of expression since the morning, opened the prayer-meeting with a psalm. He then read passages from the two sacred books he had brought with him; and he wound up the service by an extemporaneous discourse, which drew tears from the eyes of his audience.

"The prayer-meeting being over, an elderly lady felt herself so overcome with my father's convincing eloquence, that a considerate old gentleman sent for a bottle of gin; and thus my father's 'call' was duly celebrated.

"To be brief—so well did my father play his cards, that he soon gathered about him a numerous congregation; a chapel was hired somewhere in Goodman's Fields; and he was now a popular minister. His flock placed unbounded confidence in him—nay almost worshipped him; so that, thanks to their liberality, he was soon provided with a nicely-furnished house in the immediate vicinity of the chapel. Next door to him there dwelt a poor widow, named Ashford, and who had a very pretty daughter called Ruth. These females were amongst the most devoted of my father's flock; and in their eyes the reverend preacher was the pattern of virtue and holiness. The widow was compelled to take a little gin at times 'for the stomach's sake;' but one day she imbibed too much, fell down in a fit, and died. My father preached a funeral sermon, in which he eulogised her as a saint; and he afforded an asylum to the orphan girl. Ruth accordingly became an inmate of my father's house.

"And now commences the most extraordinary portion of the history of my father's life. You will admit that the suddenness of his 'call' was remarkable enough; but this was nothing to the marvellous nature of a vision which one night appeared to him. Its import was duly communicated to Miss Ashford next day; and the young lady piously resigned herself to that fate which my father assured her was the will of heaven. In a few months the consequences of the vision developed themselves; for Miss Ashford was discovered to be in the family way. My father's lawful wife raised a storm which for some time seemed beyond the possibility of mitigation; the deacons of the chapel called, and the elders of the congregation came to investigate the matter. My father received them with a countenance expressive of more than ordinary demureness and solemnity. A conclave was held—explanations were demanded of my father. Then was it that the author of my being rose, and, in a most impressive manner, acquainted the assembly with the nature of his vision. 'The angel of the Lord,' he said, 'appeared to me one night, and ordered me to raise up seed of righteousness, so that when the Lord calls me unto himself, fitting heirs to carry on the good work which I have commenced, may not fail. I appealed to the angel in behalf of my own lawfully begotten offspring; but the angel's command brooked not remonstrances, and willed that I should raise up seed of Ruth Ashford: for she is blessed, in that her name is Ruth.'—This explanation was deemed perfectly satisfactory: and, when the deacons and elders had departed, my father succeeded some how or another not only in pacifying his wife, but also in reconciling her to the amour which he still carried on with Miss Ashford.[19]

"Thus my father preserved both his mistress and his sanctity—at least for some considerable time longer. The fruit of that amour was myself; and my name is consequently Ashford—James Ashford—although my father insisted upon calling me Cuffin. Time wore on; but by degrees the jealousies which my father had at first succeeded in appeasing, developed themselves in an alarming manner between the wife and the mistress. Scenes of violence occurred at the house of his Reverence; and the neighbours began to think that their minister's amour was not quite so holy in its nature as he had represented it. The congregation fell off; and my father's reputation for sanctity was rapidly wearing out. Still he would not part with my mother and me; and the result was that his lawful wife left the house with all her own children. My father refused to support them; the parish officers interfered; and the scandal was grievously aggravated. Death arrived at this juncture to carry away the principal bone of contention. My mother became dangerously ill, and after languishing in a hopeless condition for a few weeks, breathed her last.

"Having thus stated the particulars of my birth, it will not be necessary to dwell on this portion of my narrative. I will only just observe that, at the death of Miss Ashford, a reconciliation was effected between my father and his wife; and that the former contrived to maintain his post as minister of the chapel—though with a diminished flock, and consequently with a decreased revenue. Nevertheless, I obtained a smattering of education at the school belonging to the chapel, and was treated with kindness by my father, although with great harshness by his wife. Thus continued matters until I was fifteen, when my father died; and I was immediately thrust out of doors to shift for myself.

"I was totally friendless. Vainly did I call upon the deacons and elders of the congregation; even those who had adhered to my father to the very last, had their eyes opened now that he was no longer present to reason with them. They spurned me from their doors; and I was left to beg or steal. I chose the former; but one night I was taken up by a watchman (there were no police in those times) because I was found wandering about without being able to give a satisfactory account of myself. You may look astonished; but I can assure you that when a poor devil says, '*I am starving—houseless—friendless—pennyless*,' it is supposed to mean that he can't give a satisfactory account of himself! In the morning I was taken before the magistrate, and committed to the House of Correction as a rogue and vagabond.

"In prison I became acquainted with a number of young thieves and pickpockets; and, so desperate was my condition, that when the day of emancipation arrived, I was easily persuaded to join them. Then commenced a career which I would gladly recall—but cannot! Amongst my new companions I obtained the nickname of '*Crankey*,' because I was subject to fits of deep despondency and remorse, so that they fancied I was not right in my head. In time I became the most expert housebreaker in London—Tom the Cracksman alone excepted. My exploits grew more and more daring; and on three occasions I got into trouble. The first and second times I was sent to the hulks. I remember that on my second trial a pal of mine was acquitted through a flaw in the indictment. He was charged with having broken into and burglariously entered a jeweller's shop. It was, however, proved by one of the prosecutor's own witnesses that the shop door had been accidentally left unlocked and unbolted, and that consequently he had entered without any violence at all. Thanks to the laws, he escaped on that ground, although judge and jury were both convinced of his guilt. Time wore on; and I formed new acquaintances in the line to which I was devoted. These were Tom the Cracksman, Bill Bolter, Dick Flairer, the Buffer, and the Resurrection Man. With them I accomplished many successful burglaries; but at length I got into trouble a third time, and a stop was put to my career in London. It was in the year 1835 that the Resurrection Man and I broke into a jeweller's shop in Princes Street, Soho. We got off with a good booty. The Resurrection Man went over to the Mint: I let Dick Flairer into the secret, gave him a part of my share in the plunder, and then took to a hiding-place which there is in Chick Lane, Smithfield. Now I knew that Dick was stanch to the back-bone; and so he proved himself—for he brought me my food as regularly as possible; and at the end of a week, the storm had blown over enough to enable me to leave my hiding-place. I hastened to join the Resurrection Man in the Mint, where I stayed two or three days. Then the miscreant sold me, in order to save himself; and we were both committed to Newgate. Tidkins turned King's Evidence; and I was sentenced to transportation for life. The Resurrection Man was discharged at the termination of the business of the sessions.

"Myself and several other convicts, who were sentenced at the same session, were removed from Newgate to the Penitentiary at Millbank. Amongst the number were two persons whose names you may have heard before, because their case made a great noise at the time. These were Robert Stephens and Hugh Mac Chizzle, who were the principal parties concerned in a conspiracy to pass a certain Eliza Sydney off as a young man, and defraud the Earl of Warrington out of a considerable property. We remained about a fortnight in the Penitentiary, and were then transferred to the convict-ship at Woolwich. But before we left Millbank, we were clothed in new suits of grey, or pepper-and-salt, as we called the colour; and we were also ironed. The convict-ship was well arranged for its miserable purpose. On each side of the between-decks were two rows of sleeping-berths, one above the other: each berth was about six feet square, and was calculated to hold four convicts, eighteen inches' space to sleep in being considered ample room enough for each individual. The hospital was in the fore-part of the vessel, and was separated from the prison by means of a bulk-head, in which partition there were two strong doors, forming a means of communication between the two compartments. The fore and main hatchways, between decks, were fitted up with strong wooden stanchions round them; and in each of those stanchions there was a door with three padlocks, to let the convicts in and out, and secure them effectually at night. In each hatchway a ladder was placed, for us to go up and down by; and these ladders were always pulled on deck after dusk. Scuttle-holes, or small ports to open and shut for the admission of air, were cut along the vessel's sides; and in the partition between the prison and the hospital was fixed a large stove, with a funnel, which warmed and ventilated both compartments at the same time. When we were placed on board the convict-ship, we had each a pair of shoes, two pairs of trousers, four shirts, and other warm clothing, besides a bed, bolster, and blanket. Of Bibles, Testaments, and Prayer-Books, there was also plenty.

"The moment the surgeon came on board, he arranged the mess-berths and mess-tables. All the clothing, linen, bedding, and other articles were marked with consecutive numerals in black paint, from No. 1. up to the highest number of convicts embarked. Thus, we messed and slept along the prison-deck in regular numerical progression. In food we were not stinted: each man had three-quarters of a pound of biscuit daily; and every day, too, we sate down to beef, pork, or pease-soup. Gruel and cocoa were served out for breakfast and supper. Every week we received a certain quantity of vinegar, lime-juice, and sugar, which were taken as preventatives for scurvy. Each mess selected a head, or chairman, who saw the provisions weighed out, and that justice was done in this particular to each individual at his table.

"The surgeon selected six of the most fitting amongst the convicts to act the part of petty officers, whose duty it was to see his orders punctually executed, and to report instances of misconduct. Four of these remained in the prison; and the other two were stationed on deck, to watch those convicts who came up in their turns for airing. The *Captains of the Deck*, as the officers were called, had some little extra allowance for their trouble, and were moreover allowed a certain quantity of tobacco.

"It was in January, 1836, that we sailed for Sydney. Although I had no wife,—no children,—and, I may almost say, no friend that I cared about,—still my heart sank within me, when, from the deck of the convict-ship, I caught a last glimpse of the white cliffs of Old England. Tears came into my eyes; and I, who had not wept since childhood, wept then. But there were several of my companions who had left wives and children, or parents, behind them; and I could read on their countenances the anguish which filled their inmost souls!

"The surgeon was a kind and humane man. The moment we were out of sight of land, he ordered our chains to be taken off; and he allowed us to enjoy as much air upon deck as we could possibly require. The guard, under the command of a commissioned officer, consisted of thirty-one men, and did duty on the quarter-deck in three alternate watches. A sentry, with a drawn cutlass, stood at each hatchway; and the soldiers on watch always had their fire-arms loaded.

"When we had been to sea a little time, most of the convicts relapsed into their old habits of swearing, lying, and obscene conversation. They also gambled at pitch and toss, the stakes being their rations. Thieving prevailed to a very great extent; for the convict who lost his dinner by gambling, was sure to get one by stealing. They would often make wagers amongst themselves as to who was the most expert thief; and when the point was put to a practical test, dreadful quarrels would arise, the loser of the wager, perhaps, discovering that he himself was the victim of the trial of skill, and that his hoard of lime-juice, sugar, tobacco, or biscuit had disappeared. Stephens, who was at the same mess with myself, did all he could to discourage these practices; but the others pronounced him '*a false magician,*' and even his friend, Mac Chizzle, turned against him. So at last he gave up the idea of introducing a reformation amongst his brethren in bondage. The fact is, that any convict who attempts to humbug the others by pretensions to honesty, or who expresses some superior delicacy of sentiment, which, of course, in many instances is actually experienced, had better hang himself at once. The equality of the convict-ship is a frightful equality,—the equality of crime,—the levelling influence of villany,—the abolition of all social distinctions by the hideous freemasonry of turpitude and its consequent penalties! And yet there is an aristocracy, even in the prison of the convict-ship,—an aristocracy consisting of the oldest thieves, in contra-distinction to the youngest; and of *townies,*[20] in opposition to *yokels.*[21] The deference paid by the younger thieves to the elder ones is astonishing; and that man who, in relating his own history, can enumerate the greatest number of atrocities, is a king amongst convicts. Some of the best informed of the convicts wrote slang journals during the passage, and read them once a-week to the rest. They generally referred to the sprees of the night, and contained some such entries as this:—'*A peter cracked and frisked, while the cobbles dorsed; Sawbones came and found the glim doused; fadded the dobbins in a yokel's crib, while he blew the conkey-horn; Sawbones lipped a snitch; togs leered in yokel's downy; yokel screwed with the darbies.*' The exact meaning of this is:—'A chest broken open and robbed while the convicts slept: surgeon came in and found the lamp put out; the thief thrust the clothes which he had stolen into a countryman's berth, while he was snoring fast asleep; the surgeon ordered a general search; the clothes were found in the countryman's bed; and the countryman was put into irons.'

"I must observe, that while the ship was still in the Thames, none of the convicts would admit that they deserved their fate. They all proclaimed themselves much-injured individuals, and declared that the Home Secretary was certain to order a commutation of their sentence. The usual declarations were these:—'I am sure never to see New South Wales. The prejudice of the judge against me at the trial were evident to all present in the court. The jury were totally misled by his summing-up. My friends are doing every thing they can for me; and I am sure to get off.'—Out of a hundred and ten convicts, at least a hundred spoke in this manner. But the ship sailed,—England was far behind,—and *not one single convict* had his hopes of a commuted sentence gratified. Then, when those hopes had disappeared, they all opened their budget of gossip most freely, and related their exploits in so frank a manner, that it was very easy to perceive the justice of the verdicts which had condemned them.

"The voyage out was, on the whole, a tolerably fine one. It lasted four months and a half; and it was, consequently, in the middle of May that we arrived in sight of Sydney. But, when thus at the point of destination, the sea became so rough, and the wind blew such 'great guns,' that the captain declared there was mischief at hand. The convicts were all ordered into the prison, the ports of which were closed; and the heat was stifling. The tempest came with appalling violence. Crash went every loose thing on board,—the timbers creaked as if they would start from their settings,—the ropes rattled,—and the wind whistled horribly through the rigging. The ship was lifted to an immense height, and then by the fall of the mountain wave, was plunged into the depths of the trough of the sea;—at one moment dipping the studding-sail boom into the water,—and the next lying nearly on its beam-ends on the opposite side. I afterwards learnt from a sailor, that the waves were forty feet high, twenty below the ordinary level of the sea, and twenty above it. Thus, when we were in the trough, they were forty feet above our heads! Towards evening the storm subsided; and early next morning Sydney broke more clearly upon our view.

"Sydney is beautifully situated. It possesses a fine ascent from a noble harbour; and its bays, its coves, its gardens, its gentlemen's seats, form a pleasing spectacle. Then its forests of masts—the Government-house, with its beautiful domain—the numerous wharfs—the thousands of boats upon the glassy water—and Wooloomooloo, with its charming villas and its windmills,—all these combine to enhance the interest of the scene. The town itself is far more handsome than I had expected to find it. The shops are very fine—particularly the silversmiths', the haberdashers', and confectioners', which would not disgrace the West End of London. They are mostly lighted with gas, and in the evening have a brilliant appearance. There is an astonishing number of grog-shops—nearly two hundred and fifty, for a population of 30,000 souls. George Street and Pitt Street are the principal thoroughfares: and the rents are so high that they average from three to five hundred pounds a-year. There are no common sewers in Sydney; and, although the greater portion of the town stands upon a height, yet many of the principal streets are perfectly level, and the want of a vent for the foul water and other impurities is sadly felt. I may add, that the first appearance of Sydney and its inhabitants does not impress a stranger with the idea of being in a country so far away from Europe; the language, the manners, and the dress of the people being so closely similar to those of England. But wait a little while, and a closer observation produces a different effect. Presently you will see the government gangs of convicts, marching backwards and forwards from their work in single military file,—solitary ones straggling here and there, with their white woollen Paramatta frocks and trousers, or grey or yellow jackets with duck overalls, all daubed over with broad arrows and initial letters to denote the establishment to which they belong,—and then the gaol-gang, moving sulkily along with their jingling leg-chains,—all these sad spectacles telling a tale of crime and its effects, and proclaiming trumpet-tongued the narrative of human degradation!

"The ship entered the harbour; our irons had already been put on again some days previously; and we were all landed under the care of the guard. We were marched to the gaol-yard; and there our clothes were all daubed over with broad arrows and the initials P. S.—meaning '*Prisoners' Barracks*,' to which establishment we were conducted as soon as the ceremony of painting our garments was completed. This barrack had several large day-rooms and numerous sleeping wards, the bedsteads being arranged in two tiers, or large platforms, but without separation. In every room there was a man in charge who was answerable for the conduct of the rest; but no one ever thought of complaining of the misbehaviour of his companions. A tread-mill was attached to the building: there were moreover several solitary cells—a species of punishment the horrors of which no tongue can describe.

"In the course of a few days we were all divided into sections, according to the degrees of punishment which we were to undergo. Stephens and Mac Chizzle were kept at Sydney: I was sent with some thirty others to Port Macquarie—a place about two hundred and sixty miles, as the crow flies, to the north of Sydney.

"The scenery is magnificent in the neighbourhood of Macquarie Harbour: but the life of the convict—oh! that is fearful in the extreme! I know that I was a great criminal—I know that my deeds demanded a severe punishment; but death had been preferable to a doom like that! Compelled to endure every kind of privation,—shut out from the rest of the world,—restricted to a very limited quantity of food, which *never* included fresh meat,—kept in chains and under a military guard with fixed bayonets and loaded fire-arms,—with no indulgence for good conduct, but severe penalties, even flogging or solitary confinement, for the smallest offences,—constantly toiling in the wet, at felling timber and rolling it to the water,—forced to support without murmuring the most terrible hardships,—how did I curse the day when I rendered myself liable to the discipline of this hell upon earth! I will give you an idea of the horrors of that place:—during the six months that I remained there, nineteen deaths occurred amongst two hundred and twenty convicts; and of those *nineteen*, only five were from natural causes. Two were drowned, four were killed by the falling of trees, three were shot by the military, and five were murdered by their comrades! And why were those murders perpetrated? Because the assassins were tired of life, but had not the courage to commit suicide; and therefore they accomplished crimes which were sure to be visited by death upon the scaffold!

"The chain-gang to which I belonged was stationed at Philip's Creek; and our business was to supply timber for the ship-builders on Sarah's Island. We were lodged in huts of the most miserable description; and though our toils were so long and arduous, our rations were scarcely sufficient to keep body and soul together. The timber we cut was principally Huon pine; no beasts of burden were allowed; and we had to roll the trunks of trees to an immense distance. What with the humid climate, the want of fresh meat, and the severity of the labour, no man who fell ill ever entertained a hope of recovery. Talk of the civilised notions of the English—talk of the humane principles of her penal laws,—why, the Inquisition itself could not have been more horrible than the doom of the convict at Macquarie Harbour! Again I say, it was true that we were great criminals; but surely some adequate mode of punishment—some mode involving the means of *reformation*—might have been devised, without the application of so much real physical torture! I have heard or read that when the Inquisition put its victims to the rack, it afterwards remanded them to their dungeons, and allowed them leisure to recover and be cured;—but in the penal settlement of Port Macquarie those tortures were renewed daily—and they killed the miserable sufferers by inches!

"Our rations consisted daily of one pound and a half of flour, from which twelve per cent. of bran had been subtracted, one pound and a half of salt meat, and half an ounce of soap. No tea—no vegetables. The flour was made into cakes called *damper*, cooked in a frying-pan; and this wasteful mode of preparing it greatly diminished its quantity. Besides, divide those rations into three parts, and you will find that the three meals are little enough for men toiling hard from sunrise to sunset. The convict who did not keep a good look-out on his provisions was certain to be robbed by his comrades; and some men have been plundered to such an extent as actually to have been on the very verge of starvation.

"I had not been at Macquarie Harbour more than five months, when Stephens and Mac Chizzle arrived, and were added to our chain-gang. This punishment they had incurred for having endeavoured to escape from Sydney, where they had been treated with some indulgence, in consequence of their station in life previous to their sentence in England. So miserable was I, with hard work and scanty food, that I resolved to leave the place, or perish in the attempt. I communicated my design to Stephens and Mac Chizzle; and they agreed to accompany me. Escape from Macquarie was known to be a most difficult undertaking; and few convicts who essayed it were ever able to reach the settlements in other parts of the Colony. They were either murdered by their comrades for a supply of food, or perished in the bush. Formidable forests had to be traversed; and the chance of catching kangaroos was the only prospect of obtaining the means of existence. Nevertheless, I resolved to dare all those horrors and fearful risks, rather than remain at Philip's Creek. Five or six others, in addition to Stephens and Mac Chizzle, agreed to adopt this desperate venture with me; and one night we stole away—to the number of ten—from the huts.

"Yes—we thus set out on this tremendous undertaking, each individual possessing no more food than was sufficient for a single meal. And ere the sun rose all our store was consumed; and we found ourselves in the middle of a vast forest—without a guide—without victuals—almost without a hope! Convicts are not the men to cheer each other: misfortunes have made them selfish, brutal, and sulky. We toiled on in comparative silence. One of my companions, who had been ten years at Macquarie Harbour, was well acquainted with the mode in which the natives search for traces of the opossum; and, when hunger began to press upon us, he examined every tree with a hollow limb, and also the adjacent trees for marks of the opossum's claws. For, I must tell you, that this animal is so sagacious, that it usually runs up a neighbouring tree and thence jumps to the one wherein its retreat is, in order to avoid being traced. The convict to whom I have alluded, and whose name was Blackley, at length discovered the trail of an opossum, and clambered up the tree in which its hole was found, by means of successive notches in the bark, to place the great toe in. Having reached the hole, he probed it with a long stick, and found that there actually was an opossum within. Thrusting in his hand, he seized the animal by the tail, pulled it out, and killed it by a swinging dash against the trunk of a tree. But this was little enough among so many. We, however, made a fire, cooked it, and thus contrived just to mitigate the terrible cravings of hunger. The flesh of the opossum is like that of a rabbit, and is therefore too delicate to enable a hearty appetite to make a good meal on a tenth portion of so small an animal.

"On the following day Blackley managed to kill a kangaroo, weighing about sixty pounds; and thus we were supplied with food for three or four days, acting economically. The flesh of the kangaroo is much like venison, and is very fine eating. We continued our way amidst the forest, which appeared endless; and in due time the kangaroo's flesh was consumed. Blackley was unwearied in his exertions to provide more food; and, so much time was wasted in these endeavours, that we made but little progress in our journey. And now, to our terror, Blackley could find no more opossums—could kill no more kangaroos. We grew desperate: starvation was before us. Moody—sulky—glaring on each other with a horribly significant ferocity, we dragged ourselves along. Four days elapsed—and not a mouthful of food had we touched. On the fifth night we made a fire, and sate round it at considerable distances from each other. We all endeavoured to remain awake: we trembled at the approach of drowsiness—*for we knew the consequences of sleep in our desperate condition*. There we sate—none uttering a word,—with cracked and bloody lips—parched throats—eyes glowing with cannibal fires,—our minds a prey to the most appalling thoughts. At length Mac Chizzle, the lawyer, fell back in a sound slumber, having no doubt found it impossible to bear up against the weariness which was creeping over him. Then

Blackley rose, and went farther into the wood. It required no ghost to tell us that he had gone to cut a club for a horrible purpose. The most breathless silence prevailed. At length there was a strange rustling amongst the trees at a little distance; and then cries of indescribable agony fell upon our ears. These tokens of distress were in the voice of Blackley, who called us by name, one after another. A vague idea of the real truth rivetted us to the spot; and in a short time the cries ceased altogether. Oh! what a night of horror was that! An hour had elapsed since Blackley's disappearance; and we had ceased to trouble ourselves concerning his fate:—our own intolerable cravings for food were the sole objects of our thoughts. Nor was Mac Chizzle doomed to escape death. A convict named Felton determined to execute the purpose which Blackley had entertained—though in a different manner. Afraid to venture away from the party to cut a bludgeon, he drew a large clasp-knife from his pocket, and plunged the long sharp blade into the breast of the sleeper. A cry of horror burst from Stephens and myself; and we rushed forward—now that it was unfortunately too late—to save the victim. We were well aware of the man's intentions when he approached his victim; but it was not until the blow was struck that we had the courage to interfere. It was, however, as I have said—too late! Mac Chizzle expired without a groan.

"I cannot dwell upon this scene: depraved—wicked—criminal as I was in many respects, my soul revolted from the idea of cannibalism, now that the opportunity of appeasing my hunger by such horrible means was within my reach. Stephens and I retired a little from the rest, and turned our backs upon the frightful work that was in progress. Again I say—oh! the horrors of that night! I was starving—and food was near. But what food? The flesh of a fellow-creature! In imagination I followed the entire process that was in operation so close behind me; and presently the hissing of the flesh upon the embers, and the odour of the awful cookery, convinced me that the meal would soon be served up. Then how did I wrestle with my own inclinations! And Stephens, I could well perceive, was also engaged in a terrific warfare with the promptings of hunger. But we resisted the temptation: yes—we resisted it;—and our companions did not trouble themselves to invite us to their repast.

"At length the morning dawned upon that awful and never-to-be-forgotten night. The fire was now extinguished; but near the ashes lay the entrails and the head of the murdered man. The cannibals had completely anatomised the corpse, and had wrapped up in their shirts (which they took off for the purpose) all that they chose to carry away with them. Not a word was spoken amongst us. The last frail links of sympathy—if any really had existed—seemed to have been broken by the incidents of the preceding night. Six men had partaken of the horrible repast; and they evidently looked on each other with loathing, and on Stephens and myself with suspicion. We all with one accord cut thick sticks, and advanced in the direction whence Blackley's cries had proceeded a few hours previously. His fate was that which we had suspected: an enormous snake was coiled around the wretch's corpse—licking it with its long tongue, to cover it with saliva for the purpose of deglutition. We attacked the monstrous reptile, and killed it. Its huge coils had actually squeezed our unfortunate comrade to death! Then—for the first time for many, many years—did a religious sentiment steal into my soul; and I murmured to myself: '*Surely this was the judgment of God upon a man who had meditated murder.*'

"That same day Stephens and myself gave our companions the slip, and struck into another direction together. We were fortunate enough to kill a kangaroo; and we made a hearty meal upon a portion of its flesh. Then how did we rejoice that we had withstood the temptation of the cannibal banquet! Stephens fell upon his knees and prayed aloud: I imitated his example—I joined in his thanksgiving. We husbanded our resources as much as possible; and God was merciful to us. We succeeded in killing another kangaroo, even before the first was entirely consumed; and this new supply enabled us to reach a settlement without further experiencing the pangs of hunger. Prudence now compelled us to separate; for though we had rid ourselves of our chains, we were still in our convict garb; and it was evident that two persons so clad were more likely to attract unpleasant notice, than one individual skulking about by himself. We accordingly parted; and from that moment I have never heard of Stephens. Whether he succeeded in escaping from the colony altogether, or whether he took to the bush again and perished, I know not:—that he was not retaken I am sure, because, were he captured, he would have been sent to Norfolk Island; and that he did *not* visit that most horrible of all the penal settlements—at least during a period of eighteen months after our escape from Macquarie—I am well aware, for reasons which I shall soon explain.

"In fact, I was not long at large after I separated with Stephens. My convict-dress betrayed me to a party of soldiers: I was arrested, taken to Sydney, tried, and sentenced to transportation to Norfolk Island. Before I left England in 1836, and since my return towards the end of 1839, I have heard a great many persons talk about Norfolk Island; but no one seemed to know much about it. I will therefore tell you something concerning it now.

"A thousand miles to the eastward of Sydney there are three islands close together. As you advance towards them in a ship from Sydney, Philip Island, which is very high land, and has a bold peak to the south, comes in view: close beyond it the lower hills of Norfolk Island, crowned with lofty pines, appear in sight; and between those two islands is a small and sterile speck called Nepean Island. Norfolk Island is six miles and a half long, and four broad—a miserable dot in the ocean compared to the vast tract of Australia. The soil is chiefly basaltic, and rises into hills covered with grass and forest. Mount Pitt—the loftiest eminence in the island—is twelve hundred feet above the level of the sea. The Norfolk Island pine shoots to a height of a hundred feet,—sometimes growing in clumps, elsewhere singly, on the grassy parts of the island, even to the very verge of the shore, where its roots are washed by the sea at high water. The apple-fruited guava, the lemon, grapes, figs, coffee, olives, pomegranates, strawberries, and melons have been introduced, and are cultivated successfully. The island is every where inaccessible, save at an opening in a low reef fronting the little bay; and that is the point where the settlement is situated. The Prisoners' Barracks are pretty much upon the same plan as those at Sydney, and which I described to you just now. There is a room, called the Court-House, where the Protestant prisoners meet on Sunday to hear prayers; and there is another, called the Lumber-Yard room, for the Roman Catholics. The prayers in both places are read by prisoners. The principal buildings in the settlement are the Commandant's Residence, the Military Barracks, the Penitentiary, the Gaol, and the Hospital. The convicts are principally employed in quarrying stone; and as no gunpowder is used in blasting the rocks, and the stone is raised by means of levers, the labour is even more crushing than that of wood-felling at Port Macquarie. The prisoners, moreover, have to work in irons; and the food is not only insufficient, but bad—consisting only of dry maize bread and hard salt meat. Were it not for the supply of wild fruits in the island, the scurvy would rage like a pestilence. Between Macquarie Harbour and Norfolk Island I can only draw this distinction—that the former is *Purgatory*, and the latter *Hell!*

"There is no attempt to reform the prisoners in Norfolk Island, beyond prayer-reading—and this is of scarcely any benefit. The convicts are too depraved to be amended by mere moral lessons: they want *education*; they require to be *treated like human beings*, instead of brute beasts, criminal though they are; they need *a sufficiency of wholesome food*, to enable them to toil with something approaching a good will; they ought to be *protected against the tyranny of overseers*, who send them to gaol for the most trivial offences, or on the slightest suspicions; they should not be *forced to labour in chains which gall their ankles almost to the bone*, when a guard with loaded muskets is ever near, and seeing that shackles on the legs would not prevent violence with the hands were they inclined to have recourse to it; nor should they be *constantly treated as if they were merely wild beasts whom it is impossible to tame save by means of privation, heart-breaking toil, and the constant sense of utter degradation*. How can men be redeemed—reclaimed—reformed by such treatment as this? Let punishment be terrible—not horrible. It is monstrous to endeavour to render the criminal more obstinate—to make the dangerous one more ferocious—to crush in the soul every inducement to amend—to convert vice into hardened recklessness. The tortures of semi-starvation and overwhelming toil, and the system of retaining men's minds in a state of moral abasement and degradation in their own eyes, will never lead to reform. When at Macquarie Harbour, or at Norfolk Island, I have often thought how comparatively easy it would be to reclaim even the very worst among the convicts. Teach them *practically* that while there is life there is hope,—that it is *never too late to repent*,—that man can show mercy to the greatest sinner, even as God does,—that the most degraded mind may rise from the depths of its abasement,—that society seeks reformation and prevention in respect to crime, and not vengeance,—that the Christian religion, in a word, exists in the heart as well as in a book. But what sentiments do the convicts entertain? They are taught, by oppressive treatment, to lose sight of their own turpitude, and therefore to consider that all mankind is bent on inflicting a demoniac vengeance upon them;—they look upon the authorities as their persecutors;—they begin to fancy that they are worms which are justified in turning on those who tread them under foot;—they swear, and blaspheme, and talk obscenely, *merely because there is no earthly solace left them save in hardening their own hearts against all kindly sympathies and emotions*;—they receive the Word of

God with suspicion, because man does not practically help them to a belief in the divine assurance relative to the efficacy of repentance;—they are compelled by terrific and unceasing hardships to look upon the tears of a contrite heart as the proofs of moral weakness:—and, in a word, they study how to avoid reflections which can lead, so far as they can see, to no beneficial end. They therefore welcome hardness of heart, obstinacy, and recklessness of disposition as an actual means of escape from thoughts which would, under favourable circumstances, lead to moral amendment and reformation.

"You may be surprised to hear such ideas from my lips; but I have pondered much and often upon this subject. And if ever these words which I am now uttering to you, Henry Holford, should find their way into print,—if ever my narrative, with its various reflections, should go forth to the world,—be you well assured that these ideas will set people thinking on the grand point—*whether society punishes to prevent crime and to reclaim the offender, or merely to avenge itself upon him*?

"My own prospects were gloomy enough. My life was to be passed in exile, misery, and torture. I loathed my associates. They took all possible pains to tease and annoy each other. They converted a beautiful spot—one of the loveliest islands in the world—into a perfect hell upon earth;—and seemed determined to supply any deficiency which the authorities had left in the sum of our unhappiness. They concocted various schemes of mischief, and then the most hardened would betray their comrades merely for the pleasure of seeing them flogged! I never shall forget a convict saying to me one day, 'I doubt the existence of a God; but I wish, if there is one, that he would take away my life, for I am so very miserable. I have only six years more to serve; and I am determined either to escape, or to murder some one and get hanged for it.'—This man's name was Anson; and from that moment he and I had frequent conversations together relative to an escape from the island. But how few were our hopes? Surrounded by the ocean—pent up in so narrow a space, as it were—so distant from all other lands—fearful to confide in our companions—and unable to carry our scheme into effect without assistance, we were frequently induced to give it up in despair.

"Not very far from the Commandant's house was a singular little cave, hollowed in the rugged limestone that forms two low hills,—the flat and the reef on the south of the island. This cave was near a lime-kiln, and was concealed by a stone drawn over its mouth. I had been nearly eighteen months on the island, (during which time, as I before said, Stephens was not sent to join the gangs; and therefore I concluded that he either perished in Australia, or effected his escape to Europe,)—eighteen months, I say, had elapsed, when Anson and I were one day at work in the lime-kiln, with a small gang. When the mid-day meal-time came, he and I strolled apart from the rest; and none of the sentries took any notice of us, because escape from that point in the broad daylight was impossible. As we were walking along and conversing, we discovered the cave. This circumstance gave a new impulse to our ideas, and to our hopes of an escape; and a few days afterwards, we put our plan into execution. We enlisted two other convicts in the scheme,—two men in whom we imagined that more confidence was to be placed than in any of the rest. By their aid we contrived to purloin at dusk a sack of biscuits; and this we conveyed to the cave. On the next night one of our new accomplices contrived to rob a small house of entertainment for seamen, of three suits of sailors' clothes; and these were conveyed to the cave. Our plans were now all matured. A small decked yacht, cutter-rigged, and belonging to the Commandant, lay close by the shore; and we knew that there were only a man and a boy on board at that time. Our project was a desperate one; but the risk was worth running, seeing the result to be gained—namely, our freedom. When our arrangements were completed, we all four one evening absconded as we were returning home from the day's toils, and took refuge in the cave. No time was to be lost. About midnight, Anson and I swam off to the yacht, contrived to get on board, seized each a windlass-bar, and, descending to the cabin, mastered the man and the boy. We bound them in such a way that they could not leave their hammocks; and then we fastened down the hatchway to drown their cries in case they should shout for assistance. We next lowered the little skiff, and returned to land. Our companions joined us, with the bag of biscuit and the clothes, at a point previously agreed upon; and we all succeeded in reaching the cutter in safety. Then we set sail; and, favoured by the darkness of the night, got clear away without having excited on shore a suspicion that the yacht had moved from its moorings.

"As we had conjectured, there was very little provision on board; for the Commandant never used the yacht for more than a few hours' trip at a time. We had therefore done wisely to provide the biscuit; but there was not two days' supply of meat on board. We accordingly steered for the back of Philip Island, which we knew to abound in pigs and goats, and to be uninhabited by man. Anson and another of our companions went on shore with fire-arms, which we had found in the cutter; and within two hours after day-light they shot four pigs and thirteen goats. Myself and the other convict, who remained on board to take care of the vessel and guard the seaman and the boy, caught several king-fish and rock-cod. We were thus well provisioned; and another trip to the shore filled our water-casks. We next proposed to the seaman and boy either to join us, or to take the skiff and return to Norfolk Island as best they might. They preferred the latter offer; and we accordingly suffered them to depart, after compelling the sailor to exchange his clothes for one of our convict suits; so that we had now a proper garb each. In their presence we had talked of running for New Caledonia—an Island to the north of Norfolk Island; but the moment they were gone, we set sail for New Zealand, which is precisely in a contrary direction—being to the south of Norfolk Island. Our craft was but little better than a cockle-boat: it was, however, decked; fine weather prevailed; and moreover, it was better to die by drowning than perish by the gradual tortures of a penal settlement.

"We were in sight of New Zealand, when a fearful storm came on suddenly at an early hour on the thirteenth morning after we had quitted Norfolk Island. A tremendous sea broke over our little craft, and washed poor Anson over-board. The other two convicts and myself did all we could to save the vessel, and run her into a bay which we now descried in the distance; but our inexperience in nautical matters was put to a severe test. When our condition was apparently hopeless, and we expected that the sea would swallow us up, a large bark hove in sight. We made signals of distress; and the vessel steered towards us. But a mountainous wave struck the stern of the cutter, and stove in her timbers. She immediately began to fill. We cut away the boom, and clung to it as to a last hope. The vessel went down; and, small as it was, it formed a vortex which for a few moments sucked us under, spar and all. But we rose again to the surface, clinging desperately to the boom. Suddenly one of my comrades uttered a fearful cry—a cry of such wild agony that it rings in my ears every time I think of that horrible incident. I glanced towards him: the water was for an instant tinged with blood—a shark had bitten off one of the wretched man's legs! Oh! what an agony of fear I experienced then. The poor creature continued to shriek in an appalling manner for a few seconds: then he loosened his hold upon the spar, and disappeared in the raging element. My only surviving companion and myself exchanged looks of unutterable horror.

"We were drifting rapidly in the direction of the bark, which on its side was advancing towards us. When within hail, it lowered a boat. But I was destined to be the only survivor of the four convicts who had escaped from Norfolk Island. When only a few yards from the boat, my companion suddenly relaxed his hold upon the spar, and sank with a loud cry—to rise no more. The water was not tinged with blood—and therefore I do not suppose that he was attacked by a shark: most probably a sudden cramp seized him;—but, whatever the cause, he perished! I was dragged in an exhausted state into the boat, and was speedily safe on board the bark.

"The vessel was a trading one, and bound for Hobart Town, whence it was to sail for England. I gave so plausible an account of the shipwrecked cutter, that the real truth was not suspected, especially as I was attired in a sailor's dress; and as the bark was not to remain many days at Hobart Town, where, moreover, I was not known, I entertained the most sanguine hopes of being able to ensure my safe return to England. In three weeks,—after encountering much bad weather—we entered the Derwent; and, taking in a pilot, were carried safe up to Sullivan's Cove.

"Hobart Town is the capital of Van Diemen's Land, and is beautifully placed on the banks of an estuary called the Derwent. The streets are spacious: the houses are built of brick; and the roofs, covered with shingles, have the appearance of being slated. Mount Wellington rises behind the town to the height of 4000 feet, and is almost entirely clothed with forests. There is in Hobart Town a spacious House of Correction for females: it is called the Factory, and contained at that time about two hundred and fifty prisoners. They were employed in picking and spinning wool, and in washing for the Hospital, Orphan-School, and other institutions. The women were dressed in a prison garb, and had their hair cut close, which they naturally considered a grievous infliction of tyranny. When they misbehaved themselves, they were put into solitary confinement; and I heard that many of them had gone raving mad while enduring that horrible mental torture. I saw a chain-gang of a hundred and ten convicts, employed in raising a causeway across a muddy flat in the Derwent: they looked miserably unhealthy, pale, and emaciated, being half-starved, over-worked, and compelled to drink very bad water. The Government-House is a fine building, on the banks of the Derwent, and about a mile from the town. The Penitentiary at Hobart Town contains about six hundred prisoners, and is the principal receptacle for newly-arrived convicts. They are sent out in gangs, under overseers and guards, to work on the roads, or as carpenters, builders, sawyers, or masons, in the various departments.

"After remaining almost a fortnight at Hobart Town, the bark sailed for England, by way of Cape Horn; and I was now relieved from all fears of detection—at least for the present. As I have spoken of the condition of the female convicts in Hobart Town, I may as well give you some account of how transportation affects women; for you may be sure that I heard enough of that subject both at Sydney and at Macquarie Harbour. A female-convict ship is fitted up on precisely the same plan as that of the men, with the addition of shelves whereon to stow away the tea-crockery. The women's rations are the same as the men's, with the extra comforts of tea and sugar. This they have for breakfast, and oatmeal for supper. No guard of soldiers is required on board: nor is there a bulk-head across the upper deck in mid-ships. Instead of *captains of the vessel*, there are matrons appointed by the surgeon to take care of the *morals* of the rest; and these matrons are usually old brothel-keepers or procuresses, who know how to feign a sanctity which produces a favourable impression in their behalf. Women convicts are dreadfully quarrelsome; and their language is said to be more disgusting and filthy than that of the men. However vigilant the surgeon may be, it is impossible altogether to prevent intercourse between the females and the sailors; and it often happens that some of the *fair ones*, on their arrival in the colony, are in a way to increase the Australian population. Perhaps the surgeon himself may take a fancy to one or two of the best-looking; and these are sure to obtain great indulgences—such as being appointed nurses to the sick, or being permitted to remain on the sick-list throughout the voyage, which is an excuse for allowing them wine and other little comforts. The women always speak *to* and *of* each other as *ladies*; and the old procuresses, when chosen as matrons, are treated with the respectful *Mrs*. Thus it is always, '*Ladies*, come for'ard for your pork;' or '*Ladies*, come up for your biscuit;' or '*Ladies*, the puddings are cooked.' Of an evening they dance or sing,—and as often quarrel and fight. This cannot be wondered at, when it is remembered that there is no attempt at classification; and women who may have been chaste in person, though criminal in other respects, are compelled to herd with prostitutes of all degrees, from the lowest trull that skulks in the courts leading out of Fleet Street to the fashionable nymph who displays her charms at the theatre. The very chastity of a woman who has been sentenced perhaps for robbing furnished lodgings, or plundering her master in her capacity of servant, or for committing a forgery, is made a reproach to her by the prostitutes and old procuresses; and her life is miserable. Moreover, it is next to impossible that she can escape a contamination which prepares her for a life of profligacy when she reaches the colony.

"Before the female convict-ship leaves the Thames, numbers of old procuresses and brothel-keepers go on board to take leave of the girls with whom they are acquainted. These hags, dressed out in their gayest garb, and pretending to be overwhelmed with grief (while they really are with gin), represent themselves to be the mothers or aunts of the '*poor dear creatures*' who have got into trouble, and assure the surgeon that their so-called daughters or nieces were most excellent girls and bore exemplary characters previous to their present '*misfortune.*' The surgeon—if a novice, or a humane man—believes the tale, and is sure to treat with kindness the '*poor creatures*' thus recommended to him. About twenty years ago a Religious Society in London sent out, in an emigrant ship, twelve '*reclaimed unfortunate girls*,' with the hope that they might form good matrimonial connexions among the free settlers in the colony; there always having been—especially at first—a great dearth of European females in Australia. These girls were called the *Twelve Apostles*; and all England rang with the good work which had been accomplished by the Religious Society. But on the arrival of the Twelve Apostles at Sydney, seven of them were found to be in the family way by the sailors; and the others immediately entered on a course of unbounded licentiousness.[22]

"A few days before the female convict-vessel arrives at Sydney, the women—old and young—busy themselves in getting ready their finery for landing. The debarkation of female convicts always takes place with great effect. The prostitutes appear in their most flaunting attire; and many of them have gold ornaments about them. They are then sent to the Paramatta Factory. This establishment cannot be looked on as a place of punishment—nor as a place of reformation. The inmates are well fed, and are put to no labour. There is an extensive garden, in which they can walk at pleasure. Some of them are allotted to free settlers requiring servants; but the grand hope of the female convict is to marry. This prospect is materially aided by the fact that both free settlers and ticket-of-leave convicts are allowed to seek for help-mates in the Factory. When they call for that purpose, the fair penitents are drawn up in a row; and the wife-seeking individual inspects them as a general does his army, or a butcher the sheep in Smithfield Market. If he fancies one of the candidates, he beckons her from the rank, and they retire to a distance to converse. Should a matrimonial arrangement be made, the business is soon finished by the aid of a clergyman; but if no amicable understanding is come to, the nymph returns to the rank, and the swain chooses another—and so on, until the object of his visit is accomplished. So anxious are the unmarried free settlers or the ticket-of-leave convicts to change their single state of blessedness, and so ready are the fair sex to meet their wishes, that few women whose husbands die remain widows a couple of days; some not more than four-and-twenty hours. A few years before I was in the colony, an old settler saw a convict-girl performing penance on a market-day, with her gown-tail drawn over her head, for drunkenness and disorderly conduct in the Factory. He walked straight up to her—regardless of the hootings of the crowd—and proposed marriage. She was candid enough to confess to him that she was five months gone in the family way by a master to whom she had been allotted ere she returned to the Factory; but the amorous swain, who was nearly sixty, was so much struck by her black eyes and plump shape, that he expressed his readiness to take her 'for better or worse;' and she had not left the place of punishment an hour, ere she was married to one of the richest settlers in the colony.[23]

"I will tell you one more anecdote relative to Australian marriages. A very handsome woman was transported for shop-lifting—her third offence of the kind. She left a husband behind her in England. On her arrival at Sydney she was allotted to an elderly gentleman, a free settler, and who, being a bachelor, sought to make her his mistress. She, however, resisted his overtures, hoping that he would make her his wife, as he was not aware that she had a husband in her native country. Time wore on, he urgent—she obstinate,—he declining matrimonial bonds. At length she received a black-edged letter from her mother in England; and upon being questioned by her master, she stated '*that its contents made a great alteration in her circumstances.*' More she would not tell him. He was afraid of losing his handsome servant; and agreed to marry her. They were united accordingly. When the nuptial knot was indissolubly tied, he begged his beloved wife to explain the nature of the black-edged letter. '*There is now no need for any further mystery,*' she said, '*The truth is, I could not marry you before, because I had a husband living in England. That black-edged letter conveyed to me the welcome news that he was hanged five months ago at the Old Bailey; and thus nothing now stands in the way of our happiness.*'—And that woman made the rich settler a most exemplary wife.

"I have now given you an insight into the morals of the female, as well as those of the male convicts; and you may also perceive that while transportation is actually a means of pleasing variety of scene and habits to the woman, it is an earthly hell to the man. I know that transportation is spoken of as something very light—a mere change of climate—amongst those thieves in England who have never yet crossed the water; but they are woefully mistaken! Transportation was *once* a trivial punishment, when all convicts were allotted to settlers, and money would purchase tickets-of-leave; or when a convict's wife, if he had one, might go out in the next ship with all the swag which his crimes had produced, and on her arrival in the colony apply for her husband to be allotted to her as her servant, by which step he became a free man, opened a public-house or some kind of shop, and made a fortune. Those were glorious times for convicts; but all that system has been changed. Now you have Road-Gangs, and Hulk-Gangs, and Quarrying-Gangs,—men who work in chains, and who cannot obtain a sufficiency of food! There is also Norfolk Island—a Garden of Eden in natural loveliness, rendered an earthly hell by human occupation. Oh! let not the opinion prevail that transportation is no punishment; let not those who are young in the ways of iniquity, pursue their career under the impression that exile to Australia is nothing more than a pleasant change of scene! They will too soon discover how miserably they are mistaken; and when they feel the galling chain upon their ankles,—when they find themselves toiling amidst the incessant damps of Macquarie, or on the hard roads of Van Diemen's Land, or in the quarries of Norfolk Island,—when they are labouring in forests where every step may arouse a venomous snake whose bite is death, or where a falling tree may crush them beneath its weight,—when they are exposed to the brutality of overseers, or the still more intolerable cruelty of their companions,—when they sleep in constant dread of being murdered by their fellow-convicts, and awake only to the dull monotony of a life of intense and heart-breaking labour,—then will they loathe their very existence, and dare all the perils of starvation, or the horrors of cannibalism, in order to escape from those scenes of ineffable misery!

"But I need say no more upon this subject. The bark, in which I worked my passage to Europe, reached England in safety; and I was once more at large in my native country. Yes—I was free to go whithersoever I would—and to avenge myself on him who had betrayed me to justice! The hope of some day consummating that vengeance had never deserted me from the moment I was sentenced in the Central Criminal Court. It had animated me throughout all the miseries, the toils, and the hardships which I have related to you. It inspired me with courage to dare the dangers of an escape from Macquarie: its effect was the same when I resolved upon quitting Norfolk Island. I have once had my mortal foe within my reach; but my hand dealt not the blow with sufficient force. It will not fail next time. I know that vengeance is a crime; but I cannot subdue those feelings which prompt me to punish the man whose perfidy sent me into exile. In all other respects I am reformed—completely reformed. Not that the authorities in Australia or Norfolk Island have in any way contributed to this moral change which has come over me: no—my own meditations and reflections have induced me to toil in order to earn an honest livelihood. I will never steal again: I will die sooner. I would also rather die by my own hand than return to the horrors of Macquarie or Norfolk Island. But my vengeance—Oh! I must gratify my vengeance;—and I care not what may become of me afterwards!"

Crankey Jem then related so much of his adventures with the gipsies as did not involve a betrayal of any of their secrets, and concluded his recital by a concise account of his sudden meeting with, and attack upon, the Resurrection Man *at a certain house in St. Giles's.*

19. This episode is founded on fact. The newspapers of 1840, or 1841, will in this instance furnish the type of Mr. Robert Cuffin in the person of a certain Reverend who obtained much notoriety at Rickmansworth.

20. Londoners.

21. Countrymen.

22. Fact.

23. Fact.

CHAPTER CXCII.

THE MINT.—THE FORTY THIEVES.

Reader, if you stroll down that portion of the Southwark Bridge Road which lies between Union Street and Great Suffolk Street, you will perceive, midway, and on your left hand, a large mound of earth heaped on an open space doubtless, intended for building-ground.

At the southern extremity of this mound (on which all the offal from the adjacent houses is thrown, and where vagabond boys are constantly collected) is the entrance into an assemblage of miserable streets, alleys, and courts, forming one of the vilest, most dangerous, and most demoralised districts of this huge metropolis.

The houses are old, gloomy, and sombre. Some of them have the upper part, beginning with the first floor, projecting at least three feet over the thoroughfares—for we cannot say over the pavement. Most of the doors stand open, and reveal low, dark, and filthy passages, the mere aspect of which compels the passer-by to get into the middle of the way, for fear of being suddenly dragged into those sinister dens, which seem fitted for crimes of the blackest dye.

This is no exaggeration.

Even in the day-time one shudders at the cut-throat appearance of the places into the full depths of whose gloom the eye cannot entirely penetrate. But, by night, the Mint,—for it is of this district that we are now writing,—is far more calculated to inspire the boldest heart with alarm, than the thickest forest or the wildest heath ever infested by banditti.

The houses in the Mint give one an idea of those dens in which murder may be committed without the least chance of detection. And yet that district swarms with population. But of what kind are its inhabitants? The refuse and the most criminal of the metropolis.

There people follow trades as a blind to avert suspicions relative to their real calling: for they are actually housebreakers or thieves themselves, or else the companions and abettors of such villains.

In passing through the mazes of the Mint—especially in Mint Street itself—you will observe more ill-looking fellows and revolting women in five minutes than you will see either on Saffron Hill or in Bethnal Green in an hour. Take the entire district that is bounded on the north by Peter Street, on the south by Great Suffolk Street, on the east by Blackman Street and High Street, and on the west by the Southwark Bridge Road,—take this small section of the metropolis, and believe us when we state that within those limits there is concentrated more depravity in all its myriad phases, than many persons could suppose to exist in the entire kingdom.

The Mint was once a sanctuary, like Whitefriars; and, although the law has deprived it of its ancient privileges, its inhabitants still maintain them, by a tacit understanding with each other, to the extent of their power. Thus, if a villain, of whom the officers of justice are in search, takes refuge at a lodging in the Mint, the landlord will keep his secret in spite of every inducement. The only danger which he might incur would be at the hands of the lowest description of buzgloaks, dummy-hunters, area-sneaks, and vampers who dwell in that district.

There is no part of Paris that can compare with the Mint in squalor, filth, or moral depravity;—no—not even the street in the Island of the City, where Eugene Sue has placed his celebrated *tapis-franc*.

Let those who happen to visit the Mint, after reading this description thereof, mark well the countenances of the inhabitants whom they will meet in that gloomy labyrinth. Hardened ruffianism characterises the men;—insolent, leering, and shameless looks express the depravity of the women;—the boys have the sneaking, shuffling manner of juvenile thieves;—the girls, even of a tender age, possess the brazen air of incipient profligacy.

It was about nine o'clock in the evening when the Resurrection Man, wrapped in a thick and capacious pea-coat, the collar of which concealed all the lower part of his countenance, turned hastily from the Southwark Bridge Road into Mint Street.

The weather was piercingly cold, and the sleet was peppering down with painful violence: the Resurrection Man accordingly buried his face as much as possible in the collar of his coat, and neither looked to the right nor left as he proceeded on his way.

To this circumstance may be attributed the fact that one so cautious and wary as he, should now fail to observe that his motions were watched and his steps dogged by a lad whose countenance was also well concealed by a high collar which was drawn up to his ears.

In order to avoid unnecessary mystification, we may as well observe that this youth was Henry Holford.

The Resurrection Man pursued his way along Mint Street, and suddenly turned into a small court on the left-hand side. There he knocked at a door in a peculiar manner, whistling a single sharp shrill note at the same time; and in another moment Holford saw him enter the house.

"Well, Mr. Tidkins," said a boy of about fourteen, who had opened the door to admit the formidable individual with whom he was evidently well acquainted: "a preshus cold night, arn't it?"

"Very, my lad," answered the Resurrection Man, turning down his collar, so that the light of the candle which the boy held, gleamed upon his cadaverous countenance. "Is the Bully Grand at home?"

A reply in the affirmative was given; and the boy led the way, up a narrow and dilapidated staircase, to a large room where a great number of youths, whose ages varied from twelve to eighteen, were seated at a table, drinking and smoking.

The organisation of this society of juvenile reprobates requires a detailed notice.

The association consisted of thirty-nine co-equals and one chief who was denominated the Bully Grand. The fraternity was called *The Forty Thieves*;—whether in consequence of the founders having accidentally amounted to precisely that number, or whether with the idea of emulating the celebrated heroes of the Arabian tale, we cannot determine.

The society had, however, been established for upwards of thirty years at the time of which we are writing,— *and is in existence at this present moment.*

The rules of the association may thus be briefly summed up:—The society consists of Forty Members, including the Bully Grand. Candidates for admission are eligible at twelve years of age. When a member reaches the age of eighteen, he must retire from the association. This rule does not, however, apply to the Bully Grand, who is not eligible for that situation until he has actually reached the age of eighteen, and has been a member for at least four years. Each candidate for membership must be guaranteed as to eligibility and *honour* (that *honour* which is necessary amongst thieves) by three members of good standing in the society; and should any member misconduct himself, or withhold a portion of any booty which he may acquire, his guarantees are responsible for him. The Bully Grand must find twelve guarantees amongst the oldest members. His power is in most respects absolute; and the greatest deference is paid to him.

The modes of proceeding are as follow:—The metropolis is divided into twelve districts distinguished thus:— 1. The Regent's Park; 2. Pentonville; 3. Hoxton; 4. Finsbury; 5. City; 6. Tower Hamlets; 7. Westminster; 8. Pimlico; 9. Hyde Park; 10. Grosvenor Square; 11. Lambeth; 12. The Borough. Three members are allotted to each district, and are changed in due rotation every day. Thus the three who take the Regent's Park district on a Monday, pass to the Pentonville district on Tuesday, the Hoxton district on Wednesday, and so on. Thus thirty-six members are every day employed in the district-service. The Bully Grand and the three others in the meantime attend to the disposal of the stolen property, and to the various business of the fraternity. In every district there is a public-house, or boozing-ken, in the interest of the association; and to the landlords of these flash cribs is the produce of each day's work consigned in the evening. The house in the Mint is merely a place of meeting once a fortnight, a residence for the Bully Grand, and the central depôt to which articles are conveyed from the care of the district boozing-kens.

The minor regulations and bye-laws may be thus summed up:—Of the three members allotted to each district, the oldest member acts as the chief, and guides the plan of proceedings according to his discretion. Should any member be proved to have secreted booty, his guarantees must pay the value of it; and with them rests the punishment of the defaulter. General meetings take place at the head-quarters in the Mint on the first and third Wednesday in every month; but if the Bully Grand wishes to call an extraordinary assembly, or to summon any particular member or members to his presence, he must leave notices to that effect with the landlords of the district houses-of-call. The members are to effect no robberies by violence, nor to break into houses: their proceedings must be effected by sleight of hand, cunning, and artifice. All disputes must be referred to the Bully Grand for settlement. The booty must be converted into money, and the cash divided fairly between all the members every fortnight, a certain percentage being allotted by way of salary to the Bully Grand.

Such are the principles upon which the association of the Forty Thieves is based. Every precaution is adopted, by means of the guarantees, to prevent the admission of unsuitable members, and to ensure the fidelity and *honour* of those who belong to the fraternity. When a member "gets into trouble," persons of apparent respectability come forward to give the lad a character; so that magistrates or judges are quite bewildered by the assurances that "it must be a mistake;" "that the prisoner is an honest hard-working boy, belonging to poor but respectable parents *in the country*;" or "that so convinced is the witness of the lad's innocence, that he will instantly take him into his service if the magistrate will discharge him." While a member remains in prison previous to trial, the funds of the association provide him with the best food allowed to enter the gaol; and, if he be condemned to a term of incarceration in the House of Correction, he looks forward to the banquet that will be given in the Mint to celebrate the day of his release. Moreover, a member does not lose his right to a share of the funds realised during his imprisonment. Thus every inducement is adopted to prevent members who "get into trouble" from peaching against their comrades, or making any revelations calculated to compromise the safety of the society.

It was a fortnightly meeting of the society when the Resurrection Man visited the house in the Mint, on the occasion of which we were ere now speaking.

The Forty Thieves were all gathered round a board formed of several rude deal tables placed together, and literally groaning beneath the weight of pewter-pots, bottles, jugs, &c.

The tallow-candles burnt like stars seen through a mist, so dense was the tobacco-smoke in the apartment.

At the upper end of the table sate the Bully Grand—a tall, well-dressed, good-looking young man, with a profusion of hair, but no whiskers, and little of that blueish appearance on the chin which denotes a beard. His aspect was therefore even more juvenile than was consistent with his age, which was about twenty-five. He possessed a splendid set of teeth, of which he seemed very proud; and his delicate white hand, which had never been applied to any harder work than picking pockets, was waved gently backward and forward when he spoke.

Around the table there were fine materials for the study of a phrenologist. Such a concatenation of varied physiognomies was not often to be met with; because none of the charities nor amenities of life were there delineated;—those countenances were indices only of vice in all its grades and phases.

The Resurrection Man was welcomed with a hum of applause on the part of the members, and with out-stretched hands by the Bully Grand near whom he was invited to take a seat.

"The business of the evening is over, Mr. Tidkins," said Mr. Tunks,—for so the Bully Grand was named; "and we are now deep in the pleasures of the meeting, as you see. Help yourself! There are spirits of all kinds, and pipes or cigars—whichever you prefer."

"Have you any information to give me?" inquired Tidkins in a low tone.

"Plenty—but not at this moment, Mr. Tidkins. Take a glass of something to dispel the cold; and by-and-bye we will talk on matters of business. There is plenty of time; and many of my young friends here would no doubt be proud to give you a specimen of their vocal powers. Let me see—who's turn is it?"

"Leary Lipkins's, sir," whispered a boy who sate near the Bully Grand.

"Oh! Leary Lipkins—is it?" said Tunks aloud. "Now, brother Lipkins, the company are waiting for an opportunity to drink to your health and song."

Mr. Lipkins—a sharp-looking, hatchet-faced, restless-eyed youth of about sixteen—did not require much pressing ere he favoured his audience with the following sample of vocal melody:—

THE SIGN OF THE FIDDLE.

There's not in all London a tavern so gay,

As that where the knowing ones meet of a day:

So long as a farthing remains to my share,

I'll drink at that tavern, and never elsewhere.

Yet it is not that comforts there only combine,

Nor because it dispenses good brandy and wine;

'Tis not the sweet odour of pipe nor cigar—

Oh! no—'tis a something more cozie by far!

'Tis that friends of the light-fingered craft are all nigh,

Who'd drink till the cellar itself should be dry,

And teach you to feel how existence may please,

When pass'd in the presence of cronies like these.

Sweet Sign of the Fiddle! how long could I dwell

In thy tap full of smoke, with the friends I love well;

When bailiffs no longer the alleys infest,

And duns, like their bills, have relapsed into rest.

"Bravo!" "Brayvo!" "Bra-ah-vo!" echoed on all sides, when this elegant effusion was brought to a close.

The Bully Grand then rose, and spoke in the following manner:—

"Gentlemen, in proposing the health of our excellent brother Leary Lipkins, I might spare eulogy, his merits being so well known to us all. But I feel that there are times when it is necessary to expatiate somewhat on the excellent qualities of the leading members of our honourable Society—in order to encourage an emulative feeling in the breasts of our younger brethren. Such an occasion is the present one, when we are all thus sociably assembled. Gentlemen, you all know Leary Lipkins! (Cheers, and cries of "We do! we do!") You all know that he is indeed leary in every sense of the word. (Hear! hear!) He can see through the best bit of broad cloth that ever covered a swell's pocket. There seems to be a sort of magnetic attraction between his fingers and a gold watch in the fob of a Bond Street lounger. (Cheers.) Talk of mesmerism! why—Leary Lipkins can send a gentleman into a complete state of *coma* as he walks along the streets, so that he never can possibly feel Leary's hands in his pockets. Gentlemen, I hold Leary Lipkins up to you as an excellent example; and beg to propose his very good health."

The toast was drunk with "three times three."

Mr. Lipkins returned thanks in what a newspaper-reporter would term "a neat speech;" and he then exercised the usual privilege of calling upon a particular individual for a song.

A certain Master Tripes Todkinson accordingly indulged his companions in the following manner:—

THE COMPASSIONATE LADY AND THE CHIMNEY-SWEEP.

"Pray, who's the little boy that is dancing so nimbly?

Come, Mary, bring a halfpenny down.—"

"Please, ma'am, I'm the feller as swept your chimbley,

And I'm very much obleeged for the brown.—"

"Alas! how his schooling has been neglected!

But perhaps his kind father's dead?—"

"No, ma'am; he's a tinker as is wery much respected

And this mornin' he's drunk in bed.—"

"Perchance 'tis a motherless child that they've fixed on

To dance. Does your mamma live still?—"

"Yes, ma'am; at this moment she's stayin' at Brixton,

Vith a gen'leman as keeps a mill.—"[24]

"Poor child, he is miserably clad! How shocking!

Not to give him some clothes were a sin!—"

"Thank'ee, ma'am; but I doesn't want no shoe nor stocking,

I'd rayther have a quartern o' gin!"

The Bully Grand proposed the health Of Master Tripes Todkinson, in a speech which was mightily applauded; and Master Tripes Todkinson, having duly returned thanks, called on Master Bandy-legged Diggs to continue the vocal harmony.

This invitation was responded to with as much readiness as Master Diggs would have displayed in easing an elderly gentleman in a crowd of his purse; and the air with which he favoured his audience ran thus:—

THE LAST OATH.

Upon the drop he turned

To swear a parting oath;

He cursed the parson and Jack Ketch,

And he coolly damned them both.

He listened to the hum

Of the crowds that gathered nigh;

And he carelessly remarked,

"What a famous man am I!"

Beside the scaffold's foot

His mistress piped her eye:

She waved to him her dirty rag,

And whimpering said, "Good bye!"

She mourned the good old times

That ne'er could come again,

When he brought her home a well-lined purse;—

But all her tears were vain!

Poor Jack was soon turned off,

And gallantly was hung:

There was a sigh in every breast,

A groan on every tongue.

Go—gaze upon his corse,

And remember then you see

The bravest robber that has been,

Or ever more shall be!

We need scarcely observe that this chant was received with as much favour as the preceding ones. The Resurrection Man was, however, growing impatient; for the reader doubtless comprehends enough of his character to be well aware that Tidkins was not one who loved pleasure better than business. He looked at his watch, and cast a significant glance towards the Bully Grand.

"What o'clock is it, Mr. Tidkins?" inquired that great functionary.

"Half-past ten," was the answer.

"Well, I will devote my attention to you in a few minutes," said Tunks. "You may rest perfectly easy—I have obtained information on every point in which you are interested. But—hark! Shuffling Simon is going to speak!"

A lad of about seventeen, who had a weakness in the joints of his knees, and walked in a fashion which had led to the nickname mentioned by the Bully Grand, rose from his seat, and proposed the health of Mr. Tunks, the chief of the society of the Forty Thieves.

Then followed a tremendous clattering of bottles and glasses as the company filled up bumpers in order to pay due honour to the toast; and every one, save the Grand himself, rose. The health was drunk with rounds of applause: a pause of a few moments ensued; and then Shuffling Simon commenced the following complimentary song, in the repetition of which all the other adherents of the Chief vociferously joined:—

PROSPER THE GRAND.

Prosper our Bully Grand,

Great Tunks, our noble Grand;

Prosper the Grand

Send him good swag enough,

Heart made of sterling stuff,

Long to be up to snuff;—

Prosper the Grand.

Save him from all mishaps,

Scatter blue-bottle traps

Throughout the land

Confound the busy beak,

Flourish the area-sneak;

In Tunks a chief we seek;—

Prosper the Grand!

The best lush on the board

To Tunks's health be poured

By all the band!

May he continue free,

Nor ever tread-mill see;

And all shall shout with glee,

Prosper the Grand!'

It was really extremely refreshing for the Resurrection Man to contemplate the deep manifestation of loyalty with which the thirty-nine thieves sang the preceding air.

Nor less was it an imposing spectacle when the object of that adoration rose from his seat, waved his right hand, and poured forth his gratitude in a most gracious speech.

This ceremony being accomplished, the Grand (what a pity it was that so elegant and elevated a personage had retained his unworthy patronymic of *Tunks!*) took a candle from the table, and conducted the Resurrection Man down stairs into a back room, which the Chief denominated his "private parlour."

"Now for your information," said the Resurrection Man, somewhat impatiently. "In the first place, have you discovered any thing concerning Crankey Jem Cuffin?"

"My emissaries have been successful in every instance," answered Tunks, with a complacent smile. "A man exactly corresponding with your description of Crankey Jem dwells in an obscure court in Drury Lane. Here is the address."

"Any tidings of Margaret Flathers?" inquired Tidkins.

"She has married a young man who answers to your description of Skilligalee; and they keep a small chandlery-shop in Pitfield Street, Hoxton Old Town. The name of Mitchell is over the door."

"Your lads are devilish sharp fellows, Bully Grand," said the Resurrection Man, approvingly.

"With thirty-six emissaries all over London every day, it is not so very difficult to obtain such information as you required," returned Tunks. "Moreover, you paid liberally in advance; and the boys will always be glad to serve you."

"Now for the next question," said Tidkins. "Any news of the old man that Tomlinson goes to see sometimes?"

"Yes—he lives in a small lodging in Thomas Street, Bethnal Green," was the answer. "There is his address also. His name is Nelson:—you best know whether it is his right one or not. That is no business of mine. Mr. Tomlinson regularly calls on him every Sunday afternoon, and passes some hours with him. The old man never stirs out, and is very unwell."

"Once more I must compliment your boys," exclaimed Tidkins, overjoyed with this intelligence. "Have you been able to learn any thing concerning Katherine Wilmot?"

"There I have also succeeded," replied Mr. Tunks. "My boys discovered that, after the trial of Katherine, she lunched with some friends at an inn in the Old Bailey, and shortly afterwards left in a post-chaise. She was accompanied by an old lady; and the chaise took them to Hounslow."

"And there, I suppose, all traces of them disappear?" said the Resurrection Man, inquiringly.

"Not at all. I sent Leary Lipkins down to Hounslow yesterday; and he discovered that Miss Wilmot is staying at a farm-house belonging to a Mr. and Mrs. Bennet."

"Precisely!" exclaimed the Resurrection Man. "That Mrs. Bennet was a witness on the trial. I remember reading all about it. She was the sister of the woman whom Reginald Tracy murdered."

"The farm is only a short distance from Hounslow," observed the Bully Grand: "any one in the town can direct you to it. Most probably it was with this Mrs. Bennet that Miss Wilmot travelled in the post-chaise."

"Evidently so," said the Resurrection Man. "But of that no matter. All I required was Katherine Wilmot's address; and you have discovered it. Now for my last question. Have you ascertained whether it will be possible to bribe the clerk of the church where Lord Ravensworth and the Honourable Miss Adeline Enfield were married, to tear out the leaf of the register which contains the entry of that union?"

"I have learnt that the clerk is open to bribery: but he is a cautious man, and will not allow himself to be sounded too deeply in the matter," was the answer.

"Then that business must regard me," observed the Resurrection Man. "You have served me well in all these matters. Twenty pounds I gave you the other day: here are twenty pounds more. Are you satisfied?"

"I have every reason to be pleased with your liberality," returned the Bully Grand, folding up the bank-notes with his delicate fingers. "Have you any further commands at present?"

"Yes," replied the Resurrection Man, after a few moments' consideration: "let one of your lads take a couple of notes for me."

While the Bully Grand proceeded to summon Leary Lipkins, the Resurrection Man seated himself at a desk which there was in the room, and wrote the following note:—

"The news I have just received are rather good than bad. The clerk is open to bribery, but is cautious. I will myself call upon him the day after to-morrow; and I will meet you afterwards, at our usual place of appointment, in the evening between six and seven. But you must find money somehow or another: I am incurring expenses in this matter, and cannot work for nothing. Surely Greenwood will assist you?"

This letter was sealed and addressed to "GILBERT VERNON, ESQ., No.—*Stamford Street.*"

The Resurrection Man then penned another note which ran thus:—

"I have discovered Katherine's address, and shall call upon you the day after to-morrow at nine o'clock in the evening. Remain at home; as you know the importance of the business."

By the time he had concluded his correspondence, the Bully Grand had returned with Leary Lipkins.

"My good lad," said the Resurrection Man, addressing the latter, "here are two notes, which you must deliver this night—*this night, mind.* The first is addressed; and the person for whom it is intended never retires to bed until very late. He will be up, when you call at the house where he lodges in Stamford Street. Give the letter into his own hand. You must then proceed to Golden Lane; and in the third court on the right-hand side of the way, and in the fourth house on the left-hand in that court, an old woman lives. You must knock till she answers you; and give her this second letter. I actually do not know her name, although I have dealings with her at present."

Leary Lipkins promised to fulfil these directions, and immediately departed to execute them.

Shortly afterwards the Resurrection Man took his leave of the Bully Grand, and left the head-quarters of the Forty Thieves.

Henry Holford, who had never lost sight of the door of that house since he had seen the Resurrection Man enter it, and who had remained concealed in the shade of an overhanging frontage opposite for more than two hours, resumed his task of dogging that formidable individual.

The Resurrection Man passed down Mint Street, into the Borough, and called a cab from the nearest stand, saying to the driver, "New Church, Bethnal Green."

The moment Tidkins was ensconced within, and the driver was seated on his box, Henry Holford crept softly behind the cab. In that manner he rode unmolested until within a short distance of the place of destination, when he descended, and followed the vehicle on foot.

The cab stopped near the railings that surround the church; and the Resurrection Man, having settled the fare, hurried onwards into Globe Town, Holford still dogging him—but with the utmost caution.

Presently Tidkins struck into a bye-street at the eastern extremity of the Happy Valley (as, our readers will remember, Globe Town is denominated in the gazetteer of metropolitan thieves), and stopped at the door of a house of dilapidated appearance. In a word, this was the very den where we have before seen him conducting his infamous plots, and in the subterranean vaults of which Viola Chichester was imprisoned for a period of three weeks.

Holford saw the Resurrection Man enter this house by the front door communicating with the street. He watched the windows for a few moments, and then perceived a light suddenly appear in the room on the upper floor.

"I have succeeded!" exclaimed Holford, aloud, "the villain lives there! I have traced him to his lurking-hole; and Jem may yet be avenged!"

Then, in order to be enabled to give an accurate description of the house to the returned convict, Holford studied its situation and appearance with careful attention. He observed that it was two storeys high, and that by the side was a dark alley.

At length he was convinced that he should be enabled to find that particular dwelling again, or to direct Crankey Jem to it without the possibility of error; and, rejoicing at being thus enabled to oblige his new friend, the young man commenced his long and weary walk back to Drury Lane.

---

24. The tread-mill.

CHAPTER CXCIII.

ANOTHER VISIT TO BUCKINGHAM PALACE.

It was the evening following the one the incidents of which occupied the preceding chapter.

Beneath a sofa in the Ball Room of Buckingham Palace, Henry Holford lay concealed.

It would be a mere repetition of statements made in former portions of this work, were we to describe the means by which the young man obtained access to the most private parts of the royal dwelling. We may, however, observe that he had paid frequent visits to the palace since the occasion when we first saw him enter those sacred precincts at the commencement of January, 1839; and that he was as familiar with the interior of the sovereign's abode, even to its most retired chambers, as any of its numerous inmates.

He had run many risks of discovery; but a species of good fortune seemed to attend upon him in these strange and romantic ventures; and those frequent alarms had never as yet terminated in his detection. Thus he became emboldened in his intrusions; and he now lay beneath the sofa in the Ball Room, with no more apprehension than he would have entertained if some authority in the palace had actually connived at his presence there.

It was nine o'clock in the evening; and the Ball Room was brilliantly illuminated.

But as yet the low-born pot-boy was its sole occupant.

Not long, however, was he doomed to that solitude. By a strange coincidence, the two noble ladies whose conversation had so much interested him on the occasion of his first visit to the palace, entered the room shortly after nine o'clock. He recognised their voices immediately; and he was delighted at their arrival, for their former dialogues had awakened the most lively sentiments of curiosity in his mind. But since his intrusion in January, 1839, he had never seen nor heard them in his subsequent visits to the royal dwelling, until the present occasion; and now, as they advanced through the room together, he held his breath to catch the words that fell from them.

"The dinner-party was tiresome to-day, my dear countess," observed the duchess: "her Majesty did not appear to be in good spirits."

"Alas!" exclaimed the lady thus addressed, "our gracious sovereign's melancholy fits occur at less distant intervals as she grows older."

"And yet her Majesty has every earthly reason to be happy," said the duchess. "The Prince appears to be devotedly attached to her; and the Princess Royal is a sweet babe."

"Worldly prosperity will not always ensure felicity," returned the countess; "and this your grace must have perceived amongst the circle of your acquaintance. Her Majesty is a prey to frequent fits of despondency, which are distressing to the faithful subjects who have the honour to be near the royal person. She will sit for an hour at a time, in moody contemplation of that sweet babe; and her countenance then wears an expression of such profound—such plaintive—such touching melancholy, that I have frequently wept to behold her thus."

"What can be the cause of this intermittent despondency?" inquired the duchess.

"It is constitutional," answered the countess. "The fit comes upon her Majesty at moments when she is surrounded by all the elements of pleasure, happiness, and joy. It is a dark spirit against which no mind, however powerful, can wrestle. The only method of mitigating the violence of its attacks is the bustle of travelling:—then novelty, change of scene, exercise, and the demonstrations of popular devotion seem to relieve our beloved sovereign from the influence of that morbid, moody melancholy."

"I believe that when we conversed upon this topic on a former occasion,—it must be at least two years ago,—your ladyship hinted at the existence of hereditary idiosyncrasies in the Royal Family?" observed the duchess, inquiringly. "Indeed," added her grace, hastily, "I well remember that you alluded to the unfortunate attachment of George the Third for a certain Quakeress——"

"Yes—Hannah Lightfoot, to whom the monarch, when a prince, was privately united," answered the countess. "His baffled love—the necessity which compelled him to renounce one to whom he was devotedly attached—and the constant dread which he entertained lest the secret of this marriage should transpire, acted upon his mind in a manner that subsequently produced those dread results which are matters of history."

"You allude to his madness," said the duchess, with a shudder.

"Yes, your grace—that madness which is, alas! hereditary," replied the countess solemnly. "But George the Third had many—many domestic afflictions. Oh! if you knew all, you would not be surprised that he had lost his reason! The profligacy of some of his children—most of them—was alone sufficient to turn his brain. Many of those instances of profligacy have transpired; and although the public have not been able to arrive at any positive proofs respecting the matters, I can nevertheless assure your grace that such proofs *are* in existence—and in my possession!"

"Your ladyship once before hinted as much to me; and I must confess that without having any morbid inclination for vulgar scandal, I feel some curiosity in respect to those matters."

"Some day I will place in your hand papers of a fearful import, in connexion with the Royal Family," returned the countess. "Your grace will then perceive that profligacy the most abandoned—crimes the most heinous—vices the most depraved, characterised nearly all the children of George the Third. There is one remarkable fact relative to that prince's marriage with Hannah Lightfoot. The Royal Marriage Act was not passed until *thirteen years after this union*, and could not therefore set it aside; and yet *Hannah Lightfoot was still living when the prince espoused Charlotte Sophia Princess of Mecklenburgh Strelitz in 1761.*"

"Is this possible?" exclaimed the duchess, profoundly surprised.

"It is possible—it is true!" said the countess emphatically. "In 1772 the Royal Marriage Act[25] was passed, and provided that no member of the Royal Family should contract a marriage without the sovereign's consent. This measure was enacted for several reasons; but principally because the King's two brothers had formed private matrimonial connexions,—the Duke of Cumberland with Mrs. Horton, a widow—and the Duke of Gloucester with the widow of the Earl of Waldegrave."

"The act certainly appears to me most cruel and oppressive," said the duchess; "inasmuch as it interferes with the tenderest affections and most charming of human sympathies—feelings which royalty has in common with all the rest of mankind."

"I cordially agree with your grace," observed the countess. "The law is barbarous—monstrous—revolting; and its evil effects were evidenced by almost every member of the family of George the Third. In the first place, the Prince of Wales (afterwards George the Fourth) was privately united to Mrs. Fitzherbert, at the house of that lady's uncle, Lord Sefton. Fox, Sheridan, and Burke were present at the ceremony, in addition to my mother and several relations of the bride. Mr. Fox handed her into the carriage; and the happy pair proceeded to Richmond, where they passed a week or ten days. Queen Charlotte was made acquainted with the marriage: she sent for her son, and demanded an explanation. The prince avowed the truth. Your grace has, of course, read the discussion which took place in connexion with this subject, in the House of Commons, in 1787. Mr. Rolle, the member for Devonshire, mysteriously alluded to the union: Mr. Fox rose up, and denied it; but from that day forth Mrs. Fitzherbert never spoke to Fox again. Sheridan let the truth escape him:—he said, '*A lady who has been alluded to, is without reproach, and is entitled to the truest and most general respect.*' How would Mrs. Fitzherbert have been without reproach, or entitled to respect, if she were *not* married to the prince? But I have proofs—convincing proofs—that such an union did actually take place, although it was certainly null and void in consequence of the Marriage Act."

"It nevertheless subsisted according to the feelings and inclinations of the parties interested," said the duchess; "and it was based on *honour*, if on no legal principle."

"Alas!" whispered the countess, casting a rapid glance around; "the word *honour* must not be mentioned in connexion with the name of George the Fourth. It pains me to speak ill of the ancestors of our lovely queen: but—if we converse on the subject at all—truth must influence our observations. The entire life of George the Fourth was one of profligacy and crime. Often have I marvelled how one possessing a soul so refined as

Georgiana, the beautiful Duchess of Devonshire, could have resigned herself to such a degraded voluptuary—such a low debauchee. Yet she was his Queen of Love, surrounded by her graces, who, however, bore the modern names of Craven, Windham, and Jersey."

"Carlton House has, indeed, beheld strange and varied scenes," said the duchess; "low orgies and voluptuous revels—music floating here—dice rattling there—the refinements of existence in one room, and the most degraded dissipation in another."

"Such was the case," observed the countess. "But let us return to the consequences of the Royal Marriage Act. Rumour has told much in connexion with the coupled names of the Duke of York and Mrs. Clarke—the late King William and Mrs. Jordan; and so well known are these facts that I need not dwell upon them. The matrimonial connexions of the Duke of Sussex—first with Lady Augusta Murray, and afterwards with Lady Cecilia Underwood,[26] are all matters resting upon something more solid than mere conjecture."

"And the Duke of Cumberland—the present King of Hanover?" said the duchess inquiringly.

"It is dangerous to speak of *him*," whispered the countess; "because it is impossible to utter a word in his favour."

"You surely cannot believe all the tales that have been circulated against him?" exclaimed the duchess, earnestly watching the countenance of her companion, as if to anticipate her reply.

"Does your grace particularly allude to the death of Sellis?" asked the countess, turning her head so as to meet the glance of her friend. "Because," continued she, without waiting for a reply, "I should be sorry—nay, nothing should induce me—to state in plain terms my impression relative to that event. I may, however, allude to a few material points. Sir Everard Home, the medical attendant of the Duke of Cumberland, frequently observed, '*that too much pains were taken to involve that affair in mystery;*' and another eminent physician, since dead, declared that '*the head of Sellis was nearly severed from his body, and that no man could inflict upon himself a wound of such a depth.*' The Duke of Cumberland stated that his valet, Sellis, entered his bed-chamber and attacked him with a sword; and that having failed in his murderous purposes, he retired to his own room and committed suicide. Sir Everard Home distinctly proved, on the inquest, that the corpse was found lying on its *side* on the bed; and yet '*he had cut his own throat so effectually that he could not have changed his position after inflicting the wound.*' I will not, however, make any observations upon *that* fact and *this* statement which seem so conflicting: the subject is almost too awful to deal with. There is still one remarkable point to which the attention of those who discuss the dark affair should be directed:—the hand-basin in Sellis's room was half full of blood-stained water, and it is very clear that the miserable wretch himself could not have risen to wash his hands *after* the wound was inflicted in his throat. But let us not dwell on this horrible event: the mere mention of it makes me shudder."

"The King of Hanover has been, at least, unfortunate in many circumstances of his life, if not guilty," observed the duchess; "because his enemies have insisted strongly upon the suspicious nature of the incident of which we have been speaking."

"The more so, because it was known that the Duke of Cumberland had intrigued with the wife of Sellis," returned the countess. "As your grace declares, that exalted personage has been indeed unfortunate—if nothing more. In 1830 Lord Graves committed suicide; and the improper connexion existing between the Duke of Cumberland and Lady Graves was notorious."

"I well remember," said the duchess, "that the conduct of the Duke and Lady Graves was far from prudent, to say the least of it, after that melancholy event. Scarcely were the remains of the self-slain nobleman cold in the tomb, ere his widow and her illustrious lover were seen driving about together in the neighbourhood of Hampton Court, where Lady Graves had apartments."

"True," exclaimed the duchess. "But we have travelled a long way from our first topic—the Royal Marriage Act. We were speaking of its pernicious effects in respect to the family of George the Third. And that was a fine family, too! My deceased mother often expatiated—and her secret papers dwell at length—upon the charms of the princesses. Alas! how sorrowfully were they situated! In the bloom of youth—in the glow of health—with warm temperaments and ardent imaginations, which received encouragement from the voluptuous indolence of their lives—they were denied the privileges of the meanest peasant girl in the realm:—they were unable to form matrimonial connexions where their inclinations prompted them. The consequences were those which might have been anticipated: the honour of the princesses became sacrificed to illicit passion—passion which was still natural, although illicit! Those amours were productive of issue; but the offspring of none has created any sensation in the world, save in the instance of Captain Garth, the son of the Princess Sophia. Relative to the mysterious birth of that individual, the secret papers left by my mother—and the existence of which is even unknown to my husband—contain some strange, some startling facts. Conceive the embarrassment—the perilous nature of the situation in which the princess was suddenly involved—when, during a journey from London to some fashionable watering-place, she found herself overtaken with the pangs of premature maternity—she, who up to that moment had managed to conceal her condition even from the attendants upon her person! Then imagine this princess—a daughter of the sovereign of the realm—compelled to put up at a miserable road-side inn—forced to make a confidant of her lady in attendance, and obliged also to entrust her secret to the surgeon of the village where her child was born! But you shall read the narrative, with all its details, in my private papers."

"What opinion has your ladyship formed relative to the circumstances which led to the Bill of Pains and Penalties instituted against Queen Caroline, the spouse of George the Fourth?" inquired the duchess.

"I firmly believe that most unfortunate and most persecuted princess to have been *completely innocent*," answered the countess, with solemn emphasis. "From the first she was hateful to her husband. When the Earl of Malmsbury, who was sent to Germany to escort the Princess to England, arrived with her in London, the Prince of Wales repaired instantly to pay his respects to his intended bride. But scarcely had he set eyes on her when he conceived a feeling of ineffable dislike; and, turning towards the Earl, he said, 'Harris,[27] a glass of brandy—I am ill!' Your grace has heard of love at first sight: here was hatred at first sight. Every thing attending that marriage was inauspicious: for if the Princess had the misfortune to make an unfavourable impression on the Prince, his Royal Highness wantonly wounded her feelings by grossly manifesting his dislike towards her on all occasions. On the bridal night he drank so deeply that he fell on a sofa in the nuptial chamber, and there slept with his clothes on. But to pass over many years, let us come to the circumstances which led to the memorable trial of Queen Caroline. During her continental travels, Baron Bergami was presented to her. He was a man of honourable character, good family, but ruined fortunes. His condition excited the compassion of the generous-hearted Caroline; and she gave him a situation in her household. His conversation was fascinating; and he was frequently her companion inside the travelling chariot. Perhaps an English lady would have acted with more prudence; but your grace will remember that there is a wide distinction between our manners and customs and those of the Continent. *We* see improprieties in actions which foreigners view as harmless courtesies or innocent proofs of friendly interest. *We* also seem ready to meet suspicions of evil half-way: foreigners, with more generous frankness and candour, say, '*Evil be to him who evil thinks.*' But the marriage was hateful to King George the Fourth; and he was determined to dissolve it. He was resolved to sacrifice his wife to his aversions. She was to be made a victim. Then commenced that atrocious subornation of perjured witnesses which gave a colour to the proceedings against the unfortunate Queen. Her slightest levities were tortured into proofs of guilt: her generosity towards Bergami was branded as an illicit passion. The witnesses made statements which proved how well they had been tutored: they over-acted their parts; and, in their zeal to serve a master who paid them for their perjury, they deposed to more than they could possibly have known, even if the main accusation had been true. The nation was indignant—for *the people*, your grace, are possessed of much chivalry and noble generosity of character. Then, too, rose the portentous voices of Denman and Brougham, calling upon the hidden accuser to come forth and confront his victim. Oh! it was a vile proceeding; and I, as a woman—as a wife, feel my blood boiling in my veins when I think of all the foul wrongs which were heaped upon the most injured of my sex!"

"That trial," said the duchess, who was naturally of a more cautious disposition than her companion,—"that trial was certainly a dark blot on the page which records the annals of George the Fourth's reign."

"Say rather, your grace," exclaimed the countess, "the blackest of the innumerable black deeds which characterised his existence. Before the accusation in respect to Bergami was ever thought of, a charge was concocted against that injured lady, and commissioners were appointed to investigate it. Thus, your grace perceives, her bad husband was determined to ruin her. That charge accused her of having been delivered of a male child at her abode at Blackheath; and the affair certainly appeared suspicious at first. But how triumphantly was it met? how readily was it refuted? how easily was it explained! The injured lady had taken a fancy to the infant of poor but respectable people named Archer, living in that neighbourhood; and she had undertaken to adopt and provide for the boy. The unfortunate Princess felt the necessity of loving something—since her own child was taken from her. Thus was her goodness towards William Archer converted into a weapon wherewithal to assail her in the most tender point. Her husband's agents circulated the most odious calumnies concerning her, and even improperly coupled her name with that of Sir Sydney Smith, the hero of Acre. But the Archer story fell to the ground; and the Bergami scandal was subsequently propagated with a zeal which evinced the determination of George the Fourth to ruin Caroline of Brunswick."[28]

There was a pause in the conversation.

The duchess, who was possessed of a strong inclination for the mysterious or scandalous narratives connected with the family of George the Third, was so impressed by the vehemence and confident emphasis with which her companion had denounced the profligacy of George the Fourth, that a species of awe—an undefined alarm came over her:—it suddenly appeared as if it were a sacrilege thus to canvass the character of that deceased monarch within the very palace where he himself had dwelt;—and she hesitated to make any remark or ask any question that might lead to a continuation of the same topic.

On her side, the countess—who was much older than the duchess, and more deeply initiated in the mysteries of Courts—had become plunged into a deep reverie; for she possessed a generous mind, and never could ponder upon the wrongs of the murdered Queen Caroline without experiencing the most profound indignation and sorrow.[29]

The reader may probably deem it somewhat extraordinary that ladies attached to the Court should thus freely discuss the most private affairs, and canvass the characters of deceased members of the Royal Family. But we can positively assert that nowhere are scandal and tittle-tattle more extensively indulged in, than amongst the members of that circle of courtiers and female sycophants who crowd about the sovereign.[30]

The conversation of the duchess and countess was not renewed on the present occasion; for while they were yet plunged each in the depths of her own particular meditations, the regal train entered the Ball Room.

And all this while Henry Holford remained concealed beneath the sofa!

Victoria leant upon the arm of her consort; and the illustrious party was preceded by the Lord Chamberlain and the Lord Steward. The Queen and the Prince proceeded to the reserved seats which were slightly elevated in a recess, and were covered with white satin embroidered in silver.

Then the magnificent Ball-Room presented a truly fairy spectacle. Plumes were waving, diamonds were sparkling, bright eyes were glancing, and music floated on the air. The spacious apartment was crowded with nobles and gentlemen in gorgeous uniforms or court-dresses; and with ladies in the most elegant attire that French fashions could suggest or French milliners achieve. All those striking or attractive figures, and all the splendours of their appearance, were multiplied by the brilliant mirrors to an illimitable extent.

The orchestra extended across one end of the Ball-Room; and the musicians had entered by a side-door almost at the same moment that the royal procession made its appearance.

In the rooms adjoining, the Corps of Gentlemen-at-arms and the Yeomen of the Guard were on duty; and in the hall the band of the Royal Regiment of Horse Guards was in attendance.

The Queen and the Prince danced in the first quadrille; and afterwards they indulged in their favourite waltz—the *Frohsinn mein Ziel*. At the termination of each dance the royal party passed into the Picture Gallery, where they promenaded amidst a wilderness of flowers and aromatic shrubs. Then indeed the odour-breathing exotics—the whispering leaves—the light of the pendent lamps, mellowed so as to give full effect to the portraits of those who were once famous or once beautiful—the ribboned or gartered nobles—the blaze of female loveliness—the streams of melody—the presence of all possible elements of splendour, harmony, and pleasure, combined to render the whole scene one of enchantment, and seemed to realize the most glowing and brilliant visions which oriental writers ever shadowed forth!

The dancing was renewed in the Ball-Room: and as the beauteous ladies of the court swam and turned in graceful mazes, it appeared as if the art had become elevated into the harmony of motion. Dancing there was something more than mechanical: it was a true, a worthy, and a legitimate sister of poetry and music.

At twelve o'clock the doors of the supper-room were thrown open; and in that gorgeous banqueting-hall the crimson draperies, the service of gold, and the massive table ornaments were lighted up by Chinese lanterns and silver candelabra of exquisite workmanship. A splendid row of gold cups was laid on each side of the table. On the right of each plate stood a decanter of water, a finger-glass half filled with tepid water, a champagne glass, a tumbler, and three wine-glasses. Numerous servants in magnificent liveries were in attendance. No one asked for any thing: the servants offered the various dishes, of which the guests partook or which they rejected according to their taste. No healths were drunk during the Queen's presence; nor was the ceremony of taking wine with each other observed—not even on the part of the gentleman with the lady whom he had handed into the room. The domestics whose especial duty it was to serve the wine, never filled a glass until it was quite empty; nor did any guest ask for wine, but, when the servant approached him, merely stated the kind of wine he chose.

After sitting for about an hour, the Queen rose, and was conducted to the Yellow Drawing-Room by Prince Albert, the guests all rising as the royal couple retired.

Then the servants filled the glasses, and the Lord Steward said, "The Queen!" The health was drunk standing, in silence, and with a gentle inclination of the head. In a few minutes afterwards the gentlemen conducted the ladies into the Yellow Drawing-Room, where coffee and liqueurs were served.

The harp, piano, and songs by some of the ladies, occupied another hour; at the expiration of which the guests took their departure.

Holford had now been concealed nearly five hours beneath the sofa in the ball-room; and he was cramped, stiff, and wearied. During that interval he had experienced a variety of emotions:—wonder at the strange revelations which he had heard from the lips of the countess,—ineffable delight in contemplating the person of his sovereign,—envy at the exalted prosperity of Prince Albert,—thrilling excitement at the fairy-like aspect of the enchanting dance,—sensations of unknown rapture occasioned by the soft strains of the music,—and boundless disgust for his own humble, obscure, and almost serf-like condition.

During those intervals when the royal party and the guests were promenading in the Picture-Gallery or were engaged in the supper-apartment and the drawing-room, Holford longed to escape from his hiding-place and retreat to the lumber-closet where he was in the habit of concealing himself on the occasion of his visits to the palace; but there were too many persons about to render such a step safe.

It was not, therefore, until a very late hour,—or rather an early one in the morning,—that he was able to enter the supper-room and help himself to some of the dainties left upon the board; having done which, he retreated to his nook in the most retired part of the palace.

---

25. This Act was denounced at the time as "one calculated only to encourage fornication and adultery in the descendants of George the Second."

26. Now Duchess of Inverness.

27. The family name of the Earl of Malmsbury.

28. We had the honour of enjoying the friendship of Sir Sydney Smith in Paris during the years 1834-7; and the misfortunes of Queen Caroline frequently became the topic of discourse between us. Sir Sydney Smith assured us on several occasions and in the most solemn manner, that the reports which had been circulated relative to himself and that injured lady, during her residence at Blackheath, were vile calumnies. "Queen Caroline had certainly much levity of manner, and was very thoughtless and inexperienced," he would observe; "but her

virtue was never for a moment suspected by me." The following passage occurs in a letter which Queen Caroline wrote to the Countess de C——, shortly before the commencement of the Trial, and which autograph letter (*together with numerous important papers concerning George the Third and his family*) is in our possession:—"This letter will be delivered to you by an individual who is persecuted because he has served me faithfully. I recommend him to your kindness. The Baron Bergami is of high birth. He has been unfortunate: I perceived the excellence of the qualities he possesses—I have ameliorated his condition in a pecuniary point of view—and thus have I secured him as my friend. The fury of my adversaries pursues him—I tremble for his very existence—my royal husband is *capable of any crime* to ensure the gratification of his revenge. I therefore crave your protection for Bergami, and hope that by your influence you will so arrange matters that he shall not be molested in Paris. I do not ask you to admit him into your society, unless agreeable to yourself; at the same time, my dear Countess, you must be aware that pride is folly. We must judge mankind by the scale of merit, and not by the grandeur of titles. This is the course I have adopted through life, and am well pleased with my line of conduct. Recollect this precept: you will perceive its wisdom when you grow old."

29. The last and fatal illness of Queen Caroline was caused by a stoppage in the bowels. Doctors Maton and Warren (the king's physicians) attended upon the illustrious lady; and various remedies were prescribed by them—but in vain. One morning, a bottle of *croton oil* was sent to an individual of Her Majesty's household, accompanied by the following letter:—

"SIR,—I am aware that nothing but the great—the very great—danger Her Majesty is in, would excuse this unauthorised intrusion. Having, however, learnt from the papers the nature of Her Majesty's complaint, I have taken the liberty to forward to you, with a view of having it handed to Dr. Maton or Dr. Warren, a medicine of strong aperient properties, called *croton oil*—one drop of which is a dose. It is most probably known to some of Her Majesty's advisers; but it has only been recently brought into this country. It may be proper to observe that Doctor Pemberton has *himself* taken it; and I have administered it to more than one person. Its operation is quick and certain. Two drops, when made into pills with bread, usually produce saving effects in half or three quarters of an hour. It has struck me that this medicine might be successfully administered to Her Majesty. At all events I can have done no harm in taking the liberty to suggest it; but, unwilling to appear anxious to make myself obtrusive, or to seem influenced by any other than the most disinterested motives, I have declined giving my name.

"Yours respectfully,

A CHEMIST."

This letter, and the medicine, were forwarded to Dr. Pemberton, of Great George Street, Hanover Square, who had at one time been Her Majesty's principal medical attendant. Dr. Pemberton's answer was this:—"I have myself taken *two* drops of the *croton oil*, on several occasions; and the Queen may safely take *one*." The royal physicians obtained an interview with George the Fourth, and the result was a declaration on their part, "*that they did not consider themselves justified in administering the medicine to Her Majesty.*" Comment is unnecessary.

30.

But, ah! while of Victoria's court I'm singing,
What solemn music echoes from the lyre!
And wherefore does a passing bell seem ringing,
And melancholy thoughts my soul inspire?

See where the raven now his flight is winging—

Hark to the anthem of the funeral choir—

List to the curfew's note of death-like gloom—

And drop a tear o'er Flora Hastings' tomb!

—*Sequel to Don Juan.*

CHAPTER CXCIV.

THE ROYAL BREAKFAST.

Holford did not immediately close his eyes in slumber.

Although his education had been miserably neglected, he possessed good natural abilities; and his reflections at times were of a far more philosophical nature than could have been anticipated.

The gorgeous scenes which he had just witnessed now led him to meditate upon the horrible contrasts which existed elsewhere, not only in the great metropolis, but throughout the United Kingdom,—and many, very many of which he himself had seen with his own eyes, and felt with his own experience.

At that moment when festivity was highest, and pleasure was most exciting in the regal halls, there were mothers in naked attics, dark cellars, or even houseless in the open streets,—mothers who pressed their famished little ones to their bosoms, and wondered whether a mouthful of food would ever pass their lips again.

While the royal table groaned beneath the weight of golden vessels and the choicest luxuries which earth's fruitfulness, heaven's bounty, or man's ingenuity could supply,—while the raciest produce of fertile vineyards sparkled in the crystal cups,—at that same period, how many thousands of that exalted lady's subjects moistened their sorry crust with tears wrung from them by the consciousness of ill-requited toil and the pinching gripe of bitter poverty!

Delicious music here, and the cries of starving children there;—silver candelabra pouring forth a flood of lustre in a gorgeous saloon, and a flickering rushlight making visible the naked and damp-stained walls of a wretched garret;—silks and satins, rags and nudity;—luxurious and pampered indolence; crushing and ill-paid labour;—homage and reverence, ill-treatment and oppression;—the gratification of every whim, the absence of every necessary;—not a care for to-morrow here, not a hope for to-morrow there;—a certainty of a renewal of this day's plenty, a total ignorance whence the next day's bread can come;—mirth and laughter, moans and sorrowing;—a palace for life on one hand, and an anxiety lest even the wretched hovel may not be changed for a workhouse to-morrow;—these are the appalling contrasts which our social sphere presents to view!

Of all this Holford thought as he lay concealed in the lumber-room of the royal dwelling.

But at length sleep overtook him.

It was still dark when he awoke. At first he thought that he must have slumbered for many hours—that a day had passed, and that another night had come;—but he felt too little refreshed to remain many instants in that opinion. Moreover, as he watched the window, he observed a faint, faint gleam of light—or rather a mitigation of the intenseness of the gloom without—slowly appearing; and he knew that the dawn was at hand.

He was nearly frozen in that cheerless room where he had slept: his teeth chattered—his limbs were benumbed. He longed for some new excitement to elevate his drooping spirits, and thus impart physical warmth to his frame.

Suddenly a thought struck him: he would penetrate into the royal breakfast-room! He knew that the Queen and Prince Albert frequently partook of the morning meal together; and he longed to listen to their conversation when thus *tête-a-tête*.

Scarcely had he conceived this project when he resolved to execute it. The interior of the palace—even to its most private apartments and chambers—was as we have before stated, perfectly familiar to him. Stealing from the place where he had slept, he proceeded with marvellous caution to the point of his present destination; and in about ten minutes he reached the breakfast-room in safety.

The twilight of morning had now penetrated through the windows of this apartment; for the heavy curtains were drawn aside, a cheerful fire burnt in the grate, and the table was already spread.

A friendly sofa became Holford's hiding-place.

Shortly after eight o'clock a domestic entered with the morning Ministerial paper, which he laid upon the table, and then withdrew.

Five minutes elapsed, when the door was thrown open, and the Queen entered, attended by two ladies. These were almost immediately dismissed; and Victoria seated herself near the fire, to read the journal. But scarcely had she opened it, ere Prince Albert made his appearance, followed by a gentleman in waiting, who humbly saluted her Majesty and retired.

Servants immediately afterwards entered, and placed upon the table the materials for a sumptuous breakfast, having performed which duty they immediately left the room.

The Queen and her consort were now alone—or at least, supposed themselves to be so; and their conversation soon flowed without restraint.

But such an empire—such a despotism does the habitual etiquette of Courts establish over the natural freedom of the human mind, that even the best and most tender feelings of the heart are to a certain extent subdued and oppressed by that chilling influence. The royal pair were affectionate to each other: still their tenderness was not of that lively, unembarrassed, free, and cordial nature which subsists at the domestic hearth elsewhere. There seemed to be a barrier between the frank and open interchange of their thoughts; and even though that barrier were no thicker than gauze, still it existed. Their words were to some degree measured—scarcely perceptibly so, it is true—nevertheless, the fact *was* apparent in the least, least degree; and the effect was also in the least, least degree unpleasant.

The Queen was authoritative in the enunciation of her opinion upon any subject; and if the Prince differed from her, he expressed himself with restraint. In fact, he did not feel himself his wife's equal. Could a listener, who did not see them as they spoke, have deadened his ear to those intonations of their voices which marked their respective sex, and have judged only by their words, he would have thought that the Queen was the *husband*, and the Prince the *wife*.

The Prince appeared to be very amiable, very intelligent; but totally inexperienced in the ways of the world. The Queen exhibited much natural ability and an elegant taste: nevertheless, she also seemed lamentably ignorant of the every-day incidents of life. We mean that the royal pair manifested a reluctance to believe in those melancholy occurrences which characterize the condition of the industrious millions. This was not the result of indifference, but of sheer ignorance. Indeed, it would necessarily seem difficult for those who were so surrounded by every luxury, to conceive that such a fearful contrast as literal starvation could possibly exist.

But let us hear that illustrious pair converse: their language will to some extent serve as an index to their minds.

"Melbourne informed me last evening," said the Queen, "that he trembles for the safety of his Cabinet during the approaching session. The Carlton Club is particularly active; and the Conservative party has acquired great strength during the recess."

"What would be the consequence of a Ministerial defeat?" inquired Prince Albert.

"A dissolution, of course," answered the Queen. "I must candidly confess that I should regret to see the Conservative party succeed to power. All the principal lords and ladies of our household would be immediately changed. The Whigs, however, have certainly grown unpopular; and there appears to be some distress in the country. The very first article on which my eyes rested when I took up this newspaper ere now, is headed '*Dreadful Suicide through Extreme Destitution.*' Beneath, in the same column, is an article entitled '*Infanticide, and Suicide of the Murderess, through Literal Starvation.*' The next column contains a long narrative which I have not had time to read, but which is headed '*Suicide through Dread of the Workhouse.*' On this page," continued the Queen, turning the paper upon the table, "there is an article entitled '*Death from Starvation;*' another headed '*Dreadful Condition of the Spitalfields' Weavers;*' a third called '*Starving State of the Paisley Mechanics;*' a fourth entitled '*Awful Distress in the Manufacturing Districts;*' and I perceive numerous short paragraphs all announcing similar calamities."

"The English papers are always full of such accounts," observed the Prince.

"And yet I would have you know that England is the richest, most prosperous, and happiest country on the face of the earth," returned the Queen, somewhat impatiently. "You must not take these accounts literally as you read them. My Ministers assure me that they are greatly exaggerated. It appears—as the matter has been explained to me—that the persons who furnish these narratives are remunerated according to quantity; and they therefore amplify the details as much as possible."

"Still those accounts must be, to a certain extent, based on truth?" said Prince Albert, half inquiringly.

"Not nearly so much as you imagine. My Ministers have satisfied me on that head; and they must know better than you. Take, for instance, the article headed '*Dreadful Condition of the Spitalfields' Weavers*.' You may there read that the weavers are in an actual state of starvation. This is only newspaper metaphor: the writer means his readers to understand that the weavers are not so well off as they would wish to be. Perhaps they have not meat every day—perhaps only three or four times a week: but they assuredly have plenty of bread and potatoes—because bread and potatoes are so cheap!"

"I thought that you intended to discountenance the importation of foreign silks, by ordering all the ladies of the Court to wear dresses of English material?" observed Prince Albert, after a pause.

"Such was my intention," answered the Queen; "but the ladies about me dropped so many hints on the subject, that I was compelled to rescind the command. I must confess that I was not sorry to find an excuse for so doing; for I greatly prefer French silks and French dressmakers. But let me make an observation upon this article which is headed '*Suicide through Dread of the Workhouse*.' I spoke to the Secretary of State a few days ago upon the subject of workhouses; and he assured me that they are very comfortable places. He declared that the people do not know when they are well off, and that they require to be managed like refractory children. He quite convinced me that all he said was perfectly correct; and I really begin to think that the people are very obstinate, dissatisfied, and insolent."

"They are most enthusiastic in their demonstrations towards their sovereign," remarked the Prince.

"And naturally so," exclaimed Victoria. "Am I not their Queen? are they not my subjects? do I not rule over them? All the happiness, prosperity, and enjoyments which they possess emanate from the throne. They would be very ungrateful if they did not reverence—nay, adore their sovereign."

"Oh, of course!" said Prince Albert. "In Germany, any individual who exhibits the least coldness towards his sovereign is immediately marked as a traitor."

"And in this country the Home Secretary keeps a list of disaffected persons," observed the Queen; "but, thank God! their number is very limited—at least, so I am assured. My Ministers are constantly informing me of the proofs of loyalty and devotion which the people manifest towards me. If this were a Roman Catholic nation, they would no doubt place my image next to the Virgin in their chapels; and if it were an idolatrous country, my effigy would assuredly stand amongst the gods and goddesses. It is very pleasant, Albert, to be so much loved by my subjects—to be positively worshipped by them."

The Prince replied with a compliment which it is not worth while to record.

The Queen smiled, and continued:—

"You remember the paragraph which the Secretary of State pointed out a few days ago: it was in the *Morning Post*, if you recollect. That journal—which, by the bye, circulates entirely amongst the upper servants of the aristocracy, and nowhere else—declared '*that so great is the devotion of my loyal, subjects that, were such a sacrifice necessary, they would joyfully throw themselves beneath the wheels of my state-carriage, even as the Indians cast themselves under the car of Juggernaut.*'[31] I never in my life saw but that one number of the *Post*: its circulation, I am told, is confined entirely to the servants of the aristocracy; still it seems in that instance to express the sentiments of the entire nation. You smile, Albert?"

"I was only thinking whether the paragraph to which you have alluded, was another specimen of newspaper metaphor," answered the Prince, with some degree of hesitation.

"Not at all," returned the Queen, quickly; "the Editor wrote precisely as he thought. He must know the real sentiments of the people, since he is a man of the people himself. I have been assured that he was once the head-butler in a nobleman's family: hence his success in conducting a daily newspaper exclusively devoted to the interests and capacities of upper-servants."

"I thought that English Editors were generally a better class of men?" observed the Prince.

"So they are for the most part," replied the Queen: "graduates at the Universities—barristers—and highly accomplished gentlemen. But in the case of the *Morning Post* there seems to be an exception. We were, however, conversing upon the distress in the country—for there certainly is some little distress here and there; although the idea of people actually dying of starvation in a Christian land is of course absurd. I am really bewildered, at times, with the reasons of, and the remedies proposed for, that distress. If I ask the Home Secretary, he declares that the people are too obstinate to understand what comfortable places the workhouses are;—if I ask the Colonial Secretary, he assures me that the people are most wilfully blind to the blessings of emigration: if I ask the Foreign Secretary, he labours to convince me that the distracted state of the East reacts upon this country; and if I ask the Bishop of London he expresses his conviction that the people require more churches."

"For my part, I do not like to interfere in these matters," said the Prince; "and therefore I never ask any questions concerning them."

"And you act rightly, Albert, for you certainly know nothing of English politics. I observe by the newspapers that the country praises your forbearance in this respect. You are a Field-Marshal, and Chief Judge of the Stannaries Court—and———"

"And a Knight of the Garter," added the Prince.

"Yes—and a Learned Doctor of Laws," continued the Queen: "any thing else?"

"Several things—but I really forget them all now," returned the Prince.

"Never mind," exclaimed the Queen. "I intend to obtain for you higher distinctions yet. I do not like the mere title of *Prince*, and the style of *Royal Highness*: you shall be *King-Consort* and *Your Majesty*. Then, when a vacancy occurs, you must be appointed Commander-in-Chief."

"I feel deeply grateful for your kind intentions," returned the Prince, with a smile; "but you are well aware that I am totally ignorant of every thing connected with the army."

"That is of no consequence in England," replied the Queen. "You will have subordinates to do your duty. I must speak to Melbourne about all this. And now, as I intend to take these steps in your behalf, pray be a little more cautious relative to your private amusements; and let me hear of no more burying of dogs with funeral honours. That little affair of the interment of *Eos* at Windsor has attracted the notice of the press, I understand. It was indiscreet."

"If I adapt my conduct entirely according to the English notions," returned the Prince, "I should be compelled to give up those *battues* to which I am so devotedly attached."

"We must consult Melbourne on that head," observed the Queen.

The royal pair then conversed upon a variety of topics which would afford little interest to the reader; and shortly after nine her Majesty withdrew.

Prince Albert remained in the room to read the newspaper.

Henry Holford had listened with almost breathless attention to the conversation which we have recorded.

The Prince had drawn his chair more closely to the fire, after the Queen left the room; and he was now sitting within a couple of yards of the sofa beneath which Holford lay concealed.

The pot-boy gently drew aside the drapery which hung from the framework of the sofa to the floor, and gazed long and intently on the Prince. His look was one in which envy, animosity, and admiration were strangely blended. He thought within himself, "Why are you so exalted, and I so abased? And yet your graceful person—

your intelligent countenance—your handsome features, seem to fit you for such an elevated position. Nevertheless, if I had had your advantages of education———"

The meditations of the presumptuous youth were suddenly and most disagreeably checked:—the Prince abruptly threw aside the paper, and his eyes fell on the human countenance that was gazing up at him from beneath the sofa.

His Royal Highness uttered an exclamation of surprise—not altogether unmingled with alarm; and his first impulse was to stretch out his hand towards the bell-rope. But, yielding to a second thought, he advanced to the sofa, exclaiming, "Come forth—whoever you may be."

Then the miserable pot-boy dragged himself from his hiding-place, and in another moment stood, pale and trembling, in the presence of the Prince.

"Who are you?" demanded his Royal Highness in a stern tone: "what means this intrusion? how came you hither?"

Henry Holford fell at the feet of the Prince, and confessed that, urged by an invincible curiosity, he had entered the palace on the preceding evening; but he said nothing of his previous visits.

For a few moments Prince Albert seemed uncertain how to act: he was doubtless hesitating between the alternatives of handing the intruder over to the officers of justice, or of allowing him to depart unmolested.

After a pause, he questioned Holford more closely, and seemed satisfied by the youth's assurance that he had really entered the palace through motives of curiosity, and not for any dishonest purpose.

The Prince accordingly determined to be merciful.

"I am willing," he said, "to forgive the present offence; you shall be suffered to depart. But I warn you that a repetition of the act will lead to a severe punishment. Follow me."

The Prince led the way to an ante-room where a domestic was in waiting.

"Conduct this lad as privately as you can from the palace," said his Royal Highness. "Ask him no questions—and mention not the incident elsewhere."

The Prince withdrew; and the lacquey led Henry Holford through various turnings in the palace to the servants' door opening into Pimlico.

Thus was the pot-boy ignominiously expelled from the palace; and never—never in his life had he felt more thoroughly degraded—more profoundly abased—more contemptible in his own eyes, than on the present occasion!

---

31. Such a disgustingly fulsome, and really atrocious paragraph did actually appear in the *Morning Post* three or four years ago.

CHAPTER CXCV.

THE ARISTOCRATIC VILLAIN AND THE LOW MISCREANT.

On the northern side of the Thames there is no continuously direct way along the bank for any great distance: to walk, for instance, from London Bridge to Vauxhall Bridge, one would be compelled to take many turnings, and deviate materially from the course shaped by the sinuosity of the stream. But on the southern side of the Thames, one may walk from the foot of London Bridge to that of Vauxhall, without scarcely losing sight of the river.

In this latter instance, the way would lie along Clink Street, Bankside, and Holland Street, to reach Blackfriars Bridge; the Commercial Road to Waterloo Bridge; the Belvidere Road, and Pedlar's Acre, to Westminster Bridge; and Stangate, the Bishop's Walk, and Fore Street, to reach Vauxhall Bridge.

This journey would not occupy nearly so much time as might be supposed ere a second thought was devoted to the subject; and yet how large a section of the diameter of London would have been traversed!

A portion of the path just detailed is denominated Pedlar's Acre; and it lies between Westminster and Hungerford Bridges. Adjoining the thoroughfare itself is an acre of ground, which is the property of the parish, and is let as a timber-yard. Tradition declares that it was given by a pedlar to the parish, on condition that the picture of himself and his dog be preserved, in stained glass, in one of the windows of Lambeth church; and in support of this legend, such a representation may indeed be seen in the south-east window of the middle aisle of the church just mentioned. Nevertheless, one of those antiquaries whose sesquipedalian researches are undertaken with a view to elucidate matters of this kind,—a valueless labour,—has declared that the land was bequeathed to the parish, in the year 1504, by some person totally unknown. Be the origin of the grant and the name of the donor as they may, there *is* such a place as Pedlar's Acre; and it is to a public-house in this thoroughfare that we must now request our readers to accompany us.

Seated in a private room on the first floor was a gentlemanly-looking man, of about six-and-thirty years of age. His face was decidedly handsome; but it had a downcast and sinister expression little calculated to prepossess a stranger in this person's favour. There was also a peculiar curl—more wicked than haughty—about his lip, that seemed to speak of strongly concentrated passions: the deep tones of his voice, the peculiar glance of his large grey eyes, and the occasional contraction of his brow denoted a mind resolute in carrying out any purpose it might have formed.

He was dressed with some degree of slovenliness; as if he had not leisure to waste upon the frivolity of self-adornment, or as if his means were not sufficient to permit that elegance of wardrobe which could alone stimulate his pride in the embellishment of his person.

A glass of steaming punch stood untouched near him.

It was six o'clock in the evening; and he was evidently waiting for some one.

His patience was not, however, put to a very severe test; for scarcely had five minutes elapsed after his arrival, when the door opened, and the Resurrection Man entered the room.

"Good evening, Mr. Vernon," he said, as he carefully closed the door behind him: then, taking a seat, he observed, "I hope I have not kept you waiting."

"Oh! never mind that," exclaimed Vernon, impatiently. "Have you any good news to communicate?"

"I am sorry to say that I have not. I called this morning upon the clerk of the parish church where your brother was married, and tried him in all ways."

"And he refused?" said Vernon, with an angry tone.

"He refused," answered Tidkins. "He is timid and old; and, after having first entertained the subject, at length backed out of it altogether."

"Because you did not offer him enough," cried Vernon, savagely: "because you did not show him gold! You are only lukewarm in this affair: you are afraid to risk a few miserable pounds in the business. This is not the way to conduct a grand project of such a nature. It is true that I am fearfully embarrassed for funds at this moment; but if you had acted with liberality—if we eventually succeeded—you *must* be well aware that my generosity would know no bounds."

"Mr. Vernon," said the Resurrection Man, coolly, "if you have nothing better than reproaches to offer as the reward of my exertions in your behalf, we should do well to separate at once. I was *not* niggard in my offers to the clerk: I spread fifty golden sovereigns before him—told him to take them, and promised as much more when he had done the job. But he hesitated—reflected—and at length positively refused altogether."

"And you really believe there is no hope in that quarter?" said Vernon, anxiously.

"None. If the old clerk would ever agree to serve us, he would have consented this morning. I know the man now: he is too timid to suit our purposes. But let us look calmly at the whole business, and devise another mode of proceeding," added the Resurrection Man. "You are still determined, by some means or other, to get possession of the estates of your elder brother?"

"My resolution is even increased by every fresh obstacle," replied Vernon. "I have two powerful objects to accomplish—revenge and ambition. Lord Ravensworth has treated me with a cruelty and a contempt that would goad the most meek and patient to study the means of vengeance. Our late father always intended the ready money, of which he *could* dispose, to come to me, because the estates were entailed upon my brother. But my father died suddenly, and intestate; and my brother, although he well knew our parent's intentions, grasped all—gave me nothing! No—I am wrong," added Vernon, with exceeding bitterness of tone and manner; "he agreed to allow me five hundred pounds a-year, as a recompense for the loss of as many thousands!"

"And you accepted the offer?" said the Resurrection Man.

"I accepted it as a beggar receives alms sooner than starve," continued Vernon: "I accepted it because I had nothing: I had not the means of existence. But I accepted it also as an instalment of my just due—and not as a concession on the part of his bounty. My habits are naturally extravagant: my expenses are great—I cannot check myself in that respect. Thus am I perpetually obtaining advances from my brother's agent; and now I have not another shilling to receive until next January."

"Nearly a year!" exclaimed the Resurrection Man. "But if you was to call on the agent——"

"Absurd!" ejaculated Vernon. "Have I not told you that my brother believes me still to be in the East—still travelling in Turkey? So long as he supposes me far away, I can carry on my projects in London with far greater security. In a word, it is much safer that my presence in this country should remain a profound secret. He will die shortly—he *must* die—he is daily, steadily parting with vitality. He is passing out of existence by a sure, a speedy, and yet an inexplicable progression of decay. Of *his* death, then, I am sure; and when it shall occur, how can suspicion attach itself to me—since I am supposed to be abroad—far away?"

"You are certain that your brother is hastening towards the grave?" said the Resurrection Man. "The great obstacle—the greatest, I mean—will be thereby removed. Suppose that Lady Ravensworth should be delivered of a boy, would it not be equally easy——"

"Yes—it would be easy to put it out of the way by *violence*," was the rapid reply; "but, then, I should risk my neck at the same time that I gained a fortune. No—that will not do! I could not incur a danger of so awful a nature. The infant heir to vast estates would be jealously protected—attentively watched—surrounded by all wise precautions:—no—it were madness to think of practising aught against its life."

"Could not the same means by which—even though at a distance—you are undermining the life of your brother——"

"No—no," replied Vernon, impatiently. "It is not necessary that I should explain to you the precise nature of the means by which I succeed in effecting Lord Ravensworth's physical decay; suffice it to state that those means could not be applied to a child."

"Nevertheless," continued the Resurrection Man, "you must have an agent at Ravensworth Park; for if—as I suppose—your brother is dying by means of slow poison, there is some confidential creature of your own about his person to administer the drugs."

"I have no agent at Ravensworth;—I have no confidential creature about my brother's person;—and I have so combined my measures that Lord Ravensworth *is actually committing suicide—dying by his own hand*! Another time I will expound all this to you; for to *you* alone have I communicated my projects."

"Have you not explained yourself to Greenwood?" demanded the Resurrection Man. "I thought you told me, the last time we met, that he knew you well—and knew also that you are in England?"

"I was acquainted with him some four or five years ago, when he was not so prosperous as he is—or as he appears to be—at present," replied Vernon; "but having been abroad since that time until my return last week, I had lost sight of him—and had even forgotten him. It was not a little provoking to run against him the very first day of my arrival in London; and, though I endeavoured to avoid him, he persisted in speaking to me."

"You are not afraid that he will gossip about your presence in London?" said the Resurrection Man.

"He promised me most faithfully to keep the fact a profound secret," returned Vernon.

"And will he not advance you a small sum for your present purposes?" demanded Tidkins.

"I called on him last evening, in consequence of the suggestion contained in your note;—I requested a loan for a particular purpose;—but he refused to oblige me," added Vernon, his brow contracting. "I wish that I had not so far humbled myself by asking him."

"No matter for that," said Tidkins: "we are wandering from our subject. Here is the substance of the whole affair:—Lord Ravensworth will soon be gathered to his fathers, as they say: but in the meantime Lady Ravensworth may have a child. If it is a daughter, you are all safe; if it is a son you are all wrong. I don't know how it is—I'm not superstitious—but in these matters, where a good fellow like yourself is within reach of a fortune, and whether you are to get it or not depends on the sex of an expected infant,—in such cases, I say, the card generally does turn up wrong. Now if the child should be a boy, what will you do?"

"I cannot consent to abandon the plan of bribing the clerk to destroy the leaf in the register," answered Vernon.

"Pshaw! the project is bad—I told you so all along. See how the matter would stand," continued Tidkins:—"Lord Ravensworth dies and leaves, we will suppose, an infant heir—a son. Then you suddenly make your appearance, and demand proofs of your brother's marriage. The register is searched—a leaf is missing—it is the one which contains the record of the union celebrated between Lord Ravensworth and Miss Adeline Enfield! Would not this seem very extraordinary? would it not create suspicions that Lord Ravensworth may not have died fairly? No—your project, Mr. Vernon, will never do: It is baseless—shallow—childish. It is unworthy of you. If you persist in it, I shall wash my hands of the business:—if you will follow my advice, you shall be Lord Ravensworth before you are a year older."

Vernon could not conceal a sentiment of admiration for that man who thus dexterously reasoned on his plans, and thus boldly promised that consummation to which he so fondly aspired.

"Speak, Mr. Tidkins," he said; "we have met to consult on the necessary course to be adopted."

"Let us come, then, boldly to the point," continued the Resurrection Man, sinking his voice to a whisper: "rest patiently for the confinement of Lady Ravensworth, which, you have learnt, is expected to take place in six weeks;—if the issue is a girl, you need trouble yourself no more in the business, but calmly wait till death does its work with Lord Ravensworth."

"And if the issue be a boy?" said Vernon, gazing fixedly on his companion's countenance.

"It must be put out of the way," answered the Resurrection Man, in a low, but stern tone; "and you may trust to me that the business shall be done in such a manner as to endanger no one's neck."

"You think—you imagine that it can be done——" said Vernon, hesitatingly—but still with that kind of hesitation which is prepared to yield and to consent.

"I do not speak upon thoughts and imaginings," replied Tidkins: "I argue on conviction. Leave the whole affair to me. I have my plan already settled—and, when the time comes, we will talk more about it. For the present," continued the Resurrection Man, drawing a bill-stamp from his pocket, and handing it to his companion, "have the goodness to write the name of *Ravensworth* at the bottom of this blank. I shall not use it until you are really Lord Ravensworth, when the signature will be your proper one."

Vernon cast a hasty glance over the bill, and observed, "It is a five-and-twenty shilling stamp."

"Yes—to cover three thousand pounds," returned the Resurrection Man. "That will not be too much for making you a peer and a rich man. Besides, I intend to advance you a matter of fifty pounds at once, for your immediate necessities."

"And if I should happen to fail in obtaining the title and estates of Ravensworth," said Vernon, "this document would enable you to immure me in a debtor's prison."

"Ridiculous!" ejaculated Tidkins, impatiently. "In that case your name would not be *Ravensworth*; and it is the name of *Ravensworth* which I require to this bill. As for throwing your person into a prison, what good could that do me? A dead carcass is of more value than a living one," he added, in a muttering tone.

Vernon did not overhear this remark—or, if he did, he comprehended not the allusion; but he signed the bill without farther hesitation.

The Resurrection Man consigned it to his pocket-book, and then drew forth a purse filled with gold, which he handed to his companion.

Vernon received it with a stiff and haughty inclination of the head:—his necessities compelled him to accept the succour; but his naturally proud feelings made him shrink from its source.

Having so far arranged the matters which they had met to discuss, the aristocratic villain and the low miscreant separated.

Vernon returned to his lodging in Stamford Street; and the Resurrection Man proceeded into the Westminster Road, where he took a cab, saying to the driver, "Golden Lane, Saint Luke's."

CHAPTER CXCVI.

THE OLD HAG AND THE RESURRECTION MAN.

The Old Hag, who has so frequently figured in former portions of our narrative, had latterly become more prosperous, if not more respectable, than when we first introduced her to our readers.

From having been the occupant of only one room in the house in the court leading from Golden Lane, she had become the lessee of the entire dwelling. The commencement of this success was owing to her connexion with Lady Cecilia Harborough in the intrigue of the "living statue;" and from that moment affairs seemed to have taken a new turn with her. At all events her "business" increased; and the sphere of her infamy became enlarged.

She would have taken another and better house, in some fashionable quarter, and re-commenced the avocation of a first-rate brothel-keeper—the pursuit of the middle period of her life;—but she reasoned that she was known to a select few where she was—that the obscurity of her dwelling was favourable to many of the nefarious projects in which her aid was required—and that she was too old to dream of forming a new connexion elsewhere.

It would be impossible to conceive a soul more diabolically hardened, more inveterately depraved, than that of this old hag.

In order to increase her resources, and occupy, as she said, "her leisure time," she had hired or bought some half-dozen young girls, about ten or twelve years old;—hired or bought them, whichever the reader pleases, of their parents, a "consideration" having been given for each, and the said parents comforting themselves with the idea that their children were well provided for!

These children of tender age were duly initiated by the old hag in all the arts and pursuits of prostitution. They were sent in pairs to parade Aldersgate Street, Fleet Street, and Cheapside; and their special instructions were to practise their allurements upon elderly men, whose tastes might be deemed more vitiated and eccentric than those of the younger loungers of the great thoroughfares where prostitution most thrives.

A favourite scheme of the old woman's was this:—One of her juvenile emissaries succeeded, we will suppose, in alluring to the den in Golden Lane an elderly man whose outward respectability denoted a well-filled purse, and ought to have been associated with better morals. When the wickedness was consummated, and the elderly gentleman was about to depart, the old hag would meet him and the young girl on the stairs, and, affecting to treat the latter as a stranger who had merely used her house as a common place of such resort, would seem stupefied at the idea "*of so youthful a creature having been brought to her abode for such a purpose.*" She would then question the girl concerning her age; and the reply would be "*under twelve*" of course. Thus the elderly voluptuary would suddenly find himself liable to punishment for a misdemeanour, for intriguing with a girl beneath the age of twelve; and the virtuous indignation of the old hag would be vented in assertions that though she kept a house of accommodation for grown-up persons, she abhorred the encouragement of juvenile profligacy. The result would be that the hoary old sinner found himself compelled to pay a considerable sum as hush-money.

We might occupy many pages with the details of the tricks and artifices which the old hag taught these young girls. And of a surety, they were subjects sufficiently plastic to enable her to model them to all her infamous purposes. Born of parents who never took the trouble to inculcate a single moral lesson, even if they knew any, those poor creatures had actually remained ignorant of the meaning of right and wrong until they were old enough to take an interest in the events that were passing around them. Then, when they missed some lad of their acquaintance, and, on inquiry, learnt that he had been sent to prison for taking something which did not belong to him, they began to understand that it was *dangerous* to do such an act—but it did not strike them that it was *wrong*. Again, if by accident they heard that another boy whom they knew, had got a good place, was very industrious, and in a fair way to prosper, they would perceive some *utility* in such conduct, but would still remain unable to appreciate its *rectitude*.

Most of the girls whom the old hag had enlisted in her service, had been born and reared in that dirty warren which constitutes Golden Lane, Upper Whitecross Street, Playhouse Yard, Swan Street, and all their innumerable courts, alleys, and obscure nooks, swarming with a ragged and degraded population. Sometimes in their infancy they creeped out from their loathsome burrows, and even ventured into Old Street, Barbican, or Beech Street. But those excursions were not frequent. During their childhood they rolled half-naked in the gutters,—eating the turnip-parings and cabbage-stalks which were tossed out into the street with other offal,—poking about in the kennels to find lost halfpence,—or even plundering the cat's-meat-man and the tripe-shop for the means of satisfying their hunger! This mode of life was but little varied;—unless, indeed, it were by the more agreeable recreations of particular days in the year. Thus, for instance, November was welcomed as the time for making a Guy-Fawkes, and carrying it round in procession amidst the pestilential mazes of the warren; August gave them "oyster day," to be signalised by the building of shell-grottoes, which were an excuse for importuning passengers for alms; and the December season had its "boxing-day," on which occasion the poor ragged creatures would be seen thronging the doors of the oil-shops to beg for Christmas-candles!

These had been the only holidays which characterised the childhood of those unfortunate, lost, degraded girls whose lot we are describing. Sunday was not marked by cleanlier apparel, nor better food: if it were singled out at all from the other days of the week, the distinguishing sign was merely the extra drunkenness of the fathers of the families. Good Friday brought the little victims no hot-cross buns, nor Christmas Day its festivities, nor Shrove Tuesday its pancakes:—they had no knowledge of holy periods nor sacred ceremonies;—no seasonable luxury reminded them of the anniversaries of the birth, the death, or the resurrection of a Redeemer.

No—in physical privations and moral blindness had they passed their infancy:—and thus, having gone through a complete initiation into the miseries and sufferings of life, they were prepared at the age of ten to commence an apprenticeship of crime. And the old hag was an excellent mistress: were there an University devoted to graduates in Wickedness, this horrible wretch would have taken first-class Degrees in its schools.

Thus, be it understood, up to the age of ten or eleven, when those poor girls were transferred by their unfeeling parents (who were glad to get rid of them) to the care of the old woman, they had scarcely ever been out of the warren where they were born. Now a new world, as it were, dawned upon them. They laid aside their fetid rags, and put on garments which appeared queenly robes in their eyes. They were sent into streets lined with splendid shops, and beheld gay carriages and equipages of all kinds. Hitherto the principal gin-shop in their rookery had appeared the most gorgeous palace in the world in their eyes, with its revolving burners, its fine windows, and its meretriciously-dressed bar-girls:—now they could feast their gaze with the splendours of the linen-drapers' and jewellers' establishments on Ludgate Hill. Their existence seemed to be suddenly invested with charms that they had never before dreamt of; and they adored the old hag as the authoress of their good fortune. Thus she established a sovereign dominion over her poor ignorant victims through the medium of their mistaken gratitude; and when she told them to sin, they sinned—sinned, too, before they even knew the meaning of virtue!

Such was the history—not of one only—but of all the young girls whom this atrocious old hag had bought from their parents!

To many—to most of our readers, the details of this description may seem improbable,—nay, impossible.

The picture is, alas! too true.

Poor fallen children! the world scorns you—society contemns you—the unthinking blame you. But, just heaven! are ye more culpable than that community which took no precaution to prevent your degradation, and which now adopts no measures to reclaim you?

As for ourselves, we declare most solemnly that we believe no age to have been more disgraced than the present one, and no country more culpable than our own. In this age of Bibles and country of glorious civilisation,—in this epoch of missions and land of refinement,—in this period of grand political reform, and nation of ten thousand philanthropic institutions,—in the middle of the nineteenth century, and with all the advantages of profound peace,—and, what is worst of all, in that great city which vaunts itself the metropolis of the civilised world, there are thousands of young children whose neglected, hopeless, and miserable condition can only be looked upon as an apprenticeship calculated to fill our streets with prostitutes of finished depravity—to people our gaols, hulks, and penal colonies with villains familiar with every phase of crime—and to supply our scaffolds with victims for the diversion of a rude and ruthless mob!

It was nine o'clock in the evening; and the old hag was seated in the same room where we have before frequently seen her.

She was, however, surrounded by several additional comforts. She no longer burnt turf in her grate, but good Wall's End coals. She no longer placed her feet on an old mat, but on a thick carpet. She no longer bought her gin by the quartern or half pint, but by the bottle. She sweetened her tea with lump sugar, instead of moist; and in the place of a stew of tripe or cow-heel, she had a joint cooked at the bake-house, or a chicken boiled on her own fire.

Her select patrons had contributed much towards this improvement in her circumstances; but the luxuries in which she could now indulge, were provided for her by the prostitution of her young victims.

She was now dozing in her arm-chair, with her great cat upon her lap; but even in the midst of her semi-slumber, her ears were awake to the least motion of the knocker of the house-door—that sound which was the indication of business!

Thus, when, true to the time appointed in his note, the Resurrection Man arrived at the house, not many moments elapsed ere he was admitted into the hag's parlour.

"So you have discovered the address of Katherine Wilmot," said the hag. "Where does she reside?"

"No matter where," returned the Resurrection Man; "it is sufficient that I can communicate with her, or bring her up to London, when it suits me. I have come now to have a full understanding with you on the subject; and if we play our cards well, we may obtain a round sum of money from this girl—that is, supposing she is really the child of the Harriet Wilmot whom you knew."

"There can be no doubt of it—there can be no doubt of it," exclaimed the old hag, rocking herself to and fro. "She is the daughter of that Harriet Wilmot whom I knew, and whose image sometimes haunts me in my dreams."

"But what proofs have you of the fact?" demanded the Resurrection Man. "It will not suit me to take any more trouble in the matter, unless I know for certain that I am not running a wild-goose chase."

"I shall not tell you how I came to know Harriet Wilmot seventeen years ago, nor any thing more about her than I can help," said the old hag resolutely. "I was, however, well acquainted with her—I knew all about her. With her own lips she told me her history. She was for some time engaged to be married to a young man—young at that period—at Southampton. His name was Smithers. Circumstances separated them before the realisation of their hopes and wishes; and she came to London with her father, who soon afterwards died of a broken heart through misfortunes in business."

"Broken heart!" exclaimed the Resurrection Man contemptuously: "who ever died of a broken heart? But never mind—go on."

"Harriet was alone in the world—an orphan—unprotected—and without friends or resources," continued the hag. "She was accordingly compelled to go out to service. A wealthy gentleman saw her, and fell in love with her—but I shall not tell you all about *that*! No—I shall not tell you about *that*! Harriet's was a strange fate—a sad fate; and I do not like to think of the part I acted in some respects towards her," added the old woman, shaking her head, as if it were in regret of the past.

"Go on," said the Resurrection Man. "If you have got any thing unpleasant in your memory, all the shakings of heads in the world won't drive it out."

"Alack! you speak the truth—you speak the truth," muttered the old woman. "It was the blackest deed I ever committed—I wish it had never occurred: it troubles me very often; and when I cannot sleep at night, I am constantly thinking of Harriet Wilmot."

"What is all this to lead to?" demanded Tidkins, impatiently.

"I shall not trouble you with many more of my reflections," said the hag. "Harriet became a mother: she had a daughter, on whom she bestowed the name of Katherine. Three or four years afterwards I lost sight of her, and never beheld her more. From that time all traces of herself and her child were gone until last year, when the murder of Reginald Tracy's housekeeper placed the name of Katherine Wilmot before the public. That name immediately struck me: the newspapers said she was sixteen years old—precisely the age that Harriet's daughter must have been. Then the name of Smithers was mixed up in the proceedings which ensued: I saw it all—Harriet must be dead, and Smithers had adopted her child as his niece! But, to convince myself still further, I went to the Old Bailey—I saw Katherine in the dock: you might have knocked me down with a feather, so strong was the resemblance between the young girl and her deceased mother! I came home—I was very ill: methought I had seen the ghost of one whom I had deeply, deeply injured!"

"And now you have so far forgotten your remorse that you are desirous to turn your knowledge of Katherine's parentage to a good account?" said the Resurrection Man, with a sneering laugh. "But how do you know that she is not well informed on that head already?"

"She cannot be—she cannot be," answered the old hag; "she would not bear the name of *Wilmot* if she was. Besides, I have since ascertained that her mother died when she was only four years old; and therefore Katherine was too young to receive any revelation from her parent's lips. No—no: I have good reason to believe that Katherine knows nothing of her paternal origin."

"I am now perfectly satisfied, from all you have told me, that Katherine Wilmot is the daughter of the Harriet whom you knew," said the Resurrection Man; "and as you seem so positive that she is unaware of many important particulars concerning her birth, I will proceed in the business you have proposed to me."

"Where is she living?" inquired the old woman.

"If I tell you that," said Tidkins, "what guarantee have I got that you will not post off alone to her, extort the purchase-money for your secrets, and chouse me out of my reglars? Look you—I have been at the trouble and expense of finding her out—which you never could have done—and I must go halves with you in the produce of the affair."

"So you shall—so you may," returned the old woman. "But I will not speak to her in your hearing. I don't know how it is that I have a strange superstitious awe in connexion with all that concerns Harriet Wilmot's memory and the existence of her child. I cannot help the feeling—I cannot help it."

"By Satan," exclaimed the Resurrection Man, darting a furious glance upon the hag, "you are either a drivelling fool, or you are deceiving me. You entertain compunction about these Wilmots—and yet you purpose to obtain money from the girl. Now is this consistent? Take care how you play with me; for—if I catch you out in any of your tricks—I will hang you up to your own bedpost as readily as I would wring the neck of that damned old cat."

"You shall see whether I will deceive you—you shall see," cried the old hag, with some degree of alarm. "Arrange the business as you will, so long as I may have speech of Katherine without being overheard; but you shall be present when she pays me for the secret which I have to communicate."

"Let that be the understanding, and I am agreeable," observed the Resurrection Man. "Will it suit you to go a few miles out of town with me to-morrow."

"Is it to see Katherine?" inquired the hag.

"What the devil else do you think I want your company for?" cried Tidkins: "to take you to dine at Greenwich or Blackwall—eh? Not quite such a fool as that! However, to-morrow morning you may expect me at seven o'clock——"

"It is not light at that hour," observed the hag.

"I prefer the dusk of either morning or evening," answered the Resurrection Man. "It suits me better—because I have a few enemies in London. But, as I was saying, I shall call for you at seven to-morrow morning; a friend of mine—one Banks of Globe Town—has a covered spring-cart and a capital bit of horse-flesh. He will drive us to where we have to go, in no time. So don't keep us waiting—as the vehicle will be at the bottom of the lane by a quarter to seven."

The old hag promised to be punctual; and the Resurrection Man took his departure from her den.

CHAPTER CXCVII.

ELLEN AND KATHERINE.

Turn we now to the farm-house of the Bennets near Hounslow—the residence of Katherine Wilmot.

The morning was dry and beautiful—one of those mornings which sometimes cheer us towards the end of January, and give us a short foretaste of the approaching spring.

It was nine o'clock, when the door of the farm-house opened, and two young females came forth to enjoy the fresh air of a charming day.

These were Ellen Monroe—(for by her maiden name must we continue to call her, as she herself maintained it for the present)—and Katherine Wilmot.

Never had Ellen appeared more beautiful; nor Katherine more sweetly interesting.

They had evidently been conversing on a subject which gave them pleasure; and they were both intent on continuing the same delightful topic during their walk.

The subject of that discourse had inspired Ellen with emotions of pride, as well as of joy. She walked with a dignity and yet an elegance of motion which denoted the vigour of that vital system which was so highly developed in her voluptuous style of beauty. The generous and noble feelings of the heart shone in the light of her deep blue eyes, and in the animation of that countenance where the fair and red were so exquisitely blended. They were indicated, too, by the expression of that short and somewhat haughty upper lip which belonged to the classic regularity of her features, and in the dilation of the rose-tinted nostrils.

Ellen was a finer and far lovelier creature than Katherine;—but the latter was characterised by more of that tender sensibility and touching interest which physiologists deem the development of the intellectual system. The eyes were intensely expressive; and over her features a soft, pale, and modest light seemed to be shed. Her figure was delicate and slight, and contrasted strongly with that luxuriant expansion which constituted the fine and not less symmetrical proportions of Ellen.

"I shall really experience deep regret to leave your dwelling-place, dear Katherine," observed Ellen, as they entered a hard and dry pathway leading through the fields; "for even at this season, it possesses many attractions superior to the vicinity of a great city."

"In the warmer months it is a beautiful spot," returned Katherine. "But you will not leave me to-day? Consider—you have only been here a few hours——"

"Since yesterday morning," exclaimed Ellen, with a smile; "and in that time we have formed a friendship which may never, I hope, be interrupted."

"Oh! never," said Katherine warmly. "It was so kind of you to come and find me out in my seclusion—so considerate to make me acquainted with all those wonderful events which have occurred to my benefactor———"

"Nay—neither kind nor considerate," again interrupted Ellen. "Richard's letter, dated from the city of Abrantani on the 10th, and received by my father the day before yesterday, enjoined him to send me to see you—to make your acquaintance—to assure myself that you are well and happy—and to communicate to you tidings which Richard feels will be welcome to all his friends."

"Oh! welcome indeed!" exclaimed Katherine, with grateful enthusiasm. "How much do I owe to him—and how worthy is he of that rank which has rewarded his grand deeds! Such a man could not long remain a humble individual: his great talents—his noble heart—his fine qualities were certain to elevate him above the sphere in which he was born."

"And now will the name of Markham go down to posterity," said Ellen, proudly: "and the glory which Richard has thrown around it, will be to some degree shared by all who bear it. Oh! this was prophesied to me but a little while ago;—and yet, *then* how far was I from suspecting that the realisation of the prediction was so near at hand, especially too, as that prediction was not uttered with any reference to Richard—but to another,—*that other alluding to himself*!"

Katherine cast a glance of surprise towards her companion, whose last words were unintelligible to her; and Ellen, apparently recollecting herself, hastened to add, "But I was speaking of matters which are yet unknown—yet strange to you. Think no more of my observations on that topic. There are times when the soul is lost and bewildered in the contemplation of the world's strange events and marvellous vicissitudes; and such has often been the case with me during the last few days. It was on the 16th of January that we received the letter which imparted us the tidings of Richard's first exploit—the capture of Estella. Oh! how sincerely I prayed for his success—and yet I trembled for him! My father, too, had some misgivings; but we endeavoured to reassure each other, mutually concealing our fears. Two or three days afterwards we received the news of his triumphant entry into Villabella;—another interval of a few days, and we had a letter from him, giving us a brief account of the Battle of Piacere. Our fears were almost entirely dissipated by the tidings of this glorious achievement; and if any doubts yet lingered, they were completely dispelled by the news of the great victory of Abrantani. Oh! how well has he earned that coronet which now adorns his brow!—how well does that proud title of Marquis become the great, the generous, and the good!"

"Would that his struggles were over, and that the civil war was put an end to in Castelcicala!" exclaimed Miss Wilmot—for the news of the great victory beneath the walls of Montoni were yet unknown in England.

"I have no fears for the result," said Ellen: "a conqueror has he hitherto been—and a conqueror will he remain! Heaven itself prospers him in this undertaking: the wise dispensations of Providence are apparent throughout his career in the Grand Duchy. Had the first expedition, which landed at Ossore, succeeded, there were great chiefs—Grachia and Morosino—who would have taken the lead in the State. But the enterprise failed—and those patriots were numbered with the slain. The idea of releasing from their captivity his companions in that fatal affair, led Richard to the attack of Estella. He succeeded—and he stood alone at the head of the movement. There was not a chief amongst the patriots to dispute his title to that elevated situation."

"Yes—the finger of heaven was assuredly visible in all those circumstances which led to my benefactor's greatness," remarked Katherine. "Methinks that when I see him again, I shall be strangely embarrassed in his presence:—instead of addressing him by the familiar name of *Mr. Markham*, my lips must tutor themselves to breathe the formal words '*My Lord*,' and '*Your Lordship*;' and——"

"Oh! you wrong our noble-hearted friend—our mutual benefactor," interrupted Ellen. "Rank and distinction—wealth and glory cannot change *his* heart: he will only esteem them as the elements of an influence and of a power to do much good."

The young ladies paused in their conversation, because two persons were approaching along the pathway.

A man muffled in a large cloak, and with a countenance of cadaverous repulsiveness scowling above the collar, advanced first; and behind him walked a female whose bowed form denoted the decrepitude of old age. There was an interval of perhaps a dozen yards between them; for the woman was unable to keep pace with the more impatient progress of the man.

"Is this the way, young ladies, to Farmer Bennet's?" demanded the foremost individual, when he was within a few feet of Ellen and Katherine.

"It is," replied Kate. "You may see the roof appearing from the other side of yonder eminence. Mr. Bennet is not, however, within at this moment: he has gone to a neighbouring village on business, and will not return till two o'clock."

"Then you know Farmer Bennet?" exclaimed the Resurrection Man—for he was the individual who had addressed the young ladies.

But before Katherine could give any reply, an exclamation of astonishment broke from the lips of Ellen, whose eyes had just recognised the countenance of the old hag.

"Well, Miss—do I have the pleasure of meeting you once more?" said the detestable woman, with a leer comprehensively significant in allusion to the past: then, as her eyes wandered from Ellen's countenance to that of Katherine, she suddenly became strangely excited, and exclaimed, "Ah! Miss Wilmot!"

"Is *this* Miss Wilmot?" demanded the Resurrection Man, with an impatient glance towards Katherine, while he really addressed himself to the old hag.

"My name is Wilmot," said Kate, in her soft and somewhat timid tone. "Was it for me that your visit to the farm was intended?"

"Neither more nor less, Miss," answered the Resurrection Man. "This person," he continued, indicating his horrible companion, "has something important to say to you."

"Yes—and we must speak alone, too," said the hag.

"No!" ejaculated Ellen, hastily and firmly; "that may not be. I am Miss Wilmot's friend—the friend, too, of one in whom she places great confidence; and whatever you may have to communicate to her cannot be a secret in respect to me."

And, as she uttered these words, she glanced significantly at her young companion.

"Yes," said Kate, who understood the hint conveyed in that look, although she was of course entirely ignorant of the motives of Ellen's precaution: "yes—whatever you may wish to communicate to me must be told in the presence of my friend."

"But the business is a most delicate one," cried the Resurrection Man.

"Oh! I have no doubt of that," exclaimed Ellen, with a contemptuous smile which the hag fully comprehended.

"Do you know this young lady?" asked the Resurrection Man, in an under tone, of the old woman, while he rapidly indicated Ellen.

"I know that young lady well," said the hag aloud, and with a meaning glance: "I know you well,—do I not, Miss Monroe?"

"I am not disposed to deny the fact," replied Ellen, coolly; "and I can assure you that my disposition is as resolute and determined as you have always found it to be. Therefore, if you have aught to communicate to Miss Wilmot, say it quickly—or come with us to the farm, where you will be more at your ease: but, remember, I do not quit this young lady while you are with her."

"You will repent of this obstinacy, Miss—you will repent of this obstinacy," muttered the hag.

"It may be so," said Ellen: "nevertheless, menaces will not deter me from my purpose."

"If you thwart me, I can proclaim matters that you would wish unrevealed," retorted the hag, but in a whisper apart to Ellen.

"Act as you please," exclaimed this young lady aloud, and with a superb glance of contemptuous defiance. "Your impertinence only convinces me the more profoundly of the prudence of my resolution to remain with Miss Wilmot."

The hag made no reply: she knew not how to act.

Tidkins was not, however, equally embarrassed. He saw that Ellen was acquainted with the old woman's character, and that she entertained suspicions of a nature which threatened to mar the object of his visit to that neighbourhood.

"Miss Monroe," he said,—"for such, I learn, is your name,—I beg of you to allow my companion a few moments' conversation with your young friend. They need not retire a dozen yards from this spot; and your eye can remain upon them."

"No," returned Ellen, positively: "your companion shall have no private conference with Miss Wilmot. Miss Wilmot's affairs are no secret to me;—she has voluntarily made me acquainted with her past history and her present condition—and she cannot now wish me to remain a stranger to the object of your visit, however delicate be the nature of that business."

"I am desirous that Miss Monroe should hear your communications," added Kate.

"I will not speak to Miss Wilmot in the presence of witnesses," said the old hag.

"Then we have nothing farther to prevent us from returning to the farm immediately," exclaimed Ellen; and, taking Katherine's arm, she turned away with a haughty inclination of her head.

"Neither need we remain here any longer, Mr. Tidkins," said the hag.

"Tidkins!" repeated Ellen, with a convulsive shudder—for the name reached her ear as she was leading her young friend homeward:—"Tidkins!" she murmured, the blood running cold in her veins; "my God! what new plot can now be contemplated?"

And she hurried Katherine along the path, as if a wild beast were behind them.

"Do you know those people?" asked Miss Wilmot, alarmed by her companion's tone and manner.

"Unfortunately," replied Ellen, in a low voice and with rapid utterance,—"unfortunately I can attest that the woman whom we have just met, is the vilest of the vile; and the mention of that man's name has revealed to me the presence of a wretch capable of every atrocity—a villain whose crimes are of the blackest dye—an assassin whose enmity to our benefactor Richard is as furious as it is unwearied. Come, Katharine—come: hasten your steps;—we shall not be in safety until we reach the farm."

And the two young ladies hurried rapidly along the path towards the dwelling, every now and then casting timid glances behind them.

But the Resurrection Man and the old hag had not thought it expedient to follow.

CHAPTER CXCVIII.

A GLOOMY VISITOR.

As soon as the two young ladies had reached the farm-house, Ellen addressed Katherine with alarming seriousness of manner.

"My dear friend," she said, "some plot is in existence against your peace. That fearful-looking man and that horrible old woman are perfect fiends in mortal shape."

"But what cause of enmity can they entertain against me?" asked Katharine, drawing her chair close to Ellen's seat with that sweet confidence which a younger sister would have been expected to show towards an elder one. "I never saw them before in my life, to my knowledge; and I certainly never can have injured them."

"You are rich—and that is a sufficient motive to inspire the man with designs against you: you are pretty—and that is a sufficient reason for inducing the woman to spread her nets in your path. The man," continued Ellen, "has more than once attempted the life of our generous benefactor Richard; and that old hag, Katherine, is a wretch who lives upon the ruin of young females."

At this moment Mrs. Bennet entered the room; and, observing the disturbed countenances of Ellen and Katherine, she felt alarmed.

Ellen immediately communicated to her the particulars of the adventure just related, and concluded with these observations:—"The person of the man was previously unknown to me; but Mr. Markham had made me familiar with his name. Thus, when I heard that name breathed by his infamous companion, I recognised in him the monster of whose crimes my benefactor has related so dread a history. As for the woman," added Ellen, after a moment's hesitation, "she has been pointed out to me as one of those vile wretches who render cities and great towns dangerous to young females. Indeed, she once practised her arts upon me:—hence I am well aware of her true character."

Mrs. Bennet was dreadfully frightened at the incident which had occurred; but, like Katherine, she was somewhat at a loss to conceive what possible object the two bad characters whom Ellen so bitterly denounced, could have in view with respect to her young charge.

The trio were still conversing upon the mysterious occurrence, when Farmer Bennet entered the room.

Of course the narrative had to be repeated to him; and he was much troubled by what he heard.

The dinner was served up; but none of those who sate down to it ate with any appetite. A vague and uncertain consciousness of impending danger or of serious annoyance oppressed them all.

The table was cleared; and Mrs. Bennet had just produced a bottle of excellent home-made wine, "to cheer their spirits," as she said, when the servant entered to announce that a person desired to speak to Mr. Bennet. The farmer ordered the individual in question to be admitted; and the servant, having disappeared for a few moments, returned, ushering in an elderly man dressed in shabby black, and wearing a dingy white cravat with very limp ends.

"Your servant, ma'am—your most obedient, young ladies," said he: then, starting with well-affected surprise, he ejaculated, "Ah! if my eyes doesn't deceive me in my old age, that's Miss Kate Wilmot, werily and truly!"

"Mr. Banks!" said Katherine, in a tone expressive of both surprise and aversion; for she remembered that the undertaker used to call upon Smithers to purchase the rope by means of which criminals had been executed.

"Yes, my dear—my name is, as you say, Banks—Edward Banks, of Globe Lane, London—Furnisher of Funerals on New and Economic Principles—Good Deal Coffin, Eight Shillings and Sixpence—Stout Oak, Thirty-five Shillings—Patent Funeral Carriage, One Pound Eleven—First Rate Carriage-Funeral, Mutes and Feathers, Four Pound Four—Catholic Fittings——"

"Really, sir," exclaimed Mr. Bennet, impatiently, "this is not a very pleasant subject for conversation; and if you have come upon no other business than to recite your Prospectus———"

"A thousand apologies, sir—a thousand apologies," interrupted Mr. Banks, calmly sinking into a seat. "But whenever I see a few or a many mortal wessels gathered together, I always think that the day must come when they'll be nothink more than blessed carkisses and then, Mr. Bennet," added the undertaker, shaking his head solemnly, and applying a dirty white handkerchief to his eyes, "how pleasant to the wirtuous feelings must it be to know where to get the funeral done on the newest and most economic principles."

"Katherine, do you know this person?" inquired the farmer, irritated by the intruder's pertinacity in his gloomy topic.

"I have seen him three or four times at Mr. Smithers' house in London," was the answer; "but Mr. Banks well knows that I never exchanged ten words with him in my life."

"Then you do not come to see Miss Wilmot?" demanded Mr. Bennet, turning towards the undertaker.

"No, sir—no," answered Banks, heaving a deep sigh. "Did you not perceive, sir, that I was quite took at a nonplush when I set my wenerable eyes on the blessed countenance of that charming gal? But pardon me, sir—pardon me, if I am someot long in coming to the pint:—it is, however, my natur' to ramble when I reflects on the pomps and wanities of this wicked world; and natur' is natur,' sir, after all—is it *not*, ma'am?"

Here he turned with a most dolorous expression of countenance towards Mrs. Bennet.

"I really do not understand you, sir," was her laconic reply:—nor more she did, good woman! for it was not even probable that Mr. Banks quite understood himself.

"Now, sir, will you have the goodness to explain the nature of your business with me—since it is with *me*, no doubt, that you have business to transact?" said the farmer, in a tone which showed how disagreeable the undertaker's whining nonsense was to him.

"Something tells me that this man's visit bears reference to our adventure of the morning," whispered Ellen to Katherine. "Do not offer to leave the room: let us hear all he has to say."

Katherine replied by a meaning look, and then glanced with suspicious timidity towards Banks, who was again speaking.

"My business isn't to be explained in a moment, sir," said the undertaker; "and I must beg your patience for a little while."

"Go on," exclaimed the farmer, throwing himself back in his seat, and folding his arms with the desperate air of a man who knew that he could only get rid of a troublesome visitor by allowing him to tell his story in his own way.

"You're in mourning, ma'am, I see," observed Mr. Banks, turning towards Mrs. Bennet. "Ah! I remember—that wexatious affair of the Rector of Saint David's. Pray, ma'am, who *undertook* the funeral of your blessed defunct sister?"

"Sir!" exclaimed Mrs. Bennet, tears starting into her eyes.

"No offence, ma'am—no offence. Only I should like it to be known in these here parts that Edward Banks—of Globe Lane, London, undertakes on new and economic principles, and doesn't mind distances. S'pose, sir," continued this most disagreeable visitor, again addressing the farmer, "s'pose you come to me some fine morning and says, '*Banks*,' says you, '*my dear wife has just become a blessed defunct*——'"

"This is too much!" ejaculated Mr. Bennet, starting from his seat. "Have you, or have you not, any business to engage my attention?"

"I'm coming to the pint—I'm coming to the pint this moment," said Banks. "Pray sit down for a few minutes—I shan't ingross much more of your wallyable time; for time really *is* wallyable in this sublunary speer;"—and the undertaker shook his head so mournfully that worthy Mrs. Bennet could not help thinking he was a very good and humane, though somewhat a prosy individual. "When we look around us, and behold how many benighted creeturs lives in total recklessness for the futur'—without putting by in an old stocking or any where else a single penny towards buying 'em a decent coffin—it's enough to make one's hair stand on end. But I see you are growing impatient, sir:—well—perhaps my feelings does carry me away. Still I don't mean no harm. Howsomever—business is business, as coffins is coffins, or carkisses is carkisses; and so here's to business in a jiffy."

With these words Mr. Banks drew from his capacious coat-pocket a brown-paper parcel, about a foot long, three inches wide, and as many deep.

Then he began, with most provoking deliberation of manner, to unroll the numerous folds of paper in which the precious object of so much care was wrapped; and, while he thus aroused the curiosity of his spectators to the utmost, he continued talking in a more lachrymose style than ever.

"There is dooties which we owe to heaven—and there is dooties which we owe to our fellow-creeturs. To heaven, ma'am, we owes a obligation of wirtue: to our fellow-creeturs we owes respect and decency when they're no more. Wirtues, ma'am, is like the white nails on a black-cloth covered coffin: the more there is of 'em, the stronger is the coffin, and the better it looks. Wices, ma'am, is like the knots in a common deal coffin: the more there is of 'em, the veaker is the coffin, and the wuss it looks. I'm now a-going to show you, ma'am—and you, too, sir—and you also, young ladies—a object of the deepest interest to us poor mortal wessels. I've wrapped it up in this wise, 'cause I've paytented it, and this is the only model I've got. When once it's generally known, the whole world will thank me for the inwention; and posterity will remember with gratitude the name of Banks of Globe Lane—Furnisher of Funerals on New and Economic Principles. You see, the parcel is gettin' smaller and smaller—'cause the blessed object was as well wrapped up as a young babby. However—here's the last fold:—off with the paper—and there's the concentrating focus of all interest!"

As Mr. Banks wound up with this beautiful peroration, he disengaged from the last fold of paper a miniature model of a coffin, about eight inches long, and wide and deep in proportion. It was covered with black silk, and was studded with innumerable white nails.

But as he placed it, with a glance of almost paternal affection, upon the table, the farmer started up, exclaiming, "I have already put up with your insolence too long. What does this unwarrantable intrusion upon my privacy mean? Speak, sir: have you any thing to say to me?"

"I am now coming to the pint at length," answered the undertaker, but little abashed by this rebuff. "In one word," he continued, producing a small memorandum-book and preparing to write with a pencil,—"in one word, I want you and your family to let me put down each of your names——"

"For what?" demanded Bennet, impatiently.

"For a Paytent Silk-covered Silver-nailed Indestructible Wood-seasoned Coffin," was the calm reply. "It's warranted to keep as good as new till you want it."

Mr. Bennet fell back into his seat, completely stupefied by this extraordinary announcement;—Mrs. Bennet cast horrified glances at the undertaker, as if she thought he was mad;—Ellen cast a look of deep indignation on the individual who had produced this excitement;—and Katherine started on her seat, exclaiming, "What have you done, Mr. Banks? Mrs. Bennet is fainting!"

This was really the case—such an effect did the sudden display of the coffin and the cool demand of patronage made by the undertaker, produce upon one whose mind had not yet quite recovered from the severe shock occasioned by the murder of her sister.

"Water, Katherine!—quick!" exclaimed the farmer, hastening towards his wife.

Kate instantly hurried from the room to fetch water; while Ellen, on her part, proffered the necessary attentions to the fainting woman.

Mr. Banks was thus for a moment forgotten; and this was exactly the condition of things that suited his purpose. Hastily thrusting the model coffin into his pocket, he seized his hat and hurried from the parlour, closing the door behind him.

In the passage he met Kate, who was hastening back to the room, with a jug of water in her hand.

"One moment—only one moment—*as you value the memory of your deceased mother*,"—whispered Banks, speaking more rapidly and with less whining affectation than he had done for many years. "Take this note—read it in private—its contents deeply concern you and your *blessed defunct parent*. If you breathe a word concerning it to a soul *you will for ever lose the opportunity of knowing who was your father*."

Banks thrust a note into the girl's hand, and hastily left the house.

The words which he had uttered, produced—as might naturally be supposed—so strange an effect upon Katherine,—that sudden allusion to her mother took her so much by surprise,—and then that mysterious mention of her father increased her bewilderment to such an extent, that she mechanically grasped the note with a mixture of awe and gratitude, and, prompted by the same impulses, thrust it into the bosom of her dress.

All this was the work of scarcely a quarter of a minute; and the moment she had thus received and concealed the note, she re-entered the parlour, where the aid of the fresh water soon brought Mrs. Bennet to herself.

"Where is that scoundrel?" cried the farmer, now finding leisure to think of the cause of his wife's sudden indisposition.

"He is gone," returned Katherine.

Then, seating herself near the window, the young girl fell into a profound reverie.

"Gone!" ejaculated Bennet. "But it is better that he should have gone—or I might be tempted to do him a mischief."

"That man came hither with some sinister design," said Ellen. "From the first moment of his appearance, my suspicions associated his visit with the adventure of the morning."

"But what object could he have?" cried the farmer. "He seemed only anxious to intrude himself as long as possible."

"Perhaps he was waiting for an opportunity to speak to Katherine alone," observed Ellen. "He certainly appeared to be talking against time."

"Yes, dear friends," exclaimed Katherine, rising from her seat, and advancing towards those whom she thus addressed; "that man *did* desire to speak to me alone—and he succeeded in his object. Pardon me if for a few moments I hesitated whether to obey his solemn injunction of silence, or to communicate the incident to you who wish me well. But the words which he spoke, and the earnestness of his manner, bewildered me. It however only required a short interval of sober reflection to teach me my duty."

Katherine then repeated the words that Banks had whispered in her ears, and produced the note which he had thrust into her hand.

"You have acted prudently in revealing these particulars, dear Kate," said Ellen. "A man who is compelled to effect his purposes by such low devices as those employed by him who has just left us, cannot mean well."

"Let us hear the contents of the letter," cried Farmer Bennet: "we may then, perhaps, see more clearly into the mystery."

"Read it, Ellen," said Kate. "I must confess to a profound curiosity to become acquainted with its contents."

Ellen accordingly opened the note, and read as follows:—

"Silence and secrecy,—if you respect the memory of your deceased mother! Be not deluded by the advice of Miss Monroe, who has her own reasons for prejudicing you against me. I am well acquainted with all the particulars of your birth:—I can impart facts that it behoves you to learn. You will bitterly repent any distrust in this matter. Have you no inclination to hear more concerning your mother's history than you can possibly now know? would you not go far, and sacrifice much, to glean something with regard to *your father?* This evening—at seven precisely—I shall be at the foot of the hill where I met you just now. If you come alone, you will learn much that nearly and deeply concerns you: if you appear accompanied by a soul, my lips will remain sealed.

"THE FEMALE YOU SAW JUST NOW."

"I have so far my own reasons for counselling you against that wicked woman," said Ellen, indignantly, "inasmuch as I would save you from danger. But if you really believe that there can be any thing serious in this promise of important communications, I should advise you to meet that female—for precautions can be adopted to protect you from a distance."

Katherine glanced inquiringly towards the farmer.

"I see that you are anxious to meet this woman, Kate," said he, after a pause; "and it is natural. She promises communications on subjects that cannot be otherwise than dear to you. Miss Monroe and I can keep watch at a distance; and on the slightest elevation of voice on your part, we will hasten to your assistance."

This project was approved of even by the timid Mrs. Bennet; and Katherine Wilmot anxiously awaited the coming of the appointed hour.

CHAPTER CXCIX.

THE ORPHAN'S FILIAL LOVE.

The evening was calm, fresh, and dry: the heavens were covered with stars; and objects were visible at a considerable distance.

A few minutes before the wished-for hour, Katherine, Ellen, and the farmer reached the hill at the foot of which was the place of appointment.

Then Kate left them and proceeded alone, while her two friends hastened by a circuitous route to gain a clump of trees which would enable them to remain concealed within a distance of fifty yards of the spot where Kate was to meet the old woman.

The young girl pursued her way—her heart palpitating with varied emotions,—vague alarm, exalted hope, and all the re-awakened convictions of her orphan state.

She reached the foot of the hill, and in a few minutes beheld a human form emerging, as it were, from the obscurity at a distance—the dim outline gradually defining itself into a positive shape, and at length showing the figure of the old woman whom she had seen in the morning.

"You have done well to obey my summons, Miss," said the hag, as she approached the timid and trembling girl. "But let me look well on your countenance—let me be satisfied that it is indeed Katherine Wilmot."

Then Kate turned towards the moon, and parted the light chesnut hair: which clustered around her countenance; so that a pure flood of silvery lustre streamed on all the features of that sweetly interesting face—a sight too hallowed for the foul-souled harridan to gaze upon!

It was as if the veil of the Holy of Holies, in the Jewish temple, were lifted before some being fresh from the grossest pollutions of the world.

"Yes—I am satisfied!" murmured the hag. "You are Katherine Wilmot—the Katherine whom I saw and recognised this morning. I feared lest your artful friend, Ellen Monroe, less timid than yourself, might have come to play your part."

"Wherefore should you speak ill of Miss Monroe?" inquired Katherine, mildly. "Malicious allusions to my friends will not serve as a passport to my confidence."

"Well, well," said the hag, "we will speak no more on that subject. It was for other purposes that I sought this interview. Tell me, Miss—do you remember your mother?"

"I remember her, with that faint and dim knowledge which consists only of many vague and dubious impressions," replied Kate, in a deeply plaintive tone. "I was but four years of age when God snatched her from me; and it was not until I was old enough to feel her loss, that my memory began to exert itself to the utmost to recall every incident which I could associate with her kindness towards me. For kind she must have been—because every reminiscence which my mind has ever been able to shadow forth concerning her, fills my heart with grateful tenderness and love. Oh! I have sate for hours—in the solitude of my own chamber—endeavouring to fix the volatile ideas which at times flash through my memory in reference to the past,—until I have seemed to connect them in a regular chain;—and then I have fancied that at the end of the vista of years through which my mental glances retrospected, I could define a beautiful but melancholy countenance—the mild blue eyes weeping, and the lips smiling sweetly, over me—the gentle hand smoothing down my hair, and caressing my cheeks,—and all this in a manner so touching, so plaintive, so softly sorrowful, that the picture fills my soul with sad fears lest my mother was not happy! And there have been times, too," continued Kate, tears trickling down her cheeks, "when it appeared to me, that I could remember the fervent tenderness with which my mother clasped me in her arms—fondled me—played with me—did all she could to make me laugh—and then wept bitterly, because my infantine joy was so exuberant! Yes—these and many other things of the same kind have I pondered on and treasured up as holy memories of the past;—and then the dread thought has suddenly flashed to my brain, that I have been merely worshipping the images of my own fond creation. At such times, I have gone down upon my knees—I have prayed that these ideas might really be reflections of the long-gone truth,—bright reflections which had been cast in the mirror of my mind during the days of my infancy! Oh! it would grieve me sadly—it would wring my soul with anguish—it would fill my heart with desolation, were I to be led to the fearful conviction that all those pleasing-painful glimpses of my mother's presence and my mother's love are not the reminiscences of reality, but the creations of a fond and credulous imagination."

"Your memory has not deceived you, Miss," said the old woman. "Your mother fondled and caressed you—smiled and wept over you, in the manner you have described."

"Oh! thank you—thank you for that assurance!" exclaimed Katherine, forgetting, in the enthusiasm of her filial, but orphan, love, all her late repugnance to that old woman: "again, I say, thank you! You know not the consolation you have imparted to me! Oh! were it possible to recall from the tomb that dear mother who fondled and caressed me—smiled and wept over me, I would give all the remainder of my life for one day of her presence here—one day of her love! When I think that she is really gone for ever—that no tears and no prayers can bring her back—ah! it seems as if there were an anguish in my heart which no human sympathy can ever soothe. But you knew my mother, then?" added Kate, suddenly; "you knew her—did you not? Oh! tell me of her: I could never weary of hearing you speak of her."

"Yes—I knew your mother well," was the answer: "I knew her before you were born."

"And was she happy?" demanded Katherine, trembling at the question she thus put, for fear the reply should not be as she would wish it.

"She knew happiness—and she was also acquainted with sorrow," said the hag: "but that is the lot of us all—that is the lot of us all!"

"Poor mother!" murmured the young girl, with a profound sob: "it is then true that, in my infancy, I saw her weep as well as smile! Wherefore was she unhappy? Was she betrayed and neglected? But, oh! I tremble to ask those questions, which—"

"To explain the cause of her sorrows would be to tell you all her history," answered the old woman; "and, ere I can do that, I have some questions to ask you, and—and some conditions to—to propose."

The hag hesitated:—yes, even *she*, with her soul so hardened in the tan-pits of vice, as to be on all other occasions proof against the dews of sympathy,—even *she* hesitated, as if softened by the ingenuous and holy outpourings of that young orphan's filial love.

"Speak—say quickly what you require of me," exclaimed Katherine; "and hasten to tell me of my parents—for in your letter you spoke of both my father and my mother."

As Katherine entertained not the slightest recollection of her father, all her thoughts had ever been fixed on the memory of her mother;—but when she coupled the two names together—when she found her lips pronouncing the sacred denominations of *father* and *mother* in the same breath, there arose in her soul such varied and overpowering emotions that she dissolved into a violent agony of weeping.

But that efflux of tears relieved the surcharged heart of the orphan; and, composing herself as quickly as she could, she exclaimed, "Speak, good woman—name your conditions: I am rich—and they shall be complied with,—so that you hasten to tell me of my parents!"

"Did your mother leave no papers behind her—no letters—no private documents of any kind?" inquired the old hag.

"Nothing,—nothing save the fragment of a note which she commenced when in a dying state, and which death did not permit her to finish," answered Katherine.

"And that fragment—did it suggest no trace—"

"Stay—I will repeat its contents to you," exclaimed Katherine: "the words are indelibly fixed upon my memory——Oh! how were it possible that I could ever forget them? Those words ran thus:—'*Should my own gloomy presages prove true, and the warning of my medical attendant be well founded,—if, in a word, the hand of death be already extended to snatch me away thus in the prime of life, while my darling child is*——:' there," continued Katherine, "is a blank, occasioned—alas! by the tears of my poor mother! Two or three lines are thus obliterated; and then appears a short—disjointed—but a most mysterious portion of a sentence, written thus:—'*and inform Mr. Markham, whose abode is*——.' There's not another word on the paper!" added the orphan.

"Markham—Markham!" repeated the hag, as if sorely troubled by some reminiscence; "she mentioned the name of Markham in the letter she wrote on her death-bed? Young lady, did you ever hear more of that Mr. Markham?"

"Inquiries were instituted at my mother's death," replied Kate; "but the Mr. Markham alluded to in the note could not be discovered. The name—the very name, however, seems to be of good omen to me; for one of that name,—who is now a noble of exalted rank, and the commander of a mighty army in a foreign land,—has been my best friend—my benefactor—my saviour. Yes—it is to Richard Markham——"

"Ah! now I comprehend the cause of your intimacy with Miss Monroe," said the hag, hastily: "she resides with her father at the house of Mr. Richard Markham. And so," she continued in a musing tone,—"and so that same Mr. Richard Markham is your friend—your benefactor?"

"Oh! what should I have been without him?" ejaculated Katherine. "When I was involved in that fearful situation, of which you have no doubt heard, *he* was the only one who came to me and said, '*I believe you to be innocent*!' May heaven ever prosper him for that boundless philanthropy—that noble generosity which induced him to espouse the orphan's cause! Yes—to him I owed the development of my innocence—the unravelling of that terrible web of circumstantial evidence in which I was entangled. He employed an active agent to collect evidence in my favour; and the measures which he adopted led to the results which must be known to you."

"It is, then, as I thought," said the old woman, scarcely able to subdue a chuckle of delight. "You know but little concerning your mother—and nothing relative to your father."

"And it is to receive precious communications on those points that I have met you now," exclaimed Katherine. "Let us lose no more time—my friends will grow uneasy at my prolonged absence! Speak—in the name of heaven, speak on a subject so near and dear to my heart."

"Listen attentively, young miss, to what I am about to say—listen attentively," returned the hag. "Now do not be alarmed at my words: you will see that I am disposed to act well towards you. The man who was with me this morning—," and here the old woman cast a rapid glance around, and lowered her voice to a whisper,—"that man is a bad one, and he knows I am acquainted with all that concerns your parentage. He is avaricious, and desires to turn my knowledge to a good account."

"I understand you," said Katherine: "he requires money. But are you influenced by him?"

"I cannot explain all that, Miss: attend to what I choose to tell you—or *may* tell you—and you will act wisely," returned the old woman. "He is a desperate man—and I dare not offend him. He wants money; and money he must have—money he must have!"

"How much will satisfy him?" asked Katherine. "And if I procure the sum that he needs, will you then tell me all you know in connexion with my parents?"

"Wait a moment—wait a moment, Miss," said the hag. "I am but a poor—miserable—wretched—oppressed—starving creature myself——"

"Again I understand you," interrupted Katherine, unable to subdue a tone expressive of contempt. "You declare yourself to be the possessor of a secret which nearly and dearly concerns me; and you intend to barter it for gold? But if I meet your demands in all respects,—if I satisfy that man who exercises such influence over you, and if I reward yourself,—what security can you give me that you are really acquainted with those particulars which you offer to communicate? what guarantee can you show that this first concession on my part will not be followed by increased demands on yours?"

"I will convince you of my good faith," was the old woman's ready reply. "Give me wherewithal to satisfy that man; and the reward you intend for me need not be bestowed until I have told you all I know."

"How much will that man require?" asked Katherine, wearied by this mercenary trading in matters which to her appeared so sacred.

"Give him a hundred pounds:—you are rich and can well afford it—for report says that you inherited the fortune of Reginald Tracy," exclaimed the hag.

"And for yourself?" said Kate, impatiently.

"Alack! I am a poor, starving old creature," was the answer; "I am miserable—very miserable! Give me wherewith to make my few remaining days happy—as I shall be able to show you great sources of comfort in the news I have to impart."

"Listen, now, to me," said Kate, after a moment's hesitation. "I will give you that sum of one hundred pounds to enable you to satisfy the man of whom you speak; and, afterwards—if your communications should really and truly prove a source of comfort to me—I will reward you with a liberality surpassing your most sanguine expectations. But, alas! some delay must take place ere I can procure the funds from the solicitor who has my affairs in his charge; and, oh! I shall know no peace until your lips reveal those secrets which are to prove such sources of comfort to me."

There was a temporary pause:—the old woman seemed to be reflecting upon the orphan's words; and the young girl herself was rapidly conjecturing of what nature the promised revelations could be. But how vain were all her attempts to assign a satisfactory solution to that enigma which the hag, like some horrible sphynx, had set before her!

During this prolonged interview the early loveliness of the evening had yielded to one of those sudden variations peculiar to our island-climate at that season of the year:—the sky had become overcast—the moon no longer poured forth a flood of sweet silver lustre to light up the innocent countenance of the maiden, or to mock with its chaste halo the wrinkled expression of the foul hag.

"But perhaps your solicitor may refuse you the advances which you need?" said the old woman at length.

"No: he will not cast an obstacle in the way of aught which is to contribute to my happiness," answered Katherine. "I have seen him but twice, and, inexperienced as I am in the ways of life, I feel confident that he possesses a kind and generous heart. Oh! if Richard—I mean, the Marquis of Estella—were in England now, I should not be compelled to wait many hours in suspense for the want of this money which you require."

"The Marquis of Estella!" exclaimed the hag, in astonishment: "who is he? and what connexion can he have with you?"

"Have you not heard or read the news which have doubtless appeared in all the London journals?" inquired Katherine;—"those glorious news———"

"Alack! dear Miss—I never read a newspaper," said the hag.

"Then you are ignorant that the Richard Markham of whom we have been speaking, is a great noble—a peer of a foreign realm,—that the coronet of a Marquis has been conferred upon him for his gallant deeds———"

"Well-a-day! this world sees strange ups and downs!" interrupted the hag. "Ah! Miss—lose no time in satisfying that man who was with me this morning, and I will tell you a secret that will be well worth all the gold you will have to give for its purchase. But what was that noise? did you not hear something?"

"It seemed to me that there was a rustling along the path," replied Katherine, in a hasty and timid whisper. "Oh! you would not do me any harm—you have not been deceiving me? My God! how cruel would it be to lead the orphan into danger, by the allurements of fond hopes respecting the memory of her parents!"

"Silence, Miss—listen!" said the hag, in a subdued but earnest tone: "I mean you no harm."

Then they both held their breath;—but all was still—not a sound met their ears, save the low murmur of the breeze which had sprung up within the last few minutes.

"It is nothing," observed the old woman. "But why should you mistrust me?"

"Pardon me if I wrong you," returned Kate:—"you are a stranger to me—and, although you may mean to serve me, your proceedings are conducted with so much mystery—so much secrecy—that I must be forgiven if vague suspicions——"

"I know it—I know it," interrupted the old woman; and after a short pause, she added, "Yes—I will ensure your confidence, Miss; and then you will understand my sincerity. That man who was with me this morning discovered your place of abode at my desire. He demanded to be present at our interview but I refused—for reasons of my own. I assured him I would speak to you alone, or not at all. I was therefore compelled, this morning, in his presence, to insist on having none by to overhear the business that made me seek you; and the same reason forced me to stipulate that you should meet me this evening unaccompanied by any of your friends. For if I had permitted one to be present at our interview, then there was no reason to exclude another; and that man might have insisted on being a witness as well as any companion of yours."

"If that be the only reason for this mystery," observed Katherine, considerably relieved by the old woman's explanation, "you cannot object to Miss Monroe accompanying me on the next occasion of our meeting."

"No," answered the old woman; "that may not be, for the man who is to be satisfied with money will watch me at a distance when we meet again. But, afterwards—at any future interview that may be necessary—Miss Monroe may accompany you."

"I understand you," said Kate. "To-morrow evening I will meet you again—here—and at the same hour. I shall then doubtless be prepared to give you the amount necessary to satisfy that man's avarice; and his interference will be disposed of. It will afterwards remain for *you* to satisfy *me*—and for *me* to reward *you*."

"Agreed, young lady—agreed!" answered the old woman. "We have now no more to say—except," she added, as a sudden thought struck her,—"except that, should the man insist on speaking to you to-morrow evening, you need not tell him that you have any intention of bestowing a separate recompense on me."

"I hope that he will not dare to approach me," said Katherine, indignantly; "and, were he to force his disagreeable presence upon me, I should scarcely permit myself to be catechised by him."

"'Tis well, Miss," returned the hag, apparently well pleased with the resolute manner of the young orphan.

They then separated.

The old woman went one way; and Katherine proceeded direct to the clump of trees where Ellen and the farmer were concealed;—for it was now so dark that there was no fear of the direction she took being observed.

It may be naturally supposed that Ellen and Mr. Bennet were deeply anxious to be made acquainted with the particulars of an interview concerning which they had some few misgivings.

On the return of the trio to the farm-house, they found Mrs. Bennet very uneasy on Kate's account. The appearance of the young maiden reassured the good-hearted woman; and Katherine then gave a detailed account of all that had passed between herself and the hag.

The impression produced was, that there was really a legitimate foundation for the old woman's proceedings, and that she was actually possessed of secrets touching Kate's parentage. The agreement that the recompense was only to be awarded to her after she had made the promised communications, was considered a proof of good faith; and Kate's promise to supply the sum demanded in the first instance to satisfy the avarice of the Resurrection Man, met with the approval of her friends.

"To-morrow, then," said Kate, "I must repair to London, and procure the necessary funds from Mr. Wharton. You will accompany me, Ellen?"

"That journey is not requisite," observed the farmer. "Mr. Wharton would demand an explanation of the business for which the money is intended; and he would only view it with the calm and severe eye of a lawyer. He might even go so far as to insist upon having those persons arrested as extortioners. He might not fully appreciate your filial anxiety, Kate, to risk every chance to know more of the authors of your being. I can well comprehend your feelings; and, after all, the venture is but a hundred pounds—for the old woman is to make her revelations before she receives a recompense. No—you shall say nothing to Mr. Wharton on the subject. I am going to London to-morrow; and on my return I will supply you with the sum required."

It is needless to say that Katherine expressed her gratitude to Mr. Bennet for his goodness; and Ellen readily promised to stay at the farm for a day or two longer, until the pending mysteries should be cleared up. Mr. Bennet moreover undertook to call at Markham Place, with a note from Ellen to relieve Mr. Monroe of any anxiety which he might feel on her account, as her absence from home would be protracted beyond the time originally contemplated.

CHAPTER CC.

A MAIDEN'S LOVE.

The two young ladies had now retired to the bed-chamber which Kate occupied at the farm, and which Ellen shared with her during her visit.

The respective characters of those two charming creatures were then incidentally contrasted and powerfully set forth, each in its peculiar phase, by means of occurrences apparently trivial to a degree, but which were nevertheless significant in the eyes of those who closely observed the nature of the human mind.

While Ellen was disrobing herself, she stood, in all the pride of her glorious beauty, before the mirror; in the reflection of which she also arranged her long, luxuriant hair previously to retiring to rest.

But Katherine, in the semi-obscurity of the remotest corner, laid aside her vestment; nor did she once think of approaching the glass.

Whence arose this discrepancy,—this pride on the one hand, and this bashfulness on the other?

It was that Ellen had been placed in those circumstances which had taught her the value and led her to appreciate the extent of her almost matchless charms:—her lovely countenance had served as a copy, and her exquisitely modelled form as a pattern for artists and sculptors;—during her brief dramatic career, she had been the object of unceasing adulation;—and when she forced Greenwood to espouse her, the splendour of her beauty had disarmed him of the resentment which he would otherwise have experienced in being compelled to sacrifice for her all his hopes of a brilliant matrimonial alliance. Hers was the pride of a loveliness which had produced her bread in the hour of her bitter need,—which was perpetuated in great works of art,—which had elicited the heart-felt admiration of many suitors of rank and name,—and which was still in all the freshness of health and youth. Still that pride was never obtrusive—not even conspicuous; for it was attempered by a natural generosity, an innate loftiness of soul which rendered her as adorable for her disposition as she was desirable for her beauty.

Katherine had long languished in a condition which compelled her to retire from observation. While she dwelt with the late executioner, she was glad to be able to shroud herself from public view. She was always neat and cleanly from principle, but not from pride. The germinations of self-complacency had been checked in their nascent state, though not completely obliterated; and now, if they were slightly expanding in the genial atmosphere of the improved circumstances which surrounded her, it was with a legitimate growth, such as no female mind should remain unacquainted with. For a certain degree of proper pride is necessary to woman,—to preserve her self-esteem, and to maintain her soul so happily poised that it may not fall into over-weening confidence on the one side, nor into an awkward and repulsive reserve on the other.

That chamber-scene would have made a fine and deeply interesting subject for the pencil of the artist, who would have delighted to shadow forth the variety of the female character,—here the glorious loveliness of the wife who dared not avow that sacred name,—there the retiring beauty of the young virgin.

But Katherine had not altogether escaped the influence of that blind deity who exercises so important a control over the destinies of us mortals.

How this happened we must leave her to describe in her own artless manner.

"I have been thinking, dear Kate," said Ellen, as she stood combing her long and silky hair, on which a lamp's reflection in the mirror shed a bright glory,—"I have been thinking that this is a dull and lonely place for you. Mr. and Mrs. Bennet are very kind and amiable people; but it will not be suitable for one whose worldly prospects are so good as yours, to remain in this solitude. You are literally buried here! I am almost inclined to take you with me to Markham Place for a short time, when the business with that old woman is decided. I am sure Richard would be pleased with such an arrangement."

"I should like to be with you, Ellen," was the reply: "but—for the present—I must remain here," added Katherine, with some little hesitation.

"Oh! no—you must come with me to Markham Place," exclaimed Ellen; "and the change of scene will please you. Besides—I have a secret to tell you, Kate."

"A secret!" repeated the maiden.

"Yes—a secret that will surprise you," continued Ellen. "I shall reveal it to you now; but you must not mention it to any one here—for particular reasons which I cannot explain to you at present. What should you think if I were to tell you that I am married?"

"You!—married!" exclaimed Katherine. "Then why are you still called Miss Monroe?"

"There are certain circumstances which compel me to keep my marriage a secret. When you come to Markham Place—as you must—you will see my father; but never in his presence, nor in that of Richard when he returns home, may you speak of me as a wife. And now do you know why I have told you this? Because, as I am determined that you shall come and pass at least a few days with me you will see my child——"

"Oh! Ellen, are you indeed a mother?" cried Katherine. "Are you not devotedly attached to your child? do you not fondle—play with it?"

"I am never wearied of its little company," answered Ellen. "It is a boy, and named after our mutual benefactor Richard. And now you know my secret. But tell me, Kate, wherefore you wish to remain pent up in this secluded dwelling? Has some happy youth in the neighbourhood touched your heart? You do not answer me. I cannot see you where you are; but I'll wager that you are blushing. Oh! if there be any truth in my suspicion, let it be revelation for revelation. We are friends—and you may confide in me."

"I know not how to answer you, Ellen;—and yet——"

"And yet you *have* a secret," returned the young wife, laughing; "oh! yes—you *have* a secret—and you must make me your confidant."

"I am willing to tell you all that relates to this foolish affair," said Katherine; "but that *all* is very little."

And she hesitated,—suffused with blushes even in the nook whither Ellen's eyes were not directed!

"Nay, continue," exclaimed Ellen. "I perceive that you are about to interest me with the commencement of a charming little love-tale. Seriously speaking, Kate—you will lose nothing by entrusting your secret to one who may be enabled to give you some useful counsel in a matter which is of far greater moment than young persons of our sex are induced to believe?"

"I will conceal nothing from you, Ellen," returned Katherine, in a low and timid tone. "It was only at the commencement of last week that I was rambling in the neighbourhood—on as fine a day as this one has been—when I met a young gentleman, who was crossing the same field as myself, but in an opposite direction. The path was very narrow; and he stood on one side to allow me to pass. I bowed in acknowledgment of his politeness, and he raised his hat. The glance that I threw upon him was of course only momentary; and I passed on. I thought no more of the incident——"

"He is doubtless very handsome," said Ellen, laughing. "All heroes of such romantic adventures are."

"Nay—hear me to the end," continued Katherine; "for since I have begun this silly tale, I may as well terminate it. The following day was fine; and I walked out again—as indeed I always do, when the weather will permit. I was proceeding through the same field——"

"The same field," observed Ellen slily.

"Oh! I can assure you, my dear friend, that you do me an injustice by the suspicion which your words imply," exclaimed Katherine. "I had totally forgotten the trifling incident of the preceding day; but I chose that path,—it was the same which we took this morning,—because it was dry and hard. To my surprise I again met that gentleman; and when he made way as before, to let me pass, he looked at me with an attention not rude, but still earnest. Our eyes met—and I passed hastily on. I felt myself blushing—I knew not why—to the very verge of my forehead. And yet I had done no wrong. I had glanced towards him as I acknowledged his politeness in stepping aside to allow me to pass; and it was by accident—at least on my part—that our eyes thus met. When I became more composed, I was angry at having been annoyed with myself. I then found myself involuntarily reflecting upon the handsome countenance,—for he *is* handsome, Ellen,—of which I had only so hasty a glimpse. I must admit that I thought of him more than once during the remainder of that day."

"Love at second sight, we must denominate it," observed Ellen, with a smile. "I will hazard a guess that the next day was fine,—for the weather is usually favourable in such circumstances,—and that you unwittingly found yourself rambling in the same path."

"Ah! Ellen, I am afraid that I was wrong—but all happened as you have described," said Kate, in a soft and melancholy tone; "and I obeyed some impulse for which I could not account. I candidly confess that I wondered, as I walked along, whether *he* would be there again; and when I did not perceive him, I experienced a sentiment of vexation. At length he appeared at the extremity of the field—he drew near—nearer and nearer. I felt ashamed of myself: it suddenly struck me that he must suppose I came thither on purpose to see him again. I never thought so little of myself—no, not even when I was pointed at as the presumed relative of an executioner. I turned abruptly round, and began to retrace my way towards the farm. I reached the low stile on the brow of the hill: at that moment I heard steps behind me. I cannot describe the sensations which I then experienced—a few short seconds of pleasing, painful suspense. Ere a minute had elapsed, the stranger stood by my side; and with a low bow he extended his hand to assist me in crossing the barrier. My head seemed to swim round; and I mechanically gave him my hand. He held it but for an instant as I passed into the next field;—and yet he pressed it gently—very gently;—still he pressed it! I know not whether I bowed or hurried abruptly on—I was so confused!"

"And during the remainder of that day you pondered on the incident," observed Ellen.

"Oh! how well you seem to divine all my thoughts—all my emotions!" exclaimed Katherine.

"Love has the same emblems—the same symbols, throughout the world," answered Ellen; "and it also has the same unvarying worship. Of the true nature of the great God there are many conflicting opinions; and different nations offer up their adoration in different manners. But to that blind deity whom we call Love, there is only one incense—and that is common to all humanity!"

"Then it was not wrong on my part to experience those emotions which I have explained to you?" said Katherine, with the most amiable *naïveté*.

"Wrong, dearest girl! oh, no!" exclaimed Ellen. "That heart must be a cold—a callous—a worldly-minded one, which never feels those most beautiful and holy of all sympathies! But go on with your narrative, Kate; for I feel convinced that you have seen your handsome lover since the day mentioned."

"I will tell you how we met again," said Katherine. "On the following day I did not stir abroad: I wished to take my usual ramble—but I feared that I should be doing wrong to incur the chance of meeting *him* again. As I was sitting at the parlour window, he passed. I was so taken by surprise—he appeared so unexpectedly,—ah! no—I am deceiving myself—I am deceiving you;—he came not altogether unexpectedly—for I had found myself wondering more than once whether he would again revisit this neighbourhood. He passed the window, then—as I have said; and I did not turn away until it was too late. He saw me—he seemed pleased: he bowed—and I slightly responded to his salutation. Then I retreated from the window, and did not approach it again during the rest of that day. The next day was wet and gloomy; and I felt persuaded that I should not see him. Will you blame me if I say that I was vexed at this circumstance? would you believe me if I declared that I treated it with indifference? But, ah! my annoyance was soon dissipated:—he passed the house at the same hour as on the preceding day! He was wrapped in a long military cloak; and when he saw me, he bowed with the same courtesy as heretofore;—but methought he smiled, as if with satisfaction at seeing me. And now you will say that I am a vain and foolish girl;—but, dearest Ellen, I an faithfully detailing to you all that occurred, and all the emotions I have experienced."

"Proceed, Katherine," said Ellen. "I become deeply interested in your narrative."

"The next day was fine once more; and I felt indisposed for want of exercise," continued the maiden. "I accordingly walked out—but in another direction. How I trembled at the slightest sound which resembled a footstep! How my heart beat when a bird flew past me! But my alarms—if I can honestly so call them—were without foundation: I beheld not the stranger that day. On the ensuing one I walked out again in the same direction; and, lost in thought, I rambled to a considerable distance. But at length I turned homewards once more; and when in sight of the farm, I suddenly beheld the stranger advancing towards me across a field. He was pursuing no direct path:—my heart beat violently—for something told me that he was coming that way only on my account! In a few moments we met: he bowed—I returned his salutation;—he suddenly took my hand, and pressed it—I hastily withdrew it—and passed rapidly on."

"This mute declaration of love is truly romantic," said Ellen, laughing, as she threw herself, half undressed, into an easy chair, and began to unlace the boots which enclosed her pretty feet.

Katherine had emerged from her nook, and was sitting on the side of the bed which was farthest removed from Ellen; and there, veiling her blushes behind the curtain, the young maiden continued her artless narrative.

"I know not how it was," she said: "but that gentle pressure seemed to remain upon my hand. I can even feel it now, when I think of it. Is not this very foolish, Ellen? But you wish me to tell you every thing; and therefore you must expect to be wearied with my frivolous details. The incident which I have just related made a profound impression upon me. The image of the stranger was constantly present to my memory throughout that day. I fancied that there was something sincere—and yet extremely respectful,—something fervent—and yet quite inoffensive,—in his manner towards me when he seized and pressed my hand. But I have forgotten to give you some idea of his appearance. He is young—tall—slight—and of a dark complexion. He seems to be of a foreign nation. His eyes are black and animated, and on his lip he wears a small moustache. His gait is elegant; and his manners are evidently those of a polished gentleman."

"And his name?" said Ellen. "He has doubtless communicated that?"

"He has never spoken a word to me," answered Katherine, with the most ingenuous seriousness. "We have not exchanged a syllable. I think, indeed, that I have already been sufficiently imprudent in allowing him to touch my hand. Still I could not have prevented him—he took it so suddenly!"

"And you have not exchanged a syllable!" exclaimed Ellen. "But it is as well that matters have remained where they appear to be. I will, however, give you my advice presently. In the meantime, continue your narrative."

"I have little more to say," answered Katherine, with a sigh. "On the following morning I met him once more—that was three days ago; and he accosted me evidently with the intention of speaking. But I hurried on; and he stopped. When I was at some distance, I cast a rapid glance round: he was still standing where I had left him. He saw that I threw that hasty look behind me; for——but, no——I cannot tell you the indiscretion of which he was guilty. It pains me to think of it; and perhaps he himself is conscious of his impropriety, for I have not seen him since."

"What, in heaven's name, did he do?" asked Ellen, surprised by the thoughtful seriousness of her young friend's manner.

"Do you wish me to tell you?" exclaimed Katherine. "Well—I must confess all! He kissed his hand to me."

"Were I not afraid of wounding your feelings, I should laugh immoderately, Kate," said Ellen. "Here was I on the tenter-hooks of expectation—awaiting some truly mortifying disclosure; and I find that the only fault which your swain has committed, is a delicate and mute declaration of his attachment. But to speak seriously once more. If you really entertain any sentiment of interest in behalf of this handsome stranger, you must allow time and circumstances to serve you. These romantic meetings, dear Katherine, are calculated to fill your young heart with hopes which may be cruelly disappointed. If he really experience a tender feeling towards you, he will find means to make it known in a more satisfactory, if not more intelligible manner. Then will be the proper time for your friends to ascertain who he is. For the present I cannot,—as I wish you well,—counsel you to incur the chance of meeting him in that wild way again. I am glad you have imparted this secret to me. It shall be sacred. But, oh! I am too intimately acquainted with the world to treat lightly or neglectfully a matter that may so nearly touch,—that does, perhaps, already to some extent concern,—your happiness; more than ever do I now desire that you should pass a few days with me at Markham Place. If your stranger really wishes to know more of you,—if his views be honourable, and his pretensions feasible, he will soon institute inquiries at the farm regarding you. Mr. Bennet will then know how to act. In the meantime there is no necessity to mention the affair to either him or his wife."

The tender interest of the subject had so completely absorbed all other ideas in the mind of Katherine, that—no longer under the restraint of the extreme bashfulness which had driven her into the obscure part of the chamber in order to lay aside her vesture—she had emerged from the concealment of the curtain, and gradually approached nearer and nearer towards Ellen, while the latter was affectionately offering her counsel.

The scene was now a most touching one.

In the large arm-chair reclined the young wife, her luxuriant hair, not yet arranged for repose, flowing in shining waves over her ivory shoulders, and forming a dark curtain behind her arching neck, the dazzling whiteness and graceful contour of which were thus enhanced with an effect truly enchanting;—while a stray curl of the glossy hair, detached from the mass behind, and more fortunate than its companions, fell on the glowing bosom which was without shame revealed in the sanctity of that chamber.

And, standing meekly before the young wife,—with downcast eyes and blushing cheeks,—was the young virgin,—her white arms supporting the loosened garments over her bosom in that sweet attitude of modesty which so many great masters have loved to delineate in their marble representations of female beauty.

It seemed as if Venus, the Queen of Love, were enthroned in the voluptuous negligence of the boudoir, and had suddenly assumed a demeanour befitting her sovereign sway, while she tutored one of her attendant Graces in some lesson whose importance demanded that unusual seriousness.

"And now, dearest Katherine," added Ellen, after a moment's pause, "I have given you the best advice which my humble capacity allows me to offer; and I think so well of you that I feel convinced of your readiness to follow it."

"I should be unworthy of your good opinion—I should despise myself, were I to hesitate a moment what course to pursue," returned Kate; and, yielding to the generous emotions of friendship, she threw herself on the bosom of her whom she had made the confidant of her young love.

"And you will consent to pass a short time with me at Markham Place?" said Ellen, embracing her affectionately.

"I will follow your counsel in all things, dear Ellen," replied the maiden, weeping from emotions of gratitude and love.

Human nature has no essence more pure,—the world knows nothing more chaste,—heaven has endowed the mortal heart with no feeling more holy, than the nascent affection of a young virgin's soul. The warmest language of the sunny south is too cold to shadow forth even a faint outline of that enthusiastic sentiment. And God has made the richest language poor in the same respect, because the depths of hearts that thrill with love's emotions are too sacred for the common contemplation. The musical voice of Love stirs the source of the sweetest thoughts within the human breast, and steals into the most profound recesses of the soul, touching chords which never vibrated before, and calling into gentle companionship delicious hopes till then unknown!

Yes—the light of a young maiden's first love breaks dimly but beautifully upon her as the silver lustre of a star glimmers through a thickly-woven bower; and the first blush that mantles her cheek, as she feels the primal influence, is faint and pure as that which a rose-leaf might cast upon marble. But how rapidly does that light grow stronger, and that flush deeper,—until the powerful effulgence of the one irradiates every corner of her heart, and the crimson glow of the other suffuses every feature of her countenance.

CHAPTER CCI.

THE HANDSOME STRANGER.—DISAPPOINTMENT.

On the ensuing morning Farmer Bennet departed early for London.

After breakfast, Ellen said, with a significant smile: "The weather is fine, Kate: let us take advantage of it. Your country air does me so much good."

Katherine blushed, and then smiled also; but she offered no objection to the proposed walk.

The toilette of the young ladies was soon complete; and they sallied forth on their little excursion.

"Mr. Bennet has promised to call at Markham Place," observed Ellen. "I have written a note to my father, stating that I shall return to-morrow, or next day at latest; and I have intimated my intention of bringing you with me. I most sincerely hope that some fresh tidings have been received from Richard."

"And in that wish I earnestly partake," said Katherine. "But wherefore do you choose this path?" she added in a tremulous tone, and with downcast eyes.

"Because it is the most pleasant," answered Ellen, laughing. "It seems, moreover, that your handsome stranger was determined to seek you in one direction, as well as in another; and if he be in the neighbourhood this morning, rest assured that he will see you—whichever way you may pursue. Love has as many eyes in this respect as Argus. I am with you, dear Kate—you have a companion; and there is no indiscretion in even taking this very path where you have on most occasions met your unknown. Besides, should he be here to-day, I am anxious to catch a glimpse of him. To-morrow or next day you will leave this vicinity of pleasant memories—at least for a time; and——"

"Ellen, Ellen!" murmured Kate, suddenly; and she caught her companion by the arm.

"Ah! I understand!—compose yourself, Katherine—compose yourself," was the rapid reply. "It would be improper to betray any emotion. See—he is approaching slowly;—in the name of heaven compose yourself!"

And, in effect, a handsome young man,—with a dark complexion, fine and expressive eyes, and a graceful figure,—was advancing in the opposite direction. But he came slowly, as if anxious to keep some favourite object as long in view as possible!

How the pulse of the maiden's young heart quickened, as she beheld her unknown lover approaching.

And now the handsome stranger came near:—and Katherine drew close to her companion, as the timid fawn relies for protection on the stately deer.

The look of the stranger was cast for a moment upon Ellen; but not the bright glance of her eye—nor the rich colouring of her cheeks, framed as they were in masses of glossy hair—nor that symmetry of swelling bust, delicate waist, and matchless proportions of a finely-moulded form,—not this assemblage of charms induced the stranger to dwell for more than an instant on Katherine's companion. No:—it was to Katherine herself that his eyes reverted with adoring glance; and though he gazed fixedly upon the retiring maiden, yet there was something so respectful in his manner, that it was impossible to take offence at it.

He made way for the two ladies, and raised his hat as they passed.

Katherine returned the salutation without turning her eyes towards him.

"Your stranger is not only handsome," observed Ellen, when they were at such a distance as to incur no danger of being overheard; "but he is also of an appearance so respectable—so superior,——I had almost said noble,——that I cannot for a moment suppose his intentions to be dishonourable. At the same time, why does he not address you? He might, without impropriety, have taken advantage of my presence to speak to you; and, to tell you the truth, it was to afford him such an opportunity that I brought you in this direction."

We need not record the conversation that ensued: the reader does not require to be informed that its principal topic was the love of the young maiden—a theme on which she was naturally pleased to speak, and in the discussion of which Ellen indulged her;—not, however, with the view of fanning the flame of incipient passion; but with the affectionate motive of warning her against the encouragement of hopes which might never be fulfilled.

The walk was prolonged until two o'clock, when the young ladies retraced their steps to the farm. Mr. Bennet had not yet returned from London: dinner was however served up. The fresh air had given Ellen an appetite; but Katherine ate little, and was somewhat pensive.

Indeed, the maiden had sufficient to engage the meditation of her young mind. The evident impression which the handsome stranger had made upon her, and the hope that evening would bring her the much-desired information relative to her parents, divided her thoughts.

But of what nature would the old woman's secrets prove? in what manner were they to be a source of comfort to her? It will be remembered that Smithers had made her acquainted with certain particulars relative to her mother; and the sad inference had been that Katherine was of illegitimate birth. Would the tendency of the old woman's communications be to clear up this mystery in a manner satisfactory to the young maiden? As yet all was doubt and uncertainty; and conjecture was vain!

It was about four o'clock when the farmer made his appearance.

He entered the parlour, where Ellen, Katharine, and Mrs. Bennet were sitting, with a countenance expressive of supreme satisfaction.

"I have glorious news for you, young ladies," he exclaimed; "and, indeed, all who know Mr. Markham———I beg his pardon, the Marquis———must be rejoiced."

"Oh! what of him?" ejaculated Ellen and Kate, as it were in one breath.

"Patience for a moment," said the farmer. "Here is a letter from Mr. Monroe to you, Miss,"—addressing Ellen; "and that will explain every thing yet known of the affair."

Ellen hastily tore open her father's note, and began to read its contents aloud:—

"*January 29th, 1841.*

"You will be supremely delighted, dearest Ellen, to hear the joyful tidings which I am about to communicate. This morning's newspapers publish a *Telegraphic Despatch* from Toulon, stating that a grand and decisive battle took place beneath the walls of Montoni on the 23d. Richard was completely victorious. The Austrian army was routed with tremendous loss; the Grand Duke fled; and the capital was delivered. Our dear benefactor is safe. The steamer which conveyed these tidings to Toulon left Montoni in the afternoon of the 24th, at the moment when Richard was entering the city—as the Regent of Castelcicala!

"Nothing more is known at present; but this is enough not only to reassure us all—but to fill our hearts with joy. My blood glows in my veins, old as I am, when I think of Richard's grand achievements. To what a proud height has he raised himself—second only to a sovereign! As I looked forth from the casement ere now, and beheld the two trees on the hill-top, I could not avoid a sorrowful reflection concerning Eugene. What can have become of him? I———"

"Heavens! dearest Ellen, are you ill?" exclaimed Katherine, seeing that her friend suddenly turned ashy pale.

"No, Kate: it is nothing! The abruptness with which we have received these tidings———"

"Yes—you *are* unwell," persisted Katherine; and she hastened to procure water.

Ellen drank some; and the colour slowly returned to her cheeks.

"I am better now, Kate," she said. "Do you terminate the perusal of my father's letter."

Katherine, perceiving that her friend really seemed to have revived, read the remainder of the note in the following manner:—

"I fear that he will not be enabled to tell so glorious a tale as his younger brother,—even if the appointment be really kept on his part! But enough of that. You speak of bringing Miss Wilmot, to pass a few days at the Place. I entirely approve of the project, if the excellent people with whom she is living, and of whom Richard has spoken to us so highly, be willing to part with her.

"I must not forget to mention that poor Whittingham is nearly crazed with joy at Richard's success. You remember his extravagant but unfeigned manifestation of delight when we received the tidings of the battle of Abrantani and its results. Then the worthy fellow danced and capered madly, exclaiming, *Master Richard a Markis!* all day long. But when I read him the Telegraphic Despatch this morning, he took his hat and kicked it all round the room,—a new hat too,—until it was battered into a state beyond redemption,—shouting all the time, *Here's a glorious cataplasm!*—(meaning 'catastrophe,' no doubt):—*Master Richard a Markis, and a Regency! I'll get drunk to-night, sir: I haven't been intoxicated for many a year; but I'll get drunk to-night, in spite of all the Teetotalers in London! Thank God for this glorious cataplasm!* And he rushed out of the room to communicate the news in his own way to Marian. But conceive my surprise when I presently heard the report of fire-arms: I listened—a second report followed—a third—a fourth. I became alarmed, and hastened into the garden. There was Whittingham firing a salute with his old blunderbuss; and Marian's new plaid shawl was floating, by way of a banner, from the summit of a clothes' prop fixed in the ground. Poor Marian did not seem to relish the use to which her Sunday shawl was thus unceremoniously converted; but all the satisfaction she could obtain from Whittingham was, *It's a glorious cataplasm! Master Richard's a Regency!* And away the old blunderbuss blazed again, until the salute was complete. I do really believe the excellent-hearted old man intends to illuminate the Place this evening; and I shall not interfere with the ebullition of his honest joy.

"I write this long letter while Mr. Bennet partakes of some refreshment.

"Trusting to see you and your young friend to-morrow or next day at latest, I am, dearest Ellen," &c. &c.

It is unnecessary to state that the news from Montoni diffused the most lively joy amongst the party assembled in the parlour of the farm-house.

Ellen speedily recovered her usual flow of excellent spirits, and expressed her sincere satisfaction at that remarkable elevation on the part of Richard which had excited the enthusiasm of her father.

Mr. and Mrs. Bennet offered no objection to the proposal that Kate should pay a visit to Markham Place: on the contrary, though grieved to part with her, they considered that change of scene could not do otherwise than benefit her.

And now the appointed hour for the meeting with the old woman drew near; and Mr. Bennet provided Kate with the necessary funds for her purpose.

Shortly before seven, the farmer (provided with a brace of loaded pistols) and Ellen repaired to the same hiding-place which they had occupied on the preceding evening; and, with a beating heart, Katherine hastened to the spot where she expected to encounter one who had promised to reveal secrets so nearly concerning her.

The old woman did not, however, make her appearance.

The minutes passed slowly away—and still she came not.

Katherine's anxiety was intense.

Half an hour had elapsed: still there was no sign of the hag.

The young maiden waited until past eight o'clock; and at length she suddenly perceived two persons advancing towards her at a little distance.

For a moment she felt afraid; but the farmer's voice speedily reassured her.

Ellen and he were alarmed at Katherine's prolonged absence, and had come to seek her.

Finding that the old woman had not made her appearance, they began to view the entire affair with some suspicion; and Kate was compelled to return with them to the farm—a prey to the most cruel disappointment.

"If the old woman was prevented, by any unforeseen circumstance, from meeting you," said the farmer, "she will communicate with you early to-morrow. Perhaps we may be favoured with another visit from her emissary, Mr. Banks; but should he come, I shall take good care that he treats us to a sight of no more model-coffins."

During the remainder of the evening Kate was pensive and melancholy; nor could all Ellen's affectionate endeavours wean her from her sorrowful thoughtfulness.

They retired to rest early; and Katherine rose next morning with the hope of receiving tidings from the old woman.

But hour after hour passed without gratifying her wish.

Ellen purposely delayed their departure for London, to afford a fair opportunity for the arrival of any intelligence which the old woman might forward; but three o'clock came, and still all was blank disappointment and mystery in respect to the affair.

Then Kate herself saw the inutility of tarrying longer; and, having taken an affectionate farewell of Mrs. Bennet, the young ladies were accompanied by the farmer to Hounslow. There they obtained a conveyance for the capital, and Mr. Bennet saw them depart in safety.

CHAPTER CCII.

THE PRINCESS ISABELLA.

We must now succinctly record a few incidents which occurred at the mansion of Prince Alberto in the vicinity of Richmond, from the period when Richard bade adieu to Isabella ere his departure for Castelcicala in the month of October, 1840, until the end of January, 1841—that is, up to the date at which we have brought our narrative in the preceding chapter.

The Princess Isabella declared, at her farewell meeting with Richard, that wild hopes and exalted visions filled her imagination when she contemplated the enterprise on which her lover was about to embark. So well did she read the true character of our hero, and so elevated was her opinion of his high qualifications, that she felt persuaded he only required an opportunity to open for himself a grand and brilliant career.

Her boundless affection for Richard Markham aided her not only in fostering these convictions, but also in shadowing forth and defining the elements of a glorious success and rapid rise on the part of one to whom her first and undivided love was given.

But when she tore herself away from his last embrace,—when she breathed the mournful word "Farewell," and then separated from the generous, the high-minded, and handsome young man who possessed her heart,—oh! how acute was the anguish that filled her soul!

For some minutes—when he was no longer in sight—all her golden dreams and glorious visions fled from her imagination;—she strove to recall them, as a drowning person in the dark hour of night struggles to gain the surface of the waters once more to catch another glimpse of the bright stars above;—but hope seemed to have yielded to blank despair.

The Princess, however, possessed a firm mind; and when the primal burst of anguish was over, she wrestled with her gloomy imaginings, until she gradually triumphed over their mournful influence.

Having purposely prolonged her walk homewards, in order to compose herself, Isabella did not re-enter the mansion until she had collected her scattered thoughts and had wiped away the traces of her tears.

Her father had all along discountenanced the expedition to Castelcicala, so far as he was concerned; although he could not do otherwise than wish it success. Indeed, as he himself had intimated to General Grachia, he would no doubt have joined in it, had he been differently situated. It was therefore with feelings of admiration that the Prince had from the first heard of Markham's enthusiasm in the Constitutional cause: and at that period he frequently found himself dwelling attentively upon all the good points in Richard's character which had once made our hero so welcome a guest at the mansion.

As for Isabella's mother, this Princess was more than ever favourable towards Markham; for she saw in his present conduct nothing save a profound devotion to the cause of her illustrious husband, and a laudable ambition to render himself worthy of her daughter's love—that love which was no secret to the parents of the amiable girl!

When Isabella returned to the drawing-room after her interview with Richard, her still melancholy demeanour attracted the notice of her affectionate parents.

"Where have you been, Isabel?" inquired the Prince, eyeing her attentively.

"My dear father," was the instantaneous reply, "I went for my usual walk in the adjacent fields, and I met Mr. Markham."

"Ah!" exclaimed the Prince, a little impatiently.

"I do not pretend that it was accidentally on *his* part," continued Isabella, in a tone expressive of the pride of truth; "because he is the last person in the world to sanction duplicity of any kind. It was, however, accidental in reference to myself—for I knew not of his intention to seek an interview with me this day."

"But you have met?" said the Prince, in a softening voice, and with a manner which denoted how justly proud he was of the upright mind of his daughter.

"We have met, dear father," answered Isabel, wiping away a tear; "and—we have separated—perhaps," she added in a faltering tone, "never to meet again. Oh! be not angry with *him*—nor with *me*, my dearest parents,—especially not with *him*!"

"No—we are not angry, my child," said the Princess of Castelcicala, hastily. "Indeed, for my part, I wish that Mr. Markham had come to wish us all farewell. But perhaps he will write———"

"I did not refuse his request on that subject," murmured Isabella, casting down her eyes and blushing: "Oh! no—I could not! And now, my dear parents, you know all. If I have done wrong, I am deeply grieved;—but my conscience tells me that I have not outraged the devotion and love that I owe to you."

The Prince made no reply: but the expression of his countenance was not severe; and the Princess of Castelcicala embraced her daughter affectionately.

From that time the mansion contained three anxious hearts; for the exiled family was deeply interested in the results of the expedition to Castelcicala.

Who, then, can depict the disappointment with which the tidings of the fatal affair of Ossore were received, at the end of November, in that dwelling?

The Prince and Princess perceived in the failure of the enterprise a deep blow to their own cause in the Duchy, inasmuch as it was calculated to afford the supporters of the Grand Duke an excuse for heaping opprobrium on the name of Alberto, whom they would point out as the instigator of the invasion;—and Isabella was overwhelmed with grief by the mystery which at that period enveloped the fate of Richard.

Several days of heart-breaking suspense elapsed: the colour forsook the maiden's cheek; and her countenance became expressive of a deep melancholy.

Nor was this terrible uncertainty concerning Richard's fate the only cause of affliction which she was now doomed to experience. Her father was so profoundly affected by the failure of the expedition, and the evils which he believed would result to his own interests in many respects, that he became ill, and was soon unable to leave his bed.

Then how assiduous was the poor girl to her parent, while her own heart was often well-nigh breaking! The Prince grew irritable and impatient, and even reproached his daughter for fretting on account of one who, as he declared, "had helped to hurry the Constitutional cause,—a cause that might have triumphed in time,—to a most ruinous catastrophe." But Isabella bore all this without a murmur; and as her father grew more harsh, her attentions towards him were redoubled. In her mother's kindness and sympathy the afflicted maiden found a consolation; but she could with difficulty bear up against the agony of suspense and alarm which she experienced on account of her lover.

At length,—about a week after the receipt of the fatal tidings connected with the battle of Ossore,—Whittingham called at the mansion, and placed in Isabella's hand a letter from Richard.

"He lives! he lives!" were the maiden's first words of reviving hope; "heaven be thanked—he lives!"

But Isabella's joy was speedily overclouded once more; for she saw, by the guarded manner in which he wrote and by the omission of his signature, that her lover was in danger.

Nevertheless—"where there is life, there is hope," as the proverb says; and, somewhat consoled by his conviction, she was less miserable than before!

And now came another tedious interval of suspense, the wretchedness of which was enhanced by the increasing indisposition of the Prince.

At length—at the expiration of about three weeks—the Princess Isabella received a letter from Signora Viviani, the nature of which, as already known to our readers, was not extremely well calculated to reassure the affectionate girl relative to her lover. It was true that she was informed of Richard's safe arrival at Pinalla, where he was in the society of kind friends; but vague and torturing fears were aroused by the fact that he himself had been unable to write to her.

Again was there a weary interval of silence; but this was suddenly broken in a manner calculated to re-awaken all the bright hopes which Isabella had once entertained relative to the future greatness of Richard Markham. On the 16th of January, the news of the glorious exploit at Estella reached the mansion of the exiled family in England; and inspired the young Princess with the most enthusiastic feelings of admiration towards him whom she loved so fondly, and of whom she had always thought so well.

"Oh! why am I bound to this bed of sickness?" exclaimed the Prince, when Signor Viviani's letter narrating that event was read to him. "Why am I not permitted to hasten to my native country, and take part with that gallant youth! No consideration of policy or delicacy should now restrain me; for the Austrian is in the land, and every true Castelcicalan should draw the sword and fling away the scabbard!"

"Compose yourself, dearest father," said Isabella, enraptured at the manner in which he had spoken of her lover: "excitement will only delay your recovery;—and something tells me that Castelcicala will soon demand your presence!"

But the Prince could *not* tranquillize his mind: the thraldom of a sick bed had become more intolerable to him than ever; and, although he now ceased to reproach his daughter, his irritability of temper painfully increased.

Three days afterwards letters were received at the mansion announcing Richard's entry into Villabella. Then the colour came back again to the cheeks of the charming Italian maiden; and her eyes shone with all their wonted brilliancy. Forgotten were her recent sorrows—gone was her agonising suspense—banished was the memory of her cruel doubts;—her lover was already a hero—and hope was once more enthroned in her heart.

The Prince now began to perceive the absolute necessity of avoiding the excitement of useless repinings at that illness which still chained him to his bed. Richard's letters told him how the inhabitants of Villabella had shouted the thrilling words "Long live Alberto!"—and the Prince was inspired with hopes the extent of which he did not seek to conceal.

Four days elapsed; and when the postman was again descried by the watchful Isabella advancing through the shrubbery towards the mansion, how quickly beat the hearts of the illustrious exiles!

Yes—there were letters from Castelcicala:—never were sealed documents more quickly torn open! And, oh! what joyous news did they contain—the victory of Piacere!

Isabella's feelings found vent in tears:—she was so happy—that she wept!

"These are indeed glorious tidings!" said the Prince, raising himself upon his pillow; then, after a moment's pause, he exclaimed warmly, "Richard Markham is a hero!"

Ah! how touchingly grateful was the glance which Isabella cast upon her father through her tears, to thank him for that generous sentiment relative to one in whom she felt so deep an interest!

Another short interval now occurred; and then fresh letters came, bringing farther tidings of success. The battle of Abrantani was a worthy sequence to that of Piacere!

"Oh! my beloved Isabella," now exclaimed the Prince, pressing her to his heart, "can you forgive me for the reproaches I have so unjustly—so wantonly uttered relative to Richard Markham?"

"Think not of the past, dearest father," answered the maiden: "the present is so full of joy, and hope, and glory, that we should not feel wearied of contemplating it."

"And, whatever may be the result of this contest," observed the Princess of Castelcicala to her husband, "you will always acknowledge that Richard is a hero?"

"He is a young man whom the greatest sovereign in the world might be proud to claim as a son!" ejaculated the Prince, enthusiastically.

Isabella pressed her mother's hand tenderly for having obtained this most welcome avowal.

The health of Prince Alberto now rapidly improved; and in a few days he was enabled to leave the couch to which he had been confined for many weary weeks.

And Isabella—Oh! all the charming carnation tinge had come back to her cheeks; and her eyes were brilliant with the purest rays of happiness and hope. Her fondest dreams—her brightest visions were all but realised: her lover was accomplishing those grand destinies of which her mental vision had caught glimpses ere his departure from England; and the world was already busy with his name. And now, too, was that name ever upon the tongue of her father, who pronounced it with admiration and respect.

A few days after the arrival of the intelligence of the decisive victory of Abrantani, the newspapers acquainted the illustrious Italian family with the fact that the Committee of Government at Montoni had bestowed the title of Marquis of Estella upon the youthful Commander-in-Chief of the Armies of Castelcicala.

Oh! with what joyous feelings—with what ineffable emotions of enthusiasm, did the charming Isabella read aloud to her parents that account of her lover's elevation,—an elevation which, as he himself had felt convinced, must remove one grand obstacle that had hitherto existed in the way of their happiness.

And how did her young heart beat and her bosom heave, when her father exclaimed, in an emphatic tone, "Yes—Richard is now a Marquis, and may take his rank amongst the proudest peers in the universe;—but there is a higher grade which he yet may reach—and it will be a happy day for us all when I shall say to him, '*Receive my daughter as the reward of your achievements, and become a Prince!*'"

Isabella threw herself at her father's feet, and pressed to her lips the hand which she also moistened with her tears. She endeavoured to murmur words of gratitude for that most welcome assurance; but her heart was too full—she could only weep!

It was a most touching scene; and, perhaps, never had that exiled family experienced more perfect happiness than on this occasion.

But the sentiment was soon destined to give way to new fears and fresh anxieties. It was well-known that Montoni was besieged by an immense Austrian force; and the English newspapers, in commenting upon the position of the Constitutionalists, declared that though the moral effects of so decisive a victory as that of Abrantani must be very great, there was nevertheless much room to doubt whether the Marquis of Estella would be able to assemble an army sufficiently strong to march to the relief of the capital.

Prince Alberto trembled as he read these observations; because he not only comprehended their justice, but was also well aware that the fate of Castelcicala could be alone decided by a pitched battle between the Austrians and the Constitutionalists.

He endeavoured to conceal his misgivings from his wife and daughter: but they saw what was passing in his mind;—and thus all was still anxiety and hope—uncertainty and fervent aspiration, at the mansion of the Prince.

Thus did a few days pass; and Alberto suffered a slight relapse, in consequence of the nervous state of doubt in which he was plunged.

All his hopes—all his interests—all his prospects were at stake. If the Constitutionalists were successful, a crown awaited him: if the Austrians triumphed, the Grand Duke Angelo had pledged himself to adopt a scion of the imperial family of Vienna as the heir to the throne. Thus Prince Alberto hovered between a glorious elevation or a fatal fall.

The Princess, his wife, entertained sanguine hopes that a campaign so successfully begun, would terminate in triumph; and Isabella called every argument to her aid to convince her father and mother that all must end well! Nevertheless, poor girl! she also had her intervals of doubt and alarm; and many were the tears which she shed in secret as she prayed for the safety of her lover.

And now how eagerly was the arrival of the postman looked for every day; how anxiously was the presence of the newspaper awaited!

At length, on the morning of the 29th of January, all doubts were cleared up—all uncertainties terminated.

The illustrious family was seated at the breakfast table—a mere ceremonious mockery, for they were unable to eat a morsel.

Presently a servant entered, and presented the morning paper to the Prince.

Alberto opened it with a trembling hand: his wife and daughter watched him attentively.

Suddenly he started—his eyes were lighted up with their wonted fires—a flush appeared on his pale cheek—and he exclaimed in a fervent tone, "O God! I thank thee!"

He could say no more: his emotions nearly overpowered him, weakened as he was by a long illness.

Isabella caught the paper as it was falling from his hands. One glance was sufficient: it told her all! For there—conspicuously displayed at the head of a column—was the following glorious announcement:—

"CASTELCICALA.

"TOTAL DEFEAT OF THE AUSTRIANS—DELIVERANCE OF MONTONI.

"The French Government have received the following Telegraphic Despatch from Toulon:—

"'*The Castelcicalan steamer* Torione *has just arrived. The Austrians were completely routed on the 23rd. Montoni is delivered. The Grand Duke has fled.* THE MARQUIS OF ESTELLA *entered the capital at three o'clock on the 24th. He has been appointed Regent until the arrival of* ALBERTO I. *The* Torione *left while the cannon were saluting the presence of the* MARQUIS.'"

"Let me be the first to congratulate your Serene Highness on this glorious result!" exclaimed Isabella, falling at the feet of her father, and pressing his hand to her lips.

"No—not on your knees, dearest Isabel!" cried Alberto, now Grand Duke of Castelcicala: "but come to my arms, sweet girl—and you also, beloved companion of my banishment," he added, turning towards his wife, who was nearly overcome by these sudden tidings of joy:—"come to my arms—for we are no longer exiles—we shall once more behold our native land!"

How sweet—how sweet were the caresses which those three illustrious personages now exchanged:—how unalloyed was that happiness which they now experienced!

And when they were enabled to compose their feelings so far as to discourse upon the triumphant result of the Constitutional cause, the name of Richard Markham was not forgotten!

CHAPTER CCIII.

RAVENSWORTH HALL.

In the immediate neighbourhood of Kilburn on the gentle acclivity rising towards Wilsden Green, stood a noble mansion in the midst of a spacious park.

Every thing about that vast structure, within and without, denoted aristocratic grandeur combined with exquisite taste.

The adjunction of no modern buildings had spoiled the antique and time-honoured appearance of Ravensworth Hall: the hand of the mason, when repairing the ravages of years, had successfully studied to preserve the effect of the beautiful Elizabethan architecture.

Thus the splendid mansion,—with its numerous gables, its tall chimneys, its picturesque belfry, its immense windows with small diamond-shaped panes, and its ample portals approached by a flight of twenty steps,—seemed well adapted for the residence of a peer who could trace his family back to the epoch of the Conquest, and who preserved as much feudal state and grandeur as modern systems and habits would permit.

It was the 1st of February; and as early as six o'clock on that morning—before it was light—Ravensworth Hall was a scene of bustle and excitement.

Some grand event was evidently about to take place.

The chimneys belonging to the kitchen and servants' offices in the rear of the building, sent forth dense columns of smoke, which seemed to imply that extensive culinary preparations were in progress.

The butler,—a venerable old man with hair as white as snow, but with a stately portliness of form that was scarcely bent by age,—was busy in selecting the choicest wine from the immense stock of which he was the guardian. The female domestics were early employed in preparing the grand apartments of the mansion for the reception of a brilliant company:—windows were cleaned, coverings removed from the velvet cushions of chairs and sofas, heavy hangings and curtains arranged in the nicest folds so as to display the richness of their texture to the best advantage, and China ornaments carefully dusted.

Lord Ravensworth rose earlier than he had done for some weeks; for before the clock struck eight he descended from his dressing-room to a chamber which he denominated his "cabinet."

He was a man of about fifty years of age, and had evidently been very handsome. But his countenance was now colourless, haggard, and painfully indicative of some deeply seated disease which was preying upon his vitals. His eyes were sunken and lustreless: his cheeks were hollow,—and yet seldom had an individual of his age possessed so splendid a set of teeth, the whole of which were perfect. So thin and wasted was his form, that, although he was naturally of a powerful and portly structure, the dressing-gown which he had on hung as loosely about him as if on a skeleton.

And how rapidly had these ravages of an unknown and unaccountable malady worked their terrific influence on a man who had lately appeared to possess that constitutional vigour and robustness of health which predicate a long life!

Three months previously to the time of which we are writing had Lord Ravensworth first experienced a change in his physical energies which began to alarm him. He was then staying, with his young and beautiful wife, to whom he had only then been married half-a-year, at his town-mansion; and when the primal symptoms of his malady appeared,—evidencing themselves in want of appetite, intervals of deep lethargic languor, and an apathetic listlessness in respect to every thing passing around him,—his physicians advised him to essay the bracing air and change of scene of Ravensworth Park. His lordship was, however, unwilling to remove his young wife—the lovely Adeline—from the gaieties of London, at that season when all the fashionable world was returning to the metropolis after the autumnal visits to their country seats or favourite watering-places; and he had accordingly persisted in passing the Christmas holidays at his town-residence.

But he rapidly grew worse:—his appetite totally failed him; and it was with the greatest difficulty that he could force himself to take the sustenance necessary to sustain life. He had always been a great smoker; and his only solace now appeared to be his meerschaum. Alone in his own private apartment, he would sit for hours with no other companion than the eternal pipe. He was fond of oriental tobacco, because the Turkish and Persian weeds possessed a peculiar aroma which rendered their use a habit comparatively inoffensive to others. And here we may observe that the only reciprocal attentions which had taken place for years between Lord Ravensworth and his younger brother, the Honourable Gilbert Vernon, consisted in the annual interchange of presents:—thus, as Gilbert had resided in oriental climes, he was in the habit of sending Lord Ravensworth every year a small chest containing the most rare and excellent samples of tobacco grown in Asia Minor and Persia; and in return he received from his elder brother a box filled with all the newest English publications, and a variety of choice articles for the toilette, such as Gilbert could not have procured in the East.

Thus was it that, when the nobleman found a strange and insidious malady growing upon him, he naturally sought relief, both mental and physical, in his favourite recreation; and never had the present of his brother seemed more valuable to him than when he forgot his ailments in the soothing enjoyments of the aromatic Turkish or mildly-flavoured Persian tobacco.

For two months had he been subject to a mysterious and deeply-rooted disease,—which one physician treated as atrophy, and which another honestly confessed he could not comprehend,—when about the beginning of the year, he had yielded to the entreaties of his wife and removed to Ravensworth Hall.

There he appeared to rally for a few days,—taking powerful exercise on horseback and on foot, and indulging but little in the luxury of the meerschaum. One day, however, the weather was so intemperate that he could not stir abroad; and he passed several hours in his "cabinet," with his favourite meerschaum. From that period the apathy which he had to some extent shaken off, returned with increased power: his manner seemed more lethargic and indifferent than it had yet been; and the companionship of his pipe grew more welcome to him than ever. He now spent the greater portion of each day in his cabinet, with positive orders that he was not to be disturbed; and there he enjoyed that baleful comfort which is experienced by the *Teryaki*, or oriental opium-eaters. Reclining in a capacious arm-chair, with the tube of his meerschaum between his lips, Lord Ravensworth forgot the world without,—remembered not his wife,—thought not of the infant that she bore in her bosom,—and even seemed insensible to the fearful wasting away which his physical strength was rapidly undergoing. He refused to allow his physician to prescribe for him; and though the work of enfeeblement and decay progressed with alarming velocity, he seldom appeared to reflect that he must shortly be numbered with the dead.

It is due to Adeline to state that,—attached to pleasure and gaiety, and fond of society as she was,—she endeavoured to arouse her husband as much as she could from that mortal apathy which, even in her presence, shrouded all his sensibilities as it were in a premature grave. His case presented the remarkable and mysterious anomaly of a man in the noon of lusty-hood, and without any apparent ailment of a specific kind, passing out of existence by a geometrical progression of decay.

Such was the condition of Lord Ravensworth at the period when we introduce our readers to the Hall.

A few words will explain the motive which had induced him to rise at so unusually early an hour on the 1st of February, and which also led him to a temporary, and, alas! very feeble exertion to shake off the torpor of listlessness and the opiate influence of his mortal apathy.

Lady Ravensworth's cousin, the Honourable Miss Maria Augusta Victoria Amelia Hyacintha Villiers, was, in fashionable language, "to be that morning led to the hymeneal altar." This young lady was rich only in her names: she was a portionless orphan; and the cold calculation of her guardian, Lord Rossville (Adeline's father), had induced him to consent to the sacrifice of the poor girl to a suitor whose wealth and title of Baronet were his only recommendations.

Miss Maria Augusta Victoria Amelia Hyacintha Villiers had been residing with her cousin Adeline, ever since the marriage of the latter with Lord Ravensworth; and it was to consummate the sacrifice ere now alluded to that all the grand preparations before mentioned were in progress. Lord and Lady Rossville and Lady Ravensworth all conceived that Lord Ravensworth would be benefited by the excitement attending the assemblage of a marriage party at the Hall; and their expectations appeared to be in some measure justified. His lordship descended at an unusually early hour to his cabinet, and, instead of having recourse to his meerschaum, he summoned the butler, to whom he gave instructions relative to the service of particular wines.

For nearly a month past his lordship had not meddled in any of the affairs of the household; and the venerable servant was overjoyed to think that his noble master was giving unequivocal signs of recovery. This idea seemed to acquire confirmation from the circumstance that the nobleman afterwards returned to his dressing-room without smoking a single pipe, and, aided by his valet, attired himself with unusual precision and care.

"Your lordship is better this morning," observed the valet, deferentially.

"Yes—I am a little better, Quentin," returned the nobleman; "and yet I hardly know that I have ever felt actually ill. Want of appetite is the principal ailment which affects me. It makes me grow thin, you perceive:—but am I so *very* thin, Quentin?"

"Oh! no, my lord," answered the valet, who belonged to a class that never tell disagreeable truths so long as their wages are regularly paid. "Your lordship is certainly not so stout as your lordship was; but——"

"But what, Quentin?"

"I think—if your lordship would not be offended—that I am acquainted with the cause of that want of appetite, which prevents your lordship from taking proper sustenance."

"Go on, Quentin: I shall not be offended. I know you are a faithful fellow," exclaimed the nobleman. "What do you think is the cause?"

"With your lordship's permission, I should say that smoking too much—" began the valet, timidly.

"Pooh! pooh!—nonsense!" interrupted Lord Ravensworth, impatiently. "I have always been a great smoker: you know I have. I began to smoke when I was only fourteen; and as I was so long a bachelor—during the best years of my life, indeed—I had no reason to curb myself in my favourite recreation. It would be different, perhaps, if I used the filthy tobacco which you buy in England—or if I smoked strong Havannah cigars. But that mild and aromatic plant, which is reared in the East, cannot injure a soul:—a child might smoke it."

"Your lordship knows best," observed the valet, feeling that he was treading on delicate ground. "But I think your lordship has smoked more lately than——"

"I dare say I have," again interrupted the nobleman, with some little petulance. "But the last chest of tobacco which my brother sent me is so much better than all the former ones; and there is such a delightful soothing influence in the samples of Turkish and Persian, that I cannot lay aside my pipe when once I take it up. Let me see! It was only last October—yes, and at the end of October, too—that I received the chest; and I have already made a deep inroad into it."

"Is the Honourable Mr. Vernon still in Turkey, my lord?" inquired the valet.

"Yes: at least, when I heard from him last—that was when he sent me the chest of tobacco in October—he stated in his letter that he should yet remain abroad for two or three years. He seems devoted to the East. But you know, Quentin, that he and I are not upon the very best of terms, although we occasionally correspond and interchange little civilities every now and then. However, I can scarcely blame myself for any coldness that may subsist between us. I have behaved to him as an elder brother ought to a younger one;—and because I would not consent to minister to his extravagant propensities he took umbrage. When I espoused her ladyship last May, I wrote to Mr. Vernon, who was then at Beyrout, acquainting him with that event; and his reply, which accompanied the chest of tobacco in October, was more kind and conciliatory than I could have expected, considering his gloomy and morose character."

"I am glad that he exhibited a proper feeling towards your lordship," said Quentin, by way of making some observation, because his master had paused.

"And so am I," continued the nobleman. "Then I wrote to him again in November, to inform him that Lady Ravensworth was in a way that gave promise of a continuation of our name,—the name of Ravensworth is a very ancient one, Quentin——"

"Yes, my lord. I believe your lordship can trace it back to the invasion of Britain by the Romans?"

"No—not quite that," returned the nobleman; "but to the conquest by William the Norman. However, I wrote to my brother, as I have informed you; and I received no answer. I therefore conclude that he has renewed his travels through Asia-Minor."

The toilet of Lord Ravensworth was now complete; and he hesitated for a moment whether he should repair to his cabinet and take "just one little pipe," or whether he should hasten to the drawing-room at once.

The valet understood what was passing in the nobleman's mind; but as he was really attached to his master, and moreover entertained a belief that the too liberal use of tobacco had reduced him to his present wretched physical condition, he hastened to exclaim, "The company are already assembled, my lord, in the drawing-room; and her ladyship will be quite delighted to see your lordship looking so very well to-day."

Once more Lord Ravensworth, who for a moment was about to relapse into a state of listless apathy, brightened up, and wrestled with the fatal influence that was creeping over him; and in this improved state of mind and body he proceeded to the drawing-room.

CHAPTER CCIV

THE BRIDE AND BRIDEGROOM.

A brilliant assembly was collected in the principal saloon of Ravensworth Hall.

Lord Rossville,—a tall, thin, stern-looking man,—and Lady Rossville,—a very short, stout, and affected dame,—were amongst the most conspicuous by rank and station.

Lady Ravensworth seemed as beautiful as Lydia Hutchinson had described her; and, as she was rather pale and delicate in consequence of being in an "interesting situation," she was really a being who might be termed, without any poetical exaggeration, sweetly fascinating. But no one who there beheld the elegant and proud peeress, doing the honours of her splendid mansion to a circle of noble guests, would have imagined that, when plain Miss Adeline Enfield, she had played the wanton at so tender an age, and given birth to a child in a miserable garret!

The Honourable Miss Maria Augusta Victoria Amelia Hyacintha Villiers was a beautiful, but timid and retiring, girl of seventeen;—and as she now appeared in the virginal white which custom had compelled her to assume for the consummation of a sacrifice which she felt—Oh! how keenly felt,—it was easy for a benevolent eye to perceive that she was a victim to cold calculation, and not a happy bride about to accompany to the altar one whom she loved.

But there were no benevolent eyes there:—there seldom are in fashionable life and in such cases. The expression of blank despair which marked the countenance of the young bride was regarded only as the token of maidenly reserve and bashfulness.

Not that she loved another: no—her heart was entirely her own;—but she was about to be given to a man whom she abhorred.

"Why did she not remonstrate with her guardian?" asks the innocent reader. Remonstrate with a stanch Tory and High-Church-supporting peer like Lord Rossville? Ridiculous! He who believed that the people are mere machines formed to toil for the aristocracy, was not likely to listen with even common patience to the remonstrances of a young maiden for whom he believed he had arranged a splendid destiny.

"But, then, poor Maria might have opened her heart to Lady Rossville?" says that self-same innocent reader. Equally ridiculous! A mother who had intrigued so well as to foist her own daughter upon an elderly noble like Lord Ravensworth, and who imagined that matrimony was nothing more nor less in respect to young ladies than "catching at the first rich man who offered himself," was very far from being the proper person at whose hands the orphan and portionless Maria could obtain a reprieve of the death-sentence which had been pronounced upon her heart.

In high life how many matrimonial connexions are based on the calculations of sordid interest, instead of the sympathies of the soul! And then the hoary peer or the decrepid nabob is surprised that his young wife proves unfaithful to his bed, and declaims against the profligacy of her conduct in yielding to the temptations of a deeply-seated love for another—a love which was perhaps engendered before the ignominious sacrifice of her person to the sexagenarian husband was ever thought of!

But to return to the drawing-room at Ravensworth Hall.

Amongst the select party assembled, we must especially mention the Honourable Miss Wigmore and the Honourable Miss Helena Sophia Alexandrina Wigmore—the bridesmaids, who looked as if they had much rather have been principal instead of secondary actresses in the matrimonial ceremony. There also was the newly-appointed Bishop of the Carribbee Islands—solemn in lawn sleeves, and pompous in the display of his episcopal importance. Lounging near the chair of a very pretty girl, with whom he was conversing, stood Count Swindeliski—a refugee who sported enormous whiskers, who had found his way into fashionable society no one exactly knew how, and who had the extraordinary but not altogether uncommon knack of living at the rate of five thousand a-year—upon nothing! Then there were several Members of Parliament who had collected together near a window, and were disputing with all their talent whether there ought to be a duty of one halfpenny or three-farthings per hundred on foreign brick-bats. Near an open piano was gathered a group of very young ladies, engaged in an edifying discussion on the character of some other very young lady who was not present. Conversing with Lord Rossville was the owner of half a county, who could return six Members to Parliament with the greatest ease, but could not for the life of him return a sensible answer to even the plainest question. Standing apart from all the rest, was a young country clergyman, who kept turning up the whites of his eyes as if in a constant agony of some kind or another—but really because he was in the presence of a Bishop, although the said Bishop never once cast his reverend eyes that way. Then there was the Dowager Countess of Brazenphace, who had "got off" seven out of nine red-haired daughters, and had brought the two remaining single ones with her just to see if they could not make an impression somewhere or another. There also was the celebrated German philosopher Baron Torkemdef, who had written a work in fourteen quarto volumes to prove that there is no such thing as matter—that we do not really exist—but that we ourselves and every thing else are mere ideas. This learned man was, as might be supposed, a very valuable acquisition to a bridal party. Seated next to Lady Rossville was the Honourable Mrs. Berrymenny, who had seen five husbands consigned to the tomb, and was looking out for a sixth. It was, however, probable that she was doomed to look long enough, inasmuch as she had no fortune, and had already reached the comfortable age of fifty-three. Lastly, there was the elegant and accomplished Miss Blewstocken, who was known to have written a volume of poems which had an excellent circulation (amongst the butter-shops), and who was suspected of having perpetrated a novel.

These are all the stars whom it is worth while to signalise amidst a galaxy of some fifty personages.

The bridegroom had not yet arrived: he was expected to make his appearance at about half-past eight.

When Lord Ravensworth entered the room, every one who had not lately seen him was shocked at the dreadful change which had taken place in him; but of course the guests, one and all, assured him that they had never seen him look so well before.

Adeline sighed deeply—for she could not help thinking that it was a miserable mockery for a gaunt and almost fleshless skeleton thus to deck itself out in an apparel befitting a bridal:—moreover, the idea that if her yet unborn offspring should prove a girl, the broad lands and noble Hall of Ravensworth would pass away to another, was ever uppermost in her mind.

To conceal her emotions, she hastened to the side of poor Maria Villiers, to whom she said, "It is very strange that the lady's-maid whom you have hired did not come last evening, as promised."

"It is, indeed, very annoying," observed Maria, whose sorrows were, however, too deep to permit her mind to be even ruffled by that trifling source of vexation.

"But never mind," continued Lady Ravensworth, in a whisper; "you shall take my maid Flora with you, and I will either find another at my leisure, or keep the one whom you have engaged, should she make her appearance after you have left."

"This is very kind of you, Adeline," said Maria, mechanically.

"I am afraid you did not manage well in your first essay in choosing dependants, dear Maria," observed Lady Ravensworth. "You were attracted by the advertisement in the *Morning Herald*; whereas I never should think of taking a lady's-maid who advertises. Then, as you yourself told me, you went to some out-of-the-way place in the City for the young woman's character."

"Oh! I was perfectly satisfied, Adeline," interrupted Maria, to whom this conversation appeared trivial in the extreme on an occasion so fraught with solemnity to herself.

Lady Ravensworth was about to make some reply, when Lord Rossville, who had been standing at the window for the last few moments, exclaimed, "Here's the bridegroom!"

A cold shudder passed over Maria's frame; and it seemed as if her heart had been suddenly swathed in ice.

She alone retained her place: all the other persons present hurried to the window.

And, sure enough, the bridegroom was in view; and a very funny view it was. Perched upon the back of an enormous bright bay horse, the "happy man" never appeared more miserable in his life. He was tugging at the reins with all his might; but the huge animal galloped furiously along in spite of the efforts made to restrain its speed. The bridegroom's feet were thrust as far as they could go into the stirrups: his hat was rammed tight down over his eyes, to prevent it from blowing away;—his form was bent, or rather crouched up, like that of a monkey;—with his right hand he held fast by the horse's mane;—and with his left he continued tugging at the bit and bradoon. The poor animal itself seemed to wonder, like John Gilpin's steed, what sort of a thing it had got upon its back; for its eyes glared, and its nostrils dilated with affright: while its whole body was covered with a greasy perspiration, and white flakes of foam kept falling from its mouth.

In this manner did the bridegroom rush madly, but with involuntary speed, through the spacious Park towards the Hall. At a short distance behind him rode another cavalier, who managed his horse well, and amused himself by maintaining a succession of shouts and hurrahs after the bridegroom, whereby that unfortunate individual's steed was only affrighted all the more. A third person on horseback appeared at a greater distance still; but this was the bridegroom's servant.

"A most un-christianlike and decidedly unhallowed manner for a bridegroom to comport himself," said the Bishop of the Carribbee Islands, as he contemplated this ludicrous display of horsemanship.

"It certainly is strange," observed Lord Rossville. "But perhaps our young friend is anxious to display his skill———"

"No such a ting, milor—no such a ting!" ejaculated Count Swindeliski, caressing his whiskers. "Dat young gentleman's von great homebogue; and if me was dere, me hit him some kick for his pain."

"Ah! he doesn't ride so well as my poor dear *fourth*," said Mrs. Berrymenny, with a profound sigh, as she thus alluded to one of her husbands.

"It's all vanity and vexation of spirit," observed the young clergyman, glancing deferentially towards the Bishop.

"No, sir—it is not, sir," said the Bishop sternly: "it is sheer bad riding, sir—and nothing else."

The Right Reverend Father in God had been a fox-hunter in his time.

"For my part," cried a Member of Parliament, "I move that we repair to the young gentleman's assistance."

"And I beg to second the motion," said another Member.

"Ah! by heaven, that's serious!" ejaculated Lord Rossville, turning abruptly away from the window.

And so it seemed; for the horse suddenly stopped near the entrance of the mansion, and pitched the bridegroom clean over its head into a clump of evergreens.

All the ladies who beheld this catastrophe screamed aloud.

But at the very next moment he rose from his ignominious position, and with difficulty removing his battered hat from over his eyes, saluted the company assembled at the windows of the drawing-room.

"It's noting at all," said Baron Torkemdef: "he only tink himself hurted—you only tink dat a horse what did seem to run way wid him:—it all de idea—all de fancy."

Then, while Lord Rossville and others hastened to meet the bridegroom and assure themselves that he was not hurt, Baron Torkemdef caught hold of the great county landowner by the button-hole, and began to expatiate upon the folly of yielding to sensations of pain and other afflictions, as not only those sensations but also we ourselves were only so many unsubstantial ideas.

Meantime, poor Maria Villiers had remained in a sort of listless reverie in her seat; and it was only when Lady Ravensworth assured her that the bridegroom had sustained no injury, that she learnt he had been in any peril at all.

In ten minutes the door opened, and Lord Rossville returned to the room, ushering in the bridegroom, who had been cleansed in the meantime from the effects of his fall, and who endeavoured to put a smiling face upon the matter, although still terribly disconcerted.

Then Lady Adeline advanced to meet him, and said in a most gracious tone, "We have been painfully excited on your account, Sir Cherry Bounce."

CHAPTER CCV.

THE BREAKFAST.

Yes—it was to this individual that Maria Villiers was to be sacrificed:—it was to him that the cold and selfish policy of Lord Rossville was about to consign a beautiful, an artless, and an amiable girl.

Sir Cherry's mother had paid the debt of nature about a year previously; and the young baronet found himself the possessor of an immense fortune.

Lord Rossville only looked upon his orphan niece Maria as an encumbrance while she remained single, or as a means of increasing the *wealth* (and in his idea, the *strength*) of the family when she married. Sir Cherry had met her in the brilliant sphere of the West-End society: he had courted her; and, the moment Lord and Lady Rossville observed his attentions, they *commanded* her to receive them with favour. She—poor timid, friendless girl!—was half persuaded into the idea that the match was really to her advantage, and half bullied (for we can actually use no other term) into an acquiescence in the views of her guardian.

Thus she had not dared to utter a negative when the effeminate and insipid baronet had solicited her hand; and, her silence being taken for a ready consent, the preliminaries were hurried on, without any further reference to the inclinations or wishes of the victim!

"We have been painfully excited on your account, Sir Cherry Bounce," said Lady Ravensworth, advancing to receive the bridegroom.

"The twuth wath that my fwiend Thmilackth inthithted on my widing the new horth I bought yethterday," exclaimed the baronet; "and ath he don't theem to be veway well bwoken in, the wethult wath that I nearly got a bwoken head."

"I never saw such a Guy on a horse before—strike me!" ejaculated Major Smilax Dapper, who had followed his friend into the room. "He would keep in advance of me the whole way; and although I called after him to rein in—strike him!—he would not listen to me."

"It wath that thouting and hoowaying that fwightened my horth," observed Sir Cherry, casting a sulky look towards Smilax.

"At all events you are not hurt—and that is the essential," said Lord Rossville.

"Hurted! no—of course de good gentleman's not hurted," exclaimed Baron Torkemdef: "it noting at all but de idea—de fancy. You know vare well, sare, dat you not really exist—dat you only tink you do exist———"

Sir Cherry Bounce, to whom these words were addressed, cast so ludicrous a look of surprise mingled with dismay upon the philosopher, that Major Smilax Dapper burst into an immoderate fit of laughter; so that Baron Torkemdef was for a moment disconcerted.

Lord Rossville seized this opportunity to lead Sir Cherry Bounce towards Miss Villiers, who received her intended husband with a manner which to the superficial observer might appear excessive bashfulness, but which to the penetrating eye was the expression of blank—dumb—soul-crushing despair.

"I was just as timid with my *first* as Maria is," whispered Mrs. Berrymenny to the Countess of Brazenphace: "with my *second* I was a leetle more gay;—with my *third*———"

"Dear Mrs. Berrymenny," interrupted the Countess, impatiently; "pray do not talk of your *seconds* and *thirds*, when here are my two youngest daughters who haven't even yet got their *firsts*."

Two footmen, in gorgeous liveries, now entered the room and threw open a pair of folding-doors, thus revealing an inner apartment where the nuptial ceremony was to take place by special license.

Then Sir Cherry Bounce took Maria's hand, and led her slowly into the next room, the Honourable Misses Wigmore attending her in the capacity of bridesmaids.

The remainder of the company followed in procession.

And now the Bishop takes his place near the table, and opens the book.

The ceremony begins.

Pale as marble, and almost insensible to what is passing around her, Maria Villiers hears a sort of droning mumbling, but cannot distinguish the words.

And yet the Bishop read the prayers in a clear, distinct, and impressive manner.

One of the bridemaids whispered in Maria's ear; and the young victim mechanically repeated the answer thus prompted.

But she was scarcely aware of the tenour of what she had said: every moment the scene became less comprehensible to her mind—and she was on the point of uttering a wild cry, so alarming was the confusion of her thoughts, when there was a sudden movement amongst the assembly—warm lips touched her forehead for a moment and were instantly withdrawn—and then her ears rang with the congratulations of her *friends*!

The chaos of her ideas was immediately dispelled; and the appalling truth broke suddenly on her.

The ceremony was over—and she was a wife:—upon her marble brow the kiss of a husband had been imprinted.

By one of those strange efforts of which the soul is sometimes capable, when "the worst" has arrived and "the bitterness of death" has passed, Maria recovered her presence of mind, and even smiled faintly in acknowledgment of the congratulations which she received.

"Dat young lady seem vare happy now," whispered the German philosopher to Mrs. Berrymenny; "but it all noting more dan de idea. We all idea—dat reverend Bischop—dis room—dat book what he was read in—every ting!"

"Do you mean to persuade me, sir," asked Mrs. Berrymenny, with an indignant glance at Baron Torkemdef, "that it is all mere fancy on my part that I have had five husbands? If so, sir, all I can say is that I should like to have a sixth opportunity of putting your theory to the test."

And with these words the widow of five experiments of the marriage-state joined the procession which was now on its way to the breakfast-room.

The table in this apartment was spread with all the delicacies which were calculated to tempt the appetite even of satiety.

Sir Cherry thought it necessary to whisper some soft nonsense in the ears of his bride, as he conducted her to a seat; and Maria turned upon him a vacant glance of surprise;—then, suddenly recollecting the relation in which she stood towards him, her head drooped upon her bosom, and she made no reply.

"Cherry," whispered Major Dapper, "you are not half lively enough—blow you! You look like a fool—but I suppose you can't help it."

"Hold your tongue, Thmilackth," returned Sir Cherry, colouring to such an extent that the deep red was visible beneath his light hair. "You than't tweat me like a child any more."

And now began the bustle of the breakfast-table, and the excitement of the scene appeared to produce the most beneficial effects upon Lord Ravensworth, who did the honours of the table, conjointly with Adeline, in a manner indicative of more gaiety and spirit than he had exhibited for some time.

"Lord Ravensworth is certainly improving," said the Countess of Brazenphace apart to Mrs. Berrymenny.

"My *second* used to deceive me in the same manner," was the reply, also delivered in an under tone. "He was always dying—and always getting better, for at least three years before he went off altogether. My *fourth*———"

"Oh! you have told me all about him before," hastily interrupted the Countess, who was alarmed lest the widow should inflict upon her a narrative of oft-experienced tediousness.

"Dat vare excellent bird—how you call him? Peasant—ah!" observed Baron Torkemdef to the young clergyman, who, like a child, saw, heard, but said nothing. "But after all it no use for to praise one ting or to blame anoder—'cause dem each de idea—de fancy. Dere really no table—no peasant—no wine—no peoples: it all de imagination."

And while the philosopher went on expatiating in this manner, the viands disappeared from his plate and the wine from the decanter near him with a marvellous rapidity; so that the young clergyman could not help muttering to himself, "I wonder whether the Baron's appetite is an idea also."

"Seraphina," whispered the Countess of Brazenphace to one of her daughters, "if you look so much at Count Swindeliski, I shall be very angry. He has got no money, and is not a match for you. There is the Member for Buyemup-cum-Rhino sitting on your right, and he is a wealthy bachelor."

"But, dear mamma," returned Miss Seraphina, also in a whisper, "he is at least sixty."

"So much the better," was the prompt reply: "he is the easier to catch. Now mind your p's and q's, Miss."

This maternal advice was duly attended to; and, by the time he had tossed off his third glass of champagne, the Member for Buyemup-cum-Rhino had grown very tenderly maudlin towards the red-haired young husband-hunter.

"Miss Blewstocken, dear," cried the elder Miss Wigmore, "have you composed nothing appropriate for the present occasion?—no sweet little poem in your own fascinating style?"

"Oh! dear Miss Wigmore, how unkind!" said the literary young lady, in an affected and languishing manner. "I could not have believed it of you—to appeal to me before so many! If I have told you in confidence, or if it be indeed generally known that '*The Poetic Nosegay*' was written by me—and if it had a very large circulation—I do not think it is fair to expect——"

"Ah! Miss Blewstocken," exclaimed Miss Wigmore, "we are all aware that your pen is seldom idle."

"It is really quite provoking to find oneself known to Fame," said the literary lady, with increasing affectation of manner, and in a drawling, insipid tone. "I wish I had never written at all:—not that I have ever been induced to acknowledge the authorship of that novel which was so successful last year—'*The Royal Fiddlestick*,' I mean. No:—but the time *may* come——"

And here the literary lady shook her head in so mysterious a way that if she intended to be incomprehensible, she certainly was most successful in the endeavour.

"Who is that lady?" inquired the Bishop of Lord Rossville.

"Miss Blewstocken, the celebrated authoress," was the reply.

"Oh!" said the Bishop, in a dry laconic way, which proved that, however celebrated Miss Blewstocken might be, the trumpet of her renown had never sounded in his ears before.

"Talk of de poetry and de novel," exclaimed the German Baron, "what are all dem to de researches of de philosoph? Was your lordship ever read my von grand vork on de '*Ideality of de Universe*?'"

"I cannot say that I have ever read it, sir," answered the Bishop, with a frown. "I have heard of it, sir—and I consider its doctrines to be opposed to the Bible, sir. I believe it is in fourteen large volumes, sir? Well, sir—then all I have to observe upon it is that so many quartos are themselves too substantial to be a mere idea."

"But dey are von idea!" exclaimed the Baron, angrily. "Dey do not really exist, milor—in spite of what your lordship shall say. Every ting is de idea—we be ourselves all de walking, moving idea: dere no such ting as joy—no such ting as pain—dey mere sensation—"

At this moment the learned philosopher started from his seat with a yell of agony, and began stamping on the floor in a furious manner.

The fact was that while he was gesticulating in order to bestow additional emphasis on the enunciation of his principles, his hand, raised in the air, came in contact with a cup of coffee which a domestic was about to place before the young clergyman; and the scalding fluid was poured forth on the bald head and down the back of the philosopher.

"Pray do not mind it, sir," said the Bishop, drily: "it is merely an idea."

"Yes—it de idea, no doubt!" ejaculated Baron Torkemdef, as he wiped his head with his pocket-handkerchief, while the domestic murmured an apology and slunk away: "but de idea was come in de unpleasant shape—dat noting against my doctrine—tousand devils, how him do burn!"

And, particularly disconcerted, the learned man sank back into his seat, where he consoled himself with a renewed application to the decanter near him.

Meantime Count Swindeliski was rendering himself very amiable to the Honourable Miss Helena Sophia Alexandrina Wigmore, next to whom he sate.

"Poland, then, must be a very beautiful country?" said the young lady, duly impressed by a most graphic description which the Count had just terminated.

"It vare fine—vare fine," returned the fascinating foreigner. "De ancestral castle of the Swindeliskis vare grand—touch de clouds—so long dat when you do stand at de von end you shall not see de oder—so wide dat horses shall always be kept saddled for to cross de court. My father was keep tree tousand dependants: me not choose for to spend de revenue in dat vay—me only may keep von tousand."

"And can you prefer England to your own beautiful country?" inquired Miss Helena Wigmore.

"Me shall not prefare England," answered the Count: "me shall choose wife of de English ladies—dey vare beautiful—vare fine—vare clevare. Den me take my wife to Poland, where she shall be von vare great lady indeed."

And, as he spoke, he threw a tender glance at his fair companion.

But Miss Helena Sophia Alexandrina Wigmore knew full well that every word the Count uttered concerning his fortune and castle was false. She was, however, too polite not to seem to believe him; and she was, moreover, pleased at engrossing the attentions of the handsomest man in the room. She therefore permitted herself to flirt a little with him; especially as her mother was not present to control her actions; but, like all young ladies in fashionable circles, she was too astute and wary to entertain the least idea of a more serious connexion.

The breakfast was now over; a carriage and four drove up to the front of the mansion; and the hour of departure had arrived for the "happy couple."

Maria withdrew for a few moments in company with Lady Ravensworth and the two bridemaids and when she returned she was dressed for travelling.

"Happy fellow!" whispered Major Dapper to his friend; "blow you!"

"Fooleth Thmilackth!" returned Sir Cherry Bounce. "But I am weally veway happy—ekthepth that curthed wide on the fatht twotting horth. Good bye: I thall wite to you in a few dayth."

The farewells were all said; and Maria resigned her hand to him who was about to bear her away from the Hall.

She wept not—she sighed not: but despair was written on her marble visage—though none present could read that sombre and melancholy language.

"I have directed Flora to accompany you," whispered Lady Ravensworth; "and you can keep her altogether, if you choose. Should the young woman whom you have hired, make her appearance, I will retain her, and give her a trial. But what is her name? I had forgotten to ask you."

Maria gave an answer; but there was such a bustle in the room at the moment and such a confused din of many voices, that the name escaped Adeline's ears.

Sir Cherry at the same instant led Maria towards the stairs; and in a few minutes the carriage, containing the newly-married pair, was rolling away from Ravensworth Hall on its journey to Cherry Park in Essex.

"I wish I was bound on a similar trip with a *sixth*," thought Mrs. Berrymenny, as she watched from the window the departure of the carriage.

"I wish I could get off my *eighth* and *ninth* as easily as the Rossvilles have done with Maria," thought the Countess of Brazenphace. "But I am afraid that the member for Buyemup-cum-Rhino will not bite."

"I wish I had not eulogised the single state in my poems," thought Miss Blewstocken, with a profound sigh.

"Me wish me shall soon find de agreeable lady dat will make me de von happiest of men," said Count Swindeliski to Miss Helena Sophia Alexandrina Wigmore.

"After all," said Baron Torkemdef, who had recovered his equanimity, by dint of frequent libations, "de marriage only de idea—de fancy, like any oder ting. Dat handsome chariot do not actually exist—it only de idea; and dat loving pair what shall sit in it are only idea as well. All is idea—me an idea—and dat Lord Bischop wid de lawn-sleeves only an idea."

"Where is Lord Ravensworth?" inquired Adeline of a domestic.

"His lordship felt suddenly unwell a few moments ago, my lady, and has retired to his cabinet."

"Ah! a reaction—a recurrence to the meerschaum!" murmured Lady Ravensworth, a cloud passing over her brow.

"Please your ladyship," said the servant, "a young woman has just arrived from London. She says that she was hired by Miss Villiers—I beg pardon Lady Bounce—and that an accident to the vehicle in which she came to the Hall has delayed her."

"Oh! she is to remain with me," returned Adeline. "Tell her that I will take her into my service on the same terms that were arranged between her and Lady Bounce. She is to replace Flora."

"Very good, my lady;"—and the servant was about to retire.

"One moment, William," said Adeline, beckoning him back. "Did this young woman mention her name—for as yet I am really ignorant of it?"

"Yes, my lady," answered the domestic: "her name is Lydia Hutchinson."

And the servant withdrew.

"Lydia Hutchinson!" murmured Lady Ravensworth, turning deadly pale, and tottering to a seat.

"Are you unwell, Adeline?" inquired Lady Rossville, approaching her daughter.

"No—a sudden indisposition—it is nothing!" replied Adeline; and she hastened from the room.

CHAPTER CCVI.

THE PATRICIAN LADY AND THE UNFORTUNATE WOMAN.

Lady Ravensworth retired to her boudoir; and, throwing herself upon a voluptuous ottoman, she burst into a flood of tears.

The wife of one of England's wealthiest nobles,—mistress of a splendid mansion and numerous household,—young, beautiful, and admired,—with a coronet upon her brow, and all the luxuries and pleasures of the world at her command,—this haughty and high-born lady now trembled at the idea—now shrunk from the thought—of meeting an obscure young woman who was forced to accept a menial place in order to earn her daily bread!

It was a strange coincidence that thus brought Lydia Hutchinson beneath the roof of Lady Ravensworth, whom the young woman was very far from suspecting to be that same Adeline Enfield who had been her companion—nay, her tutoress—in the initiative of wantonness and dishonour.

Mrs. Chichester had manifested a sisterly kindness towards the unfortunate Lydia; and, instead of shrinking in disgust, as so many others would have done, from the young woman who had been urged by stern necessity to ply a loathsome trade, she had endeavoured, by the most delicate attentions, to reclaim the mind of society's outcast from the dark ocean of despair in which it was so profoundly plunged.

The reader has doubtless seen that Lydia Hutchinson had never courted vice for vice's sake. She was not naturally of a depraved nor lascivious disposition. Circumstances—amongst which must be reckoned the treachery exercised by Lord Dunstable to accomplish her seduction, and the accident which threw the poor creature upon the tender mercies of Mrs. Harpy,—had conspired,—fearfully conspired, to brand her with infamy, and to drag her through the filth and mire of the various phases which characterise the downward path of a career of prostitution. Necessity had made her what she was!

Mrs. Chichester comprehended all this; and she was not one of those who believe that there is no sincere penitence—no reformation for the lost one. She longed to afford Lydia an opportunity of entering on a course of virtue and propriety. She would have willingly afforded the poor creature a permanent asylum, as a matter of charity, and even to insure a companion to cheer her own species of semi-widowed loneliness; but she was well aware that eleemosynary aid of such a kind, by retaining its object in a condition of idleness and of dependence, was of a most demoralising nature. She wished to give Lydia an opportunity of retrieving her character in her own estimation, and of regaining a proper confidence in herself; and she resolved that no excess of indulgence, nor extreme of charity, on her part, should permit the young woman to live in an indolence that might unfit her for any occupation in case of ultimate necessity, and that would thus fling her back upon the last and only resource—a recurrence to the walks of ignominy and crime. To reclaim and reinstate, as it were the unfortunate Lydia Hutchinson, was Viola Chichester's aim; and the object of this humane solicitude was deeply anxious to second, by her own conduct, the intentions of her generous benefactress.

As time wore on, Lydia improved greatly in mental condition and personal appearance: her thoughts became settled and composed, and her form resumed much of the freshness which had characterised her youth. She speedily began to express a desire to exert herself in some honest employment to gain her livelihood;—she also felt that indolence and dependence, even in the presence of the best moral examples, produce a vitiated frame of mind;—and she revolted from the mere idea of a relapse into the horrible path from which a friendly hand had redeemed her, as the most appalling catastrophe that her imagination could conceive.

Mrs. Chichester felt so persuaded of Lydia's firmness of purpose in pursuing a career of rectitude, that she resolved to take a step which only the extreme urgency of the case and a settled conviction of the young woman's inclination to do well, could justify. This was to obtain her a situation in some family. Lydia was overjoyed at the proposal. An advertisement was accordingly inserted in a newspaper; and a few days brought many written answers. Miss Villiers—now Lady Bounce—called personally, and was so pleased with Lydia's manner that she put no special questions to Mrs. Chichester.

Viola, however, addressed Miss Villiers thus:—"The young woman who now stands before you has been unfortunate—very unfortunate; and hers has been the fate of the unfortunate. She is most anxious to eat the bread of industry and honesty. I am persuaded that a kind hand stretched out to aid her in this desire, will raise her to happiness, and ensure her lasting gratitude."

Miss Villiers was a young lady of an excellent heart: she did not completely understand all that Mrs. Chichester meant; but she comprehended enough to render her willing to assist a fellow-creature who sought to earn her livelihood honourably, and who seemed to possess the necessary qualifications for the employment desired. Thus the bargain was hastily concluded; and when Miss Villiers desired Lydia to join her on a certain day at Ravensworth Hall, the young woman entertained not the least idea that her school friend Adeline Enfield was Lady Ravensworth, the mistress of that lordly habitation.

We will now return to Adeline, whom we left weeping in her boudoir.

The presence of Lydia in that house was indeed enough to alarm and embarrass her. Not that she precisely feared exposure at Lydia's hands in respect to the past—especially as it would be so easy to deny any derogatory statement of the kind. But Adeline felt that she should now possess a dependant before whom her dignity and self-confidence would ever be overwhelmed by the weight of that dread secret of which Lydia's bosom was the depository. Such a prospect was most galling—most humiliating—most degrading to the mind of the haughty peeress.

"But of what avail are tears?" said Adeline, suddenly. "The danger is here—the evil is before me. We must meet:—it were better that I should see her at once! Doubtless she is unaware in whose abode she is now a menial!"

Adeline wiped her eyes, rang the bell, and reseating herself, assumed as composed a manner as possible under the circumstances.

In a few moments she heard footsteps approaching.

"This is my lady's apartment," said the housekeeper in the passage.

"Thank you," replied another voice.

Oh! how Adeline's heart beat,—the well-remembered tones of Lydia Hutchinson had just met her ears.

Then she heard the retreating sounds of the housekeeper's footsteps; and there was a gentle knock at the door of their boudoir.

"Come in," said Adeline, in a half-stifling voice.

The door opened, and Lydia Hutchinson entered the room.

Lady Ravensworth's countenance was averted towards the fire; and it was not until she heard the door close that she turned towards Lydia, who was in a state of trembling anxiety, mingled with curiosity, as to what might be the disposition of her mistress.

But no pen can describe the astonishment of the young woman, when by that pale but beautiful countenance, which was now suddenly turned towards her, she recognised her whom she had so much reason never to forget.

Staggering towards the mantel for support, and with her eyes fixed almost wildly upon her mistress, she exclaimed, "Miss Enfield! Is it indeed you?"

"I am Lady Ravensworth," was the somewhat haughty answer.

"Oh! now I understand it all!" cried Lydia, an expression of sincere gratitude animating her countenance, while she clasped her hands fervently together: "you have taken compassion on me at length,—you discovered where

I was residing,—you sent some friend to engage me as if for herself,—and you were determined to surprise me by this proof of your goodness—this token of your kind remembrance of me!"

"No," returned Adeline: "accident alone has brought you into my service: and you must well understand that I am not over well pleased with the coincidence. In a word, name the sum that will satisfy you for the loss of a good place—and take your departure. You can leave to me the invention of some proper excuse———"

"Is it possible?" ejaculated Lydia; "this cold—heartless—ungrateful reception———"

"Do you recollect to whom you are speaking?" demanded Adeline, the colour mounting to her cheeks.

"Oh! yes,—I know that full well—too well," said Lydia, again clasping her hands, and casting her eyes upwards, as if in appeal to heaven against the ingratitude of the world. "I stand in the presence of one to save whose good fame I sacrificed my own—to shield whom from the finger of scorn and reproach, I allowed myself to be made a victim! Yes, proud lady of Ravensworth—so many years have not elapsed since, in my cold and cheerless garret, in the depth of a winter night, you gave birth———"

"Silence, Lydia!" ejaculated Adeline, her lips quivering, and the colour coming and going on her cheeks with rapid alternations. "Let us not refer to the past. The present———"

"No," interrupted Lydia, in a solemn tone: "you *can* not—you *shall* not deter me from talking of the past. For you, lady, are so highly exalted above myself, that it is almost impossible for you to shape the least—the faintest—the most remote idea of the depth of misery into which I have been plunged. And yet I pant—I long—I feel a burning desire to make you comprehend all I have suffered;—because to my acquaintance with you—to my fatal connexion with you at the seminary—may be traced all the sorrows—the profound, ineffable woes—the degradations—the terrible afflictions that have since marked my career!"

"I will not hear more;—I cannot permit you thus to insult—to upbraid me," faltered Lady Ravensworth, her bosom agitated with the most cruel emotions.

"Oh! I have longed for this opportunity to meet you face to face, and tell you all I have suffered, and all I now feel!" exclaimed Lydia; "and it is not likely that I will abandon so favourable an occasion. No—you have triumphed over me long enough: you have used me as a tool when it suited your convenience—and you spurned me when I had ceased to be useful. Though maintaining your own outward respectability, honour, and good name upon the wreck of mine, you dare to treat me with the blackest ingratitude! Lady Ravensworth, I said that all I have endured was traceable to you! When I first met you at the Kensington seminary, I was pure, artless, innocent:—you were already initiated in the secrets of intrigue—you were even then, at that tender age, a wanton in your heart."

"Lydia—Miss Hutchinson! Oh! my God!" exclaimed Adeline, covering her face with her hands.

"Yes—you were already trembling on the verge of dishonour—you were courting seduction and all its consequences!" continued the unfortunate woman, upbraiding that proud peeress with a remorselessness, a bitterness, and a feeling of delighted vengeance that made her language the more terrible and its effect more overwhelming. "I even remember still—oh! how well I remember—that you were the first who opened my eyes to the existence of female frailty. Yes—I, who went to that school as a teacher, was taught by a pupil! And merciful heavens! what did you teach me? You led me on step by step in the path of duplicity and dishonour: you made me the companion of your own amours; and we became victims to our seducers on the same day!"

"Oh! spare me—spare me!" moaned Adeline. "My God! if we were overheard! I should be lost—ruined—undone!"

"Rest tranquil on that head:—it does not suit my present purposes to betray you—and I will explain my reason shortly. In the meantime," continued Lydia Hutchinson, "I must recall to your recollection all those circumstances which led me to sacrifice myself to save you."

"No—no: I remember everything. Say no more, Lydia," cried Lady Ravensworth. "Tell me what you require—what I can do for you! Will you have money? or———"

"Peace!—silence!" said Lydia, eyeing the patrician lady with a glance of ineffable scorn. "Oh!" she added, almost wildly, "I *have* sold myself for gold;—but never—never may that occur again; either bodily or morally! Your ladyship declares you remember all that has ever passed between us? Then does your ingratitude become infinitely the more vile and contemptible. For when you lay writhing in the agonies of maternity, I was there,—there in that cold and cheerless garret,—to minister unto you! And when the lifeless form of your babe was discovered concealed amongst my clothes—in my room—and in my box,—I did not turn to the school-mistress and say, '*It is not mine: it is Miss Adeline Enfield's!*'—When, too, I saw that you were so weak, so feeble, and so suffering that the cold night air would kill you, I took your child, and, like a thief, stole away from the house to sink the corpse in a distant pool. For you had said to me, '*Keep my secret, dearest Lydia: the honour of a noble family depends upon your prudence!*'—My prudence! Oh! no:—the honour of your family depended on the sacrifice of *mine*! And I *did* sacrifice my family to save you;—for to all that I did for you may be traced the broken heart of my poor father and the assassination of my brother by the hand of the duellist!"

"Oh! spare me—spare me!" again exclaimed Lady Ravensworth. "I have been very ungrateful—very unkind; but now, Lydia, I will endeavour to compensate you for all that has passed."

"One being alone can so compensate me, lady," said Miss Hutchinson in a solemn tone; "and that being is God! No human power can give me back my poor father or my much-loved brother: no human agency can obliterate from my mind those infamies and degradations to which I have been subject. What amount of gold can reward me for days of starvation and nights of painful wanderings amidst the creatures of crime, without a place to repose my aching, shivering limbs? And sometimes, amidst the overwhelming crowd of sorrows that so often drove me to the river's bank, or made me pause on the threshold of the chemist's-shop where poison was to be procured,—I saw, from time to time, your name mentioned in the newspapers. Oh! what memories did those occasions recall! On the very day that you were presented at Court, I had not a crust to eat! And twice on that day did I seek the river's brink, whence I turned away again—afraid of changing even the horrible certainties of this life's sufferings for the more appalling uncertainties of another world."

"Lydia—Lydia, you are killing me!" exclaimed Lady Ravensworth. "Pity me—if not for myself, for the sake of the innocent child which I bear in my bosom. Tell me what I can do for you—what you require——"

"My views are soon explained," interrupted Lydia. "I demand permission to remain in the service of your ladyship."

"Oh! no—no: impossible!" said Adeline, in an imploring tone.

"It must be as I say," observed Lydia, coolly.

"Insolent menial!" ejaculated Lady Ravensworth, losing all command over herself. "Leave me—quit this house—go——"

"Do you dare me?" said Miss Hutchinson. "I assured your ladyship ere now that it did not suit my present plans to expose you; because I seek to remain in your service. But, if you essay again to triumph over me—to spurn me from your presence—I will, remorselessly and fearlessly, proclaim the past."

"And who will believe you?" cried Adeline, trembling with mingled alarm and rage: "who will believe you? The whole world will denounce you as an impostress. Nay—more: I will punish you—yes, I will punish you for your insolence! I will declare that you have attempted to extort money from me by means of the most diabolical threats——"

"Think not that I am to be intimidated by your ladyship's miserable subterfuges," interrupted Lydia, who grew if possible more cold and contemptuous in her manner in proportion as the proud patrician became excited and indignant. "Are there no witnesses to speak to collateral faces? Could Cholmondeley and Dunstable prove nothing against you?"

"They would not raise their voices against a noble lady's fame," said Adeline, impatiently.

"They would speak the truth when placed on their oaths in a court of justice," exclaimed Lydia, confidently; "for it is to a court of justice that your ladyship threatens to drag me. And now, proud peeress, I dare you to the public investigation! Throw open the door—summon your domestics—send me to a gaol!—but the day of fair and searching scrutiny must come—and I should await in confidence the reply that a British judge and a British jury would give to the vile calumny of even a lady so highly exalted as yourself!"

"Enough!" cried Adeline, now almost purple with rage, and every vein on her forehead swollen almost to bursting. "I accept your challenge—for I well know that I can rely upon the honour of Lord Dunstable and Colonel Cholmondeley. Yes—yes: they would sooner perjure themselves than attaint the honour of a peeress!"

"There is one other consideration, then," said Lydia, still completely unruffled: "and perhaps the ingenuity of your ladyship will devise a means of frustrating that test also."

"To what do you allude?" demanded Adeline.

"I mean that when you summon your domestics to drag me to a gaol on a charge of extortion," replied Lydia, contemptuously, "that moment do I proclaim the history of the past! Then will medical experience speedily prove whether Lady Ravensworth now bears *her first child* in her bosom!"

Adeline uttered a faint shriek, and fell back upon the sofa, overwhelmed by this dread menace.

That shriek was accompanied by a low moan that seemed to come from the passage outside.

Lydia hastened towards the door; but ere she had half crossed the room, it was thrown violently open, and Lord Ravensworth entered the boudoir.

"My husband!" screamed Adeline, in a frantic tone: then, flinging herself on her knees before him, she cried, "Mercy! mercy!"

CHAPTER CCVII.

THE HUSBAND, THE WIFE, AND THE UNFORTUNATE WOMAN.

"Mercy! mercy!" were the words that burst from the lips of the affrighted lady, ere she paused to reflect whether the preceding conversation had been overheard or not.

"Rise," said Lord Ravensworth, his quivering lip, flashing eye, hectic cheek, heaving chest, and clenched hand denoting a more powerful excitement than he had experienced for a long, long time. "Rise, madam: this is a subject which cannot be disposed of in passionate ejaculations;—it requires a calmer deliberation—for the honour of two noble families is now at stake!"

"Then you know all!" cried Adeline, in an agonising tone, as she embraced her husband's knees.

"Yes—I overheard enough to enable me to comprehend the whole truth," returned the nobleman, who for the time being seemed to have altogether thrown off the apathetic lethargy which had characterised him lately with such few intermissions.

Then, as he was yet speaking, he forcibly raised his wife from her suppliant position, and placed her upon the ottoman.

Taking a chair near her, he pointed to another, and, glancing towards Lydia, said in a tone rather mournful than angry, "Young woman, be seated."

Lydia obeyed mechanically; for she herself was alarmed at the serious turn which the affair had taken.

"Adeline," said the nobleman, after a short pause, during which he evidently endeavoured to compose his feelings as much as possible, "before we enter upon this sad topic, I must in justice to myself observe that I did not seek your chamber to play the eaves-dropper. I felt unwell in the drawing-room ere now, and I retired to my own cabinet to solace myself in the usual manner with the meerschaum. But it struck me that I *had* been better during all the early part of the morning than for some weeks past; and, after a long struggle with myself, I resolved to renounce the pipe. On my return to the drawing-room, I heard that you were suddenly indisposed; and I came hither to inquire after you. But at the moment I reached your door, I overheard words which struck me as with a thunderbolt. Then I listened—and overheard much—too much!"

"And now you hate—you despise me!" cried Adeline, wildly: "you will thrust me forth from your dwelling—you will cover me with shame! No—no," she added hysterically, "death—death before such a fate!"

"Calm yourself, Adeline," said Lord Ravensworth, who evidently suppressed his own feelings with great difficulty: "I before observed that there is the honour of *two* families to preserve—that of Rossville and of Ravensworth. Give me your Bible."

"My Bible!" exclaimed Adeline, in astonishment mingled with alarm.

"Yes—your Bible. Where is it?"

"There—there!" said Adeline in a faint tone—for she was at a loss to divine the meaning or intention of her husband; and that mysterious uncertainty filled her with vague fears.

Lydia rose, and taking the Bible from a small book-case to which Lady Ravensworth pointed, handed it to the nobleman.

"Will you swear, Adeline," he said, in a solemn and impressive tone,—"will you swear upon this volume which contains the Word of God, that the child you now bear in your bosom is mine, and that since your marriage you have never forgotten the fidelity due to a husband? Will you swear this, Adeline?"

"I will—I will!" she exclaimed, in almost a joyful tone, as if she were satisfied that her conjugal faith should be put to such a test.

"Swear, then," said Lord Ravensworth; "and invoke God to cast you dead—dead this minute at my feet—if you swear falsely."

"I do—I do!" cried Lady Ravensworth: then, taking the holy volume in her hand, she said in a calmer and more measured tone, "I swear, as I hope for future salvation, that I have never been unfaithful, even in thought, to my marriage vow, and that the child I bear in my bosom is my husband's. This I swear by every thing sacred and holy; and if I have sworn falsely, may the great God cast me dead at your feet."

She then kissed the book.

There was a solemn pause:—Lady Ravensworth was now perhaps the most composed of the three, for she saw that her husband was satisfied in all that concerned his own honour since the day he had led her to the altar.

As for Lydia—she was overawed and even alarmed at that imposing ceremony of a husband administering an oath to his wife; and Lord Ravensworth remained for some moments absorbed in deep thought.

"Yes," he suddenly exclaimed, as if continuing aloud the thread of his silent thoughts,—"the honour of two families must be preserved! And, after all,—perhaps I am rightly served! A man of my years should have sought a partner of a fitting age; but it is the fault—the error—the curse of elderly men to believe that their rank and wealth warrant them in seeking some young girl who may thus become as it were a victim. Then mothers take advantage of that longing to obtain a wife of comparatively tender years; and those worldly-minded parents——"

"My lord—my lord, spare my feelings!" ejaculated Adeline, now painfully excited. "My mother knew not of her daughter's frailty——"

"Well—enough on that head!" said Lord Ravensworth, somewhat impatiently. "The past cannot be recalled: let us secure the honour of the future. You have erred in your girlhood, Adeline! and there," he added, indicating Lydia, "is one who knows that sad secret. You have been ungrateful to her—by *her* accusations and *your* acknowledgment; and she holds you in her power. Not *you* alone:—but she holds *your* family and *mine*—for an exposure would create a scandal that must redound upon us all!"

"I have no wish to avail myself of the possession of that secret for such an object," said Lydia. "I have two motives for desiring to remain at least a year in her ladyship's service."

"Never!" cried Adeline, emphatically. "It is you who have made all this mischief!"

"Silence, Adeline," said Lord Ravensworth, sternly; then, turning towards Lydia, he added, "Young woman, proceed—and speak frankly."

"I stated that I had two objects to serve in being anxious to remain in her ladyship's service for one year," continued Lydia. "In the first place, I have been so unfortunate—so very, very miserable, that I wish to earn my livelihood by servitude; and it is my hope to remain here until her ladyship can conscientiously give me such a character as will ensure me a good situation elsewhere."

"That is naturally understood," observed Lord Ravensworth. "What is your second motive?"

"My second motive!" repeated Lydia, with the least accent of bitterness: "oh! that I will explain to her ladyship in private—and she will be satisfied!"

"Now listen to me," said the nobleman. "Lady Ravensworth dislikes the idea that you should remain here. I will give you the means of settling yourself comfortably for life, if you will leave forthwith, and promise solemnly to preserve that fatal secret which you possess."

"My lord," answered Lydia, respectfully but firmly, "I return you my most sincere thanks for that bounteous offer which I am compelled to decline. Were I to accept your lordship's conditions, my aims would not be answered. In respect to my first object, I have determined to earn a character that may to some extent retrieve the past;—for, as your lordship must have gathered from the conversation which you overheard, I have been unfortunate—very unfortunate!"

"Merciful heavens!" exclaimed Adeline; "how can I retain you in my service? You have belonged to a class—oh! no—it is impossible—impossible!"

"I do not wish to insult your feelings, young woman," said Lord Ravensworth; "especially since you manifest so praiseworthy a desire to retrieve your character. But you must perceive the impossibility, as her ladyship observes, of retaining you in our service. You might be known—recognised———"

"I understand your lordship," interrupted Lydia, bitterly; "I might be recognised as an unhappy creature who had once earned a livelihood by parading the public streets. That is scarcely probable:—I am much changed since then. The kindness of an excellent lady has enabled me to recruit my strength and to recover a healthy appearance. Yes—I must be altered; for your lordship does not perceive in me the poor miserable starving wretch who some few months since accosted her ladyship in Saint James's Street."

"Ah! I recollect," exclaimed the nobleman, as the incident flashed to his mind. "I only observed you for a moment on that occasion; but still—so miserable was your appearance—it made an impression on my mind. Yes—you are indeed changed! Nevertheless, those who saw you in an unhappy career, before you became so reduced as you were on the occasion which you have mentioned, might recognise you. And—pardon my frankness, young woman; but the subject admits not of the measurement of words—what would be thought of me—of my wife—of all the other members of my household———"

"If I were seen in your establishment, your lordship would add," exclaimed Lydia. "I admit the truth of all your lordship states: still my wish to remain a member of that establishment is unchanged. For—as your lordship may have ere now gathered from our conversation—it was her ladyship who first placed me in those paths which led to my ruin; and it must be her ladyship who shall aid me in earning an honourable character once more."

"But this punishment is too severe!" exclaimed Adeline, almost wringing her hands; for she perceived how completely the honour of two families was in Lydia's power.

"Consider, I implore you, the position of my wife," said the nobleman: "in a few weeks she will become a mother!"

"My lord, her ladyship never had any consideration for me, from the first moment that I ceased to be useful to her," returned Lydia, with inexorable firmness; "and I cannot consent to sacrifice what I consider to be my own interests to her ladyship's wishes now."

Then Lydia Hutchinson rose, as if to intimate that her determination was unchangeable; and that obscure girl was enabled to dictate her own terms to the noble peer and the proud peeress.

"It must be so, then—it must be so," said Lord Ravensworth, with a vexation of manner which he could not conceal. "You shall have an apartment in my establishment and handsome wages:—all I exact is that you do not force your attentions on her ladyship save when she demands them."

"If I remain here, it must be in the capacity of her ladyship's principal attendant," returned Lydia: "otherwise I could not fairly earn a good character in the eyes of the other dependants of your lordship."

"Perdition! young woman," exclaimed the nobleman; "you demand too much!"

"More than I will ever concede," added Lady Ravensworth, unable to restrain a glance of malignity and desperate hate towards Lydia Hutchinson.

"Then your lordship will permit me to take my departure," said she, calmly; and she moved towards the door.

"My God! she will reveal every thing!" almost shrieked Lady Ravensworth.

"Yes—every thing," said Lydia, returning the look which Adeline had cast on her a few moments before.

"Stay, young woman—this may not be!" ejaculated Lord Ravensworth. "You exercise your power with a fearful despotism."

"The world has been a fearful despot towards me, my lord," was the firm but calm reply.

"And with your tyranny in this respect you will kill my wife—kill my yet unborn child!" exclaimed the nobleman, rising from his seat and pacing the room in a state of desperate excitement. "But the honour of the Rossvilles and the Ravensworths must be preserved—at any sacrifice—at any risk!—Yes—though you bring misery into this house, here must you remain—since such is your inflexible will. Were an exposure to take place, the consequences—my God! would be awful—crushing! The finger of ridicule and scorn would point at me—the elderly man who espoused the young and beautiful girl, and who was so proud that he had won her for a wife! And then—should the child of which she is so soon to become a mother, prove a son—although the law would recognise him as the heir to my name and fortune, yet the scandalous world would throw doubts, perhaps, on his legitimacy. Ah! the thought is maddening! And my brother—my brother too———"

Lord Ravensworth checked himself in the midst of those musings, into the audible expression of which the agitation of his mind had hurried him:—he checked himself, for the convulsive sobs which came from his wife's lips suddenly reminded him that every word he was uttering pierced like a dagger into her soul.

"Oh! God have mercy upon me!" she exclaimed, in a voice scarcely audible through the convulsions of her grief: "how dearly—dearly am I now paying for the errors of my youth!"

"Does that sight not move you, woman?" muttered the nobleman between his grinding teeth, as he accosted Lydia, and pointed to the lamentable condition of his wife.

"My lord, I lost all by serving the interests of her who is now Lady Ravensworth; and it is time that I should think only of my own."

This reply was given with a frigid—stern—and inexorable calmness, that struck despair to the heart of the unhappy nobleman and his still more wretched wife.

"Then be it all as you say—be it all as you wish, despotic woman!" cried Lord Ravensworth. "Remain here—command us all—drive us to despair—for our honour is unhappily in your remorseless hands."

With these words, the nobleman rushed from the room in a state bordering on distraction.

A few minutes of profound silence elapsed.

Lydia remained standing near the mantel, gazing with joyful triumph on Adeline, whose head was buried in her hands, and whose bosom gave vent to convulsive sobs.

Suddenly Lady Ravensworth looked up, and gazed wildly around her.

"He is gone—and you are still there!" she said, in a low and hoarse voice. "Now we are alone together—and doubtless I am to look upon you as one determined to drive me to despair. What other motive had you for insisting upon remaining here?"

"Lady, I will now explain myself," returned Lydia, speaking slowly and solemnly. "It pierced me to the heart to cause so much grief to that good nobleman, of whom you are so utterly unworthy; but for you I have no kind consideration—no mercy. Adeline, I hate you—I loathe you—I detest you!"

"Merciful heavens!" exclaimed Lady Ravensworth: "and you are to be constantly about my person!"

"Yes: and my second motive for remaining here to enjoy that privilege," continued Lydia, bitterly, "is *vengeance!*"

"Vengeance!" repeated Adeline, recoiling as it were from the terrible word, and clasping her hands frantically together.

"Vengeance—vengeance!" continued Lydia Hutchinson. "Before the rest of the world I shall appear the humble and respectful dependant—yes, even in the presence of your husband. But when alone with you, I shall prove a very demon, whose weapons are galling reproaches, ignominies, insults, and indignities."

"Oh! this is terrible!" cried Adeline, as if her senses were leaving her. "You cannot be such a fiend."

"I can—I will!" returned Lydia. "Have I not undergone enough to make me so? And all was occasioned by *you!* When I was your wretched tool, you promised me the affection of a sister; and how did you fulfil your pledge?

You came to me at a house where I was a governess, and whence I was anxious to remove from the importunities of the master; and there you threw off the mask. I then saw the hollowness of your soul. My father died of a broken heart, and my brother perished in a duel, in consequence of my iniquity. But who had made me criminal? *You!* I called upon you at Rossville House at a time when a little sympathy on your part might have still saved me; for I should have felt that I had *one friend* still left. But you scorned me—you even menaced me; and I then warned you that I was absolved from all motives of secrecy on your account. Your black ingratitude drove me to despair; and I immediately afterwards fell to the lowest grade in the social sphere—that of a prostitute! Yes—for I need use no nice language with you. All the miseries I endured in my wretched career I charge upon your head. And ere now you menaced me again: you threatened to accuse me falsely of a crime that would render me amenable to the criminal tribunals of the country. It only required *that* to fill the cup of your base ingratitude to the very brim. And think you that your malignant—your spiteful glances,—your looks of bitter, burning hate,—were lost upon me? No—you would doubtless assassinate me, if you dared! Oh! I have long detested you—long loathed your very name! But, never—never, until we met in this room ere now, did I believe that my hatred against you was so virulent as it is. And never—never until this hour did I appreciate the sweets of vengeance. At present I can revel in those feelings:—I can wreak upon you—and I *will*—that revenge which my own miseries and the death of those whom I held dear have excited in my heart! Your ladyship now knows the terms of our connexion, for one year; and at the expiration of that period you will be glad—Oh! too glad to rid yourself of me by giving me a character that will never fail to procure for me a place in future."

With these words Lydia Hutchinson left the room.

Lady Ravensworth sank back in convulsions of anguish upon the ottoman.

And Lord Ravensworth,—who throughout the morning had experienced so much lightness of heart and mental calmness that he resolved to wrestle in future with that apathy and gloom which drove him to his pipe,—had shut himself up in his private cabinet, to seek solace once more in the fatal attractions of the oriental tobacco.

Thus had the presence of Lydia Hutchinson,—once despised, scorned, and trampled on,—brought desolation and misery into that lordly dwelling.

O Adeline, Adeline! thou wast now taught a bitter lesson illustrative of the terrible consequences of ingratitude!

The aristocracy conceives that it may insult the democracy with impunity. The high-born and the wealthy never stop to consider, when they put an affront upon the lowly and the poor, whether a day of retribution may not sooner or later come. The peer cannot see the necessity of conciliating the peasant: the daughter of the nobility knows not the use of making a friend of the daughter of the people.

But the meanest thing that crawls upon the earth may some day be in a position to avenge the injuries it has received from a powerful oppressor; and the mightiest lord or the noblest lady may be placed in that situation when even the friendship of the humblest son or the most obscure daughter of industry would be welcome as the drop of water to the lost wanderer of the desert.

Yes! Most solemnly do I proclaim to you, O suffering millions of these islands, that ye shall not always languish beneath the yoke of your oppressors! Individually ye shall each see the day when your tyrant shall crouch at your feet; and as a mass ye shall triumph over that proud oligarchy which now grinds you to the dust!

That day—that great day cannot be far distant; and then shall ye rise—not to wreak a savage vengeance on those who have so long coerced you, but to prove to them that ye know how to exercise a mercy which they never manifested towards you;—ye shall rise, not to convulse the State with a disastrous civil war, nor to hurry the nation on to the deplorable catastrophe of social anarchy, confusion, and bloodshed;—but ye shall rise to vindicate usurped rights, and to recover delegated and misused power, that ye may triumphantly assert the aristocracy of mind, and the aristocracy of virtue!

CHAPTER CCVIII.

THE RESURRECTION MAN'S HOUSE IN GLOBE TOWN.

Return we to the house of the Resurrection Man in Globe Town,—that house where we have already seen such diabolical mischief concocted, and much of which was actually perpetrated,—that house where the gloomy subterraneans had echoed to the moans of Viola Chichester!

It was about seven o'clock in the evening, when the Resurrection Man suddenly emerged from that very same cell in which Viola had once been confined.

He held a lantern in his hand; and the feeble rays glanced upon a countenance convulsed and distorted with deep, malignant rage.

On the threshold of the dungeon he paused for a moment; and turning towards the interior of that living tomb, he growled in a savage tone, "By all the powers of hell! I'll find means to cure you of this obstinacy."

A hoarse and stifled moan was the only answer.

"Then try another night of it!" exclaimed the Resurrection Man.

And he closed the door violently.

The heavy bolt grated upon the ears of another victim to the remorseless cruelty of this fiend-like miscreant!

Muttering maledictions to himself, the Resurrection Man slowly left the subterranean, and extinguishing his lantern, secured the doors of the lower part of his dwelling.

As he was about to ascend the steep staircase leading to the upper floor, a person in the street called after him in a low and tremulous tone, "Mr. Tidkins! Mr. Tidkins! is that you?"

"Rather so," replied the Resurrection Man, who had immediately recognised the voice; "walk up, Mr. Tomlinson."

"I—I—if you have no objection," stammered the stock-broker, who evidently had some cause of alarm, "I would much prefer—that is, I should like to speak to you down here; because my time is precious—and——"

"And you are afraid to trust yourself with me," added the Resurrection Man, gruffly. "Why, what an infernal fool you must be! I don't suppose that you've come with your pockets full of gold: and, if you haven't, you certainly ain't worth robbing and murdering. So, walk up, I say—and no more of this gammon. Shut the door, and bolt it after you."

The stock-broker did not like to offer any farther objection, so deep was his dread of irritating a man of whom he entertained a vague and horrible apprehension.

He accordingly closed the door, and followed Tidkins up the precipitate steps to the back room on the first floor: for the Resurrection Man had converted this one into his parlour, to avoid the necessity of having a light in the front chamber, the windows of which looked upon the street—the miscreant being compelled to adopt as many precautions as possible to prevent his numerous enemies from discovering a trace of his whereabouts.

"Sit down, and don't be afraid, Mr. Tomlinson," said Tidkins. "There, sir—draw near the fire; and here's brandy, rum, or gin, if you like to take any thing."

"Nothing, I thank you," faltered the stock-broker, casting a hurried glance of alarm around him as he sank upon a chair. "You wrote to desire me to call this evening—at seven o'clock—or I might repent——"

"Yes—and so you would repent the consequences," added the Resurrection Man. "But, as you have come, it is all right. I dare say you thought I had forgotten you: you were deceived, you see; for I never lose sight of old friends. When I want to use them, I am sure to find them out again."

"And what can I do for you, Mr. Tidkins?" asked the stock-broker, in a tremulous tone; for he felt a desperate alarm lest the Resurrection Man should have discovered *the one secret* which he had taken so much pains to conceal—the secret of the abode of old Michael Martin.

"I have but two wants in the world at any time," answered the Resurrection Man, lighting his pipe: "money most often—vengeance now and then. But it is money that I want of you."

"Money—money!" murmured Tomlinson: "do you think I am made of money? I have had hard struggles—losses—expenses——"

"I dare say you have," observed the Resurrection Man, drily. "I do not mean to be hard upon you; but something I must have. You see, I have got a little amount put by—how obtained is neither here nor there; and I want to scrape together as much as I can, so that in a few months, when I have settled the different matters I have on hand, I may leave England for America, or some such place; and then you will never hear of me any more."

"That will be a great blessing," thought Tomlinson; but he did not say so.

"And under all circumstances, you must help me to make up the sum I want," added the Resurrection Man.

"You are too hard upon me, Mr. Tidkins," said Tomlinson. "If I had employed you on any business, it would be different: but——"

"But if you have a secret that I have found out, and that's worth keeping?" exclaimed Tidkins, significantly.

"Oh! then it is as I feared!" murmured Tomlinson, pressing his feverish hand to his forehead, through which a sudden pain seemed to shoot, producing a sensation as of tightness on the brain. "Surely this man must be Satan himself, who comes at intervals to goad the wicked to desperation for their sins!"

"What's that you say about Satan?" asked Tidkins.

"Nothing—nothing," replied the stock-broker, hastily: "I was only thinking to myself that Satan took a delight in persecuting me."

"I know nothing about that," observed the Resurrection Man. "All I care for is the cash that you will have the goodness to bring me down to-morrow evening at this same hour."

A sudden idea struck Tomlinson. Was the Resurrection Man really acquainted with Martin's present place of abode? or was he endeavouring to extort money merely upon the strength of his knowledge, some time previously obtained (as our readers will remember), that the old clerk, though generally believed to have absconded, had actually remained concealed in London?

"But wherefore should you press me in this way?" said the stock-broker. "Did I not satisfy your demands on a former occasion?"

"And have I not kept my pledge?" cried Tidkins. "Has a word ever escaped my lips to do you an injury? Why, there is still a reward of three thousand pounds to be got——"

"No—no," interrupted Tomlinson; "you are wrong. My affairs are all wound up in respect to the bank—and a dividend has been paid."

"A precious small one, I'll be bound," observed Tidkins. "However,—reward or no reward,—it wouldn't place you in a very comfortable situation if I was to take a policeman with me, and just call at a particular house in Thomas Street, where an old gentleman named Nelson——"

"Enough!" cried Tomlinson: "I see you know all. My God! when shall I be released from this peril? when shall I know a moment's comfort?"

"When you've brought me down a couple of hundred pounds to-morrow night," answered the Resurrection Man, knocking out the ashes from his pipe. "And, then—if you like to make it worth my while—I tell you what I'll do for you."

"What?" asked the stock-broker, gasping for breath.

"I'll entice the old fellow down here, and either lock him up in one of my cells, or else settle his hash in such a way that he shall only be fit to sell to the surgeons," returned the Resurrection Man, fixing his snake-like eyes on the stock-broker's countenance, as if to ascertain the precise impression which this proposal made.

"Monster!" ejaculated Tomlinson, shrinking from the bare idea of such an atrocity—for he was more or less attached to Michael Martin, in consequence of the immense sacrifice which the old man had made on his account: "no—never will I imbrue my hands with blood, nor suborn another to play the assassin's part for me! To-morrow evening you shall receive the amount you demand; and heaven grant that all connexion between us may cease."

"Be it so," observed the Resurrection Man, coolly, as he brewed himself a glass of grog.

"You have nothing more to say to me?" asked Tomlinson, rising to depart.

The reply was a negative; and the stock-broker hurried away from a dwelling where crime seemed to proclaim its presence trumpet-tongued,—where every look that eyes shot forth, and every word that lips uttered, and every thought that brains conceived—all, all appeared to feel the noxious atmosphere of blackest turpitude.

In a house where a person has lately died, every thing seems to exhale a sickly odour as of a corpse; and if you touch the wall with your finger, you feel a clammy and fetid moisture which makes your blood run cold within you. So was it with the dwelling of the Resurrection Man: the taint of crime impregnated the very atmosphere; and Tomlinson shook himself when he gained the open air, as if he could thus throw off some pestilential influence which had seized hold of him.

Tomlinson had not left the house many minutes, when a low, but peculiar knock at the door brought the Resurrection Man down to answer the summons.

"Who is it?" he demanded, ere he opened.

"Me," growled a voice which Tidkins immediately recognised to be that of the Lully Prig.

This individual was forthwith admitted; and when the two villains were seated by the fire in the back room, the Resurrection Man asked "What news?"

"Just as you wished," was the reply. "I called at the chandlery shop in Pitfield Street, Hoxton, and axed for a nounce of bakker. The woman served me; and I soon see that she was alone. Then says I, '*If so be no one's within 'earing, I want a word with you.*'—She looked frightened, but said nothing wotsomever.—'*All I have to tell you is just this,*' says I: '*Tony Tidkins knows where you be and all about you. But he says, says he, that if you take no notice of him in case you sees him, and says nothing to nobody in case you 'ears of him, he'll leave you alone.*'—Lor! how she did turn pale and tremble when I mentioned your name; and she seemed so glad when I told her that you wouldn't do her no harm, if so be she didn't try to do you none.—'*If he won't come near me, I'll never even breathe his name,*' she says.—'*And you'll never utter a word about the crib in Globe Town,*' says I.—'*Never, never,*' says she.—'*Well, then,*' says I, '*all will go on well; and you can sleep as sound in your bed as if there wasn't such a man as Tony Tidkins in the world. But if so be you peaches, or says a word,*' says I, '*that may get Tony into trouble, he's got plenty of friends as will avenge him, and the fust is me.*'—So she swore eyes and limbs, she'd keep all close; and in that way I left her."

"So far, so good," observed the Resurrection Man. "She's frightened, and will keep a close tongue. That's all I want. When I have finished the different things I have in hand, and don't care about staying in London any longer, I will punish her for what she did to me. But my revenge will keep for the present. Now, what about Crankey Jem?"

"He still lives in the court in Drury Lane, and stays at home all day," answered the Lully Prig. "But at night he goes out for some hours, and I can't find out where. For three evenin's follering I watched him; and every time I missed him at last somehow or another."

"Which way did he go?" demanded the Resurrection Man.

"Different ways—but always up one street and down another—now here, then there, as if he hadn't no partickler motive, but merely went out a walkin' for the fun of it."

"I tell you what it is, Lully," said the Resurrection Man, gloomily, "you're not so wide awake as I am. That fellow has some object in wandering about zigzag and crosswise in that manner. He has got a scent of me; and he's following it up. But at the same time he's afraid that I may have a scent of him; and so he dodges about. It's as clear as day-light—'cause it's just what I should do."

"And you're a downy cove enough, Tony," observed the Lully Prig; "although I do think arter all you've let that damned parley-woo French feller do us about them Bank notes."

"It's very strange the Buffer doesn't return," said the Resurrection Man. "I'd take my davy that he wouldn't chouse us out of our reglars. But time will show. Now look here, Lully,—as you've made that same remark a dozen times since the thing took place,—and just see how the matter stood. We got four thousand pounds clear———"

"Yes—a thousand a-piece," said the Lully Prig, assentingly: "and a precious jolly catch it was."

"Well," continued the Resurrection Man, "the Bank notes were of no more use to us than so much waste paper, because Greenwood was sure to stop them the moment he got back to London: at least I should think so. Now when that French fellow Lafleur offered to let you, me, the Buffer, and Long Bob share the gold, and he would go to France to smash the notes at the money-changer's that he told us about in Paris, and then take his thousand beyond his fifth share of the produce of the notes, it was the best thing we could do to accept his proposal—particularly as he said that any one of us might go with him."

"But if he sticks to the whole sixteen thousand pounds, what a deuced good pull he has over us," observed the Lully Prig.

"So he has," said the Resurrection Man; "and again I tell you that if he hadn't offered to go to France and change the notes, we must have destroyed them in the very chalk-pit where we divided the swag. They were no use to us—but a great danger. It was better to trust to the chance of Lafleur doing the thing that's right; and if he don't, the Buffer will drop down on him, in spite of all the guilloteens[32] and Johnny-darmies[33] in France."

"Well, we won't quarrel about it, Tony," said the Lully Prig. "You and the Buffer let me in for a good thing; and I ought not to grumble. You see, I've follered your advice, and kept the blunt in a safe place, without wasting it as Long Bob is doing. He's never been sober since the thing took place."

"Where is he now?" asked the Resurrection Man.

"Oh! he's knocking about at all the flash cribs, spending his tin as fast as he can," answered the Lully Prig.

"Don't let him know of this place of mine for the world," said Tidkins. "A drunken chap like that isn't to be trusted in any shape. I only hope he won't wag his tongue too free about the business that put all the money into his pocket."

"Not he!" cried the Lully Prig: "he's as close as the door of Newgate about them kind of things, even when he's as drunk as a pig. But I don't want to have nothing more to do with him; I'll stick to you and the Buffer; and when you've settled all the things you say you have in hand, we'll be off to Americky."

"So we will, Lully. But this fellow Crankey Jem annoys me. You must go on watching him. Or p'rhaps it would be better to get the Bully Grand to set some of his Forty Thieves after him?" added the Resurrection Man.

"No—no," cried the Lully Prig, whose pride was somewhat hurt at this suggestion, which seemed to cast a doubt upon his own skill and ability in performing the service required: "leave him in my hands, and I'll find out what dodge he's upon sooner or later."

Scarcely were these words uttered, when a knock at the front door fell on the ears of the two villains.

The Resurrection Man descended; and, to the usual inquiry ere the door was opened, the well-known voice of the Buffer answered, "It is me."

"Well—what luck?" demanded the Resurrection Man, hastily—his avarice prompting the question even before his accomplice in iniquity had scarcely time to utter a reply to the first query.

"Sold—regularly sold—done brown!" returned the Buffer, closing and bolting the door behind him.

"Damnation!" cried the Resurrection Man, who, now that the faint hope of obtaining a further share of the plunder of Greenwood's tin-case was annihilated, manifested a fiercer rage than would have been expected after his cool reasoning with the Lully Prig upon the special point.

"You may well swear, Tony," said the Buffer, sulkily, as he ascended the stairs; "for we never was so completely done in all our lives. That snivelling Mounseer was one too many for us."

"Ah! I see how it is," observed the Lully Prig, when the two men entered the room where he had remained; "and I can't say it's more than I expected. But how did he do it?"

"Why, he gave me the slip at last," answered the Buffer, pouring himself out half a tumbler of raw spirit, which he drank without winking, just as if it were so much water. "You see, he kept me humbugging about in Paris week after week, always saying that it wasn't prudent to begin smashing the notes yet awhile; and I stuck to him like a leech. I shan't make a long story on it now—I'm too vexed: all I'll tell you at present is that four days ago he gave me the slip; and so I twigged that it was all gammon. He'd done us brown—that was wery clear;—and so I come back."

We shall leave the three villains to discuss this disappointment, together with divers other matters interesting to themselves, and continue the thread of our narrative in another quarter.

It is, however, as well to observe that all these comings and goings at the house of the Resurrection Man were watched by an individual, who for several nights had been lurking about that neighbourhood for the purpose, but who had exercised so much caution that he was never perceived by any one of the gang.

This person was Crankey Jem.

---

32. Guillotines.

33. Gendarmes.

CHAPTER CCIX.

ALDERMAN SNIFF.—TOMLINSON AND GREENWOOD.

It was eleven o'clock in the forenoon of the day following the incidents just related.

The scene is Mr. Tomlinson's office in Tokenhouse Yard.

The stock-broker was seated at his desk. His manner was nervous, and his countenance expressive of anxiety: he had, indeed, passed a sleepless night—for he saw in the conduct of the Resurrection Man the renewal of a system of extortion which was not likely to cease so long as there was a secret to be hushed up.

The careful aspect of the stock-broker was not, however, noticed by Mr. Alderman Sniff, who was lounging against the mantel, with his back to the fire, and expatiating on his own success in life—a favourite subject with this civic functionary, who considered "success" to be nothing more nor less than the accumulation of money from a variety of schemes and representations so nearly allied to downright swindling, that it was impossible to say what a jury would have thought of them had they come under the notice of a criminal tribunal.

"But how have you managed to do it all?" asked Tomlinson, by way of saying something—although his thoughts were far removed from the topic of Mr. Alderman Sniff's discourse.

"You see I began life with plenty of money," returned the Alderman: "I mean I had a decent fortune at the death of my father, which took place when I was about two-and-twenty. But that soon went; and I was glad to accept an offer to go out to India. On my arrival at Madras I was inducted into a situation as clerk in a mercantile establishment; and there I was making some little money, when I was foolish enough to issue a prospectus for the '*General Boa-Constrictor Killing and Wild Beast Extirpation Joint-Stock Company*,'—a project which was not so well relished as I could have wished. My employers discharged me; and, deeply disgusted with the ignorance of the English settlers and the natives, who could not understand the magnitude of my designs, I came back to England. My trip to India was, however, very useful to me; for, on my return to this country, I lived splendidly on the Deccan Prize Money for four years."

"Lived on the Deccan Prize Money!" exclaimed Tomlinson: "why—what claim had you to any of it?"

"None," replied Mr. Sniff; "I never was in the Deccan in my life. But I declared that I had claims to I can't remember how many lacs of rupees; and it was very easy to obtain loans from friends and get bills cashed on the strength of the assertion. Of course this had an end: the settlement of the Deccan Prize Money affairs was interminable; but the facility for procuring cash on the strength of it was not equally lasting. However,—as I just now observed,—I lived comfortably on my alleged claims for four years; and then I started the '*Universal Poor Man's Corn-Plaster and Blister Gratuitous Distribution Society*.' I got several philanthropic and worthy men to join me in this laudable undertaking: we took splendid offices in King Street, Cheapside; and the enterprise progressed wonderfully. How well I remember our first annual meeting at Exeter Hall! The great room was crowded to excess. I was the Secretary, and it was my duty to read the *Report* of the Committee. That document had been drawn up in most pathetic language by some poor devil of an author whom I employed for the purpose; and it produced a wonderful effect. It was really quite touching to see how the ladies—poor dear creatures!—wept tears of the most refreshing philanthropy, when I enumerated the blessings which this Society had conferred upon vast numbers of individuals. Nine thousand six hundred and sixty-seven Corn-Plasters and eleven thousand two hundred and fourteen Blisters had been distributed gratuitously, during the year, to as many poor suffering creatures, who had all been thereby cured of corns previously deemed inveterate, and of chest-complaints that until then had received no medical attention. The *Report* dwelt upon the gratitude of thousands of poor families for the relief thus dispensed, and congratulated the members of the Society on the claims they possessed to the applause of the whole Christian world. Subscriptions rained in upon me in perfect torrents; and there was not a tearless eye throughout that vast hall."

"How was it that so excellent an institution became extinct?" asked Tomlinson, awaking from his reverie when the Alderman paused.

"I really can scarce tell you," was the reply. "Whether it was that the public thought there could not possibly be any more corns to cure or pulmonary complaints to heal,—or whether it was in consequence of a proposition which I made, in an unlucky hour, to extend the benefits of the Society to the poor savages in the islands of the Pacific,—I can't say: it is, however, certain that the subscribers were very 'backward in coming forward' at the third annual meeting; and so the institution dwindled into nothing. I had, nevertheless, saved some little money; and I was not long idle. My next spec. was '*The Metropolitan Poor Family's Sunday-Dinner Gratuitous Baking Association*.' You perceive that I am fond of dealing in humane and philanthropic enterprises. My idea was to establish numerous baking-houses all over London, and to cook the poor man's Sunday joint and potatoes for him, the Society reserving to itself the dripping, which being sold, and the profits added to the voluntary subscriptions received from the charitable, would support these most useful institutions. At the end of a year, however, I was compelled to dissolve the Association, after having gone to the expense of building no less than sixty enormous ovens in as many different parts of London."

"How came that project to fail," asked Tomlinson, "when it was calculated to benefit so many poor families?"

"Simply because so few of those poor families ever had any Sunday dinners to cook at all," replied Alderman Sniff. "Nevertheless, the subscriptions which were received paid all the outlay, and remunerated me for my trouble. I therefore met with some little encouragement in all I did for the benefit of my fellow-creatures; and, more than *that*," added the philanthropist, slapping his left breast," I enjoyed the approval, Mr. Tomlinson, of my conscience."

The stock-broker sighed:—not that he envied any inward feelings which Mr. Alderman Sniff could have experienced as the results of the speculations referred to; but the thoughts occasioned by the mere mention of the word "Conscience" aroused painful emotions in the breast of James Tomlinson.

"While I was thus engaged in the behoof of the poorer classes of the community," continued Alderman Sniff, "I was gaining influence with my fellow citizens. I became the Treasurer of no end of charitable institutions, was elected Churchwarden of my parish, and soon became Deputy of the Ward. Fortunately my parish, as you well know, is governed by a Select Vestry—properly consisting of three individuals; but as two of the last-elected trio have died, and as I have ever stedfastly and successfully opposed the nomination of other parishioners to replace the deceased, we have now a Select Vestry of *One*. This gentleman is my most intimate friend; and it would do your heart good to see the parochial solemnity and official dignity with which he annually proposes me to himself as a candidate for the place of Churchwarden, and then proceeds to second the nomination, put the question, lift up his hand, and declare me duly elected *without a dissentient voice*. In due time I was chosen Alderman of the Ward; and every thing has gone well with me. I have been eminently successful. My '*British Marble Company*' was a glorious hit, as you well know."

"Yes—a glorious hit for you," said Tomlinson, with a faint smile. "You yourself were Managing Director, and you sold your quarry—or rather your supposed quarry—*to* yourself;—you were Auditor and Secretary, and consequently examined and passed your own accounts;—you were also the Treasurer, and paid yourself. You had the best of it in every way."

"Come, Mr. Tomlinson," exclaimed Sniff, chuckling audibly, "I allowed you to reap a decent profit on the shares which you sold; so you need not complain."

"Oh! I do not complain," observed the stock-broker. "But how do you get on with the accounts of your parish?"

"Mr. Tomlinson," said the Alderman, almost sternly, "I never will give any accounts at all to those refractory parishioners of mine. The Select Vestry of One has met regularly every year, and resolved himself into a Committee to investigate my accounts—and that is sufficient. And, after all," added the civic functionary, sinking his voice to a mysterious whisper, "even if the accounts *were* produced,—although they run over such a long period of years, you might put them all into your waistcoat-pocket without finding it stick out more than it now does with your small French watch."[34]

With these words, Mr. Alderman Sniff, who had merely looked in to have a chat and talk of himself to one with whom there was no necessity to maintain any secrecy in respect to his antecedents,—Mr. Alderman Sniff retired.

A few minutes afterwards Mr. Greenwood was introduced.

"My dear Tomlinson," he said, "I am quite delighted to find you within. I have made a hit, and shall retrieve myself with ease. The ten thousand pounds which Holmesford lent me are now twenty thousand."

"You are a lucky fellow," observed Tomlinson, with a sigh. "Adversity has no effect upon you; whereas with me——"

"Why—what is the matter now?" interrupted Greenwood. "Always complaining?"

"I have good cause for annoyance," returned the stock-broker. "That precious acquaintance of yours——"

"Who?" demanded Greenwood, sharply.

"The lunatic-asylum keeper, as your friend Chichester supposed him to be—but the resurrectionist, thief, extortioner, villain, and perhaps murderer, as I take him to be," said Tomlinson,—"that scoundrel Tidkins, in a word, has discovered poor old Michael's address, and menaces me."

"Ah!" said Greenwood, coolly; "it is your own fault: you should have got Martin out of the way—even if you had painted him black, shipped him to the United States, and sold him as a slave."

"Ridiculous!" cried Tomlinson, sternly. "I never will cease to be a friend—a grateful friend—to that poor old man."

"Well," observed Greenwood, after a pause, "I can do you a service in this respect. I was at Rottenborough yesterday—amongst my intelligent and independent constituents; and I learnt that the situation of porter to the workhouse in that truly enlightened town is vacant. Now, if——"

"Enough of this, Greenwood!" exclaimed Tomlinson. "I was wrong to mention the old man's name to *you*.—What can I do for you this morning? Have you made up your mind to take the loan which my friend consented to advance to you about a month ago, and which you——"

"Which I declined then, and decline now," said Greenwood, hastily—as if the allusion awoke unpleasant reminiscences in his mind.

"I never could understand your conduct on that evening," observed Tomlinson, in his quiet manner: "you came at the appointed hour to terminate the business: the money was ready—the deed was prepared—my friend was here,—and when you put your hand into your pocket for the securities, you turned on your heel and bolted off like a shot."

"Yes—yes," said Greenwood, with increased impatience; "I had lost my pocket-book. But——"

"And have you found it since?" asked the stock-broker.

"I have. But I do not require the loan," returned Greenwood, shortly. "So far from that, I wish you to lay out these seven thousand pounds for me in a particular speculation which I will explain to you. I have prepared the way for certain success, but cannot appear in it myself."

Greenwood then counted the Bank notes upon the table for the sum named, and gave Tomlinson the necessary instructions for the disposal of the amount.

"Any news to-day?" he asked, when this business was concluded.

"Here is a second edition of *The Times* with another Telegraphic Despatch from Castelcicala," said Tomlinson. "I know you are interested in the affairs of that country, by the way you have lately spoken to me on the subject."

"Yes:—I am—I am indeed," exclaimed Greenwood, earnestly, as he seized the paper, in which the following article appeared in a bold type:—

"CASTELCICALA.

"PROCLAMATION OF ALBERTO I.—FORMATION OF

THE NEW MINISTRY.

"The French Government have received the following Telegraphic Despatch from Toulon:—

"'*The* Alessandro *steamer has just arrived from Montoni.* THE MARQUIS OF ESTELLA *proclaimed the* GRAND DUKE ALBERTO I. *in the evening of the 24th, instead of in the morning of that day, which was his original intention. This was merely occasioned by the delay of the Marquis in entering the capital. The Marquis has formed the following Ministry:—*

- "*Prime Minister, and Minister of Foreign Affairs*, SIGNOR GAËTANO.
- *Minister of the Interior*, SIGNOR TERLIZZI.
- *Minister of War*, COLONEL COSSARIO.
- *Minister of Marine*, ADMIRAL CONTARINO.
- *Minister of Finance*, SIGNOR VIVIANI.
- *Minister of Justice*, BARON MANZONI.
- *Minister of Commerce*, CHEVALIER GRACHIA.'"

The Times newspaper, commenting upon this Administration, reminded its readers that Signors Gaëtano and Terlizzi were the Chiefs of the Provisional Committee of Government during the Revolution in Castelcicala; that Colonel Cossario was the second in command of the glorious army that had achieved Castelcicalan freedom; that Signor Viviani was the well-known banker of Pinalla; and that the Chevalier Grachia was the nephew of the deceased general of that name.

"Thus is it that Richard can now make a Ministry in a powerful State!" murmured Greenwood to himself. "Oh! what a sudden elevation—what a signal rise! And I——"

"What are you muttering about to yourself, Greenwood?" asked Tomlinson.

"Ah!" cried the Member of Parliament, suddenly, and without heeding the stock-broker's question,—for his eyes, wandering mechanically over the surface of the paper which he held in his hand, had settled upon a paragraph that excited the liveliest emotions of surprise:—who could have believed it? Oh! now I recall to mind a thousand circumstances which should have made me suspect the truth!"

"The truth of what?" demanded Tomlinson.

"That Count Alteroni and Prince Alberto were one and the same person," exclaimed Greenwood; "and he is now the Grand Duke of Castelcicala!"

"Then you have had the pleasure of including a sovereign-prince amongst the number of your victims," observed the stock-broker, coolly.

Greenwood made no reply, but remained plunged in a deep reverie, the subject of which was the brilliant destiny that appeared to await Richard Markham.

As soon as he had taken his leave, Tomlinson also began musing; but it was upon a far different topic!

"Oh! what a hollow-hearted wretch is that Greenwood!" he said within himself: "and how would he have treated Michael Martin, had the poor old man been dependent upon him! Greenwood would indeed be capable of sending him to the United States as a slave, were such a course practicable. Ah!—the United States!" cried Tomlinson, aloud, as a sudden idea was created in his mind by the mention of the name of that glorious Republic:—"and why should *not* Michael Martin visit the States—and with me too? Yes! I am wearied of London,—wearied of this city where all hearts seem to be eaten up with selfishness,—wearied of supporting the weight of that secret which the merest accident may reveal, and which places me at the mercy of that ferocious extortioner! Oh! if that secret were discovered—if it were ascertained that Michael Martin was really in London,—he would be dragged before the tribunals—and I must either appear against him as a witness, or proclaim his innocence and thereby sacrifice myself! No—no—I could not do either:—never—never! I know that I am weak—vacillating—timid! But God also knows how unwillingly I have departed from the ways of rectitude—how many bitter tears have marked the paths of my duplicity! And now I will be firm—yes, firm to commit one last crime! Oh! I will prove myself a worthy pupil of my great master Greenwood! He shall be amply repaid," continued the stock-broker, bitterly, "for all the kind lessons he has given me in the school of dishonour—yes, and repaid, too, in his own coin. Seven thousand pounds—added to my own little stock,—this will be a sufficient fund wherewith to begin an honourable avocation in another clime. Yes—America is the country for me! There I can begin the world again as a new man—and perhaps I may retrieve myself even in my own estimation!"

Tomlinson's resolution was now irrevocably fixed.

He would emigrate to the United States, accompanied by his faithful old clerk!

Greenwood's money should constitute the principal resource to which he must trust as the basis whereon to establish a fortune in the place of the one he had lost.

Nor did he hesitate a moment—weak, timid, and vacillating as he was in ordinary circumstances—to self-appropriate those funds thus entrusted to him.

He had no sympathy for Greenwood;—and, moreover, he had many an act of insolence on the part of that individual—many an instance of oppression, to avenge. Ere the failure of the bank, Greenwood had taken advantage of his necessities to wring from him enormous interest for loans advanced, and had, moreover, made him his instrument in defrauding the Italian prince. Since the establishment of the office in Tokenhouse Yard,

Greenwood had continued to use Tomlinson as a tool so long as his own fortunes had remained prosperous;—and even latterly—since the condition of Greenwood's finances had levelled some of those barriers which the necessities of the one and the wealth of the other had originally raised between them,—even latterly, the manner of the Member of Parliament towards the fallen banker had been that of patronage and superiority. Then the frequent and heartless allusions which Greenwood made to the poor old clerk, rankled deeply in the mind of Tomlinson; and all these circumstances armed that naturally weak and timid man with a giant strength of mind when he contemplated the possibility of at length punishing Greenwood for a thousand insults.

Tomlinson was not naturally a vindictive man:—persons of his quiet and timid disposition seldom are. But there are certain affronts which, when oft repeated and dwelt upon in their aggregate, form a motive power that will arouse the most enduring and the weakest mind to action—especially, too, when accident throws a special opportunity of vengeance in the way.

James Tomlinson was a strange compound of good and bad qualities—the latter arising from his constitutional want of nerve, and his deficiency in moral energy. Had he been mentally resolute, he would have proved a good and great man. The conflicting elements of his character were signally demonstrated on this occasion, when he had determined to fly from the country.

Having given his clerks positive orders that he was not to be interrupted for some hours, he sealed up in different parcels the small sums of money which his various clients had placed in his hands to purchase scrip or other securities, and addressed the packets to those to whom the sums respectively belonged,—omitting, however, Greenwood in this category. He next computed the salaries due to his clerks, and set apart the amount required to liquidate those obligations also. These duties being accomplished, he locked all the parcels up in one of the drawers of his writing-table, and placed the key in his pocket. Greenwood's deposit he secured about his person.

When it grew dusk in the evening, he repaired to the lodging which Michael Martin occupied in Bethnal Green.

As soon as Tomlinson had made known his scheme to the old man—(but, of course, without betraying the fact of his intention to self-appropriate Greenwood's money)—Michael took a huge pinch of snuff, and reflected profoundly for some minutes.

"And what's the meaning of this all of a sudden?" demanded the ex-cashier at length.

Tomlinson explained, with great frankness, that the Resurrection Man had by some means discovered the secret of Michael's abode, and was again playing the part of an extortioner. He, moreover, expressed his invincible dislike for a city where he had experienced such painful reverses; and declared his resolution of no longer living in such a state of suspense and anxiety as he was kept in by the constant dread of an exposure in respect to his faithful old clerk.

"You need not leave London on that account," said Martin, gruffly: "I have long made up my mind how to act in case of detection."

"How?" asked Tomlinson, with a foreboding shudder.

"I should put an end to my life," returned the old man, filling his nose with snuff. "I am well aware that you would not have the courage to appear against me in a court of justice and boldly accuse me of having embezzled your funds——"

"The courage!" exclaimed Tomlinson, wiping away a tear: "no—nor the heart! My good—faithful old friend———"

"Well—well: don't be childish, now," said Michael, who was obliged to take several pinches of snuff to conceal his own emotions: "if you are really desirous to leave England and go to America, I will accompany you. Of course I will—you know I will," he added, more hastily than he was accustomed to speak.

"There is no time for delay," said Tomlinson, rejoiced at this assent which he had wrung from his faithful servitor. "We will repair to Dover this very night, and thence proceed to France. The distance from Calais to Havre is not very great: and from the latter port ships are constantly sailing for America."

"Let me proceed alone to Havre," said old Martin; "and you can follow me openly and at your leisure."

"No," replied Tomlinson; "that would only be to compromise *your* safety, perhaps. We will part no more."

The advice of the stock-broker was acted upon; and the fugitives succeeded in leaving the kingdom in safety.

But that night the Resurrection Man vainly awaited the arrival of James Tomlinson.

And on the following day, Mr. Greenwood discovered, to his cost, that the effects of those lessons of duplicity and dishonour which he had inculcated in respect to the stock-broker, practically redounded upon himself!

---

34. The readers must not for a moment suppose that we intend Mr. Sniff to be a type of *all* the city aldermen. Far from it. There are some excellent, honourable, and talented men amongst the civic body. Mr. Sniff is as different from what Sir Peter Laurie *is*, or Mr. Harmer *was*, as light differs from darkness. There are, however, some individuals wearing civic gowns, who are a disgrace to the great city of which they have the unaccountable effrontery to remain magistrates.

CHAPTER CCX.

HOLFORD'S STUDIES.

It was midnight.

In a garret, belonging to a house in the same court where Crankey Jem resided, sate Henry Holford.

He was alone. His elbow rested on the table, and his hand supported his feverish head—for dark thoughts filled the brain of that young man.

The flickering light of a single candle fell upon the pages of an old volume, which he was reading with intense interest.

His cheeks were pale,—his lips were dry,—his throat was parched,—and his eye-balls glared with unnatural lustre.

He did not feel athirst—else there was water handy to assuage the craving:—nor did he hear his heart beating violently, nor experience the feverish and rapid throbbing of his temples.

No:—his whole thoughts—his entire feelings—his every sensation,—all were absorbed in the subject of his study.

And that the reader may fully comprehend the nature of those impulses which were now urging this strange young man on to the perpetration of a deed that was destined to give a terrible celebrity to his name, we must quote the passage on which his mind was so intently fixed:—

"THE ASSASSINATION OF GUSTAVUS III., OF

SWEDEN.[35]

"The nobles were discontented with the general conduct of the King; and a conspiracy was planned against him under his own roof. His wars had compelled him to negotiate large loans, and to impose upon his subjects heavy taxes. The nobles took advantage of that circumstance to prejudice the minds of many of the people against the sovereign who had laboured so long for their real good. On the 16th of March, 1792, he received an anonymous letter, warning him of his immediate danger from a plot that was laid to take away his life, requesting him to remain at home, and avoid balls for a year; and assuring him, that if he should go to the masquerade for which he was preparing, he would be assassinated that very night. The King read the note with contempt, and at a late hour entered the ball-room. After some time he sat down in a box with the Count of Essen, and observed he was not deceived in his contempt for the letter, since, had there been any design against his life, no time could be more favourable than that moment. He then mingled, without apprehension, among the crowd; and just as he was preparing to retire with the Prussian ambassador, he was surrounded by several persons in masks, one of whom fired a pistol at the back of the King, and lodged the contents in his body. A scene of dreadful confusion ensued. The conspirators, amidst the general tumult and alarm, had time to retire to other parts of the room; but one of them had previously dropped his pistols and a dagger close by the wounded King. A general order was given to all the company to unmask, and the doors were immediately closed; but no person appeared with any particular distinguishing marks of guilt. The King was immediately conveyed to his apartment; and the surgeon, after extracting a ball and some slugs, gave favourable hopes of his Majesty's recovery.

"Suspicions immediately fell upon such of the nobles as had been notorious for their opposition to the measures of the court. The anonymous letter was traced up to Colonel Liljehorn, Major in the King's Guards, and he was immediately apprehended. But the most successful clue that seemed to offer was in consequence of the weapons which had fallen from the assassin. An order was issued, directing all the armourers, gunsmiths, and cutlers, in Stockholm, to give every information in their power to the officers of justice, concerning the weapons. A gunsmith who had repaired the pistols readily recognised them to be the same which he had repaired some time since for a nobleman of the name of Ankarstrom, a captain in the army; and the cutler who had made the dagger, referred at once to the same person.

"The King languished from the 17th to the 29th of March. At first, the reports of his medical attendants were favourable; but on the 28th a mortification was found to have taken place, which terminated his existence in a few hours. On opening his body, a square piece of lead and two rusty nails were found unextracted within the ribs.

"During his illness, and particularly after he was made acquainted with the certainty of his approaching dissolution, Gustavus continued to display that unshaken courage which he had manifested on every occasion during his life. A few hours before his decease, he made some alterations in the arrangement of public affairs. He had before, by his will, appointed a council of regency, but convinced, by recent experience, how little he could depend on the attachment of his nobles, and being also aware of the necessity of a strong government in difficult times, he appointed his brother, the Duke of Sudermania, sole regent, till his son, who was then about fourteen, should have attained the age of eighteen years. His last words were a declaration of pardon to the conspirators against his life. The actual murderer alone was excepted; and he was excepted only at the strong instance of the regent, and those who surrounded his Majesty in his dying moments. Immediately on the death of the King, the young prince was proclaimed by the title of Gustavus IV.

"Ankarstrom was no sooner apprehended, than he confessed with an air of triumph, that he was the person 'who had endeavoured to liberate his country from a monster and a tyrant.' Suspicions at the same time fell on the Counts Horn and Ribbing, Baron Pechlin, Baron Ehrensvard, Baron Hartsmandorf, Von Engerstrom the Royal Secretary, and others; and these suspicions were confirmed by the confession of Ankarstrom. After a very fair and ample trial, this man was condemned to be publicly and severely whipped on three successive days, his right hand and his head to be cut off, and his body impaled: which sentence he suffered on the 17th of May. His property was given to his children, who, however, were compelled to change their name."

"Ankarstrom was a martyr—a hero!" exclaimed Holford, aloud; his imagination excited by the preceding narrative, and all the morbid feelings of his wrongly-biassed mind aroused at the idea of the terrible renown that attached itself to the name of a regicide.

Then,—although the garret in which he sate was so cold that ice floated on the water in the pitcher, and the nipping chill of a February night came through the cracked panes and ill-closed lattice, while the snow lay thick upon the slanting tiles immediately above his head,—that young man's entire frame glowed with a feverish heat, which shone with sinister lustre in his eyes, and appeared in the two deep-red hectic spots which marked his cheeks.

"Yes—Ankarstrom was a hero!" he exclaimed. "Oh! how he must have despised the efforts of the torturers to wring from him a groan:—how he must have scorned the array of penalties which were sought to be made so terrible! And Ravaillac—the regicide beneath whose hand fell Henry IV. of France—oh! how well is every word of his history treasured up in my mind. But Francis Damien—ah! his fate was terrible indeed! And yet I am not afraid to contemplate it—even though such a one should be in store for me."

Then hastily turning to the "History of France," in the volume which he was reading, he slowly and in measured terms repeated aloud the following passage:—

"ATTEMPTED ASSASSINATION OF LOUIS XV.,

OF FRANCE.

"In the year 1757, one Francis Damien, an unhappy wretch, whose sullen mind, naturally unsettled, was inflamed by the disputes between the King and his Parliament concerning religion, formed the desperate resolution of attempting the life of his Sovereign. In the dusk of the evening, as the King prepared to enter his coach, he was suddenly, though slightly, wounded, with a pen-knife, between the fourth and fifth ribs, in the presence of his son, and in the midst of his guards. The daring assassin had mingled with the crowd of courtiers, but was instantly betrayed by his distracted countenance. He declared it was never his intention to kill the King: but that he only meant to wound him, that God might touch his heart, and incline him to restore the tranquillity of his dominions by re-establishing the Parliament, and banishing the Archbishop of Paris, whom he regarded as the source of the present commotions. In these frantic and incoherent declarations he persisted, amidst the most exquisite tortures; and after human ingenuity had been exhausted in devising new modes of torment, his judges, tired out with his obstinacy, consigned him to a death, the inhumanity of which might fill the hearts of savages with horror: he was conducted to the common place of execution, amidst a vast concourse of the populace; stripped naked, and fastened to the scaffold by iron manacles. One of his hands was then burnt in liquid flaming sulphur; his thighs, legs, and arms, were torn with red hot pincers: boiling oil, melted lead, resin, and sulphur, were poured into the wounds; and, to complete the terrific catastrophe, he was torn to pieces by horses!"

"And they call him an unhappy wretch!" exclaimed Holford, pushing the book from him: "no—no! He must have had a great and a powerful mind to have dared to attempt to kill a King! And his name is remembered in history! Ah! that thought must have consoled him in the midst of those infernal torments. What is more delightful than the conviction of emerging from vile obscurity, and creating a reputation—although one so tarnished and disfigured that the world shrinks from it with loathing? Yes:—better to be a Turpin or a Barrington—a Claude du Val or a Jack Sheppard, than live unknown, and die without exciting a sensation. But it would be glorious—oh! how glorious to be ranked with Ankarstrom, Ravaillac, Damien, Felton, Guy Fawkes, Fieschi, and that gallant few who have either slain, or attempted the lives of, monarchs or great men! I am miserable,—poor,—obscure,—and without a hope of rising by legitimate means. I have seen the inside of a palace—and am doomed to drag on my wretched existence in this garret. I have partaken of the dainties that came from the table of a sovereign—and, were I hungry now, a sorry crust is all that my cupboard would afford. I have listened to the musical voice of that high-born lady whose name I scarcely dare to breathe even to myself—and now the cold blast of February comes with its hoarse sound to grate upon my ears in this miserable—miserable garret! Oh! why was my destiny cast in so lowly a sphere? What has been my almost constant occupation—with some few brighter intervals—since I was twelve years old? A pot-boy—a low, degraded pot-boy: the servant of servants—the slave of slaves—forced to come and go at the beck and call of the veriest street-sweeper that frequented the tap-room! Ah! my God—when I think of all this humiliation, I feel that my blood boils even up to my very brain—my eyes and cheeks appear to be upon fire—I seem as if my senses were leaving me!"

And, as he spoke, he clenched his fists and ground his teeth together with a ferocious bitterness, which indicated the fearfully morbid condition of his mind.

For he was enraged against fortune who had made him poor and humble—against the world for keeping him so—and against royalty and aristocracy for being so much happier and so incomparably more blessed than the section of society to which he belonged.

And in his vanity—for his soaring disposition made him vain—he conceived that he possessed elements of greatness, which the world, with a wilful blindness, would not see; or which adverse circumstances would not suffer to develop themselves.

He deemed himself more persecuted than others moving in the same sphere: his restless, diseased, and excited mind, had conjured up a thousand evils to which he thought himself the marked—the special prey.

He had seen, in his visits to the palace, so much of the highest eminence of luxury, pleasure, happiness, and indolent enjoyment, that he looked around with horror and affright when he found himself hurled back again into the lowest depths of obscurity, privation, and cheerlessness of life.

He had at intervals feasted his eyes so greedily with all the fascination, the glitter, the gorgeousness, the splendour, the ease, and the voluptuousness, of the Court, that he could not endure the contemplation of the fearful contrast which was afforded by the every-day and familiar scenes of starvation, penury, misery, and ineffectual toil that marked the existence of the people.

The moral condition of Henry Holford was a striking proof of the daring flights of which the human mind is capable. On the very first occasion of his visit to the palace, he had allowed himself to be carried away by all the wildest emotions and the strangest impressions that were produced by the novelty of what he then saw and heard. Royalty had been ever associated, in his vulgar conception, with something grand and handsome in man, and something wonderfully beautiful in woman. Thus, when he first saw the Queen, he was prepared to admire her:—he admired her accordingly; and that feeling increased to a degree the insolence of which at times overawed and terrified even himself.

By another wayward inclination of his unhealthy but enthusiastic mind, he had from the first been prepared to dislike the Prince; and this feeling increased in violence with those circumstances which each successive visit to the royal abode developed. At length—as if his evil destiny must infallibly hurry him on to some appalling catastrophe—he was discovered by the Prince in the detestable condition of an eaves-dropper, and was ignominiously driven forth from that dwelling where his mind had gradually collected the elements of a most unnatural excitement.

He knew that any attempt to repeat his visits would be frustrated by the precautions which were certain to have been adopted to prevent future intrusions of a like nature; and he now felt precisely as one who is compelled suddenly to abandon a habit to which he had become wedded. Strange as it may appear, the morbid excitement attendant upon those visits to the palace was as necessary to Holford's mental happiness as tobacco, opium, snuff, or strong liquors are to so many millions of individuals.

With a person in such a state of mind, the first impulse was bitter hatred against the one who had deprived him of a source of pleasurable excitement; and in that vengeful feeling were absorbed all those rational reflections which would have convinced him that his own insolent intrusion—his own unpardonable conduct—had provoked the treatment he had received. He never paused to ask himself by what right he had entered the palace and played the ignoble part of a listener to private conversation and a spy upon the hallowed sanctity of domestic life:—the dominant idea in his mind was his ignominious expulsion.

"Fate has now filled my cup of bitterness to the brim," he would say to himself; "and all that remains for me to do is to avenge myself on him whom my destiny has made the instrument of this crowning degradation."

By degrees the mind of that young man found its gloomy broodings upon vengeance associating themselves with other sentiments. He gradually blended this idea of revenge with the ardent desire of breaking those trammels which kept his name imprisoned in the silent cavern of obscurity. The two sentiments at length united in his imagination; and his pulse beat quickly—and his eyes flashed fire, when he surveyed the possibility of gratifying his thirst for vengeance and suddenly rendering his name notorious at the same moment, and by one desperate—fearful deed!

The reader cannot now be at a loss to comprehend how this wretchedly mistaken young man was brought to study the history of those regicides who have gained an infamous renown in the annals of nations.

And as he dwelt with an insane enthusiasm upon those narratives, the feeling of admiration—nay, adoration—which he had once experienced towards the Queen, was merged in the terrible longing for a diabolical notoriety that now became his predominating—his all-absorbing passion!

"Yes!" he exclaimed, as he pushed the book away from him, that night on which we have introduced the reader to his garret: "I will be talked about—my name shall be upon every tongue! Obscurity shall no longer enshroud me: its darkness is painful to my soul. I will do a deed that shall make the Kingdom ring from one end to the other with the astounding tidings:—the newspapers shall struggle with all the eagerness of competition to glean the most trivial facts concerning me;—and when the day arrives for me to appear before my judges, the great nobles and the high-born ladies of England shall crowd in the tribunal to witness the trial of the pot-boy Henry Holford!"

The act on which the young man was now resolved, appeared not to him in its real light as an atrocious crime—a damnable deed that would arouse a yell of execration from one end of the land to the other:—it seemed, on the contrary, a glorious achievement of which he would have reason to be proud.

Alas! how strangely constituted is the human mind, which, in any state of being, could cherish such monstrous delusions—such fatal aspirations!

But is there no blame to be attached to society for this development of ideas so morbid even on the part of one single individual? is there nothing in the constitution of that society which gives encouragement, as it were, to those detestable sentiments?

Let us see.

Enough has been said in the more serious and reasoning parts of this work to prove that society is in a vitiated—a false—and an artificial condition. The poor are too poor, and the rich too rich: the obscure are too low, and the exalted too high. The upper classes alone have opportunities of signalising themselves: the industrious millions have no chance of rising in the State. Interest procures rank in the Navy—money buys promotion in the Army—and interest and money united obtain seats in the Legislative Assembly. Interest and money, then, remain to the exclusive few: the millions have neither—nor are they even stimulated by a national system of Education. An aristocrat of common abilities may rise to eminence in some department of the State, with but little trouble: but a son of toil, however vast his natural talents, has not a single chance of starting from obscurity through the medium of their proper development.

This is true: and we defy the most subtle reasoner on behalf of the oligarchy to refute those positions.

Now, such being the case,—with a dominant aristocracy on one hand, and the oppressed millions on the other,—is it not evident that every now and then some member of the latter class will brood upon the vast, the astounding contrast until feelings of a deplorably morbid nature become excited in his mind? How could it be otherwise? Ireland, with its agrarian outrages and its frequent instances of assassination, proves the fact. England, with its incendiary fires in periods of deep distress, affords additional corroboration.

We deplore that such should be the case; and not for a moment do we advocate such means of vindicating just rights against the usurpers thereof.

But if these instances of outbreaking revenge—if these ebullitions of indomitable resentment *do* now and then occur, no small portion of the blame must be charged against that aristocracy which maintains itself on an eminence so immeasurably above the depths in which the masses are compelled to languish. And when the poor creature who is goaded to desperation, *does* strike—can we wonder if, in the madness of his rage, he deals his blows indiscriminately, or against an innocent person? He may even aim at royalty itself—although, in every really constitutional country, the sovereign is little more than a mere puppet, the Prime Minister of the day being the virtual ruler of the nation.

From what we have said, it is easy to perceive how the contemplation of the splendid luxury of the palace first unhinged and unsettled the mind of Henry Holford.

We must now go a step farther.

Society manifests a most inordinate and pernicious curiosity in respect to criminals who perpetrate an unusual offence. This curiosity passes all legitimate bounds. The newspapers, with a natural attention to pecuniary interests, obey the cravings of that feeling by serving up the most highly-seasoned food to suit the peculiar appetite. Portraits of the guilty one are exhibited in every picture-shop. Apposite allusions are introduced into dramatic representations; and even the presiding genius of a "Punch and Judy show" mingles the subject with his humorous outpourings. If the criminal make an attack upon royalty, he goes through the important but mysterious ordeal of an examination at the Home Office, whence the reporters for the press are excluded. On his appearance at Bow Street, the magisterial tribunal is "crowded with gentlemen and ladies, who were accommodated with seats upon the bench," as the journals say; and when the finale comes at the Central Criminal Court, the fees for admission to the gallery rise to two or three guineas for each individual.

Thus the criminal is made into a hero!

Now is not all this sufficient to turn the head of one whose mind is already partially unhinged?

Society, then, is to blame in many ways for the development of those morbid feelings which, in the present instance, actuated Henry Holford in his desperate purpose.

---

35. From Evans' and Forbes' "Geographical Grammar." Edition of 1814.

CHAPTER CCXI.

THE DEED.

Crankey Jem was at dinner, in the afternoon of the day which followed the night of Holford's sad historical studies, when the young man entered his room.

"Oh! so you've turned up at last," said Jem, pointing to a seat, and pushing a plate across the table in the same direction. "What have you been doing with yourself for the last two days? But sit down first, and get something to eat; for you look as pale and haggard as if you'd just been turned out of a workhouse."

"I am not well, Jem," replied Holford, evasively; "and I cannot eat—thank you all the same. But I will take a glass of beer: it may refresh me."

"Do. You really seem very ill, my poor lad," observed Crankey Jem, attentively surveying Holford's countenance, which was sadly changed. "If you have got no money left, my little store is at your service, as far as it goes; and you need not think of working in any way till you are better. I can easily make another boat or two more during the week; and so you shall not want for either medicine or good food."

"You are very kind to me, Jem," said Holford, wiping away a tear. "If it hadn't been for you I don't know what I should have done. You have supplied me with the means of getting a lodging and——"

"And you served me well by tracing the villain Tidkins to his nest in Globe Lane," interrupted the returned transport. "I have watched about that neighbourhood every night since you followed him there, and have seen something that has made me hesitate a little before I pay him the debt of vengeance I owe him. Now that he is in my power, I don't care about waiting a while. Besides, if I can find him out in something that would send him to the gibbet, I would sooner let him die that way—as a dog, with a halter round his neck—than kill him outright with my dagger."

"And you suspect——" began Holford.

"Yes—yes: but no matter now," cried Jem, hastily. "You are not in the right mood to-day to listen to me: but, either I am very much mistaken, or *murder* has been committed within the last few days at that house in Globe Town. At all events, I saw a person taken by force into the place one night; and that person has never come out again since."

"How do you know?" said Holford. "You only watch about the neighbourhood by night."

"And is it likely that a person who was conveyed into that house by force during the night, would be allowed to walk quietly out in the day-time?" demanded Crankey Jem. "No such thing! Tidkins is not the chap to play such a game. The person I speak of was blindfolded—I could see it all as plain as possible, for the moon was bright, though I kept in the shade. Now, being blindfolded," continued Jem, "it was to prevent her——"

"What? was the person a woman?" cried Holford, his interest in Jem's conversation somewhat increasing, in spite of the absorbing nature of his own reflections.

"Yes. And, as I was saying, the blindfolding was of course to prevent her knowing whereabouts she was: so it isn't likely that Tidkins would let her go away again in the broad day-light."

"Neither does it seem probable that he took her there to make away with her," said Holford; "for, as the dead tell no tales, there was not any use in binding her eyes."

"*That* also struck me," observed Crankey Jem; "and it's all those doubts and uncertainties that make me watch him so close to find out what it all means. And, mark me, Harry—I *will* find it all out too! I'm pretty near as cunning as he is! Why—what a fool he must take me for, if he thinks I can't see that he has got a great hulking chap to dog me about. But I always give him the slip somehow or another; and every evening when I go out I take a different direction. So I'll be bound that I've set Tidkins and his man at fault. The night afore last I saw the spy, as I call him—I mean the chap that is set to dog me—go to Tidkins's house; and about an hour afterwards a man I once knew well—one Jack Wicks, who is called the Buffer—went there also. Ah! there's a precious nest of them!"

"I say, Jem," exclaimed Henry Holford, abruptly, "I wish you would lend me your pistols for a few hours."

"And what do you want with pistols, young feller?" demanded the returned convict, laying down his knife, and looking Holford full in the face.

"A friend of mine has made a wager with another man about hitting a halfpenny at thirty paces," said Henry, returning the glance in a manner so confident and unabashed, that Jem's suspicions were hushed in a moment.

"Yes—you shall have the pistols till this evening," said he: "but mind you bring 'em back before dusk."

With these words, he rose, went to a cupboard, and produced the weapons.

"I'll be sure to bring them back by the time you go out," said Holford. "Are they loaded?"

"No," answered Jem. "But here's powder and ball, which you can take along with you."

"I wish you would load them all ready," observed Holford. "I—I don't think my friend knows how."

"Not know how to load a pistol—and yet be able to handle one skilfully!" ejaculated Jem, his vague suspicions returning.

"Many persons learn to fire at a mark at Copenhagen House, or a dozen other places about London," said the young man, still completely unabashed; "and yet they can't load a pistol for the life of them."

"Well—that's true enough," muttered Jem.

Still he was not quite reassured; and yet he was unwilling to tax Holford with requiring the pistols for any improper purpose. The young lad's reasons might be true—they were at least feasible; and Jem was loth to hurt his feelings by hinting at any suspicion which the demand for the weapons had occasioned. Moreover, it would be churlish to refuse the loan of them—and almost equally so to decline loading them;—and the returned convict possessed an obliging disposition, although he had been so much knocked about in the world. He was also attached to Henry Holford, and would go far to serve him.

Nevertheless, he still hesitated.

"Well—won't you do what I ask you, Jem?" said Holford, observing that he wavered.

"Is it really for your friends?" demanded the man, turning short round upon the lad.

"Don't you believe me?" cried Holford, now blushing deeply. "Why, you cannot think that I'm going to commit a highway robbery or a burglary in the day-time—even if I ever did at all?"

"No—no," said Jem; "but you seemed so strange—so excited—when you first came in——"

"Ha! ha!" cried Holford, laughing: "you thought I was going to make away with myself! No, Jem—the river would be better than the pistol, if I meant *that*."

"Well—you must have your will, then," said Crankey Jem; and, turning to the cupboard, he proceeded to load the pistols.

But still he was not altogether satisfied!

Holford rose from his seat with an assumed air of indifference, and approached the table where the little models of the ships were standing.

A few minutes thus elapsed in profound silence.

"They're all ready now," said Jem, at length; "and as your friends don't know how to load them, it's no use your taking the powder and ball. I suppose they'll fire a shot each, and have done with it?"

"I suppose so," returned Holford, as he concealed the pistols about his person. "I shall see you again presently. Good bye till then."

"Good bye," said Jem.

But scarcely had Holford left the room a minute, when the returned convict followed him.

The fact was that there shot forth a gleam of such inexpressible satisfaction from Holford's eyes, at the moment when he grasped the pistols, that the vague suspicions which had already been floating in the mind of Crankey Jem seemed suddenly to receive confirmation—or at least to be materially strengthened; and he feared lest his young friend meditated self-destruction.

"The pistols are of no use to him," muttered Jem, as he hastened down the stairs, slouching his large hat over his eyes; "but if he is bent on suicide, the river is not far off. I don't like his manner at all!"

When he gained the street, he looked hastily up and down, and caught a glimpse of Holford, who was just turning into Russell Street, leading from Drury Lane towards Covent Garden.

"I will watch him at all events," thought Crankey Jem. "If he means no harm, he will never find out that I did it; and if he does, I may save him."

Meantime, Holford, little suspecting that his friend was at no great distance behind him, pursued his way towards St. James's Park.

Now that his mind was bent upon a particular object, and that all considerations had resolved themselves into that fixed determination, his countenance, though very pale, was singularly calm and tranquil; and neither by his face nor his manner did he attract any particular notice as he wandered slowly along.

He gained the Park, and proceeded up the Mall towards Constitution Hill.

Crankey Jem followed him at a distance.

"Perhaps, after all, it is true that he has got some friends to meet," he muttered to himself; "and it may be somewhere hereabouts that he is to join them."

Holford stopped midway in the wide road intersecting Constitution Hill, and lounged in an apparently indifferent manner against the fence skirting the Green Park.

There were but few persons about, in that particular direction, at the time,—although the afternoon was very fine, and the sun was shining brightly through the fresh, frosty air.

It was now three o'clock; and some little bustle was visible amongst those few loungers who were at the commencement of the road, and who were enabled to command a view of the front of the palace.

They ranged themselves on one side:—there was a trampling of horses; and in a few moments a low open phaeton, drawn by four bays, turned rapidly from the park into the road leading over Constitution Hill.

"They are coming!" murmured Holford to himself, as he observed the equipage from the short distance where he was standing.

Every hat was raised by the little group at the end of the road, as the vehicle dashed by—for in it were seated the Queen and her illustrious husband.

By a strange coincidence Her Majesty was sitting on the left hand of Prince Albert, and not on the right as usual: she was consequently nearest to the wall of the palace-gardens, while the Prince was nearest to the railings of the Green Park.

And now the moment so anxiously desired by Holford, was at hand:—the phaeton drew nigh.

He hesitated:—yes—he hesitated;—but it was only for a single second.

"Now to avenge my expulsion from the palace!—now to make my name a subject for history!" were the thoughts that, rapid as lightning, flashed across his mind.

Not another moment did he waver; but, advancing from the railings against which he had been lounging, he drew a pistol from his breast and fired it point-blank at the royal couple as the phaeton dashed past.

The Queen screamed and rose from her seat; and the postillions stopped their horses.

"Drive on!" cried the Prince, in a loud tone, as he pulled Her Majesty back upon the seat; and his countenance was ashy pale.

Holford threw the first pistol hastily away from him, and drew forth the second.

But at that moment a powerful grasp seized him from behind,—his arm was knocked upwards,—the pistol went off into the air,—and a well-known voice cried in his ears, "My God! Harry, what madness is this?"

Several other persons had by this time collected on the spot; and the most cordial shouts of "God save the Queen!" "God save the Prince!" burst from their lips.

Her Majesty bowed in a most graceful and grateful manner: the Prince raised his hat in acknowledgment of the sympathy and attachment manifested towards his royal spouse and himself;—and the phaeton rolled rapidly away towards Hyde Park, in obedience to the wishes of the Queen and the orders of the Prince.

"What madness is this, I say, Harry?" repeated Crankey Jem, without relaxing his hold upon the would-be regicide.

But Holford hung down his head, and maintained a moody silence.

"Do you know him?" "Who is he?" were the questions that were now addressed to Crankey Jem from all sides.

But before he could answer his interrogators, two policemen broke through the crowd, and took Holford into custody.

"We must take him to the Home Office," said one of the officers, who was a serjeant, to his companion.

"Yes, Mr. Crisp," was the reply.

"And you, my good feller," continued the serjeant, addressing himself to Crankey Jem, "had better come along with us—since you was the first to seize on this here young miscreant."

"I'd rather not," said Jem, now terribly alarmed on his own account: "I——"

"Oh! nonsense," cried Mr. Crisp. "The Home Secretary is a wery nice genelman, and will tell you how much obleeged he is to you for having seized——But, I say," added Mr. Crisp, changing his tone and assuming a severe look as he gazed on the countenance of the returned convict, "what the deuce have we here?"

"What, Mr. Crisp?" said the policeman, who had charge of Holford.

"Why! if my eyes doesn't deceive me," cried the serjeant, "this here feller is one James Cuffin, generally known as Crankey Jem—and he's a 'scaped felon."

With these words Mr. Crisp collared the poor fellow, who offered no resistance.

But large tears rolled down his cheeks!

Policemen and prisoners then proceeded across the park to the Home Office, followed by a crowd that rapidly increased in numbers as it rolled onwards.

CHAPTER CCXII.

THE EXAMINATION AT THE HOME OFFICE.

On the arrival of the two prisoners and the two policemen at the Home Office, they were shown into a small room joining the one in which the Secretary of State for that Department was accustomed to receive individuals or deputations, and where we have already seen him in an earlier portion of this work.

But on the present occasion the Home Secretary had to be fetched from the Foreign Office, where he was sitting with his colleagues in a Cabinet Council.

The police officers and the prisoners were therefore left alone together for nearly half an hour in the room to which some subordinate official had ordered them to be conducted, upon the motives of their presence there being made known to him.

The crime of which Holford was accused seemed too grave and serious for even the tamperings of policemen: still as these gentry are not merely content with having a finger in almost every pie, but must thrust a whole hand in when once they find the opportunity, it was impossible that either Mr. Crisp or his colleague could leave Crankey Jem as well as the would-be regicide unassailed with questions.

The common policeman placed a chair against the outer door of the room, and seated himself in it with the air of a man who meant to say as plainly as he could, "Escape now if you can."

Holford sank upon a seat and fell into a profound reverie; but it was impossible to gather the nature of his thoughts from the now passionless and almost apathetic expression of his countenance.

Crankey Jem also took a chair; but his nervous manner, the pallor of his face, the quivering of his lip, and the unsettled glances of his eyes, betrayed the fearful condition of his mind. The poor wretch already imagined himself transported back amongst the horrors of Norfolk Island!

As for Mr. Crisp, he walked once or twice up and down the room, surveying himself complacently in a mirror, and then advancing towards Crankey Jem, said with a sort of official importance, "Well, my fine feller, you've done it pretty brown again—you have."

Jem Cuffin cast upon him a look of deep disgust.

"Remember," continued Mr. Crisp, in no way abashed at this unequivocal expression of feeling, "whatever you says to me now will probably trans-peer in another place, as we officials express it; but if you choose to tell me anything by way of unbuzziming yourself and easing your conscience, why, I don't think there'd be no harm in it, and it might do you good with the 'thorities. At the same time it's no part of my dooty to pump you."

"I have nothing to say to *you*," observed Crankey Jem.

"Well—p'rhaps that's prudent,—'cos I'm official after all," said Mr. Crisp. "But if so be you was to tell me how you got away from transportation, how long you've been in England, and what you've been doing with yourself since your return, I don't see that you could prejjudidge yourself."

"As you've had the trouble of taking me, policeman, you'd better go to the extra trouble of finding out what you want to know about me," said Jem.

"You needn't be uppish with me, because I did my dooty," returned Mr. Crisp. "Remember, I don't ask—but I s'pose you've been living in London—eh?"

"Well—and if I have——"

"There! I knowed you had," cried Crisp.

"I didn't say so," observed Jem Cuffin, angrily.

"No—but you can't deny it, though. Well, then—as you *have* been living in London, *according to your own admission*," continued Mr. Crisp, "in course you must have hung out in some partickler quarter. Remember, I don't ask you—but I des say it was in the Holy Land."

"I dare say it wasn't," returned Jem, drily.

"Then it was in the Mint, I'll be bound," cried Crisp. "I don't ask, you know—but wasn't it in the Mint?"

"No—it wasn't," said Crankey Jem, with a movement of impatience.

"Not the Mint—eh? Well, if you says so, it must be true—'cos you should know best. But I s'pose you won't deny that it was somewhere in Clerkenwell?"

"You're out again," returned Crankey Jem.

"The devil I am!" exclaimed Crisp, rubbing his nose. "And yet I'm a pretty good hand at a guess too. Now it isn't my wish or my dooty to pump a prisoner—but I should like to be resolved as to whether you haven't been living in the Happy Valley?"

"No," cried Jem; "and now leave me alone."

"Not the Happy Valley—eh?" proceeded the indefatigable Mr. Crisp: then, perceiving that his endeavours to find out the prisoner's place of abode were useless, he went upon another tack. "Well—it isn't my business to pump you; but I am really at a loss to think how you could have been such a fool as to go back to your old tricks and break into that house there—down yonder, I mean—you know where? Come now?"

And Mr. Crisp fixed a searching eye upon Crankey Jem's countenance.

"I tell you what it is," exclaimed the prisoner, seriously irritated at length; "you want to entrap me, if you can—but you can't. And for a very good reason too—because I haven't broken into any house at all, or done a thing I'm ashamed of since I came back to England."

With these words, Crankey Jem turned his back upon the baffled Mr. Crisp, and looked out of the window.

Almost at the same moment an inner door was thrown open, and one of the Under Secretaries for the Home Department beckoned Mr. Crisp into the adjacent room, where the principal Secretary was already seated, he having arrived by the private entrance.

Crisp remained with the Minister for about ten minutes, and then returned to the ante-room, but it was merely to conduct Henry Holford and Crankey Jem into the presence of the Home Secretary and the Chief Magistrate of Bow Street.

"You may withdraw, Mr.——ahem?" said the Home Secretary, addressing the police-officer.

"Crisp, my lord—Crisp is my name."

"Oh! very good, Mr. Frisk. You may withdraw, Mr. Frisk," repeated the Minister.

And the police-officer retired accordingly, marvelling how the examination could possibly be conducted in a proper manner without his important presence.

The magistrate commenced by informing Henry Holford of the accusation laid against him by Crisp, and then cautioned him in the usual manner to beware of what he said, as anything he uttered might be used in evidence against him.

"I have no desire to conceal or deny a single particle of the whole truth," returned Holford. "I acknowledge that I fired at the Queen and Prince Albert—and with pistols loaded with ball, too."

"No—there you are wrong," exclaimed Jem; "for I loaded the pistols myself, and I took good care only to put powder into them."

Holford cast a glance of unfeigned surprise on his friend.

"Yes," continued the latter, "what I say is the truth. Your manner was so strange when you came to me to borrow the pistols, that I feared you meant to make away with yourself. I did not like to refuse to lend you the weapons—particularly as I knew that if you was really bent on suicide, you could do it in other ways. But I was resolved that my pistols should not help you in the matter; and I only charged them with powder. Then I followed you all the way down to the Park; and as you did not stop anywhere, I know that you couldn't have either bought balls or altered the charge of the pistols."

"This is important," said the magistrate to the Home Secretary.

"Very important," answered the latter functionary, who, from the first moment that Holford entered the room, had never ceased to gaze at him in the same way that one would contemplate an animal with two heads, or four tails, in the Zoological Gardens.

"It is very evident that the man was no accomplice in the proceeding," remarked the magistrate, in an under tone.

The words did not, however, escape Holford's ears.

"He an accomplice, sir!" cried the youth, as if indignant at the bare idea. "Oh! no—he has been a good friend to me, and would have advised me quite otherwise, had I mentioned my purpose to him. He was the first to rush upon me, and—I remember now—knocked up my arm when I was about to fire the second pistol."

Crisp and the other policeman were called in separately, and examined upon this point. Their evidence went entirely to prove that James Cuffin could not have been an accomplice in the deed.

When the policemen had withdrawn, the Home Secretary and the magistrate conversed together in a low tone.

"This man Cuffin's evidence will be absolutely necessary, my lord," said the magistrate; "and yet, as a condemned felon, and with another charge—namely, that of returning from transportation—hanging over him, he cannot be admitted as a witness."

"You must remand him for farther examination," returned the Home Secretary; "and in the mean time I will advise Her Majesty to grant him a free pardon."

"And Henry Holford will stand committed to Newgate, my lord?" said the magistrate, inquiringly.

The Minister nodded an assent.

The policemen were re-admitted, the depositions were signed, and the necessary instructions were given for the removal of the prisoners.

Two cabs were procured: Holford was conducted to one, and conveyed to Newgate,—but not before he had shaken hands with Crankey Jem, who shed tears when he took so sad a farewell of the lad, whom he really liked.

He himself was shortly afterwards removed in the other cab to the New Prison, Clerkenwell.

CHAPTER CCXIII.

THE TORTURES OF LADY RAVENSWORTH.

A week had now elapsed since Lydia Hutchinson entered the service of Lady Ravensworth.

The service! Oh! what a service was that where the menial had become the mistress, and the mistress had descended to the menial.

From the moment that Lydia had expressed her unalterable resolution to remain at the Hall, Lord Ravensworth scarcely ever quitted his private cabinet. He had a bed made up in an adjoining room, and secluded himself completely from his wife. Vainly did Adeline seek him—go upon her knees before him—and beseech him, with the bitterest tears and the most fervent prayers, to return to an active life:—he contemplated her with an apathetic listlessness—as if he were verging, when but little past the prime of life, into second childhood. Or if he did manifest a scintillation of his former spirit, it was merely to command his wife to leave him to his own meditations.

And again did he have recourse to the pipe: in fact he was never easy now save when he lulled his thoughts into complete stupefaction by means of the oriental tobacco. Even when, in the midst of her earnest prayers, his wife implored him to come forth again into the world—to *live*, in fine, for the sake of his as yet unborn babe, the fire that kindled in his eyes was so evanescent that an acute observer could alone perceive the momentary—and only momentary—effect which the appeal produced.

The guests had all taken their departure the day after the bridal; and the splendid mansion immediately became the scene of silence and of woe.

To all the entreaties of his wife—to all the representations of his favourite page Quentin, that he would engage eminent medical assistance, Lord Ravensworth turned a deaf ear, or else so far roused himself as to utter a stern refusal, accompanied with a command that he might be left alone.

Thus was he rapidly accomplishing his own destruction,—committing involuntary suicide by slow, certain, and yet unsuspected means,—even as his brother, the Honourable Gilbert Vernon, had declared to the Resurrection Man.

Adeline had no inclination to seek the bustle and excitement of society. Her love of display and ostentation was subdued—if not altogether crushed. She was so overwhelmed with sorrow—so goaded by the tyranny of Lydia Hutchinson—so desperate by the mere fact of having to submit to that oppression, and by the consciousness that she dared not unbosom her cares to a single sympathising heart,—that she at times felt as if she were on the point of becoming raving mad, and at others as if she could lay herself down and die!

We will afford the reader an idea of the mode of life which the once proud and haughty Lady Ravensworth was now compelled to lead beneath the crushing despotism of Lydia Hutchinson.

It was on the seventh morning after the arrival of the latter at Ravensworth Hall.

The clock had struck nine, when Lydia repaired to the apartment of her mistress——her mistress!

Until she reached the door, her manner was meek and subdued, because she incurred a chance of meeting other domestics in the passages and corridors.

But the moment she entered Adeline's apartment—the moment the door of that chamber closed behind her—her manner suddenly changed. No longer meek—no longer subdued—no longer wearing the stamp of servitude Lydia assumed a stern expression of countenance—so terrible in a vengeful woman—and in an instant clothed herself, as it were, with an appearance of truly fiend-like malignity.

Adeline slept.

Approaching the bed, Lydia shook her rudely.

Lady Ravensworth awoke with a start, and then glanced hastily—almost franticly—around.

"Ah! *you* here again!" she murmured, shrinking from the look of bitter hatred which Lydia cast upon her.

"Yes—I am here again," said the vindictive woman. "It is time for you to rise."

"Oh! spare me, Lydia," exclaimed Adeline; "allow me to repose a little longer. I have passed a wretched—a sleepless night: see—my pillow is still moist with the tears of anguish which I have shed; and it was but an hour ago that I fell into an uneasy slumber! I cannot live thus—I would rather that you should take a dagger and plunge it into my heart at once. Oh! leave me—leave me to rest for only another hour!"

"No:—it is time to rise, I say," cried Lydia. "It has been my destiny to pass many long weary nights in the streets—in the depth of winter—and with the icy wind penetrating through my scanty clothing till it seemed to freeze the very marrow in my bones. I have been so wearied—so cold—so broken down for want of sleep, that I would have given ten years of my life for two hours' repose in a warm and comfortable bed:—but still have I often, in those times, passed a whole week without so resting my sinking frame. Think you, then, that I can now permit *you* the luxury of sleep when your body requires it—of repose when your mind needs it? No, Adeline—no! I cannot turn you forth into the streets to become a houseless wanderer, as I have been:—but I can at least arouse you from the indolent enjoyment of that bed of down."

With these words Lydia seized Lady Ravensworth rudely by the wrist, and compelled her to leave the couch.

Then the revengeful woman seated herself in a chair, and said in a harsh tone, "Light the fire, Adeline—I am cold."

"No—no: I will not be *your* servant!" exclaimed Lady Ravensworth. "You are *mine*—and it is for you to do those menial offices."

"Provoke me not, Adeline," said Lydia Hutchinson, coolly; "or I will repair straight to the servants' hall, and there proclaim the astounding fact that Lord Ravensworth's relapse has been produced by the discovery of his wife's frailty ere their marriage."

"Oh! my God—what will become of me?" murmured Adeline, wringing her hands. "Are you a woman? or are you a fiend?"

"I am a woman—and one who, having suffered much, knows how to revenge deeply," returned Lydia. "You shall obey me—or I will cover you with shame!"

Adeline made no reply; but, with scalding tears trickling down her cheeks, she proceeded—yes, she—the high-born peeress!—to arrange the wood in the grate—to heap up the coals—and to light the fire.

And while she was kneeling in the performance of that menial task,—while her delicate white hands were coming in contact with the black grate,—and while she was shivering in her night gear, and her long dishevelled hair streamed over her naked neck and bosom,—there, within a few feet of her, sate the menial—the servant, comfortably placed in an arm-chair, and calmly surveying the degrading occupation of her mistress.

"I have often—oh! how often—longed for a stick of wood and a morsel of coal to make myself a fire, if no larger than sufficient to warm the palms of my almost frost-bitten hands," said Lydia, after a short pause; "and when I have dragged my weary limbs past the houses of the rich, and have caught sight of the cheerful flames blazing through the area-windows of their kitchens, I have thought to myself, '*Oh! for one hour to sit within the influence of that genial warmth!*' And yet you—*you*, the proud daughter of the aristocracy—recoil in disgust from a task which so many thousands of poor creatures would only be too glad to have an opportunity of performing!"

Adeline sobbed bitterly, but made no reply.

The fire was now blazing in the grate: still the high-born peeress was shivering with the cold—for ere she could put on a single article of clothing, she was forced to wash the black dirt from her delicate fingers.

Then that lady, who—until within a week—had never even done so much as take, with her own hands, a change of linen from the cupboard or select a gown from the wardrobe, was compelled to perform those duties for herself;—and all the while her servant,—her hired servant, to whom she had to pay high wages and afford food and lodging,—that servant was seated in the arm-chair, warming herself by the now cheerful fire!

"Do not be ashamed of your occupation, madam," said Lydia. "It is fortunate for you that there is a well-stocked cupboard to select from, and a well-provided wardrobe to have recourse to. Your linen is of the most delicate texture, and of the most refined work: your feet have never worn any thing coarser than silk. For your gowns, you may choose amongst fifty dresses. One would even think that your ladyship would be bewildered by the variety of the assortment. And yet you are indignant at being compelled to take the trouble to make your selections! For how many long weeks and months together have I been forced, at times, to wear the same thin, tattered gown—the same threadbare shawl—the same well-darned stockings! And how many thousands are there, Adeline, who dwell in rags from the moment of their birth to that of their death! Ah! if we could only take the daughters of the working classes, and give them good clothing,—enable them to smooth their hair with fragrant oil, and to wash their flesh with perfumed soaps,—and provide them with all those accessories which enhance so much the natural loveliness of woman, think you not that they would be as attractive—as worthy of homage—as yourself? And let me tell you, Adeline, that such black ingratitude as I have encountered at your hands, is unknown in the humble cottage:—the poor are not so selfish—so hollow-hearted as the rich!"

While Lydia Hutchinson was thus venting her bitter sarcasm and her cutting reproach upon Lady Ravensworth, the latter was hurriedly accomplishing the routine of the toilet.

She no longer took pride in her appearance:—she scarcely glanced in the mirror as she combed out those tresses which it was Lydia's duty to have arranged;—her sole thought was to escape as speedily as possible from that room where insults and indignities were so profusely accumulated upon her.

But her ordeal of torture was not yet at its end.

So soon as Lady Ravensworth was dressed, Lydia Hutchinson said in a cool but authoritative tone, "Adeline, you will comb out my hair for me now."

"Provoke me not, vile woman—provoke me not beyond the powers of endurance!" almost shrieked the unhappy lady; "or I shall be tempted—oh! I shall be tempted to lay violent hands upon you. My God—my God! what will become of me?"

"I am prepared to stand the risk of any ebullition of fury on your part," said Lydia, in the same imperturbable manner in which she had before spoken. "Lay but a finger upon me to do me an injury, and I will attack you—I will assault you—I will disfigure your countenance with my nails—I will tear out your hair by handfuls—I will beat your teeth from your mouth;—for I am stronger than you—and you would gain nothing by an attempt to hurt me."

"But I will not be your servant!" cried Adeline, fire flashing from her eyes.

"I tended your ladyship when you lay upon the humble couch in my garret, in the agonies of maternity," replied Lydia; "and your ladyship shall now wait upon me."

"No—no! You would make me a slave—a low slave—the lowest of slaves!" ejaculated Adeline, wildly. "You degrade me in my own estimation—you render me contemptible in my own eyes——"

"And you have spurned and scorned me," interrupted Lydia; "you have made me, too, the lowest of slaves, by using me as an instrument to save you from shame;—and now it is time that I should teach you—the proud peeress—that I—the humble and friendless woman—have *my* feelings, which may be wounded as well as *your own*."

"Lydia—I beg you—I implore you—on my knees I beseech you to have mercy upon me!" cried Adeline, clasping her hands together in a paroxysm of ineffable anguish, and falling at the feet of the stern and relentless woman whom she had wronged.

"I can know no mercy for *you*!" said Lydia Hutchinson, now speaking in a deep and almost hoarse tone, which denoted the powerful concentration of her vengeful passions. "When I think of all that I have suffered—when I trace my miseries to their source—and remember how happy I might have been in the society of a fond father and a loving brother,—when I reflect that it was you—*you* who led me astray, and having blighted all my prospects—demanding even the sacrifice of my good name to your interests,—thrust me away from you with scorn,—when I ponder upon all this, it is enough to drive me mad;—and yet you ask for mercy! No—never, never! I cannot pity you—for I hate, I abhor you!"

"Do not talk so fearfully, Lydia—good Lydia!" cried Adeline, in a voice of despair, while she endeavoured to take the hands of her servant, at whose feet she still knelt.

"Think not to move me with a show of kindness," said Lydia, drawing back her hands in a contemptuous manner: "*your overtures of good treatment come too late!*"

"But I will make amends for the past—I will henceforth consider you as my sister," exclaimed Adeline, raising her eyes in an imploring manner towards the vengeful woman. "I will do all I can to repair my former ingratitude—only be forbearing with me—if not for *my* sake, at least for the sake of my unborn babe!"

"Your maternal feelings have improved in quality of late," said Lydia, with a scornful curl of the lip; "for—as you must well remember—your *first babe* was consigned to me to be concealed in a pond, or thrust into some hole—you cared not how nor where, so long as it was hidden from every eye."

"Of all the agonies which you make me endure, detestable woman," ejaculated Adeline, rising from her knees in a perfect fury of rage and despair, "that perpetual recurrence to the past is the most intolerable of all! Tell me—do you want to kill me by a slow and lingering death? or do you wish to drive me mad—*mad*?" she repeated, her eyes rolling wildly, and her delicate hands clenching as she screamed forth the word.

The scene was really an awful one—a scene to which no powers of description can possibly do justice.

The stern, inflexible tyranny of Lydia Hutchinson forced Lady Ravensworth to pass through all the terrible ordeal of the most tearing and heart-breaking emotions.

Did the miserable peeress endeavour to screen herself within the stronghold of a sullen silence, the words of Lydia Hutchinson would gradually fall upon her, one after the other, with an irritating power that at length goaded her to desperation. Did she meet accusation by retort, and encounter reproach with upbraiding, the inveteracy of Lydia's torturing language wound her feelings up to such a pitch that it was no wonder she should ask, with an agonising scream, whether the avenging woman sought to drive her mad? Or, again, did she endeavour to move the heart of her hired servant by self-humiliation and passionate appeal, the coldness, or the malignant triumph with which those manifestations were received awoke within her that proud and haughty spirit which was now so nearly subdued altogether.

"Do you wish to drive me mad?" Lady Ravensworth had said:—then, when the accompanying paroxysm of feeling was past, she threw herself on a chair, and burst into an agony of tears.

But Lydia was not softened!

She suffered Adeline to weep for a few minutes; and when the unhappy lady was exhausted—subdued—spirit-broken—the unrelenting torturess repeated her command—"You can now arrange my hair."

Oh! bad as Adeline was at heart—selfish as she was by nature and by education,—it would have moved a savage to have seen the imploring, beseeching look which, through her tears, she cast upon Lydia's countenance.

"My hair!" said Lydia, imperatively.

Then Lady Ravensworth rose, and meekly and timidly began to perform that menial office for her own menial.

"I never thought," observed Lydia, "while I was a wanderer and an outcast in the streets,—as, for instance, on the occasion when I accosted you, in the bitterness of my starving condition, in Saint James's Street, and when your lacqueys thrust me back, your husband declaring that *it was easy to see what I was*, and your carriage dashing me upon the kerb-stone,—little did I think *then* that the time would ever be when a peeress of England should dress my hair—and least of all that this peeress should be *you*! But when, in your pride, you spurned the worm— you knew not that the day could ever possibly come for that worm to raise its head and sting you! Think you that I value any peculiar arrangement which you can bestow upon my hair? Think you that I cannot even, were I still vain, adapt it more to my taste with my own hands? Yes—certainly I could! But I compel you to attend upon me thus—I constitute myself the mistress, and make you the menial, when we are alone together—because it is the principal element of my vengeance. It degrades you—it renders you little in your own eyes,—you who were once so great—so haughty—and so proud!"

In this strain did Lydia Hutchinson continue to speak, while Lady Ravensworth arranged her hair.

And each word that the vindictive woman uttered, fell like a drop of molten lead upon the already lacerated heart of the unfortunate Adeline.

At length the ordeal—that same ordeal which had characterised each morning since Lydia Hutchinson had become an inmate of Ravensworth Hall—was over; and Adeline was released from that horrible tyranny—but only for a short time.

CHAPTER CCXIV.

THE DUELLISTS.

When Lady Ravensworth descended to the breakfast parlour, she summoned her husband's principal valet, Quentin, to her presence, and desired him to hasten and inform his lordship that the morning meal was served up.

Quentin bowed and retired.

But both Lady Ravensworth and the valet were well aware that this was a mere idle ceremonial which would only lead to the same ineffectual result as on the six preceding mornings—indeed, ever since the arrival of Lydia Hutchinson at the Hall. At the same time, the servant was very far from suspecting how large a share the new lady's-maid enjoyed in the relapse of his master and the increasing sorrows of his mistress.

In a few minutes Quentin returned.

"His lordship requests you, my lady, to excuse his absence," was the message which he delivered—a message as formal as the one that had evoked it.

"How is your lord this morning?" asked Adeline, with a profound sigh.

"His lordship does not appear to be improving, my lady," was the answer.

Adeline sighed once more, and remained silent.

The valet withdrew; and the unhappy lady endeavoured to eat a morsel of food: but she had no appetite—her stomach seemed to loathe all solid nourishment; and she pushed her plate from her.

She then endeavoured to while away an hour or two with the most recently published novel and the morning's newspapers; but she found her imagination ever wandering to other and sadly painful topics.

It was about mid-day, when, as she was standing listlessly at the window, which commanded a view of the park, she suddenly caught sight of a carriage that was advancing rapidly towards the mansion.

The livery of the servants belonging to it was unknown to her; and she hastily summoned a domestic to instruct him that "she was not at home to any visitors."

The vehicle drove up to the principal entrance of Ravensworth Hall; and although the domestic delivered the answer commanded by his mistress, it did not seem sufficient to cause the departure of the carriage.

There was some conversation between the servant who gave that answer and the occupants of the vehicle;—but Lady Ravensworth could not overhear a word that was said.

In a few minutes, however, the domestic returned to Adeline's presence.

"Please your ladyship," he said, "there is a gentleman below who has just been dangerously wounded in a duel; and his companions earnestly request——"

"I understand you," interrupted Lady Ravensworth. "This is quite another consideration. You must admit them by all means."

The domestic once more hurried away; and Adeline shortly beheld, from the window, two gentlemen alight from the carriage, and then carefully remove a third, who appeared to be in a helpless condition. She did not, however, catch a glimpse of either of their faces.

Lady Ravensworth now felt herself to be in a most unpleasant situation. Her husband, she knew, would not come forth from his private cabinet to do the honours of his mansion; and delicacy prevented her from hastening to receive persons who might be total strangers to her, and who arrived under such extraordinary circumstances.

She did not, however, long hesitate how to act. Ringing the bell, and summoning Quentin to her presence, she said to him, "You must make a fitting excuse for the non-appearance of Lord Ravensworth, and see that the wounded gentleman be conveyed to a chamber. Then assure his friends that they may command every thing they require in this house; and state that I shall be happy to receive them in the drawing-room in half an hour."

Quentin retired to execute this commission. He had the wounded man borne to a bed-room, and offered to send a messenger on horseback to procure medical assistance, from the nearest village; but one of the other two gentlemen proved to be a surgeon, whose services had been engaged in the usual manner by the duellists.

In the meantime, Lady Ravensworth repaired to her boudoir, to change her dress.

She was immediately followed thither by Lydia Hutchinson.

"I do not require your attendance," said Adeline, with a visible shudder, as the lady's-maid closed the door behind her.

"I care not for your wishes or aversions," returned Lydia. "Appearances compel me to wait upon you—or to have the semblance of waiting upon you;—and, moreover, I have something important to communicate. Oh! I feel such pleasure in being the bearer of good news to *you*!"

"What new torture have you in store for me, horrible woman?" cried Lady Ravensworth, affrighted by the malignant bitterness with which these last words were uttered.

"Know you to whom your princely mansion has just afforded its hospitality?" demanded Lydia.

"To a wounded duellist and his friends," replied Adeline. "Is *this* circumstance to be in any way rendered available to your fearful purposes of torture in respect to me?"

"And that wounded duellist and one of his companions are well known to you," said Lydia, impressively.

"Known to me!" ejaculated Adeline, who felt convinced that some fresh cause of anguish to herself lurked in the mysterious language of her torturess.

"Oh! yes—known too well to yourself and to me also!" said Lydia, as if shuddering with concentrated rage.

"Ah! my God—it would require but *that* to drive me to desperation!" exclaimed Adeline, a terrible suspicion darting across her mind.

"Then despair must be your lot," said Lydia, fixing her eyes with malignant joy upon her mistress: "for—as sure as you are called Lady Ravensworth—Lord Dunstable and Colonel Cholmondeley are inmates of this mansion!"

"May God have mercy upon me!" murmured Adeline, in a low but solemn tone.

And she sank almost insensible upon the sofa.

"Yes," continued the unrelenting Lydia, "*he* to whom you gave your honour, as one child might give a toy of little value to another—and *he* who stole my honour as a vile thief plunders the defenceless traveller upon the highway,—those two men are beneath this roof! The villain who ruined me and slew my brother, is now lying upon a bed from which he may never more be removed save to the coffin. His second was the gay seducer who rioted awhile upon your charms, and then threw you aside,—yes, *you*—the daughter of one of England's proudest peers—as he would a flower that had garnished his button-hole for an hour, and then failed to please any longer. These two men are beneath your roof!"

"Oh! if my errors have been great, surely—surely my punishment is more than commensurate!" murmured Adeline, in the bitterness of her heart.

"Your punishment seems only to have just begun," retorted Lydia, ever ready to plunge a fresh dagger into the soul of the unhappy lady.

"My God! you speak but too truly!" ejaculated Adeline, clasping her hands together. "Oh! that I could pass the latter half of my life over again—oh! that I could recall the years that have fled!"

"The years that have fled have prepared a terrible doom for those that are to come," said Lydia. "But hasten, my lady,—*this time* I will aid you to change your dress," she added sneeringly; "for I long to see your meeting with Colonel Cholmondeley."

"*See* our meeting!—*you!*" cried Lady Ravensworth, springing from the sofa in alarm.

"Yes—I shall contrive that pleasure for myself," observed Lydia, calmly.

Adeline made no reply: she felt convinced that all remonstrance would be useless.

She accordingly addressed herself to the toilet, Lydia assisting her in that ceremony for the first time.

"I have chosen the attire that best becomes you—and I have arranged your hair in the most attractive manner," said Lydia; "for I should be vexed were you not to appear to advantage in the presence of him who made you his mistress during pleasure."

"Wretch!" cried Adeline, turning sharply round upon Lydia, whose bitter taunt touched the most sensitive fibre of her heart.

"If I be a wretch, it is you who made me so," said Lydia, with imperturbable coolness.

Adeline bit her lips almost till the blood came, to suppress the rage that rose as it were into her throat.

She then hastily left the boudoir, followed at a short distance by Lydia Hutchinson.

Lady Ravensworth knew that her torturess was behind her,—knew also that it was vain to reason with her in respect to any particular line of conduct that she might choose to adopt.

As the unhappy lady proceeded towards the drawing-room, she endeavoured to compose both her countenance and her mind as much as possible: but she felt herself blushing at one moment and turning pale the next,—now with a face that seemed to be on fire—then with an icy coldness at the heart.

Since she was at school at Belvidere House she had never met Colonel Cholmondeley. He had been much abroad; and, when he was in London, accident had so willed it that he did not once encounter the partner of his temporary amour.

But that same chance was not for ever to be favourable to Adeline in this respect; and now she was at length about to meet that man of all the species in whose presence she had most cause to blush.

Such an encounter was however necessary, for the sake of appearances. What would her servants think if she remained in the solitude of her own chamber while visitors were at the mansion? what would the surgeon, who attended the wounded duellist, conjecture if she refused the common courtesy which became the mistress of the mansion? The total retirement of Lord Ravensworth was already a sufficient reason to provoke strange surmises on the part of the newly-arrived guests, although the existence of his extraordinary and unaccountable malady was well known in the fashionable world: but if to that fact were superadded the circumstance of a similar seclusion on the part of Lady Ravensworth, the most unpleasant rumours might arise. Thus was Adeline imperatively forced to do the honours of her house on this occasion.

And now she has reached the door of the drawing-room.

She pauses for a moment: how violently beats her heart!

"This is foolish!" she murmurs to herself: "the ordeal must be passed;—better to enter upon it at once!"

And she entered the drawing-room.

One only of the guests was there; and he had his back towards the door at the moment.

But full well did she recognise that tall, graceful, and well-knit frame.

The sound of light footsteps upon the thick carpet caused him to turn hastily round;—and then Adeline and her seducer were face to face.

"Lady Ravensworth," said the Colonel, rather averting his glance as he spoke—for he experienced the full embarrassment of this encounter,—"necessity, and not my wish, has compelled me to intrude upon your hospitality. My friend Lord Dunstable and another officer in the same regiment had an altercation last evening, which would permit of none other than a hostile settlement. The choice of time and place, fell by the laws of honour, to Lord Dunstable's opponent; and the vicinity of your abode was unfortunately fixed upon as the spot for meeting. My friend was grievously wounded with the first shot; and I had no alternative but to convey him to the nearest habitation where hospitality might be hoped for. Your ladyship can now understand the nature of that combination of circumstances which has brought me hither."

"I deeply regret that Lord Ravensworth should be too much indisposed to do the honours of his house in person," said Adeline, with her eyes fixed upon the ground, and a deep blush upon her cheeks. "Is your friend's wound dangerous?"

"Mr. Graham, a surgeon of known skill, is now with him," answered the Colonel; "and entertains great hopes of being enabled to extract the ball, which has lodged in the right side. It is true that I incur some risk by remaining in the neighbourhood of the metropolis; but I cannot consent to abandon my friend until I am convinced that he is beyond danger."

"*It is the fashion in the aristocratic world to adhere to a friend, but to abandon the seduced girl when she no longer pleases,*" said Lydia Hutchinson, who had entered the room unperceived by either Colonel Cholmondeley or Lady Ravensworth, and who now advanced slowly towards them.

The Colonel stared at Lydia for a few moments: but evidently not recognising her, he turned a rapid glance of inquiry upon Adeline, who only hung down her head, and remained silent.

"I see that you do not know me, sir," continued Lydia, approaching close to Colonel Cholmondeley: then, fixing her eyes intently upon him, she said, "Do you remember me now?"

"My good young woman," replied the Colonel, with a mixture of hauteur and bantering jocularity, "I really do not think that you have served in any family which I have had the honour to visit: and, even if you had, I must candidly confess that my memory is not capacious enough to retain the image of every lady's-maid whom I may happen to see."

"And yet it is not every lady's-maid," said Lydia, with a scornful glance towards Adeline, who, pale and trembling, had sunk upon a seat,—"it is not every lady's-maid that can venture to talk thus openly—thus familiarly in the presence of her mistress."

While she was yet speaking, a light broke upon the Colonel's mind. Who but one acquainted with Lady Ravensworth's secret could be capable of such extraordinary conduct? This idea led him to survey Lydia Hutchinson's countenance more attentively than before;—and, although it was much altered,—although it no longer bore the blooming freshness which had characterised it when he first knew her,—still the expression and the features enabled him to recognise the young woman who had become the victim of his friend Lord Dunstable.

"Ah! you know me now," continued Lydia, perceiving by a sudden gesture on the part of the Colonel that he *had* at length remembered her. "Think you that I have no reproaches to hurl at you, sir? Was it not at your house that my ruin was consummated? and were you no party to the infamous treachery which gave me to the arms of your friend? But you have no shame:—you are a fashionable gentleman—a *roué*—one who considers seduction an aristocratic amusement, as well as wrenching off knockers or breaking policemen's heads. What to such as you are the tears of deceived and lost girls? what to you are the broken hearts of fond parents? Nothing—nothing: I know it well! And therefore it were vain for me to say another word—unless it be that I shall now leave you to make your peace as best you may with your cast-off mistress *there!*"

And pointing disdainfully at Adeline, who uttered a low scream and covered her face with her hands as those terrible words fell upon her ears, Lydia slowly quitted the room.

Frightfully painful was now the situation of Lady Ravensworth and Colonel Cholmondeley.

The former was crushed by the terrible indignity cast upon her: the latter was so astounded and at the same time so hurt by all that had just occurred, that he knew not how to act.

He felt that any attempt to console Lady Ravensworth would be an insult; and yet he experienced an equal inability to permit the scene to pass without some comment.

Fortunately for them both, Mr. Graham, the surgeon, entered the room at this juncture.

Adeline composed herself by one of those extraordinary efforts which she had lately been so often compelled to exert; and Cholmondeley, with the case of a man of fashion (who must necessarily be a thorough hypocrite), instantly assumed a manner that would even have disarmed suspicion, had any been excited.

Having uttered a few ceremonial phrases upon his introduction to Lady Ravensworth, Mr. Graham said, "I am happy to state that Lord Dunstable is in as favourable a state as under the circumstances could be expected. I have succeeded in extracting the ball—and he now sleeps."

"Thank God!" exclaimed Cholmondeley,—not with any real piety, but merely using that common phrase as expressive of his joy to think that the matter was not more serious than it now appeared to be.

"I am, however, afraid," continued the surgeon, turning towards Adeline, "that my patient will be compelled to trespass for some few days upon the kind hospitality of your ladyship."

"In which case Lord Dunstable shall receive every attention that can be here afforded him," observed Adeline. "It would be but an idle compliment to you, sir, under the circumstances, to say that Ravensworth Hall will be honoured by your presence so long as you may see fit to make it your abode."

The surgeon bowed in acknowledgment of this courteous intimation.

"For my part," Colonel Cholmondeley hastened to say, "I shall not trespass upon her ladyship's hospitality; for—since I am assured that my friend is no longer in danger—I must attend to certain pressing business which calls me elsewhere."

Adeline threw a glance of gratitude upon the Colonel for this expression of his intention to relieve her from the embarrassment of his presence; and accordingly, after partaking of some luncheon, Cholmondeley took his departure.

But ere he left, Lydia Hutchinson had secretly placed a letter, containing a key, upon the seat of the carriage which bore him away.

CHAPTER CCXV.

THE VOICES IN THE RUINS.

It would be impossible to conceive the existence of a more wretched woman than Adeline Ravensworth.

Though wealth and title were hers,—though every luxury and every pleasure were within her reach,—though with jewels of inestimable value she might deck herself at will, and thus enhance her natural charms,—still, still was she the prey to a constant agony of mind which rendered life intolerable.

For it is not all the wealth of India,—nor all the luxuries and pleasures of oriental palaces,—nor all the diamonds that ever sparkled over the brow of beauty,—it is not these that can impart tranquillity to the soul, nor give peace to the conscience.

Such was the bitter truth that Adeline was now compelled to acknowledge!

Shortly after the departure of Colonel Cholmondeley, which occurred at about four o'clock in the afternoon, Lady Ravensworth felt so deeply the want of undisturbed solitude for her meditations and of fresh air to relieve the stifling sensation which oppressed her, that she determined to take a long walk through the quiet fields.

Hastily slipping on a plain straw bonnet and a thick warm shawl, she left the house unperceived by her torturess—Lydia Hutchinson.

Passing through the spacious gardens at the back of the mansion, she gained the open fields, where the cold fresh breeze somewhat revived her drooping spirits.

"Heaven grant that the babe which now agitates in my bosom may prove a son!" she thought, as she cast a hasty but proud glance around: "or else the broad lands which I now behold, and the soil on which my feet now tread, will stand but a poor chance of remaining long beneath my control. Yes—they would pass away to one whom I have never seen—whom I have never known save by name—and who could not possibly be supposed to entertain any sympathy for me! But if my babe should prove a boy—if he should live, too—then adieu to all thy hopes and chances, Gilbert Vernon."

These reflections led to a variety of others—all connected with Adeline's interests or her sorrows.

So profoundly was she plunged in her painful reverie, and at the same time so invigorated did she feel by the freshness of the air, that she insensibly prolonged her walk until the shades of evening gathered around her.

She had now reached the ruined remains of a gamekeeper's lodge which marked the boundary of the Ravensworth estate in that direction.

Feeling a sudden sensation of weariness come over her, she seated herself on a bench which still existed near the dilapidated remnant of the cottage-portico.

Scarcely had she taken that place, when a voice from the other side of the ruined wall caused her to start with sudden affright: but the words that met her ears conquered this first feeling of alarm, and inspired one of curiosity.

She accordingly lingered where she was; and as the darkness was every moment growing more intense, she knew there was but little danger of being perceived.

"I tell you that I am a man capable of doing any thing for money," said the voice, in an impatient tone. "If you think there is any squeamishness about me, you are deucedly mistaken. What I have promised you, I will perform, when the time comes, and if there should be a necessity for such a step. I value a human life no more than I do that of a dog. If any one came to me and said, '*There is my enemy, and here is your price—now go and kill him*,' I should just count the money first to see that it was all right, and the remainder of the job would soon be done, I can assure you."

"Well—well, I believe you," said another voice, whose deep tones rolled solemnly upon the silence of the dark evening. "To all that you have proposed I must assent—I have gone too far to retreat. But we must now separate."

"And when shall I see you again?" demanded the first speaker: "because now that you have made me acquainted with the whereabouts, I shall constantly be ascertaining how things go on, and I ought therefore to be able to communicate very often with you. That is—I ought to see you frequently; for I hate doing business by letter."

"Can you not give me your own private address?" asked the individual with the deep-toned voice; "and then I might call upon you every other evening."

"Well said," exclaimed the first speaker: then, after a pause, during which Adeline distinctly heard the rustling sound of paper, he said, "Have you got a pencil in your pocket? for I can *feel* to write a few words in the dark."

"Yes—here is a pencil," returned the deep-toned voice.

There was another short pause.

"All right!" cried the first speaker, at length. "That bit of paper contains the name and address of the most daring fellow that London ever produced," he added with a low chuckle. "Talk of your bravos of Spain or Italy—why, they are nothing to me! And isn't it odd, too, that whenever a rich or great person wants any thing queer done for him, it is sure to be me that he gets hold of somehow or another?"

"I have no doubt that you enjoy a most extensive patronage," said the deep-toned voice, rather impatiently—and even haughtily. "But we must now separate. The day after to-morrow—in the evening—I shall call upon you."

"Good: I shall expect you," returned the other.

The two individuals then separated—each taking a different way; but one came round the angle of the ruined wall, and passed so close to Adeline that she shrank back in a dreadful state of alarm lest her presence there should be discovered;—for, mysterious as was the conversation which she had just overheard, there was one fact which it too intelligibly revealed—and this was the desperate nature of those two men's characters.

But the individual who passed so closely, did not observe her—for the evening was very dark, and she moreover was sitting in the still deeper obscurity of the ruined portico.

Neither was she enabled to obtain a glimpse of his countenance: the outline of a tall and somewhat stout figure, as he hurried by her, was the extent of the view which she caught of him.

In a few moments all was again silent: the sounds of the retreating footsteps no longer met her ears.

She did not immediately leave the ruins: she paused to reflect upon the strange conversation which she had overheard. But all its details were dark and mysterious—save that one man was a wretch who gloried in his readiness to perform any crime for a commensurate reward, and that the other was either his accomplice or his employer in some fearful plot that was in progress.

There was one expression that had fallen from the lips of the former miscreant, and on which Lady Ravensworth principally dwelt:—"*Now that you have made me acquainted with the whereabouts, I shall be constantly ascertaining how things go on.*"

Could the *whereabouts*, or locality, alluded to, have any connexion with that neighbourhood? And, if so, did the observation refer to the Ravensworth estate? Or were the two men merely discussing, in those ruins, matters which regarded some other and totally distinct spot?

"The latter supposition must be the right one," said Adeline to herself, after a long meditation upon the subject. "The only person in the world who could have any interest in learning '*how things were going on*' in this neighbourhood, is Gilbert Vernon; and he is in Turkey. Moreover—even were he in England—he would have no need to spy about in the dark: he is on friendly terms with his brother, and might present himself boldly at the Hall."

Thus reasoning against the vague and temporary fears which had arisen in her mind, Adeline rose from the bench and was about to retrace her steps homewards, when the moon suddenly appeared from behind a cloud, and its rays fell upon a small white object that lay at the lady's feet.

She mechanically picked it up:—it was a piece of paper on which she could perceive, by the moonlight, that a few words were written; but she could not decypher them.

Nevertheless, the mode in which the short lines were arranged struck her with the idea that this paper contained an address; and a natural association of facts immediately encouraged the belief that she held in her hand the one which the self-vaunted bravo had given ere now to his companion, and which the latter might probably have dropped by accident.

Hastily concealing it in her bosom, Adeline retraced her steps to Ravensworth Hall.

On her arrival she hurried to her boudoir, lighted the wax tapers, and examined the paper ere she even laid aside her bonnet and shawl.

Yes—it contained an address; and the words were scrawled as they would be if written in the dark.

There could, then, be no doubt that this was the address which one of the men had given to his companion in the ruins of the gamekeeper's lodge.

"It is useful to know that such a villain as this can be hired for money!" muttered Adeline to herself, as she concealed the paper in one of her jewel-caskets. "What did he say? That if any one went to him and whispered, '*There is my enemy, and here is your price—now go and kill him*,' he would take the bribe and do the deed. And did he not boast that he was employed by the rich and the powerful? In what manner could such persons require his aid? Assuredly in no good cause! Ah! Lydia—Lydia," continued Adeline, her brows contracting and a dark cloud passing over her countenance as she spoke, "be not too confident! You are now in *my* power!"

But scarcely was the fearful thought thus implied, when Adeline seemed to recoil from it with horror: for, covering her face with her hands, she almost shrieked out, "No—no! I could not do it!"

"What can you not do, dearest?" said a low voice close by her ear; and almost at the same instant she was clasped in the arms of Colonel Cholmondeley.

"Release me—release me!" exclaimed Adeline, struggling to free herself from his embrace.

"Not till I have imprinted another kiss upon, those sweet lips," returned the Colonel: "not till I have made my peace with you, dearest Adeline, in respect to the past:—else wherefore should I have come hither?"

And as he uttered these words, he glued his lips to hers, although she still continued to resist his insolence to the utmost of her power.

"Oh! my God!" she murmured in a faint tone "am I to submit to this new indignity?"

Cholmondeley supported her to the sofa; then, throwing himself at her feet, he took her hands in his, and said in a fervent tone, "Adeline—dearest Adeline, wherefore do you receive me thus coldly? Is it possible that you can have altogether forgotten those feelings which animated our hearts with a reciprocal affection some years ago? But perhaps my conduct—my ungrateful, my ungenerous conduct—has completely effaced all those emotions, and excited hatred and disgust instead? Oh! I admit—I acknowledge that my conduct *was* ungrateful—*was* ungenerous! I abandoned you at a moment when you most required my counsel—my assistance! But was my fault so grave that it is beyond the possibility of pardon? When I found myself this morning brought by an imperious necessity—or rather by a strange chance—to this mansion, I thought within my breast, '*I shall now see Adeline once again: but we must be strangers unto each other. Cold ceremony must separate hearts that once beat in the reciprocities of love.*'—And you know, Adeline, with what formal respect I sought to treat you. But when I beheld you so beautiful, and yet so unhappy,—when I saw that the lovely girl had grown into the charming woman,—oh! I was every moment about to dash aside that chilling ceremony and snatch you to my breast. And now, Adeline, will you forgive me?—will you say that you do not quite detest me—even if you cannot call me your lover—your friend?"

With her head drooping upon her bosom,—with tears trembling upon her long dark lashes,—and with her hands still retained in those of Colonel Cholmondeley, did Adeline listen to this specious appeal.

The words "*your friend*" touched a chord which vibrated to her heart's core.

"Oh! yes—I do require a friend—a friend to advise and console me," she exclaimed; "for I am very—very miserable!"

Cholmondeley was man of the world enough to perceive that his appeal was successful—that his victory was complete; and, seating himself by Adeline's side, he drew her towards him, saying, "I will be your friend, dearest—I will advise you—I will console you. You shall pour forth all your sorrows to me, as if I were your brother: and I swear most solemnly, beloved Adeline, that if it be your wish, I will never seek henceforth to be more to you than a brother!"

"Oh! if that were true—if I could rely upon your word!" cried Adeline, joyfully.

"By every sacred obligation with which man can bind himself, do I vow the sincerity of that promise," returned Cholmondeley.

Then withdrawing his arm from her waist, as a tacit proof of his honourable intentions, but still retaining one of her hands in his own, he looked anxiously in her countenance to read the impression which his words and manner had created.

"Again I say that if I could believe you, I should think myself happy—nay, blest in your friendship," returned Adeline; "for I am so miserable—so very, very wretched—that I feel the burden of such an existence too heavy to bear. All that has passed between us constitutes a reason to induce me to accept you as my friend, rather than any other;—for I have lately seen so much of the fiend-like disposition of *one* woman, that I am inclined to abhor the whole sex—yes, even though it be my own! And to you, moreover, I can speak frankly of those causes which have rendered me so very wretched."

"Speak, dear Adeline—unburden your mind to me," said Cholmondeley, in a low, but tender tone. "I must, however, inform you that I am already acquainted with many of the incidents regarding the connexion between Lydia Hutchinson and yourself, from the moment when Lord Dunstable and I so dishonourably wrote to you both to state that we were going abroad. Yes—Adeline, I have learnt how you were extricated from the embarrassments of that situation in which I shamefully left you,—how, in a word, the offspring of our love was born dead and disposed of, and how your reputation was saved through the means of Lydia."

"You know all those fearful particulars?" exclaimed Lady Ravensworth, profoundly surprised at what she heard.

"Yes, dearest: for Lydia, some time after she left the school, became the mistress of my friend Dunstable; and she told him all. He related those incidents to me: it was natural that he should do—seeing that we were mutually acquainted with each-other's loves. And, oh! my dearest Adeline," continued the Colonel, "I can well understand how completely that odious woman is enabled to tyrannise over you."

"And you can also comprehend how much I stand in need of a friend?" said Lady Ravensworth; "for it is hard to be compelled to nurse one's griefs—to conceal one's sorrows—without being able to unburden to a single living soul a heart surcharged with woe."

"I will be that friend, Adeline," replied Cholmondeley.

"But, oh! what dangers do I incur by seeing you—by receiving you here!" exclaimed Adeline. "And this thought reminds me that I am even yet ignorant of the means by which you gained access to my chamber."

"Nay, Adeline," said Cholmondeley, in a tender tone, "do not attempt to disavow the encouragement which you so kindly gave me—and to which you now force me to allude."

"Encouragement!" repeated Lady Ravensworth, with a tone and manner expressive of unfeigned surprise.

"Yes, dearest. That key which I found in the post-chaise—and the few words written upon the paper which enveloped it——"

"My God! there is some fearful mistake in all this!" cried Adeline, seriously alarmed. "But explain yourself—quickly—I conjure you!"

Cholmondeley was now astonished in his turn; and hastily taking a paper from his pocket, he handed it to Lady Ravensworth, saying, "The key was enclosed in this."

Adeline cast her eyes upon the paper, and read these words:—

"The key contained herein belongs to a door on the southern side of Ravensworth Hall: and that door communicates with a private staircase leading to the passage from which my own apartments open. I wish to converse with you in secret—if only for a moment; and though I have taken this imprudent—this unpardonable step, you will surely spare my feelings, should you avail yourself of the possession of the key, by forbearing in my presence from any allusion to the means by which it fell into your hands."

"Merciful heavens!" ejaculated Adeline, when she had hurriedly glanced over the paper: "I am ruined—I am undone! It must be that fiend Lydia, who has thus paved the way for my utter destruction!"

There was the wildness of despair in the manner of Lady Ravensworth, as she uttered these words; and Cholmondeley could not for another moment imagine that her distress was feigned.

"What do you mean, Adeline?" he said: "did you not send me the key?—did you not pen those lines? Surely—surely the handwriting is yours?"

"As God is my judge, Cholmondeley," she answered, emphatically, "I never sent you the key—I never penned those lines! No—it is Lydia who has done it: she knows my writing well—she has imitated it but too faithfully! Go—fly—depart, Cholmondeley: ruin awaits me—perhaps both!"

The Colonel dared not delay another moment: the almost desperate wildness of Adeline's manner convinced him that she spoke the truth—that she had *not* invited him thither.

"At least let me hope to see you soon again—or to hear from you," he said, imprinting a hasty kiss upon her forehead.

"Yes—yes—any thing you will, so that you now leave me," she cried, in a tone of agonising alarm.

Cholmondeley rushed to the door:—Adeline followed him into the passage, bearing a candle in her hand.

The reader may conceive the relief which she experienced, when, upon casting a rapid glance up and down, she found that her torturess was not there either to expose her completely, or to triumph over her alarms.

"Farewell," whispered Cholmondeley; and he disappeared down the staircase.

Adeline remained at the top, until she heard the private door at the bottom carefully open and as gently close.

Then she breathed more freely, and re-entered her own chamber.

"What could Lydia mean by this perfidious plot?" she murmured to herself, as she sank upon the sofa, exhausted both mentally and bodily. "She was not there to enjoy my confusion; she did not come with the servants to behold what might have been considered the evidence of infidelity towards my husband:—what, then, *could* she mean?"

Scarcely had these words passed Adeline's lips, when the door opened, and her torturess entered the room.

CHAPTER CCXVI.

THE PROGRESS OF LYDIA HUTCHINSON'S VENGEANCE.

"What means this new device, terrible woman?" cried Adeline, advancing towards Lydia Hutchinson, and giving vent to the question which was uppermost in her mind.

"Ah! you have already detected my handiwork in the new source of torment which is now open against you?" said Lydia, with a smile of triumphant contempt.

"I know that you have forged a letter in imitation of my writing——" began Adeline.

"And that letter has already produced the desired effect," interrupted Lydia, coolly; "for five minutes have scarcely elapsed since Colonel Cholmondeley stole from the private door opening upon the garden."

"Then you were watching the results of your detestable scheme," cried Lady Ravensworth, in a tone bitter with rage.

"Not only I—but half a dozen of the other dependants of the household," returned Lydia.

"Merciful God! you have done this, vile woman?" screamed Lady Ravensworth. "No—no: you surely could not have been so wicked?"

"I have done it," replied Lydia, in her calm, impassive manner.

"Then it is now for *me* to think of vengeance!" said Adeline, conquering the turbulent emotions of passion which agitated within her, and flinging herself once more upon the sofa, while her thoughts wandered to the address concealed in the casket of jewels.

"*You* think of vengeance!" repeated Lydia, scornfully. "Oh! I should rejoice if you were to meet me with my own weapons—for such conduct on *your* part would afford *me* scope and excuse for augmenting the means of punishment which I employ. And now listen to the details of that scheme by which I have this evening so successfully degraded you."

"Wretch!" muttered Adeline, hoarsely between her teeth.

"Hard names break no bones, my lady," said Lydia. "But again I enjoin you to listen to what I have to tell you. I knew your handwriting well—and it was no difficult thing to imitate it. I penned that letter which the Colonel ere now showed you—and I enclosed the key. In the note I desired that no allusion might be made by him to that letter, because I wished the interview to be a long one, and I suspected that the suddenness and boldness of his unexpected intrusion would cause a protracted conversation ere any question on your part would elicit from him the means by which he had obtained access to your privacy. Nor was I mistaken."

"Then you listened—you overheard all that passed between us?" cried Adeline.

"Nearly every word," answered Lydia: "I only quitted the door of this chamber when he was about to leave it."

"And therefore you are well aware that he received no criminal encouragement on my part?"

"Oh! is there nothing criminal in the fact of a lady accepting her seducer—her former lover—the father of her first child, as her friend? And such a friend as Cholmondeley would prove!" continued Lydia, in a tone of the most mordent sarcasm: "such a friend! Good heavens! does your ladyship suppose that that man who is so selfish in his pleasure—so unprincipled in his adoption of means to procure the gratification of his wishes—would content himself with the cold title and small privileges of a friend? No—no! Were you to encourage his visits to this boudoir, ere the third were passed, you would become criminal again!"

"And was it to render me criminal again that you inveigled him hither by an atrocious forgery?" exclaimed Adeline.

"Such was not my object," replied Lydia; "although I have no interest in protecting your virtue! *Your virtue*—the virtue of Adeline Enfield—the virtue of Lady Ravensworth! Where was ever virtue so immaculate?"

"Beware lest you destroy every particle of virtue—that is, of forbearance—remaining within me," cried Adeline, her thoughts again reverting to the address which she had concealed in her jewel-casket.

"Could you kill me, I believe you capable of laying violent hands upon me," returned Lydia; "for I know how you must hate *me*—even as sincerely as I loathe *you*! But I have before told you that I am stronger than you!"

Adeline made no answer: her mind now dwelt with less horror than before upon the possible use which she might be driven to make of the address in the casket.

"Oh! brood—brood over plans of vengeance," exclaimed Lydia; "and remember that I defy you! All the dark malignity which is now expressed in your lowering countenance, does not terrify me. But listen to the conclusion of the narrative which I ere now began. My object in effecting the prolongation of the interview between Cholmondeley and yourself, was to afford me leisure to warn those of your servants to whom I had already hinted my suspicions of your infidelity."

Adeline started convulsively, but checked the reply which rose to her lips.

"I stationed myself in the garden, accompanied by the housekeeper," continued Lydia; "for I suspected that your Colonel would not allow one evening to elapse ere he availed himself of the invitation which he supposed to have come from you. Nor was I mistaken. We saw him creep stealthily along towards the private door: we saw him enter. Then, while I flew hither to listen in the passage to what might pass between you, the housekeeper hastened to fetch Quentin——"

"Quentin!" cried Adeline, with a shudder.

"Yes—your husband's principal valet and four of the other servants, that they might watch your supposed lover's departure," continued Lydia. "But fear not that the tidings will reach your husband. No: my vengeance does not seek to wound him:—I pity him too much for that! My sole object was to degrade *you* in the eyes of your domestics, as *I* have been degraded in the eyes of the world; for I must reduce *your* situation as nearly as I can to the level of what *mine* so lately was—that you may understand how much I have suffered, and how strong is my justification in avenging myself on the one whose bad example and ungrateful heart threw me into the ways of vice and sorrow."

"And how can *you*, detestable woman, prevent my servants from circulating this terrible scandal?" cried Lady Ravensworth, trembling as she beheld ruin and disgrace yawning like a black precipice at her feet, ready to engulph her: "how can *you* seal the lips of Quentin, so that this same scandal shall not reach the ears of my husband?"

"I have enjoined them all to secrecy on many grounds," answered Lydia: "I have pointed out to them the necessity of waiting for ampler proofs of your guilt—I have represented to them the propriety of sparing you in your present position, so near the time of becoming a mother as you are—and I have also conjured them to exercise forbearance on account of their lord, for whom they all feel deeply."

"Oh! how kind—how considerate were you in my behalf!" exclaimed Adeline, bitterly: "and yet—were I already a mother—you would not hesitate, doubtless, to wreak your fiend-like vengeance upon my poor innocent babe."

"God forbid!" cried Lydia, emphatically: "no—it is enough that I punish *you*."

"And yet every taunt you throw in my teeth—every indignity you compel me to undergo—every torture you inflict upon me, redound in their terrible effects upon the child which I bear in my bosom," said Lady Ravensworth, pressing her clasped hands convulsively to her heart.

"I know it—and I regret it," returned Lydia coldly: "but I cannot consent to forego one tittle of all the tortures which my mind suggests as a punishment for such a bad and heartless creature as yourself. I shall now leave you; for I have more work in hand. I have undertaken to sit up during the first half of the night, in the chamber of the wounded Lord Dunstable. The housekeeper will relieve me for the second half."

"Heavens! have you found another object whereon to wreak your vengeance?" exclaimed Adeline. "Then may God have mercy upon the unhappy man!"

"Yes—pray for him, Adeline: he will have need of all your sympathy!"

With these words Lydia Hutchinson left the boudoir.

It was now nine o'clock in the evening: Mr. Graham had been left to dine alone; and Adeline felt the necessity of proceeding to the drawing-room, to join her guest in partaking of coffee.

A plea of indisposition was offered for her absence from the dinner-table; and to her questions concerning his patient, Mr. Graham replied favourably.

The evening dragged its slow length wearily along; for Adeline was too much depressed in spirits to prove a very agreeable companion. She moreover fancied she beheld an impudent leer upon the countenances of the domestics who served the coffee; and this circumstance, although in reality imaginary, only tended to complete her confusion and paralyse her powers of conversation.

Were it not that *she* now dreamt of vengeance in her turn,—were it not that she beheld a chance of speedily ridding herself for ever of the torturess whom circumstances had inflicted upon her,—she could not possibly have endured the weight of the last indignity forced upon her.

To be made the object, as she deemed herself to be, of her very servants' scandalous talk and insulting looks, was a position so utterly debasing, that she would have fled from it by means of suicide, had she not consoled herself by the idea that a terrible vengeance on the authoress of her degradation was within her reach.

Crime is like an object of terror seen dimly through the obscurity of night. When afar off from it, the appearance of that object is so vaguely horrible—so shapelessly appalling, that it makes the hair stand on end; but the more the eye contemplates it—the more familiar the beholder grows with its aspect—and the nearer he advances towards it, the less terrible does it become; until at length, when he goes close up to it, and touches it, he wonders that he was ever so weak as to be alarmed by it.

We have seen Lady Ravensworth recoiling with horror from the bare idea of perpetrating the crime which the possession of the self-vaunted bravo's address suggested to her imagination:—the next time it entered her thoughts, she was less terrified;—a few hours passed—and she was now pondering calmly and coldly upon the subject.

O God! what is the cause of this? Is there implanted in the heart of man a natural tendency towards even the blackest crimes—a tendency which only requires the influence of particular circumstances to develop it to its dark and terrible extreme?

We may here explain the motives which had induced Colonel Cholmondeley to endeavour to renew his connexion with Adeline.

Of love remaining for her he had none—even if he had ever experienced any at all. But his interests might have been probably served by the restoration of his former influence over her.

He was a man of ruined fortunes—having dissipated a large property; and although he still contrived to maintain appearances, the struggle was a severe one, and only kept up with the desperate view of "hooking an heiress."

Thus, when he found the letter and the key in the carriage—naturally presuming that Adeline had herself thereby intimated her readiness to renew their former *liaison*,—he began to reflect that Lord Ravensworth was dying—that Lady Ravensworth might, should she have a son, be speedily left a wealthy widow—or that at all events she must acquire some fortune at her husband's decease,—and that he should be acting prudently to adopt all possible means to regain his ancient influence over her.

This explanation will account for his readiness to act in accordance with the hint which he had fancied to have been conveyed by Adeline through the medium of the letter and the key: it will also show wherefore he humoured her, during their interview, in respect to accepting the colder denomination of *friend*, instead of the warmer one of *lover*.

The reader may imagine his confusion, when an explanation took place relative to the letter and the key; nor need we describe the bitter feelings with which he beat his ignominious retreat.

It was eleven o'clock at night.

Mr. Graham had just left his patient in a profound sleep, and had retired to the bed-room allotted to him, Lydia Hutchinson having already come to keep the promised vigil by the couch of the wounded nobleman.

The curtains were drawn around the bed: waxlights burnt upon the mantel.

A deep silence reigned throughout the mansion.

Lydia Hutchinson threw herself back in the arm-chair, and gave way to her reflections.

"Thus far has my vengeance progressed: but it is not yet near its termination. It must fall alike upon the woman who first taught me the ways of duplicity and vice, and on him who used the blackest treachery to rob me of my innocence. Oh! who would have ever thought that I—once so humane in disposition—once possessed of so kind a heart that I sacrificed myself to save a friend,—who would have thought that I could have become such a fiend in dealing forth retribution? But my heart is not yet completely hardened: it is only towards those at whose hands I have suffered, that my sympathies flow no longer. And even in respect to the hateful Adeline, how often—oh! how often am I forced to recall to mind all my wrongs—to ponder, to brood upon them—in order to nerve myself to execute my schemes of vengeance! When she spoke this evening of her unborn child, she touched my heart:—I could have wept—I could have wept,—but I dared not! I was compelled to take refuge in that freezing manner which I have so well studied to assume when I contemplate her sufferings. My God! thou knowest how great are my wrongs! A father's grey hairs brought down with sorrow to the grave impel me to revenge:—the voice of a brother's blood appeals to me also for revenge! Revenge—revenge—upon Adeline and on the perfidious nobleman sleeping here!"

She had reached this point in her musings, when Lord Dunstable moved, and coughed gently.

He was awake.

"Graham," he murmured, in a faint tone: "for God's sake give me some drink—my throat is parched!"

"Mr. Graham is not present," answered Lydia: "chance has brought *me* hither to attend upon you."

Thus speaking, she drew aside the curtains.

Lord Dunstable cast one glance up to that countenance which looked malignantly on him.

"Lydia!" he said: "is that you? or is my imagination playing me false?"

"It *is* Lydia Hutchinson, whom you betrayed—whose brother fell by your hand—and who is now here to taunt you with all the infamy of your conduct towards her," was the calm and measured reply.

"Am alone with you?—is there none else present?" asked Dunstable, in a tone of alarm.

Lydia drew the curtains completely aside; and the nobleman cast a hasty look round the room.

"You see that we are alone together," she said; "and you are in my power!"

"What would you do to me, Lydia?" he exclaimed: "you cannot be so wicked as to contemplate———"

"I am wicked enough to contemplate any thing horrible in respect to *you*!" interrupted the avenging woman. "But fear not for your life. No:—although your hands be imbrued with the blood of my brother, I would not become a murderess because you are a murderer."

"Did a man apply that name to me," said Dunstable, darting a savage glance towards Lydia's countenance, "he should repent his insolence sooner or later."

"And are you not a murderer as well as a ravisher?" cried Lydia, in a taunting tone. "By means the most vile—the most cowardly—the most detestable—the most degrading to a man, you possessed yourself of my virtue. Afterwards, when my brother stood forth as the avenger of his sister's lost honour, you dared to point the murderous weapon at him whom you had already so grossly wronged in wronging me. Ravisher, you are a cowardly villain!—duellist, you are a cold-blooded murderer!"

"Lydia—Lydia, what are *you*?" cried Lord Dunstable; "a fiend—thus to treat a wounded man who is so completely at your mercy!"

"And how did you treat me when I was at your mercy at the house of your equally abandoned friend Cholmondeley?" continued Lydia. "Was not the wine which I drank, drugged for an especial purpose? Or, even if it were not—and supposing that I was intemperate,—granting, I say, that the stupefaction into which I fell was the result of my own imprudence in drinking deeply of a liquor till then unknown to me,—did you act honourably in availing yourself of my powerlessness to rob me of the only jewel I possessed? I was poor, my lord—but I was still virtuous:—you plundered me of that chastity which gave me confidence in myself and was the element of my good name! No prowling—skulking—masked thief ever performed a more infernal part than did you on that foul night!"

"And now that years have passed, you regret the loss of a bauble—call it a jewel, indeed!—which I certainly seized an opportunity to steal, but which you would have given me of your own accord a few days later, had I chosen to wait?" said Dunstable, speaking contemptuously, and yet with great difficulty.

"It is false—it is false—it is false!" replied Lydia, in a hoarse voice that indicated the rage which these words excited in her bosom. "I never should have yielded to you: never—never! But when once I was lost, I became like all women in the same state—reckless, indifferent! Villain that you are, you make light of your crimes. Oh! I am well aware that seduction—rape, even, under such circumstances as those in which you ravished me—are not deemed enormities in the fashionable world: they are achievements at which profligates like yourself laugh over their wine, and which render them favourites with the ladies! Yon call seductions and rapes by the noble name of '*conquests*!' O glorious conqueror that *you* were, when you lay down by the side of a mere girl who was insensible, and rifled her of the only jewel that adorned her! How was your victory celebrated? By my tears! What have been its consequences? My ruin and utter degradation! Detestable man, of what have you to boast? Of plunging a poor, defenceless woman into the depths of misery—of hurrying her father to the grave with a broken heart—of murdering her brother! Those are your conquests, monster that you are!"

Weak as was the young nobleman's frame,—attenuated as was his mind by suffering and by prostration of the physical energies, it is not to be wondered at if those terrible reproaches produced a strange effect upon him,—uttered as they were, too, in a tone of savage malignity, and by a woman with whom he found himself alone at an hour when all the other inmates of the mansion were probably rocked in slumber.

That evanescent gleam of a naturally spirited disposition which had enabled him to meet her first taunts with a contemptuous reply, had disappeared; and he now found himself prostrated in mind and body—rapidly yielding to nervous feelings and vague alarms—and almost inclined to believe himself to be the black-hearted criminal which Lydia represented him.

"And when such profligates as you appear in the fashionable world, after some new conquest," proceeded Lydia, "how triumphant—how proud are ye, if the iniquity have obtained notoriety! Ye are the objects of all conversation—of all interest! And what is your punishment at the hands of an outraged society? Ladies tap you with their fans, and say slyly, '*Oh! the naughty man!* And the naughty man smiles—displays his white teeth—and becomes the hero of the party! But all the while, how many bitter tears are shed elsewhere on his account! what hearts are breaking through his villany! Such has doubtless been your career, Lord Dunstable: and I do not envy you the feelings which must now possess you. For should that wound prove fatal—should mortification ensue—should this, in a word, be your death-bed, how ill-prepared are you to meet that all-seeing and avenging Judge who will punish you the more severely on account of the high station which you have held in the world!"

"Water, Lydia—water!" murmured Lord Dunstable: "my throat is parched. Water—I implore you!"

"How could I give you so poor a drink as water, when you gave me wine?"

"Oh! spare those taunts! I am dying with thirst."

"And I am happy in the thirst which now possesses me—but it is a thirst for vengeance!"

"Water—water! I am fainting."

"Great crimes demand great penance. Do you know in whose mansion you are? This is Ravensworth Hall," added Lydia; "and Lady Ravensworth is Adeline—Cholmondely's late paramour."

"I know all that," said Lord Dunstable, faintly: "but how came you here?"

"It were too long to tell you now."

"Water, Lydia,—Oh! give me water!"

"Tell me that you are a vile seducer—and you repent."

"Oh! give me water—and I will do all you tell me!"

"Then repeat the words which I have dictated," said Lydia, imperiously.

"I am a seducer———"

"No: a *vile* seducer!"

"A vile seducer—and I repent. Now give me water!"

"Not yet. Confess that you are a ruthless murderer, and that you repent!"

"No—never!" said Dunstable, writhing with the pangs of an intolerable thirst. "Water—give me water!"

"You implore in vain, unless you obey me. Confess———"

"I do—I do!" exclaimed the miserable nobleman. "I confess that I am—I cannot say it!"

"Then die of thirst!" returned Lydia, ferociously.

"No: do not leave me thus! Give me water—only one drop! I confess that I murdered your brother in a duel—and I deeply repent that deed! Now give me to drink!"

"First swear that you will not complain to a living soul of my treatment towards you this night," said Lydia, holding a glass of lemonade at a short distance from his lips.

"I swear to obey you," murmured Dunstable, almost driven to madness by the excruciating anguish of his burning thirst.

"You swear by that God before whom you may so soon have to appear?" continued Lydia, advancing the glass still nearer to his parched mouth.

"I swear—I swear! Give me the glass."

Then Lydia allowed him to drink as much as he chose of the refreshing beverage.

At that moment the time-piece struck one, and a low knock was heard at the door.

"I now leave you," said Lydia, in a whisper, as she leant over him. "Another will watch by your side during the remainder of the night. To-morrow evening I shall visit you again. Remember your oath not to utter a complaint that may induce the surgeon to prevent me from attending on you. If you perjure yourself in this respect, I shall find other means to punish you:—and then my vengeance would be terrible indeed!"

Lord Dunstable groaned in anguish, and closed his eyes—as if against some horrific spectre.

Lydia smiled triumphantly, and hastened to admit the housekeeper.

"His mind wanders a little," she whispered to the person who thus came to relieve her in the vigil; "and he appeared to think that I wished to do him a mischief."

"That is a common thing in delirium," answered the housekeeper, also in a low tone, inaudible to the invalid. "Good night."

"Good night," returned Lydia.

She then withdrew—satisfied at having adopted a precautionary measure in case the nobleman should utter a complaint against her.

And she retired to her own chamber gloating over the vengeance which she had already taken upon the man who had ruined her, and happy in the hope of being enabled to renew those torments on the ensuing night.

We must conclude this chapter with an incident which has an important bearing upon events that are to follow.

Adeline arose early on the morning following that dread night of vengeance, and dressed herself before Lydia made her appearance in the boudoir.

Hastening down stairs, Lady Ravensworth ordered breakfast to be immediately served, and the carriage to be got ready.

When she returned to the boudoir to assume her travelling attire, Lydia was there.

"You have risen betimes this morning, madam," she said; "but if you think to escape the usual punishment, you are mistaken."

"I am going to London, Lydia, upon important business for Lord Ravensworth," answered Adeline; "and as you have frequently declared that you do not level your vengeance against *him*, I——"

"Enough, madam: I will do nothing that may directly injure the interests of that nobleman, whom I sincerely pity. When shall you return?" she demanded in an authoritative manner.

"This evening—or at latest to-morrow afternoon," was the reply, which Adeline gave meekly—for she had her own reasons not to waste time by irritating her torturess on this occasion.

"'Tis well, Adeline," said Lydia: "I shall not accompany you. *You* are always in my power—but Dunstable may soon be far beyond my reach; and I would not miss the opportunity of passing the half of another night by his bed-side."

Adeline was now ready to depart; and Lydia attended her, for appearance' sake, to the carriage.

Ere the door of the vehicle was closed, Lady Ravensworth said to Lydia, "You will prepare my room as usual for me this evening—and see that the fire be laid by eleven o'clock—as it is probable that I may return to-night."

Lydia darted upon her mistress a glance which was intended to say—"You shall soon repent the authoritative voice in which you uttered that command;"—but she answered aloud, in an assumed tone of respect, "Yes, my lady."

The footman closed the door—and the carriage drove rapidly away for the town-mansion at the West End.

And as it rolled along, Adeline mused thus:—

"Now, Lydia, for vengeance upon *you*! You have driven me to desperation—and one of us must die! Oh! I have overreached you at last! You think that I am bound upon business for my husband:—no, it is for *you*! And well did I divine that your schemes of vengeance against the poor wounded nobleman would retain you at the Hall: well was I convinced that you would not offer to accompany me! At length, Lydia, you are in my power!"

Then, as she smiled with demoniac triumph, Adeline took from her bosom and devoured with her eyes the address that she had picked up in the ruins of the gamekeeper's cottage.

There was only an old housekeeper maintained at the town-mansion, to take care of the dwelling; and thus Adeline was under no apprehension of having her motions watched.

Immediately after her arrival, which was shortly before eleven in the forenoon, she repaired to a chamber, having given instructions that as she had many letters to write, she desired to remain uninterrupted.

But scarcely had the housekeeper withdrawn, when Adeline enveloped herself in a large cloak, put on a common straw bonnet with a thick black veil, and left the house by a private door of which she possessed the key.

CHAPTER CCXVII.

THE PRISONER IN THE SUBTERRANEAN.

It was on the same morning when Adeline came to London in the manner just described, that Anthony Tidkins emerged from his dwelling, hastened up the dark alley, and entered the ground-floor of the building.

He was not, however, alone:—Mr. Banks, who had been breakfasting with him, followed close behind.

"Light the darkey, old fellow," said the Resurrection Man, when they were both in the back room; "while I raise the trap. We must bring matters to an end somehow or another this morning."

"I hope so," returned Banks. "It isn't wery probable that the poor old weasel will have pluck enow to hold out much longer. Why—it must be near upon ten days that she's been here."

"I dare say it is," observed the Resurrection Man, coolly: "but she'll never stir out till she gives us the information we want. It would be worth a pretty penny to us. The young girl was evidently dying to know about her parents, that night she met the old woman; and she can get money from her friends—she said so."

"Well," returned Banks, "let us hope that the old woman has thought better on it by this time and will make a clean buzzim of it. It would be a great pity and a wery useless crime if we was obleeged to knock the sinful old weasel on the head arter all: her corpse would fetch nothing at the surgeon's."

"Don't be afraid," said Tidkins: "it won't come to that. She was half inclined to tell every thing last night when I visited her as usual. But come along, and let's see how she is disposed this morning."

The Resurrection Man descended the stone staircase, followed by Banks, who carried the light.

In a few moments they entered the vault where their prisoner was confined.

And that prisoner was the vile hag of Golden Lane!

A lamp burned feebly upon the table in the subterranean; and the old woman was already up and dressed when the two men made their appearance.

She was sitting in a chair, dolefully rocking herself to and fro, and uttering low moans as she pondered upon her condition and the terms on which she might obtain her release.

When the Resurrection Man and Banks entered the subterranean, she turned a hasty glance towards them, and then continued to rock and moan as before.

The two men seated themselves on the side of the bed.

"Well," said the Resurrection Man, "have you made up your mind, old woman? Because me and my friend Banks are pretty tired of this delay; and if the solitary system won't do—why, we must try what good can be effected by starvation."

"Alack! I have always thought myself bad enough," said the old hag; "but you are a very devil."

"Ah! and you shall find this place *hell* too, if you go on humbugging me much longer," returned the Resurrection Man, savagely. "You have only got yourself to thank for all this trouble that you're in. If you had behaved in a straightforward manner, all would have gone on right enough. My friend Banks here can tell you the same. But you tried to get the upper hand of me throughout the business."

"No—no," murmured the hag, still rocking herself.

"But I say yes—yes," answered the Resurrection Man. "In the first place you would tell me nothing about Catherine Wilmot's parentage: you kept it all close to yourself. I suspected you—I even told you so. I declared that '*if I caught you out in any of your tricks, I would hang you up to your own bedpost, as readily as I would wring the neck of your old cat*.' And I will keep my word yet, if you refuse to give me the information I require."

"What will become of me? what will become of me!" moaned the old hag. "Alack! alack!"

"You'll very soon find out," answered Tidkins. "But I just want to prove to you that I am right in all I am doing with regard to you. In the first place you would speak to Katherine alone: that didn't look well. You said I might be a witness at a distance—or when the money was paid; but I knew that to be all humbug. However, I let you have your way at the beginning—if it was only to see how the young girl would receive you. Well, friend Banks drives us to Hounslow: we set off to the farm—we meet Katherine and another young lady—and this Miss Monroe throws cold water on the whole business. Still you won't speak before witnesses. We go back to the inn at Hounslow: we concoct the note to Kate; and friend Banks undertakes to deliver it, as it seemed he knew something of her. He managed to give it to her; and you, old woman, go off to meet her at seven. Now did you think I was so precious green as not to take advantage of the opportunity? Not I! I went after you—I crept round behind the fences near where you and Katherine met each other—and I heard every word that passed between you."

"Alack! alack!" moaned the old woman.

"Yes—I heard every thing," continued the Resurrection Man;—"enough to prove to me that the young girl would give half her fortune to learn the truth concerning her father and mother. I also understood pretty well that there is the name of *Markham* in the case; and I was struck by the manner in which you urged her to purchase your secret, when she informed you that Richard Markham—the Markham whom I know and hate— had been made a great lord. All you said in respect to the conditions on which your secret was to be sold didn't astonish me at all. It only confirmed me in the conviction that you had intended throughout to gammon me. You meant to make use of me as a tool to find out Katherine's address, and then to reserve for your own particular plucking the pigeon whose hiding-place I had detected. '*The man who was with me this morning, is a bad one,*' said you: '*he is avaricious, and desires to turn my knowledge of this secret to a good account.*'—And so I did, you old harridan; and so I mean to do now.—'*He is a desperate man, and I dare not offend him,*' you went on to say.—Egad! you've found out that you spoke pretty truly.—'*He wants money; and money he must have.*'—True again: and money I will have too. The girl tells you she is rich and anxious to purchase the secret; and when she asks you how much will satisfy me, you coolly tell her, '*A hundred pounds!*'—A hundred devils! And then, in your gammoning, snivelling way, you demand of her the '*wherewith to make your few remaining days happy!*'"

"Alas! I am a poor old soul—a poor old soul!" murmured the horrible crone, shaking her head. "Do with me what you will—kill me at once!"

"And what the devil good would your carcass be to us?" exclaimed the Resurrection Man.

"A workus coffin would be thrown away on it," added Mr. Banks.

"So it would, Ned," returned Tidkins. "But I'll just finish what I have to say to the old woman; and we'll then go to the point. I was so disgusted, and in such an infernal rage, when I heard you going on in such a rascally manner,—selling me, and taking care of yourself,—that I determined at one time to come down from behind the palings, and force you to tell Katherine Wilmot on the spot all you knew about her parents, and then trust to her generosity. And as the night had turned dark, I had moved away from the spot, and was coming towards you along the path, when you heard the rustling of my cloak. At that instant another idea struck me: I resolved to bring you *here*, and get the secret out of you. I therefore crept softly back behind the fence. Then you went on with a deal more nonsense—all of which I heard as well as the rest. I was now determined to punish you: so I got back to the inn before you—arranged it all with Banks—and we had you up to London, and safely lodged here in this pleasant little place, that very night. Now, tell me the truth, old woman—don't you deserve it all?"

"Lack-a-day!" crooned the harridan.

"She does indeed deserve it, Tony," said Banks, shaking his head with that solemnity which he had affected so long as at length to use it mechanically: "she's as gammoning an old wessel as ever stood a chance of making a ugly carkiss to be burnt in the bone-house by my friend Jones the grave-digger."

"Now, by Satan!" suddenly ejaculated the Resurrection Man, starting up, and laying his iron hand on the hag's shoulder so as to prevent her from rocking to and fro any longer; "if you don't give up this infernal croaking and moaning, I'll invent some damnable torture to make you tractable. Speak, old wretch!" he shouted in her ears, as he shook her violently: "will you tell us the secret about Katherine Wilmot—or will you not?"

"Not now—not now!" cried the hag: "another time!"

"I will not wait another hour!" ejaculated the Resurrection Man; "but, by God! I'll put you to some torture. What shall we do to her, Banks?"

"Screw her cussed carkiss down in one of my coffins for an hour or so," answered the undertaker.

"No—that won't do," said the Resurrection Man.

"I always punishes my children in that way," observed Banks; "and I find it a wery sallitary example."

"I know what we'll do," exclaimed Tidkins: "they say that Dick Turpin used to put old women on the fire to make them tell where their money was. Suppose we serve this wretched hag out in the same way?"

"I'm quite agreeable," returned Banks, with as much complacency as if a party of pleasure had been proposed to him. "I b'lieve you've got a brazier."

"Yes—up in the front room, ground-floor, where all the resurrection-tools are kept," answered Tidkins. "You go and fetch it—bring plenty of coal and wood, and the bellows—and we'll precious soon make the old woman speak out."

The undertaker departed to execute this commission; and Tidkins again reasoned with the hag.

But all he could get out of her was a moaning exclamation; and as soon as he withdrew his hand from her shoulder, she began rocking backwards and forwards as before.

It suddenly struck the Resurrection Man that she was actually losing her senses through the rigours of confinement; and he became alarmed—not on her account, but for the secret which he wished to extort from her.

As this idea flashed to his mind, he cast a rapid glance towards the old woman; and surprised her as she herself was scrutinising his countenance with the most intense interest, while she was all the time pretending to be listlessly rocking her self.

"Another gag—by hell!" ejaculated Tidkins "What *do* you take me for? You think that I am such a miserable fool as to be deluded by your tricks? Not I, indeed! Ah! you would affect madness—idiotcy—would you? Why, if you really went mad through captivity in this place, I would knock you on the head at once—for fear that if you were let loose you might preach in your ravings about my designs concerning Kate Wilmot. But if you tell me, in your sober senses, all I want to know, I'll give you your freedom in twelve hours; because I am very well aware that you would not, when in possession of your reason, attract attention to your own ways of life by betraying mine."

"And if I tell you all I know," said the hag, seeing that her new design was detected and that it was useless to persist in it,—"if I tell you all I know, why will you not allow me to go home at once?"

"Because you came here in the night—and you shall go away in the night: because you arrived blindfolded—and you shall depart blindfolded," replied the Resurrection Man, sternly. "Do you think that I would let an old treacherous hag like you discover the whereabouts of this house? Why—you have no more idea at present whether you're in Saint Giles's or the Mint—Clerkenwell or Shoreditch—Bond Street or Rosemary Lane;—and I don't intend you ever to be any wiser. But here comes Banks, with the brazier."

The undertaker made his appearance, laden with the articles for which he had been sent.

The Resurrection Man laid the wood and coals in the brazier, and applied a match. In a few moments there was a bright blaze, which he fanned by means of the bellows.

"It'll be a good fire in a minute or two," said Tidkins, coolly.

"Almost as good as Jones makes in the bone-house where he burns the blessed carkisses of wenerable defuncts," returned Mr. Banks.

"Don't blow any more, Mr. Tidkins—save yourself the trouble," said the hag, now really alarmed. "I will make terms with you."

"Terms, indeed!" growled the Resurrection Man. "Well—what have you to say?"

"If I tell you every thing, you can get what money you choose out of Katherine," continued the old woman; "and I shall not receive a penny."

"Serve you right for having tried to gammon me."

"That will be very hard—very hard indeed," added the hag. "And after all, when you go to Katherine Wilmot and reveal to her the secrets I communicate to you, she will ask you for proofs—*proofs*," repeated the old woman, with a cunning leer; "and you will have no proofs to give her."

"Then you shall write out the whole history, and sign it," said Tidkins; "and my friend Banks will witness it."

"Yes," observed the undertaker, smoothing his limp cravat-ends: "Edward Banks, of Globe Lane, Globe Town—Furnisher of Funerals on New and Economic Principles—Good Deal Coffin, Eight Shillings and——"

"Hold your nonsense, Ned," cried Tidkins: then addressing himself again to the old woman, he said, "Well—don't you think that scheme would answer the purpose?"

"Very likely—very likely," exclaimed the hag. "But proofs—*written proofs*—would not be bad companions to the statement that you wish me to draw up."

"And have you such written proofs?" demanded Tidkins, eagerly.

"I have—I have," was the reply.

"Where are they?"

"Where you cannot discover them—concealed at my own abode. No one could find them, even if they pulled the house down, except myself."

And again the hag leered cunningly.

"This only makes the matter more important," mused the Resurrection Man, now hesitating between his avarice and his desire to possess such important testimony. "Well," he continued, after a pause,—"to use your own words, we *will* make terms. I tell you what I'll do:—write out your history of the whole business in full—in full, mind; and I will give you ten guineas down. At night me and Banks will take you home—to your own place; where you shall give me up the written proofs you talk of—and I will give you another ten guineas. Now is that a bargain?"

"Alack! it must be—it must be!" said the hag. "But why not let me go home to write out the history?"

"I am not quite such a fool," returned Tidkins. "And mind you do not attempt to deceive me with any inventions for I shall deuced soon be able to tell whether your history tallies with all I overheard you and Katherine say together on the subject. Besides, the written proofs must be forthcoming—and they, too, must fully corroborate all you state. Fail in any one of these conditions—and, by Satan! I'll cut your throat from ear to ear. Do you agree?"

"I do," answered the hag. "Give me paper and pens."

Tidkins departed to fetch writing materials, food, some strong liquor, and oil for the old woman's lamp.

In five minutes he returned; and, placing those articles upon the table, said, "When will your task be completed?"

"It will take me some hours," returned the hag: "for I have much to think of—much to write!"

And she heaved a deep sigh.

"This evening I will visit you again," said the Resurrection Man.

He and Banks then fastened the huge door upon the old woman, and left the subterranean.

When they reached the street, the undertaker departed in the direction of his own house; and the Resurrection Man ascended to his apartment on the first floor.

CHAPTER CCXVIII.

THE VEILED VISITOR.

Mr. Tidkins sate down and smoked his pipe as calmly as if he were not at all afraid to be left alone to the company of the thoughts which the occupation was likely to stir up within him.

For when a man takes up his pipe, all the most important ideas in his brain are certain to present themselves to his contemplation; and think on them he must, willing or unwilling.

But Tidkins shrank not from any of those reflections: he was not one of your villains who are either afraid in the dark, or who loathe solitude;—what he did he perpetrated systematically, and reviewed coolly.

He did not have recourse to the pipe on account of its soothing qualities—for as long as he made money, he had no cares; and when he indulged in a glass, it was by no means to drown remorse—because he had no compunctions to stifle.

"A few months more in this country, and I shall be all right," he mused to himself: "then off to America—plunge into the far-west—change my name—buy land—and live comfortable for the rest of my days. This business of Katherine Wilmot must produce me something handsome:—Gilbert Vernon's affair is sure to do so, in one way or the other;—and if any other business worth taking, and speedily done, comes in the meantime, all the better. That rascal Tomlinson regularly bilked me: and yet the fellow did it cleverly! Bolted with the old man—got clean away. For my part, I wonder he didn't do it long ago. Well—perhaps I shall meet them both some day in America; for I dare say they are gone there. All run-a-ways go to America—because there's no fear of questions being asked in the back-woods, and no need of letters of introduction when a chap has got plenty of money in his pocket. With what I've got already, and what I hope to get from the things now in hand, I shall stand a chance of taking a few thousands with me. But before I do go I must pay one or two people out:—there's that hated Markham—when he comes back; then there's the Rattlesnake; and there's Crankey Jem, who, they say in the papers, will have a free pardon before the trial of that young fool Holford comes on. Well—I have got something to do, in one way or another, before I leave England; but I'm not the man to neglect business—either in the pursuit of money or to punish an enemy. Ha! that was a knock at the door! who can come to me at this hour?"

The Resurrection Man looked at his watch:—the time had passed rapidly away while he was smoking and thinking;—and it was now nearly an hour past mid-day.

The knock—which was low and timid—was repeated.

"It *is* a knock," said Tidkins; and he hastened down to the street door.

He opened it and beheld a lady, enveloped in a large cloak, and wearing a black veil which was so elaborately worked and so well arranged in thick folds that it was impossible to catch even the faintest glimpse of the countenance that it concealed.

Tidkins, however, perceived at the first glance that it was no mean person who had sought his abode; for the delicate kid gloves were drawn on the small hands with a scrupulous nicety; the foot which rested upon the door-step was diminutive to a fault; and the appearance of the lady, even disguised as she was, had something of superiority and command which could not be mistaken.

"Does Mr. Tidkins reside here?" she said, in a tremulous and half-affrighted tone.

"My name's Tidkins, ma'am—at your service," answered the Resurrection Man, in as polite a manner as he could possibly assume.

It seemed as if the lady looked at him through her veil for a few moments, ere she made a reply; and she even appeared to shudder as she made that survey.

And no wonder;—for a countenance with a more sinister expression never met her eyes; and she had moreover recognised the man's voice, which she had heard before.

"Will you step in, ma'am?" said Tidkins; seeing that she hesitated. "I am all alone;—and if you come to speak on any particular business—as of course you do—there'll be no one to overhear us."

For another instant did Adeline—(there is no necessity to affect mystery here)—hesitate ere she accepted this invitation:—then she thought of her torturess Lydia—and she boldly crossed the threshold.

But when Tidkins closed and bolted the door behind her, and she found herself ascending the steep staircase,—when she remembered that she was now alone in that house with a man concerning whom her notions were of the most appalling nature,—she felt her legs tremble beneath her.

Then again was she compelled to encourage herself by rapidly passing in mental review the horrors of those tortures and the extent of those indignities which she endured at the hands of Lydia Hutchinson!—and her strength immediately revived.

She ascended the stairs, and entered the back room, to which the Resurrection Man directed her in language as polite as he could command.

Then, having placed a chair for his mysterious visitor near the fire, he took another at a respectful distance from her—for he knew that it would be impolitic to alarm one who was evidently a well-bred lady, by appearing to be too familiar.

"I dare say you are surprised to see a—a female—alone and unprotected—visit your abode in this—in this unceremonious manner?" said Adeline, after a long pause, but still fearfully embarrassed.

"I am not surprised at any thing, ma'am, in this world," replied Tidkins: "I've seen too much ever to wonder. Besides, it is not the first time that I have had dealings with gentlemen and ladies even of the highest class. But I ask no impertinent questions, and make no impertinent remarks. One thing, however, I should like to learn, ma'am—if it would not be rude: and that is, how you came to address yourself to me for whatever business you may have in hand?"

"That I cannot explain," returned Adeline: then, after a moment's thought, she said, "Will it not be sufficient for you to know that I obtained your address from one of those high-born persons to whom you ere now alluded?"

"Quite sufficient, ma'am," answered Tidkins. "In what way can I aid you?"

"I scarcely know how to explain myself," said Lady Ravensworth. "I require a great service—a terrible one; but I am prepared to pay in proportion."

"Do not hesitate with me, ma'am," observed Tidkins, his countenance brightening up considerably at the prospect of reaping a good harvest by means of his new customer. "Of course you require something which a lawyer can't do, or else you'd go to one: therefore what you want is illegal, ma'am; and my business, in a word, is to do every thing which can be done in opposition to the law."

"But are you prepared to accomplish a deed which, if detected———Oh! I cannot explain myself! No:—let me depart—I never should have come hither!"

And Adeline was seized by a sudden paroxysm of remorse and alarm.

"Calm yourself, ma'am," said Tidkins. "If you wish to go, I cannot prevent you; but if you really need my aid—*in any way*—no matter what—speak at your leisure. I am not particular, ma'am, as to what I undertake; and don't think I mean to offend you in what I'm going to say—it's only to give you confidence towards me, and to afford you an idea of what I now and then do for great folks and others, both male and female. Suppose a lady has pawned or sold her diamonds to pay a gaming debt, she wants a sham burglary got up in the house to cover the loss of them: well, ma'am, I'm the man to break in and carry off a few trifles, besides forcing open the door of the closet or bureau *where the casket of jewels ought to be*. Or perhaps a tradesman who is about to become bankrupt, wants the stock removed to a place of safety where he can have it again after a time: there again, ma'am, I'm the individual to accomplish the whole affair in the night, and give the house the appearance of having been robbed. Or else a gentleman insures his house and furniture, and wants the money: he goes off into the country—his place is burnt to a cinder during his absence—and no one can possibly suspect him of having had any thing to do with it. Besides, the whole thing seems an accident—so cleverly do I manage it. And, to go a little farther, ma'am—if a lady should happen to want to get rid of a severe husband—an illegitimate child—an extortionate lover—or a successful rival——"

"Or a bitter enemy?" added Lady Ravensworth, hastily—for she had been enabled to collect her thoughts and compose herself while Tidkins was thus expatiating upon his exploits.

"Yes, ma'am—or a bitter enemy," he repeated;—"it's all the same to me; for,"—and he lowered his voice as he spoke—"I have either the means of imprisoning them till they're driven raving mad and can be safely removed to an asylum—or I make shorter work of it still!" he added, significantly.

"Ah! you have the means of imprisoning persons—of keeping them for ever out of the way—and yet not go to the last extreme?" said Adeline, catching at this alternative.

"I have, ma'am," was the calm reply.

"But wherefore do you speak thus freely to me? why do you tell me so much?" demanded Adeline, a vague suspicion entering her mind that this fearful man knew her. "I am a complete stranger to you——"

"Yes, ma'am: and you may remain so, if it suits your purpose," answered Tidkins, who divined the motive of her observations. "Tell me what you wish done—pay me my price—and I shall ask you no questions. And if you think that I am incautious in telling you so much concerning myself, let me assure you that I am not afraid of your being a police-spy. The police cannot get hold of such persons as yourself to entrap men like me. I *know* that you have business to propose to me: your words and manner prove it. Now, ma'am, answer me as frankly as I have spoken to you. You have a bitter enemy?"

"I have indeed," answered Adeline, reassured that she was not known to the Resurrection Man: "and that enemy is a woman."

"Saving your presence, ma'am, a woman is a worse enemy than a man," said Tidkins. "And of course you wish to get *your enemy* out of the way by some means?"

"I do," replied Adeline, in a low and hoarse tone—as if she only uttered those monosyllables with a great exertion.

"There are two ways, ma'am," said the Resurrection Man, significantly: "confinement in a dungeon, or——"

"I understand you," interrupted Lady Ravensworth, hastily. "Oh! I am at a loss which course to adopt—which plan to decide upon! Heaven knows I shrink from the extreme one——and yet——"

"The dead tell no tales," observed Tidkins, in a low and measured tone.

Adeline shuddered, and made no reply.

She fell back in the chair, and rapidly reviewed in her mind all the perils and circumstances of her position.

She wished to rid herself of Lydia Hutchinson—for ever! She was moreover anxious that this object should be effected in a manner so mysterious and secret that she might not afterwards find herself at the mercy of the agent whom she employed in her criminal purpose. She had, indeed, already settled a plan to that effect, ere she called upon Tidkins. During the whole of the preceding night had she pondered upon that terrible scheme; and so well digested was it that Lydia might be made away with—murdered, in fine—and yet Tidkins would never know whom he had thus cut off, where the deed was accomplished, nor by whom he had been employed. Thus, according to that project, all traces of the crime would disappear, without the possibility of ever fixing it upon herself.

Now this idea was disturbed by the hint thrown out relative to imprisonment in a dungeon. Were such a scheme carried into effect, Tidkins must know who his prisoner was, and by whom he was employed. A hundred chances might lead to an exposure, or enable Lydia to effect her escape. Moreover, by adopting this project, Adeline saw that she should be placing herself at the mercy of a ferocious man, who might become an extortioner, and perpetually menace her by virtue of the secret that would be in his keeping. She felt that she should live in constant alarm lest Lydia might effect her release by bribery or accident. But chiefly did she reason that she had suffered so much at the hand of one who was acquainted with a dread secret concerning her, that she shrank from the idea of so placing herself at the mercy of another.

All these arguments were reviewed by the desperate woman in far less time than we have occupied in their narration.

But while she was thus wrapped up in her awful reverie, Tidkins, who guessed to a certain extent what was passing in her mind, sate silently and patiently awaiting her decision between the two alternatives proposed—a dungeon or death!

Had he been able to penetrate with a glance through the folds of that dark veil, he would have beholden a countenance livid white, and distorted with the fell thoughts which occupied the mind of his visitor:—but never once during this interview did he obtain a glimpse of her features.

"Mr. Tidkins," at length said Adeline, in a low tone and with a visible shudder, "my case is so desperate that nothing but a desperate remedy can meet it. Were you acquainted with all the particulars, you would see the affair in the same light. Either my enemy must die—or I must commit suicide! Those are the alternatives."

"Then let your enemy die," returned the Resurrection Man.

"Yes—yes: it must be so!" exclaimed Adeline, stifling all feelings of compunction: then taking from beneath her cloak a heavy bag, she threw it upon the table, the chink of gold sounding most welcome to the ears of the Resurrection Man. "That bag contains a hundred sovereigns," she continued: "it is only an earnest of what I will give if you consent to serve me precisely in the manner which I shall point out."

"That is a good beginning, at all events," said Tidkins, his eyes sparkling with joy beneath their shaggy brows. "Go on, ma'am—I am ready to obey you."

"My plan is this," continued Adeline, forcing herself to speak with calmness:—"you will meet me to-night at the hour and place which I shall presently mention; you will accompany me in a vehicle some few miles; but you must consent to be blindfolded as long as it suits my purpose to keep you so: when the deed is accomplished, you shall receive two hundred sovereigns in addition to the sum now lying before you; and you will return blindfolded with me to the place where I shall think fit to leave you. Do you agree to this?"

"I cannot have the least objection, ma'am," answered Tidkins, overjoyed at the prospect of obtaining such an important addition to the ill-gotten gains already hoarded. "Where and when shall I meet you?"

"This evening, at nine o'clock—at the corner of the Edgeware Road and Oxford Street," replied Adeline.

"I will be punctual to the minute," said the Resurrection Man.

Lady Ravensworth then took her departure.

As soon as it was dusk, Tidkins filled a basket with provisions, and repaired to the subterranean dungeon where the old hag was confined.

"How do you get on?" he demanded, as he placed the basket upon the table.

"Alack! I have not half completed my task," returned the old woman: "my thoughts oppress me—my hand trembles—and my sight is bad."

"Then you will have to wait in this place a few hours longer than I expected," said Tidkins. "But that basket contains the wherewith to cheer you, and you need not expect to see me again until to-morrow morning, or perhaps to-morrow night. So make yourself comfortable—and get on with your work. I shall keep my word about the reward—do you keep yours concerning the true history and the written proofs of Katherine's parentage."

"I shall not deceive you—I shall not deceive you," answered the hag. "Alack! I am too anxious to escape from this horrible den."

"You may leave it to-morrow night for certain," returned Tidkins: "at least, it all depends on yourself."

He then closed the door, bolted it carefully, and quitted the subterranean.

While he was engaged in making some little changes in his toilet ere he sallied forth to his appointment with the veiled lady, he thus mused upon a project which he had conceived:—

"I have more than half a mind to get the Buffer to dog that lady and me, and find out where she takes me to. And yet if we go far in a vehicle, the Buffer never could follow on foot; and if he took a cab, it would perhaps be observed and excite her suspicions. Then she might abandon the thing altogether; and I should lose my two hundred quids extra. No:—I must trust to circumstances to obtain a clue to all I want to know—who she is, and where she is going to take me."

Having thus reasoned against the project which he had for a moment considered feasible, the Resurrection Man armed himself with a dagger and pistols, enveloped himself in his cloak, slouched his hat over his forbidding countenance, and then took his departure.

CHAPTER CCXIX.

THE MURDER.

It wanted five minutes to nine o'clock when Anthony Tidkins reached the corner of Oxford Street and the Edgeware Road.

A cab was standing a few yards up the latter thoroughfare; and as the driver was sitting quietly on his box, without endeavouring to catch a fare, it instantly struck the Resurrection Man that his unknown patroness might be the occupant of the vehicle, and was waiting for him.

He accordingly approached the window, and by the reflection of a shop gas-light, perceived the veiled lady inside.

"Is it you?" she said, unable to distinguish his countenance beneath his slouched hat.

"Yes, ma'am. All right," he cried to the driver; and, opening the door, entered the cab.

It then moved rapidly away—the driver having evidently received his instructions before-hand.

"Draw up the window," said the lady.

Tidkins obeyed.

"You remember your promise to be blindfolded?" continued Adeline.

"I have forgotten nothing that passed between us, ma'am."

He had taken off his hat upon entering the vehicle; and Adeline now drew over his head a large flesh-coloured silk cap, or bag, fitted with a string that enabled her to gather it in and fasten it round his neck—but not so tightly as to impede the free current of air.

"I am sorry to be compelled to subject you to any inconvenience," she said, loathing herself at the same time for being compelled to address this conciliatory language to such a man—a murderer by profession!

"Don't mention it, ma'am: it's all in the way of business."

A profound silence then ensued between them.

On his part the Resurrection Man, who was intimately acquainted with London and all its multitudinous mazes, endeavoured to follow in his mind the course which the vehicle was taking; and for some time he was enabled to calculate it accurately enough. But it presently turned off to the left, and shortly afterwards took several windings, which completely baffled his reckoning. He accordingly abandoned the labour, and trusted to accident to furnish him with the clue which he desired.

On her side, Adeline was a prey to the most horrible emotions. Now that she had carried the dread proceedings up to the point which they had reached, she recoiled from urging them to the awful catastrophe. Vainly did she endeavour to tranquillise herself with the specious reasoning that she would not become a murderess, since *her* hands were not to do the deed,—or that even if that name must attach itself to her, she was justified in adopting any means, however extreme, to rid herself of a remorseless enemy:—vainly did she thus argue:—the crime she was about to commit, or to have committed for her, seemed appalling! Often during this long ride was she on the point of declaring to her terrible companion that she would stop short and abandon the murderous project at once: and then would come soul-harrowing remembrances of Lydia's tyranny, accompanied by violent longings after vengeance.

Thus did nearly three quarters of an hour pass, when the cab suddenly halted.

"Put on your hat—draw up your cloak-collar—and hold down your head as you alight," said Adeline in a rapid whisper.

The Resurrection Man understood her; and the darkness of the night favoured the precautions which Lady Ravensworth had suggested to prevent the driver, who opened the door, from observing that Tidkins's face was covered with the flesh-coloured silk.

"Wait until our return," said Adeline: "we may not be back for two, or even three hours;—but in any case wait."

And she placed a piece of gold in the man's hand.

She then took the arm of Tidkins and hurried him across the fields—for such he could feel the soil upon which he was walking to be.

In this manner did they proceed for upwards of half an hour, when they reached the fence surrounding the gardens of Ravensworth Hall. Adeline opened the wicket by means of a key which she had with her, and hurried her companion through the grounds to the private door at the southern extremity of the mansion. This she also opened and locked again when they had entered. She then conducted the Resurrection Man up the staircase, and finally into her boudoir.

Guiding him to a chair, she released him from the silk cap; but when it was removed, he could perceive nothing—for the room was quite dark.

"My enemy is certain to come hither shortly," whispered Adeline: "it may be directly—or it may be in an hour;—still she is sure to come. I shall conceal you behind a curtain—in case *the wrong person* might happen to enter the room by accident. But when any one comes in, and you hear me close the door and say 'WRETCH!' rush upon her—seize her by the throat—and strangle her. Are you strong enough to do this?—*for no blood must be shed.*"

"Trust to me, ma'am," returned Tidkins. "The woman—whoever she may be—will never speak again after my fingers once grasp her neck."

Adeline then guided him behind the curtain of her bed; and she herself took her post near the door.

And now succeeded a most appalling interval of nearly twenty minutes,—appalling only to Adeline; for her hardened accomplice was thinking far more of the additional sum he was about to earn, than of the deed he was hired to perpetrate.

But, Adeline—oh, her thoughts were terrible in the extreme! Not that she dreaded the failure of the deadly plot, and a consequent exposure of the whole machination:—no—her plans were too well laid to admit that contingency. But she felt her mind harrowing up, as it were, at the blackness of the tragedy which was in preparation.

Twenty minutes, we said, elapsed:—twenty years of mental agony—twenty thousand of acute suffering, did that interval appear to be.

At length a step echoed in the corridor;—nearer and nearer it came.

Good God! what pangs lacerated the heart of Lady Ravensworth;—and even then—far as she had gone—she was on the point of rushing forward, and crying, "No! no!—spare—spare her!"

But some demon whispered in her ear, "Now is the time for vengeance!"—and she retained her post—she stifled the better feelings that had agitated within her—she nerved herself to be merciless and unrelenting.

She knew that the step approaching was that of Lydia; for Lydia allowed none of the other servants to enter her mistress's own private chamber. The reason of this must be obvious to the reader:—Lydia only repaired thither for the sake of appearances—and not to do the work which it was her duty to perform. No—that had been left for Adeline herself to execute!

And now the handle of the lock was agitated—the door opened—and Lydia, bearing a light, entered the room.

Instantly Adeline closed the door violently—exclaiming, "WRETCH, your time is come!"

Lydia started—and dropped the light.

But in another second the Resurrection Man, springing like a tiger from his lair, rushed upon her from behind the curtain—seized her throat with his iron grasp—and threw her on the floor as easily as if she were a child.

The light had gone out—and the fearful deed was consummated in the dark.

A low gurgling—a suffocating sound—and the convulsions of a body in the agony of death were the terrible indications to Adeline that the work was indeed in awful progress!

Faint and sick at heart—with whirling brain—and bright sparks flashing from her eyes—Lady Ravensworth leant against the door for support.

Two minutes thus elapsed—the gurgling sound every instant growing fainter and fainter.

Adeline felt as if her own senses were leaving her—as if she were going mad.

Suddenly a low, hoarse voice near her whispered, "It's all over!"

Then Lady Ravensworth was suddenly recalled to the consciousness of her perilous position,—awakened to the necessity of carrying out all her pre-arranged measures of precaution to the end.

"We must now dispose of the body," she said, in a low and hurried tone. "You must take it on your back, and carry it for a short distance, whither I will lead you. But, first—here is a bag: it contains two hundred and fifty sovereigns—fifty more than I promised you."

The Resurrection Man clutched the gold eagerly:—the weight was sufficient to convince him that his patroness was not deceiving him.

While he was hugging his ill-earned gains, Adeline hastily felt her way to the bureau, opened it, and took forth her casket of jewels. She left the door of the bureau open, and the key in the lock.

The Resurrection Man now suffered her to replace the silk cap over his head:—what would he not have done for one who paid so liberally!

Then, taking the body upon his back, he was led by Adeline from the boudoir.

They descended the stairs, and passed out of the mansion by the private door, which Adeline closed but left the key in the lock.

She conducted him through the grounds once more, leaving the wicket open—and proceeded across a field, in one corner of which was a large deep pond.

A pile of stones was near the brink.

"Throw the body upon the ground," said Adeline.

The Resurrection Man obeyed, and seated himself quietly by it.

Adeline averted her eyes from the pale countenance, on which a faint stream of straggling moonlight stole through the darkness of the night;—and rapidly did she busy herself to secure her casket of rich jewels and several huge stones about the corpse. This she did by means of a strong cord, with which she had provided herself; for—fearful woman!—she had not omitted one single detail of her horrible plan—nor did she hesitate to sacrifice her precious casket to aid in the assurance of her own safety.

When this labour was finished,—and it did not occupy many minutes,—Adeline rolled the body down the precipitous bank into the pond.

There was a splash—a gurgling sound; and all was still.

"By God!" murmured the Resurrection Man; "this is the cleverest woman I ever met in my life. I really quite admire her!"

The words did not, however, reach the ears of Lady Ravensworth,—or she would have recoiled with abhorrence from that fearful admiration which she had excited in the mind of such a miscreant—a resurrectionist—a murderer!

"Every thing is now finished," said Adeline, breathing more freely. "Let as depart."

She led her companion across the fields:—her delicate feet were wet with the dew;—and though she felt wearied—oh! so wearied that she was ready to sink,—yet that woman—within a few weeks of becoming a mother—was armed with an almost superhuman energy, now that it was too late to retreat and her enemy was no more.

When they reached the cab, the driver was sleeping on his box; and before he was well awake, the Resurrection Man had entered the vehicle.

"Back to the place where you took up my companion," said Adeline, as she followed Tidkins into the cab.

And now she was journeying side by side with one who had just perpetrated a cold-blooded murder,—she the promptress—he the instrument!

In three quarters of an hour they again stopped at the corner of the Edgeware Road, Adeline having removed the cap from the Resurrection Man's head a few minutes previously.

The cab was dismissed:—Tidkins had vainly looked to discover its number. Adeline, by bribing the driver, had provided against *that* contingency also!

"Any other time, ma'am," said Tidkins, "that you require my services—or can recommend me to your friends——"

"Yes—certainly," interrupted Adeline. "Good night."

And she hastened rapidly away.

"It's no use for me to attempt to follow her," murmured the Resurrection Man to himself: "she is too wary for that."

He then pursued his way homewards, well contented with his night's work.

And Adeline regained admittance to her town-mansion, having so well contrived matters that the housekeeper never suspected she had once quitted it during the day or night.

Between three and four o'clock in the morning the rain began to pour down in torrents, and continued until past eight,—so that Lady Ravensworth was enabled to assure herself with the conviction that even the very footsteps of herself and Anthony Tidkins were effaced from the grounds belonging to the Hall, and from the fields in one of which was the pond to whose depths the corpse of the murdered victim had been consigned.

CHAPTER CCXX.

THE EFFECT OF THE ORIENTAL TOBACCO.—THE OLD HAG'S PAPERS.

Scarcely had Lady Ravensworth risen from the table, whereon stood the untasted morning meal, when the housekeeper of the town-mansion entered the room, and informed her mistress that Quentin had just arrived on horseback from the Hall, and requested an immediate audience of her ladyship.

Adeline was not unprepared for some such circumstance as this; she however affected to believe that the sudden appearance of Quentin in town bore reference to the illness of her husband; and when the valet entered the apartment, she hastened to meet him, exclaiming, with well-assumed anxiety, "Is any thing the matter with your lord? Speak, Quentin—speak!"

"His lordship is certainly worse this morning, my lady: but——"

"But not dangerously so, Quentin?" cried Adeline, as if tortured by acute suspense and apprehension.

"My lord is far—very far from well," returned Quentin: "but that is not precisely the object of my coming to town so early. The truth is, my lady, that Lydia Hutchinson has decamped."

"Lydia gone!" exclaimed Lady Ravensworth.

"Yes—my lady. But permit me to ask whether your ladyship brought your jewel-casket to town with you yesterday morning."

"Certainly not, Quentin: I merely came for a few hours—or at least until this morning——"

"Then our worst fears are confirmed!" ejaculated the valet. "Lydia has decamped with your ladyship's jewel-case."

"The ungrateful wretch!" cried Adeline, feigning deep indignation. "Was she not well treated at the Hall? was I a severe mistress to her?"

"She was not a favorite with the other dependants of your ladyship's household," observed Quentin.

"And when did this happen? how did you discover her flight?" demanded Lady Ravensworth.

"She was not missed until this morning, my lady; although there is every reason to believe that she must have taken her departure last evening. She had agreed with the housekeeper to take the first half of the night in watching by the side of Lord Dunstable's bed; but as she did not make her appearance at the proper time, it was concluded she had gone to rest, and another female domestic took her place. This morning, the gardener found the wicket of the southern fence open, and the key in the lock: this circumstance excited his suspicions; and, on farther investigation, he also found the key in the lock of the private door at the same end of the building. He gave an alarm: a search was instituted; and, after a time, your ladyship's chamber was visited, when the bureau was discovered to be open and the casket of jewels was missed. The servants were mustered; but Lydia had disappeared; and it was subsequently ascertained that her bed had not been slept in all night. Moreover, the candlestick which Lydia was in the habit of using when she waited upon your ladyship, was found lying in the middle of your ladyship's boudoir, as if it had been hastily flung down—probably in a moment of alarm."

"And has nothing been missed save my jewels?" demanded Adeline, whose plan had succeeded in all its details precisely as she had foreseen.

"Nothing—at least so far as we had been enabled to ascertain before I left for town, my lady," answered Quentin. "And what is more remarkable still, is that Lydia took none of her own things with her. It seems as if she had gone to your ladyship's boudoir, discovered the key of the bureau, and finding the jewel-casket there, was suddenly impelled by the idea of the theft; so that she decamped that very moment—for it does not appear that she even took a shawl, or a cloak, or a bonnet with her; although, of course, as she had been so short a time in your ladyship's service, the other female servants scarcely knew what clothes she possessed."

"But the keys of the private door and the wicket?" exclaimed Adeline: "how came she with them?"

"They might have been in your ladyship's room—by some accident," answered Quentin, with a little embarrassment of manner.

"Yes—I believe they were," said Adeline, blushing deeply—for she guessed the cause of the valet's hesitation: he was evidently impressed with the idea that his mistress had possessed herself of those keys to favor her supposed amour with Colonel Cholmondeley.

But she willingly incurred even this suspicion, because, by apparently accounting for the keys being in her room, it made the evidence stronger against Lydia Hutchinson.

"Does his lordship yet know of this event?" inquired Adeline, after a short pause.

"I communicated the fact to his lordship," answered Quentin; "but he treated it with so much indifference, that I did not enter into any details. I shall now, with your ladyship's permission, repair to Bow Street, and lodge information of the robbery."

Lady Ravensworth suffered the valet to reach the door ere she called him back; for nothing was more opposed to her plan than the idea of giving any notoriety to the transaction, inasmuch as such a course might afford Anthony Tidkins a clue to the entire mystery of the transaction in which he had played so important a part.

Accordingly, as if impelled by a second thought, she said, "Stay, Quentin: this step must not be taken."

"What, my lady?" cried the valet, in astonishment.

"I must show leniency in this respect," was the answer.

"Leniency, my lady, towards one who has robbed your ladyship of jewels worth, as I understand, at least two thousand pounds!" ejaculated Quentin, his surprise increasing.

"Yes—such is my desire, upon second thoughts," she continued. "My dear cousin Lady Bounce is deeply interested—I scarcely know exactly why—in this young woman; and I feel convinced that she would rather induce her husband Sir Cherry to repay me for the loss of my jewels, than see Lydia Hutchinson, bad though she must be, involved in so serious a dilemma. I shall therefore feel obliged to you, Quentin, to keep the affair as secret as possible—at least until I have communicated with Lady Bounce."

"Your ladyship's commands shall be obeyed," said the obsequious valet, with a bow. "In this case, I may return immediately to the Park."

"Let the carriage be got ready, and I will myself hasten thither," answered Adeline; "as you say that his lordship is somewhat worse."

Quentin retired, well persuaded in his own mind that the leniency of his mistress was caused by her fears lest the presumed fact of the keys of the private door and the wicket having been kept in her room might lead to inquiries calculated to bring to light her supposed amour with Colonel Cholmondeley.

Thus was it that one of the engines of Lydia's vengeance,—namely, the trick by which she had induced the Colonel to enter her mistress's boudoir, and the fact of making the other servants privy to that visit,—now materially served the purposes of Adeline.

In a quarter of an hour the carriage was ready; and Lady Ravensworth was soon on her way back to the Hall.

On her arrival, she found that the circumstance of Lydia Hutchinson's disappearance had yielded in interest to one of a more grave and absorbing character.

Lord Ravensworth was dying!

She hastened to his apartment, and found him lying in bed—in a state of complete insensibility—and attended by Mr. Graham, who had sent off an express to town (by a shorter way than the main road by which Adeline had returned) for eminent medical assistance.

It appeared that about an hour previously the nobleman's bell had rung violently; and when the servants hurried to the room, they found their master in a fit. He had probably felt himself suddenly attacked with an alarming symptom, and staggered from his chair to the bell-rope, and had then fallen upon the floor. Mr. Graham had been immediately summoned; and by his orders Lord Ravensworth was conveyed to bed.

But he had continued insensible—with his eyes closed; and the only sign of life was given by his faint, low breathing.

It is scarcely necessary to state that Mr. Graham exerted all his skill on behalf of the dying man.

Adeline affected the deepest sorrow at the condition in which she found her husband;—but the only grief which she really experienced was caused by the prospect of being shortly compelled to resign all control over the broad lands of Ravensworth, in case her as yet unborn child should prove a daughter.

In the course of the day two eminent physicians arrived from London; but the condition of Lord Ravensworth was hopeless: nothing could arouse him from the torpor in which he was plunged; and in the evening he breathed his last.

Thus was it that this nobleman had at length accomplished—involuntarily accomplished—his self-destruction by the use of the oriental tobacco sent to him by his brother Gilbert Vernon!

On the first day of February there had been a marriage at Ravensworth Hall: on the sixteenth there was a funeral.

How closely does mourning follow upon the heels of rejoicing, in this world!

On the same night when Lord Ravensworth breathed his last, the following scene occurred in London.

It was about eleven o'clock when the Resurrection Man and Mr. Banks entered the cell in which the old woman was confined.

"Is your labour done?" demanded Tidkins, in a surly tone, as if he expected a farther delay in the business.

"God be thanked!" returned the foul hag; "it is complete."

And she pointed to several sheets of paper, written upon in a hand which showed that the harridan had been no contemptible pen-woman in her younger days.

The Resurrection Man greedily seized the manuscript, and began to scrutinise each consecutive page. As he read, his countenance displayed grim signs of satisfaction; and when, at the expiration of a quarter of an hour, he consigned the papers to his pocket, he said, "Well, by what I have seen this really looks like business."

"The old wessel has done her dooty at last," observed Mr. Banks, shaking his head solemnly; "and what a blessed consolation it must be for her to know that she has made a friend of you that's able to protect her from her enemies while she lives, and of me that'll bury her on the newest and most economic principles when she's nothing more than a defunct old carkiss."

"Consolation, indeed!" cried Tidkins: then, counting down ten sovereigns upon the table, he said, "Here's what I promised you, old woman, for the fulfilment of the first condition. Now me and Banks will take you home again; and when you give me up the written proofs you spoke of, you shall have t'other ten quids."

"Alack! I've earned these shining pieces well," muttered the hag, as she wrapped the sovereigns in a morsel of paper, and concealed them under her clothes.

The Resurrection Man now proceeded to blindfold her carefully; and the operation reminded him of the process to which he had submitted on the preceding night, at the hands of his veiled patroness. He next helped the old woman to put on her cloak, the hood of which he threw over her bonnet so that a portion of it concealed her face; and Banks then led her away from the subterranean, while Tidkins remained behind them for a few moments to secure the doors.

The party now proceeded, by the most unfrequented streets, through Globe Town into Bethnal Green; but it was not until they reached Shoreditch, that the Resurrection Man removed the bandage from the old hag's eyes.

Then she gazed rapidly around her, to ascertain where she was.

"Ah! you'll never guess where you've been locked up for the last ten or twelve days," said the Resurrection Man, with a low chuckle.

"Never—as sure as she's a sinful old creetur'!" remarked Banks.

The worthy trio then pursued their way to Golden Lane.

On their arrival at the court, the hag uttered an exclamation of delight when she beheld the filthy place of her abode once more: but her joy was suddenly changed into sadness as a thought struck her; and she exclaimed, "I wonder what has become of the poor dear children that are dependant on me?"

She alluded to the juvenile prostitutes whom she had tutored in the ways of vice.

Heaving a deep sigh at the reflection, she took a key from her pocket, and opened the door of her house.

A little delay occurred in obtaining a light; but at length she found a candle and matches in a cupboard at the end of the passage.

Mr. Banks now officiously opened the door of the old woman's parlour; but this act was followed by a sweeping, rustling noise—and the undertaker started back, uttering a yell of agony.

The hag screamed too, and nearly dropped the light; for her large black cat had flown at Banks as he entered the room.

The fact was that the poor animal had been left in that apartment, when the old woman first set out with the Resurrection Man and the undertaker for Hounslow; and it had gone mad through starvation.

Tidkins rushed forward the moment his friend gave vent to that scream of anguish, and caught the cat by the neck and hind legs with his powerful fingers, as it clung, furious with rage, to the breast of the undertaker, whose dingy shirt frill and front its claws tore to rags.

"Don't strangle it—don't strangle it!" cried the hag, with unfeigned anxiety—for the only thing she loved in the world was her huge black cat.

"Stand back, old witch!" exclaimed Tidkins: "this beast is capable of tearing you to pieces."

And in spite of the violent pressure he maintained with his fingers upon its throat, the animal struggled fearfully.

"They say the cussed wessel has nine lives," observed Mr. Banks, dolefully, as he beheld the tattered state of his linen and smarted with the pain of the cat's scratches upon his chest.

"Don't kill it, I say!" again screamed the hag: "it will be good with me—it will be good with me."

"Too late to intercede," said the Resurrection Man, coolly, as he literally wrung the cat's neck: then he tossed the carcass from him upon the stairs.

"Poor thing!" murmured the old woman: "poor thing! I will bury it decently in the yard to-morrow morning."

And she actually wiped away a tear,—she who felt no pity, no compunction, no sympathy in favour of a human soul!

"She'll bury it, will she?" muttered Banks, endeavouring to smooth his linen: "on economic principles, I suppose."

The trio then entered the parlour: but before she could compose herself to attend to business, the old hag was compelled to have recourse to her gin; and fortunately there was some in her bottle. Her two companions refreshed themselves in a similar manner; and Tidkins then said, "Now for the proofs of all you've said in your history."

"Not all—not all: I never said all," cried the hag; "only of a part. And so, if you will lay the other ten sovereigns on the table, you shall have the papers."

The old woman spoke more confidently now; for she felt herself to be less in the power of her two companions than she so lately was.

The Resurrection Man understood her, and smiled grimly, as he counted the money before her.

She then took a pair of scissors, cut a small hole in the mattress of her bed, and drew forth a pocket-book, which she handed to Tidkins.

It was tied round with a piece of riband—once pink, now faded to a dingy white; and its contents were several letters.

The Resurrection Man glanced over their superscriptions, muttering to himself, "Well, you have not deceived me: I have brought you to reason—I thought I should. Ha! what have we here? '*To Mr. Markham, Markham Place, Lower Holloway.*'—And here is another to him—and another.—But this next is different. '*To the Marquis of Holmesford, Holmesford House.*'—Slap-up fellow, that—a regular old rake: keeps a harem, they say.—And here is another to him.—Then we have one—two—three, all directed alike—to '*Mrs. Wilmot,*' and no address: conveyed by hand, I suppose. And that's all."

With a complacent smile—as complacent as a smile on such a countenance could be—the Resurrection Man secured the pocket-book with its contents about his person.

He and Banks then took their leave of the old woman.

CHAPTER CCXXI.

THE RETURN TO ENGLAND.

It was on a beautiful morning, in the first week of March, that a large war-steamer passed Gravesend, and pursued its rapid way towards Woolwich.

She was a splendid vessel, rigged as a frigate, and carrying twelve carronades. Her hull was entirely black, save in respect to the gilding of her figurehead and of her stern-windows; but her interior was fitted up in a style of costly magnificence. Large mirrors, chaste carving, rich carpets, and soft ottomans gave to the chief cabin the air of a princely drawing-room.

On the deck every thing denoted the nicest order and discipline. The sailors performed their duties with that alacrity and skill which ever characterise men-of-war's men who are commanded by experienced officers; and two marines, with shouldered firelocks, paced the quarter-deck with measured steps.

The white sails were all neatly furled; for the gallant vessel was now progressing by the aid of that grand power which has achieved such marvellous changes on the face of the earth. The tall chimney sent forth a volume of black smoke; and the bosom of the mighty river was agitated into high and foam-crested billows by the play of the vast paddle-wheels.

From the summit of the main-mast floated the royal standard of Castelcicala.

And on the deck, in the uniform of a general officer, and with a star upon his breast, stood the Marquis of Estella, conversing with his *aides-de-camp*.

At a short distance was Morcar—in plain, private clothes.

Richard was now returning to his native shore—occupying in the world a far more exalted position than, in his wildest imaginings, he could ever have hoped to attain. He had left England as an obscure individual—a subordinate in a chivalrous expedition—under the authority of others:—he came back with a star upon his breast—having achieved for himself a renown which placed him amongst the greatest warriors of the age! Unmarked by title, unknown to fame, was he when he had bade adieu to the white cliffs of Albion a few months previously:—as the Regent of a country liberated by himself—as a Marquis who had acquired nobility by his own great deeds, did he now welcome his native clime once more.

Tears of joy stood in his eyes—emotions of ineffable bliss arose in his bosom, as he thought of what he had been, and what he now was.

But vanity was not the feeling thus gratified: at the same time, to assert that our hero was not proud of the glorious elevation which he had reached by his own merits, would be to deny him the possession of that laudable ambition which is an honour to those who entertain it. There is, however, a vast distinction between vanity and a proper pride: the former is a weakness—the latter the element of moral strength.

Yes: Richard *was* proud—but not unduly so—of the honours which were now associated with his name;—proud, because he had dashed aside every barrier that had once seemed insuperable between the Princess and himself.

And, oh! he was happy, too—supremely happy; for he knew that when he landed at Woolwich he should behold her whom we have before declared to be the only joy of his heart—the charming and well-beloved Isabella!

The gallant steamer pursued its way: Erith is passed;—and soon Woolwich is in sight.

And now the cannon roars from the English arsenal: the volumes of white smoke sweep over the bosom of the Thames;—the artillery salutes the royal standard of Castelcicala.

The troops are drawn up in front of the barracks to do honour to their heroic fellow-countryman, who retains his almost sovereign rank until the moment when he shall resign it into the hands of that Prince on whose brow he has come to place a diadem.

It is low water; and the Castelcicalan steamer drops her anchor at some little distance from the wharf. Then, under a salute from the cannon of the gallant vessel, the Marquis of Estella descends into a barge which has been sent from the arsenal to waft him ashore.

But while he is still at a distance from the wharf his quick eye discerns well-known forms standing near the spot where he is to land. There are the Grand-Duke Alberto and the Grand-Duchess, attended by the commandant of Woolwich and his staff; and leaning on her father's arm, is also the Princess Isabella.

The Grand-Duke is in plain clothes: he has come as it were incognito, and as a friend, to receive him to whom he is indebted for that throne which awaits him; and he is moreover anxious that all the honours proffered on this occasion shall be acknowledged by him who still bears the rank of Regent of Castelcicala.

The barge touches the steps: Richard leaps ashore. He hurries up the stairs—he stands upon the wharf; and, while the guard of honour of British soldiers presents arms, he is affectionately embraced by the Grand-Duke.

"Welcome—welcome, noble youth!" exclaimed Alberto, straining him to his breast, as if he were a dearly beloved son.

"I thank heaven, that you, most gracious sovereign, are pleased with my humble exertions in favour of Castelcicalan freedom," replied Markham, whose heart was so full that he could with difficulty give utterance to those words.

"Humble exertions do you call them!" cried the Grand-Duke. "At all events they have deserved the highest reward which it is in my power to offer."

And, as he thus spoke, Alberto placed the hand of our hero in that of the beauteous Isabella, while the Grand-Duchess said in a voice tremulous with joyful emotion, "Yes, dear Richard—you are now our son!"

Markham thanked the parents of his beloved with a rapid but expressive glance of the deepest gratitude; and he and Isabella exchanged looks of ineffable tenderness, as they pressed each other's hand in deep silence—for their hearts were too full to allow their lips to utter a syllable.

But those looks—how eloquent were they! They spoke of hopes long entertained—often dim and overclouded—but never completely abandoned—and now realized at last!

To appreciate duly the sweets of life, we should have frequently tasted its bitters; for it is by the influence of contrast, that the extent of either can be fully understood. Those who have been prosperous in their loves,—who have met with no objections at the hands of parents, and who have not been compelled to wrestle against adverse circumstances,—are incapable of understanding the amount of that bliss which was now experienced by Richard and Isabella. It was indeed a reward—an adequate recompense for all the fears they had entertained, the sighs they had heaved, and the tears they had shed on account of each other!

And we ourselves, reader, pen these lines with heart-felt pleasure; for there are times—and the present occasion is one—when we have almost fancied that our hero and heroine were real, living characters, whom we had seen often and known well;—and we are vain enough to hope that this feeling has not been confined to our own breast. Yes—we can picture to ourselves, with all its enthusiasm, that delightful scene when the handsome young man,—handsomer than ever in the uniform which denoted his high rank,—exchanged those glances of ineffable tenderness and devoted love with the charming Italian maiden,—more charming than ever with the light of bliss that shone in her eyes, made her sweet bosom heave, and brought to her cheeks a carnation glow beneath the faint tint of *bistre* which denoted her southern origin without marring the transparency of her pure complexion.

And now, the first delights of this meeting over, Richard presented his *aides-de-camp* to the illustrious family; then, beckoning Morcar towards him, he took the gipsy by the hand, saying, "It is to this faithful friend that

Castelcicala is indebted for the first step in that glorious career which was finally crowned with triumph beneath the walls of Montoni."

"And I, as the sovereign of Castelcicala," returned the Grand-Duke, shaking Morcar warmly by the hand, "shall find means to testify my gratitude."

"Your Serene Highness will pardon me," said Morcar, in a firm but deferential manner, "if I decline any reward for the humble share I enjoyed in those successes of which his lordship ere now spoke. No:—the poor Zingaree has only done his duty towards a master whom he loved—and loves," continued Morcar, looking at Richard and dashing away a tear at the same time; "and it only remains for him to return to his family—and to his roving life. The sole favour I have to ask at the hands of these whom I have now the honour to address, is that when they hear—as they often may—the name of *Gipsy* vilified and abused, they will declare their belief that there are a few favourable exceptions."

"But is it possible that I can do nothing to serve you?" exclaimed the Duke, struck by the extreme modesty and propriety of the Zingaree's words and manner. "Consider how I may ameliorate your condition."

"I require nothing, your Highness," answered Morcar, in the same respectful but firm tone as before,—"nothing save the favour which I have demanded at your hands. No recompense could outweigh with me the advantage which I have received from the contemplation of a character as good as he is great—as noble by nature as he now is by name," continued the gipsy, once more looking affectionately towards Markham;—"and, from the moral influence of his society and example, I shall return to my people a new man—a better man!"

Having thus spoken, Morcar wrung the hand of our hero with a fraternal warmth, and was about to hurry away,—leaving all his hearers deeply affected at the words which he had uttered,—when Isabella stepped forward, caught him gently by the arm, and said in her sweet musical voice, now so tremulously clear,—"But you have a wife, Morcar; and you must tell her that the Princess Isabella is her friend! Nor will you refuse to present her with this small token of that regard which I proffer her."

Thus speaking, the Princess unfastened a gold chain from her neck, and forced it upon Morcar.

"Yes, lady," said the gipsy, "Eva shall accept that gift from you; and she shall pray morning and night for your happiness. Nay, more," he added, sinking his voice almost to a whisper, "she shall hold up to her son the example of him who is destined, lady, to make you the happiest woman upon earth."

With these words, Morcar hurried away—hastened down the steps, leapt into a wherry, and directed the rowers to push the boat instantly from the wharf.

When it was some yards distant, Morcar turned his head towards the group upon the quay, and waved his hand in token of adieu;—and every member of that group returned his salutation with gestures that expressed the kindest feelings towards him.

The party now proceeded to the residence of the commandant, where a splendid *déjeuner* was served up. Richard sate next to his Isabella, and was supremely happy.

"Oh! how rejoiced shall I feel," he whispered to her, "when we can escape from all the ceremony which accompanies rank and power, and indulge uninterruptedly in that discourse which is so dear to hearts that love like ours! For I have so much to tell you, beloved one; and now that all the perils of war and strife are past, I can look with calmness upon that series of events of which I was only enabled to send you such slight and rapid accounts. But, believe me, Isabella—I would much rather have come back to my native shores unattended by all that ostentation and formal observance which have accompanied my return: nevertheless, the high office with which I was invested, and the respect due to your father by the one who came to announce with befitting ceremony that a throne awaited him, demanded the presence of that state and required that public demonstration. You must not, however, imagine, dearest one, that a sudden elevation has made me vain."

"I have too high an opinion of your character, Richard," answered Isabella, "to entertain such an idea for a single moment. I know that you are not unduly proud; but I, Richard, am proud—proud of you!"

"And yet, dear girl," whispered our hero, "all I have done has been but through the prompting of your image; and so did I write to you in the evening after that dreadful battle which decided the fate of Castelcicala."

"Ah! Richard, you know not the deep suspense which we experienced, and the moments of indescribable alarm which *I* felt, during the intervals between the letters announcing your several successes," said the Princess. "But all fear has now vanished—and happiness has taken its place. When we glance at the past, it will only be to rejoice at those events which have prepared so much joy for the future. Do you not remember how often I bade you hope, when you were desponding? Oh! heaven has indeed rewarded you, by placing you in so proud a position, for all the misfortunes which you have endured."

"Rank and honours were nothing in my estimation," answered Richard, "had they not removed the obstacles which separated me from you!"

A domestic now entered and stated that the carriages were in readiness; and the illustrious party, having taken leave of the commandant and officers of the garrison, proceeded to the mansion at Richmond.

Alberto and Richard Markham were then closeted for some time together. Our hero presented his Highness with the official despatches from the Ministers announcing his proclamation as Grand-Duke, and inviting him to return to Castelcicala to take possession of the throne.

"Your Serene Highness will not deem me presumptuous," said Richard, when these documents had been perused, "in accepting the executive sway immediately after the battle of Montoni. My object was to ensure the tranquillity of the country, and to lay the foundation of that liberal system of government which I knew to be congenial to the sentiments of your Highness. I appointed a Ministry formed of men who had shown their devotion to the Constitutional cause, and who were worthy of the confidence thus reposed in them. With respect to the late sovereign, Angelo III., I learnt a few hours ere my departure, that he had taken refuge in Austria; but in reference to the Grand-Duchess Eliza I have obtained no tidings."

"I cordially approve of every step you have taken, my dear Richard," replied the Grand-Duke: "your conduct has been beyond all praise. I expressed that opinion in the letter which I wrote to you, and wherein I informed you that I should wait in England until you came in person to announce to me the desire of the Castelcicalans that I should become their sovereign. I have, as I told you in my communication, only just recovered from a severe illness; but my duty to my country requires that I should return thither as soon as possible. In four days I shall embark on board the ship that brought you to England."

"So soon, my lord?" cried Markham, somewhat uneasily.

"I should leave England to-morrow, had I not one solemn but joyful task to accomplish," answered the Duke with a smile. "Fear not, dear Richard, that I shall delay your happiness any longer; for if you yourself do not consider the haste indelicate, I purpose to bestow Isabella upon you the day after to-morrow."

"Oh! my lord—what happiness!—and what deep gratitude do I owe you!" exclaimed Richard, falling upon his knees, and pressing the sovereign's hand to his lips.

"Rise, Richard—rise," said the Grand-Duke: "you owe me no gratitude—for you forget how deeply I am your debtor! You have delivered my native land from an odious tyranny—although it be of my own relative of whom I am compelled to speak thus severely; and you have given me a throne. In return I bestow upon you the dearest of all my earthly treasures—my daughter!"

"And the study of my life shall be her happiness," replied our hero. "But I have one great and signal favour to implore of your Highness; and I tremble to ask it—lest you should receive my prayer coldly."

"What is there that you should hesitate to ask or that I could refuse to grant?" exclaimed the Grand-Duke. "Speak, Richard:—the favour—if favour it be—is already accorded."

"Your Highness must be informed," continued Richard, thus encouraged, "that I have various duties to accomplish, which demand my presence for some time in England. I have an old friend and his daughter dependant upon me: I must settle them in a comfortable manner, to ensure their happiness. There is also a young female named Katherine Wilmot,—whose history I will relate to your Highness at a more convenient period,—but to whom I have been in some measure left guardian. By letters which I received a few days before my departure, I learnt that she is residing at my house, with my old friend and his daughter. It will be my duty to arrange plans for the welfare of Katherine. This I should wish to do in concert with Isabella. Lastly, my lord, I have the hope of meeting my brother—should he be still alive," added Richard, with a sigh. "Your Highness is aware of our singular appointment for the 10th of July, 1843."

The Grand-Duke reflected profoundly for some minutes; and Richard awaited his answer with intense anxiety.

"You shall have your will, noble-hearted young man!" at length cried Alberto: "I was wrong to hesitate even for a moment; but you will pardon me when you remember that in granting your request, I consent to a long—long separation from my daughter."

"But when the time for the appointment with my brother shall have passed," said Richard "Isabella and myself will hasten to Montoni; and then, God grant that you may be parted from your daughter no more in this life."

"Would it be impossible for you to effect a species of compromise with me in this way?" returned Alberto, with a smile. "Provide for those who are dependant on you; and when that duty is accomplished, pass at Montoni the interval until the period of the appointment with your brother shall demand your return to London."

"I would submit to your Highness this fact," answered Richard,—"that I live in constant hope of the reappearance of my brother ere the stated time; and should he seek me in the interval—should he be poor or unhappy—should he require my aid or consolation—if I were far away———"

"I understand you," interrupted the Grand-Duke. "Be it as you say. Provided Isabella will consent," he added, smiling, "you shall remain in England until the autumn of 1843."

"Much as the Princess will grieve to separate from her parents———"

"You think she will be content to stay in this country with you," again interrupted the Duke, laughing. "I see that you have already planned every thing in your own way; and both the Grand-Duchess and myself are too much pleased with you—too willing to testify our regard for you—and too anxious to make reparation for the past," added his Serene Highness significantly, "to oppose your projects in the slightest degree. It shall be all as you desire."

"Your Highnesses will then render me completely happy," exclaimed Richard, again pressing the Duke's hand to his lips.

Alberto then rang the bell, and commanded the domestic who answered the summons to request the presence of the Grand-Duchess and the Princess.

Those illustrious ladies soon made their appearance—Isabella's heart fluttering with a kind of joyful suspense, for she full well divined at least *one topic* that had been discussed during the private interview of her father and her lover.

The two latter rose as the ladies entered the room.

Then the Grand-Duke took his daughter's hand, and said, "Isabella, our duty towards our native land requires that your mother and myself should return thither with the least possible delay. But before we depart, we must ensure the happiness of you, beloved child, and of him who is in every way worthy of your affections. Thus an imperious necessity demands that the ceremony of your union should be speedily accomplished. I have fixed the day after to-morrow for your bridal:—but you, dearest Isabel, will remain in England with your noble husband. He himself will explain to you—even if he has not already done so—the motives of this arrangement. May God bless you, my beloved children! And, oh!" continued the Grand-Duke, drawing himself up to his full height, while a glow of honourable pride animated his countenance, "if there be one cause rather than another which makes me rejoice in my sovereign rank, it is that I am enabled to place this excellent young man in a position so exalted—on an eminence so lofty—that none acquainted with his former history shall ever think of associating his name with the misfortunes that are past! And that he may give even a title to his bride and accompany her to the altar with that proper independence which should belong to the character of the husband, it is my will to create him PRINCE OF MONTONI; and here is the decree which I have already prepared to that effect, and to which I have affixed my royal seal."

With these words the Grand-Duke took from the table a paper which he presented to our hero, who received it on his bended knee.

He then rose: Alberto placed the hand of Isabella in his; and the young lovers flew into each other's arms.

The parents exchanged glances of unfeigned satisfaction as they witnessed the happiness of their charming daughter and of him whom she loved so faithfully and so well.

Dinner was shortly announced; and around the table were smiling faces gathered that evening.

At nine o'clock Richard took his departure alone in the Grand-Duke's carriage; for he had transferred his own *aides-de-camp* to the service of their sovereign.

But when he bade farewell to Isabella on this occasion, it was with the certainty of seeing each other again in a short time; and they inwardly thanked heaven that their meeting was no longer clandestine, and that their attachment was at length sanctioned by the parents of the charming maiden.

CHAPTER CCXXII.

THE ARRIVAL AT HOME.

On the same evening Mr. Monroe, Ellen, and Katharine were assembled in the drawing-room at Markham Place.

The lamp burnt bright, and there were books open upon the table; but none of the little party had any inclination to read:—some event of importance was evidently expected.

"He will assuredly return this evening," observed Mr. Monroe, after a long pause in the conversation. "The last letter he wrote to us was positive in naming the day when he calculated upon arriving in England."

"But as he said that he should be compelled to come back to his native land in one of the government steamers of Castelcicala," said Ellen, "it is impossible to conjecture what delay adverse weather may have caused."

"True," exclaimed Mr. Monroe; and he walked to the window, whence he looked forth into the bright clear night.

It is a strange fact that whenever people are expecting the arrival of some one near or dear to them, they invariably go to the windows, where they watch with a sort of nervous agitation—as if by so doing they could hasten the coming which they anticipate.

The two young ladies drew close to each other on the sofa, and exchanged a few words in whispers.

"You seem low-spirited, dearest Kate," said Ellen; "and yet our benefactor is about to return to us. I feel convinced that you are more annoyed than you choose to confess, on account of the, non-appearance of the handsome stranger."

"I should be telling you an untruth, Ellen," answered Kate, blushing deeply, "were I to declare that I do not sometimes think of him whom you alluded to. But have I not another cause of vexation? do you imagine that the recent interview which I had with that odious Mr. Banks——"

"Yes, dear Kate: all that he told you was well calculated to render you anxious and unsettled in mind," interrupted Ellen. "But it was necessary to await the return of him who can best counsel you; and the time now approaches when you may communicate to Richard all that has passed."

Katherine was about to reply, when Mr. Monroe, who was still watching at the window, suddenly exclaimed, "A carriage—at last!"

The two young ladies hurried to the casement, and beheld the lamps of the vehicle rapidly approaching, while the sound of its wheels also reached their ears.

Then they both hastened from the room, followed by Mr. Monroe, to receive Markham the moment he should alight.

Whittingham and Marian joined them; and the whole party was stationed on the steps of the front door when the carriage drove up.

In another moment Richard was amongst them; and there were such congratulations—such shaking of hands—and such proofs of joy as were seldom known or seen even on occasions of similar happiness.

As for the old butler, he was literally mad with the excitement of his feelings. He hugged his young master with a warmth that could not possibly have been exceeded had they stood in the relation of father and son, and the fervour of which considerably deranged the position of our hero's epaulettes and aiguillettes—for he was in his uniform, as the reader will remember. Then, when Whittingham had thus far testified his joy at his master's return, he seized upon Marian and compelled her to perform three or four rapid pirouettes with him in the hall—to the infinite peril of that good woman's equilibrium. She disengaged herself from him with considerable difficulty; and the old man, quite overcome by his feelings and performances, sate down in one of the hall-chairs, and began to whimper like a child—exclaiming as well as he could, "Don't mind me—don't mind me! I can't help it! It's the unavoidable commotions here!" and he slapped his breast. "Master Richard's come back to the home of his successors; and he's a great man too—in spite of all that them willains Marlborough and Axminster once did to him!"

"Compose yourself, my excellent old friend," said the young Prince, pressing Whittingham's hand: "I am indeed come back—and to remain, too, for a long—long time."

The footman who attended upon the Grand-Duke's carriage now approached our hero, and with head uncovered, said in a tone of extreme deference, "Is it the pleasure of your Highness that the chariot should remain, or return to Richmond?"

"I wish you to stay here until the morning," answered Richard; "as I shall visit his Serene Highness to-morrow."

The footman bowed, and retreating to the hall-steps, cried aloud to the coachman, "The Prince commands us to remain."

"Hey! what's that?" ejaculated Whittingham, who, together with the others present, had caught those swelling titles. "I heerd, Master Richard, that you was a Markiss; but——"

"It has pleased the gracious sovereign to whose service I have the honour to belong, to invest me with the rank which has surprised you," answered Richard, laughing at his old dependant's bewilderment: "at the same time I can assure you that you will please me best by addressing me ever as you have been accustomed to do from my childhood."

The butler seemed to reflect profoundly for a few moments, with his eyes fixed on the marble floor then, suddenly raising his head, he exclaimed, "No, Master Richard—it can't be done! It would be to treat you as if you was still a boy. There's such a thing in the world as epaulette—etiquette, I mean; and I know myself better than to lose sight on it. Besides, Master Richard—it isn't every one as is butler to a Prince; and I'm proud of the office. So now I've called you *Master Richard* for the last time. Marian, bustle about the supper—and see that the servants with the carriage is well taken care of. You can show 'em round to the stables; while I light his Highness to the drawing-room."

Having issued these commands in a tone of pompous importance which the old man had not adopted for some years past, he seized a candle and led the way in a solemn and dignified manner up stairs.

"Poor Whittingham scarcely knows whether he stands on his head or his feet," whispered Richard, laughing, to Ellen and Katharine, as he placed himself between them, and gave them each an arm. "Let us, however, humour the good old man, and ascend with due ceremony to the drawing-room."

The reader will not require us to detail all the conversation which ensued. Markham had so much to tell, and his hearers so much to learn, that the time slipped away with lightning speed. Our hero not only related at length all that had occurred to him in Italy, but also entered upon explanations which he had never broached before relative to his attachment to Isabella. He made Whittingham sit down and listen to all he had to say; and he concluded by acquainting those present with his intended marriage.

"But," he hastened to add, "this event will make no difference in regard to the dear friends by whom I am surrounded. You, Mr. Monroe and Ellen, must continue to dwell with me; and you, Katherine, must look upon this house as your home. It is large enough for us all—even for those servants whom it will now be necessary to add to our establishment, and who will increase the department over which you, my faithful friend,"—addressing himself to Whittingham,—"preside so ably."

"I shall know how to distrain 'em all in order, my lord," said the butler, with an air of considerable importance.

Ellen's countenance had suddenly become thoughtful, when she heard that Richard was so shortly to be married.

Leaning towards him, as she sate by his side, she murmured in a hasty whisper, "Tell Whittingham to leave the room: I wish to speak to you and my father immediately."

Markham requested the old man to see that the servants of the Grand-Duke were well cared for; and Whittingham accordingly withdrew.

Richard then glanced inquiringly towards Ellen, who rose and whispered to Katherine, "Leave us, my sweet friend, for a few moments: I wish to speak to Richard and my father on a subject which nearly concerns myself."

Kate cheerfully complied with this request, and retired.

"What does this mean, Ellen?" inquired Richard with some degree of anxiety. "God grant that no cause of unhappiness may interrupt the joy of my return!"

"No—reassure yourself on that head," said Ellen. "My dear benefactor—and you, beloved father—listen to me for a few moments. You, Richard, are about to bring home a bride whom you love—whom you respect—and who must be respected,—a lady endowed with every quality that can render her worthy of you,—pure, chaste, and stainless as snow. Richard, she must not be placed in the companionship of one who occupies an equivocal situation in society—like myself!"

"Ellen, my Isabella is of too generous—too charitable a mind——" began Richard, deeply affected by these words, which recalled so many unpleasant reminiscences with respect to Monroe's daughter.

"Nay—hear me out," continued Ellen, with a sweet smile of gratitude for the sentiment which Markham had half expressed: "I shall not keep you in suspense for many moments. You wish me to be the companion of your Isabella, Richard?—I will be so—and not altogether unworthily either in respect to her or to myself. And now I am about to communicate to you both a secret which I should have treasured up until the proper time to elucidate it had arrived—were it not for the approaching event which has compelled me to break silence. But in imparting this secret, I must confide in your goodness—your forbearance—not to ask me more than I dare reveal. Richard—father—I am married!"

"Married!" repeated our hero, joyfully.

"Come to my arms, Ellen!" cried Mr. Monroe: "let me embrace you fondly—for now indeed are you my own daughter for whom I need not blush!"

And he pressed her to his heart with the warmest enthusiasm of paternal affection.

"Yes," continued Ellen, after a short pause, "I am married—married, too, to the father of my child;—and that is all that I dare reveal to you at present! I implore you—I beseech you both to ask me no questions; for I could not respond truly to them, and be consistent with a solemn promise of temporary secrecy which I have pledged to my husband! The motives of that mystery are not dishonourable, and do not rest with me. In two or three years there will be no necessity to keep silent. And now tell me, dear father—tell me, Richard—have you sufficient confidence in me, to believe what I have unfolded you, without knowing more?"

"Believe you, Ellen!" exclaimed Markham: "oh why should I doubt you? Your motive in revealing the happy fact of your marriage—a motive instigated by delicacy towards her who is so soon to accompany me to the altar—is so generous, so pure, so noble, that it speaks volumes in your favour, Ellen; and I love you as a sister—a very dear sister."

"Yes—it is with a brother's love that you must regard me," exclaimed Ellen, emphatically and joyfully; "and you know not what happiness your assurance imparts to me! Let me not, however, be misunderstood in any thing that I have already stated. I would not have you infer that I have been married long—nor that I was a wife when I became a mother," continued Ellen, casting down her eyes, and blushing deeply. "No—it was only on the 3d of January, in the present year, that I was united to him who will one day give a father's name to his child."

"I care not to know more, Ellen!" exclaimed Mr. Monroe. "You are a wife—and your son, as he grows up, need never be made acquainted with the true date of his parents' union. That innocent deception will be necessary."

"Your father is satisfied—and I am satisfied, dear Ellen," said Richard: "we should be wrong to seek to penetrate into a secret which your good sense would not induce you to retain inviolable without sufficient motives. I cannot express to you my joy at the revelation which you have made; and, believe me, you will now have no cause to blush in the presence of my Isabella."

"Father—Richard," murmured Ellen, pressing their hands affectionately in her own, "you have made me happy—because you have placed confidence in my word!"

And as tears of joy stood in her large melting blue eyes, and her face and neck were suffused in blushes, how beautiful did she appear—sweet Ellen!

"You have banished your young friend from the room," said Markham, after a short pause.

"But I will speedily summon her hither again," answered Ellen; "for she also has something important to reveal to you."

"A continuation, doubtless, of the narrative of the mysterious proceedings of the vilest of men and his female accomplice, and concerning which you wrote me full details some weeks ago?" observed Richard.

"Yes—there is another chapter in that strange history for you to hear," replied Ellen.

She then hurried from the room, and in a short time returned with Katherine.

"Tell Richard the remainder of your story in your own way, dear Kate," said Ellen, as the young ladies seated themselves side by side upon the sofa.

"It was nearly a week ago," began Katherine "that I rambled forth a little way alone. Ellen was somewhat indisposed and unable to accompany me; and Mr. Monroe had gone into town upon some business. I ascended the hill, and, having enjoyed the prospect for a short time, passed down on the opposite side, and walked through the fields. I was thinking of various matters,—but chiefly of the cruel disappointment which I had experienced in my recently awakened hopes of obtaining information relative to my parentage,—when I suddenly observed a person approaching; and I was somewhat alarmed when I perceived that it was that odious Mr. Banks, the undertaker, whom Ellen mentioned to you in the letter which related all that had taken place at the farm. I was about to retrace my steps, when Mr. Banks called after me, assuring me that I had no reason to be afraid of him, and declaring that he had important news to communicate. My hopes were revived—I felt convinced that his business was to renew those negotiations between myself and the old woman which had been so suddenly interrupted; and I no longer experienced any alarm. He accosted me, and, in his peculiar phraseology—an imitation of which I shall not inflict upon you—declared that a friend of his possessed certain papers which would entirely clear up the mystery wherein my parentage was involved. You may conceive the emotions which this communication excited within me: I trembled to put implicit faith in what I heard—in case of disappointment—in case of deception; and yet I clung—oh! I clung to the hope of at length being enlightened in matters so dear to my heart. Mr. Banks spoke candidly and intelligibly—though with wearisome circumlocution and a mass of hypocritical cant. He said that his friend had purchased the papers of the old woman for a large sum; and that he would only part with them for a larger sum still. In a word, he demanded five hundred pounds; and he assured me that I should not regret the bargain—for there were letters in my poor mother's own handwriting."

Kate wiped away the tears that had started into her eyes as she thus alluded to her maternal parent.

"I represented to Mr. Banks," she continued, after a pause, "that I was unpossessed of the immediate command of the sum demanded, and that I must either apply to the solicitor who had the management of my affairs, or wait until your return, Richard, from Italy. I moreover explained to him the extreme improbability that either Mr. Wharton or yourself would permit me to pay so large an amount for the papers, unless they were previously ascertained to be of the value represented. He seemed prepared for this objection; for he immediately declared that if I would name a day and an hour when I would call upon him, accompanied by any one friend, male or female, whom I might choose to select, he would have the papers in readiness, and that I might glance over them in order to satisfy myself of their value and authenticity."

"That was certainly a fair proposal for such a gang of villains to make," observed Richard; "and it invests the entire affair with the utmost importance. Did you give the man any definite answer?"

"I assured him that I could do nothing without consulting my friends; but that I would write to him in the course of a day or two. He advised me to lose no time; as his friend was not a person to be trifled with."

"And that friend," said Markham, "is the villain Anthony Tidkins—beyond all doubt. He does not dare appear actively himself in this business, for fear of affording me a clue to his haunts; and therefore he employs this Banks as his agent. The whole scheme is as transparent as possible."

"Before I parted from the undertaker," observed Katherine, "I objected to visit his house, and proposed to him that, in the event of my friends permitting me to purchase the papers, he should allow the cursory inspection of them either at Mr. Wharton's office or at Markham Place. But to this arrangement he expressed his entire hostility, stating emphatically that the documents must be examined and the purchase-money paid at his own house—and that, too, with four-and twenty-hours' notice of the time which I should appoint for the purpose."

"I see through it all!" exclaimed Richard. "Tidkins is afraid to trust his own agent with the papers or with the money paid for their purchase; and he will be concealed somewhere in Banks's house when the appointment takes place. Hence the notice required. It is as clear as the noon-day sun."

"On my return to the Place," continued Katherine, "I acquainted Mr. Monroe and Ellen with the particulars of the interview between the undertaker and myself; and as your letter, announcing the day when you hoped to set foot on the English soil again, had arrived that very morning, it was arranged that no decisive step should be taken until you were present to advise and to sanction the course to be adopted. I accordingly wrote a note to Mr. Banks, stating that I would communicate with him in a positive manner in the course of a week or ten days."

"You acted wisely, dear Kate," said Richard; "and I now question whether the Resurrection Man has not allowed his suspicious avarice to get the better of his prudence. But of that we will speak on a future occasion. You shall purchase the documents, Katherine—and without troubling Mr. Wharton upon the subject. Thanks to the liberality of the Castelcicalan government, my fortune is now far more ample than that which I lost; and pecuniary vexations can never again militate against my happiness. Yes, Katherine, we will yield to the extortion of these villains who are trading in the dearest ties and holiest sympathies of the human heart; but I must tax your patience somewhat—for you can well understand that for a few days I shall be unable to devote myself to even an affair so important as this. To-morrow you can write to Mr. Banks, and fix an appointment at his own house—one week hence—the hour to be eight o'clock in the evening, for it is then dark."

Katherine expressed her gratitude to our hero for this additional proof of his kindness towards her.

The happy party remained in conversation until a late hour—unconscious of the rapid lapse of time, so deeply were they interested in the various topics of their discourse.

It was, indeed, nearly two o'clock in the morning when the last light was extinguished in Markham Place.

Nevertheless, the inmates of that happy dwelling rose at an early hour—for there was much to be done that day, and little time for the purpose.

Ellen and Mr. Monroe repaired to town the moment breakfast was over, to make a variety of purchases in order to render the mansion as complete in all its arrangements as possible for the reception of the bride. Money is endowed with a wondrously electric power to make tradesmen bustling and active; and in spite of the little leisure left for choice and selection, the business-habits of Mr. Monroe and the good taste of his daughter enabled them to accomplish their task in a manner satisfactory to all concerned. Thus, in the afternoon, waggons piled with new and costly furniture, carts laden with chinaware and glass, and others containing carpets, curtains, and handsome hangings for the windows, were on their way to Markham Place.

And at the mansion, in the meantime, all was bustle and activity. Richard had departed early in the Grand-Duke's carriage for Richmond; but Katherine superintended all the domestic arrangements; Marian obtained the assistance of two or three char-women in her special department; and Whittingham forthwith added to the establishment, upon his own responsibility, two footmen and a page, all of whom were well known to him and happened to have been out of place at the moment.

Thus, by the time the young Prince returned home to dinner at five o'clock, the old mansion exhibited an appearance so changed, but withal so gay and tastefully handsome, that he was unsparing in his praises of those who had exhibited so much zeal in rendering it fit to receive his bride on the following day.

CHAPTER CCXXIII.

THE MARRIAGE.

The happy morning dawned.

The weather was mild and beautiful; the sky was of a cloudless azure; and all nature seemed to smile with the gladness of an early spring.

Markham rose at seven o'clock, and dressed himself in plain clothes; but upon his breast he wore the star which denoted his princely rank.

And never had he appeared so handsome;—no—not even when, with the flash of his first triumph upon his cheeks, he had entered the town of Estella and received the congratulations of the inhabitants.

When he descended to the breakfast-room, he found Mr. Monroe, Ellen, and Katherine already assembled: they too were attired in a manner which showed that they were not to be omitted from the bridal party.

At eight o'clock the Grand-Duke's carriage drove up to the door; and in a few minutes our hero and his friends were on their way to Richmond.

"Strange!" thought Ellen to herself; "that I should have passed my honeymoon of twenty-four hours with *him* in the same neighbourhood whither Richard is now repairing to fetch his bride."

The carriage rolled rapidly along; and as the clock struck nine it dashed up the avenue to the door of the now royal dwelling.

Richard and his companions were ushered into the drawing-room, where the Grand-Duke and the Duchess, with the *aides-de-camp*, and a few select guests, were awaiting their arrival. The reception which Mr. Monroe, Ellen, and Katherine experienced at the hands of the royal pair was of a most cordial kind, and proved how favourably our hero had spoken of them.

In a short time Isabella made her appearance, attended by her bridesmaids—the two daughters of an English peer.

Richard hastened to present his friends to the Princess; and the cordiality of the parents underwent no contrast on the part of the daughter;—but if she were more courteous—nay, kind—in her manner to either, that preference was shown towards Ellen.

And it struck the young lady that such slight preference was evinced towards her; for she turned a quick but rapid glance of profound gratitude upon Richard, as much as to say, "'Tis you whom I must thank for this!"

How lovely did Isabella seem—robed in virgin white, and her cheeks suffused with blushes! There was a charm of ineffable sweetness—a halo of innocence about her, which fascinated the beholder even more than the splendour of her beauty. As she cast down her eyes, and the long slightly-curling black fringes reposed upon her cheeks, there was an air of purest chastity in her appearance which showed how nearly allied her heart was to the guilelessness of angels. And then her loveliness of person—Oh! that was of a nature so ravishing, so enchanting, as to inspire something more than mere admiration—something nearer resembling a worship. Poets have compared eyes to stars—teeth to ivory—lips to coral—bosoms to snow;—they have likened symmetry of form to that of sylphs, and lightness of step to that of fairies;—but poor, poor indeed are all similitudes which we might call to our aid to convey an idea of the beauty of this charming Italian maiden, now arrayed in her bridal vestment!

The ceremony was twofold, Richard being a Protestant and Isabella a Roman Catholic. A clergyman of the Church of England therefore united them, in the first instance, by special licence, at the Grand-Duke's mansion. The bridal party immediately afterwards entered the carriages, which were in readiness, and repaired to the Roman Catholic chapel at Hammersmith, where the hands of the young couple were joined anew according to the ritual of that creed.

And now the most exalted of Richard's earthly hopes were attained;—the only means by which his happiness could be ensured, and a veil drawn over the sorrows of the past, were accomplished. When he looked back to the period of his first acquaintance with Isabella,—remembered how ridiculously insignificant was once the chance that his love for her would ever terminate in aught save disappointment,—and then followed up all the incidents which had gradually smoothed down the difficulties that arose in his path until the happy moment when he knelt by her side at the altar of God,—he was lost in astonishment at the inscrutable ways of that Providence which had thus brought to a successful issue an aspiration that at first wore the appearance of a wild and delusive dream!

On the return of the bridal party to the mansion near Richmond, a splendid banquet was served up; and if there were a sentiment of melancholy which stole upon the happiness of any present, it was on the part of Isabella and her parents at the idea of separation.

At length the *déjeuner* is over; and Isabella retires with her mother and bridemaids to prepare for her departure. The Grand-Duke takes that opportunity to thrust a sealed packet into our hero's hand. A few minutes elapse—Isabella returns—the farewells take place—and the bridegroom conducts his charming bride to the carriage. Mr. Monroe, Ellen, and Katherine follow in a second chariot.

It was four o'clock in the afternoon when Richard assisted his lovely young wife to alight at the door of his own mansion; and now Markham Place becomes the residence of the Prince and Princess of Montoni.

Vain were it to attempt to describe the delight of the old butler when he beheld his master bring home that beauteous, blushing bride; and—as he said in the course of the day to Mr. Monroe, "It was only, sir, a doo sense of that comportance which belongs to a man in my situation of authority over the servants that perwented me from collapsing into some of them antics that I indulged in when we heerd of Master—I mean of his Highness's successes in Castle Chichory, and when he came home the day before yesterday. But I won't do it, sir—I won't do it; although I don't promise, Mr. Monroe," he added, in a mysterious whisper, "that I shan't go to bed rayther jolly to-night with champagne."

It was eleven o'clock that night when Ellen cautiously issued from the back door of the mansion.

She passed rapidly through the garden, passed out of the gate, and hastily ascended the hill on whose summit were the two trees.

A man was seated on the bench.

Ellen approached him, threw her arms round his neck, and embraced him with a tenderness that even appeared to surprise him by its warmth.

She placed herself by his side; he drew her towards him—and kissed her almost affectionately.

"You are not happy?" said Ellen, in a plaintive and anxious tone. "I knew *that* by the contents of the note which Marian gave me just now; and your manner confirms me in the opinion."

"I know not how it is," replied Greenwood, without answering her question in a direct way, "but you never seemed dear to me, Ellen, until this evening."

"And am I dear to you now?" she asked, in a tone tremulous with joy.

"You are—you are," exclaimed Greenwood, speaking nevertheless in a manner which seemed to indicate that he was giving way to a feeling of weakness which he could not conquer, but of which he was ashamed; "you are dear to me—for my heart appears as if it required something to love, and some one to love me."

"And do I not love you?" cried Ellen, pressing her lips to his. "Oh! there was a time when I never thought I could love you—when I only sought you as a husband because you were the father of my child:—but since we have been united in holy bonds, I have learnt to love you—and I *do* love you—I *do* love you—in spite of all that has passed!"

"You are a good girl, Ellen," said Greenwood, upon whose lash a tear stood: but he hastily dashed it away, exclaiming, "This is unlike me! What can be the cause of these emotions—hitherto unknown? Is it that I am envious of *his* happiness? Is it that I pine for that sweet domesticity which he will now enjoy? Or is it that I am wearied of a world false and hollow-hearted?"

"Alas!" cried Ellen, the tears streaming from her eyes: "is the world really false and hollow-hearted? or have you sought only that sphere which wears the appearance that you deplore? Look yonder," she continued, pointing towards the mansion; "no falsehood—no hollow-heartedness are there! And why? Because he who rules in that abode has encouraged every sweet sympathy that renders life agreeable—every amenity which inspires confidence and mutual reliance between a number of persons dwelling together. The sphere that he has chosen is purified by his own virtues: the light of his excellence is reflected from the hearts of all around him. All are good, or strive to be good in his circle—because he himself is good. Where you have moved—ever agitating amidst the selfish crowd, as in troubled waters—none are good, because no one sets a good example. Every thing in *your* world is SELF: in Richard's world *he* sacrifices SELF unto others. Hence *his* prosperity—*his* happiness——"

"And hence my adversity—my dissatisfied spirit!" exclaimed Greenwood, impatiently. "But talk not thus, Ellen, any more: you will drive me mad!"

"Oh! my dear husband, what makes you thus?" cried Ellen, in alarm: "I never saw you so before. You who were ever so cool—nay, pardon me, if I say so chilling,—so calculating—so inaccessible to the tenderest emotions,—you are now an altered being! But God grant that your heart is touched at last, and that you will abandon those paths of selfishness which, as you have by this time learnt, are not those of permanent prosperity! Do not be offended with me:—heaven knows I would not wound your heart; for I love you ten thousand times better to-night than ever I did before—and solely because you *are* changed, or appear to be. Oh! let me implore you to cast aside your assumed name—to throw off all disguise—to return to that home where the arms of sincerest affection will be extended to welcome you——"

"No—no, Ellen!" cried Greenwood, almost furiously: "my pride will not permit me to do that! Speak no more in this way—or I will quit you immediately. I will fulfil my destiny—whatever it may be. Not a day—not an hour before the appointed time must *he* and I meet! No—broken though my fortunes be, they are not irreparable. Had it not been for the flight of that villain Tomlinson, I should have retrieved them ere now. I must not, however, despair: my credit is still good in certain quarters; and I possess talents for finance and speculation of no mean order."

"But you will not again embark in any such desperate venture as—as——"

"As the forged bills, you would say, Ellen," added Greenwood, hastily. "No:—be not alarmed on this head. I will not sully that name which *he* has rendered great."

"Oh! do you not remember," cried Ellen, as a sudden reminiscence shot through her brain, "that on the morning when our hands were united, you promised *that the name which you then gave me should go down to posterity*?"

"It will—it will: the prediction is already fulfilled, Ellen," said Greenwood, hastily;—"but not by me!" he added mournfully. "I know not why I feel so low spirited to-night; and yet your presence consoles me! Richard now clasps his lovely bride in his arms—and we are forced to snatch this stolen interview, as if we had no right to each other's society!"

"And whose fault is that?" asked Ellen, somewhat reproachfully. "Is it not in your power to put an end to all this mystery?"

"I cannot—I will not," returned Greenwood, with renewed impetuosity. "No—let us not touch upon the topic again. My resolves are immoveable on that point. If you love me, urge me not to inflict so deep a wound upon my pride. This lowness of spirits will soon pass away: I am afraid that envy—or jealousy, rather—has in some degree depressed me. And yet envy is not the term—nor does jealousy express the true nature, of my sentiments. For, in spite of all my faults, I have loved *him*, Ellen—as you well know. But it is that I feel disappointed—almost disgusted:—I have as yet toiled for naught! I contrast my position with *his*—and that makes me mournful. Still I am proud of him, Ellen:—I cannot be otherwise."

"That is a generous feeling," said Ellen, again embracing her husband: "it does me good to hear you express such a sentiment."

"I scarcely know what I have been saying," continued Greenwood: "my mind is chaotic—my ideas are confused. Let us now separate; we will meet again shortly—and I will tell you of my progress towards the fortune which I am resolved to acquire."

"Yes—let us meet again soon," said Ellen; "but not here," she added, glancing towards the trees. "It makes you melancholy."

"Well—well: I will find another spot for our interviews. Farewell, Ellen—dearest Ellen."

"Farewell, my dearest husband."

They embraced, and separated—Ellen retracing her steps towards the mansion, and Greenwood remaining on the hill.

On the following morning, after breakfast, Richard conducted his lovely bride over the grounds belonging to the Place; and when they had inspected the gardens, he said, "I will now lead you to the hill-top, beloved Isabella, where you will behold those memorials of affection between my brother and myself, which mark the spot where I hope again to meet him."

They ascended the eminence: they stood between the two trees.

But scarcely had Richard cast a glance towards the one planted by the hand of Eugene, when he started, and dropped Isabella's arm.

She threw a look of intense alarm on his countenance; but her fears were immediately succeeded by delight when she beheld the unfeigned joy that was depicted on his features.

"Eugene is alive! He has been hither again—he has revisited this spot!" exclaimed Richard. "See, Isabella—he has left that indication of his presence."

The Princess now observed the inscriptions upon the tree.

They stood thus:—

EUGENE.

Dec. 25, 1836.

EUGENE.

May 17th, 1838.

EUGENE.

March 6, 1841.

"Eugene was here yesterday," said Richard. "Oh! he still thinks of me—he remembers that he has a brother. Doubtless he has heard of my happiness—my prosperity: perhaps he even learnt that yesterday blest me with your hand, dearest Isabel; and that inscription is a congratulation—a token of his kind wish alike to you and to me."

Isabella partook of her husband's joy; and after lingering for some time upon the spot, they retraced their steps to the mansion.

The carriage was already at the door: they entered it; and Richard commanded the coachman to drive to Woolwich.

On their arrival at the wharf where Richard had landed only two days previously, they found a barge waiting to convey them on board the Castelcicalan steamer.

The Grand-Duke and Grand-Duchess, with their suite, received them upon the deck of the vessel.

The hour of separation had come: Alberto and his illustrious spouse were about to return to their native land to ascend a throne.

The Grand-Duke drew Richard aside, and said, "My dear son, you remember your promise to repair to Montoni so soon as the time of appointment with your brother shall have passed."

"I shall only be too happy to return, with my beloved Isabella, to your society," answered Markham. "My brother will keep his appointment; for yesterday he revisited the spot where that meeting is to take place, and inscribed his name upon the tree that he planted."

"That is another source of happiness for you, Richard," said the Grand-Duke; "and well do you deserve all the felicity which this world can give."

"Your Serene Highness has done all that is in mortal power to ensure that felicity," exclaimed Markham. "You have elevated me to a rank only one degree inferior to your own;—you have bestowed upon me an inestimable treasure in the person of your daughter;—and you yesterday placed in my hands a decree appointing me an annual income of twenty thousand pounds from the ducal treasury. Your Serene Highness has been too liberal:—a fourth part will be more than sufficient for all our wants. Moreover, from certain hints which Signor Viviani dropped when I was an inmate of his house at Pinalla—and subsequently, after his arrival at Montoni to take the post of Minister of Finance which I conferred upon him, and which appointment has met the approval of your Serene Highness—I am justified in believing that in July, 1843, I shall inherit a considerable fortune from our lamented friend Thomas Armstrong."

"The larger your resources, Richard, the wider will be the sphere of your benevolence," said the Grand-Duke; then, by way of cutting short our hero's remonstrances in respect to the annual revenue, his Serene Highness exclaimed, "But time presses: we must now say farewell."

We shall not dwell upon the parting scene. Suffice it to say that the grief of the daughter in separating from her parents was attempered by the conviction that she remained behind with an affectionate and well-beloved husband; and the parents sorrowed the less at losing their daughter, because they knew full well that she was united to one possessed of every qualification to ensure her felicity.

And now the anchor was weighed; the steam hissed through the waste-valves as if impatient of delay; and the young couple descended the ship's side into the barge.

The boat was pushed off—and the huge wheels of the steamer began to revolve on their axis, ploughing up the deep water.

The cannon of the arsenal thundered forth a parting salute in honour of the sovereign and his illustrious spouse who were returning to their native land from a long exile.

The ship returned the compliment with its artillery, as it now sped rapidly along.

And the last waving of the Grand-Duchess's handkerchief, and the last farewell gesture on the part of the Grand-Duke met the eyes of Isabella and Richard during an interval when the wind had swept away the smoke of the cannon.

The Prince and Princess of Montoni landed at the wharf, re-entered their carriage, and were soon on their way back to Markham Place.

CHAPTER CCXXIV.

MR. BANKS'S HOUSE IN GLOBE LANE.

The evening appointed by Katherine, in her note to Mr. Banks, for the purchase of the papers relating to her birth, had now arrived.

It was nearly eight o'clock.

The undertaker was at work in his shop, the door of which stood open; and several idle vagabonds were standing near the entrance, watching the progress that was made in bringing a new coffin to completion. Somehow or another, people always do stop at the doors of undertakers' workshops—doubtless actuated by feelings of the same morbid nature as those which call crowds of faces to the windows in a street along which a funeral is passing.

Mr. Banks had laid aside his coat, and appeared in his dingy shirt sleeves: he wore a paper cap upon his head; and a long apron was tied very high up above his waist—reaching, indeed, almost to the waistcoat pockets. As the gas was not laid on in his establishment, he was working by the light of a couple of tallow candles, that flickered in a most tantalising manner with the draught from the open door—leaving Mr. Banks every other minute in a state of exciting suspense as to whether they were about to be extinguished or to revive again. Still he did not choose to adopt the very natural precaution of closing the shop-door, because he considered it business-like to have a group of idlers collected at the entrance.

And there *was* an air of business about Mr. Banks's establishment. There were shining white coffin-plates hanging along one row of panes in the window; and black japanned ones suspended along another row. At a central pane hung a miniature coffin-lid, covered with black cloth, and studded with nails in the usual manner. The shop itself was crowded with coffins, in different stages towards completion: the floor was ankle deep in shavings and sawdust; and carpenters' tools of all kinds lay scattered about. But, pre-eminently conspicuous amongst all those objects, was a glass-case standing upon a little shelf, and enclosing that very miniature model of the patent coffin which he had displayed at the farm-house near Hounslow.

Mr. Banks was busily employed in fitting a lid to a coffin which stood upon trestles in the middle of the shop; and his two eldest boys, one fifteen and the other thirteen, were occupied, the first in planing a board, and the second in sawing a plank.

"Well," mused Mr. Banks to himself, as he proceeded with his work, "I hope Miss Kate won't fail to keep her appintment—partickler as Tidkins seems so sure of the job. That other feller which came yesterday to look at my first floor front as is to let, never returned. And yet he appeared to like the blessed place well enow. Goodness knows he asked questions by the dozen, and looked in every cranny about the house. What did he want to bother his-self like that as to whether there was a good yard for his missus to hang her clothes in on washing days? He should have sent her to see all about that. Then he would see where the yard-wall looked—and whether there was a yard or a street t' other side—and all about it. I raly thought he would have taken the rooms. But p'rhaps he didn't like the coffins: p'rhaps his missus don't fancy that there constant hammering. Ah! it's a sinful world!"

And, as if deeply impressed by this conviction, the undertaker shook his head solemnly.

He then continued his employment for some time without musing upon any one topic in particular.

At length he broke silence altogether.

"Now, Ned," said he to his eldest-born (he had five or six smaller specimens of the Banks' breed indoors), as he raised his head from his work, and looked severely round towards the lad; "that's quite planing enow: the board'll be veared as thin as a egg-case before it's used. Make it on economic principles, boy—economic principles, I say, mind!" added Mr. Banks, sternly.

"It ain't economic principles to turn out coffins as rough as if they didn't know what planing is," returned the youth; "'cause the friends of the defuncks'll only send them back again."

"The friends of the defuncts will do no such a thing to a 'spectable furnisher of funerals like me, as has lived, man and boy, in the same house for fifty year, and paid his way reglar," responded Mr. Banks. "If we adopts economic principles, we can't waste wood or time either."

"And do you mean to say, father," cried the boy, "that this here plank is planed enow? Pass your hand along it, and it'll get kivered with splinters—stuck all over like a porkipine."

"It will do exceeding well for the blessed carkiss that'll rejice in such a lid as that board will help to make him," said Banks, sweeping his horny palm over the plank. "That's good enow—that's economic principles."

"Then economic principles is a fool and a humbug," returned the lad, sulkily: "that's all I can say about the matter."

"Oh! that's it—is it?" cried Banks, assuming a threatening attitude.

"Yes—with a wengeance," added his son.

"No—that's the wengeance," said Mr. Banks, coolly, as he dealt his heir a tremendous box on the ear, which forced the young man nearly over the plank that had caused the dispute; but as the lad was not quite floored, his father bestowed on him a kick which, speedily succeeding the slap, levelled the youthful coffin-maker altogether.

"Brayvo!" shouted the idlers at the door.

The discomfited son of Mr. Banks got up, retreated to the farther end of the shop, and was about to discharge a volley of insolence at his father when a gentleman and lady suddenly appeared on the threshold of the shop.

"Ah! Miss Wilmot," exclaimed Mr. Banks: "punctual to the time! Your most obedient, sir," he added, turning towards Kate's companion, whom he did not know personally, but who was really Richard Markham. "Walk in, Miss—walk in, sir."

Then, without farther ceremony, the undertaker banged the door violently in the faces of the loungers at the shop-entrance.

"Please to come this way," he said, again turning to his visitors. "Take care of that lid, Miss; it'll soon cover a blessed defunct as a widder and seven small childern is now a-weeping for. I'm doing it cheap for 'em, poor things—eighteen-pence under the reg'lar charge, 'cause they had to sell their bed to pay for it—in adwance. This way, sir: mind them trestles. Ah! a many coffins has stood on 'em—all made on the newest and most economic principles; for my maxim is that a cheap and good undertaker is a real blessin' to society—a perfect god-send in this world of wanity and wexation. What would the poor sinful wessels in this neighbourhood do without me?—what indeed?"

Thus talking, and shaking his head in a most solemn manner, Mr. Banks led the way to a parlour behind the shop: and when his two visitors had entered it, he closed the door to prevent the intrusion of his sons.

"Pray, sit down, Miss—sit down, sir," said the undertaker, doing the honours of his abode with all the politeness of which he was master. "I am truly glad to behold your blessed countenance again, Miss;—for it's a sinful world, and blessed countenances is scarce—wery scarce. And this gentleman is Mr.—Mr.—ahem!—I haven't the pleasure of knowing him."

"It's no matter who I am," said Richard. "The agreement between Miss Wilmot and yourself was that she should visit you, accompanied by a friend:—I am that friend. Let us now proceed to business."

And as he spoke, our hero coolly produced a brace of pistols, which he laid upon the table.

"Sir—Miss Kate—I—I hope———" stammered the undertaker, turning pale, and recoiling in alarm.

"Fear nothing," said Markham: "it is merely a necessary precaution. This young lady and myself are in a strange neighbourhood:—I have about me a considerable sum of money, for the purpose of buying certain papers which you profess to have; and you will pardon me if I have thought fit to adopt every precaution—yes, *every precaution*," he added emphatically, "to guard against treachery."

"But surely that dear creetur, Miss Katherine, with her angelic countenance," said Banks, "must have told you, sir, that I'm a 'spectable man as was well known to Mr. Smithers, and that I should scorn to act dishonourable to any blessed living wessel."

"We will not dispute upon the point, sir," returned our hero, in an authoritative tone. "I have my reasons for acting with caution. If you intend us no harm—none can befall you. Where are these papers?"

"The papers, sir? Oh! the papers is safe enow," said Banks, still hesitating; "but them pistols———"

"Will remain there until the bargain is concluded," added Markham. "Again I say that I mean fairly if you do."

Thus speaking, he drew forth a pocket-book, and, opening it, displayed to the undertaker's eager eyes a number of Bank notes.

"Business—it looks like business," murmured Banks; "in spite of them bles———cussed pistols. You see, dear pretty Miss—and you, good sir,—that a man moving in such a important speer as myself sees so much of the pomps and wanities———"

"A truce to these unnecessary observations, Mr. Banks," said Markham, somewhat sternly; "or you will compel me to think that you are only talking to gain time—which could not be for any proper motive. In one word, then—have you the papers which relate to this young lady's parentage?"

"I have, sir—I have indeed," returned the undertaker.

With these words, he slowly unlocked an old walnut-wood desk, which stood in a recess; and thence he took a brown-paper parcel, tied round with coarse string and sealed in several places.

"This is just as I received the blessed dokiments from my friend," he said, leisurely advancing towards the table: then, taking a seat, he handed the parcel to Markham, observing, "You may break it open, and satisfy yourself that its contents is geniwine. Two minutes will be enow for that—and two minutes is all my friend told me to give for the purpose. I haven't read a line of them myself; and I know nothink of what they say;—but my friend is as sharp a feller as here and there one; and he assures me they're going dirt cheap—like workus coffins."

While Banks was thus indulging his garrulity, Markham had opened the parcel by the aid of a pair of scissors which lay upon the table; and the first thing which struck him was a letter addressed to "*Mr. Markham, Markham Place.*"

Katherine, who watched him attentively, without, however, looking at the papers herself, observed him start as if with sudden surprise: then he tore open the letter with almost a wild precipitation, and glanced rapidly over the contents. As he read, his countenance became flushed, and his features expressed mingled joy and astonishment—joy the most fervent, astonishment the most profound.

"My God!" he exclaimed, throwing down the letter, ere he had fully perused it: "how wondrous are thy ways! Katherine, dearest girl—come to my arms—for you are my sister—my own sister!"

"Your sister, Richard!" murmured the young maiden, as she sank almost fainting upon her brother's breast.

"Yes—my sister, Kate—my own sister!"—and he embraced her tenderly. "Compose yourself, dear girl—compose yourself: this is no place for explanations! But you are not the less my sister—and I thank God for it! I have now a natural right to be your protector—and a protector as well as an affectionate brother will you ever find me!"

"Oh! Richard—this sudden—this unexpected happiness is too much!" exclaimed Katherine, weeping through varied but ineffable emotions. "Is it possible that he whom I have known as a benefactor is indeed a brother!"

"I cannot doubt it—I do not wish to doubt it," returned Markham. "No—I am happy that I have found a sister in her whom I already loved as one!"

And again he embraced her tenderly.

"And I to find a brother in the noblest and best of men!" murmured Katherine: "it appears to be a dream—a delicious dream!"

"It is a reality," said Richard; "and we shall now all be happier than ever. Oh! what a surprise for those at home!"

"Then you perceive, my lord, that the dokiments is of some wally," observed Mr. Banks, wiping his eyes with the limp ends of his cravat, as if deeply affected by the scene. "I knowed they was; and I now begin to think that I have found out your name. I'm sure it's a unspeakable honour that a great lord and prince like you has done my poor house by setting foot in it—and all amongst the coffins too!"

"Let us now conclude this business, sir," exclaimed Richard, with whom the undertaker's remarks passed unheeded, so absorbed were his thoughts in the signal discovery which he had just made. "These papers are mine; and this pocket-book is yours. You may examine its contents."

"Oh! I've no doubt they're all right, my lord," said Banks, grasping the treasure now handed to him; "but I'll just look over 'em—merely for form's sake. It's more business-like. And nice new flimsies they are, too," continued the undertaker, as he scrutinised the notes one by one. "Ah! what miserable wessels we should be without money, my lord—in this wicked world;—and what would become of us if our friends had no cash to buy us nice coffins when we are blessed defunct carkisses? It's awful to think of! Four fifties—two hundreds—and ten tens: that's five hundred—sure enow."

And Mr. Banks proceeded to lock up the pocket-book, with its valuable contents, in his desk.

Richard and Katherine rose, as if to depart.

"May be, your lordship and this pretty young lady will just wash your mouths out," said Mr. Banks, attempting a pleasant smile. "A leetle drop of wine—one glass; and I'll step myself to the public-house to fetch it."

"Do so," returned Markham, throwing a sovereign upon the table.

Katherine looked at her brother in astonishment; but he affected not to perceive the impression which his strange conduct had thus created.

Banks seemed overjoyed at the affability of the nobleman; and gathering up the piece of gold, the change out of which he already considered as his own perquisite, he hastened to execute the commission;—but not without trying the lid of the desk ere he left the room, to convince himself that it was securely locked.

He passed through the shop, which was empty; and, muttering to himself something about "his unnat'ral boys who had gone off to the public without finishing the economic coffins," opened the street door and went out.

The moment he was gone, Richard seized his pistols, and saying in a hurried tone to Katharine, "Remain here, dear sister, for a few moments," hastened from the room by a door leading to the inner part of the dwelling.

He rushed down a passage, and entered the yard—as if well acquainted with the undertaker's premises.

The moment he set foot in the yard, he whistled in a peculiar manner.

"Damnation!—treachery!" cried a man, darting forward from the corner near the window.

"Stand—or I fire!" exclaimed Markham, advancing towards him, and presenting a pistol.

"Fool!" said the man; and he threw himself with desperate fury upon our hero.

But Richard, maintaining his footing gallantly, closed with his assailant, and threw him to the ground, his pistol going off with the shock—without, however, inflicting any injury.

And at the same moment three police-officers leapt over the wall, in time to put an end to the struggle between Markham and his opponent, the latter of whom they made their prisoner and immediately bound with strong cords.

"Is your Highness hurt?" asked one of the officers.

"No, Benstead," was the reply: "a little bruised, perhaps—but it is nothing. Bring the prisoner this way."

The whole transaction,—from the moment when Richard left the undertaker's parlour to that when he re-entered it, followed by the policemen with the captive,—had not occupied two minutes.

He found Katherine reclining back in her chair—half fainting and paralysed by terror, so deeply had the report of the pistol and the concomitant scuffle in the yard alarmed her.

But the moment she heard her brother's voice, she started up, gazed wildly around, and threw herself into his arms.

"You are not hurt, Richard? Oh! tell me—that pistol!" she exclaimed, terror still depicted on her countenance.

"No, dear sister—I am not hurt," exclaimed Richard. "Calm yourself. Every thing has resulted according to my expectations. Look, Kate—that terrible man is at length in the hands of the officers of justice."

Katherine turned a rapid glance towards the group on the other side of the room, and beheld the sinister and ferocious countenance of the individual whom she had seen in the company of the old hag near Bennet's farm.

At this moment the door communicating with the shop opened, and Mr. Banks made his appearance, carrying a bottle in his hand.

He started back in astonishment and alarm when his eyes encountered the police-officers, with his friend Anthony Tidkins securely bound in the midst of them.

But as his glances wandered from one to another, he suddenly appeared to recollect something; and, fixing his eyes on Benstead, he exclaimed, "Ah! now I twig it all. What a cussed fool I was not to know a trap even in plain clothes! But I was blind, 'cause I thought I'd got a 'spectable man coming as a fust floor lodger. No wonder you poked your nose in every hole and corner—'specially the yard. I was a idiot—a ass—a addle-pated old wessel! But p'rhaps the gen'lemen will take a glass of wine, since they're here?" added Mr. Banks, with a smirking countenance.

This semi-pleasantry on his part was only assumed; for his own life had not been so immaculate as to preclude the existence of certain fears when he found himself in the dangerous vicinity of the police.

He was, however, speedily reassured on this head.

"Keep your wine, sir," exclaimed Markham, "for those who can enjoy it in your company; and consider yourself fortunate that, in becoming the agent of that man,"—pointing with deep disgust towards Tidkins,—"you have not committed yourself in any way which at present endangers your safety. I see that you glance uneasily at your desk:—you need not fear that I shall attempt to deprive you of the sum which you have extorted as the purchase-money for the papers now in my possession. No:—although I do not envy you the feelings which could prompt you thus to lend yourself to make a market of secrets so sacred as those which the documents contain, I cannot question your right thus to act, seeing that the papers were in your possession. And were I compelled to pay a thousand times the sum given to obtain them, I should consider they were cheaply bought, inasmuch——But *you* cannot understand such feelings!" he added, addressing these words to the undertaker, but glancing affectionately towards Katherine.

"I hope there's no offence, my lord," said Banks, shaking in every limb with vague fears and suspicions. "I'm a poor man, which tries to live honestly by *undertaking* on the most economic principles; and there isn't a carkiss as goes through my hands that wouldn't sign a certifikit in my favour if it could."

Richard turned his back contemptuously upon Mr. Banks, and, addressing himself to Benstead, asked where he intended to lodge the prisoner for the night.

"There isn't a station-house in London that would be safe to put such a desperate feller in," was the reply. "He'd get out as sure as my name is Morris Benstead. I shall take him direct to Coldbath Fields, where the keeper will be sure to give him accommodation. To-morrow your Highness will be so kind as to appear against him at Lambeth Street."

Markham promised compliance with this request. A cab was sent for; and the Resurrection Man, who had maintained a moody silence, although he never ceased from looking vindictively upon our hero, from the moment he was arrested, was now removed in safe custody.

The Prince then conducted Katherine to the carriage that was waiting for them in another street; and shortly after ten o'clock they reached Markham Place.

We shall pass over all elaborate details of the surprise and joy with which Isabella, Ellen, and Mr. Monroe received the intelligence that Katherine was our hero's sister,—his sister without what the world calls the *stigma* of illegitimacy! Suffice it to say, that the discovery produced the most unfeigned pleasure in the breasts of all, and that Kate became the object of the sincerest congratulations.

Richard then related as succinctly as possible,—for he longed to peruse the precious documents in his possession,—the capture of the Resurrection Man and the scheme by which he had placed that villain in the hands of the officers of justice.

"I felt persuaded," he said, "that Tidkins did not put implicit confidence in Banks, and that he intended to watch the negotiation. His avarice engendered suspicions and got the better of his prudence. I communicated my views yesterday morning to a faithful officer whom I know; and Morris Benstead—the person to whom I allude—visited the undertaker's house on a pretence of hiring apartments which were to let. By those means he was enabled to *reconnoitre* the premises, and adopt measures accordingly. The result has answered my anticipations; and that consummate villain, who twice attempted my life, and whose atrocities are numerous as the hairs on his head, is at length in custody."

"Ah! dearest Richard," said Isabella, "wherefore should you have thus perilled your precious life?"

"Do not chide me, Isabel," exclaimed the Prince, kissing her tenderly. "I only performed a duty that I owed alike to society and to myself. Let us now examine these documents which have already made so strange, and yet so welcome a revelation."

The members of that happy party drew round the table; and Richard began by reading the various letters that accompanied the old woman's narrative. But as those epistles merely corroborated the main points of her tale, we shall not quote them.

The narrative itself will explain all; and that important document may be found in the ensuing chapter.

CHAPTER CCXXV.

THE OLD HAG'S HISTORY.

"I must carry my recollection back between seventeen and eighteen years. Not that it requires any effort to call to mind the leading facts in this sad history; no—no—they are too well impressed upon my memory;—but there are certain details connected with my own position at the time which will need the fullest explanation, in order to show how one like me could have become the friend of Harriet Wilmot.

"At that epoch I kept a boarding-house—a fashionable boarding-house, in a fashionable street at the West End. I was not then ugly and withered as I am now: I had the remains of great beauty—for I *was* very beautiful when young! I was also of pleasant and agreeable manners, and knew well how to do the honours of a table. You will not therefore be surprised when I tell you that I was a great favourite with the persons who lodged at my establishment, and with the still more numerous visitors. It is true that this establishment was a boarding-house; and it was conducted to all outward appearances, in a most respectable manner. But it had its interior mysteries as well as many other dwellings in this metropolis. The fact is, that I was well known to a large circle of nobles and gentlemen who employed all their leisure time in intrigues and amours. Having been gay myself from fifteen to forty, I was deeply versed in the various modes of entrapping respectable young persons, and even ladies, in the meshes artfully spread to ensure a constant supply of new victims to the lust of those men of pleasure. Having changed my name and thrown a veil as it were over the past, I opened the boarding-house by means of the funds supplied by my patrons, and soon experienced great success. By paying all my tradesmen with the utmost punctuality, I acquired a good character in the neighbourhood; for your tradesmen can always make or mar you, their shops being the scandal-marts where all reports, favourable or unfavourable, are put into circulation; and as they consider that those who pay well *must* necessarily be respectable, regularity on that point is certain to ensure their advantageous opinion. Having thus founded the *respectability* of my establishment, the rest was easy enough. The calculations made by myself and patrons were these:—Boarding-houses are usually inhabited by ladies possessing incomes which, though derived from sources that are sure, are too small to enable them to set up in housekeeping for themselves. Elderly widows with their daughters,—young widows who, coming from the country or from abroad, are strangers in London, but who wish to marry again, and therefore seek that society which is most easily entered,—friendless orphans who possess small annuities,—aunts and their nieces,—grandmothers with their grand-daughters,—these are the class of ladies who principally support boarding-houses. Thus there is always a large proportion of *young ladies* in those establishments; and out of a dozen there are sure to be three or four very good-looking. There can now be no difficulty in understanding the motives which induced my patrons to place me at the head of a boarding-house.

"I must now record the plan of operations. In all boarding-houses the number of ladies preponderates greatly over that of gentlemen. My average was usually about twenty ladies and four or five gentlemen. Three times every week we had music and dancing in the evening; and as there was a lack of *beaux*, I of course supplied the deficiency by inviting '*some highly respectable gentlemen with whom I had the honour to be acquainted.*' These were of course my patrons; and when they were at the house they always took care to treat me with a proper politeness, as if all they knew of me was highly to my credit and honour. They thus became constant visitors, and were enabled to improve their acquaintance with any of the young ladies whom they fancied. As they were very attentive also to the elderly ladies, and as good wine and negus were never spared upon those occasions, the mammas, aunts, and grandmammas were very fond of our evenings' entertainments, and considered the gentlemen whom I invited to be '*the most delightful creatures in the world.*' Sometimes rubbers of whist would vary the amusements; and as my patrons were not only all rich, but had their own private purposes to serve in frequenting my house, they allowed the old ladies to cheat them without manifesting the least ill will; or else they actually played badly to enable the said old ladies to win. It was therefore impossible that they could have failed to become especial favourites; and of these advantages they availed themselves in their designs upon the young ladies.

"The lodgers in boarding-houses are always mean and avaricious. The smallness of their incomes does not permit them to indulge largely in their natural taste for dress; and yet nowhere do females maintain such desperate struggles to appear fine in their apparel. Thus the ladies in boarding-houses can easily be persuaded to accept of presents; and of these my patrons were by no means sparing. A gold chain was a certain passport to a young lady's favour; and a velvet or silk dress would secure the good opinion of the aunt or grandmamma, and even of the mamma. Moreover, when one of my patrons appeared particularly attentive to any young lady, she concluded of course that his intentions were honourable; and in a very short time she became his victim. In a word, my boarding-house, though ostensibly so respectable, was nothing more nor less than a brothel conducted with regard to outward decencies, and carefully hushing up scandals that occurred within.

"I must now proceed to the principal topic of my history. It was, as I said, between seventeen and eighteen years ago, that the Marquis of Holmesford, who was one of my best patrons, called upon me and said that he had seen a beautiful young woman enter a humble lodging-house in a street not far from my own; and he directed me to institute inquiries concerning her. I did so; and in due course ascertained that her name was Harriet Wilmot—that she lived with her father in poor lodgings—and that they were by no means well off. I managed to get acquainted with Harriet, and called upon her. Her father was very ill—dying, indeed, of a broken heart, through losses in business. It moreover appeared that he had arrived in London only a short time before, and with a small sum of ready money, which he embarked in a little speculation that totally failed. They were sorely pressed by penury when I thus sought them out; and as I then knew well how to offer assistance in a delicate manner that could give no offence, I was looked upon by the poor young woman as an angel sent to minister to the wants of her dying father. The Marquis supplied me liberally with the means of thus aiding them; and I called regularly every day.

"My plan was to instil into Harriet's mind elevated notions of the position which she ought to reach through the medium of her personal attractions. I told her of great lords who had fallen in love with females in obscure stations, and who had married them; and as I also supplied Harriet with clothes, I took good care that they should be of such a nature as was calculated to engender ideas of finery. But all my arts failed to corrupt the pure mind of Miss Wilmot: she listened to me with respect—never with interest;—she wore the garments that I gave her, because she had none others. I saw that it was no use to think of introducing the Marquis to her immediately; and such was the passion he had conceived for her, that he did not become lukewarm with delay.

"In three weeks after I first became acquainted with the Wilmots, the old man died. The purse of the Marquis supplied, through my agency, the means of respectable interment; and when the first week of mourning was over, I touched gently upon Harriet's situation. She threw herself into my arms, called me her benefactress and only friend, and thanked me for my kindness towards her deceased father and herself, in such sincere—such ardent—and yet such artless terms, that for the first time in my life I experienced a remorse at the treacherous part I was playing. Harriet declared that she could not possibly think of being a burden to me, and implored me to follow up my goodness towards her by procuring her a menial situation—as she was determined to go out to service. I told her I would consider what I could do for her; and I went away more than half resolved to gratify her wish and place her beyond the reach of the Marquis by obtaining for her a situation through the means of my tradesmen. But when I reached my own house, I found the Marquis waiting for me; and he was so liberal with his gold, and so useful to me as my best patron, that I did not dare offend him. I accordingly hushed my scruples, and communicated to him all that had just occurred. He directed me to get Harriet into my house on any terms, and leave the rest to him. I was over-persuaded; and the next day I went to Harriet, and said to her 'My dear child, I have been thinking of your wish to earn your own living; and I have a proposal to make to you. I require a young person to act as my housekeeper: will you take the place? You shall have your own room to yourself; and I will make you as comfortable as I can.' The tears of gratitude and the tokens of affection towards me, with which that friendless young woman met my offer, actually wrung my heart. I wept myself—yes, I wept myself! And I weep now, too, as all those memories return to me with overwhelming force.

"Harriet Wilmot thus entered my service. But the very same day that she came into my house, I was attacked with a sudden and malignant fever, which threw me upon a sick bed. For ten days I was insensible to all that was passing around me; and when I awoke from that mental darkness, I found Harriet by my bed-side. For ten days and ten nights had she watched near me, scarcely snatching a few moments' repose in the arm-chair. She was pale and wan with long vigils; but how her beautiful countenance lighted up with the animation of joy, when the physician declared that I should recover. And this same physician assured me that I owed my life more to the care of the faithful Harriet than to his skill. I was overwhelmed by this demonstration of so much gratitude on her part; and I determined to place her beyond the reach of danger the moment I was convalescent.

"But when I recovered, and was once more involved in the bustle and intrigues of my business, my good resolutions rapidly vanished—for the gold and the patronage of the Marquis of Holmesford were so necessary to me! The Marquis now became a more constant visitor than ever at the house; and he found opportunities to pay his attentions to Harriet. But she did not comprehend his hints; and he soon spoke more boldly. Then she grew alarmed: still, as she afterwards told me, she did not choose to annoy me by complaints; and she contented herself by shunning the Marquis as much as possible. At length, one evening, when inflamed with wine, he forced his way into her chamber, and declared his views in such unequivocal terms, that the poor creature could no longer support his importunities. She indignantly commanded him to leave her: he grew bolder, and attempted violence. She escaped from him, and quitted the house. From a lodging which she immediately took, she wrote me a letter, detailing the insults she had endured, reiterating all her former expressions of gratitude towards me, acquitting me of all blame in the transaction, but declaring that, as she supposed I could not prevent the Marquis from visiting at the house, she must respectfully but firmly decline remaining in my service. I hastened to her, and was not very urgent in my desire that she should return; for I remembered her goodness to me when I was ill, and my heart was softened in her favour. By means of one of my tradesmen she almost immediately obtained a situation as nursery-maid in a family residing at Lower Holloway. I kept this circumstance concealed from the Marquis of Holmesford, to whom I declared that I knew not whither she was gone; and it was impossible that he could now blame me, as he himself had driven her by his rashness from my house.

"I must observe that all these incidents,—from the first moment of my acquaintance with Harriet until she thus quitted my house,—occurred within a period of three months.

"Harriet was not happy in her new place. She found that her mistress was an ill-tempered vixen, and her master a despotic upstart. But an event occurred which entirely changed her gloomy prospects, and enabled her to leave her situation without the necessity of seeking for another. During her walks with the children whom she had to attend upon, she met with a gentleman of middle age, but handsome person and agreeable manners; and some accident, which I have forgotten, made them acquainted. From that time they met every day: the gentleman became deeply enamoured of her, but never once did he make a dishonourable proposal. She told him that she was a poor friendless orphan and he pitied her:—in a short time he learnt to appreciate the purity of her mind—and he loved her. He offered her his hand;—but his pride imposed a condition. He was wealthy—he was a widower—he had two children; and he probably disliked the idea of introducing to the world as his wife one who had been a servant. She was unhappy in her place—without friends—without protectors; and she yielded to his solicitations for a private union. They were married—married at Norwood, where the register will doubtless attest the fact!

"This gentleman was Mr. Markham, of Markham Place. I never was in the neighbourhood of that mansion until about a year ago; then I saw it for the first time, and I sighed as I thought of Harriet Wilmot! For she ought to have become the mistress of the spacious dwelling;—and so she doubtless would have become, had not my treachery blighted all her hopes—all her prospects! But I must go back to resume the thread of my history in due course.

"Mr. Markham took a comfortable lodging for his young bride in a street somewhere near Brunswick Square. Precisely ten months after their union Katherine was born; and Mr. Markham now seriously thought of acknowledging his wife and child. She had hitherto passed by the name of Mrs. Wilmot since the marriage; and the husband regretted that he had not at once boldly proclaimed his second matrimonial connexion to the world. All these facts I subsequently learnt from Harriet's own lips.

"It was about three months after the birth of Katherine that I met Harriet one day in the street; and she seemed to me more beautiful than ever. She had written to announce to me that she was married, but without saying to whom, nor indicating where she lived. When I thus encountered her, holding her babe in her arms, she invited me to her lodgings, for she said, 'My husband will not be offended with me for communicating all the particulars of my happiness to you; since you were the only friend I found in the time of my poverty and, when my poor father was on his death-bed. Besides,' she added, with a smile of infinite satisfaction, 'my husband is about to acknowledge me as his wife and take me to his own home.' While we were yet speaking, the Marquis of Holmesford rode by on horseback; and, as he turned to nod to me, he instantly recognised Harriet. She also knew him, and hurrying along with some alarm, entered her lodging, which was close by. I followed her: the incident which had disturbed her was soon forgotten; and she then told me all the particulars of her first meeting and her subsequent marriage with Mr. Markham. And how she doted upon her child! Never did I behold a mother so enthusiastic in her tenderness towards the offspring which she loved—and in which she felt pride!

"I took leave of her, and promised to call soon again. On my return home I was by no means disappointed to find the Marquis waiting for me. He said, 'You are acquainted with Harriet's abode. How happens it that you have kept it secret from me?'—I assured him that I had only just discovered it—'Well, it may be as you assert,' he continued; 'but do not deceive me in what I now require at your hands. Harriet looks more lovely than ever; and all my passion for her is revived. She must be mine; and to you I look for aid in obtaining for me the gratification of my wishes.'—I told him that Harriet was married, and that the child he had seen in her arms was her own; but I did not mention the name of her husband.—'I care nothing for her marriage or her maternity,' said the Marquis: 'she is charming, and that is all I choose to think of. When money and cunning can produce any thing in this city, it is not probable that I should entertain ridiculous scruples. The money I possess; and if cunning were wealth, you would be the richest woman in England.'—I remember this conversation as well as if it only occurred yesterday. Vainly did I represent to his lordship the difficulty of accomplishing the design he had in view. I assured him that Harriet's virtue was beyond the possibility of corruption: he replied that artifice could not fail to succeed, and that if I appeared cold in the cause, he would employ another and less scrupulous agent. I trembled lest I should lose his patronage and that of his friends; and I promised to do my best. The Marquis left me, saying, 'Within a week I shall expect that you will have matured some scheme that may make her mine; and your reward shall be liberal.'

"I was now sorely perplexed: I no longer hesitated to obey the Marquis, because my own interests were concerned; but I knew not what project to devise. At length, after having racked my brain for some short time, I hit upon a device which seemed to be the most feasible my ingenuity could suggest; but I resolved to cultivate the intimacy of Harriet for nearly a week ere I put it into execution. I accordingly contrived to be almost constantly with her for the next five days, saving when she expected her husband. Of his coming she was usually made aware by letters from him: some of those epistles she read to me, in the ingenuous confidence of her pure soul; and well might she rejoice in them—well might she treasure them,—for they were replete with tenderness and love. I know not exactly now what it was that prompted me to possess myself of some of those letters, in which Mr. Markham spoke of Harriet as his wife and the infant Katherine as his own child;—but I most probably thought that my knowledge of that secret union and its fruit might be turned to advantage, especially as I saw that a wealthy and well-born man was struggling with his pride whether to proclaim to the world his marriage with an obscure servant or whether he should continue to keep the affair secret. At all events I cannot conceal the fact that I abstracted, during a temporary absence of Harriet from the room on one occasion when I called, three of the letters from her desk,—three epistles in which Mr. Markham alluded in the most unequivocal terms to his private marriage with Harriet and the existence of the fruit of that union. These letters were addressed simply '*Mrs. Wilmot*,' and without the mention of her abode on the envelope; because, as I learnt from Harriet, Mr. Markham always sent them by a messenger from a tavern in Lower Holloway—never from his own house, nor by any one of his servants; and by omitting the address, no clue could be afforded to impertinent curiosity should a letter thus sent happen to be lost.

"But to return to the scheme which I had formed for the ruin of Harriet. During the five days that we were so constantly together, as I have stated above, I professed the most sincere friendship for Harriet; and she declared that the feeling was not only reciprocal, but that on her part '*it was founded on the most sincere gratitude for my former kindness.*' And grateful she really was. It was her nature to be grateful and good towards any one who was good—or seemed good—to her. But she could not even have hated her bitterest enemies, had she known any persons who were openly and avowedly her foes. She was all gentleness and amiability—all ingenuousness and candour. But why do I thus dwell upon her excellent qualities—since the more blameless was she, the less pardonable was I!

"When I took leave of her on the fifth evening she said to me, 'Mr. Markham will not be able to visit me at all to-morrow: you would afford me pleasure by dining with me and passing a long evening.'—The invitation exactly suited my purposes; and I readily accepted it. But on the following day, instead of repairing to Harriet's lodging at four o'clock, as promised, I went straight to Holmesford House. The Marquis was at home: he awaited my coming—for I had communicated my design to him by note on the preceding evening.

"Holmesford House has long been notorious for the debaucheries of its lordly owner. Separated from his wife, and enjoying an immense fortune, the Marquis has for many years led a life which, were he a private individual, would exclude him from society, but which does not in the least degree injure him in the elevated sphere wherein he moves. His dwelling is fitted up in the most luxurious—the most voluptuous manner, and is provided with all possible means to facilitate his designs upon those virtuous females who may be entrapped into his mansion, but who will not yield to him save when overcome by violence. And to that extreme measure has the Marquis never hesitated to resort;—for who would think, however great her wrongs, of appealing to the law against a nobleman so powerful, so wealthy, and so unprincipled as the Marquis of Holmesford?

"There was one room in Holmesford House which I must particularly describe. It was a bed-chamber—small, but furnished in the most sumptuous manner. It had no side windows; but there was a sky-light on the roof; and double sets of panes were fixed in the ample wood-work, with an interval of perhaps four inches between each pair. Thus no screams—no shrieks could penetrate beyond that strangely-contrived window: the double panes deadened every sound which transpired in that room. Similar precautions were adopted in respect to the other parts of the chamber. The doors were double, and covered with thick baize, so that they fixed tightly in their setting. The walls were also double, with a considerable interval between them: there was even a false floor half a foot above the proper one; and carpets were spread so thickly that not even a footstep echoed in that chamber.

"I shall now continue the narrative of my project against Harriet. Immediately upon my arrival at Holmesford House, I wrote a note to the intended victim: it was thus worded:—'*Come to me, dearest Harriet, without an instant's delay after the receipt of this. I am in sad tribulation—at the house of a friend; but I cannot spare a moment to give you an idea of the sudden misfortune which has overtaken me. If you ever loved me—and if I have the slightest claim upon your kindness—come! The bearer of this note will conduct you to the friend's house where I am!*'—Poor Harriet! she naturally conceived that it must be some serious event which could prevent me from keeping my engagement with her; and she hesitated not to accompany the female servant who delivered the note to her. She took her child in her arms: the servant of the Marquis suggested that she should leave the babe in the care of Harriet's own domestic; but Harriet would never separate herself from her beloved infant! The servant could not offer further remonstrance on this point; and Harriet entered the hackney-coach which was waiting to convey her to destruction!

"It was in the very depth of winter and consequently quite dark when Harriet reached Holmesford House. The lamps over the entrance had been purposely left unlighted; and thus the poor young woman did not observe the vast exterior of the mansion to which she had come. But when the front door had closed behind her, and she found herself in the hall, she exhibited some alarm; for, dimly as it was seen by the lustre of one faint lamp, she observed enough to convince her that she was in no common dwelling. The servant (who had of course received her cue) noticed the impression thus made upon her, and hastened to say something of a re-assuring nature. Thus, in a few minutes, Harriet was inveigled into the chamber which I have before described. 'Permit me to hold the baby, madam,' said the servant; 'your friend is ill in that bed.'—Harriet, doubtless bewildered at the strangeness of the whole proceeding, mechanically passed the child to the servant, and advanced towards the bed, the curtains of which were drawn around. She heard the doors close: she looked round—the servant had disappeared with the babe;—and Harriet was now alone with the Marquis of Holmesford!

"Two hours elapsed! I was awaiting, in a distant part of the mansion, the issue of that foul plot. Wine and generous cordials were on the table; and I drank deeply of them to drown the sad thoughts which oppressed me. Never had I before experienced—never have I since known such terrible emotions! All the particulars of my connexion with Harriet rushed to my mind. I remembered how I first beheld her, affectionately tending the dying bed of her father,—how she sate day and night by my side, ministering unto me in my malady as if she was my daughter,—how I had seen her a happy wife, content with retirement and privacy—content even with being, as it were, an unacknowledged wife, so long as she enjoyed her husband's love,—and how she had conducted herself as a tender mother, fondling and nursing her innocent little one! I thought of all this; and at the same time I was almost distracted with the idea of the infernal treachery which had now ensnared her! Years have passed since that foul night; and its memory haunts me still. I have made many—many lovely girls victims to the lust of my employers;—but none—no, not one—do I regret, save Harriet Markham!

"Two hours elapsed, I say; and at length the Marquis of Holmesford made his appearance. He was dreadfully frightened: his manner was wild and excited. I could not gather, from the expression of his countenance, whether he had triumphed or lost the victory to which he aspired over a virtuous and defenceless woman. I interrogated him with a gesture of impatience. '*Damnable woman!*' he exclaimed; '*if there were not such creatures as you, there would be less scope for the vices of men like me. Begone! I would not endure another such scene—no, not were I offered a sovereign crown!*'—I made some observation; but he interrupted me fiercely, and commanded me to depart. I dared not disobey—his manner was actually terrific. He appeared as if he had just witnessed some horrible spectre, or had perpetrated a dreadful crime. I returned home; and never did I pass such a miserable night.

"All next day I waited in expectation of hearing from the Marquis; but no communication arrived. In the evening I went to Harriet's lodging, and saw the landlady. In answer to my inquiries, she said, 'Mrs. Wilmot remained out until a very late hour last night, or rather this morning. It was nearly one when she came home with her child. She was in almost a frantic state, and talked so wildly and incoherently that I could not comprehend her. I persuaded her to retire to her chamber, and offered to sit up with her. She allowed me to conduct her to her room, but insisted on remaining alone. Poor thing! I heard her walking up and down the chamber until past five; and then all became quiet. I supposed she had retired to bed. When I rose at eight, I learnt from the servant that she had gone out with her child half an hour previously. She has not been back since; and I feel alarmed at her absence.'—'Some sudden calamity has perhaps overtaken her,' I said, terribly frightened at these tidings. 'Have the kindness to send your servant to let me know when she returns; but you need not tell her that you do so. I have my reasons.' The landlady, believing me to be an intimate friend of Harriet, readily promised compliance with my request. I was about to depart, when she suddenly recollected something, and said, 'I had nearly forgotten to tell you that about an hour ago, the messenger that usually comes from the gentleman who visits Mrs. Wilmot, and who she says is her husband—'—'Yes, yes,' cried I impatiently.—'The messenger has left a small packet for her,' continued the landlady.—'Let me see it,' I said, thinking that its contents might afford some clue to the mystery of Harriet's disappearance: 'I am acquainted with all Mrs. Wilmot's affairs, for you know how intimate we are.'—The landlady showed me the packet without the least hesitation, and I instantly recognised in the address the handwriting of Mr. Markham. I longed to open the parcel, but dared not. So I took my departure, having reiterated my desire to be informed of Harriet's return, the moment it might happen.

"The next evening came, and I had neither heard from the landlady, nor seen the Marquis. I sent a note to the latter; but he had left town on the previous day. A thought struck me: could he have persuaded Harriet to accompany him? Had he so far overcome the virtue of that pure-minded creature? I thought of the packet from Mr. Markham, and longed to ascertain its contents. A strong suspicion lurked in my mind that it was connected with the affair in some way or another. I however waited a week; and, hearing no tidings of any kind concerning Harriet, went boldly to her lodgings. 'Mrs. Wilmot's disappearance is so strange,' I said to the landlady, 'that, having consulted my legal adviser, and acting on the plea of being her intimate friend, I am determined to open that packet which was sent for her, and which I think must afford some clue to her absence.'—The landlady gave me the packet, saying, 'If you take the responsibility on yourself, well and good; but I will have nothing to do with the business.'—This was better than I had even expected; and I departed with the parcel.

"I was not long in returning to my house, and the moment I had reached my own chamber, I tore open the parcel. It contained four letters: but the contents of one will explain the presence of the other three. That one was from Mr. Markham, and ran as nearly as I can recollect thus: 'After the terrible discovery which I made last night, I can never see you more. You have wantonly betrayed the confidence and affection of a man who descended from his eminence to court your love in your social obscurity. But the moral bond that united us is riven asunder; and the legal one shall be equally broken should you dare to represent yourself as my wife. The most horrible suspicion now haunts me that even *your* child may not be *mine*. Keep that infant, then; and be good to it, if your depraved heart will allow you. And that you may not sink into the lowest grades of crime from the embraces of the noble libertine to whom you have abandoned yourself, I have instructed my banker to pay to you, as *Mrs. Wilmot*, a monthly stipend of ten pounds. I have destroyed all your letters, save the *three* which I enclose; and I return them to you in the hope that a re-perusal of them will place before you in all its glaring flagrancy the contrast between your protestations and your deeds.

"This terrible document bore no signature: but it was impossible, either by its nature or the handwriting, that it could have emanated from any one save Mr. Markham. The three letters accompanying it contained expressions of sincere gratitude and fervent affection towards Mr. Markham, and denoted three particular phases in Harriet's connexion with him: namely, her assent to their union, the fact that she was in a way to become a mother, and the announcement of approaching maternity. I wept as I read them:—I wept as I thought of all I had done in accomplishing the ruin of poor Harriet!

"The Marquis came no more to my house;—I saw by the newspapers that he had returned to London, a few weeks after the sad incidents just described;—again I sought an interview with him, but he would neither see nor correspond with me. My other patrons deserted me: they had been introduced by the Marquis; and, finding that he had some private reason to shun me, they fell off rapidly. I was compelled to break up my establishment: it ruined me in pocket, as it had ruined many, many young females in virtue. But for none of my victims did I reck—no, not one, save Harriet Markham.

"I fell gradually lower and lower in the scale of my avocations; but still I contrived to gain a living in various ways which have no connexion with the object of this narrative. It was about a year after the sad events above recorded, that I one day met Harriet Wilmot face to face in the neighbourhood of Bloomsbury. She was poorly clad and sickly in appearance; and her countenance was expressive of profound mental dejection. She held a letter in her hand; but she had not her child with her; and she was hurrying rapidly along—most probably to the post-office. 'Harriet!' I exclaimed, catching her by the hand.—She started at being thus accosted; but the moment her eyes fell on my countenance, she shuddered visibly, and cried out, '*You!*'—then she darted away as if in affright, dropping the letter upon the pavement. For some moments I was so stupefied by her abrupt flight, that I stood as it were paralyzed. But seeing the letter upon the pavement, I recovered the use of my limbs, and hastened to pick it up. It was addressed '*To the Marquis of Holmesford, Holmesford House.*' I hurried away with it, saying to myself, 'Now I shall discover how far the connexion between Harriet and the Marquis went.'—But I was disappointed: the letter merely contained, as far as I can remember, these words:—'I ought not to address your lordship, under the peculiar—the distressing circumstances which made us acquainted; but necessity compels me to appeal to your lordship's bounty. It is not for myself, however, that I implore your aid; but for the sake of my child, who is starving! Oh! my lord, if you only knew what the feelings of a mother are when she beholds her infant shrieking for food, and turning its eyes towards her countenance in so piteous a manner that they speak the language of famine far more eloquently than its tongue could possibly do, were it able to express its wants in words,—if you could understand these feelings, you would not think ill of me because I thus appeal to your bounty!'—An address was given in an obscure street in Bloomsbury; and the letter was signed '*Harriet Wilmot.*'

"Again I felt for that poor creature, who was now reduced, with her poor infant of fifteen months old, to such a state of penury; and I do not say it to render myself less despicable than I must appear in the eyes of those who may peruse this narrative,—but I merely state it as a fact, that I hastened home, gathered together the few shillings which I possessed, and hurried off to the address mentioned in Harriet's letter. But when I reached the house indicated, I learnt from the landlady that Mrs. Wilmot had suddenly departed half an hour before. 'She was very poor,' observed the woman; 'but she was honest. She strove hard to maintain herself with her needle, and starved herself to feed her infant. She thought herself quite happy when she earned five shillings in a week. Night after night did the poor creature sit up till she was nearly blind, toiling constantly at her work. And when she went away so suddenly just now, she offered me her shawl in payment of the little arrears of rent due. My God! I would sooner have given her all I had than have taken a rag from her! Ah!' added the woman, wiping her eyes, 'there's something very wrong somewhere in the country when such good mothers are allowed to die by inches through sheer famine!'

"I went away, very miserable. I felt convinced that Harriet, when she perceived she had lost her letter, suspected that it might fall into my hands, and that I should thereby learn her place of abode. And it was clear that she had departed so abruptly to avoid me! I have kept that letter—as well as all the others to which I refer in my history.

"As nearly as I can recollect, two years and three quarters passed away; and I again saw Harriet. It was in the month of January, about noon on a bitter cold day; and I was walking through Long Acre, when I suddenly perceived her enter a house, which was evidently let in lodgings to poor families. She did not observe me; but I felt a violent longing to make my peace, if possible, with that unfortunate victim of my treachery. The door stood open for the accommodation of the various inmates; and I hurried up the staircase. I heard footsteps before me—and I followed them to the very top of the house: then I caught a glimpse of Harriet entering a back garret. I advanced to the door, and knocked gently. Harriet immediately opened it; but when she beheld me, she recoiled with such an expression of horror and alarm upon her death-like countenance, that I was dreadfully embarrassed. 'My dear friend,' I said, at length: 'pray—in the name of heaven! hear me!'—'*You!*' she cried, in that shrieking kind of tone which had marked her utterance of the word when we met before, and which showed her utter abhorrence of me—a sentiment I well deserved: 'hear *you!* Oh! no—no!'—and she closed the door violently. I knew not how to act. I felt convinced that she had never communicated with Mr. Markham since the period when he made that mysterious but '*terrible discovery*' to which he alluded in his letter that fell into my hands. I thought I would acquaint her with the existence of that letter and the nature of its contents; because it promised an income which would have placed her above want. So I sate down upon the stairs to reflect how I should proceed to induce her to hear me. In a few minutes the door opened quickly, and Harriet, with her child (who was then four years old) in her arms and a small bundle in her hand, appeared on the landing. She shrank back when she saw me—she evidently thought I was gone. Then, recovering herself, she exclaimed, '*Wretch! why do you haunt me? Have you not injured me enough already? Will you not even let me die in peace?*'—I started up, saying, 'Do hear me! You know not how important——.'—But ere I could utter another word, she rushed wildly past me, and ran down the stairs with a precipitation which manifested her profound horror at my presence.

"Thus had I involuntarily driven her a second time from her humble home! I was sorely afflicted, for many reasons—but chiefly because my motives were not on either occasion wrong. I was about to take my departure, when I thought I would cast a look at the interior of the chamber which she had inhabited. By its appearance I hoped to judge of her circumstances, which I sincerely wished might be improved. I entered the room: it was evidently a ready-furnished garret. I am able to recognise such facts at a glance. Though not absolutely wretched, it was mean—very mean—too mean to permit the idea that she, poor creature! was comfortable in her resources. Several papers were burning in the grate: she had evidently set fire to them the moment ere she left the room in the precipitate manner described. I hastened to extinguish the smouldering flames, but redeemed the fragment of only one important paper. It contained the commencement of a letter evidently written that morning, as I discovered by the date. Strange to say, it was another epistle addressed '*To the Marquis of Holmesford, Holmesford House.*' Its contents were to this effect:—'Your lordship will pardon me for again intruding myself upon your notice; but a deep sense of the duty I owe to my child, and the dread of leaving the poor innocent girl to the mercy of strangers—for the hand of Death seems to be already upon me—must serve as my excuse for thus troubling you. And when your lordship reflects that it is to you that I owe all the hideous misery which has been my lot for nearly four years,—through you that I lost the love and confidence of my husband,—your lordship's heart will not allow this appeal to be made in vain. Hitherto your lordship has remained unacquainted with the name of that husband of whom I speak; but now it is my duty to reveal it to you, that your lordship may see him and ex——'

"The remainder had been so scorched that it was illegible. Conjecture relative to the termination of the sentence was vain. Was the unfinished word *explain*? Or was it *express*? Often—often have I sate and wondered what the end of the passage originally was, ere the flames singed that sad letter. *She felt the hand of Death already upon her*; and I had driven her from the place where she wished *to die in peace*! Wretch—wretch that I was!

"From that time forth I never saw her more!

"All that I know of Harriet Markham is now told. The only link that is missing in the chain of my narrative is the detailed account of the mode in which Mr. Markham discovered that his wife had become the victim of the Marquis of Holmesford. That mystery the Marquis himself may be enabled to explain.

"My task is terminated: nor would I for worlds be compelled to accomplish it over again. It has given additional poignancy to thoughts that frequently oppress me, and has aroused others equally painful, but which had slumbered for years and years until now. And where I write—I dare not name the place, nor even those at whose command I write—there is a fearful gloom that is congenial, too congenial with those appalling reminiscences. Perhaps I should have felt and expressed less remorse for the past, had I written under more pleasant circumstances; perhaps, in that case, many of those dread images which *here* haunt my mind and are reflected in the bewailings and self-reproaches which appear in these pages, would not have visited me: still, had I performed this task in a cheerful chamber and in the gladdening sun-light,—even then I must have felt *some* remorse—for of all the bad deeds of my life, the treachery which I perpetrated towards Harriet is the blackest!

"May her sweet daughter Katharine be more happy—more fortunate!"

CHAPTER CCXXVI.

THE MARQUIS OF HOLMESFORD.

It was eleven o'clock on the following day, when the Marquis of Holmesford rose from the arms of one of the houris who formed his harem.

He thrust his feet into a pair of red morocco slippers, put on an elegant dressing-gown of gay-coloured silk, and passed from the room of his charmer to his own chamber.

There he entered a bath of warm milk; and, while luxuriating in the tepid fluid which imparted temporary vigour to a frame enfeebled by age and dissipation, he partook of a bowl of the richest French soup, called *consommée*, which his valet presented on a massive silver salver.

Having finished a broth that was well calculated to replenish the juices of his wasting frame, the hoary voluptuary left the bath, which was immediately wheeled into an adjacent chamber.

Every morning was a certain quantity, consisting of many gallons, of new milk supplied for the use of the Marquis of Holmesford; and when it had served him for one bath, it became the perquisite of his valet.

And what did this domestic do with it? Had he possessed hogs, he would not have given to those unclean beasts the fluid which had washed off all the impurities of his master's person:—no—he would not have allowed the very pigs to partake of the milk with which the disgusting exudations of the old voluptuary's body had commingled!

But he contracted with a milk-man whose "walk" was in a very poor neighbourhood; and that milk-man paid the valet a certain sum daily for the perquisite.

It was then retailed to the poor as the best "country grass-fed milk!"

Let us, however, return to the Marquis.

Upon quitting his bath, he commenced the mysteries of the toilet,—that ceremony which involves so many repulsive details when connected with old men or old women who have recourse to cosmetics or succedaneous means to render less apparent the ravages of time and debauchery.

Taking out his complete set of false teeth, he placed them in a glass filled with pure lavender water. His dressing-case supplied a silver instrument to scrape the white fur from a tongue that denoted the fever produced by the previous evening's deep potations; a pair of silver tweezers removed the hairs from his nostrils; and, in the meantime, his wig, stretched upon a block, was skilfully dressed by the valet.

It was past mid-day when Lord Holmesford quitted his chamber, looking as well as all the artificial means which he adopted towards the improvement of his person, and all the accessories of faultless clothes, whitest linen, and richest jewellery, could render an old worn-out beau of sixty-four.

As he was descending the stairs, a servant met him, and said in a profoundly respectful tone, "Mr. Greenwood, my lord, is in the drawing-room."

The Marquis nodded his head, as much as to say that he heard the announcement, and proceeded to the apartment where the Member for Rottenborough was waiting.

"Well, Greenwood, my boy," cried the Marquis, affecting the sparkling hilarity of youth, and endeavouring to walk with a jaunty and easy air, just as if his old bones did not move heavily in their sockets like a door on rusty hinges; "how goes the world with you? As for me, by God! I really think I am growing young again, instead——"

"Your lordship *does* look uncommonly well," said Greenwood, who had his own purposes to serve by flattering the nobleman; "and for a man of fifty-two——"

"Come, Greenwood—that won't do!" cried the Marquis. "Fifty-one, if you please, last birth-day."

"Yes—I meant in your fifty-second year, my lord," said Greenwood, with admirable composure of countenance, although he well knew that the hoary old sinner would never see sixty-four again:—"but, as I was observing, you are really an astonishing man; and if I were married—egad! I should deem it but prudent to request your lordship not to call at the house except when I was at home!"

"Ah! you rogue, Greenwood!" exclaimed the Marquis, highly delighted at the compliment thus conveyed—for with debauchees in fashionable life such a degrading assertion *is* a compliment, and a most welcome one, too:—"no—no—not so bad as that, either, Greenwood. Friendship before every thing!"

"No, my lord—*love* before every thing with your lordship!" cried Greenwood, gravely sustaining the familiar poke in the chest which his former compliment had elicited from the old nobleman. "You are really terrible amongst the women; and, some how or another, they cannot resist you. By the bye, how gets on the action which Dollabel has against you?"

"What! Dollabel, the actor at the Haymarket!" ejaculated the Marquis. "Oh! settled—settled long ago. My lawyer ferreted out an overdue bill of his, for ninety-odd pounds, bought it up for seven guineas, sued him on it, and threw him into some hole of a place in the City, that they call Redcross——"

"No—Bluecross, I think," suggested Greenwood, doubtingly—although he knew perfectly well to what place the Marquis was alluding.

"No—no—that isn't it either," cried the nobleman: "Whitecross Street—that's it."

"Ah! Whitecross Street—so it is!" exclaimed Greenwood. "What a memory your lordship has!"

"Yes—improves daily—better than when I was a boy," said the Marquis. "But as I was observing, my solicitor threw Dollabel into Whitecross Street gaol, and starved him into a compromise. I consented to give him his discharge from the debt and a ten-pound note to see his way with when he came out. But his wife was really a nice woman!"

"She was—a very nice woman," observed Greenwood. "You got out of that little *crim. con.* very nicely. Then there was Maxton's affair——"

"What! the tea-dealer in Bond Street!" exclaimed the Marquis, chuckling with delight as his exploits in the wars of love were thus recalled to his mind. "Oh! that was not so easily settled, my dear fellow. It went up to within a week of trial; and then Maxton agreed to stop all further proceedings and take his wife back if she came with a cool two thousand in her pocket. Well, my lawyer—knowing fellow, that!—drew him into a correspondence, and got him to receive his wife. Home she went:—Maxton met her with open arms—declared before witnesses that he was at length convinced of her innocence—(this he said to patch up her reputation)—and all was well till next morning, when he asked her to give him the two thousand pounds, that he might take them to the Bank. Then she laughed in his face—and he saw that he was done. *Condonation*, the civilians call it—and so he could not go on with the suit. Capital—wasn't it?"

"Capital, indeed!" ejaculated Greenwood, nearly dying with laughter.

The Marquis never for a moment suspected it to be all forced, but rubbed his hands together so briskly and chuckled so heartily, that a violent fit of coughing supervened, and he was compelled to turn aside to hold in his false teeth.

"Your lordship has caught a little cold," said the Member for Rottenborough. "But it is nothing—a mere nothing: I often have a cough like that. I've known many young men—much younger than your lordship—have worse coughs."

"Oh! I know that it's nothing," cried the Marquis, still stammering with a diabolical irritation in the throat.

"By the bye," said Greenwood, imagining that he had now so effectually worked himself into the old nobleman's good graces that he might safely explain the business that had brought him thither; "you are not in any hurry for the ten thousand I borrowed of you at the beginning of the year?"

"Not in the least, my dear fellow," returned the Marquis. "But, while I think of it, what has become of the fair Georgian—the blue-eyed Malkhatoun?"

"I handed her over to Dapper some time ago," answered Greenwood. "We were, however, speaking of those ten thousand pounds——"

"A trifle—a mere trifle. Say no more about it," cried the nobleman.

"I expected as much from your lordship's generous friendship," said Greenwood, obsequiously. "In fact, I came to tax you for a further loan—just for a few days——"

"Impossible at present, my dear fellow!" interrupted the Marquis, rather peremptorily; for he had entertained doubts of his friend's prosperity for some time past; and this application only tended to confirm his suspicions. "I am really so pressed at this moment——"

The dialogue was interrupted by the sudden entrance of a servant, who said, "My lord, the Prince of Montoni requests an interview with your lordship."

"The Prince—Richard—*here*!" exclaimed Greenwood, thrown off his guard.

"Show his Highness up immediately," said the Marquis, in the tone of a man who was surprised but not alarmed at this visit.

"My lord," interrupted Greenwood, speaking in a hurried and thick tone, "I have the most urgent reasons for not meeting the Prince of Montoni—for not even being seen by him. I implore you not to say that I am here—not even to allude to me."

And having uttered this hasty injunction, Greenwood passed into a back drawing-room, which was separated from the front one by folding-doors.

But it was easy to overhear in the former apartment all that was said in the latter.

Scarcely had the Member for Rottenborough thus retreated, when the Prince was ushered into the presence of the Marquis of Holmesford.

Those two personages had never met before; and the moment they thus found themselves face to face, they surveyed each other with rapid but scrutinising glances.

On one side Richard Markham was naturally curious to behold the man,—the monster in human form,—who could have practised so much villany against so much virtue—who, in a word, had destroyed the happiness of the deceased and lamented mother of Katharine.

On the other hand, the Marquis was struck by the handsome and noble appearance of that fine young man, who had raised himself from a sphere comparatively humble to an exalted position—who had led armies to a crowning triumph through the deadly strife of battle—and who was himself the personification of that generous spirit of political freedom which now influences the civilised world from the banks of the Thames to the waters of the Volga.

And, oh! what a contrast was formed in that splendid drawing-room where a great Prince and a wealthy peer now met for the first time:—the one possessing a heart beating with all the generous emotions that can redeem frail humanity from some of the dire consequences of the Primal Fall; the other accustomed to sacrifice all and every thing to his own selfish lusts and degrading debaucheries:—the one endowed with that manly beauty which associates so well with the dignity of high rank and the aristocracy of virtue; the other sinking beneath the infirmities of age and the ravages of dissipation:—the one noble alike by nature and by name; the other noble only by name:—the one carrying his head erect, and well able to meet the glance of every eye that would seek to penetrate into the recesses of his soul; the other conscious of having outraged so many hearts, that he quailed beneath the look of every visitor whose business was not immediately announced:—the one, in a word, the type of all that is great, good, chivalrous, and estimable; the other a representative of a vicious hereditary aristocracy!

The Marquis requested our hero to be seated, and, having himself taken a chair, waited for an explanation of the motives of this visit.

"I have called upon you, my lord," said Richard, "for the purpose of requesting one half-hour's serious conversation on a subject which deeply interests me and an amiable girl whom I only yesterday discovered to be my sister. My name is not unknown to your lordship——"

"I have heard much of your Highness," interrupted the nobleman; "and am well acquainted with those great achievements which have covered you with glory."

"When I said that my name was not unknown to your lordship," continued Richard, bowing coldly in acknowledgment of the compliment thus paid him, "I did not allude to that title by which the forms of ceremony compelled me to announce myself: I intended you to understand that the name of *Markham* must occupy no agreeable place in your lordship's memory."

"Your Highness oversteps the bounds of courtesy in undertaking to answer for the state of my feelings," exclaimed the Marquis, with evident signs of astonishment: "your Highness insinuates that I have reason for self-reproach; and this between strangers——"

"Pardon me for interrupting your lordship," said our hero, calmly but firmly: "if we were personally strangers to each other until now, the name of my deceased father was not unknown to you; nor am I unacquainted with your conduct towards one who was dear to *him*. And now, my lord, let us understand each other. I came not hither on an inimical errand—scarcely even to reproach you. You are an old man—and it would be unseemly in me, who am a young man, to assume a tone of intimidation or of menace. But I come to request an explanation of a certain affair which is to some degree enveloped in doubt and mystery—although, alas! I dread the very worst:—I come as one gentleman seeks another, to demand the only atonement that can be made for wrongs inflicted years ago on him who was the author of my being;—and that atonement is a full avowal of the past, so that no uncertainty even as to the worst may dwell in the minds of those who are now interested in the subject to which I allude."

"Your Highness is labouring under some extraordinary error," said the Marquis of Holmesford, warmly. "I declare most solemnly that the name of your father was totally unknown to me: indeed, I never heard of your family until the newspapers first became busy with your own exploits in Italy."

"Is this possible?" cried Richard: then, as a sudden reminiscence struck him, he said in a musing tone, "Yes—it may be so. In her last letter addressed to the Marquis of Holmesford poor Harriet intimated that the name of her husband was unknown to him—and that letter was never sent!"

Although the Prince uttered those words rather in a musing tone to himself than in direct address to the Marquis, the latter caught the name of *Harriet*, and instantly became deeply agitated.

"Harriet, my lord?—did your Highness mention the name of Harriet?" murmured the nobleman.

"Yes, my lord," continued Richard: "I see that I have hitherto been speaking in enigmas. But I will now explain myself better. It is of one whom you knew as Harriet Wilmot that I require explanations at your hands."

"Harriet Wilmot!—yes—I knew her," said the Marquis, faintly: "I did her grievous wrong! and yet——"

"Your lordship will understand wherefore I feel interested in all that relates to Harriet Wilmot," interrupted Markham,—"when I declare to you that she was secretly married to my own father—and it is her child whom I yesterday embraced as a sister!"

"As there is a God in heaven, my lord," exclaimed the Marquis of Holmesford, emphatically, "I never until this moment knew the name of Harriet's husband; and with equal solemnity would I assert on my death-bed that she was innocent, my lord—she was innocent!"

"Oh! if I could believe—if I were assured——"

Richard could say no more: he pressed his hand to his brow, as if to steady his brain and collect his thoughts; and tears trembled on his long black lashes.

"Prince of Montoni," cried the Marquis, rising from his seat, and speaking with more sincerity and more seriousness than had characterised his tone for many, many years; "I am a man of pleasure, I admit—a man of gallantry, I allow; but I have no inclination to gratify, no interest to serve, by uttering a falsehood now. Again I declare to you—as God is my judge—that Harriet was innocent in respect to myself,—and I believe—nay, I would venture to assert—innocent also with regard to others—and faithful to her husband!"

"My lord," said Richard, in a voice tremulous with mingled emotions of joy and doubt; and as he spoke, he also rose from his seat, and took the nobleman's hand, which he pressed with nervous force,—"my lord, prove to me what you have just stated—explain all that took place between yourself and Harriet on that night which appears to have been so fatal to her happiness,—show me, in a word, that she *was* innocent,—and I will banish from my mind all angry feelings which may have been excited by the knowledge of your intrigues to undermine her virtue!"

"I cannot for a moment, hesitate to satisfy you in this respect," said the Marquis. "Resume your seat, my lord—and I will narrate, as calmly and distinctly as I can, all that transpired on the night when she was inveigled to my house;—for I perceive that you are well acquainted with many details concerning her."

"It is but right to inform you," observed Richard, "that the old woman who aided your designs with regard to her whom I must consider to have been my step-mother, has committed to paper a narrative of all which she knew relative to that unfortunate young woman. But there is one gap which your lordship must fill up—one mystery which is as yet unrevealed. I allude to the incidents of that fatal night, when, even if Harriet escaped innocent from this house, she, by some strange combination of untoward circumstances, lost the confidence of my father—her husband—and appeared guilty in his eyes."

"And yet she *was* innocent!" exclaimed the Marquis, emphatically. "Listen, Prince, to what I am about to say. The old woman to whom you have alluded, inveigled Harriet to my house—and, I confess, by my instructions. I knew that she was married; but the old woman told me not to whom—even if she knew."

"She *did* know," remarked our hero; "but the marriage was kept secret———"

"And I never asked the vile procuress any particulars concerning it," interrupted the Marquis. "All I coveted was Harriet's person: I cared nothing for her connexions or circumstances. The young mother came hither, with her child in her arms. One of my female servants took the babe from her, and locked her in a room where she expected to find the woman whom she believed to be her friend. But she was alone with me! She knew me—and the conviction that she was betrayed flashed to her mind the moment her eyes met mine. Then she fell upon her knees, and implored me to save her—to spare her. I was inflamed with wine—maddened with desire; and I heeded not her prayers. I attempted to reason with her;—but not all the tempting offers I made her—not all the promises I uttered—not all the inducements I held out, could persuade her to submit to my wishes. I was already a widower, and I even swore to make her my wife, so soon as a divorce could be obtained between herself and her husband, if she would become my mistress. No:—she wept and shrieked—she prayed and menaced—she grew violent and imploring, by turns. At length—for I must tell you all—I had recourse to violence: I was no longer able to master my passions. But she resisted me with a strength and energy that surprised me. I was completely baffled—and Harriet remained innocent!"

"Thank God—thank God!" exclaimed Markham, fervently clasping his hands together.

"Yes, my lord—she remained innocent," continued the Marquis; "and, when I myself grew more cool, I felt ashamed—humiliated—cast down, in the presence of that young woman who had preserved her virtue from my violence,—the first who ever entered that room and conquered *me*! I suddenly experienced an admiration for her—such as I had never known till then on behalf of any female! I approached her—in my turn I became a suppliant;—but it was for pardon! I deplored the outrage I had committed—I went upon my knees to ask her forgiveness.—'*My child!* she suddenly exclaimed, as if awaking from a profound reverie.—I rang the bell, and received her child at the door: in my own arms I carried the babe to her. She covered it with kisses; and my manner touched her—for she declared that she would pardon me, if I never molested her more. I called heaven to witness the sincerity of the oath that I then pledged to observe this condition. Two hours had thus elapsed; and when she was composed, I rang the bell and ordered a hackney-coach to be fetched. When the vehicle arrived, I escorted her to it. But as I handed her down the steps of the front door, a gentleman, who was passing at the moment, caught sight of her countenance.—'*Harriet!* he exclaimed, in a voice of mingled astonishment, rage, and despair.—'*My husband!* she cried, with a wild shriek; and she would have fallen on the pavement, had I not caught her in my arms.—'*Sir,*' I said to the stranger, '*this lady is innocent, although appearances may be against her.*'—'*Innocent!* he repeated, in a tone of bitterness and grief: '*innocent when she comes calmly from the house of the Marquis of Holmesford, and sinks into the Marquis of Holmesford's arms! No: I am not to be deceived! Harriet, vile woman, I cast you off for ever!*—And, with these words, the stranger hurried away."

"Alas! that was my poor father!" said Markham, the tears trickling down his cheeks.

"I had no opportunity to explain the circumstances that had occurred," continued the nobleman, after a pause. "Your father disappeared with the rapidity of lightning; and the moment he was gone, Harriet burst from my arms, evidently in pursuit of him. I was so bewildered with the suddenness of these events, that I remained transfixed as it were to the spot. At length I hurried down the street after Harriet;—but I could not overtake her. Distressed beyond measure, I returned home, vented my wrath upon the old woman, whom I loathed as the authoress of this misfortune, and drove her from my house. The wretch wrote to me afterwards, and even endeavoured to obtain an interview with me; but I would never see her more."

"And did your lordship lose sight of poor Harriet altogether?" asked Richard.

"I once received a letter from her," was the reply: "I think it must have been about a year after the occurrences which I have just related. She wrote in a mild and respectful tone—declaring that the sufferings of her half-famished child could alone have induced her to apply for assistance to me. I enclosed her a hundred pounds, and desired her in my letter of reply never to hesitate to avail herself of my purse—as I should not attempt to take any advantage of the assistance which I might render her. But to my astonishment she sent back eighty pounds—retaining only twenty, and declaring in a brief note that she felt ashamed of being even compelled to accept that sum. I never heard from her again; but I gather from your Highness's observations that she is no longer living!"

"She died unhappily,—miserably upwards of thirteen years ago," said Richard. "A strange combination of circumstances threw me in the way of her daughter,—the orphan whom she left—about fifteen months ago; and it was only last night that I discovered a sister in her whom I had known as Katherine Wilmot."

"Katherine Wilmot!" exclaimed the Marquis: "surely that name is known to me?"

"My sister was accused of a crime which the Rev. Reginald Tracy had in reality perpetrated; and——"

"I remember the occurrence full well," interrupted the Marquis. "When that exposure of the rector of Saint David's took place, I was struck by the name of Wilmot; but I suspected not for a moment that the Katherine Wilmot, who was concerned in that affair, and whose innocence transpired so clearly, was the daughter of poor Harriet."

"Katharine Markham—for such is now her name," said Richard, "was for a period the victim of circumstantial evidence—even as a combination of unfortunate circumstances had persecuted her mother before her. Yes—it was evidence of that kind which ruined Harriet in the eyes of my father! But I shall intrude no longer upon your lordship—unless it be to say that your candid explanation this day has gone far to retrieve the past in my estimation. For, oh! my lord—you can perhaps understand how welcome to me is the conviction that the mother of my newly-discovered sister was virtuous:—and to her, poor girl! the assurance of her parent's innocence will be joyful indeed! Every thing is now cleared up—and the narrative of Katherine's parentage is complete. Its truth is proved by the fact that certain letters now in my possession are in the handwriting of my father; and some which Harriet also wrote, correspond with a fragment of a note that the poor creature commenced on her death-bed, and which has remained in her daughter's possession. One link was alone wanting to make the history perfect—the occurrence of that night which was so fatal to my step-mother's happiness. That link your lordship has supplied;—and I thank you."

The Prince then took his leave of the Marquis.

Scarcely had Richard left the room, when Greenwood re-entered it from the back apartment.

His countenance was pale—his manner was agitated.

"What is the matter with you?" demanded the Marquis, astonished at his friend's altered mien.

"Your lordship cannot divine how nearly all that I have overheard concerns *me*," was the answer.

And Greenwood left the house abruptly.

We must leave the reader to imagine the joy that prevailed at Markham Place, when the Prince returned thither, the bearer of those happy tidings which proved the legitimacy of Katherine and the innocence of her departed but not unlamented mother.

CHAPTER CCXXVII.

COLDBATH FIELD'S PRISON.

Return we now to the Resurrection Man,—that incarnate fiend whose crimes were so numerous, and all of so black a dye.

Firmly bound, and guarded by three officers, who kept their bludgeons in their hands, the miscreant saw that all resistance was vain: he accordingly threw himself back in the cab that was bearing him to prison, and gave way to his saturnine reflections.

"If I had only thought that Richard Markham would have accompanied that young girl Katharine,"—it was thus he mused,—"a very different song would have been sung. But I knew that he was married only a week ago, and never dreamt that *he* would leave his pretty wife to poke his nose into Banks's crib. What an infernal oversight on my part! And now—here I am, regularly lumbered; and all the swag arising from Kate Wilmot's business is in the hands of that canting sneak Banks! Damnation to Richard Markham! I shall swing for this if I don't take precious good care. He'll swear to two different attempts on his life—one at the old house near Bird-cage Walk, and t'other at Twig Folly. What a cursed—ten times cursed fool I was to let myself tumble into a snare in this way! Some one else will find the gold that I have saved up; and when I shall be cold and stiff under the pavement of Newgate, others will riot on my treasure! But, no—it can't happen in that way: it's impossible that my time is come yet—impossible! I shall escape somehow or another;—I *must* escape—I *will* escape! But how? That question is the devil of the difficulty. Never mind—escape I will;—so I mustn't be down-hearted!"

These and numberless other reflections, in which despondency and hope alternately asserted a predominant influence, occupied the mind of Anthony Tidkins as the cab proceeded rapidly through Bethnal-Green and Shoreditch,—then along Old Street—up the Goswell Road—through Northampton Square—and lastly along Exmouth Street, in its way to Coldbath Fields' Prison.

At length the cab turned into the short road which forms the approach, within the wooden railings in front of the governor's dwelling, to the great gates of the gaol,—those gates over which may be read in large letters, "MIDDLESEX HOUSE OF CORRECTION."

A shudder crept over even the iron frame of Anthony Tidkins, as those huge portals, towering high above the cab which now drew up close to them, seemed to frown upon him like a colossal genius of evil amidst the obscurity of night.

Benstead leapt from the cab, and knocked loudly at the gate.

The iron din was responded to by gloomy echoes from the courts inside.

In a few minutes heavy chains fell, and the wicket was opened by a man bearing a lantern.

Benstead whispered to him for a few moments; and Tidkins was conducted into a little lobby on the left hand.

The turnkey, who had opened the gate, then proceeded to the governor's house, which was close by within the walls; and, after an absence of ten minutes, he returned with an affirmative answer to Benstead's request that the prisoner might be retained in custody in that gaol until a magistrate should otherwise dispose of him.

The turnkey accordingly led the way through the wicket of a strong iron grating, across a yard where a watchman armed with a loaded blunderbuss was stationed, and thence into a building, up the narrow stone staircase of which the party proceeded, until they reached a cell, where the Resurrection Man, who was now released from his bonds, was left.

Tidkins threw himself upon the bed and soon fell asleep. He was not an individual to whom danger or even the prospect of death could bring remorse: darkness and solitude had no alarms for him;—and, thus, in spite of the profound vexation he experienced at his present predicament, he yielded to the influence of fatigue and slept soundly.

On the following morning a bowl of gruel and a piece of bread were supplied for his breakfast; and he washed at the common sink belonging to that department of the gaol.

At ten o'clock Benstead and two other officers arrived, placed manacles upon him, and conveyed him to a cab, in which they seated themselves with him.

In about half an hour the Resurrection Man was placed in the dock at the Lambeth Street Police Office.

The Prince of Montoni, attended by his solicitor, Mr. Dyson, had entered the court a few moments before; and the magistrate, upon being made acquainted with his name and rank, immediately threw down the newspaper, saying, "It is by no means necessary that your Highness should enter the witness-box: your Highness will do me the honour to accept a seat on the bench; and the clerk will take down your Highness's evidence at your Highness's leisure. Make room there, for his Highness: usher, clear the way for his Highness."

Scarcely able to conceal his disgust at this fulsome behaviour of the magistrate, the Prince coldly said, "I thank you, sir, for your politeness: but I cannot consent to receive a favour which would not be shown to a poor and obscure individual."

The magistrate turned very red, and bowed meekly, but without repeating his offer.

The case was then entered upon.

The Prince detailed the particulars of that adventure at the Resurrection Man's house in the neighbourhood of the Bird-cage Walk, with which the reader is already acquainted: and he also related the subsequent circumstances connected with the blowing up of the den—a deed which had cost several persons their lives, and which (added Markham) was no doubt perpetrated by Tidkins himself.

When these depositions were taken down, the Prince was about to enter upon his second charge—namely, the attack made upon him at Twig Folly: but the magistrate thought the first case had better be previously completed, and resolved upon remanding the prisoner for three days, in order to allow time to procure the evidence of those surviving policemen who had witnessed the fate of their brother-officers on the occasion of the blowing up of the house.

Tidkins was accordingly remanded to Coldbath Fields' Prison; and the Prince of Montoni immediately repaired in his carriage to Holmesford House—the particulars of which visit have been detailed in the preceding chapter.

On his return to the gaol, Tidkins was allowed to walk for an hour in the tread-wheel yard nearest to the entrance of the prison. There are several tread-mill yards in Coldbath Fields' gaol, alike for males and females; but we specify the particular yard in which the Resurrection Man was permitted to take exercise, because it has relation to a certain event which is to follow. It is also of the wheel in this yard that the fan, or balance, is seen above the wall near the south-western angle of the prison, by persons passing through Coldbath Square.

The tread-wheel is an enormous drum, or cylinder, with ranges of steps all round it, at a distance of about a foot and a half from each other. Between forty and fifty persons can work on the wheel at one time. It moves slowly round towards the prisoners placed upon it; and thus the step on which the foot stands descends, while the next step presents itself. A platform is built to half the height of the wheel; and from this platform the prisoners step upon the wheel itself. They support themselves by a railing, and their weight keeps the wheel in motion. Thus they *must* sink *with all their weight*, as they work on that rotatory engine of diabolical torture. The action is that of going up stairs, without, however, actually rising higher; for every step so reached sinks beneath the feet, and the prisoner is compelled to get upon the next one in its descent. Those prisoners who wait their turns to go on, sit upon the platform; and the task-master in the yard directs the intervals of labour and those of rest.

And upon this engine of torture, as we ere now denominated the tread-mill, not only boys of twelve years of age are placed, but even women!

Yes:—in this civilised country,—in this land where novelists and poets celebrate the chivalrous devotion which should be paid to the softer sex,—in this great city, where the pseudo-saints blurt forth their nauseating hypocrisy at Exeter Hall, and swindle the charitable of alms for the purpose of improving the condition of savages thousands of miles off, while there is such an awful want of instruction and moralising elements at home,—in the very centre of the English capital are women subjected to the ferocious torture of the tread-mill!

The food is scanty;—and yet the labour thus forced upon the poor sickly, half-starved wretches, is horribly severe.

Three-quarters of the crimes which send prisoners to Coldbath Fields, are larcenies and robberies caused by dire penury and pinching want: the miserable beings are half-famished already when they enter that gaol; but they are nevertheless retained in something closely bordering on that state of constant hunger, while the hardest possible labour is required from them!

Remember, reader, that we do not wish idleness to prevail in a prison. It is just the place where habits of industry should be inculcated. We therefore approve of the system of workshops established in Coldbath Fields: we admire the oakum-room—the room, too, where shoe-making is taught—and that department of the prison in which rugs are manufactured for a wholesale warehouse that contracts for the purchase of the same.

But we abhor torture—we detest cruelty; and the tread-wheel is alike a torture and a cruelty!

It makes the heart bleed in the breast of the visitor to the female-division of Coldbath Fields, to behold women nursing their babes at one moment, and then compelled to deliver their sucklings to the care of their fellow-prisoners, while they themselves repair to take their turn upon the tread-mill!

Talk of the despotism of Turkey, Russia, Austria, or Prussia,—talk of the tyranny of those countries where the will of one man is a law, be it for good or evil,—we solemnly and emphatically cry, "*Look at home*!"

Flogging in the Army and Navy, private whipping in prisons, semi-starvation in workhouses and gaols, and the tread-wheel,—these are the tortures which exist in this land of boasted civilisation—these are the instances in which our rulers seek to emulate the barbarism of past ages and the wanton inhumanity of foreign autocrats!

We must in justice observe that Coldbath Fields' Prison is kept in a most cleanly state. Perhaps the ventilation is not as perfect as it might be; and certainly the stone cells must be awfully cold in winter, for there are no means of imparting to them any artificial warmth. But as far as wholesome cleanliness is concerned, there is not the slightest ground whereon to raise a cavil against the establishment.

The discipline maintained in that gaol is on the Silent System. There it no separation—no classification—during the day; but the plan of silence prevents the corruption of the only moderately bad by the inveterately wicked. At night each individual sleeps apart in a cell.

Anthony Tidkins walked about the yard, affecting a moody and sullen air of indifference, but in reality catching with rapid glance every point of the buildings around him—every object within the range of his vision; so that he committed to memory a complete map of that division of the prison where he was now taking exercise.

Having walked an hour, he was re-conducted to his room where a bowl of pease-soup with a slice of bread was given to him for his dinner. In the evening he was supplied with a basin of gruel and another piece of bread, and was then locked in for the night.

CHAPTER CCXXVIII.

A DESPERATE ACHIEVEMENT.

It was, as the readers must remember, in the middle of the month of March when these events occurred. At that season of the year the sun sets at about six o'clock; and it is consequently dark at seven.

The Resurrection Man was no sooner left undisturbed for the night, when he commenced the arduous and almost desperate attempt of an escape from the prison.

Taking off his coat, he tore open the lining of the collar, and drew forth two files scarcely larger than watch-springs, and made of steel of an equally fine temper.

"Thanks to my precaution in never moving away from home without such tools as these about me!" he exclaimed, as he bent the files almost double to try their elasticity, and then drew them over one of his nails to test the keenness of their teeth.

It is not an uncommon circumstance for the police-magistrates at the offices not within the City of London to remand prisoners accused of heinous crimes to Coldbath Fields' gaol; and as such persons cannot, according to the law, be deemed guilty until they be declared so by a jury, they are not lodged in the common dark cells allotted to misdemeanants or criminals sentenced to imprisonment within those walls. There is a room specially appropriated to the use of untried individuals who are sent to Coldbath Fields. That chamber is capable of holding four or five beds, and has two windows looking upon the prison-grounds.

Those windows are, however, secured by strong iron bars outside the casements, which are made to open for the purpose of airing the room in the day-time.

Tidkins had already carefully examined these bars, and had calculated to a nicety the exact time which it would occupy him to remove two of them by means of his files.

It was seven o'clock when he commenced his labour; and as the clock of the church on Clerkenwell Green struck eleven, that portion of his task was accomplished.

"True to a minute!" muttered the Resurrection Man to himself, with a low chuckle of triumph: "I reckoned on four hours to do it in!"

But his fingers were cut and lacerated with the process: he, however, assuaged the pain by greasing the flesh with the remainder of the gruel left in his bowl.

The next proceeding was to tear his bedding into slips, wherewith to form a rope; and this was accomplished in about half an hour.

The window was not very high from the ground; and he did not dread the descent:—but the moon was shining brightly—and he knew that watchmen, carrying fire-arms, kept guard in the prison-grounds.

He looked up at the lovely planet of the night, whose chaste splendour was at that moment blessed by so many travellers alike upon the land and on the ocean; and he uttered a fearful imprecation against its pure silvery lustre.

But he did not hesitate many minutes: his case was desperate—so was his character.

"Better receive an ounce of lead in the heart than dance on nothing in six weeks or so," he said to himself, as he fastened the rope to the bar which stood next to the place of the two that he had removed.

Then he passed his legs through the window; and clinging by his hands and feet, slid slowly and safely down the rope.

He was now in the grounds belonging to the prison; but the high wall, that bounded the enclosure, separated him from the street.

Cautiously and noiselessly did he creep along, beneath the shade of the building—directing his steps towards the tread-wheel yard in which he had been permitted to take exercise, as above stated.

Suddenly the noise of footsteps and of voices fell upon his ears; and those ominous sounds were approaching.

"Perdition!" thought the Resurrection Man, as he crouched up close beneath the building: "I could have managed one—I could have sprung upon him—strangled him in a moment. But two—*two*———"

And he ground his teeth with rage.

"And so you was at the Old Bailey to-day?" said one of the watchmen to his companion, as they advanced round that part of the prison.

"Yes: it was my half-holiday," was the reply; "and so I thought I might as well go and hear the trial of that young Holford, you know, who shot at the Queen. The jury had a good deal of trouble at coming to a verdict; but at last they acquitted him on the ground of insanity."

"Ah!" said the first speaker: "then he's let out again?"

"Deuce a bit of that!" exclaimed his companion. "The judge ordered him to be detained till the royal pleasure should be known; and so he'll get sent to Bedlam for the rest of his life."

"And d'ye think he's mad? did he look mad?"

"Not he! He's no more mad than me. He seemed a little gloomy and sulky—but not mad. The only time he showed any interest in the proceedings, was when a witness called Jem Cuffin was examined; and this chap said all he could in favour of the youngster, although he wasn't able to deny that he saw him fire at the Queen and Prince Albert. But the best of it was, this Jem Cuffin proved that the pistols wasn't loaded at all. Holford did not, however, know *that* when he fired them. So the young feller has managed to get board and lodging for life; and Jem Cuffin, who is a returned transport, it seems, and had been in custody for some time, was discharged on a full pardon granted by the Home Secretary."

"It must have been an interesting trial," observed the first speaker.

"Yes," said his companion; "but I'll tell you what will be more interesting still—and that is the trial of Tony Tidkins, whenever it comes on. Lord! what things that feller *has* done in his time! Talk of Jack Sheppard, or Dick Turpin, or any of the old criminals—why, they're nothing at all compared with this Tidkins. Ah! some rum things will come out when he goes up afore the nobs at the Old Bailey!"

The two men had stopped within half a dozen yards of the place where the Resurrection Man was crouched up in the deep shade of the building; and every word of the above conversation met his ears. In spite of the peril of discovery which now seemed inevitable, the miscreant experienced a momentary feeling of pride and triumph as he listened to the observations which were made concerning himself.

"Well, I must go round t'other way," said one of the watchmen, after a short pause: "we should get blowed up if we was found together—'specially talking in a prison on the *silent system*."

This was meant as a joke; and so the two men chuckled at it.

Tidkins also chuckled within himself; because he had just learnt that the watchmen intended to separate, and that consequently only one would pass him. He was still menaced with a fearful peril; but he considered it to be only one half so great as it had seemed a few moments previously.

Midnight was now proclaimed by the iron tongue of Clerkenwell Church; and the two watchmen parted—one retracing his steps round the building; and the other slowly advancing towards Tidkins.

"I must spring upon him and throttle him in a moment," thought the Resurrection Man, clenching his fingers as if they already held the intended victim's neck in their iron grasp.

But Providence saved the miscreant from that additional crime:—the watchman struck abruptly away from the neighbourhood of the building, and walked towards the boundary wall.

His back was now turned upon Tidkins, who lost no time in availing himself of this unexpected relief from the danger which had threatened him. In fact, the very circumstance of the two watchmen having advanced so close to him in each other's company,—which circumstance had menaced him with a detection that seemed unavoidable,—now proved most advantageous to his scheme; for as he hurried rapidly on towards the first tread-wheel yard, he passed between the two watchmen, each of whom was retreating farther from him, the one by retracing his steps round the building, and the other by lounging towards the wall.

Thus, while their backs were turned upon him, he gained in safety the tread-wheel yard where he had taken exercise, and every point of which he had accurately committed to memory.

His movements were now executed with the rapidity of one who had well weighed and pre-considered them.

Taking from a corner a gardener's basket, which he had previously noticed there, and which was used to convey the potatoes that were dug up in the prison-grounds, he turned it bottom upwards against a low building, or out-house, which abutted with a shelving slate roof against the high wall. By means of the basket, he raised himself upon this roof—crept up on it—and with one nimble spring upwards was enabled to catch at the *chevaux-de-frise*, or revolving iron spikes, which were fixed near the top of the wall, and which thus hung over the out-house.

Careless of the wounds which he received from the *chevaux-de-frise*, he scrambled over them, and gained the top of the wall.

The wall was much too high to permit him to drop into the street with any chance of escaping a broken limb. This he had previously reflected upon; and he now commenced the desperate feat of walking along the summit of that lofty wall—with a bright moon shining above, and the almost positive certainty of being observed by the watchmen inside the prison.

To increase the personal danger incurred by this extraordinary undertaking, the wall is irregular on the top, breaking into sudden and abrupt falls towards the south-western angle, and then rising with elevations equally abrupt from that point to the north-western angle.

This peculiarity of structure is caused by the unevenness of the ground on which the entire establishment with all its enclosures stands.

The journey along the top of the walls was not even a short one. The object of the Resurrection Man was to reach the houses in Guildford Place, which join the prison-wall on the eastern side. The point where he ascended was nearly at the middle of the southern wall; but between him and the south-eastern angle stood the gates and the governor's house, which he could not pass. He therefore had to make a circuit comprising nearly half the southern wall—all the western wall—all the northern wall—and then a part of the eastern wall;—and this in the largest prison in England!

It was a desperate venture: but—as we have before said—Tidkins was a desperate man—and his case was also desperate!

Fortune often aids the unworthy; and she did so upon this occasion.

Scarcely had the Resurrection Man proceeded twenty yards along the wall, when the moon—hitherto so lovely—became suddenly obscured; and a huge black cloud swept over its face.

Tidkins cast one rapid glance upwards; and his heart leapt within him, as he said to himself, "It will be dark like this long enough for my purpose."

On he went—walking upright, and rapidly—with scarcely an unusual effort to balance himself upon that giddy height,—and stooping only when he reached any of those abrupt descents or ascents in the structure of the wall which we have ere now noticed.

And now he has gained—safely gained—the north-western angle: he is pursuing his way along the wall which looks upon Calthorpe Street.

At the slightest signal of alarm he is prepared to risk his life by leaping from the wall.

But no one observes him: it is now quite dark;—he is far away from that part of the prison where the watchmen walk;—and the street beneath is empty.

Here and there are lights in the upper windows of the adjacent houses: he can almost see into those rooms, above the level of which he is placed.

Looking to his right, he perceives the dark outlines of the prison-buildings, between which and the northern wall, whereon he is now walking, there is a considerable interval, the intermediate space being occupied by the gaol-gardens.

His heart beats joyfully—triumphantly: he has gained the north-eastern angle!

A glance to the left shows him the lights of Bagnigge Wells: before him are those of Wilmington Square; and to his right is Guildford Place.

He felt that he was beyond the reach of danger; and so exhilarating was his joy, that a momentary dizziness seized upon him—and he nearly fell over within the precincts of the gaol.

But recovering his balance by an extraordinary exertion, he planted his feet more firmly than ever on the wall, and continued his walk along the dizzy height.

He was now again in danger of discovery; for he had reached that part of the eastern wall against which the buildings and tread-wheel yards of the females' department stood, and in the immediate vicinity of which a watchman was stationed.

Nevertheless, the houses in Guildford Place were near; and their back premises abutted against the outer side of the wall along which he was now proceeding.

"One minute more of that dark cloud upon the moon—and I am safe!" he said to himself, as he cast a rapid glance upwards.

But, no—the cloud passes!

It has passed;—and the bright moon suddenly bursts forth with a flood of silver light.

Almost at the same instant, a loud voice raises an alarm within the precincts of the gaol: the sharp crack of a blunderbuss is heard—and a bullet whistles past the Resurrection Man, whose dark form, as seen by the watchman near the females' department, stands out in strong relief against the moon-lit sky.

The cry of the watchman is echoed by other voices on the prison side of the wall; and Tidkins mutters a terrible curse as he hurries forward.

But his courage does not fail him:—no—he is determined to sell his life as dearly as possible!

In less than a minute after the watchman within the enclosure had raised the alarm, the Resurrection Man reached the backs of the houses in Guildford Place;—and now the clear moonlight was of the utmost service to him, in enabling him to execute his movements with security and caution.

He lowered himself from the prison-wall to the roof of an out-house, and thence alighted in a yard attached to a dwelling.

The back-door of the house was locked and bolted inside: but this was a small obstacle in the way of one who had just escaped from the Middlesex House of Correction.

Unable to waste time by proceeding with caution, and compelled to risk the chance of alarming the inhabitants of the dwelling, the desperate man threw himself with all his strength against the door, which broke inwards with a loud crash.

The noise was followed by ejaculations of alarm in the house; footsteps were heard overhead; windows were thrown open—and the cry of "Thieves!" echoed along the street.

Tidkins paused not to reflect:—he dashed through the house—along the passage to the front door, the bolts of which he drew back in a moment. The key was in the lock:—every thing now appeared to favour the escape of the Resurrection Man!

The front-door was opened in a few moments, just as the inmates of the dwelling were rushing down the stairs.

But when they reached the passage, the door closed violently behind the intruder who had caused their alarm.

The Resurrection Man was safe in the open street; and he knew that he had a good start of the prison watchmen, who would have to make a considerable circuit from the vicinity of the females' department to the gates, and from the gates round the south-eastern angle, ere they could reach the point from which he was now departing.

Swift as an arrow he scud up Guildford Place—turned to the right—and slackened his pace only when he had passed through Wilmington Square. He gained the City Road, along which he walked somewhat leisurely towards Finsbury—well aware that his pursuers would not think of looking for him in a wide and open thoroughfare, but would rather prosecute their searches in the narrow lanes and low districts in the immediate neighbourhood of the gaol.

His object was to gain his den in Globe Town; for not a word had transpired during his examination before the magistrate at Lambeth Street, to show that the police had any clue to his place of abode; and he felt certain that Banks would not have betrayed him. The undertaker, he knew, was too deeply concerned in many of his plots and schemes to risk a general smash of the whole gang, by making any unpleasant revelations.

The Resurrection Man struck from the City Road into Old Street, and speedily reached Shoreditch.

As he passed down one of the horrible lanes which lie behind Shoreditch Church, he observed the door of a public-house to be open. He was well aware of the flash character of the place, but did not happen to be known by the people who kept it.

He entered this low boozing-ken, ordered a glass of something at the bar, and inquired for the evening paper. It was immediately handed to him; for all flash houses of that description take an evening as well as a morning journal, that their customers may receive the earliest intelligence of each day's Police or Old Bailey proceedings—matters in which the generality of them are very frequently interested.

Tidkins turned to the most recent Police Intelligence, and found his own case duly reported. Nothing, however, was said in that or any other department of the paper, which tended to excite an alarm lest his house in Globe Town had been discovered or any of his accomplices in his various crimes had been traced.

Thus reassured, he drank off the contents of his glass, and then recollected that he had no money in his pocket to pay for it. All he had about him when he was arrested, had been taken from him, according to custom, on his removal to Coldbath Fields.

Scarcely had this new embarrassment presented itself to his mind, when the door of the tap-room opened, and a man came forth. To Tidkins's infinite relief it proved to be the Buffer, who started when he saw his old friend at liberty.

The Resurrection Man placed his finger upon his lip; and the Buffer instantly checked the ejaculation of astonishment which had risen to his tongue.

The trifling debt incurred for the liquor was immediately settled by the Resurrection Man's friend; and the precious pair left the boozing-ken together.

As they walked along towards Globe Town, Anthony Tidkins related the particulars of his escape, at which the Buffer was monstrously delighted. Then, in reply to the Resurrection Man's questions, the other stated that he had seen Banks on the previous afternoon, and that no inquiries of a suspicious nature had been made at that individual's abode.

When they reached the door of the Resurrection Man's house in Globe Town, the Buffer took leave of his friend, with a promise to call in the course of the day and bring the morning's newspapers.

Tidkins was overjoyed when he again set foot in his back room on the first floor: and finding some gin in the cupboard, he celebrated his escape and return with a copious dram.

He did not immediately retire to bed, although he was sadly fatigued and bruised by the achievements of the night; but, taking down a bundle of keys from a shelf, he paid a visit to the subterranean department of his establishment.

The moment he placed the key in the lock of the private door up the narrow alley, he uttered a curse, adding, "This lock has been tried—tampered with! I know it—I could swear to it: I can tell by the way that the key turns!"

And the perspiration ran down his countenance:—for he trembled for the safety of his treasure!

With feverish impatience he opened the door, and entered that part of his strangely-built house.

Having obtained a light, a new circumstance of alarm struck him: the door of the back room was standing wide open!

"And I can swear that I closed it the last time I ever came here!" he cried aloud. "Some one has been to this place;—and that some one must be Banks! The sneaking scoundrel! But he shall suffer for it."

With a perception as keen as that of the North American Indian following the trail of a fugitive foe, did the Resurrection Man examine the floor of the room; and his suspicions that some one had been thither were confirmed by the appearance of several particles of damp dirt, which had evidently been left by the feet of an intruder within the last few hours.

"Worse and worse!" thought the Resurrection Man. "And, by Satan! the trap has been raised!"

This was evident; for the brick which covered the iron ring in the masonry of the chimney, had not been restored to its place.

"I could not have left it so!" cried Tidkins, aloud: "no—it is impossible! Some one *has* been here!"

With almost frantic impatience he raised the trap, and descended into the subterranean.

Entering one of the cells,—not the same whence the Rattlesnake had stolen his treasure,—he raised a stone, and then almost shrank from glancing into the hollow thus laid open.

But mastering his fears,—those fears which owned the influence of avarice far more than that of danger or of crime,—he held the lantern over the hole, and plunged his eyes into its depth.

"Safe!—all safe—by God!" he exclaimed, as four or five canvass bags met his view.

Then, in order to convince himself of the reality of the presence of his treasure, he opened the bags one after the other, and feasted his sight upon their glittering contents.

"It can hardly be Banks who has been here," he mused to himself, as he restored the bags to their place of concealment, and then rolled the stone back into its setting: "nothing could escape the keenness of his scent! He would have pulled up all the pavement sooner than have missed what he came to look for. And then, too, he is not the man to leave the brick out of its place, so as to show the secret of the stone-trap to any other curious intruder that might find his way here. No—no: Master Banks would pay a second and a third visit to this place, if he felt sure of finding any thing concealed here; and he would leave every thing close and snug after each search. But some one *has* been here! Unless—and I might have done such a thing as to forget to replace the brick,—I *might* have done so;—and yet it is barely possible!" continued Tidkins, in deep perplexity, and almost as much alarmed as Robinson Crusoe was upon discovering the print of the human foot upon the sand of his island. "Then there is that damp mud, too—and the door that was open—and the lock that has been tampered with! But suppose the mud came from my own shoes the last time I was here? the place is very damp—and it mayn't have got dry. It might also have been myself that left the door open;—and as for the lock—it is an old one, and may begin to work badly. Besides—I remember—the last time I was here, I was in a deuce of a hurry: it was just before I went down to Banks's to see him settle that job with Kate Wilmot. So, after all—my fears may be all idle and vain! However, I shall send for Banks presently, when the Buffer comes again; and I'll precious soon tell by his sneaking old face whether he has been here, or not, during my absence!"

Thus reasoning against the feasibility of his fears,—as men often do in cases of doubt and uncertainty, and when they are anxious to persuade themselves of the groundlessness of their alarms,—Tidkins left the subterranean, and returned to his chamber, where he immediately went to bed.

But his fears *were* well founded: some one *had* visited the subterranean during the hours while he himself was occupied in escaping from Coldbath Fields' Prison.

That intruder was not, however, Banks—nor any one of the Resurrection Man's accomplices in crime.

CHAPTER CCXXIX.

THE WIDOW.

We must now return to that beautiful little villa, in the environs of Upper Clapton, to which we introduced our readers in the early portion of this history, and where we first found Eliza Sydney disguised in the garb of a man.

Nothing was altered in the appearance of that charming suburban retreat, either externally or internally,—unless it were that there were no dogs in the kennels nor horses in the stables, and that the elegant boudoir no longer displayed articles of male attire.

But the trees around were green with the verdure of Spring; the fields, stretching behind far as the eye could reach, were smiling and cultivated; and umbrageous was the circular grove that bounded the garden.

In the parlour on the ground-floor still hung the miniatures of Eliza and her dead brother—that brother whom she had personated with such fatal consequences to herself!

And now on the sofa in that parlour sate Eliza Sydney herself,—dressed in deep mourning.

She was pale—but beautiful as ever!

The snow-white widow's cap concealed her bright chesnut hair, save where the shining masses were parted, glossy and smooth, over her lofty and polished forehead.

The high black dress and plain collar covered the snowy whiteness of her neck, but still displayed the admirable *contours* of her bust.

Her countenance bore a somewhat melancholy but resigned expression; and the amiability of her soul shone in her large, soft, melting hazel eyes.

It was noon—about a week after the date of the incidents related in the preceding chapter.

Scarcely had the time-piece upon the mantel proclaimed the mid-day hour, when a carriage drove up to the front door of the villa.

A few moments elapsed; and three visitors were ushered into the parlour where Eliza awaited them.

These were the Prince and Princess of Montoni and Katherine Markham.

Eliza extended her hand with ingenuous courtesy towards Richard, saying, "Prince, no selfish feelings can prevent me from congratulating you on that proud position which your prowess and your virtues have achieved for yourself." Then, offering her hand to Isabella, she added, "Nor need I wait for a formal introduction to one whom I now see for the first time, but of whom I have heard so much that I am well prepared to become her friend—if her Highness will permit me."

There was something so sweet and touching—something so frank and sincere—in the manner of the exiled Grand-Duchess of Castelcicala, that Isabella's heart was instantaneously warmed towards her. Moreover, the young Princess felt all the noble generosity of that conduct on the part of one who had lost a throne by the events which had led to the happiness of herself and her husband, and which had achieved the exaltation of her parents.

Thus were those two beauteous creatures attracted to each other the instant they met; and Isabella, instead of receiving the out-stretched hand that was offered as the pledge of friendship, threw herself into Eliza's arms.

It was a touching picture,—the embrace of that charming bride and that scarcely less charming widow!

In due course Markham presented his sister to the exiled Grand-Duchess, who received her in the most affable and cordial manner.

When the first excitement of this meeting was over, and they were all seated, Eliza broke a temporary silence which ensued.

"The last time we met, Prince," she said, addressing herself to our hero, "no human foresight could have divined the great events that were so shortly to ensue—the brilliant destinies that were in waiting for yourself."

"And if there be one regret which I have experienced," observed Richard, "arising from those events, it is that they deprived an amiable lady of that throne which her virtues embellished. But the cause of Castelcicalan freedom outweighed all other considerations; and the duty imposed upon me by those adherents who made me their Chief, was stern, solemn, and imperative."

"You need not reproach yourself," exclaimed Eliza: "you need not entertain a moment's regret on my account! All that occurred was inevitable—and it was for the best. Castelcicala panted for freedom—and she had a right to claim it. This I may assert without injustice—without insult to the memory of my husband. And had no such reclamation been made by the people of Castelcicala—had no revolution occurred—had Angelo been more prudent, and less severe—Alberto would still at this moment be the sovereign of that country. For my husband had long been afflicted with a disease of the heart that was incurable, and that must inevitably have terminated in a sudden death. As I informed you in my letter of yesterday, he had scarcely reached the city of Vienna, where he was received as became his rank, and lodged in one of the imperial palaces, when he was taken ill, and in a few hours breathed his last. His misfortunes could not have accelerated an event which his physicians had previously seen to be near at hand—although this prescience was all along religiously concealed from me. You have therefore, Prince, naught wherewith to reproach yourself on that head."

"Your kind assurances are conveyed in a spirit worthy of your generous heart," said Richard;—and Isabella, who was greatly affected by the noble behaviour of Eliza, enthusiastically echoed her husband's sentiments.

"It was but a week ago," continued Eliza, "that I received the tidings of the late Grand-Duke's death. He had misunderstood me—he had suspected me—and we had parted in anger: nay—I had fled to save myself from his fury!"

"May I hope—and yet I dare not—that the generous behaviour of your Serene Highness towards me," observed Richard, "proved not the cause of that lamentable misunderstanding?"

"Oh! I should be grieved—deeply grieved, were such indeed the case!" exclaimed Isabella; "for Richard has made me acquainted with all the details of your Serene Highness's noble conduct towards him after he was taken prisoner at Ossore."

"I will explain all," said Eliza. "But, in the first place," she added, with a sweet smile, "let me entreat a favour of you all. You style me by that title which became mine when I was honoured with the hand of the late Grand-Duke Angelo, and which still is mine, did I choose to adopt it;—for the new Government has passed no decree to deprive me of it."

"Nor ever will!" exclaimed Richard, warmly.

"And yet I now value it not," continued the royal widow. "Thanks for that assurance, Prince;—but it is unnecessary. I was ever happier as Eliza Sydney, than as the Marchioness of Ziani, or as the Grand-Duchess of Castelcicala. As Eliza Sydney I left England: as Eliza Sydney I returned to England;—and by that name do I wish to be known. Nay—I implore you not to interrupt me: if you would please me—if you would do aught to contribute to my happiness—if you value my poor friendship,—that friendship, which, poor as it is, I so cordially offer to you all,—let me henceforth be Eliza Sydney, as I once was. When I came back three months ago to my native land, I re-entered this house—which is my own—with feelings of a far more peaceful happiness than those which I experienced when I first set foot as its mistress in the palace of Montoni. Here do I hope to pass the remainder of my days; and if you will sometimes come to cheer my solitude, I shall require no other source of felicity—no other society."

"We will visit you often, dearest Eliza—for so you will permit me to call you," said Isabella; "and you must come to our dwelling frequently—very frequently! It shall be the care of my husband, his dear sister Katherine, and myself, and also of the friends who dwell with us, to contribute to your happiness to the utmost of our power!"

Eliza pressed Isabella's hand, and smiled sweetly upon her and Katherine through the tears that stood upon her lashes.

"But I promised you an explanation of those events which led to my precipitate departure from Castelcicala," continued Eliza, after a short pause. "You must know that the loss which the ducal troops experienced at Ossore—chiefly through your prowess, Prince—overwhelmed my late husband with a fury which rendered him terrible to all around. He threatened the most deadly vengeance against the Constitutional prisoners, and was only persuaded by my entreaties and prayers to relinquish the extreme measures which he at first conceived against them. It was, I think, on the fourth day after you, Prince, left Montoni, disguised as an artist, and with a passport made out in a fictitious name, that the usher who had admitted you into the palace, and who, it appeared, had listened at the door of the room where our interview took place, betrayed the whole circumstances to the Grand-Duke. The Grand-Duke came immediately to my apartment, overwhelmed me with reproaches, and levelled the most unjust accusations against me. But I will not insult you nor your amiable bride by repeating all that the Duke said on that occasion. Never were suspicions more cruel: never was woman's conduct so thoroughly misunderstood—so unjustly interpreted! His Serene Highness commanded me to keep my own chamber—to consider myself a prisoner! An hour afterwards, Signor Bazzano contrived to obtain access to me, unperceived by the spies set to watch me. His uncle was, as I think I informed you when we met at Montoni, Prince, the Under-Secretary of State for the Home Department; and from that relative Bazzano had learnt the fearful tidings which he came to impart to me. It appeared that the Grand-Duke intended to appoint a Commission of Judges and Councillors of State to try me—*me*, his wife! All his former affection for me had suddenly changed, beneath the weight of his injurious suspicions, into the most unbounded hatred. I knew that he would form the Commission of men rather inclined to do the royal bidding than to investigate the entire matter with justice and impartiality. He was a prince who knew no other law than his own sovereign will! Alas! that was his failing; and it triumphed over all the better feelings of a mind naturally generous! Signor Bazzano also informed me that spies had been sent out all over the country to track you, Prince; and that your death, should you be captured, was determined upon. Fortunately, however, you escaped the pursuit of your foes!"

"And yet what danger must you have incurred!" exclaimed Isabella, gazing with tearful affection at her husband.

"Providence shielded you, dearest brother," murmured Katherine.

"Yes—Providence shielded him for its own wise and good purposes," added Eliza Sydney. "To continue the thread of my narrative, I must observe that the information brought me by the faithful Bazzano filled me with alarm. I already saw myself disgraced by an unjust verdict:—my life was even in danger. I was not compelled to implore Signor Bazzano to assist me to escape: he proposed the step as the only means of safety alike to myself and to him—for he was already endangered by the revelations of the usher, although the influence of his uncle had served to shield him from the immediate vengeance of the Grand-Duke. A post-chaise was procured by Bazzano that same afternoon; and I managed to escape from the palace, accompanied by Louisa—a faithful Englishwoman who has been in my service for some years. At Friuli Signor Bazzano met you, Prince, and gave you a timely warning, the nature of which you can now understand. For it was known that you had quitted Montoni, attended by a servant of dark complexion; and the spies sent after you were therefore led to inquire for *two persons* answering a certain description, and journeying together. Thence the recommendation to separate company, which Bazzano so wisely gave you; and perhaps to that circumstance of thus parting from your servant you each owed your safety. In reference to my own flight it only remains for me to say that we proceeded to Montecuculi, having left behind us at Friuli an impression that we were going in quite another direction. Arrived in safety at Montecuculi, we sent back the chaise to Montoni, and secured places in a public vehicle for the nearest town in the Roman States. Our perils were soon over:—we travelled day and night until we reached Leghorn, in Tuscany, whence we embarked on board a vessel bound for England. Shortly after my arrival here, the news of the Castelcicalan insurrection reached this country; and then I heard, Prince, that you were at the head of the Constitutionalists."

"But I did not violate my promise to you," observed Richard. "I pledged myself, on the occasion of our interview at Montoni, never to draw the hostile weapon in Castelcicala, save at the command of Alberto and in a just cause, or to relieve the Grand-Duchy from a foreign invader."

"Yes, Prince," returned Eliza; "you kept your word—for the Austrians were in the land when you became the champion of the Constitutionalists. I have now but a few words more to say in reference to myself. When the news of the battle of Montoni reached England, accompanied with the statement that the Grand-Duke Angelo had fled into the Roman States, I felt persuaded that he would repair to Vienna, the Austrian Emperor being his near relative. I accordingly wrote to my husband, addressing my letters to him in that city. I explained all that had occurred between yourself, Prince, and me at our interview immediately after the defeat of the Constitutionalists at Ossore: I told him how deeply he had wronged me with the most injurious suspicions; and I implored him to allow me to join him, and comfort him in his exile—in his misfortunes! The answer I received was satisfactory—was in itself all I could wish;—but it was accompanied by the tidings of his death! On the bed from which he never rose again, he recognised my innocence—he acknowledged his injustice—he besought me to forgive him!"

"Heaven be thanked that, through your goodness towards me, you were not doomed to undergo the additional torment of his dying enmity!" ejaculated the Prince, fervently.

"Rest tranquil on that head," returned Eliza. "I have now told you all that concerns myself. I may, however, observe that I should have sought an interview with you sooner, only I was unwilling to disturb the first few days of your happiness with your charming bride."

"Would that you had written to me the moment I arrived in England!" cried Richard. "The parents of Isabella would have been rejoiced to obtain your friendship! But you have not yet told us what has become of the faithful Mario Bazzano. I owe him a debt of deep gratitude; and if he be in this country still——"

"He *is* in England," interrupted Eliza; "and as I felt persuaded that you would comply with the request contained in my letter of yesterday, and come hither to-day, I wrote to Signor Bazzano to request his presence in the afternoon. We may, therefore, expect him shortly. He has grown very melancholy of late—I know not why: some secret care appears to oppress him! On our arrival in England, he hired apartments at the West-End; but shortly afterwards he encountered an English officer with whom he had formed an acquaintance some years ago in Montoni. It appears that this officer was travelling at that time in Italy: and during his temporary stay in the Castelcicalan capital, he and Signor Bazzano grew intimate. When they met at the West-End two or three months ago, this officer pressed Signor Bazzano to stay with him at some town near London, where his regiment is stationed. Signor Bazzano accepted the invitation; and for some weeks I saw nothing of him. Since his return to London he has not appeared to be the same being. It is true that I see him but seldom: still that change has not escaped my notice. He is fond of solitude and long lonely walks, in which he employs the greater portion of his time—save those hours which he devotes to the study of English by the aid of a master; and I can assure you that his progress in acquiring our language has been truly remarkable."

"Perhaps his melancholy is produced by absence from his native land," said Richard. "There can be no possible reason for him to remain in exile against his inclination; and should he wish to return to Italy, I will provide him with strong recommendations to the Grand-Duke."

"No—he does not desire to leave England," answered Eliza; "for I myself have questioned him upon that subject. I am rather inclined to believe that some motive of a more tender nature—some hopeless attachment, perhaps—has produced in him the alteration which I have seen and deplored. But he will be here shortly; and——"

Eliza was interrupted by a loud knock at the front door.

Katherine sighed: for the words of the royal widow had aroused within her gentle breast painful remembrances of her own romantic and apparently hopeless attachment!

The door opened; and Signor Bazzano was introduced.

Richard immediately hastened forward to greet him.

But—how strange!—a cry of wild delight burst from the lips of the handsome Castelcicalan, as his eyes encountered *one* particular countenance in that room;—and at the same moment Katherine clung convulsively to Isabella's arm, as if to save herself from falling from the sofa.

For Mario Bazzano was the hero of the young maiden's romantic adventures at Hounslow!

Katherine, with the ingenuous confidence of a sister, had revealed to her brother, and also to Isabella, the particulars of those strange meetings with the "handsome unknown," and had not attempted to disguise the impression made upon her heart by that individual,—an impression against which she had vainly endeavoured to struggle.

Thus, when those tokens of recognition were manifested alike by Mario Bazzano and Katherine Markham, both Richard and Isabella instantly divined the cause.

"Pardon me, your Highness," exclaimed the Castelcicalan officer, endeavouring to throw off the trammels of embarrassment, and speaking in excellent English; "but—that young lady—I think I have seen her——before——I——"

"Perhaps," interrupted the Prince, laughing. "At all events I will introduce her to you now—for she is my sister."

"Your sister, my lord!" cried Mario, in a tone which expressed some degree of vexation at this announcement—as if he dared not aspire to so near a relative of a personage of our hero's rank.

"Throw aside all ceremony with me, Bazzano," said Richard, shaking him warmly by the hand. "I am your debtor—deeply your debtor. You saved my life after the defeat of Ossore: your conduct was too generous—too noble ever to be lightly valued. But, say—was it near Hounslow that you have met my sister?"

And as he spoke, he glanced slily towards the blushing Katherine, who was half hiding her countenance behind Isabella.

"It was—it was!" exclaimed Mario. "And will your Highness be offended if I confess that your charming sister made a profound impression upon my mind? Although believing her to be only the daughter of the tenants of that farm-house near which I encountered her in her walks, I felt myself irresistibly attracted towards her! And,—but your Highness will laugh at my romantic dreams,—I determined to acquire the English language for her sake—that I might speak to her—that I might render myself intelligible to her!"

"We will give you an opportunity of convincing her of your proficiency in our native tongue, Mario," said the Prince, again smiling—but with kindness, and in a manner well calculated to reassure the young Italian officer, whom he led towards Katherine.

And, oh! how the bashful maiden's heart beat, and how crimson became her sweet countenance, as she felt her hand pressed in that of him who had now for some months occupied so large a portion of her thoughts!

"You guessed rightly as to the cause of Signor Bazzano's melancholy and altered appearance," whispered Isabella to Eliza, as they walked towards the window from which Richard was now gazing upon the prospect spread before the villa.

Then Mario and Katherine began to converse,—timidly and with frequent intervals of silence at first: but by degrees those intervals became shorter and shorter;—and at length the young officer found himself describing how he had felt deeply grieved at being unable to utter a word to her in her own tongue when they had met in the fields near the farm,—how he had torn himself away from the spot and returned to London to study English,—how he had gone back to Hounslow a few days afterwards, and vainly wandered about in those fields with the hope of seeing her,—how he conceived at length that she must purposely remain within the house to avoid him, the idea that she had left the neighbourhood never entering his mind,—how he had returned again to London and pursued his English studies under the romantic impression that they would some day serve him in respect to the attachment he had formed for her,—and how he paid frequent visits to the vicinity of the farm, and was at length almost compelled to abandon the hope of ever seeing her again.

All this he suddenly found himself telling her; and she as suddenly found herself listening to him with attention,—neither quite recollecting how the subject had first been touched upon.

Their pleasant *tête-a-tête* was at length interrupted by Eliza Sydney, who tapped them each on the shoulder, with the laughing assurance that the servant had already announced luncheon three times; and then Kate's countenance was again suffused with blushes, as she took the proffered arm of her lover to repair to the apartment where an elegant collation was served up.

The afternoon passed speedily away; and all were so happy that they were in no haste to break up such a pleasant party. Eliza accordingly insisted that her guests should remain to dinner—an invitation which was accepted.

Indeed, it was eleven that night ere the Prince's carriage and Mario's horse were ordered round to the door.

And when the young officer separated from Katharine, it was not without an assurance from her brother that he would always be a welcome guest at Markham Place.

Great was the surprise, but not less the joy, of Ellen Monroe, when Katherine, on her return home and ere the two young ladies sought their couch, made her friend acquainted with the elucidation of the mystery of "the handsome stranger."

CHAPTER CCXXX.

BETHLEM HOSPITAL.

What contrasts does mortal existence present to view!

While some are joyous and happy in one place, others are overwhelmed with sorrow and affliction elsewhere! At the same moment that the surgeon ushers a new being into life, the hand of the executioner cuts short the days of another. *Here* the goblet sparkles with the ruby wine—*there* the lip touches the poisoned glass of suicide:—in *this* abode a luxurious banquet is spread upon the table—in *that* the wretched inmate has not a crust to stay the cravings of famine!

Thus was it that while the hostess and the guests were blithe and happy in the villa near Clapton, a painful scene was in process of enactment elsewhere.

It was about five o'clock on that same evening when a cab stopped at the prisoners' gate of Newgate; and from the vehicle stepped a tall, powerfully-built, and rather good-looking man dressed in plain clothes. He was accompanied by a Superintendent and Serjeant of Police.

They were immediately admitted into the lobby of the gaol; and the turnkey, after bestowing upon them a nod of recognition, said, "You needn't tell me to guess what you're come about. So the youngster is to go over, then—after all?"

"Yes," replied the tall man in plain clothes. "The Secretary of State's warrant was sent down here about an hour ago. I suppose Cope is in?"

"Step into the office, Mr. Busby, and see," answered the turnkey.

The tall man, who responded to the name of Busby, accordingly passed from the lobby into the governor's office.

"Any thing new?" asked the turnkey, rubbing his nose with the end of the massive emblem of his office, and accosting the two police authorities, who had seated themselves on the bench facing the gate.

"Not that I know on," returned the Serjeant; "leastways nothink partickler—unless it is that my Superintendent here is doing someot in the littererry line, and writing a book about Great Criminals, and Police, and Prisons, and all that there kind of thing."

"You don't say so?" ejaculated the turnkey.

"Yes, sir—Mr. Crisp is quite right," said the Superintendent, pompously: "I *ham* getting up a work on them subjects; but my official po-sition will compel me to publish it enonnymusly, as they say. And while we're here, Crisp, we may as well take down a few notes—for I must inform you," continued the Superintendent, addressing himself once more to the turnkey, "that my friend and subordingate Mr. Crisp is helping me in this here labour of love."

"Well, sir," returned the gaol functionary, "any information that I can give you, I shall be most happy to furnish you with, I'm sure."

"Thank'ee kindly," said the Superintendent. "Now, Crisp, out with your note-book, and fall to. Busby will be half an hour or so in the office. Pray, sir, what may be the anniwal average of prisoners, male and female, in Newgate?"

"About three thousand males and eight hundred females," answered the turnkey.

"Put that down, Crisp. I suppose in the males you includes boys, and in the females you comprises gals?"

"Certainly," was the reply.

"Put that down, Crisp. Now what's the state of discipline here?" asked the Superintendent. "I've heerd a good deal about it, in course; but I'd rayther have it direct from a 'ficial source."

"Why, there isn't much to say on that point," returned the functionary thus appealed to. "We let the prisoners have pretty much their own way: they gamble, play at ball, fight, swear, sing, and lark in the wards just as they like."

"Put that down, Crisp. It's a blessing to think of the state of freedom one enjoys even in the gaols of this enlightened and liberal nation."

"To be sure it is," said the turnkey. "The young thieves consider Newgate to be a capital school for improvement in their profession: when they're at chapel, they're always practising pick-pocketing on each-other."

"What's bred in the bone will never go out of the flesh," observed the Superintendent. "But the poor creeturs must have some diwersion. Put that down, Crisp."

"Ah! Newgate has seen some rum things in its time," moralised the turnkey. "It has been a felon's gaol for well-nigh seven hundred years."

"Has it, though?" cried the Superintendent. "Now, then, Crisp—put that down."

"And ever since I first come here," continued the turnkey, "there have been constant *Reports* drawn up about the state of discipline; but I never see that any change follows."

"Put that down, Crisp. When *my* book is published, my good fellow, you'll jist see what the world will say about a change! There's no need of change—and that I'll undertake to prove. Newgate is the very palace of prisons. Lord bless us! it would do half the Aldermen themselves good to pass a few days in such a pleasant place."

"Sometimes we have a few discontented fellows here that don't like to associate with the rest," proceeded the turnkey; "and then they ask to be thrown into solitary cells."

"Put that down, Crisp. I suppose they're always gratified in their wishes?" asked the Superintendent.

"Oh! always," replied the turnkey. "But the worst of all is that the chaplain here is nothing more or less than a regular spy upon the governor and the officials, and constantly reports to the Home Office every thing that occurs."

"Put that down, Crisp. Such conduct is shameful; and I wonder the Gaol Committee of Aldermen don't take the matter up."

"So they will," rejoined the turnkey. "But here comes Busby."

And, as he spoke, the tall man in plain clothes re-entered the lobby.

"All right?" asked the Superintendent.

"Yes. We'll take him over at once," was the reply.

The turnkey stepped into a passage leading to the interior of the gaol, and gave some instructions to a colleague who was stationed there.

A few minutes afterwards Henry Holford, dressed in his own clothes, and not in the prison-garb, was led into the lobby by the official to whom the turnkey had spoken.

The youth was well in health, and by no means cast down in spirits. His face, at no period remarkable for freshness of colour, was less pallid than it ever before had been. There were, however, a certain apathy and indifference in his manner which might have induced a superficial observer to conclude that his reason was in reality affected; but a careful examination of the expression of his countenance and a few minutes' study of his intelligent dark eyes, would have served to convince even the most sceptical that, however morbid his mind might for an interval have become, that excitement or disease had passed away, and he was now as far removed from insanity as the most rational of God's creatures.

"Come, young man," said Mr. Busby, with great kindness of manner, as if he were endeavouring to conciliate an individual whom he actually deemed to be of disturbed intellects; "you are going along with me—and I'll take you to a nice house with a pleasant garden, and where you'll be well treated."

"I am at no loss to imagine the place to which you allude," said Holford, an expression of slyness curling his lip. "Better Bedlam than Newgate."

"He's no more mad than me, Crisp," whispered the Superintendent to the Serjeant.

"Not a bit, sir," was the reply.

"You may put that down, Crisp," continued the Superintendent, still speaking aside to his subordinate. "It will all do to go into our report to the Home Secretary. How capital that turnkey allowed himself to be pumped by me, to be sure! Don't you think I did it very well?"

"Very well, sir, indeed," returned Crisp. "But I introduced the subject for you, by saying that you was okkipied in writing a book."

"Good hidear, that, Crisp," rejoined the Superintendent. "The turnkey little thought we was spies, while he blowed up about the chaplain."

"In course you'll make out Newgate a horrid place, sir?" said Crisp.

"In course I shall," answered the Superintendent, emphatically; "'cos it'll please the Home Secretary. But there's Busby a-calling after us."

This was indeed the case; for while the two police-officers were thus engaged in the interchange of their own little private sentiments, Mr. Busby had conducted Holford to the cab, and had ensconced himself therein by the side of the prisoner.

The Superintendent followed them into the vehicle; and, at the suggestion of Busby, who declared in a whisper to that functionary that three men were not needed to take care of one boy, the farther services of Crisp were dispensed with.

And now the cab rolled rapidly along the Old Bailey, turned down Ludgate Hill, thence into Bridge Street, and over Blackfriars Bridge, in its way to Bethlem.

How strange to Holford appeared the busy, bustling streets, and that river—"the silent highway"—on whose breast all was life and animation,—after the seclusion of several weeks in Newgate!

But—ah! did he not now behold those scenes for the last time? would not he thenceforth become dead to the world? was he not about to be immured in a living tomb?

Never—never more would the echoes of the myriad voices of the great city meet his ears! He was on his way to the sepulchre of all earthly hopes—all mundane enjoyments—all human interests!

Henceforth must that bright sun, which now steeped pinnacle, dome, tower, and river in a flood of golden lustre, visit him with its rays only through the grated window of a mad-house!

For the last time was he crossing that bridge—for the last time did he behold that crowded thoroughfare leading to the obelisk:—on the gay shops, the rapid vehicles, and the moving multitudes, was he also now gazing for the last time!

The last time! Oh! those three monosyllables formed a terrible prelude—an awful introduction to an existence of monotony, gloom, and eternal confinement! Ah! could he recall the events of the last few weeks!—But, no—it was impossible:—the die was cast—the deed was done—and justice had settled his destiny!

The last time! And he was so young—so very young to be compelled to murmur those words to himself. The sky was so bright—the air of the river was so refreshing—the scene viewed from the bridge was so attractive, that he could scarcely believe he was really doomed never to enjoy them more! And there was a band of music playing in the road—at the door of a public-house! What was the air? "*Britons never shall be slaves!*" Merciful

God!—he was now a slave of the most abject description! The convict in the hulks knew that the day of release must come—the transported felon might enjoy the open air, and the glorious sun, and the cheering breeze:—but for *him*—for Henry Holford—eternal confinement within four walls!

The last time! Oh! for the pleasures of life that were now to be abandoned for ever! For the last time did his eyes behold those play-bills in the shop windows—and he was so fond of the theatre! For the last time did he see that omnibus on its way to the Zoological Gardens—and he was so fond of those Gardens! Ah! it was a crushing—a stifling—a suffocating sensation to know that in a few minutes more huge doors, and grated windows, and formidable bolts and bars must separate him from that world which had so many attractions for one of his age!

Yes:—he now beheld those houses—those shops—those streets—those crowds—those vehicles—*for the last time*!

And now the cab has reached the iron gate in front of Bethlem Hospital.

There was a temporary delay while the porter opened that gate.

Holford looked hastily from the windows; and his lips were compressed as if to subdue his feelings.

Again the vehicle rolled onward, and in a few moments stopped at the entrance of the huge mad-house.

The Superintendent alighted: Holford was directed to follow; and Busby came close after him.

The great folding doors leading into the handsome hall of the establishment stood open:—Holford paused on the threshold for an instant—cast one rapid but longing look behind him—*a last look*—and then walked with firm steps to a waiting-room commanding a view of the grounds at the back of the building.

On the table lay a book in which visitors to the institution are compelled to enter their names and places of abode. Holford turned over the leaves—carelessly at first; but when he caught sight of several great names, he experienced a momentary glow of pride and triumph, as he murmured to himself, "*How many will come hither on purpose to feast their eyes on me!*"

Busby, who was one of the principal officers connected with the establishment, of which Sir Peter Laurie is the intelligent and justly-honoured President, left the room for a short time, Holford remaining in the charge of the Superintendent. When the first-mentioned functionary returned, it was to conduct the youth to his future place of abode.

Busby led the way through a long and well ventilated passage, in which about a dozen miserable-looking men were lounging about.

Holford cast a glance of ill-concealed terror upon their countenances, and read *madness* in their wild eyes. But, to his astonishment, he beheld no horrifying and revolting sights,—no wretches writhing in chains—no maniacs crowning themselves with straws—no unhappy beings raging in the fury of insanity. He had hitherto imagined that madhouses were shocking places—and Bethlem worse than all: but distressing though the spectacle of human reason dethroned and cast down must ever be, it was still a great relief to the young man to find, upon inquiry of the officer, that there were no scenes throughout the vast establishment one tittle worse than that which he now beheld.

On one side of that long passage were the cells, or rather little rooms, in which the inmates of that department of the asylum slept, each being allowed a separate chamber. The beds were comfortable and scrupulously cleanly in appearance; and the officer informed Holford that the linen was changed very frequently.

From the other side of the passage, or wide corridor, opened the rooms in which the meals were served up; and here we may observe that the food allowed the inmates of Bethlem Hospital is both excellent in quality and abundant in quantity.

There was a very tall officer,—indeed, all the male keepers throughout the institution are tall, strong, and well-built men,—walking slowly up and down the passage of which we are speaking; and when any of the unhappy lunatics addressed him, he replied to them in a kind and conciliatory manner, or else good-naturedly humoured them by listening with apparent interest and attention to the lamentable outpourings of their erratic intellects.

It is delightful to turn from those descriptions of ill-disciplined prisons and of vicious or tyrannical institutions, which it has been our duty to record in this work,—it is delightful to turn from such pictures to an establishment which, though awakening many melancholy thoughts, nevertheless excites our admiration and demands our unbounded praise, as a just tribute to the benevolence, the wisdom, and the humanity which constitute the principles of its administration.

Oh! could the great—the philanthropic Pinel rise from the cold tomb and visit this institution of which we are speaking,—he would see ample proof to convince him that, while on earth, he had not lived nor toiled in vain.

Connected with the male department of Bethlem, there are a library and a billiard-room, for the use of those who are sufficiently sane to enjoy the mental pleasures of the one or the innocent recreation of the other. The books in the library are well selected: they consist chiefly of the works of travellers and voyagers, naval and military histories and biographies, and the leading cheap periodicals—such as *The London Journal*, Chambers's *Information for the People*, Knight's *Penny Magazine*, &c.

Communicating with the female department of the asylum, is a music-room,—small, but elegantly fitted up, and affording a delightful means of amusement and solace to many of the inmates of that division of the building.

When these attentions to the comforts and even happiness,—for Bethlem Hospital exhibits many examples where "ignorance is bliss,"—of those who are doomed to dwell within its walls, are contrasted with the awful and soul-harrowing spectacle which its interior presented not very many years ago, it is impossible to feel otherwise than astonished and enraptured at the vast improvements which civilisation has introduced into the modern management of the insane!

But let us return to Henry Holford.

We left him threading the long passage which formed a portion of his way towards the criminal department of the hospital,—that department which was thenceforth to be his abode!

It may be readily imagined that he gazed anxiously and intently on all he saw,—that not a single object of such new, strange, and yet mournful interest to him escaped his observation.

Suddenly he beheld a man leaning against the wall, and staring at him as he passed in a wild and almost ferocious manner. There seemed to be something peculiar in that poor creature's garb:—Holford looked again—and that second glance made him shudder fearfully!

The man had on a strait-waistcoat,—a strong garment made of bed-ticking, and resembling a smock that was too small for him. The sleeves were *beneath*, instead of *outside*, and were sewn to the waistcoat—a contrivance by which the arms of the unhappy wretch were held in a necessary restraint, but without the infliction of pain.

"Merciful God!" thought Holford, within himself; "if a residence within these walls should drive me really mad! Oh! if I should ever come to such an abject state as *that*!"

His miserable reflections were strangely interrupted.

One of the lunatics abruptly drew near and addressed him in a wild and incoherent tone.

"The nation is falling," he said; "and the worst of it is that it does not know that it is falling! It is going down as rapidly as it can; and I only can save it! Yes—the nation is falling—falling——"

Holford felt a cold and shuddering sensation creep over him; for these manifestations of a ruined intellect struck him forcibly—fearfully,—as if they were an omen—a warning—a presage of the condition to which he himself must speedily come!

He was relieved from the farther importunities of the poor lunatic, by the sudden opening of a door, by which Busby admitted him into a narrow passage with two gratings, having a small space between them. The inner grating was at the bottom of a stone staircase, down which another keeper speedily came in obedience to a summons from Busby's lips.

This second keeper now took charge of Henry Holford, whom he conducted up the stairs to a gallery entered by a wicket in an iron grating, and divided by a similar defence into two compartments.

One of these compartments was much larger than the other, and contained many inmates and many rooms: the smaller division had but six chambers opening from it.

The entire gallery was, however, devoted to those persons who, having committed dread deeds, had been acquitted on the ground of insanity.

It was to the lesser compartment that Holford was assigned.

And now he was an inmate of the criminal division of Bethlem Hospital,—he who was as sane as his keeper, and who could, therefore, the more keenly feel, the more bitterly appreciate the dread circumstances of his present condition!

And who were his companions? Men that had perpetrated appalling deeds—horrible murders—in the aberration of their intellects!

Was this the triumph that he had achieved by his regicide attempt? had he earned that living tomb as the sacrifice to be paid for the infamous notoriety which he had acquired?

Oh! to return to his pot-boy existence—to wait on the vulgar and the low—to become once more a menial unto menials,—rather than stay in that terrible place!

Or else to be confined for life in a gaol where no presence of madness might tend to drive him mad also!—Yes—that were preferable—oh! far preferable to the soul-harrowing scene where man appeared more degraded and yet more formidable than the brutes!

Yes—yes: transportation—chains—the horrors of Norfolk Island,—any thing—any thing rather than immurement in the criminal wards of Bethlem!

Vain and useless regrets for the past!—futile and ineffective aspirations for the future!

CHAPTER CCXXXI.

MR. GREENWOOD AND MR. VERNON.

It was in the middle of April, and about two o'clock in the afternoon, when the Honourable Gilbert Vernon knocked at the door of Mr. Greenwood's mansion in Spring Gardens.

He was immediately admitted by a footman in livery; and Filippo, the Italian valet, who was lounging in the hall at the moment, conducted him to the elegant drawing-room where the Member for Rottenborough was seated.

As soon as Filippo had retired, Mr. Vernon said in a somewhat impatient tone, as he fixed his large grey eyes in a scrutinising manner upon Greenwood's countenance, "May I request to know, with as little delay as possible, the reason that has induced you to demand this interview?"

"Sit down, Mr. Vernon," was the reply; "and listen to me calmly. In January last I met you accidentally in London; and you implored me not to breathe to a soul the fact that you were in this country."

"And if I had private—urgent motives for so acting, Mr. Greenwood," exclaimed Vernon, "I cannot suppose that it cost you any effort to maintain my secret."

"I set out by requesting you to listen to me attentively," returned the Member of Parliament, with the coolness of a man who knows he is dictating to one completely in his power.

"Proceed," said Vernon, biting his lip. "I will not again interrupt you: that is—unless———"

"I need scarcely state that I *did* keep your secret," continued Greenwood, without appearing to notice the hesitation with which his visitor gave the promise of attention. "You shortly afterwards called upon me to request a loan, which it was not convenient for me to advance at the moment. On that occasion you reiterated your request of secrecy relative to your presence in London. I renewed my pledge of silence—and I kept it; but I felt convinced that there were some cogent reasons which prompted that anxiety for concealment. Knowing much of your circumstances, I instituted inquiries in a certain quarter; and I learnt that Lord Ravensworth was dying—dying gradually—in a most mysterious manner—and of a disease that baffled all the skill of his physicians. I also ascertained that he was a slave to the use of a particular tobacco which you—his brother—had *kindly* sent him from the East!"

"Mr. Greenwood!" ejaculated Vernon, his face assuming so dark—so foreboding—so ferocious an expression that the Member of Parliament saw his dart had been levelled with the most accurate aim.

"Pray, listen, Mr. Vernon!" said Greenwood, playing with his watch-chain in a calm and quiet manner, as if he were discoursing upon the most indifferent topics. "Having made those discoveries,—which, indeed, were so generally known in the fashionable world, that the most simple inquiry induced any West-End gossip or newsmonger of the Clubs to descant upon them,—I began to view them in a particular light———"

"Mr. Greenwood," cried Vernon, starting from his seat, his countenance red with indignation, "do you pretend for one moment to insinuate that I—I, the brother of the late Lord Ravensworth———"

"I insinuate nothing," interrupted the Member, with the most provoking calmness: "but I will presently explain to you in broad terms, if you choose, the *facts* of which I am *convinced*. I promise you that you will do well to hear me patiently."

"But is my character to suffer by the scandal of superannuated dowagers and the tattle of Club *quid nuncs*?" demanded Vernon, rage imparting a terrible emphasis to his deep-toned voice.

"Your character has in no way suffered with those parties," answered Greenwood. "All that they relate is mere idle gossip, without an object or an aim. *They* have no suspicion: circumstances have aroused none in *their* minds. But when I heard all that they state as mere matter of conversation, *I* viewed it in a different light, because my suspicions *were* aroused by the knowledge of your presence in England, and your anxiety to conceal that fact. And, if any thing were wanting to confirm those suspicions, the company in which I saw you the evening before last——"

"Ah! you saw me—with some one?" cried Vernon, hastily, and for the moment thrown off his guard.

"Yes: I saw you in conversation with a man of the most desperate character—a man who only last month escaped from the Middlesex House of Correction——"

"Then, in a word, Mr. Greenwood," interrupted Vernon, subduing his vexation and rage with a desperate mental effort, and resuming his seat, "how came you to discover my address in Stamford Street? and wherefore did you yesterday write to me to call on you to-day?"

"I overheard you say to Anthony Tidkins, '*The day after to-morrow I shall proceed to Ravensworth Hall, as if I had only just returned to England in consequence of letters sent to Beyrout to announce to me my brother's death; and you will join me in the capacity agreed upon.*' This I overheard you say, Mr. Vernon," continued Greenwood, fixing upon his visitor a glance of triumphant assurance; "and I then felt convinced that all my previous suspicions were well founded! I accordingly followed you when you separated from that individual who bears the odious name of *the Resurrection Man*; and I traced you to your lodgings in Stamford Street."

"But for what purpose? with what view?" demanded Vernon, who saw that he was completely in Greenwood's power.

"I will come to that presently," was the calm reply. "You do not even give me credit for the delicacy with which I acted in bringing about this interview?"

"Delicacy!" repeated Vernon, his lip curling haughtily.

"Yes—delicacy," added Greenwood. "I knew not whether you passed at your lodging by your proper name; and therefore I would not call in person to inquire for you—fearful of betraying you."

"But I *do* pass there in my proper name," said Vernon; "for the old widow who keeps the house nursed me in my infancy, and I can rely upon her."

"Thank you for this admission, Mr. Vernon," rejoined Greenwood, complacently: "wherever reliance is to be placed, it is clear that there is something which might be betrayed. You have confirmed the strength of my previous convictions."

"Do not think that I made that admission unguardedly," said Vernon, nettled by Greenwood's manner. "No: I see that I am in your power—I admit it; and therefore I no longer attempted to mislead you."

"And you acted wisely," returned Greenwood. "It were far better for you to have me as a friend, than as an enemy. But, as I was ere now observing, it was to avoid the chance of betraying you that I sent my faithful valet, Filippo, to loiter about Stamford Street last evening, and slip my note into your hands. I described your person to him—and he executed my commission well."

"Then you have no inimical motive in seeking me out—in telling me all that you suspect?" said Vernon, looking suspiciously at Greenwood from beneath his dark brows.

"Not the slightest! How can I have such a motive?" exclaimed Greenwood. "A secret falls in my way—and I endeavour to profit by it. That is all."

"I scarcely comprehend you," observed the guilty man, his countenance again becoming overcast.

"In one word, Mr. Vernon," continued Greenwood, emphatically, "you come to England privately—upon some secret and mysterious errand. Still you pass by your own name at your lodging. That circumstance to superficial observers might seem to involve a strange want of precaution. To me it appears a portion of your plan, and the result of a judicious calculation. You return privately to England, I say—but you retain your own name at a place where you know it will not be betrayed unless circumstances should peremptorily demand its revelation; and then, should certain suspicions attach themselves to you, you would say boldly and feasibly also—'*It is true that I came to England to live quietly; but I attempted no disguise—I assumed no fictitious name.*' Ah! I can penetrate further into the human heart than most people: my experience of the world is of no common order."

"It would seem not," said Vernon: "especially as *you* also appear to know Anthony Tidkins, since you recognised him in my society the other night."

"There are few men at all notorious for their good or evil deeds, in this great city, who are unknown to me," observed Greenwood, calmly. "But permit me to continue. You are here—in this country, while really deemed to be abroad—under circumstances of no ordinary mystery; your brother smokes the tobacco you so kindly sent him—*and dies*; your associate the Resurrection Man and you are now about to proceed to Ravensworth Hall—doubtless convinced that you have allowed a sufficient interval to elapse since your brother's death in the middle of February, to maintain the belief—where such belief suits your purposes—that you have only just had time to receive that intelligence in the East, and thence return to England. Can you deny one tittle of my most reasonable conjectures?"

"Greenwood, you are an extraordinary man," cried Vernon, affecting an ease which he did not feel and a sudden familiarity which he did not like. "Did I not before say that I would no longer attempt to mislead you? And I am willing to secure you as my friend."

"You now speak to the point. I candidly confess that I have told you all I suspect or know concerning yourself and your affairs," proceeded Greenwood; "and I am perfectly indifferent as to whether you choose to enlighten me farther, or not. Doubtless you have some defined course to pursue; or else the aid of the Resurrection Man would be unnecessary. But whether you hope to inherit largely under your deceased brother's will; or whether you can establish claims that may benefit you, in spite of the existence of the infant heir of Ravensworth, who was born a month ago——"

"Ah! the birth of that heir has well-nigh destroyed all my hopes!" interrupted Vernon, again rising from his seat. "But, tell me—what do you require at my hands? how am I to secure you as my friend? how am I to purchase your continued silence concerning all you have divined or now know?"

"With money," replied Greenwood: "with that article which buys every thing in this world!"

"Money!—I have none!" exclaimed Vernon. "But ere long——"

"Stay!" cried Greenwood: "tell me nothing of your schemes—nothing of your projects! I would rather remain in ignorance of the designs you may have in view; for, look you, Mr. Vernon,—though, between ourselves, I am not over nice in some matters, as you may probably suppose from the fact that Anthony Tidkins is known to me, as well as from my readiness to receive a bribe to ensure my secrecy in respect to your proceedings,—yet I do not care if I tell you that I shudder when I think of the lengths to which you have already gone—to which, perhaps, you are still prepared to go!"

"Was it to read me a moral lecture that you sought this interview?" demanded the Honourable Gilbert Vernon, with a contemptuous curl of the lip.

"No—far from that!" responded Greenwood. "And therefore enough of this style of discourse on my part. Still the observations were not unnecessary; for they serve to explain the relative positions in which we stand. *You* have already committed *one* fearful crime—and I know it: perhaps you meditate *another*—and I suspect it. But it is not for me to betray you—nor to reason with you:—I am not inclined to do either—provided you are grateful."

"Mr. Greenwood," said Vernon, speaking thickly between his set teeth, "you shall have a noble reward, if you religiously keep my secret."

"Such is the understanding at which I was desirous to arrive," observed Greenwood.

Gilbert Vernon then took his leave, in no very enviable state of mind under the conviction that his crimes had placed him so entirely in the power of such an extortioner as the Member for Rottenborough.

We must observe, ere we conclude the chapter, that Filippo, the Italian valet, had listened at the door of the drawing-room where this interview took place; and that not a syllable of the whole conversation was lost upon him.

In the evening Filippo obtained leave of absence for a few hours; and he availed himself of this license to repair to the villa in which Eliza Sydney dwelt.

CHAPTER CCXXXII.

SCENES AT RAVENSWORTH HALL.

It was about five o'clock in the afternoon of the same day on which the interview between George Montague Greenwood and the Honourable Gilbert Vernon took place, that a post-chaise advanced rapidly through Ravensworth Park, towards the Hall.

In a few minutes it stopped at the principal entrance of the mansion; and the Honourable Mr. Vernon alighted.

Quentin, who received him, made some inquiry in a respectful tone concerning his baggage.

"My valet will be here in the evening with my trunks," replied Vernon, abruptly.

Thus, without committing himself by a positive assertion, he led Quentin and the other domestics who were present to infer that he had only just arrived in England, and had left his servant in London to clear his baggage at the Custom-House.

Quentin bowed as he received that answer, and hastened to conduct Mr. Vernon to the drawing-room where Lady Ravensworth was seated.

The widow and her brother-in-law now met for the first time.

Vernon saw before him a young and beautiful woman, very pale, and with a countenance whose expression denoted much suffering—mental rather than physical. It was true that she had only lately become a mother,—that little more than a month had elapsed since she had given birth to an heir to the proud title and broad lands of Ravensworth;—and though the pallor of her face was the natural consequence of so recent an event, yet the physical languor which usually follows also, had given place to a nervousness of manner—a restlessness of body—a rapid wandering of the eyes—and an occasional firm compression of the lips, which indicated an uneasy mind.

Alas! upon that woman's soul lay a crime, heavy and oppressive as a weight of lead! The voice of the murdered Lydia was ever ringing in her ears;—the countenance of the murdered Lydia was ever staring her in the face—ghastly, distorted, and livid in appearance;—the form of the murdered Lydia was ever standing before her! At night the spectre placed itself between the opening of the curtains, and seemed more palpable—more horrible—more substantial in the hours of darkness.

No wonder, then, that her mind was restless—that her manner was nervous—and that her looks were wandering and unsettled!

But let us continue the thread of our narrative, taking it up at the moment when the Honourable Gilbert Vernon entered the apartment where Lady Ravensworth rose to receive him.

Extending her hand towards him, she said, "Welcome to this mansion: it is kind of you to answer so speedily in person the letters which it was my painful duty to address to you at Beyrout."

These words reassured Vernon on one important point: they proved that letters *had been* sent, conveying the intelligence of his brother's death.

"Accept my gratitude for the cordiality with which you receive me, sister—for such you will permit me to call you," answered Vernon; "and believe me——. But, good God! what ails you? what is the matter, Lady Ravensworth? You are ill—you——"

"That voice—that voice!" shrieked Adeline, staggering towards a chair, on which she sank helplessly. "Oh! Mr. Vernon——"

Gilbert was astounded at the affrighted manner and strange ejaculations of his sister-in-law;—but, seeing that she was on the point of fainting, he snatched from the table a small bottle of powerful scent, and handed it to her.

She inhaled the perfume, which acted as a slight restorative; but it was chiefly to the natural vigour of her mind, and to the imperious necessity in which dread circumstances had placed her of constantly maintaining as much command over herself as possible, that she was indebted for her almost immediate recovery from the state into which sudden surprise and profound alarm had thrown her.

"Perhaps your ladyship is desirous that I should withdraw?" said Vernon. "There may be something in my countenance—my manner—or my voice that recalls to your mind painful reminiscences of my lately-departed brother:—it is natural that you should experience these feelings;—and I will leave you for the present."

"No, Mr. Vernon—stay!" exclaimed Adeline, in a tone which denoted the most painful excitement and agitation.

"Compose yourself, then: attempt not to pursue the conversation immediately," said Gilbert; "for as—with your permission—it is my intention to become your guest for a few weeks——"

"My guest!" repeated Adeline, with a shudder.

"Really, my dear sister," exclaimed Vernon, somewhat impatiently; "I am at a loss to understand the meaning of this excitement on your part. It is *not* caused by those reminiscences to which I ere now alluded: it begins to assume the aspect of aversion towards myself. Pardon me if I speak thus plainly; but if I be indeed hateful to you—if slanderous tongues have wronged me in your estimation—if even my own brother were cruel enough to malign me to his wife——"

"Mr. Vernon," interrupted Adeline, with a kind of feverish haste, "your conjectures will never lead you to discover the true cause of that agitation which I could not conquer, and which has offended you. The moment you addressed me, I was seized with a strange surprise—a wild alarm; and those feelings still influence me to some extent,—for methinks that I have heard your voice before!"

And she fixed her eyes in a penetrating manner upon his countenance.

"It may be," answered Vernon, quailing not beneath that look—for he had so desperate a part to play at Ravensworth Hall, that he knew how much depended upon a self-command and a collectedness of ideas that might avert suspicion,—"it may be, sister, that some years ago—ere I left England—we met in those circles in which we both move by right of birth and social position; and, although I do not remember that I ever had the pleasure of seeing you until now, still such a meeting may have occurred, and your mind may have retained certain impressions——"

"No, Mr. Vernon," again interrupted Adeline; "that surmise—even if correct—will not account for the cause of my agitation. To speak candidly, my impression was—and still *is*,—and yet," she added, suddenly recollecting herself, "if that impression should be indeed erroneous, I should insult you—insult you grossly by explaining it——"

"Proceed, dear sister," said Vernon, gaining additional assurance, in proportion as Lady Ravensworth hesitated. "State to me candidly the impression which you received; and I will as candidly answer you."

"Yes—I *will* tell you the reason of that excitement which nearly overcame me," cried Adeline, whose suspicions were robbed of much of their strength by the calm and apparently open manner of her brother-in-law.

"And believe me when I declare that I shall readily pardon you, however injurious to myself may be the impression my voice has unfortunately made upon you. I can make ample allowances for one who has lately lost a beloved husband, and whose anxieties have been increased by the duties of maternity," added Gilbert.

"In one word, then, Mr. Vernon," continued Adeline, "it struck me that on a certain evening—in the month of February—I heard your voice,—yes, your voice in conversation with another person, in a ruined cottage which stands on the verge of the Ravensworth estate."

And, as she spoke, she again studied his countenance with the most earnest attention.

Desperate was the effort which the guilty man exerted over the painful excitement of feeling which this declaration produced within him:—in a moment he recalled to mind all the particulars of his meeting with the

Resurrection Man at the ruined lodge; and he also remembered that he had lost on the same occasion the scrap of paper on which was written the address of his terrible agent in crime. But he *did* succeed in maintaining a calm exterior:—steadily he met the searching glance fixed upon him;—and though his heart beat with fearful emotions, not a muscle of his countenance betrayed the agitation that raged within his breast.

"My dear sister," said Vernon, in a cool and collected tone, "you are labouring under a most extraordinary delusion. Think you that there is not another voice in the world like mine? Believe me, had I been in this country at the time to which you allude, I should have only felt too much rejoiced to have paid my respects to you at an earlier period than the present."

Adeline listened to the deep tones of that voice which now rolled upon her ear like a perpetuation of the echoes of the one which she had heard in the ruins;—and she was still staggered at the resemblance! She also remembered that, in spite of the darkness of the night, she had on that occasion caught a glimpse of the tall and somewhat stout form which had passed near her, and which she knew not to have been that of the Resurrection Man, whom she had since seen:—and she was bewildered more and more.

But the calmness with which Vernon denied the circumstance of being in England at that time,—the steady, honest manner with which he declared that she was labouring under a delusion in identifying his voice with the one she had heard in the ruined lodge,—and the absence of any motive which she could conjecture for his maintaining his presence in this country (even were he really here at the period alluded to) so profoundly secret,—these arguments staggered her still more than even her contrary suspicions.

On his side, Vernon was congratulating himself on the evident embarrassment of his sister-in-law; and he felt convinced that the sound of his voice alone—and nothing that had passed between him and Tidkins in the ruined cottage—had produced an impression upon her.

"You will then forgive me for a momentary suspicion that was injurious to you?" said Adeline, after a short pause, and now adopting the only course open to her in the matter.

"I have come to England to form your acquaintance—your friendship,—to see if I can be of service to you in the position in which my brother's death and the birth of a son have placed you,—to aid you in the settlement of any affairs which may require the interference of a relative," answered Vernon; "for these purposes have I come—and not to vex you by taking umbrage at impressions which, however painful to me, are pardonable on the side of one in your situation."

"Then let us banish from our conversation the disagreeable topic which has hitherto engrossed it," exclaimed Adeline. "It is my duty to give you some information in respect to certain matters; and the family solicitor will, when you may choose to call upon him, enter into more elaborate details. You are aware that your poor brother died ere his child was born. But so far back as last November his lordship made a will the provisions of which were so prudentially arranged as to apply to the welfare of either male or female progeny, whichever might be accorded by Providence. Two distinguished noblemen are now my son's guardians, under that will, and consequently the trustees of the entailed estate."

Vernon bit his lip with vexation.

"In reference to his personal property," continued Adeline, "my lamented husband has left me sole executrix."

A dark cloud passed over the countenance of the brother-in-law.

"But, by a special clause in his will," added Lady Ravensworth, who did not observe those manifestations of feeling on the part of Gilbert Vernon, "your deceased brother has ensured in your behalf double the amount of that pension which has hitherto been paid to you."

"Thus my brother deemed me unworthy to be the guardian of his child;—he also considered it prudent to exclude me from any share in the duty of carrying his wishes into effect;—and he has provided me with a pittance of one thousand pounds a-year."

In spite of the necessity of maintaining the most complete self-command over himself, in order to carry out his plans successfully, Gilbert Vernon could not avoid those bitter observations which showed how deeply he was galled at the total want of confidence displayed in respect to him by his deceased brother.

Adeline felt that the point was a delicate one, and made no reply.

Fortunately for them both, each being much embarrassed by the present topic of discourse, a servant now entered to announce that dinner was served up.

Gilbert Vernon and Lady Ravensworth accordingly repaired to the dining-room.

We may here observe that Lord Dunstable and Mr. Graham had left the mansion some weeks previously, the young nobleman having recovered from the wound which he had received in the duel.

When dinner was over, Vernon and his sister-in-law returned to the drawing-room, where coffee was served up. Adeline directed that the infant heir—then scarcely more than a month old—should be brought in, Gilbert having hypocritically expressed a desire to see his newly-born nephew. The request was granted:—the nurse made her appearance with the babe; and Vernon passed upon it the usual flattering encomiums which are so welcome to a mother's ears.

But there was no falsehood in those praises,—however insincere might be the manner in which they were uttered:—for the infant was a remarkably fine one, and appeared sweetly interesting as it slept in the nurse's arms.

Vernon flattered the mother's vanity so adroitly, by distant but by no means unintelligible allusions to her own good looks, as he spoke of the child, that she began to consider him a far more agreeable man than she had at first supposed he could possibly prove to be.

Shortly after the nurse had retired with the child, Quentin entered the drawing-room, and, addressing himself to Vernon, said, "Your valet has just arrived, sir, with your baggage."

"If her ladyship will permit me," returned Gilbert, "I will withdraw for a few moments to give my servant some instructions."

"I am about to retire to my own chamber, Mr. Vernon," observed Adeline, "and shall leave you in undisturbed possession of this apartment. Your valet can therefore wait upon you here."

Quentin withdrew for the purpose of sending Mr. Vernon's domestic to the drawing-room; and Lady Ravensworth, having remained for a few moments to finish her coffee, also retired.

On the landing she heard hasty steps approaching and almost immediately afterwards Quentin appeared, followed by the Honourable Gilbert Vernon's valet.

They passed Lady Ravensworth as she was about to ascend the stairs leading from the brilliantly lighted landing to the floor above.

But—O horror!—was it possible?—did her eyes deceive her?—was she the sport of a terrible illusion?

No:—a second glance at the countenance of the false valet was sufficient to confirm the appalling suspicion which the first look in that direction had suddenly excited within her.

For *his* was a countenance which, once seen—if only for a moment—could never be forgotten;—and in spite of the new suit of complete black which he wore,—in spite of the care that had been bestowed upon his person,—in spite of the pains which a Globe Town barber had devoted to his usually matted hair—it was impossible not to recognise in this individual so disguised, the instrument of Adeline's own crime—the terrible Resurrection Man!

CHAPTER CCXXXIII.

A WELCOME FRIEND.

As if struck by a flash of lightning, Adeline fell insensible upon the stairs.

When she awoke, she found herself in bed,—not in the chamber where the murder of Lydia Hutchinson had been perpetrated: no—never since that fatal night had Lady Ravensworth dared to sleep in her boudoir;—but she had adopted as her own apartment, one quite at the opposite end of the building.

Yet, vain—oh! passing vain were the endeavours of the murderess to escape from the phantom of her victim:—had she fled to the uttermost parts of the earth—had she buried herself amidst the pathless forests of America, or made her abode on the eternal ice of the northern pole,—even thither would the spectre have pursued her!

It was midnight when Lady Ravensworth awoke in her chamber, after having fainted upon the stairs.

An ejaculation of terror escaped her lips—for she instantly recollected all that had passed.

The curtains were immediately drawn aside; and a charming female countenance, but totally unknown to Adeline, beamed upon her.

"Tranquillise yourself, lady," said the stranger: "it is a friend who watches by your side."

"A friend!" repeated Adeline, with a profound sigh: "have I indeed a friend? Oh! no—no: I am surrounded by enemies!"

And covering her face with her hands, she burst into an agony of tears.

"Pray compose yourself, Lady Ravensworth," said the stranger, in so sweet and musical a tone that it carried to the heart conviction of friendly intentions.

"And who are you that thus feel an interest in one so woe-begone as I?" asked Adeline, relieved by her tears.

Then she turned her still streaming eyes towards the stranger who spoke in so kind, so soothing, so convincing a manner; and she beheld, by the mellowed light of the lamps that burnt in the chamber, a female of lovely person, but clad in deep black, and wearing the peculiar cap which bespeaks the widow.

The respectability of this garb combined with the softness of the lady's tone and manner, and the sweet amiability of her fine countenance, to produce the most favourable impression upon the wretched Adeline,—wretched alike through her own misdeeds and those of others!

"You ask me who I am," answered the stranger:—"rather seek to know wherefore I am here! Compose yourself, and I will explain the latter mystery in a few words. This evening I received tidings—from an authority which I cannot doubt, but which I dare not name—of a fearful conspiracy that is in progress against you,—not only against *you*, but I fear also against your child."

"Oh! heavens—I begin to understand it all!" shrieked Lady Ravensworth, the presence of Gilbert Vernon and Anthony Tidkins in that mansion, and evidently leagued together, recurring to her mind. "But how did you hear this! how did you learn the terrible tidings which other circumstances proclaim so fatally to be, alas! too true?"

"Lady, ask me not for my authority," was the reply. "Were I to reveal it, I should incur the chance of ruining a source of intelligence which may enable me to frustrate other diabolical schemes that might be conceived, even as I hope to baffle the one that is now in progress against yourself. You are no doubt watched by enemies of a desperate character—one of whom has every thing to gain by the death of your child."

"Oh! you allude to Gilbert Vernon—my brother-in-law!" exclaimed Adeline. "He is already in this house—accompanied by his valet, who——"

She checked herself ere she uttered another word that might have led her new friend to marvel how she could possibly have obtained any previous insight into the character of that attendant upon her brother-in-law.

"And that valet, by all I have heard," said the strange lady, "is a man of the most fiend-like soul—the most remorseless disposition,—a man capable of every atrocity—every crime,—and who is so ready to accomplish any enormity for gain, that were there another Saviour to betray, he would become another Judas."

"Oh! what a picture you are drawing!" cried Lady Ravensworth, with a cold shudder—for she knew how much of that appalling description was true!

"It is not to intimidate you, that I am thus candid," was the reply; "but simply to convince you in what danger you are placed, and how deeply you need the assistance of a sincere friend."

"And that friend—" said Adeline.

"Is myself," answered the stranger. "It is true, I am but a woman—a poor, weak woman, as the lords of the creation style our sex;—but I possess the heart to aid you—the spirit to defend you—and the courage to dare every peril in your behalf!"

"Excellent woman!—heaven must have sent you to me!" cried Adeline, reassured by these words; and, as she spoke, she caught her new friend's hand and pressed it enthusiastically to her lips. "But, your name!—tell me your name!—that I may address you in terms of affection, and hereafter speak of you in those of gratitude."

"Call me by any name you will," was the reply; "but ask me no more concerning myself. In aiding you, I must impose the conditions upon which I offer to befriend you! I have no selfish motive:—my own social position places me above all interested views. No:—through the purest feelings of humanity have I sought you. Listen to me a few moments in patience. This evening I heard the principal details of the plot contrived against your peace: I learnt enough to prove that you have enemies capable of the very worst deeds to secure their own ends. I resolved upon hastening to your aid—of offering myself as your companion, your friend, until the peril be averted. I arrived at Ravensworth Hall at about nine o'clock this evening, and requested an interview with you. I was told that you had just been seized with a fit, and conveyed to your chamber. I replied that I was well known to you—that I had even come in pursuance of an invitation received from you—and that my presence was most opportune since you were so suddenly taken ill. Your lady's-maid was summoned, and, in consequence of my representations, I was admitted to your chamber. You had partially recovered, and had sunk into a sound sleep. I assured the maid that she need not remain with you, as I would watch by your side. This is the tale I have told—an innocent falsehood to ensure a good aim. If you wish me to remain with you, it will be for you to repeat to your servants the same story of our previous acquaintance. This will be necessary to account to Vernon for my presence in the mansion, and for the terms of inseparable friendship on which we must appear to be together. For from this night I shall not lose sight of yourself or your child, until the danger that threatens that innocent infant be averted. As for my name—I dare not allow it to be known here; for Vernon is acquainted with a certain individual to whom that name is not strange, and who, were he to learn that I am here, would perhaps suspect that I had some ulterior motive. Indeed, it was a conversation between your brother-in-law and that individual to whom I allude, which was overheard by a person devoted to my interests, and which discourse betrayed enough to show that one terrible deed had already been committed by Vernon, and that he was meditating another."

"One terrible deed has already been committed!" exclaimed Adeline, in affright: "to what can you allude!"

"Alas!" replied Eliza Sydney,—for she was the generous-hearted unknown,—"did the lamentable death of Lord Ravensworth excite no suspicions in your mind?"

"Oh! now I see it all!" cried Adeline, clasping her hands together, and speaking with hysterical vehemence: "Gilbert Vernon *was* in England—it *was* his voice that I heard in the ruins;—and it was he who sent the fatal and poisoned weed which carried my husband to the tomb! Monster—monster that you are, Gilbert Vernon!"

And she sank back exhausted upon the pillow, from which she had raised herself as she screamed forth that last accusation.

Several minutes elapsed ere she grew calm enough to explain to Eliza the meaning of her exclamation relative to the voice in the ruins.

"You see how well arranged have been all Vernon's plans," observed Eliza; "for, in the conversation with the individual to whom I have already alluded, he admitted that he had been some time in England. Oh! there can be no doubt that he was awaiting the effect of the poisoned weed;—for I read in the newspapers the account of your husband's strange and mysterious death after a few months of atrophy, and which fatal event was alleged to have been hastened by his passionate attachment to a peculiar oriental tobacco. It is now for you to remain retired and tranquil—to keep your child constantly with you—and to allow me to act as I shall think fit. In a short time I hope to be enabled to collect a chain of evidence that may establish Vernon's guilt. At present there is strong suspicion—but no proof—that he caused the death of his brother."

"But I will not stay here—in this lonely house," cried Adeline: "I will seek safety with my father!"

"And think you that change of dwelling will screen your child from the intrigues—the infernal intrigues and plots of a man who found means, while at a distance, to murder his brother with a fatal poison?" demanded Eliza. "No—he would accomplish his purpose, wherever you might conceal the heir of Ravensworth! But if we can obtain proofs of his past crime or of his present intention—if we can so contrive that we may place him within the reach of justice,—then—and only then will there be safety for your child. If you seek refuge with your relatives, he will see that he is suspected; and his schemes will only be prosecuted with the more caution."

"I am in your hands—I will follow your advice in all things," said Adeline: "but, in the name of heaven! devise means to bring these dangers and perplexities to a speedy issue."

"Trust to me, Lady Ravensworth," returned Eliza. "In the first place, is there still left in the house any of that oriental weed whose effects were so fatal upon your husband?"

"There is," answered Adeline; "and I think I divine your motive for asking the question. You would have the tobacco analysed and tested by a skilful chemist? That step was taken shortly after my lamented husband's death, by the desire of Mr. Graham—a medical gentleman who attended him in his last moments. Not that any suspicion against Gilbert Vernon had then arisen: no—it was curiosity and a love of science which prompted Mr. Graham thus to act."

"And the result?" said Eliza, interrogatively.

"No trace of a deleterious substance could be discovered," was the answer.

"Providence will open another road to the discovery of that man's guilt," observed Eliza. "But you must now compose yourself to sleep: the night is far advanced—and you need rest."

"Rest!—oh! not for me!" said Adeline, with a dreadful shudder, as she thought of the murdered Lydia Hutchinson.

But Eliza Sydney did not comprehend that Lady Ravensworth had any source of affliction save the machinations of her enemies.

In the morning, Eliza wrote the following letter to Filippo Dorsenni, Greenwood's valet:—

"*Ravensworth Hall, April 16th, 1841.*

"You will see by the superscription that I am on the spot where danger menaces an innocent babe of a month old. Vernon and Anthony Tidkins are both here; but Lady Ravensworth has placed herself entirely under my guidance.

"I wish you to undertake the three following commissions as speedily as possible.

"The first is to form an acquaintance with the landlady of the house in Stamford Street where Gilbert Vernon lodged, and endeavour to glean from her not only how long he lived in her dwelling, but any other particulars concerning him she may be willing to communicate. This task you must execute with great precaution, so that in case Vernon should call upon her she may not inform him that you have actually sought information at her hands. Should she be skilfully drawn into gossiping discourse upon the subject, she would not mention to Vernon that she had breathed a word in connexion with him or his affairs.

"In the second place, you must endeavour to discover the abode of the beautiful Georgian, Malkhatoun, whom, as you informed me some months ago—shortly after my arrival in England—Mr. Greenwood made over to his friend the Honourable Major Dapper.

"In the third place you must find some trusty person who will immediately set off for Beyrout. Fortunately, an extra Overland Mail departs to-morrow evening. The instructions of the individual whom you may thus employ are contained in the enclosed letter. Doubtless, amongst the few Castelcicalans who are now resident in London, you are acquainted with one who will undertake this mission, for the expenses of which I forward you a cheque upon my bankers.

"You can write to me to report the progress of these three commissions."

CHAPTER CCXXXIV.

A MIDNIGHT SCENE OF MYSTERY.

"Well," said Quentin to his fellow-domestics, as they were sitting at breakfast in the servants' hall, "the Honourable Mr. Vernon is by no means the most agreeable gentleman that ever set foot in this house; but his valet beats any thing I ever saw in the same shape."

"Did you ever see such a countenance?" exclaimed one of the maids. "I am sure it was not for his good looks that Mr. Vernon could have chosen him."

"He is just the kind of person that I should not like to meet in a lane in a dark night," observed another member of the female branch of dependants.

"He certainly cannot help his looks," said Quentin: "but heaven knows they tell amazingly against him."

"And what I think somewhat extraordinary," remarked the butler, "is that just now I found him in my pantry, balancing the silver spoons at the end of his finger, as if to tell the weight of them. So I quietly informed him that my pantry was sacred; and he took himself off with a very ill grace."

"Did you notice him last night, after supper," said the first maid who had spoken, "when we got talking about the disappearance of Lydia Hutchinson with my lady's casket of jewels, how eagerly he joined in the conversation, and how many questions he asked?"

"Yes, to be sure I did," returned another female servant: "he was as curious about the matter as if Lydia was his own sister, or daughter, or sweetheart. He wanted to learn how long ago it happened—how we knew that she had run away with the casket—and all about it; and then, when we told him what we thought of the matter, he cross-questioned us as if he was a counsel and we were witnesses at a trial. But I wonder who this widow is that came last night, and seems so intimate with my lady."

"She's a very genteel person," said Quentin; "and seems to know how to treat servants, as if she had a great many of her own. You can always tell the true breed of people by the way they behave to servants."

"I'm decidedly of your opinion, Mr. Quentin," observed a footman. "A true gentleman or true lady always says '*Thank you*,' when you hand them any thing at table, and so on. But it seems that my lady is very unwell this morning; for she and her new friend had their breakfast in my lady's own chamber."

"And the nurse and child are to remain altogether in my lady's private suite of apartments," added one of the females. "Does any one know the name of my lady's friend?"

"Mrs. Beaufort, I think the lady's-maid said," replied Quentin. "But here comes James White."

And James White did accordingly enter the servants' hall at that moment in the person of the Resurrection Man; for by the former name he now pleased to pass at Ravensworth Hall.

"Been taking a walk, Mr. White?" said Quentin, as Tidkins seated himself at the breakfast-table.

"Yes—just looking about the grounds a little," was the answer. "Handsome building this—fine park—beautiful gardens."

"It *is* a handsome building, Mr. White," said Quentin; "and as commodious as it is handsome."

"Very commodious," returned the Resurrection Man. "Nice snug little private door, too, at the southern end," he added with a strange leer.

"Why, that was the very door that Lydia Hutchinson decamped by, when she ran off with my lady's jewels," exclaimed one of the maids.

"Ah—indeed!" said the Resurrection Man, carelessly. "And wasn't her ladyship cut up at the loss of the jewels?"

"Somewhat so," was the female servant's answer. "But my lady is too rich to care very much about that."

"And was there no blue-bot—police-case, I mean, made of it?" asked Tidkins.

"None," replied the maid. "My lady possesses too good a heart to wish to punish even those who most wrong her."

"A very excellent trait in her character," observed the Resurrection Man, as he deliberately made terrific inroads upon the bread and butter and cold meat. "Was her ladyship at the Hall when that young woman bolted?"

"No: she had gone to London early in the morning of the very same day. But there's my lady's bell."

And the female servant who had been thus conversing with the Resurrection Man, hastened to answer the summons.

In a few minutes she returned, saying, "Mr. Quentin, you are wanted in the little parlour opposite my lady's room."

The valet repaired to the apartment named, where Eliza Sydney was waiting for him.

Motioning him to close the door, she said in a low but earnest tone, "Lady Ravensworth informs me that you were devoted to your late master: doubtless you are equally well disposed towards his unprotected and almost friendless wife?"

"If there is any way, madam, in which my fidelity can be put to the test, I shall be well pleased," was the reply.

"In a word, then," continued Eliza, "your mistress and the infant heir are in danger; and it behoves you to aid me in defeating the machinations of their enemies. After what I have now said, are your suspicions in no way excited?"

"I confess, madam," answered Quentin, "that the presence of a certain person in this house——"

"You allude to the Honourable Mr. Vernon," exclaimed Eliza; "and you are right! He has domiciled himself here without invitation—without apparent motive; and he is attended by an individual capable of any atrocity."

"Mr. Vernon's valet?" said Quentin, interrogatively.

"The same," was the reply. "But I dare not explain myself more fully at present. What I now require of you is to watch all the proceedings of Mr. Vernon and his attendant, and report to me whatever you may think worthy of observation."

"I will not fail to do so, madam," returned Quentin.

"And now I have to request you to give me a small portion of the tobacco which the late Lord Ravensworth was accustomed to use," continued Eliza; "and the remainder you must carefully conceal in some secure place, as it may some day be required for inspection elsewhere."

"Your directions shall all be implicitly attended to," said Quentin. "But might I be permitted to ask whether you are aware, madam, that the tobacco was sent to Lord Ravensworth by Mr. Vernon?"

"It is my knowledge of that fact which induced me to give those instructions concerning the weed—*the fatal weed*," replied Eliza, significantly.

"Ah! madam—I also have had my suspicions on that head!" exclaimed Quentin, who perfectly understood the lady's meaning. "I hinted those suspicions to the medical gentleman who attended my lord in his last moments; and he had the tobacco analysed by a skilful chemist;—but the result did not turn out as I had expected."

"Lady Ravensworth has already mentioned this fact to me," said Eliza: "I have, however, conceived a means of submitting the weed to a better test. But of this and other subjects I will speak to you more fully hereafter."

Quentin withdrew to fetch a small sample of the tobacco, with which he shortly re-appeared. Eliza renewed her injunctions to watch the movements of Vernon and his valet; and then hastened to rejoin Lady Ravensworth.

The day passed without the occurrence of any thing worth relating; but in the evening one or two little circumstances in the conduct of Mr. Vernon's valet struck the now watchful Quentin as being somewhat peculiar.

In the first place, Tidkins sought an excuse to lounge into the kitchen at a moment when the servants belonging to that department of the household were temporarily absent; and Quentin, who followed him unperceived, was not a little astonished when he saw the Resurrection Man hastily conceal three large meat-hooks about his person.

There were some silver forks and spoons lying on the table; but these Tidkins did not touch. It was consequently apparent to Quentin that Mr. Vernon's valet did not self-appropriate the meat-hooks for the sake of their paltry value: it was clear that he required them for some particular purpose.

"What, in the name of common sense! can he possibly want with meat-hooks?" was the question which the astonished Quentin put to himself.

Conjecture was vain; but the incident determined him to continue to watch Mr. Vernon's valet very closely.

When the hour for retiring to rest arrived, a female servant offered Tidkins a chamber candlestick; but he requested to be provided with a lantern, saying with a carelessness which Quentin perceived to be affected, "The truth is, I'm fond of reading in bed; and as a candle is dangerous, I prefer a lantern."

Quentin alone suspected the truth of this statement. He, however, said nothing. The lantern was given to Tidkins; and the servants separated for the night.

It so happened that the bed-room allotted to the Resurrection Man was in the same passage as that tenanted by Quentin. Suspecting that Tidkins required the lantern for some purpose to be executed that night, Quentin crept along the passage, and peeped through the key-hole of the other's chamber.

He was enabled to command a good view of the interior of that room, the key not being in the lock; and he beheld Tidkins busily engaged in fastening the meat-hooks to a stout stick about a foot and a half long. The Resurrection Man next took the cord which had secured his trunk, and tied one end round the middle of the stick. He then wound the cord round the stick, apparently to render this singular apparatus more conveniently portable.

This being done, Tidkins put off his suit of bran new black, and dressed himself in a more common garb, which he took from his trunk.

When he had thus changed his clothes, he secured the stick, with the cord and meat-hooks, about his person.

"This is most extraordinary!" thought Quentin to himself. "He is evidently going out. But what is he about to do? what can all this mean?"

The valet's bewilderment was increased when he beheld the Resurrection Man take a pair of pistols from his trunk, deliberately charge them with powder and ball, and then consign them to his pocket.

"What *can* he mean?" was the question which Quentin repeated to himself a dozen times in a minute.

The bell on the roof of the mansion now proclaimed the hour of midnight; and Tidkins, having suddenly extinguished the candle in the lantern, made a motion as if he were about to leave the room.

Quentin accordingly retreated a few yards up the passage, which was quite dark.

Almost immediately afterwards, he heard the door of Tidkins' room open cautiously: then it was closed again, and the sharp click of a key turning in a lock followed.

Tidkins was now stealing noiselessly down the passage, little suspecting that any one was occupied in dogging him. He descended the stairs, gained the servants' offices, and passed out of the mansion by a back door.

But Quentin was on his track.

The night was almost as dark as pitch; and the valet had the greatest difficulty in following the steps of the Resurrection Man without approaching him so closely as to risk the chance of being overheard. From time to time Tidkins stopped—evidently to listen; and then Quentin stood perfectly still also. So cautious indeed was the latter in his task of dogging the Resurrection Man, that this individual, keen as were his ears, and piercing his eyes, neither heard nor saw any thing to excite a suspicion that he was watched.

By degrees, black as was the night, Quentin's eyes became accustomed to that almost profound obscurity; and by the time the Resurrection Man had traversed the gardens, and clambered over the railings which separated those grounds from the open fields, the valet could distinguish—only just distinguish—a dark form moving forward before him.

"If I can thus obtain a glimpse of him," thought Quentin, "he can in the same manner catch sight of me the first time he turns round."

And the valet was accordingly compelled to slacken his pace until he could no longer distinguish the form of him whom he was pursuing.

But as the Resurrection Man, deeming himself quite secure, did not take the trouble to walk lightly along the hard path which ran through the fields, Quentin was now enabled to follow without difficulty the sounds of his footsteps.

All of a sudden these sounds ceased; and Quentin stopped short. In another minute, however, he heard the low rustling tread of feet walking rapidly over the grass; and thus he recovered the trail which was so abruptly interrupted.

The Resurrection Man had turned out of the beaten path, and was pursuing his way diagonally across the field.

Quentin followed him with the utmost caution: and in a few moments there was a bright flash in the corner of the field, the cause of which the valet was at no loss to comprehend.

Tidkins had lighted a lucifer-match—doubtless to assure himself that he was in the particular spot which he sought.

Quentin, to whom every square yard of the estate was well known, immediately remembered that there was a pond in the corner of the field where Tidkins had thus stopped; and close by was a thick hedge. The valet accordingly made a short and rapid circuit in order to gain the stile leading into the adjacent field: then, creeping carefully along the bushes, he arrived in a few moments behind that precise portion of the hedge which overlooked the pond.

The night was so dark that he could not follow with his eyes the exact movements of the Resurrection Man. He was, however, enabled to distinguish his form on the opposite bank of the pond; and not many moments after he had taken his post behind the hedge, there was a sudden splash in the water, as of some object thrown into it. Then the Resurrection Man moved slowly along the bank; and it instantly struck Quentin that he was dragging the pond.

This idea explained the purpose of the apparatus formed by the hooks, the stout stick, and the cord:—but for what could he be dragging?

The valet shuddered as this question occurred to him;—for the nature of the apparatus, the secresy of the whole proceeding, and the bad opinion which Eliza Sydney's hints had induced him to form of him whom he, however, only knew as James White,—these circumstances combined to fill Quentin's mind with a terrible suspicion that Tidkins was dragging for a dead body.

The Resurrection Man drew up his drag with a terrible oath, uttered aloud, and expressive of disappointment.

"And yet this must be the spot!" he added, as he disentangled the hooks from the cord. "I went over the whole grounds this morning—and I could swear it was here that——"

The conclusion of the sentence was muttered to himself, and therefore remained unheard by the valet.

The drag was thrown into the water a second time; and, at the expiration of a few moments, Tidkins gave utterance to an exclamation expressive of satisfaction.

Then he retreated slowly from the edge of the pond, as if dragging a heavy object out of the water.

From behind the hedge Quentin strained his eyes, with mingled feelings of curiosity and terror, to scrutinise as narrowly as possible the real meaning of this strange and mysterious proceeding. At length there was a strong gurgling of the water; and in another moment a large dark object was moving slowly and heavily up the steep bank.

A cold shudder crept over the valet's frame; for that object bore the appearance of a corpse!

He would have taken to flight—he would have escaped from the contemplation of such a strange and appalling scene—he would have hastened back to the mansion to raise an alarm;—but vague fears—ineffable horror bound him as it were to the spot—paralysed his limbs—and compelled him to remain a spectator of the dark proceeding.

The object was safely landed upon the bank: there was a sharp crack as of a match—a small blue flame suddenly appeared—and then Tidkins lighted the candle in his lantern.

This being done, he approached the object upon the bank;—and in another moment all Quentin's doubts were cleared up—for the light of the lantern now fell upon the body of a female!

He closed his eyes instinctively—and his brain was seized with a sudden dizziness. But, mastering his feelings, he again looked towards the mysterious and fearful drama which was being enacted on the opposite bank of the pond.

The light was again extinguished; and Tidkins was stooping over the corpse.

Suddenly an exclamation of joy escaped his lips; but Quentin was unable to divine the cause.

Another minute elapsed; and the Resurrection Man rolled the body back again into the water. There was a second splash a moment afterwards: it was evidently the drag which Tidkins had thrown away, its services being no longer required by him.

Then he retreated with rapid step from the bank of the pond; and Quentin, scarcely able to subdue the terror which had taken possession of him, retraced his way along the hedge,—determined, in spite of his feelings, to watch the Resurrection Man to the end——if more there were of this strange midnight drama yet to come.

Having hastily performed the short circuit that was necessary to bring him back into the field through which Tidkins was now proceeding, Quentin shortly came within sight of that individual's dark form, moving rapidly along the beaten path.

Near the railings which bounded the gardens, there were several groups of large trees; and at the foot of one of them Tidkins halted. Stooping down, he appeared to be busily employed for some minutes in digging up the earth. Quentin approached as nearly as he could without incurring the risk of discovery; and the motions of the Resurrection Man convinced him that he was indeed engaged in burying something at the foot of the tree.

This task being accomplished, Tidkins clambered over the palings, and pursued his way through the gardens towards the back gate of the Hall.

Quentin remained behind—his first impulse being to examine the spot where the Resurrection Man had been digging. But a second thought made him hesitate; and, after a few moments' reflection, he determined to wait until he had reported the whole of this night's mysterious proceedings to the lady whom he only knew as Mrs. Beaufort, and at whose instance he had been induced to watch the proceedings of Mr. Vernon's valet.

He accordingly pursued his way back to the mansion. But as the Resurrection Man had bolted the back door inside, Quentin was compelled to gain an entry through one of the windows of the servants' offices. This he effected with safety, and noiselessly returned to his own chamber.

But he closed not his eyes in slumber throughout the remainder of that night; for all he had seen haunted his imagination like a spectre.

CHAPTER CCXXXV.

PLOTS AND COUNTERPLOTS.

In the morning Eliza Sydney received the following letter from Filippo Dorsenni:—

"Your orders have been punctually obeyed.

"I have already visited the landlady in Stamford Street, under pretence of being acquainted with a gentleman who wishes to take lodgings in that street; and I have ascertained that her *last lodger*—who can be none other than Mr. Vernon—resided with her three or four months. Consequently he *has* been in England during that period.

"In the second place, I have discovered the address of the beautiful Georgian; and can communicate with her so soon as I receive your instructions to that effect.

"Thirdly, I have despatched a faithful person to Beyrout; and he will return to England the moment he shall have gleaned the information specified in your instructions."

To this letter Eliza despatched an immediate answer, praising her faithful adherent for the skill and despatch with which he had executed her orders, and giving him certain instructions in respect to Malkhatoun.

She then repaired to the parlour opposite Lady Ravensworth's own apartment; for Quentin had already sent a private message by one of the female servants, intimating that he was anxious to speak to her without delay.

When they met in the parlour, Eliza heard with profound astonishment the extraordinary narrative which the valet had to relate to her.

"Some deed of mystery and crime has been doubtless perpetrated," observed Eliza; "but it cannot possibly bear any reference to the atrocious plot which Gilbert Vernon is meditating against the happiness of his sister-in-law and the life of her child. I will now tell you that the villain who passes in this house as James White is in reality a certain Anthony Tidkins, known amongst his associates in crime as the Resurrection Man."

"I have heard of him, madam," said Quentin, with a shudder. "And, by the by—was it not this same wretch who lately escaped in so extraordinary a manner from the Middlesex House of Correction? The affair was in all the newspapers."

"He is the same person," answered Eliza.

"Oh! madam," cried Quentin, somewhat reproachfully; "it is not for me to dictate to you—but since you have discovered who this man is, how could you permit him to remain for one single day at large?—why should he be allowed to take his place at the same table with honest people?"

"I admit that such society must be abhorrent in the extreme," answered Eliza, mildly but firmly: "I also acknowledge that for a short space I am depriving justice of its due. Listen, however, to my reasons. Gilbert Vernon is a man of so desperate a character that he will hesitate at no crime which will make him master of the lands and title of Ravensworth. I have every reason to believe that he caused the death of his brother: I have equally good grounds for suspecting him of an intention to murder his nephew. As speedily as circumstances will permit am I adopting measures to collect evidence that will place his guilt beyond all doubt. But until that evidence be obtained, we must excite in his mind no suspicion that there are counter-schemes in progress. Were we to do so, it is impossible to imagine what desperate deed he might immediately risk in furtherance of his aims."

"But suspicions are already so strong against him, madam," observed Quentin, "that a magistrate would grant a warrant for his apprehension."

"And if the evidence against him were found to be incomplete and vague, as it indeed now is," answered Eliza, "he would soon be at large again to pursue his detestable machinations. No, Quentin: your good sense must show you that it is better to take no decisive step until our evidence shall be so complete that it will serve two objects—namely, to punish him for the crime he has already committed, and thereby release your lady and her son from any future danger at his hands."

"I submit to your superior judgment, madam," said Quentin. "But in respect to this Anthony Tidkins—this James White—this villain who is now quartered upon us———"

"Until you ere now communicated to me those strange and horrifying incidents of last night," interrupted Eliza, "my intention was to leave that miscreant also unmolested, for fear that by handing him over to justice Gilbert Vernon might be led to perceive that he also was suspected. But the narrative of last night's adventure involves so serious a matter that I am for a moment at a loss what course to pursue. In any case it will be better to ascertain the nature of the object which the villain buried at the foot of the tree; and probably we shall thereby discover some clue to the elucidation of this mystery. In the meantime, I conjure you to keep your lips sealed in respect to all these topics of fearful interest. Lady Ravensworth is in so nervous and agitated a state, that I shall not acquaint her with the incidents to which you were last night a spectator, until she be better able to support the terrors of so frightful a narrative. But to-night, Quentin, you must visit the spot where the villain buried some object in the earth: you will ascertain what that object is;—and we will then decide upon the proper course which we ought to pursue."

Quentin could not help admiring the strength of mind, the sagacity, and the calmness which Eliza Sydney displayed in her self-imposed task of countermining the dark plots of the Honourable Gilbert Vernon. Though but a servant, he was himself shrewd, intelligent, and well-informed; and he was not one of those obstinate men who refuse to acknowledge to themselves the superiority of a female mind, where such superiority really exists. He accordingly expressed his readiness to follow Eliza's counsel in all things connected with their present business; and he also promised that he would not by his conduct towards Tidkins excite in that individual's mind any idea that he was known or suspected.

He and Eliza Sydney then separated.

We must pause for a moment to explain the system of argument upon which this lady's present proceedings were based.

"If," she said to herself, "Tidkins be delivered up to justice, it is possible that he will not turn upon his employer Vernon, who might readily account for having such a villain in his service by declaring that he was entirely ignorant of his true character when he engaged him as a valet. Again, were Vernon immediately accused of the murder of his brother, the evidence would be slight unless it were proved not only that the tobacco was really poisoned, but also that it was the same which Vernon had sent to Lord Ravensworth. For the only positive ground of suspicion which can as yet be adduced against him, is that he has been some time in England while he represented himself to have been still dwelling in the East. But this circumstance might be disposed of by some feasible excuse on his part, and would also be inefficient unless coupled with more conclusive evidence. In a month I shall probably be able to collect all the testimony I require; and it is not likely that Vernon will immediately attempt the life of the infant heir, as such a deed following so closely upon the death of the late lord would of itself afford matter of serious inquiry and arouse suspicions against him. It is therefore necessary to remain tranquil for the present, until the day arrives when the machinations of Gilbert Vernon may be crushed for ever by the same blow that shall punish him for his past crimes."

Ravensworth Hall was now the scene of plot and counter-plot,—of fears, suspicions, and a variety of conflicting passions.

While Quentin and Eliza Sydney were engaged in the conversation above related, the following discourse took place between the Resurrection Man and Gilbert Vernon in the bed-chamber of the latter.

"I don't think I shall relish this monotonous kind of life long," said Tidkins. "Bustle and activity are what I like. Besides, I can't say that I'm altogether without fears; for that description of my person which was published after my escape from Coldbath Fields, was so infernally correct that even this white neckcloth, and bran new suit of black, and the cropping of my hair, and so on, haven't changed me enough to make all safe."

"Nonsense!" exclaimed Vernon, impatiently. "Who would think of looking for you at Ravensworth Hall? who would suspect that the valet of one in my station is what he really is?"

"But where is the use of putting the thing off for a month or six weeks?" asked Tidkins.

"Because it would appear strange—too strange that such an event should occur only a few days after my arrival at the Hall," answered Vernon. "You must be guided by me in this respect. The scheme to get rid of the brat is your own—and a good one it is too. Nothing could be better. But you really must allow me to have my own way as to the time when it is to be put into execution."

"Well, well," growled Tidkins: "be it so. For my part, however, I don't see how it is to be put into execution at all, if Lady Ravensworth remains cooped up with the brat in her own room, as she did all yesterday, and seems disposed to do again to-day, by what the servants said at breakfast just now."

"That certainly embarrasses me," observed Vernon. "It was my intention, as I before informed you, to remain here for a few weeks and ingratiate myself as much as possible with my sister-in-law, and get into the habit of fondling the child. Faugh! it almost makes me sick to think that I must take the snivelling brat from its nurse, and dandle it about for half-an-hour at a time, so as to save appearances at least. But, as you say, Lady Ravensworth seems determined that I shall have no chance of playing the amiable at all; for she keeps her room with that widow friend of hers who came so cursed inopportunely. It cannot be that Adeline suspects me? And yet the strange way in which she received me—the impression my voice made upon her——"

"Which proves that she really was concealed in those ruins, for some purpose or another, when we met there," interrupted the Resurrection Man.

"But I am convinced that nothing which then passed between us, gave her any hint concerning our projects," said Vernon; "for when I denied that it was my voice which she had heard, she afterwards became convinced that the mere coincidence of a resemblance of tones had deceived her. Had any other circumstance tended to corroborate her first impression, she would not have hesitated to mention it. But to return to what we were ere now talking of. If my sister-in-law should persist in keeping her own chamber, I shall request an interview with her; and the result will teach me how to act."

"And suppose she really is afraid of you,—suppose she suddenly leaves the Hall, and proceeds to town,—or suppose she sends for her friends and relations to keep her company here," exclaimed Tidkins; "how will you act then?"

"She will not quit the Hall," replied Vernon. "Decency compels her to live in retirement at the country-seat during the first few months of her widowhood; and Lord and Lady Rossville, her parents, are kept in London by the parliamentary duties of his lordship."

"I think I know a way to make her leave her room," said Tidkins, with some little hesitation, and after a few moments' pause.

"You!" cried Vernon, turning shortly round, and surveying his ill-favoured accomplice with astonishment.

"Yes—me," answered the Resurrection Man, coolly. "If I could only speak to her alone for a few minutes, I'm very much mistaken if I can't do what I say."

"Impossible—ridiculous!" ejaculated Vernon.

"I say that it's neither impossible or ridiculous," rejoined Tidkins, angrily.

"But how will you manage it? what will you say to her?" demanded Vernon, more and more surprised; for he knew that the Resurrection Man was not accustomed to boast without the power of performing.

"All that is my own secret," answered Tidkins. "If you question me from now till the end of next month, I won't satisfy you. That's my rule—and I always act on it. Now, all I have to say is that if you will procure me a private meeting with your sister-in-law, I'll engage that she shall leave her room—unless she really is very ill—and take her seat at the dinner-table to-day."

"But this is so extraordinary," cried Vernon, "that unless you know something wherewith to over-awe her—and let me tell you that she is not a woman to be frightened by empty menace———"

"Leave all that to me, Mr. Vernon," said the Resurrection Man, coolly. "Accept my proposal, or refuse it, as you like;—but don't question me."

"You are really a wonderful man, Tidkins," observed Gilbert, slowly; "and you are not in the habit of talking for talking's sake. If you feel convinced that you will succeed—if you do not incur the risk of spoiling all———"

"I am not such a fool as that," interrupted the other, gruffly.

"Then I will endeavour to bring about the interview which you desire," said Vernon.

And, without farther hesitation—though not entirely without misgiving—he sate down to pen a brief note to his sister-in-law, requesting an interview at her leisure.

An hour afterwards Lady Ravensworth proceeded alone to one of the drawing-rooms.

Eliza Sydney had offered no objection to this interview which Mr. Vernon had demanded with his sister-in-law: on the contrary, she was afraid that his suspicions would be excited were it refused.

On her part, Adeline was far from feeling annoyed at the request contained in Vernon's letter; for she had been a prey to the most acute suspense ever since she had recognised the Resurrection Man in her brother-in-law's valet.

Her guilty conscience led her at one moment to believe that Tidkins was certain to discover that Ravensworth Hall was the scene of the mysterious murder in which he was *her* instrument; and at another time she persuaded herself that her plans had been too prudently adopted to admit of such an elucidation.

"Oh! if that dreadful man should obtain a clue to the real truth," she thought, as she repaired to the drawing-room, "how completely should I be in his power! Nay, more—he might communicate his discovery to Vernon; and then——but I cannot dwell upon so terrible an idea! My God! in what torture do I exist! O Lydia Hutchinson, thy vengeance pursues me even from the other world! And now I am about to meet my brother-in-law again! Well—it is better that this interview should take place at once. It must relieve me from much terrible uncertainty—much agonising suspense. If Tidkins have already discovered the dread secret, I shall know the worst *now*;—and if he have not already discovered it, there is but little chance that he ever will. Let me then summon all my courage to my aid: a few minutes more, and my fate must be decided! Either I shall find myself in the power of Vernon and *that horrible man*; or my secret is safe! And if it be still safe—safe it shall remain;—for *he* could only recognise me by my voice—and I will take care never to speak in *his* presence! No—no: sooner than incur the risk of thus betraying my secret, I will shut myself up for ever in my own apartment—or I will fly far away from this house which has so many fearful recollections for me!"

Thus musing, Lady Ravensworth entered the drawing-room.

Her countenance was almost as white as marble; and this pallor was enhanced by the widow's weeds which she wore.

We must here observe that there was, as is usual in the well-furnished rooms of the mansions of the rich, a screen in one corner of the apartment; and on the same side were large folding-doors opening into an ante-chamber, which communicated with the passage and also with the suite of saloons intended for grand occasions.

The moment Adeline entered the apartment, Gilbert Vernon, who was already there, rose from a sofa and hastened to meet her.

"My dear sister," he said, taking her hand with an air of great friendship, "I was truly sorry to hear that you were so indisposed yesterday as to be compelled to keep your chamber. May I hope that you are better to-day?"

"I am very far from well, Mr. Vernon," answered Adeline coldly, as she withdrew her hand somewhat hastily; for, deeply steeped in guilt as she herself was, she shrank from the touch of one whom she looked upon as the murderer of her husband and the deadly foe of her infant child.

"You seem to avoid me purposely, Adeline," said Gilbert, fixing his large grey eyes upon her in a searching manner, though she averted her looks from him: "have I offended you? or is my presence in this house irksome to you?"

"I must candidly confess," replied Lady Ravensworth, "that I remained at the Hall, after the sad loss which I lately sustained, with a view to avoid society—to dwell in retirement;—and neither decency nor my own inclination allow me to receive company with any degree of pleasure."

"Your ladyship, then, looks upon the brother of your late husband as a stranger—a mere guest?" said Vernon, biting his lip. "And yet you have no relative who is more anxious to serve you—more ready to become your true friend———"

"My lamented husband left his affairs in such a position as to preclude the necessity of any intervention save on the part of the trustees," observed Adeline, gathering courage when she perceived that her brother-in-law was rather inclined to conciliate than to menace.

"Then, if such be your sentiments, Adeline," said Gilbert, "I need intrude upon your presence no longer."

Thus speaking, he hastily retreated from the room through the same door by which Lady Ravensworth had entered it.

"My secret is safe!" murmured Adeline, clasping her hands joyfully together, the moment Vernon had disappeared;—and she also was about to quit the apartment, when the screen was suddenly thrown back.

She cast a glance of apprehension towards the spot whence the noise had emanated; and an ejaculation of horror escaped her lips.

The Resurrection Man stood before her!

"Don't be frightened, my lady," said Tidkins, advancing towards her with a smirking smile on his cadaverous countenance: "I shan't eat you!"

"Wretch! what means this intrusion?" cried Adeline, in a feigned voice, and endeavouring to subdue her terror so as ward off, if possible, the danger which now menaced her.

"Lord, ma'am, don't be angry with me for just presenting my obscure self to your notice," said Tidkins, with a horrible chuckle. "You can't pretend not to know me, after all that's taken place between us?"

"Know you!—I know only that you are Mr. Vernon's valet, and that he shall chastise you for this insolence," cried Adeline, astonished at her own effrontery: but her case was so truly desperate!

"I always thought you was the cleverest woman I ever came near," said the Resurrection Man; "but I also pride myself on being as sharp a fellow as here and there one. If I was on the rack I could swear to your voice although it is feigned, and though when you came to my crib you kept your face out of sight. But your voice—your height—your manner,—every thing convinces me that I and Lady Ravensworth are old friends."

"You are mistaken, sir—grossly mistaken," cried Adeline, almost wildly. "I do not know you—I never saw you before you set foot in this house the other night."

"And then you recognised me so well that you fainted on the stairs," returned Tidkins, maliciously. "But if you think to put me off with denials like this, I can soon show you the contrary; for, though I was blindfolded when you brought me to the Hall on a certain night in the middle of February last, I am not quite such a fool as to have forgot the gardens we passed through—the little door leading to the private staircase at the south end of the building—and the very position of the room where the mischief was done. Why, bless you, ma'am, I began to suspect all about it the very first hour I was in this house, when the servants got talking of a certain Lydia Hutchinson who disappeared just about that time."

"You are speaking of matters wholly incomprehensible to me," said Lady Ravensworth, whose tone and countenance, however, strangely belied the words which she uttered. "It is true that a servant of mine, named Lydia Hutchinson, decamped in the month of February last; and if you know any thing concerning her——"

"By Satan!" cried the Resurrection Man, stamping his foot with impatience; "this is too much! Do you pretend that it was not Lydia Hutchinson whom you hired me to throttle in your own chamber?"

"Monster!" screamed Adeline, starting from her seat, and speaking in her proper tone, being now completely thrown off her guard: "of what would you accuse me?"

And her countenance, which expressed all the worst and most furious passions of her soul, contrasted strangely with her garb of widowhood.

"Of nothing more than I accuse myself," answered the Resurrection Man, brutally. "But if you want any other proof of what I say, come along with me, and I'll show you the very pond in which the body of Lydia Hutchinson is rotting. Ah! I found out that too, during my rambles yesterday!"

Adeline's cheeks were flushed with rage when he began to answer her last question; but as he went on, all the colour forsook them; and, pale—pale as a corpse, she fell back again upon the sofa.

"There! I knew I should bring it home to you," said the Resurrection Man, coolly surveying the condition to which he had reduced the guilty woman. "But don't be frightened—I'm not going to blab, for my own sake. I haven't even told your brother-in-law about this business. Tony Tidkins never betrays his employers."

Lady Ravensworth cast a rapid glance at his countenance as he uttered these words; and catching at the assurance which they conveyed, she said in a low and hollow tone, "You have not really acquainted Mr. Vernon with all this?"

"Not a syllable of it!" cried Tidkins. "Why should I? he wouldn't pay me the more for betraying you!"

"Then how came you here during my interview with him?" demanded Adeline, almost suffocated by painful emotions. "Was he not privy to your presence?"

"He was, my lady," answered Tidkins, in a less familiar tone than before: "but, for all that, he doesn't know what business I had with your ladyship."

"This is false—you are deceiving me!" exclaimed Adeline, with hysterical impatience.

"Not a whit of it, ma'am: I'm too independent to deceive any body," rejoined the Resurrection Man. "In plain terms, your brother-in-law has taken a fancy to this place, and means to stay here for a few weeks."

"He is very kind!" said Adeline, bitterly.

"But he doesn't like sitting down to breakfast and dinner by himself, and to lounge about in the drawing-room without a soul to speak to," continued the Resurrection Man; "for a petticoat is the natural ornament of a drawing-room. So what he wants is a little more of your society; and as he didn't exactly know how to obtain his wishes in this respect, I offered to use my interest with your ladyship."

"*Your* interest!" repeated Lady Ravensworth, disdainfully.

"Yes, ma'am—and that can't be small either," returned Tidkins, with a leer. "Now all you have to do is to show yourself more in the drawing and dining-rooms—and on my part I engage not to breathe a word of the Lydia Hutchinson affair to Mr. Vernon."

"And can you for a moment think that I shall submit to be dictated to in this manner?" cried Adeline, again becoming flushed with indignation.

"I do indeed think it, ma'am," answered Tidkins, coolly; "and what is more, I mean it, too—or, as sure as you're there, I'll drag up the body of Lydia Hutchinson, as I did last night!"

"O heavens!" shrieked Adeline: "what do you mean?"

"I mean, my lady, that when I heard the servants talking about the loss of your jewel-casket, I began to suspect that you had sacrificed it to create an idea that Lydia Hutchinson had bolted with it," answered Tidkins; "and I thought it just probable that I should find it in the pond. So last night I fished up the dead body———"

"Enough! enough!" cried Adeline, wildly: "Oh! this is too much!—you will drive me mad!"

"Not a bit of it, ma'am," returned Tidkins. "A clever and strong-minded lady like you shouldn't give way in this manner. All I wanted was the casket; and———"

"And what?" said Adeline, speaking in a tone as if she were suffocating.

"And I got it," was the answer. "But I rolled the body back again into the pond; and there it'll stay—unless you force me to drag it up once more, and bring it to the Hall."

"No: never—never!" screamed Lady Ravensworth. "Were you to perpetrate such a horrible deed, I would die that moment—I would stab myself to the heart—or I would leap from this window on the stones beneath! Beware, dreadful man—or you will drive me mad! But if you require gold—if you need money, speak: let me purchase your immediate departure from this house."

"That does not suit my book, ma'am," answered Tidkins. "Here I must remain while it suits the pleasure of my master," he added, with a low chuckling laugh.

"And what business keeps your master here? what wickedness does he meditate? why does he force his presence upon me?" cried Adeline, rapidly.

"I don't know any thing about that," answered the Resurrection Man. "All I have to say can be summed up in a word: leave your own chamber and act as becomes the mistress of the house. Preside at your own table—this very day too;—or, by Satan! ma'am, I'll take a stroll by the pond in the evening, and then run back to the Hall with a cry that I have seen a human hand appear above the surface!"

Having thus expressed his appalling menaces, the Resurrection Man hurried from the apartment.

Lady Ravensworth pressed her hands to her brow, murmuring, "O heavens! I shall go mad—I shall go mad!"

CHAPTER CCXXXVI.

WOMAN AS SHE OUGHT TO BE.

A quarter of an hour after the interview between Lady Ravensworth and the Resurrection Man, Eliza Sydney repaired to the little parlour before mentioned, in compliance with a message which had been conveyed to her from Quentin.

The moment she entered that room she was struck by the ghastly and alarming appearance of the valet.

He was pacing the apartment with agitated steps; his face was as pale as death—his eyes rolled wildly in their sockets—and his entire aspect was that of a man who had just seen some terrible spectacle, or heard some appalling revelation.

"In heaven's name, what is the cause of this excitement?" asked Eliza, advancing towards the valet, after she had carefully closed the door.

"Oh! madam—oh! Mrs. Beaufort," exclaimed Quentin, clasping his hands together through the intenseness of his mental anguish; "by playing the part of your spy I have learnt a most dreadful secret! Merciful God! this house has become the head-quarters of diabolical crime: its very atmosphere is tainted with the foul breath of murderers;—destruction lurks within its walls. Oh! accursed house, of which not one stone should be left upon another!"

"Quentin, you alarm me!" cried Eliza. "Speak—explain yourself! What mean these strange expressions?"

"Madam," said the valet, drawing close to her, and speaking in a low and hollow tone, "have you heard of a certain Lydia Hutchinson, who disappeared from this dwelling about two months ago?"

"Yes: the nurse was this morning telling me something about that event," answered Eliza; "but Lady Ravensworth hastened to change the conversation."

"And no wonder, madam—no wonder!" observed Quentin. "Oh! that I should still remain in the service of one who has perpetrated such a deed!"

"Will you explain yourself, Quentin?" cried Eliza, somewhat impatiently. "I see that you have learnt a dreadful secret: but wherefore keep me thus in suspense?"

"Pardon me, madam—forgive me," said Quentin, "I ought not to trifle with you! But, ah! madam, what will you think—how will you act, when you learn that she for whom you are so generously striving to combat the wicked plots of Gilbert Vernon,—that Lady Ravensworth, in a word, is—is———"

"Is what?" said Eliza, hastily.

"A murderess!" returned Quentin, shuddering from head to foot as he uttered the appalling word.

"Just heaven! what do I hear?" exclaimed Eliza, the colour forsaking her cheeks. "Oh! no—no: it cannot be! Recall that assertion, Quentin; for you are labouring under some strange delusion!"

"Would that I were, madam," said the valet, in a mournful tone; "but, alas! I heard too much—and that much too plainly—to entertain a doubt! Yes, Mrs. Beaufort—that lady to whom you have devoted yourself, is the murderess of poor Lydia Hutchinson!"

"Oh! this is indeed a house of crime, Quentin!" exclaimed Eliza Sydney, now greatly excited. "But tell me how you made this fearful discovery!"

"I will endeavour to collect my thoughts sufficiently to explain it all, madam," said the valet. "You must know, that about two hours ago, the miscreant Tidkins brought me a note, written by his master, and to be sent up to my lady. To this note a verbal message was returned that my lady would see Mr. Vernon in an hour in the drawing-room."

"Yes—that interview took place with my entire concurrence," observed Eliza.

"Obedient to your instructions, madam," continued Quentin, "I kept a constant watch upon Tidkins; and when the hour for the meeting between my lady and Mr. Vernon approached, I saw Tidkins accompany his master to the drawing-room. This circumstance struck me to be so singular, that I concealed myself in an ante-room, separated only by folding doors from the saloon itself. It appears that Tidkins had placed himself behind the screen; for, after a few words of little consequence had passed between my lady and her brother-in-law, the latter left the apartment—and Tidkins burst forth from his hiding-place! Oh! madam, never shall I forget the scene which followed! By means of the key-hole I could perceive, as well as hear, all that occurred in the drawing-room. With the most insolent familiarity did Tidkins address my lady; and, though for a time she steadily denied all participation in the murder of Lydia Hutchinson, at length she acknowledged it—she admitted it!"

"Miserable woman that she is!" exclaimed Eliza. "Oh! this accounts for her sleepless nights—her constant nervousness—her strange looks!"

"And it is the corpse of Lydia Hutchinson, madam," added Quentin, "which was last night dragged from the pond by that fiend who was hired by my lady to murder her!"

The valet then detailed at length all the conversation which had taken place between the Resurrection Man and Lady Ravensworth, and which explained wherefore Tidkins had fished up the body of the murdered woman.

"It is therefore clear," said Eliza, horror-struck at all she heard, "that it is the lost casket which Tidkins buried at the foot of the tree."

"Doubtless, madam. But it now remains for *you* to decide what course you will pursue," continued Quentin: "as for *me*, my mind is made up—I shall depart within an hour from this abode of crime!"

"Such will not be my conduct," said Eliza, firmly. "Dreadful as is the guilt of Lady Ravensworth, I cannot find it in my heart to abandon her to her enemies. She must have received some fearful provocation to have been driven thus to rid herself of a servant whom, under ordinary circumstances, she might have abruptly discharged."

"I think that I can penetrate into the mystery of this crime, madam," observed Quentin. "Her ladyship admitted a certain Colonel Cholmondeley to her chamber; and this intrigue was known to Lydia Hutchinson."

"Oh! crime upon crime!" ejaculated Eliza Sydney, with a shudder. "Yet will I not abandon this very guilty and very miserable woman! No:—for the sake of her babe will I still aid her in defeating her enemies! And this duty becomes the more imperious, inasmuch as if Gilbert Vernon should be made acquainted with her enormities—if the miscreant Tidkins should betray her to his master—he would obtain a hold upon her that must further all his vile schemes."

"And will you remain, madam, in the midst of these murderers?" asked Quentin, profoundly surprised at the resolution of Eliza Sydney:—"will you remain in the same house with Vernon, the murderer of his brother,—with Tidkins, who lives by murder,—and with Lady Ravensworth the murderess of Lydia Hutchinson? Can you continue to dwell in such horrible society?"

"As a matter of duty—yes," answered Eliza. "Were the infant heir of Ravensworth abandoned to the designs of those dreadful men, his life would not be worth a month's purchase; and his mother would not dare to publish the foul deed, even were he murdered before her face!"

"The protection of that child is indeed a duty," said Quentin, in a musing manner; "and my lord was always a good and kind master to me! I have eaten his bread for many years—I have amassed in his service enough to keep me in my old age! Madam," added the valet, turning abruptly round towards Eliza, "your noble example shall not be lost upon me! I will remain here—I will obey your instructions—for you are a lady of whose confidence a humble individual like myself should feel proud!"

How powerful is the moral influence of a virtuous woman, performing painful but solemn, though self-imposed duties! And, oh! had that man, who now felt and acknowledged this influence,—had he known that he stood in the presence of one whose brow had been adorned with a diadem, and who still possessed a ducal title, although she used it not,—had he known all this, he would have fallen at her feet, in homage to one so great and good!

"Your resolution, Quentin, to remain here as the protector of your lamented master's heir, does you honour," exclaimed Eliza. "And, as you are indeed deserving of my confidence, I will acquaint you with the course which I shall adopt towards Lady Ravensworth. For the sake of her family—for the sake of the memory of her deceased husband—for the sake of her child, I will spare her that exposure, and those fearful consequences of such exposure, which justice seems to demand in expiation of a crime so foul as hers. Never—never could I consent to be the means of sending one of my own sex to a scaffold! No: I will gently break to her my knowledge of her guilt; I will enjoin her to pray often—long—and fervently to that Almighty Power which can show mercy to those who truly repent, be they never so deeply stained with crime; and I will endeavour to conduct her mind to that state which shall atone for the great sin which lies so heavy on her soul!"

"Ah! madam," exclaimed Quentin, in unfeigned admiration of this excellent lady; "were there more like you in this world, there would be far less need for prisons, criminal judges, and public executioners!"

"Reformation is better than punishment, Quentin," said Eliza, impressively. "But let us now separate. I need not enjoin you to the strictest silence in respect to the awful discovery of this morning."

"Oh! madam, tell me how to act, and I would not for worlds deviate from your instructions," cried the valet.

"Thank you for this assurance," said Eliza. "Before we separate, let me ask if you will assist in the performance of a painful but solemn duty which circumstances impose upon us?"

"Speak, madam," returned Quentin: "I almost think that I can anticipate your explanation."

"The corpse of the murdered woman must not be allowed to remain in that pond," said Eliza, in a low, but emphatic tone.

"I had divined your thoughts, madam," observed the valet. "To-night I will bury it—painful, horrible though that duty be."

"And I will assist you in the sad task," returned Eliza. "Nay—offer no objection: I am determined. To-night, at eleven o'clock, I will meet you in the garden near the wicket leading into the fields. You must be provided with the necessary implements for the purpose. In respect to the casket of jewels, leave it where it is—leave it to that dreadful man who will not long remain at large to dishonour human nature with his atrocities; for he and his present master will fall together—and the same knell shall ring for them both!"

"I understand you, madam," said Quentin. "That casket could never return to the possession of Lady Ravensworth, with safety to herself."

The valet then retired; and Eliza hurried back to Adeline's apartments.

There a most painful—a most distressing scene took place.

The nurse was dismissed with the child into a remote chamber of the same suite; and when Eliza was alone with Adeline, she broke to the miserable lady her knowledge of the fearful crime which had put an end to the existence of Lydia Hutchinson.

And, oh! how gently—how delicately—and in what a purely Christian spirit of charity, did Eliza perform this most difficult—this most melancholy duty!

It was not as an avenger, menacing the thunders of the law, that Eliza spoke: it was not as one prepared to deliver up the criminal to justice, that she addressed herself to Lady Ravensworth. No:—it was as a true disciple of Him with whom is vengeance as well as mercy, that she communed with Adeline: and this wretched woman found, to her astonishment, that she possessed a friend who would pray with her, solace her, and conceal her guilt, instead of a being prepared to expose, to disgrace, and to abandon her upon the plea of performing a duty which every one owes to society!

Then, when Lady Ravensworth was sufficiently composed—when the first terrific shock was over,—she related, truly and minutely, her entire history: she revealed to Eliza all those particulars of her connexion with Lydia Hutchinson, which are known to the reader; she concealed nothing—for the unparalleled generosity of Eliza's mind and conduct aroused in Adeline's heart all the better feelings of her sex and nature.

Though the crime of murder is so horrible that there exists for it scarcely the shadow of extenuation,—still when the case of Lady Ravensworth was calmly considered,—when it was remembered how she had been goaded to madness and desperation by the conduct of Lydia Hutchinson,—when all the circumstances that united at the time to cause her reason to totter upon its seat, were dispassionately viewed,—even the well-ordered mind of Eliza Sydney was induced to admit that, if ever such shadow of extenuation did exist, it was in this most lamentable episode in the history of the human race.

And, oh! with what feelings of profound—ineffable gratitude did Adeline throw herself at the feet of that angel who seemed to have been sent from above to teach her that there was hope for even the greatest criminal, and that "*there is more joy in heaven over the repentance of one sinner than over ninety-nine just persons who need no repentance!*"

"You ask me not to leave you—not to abandon you," said Eliza: "such an idea never entered my mind. Where the plague rages, there should the physician be; and if the physician fly away through fear of infection, he is unworthy to exercise an honourable calling. For it is not the healthy who require his services. And if the rich man offer alms to those who are as wealthy as himself, his charity becomes a mere mockery, because it is only offered where he knows it will be refused. No—it is the abodes of misery which he should visit; and it is amongst those who need his assistance that he should dispense his bounty. I fear not, Adeline, that I shall be endangered by the infection which has so unhappily seized upon you: on the contrary, I hope to eradicate from your heart the seeds of the pestilence of sin! And it is also you who require the alms of sympathy and solace; for you must be very—very wretched! Do not think, then, that I will desert you: oh! no—the more guilty, the more miserable you are, the stronger shall be the bond that unites me to your interests!"

This was the holy and touching language with which Eliza Sydney sought to move the heart of Lady Ravensworth to penitence.

Could such wholesome means fail of success?

No:—and Adeline felt rejoiced that her secret had become known to one who availed herself of that knowledge for such excellent purposes!

The comprehensive mind of Eliza Sydney enabled her to embrace at a glance all the new difficulties which the crime of Adeline had conjured up. Eliza's aim, as before stated, was to take such effectual steps to stop the guilty career of Vernon, that the heir of Ravensworth should be entirely freed from any farther peril at the hands of his unnatural uncle. But the very same moment that ruined Vernon and his atrocious assistant, might bring destruction upon Adeline; for when the strong grasp of the law once fixed itself on Tidkins, there was no guarantee that he would not, in his rage, reveal the terrible mystery respecting the fate of Lydia Hutchinson.

This chance was duly weighed by Eliza Sydney; but she conceived a plan to save Adeline from the overwhelming consequences of such an exposure.

What this project was will be explained hereafter:—suffice it for the present to say that it obviated the necessity of any change in the policy already adopted to defeat and punish Gilbert Vernon and Tidkins; and that Adeline gratefully assented to the conditions which it involved.

A far more embarrassing subject for immediate consideration presented itself to the mind of Eliza Sydney. This was how to advise Lady Ravensworth to act in respect to the requisition made by Gilbert Vernon, and so energetically backed by Anthony Tidkins, relative to her presence in the drawing and dining rooms. But at length Eliza decided upon recommending Adeline to yield in this instance.

"You will suffer too much in exposing yourself, by refusal, to the menaces and constant persecutions of Anthony Tidkins," said Eliza; "and moreover, we must remain faithful to our plan of not allowing Vernon to suspect that his plots are being met by counter-schemes. I shall always be with you when you are compelled to endure his presence; and therefore it will be better thus to humour him."

"I shall be guided by you in all things," returned Adeline.

She accordingly presided at the dinner-table that very evening:—and thus was the promise, made by the Resurrection Man to his employer, fulfilled to the letter.

During the repast, Vernon endeavoured to ingratiate himself as much as possible with the two ladies: but Adeline was too unhappy even to affect any feeling beyond cold politeness; and Eliza Sydney was only distantly courteous.

Coffee was served in the drawing-room; and afterwards the ladies withdrew to their own apartments.

"One grand point is at least gained," said Vernon to himself, when he was alone: "my amiable sister-in-law has been forced to leave her nest! In a day or two I must ask to see the child. But with what spell Tidkins effected this change in Adeline's conduct, I am at a loss to imagine!"

That night, at eleven o'clock, Eliza Sydney stole from the mansion, Adeline and Quentin being alone cognisant of her proceeding.

In the garden she met the faithful valet, who was provided with a drag, a mattock, a spade, and a sack.

They repaired together to the field in which was the pond where the remains of Lydia Hutchinson were concealed.

Quentin, who had purposely reconnoitred the vicinity in the afternoon, proceeded to dig a grave in a spot where there was no grass, and at a distance of about twenty yards from the water.

This labour occupied an hour: and, when it was concluded, he proceeded with Eliza to the pond.

The drag was used successfully; and the corpse was drawn to land. It was then wrapped in a large sheet which Eliza had brought for the purpose, and carried to the grave hollowed to receive it.

Eliza breathed a prayer for the soul of her whose remains were denied Christian sepulture, while Quentin threw back the soil. The superfluous earth was conveyed in the sack to the pond; and thus all traces of this hurried burial disappeared.

Eliza and Quentin then returned to the mansion.

On the following morning, after breakfast, Eliza Sydney walked out alone, and repaired to a grove at a short distance from the mansion.

A cab, containing two persons, drove up to the same spot a few moments afterwards; and Filippo, having leapt out, assisted Malkhatoun to alight.

Eliza immediately joined them; and they all three entered the grove together.

When they had proceeded so far as to be beyond the range of the cab-driver's hearing, Eliza stopped, and, addressing herself to Malkhatoun, said, "I hope that you understand enough of the English tongue to be able to converse with me for a few minutes upon a most important subject?"

"I am well acquainted with your language, lady," was the reply, spoken with singular accuracy for an oriental foreigner.

"Now listen to me attentively," continued Eliza: "I have read in some book of eastern travel that the inhabitants of Asia Minor, Georgia, and Circassia, possess the art of steeping the tobacco-leaf in a poison of such a nature that it undermines the constitution of him who uses the plant so treated."

"It is perfectly correct, lady," answered Malkhatoun; "and the operation of steeping the plant in the opiatic poison is chiefly performed by the female slaves."

"Have you ever seen the process?" inquired Eliza.

"Frequently," was the reply. "My father was a Georgian chief,"—and as she spoke, tears started into her eyes:—"he had many slaves, and they prepared the tobacco which he purposely left in his tents, when the Persian invaders drove him from them. To poison your enemies thus, is not deemed a dishonourable mode of warfare in Georgia."

"Should you recognise tobacco so prepared, were you to see it?" asked Eliza.

"Instantaneously, lady, on the application of fire," replied Malkhatoun; "for the poison used is of so peculiar a nature that its qualities are only put into action by means of fire. The most skilful chemist cannot discover its presence in tobacco, unless he light the weed and inhale the perfume of the vapour."

"The idea of such a circumstance struck me also," observed Eliza.

As she spoke, she produced from her reticule a small galley-pot containing some of the late Lord Ravensworth's tobacco: then she drew forth a box of lucifer-matches.

Malkhatoun held the galley-pot, while Eliza procured a light; and the flame was then applied to the tobacco.

The beautiful Georgian immediately inhaled the vapour, and said, "Lady, this tobacco is so strongly impregnated with the poison, that were the strongest man to indulge freely in its use for a few months, he would sink into the tomb."

"It is as I suspected," murmured Eliza.

"Tobacco thus poisoned," continued Malkhatoun, "possesses properties of so fascinating a nature, that he who smokes it becomes irresistibly attached to it; and I have heard it said in Georgia, that men labouring under incurable maladies, or those whose life is burthensome to them, have voluntarily whiled away their existence by the use of the poisoned weed."

"I thank you sincerely for this explanation," said Eliza. "And now, pardon me if I speak a few words concerning yourself—for it is with a good motive. When you mentioned the name of your father, tears started into your eyes."

"My poor father was slain in the battle which made me and several other Georgian females the prisoners of the Persian conquerors, against whom my sire rose in rebellion," answered Malkhatoun. "I was sent to Teflis, and sold as a slave to a Turkish merchant, who carried me to Constantinople, where I was purchased for an English nobleman. I wept ere now, lady, because I have a mother, and brothers, and sisters living in my native land; and my heart yearns towards them."

"And would you be pleased, my poor girl, to return to Georgia?" asked Eliza, the tears trickling down her cheeks—for Malkhatoun's voice was soft and plaintive as she told her artless tale.

"I would give half the years that remain to me to embrace my dear mother and brothers and sisters once more," replied Malkhatoun.

"You shall return to them—oh! you shall return to them with as little delay as possible," exclaimed Eliza. "In the course of this day I will transmit by post to you, Filippo, a draft upon my banker to supply the means for this poor girl to go back to her native land."

"And it shall be my duty, madam, to see her safely on board the first ship that sails for the Levant," said Filippo.

Malkhatoun could scarcely believe her ears; but when she saw that Eliza was really in earnest, she threw herself at the feet of her benefactress, whose hand she covered with her kisses and her tears.

Eliza hastened to raise her from that posture; and when the now happy Georgian became composed, they all three retraced their steps to the cab.

Malkhatoun and Filippo returned to London; and Eliza retraced her way to Ravensworth Hall.

Nor did she forget her promise to Malkhatoun; and two days afterwards the fair Georgian embarked at Gravesend on board a ship bound for the Levant.

CHAPTER CCXXXVII.

THE JUGGLERS.

Nearly five weeks had elapsed since the day when the noble-minded Eliza Sydney first took up her quarters at Ravensworth Hall.

Time was, therefore, now verging towards the close of May, 1841.

It was at about nine o'clock in the morning of a charming day, at this period, that the Resurrection Man sauntered leisurely from the servants' offices, at Ravensworth Hall, with the air of a person about to indulge in a stroll after eating a good breakfast.

But when he was out of sight of the Hall, he quickened his pace, and proceeded somewhat rapidly towards the ruined lodge where he had once before met the Honourable Gilbert Vernon.

And it was to meet that very same individual that he now sought the place again.

But as Vernon had not yet arrived, Tidkins, after walking round the dilapidated cottage to convince himself that no stranger was near, took a seat upon a pile of bricks, and, producing a cigar-case, was speedily wrapped in the enjoyment of a mild havannah and his own delectable meditations.

With the nature of those thoughts we shall not trouble the reader: suffice it to say that they were all connected with the scheme which he and his master were carrying on at Ravensworth Hall, and the last dread act of which was now in immediate contemplation.

Tidkins had just lighted a second cigar, when he descried Vernon at a distance.

He, however, continued to smoke—for he was not the man to stand upon any ceremony with his employer, even were that employer a prince.

"Come at last?" said Tidkins, as Vernon entered the ruins. "Been doing the amiable to the ladies, I suppose?"

"I have succeeded in that task tolerably well lately," answered Vernon, with difficulty concealing an expression of disgust at the odious familiarity of his agent; but he had already learnt that crime places the menial upon a footing with the master, and compels the haughty aristocrat to brook the insolence of the vulgar desperado.

"Well, now we are drawing to the end of the play at last," continued Tidkins. "So much the better: for I was getting infernally sick of this moping kind of life. But what if this plan of ours should happen to fail?"

"Then I will try another—and even another, if necessary, until we succeed," answered Vernon, emphatically. "Yes: I am now so bent upon the deed—so resolved to become the lord and owner of these broad lands and yon proud mansion—that I will even risk my neck to attain that end."

"You speak in a plucky manner that I admire," said Tidkins. "Besides, when once you are Lord Ravensworth, who will dare to utter a suspicion—even if there should seem any ground for it?"

"No one—certainly," replied Vernon. "But have you looked about the ruins? Remember the last time we met here—there was an eaves-dropper then——"

"Don't alarm yourself," interrupted Tidkins: "I walked carefully round the place; and I'll swear no one is near. Unless, indeed," he added, with a jocular chuckle, "some very curious person has got into that great cistern up there; and I must confess I didn't climb up to look into it."

"Cease this humour," said Vernon, somewhat sternly. "If you have been round the ruins, that is sufficient. Our business is too important to allow us to waste time in idle bantering. Do the jugglers understand that they are to come up this evening?"

"Fully so," answered Tidkins, coolly inhaling the fragrant vapour of his cigar. "They are all at the *Three Kings*—that public-house which you see by the road-side yonder,—and most likely making merry with the couple of guineas that I gave them last night. It is not necessary that I should see them again before they come to the Hall."

"You mentioned to them that there was a sick lady at the mansion who would be amused with their sports?" said Vernon.

"I have already told you what representations I made," replied Tidkins, impatiently. "Where's the use of asking the question over again?"

"For the same reason that one reads a letter twice," rejoined Vernon,—"to see that nothing has been omitted which ought to be said or done. But are you sure that the fellows will understand how to use the detonating balls?"

"Nothing is easier," answered Tidkins. "And as it was merely to try one that we agreed to meet here now, suppose I just make the trial directly?"

"Yes—I am anxious to be assured of the effect," said Vernon. "We are far enough away from the Hall to do so in safety."

"Certainly we are," remarked Tidkins. "In the first place we're down in this deep valley;—in the second place there's the thick grove on the top of the hill;—and in the third place, even if there wasn't the hill at all between us and the Hall, the back windows of the mansion don't look this way. So the smoke can't be seen."

"True!" exclaimed Vernon. "And now for the test."

The Resurrection Man drew from his pocket a ball covered with coarse blue paper, and nearly as large as a cricket-ball.

Then, rising from his seat, he dashed it with some degree of violence upon the hard ground.

It exploded in the twinkling of an eye, with a din as loud as that of a blunderbuss; and both Vernon and the Resurrection Man were immediately enveloped in a dense cloud of black and sulphurous-smelling smoke.

When the dark volume had blown away, Vernon beheld the cadaverous countenance of the Resurrection Man looking towards him with a grin of ferocious satisfaction.

"Well—will that do?" cried Tidkins, triumphantly.

"Admirably," answered Gilbert, averting his face—for there was something fiend-like and horrible in the leer of his companion.

There was a short pause; and then those two villains resumed their conversation. But as the remainder of their discourse was connected with the last act of their tragic drama, which we shall be compelled to relate in detail, it is unnecessary to record in this place any more of what passed between them upon the present occasion.

After having been nearly an hour together, Gilbert Vernon and the Resurrection Man separated, in order to return by different routes to the Hall.

Five minutes after they had left the building, the head of a man looked cautiously over the brink of the empty cistern to which Tidkins had jocularly alluded, and which stood on the top of the least dilapidated portion of the lodge.

Seeing that the coast was now perfectly clear, the person who was concealed in the cistern emerged from his hiding-place and let himself drop lightly upon the ground.

This individual was the gipsy, Morcar.

Being on his way to London,—alone, and upon some business connected with his tribe,—he had stopped to rest himself in those ruins: but he had not been there many minutes, when he heard the sound of footsteps; and, almost immediately afterwards, he beheld, through a cranny in the wall behind which he was seated, the well-known form and features of the Resurrection Man.

His first impulse was to dart upon the miscreant and endeavour to make him his prisoner; but, seeing that Tidkins looked suspiciously about, Morcar instantly imagined that he had some object in seeking that place. At the same time it struck him, from his knowledge of the Resurrection Man's character, that this object could be no good one; and he resolved to watch the villain's proceedings.

Thus, while Tidkins was making the circuit of the ruins, Morcar clambered noiselessly and rapidly up to the cistern, in which he concealed himself.

The consequence was, that the gipsy overheard the entire discourse which shortly afterwards ensued between Tidkins and Vernon; and a scheme of such diabolical villany was thus revealed to him, that his hair almost stood on end as the details of the fearful plot were gradually developed by means of that conversation.

When the Resurrection Man and Gilbert Vernon had taken their departure, and Morcar had emerged from his hiding-place, his first impulse was to proceed to Ravensworth Hall and communicate every thing he had overheard to the lady of that mansion.

But, ere he took that step, he sate down, with the usual caution which characterises his race, to ponder upon the subject.

We have before stated that it is repugnant to the principles of the Zingarees to be instrumental in delivering a criminal over to any justice save their own; and Morcar knew that if he did adopt such a course, he must necessarily appear as a witness against the two villains whose dark designs he had so strangely discovered. This appearance in a court of justice would sorely damage him with his tribe, over whom he was to rule at his father's death.

It is, however, probable that the excellent effects of Richard Markham's example upon the generous-hearted Morcar would have hushed those scruples and induced him to do what his good sense told him was his duty towards society, had not the sudden reminiscence of a certain portion of the conversation he had overheard confirmed him in the opinion that he should be acting more prudently to counteract the project of the two villains at the moment it was to be put into execution, rather than deliver them up to justice ere it was attempted.

"*I am now so bent upon the deed*," had one of the miscreants said, "*so resolved to become the owner of these broad lands and yon proud mansion—that I will even risk my neck to attain that end!*"

The reasoning which these words now engendered in Morcar's mind, was coincidentally similar to that upon which Eliza Sydney's conduct had been based.

"This man," thought Morcar, "who dared to utter such sentiments, is the member of a noble family—the next heir after an infant child, to the title and lands of Ravensworth. Would the word of a wandering gipsy be for a moment credited against his indignant denial of the accusation which I should make against him, were he now delivered up to justice? And, were he to escape from that accusation, would he not commence anew his dark plots against the life of that child who seems to stand in his way? Far better will it be for me to counteract his scheme, and then proclaim his guilt when *my* evidence can be corroborated by the fact that *he* did attempt the deed of which he will stand accused! Yes—it must be so. Then will the law for ever remove him from a scene where his detestable machinations would sooner or later prove fatal to their innocent object!"

Having devised a mode of proceeding, Morcar quitted the ruins, and bent his way towards the *Three Kings* public-house, which was about a mile distant.

On his arrival at the little rustic inn, the gipsy sauntered into the tap-room, where he sate down, and ordered some refreshment.

At one of the tables five men were busily engaged in devouring bread and cheese and washing down the same with long draughts of Barclay and Perkins's Treble X. They were thin, but well-made and athletic-looking fellows; and were dressed in garments of which fustian and corduroy were the principal materials. On the bench near them were several bundles tied up in handkerchiefs, through the openings and holes of which the quick eye of the gipsy caught sight of certain nankin breeches and flesh-coloured stockings, such as are worn by itinerant mountebanks. In a corner of the room stood a large drum, and near it a wicker basket with a lid.

Morcar was convinced that these persons were the same to whom Vernon and Tidkins had alluded.

His object was now to get into conversation with them; and this was easily effected by one of those casual remarks upon the weather which invariably commence a discourse between strangers in this country.

"Fine day," said the gipsy, after quenching his thirst with half the contents of a pint of porter.

"Very, indeed," replied one of the men. "Have you walked far this morning?"

"Pretty well," returned Morcar. "I'm going to London presently," he added with apparent carelessness, "to try and astonish the people a little."

"Ah!" exclaimed another of the jugglers: "and how so? For it must be a clever feller to do that with the Londoners. But may be your people have got hold of some new way of telling fortunes—for the old one is veared out by this time, I should think."

"You suppose that because I am of the gipsy race I must be connected with women who tell fortunes," said Morcar, laughing good-naturedly. "Well, so I have been; but now I'm going to begin in a new line. In fact I don't mind telling you what it is—it's no secret; and I'm half inclined to believe that it's more or less in your way also," he added, glancing significantly towards the drum and the bundles.

"If you could only do some new trick in our line," cried one of the men, eagerly, "you'd make your fortune: but it must be a good one, mind."

"I can do a trick that, I flatter myself, no other man in England can perform," said Morcar, still speaking in a careless, indifferent kind of way. "But as you tell me that you *are* in the juggling line———"

"Yes—we are; and we ain't ashamed on't," exclaimed two or three of the men together.

"Well—then I'll explain to you what I can do," continued Morcar. "I've made a net that winds round an immense long roller, which must be raised upon two upright stakes. When the net is drawn out at dusk, or in a darkened room, it shows a thousand different figures—men, animals, fish, birds, snakes, and monsters of all kinds."

"Capital!—capital!" exclaimed the jugglers.

"But that isn't all," continued Morcar. "These figures all move about—skip—leap—dance—fly—crawl—or seem to swim, according to their nature."

"Come, come—that won't do!" said one of the men, who began to think the gipsy was bantering them.

"It's as true as you're there," answered Morcar, seriously; "and it's very easy to do, too:—only a little phosphorus and other chemical things, skilfully used in a particular way. I reckon upon setting all the young children wild with delight when they see it."

"And if you can really do what you say," observed the man who had last spoken, "you're safe to make your ten bob a-day. But, then," he added, with a sly glance towards his companions, "the trick won't take so well alone: it ought to come after the usual exhibition of chaps like us."

"That's just what I have been thinking myself," cried Morcar. "Only, as I didn't know any people in your way———"

"Well, now you know some, at all events," interrupted the spokesman of the party of jugglers; "and though I say it what shouldn't perhaps, you won't find a jollier or better set of fellers than us in all England. What should you say to making a bargain with us?"

"I have no objection," replied Morcar: "we can but give the thing a trial. But I would rather begin in the country, if possible, than in London."

"The very ticket!" cried the man: "you shall begin to-night. We're hired to perform at that great house which you see from the window; and as we are to be there about half an hour before sunset, it will just be dark enough at the end of our performances for you to show yours. What do you say?"

"Let us settle the terms," answered Morcar; "and I've no objection."

The five jugglers, who were evidently much delighted at the prospect of securing so valuable an addition to their troop, consulted together in whispers for a short period, while Morcar hummed a tune as if perfectly indifferent whether a bargain were concluded or not. The men did not fail to remark his free and off-hand manner, and took it as an unquestionable proof of his confidence in the value of his invention and the success which must attend upon its exhibition. They therefore resolved to enlist him on almost any terms.

"Well," said the spokesman of the party, at length turning towards Morcar once more, "me and my partners here have no objection to give you one-third of the earnings."

"That will suit my purpose uncommonly," replied Morcar: "so let us shake hands upon it."

"And wet it," added one of the jugglers, who, as the gipsy subsequently discovered, was the musician of the party—his instrumental harmony being composed of the huge drum and a set of Pandean pipes, vulgarly called a mouth-organ.

The process of shaking hands all round and of imbibing more strong beer was then gone through; after which the jugglers became very anxious to see the marvellous net that was to make their fortunes. They were, therefore, somewhat disappointed when Morcar informed them that one of the tribe had conveyed it to London in his cart the day before; but their elongating countenances expanded once more into smiles of satisfaction when he assured them that he would instantly set off after it, and be with them again at least an hour previously to the time when they intended to visit the mansion in the neighbourhood.

Matters being thus arranged, Morcar took his departure—rejoiced at the success of his project, though somewhat annoyed at having been compelled to utter so many falsehoods to the credulous jugglers. But this vexation was speedily dissipated by the remembrance of the important duty which he had undertaken; and he moreover intended to make the poor fellows a handsome recompense for the disappointment they were destined to experience relative to the wonderful net.

It is not necessary to follow the gipsy's footsteps to the metropolis, and back to the *Three Kings* again: suffice it to say that he made his appearance at the little public-house shortly after six o'clock in the evening—much to the joy of the five jugglers, who began to imagine that he had been hoaxing them.

But all their suspicions vanished when they beheld the gipsy return, with an iron rod, as long as a hop-pole, and round which the magic net was rolled, over his shoulder.

This rod was not much thicker than the thumb, but the bulk of the burden was considerably increased by the folds of the net.

And at that net did the jugglers stare with such eager eyes, that Morcar could hardly contain his laughter: for the net was nothing more than a common one of the very largest size, such as poachers use to drag canals and small rivers. It was, however, very strong, and when stretched out would cover a room eighteen feet long, by twelve in width.

The iron rod was about thirteen feet long, and the net was rolled round it breadthways.

"You will let us have a sight of the thing before we go?" said one of the jugglers.

"I had rather rest myself for half an hour, or so if you please," returned Morcar. "My walk to-day has been none of the shortest; and I am sadly fatigued. Your curiosity will keep till by and by; for as I have fulfilled my word in coming back, you surely can trust me when I tell you that this net, simple as it may appear, will do all I have promised. Besides, we should only have the trouble of darkening the room, which must be done with blankets, as there are no shutters."

"Let our new friend have his own way, Mike," said the musician of the troop.

"And now," continued Morcar, "I must propose a certain condition, without giving any explanation, but it belongs to my part of the performance. What I require is this:—one of you must remain entirely with me from the moment I pitch the stakes to which this net is to be fastened; and the one who so remains with me, must do just as I direct him in the arrangement of the net; because I must seize a particular time of the evening, in regard to the twilight, to unroll it."

"Well—that can be managed without difficulty," said the man who had been addressed as Mike. "It is always my business to collect the coppers after the exhibition; and I take no share in the performances. So I can remain with you—and whatever you tell me to do, shall be done."

"So far, so good," exclaimed Morcar. "And now, as it is pretty nearly time to set off, we had better begin to dress."

"Are *you* going to dress too?" demanded Mike, with mingled satisfaction and astonishment.

"Only just to disguise myself a bit," answered Morcar, taking a huge red wig from one pocket and a hideous mask from another; "because there's often a prejudice amongst people—especially young ones—against gipsies."

"So there is," observed Mike. "Besides, it's much better to go in character, as they say."

The jugglers were now in high spirits; and they speedily addressed themselves to the process of changing their common apparel for the professional costume.

CHAPTER CCXXXVIII.

THE PERFORMANCE.

The evening was serene and beautiful.

A few thin vapours floated lazily through the blue arch, the hue of which was deliciously mellowed by the golden light of the sun.

It was about seven o'clock; and the principal inmates of Ravensworth Hall were collected in the drawing-room.

Adeline, pale, emaciated, and care-worn, was reclining upon the sofa; and near her sate Eliza Sydney.

The nurse was walking up and down the apartment, with the infant heir in her arms.

Gilbert Vernon was standing outside the window, on a spacious balcony, around which were placed green wooden boxes and garden-pots containing shrubs and early flowers.

"The evening is very beautiful," said Eliza, in a low tone, to Adeline: "will you not walk with me through the Park? The nurse shall accompany us and the child can be well wrapped up. But, indeed, there are no dangers to fear—for the earth is parched with the heat of the day."

"I feel incapable of any energy," answered Adeline, mournfully—very mournfully. "Never have my spirits been so depressed as they are this evening. Methinks that a presentiment of evil near at hand, weighs upon my soul. Oh! when will this dread state of suspense terminate? For five long weeks has it now lasted——"

"Hush! lady—speak lower!" interrupted Eliza. "Mr. Vernon might suddenly enter from the balcony."

"Ah! my dear friend," returned Adeline; "do I not suffer a fearful penalty for my crimes? But human nature cannot endure this doubt—this appalling uncertainty any longer! What does he mean? what can be his plans?"

"Would that we were indeed able to read them!" said Eliza, earnestly. "But the term of this strange drama must speedily arrive," she continued, sinking her voice to a scarcely audible whisper, as she leant over the unhappy lady whom she thus addressed. "Vernon does not remain here from motives of pleasure: he has not abandoned his projects."

"Yet wherefore should he appear so affectionate towards the child?" asked Adeline. "When he first took my sweet Ferdinand in his arms, oh! how I trembled lest he should strangle him in his embrace; and had not a look from you reassured me, I should have shrieked with terror! But now I scarcely entertain a fear when I see my brother-in-law fondle my child. Tell me, dear friend—how must I account for this altered state of feelings?"

"Habit has taught you to subdue your alarms in this respect," replied Eliza Sydney. "Your brother-in-law has gradually devoted more and more of his attention to your dear Ferdinand; and as he never seeks to take him—nor even to approach him—save with your consent, you are to some extent thrown off your guard. Then, as a mother, you are naturally inclined to think better of that man since he has thus seemed to manifest an affection for his nephew. But, be not deceived, lady—his soul is deep and designing! Think you that he cares for a babe not yet ten weeks old? Oh! no—it is not probable! And when he talks in a hypocritical tone of his lamented brother's child—and expresses those apparently earnest hopes that the heir of Ravensworth may eventually prove an honour to the noble house to which he belongs, and to the ancient name which he bears,—ah! be not deceived by him, lady—I implore you: he means nothing that is good—he is playing a part, the true object of which I cannot fathom!"

"Oh! think not that I am deceived by him, dear friend," answered Lady Ravensworth: "think not that my suspicions relative to him are hushed. No—no: else wherefore should I complain of this cruel suspense? There are times, indeed, when I could throw myself at his feet—implore him to quit these walls—and beg upon my knees for mercy towards my child! Does this show that I have forgotten all those circumstances which have led us to look upon him with an abhorrence that we have alike had so much difficulty to conceal?"

"I am aware of all you must suffer," answered Eliza, with a profound sigh; for she pitied—deeply pitied the wretched but criminal woman: "still it is for your child's sake that I have tutored you to play this game of hypocrisy,—that I have induced *you* and compelled *myself* to endure the society of one who is loathsome to us both,—and that we have even condescended to veil beneath smiles our consciousness of his character and atrocious designs. This has been the sum of our hypocrisy;—and how venial it is! And now that all my plans are so nearly matured—with the exception of the return of my messenger from Beyrout———"

"And on his return?" said Adeline, anxiously.

"Have I not assured you that the moment which places in my hands the conclusive proofs of Vernon's guilt—the only link wanting to complete the chain———"

Eliza Sydney was suddenly interrupted by an exclamation which came from the lips of Gilbert Vernon.

She rose, and hastened to the window.

"Here is a troop of poor fellows who doubtless endeavour to earn an honest penny by their agility and skill," said Vernon; "and in a country where mendicity is a crime, even such a livelihood as theirs is honourably gained."

Had not Eliza Sydney's curiosity been at the moment attracted by the strange appearance of the corps of mountebanks to whom Vernon alluded, and who were advancing towards the Hall, she would have been struck with surprise at the emanation of such generous sentiments from so cold-hearted, austere, and aristocratic a person as he.

But her attention was for the time directed towards six persons, five of whom were clad in the light grotesque manner in which mountebanks appear at country-fairs, and even not unfrequently in the streets of London. They wore flesh-coloured stockings, nankin breeches, and jackets of variegated colours, as if, in respect to this latter article of their apparel, they attempted to vie with the peculiar costume of world-renowned Harlequin. The sixth was dressed in a common garb, and wore a hideous mask.

One of the jugglers carried an enormous drum slung behind his back, and had a set of Pandean pipes tucked in his neckcloth beneath his chin; and another was laden with a wicker-basket. The man who was dressed in the common garb and wore the mask, bore a long rod with a net twisted round it, upon his shoulder. A fourth carried two stout stakes; and the remaining two were empty-handed, although it was evident by their dress that they took no small share in the performances which itinerant mountebanks and conjurors of this kind are in the habit of exhibiting.

We must observe, in respect to the man who wore the mask, and who, as the reader already knows, was the gipsy Morcar, that beneath his ample straw hat, and over the edges of the mask, projected huge bushes of reddish-yellow hair, which seemed as if they had once belonged to a door-mat. He walked, a little apart from the others, in company with the man who carried the stakes.

"These conjurors evidently contemplate an exhibition upon the lawn before the windows," said Eliza Sydney, as the men drew nearer to the house. "I will send them out some money and request them to retire, as such performances are not suitable to a spot where mourning is still worn for the deceased lord."

"That were a pity, Mrs. Beaufort," returned Vernon. "These poor creatures have their little feelings as well as performers on the boards of our national theatres; and I am sure you possess too good a heart to wound them. No—let them remain; and if you can induce her ladyship to witness their sports from the balcony, she might be cheered for the moment."

"I should be sorry to wound the feelings of any living being who did not injure me," answered Eliza: "but——"

"Nay, my dear Mrs. Beaufort," interrupted Vernon, "do not refuse me this request. You cannot think that I am boy enough to care for the tricks of these jugglers; but I am well aware—setting aside any consideration on their behalf—that the most trivial and frivolous amusement will often produce a favourable impression upon the spirits. Let Lady Ravensworth come to the window."

Eliza scarcely knew how to offer any farther objection: she was, however, about to make some remark in answer to Mr. Vernon, when the point at issue was settled by that gentleman beckoning the foremost mountebank to advance under the window.

"Now, my good fellow," he exclaimed, looking over the parapet of the balcony, and tossing the man a sovereign, "let us see how well you can amuse us."

"Thank'ee, sir," cried the man, receiving the money in his straw-hat. "We'll do our best, you may depend upon it, sir."

He then returned to his companions, who had stationed themselves at a short distance on the lawn.

The mountebanks forthwith commenced their preparations.

The wicker-basket was placed upon the ground; and its contents were speedily disposed in a manner to suit the performances. A long rope was tied to two trees of about twenty yards' distance from each other: some common blue plates and a wash-hand basin were laid upon the grass; and then a number of small yellow balls were ranged in a line, and at short intervals apart, across the lawn.

While some of the men were making these arrangements, Morcar and his companion advanced to within a short distance of the balcony, and drove the two stakes firmly into the ground. To the tops of these stakes they fastened the ends of the iron rod, without however unrolling the net, but in such a manner that the rod itself would revolve with ease, and the entire net might be drawn out in a moment. They then took their posts each by one of the stakes, and there remained motionless.

In the meantime the man with the drum and the mouth-organ had commenced his instrumental harmony, such as it was; and, at the sound, the servants of the Hall flocked from their offices to the steps of the entrance, well pleased to observe that the monotony of their existence in a dwelling where no company was now received, was about to be broken by even the performances of a few wandering mountebanks.

In the drawing-room, Vernon was still stationed at the balcony; and the nurse, holding the sleeping child in her arms, had approached the open window outside of which Vernon was thus standing.

Eliza Sydney had returned to the side of Lady Ravensworth, to whom she mentioned the presence of the mountebanks and the encouragement which they had received from Mr. Vernon.

"Does he suppose that my spirits can possibly be elevated by a buffoonery of this nature?" said Adeline, her lip curling with contemptuous hauteur. "Besides, such a proceeding is most indecent—most indelicate—on the very spot where a funeral so lately passed!"

"And yet it suits not our present purpose to anger him," returned Eliza.

Lady Ravensworth was about to reply, when Quentin entered the room and placed a letter in Eliza's hands.

The valet then withdrew.

Eliza immediately recognised the writing of the faithful Filippo, and opened it in haste.

Her countenance evinced signs of satisfaction as she perused its contents; but ere she reached the end, she sighed deeply.

"You have evil tidings there," whispered Lady Ravensworth, who had attentively watched her friend's countenance. "And yet, methought you smiled at first."

"I smiled," answered Eliza, also in a low tone, "because I was rejoiced to find that the only link wanting to complete the chain of evidence against that villain"—glancing towards the window as she thus spoke—"is now complete;—and to-morrow——"

"Ah! your messenger is returned from Beyrout?" said Adeline, joyfully. "Then wherefore seem sorrowful?"

"Because the tidings which I now receive confirms the terrible suspicion that your husband was indeed murdered,—coldly—systematically—methodically murdered,—by his own brother!" answered Eliza. "Alas! for the honour of human nature that such things should be!"

Adeline became red as scarlet, and a profound sigh escaped her bosom;—for was she not also a disgrace to human nature?

Eliza forgot at the moment that her words were calculated to wound the already deeply lacerated heart of Lady Ravensworth;—else not for a moment—criminal as Adeline was—would those words have escaped her tongue.

Neither did she perceive the acute emotions which she had awakened; for she was intent upon the reflections excited by the arrival of Filippo's letter.

In the meantime the sports upon the lawn had commenced.

One of the mountebanks ascended to the tightrope, and performed many curious evolutions, much to the amusement not only of the servants assembled upon the steps at the entrance, but even of the nurse at the window.

When the dancing was over, a second juggler balanced first a blue plate, and then the basin, on the point of a long stick—making them spin rapidly round, to the especial delight of the female servants. The nurse, too, was so very much amused that she crossed the threshold of the window, and advanced a little upon the balcony, the better to view the performance.

Vernon seemed intent upon the sports, and did not appear to notice that the ladies were not spectators also. But perhaps he might have thought that they were at another window.

And all this while Morcar, with his mask and bushy yellow hair, and his assistant Mike, were stationed each by one of the stakes to which the net was fixed.

From time to time Vernon had looked over the balcony at these two men, whose presence there seemed somewhat to annoy him: and when the exhibition of the plates and basin was over, he leant forward, exclaiming, "Well, my good fellows, when does your turn come? and what are you going to do with that iron pole and net?"

"You shall see presently, sir," replied Morcar. "It will be the best trick of the whole—as I know you'll admit."

"It is all right," thought Vernon to himself. "These fellows know not the motive for which they were hired; and therefore the fact of their placing the net there can only be a coincidence. However, it is far enough away from the flag-stones to suit my purpose."

Such were the rapid reflections which passed through Vernon's brain.

And had searching eyes been fixed upon his countenance now, they would have observed that although he seemed to watch the sports with a zest passing strange in a man of his years, there were far more important matters agitating in his brain;—for his face was pale—his lips quivered from time to time—and, even while his head remained stationary as if he were looking straight towards the lawn, his eyes were wild and wandering.

Amidst the servants on the steps of the entrance stood the Resurrection Man, apparently one of the most enthusiastic admirers of the sport. But *he*—as well as his employer in the balcony—was somewhat annoyed when he beheld the iron rod and the net which was rolled round it, placed upon the stakes on the verge of the lawn almost beneath the open window of the drawing-room. Another circumstance likewise engaged his attention. This was that he had only seen five jugglers when he had first hired them for the performances; whereas there were now six present. He, however, consoled himself with the idea that the man in the mask and his companion had taken their station so near the balcony, simply because their exhibition, whatever it was, should be better viewed by the inmates of the drawing-room; and relative to the presence of the sixth juggler, he said to himself upon second thoughts, "Well, after all, the troop might have been joined by another comrade since I saw them last night."

But to continue the thread of our narrative.

The last beams of the setting sun were flickering faintly in the western horizon, when the jugglers commenced what may be termed the third act of their performances—namely, the athletic exercises. They had wrestling matches, took extraordinary leaps, and performed various other feats of strength and skill. These being over, one of the band threw himself back, supporting himself with his hands on the ground, and in this position ran on all fours along the line of yellow balls, picking them up with his mouth, one after the other, with astonishing rapidity.

This feat elicited a burst of applause from the servants on the steps; and the nurse, still holding the child in her arms, advanced close up to the parapet of the balcony.

The sun had already set when that last feat began: the twilight was, however, sufficiently strong to permit the spectators to obtain a good view of the performance. But the jugglers now paused for a few minutes to rest themselves; and during that interval the duskiness sensibly increased.

"I wonder what these men are going to do with their iron pole and net," observed Vernon. "Surely their turn must have come now?"

The nurse looked over the parapet to see whether the man in the mask and his companion were still stationed near their apparatus, the use of which puzzled her amazingly.

At that moment two of the jugglers who had advanced from the lawn towards the flag-stones that skirted the wall of the mansion, threw each a detonating-ball upon the pavement.

The explosion was loud—abrupt—startling; and a volume of dense smoke instantly burst as it were from the ground, enveloping the balcony, and pouring even into the drawing-room through the open window.

And, almost at the same instant that the explosion took place, a terrible scream pierced the air; and this was followed by agonising shrieks, mingled with frantic cries of "The child! the child!"

"Merciful heavens!" ejaculated Eliza Sydney, rushing from her seat near Lady Adeline to the window.

But she was met by the nurse, who darted in from the balcony, clasping her hands together, and still screaming wildly—"The child! the child!"

"Holy God!" cried Vernon, also rushing into the room: "the infant has fallen over! Oh! my nephew—my dear nephew!"

And he sank upon a chair, as if overcome by his grief.

"Murderer!—vile—detestable assassin!" exclaimed Eliza Sydney: "this was no accident!"

"Madam," cried Vernon, starting from his seat, "recall those words—or I will not answer for my passion!"

"No—I dare you—monster, murderer that you are!" ejaculated Eliza, as she forced the nurse, who was raving violently, to a sofa.

At that moment shouts of delight were heard from below; and loud cries of "Saved! saved!" reached all the inmates of the drawing-room—save Lady Ravensworth, who had fainted the instant the first wild scream of the nurse had struck her ears like a death-omen.

"Saved! saved!" repeated the nurse, catching at the joyous sound, and now becoming hysterical with the effects of the revulsion of emotions thereby produced.

"Oh! if it be indeed true!" cried Eliza Sydney, darting towards the balcony; but it was now too dark to distinguish any thing that was passing below.

Her suspense did not, however, endure many moments longer; for the door of the drawing-room was suddenly thrown open, and the man in the mask rushed in, crying "Saved! saved!"

Eliza Sydney hastened to meet him, and received the child in her arms.

The little innocent was indeed unhurt, to all appearance, but was crying bitterly.

"Thank God! thank God!" exclaimed Eliza, fervently, as she pressed the child to her bosom.

Quentin now made his appearance with lights: and several of the servants had followed him as far as the door of the room.

"Call the lady's-maid, Quentin, for your mistress," said Eliza, hastily: "she has fainted! Bring water—vinegar—perfume;—I dare not part with the child!"

The lady's-maid was close by; and, hastening into the room, she devoted the necessary attentions to Adeline, who, soon recovering, opened her eyes, gazed wildly around, and then exclaimed in a frantic tone, "My child! my child!"

"He is safe—he is unharmed, dear lady," said Eliza Sydney, advancing towards the sofa with the babe in her arms.

"Give him to me—to me only,—for I am his mother—and I will protect him!" cried Adeline in a shrieking tone: then, receiving the infant from her friend, she clasped it with frantic fondness to her bosom.

In the meantime—although this scene occupied but a few minutes—Gilbert Vernon had sunk upon a chair, like one intoxicated. A film came over his eyes—his brain reeled—and he could not accurately distinguish what was passing around him. Amidst the sudden chaos into which his ideas were plunged, one thought was alone clear—defined—and unobscured; and this was that the child was saved!

The moment Eliza Sidney had consigned the heir of Ravensworth to the arms of his mother, she said in a hasty whisper to Quentin, "Secure Anthony Tidkins without delay, and order the carriage immediately."

The valet quitted the room; and Eliza then advanced towards Gilbert Vernon, exclaiming in a loud tone, "Arrest this villain—hold him—keep him safely, till the officers of justice can be sent for. He murdered his brother; and ere now he has sought to murder that innocent babe!"

As these words, uttered with terrible emphasis, fell upon the ears of the servants, a cry of horror and execration burst from their lips; and Vernon, starting up, exclaimed, "Who accuses me? Wretches—you dare not say that I did such deeds!"

But the next moment he was pinioned by a pair of powerful arms; for Morcar, who had hastily thrown off his mask and wig, was prepared to secure the guilty man.

"Release me, villain!" cried Vernon, struggling furiously—but without avail; for some of the male domestics of the household now assisted the gipsy to retain him. "You shall suffer for this outrage—you shall pay dearly for your conduct! Who dares accuse me of an attempt on that child's life?"

"I!" answered Eliza Sydney, boldly.

"And I also!" echoed Morcar.

"Yes—and I too, murderous wretch!" exclaimed the nurse, stepping forward.

"This is absurd—ridiculous!" cried Vernon, ceasing to struggle, and sinking back into the chair. "You all know how I loved my nephew—how I fondled the dear infant; and you cannot—no—you cannot suppose——"

"I recollect it all now!" ejaculated the nurse, vehemently. "The sudden explosion of those fireworks frightened me dreadfully, and I loosened my hold upon the child: but—if I was standing before my God, I could declare with truth that the babe was at that very same moment pushed from my arms!—Oh! yes—I remember it all now!"

A second burst of indignation on the part of the servants struck terror to the heart of the guilty wretch, who writhed upon his chair; while the workings of his ashy pale countenance—the convulsive movements of his lips—and the wild rolling of his eyes, were terrible—terrible!

Nevertheless he mustered up courage sufficient to exclaim, "That woman speaks falsely! She dropped the child—and she would throw the blame on me!"

"She speaks truly,—vile—black-hearted man!" cried Eliza. "And now, learn that the sole object of my presence in this mansion has been to frustrate your diabolical plots, which for weeks have been known to me!"

"You!" said Vernon, quailing beneath the indignant glance of abhorrence which the royal widow fixed upon him.

"Yes," she continued: "not only have I remained here to frustrate your plots—which, alas! would have succeeded in destroying the child, had not some strange accident, as yet unaccounted for, at least to me, saved the innocent babe from being dashed to pieces against the stones beneath the balcony;—but I have also adopted those measures which will bring all your guilt most terribly home to you! Treacherous—infamous man, I denounce you as the murderer of your brother!"

"'Tis false—false as hell!" cried Vernon.

"It is, alas! too true," returned Eliza. "I have damning proofs against you!"

"Again I declare it is false!" said Gilbert, violently.

"Let us see," resumed Eliza. "You profess to have arrived from the East a few weeks ago; and you have been in England since December or January last! Lady Ravensworth heard your voice in the ruined lodge———"

"Ridiculous!—a mere coincidence—a false impression!" exclaimed Vernon.

"And your landlady in Stamford Street can prove that you lodged with her for several months," added Eliza.

"Monster!" ejaculated one of the servants who had hold upon him.

"All this proves nothing," cried Vernon, furiously.

"But the tobacco which you sent your brother was poisoned," said Eliza, with bitter emphasis.

"'Tis false! It has been submitted to tests: the surgeon who attended my brother had it analysed. All the inmates of the household can speak to this fact."

"And I also have had it analysed," returned Eliza; "and by a native of the East! Fire alone can develope its poisonous qualities; and the ablest chemists in England shall shortly test it by means of that process!"

"Even were it the rankest poison known, you cannot show that I sent it to my brother. I deny the charge—I scorn the imputation!" cried Gilbert Vernon.

"You will speak in a tone of diminished confidence," said Eliza, calmly, "when you hear that I despatched a messenger to Beyrout—that the very place where you purchased the tobacco in that town has been discovered—that the merchant who shipped it for you has made an affidavit before the British Consul at Beyrout to this effect—and that the precise time when you embarked from Beyrout for England has also been ascertained. Nay, more—the letters sent to your address in that town, announcing the death of your brother, reached their destination long after you had left, and were never opened—nor even seen by you! Yet you affected to return to England in consequence of the receipt of those letters."

"And who are you, madam, that have taken such pains to collect these particulars, which you are pleased to call evidence against me?" demanded Vernon. "Is the scion of a noble race to be maligned—outraged—accused of atrocious crimes by an unknown but meddling woman?"

"Again you speak at random," answered Eliza; "for did I choose to proclaim my title and my rank, you would admit that not even the owners of the proud name of Ravensworth possess a dignity so exalted as mine. Let me, however, return to the sad subject of my discourse: let me convince you that the evidence of your crime is so overwhelming that penitence and prayer would become you far more than obstinacy, and haughty but vain denial! For if there be farther proofs of your guilt required, seek them for yourself in those circumstances which induced you to take into your service Anthony Tidkins, the Resurrection Man!"

Vernon shuddered fearfully as these words fell upon his ears; for it seemed as if a sledge-hammer had been suddenly struck upon his brain.

"And if farther proofs are really wanting, lady," said Morcar, "it is for me to supply them. This morning I was concealed in the ruins of a cottage at no great distance from the Hall; and there my ears were astounded with the damnable plot which this man and his accomplice had conceived against the life of the infant heir of Ravensworth. Why I did not immediately betray them—why I resolved on counteracting that plot, I will explain on a more fitting occasion. But let me inform you that it was by my device the child was saved; for the instant that the arms of the jugglers were raised to throw the detonating balls upon the ground, the net was unrolled—rapid as lightning—by my companion and myself; and the babe was caught in it as he fell!"

"Excellent man!" exclaimed Eliza Sydney, while a murmur of applause passed amongst the assembled servants: "who are you? what is your name?"

"I am one of that wandering tribe called *Gipsies*, madam," was the answer: "and my name is Morcar."

"Morcar!" echoed Eliza. "Oh! I have heard of you before—often—very often! The Prince of Montoni speaks of you as a friend; and your services to him in the Castelcicalan war have become a matter of history."

"Ah! is it possible?" cried Morcar, who for some moments had been studying Eliza's features with attention—for he had seen many portraits of her during his sojourn in Italy, and a light now broke in upon his memory: "is it possible that I am in the presence of her to whom that great Prince owes his life? Oh! madam, I also have to thank your Serene Highness—humble as I am—for the safety and freedom which I experienced after the defeat at Ossore."

And, as he spoke, Morcar abandoned his hold upon Gilbert Vernon, and fell upon his knees before the royal widow.

"Rise, Morcar," she hastily exclaimed: "I have renounced for ever the proud title of Grand-Duchess, and would henceforth be known as Eliza Sydney. Moreover, this is no time for homage—even were I disposed to receive it."

"The knee of Morcar bows not to princes because they are princes," returned the gipsy, proudly and yet respectfully; "but to men or women who by their virtues deserve such homage."

At that moment a cry of alarm burst from the servants who had still retained their hold upon Vernon; and at the same instant this guilty man sprang furiously from their grasp—hurled them violently aside—and, ere a single hand could stop his mad career, rushed to the window.

Morcar bounded after him: but it was too late.

Gilbert Vernon had precipitated himself from the balcony!

The sound of his fall upon the pavement beneath,—and the sound of a human being thus falling has none other like it in the world,—struck upon every ear in that drawing-room.

Some of the servants hastened down stairs, and ran to the spot where Vernon lay.

They raised him—they bore him into the hall; but the moment the light of the lamps fell upon him, they perceived that all human aid was unavailing.

His skull was literally beaten in, and his hair was covered with his blood and brains!

Thus did he meet the fate which he had all along intended for his infant nephew.

Terrible suicide—but just retribution!

Half an hour after this dread event a travelling carriage rolled rapidly away from Ravensworth Hall.

In it were seated Adeline, with her child upon her lap, her lady's-maid, and the nurse.

The faithful Quentin, who had been induced by the persuasion of Eliza Sydney to remain in the service of Lady Ravensworth, occupied the dickey behind the vehicle.

Adeline was now on her way to Dover, whence she purposed to pass to the continent; her intention being, in pursuance of the advice of Eliza, to seek some retired spot in the south of France, where she might at least find tranquillity and repose, if not happiness, after the rude storms to which she had lately been so fearfully exposed.

Not that this self-expatriation was compulsory on account of Lady Ravensworth's *one dread crime*: it was nevertheless the project to which we have before alluded, and by which means Eliza had planned that Adeline should escape from the consequences of any revelation that might be made by the Resurrection Man in respect to the murdered Lydia Hutchinson.

But no such revelation was made, inasmuch as Tidkins had disappeared from the mansion ere Quentin received the order to secure him. For the instant the cry of "Saved! saved!" fell upon the ears of the Resurrection Man and conveyed to him the stunning fact that the scheme had failed—that the child had escaped, in some marvellous manner, the fate intended for it,—then did he know full well that Ravensworth Hall was no longer the place for him. Reckless of what might become of Vernon, and unnoticed by the servants amidst the confusion which prevailed immediately after the fall of the child from the balcony, Tidkins slipped out of the mansion by the back way, and was speedily beyond the reach of danger.

Thus terminated that terrible series of incidents which constitute so strange an episode in the annals of the family of Ravensworth.

But ere Adeline took her departure from the mansion of that noble race whose name she bore, she had learnt, with surprise and joy, that the excellent friend whom heaven had sent her, and by whose touching language and admirable example her own heart had been brought to a state of sincere and profound penitence,—she had learnt, we say, that this noble-hearted woman was one whose brow a diadem had lately graced!

We may also observe that Morcar refused the liberal recompense which both Adeline and Eliza proffered him for the most important service which he had rendered in defeating Vernon's plan at a moment when, in spite of all the precautions and the various measures adopted by Eliza, it seemed to touch upon the verge of a success fatal to the existence of the infant heir.

Satisfied with the approval of his own conscience, and attended by the blessings of a mother whose child he had saved, Morcar returned with the jugglers to the *Three Kings*, where he completely satisfied them for the disappointment they had experienced in respect to the wondrous properties of his net; and on the ensuing morning he parted from them, to pursue his own way.

Eliza Sydney passed the night at Ravensworth Hall; and, after the Coroner's Inquest had sate next day upon the body of the suicide Vernon, she returned to her peaceful villa at Clapton.

CHAPTER CCXXXIX.

THE RESURRECTION MAN'S RETURN HOME.

As the Resurrection Man hurried through the fields, amidst the darkness of the night, he vented in horrible imprecations the rage he experienced at the failure of a scheme to which he had devoted so much time and trouble.

He knew that the blank acceptance which he had extorted from Vernon, and which he had looked upon as the safe guarantee of the speedy acquisition of three thousand pounds, was now but a valueless slip of paper; and he cursed himself for having been foolish enough to advance some two or three hundred guineas of his own money to furnish his late employer with the supplies necessary for his purposes.

But as a set-off against these disappointments he had one consolation—a consolation which to a less avaricious mind would have been more than commensurate with the losses that Tidkins deplored. He was possessed of Lady Ravensworth's valuable casket of jewels, which he had removed, a few days after he had obtained it in the manner already described, to his house in Globe Town.

And it was to this den that he was now repairing. He was as yet unacquainted with the fate of Gilbert Vernon; but, supposing it probable that justice might already have that individual in her grasp, he at once determined to provide for his own safety. Abandoning, therefore, all his long-nourished schemes of vengeance against the Prince of Montoni, the Rattlesnake, and Crankey Jem, Tidkins was now intent only on securing his treasure, and taking his departure for America with the least possible delay.

It was about two o'clock in the morning when the Resurrection Man, sinking with the fatigues of his long and circuitous journey round all the northern outskirts of London, arrived at his own house.

Wearied as he was, he wasted no time in snatching a temporary repose: a glass of spirits recruited his strength and invigorated his energies; and, with his bunch of keys in his hand, he repaired from his own chamber to the rooms on the ground-floor.

It will be remembered that on a former occasion,—on his return home, in the middle of the month of March, after his escape from the Middlesex House of Correction,—the Resurrection Man had perceived certain indications which led him to imagine that the step of an intruder had visited the ground-floor and the subterranean part of his house. His suspicions had fallen upon Banks; but an interview with this individual convinced him that those suspicions were unfounded; for although he did not question him point-blank upon the subject, yet his penetration was such, that he could judge of the real truth by the undertaker's manner.

Since that period Tidkins had visited his house in Globe Town on several occasions—indeed, as often as he could possibly get away from Ravensworth Hall for the greater portion of a day; and, perceiving no farther indications of the intrusion of a stranger, he became confirmed in the belief which had succeeded his first suspicions, and which was that he had been influenced by groundless alarms.

But now, the moment he put the key into the lock of the door in the alley, he uttered a terrible imprecation—for the key would not turn, and there was evidently something in the lock!

Hastily picking the lock with one of those wire-instruments which are used for the purpose by burglars, he extracted from it a piece of a key which had broken in the wards.

Fearful was now the rage of the Resurrection Man; and when he had succeeded in opening the door, he precipitated himself madly into that department of his abode.

But what pen can describe his savage fury, when, upon lighting a lantern, he saw the trap raised, and the brick removed from the place in the chimney where it covered the secret means of raising the hearth-stone?

Plunging desperately down into the subterranean, at the risk of breaking his neck, Tidkins felt like one on whose eyes a hideous spectre suddenly bursts, when he beheld the door of a cell—the very cell in which his treasure was concealed—standing wide open!

Staggering now, as a drunken man—and no longer rushing wildly along,—but dragging himself painfully,—Tidkins reached that cell.

His worst fears were confirmed: the stone in the centre was removed from its place;—and his treasure was gone!

Yes:—money-bags and jewel-casket—the produce of heaven only knows how much atrocity and blackest crime—had disappeared.

This was the second time that his hoarded wealth was snatched from him.

Then did that man—so energetic in the ways of turpitude, so strong in the stormy paths of guilt,—then did he sink down, with a hollow groan, upon the cold floor of the cell.

For a few minutes he lay like one deprived of sense and feeling, the only indications of life being the violent clenching of his fists, and the demoniac workings of his cadaverous countenance.

Cadaverous!—never did the face of a wretched being in the agonies of strangulation by hanging, present so appalling—so hideous an appearance!

But in a short time the Resurrection Man started up with a savage howl and a terrible imprecation: his energies—prostrated for a period—revived; and his first idea, when arousing from that torpor, was vengeance—a fearful vengeance upon the plunderer.

But who was that plunderer? whose hand had suddenly beggared him?

His suspicions instantly fixed themselves upon two persons—the only two of his accomplices who were acquainted with the mysteries of the subterranean.

These were Banks and the Buffer.

He was about to turn from the cell, and repair forthwith—even at that hour—to the dwelling of the undertaker, when his eyes suddenly fell upon some letters scrawled in chalk upon the pavement, and which the position of the lantern had hitherto prevented him from observing.

He stooped down, and read the words—"JAMES CUFFIN."

The mystery was solved: his mortal enemy, Crankey Jem, had robbed him of his treasure!

Dark—terribly ominous and foreboding—was now the cloud which overspread the countenance of the Resurrection Man.

"Had I ten times the wealth I have lost," he muttered to himself, with a hyena-like growl, "I would not quit this country till I had wreaked my vengeance upon that man! But this is now no place for me: he has tracked me here—he may set the traps upon me. Let us see if the Bully Grand cannot discover his lurking hole."

With these words,—and now displaying that outward calmness which often covers the most intensely concentrated rage,—the Resurrection Man quitted the subterranean, carefully securing the doors behind him.

He purposely broke a key in the lock of the door leading into the dark alley, so as to prevent the intrusion of any of the neighbours, should their curiosity tempt them to visit the place; for he made up his mind not to return thither again so long as Jem Cuffin was alive and able to betray him.

Having provided himself with a few necessaries, he closed the up-stairs rooms, and then took his departure.

He bent his steps towards the house of the undertaker in Globe Lane; and, knocking him up, obtained admittance and a bed.

When he awoke from a sound sleep, into which sheer fatigue plunged him in spite of the unpleasant nature of his thoughts, it was broad-day-light.

He immediately rose and despatched one of Banks's boys for the morning newspaper; and from its columns he learnt the fate of the Honourable Gilbert Vernon.

"Better so than that he should have remained alive perhaps to repent, as these sentimental humbugs in high life usually do, and then blab against me," murmured Tidkins to himself. "The whole business at the Hall is evidently wrapped in considerable mystery; and there I hope it will remain. But now let me devote myself heart and soul to my search after that scoundrel Crankey Jem."

CHAPTER CCXL.

A NEW EPOCH.

Twenty months had elapsed since the events just related.

It was now the end of January, 1843.

Haply the reader may begin to imagine that our subject is well-nigh exhausted—that the mysteries of London are nearly all unveiled?

He errs; for London is a city containing such a variety of strange institutions, private as well as public, and presenting so many remarkable phases to the contemplation of the acute observer, that the writer who is resolved to avail himself fully of the heterogeneous materials thus supplied him, cannot readily lack food for comment and narrative.

The dwellers in the country, and even the inhabitants of the great provincial cities and manufacturing towns, can form no just estimate of the wondrous features of the sovereign metropolis by the local scenes with which they are familiar.

Who can judge of the splendour of the West End of London by even the most fashionable quarters of Edinburgh or Dublin?

Who can conceive the amount of revolting squalor and hideous penury existing in the poor districts of London, by a knowledge of the worst portions of Liverpool or Manchester?

Who can form a conjecture of the dreadful immorality and shocking vice of the low neighbourhoods of London, judging by the scenes presented to view in the great mining or manufacturing counties?

No:—for all that is most gorgeous and beautiful, as well as all that is most filthy and revolting,—all that is best of talent, or most degraded of ignorance,—all that is most admirable for virtue, or most detestable for crime,—all that is most refined in elegance, or most strange in barbarism,—all, all these wondrous phases are to be found, greatest in glory, or lowest in infamy, in the imperial city of the British Isles!

And shall we be charged with vanity, if we declare that never until now has the veil been so rudely torn aside, nor the corruptions of London been so boldly laid bare?

But, in undertaking this work, we were determined at the outset to be daunted by no fear of offending the high and the powerful: we were resolved to misrepresent nothing for the purpose of securing to ourselves the favour of those whom so many sycophants delight to bespatter with their sickly praises.

In the same independent spirit do we now pursue our narrative.

On the left-hand side of Brydges Street, as you proceed from the Strand towards Russell Street, Covent Garden, you may perceive a lamp projecting over the door of an establishment which, viewed externally, appears to be a modest eating-house; but which in reality is one of the most remarkable places of nocturnal entertainment in London.

Upon the lamp alluded to are painted these words——"THE PARADISE."

It was past midnight, towards the end of January, 1843, when two gentlemen, wearing fashionable Taglioni coats over their elegant attire, and impregnating the fine frosty air with the vapour of their cigars, strolled into this establishment.

Proceeding down a passage, they pushed open a door with a painted ground-glass window, and entered a spacious supper-room.

This apartment was lofty, handsomely fitted up, well furnished, and provided with boxes containing little tables, like the coffee-room of an hotel.

A cheerful fire burnt in the grate, and the numerous lights suspended around the apartment were reflected in a handsome mirror over the mantel-piece.

Above the door leading into the room was a species of gallery, forming a grotto-like opening into a suite of upper apartments, which were reached by a flight of stairs leading from the passage just now mentioned.

All was gaiety and bustle both in the coffee-room below and the chambers above. Numerous suppers were in progress, the partakers thereof consisting of gentlemen of various descriptions and gay ladies of only one particular class. Oysters, lobsters, cold fowls, ham, and kidneys, constituted the principal edibles; while liquor flowed copiously and in all gradations of luxury, from humble porter in pewter pots to sparkling champagne in green bottles.

The male portion of the guests was composed of those various specimens of "gentlemen" who either turn night into day, or who make up for the toils of the day by the dissipated enjoyments of the night.

There was an attorney's clerk, who, having picked up a stray guinea in a manner for which he would not perhaps have liked to account, was doing the liberal, in the shape of oysters, stout, and hot brandy-and-water, to some fair Cyprian whom he had never seen before, and whom he would perhaps never see again, but with whom he was on the very best possible terms for the time being; the only trifling damper to *his* enjoyment being *her* constant anxiety lest "her friend" should happen to come in and catch her at supper with the said attorney's clerk.

There was a notorious black-leg, who was regaling a couple of frail ones with champagne and looking out for flats as well; while his accomplice was doing precisely the same in the next box,—both these respectable gentlemen affecting to be total strangers to each other.

There also was a handsome young man, who, having just come of age, and stepped into the possession of a good property, was commencing his career of waste and extravagance at the Paradise. Proud of the nauseating flattery of the three or four abandoned women who had him in tow, he was literally throwing about his money in all directions, and staring around him with the vacant air of semi-intoxication, as much as to say, "Don't you think me a very fine dashing fellow indeed?"

In another box was an old man, who had reached the wrong side of sixty, but who was endeavouring to make a young girl of seventeen believe that he was but forty-four last birth-day,—a tale which she had too much tact to appear to doubt for a moment, as the antiquated beau supplied her with copious draughts of champagne to enable her to swallow the lie the more easily.

A little farther on was a dandified, stiff-necked, coxcomical individual of about six-and-twenty, sipping sherry with a fair friend, and endeavouring to render himself as polite and agreeable as possible. But, at every word he spoke, he drew out the edge of the table-cloth to precisely the extent of a yard between his fore-fingers and thumbs;—whereby it was easy to perceive that, although he assured his companion he was a captain in the Guards, he in reality exercised the less conspicuous but more active employment of a linen-draper's assistant.

Crowding near the fire were several Cyprians, who had not as yet obtained cavaliers, and were therefore hovering between the alternatives of "supper" or "no supper," the odds being, to all appearances, in favour of the latter. They did not, however, seem very unhappy while their fate, as to oysters and stout, was pending in the balance of suspense; but laughed, chattered, and larked amongst themselves; and then, by way of avoiding any thing like monotony or sameness in their recreation, two of them got up a pleasant little quarrel which terminated in a brisk exchange of blows and scratches.

Leaning over the side of the grotto-like gallery before referred to, were two individuals, whose appearance was something between that of dissipated actors and broken down tradesmen; and who were so disguised in liquor that their own mothers could scarcely have recognised them. Being most probably wearied of their own conversation, they diverted themselves by addressing their remarks to the people in the coffee-room below, whom they invited in the most condescending manner possible to "flare up," "mind their eyes," "form a union," and enact various other little social civilities of the same ambiguous nature.

Within the upper rooms were several gay ladies and jovially disposed gentlemen, all mainly intent upon the pleasures of eating or drinking, which occupations were however relieved by boisterous shouts of laughter and practical jokes of all kinds.

In justice to the proprietor of this establishment it must be observed that he conducted it upon as orderly a system as could be possibly maintained when the characters of his patrons and patronesses are taken into consideration; and the moment a disturbance occurred, either himself or his waiters adopted the most efficient means of putting an end to it, by bundling the offenders neck-and-crop into the street.

The two gentlemen who lounged, as before stated, into this celebrated night-house on the occasion alluded to, took possession of a vacant box, and throwing down their cigars, summoned the waiter.

"Yes, sir—coming, sir—*di*-rectly, sir," cried the chief functionary thus adjured, and who was busy at the moment in disputing the items of the score with the linen-draper's assistant:—but, when that little matter was duly settled to the satisfaction of the waiter and the discomfiture of the assistant aforesaid, he hurried up to the table occupied by the new comers.

"Well, what shall we have, Harborough?" asked one of the gentlemen, appealing to his companion.

"'Pon my honour, I don't care a rap," was the reply. "Order what you like, old fellow."

Thus encouraged, Mr. Chichester (for it was he) desired the waiter to bring "no end of oysters," and to follow with a cold fowl.

"Yes, sir—certainly, sir," said the domestic, hastily transferring a pepper-box from one side of the table to the other, and smoothing down the cloth: "please to order any thing to drink, gentlemen?"

"A bottle of champagne," returned Mr. Chichester; "and make haste about it."

"Yes, sir—this minute, sir:"—and the waiter glided away with that kind of shuffling, shambling motion which no living beings save waiters can ever accomplish.

When the provender was duly supplied, and the first glass of champagne was quaffed, Chichester leant across the table, and said to the baronet in a low tone of chuckling triumph, "Well, old chap, I don't think we can complain of Fortune during the last three or four months?"

"No—far from it," returned Sir Rupert Harborough. "But we musn't be idle because we happen to have a few five pound notes in our pocket. However, things will turn up, I dare say."

"Yes—if we look out for them," said Chichester; "but not unless. By the bye, who do you think I met this afternoon, as I was strolling along the Strand?"

"Can't say at all," replied the baronet. "Who?"

"Greenwood," added Chichester.

"The deuce you did! And how was he looking?"

"Not so slap-up as he used to be:—no jewellery—toggery not quite new—hat showing marks of the late rain—boots patched at the sides—and cotton gloves."

"The scoundrel! Do you remember how he served me about that bill which I accepted in Lord Tremordyn's name? Ah! shouldn't I like to pay him out for it!" said the baronet. "But how he has fallen within the last two years! Turned out of his seat for Rottenborough at the last election—obliged to give up his splendid house in Spring Gardens——"

"Well, well—we know all about that," interrupted Chichester, impatiently. "Don't speak so loud; but look into the next box—the one behind me, I mean—and tell me if you think that young fellow who is treating those girls to champagne would prove a flat or not."

The baronet glanced in the direction indicated; and immediately afterwards gave an affirmative nod of the head to his companion: then, leaning across the table he whispered, "To be sure he would; and I know who he is.

- 601 -

It's young Egerton—the son of the great outfitter, who died a few years ago, leaving a large fortune in trust for this lad. I'll be bound to say he has just come of age, and is launching out."

"Does he know you?" inquired Chichester, also speaking in a subdued tone.

"I am almost certain he does not," replied the baronet. "But sit up—we will soon see what he is made of. I will touch him on the *cross* that we have got up together."

The two friends resumed the discussion of their supper, and in a few minutes began to converse with each other in a tone loud enough to be heard—and intended also to be so heard—in the next box.

"And so you really think the Haggerstone Pet will beat the Birmingham Bruiser, Mr. Chichester?" observed the baronet, in a tone of mere friendly courtesy.

"I am convinced of it, Sir Rupert, in spite of the odds," was the answer, delivered in the same punctilious manner. "Will you take my four ponies upon the Haggerstone Pet to five?"

"Done, Mr. Chichester!" cried the baronet: then drawing out a betting-book from the breast-pocket of his coat, he proceeded to enter the wager, saying aloud and in a measured tone as he did so, "Back Birmingham Bruiser against Haggerstone Pet—five ponies to four—Honourable—Arthur—Chichester. There it is!"

This ceremony was followed on the part of Mr. Chichester, who, having produced *his* book, wrote down the wager, saying, "Back Haggerstone Pet against Birmingham Bruiser—four ponies to five—Sir—Rupert—Harborough—baronet."

"And now," exclaimed the baronet, "before we put up our books, I'll give you another chance. Will you take three hundred to one that the favourites for the fight and the *Derby* don't both win?"

"Stop, Sir Rupert!" cried Chichester. "Let me first see how I stand for the *Derby*:"—then, as if speaking to himself, he continued, "Taken even five hundred, four horses against the field, from Lord Dunstable;—seven hundred to one against *Eagle-wing*, from the Honourable Colonel Cholmondeley;—betted even five hundred, *Skyscraper* to *Moonraker*, with the Honourable Augustus Smicksmack. Well, Sir Rupert," he exclaimed, raising his head from the contemplation of the leaf on which these sham bets were entered, "I don't mind if I take you."

"It's a bargain," said the baronet; and the wager was accordingly inscribed in the little books.

The two gentlemen then refreshed themselves each with another draught of champagne; and Sir Rupert Harborough, as he drank, glanced over the edge of the glass into the next box, to ascertain the effect produced upon Mr. Egerton by the previous little display of sporting spirit.

That effect was precisely the one which had been anticipated. Mr. Egerton was not so tipsy but that he was struck with the aristocratic names of the two gentlemen in the next box; and he raised his head from the bosom of a Cyprian to take a view of Sir Rupert Harborough, Bart., and the Honourable Arthur Chichester.

So satisfactory was the result of the survey—at least to himself—that he determined not only to show off a little of his own "dashing spirit," but also, if possible, form the acquaintance of the two gentlemen; for, like many young fellows similarly circumstanced, he was foolish enough to believe that the possession of money *must* prove a passport to the best society, if he could only obtain an opening.

Therefore, having greedily devoured every word of the dialogue just detailed, and taking it for granted that nothing in this world was ever more sincere than the betting of Sir Rupert Harborough, Bart., and the Honourable Arthur Chichester, Mr. Egerton exclaimed, "Beg pardon, gentlemen, for intruding upon you; but I think I heard you staking some heavy sums on the coming fight?"

"Really, sir," said the baronet, gravely, "I was not aware that any thing which took place between me and this gentleman could be overheard;—and yet, after all," he added with a gracious smile, "I do not know that there is the least harm in a little quiet bet."

"Harm, no—and be damned to it!" ejaculated Mr. Egerton. "All I can say is, that I admire sporting men—I honour them: they're an ornament to the country. What would Old England—hic—be without her Turf—her hunting—her prize-fighting? For my part, I have a great idea of this fight—a very great—hic—idea. But I back the Birmingham Bruiser—I do."

"So do I, sir," answered the baronet "My friend here, however—the Honourable Mr. Chichester—fancies the Haggerstone Pet."

"I heard him say so," returned the young man. "But, if he hasn't made up his book, I don't mind betting him five hundred pounds—hic—to his four—that's the odds, I believe——"

"Yes—those are the odds," observed Mr. Chichester, carelessly: then, taking out his book, he said, "But I am already so deep in this fight, that I really am afraid——however, if you wish it, I don't mind——"

"Is it a bet, then, sir?" asked the young gentleman, looking round the room with an air of importance, as if he were quite accustomed to the thing, although it was in reality the first wager he had ever laid in his life.

"It shall be so, if you choose, sir," returned Chichester: then, glancing in an inquiring manner towards his new acquaintance, he said with a bland smile, "I really beg your pardon—but I have not the pleasure——"

"Oh! truly—you don't know me from Adam!" interrupted the other. "But you shall know me, sir—and I hope we shall know each other better too—hic."

He then produced his card; and Mr. Chichester, of course, affected not to have been previously aware of the young gentleman's name.

The bet between them was duly recorded—by Mr. Chichester in his little book, and by Mr. Albert Egerton on the back of a love-letter.

The latter gentleman then called for his bill, and having glanced at the amount, paid it without a murmur, adding a munificent donation for the waiter. Having effected this arrangement, by means of which he got rid of the women who had fastened themselves on him, he coolly passed round to the table at which his new acquaintances were seated, and called for another bottle of champagne.

When it was brought, he was about to pay for it; but Sir Rupert interrupted him, saying, "No—that would be too bad. If you sit at our table, you are our guest;—and here's to a better acquaintance."

The bottle went round rapidly; and Mr. Egerton became quite enchanted with the agreeable manners of Sir Rupert Harborough, Bart., and the off-hand pleasant conversation of the Honourable Arthur Chichester.

It was now past one o'clock; and the baronet proposed to depart.

"Which way do you—hic—go?" inquired Egerton.

"Oh! westward, of course," returned Harborough, in a tone of gentle remonstrance, as much as to say that there could have been no doubt upon the subject. "Will you walk with us?"

"Certainly," was the answer: "and we will smoke a—hic—cigar as we go along."

The baronet called for the bill, paid it, and led the way from the room, followed by Egerton and Chichester, the former of whom insisted upon stopping at the bar to take some soda water, as he declared himself to be "half-seas—hic—over."

While the three gentlemen were engaged in partaking each of a bottle of the refreshing beverage, Sir Rupert felt his coat-sleeve gently pulled from behind; and, turning round, he perceived a man whom he had noticed in the coffee-room. Indeed, this was one of the black-legs already alluded to as having been engaged in treating Cyprians to supper and champagne.

The baronet instantly comprehended the nature of the business which this individual had to address him upon; and making him a significant sign, he said to Chichester, "Do you and Mr. Egerton go very slowly along the Strand; and I will follow you in a few minutes. I have a word to say to this gentleman."

Gentleman, indeed!—one of the most astounding knaves in London! But vice and roguery compel the haughty aristocrat to address the lowest ruffian as an equal.

Chichester took Egerton's arm, and sauntered out of the house, attended to the door by the obsequious master of the establishment—an honour shown only to those who drink champagne or claret.

"Well, sir, what is it?" asked the baronet, taking the black-leg aside, and speaking to him in a whisper.

"Only this, Sir Rupert," returned the man: "you've got that youngster in tow, and he'll turn out profitable, no doubt. Me and my pal, which is inside the room there, meant to have had him somehow or another; and we planted our vimen on him to-night:—but we thought he wasn't drunk enough; and then you come in and take him from us. Your friend has nailed him for a bet of five hundred, which he's safe to pay; so you must stand someot for my disappointment."

"I understand you, sir," said the baronet. "Here are twenty pounds: and if the bet be paid, you shall have thirty more. Will that do?"

"Thank'ee for the twenty, which is ready," answered the black-leg, consigning the notes to his pocket. "Now never mind the other thirty; but make the best you can out of that young chap; and all I ask in return is just a word or two about the mill that's coming off."

"I don't understand you," said the baronet, colouring.

"Come, come—that won't do," continued the man. "But don't be afeard—it's all in the way of business that I'm speaking. I see you and Mr. Chichester at a public about three weeks ago along with the Birmingham Bruiser; and therefore I knowed you was the friends which deposited the money for him, but which kept in the back-ground. So all I want is the office—just a single word: is the Bruiser to win or to make a cross of it?"

"Really, my good fellow——" stammered the baronet.

"Only just one word, so that I may know how to lay my money," persisted the black-leg, "and your secret is safe with me. For my own interest it will be so, if you tell me which way it is to be."

"Can I rely on you?" said Sir Rupert. "But of course I may, if you really mean to bet. Now keep the thing dark—and you may win plenty of money. The Bruiser is to *lose*: the odds are five to four on him now—and they will be seven to four in his favour before the fight comes off. No one suspects that it is to be a cross; and the reports of the Bruiser's training are glorious."

"Enough—and as mum as a dead man, Sir Rupert," whispered the black-leg.

He then returned to the supper-room; and the baronet hastened after his friends.

CHAPTER CCXLI.

CROCKFORD'S.

Sir Rupert Harborough, Mr. Albert Egerton, and Mr. Arthur Chichester were walking arm-in-arm, and smoking cigars, along the West Strand, about ten minutes after the little incident which closed the preceding chapter, when they were met by two tall and fashionable-looking gentlemen, who immediately recognised the baronet and Chichester.

Both parties stopped; and the two gentlemen were in due course introduced to Mr. Egerton as Lord Dunstable and the Honourable Colonel Cholmondeley.

By the significant tone and manner of the baronet,—a sort of freemasonry known only to the initiated,—both Dunstable and the Colonel were given to understand that a flat had been caught in the person of Mr. Albert Egerton; and they immediately received their cue as completely as if they had been prompted by half an hour's explanation.

"What have you been doing with yourselves, gentlemen, this evening?" inquired Dunstable, as they all now proceeded together through Trafalgar Square.

"My friends and myself have been supping at the Paradise," answered the baronet, carelessly.

Mr. Egerton drew himself up an inch higher immediately, although somewhat top-heavy with the champagne and cigars;—but he felt quite proud—quite another man, indeed—at being numbered amongst Sir Rupert Harborough's *friends*, and at walking familiarly in the company of a real lord.

"Cholmondeley and I were thinking of looking in at Crockford's before we encountered you," observed Dunstable, forgetting at the moment that himself and friend were proceeding in quite a contrary direction when the meeting alluded to took place. "What say you? shall we all go to Crockford's?"

Egerton noticed not the little oversight. The word "Crockford's" perfectly electrified him. He had often passed by the great pandemonium in St. James's Street, and looked with wistful eyes at its portals—marvelling whether they would ever unfold to give admission to him; and now that there seemed a scintillation of a chance of that golden wish, which he had so often shadowed forth, being substantially gratified, he could scarcely believe that he was in truth Albert Egerton, the son of an outfitter, and having a very respectable widowed aunt engaged in the haberdashery line on Finsbury Pavement;—but it appeared as if he had suddenly received a transfusion of that aristocracy in whose company he found himself.

Already did he make up his mind to cut the good old aunt and the half-dozen of fair cousins—her daughters—for ever:—already did he vow never to be seen east of Temple Bar again. But then he thought how pleasant it would be to drop in at Finsbury Pavement on some Sunday—just at the hour of dinner, which he could make his lunch—and then astound his relatives with the mention of his aristocratic acquaintances,—no, his *friends*,—Lord Dunstable, Sir Rupert Harborough, the Honourable Colonel Cholmondeley, and the Honourable Arthur Chichester!

And what glorious names, too:—nothing plebeian about them—nothing lower than an Honourable!

Had he known how cheaply Mr. Chichester held his titular decoration, Albert Egerton would have perhaps assumed one himself: but he did not entertain the least suspicion concerning the matter, and therefore envied the pawnbroker's son almost as much as either of the others.

But to return.

Lord Dunstable had said, "Shall we all go to Crockford's?"

Deep was the suspense of Mr. Egerton until Sir Rupert Harborough replied, "With much pleasure. It would be the very thing to teach our young friend Egerton here a little of life."

"But I am not a member" he murmured, in a disconsolate tone.

"*We* are all members, however," said Lord Dunstable; "and can pass you in with ease. Let me and Harborough take charge of you."

This arrangement was rendered necessary by the fact that Mr. Chichester was *not* a member of Crockford's, and would, therefore, require to be introduced by Colonel Cholmondeley. Dunstable, Harborough, and Egerton accordingly walked on together; while the Colonel and Chichester followed at some little distance, as it was not thought worth while to allow the young flat to perceive that the Honourable Arthur Chichester must be smuggled in, as it were, as well as himself.

In this manner the two parties repaired to the celebrated—or rather notorious—Saint James's Club; and Egerton's wildest dream was realized—the acmé of his ambition was reached—the portals of Crockford's were darkened by his plebeian shadow!

Although excited by wine and by the novelty of his situation, he nevertheless maintained his self-possession so far as to avoid any display of vulgar wonderment at the brilliant scene upon which he now entered. Leaning on the arms of Lord Dunstable and Sir Rupert Harborough, he passed through the marble hall, and was conducted to the coffee-room on the right-hand side.

There they waited for a few minutes until Cholmondeley and Chichester joined them; and Egerton had leisure to admire the superb pier-glasses, the magnificent chandeliers, the handsome side-boards, the costly plate, and the other features of that gorgeous apartment.

When the Colonel and Chichester made their appearance, the party proceeded to the supper-room. There Egerton's eyes were completely dazzled by the brilliant looking-glasses, all set in splendid frames with curious designs—the crystal chandeliers—the elegant sconces—the superb mouldings—the massive plate—and the immense quantities of cut glasses and decanters. The curtains were of the richest damask silk; the walls were hung with choice pictures; and the whole magic scene was brilliantly lighted up with innumerable wax candles, the lustre of which was reflected in the immense mirrors. In a word, the voluptuousness and luxury of that apartment surpassed any thing of the kind that young Egerton had ever before witnessed.

Seated near one of the fire-places in conversation with an elderly gentleman, was an old man, somewhat inclined to stoutness, and very slovenly in his costume. His clothes were good; but they appeared to have been tossed upon him with a pitch-fork. His coat hung in large loose wrinkles over his rounded shoulders: his trousers appeared to hitch up about the thighs, as if through some defect in their cut; two or three of his waistcoat buttons had escaped from their holes, or else had not been fastened in them at all; his cravat was limp; and his shirt-frill was tumbled. His countenance was pale and sickly, and totally inexpressive of that natural astuteness and sharpness which had raised him from the most obscure position to be the companion of the noblest peers in the realm. His eyes were of that lack-lustre species which usually predicate mental dullness and moral feebleness, but which was at variance with the general rule in this instance. In a word, his entire appearance bespoke an individual whose health was wasted by long vigils and the want of needful repose and rest.

When Lord Dunstable's party entered the room, there were already three or four groups occupying supper-tables, on which the French dishes, prepared in Ude's best style steamed, with delicious odour.

"Will you take supper, Mr. Egerton?" inquired Lord Dunstable.

"No, I thank you, my lord," was the reply. "I believe Sir Rupert Harborough informed you that we had already been feeding together."

It was not true that Egerton had supped with the baronet and Chichester, as the reader knows; but Sir Rupert had already said so of his own accord, and Mr. Egerton was not the young man to contradict a statement which seemed to place him upon a certain degree of intimacy with the aforesaid baronet.

"Vot, no supper, my lord?" cried the stout gentleman, rising from his seat near the fire, and accosting Dunstable. "Yes—your lordship and your lordship's friends vill do that honour to Mosseer Ude's good things."

"No, I thank you," said Dunstable, coolly: "we shall not take any supper. We mean to step into the next room and amuse ourselves for an hour or so—eh, Mr. Egerton?"

And a significant glance, rapid as lightning, from Lord Dunstable's eyes, conveyed his meaning to the stout elderly gentleman with the sickly face.

"Wery good, my lord. I'll send some nice cool claret in; and the groom-porters is there. Valk that vay, my lord: valk that vay, gentlemen;—valk that vay, sir."

These last words were addressed to Egerton, and were accompanied by a very low bow.

Dunstable took the young man's arm, and led him into the next apartment, where there was a French hazard table.

"Who is the good-natured old gentleman that spoke so very politely, my lord?" inquired Egerton, in a whisper, when they had passed from the supper-room.

"That good-natured old gentleman!" cried Dunstable, aloud, and bursting out into a fit of laughter so hearty that the tears ran down his cheeks: "why—that's Crockford!"

"Crockford!" repeated Egerton, in astonishment; for, although he had denominated the presiding genius of the place "a good-natured old gentleman," he had not failed to observe the execrable English which he spoke, and was overwhelmed with surprise to learn that the friend of nobles was at such open hostilities with grammar.

"Yes—that is no other than the great Crockford," continued Lord Dunstable, in an under tone. "He once kept a small fishmonger's shop near Temple Bar; and he is now rich enough to buy up all the fishmongers' shops in London, Billingsgate to boot. But let us see what is going on here."

There were only three or four persons lounging about in the Hazard-Room, previously to the entrance of Dunstable, Egerton, Harborough, Cholmondeley, and Chichester; and no play was going on. The moment, however, those gentlemen made their appearance, the loungers to whom we have just alluded, and who were decoy-ducks connected with the establishment, repaired to the table and called for dice, while his croupiers took their seats, and the groom-porter instantly mounted upon his stool.

"What does he get up there for?" asked Egerton, in a whisper.

"To announce the *main* and *chance*," replied Lord Dunstable. "But don't you play hazard?"

"No, no—that is, not often—not very often," said the foolish young man, afraid of being deemed unfashionable in the eyes of his new acquaintances if he admitted that he never yet handled a dice-box in his life.

"Oh! no—not often—of course not!" exclaimed Dunstable, who saw through the artifice: "neither do I. But here comes Crockey with the bank."

And, as he spoke, Mr. Crockford made his appearance, holding in his hands an elegant rosewood case, which he placed upon the table, and behind which he immediately seated himself.

The dice-box was now taken by Lord Dunstable, who set ten sovereigns, called "five" as a main, and threw seven.

"Seven to five!" exclaimed the groom-porter.

"Three to two are the odds," said Sir Rupert Harborough to Egerton: "I'll take them of you in fifties?"

"Done," cried Egerton; and in another moment he had the pleasure of handing over his money to the baronet.

After Lord Dunstable had thrown out, Mr. Chichester took the box, and Cholmondeley in his turn ensnared Egerton into a private bet, which the young man of course lost. But he parted from his bank-notes with a very good grace; for, although considerably sobered by the soda-water which he had drunk at the Paradise, yet what with the wine and the idea of being at that moment beneath Crockford's roof, he was sufficiently intoxicated to be totally reckless of his financial affairs.

Thus, after having lost a bet to each of his friends, he was easily persuaded to take the box, and dispense a little more of his cash for the especial benefit of Mr. Crockford.

"I'll set a hundred pounds," cried Egerton, "and call five the main."

He then threw ten.

"Ten to five!" cried the groom-porter.

"Put down three fifties," said Dunstable; "and you have four fifties to three. That's right. Now go on."

Egerton threw.

"Five—trois, deuce—out!" cried the groom-porter.

And the young man's money was swept towards the bank in a moment.

"Try a *back*, Egerton," exclaimed Chichester.

"Well—I don't mind," was the reply—for the waiter had just handed round goblets of the most delicious claret, and the lights began to dance somewhat confusedly before the young victim's eyes. "I'll set myself again in two hundred; and five's the main."

"Five's the main," cried the groom-porter: "deuce, ace—out."

And away went the bank-notes to the rosewood case at the head of the table.

Colonel Cholmondeley now took the box.

"Will you set me a pony, Egerton?" he said.

"I should not mind," was the reply, given with a stammer and a blush; "but—to tell you the truth—I have no more money about me. If my cheque will do——"

Dunstable nodded significantly to Crockford.

"Oh! my dear sir," said the old hell-keeper, rising from his seat and shuffling towards Egerton, whom he drew partially aside; "I means no offence, but if you vants monies, I shall be werry 'appy to lend you a thousand or two, I'm sure."

"Take a thousand, Egerton," whispered Lord Dunstable. "You'll have better luck, perhaps, with old Crockey's money—there's a spell about it."

"I—I," hesitated the young man for a moment, as the thought of his previous losses flashed to his mind, even amidst the dazzling influence of Crockford's club and his aristocratic acquaintances: "I——"

"Glass of claret, sir?" said the waiter, approaching him with a massive silver salver on which stood the crystal goblets of ruby wine.

"Thank you;"—and Egerton quaffed the aromatic juice to drown the unpleasant ideas which had just intruded themselves upon him: then, as he replaced the glass upon the salver, he said, "Well, give me a thousand—and I'll have another throw."

Sir Rupert Harborough took the box, set himself in ten pounds, and cried, "Nine's the main."

He then threw.

"Six to nine!" exclaimed the groom-porter.

"Five to four in favour of the caster," observed Colonel Cholmondeley.

"I'll bet the odds," cried Egerton.

"'Gainst the rules, sir," said the pompous groom-porter: "you're not a setter this time."

"Pooh, pooh!" cried Crockford, affecting a jocular chuckle. "The gentleman has lost—let the gentleman have a chance of recovering his-self. Take the hodds of the gentleman."

"Then I bet five hundred to four in favour of the caster," said Egerton, now growing interested in the play as he began to understand it better.

Sir Rupert threw a few times, and at last turned up six and three.

"Nine—six, trois—out!" cried the groom-porter.

Egerton now insisted upon taking the box again; and in a few minutes he had not a fraction left of the thousand pounds which he had borrowed.

He turned away from the table and sighed deeply.

"Glass of claret, sir?" said the waiter, as composedly as if he were offering the wine through civility and not for the systematic purpose of washing away a remorse.

Egerton greedily swallowed the contents of a goblet; and when he looked again towards the table, he was astounded to find another bundle of Bank notes thrust into his hand by the obliging Mr. Crockford, who said in his blandest tones, "I think you vas vaiting, sir, for more monies."

"Take it—take it, old chap," whispered Dunstable: "you can turn that second thousand into ten."

"Or into nothing—like the first," murmured Egerton, with a sickly smile: but still he took the money.

He then played rapidly—wildly—desperately,—drinking wine after each new loss, and inwardly cursing his unlucky stars.

The second thousand pounds were soon gone; and Dunstable whispered to Crockford, "That's enough for to-night. We must make him a member in a day or two—and then you'll give me back the little I. O. U. you hold of mine."

"Certainly—certainly," answered the hell-keeper. "But mind you doesn't fail to bring him again."

"Never fear," returned Dunstable;—then turning towards his party, he said aloud, "Well, I think it is pretty nearly time to be off."

"So do I, my lord——hic," stammered Egerton, catching joyfully at the chance of an immediate escape from the place where fortunes were so speedily engulphed;—for tipsy as he now was again, the idea of his losses was uppermost in his mind.

"Well, my lord—well gentlemen," said Crockford, bowing deferentially; "I wishes you all a wery good night—or rather morning. But perhaps your friend, my lord, would just give me his little I. O. U.——"

"Oh! certainly, he will" interrupted Dunstable. "Here, Egerton, my boy—give your I. O. U. for the two thousand——"

"I'd ra-a-ther—hic—give my draft," returned the young man.

But, as his hand trembled and his visual faculties were duplicated for the time, he was ten minutes ere he could fill up a printed cheque in a proper manner.

The business was, however, accomplished at last, and the party withdrew, amidst the bows of decoy-ducks, croupiers, waiters, groom-porters, door-porters, and all the menials of the establishment.

William Crockford was the founder of the Club which so long bore his name, and which was only broken up a short time ago.

He began life as a fishmonger; and when he closed his shop of an evening, was accustomed to repair to some of the West End hells, where he staked the earnings of the day. Naturally of a shrewd and far-seeing disposition, he was well qualified to make those calculations which taught him the precise chances of the hazard-table; and a lucky bet upon the St. Leger suddenly helped him to a considerable sum of ready money, with which he was enabled to extend his ventures at the gaming-house.

In due time he gave up the fish-shop, and joined some hellites in partnership at the West End. Fortune continued to favour him; and he was at length in a condition to open No. 50, St. James's Street, as a Club.

The moment the establishment was ready for the reception of members, announcements of the design were made in the proper quarters; and it was advertised that all persons belonging to other Clubs were eligible to have their names enrolled *without ballot* as members of the St. James's. The scheme succeeded beyond even the most sanguine hopes of Crockford himself; and hundreds of peers, nobles, and gentlemen, who were fond of play, but who dared not frequent the common gaming-houses, gladly became supporters and patrons of the new Club.

In the course of a short time No. 51 was added to the establishment; and No. 52 was subsequently annexed. The rules and regulations were made more stringent, because several notorious black-legs had obtained admission; but, until the very last, any member was permitted to introduce a stranger for one evening only, with the understanding that such visitor should be balloted for in due course. The entrance-fee was fixed at twenty guineas a year; and an annual payment of ten guineas was required from every member.

The three houses, thrown into one, were soon found to be too small for the accommodation of the members: they were accordingly pulled down, and the present magnificent building was erected on their site. It is impossible to say how much money was expended upon this princely structure; but we can assert upon undoubted authority that the internal decorations alone cost ninety-four thousand pounds!

The real nature of this most scandalous and abominable establishment soon transpired. Hundreds of young men, who entered upon life with fortune and every brilliant prospect to cheer them, were immolated upon the infernal altar of that aristocratic pandemonium. Many of them committed suicide:—others perpetrated forgeries, to obtain the means of endeavouring to regain what they had lost, and ended their days upon the scaffold;—and not a few became decoy-ducks and bonnets in the service of the Arch-demon himself. Even noblemen of high rank did not hesitate to fill these ignominious offices; and for every flat whom they took to the house, they received a recompense proportionate to the spoil that was obtained. To keep up appearances with their fellow members, these ruined lacqueys of the great hellite actually paid their subscriptions with the funds which he furnished them for the purpose.

So infamous became the reputation of Crockford's, that it was deemed necessary to devise means to place the establishment apparently upon the same footing with other Clubs. A committee of noblemen and gentlemen (what precious *noblemen* and *gentlemen*, good reader!) was formed to administer the affairs of the institution; but this proceeding was a mere blind. The Committee's jurisdiction extended only to the laws affecting the introduction of new members, the expulsion of unruly ones, and the choice of the wines laid in for the use of the Club. The French Hazard Bank and all matters relating to the gambling-rooms were under the sole control of Crockford, who reaped enormous advantages from that position.

Thus was it that a vulgar and illiterate man—a professed gambler—a wretch who lived upon the ruin of the inexperienced and unwary, as well as on the vices of the hoary sinner,—thus was he enabled to make noble lords and high-born gentlemen his vile tools, and thrust them forward as the ostensible managers of a damnable institution, the infamous profit of which went into his own purse![36]

---

[36]. So far back as 1824, *The Times* newspaper thus directed attention to the atrocious nature of Crockford's Club:—

"'Fishmongers' Hall,' or the *Crock*-odile Mart for gudgeons, flat-fish, and pigeons (which additional title that 'Hell' has acquired from the nature of its 'dealings') has recently closed for the season. The opening and closing of this wholesale place of plunder and robbery, are events which have assumed a degree of importance, not on account of the two or three unprincipled knaves to whom it belongs, and who are collecting by it vast fortunes incalculably fast, but for the rank, character, and fortunes of the many who are weak enough to be inveigled and fleeced there. The profits for the last season, over and above expenses, which cannot be less than £100 a day, are stated to be full £150,000. It is wholly impossible, however, to come at the exact sum, unless we could get a peep at the Black Ledger of accounts of each day's gain at this Pandemonium, which, though, of course omits to name of whom, as that might prove awkward, if at any time the book fell into other hands. A few statements from the sufferers themselves would be worth a thousand speculative opinions on the subject, however they might be near the fact, and they would be rendering themselves, and others, a vital benefit were they to make them. Yet some idea can be formed of what has been sacked, by the simple fact that *one thousand pounds* was given at the close of the season to be divided among the waiters alone, besides the Guy Fawkes of the place, a head servant, having half that sum presented to him last January for a New Year's gift. A visitor informed me, that one night there was such immense play, he was convinced a million of money was, to use a tradesman's phrase, turned on that occasion. This sum, thrown over six hours' play of sixty events per hour, 360 events for the night, will give an average stake of £2777 odd to each event. This will not appear very large when it is considered that £10,000 or more were occasionally down upon single events, belonging to many persons of great fortunes.

"Allowing only one such stake to fall upon the points of the game in favour of the bank per hour, full £16,662. were thus sacrificed; half of which, at least, was hard cash from the pockets of the players, exclusively of what they lost besides.

"Now that there is a little cessation to the satanic work, the frequenters to this den of robbers would do well to make a few common reflections;—that it is their money alone which pays the rent and superb embellishments of the house—the good feeding and the fashionable clothing in which are disguised the knaves about it—the refreshments and wine with which they are regaled, and which are served with no sparing hand, in order to bewilder the senses to prevent from being seen what may be going forward, but which will not be at their service, they may rest well assured, longer than they have money to be plucked of; and above all, it is for the most part their money, of which are composed the enormous fortunes the two or three keepers have amassed, and which will increase them prodigiously while they are still blind enough to go. To endeavour to gain back any part of the lost money, fortunes will be further wasted in the futile attempt, as the same nefarious and diabolical practices by which the first sums were raised, are still pursued to multiply them. One of these 'Hellites' commenced his career by pandering to the fatal and uncontrollable appetites for gambling of far humbler game than he is now hunting down, whose losses and ruin have enabled him to bedeck this place with every intoxicating fascination and incitement, and to throw out a bait of a large sum of money, well hooked, to catch the largest fortunes, which are as sure to be netted as the smaller ones were. Sum up the amount of your losses, my lords and gentlemen, when, if you are still sceptical, you must be convinced of these things. Those noblemen and gentlemen, just springing into life and large property, should be ever watchful of themselves, as there are two or three persons of some rank, who themselves have been ruined by similar means, and now condescend to become 'Procurers' to this foul establishment, kept by a '*ci-devant*' fishmonger's man, and who are rewarded for their services in the ratio of the losses sustained by the victims whom they allure to it.

"They wish to give the place the character of a subscription club, pretending that none are admitted but those whose names are first submitted for approval to a committee, and then are balloted for. All this is false. In the first place, the members of different clubs at once are considered 'eligible;' and in the next, all persons are readily admitted who are 'well' introduced, have money to lose, and whose forbearance under losses can be safely relied upon. Let the visitors pay a subscription—let them call themselves a club, or whatever they choose—still the house having a bank put down from day to day by the same persons to be played against, and which has points of the games in its favour, is nothing but a common gaming-house, and indictable as such by the statutes; and in the eye of the law, the visitors are 'rogues and vagabonds.' Were it otherwise—why don't the members of this club! be seen at the large plate-glass windows of the bow front, as well as at the windows of reputable club-houses? No one is ever there but the creatures of the 'hell,' dressed out and bedizened with gold ornaments (most probably formerly belonging to unhappy and ruined players), to show off at them, and who look like so many jackdaws in borrowed plumes; the players, ashamed of being seen by the passers by, sneak in and out like cats who have burnt their tails. Some of the members of the different clubs will soon begin to display the real character of this infernal place—those who will ultimately be found to forsake their respectable club-houses, and merge into impoverished and undone frequenters to this 'hell.'"

CHAPTER CCXLII.

THE AUNT.

Albert Egerton now became the constant companion of the fashionable acquaintances whom he had accidentally picked up—or rather, who had cunningly picked up *him*.

He dined with them at Long's;—he formed with them parties to eat fish at Greenwich and Blackwall;—he became a member of Crockford's;—and every day he lost considerable sums to them in one shape of gambling or another.

They had ascertained that he was possessed, on coming of age a few weeks previously, of the handsome fortune of sixty thousand pounds; and they determined to appropriate the best portion of it to their own uses.

The Honourable Colonel Cholmondeley most obligingly acted as his Mentor in the choice of magnificent furnished apartments in Stratton Street;—Lord Dunstable was kind enough to purchase two thorough-breds for him, the price being *only* eight hundred guineas—a little transaction by which his lordship quietly pocketed three hundred as his own commission;—Mr. Chichester thought it no trouble to select a rare assortment of wines at one of the most fashionable merchants of the West End, and actually carried his good-nature so far as to see them carefully stowed away in the young dupe's cellar;—and Sir Rupert Harborough generously surrendered to him his cast-off mistress.

The four friends also conceived so violent an attachment towards Mr. Egerton, that they never lost sight of him. They managed matters so well that he had no time for compunctious reflections; for they invariably made him drunk ere they took him home to his bed; and when he awoke in the morning, the obliging Mr. Chichester was sure to be already there to give him sherry and soda-water.

Then Harborough would drop in to breakfast; and while Egerton was performing the duties of the toilette, Dunstable and Cholmondeley were sure to make their appearance.

Perhaps Egerton would complain of headach.

"Don't talk of headach, my dear fellow," Lord Dunstable exclaimed: "you were quite sober last night in comparison with me. My losses were terrific! A thousand to Cholmondeley—fifteen hundred to Chichester—and double as much to Harborough."

"It is very strange that I seldom win any thing," observed Egerton on one of these occasions: "and yet we can't all lose. Some one must be the gainer."

"Every one has his turn, my dear boy," cried Harborough. "But what shall we do to-day? Any thing going on at Tattersall's, Colonel?"

"Nothing particular," was the reply, lazily delivered. "Suppose we have some claret and cigars for an hour or two, and then play a rub of billiards till dinner-time. Of course we all dine together this evening."

"Oh! of course," chimed in Lord Dunstable. "What do you think the Duke of Highgate said of us all yesterday, Egerton?"

"I know not what he could have said of you," was the answer; "but I am sure he could have said nothing of me—for he cannot be aware that there is such a person in existence."

"Nonsense, my dear fellow!" exclaimed Dunstable: "you are as well known now in the fashionable world as any one of us. Every body is speaking of you; and it will be your own fault if you do not marry an heiress. We must introduce you at Almack's in due course. But I was speaking about my friend the Duke. His Grace met me yesterday as I was on my way to join you all at the Clarendon: and when I told him where I was going, he said with a laugh, 'Ah! I call you five the *Inseparables*!'—and away he went."

Egerton was profoundly gratified with the absurd flattery thus constantly poured in his ear; and as he really possessed a handsome person, he saw no difficulty in carrying out the idea of marrying an heiress.

And this same belief has proved fatal to thousands and thousands of young men placed in the same situation as Albert Egerton. They pursue a career of reckless extravagance and dissipation, buoying themselves up with the hope that when their present resources shall have passed away, it will be the easiest thing possible to rebuild their fortunes by means of marriage.

A month slipped away, and Egerton found himself on intimate terms with many "men about town"—one of the most popular members at Crockford's—a great favourite in certain titled but not over-particular families, where there were portionless daughters to "get off," and at whose house Lord Dunstable enjoyed the *entrée*—and the pride and delight (as he believed) of his four dear friends who had done so much for him!

And sure enough they had done a great deal in his behalf; for he had already sold out twenty thousand pounds, or one third of his entire fortune; but he was purposely kept in such an incessant whirl of excitement, pleasure, dissipation, and bustle, that he had no time for reflection.

One morning—it was about eleven o'clock—the young man awoke with aching head and feverish pulse, after the usual night's debauch; and it happened that none of his dear friends had yet arrived.

Egerton rang the bell for some white wine and soda-water to assuage the burning thirst which oppressed him; and when his livery-boy, or "tiger," appeared with the refreshing beverage, the young rake learnt that a lady was waiting to see him in the drawing-room.

"A lady!" exclaimed Egerton: "who the deuce can she be?"

"She is a stout, elderly lady, sir," said the tiger.

"And did she give no name?" inquired Egerton, beginning to suspect who his visitor was.

"No, sir," was the answer. "I assured her that you were not up yet, and that you never received any one at so early an hour; but she declared that you would see *her*; and I was obliged to show her into the drawing-room."

"Ah! it must be my aunt, then!" muttered Egerton to himself. "Bring me up some hot-water this minute, you young rascal:"—fashionable upstarts always vent their annoyances upon their servants;—"and then go and tell the lady that I will be with her in five minutes."

The tiger disappeared—returned with the hot-water—and then departed once more, to execute the latter portion of his master's orders.

Egerton felt truly wretched and ashamed of himself when he surveyed his pale cheeks and haggard eyes in the glass, and thought of the course which he had lately been pursuing. But then he remembered the flattery of his fashionable friends, and soothed his remorseful feelings by the idea that he was on intimate terms with all the "best men about town," was a member of Crockford's, and had the *entrée* of several families of distinction.

Moreover, when he was shaved and washed,—oiled and perfumed,—and attired in a clean shirt, black trousers, red morocco slippers, and an elegant dressing-gown, his appearance was so much more satisfactory to himself that he felt quite equal to the task of encountering his relative.

He accordingly proceeded, with a smile upon his lips and an easy unconstrained manner, to the drawing-room, where a respectable, motherly-looking, stout old lady was anxiously awaiting him.

"My dear Albert," she exclaimed, as he entered the apartment, "what have you been doing with yourself this last month, that you never come near us—no, not even on Sundays, as you used to do?"

And, while she spoke, the good-natured woman made a motion as if she were anxious to embrace her nephew; but he—well aware that it is improper to give way to one's feelings in the fashionable world—retreated a step or two, and graciously allowed his aunt to shake the tip of his fore-finger.

"Lor, Albert, how strange you are!" exclaimed the baffled relative. "But do tell me," she continued, quietly resuming her seat, "what you *have* been doing with yourself. Why did you leave your nice little lodging in Budge

Row? why do you never come near us? why have you moved up into this part of the town? and why didn't you even write to tell us where you was living? If it hadn't been for Storks, your stock-broker, I shouldn't have known how to find you out; but he gave me your address."

"Storks!" murmured Egerton, turning very pale. "Did he tell you—any thing———"

"Oh! yes," continued the aunt, speaking with great volubility; "he told me that you had sold out a power of money;—but when he saw that I was annoyed, he assured me that it could only be for some good purpose. And it is so, Albert dear—isn't it?"

"Certainly—to be sure, aunt—Oh! certainly," stammered the young man, as he glanced uneasily towards the door.

"Well, now—I am glad of that, Albert," said the old lady, apparently relieved of a serious misgiving. "I said to your eldest cousin Susannah Rachel, says I, '*Albert is a good young man—quiet—steady—and firm in his resolve to follow in the footsteps of his dear lamented father*':—here the aunt wiped her eyes;—'*and*,' says I, '*if he has sold out fifteen or twenty thousand pounds, depend, upon it he has bought a nice snug little estate; and he means to surprise us all by asking us to dine with him some Sunday at his country-house.*' Am I right, Albert dear?"

"Oh! quite right, aunt," exclaimed the young man, overjoyed to find that his dissipated courses were unknown to his relatives. "And that was the reason why I did not go near you—nor yet write to you. But have a little patience—and, in a few weeks, I promise you and my cousins a pleasant day———"

"Well, well—I don't want to penetrate into your little secrets, you know," interrupted the aunt. "But how late you get up. Why, it is near twelve, I declare; and I rose this morning before day-light."

"I was detained last evening———"

"Ah! by your man of business, no doubt," cried the voluble old lady. "Many papers to read over and sign—contracts to make—leases to consider—deeds to study—Oh! I understand it all; and I am delighted, Albert, to find you so prudent."

"It is quite necessary, my dear aunt," said Egerton, in a hurried and nervous tone, for a thundering double-knock at that moment reverberated through the house. "But I am afraid—that is, I think—some one is coming, who———"

"Oh! never mind me, dear Al," observed the old lady. "I shall just rest myself for half an hour or so, before I take the omnibus back to the Pavement."

"Certainly, my dear aunt—but———"

The door opened; and Lord Dunstable entered the room.

"Ah! my dear Egerton!" he exclaimed, rushing forward, with out-stretched hand, to greet his young friend: but, perceiving the lady, who had risen from the sofa, he stopped short, and bowed to her with distant politeness—for it struck him at the moment that she might be a washerwoman, or the mother of Egerton's servant, or a shirt-maker, or some such kind of person.

"How d'ye do, sir?" said the aunt, in acknowledgment of the bow; and, resuming her seat, she observed, "I find it very warm for the time of year. But then I was scrooged up in an omnibus for near an hour—all packed as close as herrings in a barrel; and that's not pleasant—is it, sir?"

"By no means, madam," answered Dunstable, in a cold tone; while Egerton bit his lips—at a loss what to do.

"Well—it is *not* pleasant," continued the garrulous lady. "And now, when I think of it, I have a call to make in Aldgate to-day; and so, when I leave here, I shall take a Whitechapel 'bus. Nasty place that Aldgate, sir?"

"Really, madam, I never heard of it until now," said Lord Dunstable, with marvellous stiffness of manner.

"Never heard of Aldgate, sir?" literally shouted the lady. "Why, you must be very green in London, then."

"I know no place east of Temple Bar, madam," was the cold reply. "I am aware that there *are* human habitations on the other side; and I could perhaps find my way to the Bank—but nothing more, madam, I can assure you."

And he turned towards Egerton, who was pretending to look out of the window.

"Well—I never!" exclaimed the lady, now eyeing the nobleman with sovereign contempt.

"My dear aunt," said Egerton, desperately resolved to put an end if possible to this awkward scene; "allow me to introduce my friend Lord Dunstable: Lord Dunstable—Mrs. Bustard."

"Oh! delighted at the honour!" cried the nobleman, instantly conquering his surprise at this announcement of the relationship existing between his young friend and the vulgar lady who complained of having been "scrooged up in an omnibus:"—"proud, madam, to form your acquaintance!"

And his features instantly beamed with smiles—a relaxation from his former chilling manner, which appeared like a sudden transition from the north pole to the tropics.

On her side, the aunt had started up from the sofa, quite electrified by the mention of the magic words—"LORD DUNSTABLE;" and there she stood, cruelly embarrassed, and bobbing up and down in a rapid series of curtseys at every word which the nobleman addressed to her. For this was the first time in her life that she had ever exchanged a syllable with a Lord, unless it were with a Lord Mayor on one or two occasions—but that was only "cakes and gingerbread" in comparison with the excitement of forming the acquaintance of a real Lord whose title was not the temporary splendour of a single year.

"I really must apologise, my dear madam," said the nobleman, now speaking in the most amiable manner possible, "for having affected ere now not to know anything of the City. I cannot fancy how I could have been so foolish. As for the Mansion House, it is the finest building in the world; and Lombard Street is the very focus of attraction. With Aldgate I am well acquainted; and a pleasant spot it is, too. The butchers' shops in the neighbourhood must be quite healthy for consumptive people. Then you have Whitechapel, madam;—fine—wide—and open: the Commercial Road—delightful proof of the industry of this great city;—and, best of all, there is the Albion in Aldersgate Street,—where, by the by, Egerton," he added, turning towards his friend, "we will all dine to-day, if you like."

"Oh! yes—certainly," said Egerton, smiling faintly.

But Dunstable was too good a judge to show that he even perceived the honest vulgarity of his friend's aunt: he accordingly seated himself near her upon the sofa, and rattled away, in the most amiable manner possible, upon the delights of the City. He then listened with great apparent interest to the long story which the old lady told him,—how she kept a haberdashery warehouse on the Pavement, and did a very tidy business,—how she had five daughters all "well-edicated gals as could be, and which was Albert's own first cousins,"—how her late husband had once been nearly an alderman and quite a sheriff,—how she and her deceased partner dined with the Lord Mayor "seven years ago come next November,"—how she had been lately plundered of three hundred pounds' worth of goods by a French Marchioness, who turned out to be an English swindler,—and how she strongly suspected that young Tedworth Jones, the only son of the great tripe-man in Bishopsgate Street Without, was making up to her third daughter, Clarissa Jemima.

To all this, we say, Lord Dunstable listened with the deepest interest; and, at the conclusion, he expressed a hope that if the anticipated match did come off between Mr. Tedworth Jones and Miss Clarissa Jemima Bustard, he should have the honour of receiving an invitation on the happy occasion.

Even Egerton himself was rendered more comfortable by the distinguished politeness with which his aunt was treated; but he was not the less delighted when she rose and took her departure.

As soon as the door was shut behind her, Dunstable hastened to observe, "There goes an estimable woman—I can vouch for it! What would England's commerce be without such industrious, plodding, intelligent persons as your aunt? Egerton, my boy, you ought to be proud of her—as I am of her acquaintance. But there is Chichester's knock, I'll swear!"

In a few moments the gentleman alluded to made his appearance; and the scene with the aunt was soon forgotten.

The day was passed in the usual profitless manner; and the greater portion of the night following was spent in gaming and debauchery.

CHAPTER CCXLIII.

THE FIGHT.—THE RUINED GAMESTER.

The day on which the fight was to take place between the Birmingham Bruiser and the Haggerstone Pet, now drew near.

Great was the excitement of the sporting world on the occasion; and all those, who were not in the secret of the "cross," felt confident that the Bruiser must win.

Indeed the odds had risen in his favour from five to four, to eleven to five. There were numerous betters, and the takers were willing.

The following paragraph appeared in *Bell's Life*, on the Sunday preceding the contest:—

"THE APPROACHING FIGHT.—The mill between the Birmingham Bruiser and the Haggerstone Pet is to come off on Thursday next, at Wigginton Bottom, near Snodsnook Park, in Essex. We are assured by persons who have seen the Bruiser in training at Bexley Heath, and the Pet at Cheshunt, that the men are in first-rate condition, and full of confidence. The Bruiser has vowed that if he is beaten in this fight, he will retire altogether from the Ring; but his friends do not for a moment apprehend that the result will be such as to occasion such a step. The admirers of this truly British sport have begun to flock to the neighbourhood of the scene of action; and every bed at Wigginton is already let. In fact we know of two guineas having been offered and refused for a mere 'shake-down' in the tap of the *Green Lion*, at that beautiful little village. The odds in favour of the Bruiser have risen within these few days to eleven to five. The Bruiser's backers are not known: they are most likely some swell nobs, who prefer keeping out of sight. Some thousands of pounds will change hands next Thursday."

On the appointed day Lord Dunstable drove his friends Egerton, Chichester, Harborough, and Cholmondeley, down to Wigginton in his four-in-hand—an equipage that he had only very recently set up, and which had been purchased and was still maintained by the coin extracted from the pocket of the credulous son of the deceased outfitter.

The scene of the contest was thronged with as miscellaneous a collection of persons as could possibly be gathered together. There were specimens of all classes, from the peer down to the beggar. The fashionable exquisite was jostled by the greasy butcher;—the sporting tradesman was crushed between two sweeps;—the flat was knocked down by one black-leg and picked up by another;—the country-squire was elbowed by the horse-chaunter;—the newspaper reporter was practically overwhelmed by the influence of the "press;"—and, in short, there was such a squeezing that many who had paid a guinea to be conveyed thither, would have gladly given ten to be removed away again.

Presently a tremendous shout of applause welcomed the arrival of Lord Snodsnook's carriage, from which leapt the Haggerstone Pet, who was immediately surrounded by his friends; and shortly afterwards a "slap-up turn-out," "tooled" by a sporting publican of the West End, to whom it belonged, brought the Birmingham Bruiser upon the scene of action, amidst renewed vociferations and another rush of supporters.

The preliminaries being all settled, the combatants stripped, entered the ring, attended by their seconds, and then shook hands. The newspapers subsequently declared that no two pugilists ever "peeled" better, nor seemed more confident.

It is not our purpose, however, to dwell upon the disgusting exhibition:—those brutal displays are loathsome to us, and, to our mind, are a disgrace to the English character.

Suffice it to say, that the Birmingham Bruiser was quite able to beat the Haggerstone Pet, if he had so chosen: but he had made his appearance there on purpose to lose. For upwards of twenty rounds, however, he secured to himself the advantage; and the general impression amongst the uninitiated was that he must win. Those who were in the secret accordingly bet heavily upon the Haggerstone Pet; and we need hardly say that, as Egerton backed the Bruiser, he found several of his dear friends perfectly willing to accept the odds at his hands.

By the twenty-fifth round, the Bruiser began to grow "groggy," and to hit at random. Of course this was mere pretence on his part: but it gave the Pet renewed courage; and in proportion as the latter acquired confidence, the former seemed to lose ground rapidly.

Many of the backers of the Bruiser now exhibited elongating countenances; and, when that champion was thrown heavily at the thirty-first round, his former supporters manifested a desperate inclination to "hedge." Egerton, however, remained confident in favour of the Bruiser; but then he knew nothing about prize-fighting—it was the first combat of the kind he had ever seen in his life—and, even if he had been inclined to hedge his bets, he would have found no persons willing at this stage of the proceeding to afford him the chance.

The Bruiser played his game so well, that even the most experienced in the pugilistic science were unable to detect the fraud that was being practised upon them; and thousands were deceived into a belief that he was really doing his best to win.

At the fortieth round he fell, apparently through sheer weakness; and it was highly ludicrous to behold the discomfited looks of those who had bet most heavily upon him.

He stood up for three rounds more; but time was called in vain for the forty-fourth—and the Haggerstone Pet was declared to be the conqueror.

The Bruiser seemed to be in a horrible plight: for some time he remained motionless upon the ground, obstinately resisting all the efforts that were made to recover him, until one of his friends thrust a huge pinch of snuff up his nose—and then he was compelled to sneeze.

He was now borne to the *Green Lion* at Wigginton, and put to bed. A surgeon in Sir Rupert Harborough's pay volunteered his services to attend upon him; and, although the Bruiser had nothing more serious the matter with him than a few bruises and a couple of black eyes, the medical gentlemen assured the multitudes who flocked to the inn, that "the poor fellow could not possibly be worse." A great deal of medicine was also purchased at the village apothecary's shop; but it was all quietly thrown away by the surgeon, and the Bruiser was regaled, in the privacy of his chamber, with a good cut off a sirloin of beef and a bottle of Port-wine.

Lord Dunstable, Mr. Chichester, Colonel Cholmondeley, and Sir Rupert Harborough divided equally amongst themselves the money won by this "cross;"—they sacked a thousand pounds each, Egerton alone having lost fifteen hundred upon the fight.

The five friends returned to town in his lordship's four-in-hand, and dined that evening at Limmer's, where Egerton speedily drowned the recollection of his heavy losses in bumpers of champagne and claret.

The party afterwards repaired to Crockford's; but just as they were ascending the steps, they beheld one of the waiters in altercation with a person of emaciated form, haggard countenance, and shabby attire, but who had evidently seen better—far better days; for his language was correct, and even beneath his rags there was an air of gentility which no tatters could conceal—no penury altogether subdue.

"Come, Major, none of this nonsense—it won't do here," said the waiter, in an insolent tone. "Be off with you—there's gentlemen coming in."

"I care not who hears me!" cried the person thus addressed: "Mr. Crockford is within—I know he is; and I must see him."

"No—he's not here—and he never comes now," returned the waiter. "If you don't make yourself scarce, I'll call a policeman. Pray walk in, my lord—walk in, gentlemen."

These last words were addressed to Lord Dunstable and his party; but, instead of entering the Club, they remained on the steps to hear the issue of the dispute.

"Call a policeman—oh! do," ejaculated the Major. "I wish you would—for I should at least have a roof over my head to-night; whereas I now stand the chance of wandering about the streets. But you dare not give me in charge—no, you dare not! You know that I should expose all the infamy of this den before the magistrate tomorrow morning. However—in one word, will you deliver my message to Mr. Crockford?"

"I tell you that he is not here," repeated the waiter, insolently.

"Did you give him my note?" asked the Major, in an imploring tone.

"Yes—and he said there was no answer," replied the menial, placing his thumbs in the arm-holes of his waistcoat.

"My God! no answer for *me*!" cried the miserable man, in a voice of bitter despair. "No answer for *me*—and I lost so much in his house! Surely—surely he could spare a guinea from the thousands which he has received of me? I only asked him for a guinea—and he does not condescend to answer me!"

"Well, I tell you what it is," said the waiter, perceiving that not only Lord Dunstable's party lingered upon the steps, but that there was also another listener—a gentleman in a military cloak—standing at a short distance:—"if you will go away now, I'll give you half-a-crown out of my own pocket, and I will undertake that Mr. Crockford shall send you up a sovereign to-morrow."

"God knows with what reluctance I accept that miserable trifle from *you*!" exclaimed the unhappy man, tears rolling down his cheeks, as he extended his hand for the pittance offered.

At the same instant Egerton, who was much moved by all he had just overheard, drew forth his purse with the intention of presenting five sovereigns to the poor Major: but the waiter, perceiving his intention, hastened to drop the half-crown into the miserable wretch's palm with a view to get rid of him at once;—for the domestic wisely argued to himself that every guinea which Egerton might give away would be so much lost to his master's bank up-stairs.

The half-crown piece had just touched the Major's hand, when the individual in the cloak sprang forward—seized it—threw it indignantly in the servant's face—and, dragging the Major away from the door, exclaimed, "No—never shall it be said that a soldier and an officer received alms from an insolent lacquey! Mine be the duty of relieving your wants."

And, leading the Major a few paces up the street, the stranger bade him enter a carriage that was waiting, and into which he immediately followed him.

The servant closed the door, received some whispered instructions from his master, and got up behind the vehicle, which immediately rolled away at a rapid pace.

But to return to Lord Dunstable and his party.

The moment that the individual in the cloak sprang forward in the manner described, and the light of the hall lamps streamed full upon his countenance, both Harborough and Chichester uttered ejaculations of surprise, and hastened precipitately into the Club, followed by Dunstable, Egerton, and Cholmondeley.

"What's the matter?" demanded Dunstable, when the baronet and Chichester were overtaken on the stairs: "and who's that person?"

"The Prince of Montoni," replied Harborough, whose countenance was very pale.

"Yes," said Chichester, hastily; "we know him well—and, as he is very particular in his notions, we did not wish him to see us coming here. But, enough of that—let us adjourn to the Hazard Room."

The conversation between the Major and the waiter, displaying as it did a fearful instance of the results of gaming, had made a deep impression upon Albert Egerton; and for some time he was thoughtful and serious.

But Dunstable attacked him so adroitly with the artillery of flattery—the waiter offered him claret so frequently—the excitement of the play appeared so agreeable—and the fear of losing ground in the good opinion of his aristocratic acquaintances was so strong in his mind, that he seized the dice-box, staked his money, lost as usual, and was conducted home in a state of intoxication at about half-past three in the morning.

In the meantime the unfortunate Major Anderson—for such was his name—had received substantial proofs of that goodness of heart which prompted the Prince of Montoni to espouse his cause against the brutal insolence of Crockford's waiter.

Immediately after the carriage rolled away from the corner of St. James's Street, Richard drew forth his pocket-book, and placed a bank-note, accompanied by his card, in the Major's hand.

"By means of this temporary relief, sir," he said, "you can place yourself in a somewhat more comfortable position than that in which I deeply regret to find you; and, when you feel inclined to see me again, be good enough to write me a note to that effect, so that I may call upon you. For, if it would not be impertinently prying into your affairs, I should wish to learn the sad narrative of those reverses which have so reduced a gentleman of your rank and station."

"Oh! sir—whoever you are," exclaimed the Major—for it was too dark to permit him to read his benefactor's card,—"how can I ever sufficiently thank you for this noble—this generous conduct? But think not that your bounty will have been bestowed in vain—think not that I would risk one sixpence of this sum—whatever be its amount—at the gaming-table! Oh! my God—who would ever play again, that had been in such misery as I? No, sir—no: I would rather throw myself headlong from one of the bridges into the silent waters of the Thames, than enter the gamblers' den!"

"Then let me tell you frankly," said Markham, much moved by the touching sincerity of the ruined officer's tone and manner,—"let me tell you frankly that my object, in wishing to see you again, was to satisfy myself that you had in reality abjured the detestable vice which has beggared you, and that you are deserving of all I am prepared to do for your benefit."

"To-morrow afternoon, sir," answered the Major, "I will take the liberty of writing to you; for by that time I shall once more be the possessor of some humble lodging. And now, with your permission, I will alight here."

Richard pulled the check-string; and the carriage stopped in Oxford Street.

The Major alighted—pressed our hero's hand fervently—and hurried away.

When the carriage had disappeared, and the poor man's feelings were somewhat composed, he stopped beneath a lamp to learn the name of his benefactor.

"The Prince of Montoni!" he exclaimed joyfully: "oh! then I am saved—I am saved; he will never let me want again! All London rings with the fame of his goodness: his whole time seems to be passed in benefiting his fellow-creatures! Wherever poverty is known to exist, thither does he send in secret his unostentatious charity! But such good deeds cannot remain concealed; and I—I for one will proclaim to all who have spurned me in my bitter need, that a stranger has saved me—and that stranger a great Prince whose shoes they are not worthy to touch!"

Such were the words which the grateful man uttered aloud in the open street; but when he glanced at the bank-note, and found himself suddenly possessed of fifty pounds, he burst into a flood of tears—tears of the most heart-felt joy!

And Richard returned home with the satisfaction of having done another charitable action:—we say *another*, because charitable deeds with him were far more common than even promises on the part of many richer men.

But Markham delighted in doing good. Often of an evening, would he repair into London, and, leaving his carriage at the corner of some street, wander about the immediate neighbourhood to succour the poor houseless wretches whom he might meet, and to discover new cases in which his bounty might be usefully bestowed. Without hesitation—without disgust, did he penetrate into the wretched abodes of want—go down even into the cellars, or climb up into the attics, where poverty was to be relieved and joy to be shed into the despairing heart.

And when he returned home, after such expeditions as these, to his beloved wife and darling child,—for he was now a father—the happy father of a lovely boy, whom he had named Alberto,—he found his reward in the approving smiles of the Princess, even if he had not previously reaped an adequate recompense in the mere fact of doing so much good.

Indeed, there was not a happier house in the world than Markham Place;—for not only was the felicity of Richard complete—save in respect to his anxiety concerning his long-lost brother Eugene,—but that of his sister was also ensured. United to Mario Bazzano, Katherine and her husband resided at the mansion—beneath the same roof where Mr. Monroe and Ellen also continued to enjoy a home!

But let us continue the thread of our narrative.

True to his promise, Major Anderson wrote on the following day to acquaint our hero with his place of abode, and to renew the expression of his most fervent gratitude for the generous conduct he had experienced at the hands of the Prince of Montoni.

In the evening Richard proceeded to the humble but comfortable lodging which the Major now occupied in the neighbourhood of the Tottenham Court Road; and from the lips of the individual whom his bounty had restored to comparative happiness, did our hero learn the following terrible narrative of a Gambler's Life.

CHAPTER CCXLIV.

THE HISTORY OF A GAMESTER.

"I was born in 1790, and am consequently in my fifty-third year. My father was a merchant, who married late in life, upon his retirement from business; and I was an only child. Your Highness may therefore well imagine that I was spoilt by my affectionate parents, whose mistaken tenderness would never permit me to be thwarted in any inclination which it was possible for them to gratify. Instead of being sent to school at a proper age, I was kept at home, and a master attended daily to give me instruction in the rudiments of education; but as I preferred play to learning, and found that if I pleaded headach my mother invariably suggested the propriety of giving me a holiday, I practised that subterfuge so constantly, that my master's place was a sinecure, and I could scarcely read two words correctly when I was ten years old.

"At that period my mother died; and my father, yielding to the representations of his friends, agreed to send me to a boarding-school. The resolution was speedily carried into effect; and during the next six years of my existence, I made up for the previously neglected state of my education. At the school alluded to, and which was in a town about fifteen miles from London, there were youths of all ages between eight and eighteen; and the younger ones thought that nothing could be more manly than to imitate the elder in all shapes and ways. Thus I was scarcely twelve when I began to play pitch and toss, odd man, shuffle-halfpenny, and other games of the kind; and as my father gave me a more liberal weekly allowance of pocket-money than any other lad of my own age possessed, I was enabled to compete with the elder youths in the spirit of petty gambling. The passion grew upon me; and that which I had at first commenced through a merely imitative motive, gradually became a pleasure and delight.

"I had just completed my sixteenth year, and was one afternoon passing the half-holiday at pitch and toss with several other boys in a remote corner of the spacious play-ground, when an usher came to inform me that my father had just arrived, and was waiting in the parlour. Thither I accordingly repaired; and in a few minutes after I had been closeted with my parent, I learnt that he had just purchased an ensign's commission for me in the —th regiment of Light Infantry, and that I was to return home with him that very day to prepare my outfit previously to joining the corps. Thus was I suddenly transformed from a raw school-boy into an officer in His Majesty's service.

"Two months afterwards I joined my regiment, which was quartered at Portsmouth. My father had intimated his intention of allowing me three hundred a-year in addition to my pay: I was therefore enabled to keep a couple of horses, and to cut a better figure in all respects than any other subaltern in the regiment. The lieutenant-colonel, who was in command of the regiment, and whose name was Beaumont, was a young man of scarcely eight-and-twenty; but his father was the member for a county, a stanch supporter of the Tories, and therefore possessed of influence sufficient to push his son on with astonishing rapidity. It was a ridiculous—nay, a cruel thing to see lieutenants of five or six-and-thirty, captains of eight-and-forty, and the major of nearly sixty, under the command of this colonel, who was a mere boy in comparison with them. But so it was—and so it is still with many, many regiments in the service; and the fact is most disgraceful to our military system.

"Colonel Beaumont was mightily annoyed when he heard that a merchant's son had obtained a commission in his regiment; for, aristocratic as military officers are even now-a-days in their opinions, they were far more illiberal and proud at the time when I entered the army. It was then the year 1807—during the war, and when the deaths of Pitt and Fox, which both occurred in the previous year, had left the country in a very distracted condition. When, however, the colonel learnt that my father was a rich man, that I had a handsome allowance, and was possessed of a couple of fine horses, his humour underwent an immediate change, and he received me with marked politeness.

"I had not been many weeks in the regiment when I discovered that several of the officers were accustomed to meet in each other's rooms for the purpose of private play; and I speedily became one of the party. The colonel himself joined these assemblies, which took place under the guise of '*wine-parties*;' and though the play was not high, the losses were frequently large enough to cause serious embarrassment to those officers whose means were not extensive. Thus they were very often compelled to absent themselves from the wine-parties for several weeks until they received fresh supplies from their agents or friends; whereas those who had capital sufficient to continue playing, were sometimes enabled to retrieve in the long run what they had previously lost. This was the case with the colonel, myself, and two or three others; and we soon obtained the credit of being the only winners. Such a reputation was by no means an enviable one; for though not a suspicion existed against the fairness of our play, we were looked upon with aversion by those officers who never joined the parties, and with something like hatred by those who lost to us. We stood in the light of individuals who made use of the advantages of superior income to prey upon those of far more slender means; and although there was no open hostility towards us, yet we certainly made many private enemies. For the very atmosphere in which gamblers live is tainted by the foulness of their detestable vice!

"One evening—when I had been about a year in the regiment—it was my turn to give the wine-party in my room; but at the usual hour of meeting no one made his appearance save the colonel. 'Well,' he said, laughing, 'I suppose we cleaned the others out so effectually last night, that they have not a feather left to fly with. But that need not prevent us from having a game together.'—I readily assented, for cards and dice already possessed extraordinary fascinations in my eyes; and we sat down to *écarté*. At first we played for small stakes, and drank our wine very leisurely; but as I won nearly every game, the colonel became excited, and made more frequent applications to the bottle. Still he lost—and the more he lost, the more wine he took; until, getting into a passion, he threw down the cards, exclaiming, 'Curse my ill-luck to-night! I have already paid over to you a hundred and seventeen guineas at this miserable peddling work; and I will have no more of it. Damn it, Anderson, if you've any pluck you'll let me set you fifty guineas at hazard?'—'Done!' cried I; and the cards being thrown aside, we took to the dice. My luck still continued: I won three hundred pounds—all the ready money the colonel had about him; and he then played on credit, scoring his losses on a sheet of paper. His excitement increased to a fearful pitch, and he drank furiously. Still we played on, and the grey dawn of morning found us at our shameful work. At length Beaumont started up, dashed the dice-box upon the floor, crushed it beneath his heel, and uttered a terrible imprecation upon his ill-luck. He drank soda-water to cool himself; and we then examined the account that had been kept. The colonel owed me four thousand four hundred pounds, in addition to the ready money he had already lost. Pale as death, and with quivering lip, he gave me his note of hand for the amount; and having enjoined me in a low hoarse voice not to mention the affair to a single soul, rushed out of the room. I retired to bed, as happy as if I had performed some great and honourable achievement.

"The colonel did not make his appearance all day—nor for several days afterwards; and the answer to all inquiries was that he was indisposed. On the evening of the sixth day after the night of his losses, I received a message requesting me to visit him at his rooms. Thither I immediately repaired, taking his note of hand with me under the pleasing supposition that I was about to be paid the amount. When I entered his sitting-apartment, I was shocked to find him ghastly pale—the cadaverous expression of his countenance being enhanced by the six days' beard which no razor had touched. He was sitting near the fire—for it was still early in Spring—wrapped in a dressing-gown. Pointing to a chair, he said in a mournful voice, 'Anderson, you must think it strange that I have not yet settled the little memorandum which you hold; but the fact is I am totally dependant upon my father, and I wrote to him confessing my loss, and soliciting the means to defray it. There is his answer:'—and he tossed me a letter which, by the date, he had received that morning. I perused it, and found that his father gave a stern refusal to the colonel's request. Mr. Beaumont stated that he had already paid his son's debts so often, and had so many drains made upon him by his other children, that he was resolved not to encourage the colonel's extravagances any farther. The letter was so positively worded that an appeal against its decision was evidently hopeless. 'You see in what a position I am placed,' continued the colonel, when I had returned the letter to him; 'and the only alternative remaining for me is to sell my commission. This I will do as speedily as possible; and until that object can be accomplished, I must request your forbearance.' Not for one moment did I hesitate how to act. 'No,' I exclaimed; 'never shall it be said that I was the cause of your ruin;' and I threw the note of hand into the fire.—He watched the paper until it was completely burnt, with the surprise of a man who could scarcely believe his own eyes; and at length, starting up, he embraced me as fervently as if I had just saved his life. He called me his saviour—his benefactor, and swore eternal friendship. We parted; and next day he appeared on parade, a little pale, but in better spirits than ever. I could not, however, avoid noticing that he encountered me with some degree of coolness and reserve, and that his manner at the mess-table in the evening was distant and constrained towards me only. But the circumstance made little impression on me at the time.

"A few days after this event the colonel obtained three months' leave of absence; and during that period the major remained in command. He was a severe, but honourable and upright man; and he intimated his desire that the wine-parties should be discontinued. Myself and the other officers who were accustomed to play, took the hint, and no longer assembled for gaming purposes in our rooms; but we had supper-parties at one of the principal taverns in the town, and the cards and dice were in as much request amongst us as ever.

"At the expiration of the three months the colonel returned; and he took the first opportunity of signifying his approval of the major's conduct in suppressing the wine-parties. This was, however, mere hypocrisy on his part, and because he did not dare encourage what an officer so near his own rank had disapproved of. His manner towards myself was more cold and distant than it was previously to his departure,—yet not so pointed in its frigidity as to authorise me to request an explanation. Besides, he was my commanding officer, and could treat me as he chose, short of proffering a direct insult."

Time passed very rapidly away, and my father purchased me a lieutenancy in the same regiment, a vacancy occurring. I would gladly have exchanged into another corps, the coldness of the colonel towards me being a source of much mortification and annoyance—the more especially as it was so little deserved on my part. I however rejoiced at my promotion, and submitted so resignedly to Beaumont's behaviour that he never had an opportunity of addressing me in the language of reprimand.

"I was now nineteen, and had been in the army three years. During that period I had gambled incessantly, but with such success that I more than doubled my income by means of cards and dice. I was completely infatuated with play, and looked upon it alike as a source of profit and recreation. About this time I formed the acquaintance of a young lady, whose name was Julia Vandeleur. She resided with her mother, who was a widow, in a neat little dwelling about two miles from Portsmouth, on the verge of South-sea common. Her deceased husband had belonged to a family of French extraction, and after passing the greater portion of his life in a government office, had died suddenly, leaving his widow, however, in comfortable though by no means affluent circumstances. Julia, at the time when I was first introduced to her at a small party given by the principal banker of Portsmouth, was a charming girl of sixteen. Not absolutely beautiful, she was endowed with an amiability and cheerfulness of disposition which, combined with the most perfect artlessness and with a rare purity of soul, rendered her a being whom it was impossible to see without admiring. Well educated, accomplished, and intelligent, she was the pride of an excellent mother, whose own good conduct through life was recompensed by the irreproachable behaviour and tender affection of her interesting daughter. Need I say that I was almost immediately struck by the appearance and manners of the charming Julia Vandeleur?

"I paid her a great deal of attention that evening, and called next day at her abode. To be brief, I soon became a constant visitor; and Mrs. Vandeleur did not discountenance my presence. Nor did her daughter manifest any repugnance towards me. The influence of that dear creature was then most salutary:—would that it had always continued so! For one year I never touched a card nor die, all my leisure time being passed at the cottage. To add to my happiness my father came down to Portsmouth to see me: he took apartments for a few weeks at the George Hotel; and I introduced him to Mrs. and Miss Vandeleur. Although Julia was no heiress, my father was too much attached to me to throw any obstacle in the way of my suit; and I was accepted as Miss Vandeleur's intended husband. Oh! what joyous days were those—days of the most pure and unadulterated happiness!

"It was settled that my father should purchase me a captaincy, and that the marriage should then take place. He accordingly returned to town to make the necessary exertions and arrangements for my promotion; and it was during his absence that my contemplated union reached the ears of Colonel Beaumont. I had kept my attachment and my engagement an entire secret from my brother officers, because I did not wish to introduce a set of profligate and dissipated men to the innocent girl who loved me, nor to her parent whom I respected. But that secret *did* transpire somehow or another; and Beaumont then found an opportunity of venting his spite upon me. He called upon Mrs. Vandeleur, sought a private interview with her, and declared that his conscience would not permit him to allow her to bestow her daughter, without due warning, upon a confirmed gamester. He then took his leave, having produced a most painful impression upon the mind of Mrs. Vandeleur. She did not, however, immediately speak to her daughter upon the subject; but when I called as usual in the evening, she took an opportunity to confer with me alone. She then calmly and sorrowfully stated the particulars of the colonel's visit. I was confounded; and my manner confirmed the truth of his accusation. Mrs. Vandeleur implored me to urge my suit with her daughter no farther—to break off the engagement where it stood—and urged me, as a gentleman, to release Julia from her promise. I threw myself at her feet—confessed that I had been addicted to play—but swore in the most solemn manner that for a year past I had renounced the abominable vice, into which my affection for her daughter would never permit me to relapse. She was moved by my sincerity—and at length she yielded to my earnest prayers. Oh! never shall I forget that excellent lady's words on this occasion. 'William,' she said, 'I will give you my daughter. But remember that the poor widow is thereby bestowing upon you the only treasure which she possesses—her only solace—her only consolation; and if you deceive her by rendering that dear child unhappy, you will break the heart of her who now addresses you!'—'Oh! my dear madam,' I exclaimed, 'the example of your virtues and the consciousness of possessing Julia's love will make me all that you can desire. And by yon pale moon I swear that never—never more will I deserve the name of a gambler. No: may this right hand wither—may the lightning of heaven strike it—if it ever touch cards or dice again!'—Mrs. Vandeleur rebuked me for the words I used; but the sincerity of my manner completely reassured her. Julia remained in ignorance of the object of the Colonel's visit and of this explanation between her mother and myself.

"Colonel Beaumont speedily found that his malignant officiousness had failed to produce the desired aim; and he called again, with some plausible pretext, upon the widow. By hypocritically affecting a merely conscientious motive in having acted as he had done, he gleaned from her the pledges I had made and the satisfaction with which she had received them. That same afternoon, at the mess-table, his manner became as kind and courteous towards me as it was wont to be when I first joined the regiment; I could not however respond with any congeniality. Still he did not seem abashed, but appeared not to notice my disinclination to accept his advances. When I was about to leave the table, for the purpose of repairing to the abode of my beloved, the Colonel said, 'Anderson, I wish to speak to you in my room.'—I bowed and accompanied him thither.—'Let us forget the past,' he said, extending his hand towards me, 'and be friendly as we were wont.'—'I am not aware, sir,' was my reply, 'that I ever offended you.'—'No; but you humiliated me,' he answered, with a singular expression of countenance; 'and *that*, to a military man and a superior officer, was most galling. Circumstances have lately changed with me. A distant relative has died and left me a considerable property; and my first duty is to pay you the four thousand pounds I owe you.'—'That debt, sir,' said I, 'has been cancelled long ago.'—'You generously destroyed the proof,' he hastily rejoined; 'but the obligation never could be annihilated, save in this manner:' and he handed me the sum which he had formerly owed.—I of course received the amount, and my opinion of him grew far more favourable, in spite of his attempt to ruin me with Mrs. Vandeleur.

"When this transaction was completed, the Colonel said, 'Anderson, we are now quits, but not exactly on equal terms. You have won a large sum from me; and though a settlement has been delayed, still that sum is now paid. As a gentleman you will give me my revenge.'—I started and turned pale.—'Of course you cannot refuse to allow me the chance of recovering myself,' he continued, calmly producing a dice-box.—'I dare not play, sir,' I exclaimed, my breath coming thickly.—'Oh! *as a gentleman*,' he repeated, 'you are bound to do so.'—'I have sworn a solemn oath never to touch cards nor dice again.'—'And if you had also sworn never to fight a duel, would that plea justify you in receiving an insult unresented, in the eyes of honourable men?' he demanded.—'Colonel Beaumont,' I said, 'in the name of heaven do not urge me to break that solemn vow!'—'Will you compel me to declare that oaths are sometimes mere matters of convenience?' cried the colonel: 'will you force me to express my conviction that Lieutenant Anderson will enrich himself by play, and will not afford the loser that opportunity of revenge which all honourable men concede?'—'Take back your money, sir,' I cried, dreadfully agitated; 'and permit me to retire.'—'Would you insult me by restoring money that I owed?' demanded the Colonel.—'Not for worlds would I insult you, sir,' was my answer: 'but do not force me to violate my promise to Mrs. Vandeleur.'—'Oh! a promise made to a lady, eh?' he exclaimed. 'I thought you more of a man than to refuse honourable satisfaction in consequence of a vow pledged under the influence of love. Come, Anderson, act fairly; and do not compel me to explain the transaction to your brother-officers.'

"Oh! what will your Highness think of me when I declare that I was alarmed by this threat, and that I yielded to the colonel's urgent solicitation! He produced wine; and I drank deeply to drown my remorse. At first I trembled as I touched the dice-box—for I remembered the solemn oath pledged only a few days previously. But in a short time the influence of the liquor and the excitement of play stifled all compunction; and I once more devoted myself to the game with all the intense interest which is experienced by the confirmed gamester. Beaumont was cool and collected: I was nervous and irritable. Fortune seemed to be bent upon giving *him* the revenge which he had solicited. I lost—we doubled our stakes: I continued to lose—and I steeped my vexation in frequent draughts of wine. In three hours I lost back again the whole amount he had paid me. The colonel then threw down the box, and said, 'I am satisfied.'—'But I am not,' I exclaimed furiously: 'let us go on.'—'As you please,' he observed calmly; and, maddened with drink—hurried on, too, by the terrible excitement which gamblers alone can know, I played—and played until I owed the colonel two thousand three hundred pounds. Then a revulsion of feeling took place; and I cursed my folly. I loathed myself: intoxicated as I was, I felt as a perjurer should feel. The colonel claimed my note of hand; and I gave it. This done, I rushed wildly from his room, and hastened to my own.

"When I awoke in the morning, I could scarcely believe that the scene of the previous night had really occurred. It seemed to me as if I were standing on the brink of a dreadful yawning gulf, which a mist hid from my sight, but which I nevertheless knew to be *there*. Then that mist gradually rolled away; and the blackness of the abyss was revealed to me with all its horrors. Terrible were my feelings. But I was compelled to reflect upon what was to be done. My mind was soon made up. The debt must be paid; and, that obligation once satisfied, I would never touch the dice again! Having written a hurried letter to Julia, stating that business of importance suddenly called me to London, and having obtained leave of absence from the colonel, I repaired in all possible haste to the metropolis. But my father, to whom it was of course my intention to apply for succour, had left town that very morning for Portsmouth; and we had therefore crossed each other on the way. An idea struck me:—could I not borrow the money I required without being compelled to reveal the truth to my father? The thought pleased me—and I even felt rejoiced that we had so missed each other. Early next morning I obtained the two thousand three hundred pounds of one Mr. Goldshig, a Jew, who received my note of hand for three thousand in return, with the understanding that he would continue to hold it so long as I paid a hundred pounds every quarter for the accommodation—such payments, however, not to be deducted from the principal, but to be regarded simply in the light of interest.

"Much relieved by this speedy and easily-effected negotiation, I returned to Portsmouth, where I arrived at about nine o'clock in the evening. I repaired straight to the George Hotel, at which, as I expected, my father had put up. But he was not within; and I accordingly hastened to the barracks to pay the money to Beaumont. The Colonel was at home, and received me with a chilling coldness for which, after all that had recently passed between us, I was little prepared. I did not however appear to notice the circumstance; but tendered him the amount due. 'Oh! Mr. Anderson,' he replied, 'the debt is paid.'—'Paid!' I exclaimed, greatly surprised at this announcement.—'Yes,' he said: 'it was settled this evening, about two hours since. Your father called on me, and redeemed the note of hand.'—'My father!' cried I, a cold chill striking to my heart: 'how came he to know that you held such a document?'—'Really, Mr. Anderson, I have no time to converse with you now,' answered the Colonel; and he bowed me out with freezing politeness.

"Strange misgivings now oppressed me; and I began to read something malignant and systematically vindictive in the conduct of the Colonel; for it was evident that he must have mentioned the fact of possessing my note of hand. Dreadfully agitated, I returned to the George. My father had just come in; and his countenance was mournfully severe, when I entered his presence. 'William,' said he, 'I am deceived in you; and you have acted in a manner which you will have cause to rue as long as you live; that is, if your attachment for Miss Vandeleur be truly sincere.'—'My God!' I exclaimed: 'what has occurred? Does Mrs. Vandeleur know of *this*?'—'She knows all; and she not only sees in you a confirmed gambler, but a wicked perjurer,' answered my father. 'Her door is closed against you for ever.'—'Oh! wretch that I am!' I cried, beating my breast in despair. 'But who can have done all this mischief?'—'Colonel Beaumont called this morning on Mrs. Vandeleur, and insultingly exhibited your note of hand, which I have ere now redeemed.'—'The villain!' I exclaimed, rushing towards the door: 'but he shall pay dearly for this!'—'Stop, sir, I command you,' cried my father. 'He is your superior officer; he evidently hates you; and, were you to challenge him, he would ruin you. No: that is not the course to pursue. I have purchased you a Captain's commission in the—the regiment, which is stationed at Chatham; and you have also three months' leave of absence. Return with me to London; and endeavour by your future conduct to atone for the misdeeds of the past.'

"In reply to my hurried and anxious questions, I learnt that any attempt to see Julia would be vain, and could have no other result than to irritate Mrs. Vandeleur the more against me. My father offered me some consolation by the assurance that if I conducted myself well for a year, there would be a hope of reconciliation with the incensed lady; and I trusted to Julia's love to ensure her fidelity. Thus, partially—though very partially—relieved from the intenseness of that pain which now pierced to my very soul, I hastened to the barracks to superintend the packing up of my things, and to take leave of my brother-officers. This being done, I was passing out of the barrack-yard, when I encountered the Colonel. The light of the lamp fell upon his countenance, which expressed fiend-like satisfaction and triumph. Catching me by the arm, as I was about to pass him in silence, he muttered between his teeth, 'Anderson, I am avenged. You humiliated me once; and I hate you for it! Know me as your implacable enemy; and renounce all hope of your Julia—for she shall be mine!'

"He then hurried away. I was so stupefied by this sudden revelation of the ferocious and most unjust enmity of this bad man, that I remained rooted as it were to the spot. Never was there such ingratitude! But his threat relative to Julia,—oh! I could have afforded to laugh at his hatred: that menace, however, rang in my ears like a deafening bell. Mournfully I turned away, and hastened back to the inn. I passed a sleepless—wretched night; and during the journey to town, scarcely spoke a word to my father the whole way.

"The money that I had borrowed of the Jew was still in my possession; and I resolved to lose no time in returning it. Accordingly, the very next day after my arrival in London, I set out on my way to his abode in the City; but meeting with some officers of my acquaintance, I agreed to dine with them at an hotel in Bridge Street, Blackfriars. In fact, I was so very unhappy that I was glad to meet with such society; and I thought that I could easily postpone my visit to the Jew until the morrow. The dinner was first-rate—the wines excellent; and I drank copiously to drown my cares. Presently some one proposed cards: I could not offer any objection; but I simply stated that I should not play. Cards, however, were brought; and *écarté* was the game. I sate looking on. In the course of half an hour I saw a most favourable opportunity for making a good bet; and, with the most wretched sophistry, I reasoned to myself that betting and playing were two very different things. I accordingly offered the wager, and won it. Encouraged by this success, I bet again; and again I won. In less than another half hour I had pocketed two hundred guineas—for the play was high and the wagers in proportion. The ice was, alas! again broken; and it did not require much persuasion to induce me to take a hand. I thought of Julia—sighed and hesitated: I looked again at the cards—sighed once more—and seized them with that desperate feeling which we experience when we know we are doing wrong. To be brief, we kept up the play until three o'clock in the morning; and I not only lost every farthing I had about me—amounting, with the Jew's money and my own, to nearly three thousand pounds—but six hundred more by note of hand. It was understood that we should meet again on the following evening at another hotel, to settle accounts; and I returned home in that state of mind which suggests suicide!

"Fortunately my father did not know at what hour I entered; and he therefore suspected nothing. After breakfast I paid a visit to the Jew—but not to repay him his money. My object was to borrow more, which he willingly lent me, as I was enabled to show him the previous evening's *Gazette* in which my promotion by purchase was recorded. I borrowed the six hundred pounds which I required, and for which I gave a bill to the amount of a thousand. At the appointed hour I repaired to the hotel where I was to meet my friends; but with the firm resolution of not yielding to any inducement to play. How vain was that determination! cards were already on the table when I entered, for I came somewhat late, having dined with my father before-hand. I strove hard to keep my vow—I wrestled powerfully against my inclinations; but a glass of champagne unsettled me—and I fell once more! Another late sitting at the card-table—another severe loss—another visit to the Jew next day!

"For the three months during which my leave of absence lasted, I pursued the desperate career of a gamester, contriving, however, so well, that my father had not a single suspicion of the fatal truth. I was now in a fearful plight,—owing nearly six thousand pounds to the Jew, and compelled to devote nearly every pound I received from my father on leaving to join my regiment, to the payment of the interest. I remained for about ten months at Chatham, and still continued to play nightly. I was, however, unsuccessful, and quite unable to keep up the settlement of the quarterly amounts of interest with the rapacious Jew. What aggravated the mental anguish which I endured, was that my father corresponded with Mrs. Vandeleur from time to time, and gave her the most favourable accounts of me. Of this he informed me in his letters, and when I occasionally repaired to town to pass a few days with him.

"At length—just when the Jew was becoming most pressing for money, and my difficulties were closing in around me with fearful rapidity—I one day received a summons to return home. On my arrival I found my father in high glee; and, after tantalising me a little, he produced a letter which he had received from Mrs. Vandeleur. That excellent lady, moved by my father's representations—touched by the drooping condition of her daughter—and also, perhaps, anxious to relieve Julia from the persecutions '*of a certain Colonel*,' as she said in her letter, '*who annoyed her with his addresses*,' had consented to our union. I was overwhelmed with joy: all my cares were forgotten—my difficulties seemed to disappear. My father had not been inactive since the receipt of that letter. He had obtained six months' leave of absence for me, and had hired and furnished a house in Russell Square for the reception of myself and Julia. Even the time and place for the celebration of the marriage had been arranged between him and Mrs. Vandeleur. The ceremony was to take place at Portsmouth on the ensuing Monday; and I was to accompany my father thither two days previously.

"Much as I longed to embrace my dear Julia, I was not sorry to be allowed a few hours' delay in London; for I felt how necessary it was to pacify the Jew. I accordingly called upon him, acquainted him with my approaching marriage, and stated that as it was my father's intention to transfer to my name a considerable sum in the public funds, the monies owing should be paid with all arrears the moment that transfer took place. Goldshig seemed quite satisfied; and I took leave of him with a light heart. But as I was issuing from his dwelling, I ran against Colonel Beaumont—my mortal enemy—who was about to enter the house. He started and was evidently much surprised: I was both surprised and annoyed. Convinced, however, that this meeting was a mere coincidence, and that his presence there had no connexion with my affairs, I was about to pass on with silent contempt, when he laid his hand on my arm—as he had done at the barrack-gate at Portsmouth thirteen months previously—and said, 'You think you will yet possess Julia: you are mistaken! She has repulsed me—but *you* know that I can avenge an insult!'—I thrust him rudely away from me, smiled contemptuously, and passed on.

"This circumstance was speedily forgotten by me amidst the bustle and excitement of the preparations for my marriage; and never did I feel more truly happy than when journeying by my father's side, in our travelling-carriage, towards the place where my beloved Julia dwelt. We alighted at the George Hotel at about five o'clock on the Saturday evening; and, as my father felt fatigued,—for he was now nearly sixty-five years of age,—I repaired alone to the cottage near South-sea Common. I shall pass over the joys—the rapturous joys of that meeting. Julia evidently loved me more than ever; and Mrs. Vandeleur received me in a manner which promised an oblivion of the past. And, oh! when I contemplated that charming girl who was so shortly to be my wife,— and when I listened to the kind language of her excellent mother,—I renewed within myself, but in terms of far more awful solemnity, the oath which I had once before taken in that very room!

"I learnt that Colonel Beaumont had, as Mrs. Vandeleur stated in her letter, persecuted my Julia with his addresses, and implored her to marry him. But her heart remained faithful to me, although circumstances had compelled her mother to explain to her the cause of our separation; and the Colonel was summarily refused.

"The happy morning dawned; and, in spite of the Colonel's threats, Julia and I were united at St. Peter's Church, Portsmouth. The ceremony was as private as possible; and as we had a long journey before us, the breakfast usually given on such occasions was dispensed with. Accordingly, on leaving the church, the bridal party repaired to the George, where the travelling-carriage and four were ready for starting. My father intended to remain in Portsmouth for a few days, for the benefit of the sea-air; and Mrs. Vandeleur was to visit us in London at the expiration of about a month, and then take up her abode with us in Russell Square altogether.

"While Julia was taking leave of her affectionate parent in a private room, a waiter entered the apartment where I and my father were conversing together, and informed me that a person desired to speak to me below. I followed the waiter to a parlour on the ground-floor; and there—to my ineffable horror—I found Mr. Goldshig. Two suspicious-looking men were standing apart in a corner. I instantly comprehended the truth. I was arrested for the debt owing to the Jew. In vain did I attempt to expostulate with him on the harshness of this proceeding. 'You know very well,' said he, 'that you and your wife are going off to the continent, and I might have whistled for my money if I had not done this. In fact, the person who gave me the information, strongly urged me to arrest you on Saturday evening immediately after your arrival; but there was some delay in getting the writ. However, you are safe in the officer's hands now; and you must go to quod if your father don't give his security.'—I was overwhelmed by this sudden disaster; and I vowed vengeance upon Beaumont, whose malignity I too well recognised as the origin of my present predicament. There was no alternative but to send for my father. His sorrow was immense; and he assured me that in settling the debt, he was moved only by consideration for the feelings of my bride and her mother, whom he would not plunge into affliction by allowing his son's conduct to reach their ears. He accordingly gave his security to the Jew; and I was once more free.

"Let me pass over the incidents of the year succeeding my marriage, and the close of which saw me blessed with a little girl. During those twelve months my behaviour was as correct as it ought to have been: the idea of gambling was loathsome to me. My father, who had not as yet transferred a single shilling to my name in the Bank, but who had allowed me a handsome monthly income, now experienced confidence in my steadiness; and to encourage me, as well as to mark his approval of my conduct since my marriage, he presented me with twenty thousand pounds the day after the birth of my daughter. Poor old man! he did not live long after that! A cold which he caught led to a general breaking up of his constitution; and he died after a short illness. But on his death-bed he implored me not to relapse into those evil courses which had originally caused so much misery; and I vowed in the most solemn manner—by all I deemed sacred, and as I valued the dying blessing of my kind parent—to follow his counsel.

"I now found myself the possessor of a fortune amounting in ready money to thirty-six thousand pounds. Mrs. Vandeleur resided with us; and, when the mournful impression created by my father's death became softened down, there was not a happier family in the universe than ours. My Julia was all that I had anticipated—amiable, affectionate, and as faultless as a wife as she was excellent as a daughter.

"Four years rolled away from the date of my father's death; and not once during that period did I touch a card nor even behold a dice-box. I had purchased a Majority, and remained unattached. I was also now the father of three children—one girl and two boys; and every thing seemed to contribute to my felicity. We had a select circle of friends—real friends, and not useless acquaintances; and our domestic economy was such as to enable us to live considerably within our income.

"Such was my position when a friend one day proposed that I should become a member of a Club to which he already belonged. Mrs. Vandeleur and Julia, seeing that I was very much at home, thought that this step would ensure me a little recreation and change of scene, and therefore advocated the propriety of accepting the offer. I was balloted for and elected. My friend was a well-meaning, sincere, and excellent man, who had not the slightest idea of placing me in the way of temptation when he made the proposal just mentioned. Neither had my mother-in-law or wife the least suspicion that play ever took place at a Club. I was equally ignorant of the fact until I became initiated; and then I perceived the precipice on which I had suddenly placed myself. But I dared not make any observation to my friend on the subject; for he was totally unaware that gaming had ever been amongst the number of my failings. To be brief, I had not been a member of the Club six weeks, when I was one evening induced to sit down to a rubber of whist with three staid old gentlemen, who only played for amusement. 'There cannot be any harm in doing this,' said I to myself; 'because no money is staked. Moreover, even if there were, I have now acquired such control over myself that I could not possibly forget my solemn vows in this respect.'—Thus endeavouring to soothe my conscience—for I knew that I *was* doing wrong, but would not admit it even to myself—I sate down. We played for an hour, at the expiration of which one gentleman left and another took his place. The new-comer proposed shilling points, '*just to render the game interesting.*' The other two gentlemen agreed: I could not possibly—at least, I thought I could not—seem so churlish or so mean as to refuse to play on those terms.

"Trifling as the amount either to be won or lost could be, the mere fact of playing for *money* aroused within me that unnatural excitement which, as I have before informed your Highness, is alone experienced by those who have a confirmed predilection for gambling. And I now discovered—when it was too late—that this predilection on my part had only been lying dormant, and was not crushed. No: for I played that evening with a zest—with an interest—with a real love, which superseded all other considerations; and I did not return home until a late hour. Next day I was ashamed of myself—I was vexed at my weakness—I trembled lest I should again fall. For a fortnight I did not go near the Club: but at the expiration of that period, a dinner took place to celebrate the fourth anniversary of the foundation of the establishment, and I found it difficult to excuse myself. I accordingly went; and in the evening I sate down to a rubber of whist. Afterwards I lounged about a table where *écarté* was being played:—I staked some money—won—and fell once more!

"I shall not linger upon details. The current of my fatal predilection—dammed up for five years and a half—had now broken through its flood-gates, and rushed on with a fury rendered more violent by the lengthened accumulation of volume and power. *Écarté* was my favourite game; and I found several members of the Club willing to play with me on all occasions. For some time I neither gained nor lost to any important amount; but one evening the play ran high, and—hurried along by that singular infatuation which prompts the gamester to exert himself to recover his losses—I staked large sums. Fortune was opposed to me; and I retired a loser of nearly two thousand pounds. The ice being once more completely broken, I plunged headlong into the fatal vortex; and my peace of mind was gone!

"My habits became entirely changed: instead of passing the greater portion of my time with my family, I was now frequently absent for the entire afternoon and the best part of the night. Julia's cheek grew gradually pale;

her manner changed from artless gaiety to pensive melancholy; and, though she did not reproach me in words, yet her glances seemed to ask wherefore I remained away from her! Mrs. Vandeleur noticed the depressed spirits of her daughter, but did not altogether comprehend the reason; because, although she observed that I was out a great deal more than I used to be, my angel of a wife never told her that it was sometimes two, three, or even four in the morning ere I returned home. The real truth could not, however, remain very long concealed from Mrs. Vandeleur. She began to be uneasy when I dined at the Club on an average of twice a week: when this number was doubled and I devoted four days to the Club and only three to my family, Mrs. Vandeleur asked me in the kindest way possible if my home were not comfortable, or if Julia ceased to please me? I satisfied her as well as I could; and in a short time I began to devote another day to the Club, and only two to Russell Square. Paler and more pale grew Julia's cheek; the spirits of the children seemed to droop sympathetically; and Mrs. Vandeleur could no longer conceal her uneasiness. She accordingly seized an opportunity to speak to me in private; and she said, 'William, for God's sake what does this mean? You are killing your poor uncomplaining wife by inches. Either you love another—or you gamble! If it be the latter, may God Almighty have pity upon my daughter!'—And the excellent lady burst into tears. I endeavoured to console her: I swore that her suspicions were totally unfounded:—but, alas! no change in my behaviour tended to corroborate my asseverations.

"I persisted in my fearful course; and, as if I were not already surrounded by elements of ruin sufficiently powerful, I became a member of Crockford's. In saying that, I mention sufficient to convince your Highness that I rushed wilfully and blindly on to the goal of utter destruction. My fortune disappeared rapidly; and when it was gone, I sold my commission, and then applied to Goldshig, who lent me money upon the most exorbitant terms. But let me pass over the incidents of three years. At the expiration of that time how was I situated? What was the condition of my family? Painful as these reminiscences are, I will not conceal the facts from your Highness. In a chamber at the house in Russell Square Mrs. Vandeleur lay upon her death-bed. Julia—pale, with haggard eyes, sunken cheeks, and appearance so care-worn that it would have moved even the heart of an overseer or master of a workhouse,—Julia hung, weeping bitterly, over the pillow. In the nursery, a servant was endeavouring to pacify the children, who were crying because they knew that their '*dear grandmamma,*' was very, very ill. In the kitchen an ill-looking fellow was dozing by the fire:—he was a bailiff's man in possession—for there was an execution levied on my property. And I—where was I? Gone to solicit Goldshig the Jew for a few days' grace, the sale having been advertised to take place next morning! Thus was this once happy home now invaded by misery and distress:—thus was an amiable wife plunged into sorrows so keen, woes so bitter, afflictions so appalling, that it was no wonder if her charming form had wasted away, and the frightful aspect of the demon of despair had chased the roses from her cheeks;—and thus, too, was an excellent lady dying prematurely with that worst of the Destroyer's plagues—a broken heart!

"It was about five o'clock in the evening when I returned, after vainly waiting six hours to see Goldshig, who was not at home. Wearied and anxious, I left a note for him at his office, and retraced my miserable way to Russell Square. On my entrance Julia hastened to meet me, for she had heard my knock. 'What tidings?' she inquired in a rapid tone.—I informed her of what I had done. Her countenance became even more wretched than it was before.—'Oh! that they will not molest my dear, dear mother on her death-bed!' she shrieked, clasping her hands franticly together. I turned aside, and shed bitter—burning tears. The children now came rushing into the room. Alas! poor innocents, they knew not of the ruin that was hanging over their heads; and when they took my hands—kissed them—and said, 'Oh! we are so glad that dear papa has come home!'—I thought my heart would break. My God! my God! had all the misery which weighed upon our house been caused by me?

"I approached my wife—I took her in my arms—I murmured, as I kissed her pale cheek, 'Can you—can you forgive me?'—'Oh! have I ever reproached you, William?' she asked, endeavouring to smile in gratitude for my caresses.—'No: never, never, poor dear afflicted creature!' I exclaimed wildly; 'and it is your resignation, your goodness which makes my conduct so black, so very black!'—She wound her arms about my neck, and said in her soft gentle tone, 'Will you not come and see my mother?'—I started back in horror. She comprehended me, and observed, 'Do not fear reproaches: but come with me, I conjure you!'—I took the hand which she extended to me: holy God! how thin that hand had become—how skeleton-like had grown the taper fingers.

Though it was my own wife's hand I shuddered at the touch. She seemed to read my thoughts; for she pressed *my* hand affectionately, and then wiped away her tears. A deep sob escaped her bosom—and she hurried me towards the sick-room. The children followed us without opposition on their mother's part; and in a few moments the mournful group approached the bed of death. I had not seen Mrs. Vandeleur for nearly a week; and I was shocked—oh! painfully shocked at the alteration which had taken place in her. From a fine, stout, handsome, healthy woman, she had wasted away to a mere shadow:—Julia was a shadow herself—but her mother seemed to be the shade of a shadow! Merciful heavens! and all this had been wrought by me!

"Kneeling by the side of the bed, I took the transparent hand that the dying woman tendered me, and pressed it to my lips. My brain seemed to whirl; and all became confusion and bewilderment around me. I remember a low and plaintive voice assuring me that heaven would yet forgive me the broken heart of the mother, if I would only be kind to the daughter:—I have a faint recollection of that dying voice imploring me to quit my evil ways, for the sake of her whom I had sworn to love and protect—for the sake of the children who were sobbing bitterly close by;—and methinks that I reiterated those solemn vows of repentance which I had before so often uttered—but to break! Then I was suddenly aroused from a sort of stupor into which I fell—kneeling as I still was,—aroused, too, by a piercing scream. Starting up, I caught the fainting form of Julia in my arms;—and a glance towards the bed showed me that her mother was no more! Her prophetic words were fulfilled: the widow, who gave me her only treasure, had died of a broken heart!

"Heaven only knows how I passed the wretched night that followed. I remember that the dawn of a cold March morning, accompanied by a cheerless drizzling rain, found me pacing the parlour in a despairing manner. I do believe I was half mad. And such horrible ideas haunted me! I thought of killing my wife and children, and then blowing out my own brains. Then I resolved to fly—and never see them more. In another minute I wept bitterly when I asked myself, 'But what would become of them?' I writhed in mental agony, as I found no response to this question; and when I pictured to myself all the amiable qualities of my wife—her gentleness—her goodness—her endearments—her unimpaired love,—and then thought of the little innocents with their winning ways, their little tricks, their pretty sayings, and their cherub countenances,——Oh! God, no words can explain how acute my sufferings were!

"From that painful reverie I was aroused by a loud commanding knock at the front door. There was an ominous insolence in that knock; and the worst fears entered my mind. Alas! they were full soon confirmed. The broker made his appearance, accompanied by his men; and the house was at the same time invaded by a posse of Jews—the usual buyers at sales effected under instructions from the Sheriff. Hastening the burst of anguish that rose to my lips, I drew the broker aside, acquainted him with the fact of my mother-in-law's death on the previous evening, and implored his forbearance for a week. He quietly took a pinch of snuff, and then observed that he was not the master—that he had no power to interfere—that the advertisements, announcing the sale, had appeared in the papers—and that the business must proceed without delay! Remonstrances—threats—prayers were all useless: the sale commenced;—and I was forced to repair to my wife's room to break the fatal news to her. She uttered no reproach—she even conquered her anguish as much as she could;—and the children were then ordered to be dressed directly. Presently Julia inquired in a meek and timid tone, if I had money enough to buy in the furniture of *the* room—she meant where her mother lay. I answered in the affirmative; but it was only to console her—for I had not a guinea—nor a friend! In a state of distraction I returned to the parlour where the sale was in progress. Merciful heavens! foremost of the buyers was Beaumont—my mortal enemy—bidding for the most costly articles that were put up. In a moment I felt as if I could fall on him, and tear him to pieces. He saw me; and, although taking no apparent notice of me, I beheld a sardonic smile of triumph upon his lips. I could bear no more: reckless of all—of every thing—I rushed from the house.

"For hours and hours did I wander about like a maniac—walking hastily along, without any defined object—and not even observing the crowds that passed me. Every thing was confused: bells seemed to be ringing in my very brain. It was dark when I thought of returning home; and then I felt shocked at the idea of having deserted my poor wife and helpless children at such a time. My ideas were now more collected; and I hastened to Russel Square. All was quiet in the house: but *they* were evidently still there—for a faint light gleamed through one of the shutters. I knocked with trembling hand. Tho door was immediately opened—by Julia. 'Oh! thank God that you have come back!' she exclaimed, sinking half-fainting into my arms: 'you know not what horrible fears have oppressed me!'—I embraced her tenderly: never—never did she seem more dear to me! The children also flocked around me; and the tender word '*Papa!*' wrung from me a flood of tears, which relieved me. I then made certain inquiries, and learnt the most heart-rending particulars. Every thing was sold and removed—even to the children's little beds;—but the worst of all was that the corse of Julia's mother lay upon the floor of the chamber where she had breathed her last!

"But let me hurry over these dreadful details. A few trinkets belonging to Julia yet remained; and the sale of those ornaments—presents made to her by me in happier days—enabled us to bury her mother decently, and to remove to a small ready-furnished lodging. Julia supported these sad afflictions and reverses with angelic resignation; and never did a single reproach emanate from her lips. Neither did she neglect the children: on the contrary, her attention to them redoubled, now that she had no longer a servant to aid her. But, alas! her strength was failing visibly: her constitution was undermined by misery and woe! And still it seemed, much though we had already suffered, as if our sorrows had only just begun. For, a few weeks after the sale of my property, and just as I had obtained a clerk's situation in a mercantile house, I was arrested for the balance of the debt due to Goldshig, the auction not having produced enough to liquidate his claims. This blow was terrible indeed, as it paralysed all my energies. I was taken to Whitecross Street prison, the only prospect of obtaining my release being the Insolvents' Court. I was accordingly compelled to apply to a philanthropic association to advance me six pounds for that purpose. The request was complied with; my wife went herself to receive the money; and she brought it to me in the prison. I compelled her to retain a sovereign for the support of herself and children; and I managed to borrow three pounds more from the only one of all my late friends who would even read a letter that came from me—so utterly was I despised by them all!

"And now—will it be believed that, such was my infatuation in respect to play, I actually gambled with my fellow-prisoners—staking the money that had been obtained with so much difficulty to pay a lawyer to conduct my business in the Insolvents' Court! Yes—while my poor wife was sitting up nearly all night to earn a trifle with her needle or in painting maps,—while my children were dependent for their daily bread upon the exertions of their poor dying mother,—I—wretch that I was—lost the very means that were to restore me to them! When the money had all disappeared, I became like a madman, and attempted to lay violent hands upon myself. I was taken to the infirmary of the prison, where I lay delirious with fever for six weeks. At the expiration of that time I recovered; and the humanity of the governor of the gaol secured the services of a lawyer to file my petition and schedule in the Insolvents' Court. The day of hearing came; and I was discharged. But, alas! I returned to the humble lodging occupied by my family without a hope—without resources. Nevertheless, the angel Julia received me with smiles; and the children also smiled with their sickly, wan, and famished countenances. Then, in the course of a conversation which Julia endeavoured to render as little mournful as possible, I learnt that Colonel Beaumont had been persecuting her with his dishonourable offers,—that he had dogged her in her way to the prison when she went thither to see me,—that he had even intruded himself upon her in her poor dwelling of one back room! Indeed, it was only in consequence of this visit that my wife mentioned the circumstance to me at all; but so pure was her soul, that she could not keep secret from me an occurrence on which, did I hear it from stranger lips, a disagreeable construction might be placed. Ill—weak—dying as she was, she was still sweetly interesting;—and I could well understand how an unprincipled libertine might seek to possess her.

"Without allowing Julia to comprehend the full extent of the impression made upon me by this information, I vowed within myself a desperate vengeance against that man who seemed to take a delight in persecuting me and mine. But for the present the condition of my family occupied nearly all my thoughts. Poor Julia was killing herself with hard—hard toil at the needle; and the children were only the ghosts of what they were in the days of our prosperity. I was, however, fortunate enough to obtain another situation, with a salary of twenty-eight shillings a week; and for some months we lived in comparative tranquillity—if not in happiness. But Julia always had smiles for me,—smiles, too, when the worm of an insidious disease was gnawing at her heart's core. And for my part, my lord, whenever I hear the discontented husband or the insolent libertine depreciating the character of Woman, the memory of my own devoted wife instantly renders me Woman's champion;—and lost—low—wretched as I have been, I have never failed—even in the vilest pot-house in which my miseries have compelled me to seek shelter—to vindicate the sex against the aspersions of the malevolent!

"Six months after my release from prison the small-pox invaded the house in which we lodged; and so virulent was the malady, that within three weeks it carried off two of my children—the girl, who was the eldest, and the younger boy. I need not attempt to describe my own grief nor the anguish of my wife. The blow was too much for *her*; and she was thrown upon a sick bed. At the same time my employer failed in business; and I accordingly lost my situation. I was returning home, one evening,—very miserable after several hours' vain search for another place,—when I met a gentleman who had once been a brother-officer in the regiment in which I first served. I made known to him my deplorable situation, assuring him that both my wife and my only remaining child were at that moment lying dangerously ill, and that I was on my way home without a shilling to purchase even the necessaries of life. He said that he had no objection to serve me; and, giving me a guinea for immediate wants, desired me to call on him next day at a particular address in Jermyn Street. I hastened joyfully home, and communicated my good fortune to poor Julia. On the following morning I repaired to Jermyn Street. My friend received me cordially, and then explained his views. To my profound surprise I learnt that he was the proprietor of a common gaming-house; and his proposal was that I should receive three guineas a week for merely lounging about the play-rooms of an evening, and acting as a decoy to visitors. My situation was so desperate that I consented; and ten guineas were given me on the spot to fit myself out in a becoming manner. I returned home; and informed Julia that I had obtained the place of a night-clerk in a coach-office. She believed me: a smile played on her sickly countenance;—and she was soon afterwards able to leave her bed.

"I entered on my new employment; and all that fatal thirst for gaming which had plunged me into such depths of misery, was immediately revived. The proprietor of the hell would not of course permit his 'decoys' to play legitimately on their own account; but we were allowed to make bets with strangers in the rooms. This I did;

and as the passion gained upon me, I visited other gambling-houses when my services were not required at the one where I was engaged. Thus I again plunged into that dreadful course; and my poor wife soon suspected the fatal truth. Our little girl died—thank God!—at this period. Start not when I express my gratitude to heaven that it was so; for what could have become of her during the period of utter destitution which soon after supervened? Yes, my lord: scarcely a year had passed, when I was hurled into the very depths of want and misery. I was accused of cheating my employer at the gaming-house: the imputation was as false as ever villanous lie could be;—and from that moment forth the door of every hell was closed against me. I was also unable to obtain an honest situation; and after Julia and myself had parted with all our wearing apparel, save the few things upon our backs, we were one night thrust forth into the streets—houseless beggars!

"It was in the middle of winter: the snow lay upon the ground; and the cold was intense. My poor wife—in the last stage of consumption, and with only a thin gown and a miserable rag of a shawl to cover her—clung to my arm, and even then attempted to console me. Oh! God—what an angel was that woman! We roved through the streets—for we dared not sit down on a door-step, through fear of being frozen to death! What my feelings were, it is impossible to explain. Morning—the cold wintry morning—found us dragging our weary forms along the Dover Road. We had no object in proceeding that way; but with tacit consent we seemed bent upon leaving a city where we had endured so much. At length Julia murmured in a faint tone, 'William, dearest, I cannot move a step farther!' And she sank, half fainting, upon a bank covered with snow.

"I was nearly distracted; but still she smiled—smiled, and pressed my hand tenderly, even while the ice-cold finger of Death touched her heart. I raised her in my arms:—my God! she was as light as a child—so emaciated in person and so thinly clad was she! I bore her to a neighbouring cottage, which was fortunately tenanted by kind and hospitable people, who immediately received the dying woman into their abode. The good mistress of the house gave up her bed to Julia, while her husband hastened to Blackheath for a doctor. And I, kneeling by the side of my poor wife, implored her forgiveness for all the miseries she had endured through me. 'Do not speak in that manner, my dearest William,' she said, in a faint tone, as she drew me towards her; 'for I have always loved you, and I am sure you have loved me in return. Alas! my adored husband, what is to become of you? I am going to a better world, where I shall meet our departed children: but, ah! to what sorrows, do I leave you? Oh! this is the pang which I feel upon my death-bed; and it is more than I can bear. For I love you, William, as never woman yet loved; and when I am no more, do not remember any little sufferings which you may imagine that you have caused me; for if there be any thing to forgive, God knows how sincerely I do forgive you! Think of me sometimes, William—and remember that as I have ever loved you, so would I continue to love you were I spared. But——'

"Her voice had gradually been growing fainter, and her articulation more difficult, as she uttered those loving words which Death rudely cut short. The medical man came: it was too late—all was over! Then did I throw myself upon that senseless form, and accuse myself of having broken the heart of the best of women. Oh! I thought, if I could only recall the past: if the last few years of my life could be spent over again—if my beloved wife, my little ones, and my fortune were still left to me—how different would my conduct be! But repentance was too late: the work was done—and the consummation of the task of ruin, sorrow, and death was accomplished! Wretch—wretch that I was!

"The poor people at whose cottage my wife thus breathed her last, were very kind to me. They endeavoured to solace my affliction, and insisted that I should remain with them at least until after the funeral. And if my poor Julia's remains received decent interment,—if she were spared the last ignominy of a parish funeral, which would have crowned all the sad memories that remained to me in respect to her,—it was through the benevolence of those poor people and the surgeon who had been called in.

"When I had followed the corpse of my poor wife to the grave, I returned to London; and, assuming another name, procured a humble employment in the City. Would you believe, my lord, that one who had held the rank of a Field Officer became the follower of a bailiff—a catchpole—a sort of vampire feeding itself upon the vitals of the poor and unfortunate? Yet such was my case: and even in that detestable capacity I experienced one day of unfeigned pleasure—one day of ineffable satisfaction; and that was upon being employed to arrest and convey to Whitecross Street prison my mortal enemy—Colonel Beaumont. Yes: he also was ruined by play, and overwhelmed with difficulties. And at whose suit was he captured? At that of Goldshig, the Jew! The Colonel was playing at hide-and-seek; but I tracked him out. Night and day did I pursue my inquiries until I learnt that he occupied a miserable lodging in the Old Bailey: and there was he taken. He languished for six months in prison—deserted by his friends—and compelled to receive the City allowance. Every Sunday during that period did I visit the gaol to gloat upon his miseries. At length he died in the infirmary, and was buried as a pauper!

"Shortly after that event, I lost my place through having shown some kindness to a poor family in whose house I was placed in possession under an execution; and from that time, until yesterday, my life has been a series of such miseries—such privations—such maddening afflictions, that it is most marvellous how I ever could have surmounted them. Indeed, I am astonished that suicide has not long ago terminated my wretched career. Your Highness saw how I was spurned from the door of that temple of infamy, which had absorbed a considerable part of my once ample means;—but that was not the first—no, nor the fiftieth time that, when driven to desperation, I have vainly implored succour of those who had formerly profited by my follies—my vices. In conclusion, permit me to assure your Highness that if the most heart-felt gratitude on the part of a wretch like me, be in any way a recompense for that bounty which has relieved me from the most woeful state of destitution and want,—then that reward is yours—for I *am* grateful—oh! God only knows how deeply grateful!"

"Say no more upon that subject," exclaimed Richard, who was profoundly affected by the history which he had just heard. "From this day forth you shall never experience want again—provided you adhere to your resolves to abandon those temples of ruin in which fortune, reputation, and happiness—yes, and the happiness of others—are all engulphed. But for the present we have both a duty to perform. Last night, at the door of Crockford's Club, I observed a young man in the society of two villains, whom I have, alas! ample cause to remember. This young man of whom I speak, drew forth his purse to assist you at the moment when I interfered."

"Yes—I saw him, and I know who he is, my lord," replied the Major. "His name is Egerton—he lives in Stratton Street—and his fortune is rapidly passing into the pockets of swindlers and black-legs. It was my intention to call upon him and warn him of the frightful precipice upon which he stands; but, alas! too well do I know that such is the infatuation which possesses the gamester——"

"Enough!" interrupted Richard. "That idea must not deter *me* from performing what I conceive to be a duty. And you must aid me in the task."

"If your Highness will show me how I can be instrumental in rescuing that young man from the jaws of destruction," exclaimed Major Anderson, "gladly—most gladly will I lend my humble aid."

"You speak as one who is anxious to atone for the misdeeds of the past," said the Prince; "and so long as such be your feelings, you will find a sincere friend in me. In respect to this foolish young man, who is rushing headlong to ruin, caution must be used; or else those arch-profligates, Chichester and Harborough, will frustrate my designs. It is for you to seek an interview with Mr. Egerton, and inform him that the Prince of Montoni is desirous to see him upon business of a most serious and of altogether a private nature."

"The wishes of your Highness shall be attended to," replied Major Anderson. "It is useless to attempt to find Egerton *alone* at this time of the day; but to-morrow morning I will call on him at an early hour."

The Prince was satisfied with this arrangement, and took his departure from the lodging of the ruined gamester.

Reader! there is no vice which is so fertile in the various elements of misery as Gambling!

CHAPTER CCXLV.

THE EXCURSION.

While Major Anderson was engaged in relating his terribly impressive history to the Prince of Montoni, Lord Dunstable and Egerton were in earnest conversation together at the lodgings of the latter gentleman in Stratton Street.

The fact was, that Albert Egerton was placed in a most cruel dilemma, as the following note, which he had received in the morning, will show:——

"*Pavement, March 28th, 1843.*

"A month has passed, dear Albert, since I saw you; and you promised to come and see us as soon as you had finished your little business about buying the estate. But you have not come; and me and the girls are quite non-plushed about it. So I tell you what we've made up our minds to do. Next Monday is a holiday; and we intend to hire a shay and go and see your new estate. But as we don't know where it is, we shall of course want you to go with us; and so you may expect us next Monday, as I say, at eleven o'clock precise. Now mind and don't disappoint us; because we've all made up our minds to go, and we won't take any refusal. If you can't go, why then we'll go by ourselves; so in that case send us the proper address, and a note to the servants. You see that me and the girls are quite determined; so no excuse.

"Your loving aunt,

"BETSY BUSTARD."

"What the deuce is to be done?" asked Egerton for the tenth time since the arrival of his friend.

"Egad! I really am at a loss to advise, my dear boy," replied Dunstable. "The affair is so confoundedly ticklish. Can't you write and put them off?"

"Impossible!" exclaimed Egerton: "you see how determined they are. Even if I were to apologise for not accompanying them, how could I refuse to give them the address of a country-seat which they so firmly believe me to possess?"

"Then write and say that, finding the house did not suit you after all, you have sold it again," suggested Dunstable.

"My aunt would see through the thing in a moment," returned Egerton. "Besides, she is intimate with Storks, my stock-broker, and would learn, from him that I had not bought in any money lately; but, on the contrary, had been selling out. I really must do something—even if I hire a country house for the purpose."

"Ah! that might be done!" cried Dunstable. "Or, stay!" he continued, a sudden idea striking him: "I have it—I have it, my dear boy!"

And his lordship seemed as overjoyed as if he himself were the individual who was unexpectedly released from a serious difficulty.

"Do not keep me in suspense," said Egerton, imploringly: "what is it that you have thought of?"

"I'll tell you in as few words as possible my boy," returned the nobleman. "It was about two years ago that I passed a short time at a place not far from London, called Ravensworth Hall. It is a splendid mansion, and has been shut up almost ever since that period. Lady Ravensworth is living somewhere on the continent, in great seclusion; and I happen to know that there is only an old gardener, with his wife, residing at the Hall."

"But I cannot understand how any thing you are now telling me bears reference to my difficulty," observed Egerton, impatiently.

"Why—don't you see!" ejaculated Lord Dunstable, slapping his friend upon the shoulder. "The gardener and his wife will not decline a five-pound note; and I dare say they are not so mighty punctilious as to refuse to allow you to call yourself the master of Ravensworth Hall for one day. What do you think of that idea?"

"I think it is most admirable," returned Egerton, his countenance brightening up—"if it can only be carried into execution."

"Will you leave it all to me?" asked Dunstable.

"I cannot possibly do better," replied Egerton. "But remember—there is no time to lose. This cursed letter must be answered to-day, or to-morrow morning at latest."

"I will ride out to Ravensworth as quickly as a thorough-bred can take me thither," said Dunstable, rising to depart. "At seven o'clock this evening I'll meet you to dine at Long's; and by that time all shall be satisfactory arranged, I can promise you."

Egerton wrung his friend's hand; and the nobleman had already reached the door of the room, when he turned back as if a sudden recollection had struck him, and said, "By the way, my dear boy, have you any cash in the house? I must make a certain payment in the neighbourhood before I go; and my agent in the country has been infernally slow lately in sending up the rents of my estate."

Lord Dunstable's estate was one of those pleasing fictions which exhibit the imaginative faculties of so many members of the aristocracy and gentry residing at the West End of London.

"Oh! certainly," was Egerton's prompt answer to the question put to him. "I have some four or five hundred pounds in my pocket-book. How much do you require?"

"Four hundred pounds will just make up the amount I have to pay," said Dunstable; and having received that sum in Bank-notes, he took his departure, humming an opera air.

It is not necessary to detail the particulars of the young nobleman's visit to Ravensworth Hall: suffice it to say that he was completely successful in his proposed arrangements with the gardener, and that he communicated this result to his friend Egerton at Long's Hotel in the evening. Chichester, Cholmondeley, and Harborough were let into the secret; and they insisted upon joining the party.

Accordingly, on the following day Egerton sent a favourable reply to his aunt's letter; but his conscience reproached him—deeply reproached him, for the cheat which he was about to practise upon his confiding and affectionate relative.

For, in spite of the dissipated courses which he was pursuing,—in spite of the gratification which his pride received from the companionship of his aristocratic acquaintances,—in spite of the lavish extravagance that marked his expenditure, this young man's good feelings were not altogether perverted; and it required but the timely interposition of some friendly hand to reclaim him from the ways that were hurrying him on to ruin!

The Monday fixed upon for the excursion arrived; and at eleven o'clock in the forenoon a huge yellow barouche, commonly called "a glass-coach," rattled up to the door of Mr. Egerton's lodgings in Stratton Street. The driver of this vehicle had put on his best clothes, which were, however, of a seedy nature, and gave him the air of an insolvent coachman; and the pair of horses which it was his duty to drive seemed as if they had been purchased at least six months previously by a knacker who had, nevertheless, mercifully granted them a respite during pleasure.

Egerton's countenance became as red as scarlet when this crazy equipage stopped at his door: but his four friends, who were all posted at the windows of his drawing-room, affected to consider the whole affair as "a very decent turn-out;" and thus the young man's mind was somewhat calmed.

By the side of the seedy coachman upon the box sate a tall, thin, red-haired young man, dressed in deep black, and with his shirt-collar turned down, over a neckerchief loosely tied, after the fashion of Lord Byron. The moment the glass-coach stopped in Stratton Street, down leapt the aforesaid seedy coachman on one side, and the thin young man on the other; and while the seedy coachman played a nondescript kind of tune upon the knocker of the house, the young gentleman proceeded to hand out first Mrs. Bustard, and then her five daughters one after the other.

This being done, and Egerton's tiger having thrown open the front door, the thin young man offered one arm to Mrs. Bustard and the other to Miss Clarissa Jemima Bustard, and escorted them into the house, the four remaining young ladies following in a very interesting procession indeed.

Egerton hastened to welcome his relatives; but from the first moment that he had set his eyes upon the red-haired young man, he had entertained the most awful misgivings;—and those fears were fully confirmed when Mrs. Bustard introduced that same young man by the name of "Mr. Tedworth Jones, the intended husband of Clarissa Jemima."

The son and heir of the wealthy tripe-man tendered a hand which felt as flabby as tripe itself; and Miss Clarissa Jemima was under the necessity of blushing deeply at her mamma's allusion to her contemplated change of situation.

Egerton gave Mr. Tedworth Jones the tip of his fore-finger, and then conducted the party up stairs to the drawing-room, where the ceremony of introducing his City relatives to his West End friends took place.

Lord Dunstable was most gallant in claiming Mrs. Bustard as "an old acquaintance;" and he even overcame his aristocratic prejudices so far as to shake hands with Mr. Tedworth Jones. Then the young ladies were introduced in due order; and, though they giggled with each other a great deal, and were dressed in very flaunting colours, they were all very good-looking; and this circumstance rendered Lord Dunstable, Sir Rupert Harborough, Colonel Cholmondeley, and Mr. Chichester particularly agreeable towards them.

"Well!" exclaimed Mrs. Bustard, throwing herself into an arm-chair, and wiping the perspiration from her fat face, "we really was scrooged up in that shay——"

"Glass-coach, mamma," said Miss Susannah Rachel, reprovingly.

"Never mind the name, my dear," returned Mrs. Bustard. "Your poor father always called it a shay; and he couldn't have been wrong. But, as I was a-saying, how we was squeeged up, to be sure! Six of us inside, and obleeged to sit on each other's knees."

"That will be just the very thing, madam, to render the trip more agreeable," said Mr. Chichester, with an affable smile.

"Provided the old lady doesn't sit on my knees," whispered Sir Rupert Harborough to Colonel Cholmondeley.

But Mr. Chichester's observation had made all the young ladies giggle, with the exception of Miss Clarissa Jemima, who blushed, and whispered to Mr. Jones something about such a remark being very unpleasant for a person "in her situation." Mr. Jones cast a sentimental glance upon his intended, and sighed very poetically as he assured Miss Clarissa that she was "a hangel."

"How are we going, Al dear?" asked Mrs. Bustard, after a pause; "and how far off is it? because I don't think the cattle in our shay are any very great shakes."

"On the contrary, aunt, I am afraid they *are* very great shakes indeed," replied Egerton, with miserable attempt at a joke. "But I think you will approve of the arrangements made."

"Oh! yes—I am sure of *that*," hastily interposed Lord Dunstable, who perceived that his young friend was very far from happy. "Your nephew's establishment is not prepared for his reception yet; but we have done all we could to make you and your amiable daughters comfortable. Materials for an elegant collation were sent out yesterday; and my four-in-hand and the Colonel's phaeton, in addition to your glass-coach, will convey us all in a very short time to your nephew's country seat."

Scarcely were these words uttered when the four-in-hand and the phaeton alluded to, dashed up the street; and the tiger entered to announce their arrival.

Egerton immediately offered his arm to his aunt, well knowing that if he did not take care of her no one else would: Mr. Tedworth Jones escorted his intended; Lord Dunstable took one of the young ladies under his protection; and the three others of course fell respectively to the lot of Colonel Cholmondeley, Sir Rupert Harborough, and Mr. Chichester.

A fair and equitable distribution of the party took place between the three vehicles; and the cavalcade moved rapidly away in a northern direction, Mrs. Bustard assuring her nephew "that it was quite a blessing to get rid of so much scrooging and squeeging as she had previously endured."

The gentlemen were very agreeable, and the young ladles very amiable—although they every now and then simpered and giggled without much apparent cause; but then it must be recollected that they suddenly found themselves for the first time in their lives in the company of a Lord, a Baronet, and two Honourables, one of whom moreover was a Colonel.

The day was very fine: the air was as mild as if it were the month of May instead of March; and the whole party were in excellent spirits—for even Egerton recovered his natural gaiety when he saw that the affair was likely to pass off without any of those annoyances which he had feared would arise from the collision of Finsbury denizens and West End fashionables.

At length the open country was gained; and in due time the stately pile of Ravensworth Hall appeared in the distance. Nothing could equal the gratification which Mrs. Bustard and the five Misses Bustard experienced when the edifice was pointed out to them as Egerton's country-seat; and, without pausing to reflect how incompatible were his means with such a grand mansion, they felt no small degree of pride at the idea of claiming the proprietor of Ravensworth Hall as their own near relation.

"What a beautiful place!" whispered Miss Clarissa to Mr. Jones, who would insist on keeping her hand locked in his during the whole ride.

"Charming, dearest—charming!" replied the enamoured swain; "and so are you."

Miss Clarissa blushed for the thirtieth time that morning; and, as if the squeeze of the hand which Mr. Jones gave her as a proof of his undivided affection were not sufficient, he planted his boot upon her foot at the same time.

This is, however, so common a token of love in all civilised and enlightened countries, that Miss Clarissa Jemima received it as such, although the tender pressure somewhat impaired the snow-white propriety of her stocking.

"Oh! what an immense building!" exclaimed Miss Susannah Rachel Bustard, as the three carriages now swept through Ravensworth Park.

"Gigantic!" said another Miss Bustard.

"Very stupendous, indeed, ladies," observed Colonel Cholmondeley, who was seated in the same vehicle with two of Mrs. Bustard's fair daughters.

"And so this great large edifisk is yours, my dear Al?" said the good lady herself, as she thrust her head from the window of the glass-coach, and surveyed the building with ineffable satisfaction. "But what a sight of chimbleys it has, to be sure!"

"Because it has a great number of rooms, aunt," replied Egerton.

"What sweet balconies!" cried the enraptured lady.

"Yes," said Egerton: "and they will look very handsome when all the shutters are opened and the windows are filled with flowers and evergreens."

"Oh! to be sure," exclaimed Mrs. Bustard, joyfully. "Well, really, it is a most charming place; and I never did see such lovely chimbley-pots in all my life. Quite picturesque, I declare!"

The three carriages now stopped before the entrance of the Hall; and Lord Dunstable's lacquey gave a furious ring at the bell.

In a short time one of the folding-doors was slowly opened to a distance of about a foot, and an old man, wearing a strange brown wig surmounted by a paper cap, thrust his head forth. Then, having surveyed the party with a suspicious air for some moments, he opened the door a little wider and revealed the remainder of his form.

"Come, my good fellow," ejaculated Dunstable, as he rushed up the steps; "don't you know your new master, who is just handing that lady out of the glass-coach?"

This was intended as a hint to make the gardener aware of the particular individual who was to be passed off as the owner of Ravensworth Hall.

"Oh! ah!" said the man, in a drawling tone, as he took off the paper cap, and made a bow to the company; "I sees him, and a wery nice gentleman he is, I've no doubt. But I hope he'll ex-kooze me for not opening the gate at fust, because———"

"Because, I suppose," hastily interposed Dunstable, "you did not know who we all were."

"No that I didn't," continued the old man; "and I'm desperate afeard of thieves."

"Thieves!" cried Lord Dunstable: "what—in the broad day-light, and riding in carriages?"

"Lor, sir," said the gardener, turning a quid of tobacco from one side of his mouth to another, so that a swelling which at first appeared in his left cheek was suddenly transferred to the right; "me and my old 'ooman is wery lonesome in this great place; and we've heerd such strange stories about the tricks of thieves, that we never know what shape they may come in."

Dunstable cut short the old man's garrulity by inquiring if the baskets, that were sent on the previous day, had arrived; and, on receiving a round-about reply in the misty verbosity of which he perceived an affirmative, the nobleman desired Egerton to do the honours of his new mansion.

"My good man," said Mrs. Bustard, advancing in a stately fashion towards the gardener, who had replaced the paper cap on his head, and had tucked up his dirty apron, so that it looked like a reefed sail hanging to his waist,—"my good man, what is your name? I don't ask through imperent curiosity; but only because I am the aunt of your new master, and all them young ladies is my daughters, your new master's fust cousins in consequence; and it's more than likely that we shall pay a many visits to the Hall. So it is but right and proper that we should know by what name we're to call you."

The gardener was a little, shrivelled, stolid-looking old man; and there was something so ludicrous in the way in which he stared at Mrs. Bustard as she thus addressed him, that Cholmondeley and Chichester were compelled to turn aside to prevent themselves from bursting into a roar of laughter.

"My good fellow," said Dunstable, hastening forward to the rescue—for Egerton was trembling like a leaf through the fear of exposure,—"this lady puts a very proper question to you; but of course her nephew, your new master, is able to answer it."

"Well, now!" cried Mrs. Bustard, struck by this observation; "and I never thought of asking Albert! Why, it's nat'ral that one should know the names of one's own servants."

"To be sure," said Lord Dunstable, hastily; "and this worthy man's name is—is—ahem?"

"Oh! yes," observed Egerton, in a faint tone, "his name is———"

"Squiggs is my name, ma'am," said the gardener: "leastways, that's the name I've bore these nine-and-sixty blessed years past, come next Aperil—Abraham Squiggs at your service. And now that I've told you my name, ma'am, p'rhaps you'll be so obleeging as to tell me your'n?"

But Dunstable hastened to cut short this somewhat disagreeable scene,—which, by the way, never would have occurred, had he adopted the precaution of previously ascertaining the name of the gardener,—by desiring Mr. Abraham Squiggs to lead the way into the drawing-room prepared to receive the company.

This request was complied with; and the old man slowly proceeded up the marble staircase, followed by the whole party.

Mrs. Bustard and her daughters were highly delighted at the splendid appearance of the mansion; and their joy was expressed by repeated exclamations of "Beautiful!"—"Charming!"—"Quite a palace!"—"Well, I never!"—"Oh! the sweet place!"—and other sentences of equally significant meaning.

"Ah! this here mansion has seen a many strange things," said the old gardener, as he admitted the company into a handsome apartment, the shutters of which were open: "this wery room is the one where Mr. Gilbert Vernon throwed his-self out of winder about two years ago."

"Threw himself out of the window!" cried Mrs. Bustard; "and what did he do that for?"

"To kill his-self, ma'am," answered the old man. "I wasn't here at the time: I'd gone down into the country to see a garden that a friend o' mine manured with some stuff that he bought in a jar at the chemist's—about a pint of it to a acre. Ah! it's a wonderful thing, to be sure, to be able to carry manure enow for a whole garden in your veskit-pocket, as one may say."

"But you was speaking about a gentleman who threw himself out of the window?" said Mrs. Bustard, impatiently.

"Ah! so I were," continued the gardener. "It was told in the newspapers at the time; but no partickler cause was given. Oh! there was a great deal of mystery about all that business; and I don't like to say much on it, 'cos Mr. Vernon is knowed to walk."

"Known to walk!" exclaimed several of the ladies and gentlemen, all as it were speaking in one breath.

"Yes," returned the gardener, with a solemn shake of the head: "Gilbert Vernon sleeps in a troubled grave; and his sperret wanders about the mansion of a night. If it wasn't that me and my wife is old and friendless, and must go to the workus if we hadn't this place, we'd not sleep another night in Ravensworth Hall."

"Why, my dear Al!" ejaculated Mrs. Bustard, casting a terrified glance around, although the sun was shining gloriously and pouring a flood of golden lustre through the windows,—"you have gone and bought a haunted house, I do declare!"

"How charmingly poetical!" whispered the tripeman's son to Miss Clarissa Jemima: "only think, dearest—a haunted house!"

"Yes, Tedworth—I do indeed think——"

"What? beloved one!" asked the sentimental swain.

"That I hope we shall leave it before it grows dusk," returned the young lady, who evidently saw nothing poetical in the matter at all.

"My dear aunt," said Egerton, in reply to the observation which his relative had addressed to him, "I am not so silly as to be frightened by tales of ghosts and spirits; and I would as soon sleep in this room as in any other throughout the mansion."

"No, you wouldn't, young man—no, indeed, you wouldn't!" exclaimed the gardener, in so earnest and impressive a manner that the young ladies huddled together like terrified lambs, and even the gentlemen now began to listen to the old man with more attention than they had hitherto shown: "I say, sir, that you would *not* like to sleep in this room—for, as sure as there is a God above us, have me and my wife seen the sperret of Gilbert Vernon standing at dusk in that very balcony which he throwed his-self from."

"Dear! dear!" whispered all the young ladies together.

"And what was he like?" asked Mrs. Bustard.

"Why, ma'am," returned the gardener, "he was dressed all in deep black; but his face were as pale as a corpse's; and when the moonbeams fell on it, me and my wife could see that it was the face of a dead man as well as I can see e'er a one of you at this present speaking."

"Egad! you have bought a nice property, Egerton," said Lord Dunstable, turning towards his young friend. "I shall propose that we return to London again before it grows dusk."

"Decidedly—since you are so disposed," returned Egerton, who was rejoiced to think that the old gardener had started a topic so well calculated to frighten his aunt and cousins away from the Hall some hours earlier than they might have otherwise been induced to leave it.

"'Pon my honour, all this is vastly entertaining!" exclaimed Sir Rupert Harborough. "But how long ago was it that you saw the ghost, my good friend?"

"How long ago?" repeated the old man, slowly: "why, I have seen it a matter of fifty—or, may be a hundred times. The fust time, me and my wife was together: we had been across the fields to a farm-house to get some milk, butter, and what not; and we was a-coming home through the Park, when we see a dark object in the balcony there. My wife looks—and I looks—and sure enow there it were.—'*What do you think it is?*' says she.—'*I think it's a thief,*' says I.—'*No it ain't,*' say she: '*it don't move; and a thief wouldn't stand there to amuse his-self.*'—'*No more he would,*' says I: '*let's go near, for no one won't harm two poor old creaturs like us.*' And we went close under the balcony, and looked up; but never shall I forget, or my old 'ooman either, the awful pale face that stared down upon us! Then we recollected that that wery balcony was the one which Mr. Vernon had throwed his-self from; and that was enow for us. We knowed we had seen his sperret!"

"Oh! dear, if it should come now!" murmured Miss Clarissa, who was so alarmed—or at least seemed to be—that she was forced to throw herself into the arms of Mr. Tedworth Jones.

"Well—this is what I call a leetle dilemmy that you're got into, Albert," said Mrs. Bustard; "for you'll never be able to live in this place."

"And no one else—unless it is such poor old helpless creaturs as me and my wife," said the gardener. "Since the fust time we see the sperret—and that's near a year and a half ago—we've seen him a many, many times; but he don't hurt us—we've got used to him, as one may say."

"If this be the room that your ghost frequents," exclaimed Colonel Cholmondeley, "why did you select it for our reception to-day, since there are so many other apartments in the mansion?"

The gardener looked confused, and made a movement as if he were about to leave the room.

"Oh! do make him tell us why he chose this apartment of all others!" whispered Mrs. Bustard to her nephew.

"My good fellow," said Egerton, thus urged on in a manner to which he could not reasonably object in his presumed capacity of owner of the mansion,—"my good fellow, did you not hear the question addressed to you by Colonel Cholmondeley?"

"Yes," replied the gardener, abruptly.

"Then, why—why do you not answer it?" said Egerton, not daring to speak in a firm or commanding tone.

"Why—if you're koorious to know, I han't no objection to tell you," responded the old gardener, after a few moments' consideration. "You see, when the establishment was broke up just after Lady Ravensworth left the Hall on a sudden, and when her lawyer come down here to discharge the servants, except me and my wife, who was put in charge o' the place, he goes through the whole building, has all the shutters shut, and locks up all the rooms——"

"Yes, yes—of course," interposed Dunstable, hastily: "because the mansion was to be sold just as it stood, with all the furniture in it."

"But he give us the keys, in course," continued the gardener; "on'y he told us to keep the rooms locked, and the shutters shut, when we wasn't dusting or cleaning. Well, the wery next day arter we see the sperret in the balcony, me and my wife come up to this room together, and sure enow the shutters was open!"

"And they had been closed before?" asked one of the young ladies, in a tremulous tone.

"As sure as you're there, Miss," replied the old man, "what I now tell you is as true as true can be. But the door was locked—and that made it more koorious still."

"It is clear that the shutters in this one particular room had been left open when all the others were closed," said Colonel Cholmondeley, with a contemptuous smile; for he began to grow weary of the old man's garrulity.

"Well—and if they was," cried Abraham Squiggs, in an angry tone,—for the Colonel's remark seemed to convey an imputation against his veracity,—"me and my wife shut 'em up again, and locked the door when we went out."

"And what followed?" inquired two or three of the Misses Bustard, speaking in low voices which indicated breathless curiosity.

"Why, that next night the shutters was opened again," answered the old man, fixing a reproachful glance upon the sceptical Colonel.

The young ladies shuddered visibly, and crowded together;—Mrs. Bustard again cast a timorous glance around;—and the gentlemen knew not what to make of the gardener's story.

"Yes," continued the old man, now triumphing in the impression which he had evidently made upon his audience; "and from that moment till now I've never set foot in this here drawing-room. But the sperret is often here; for sometimes the shutters stays open for two or three days—sometimes they're closed for weeks together."

"But what has all that to do with your bringing us to this very room on the present occasion?" asked Egerton, his aunt again prompting the question.

"Now don't be angry, sir, and I'll tell you," replied the gardener, remembering that he was to treat Mr. Egerton as the owner of the place. "The shutters has been shut for a matter of three weeks up to last night; and so when I see 'em open agen, I says to my wife, says I, '*Now's the time to see what the sperret raly wants, and why he troubles that room. There's a power of fine folks a-coming to-morrow*,' says I; '*and we'll just put 'em in the haunted-room. If so be the sperret shows his-self, they're sure to speak to him; and may be he'll tell them why he walks.*'—'Do so,' says my old o'oman: and by rights I shouldn't have said a word about the sperret at all;—but it come out some how or another; and now you know all."

"And we are very much obleeged, indeed, for being put into a haunted room," exclaimed Mrs. Bustard, bridling up.

"Oh! the joke is a capital one!" cried Cholmondeley; "and we will stay here by all means. If the ladies should be frightened, the gentlemen must take them upon their knees."

"Oh! *this* before one in my situation!" whispered Clarissa Jemima to her lover.

"It is too bad, my charmer," returned the poetical tripe-man.

But the Colonel's observation, however grievously it shocked the tender couple, had only produced a vast amount of giggling and blushing on the part of the four Misses Bustards who were *not* engaged to be married; and the result was that no serious opposition manifested itself to Cholmondeley's proposal to occupy that particular room.

"Pray be seated, ladies and gentlemen," said Egerton, now taking upon himself the duties of a host: "and excuse me for a few minutes while I ascertain that every thing necessary for your entertainment has been provided."

Egerton accordingly left the room, beckoning Abraham Squiggs to follow him.

The gardener conducted his temporary master to the kitchen, where Mrs. Squiggs was busily engaged in unpacking the hampers of wine and cold provisions sent on the preceding day. She was as like her husband as if she had been his sister instead of his wife; and therefore the reader is prepared to hear that she was a little, shrivelled, dirty old woman, possessing a face and hands apparently at open war with soap and water.

She was, however, very good-natured, and seemed quite at home in the occupation to which her attention was at present directed.

Being unaware of the approach of her husband and a stranger, she continued aloud the soliloquy in which she was engaged previous to their entrance.

"Fine turkey, stuffed with black things—truffles I've heerd 'em called by the cooks that used to be here," said the old lady, in a voice that seemed as if it sounded through a cracked speaking-trumpet; "glorious ham—four cold chicken—and tongues, reg'lar picturs! Two could pies—weal and ham most likely—leastways, unless one's beef. Six lobsters—flask of ile—and bottle of winegar. But what's this heavy feller? Cold round of biled beef;—and here's a blessed quarter of lamb. They'll want mint-sarse for that. What next? Four great German sassages—excellent eating, I'll bet a penny! No end of bread—half a Cheshire cheese—whole Stilton—and that's all in this basket."

Mrs. Squiggs had just finished the pleasing task of ranging all these succulent edibles upon the dresser, when she turned round and beheld her husband, accompanied by a stranger, who was forthwith introduced as Mr. Egerton, the temporary master of the Hall.

The old lady bobbed down and up again—thereby meaning a curtsey; for the natural good nature of her disposition was materially enhanced by the pleasing prospect of coming in for the remainder of the splendid collation which she had just been admiring.

Egerton and the gardener hastened to unpack the wine; and when this task was accomplished, the young man addressed the old one in these terms:—

"My friend Lord Dunstable gave you five pounds the other day as a slight recompense for your civility in allowing me the use of the Hall on this occasion. Here is another five-pound note for you; but pray be upon your guard should either of the ladies take it into their heads to question you concerning my right to this property. I, however, perceive that you are well disposed to aid me in this little innocent cheat upon my relations; and I really give you great credit for the ghost-story which you told to get rid of them all as soon as possible."

"Thank'ee kindly for the money, sir," exclaimed the gardener; "but as I'm a living sinner which hopes to be saved, every word I said up stairs about the sperret is as true as the Gospel."

"Ridiculous!" cried Egerton: "you cannot seriously believe in such a thing? Who ever heard of ghosts in these times?"

"Well, sir," said the man, in a solemn tone, "don't let's talk any more about it—'cos it might bring bad luck to disbelieve in ghosts where a ghost walks."

Egerton was about to reply; but he checked himself—remembering that it was useless to argue against a deeply-rooted superstition. He accordingly gave some instructions relative to the collation, which he ordered to be served up in the course of an hour; and, having renewed his injunctions as to caution in respect to his supposed ownership of the estate, he returned to the drawing-room where he had left the company.

CHAPTER CCXLVI.

THE PARTY AT RAVENSWORTH HALL.

During Albert Egerton's absence, the conversation in the drawing-room had at first turned upon the subject of the old gardener's statements respecting the ghost.

Lord Dunstable, Mr. Chichester, and Sir Rupert Harborough expressed their firm belief in the truth of the story—simply because they were anxious to serve their friend Egerton, and get the aunt and cousins back again to London as speedily as possible. For they feared that if an exposure were to take place, and if the deception relative to the ownership of the Hall were by any accident to transpire, the remonstrances, reproaches, and accompanying advice which Egerton's relations were certain to lavish upon him, might have the effect of reclaiming him entirely—a prospect by no means pleasant to the minds of those adventurers, who were resolved to pluck him to his very last feather.

Colonel Cholmondeley, although completely agreeing with his friends in all matters of this nature, nevertheless proclaimed his total disbelief of the ghost story. This he did simply because it would have appeared too pointed had all Egerton's friends combined unanimously in recommending that the party should return to London immediately after the collation.

"For my part," said Mr. Tedworth Jones, "I believe every word that the old man uttered. Love, poetry, and ghosts seem to me to go together. For what is love, unless the lover who loses her whom he loves, can soothe the agony of his mind by the conviction that she—the dear lost one—is ever near him in the shape of a disembodied spirit?"

And, having delivered himself of this splendid proof of his poetic mind, Mr. Tedworth Jones glanced triumphantly around him.

"How sweet you do talk, to be sure, my dear Tedworth!" murmured the enraptured Clarissa Jemima. "It was your conversation," she added, in a loving whisper, "that first made an impression upon my heart."

"And did my poetry have no influence, dearest?" asked Mr. Jones, in a tone of increasing mawkishness, and so far above a whisper that the words were overheard by Mr. Chichester.

"Ah! now I have found you out, Mr. Jones!" cried this gentleman, who most probably had certain reasons of his own for playing the amiable towards the wealthy tripeman's heir: "you're a poet—eh? Well—I thought so from the very first. In fact you have the air of a poet—you wear your collar like a poet—you look altogether like a poet."

Now, although Mr. Tedworth Jones looked at that precise moment, and at most other moments also, more like an ass than a poet, he nevertheless felt the compliment in its most flattering sense; and after a considerable degree of whispering on his part with Clarissa, and giggling and whispering also on hers, it transpired that Mr. Tedworth Jones had addressed to his beloved a great variety of poetical compositions.

"And I can assure you that they are very pretty too," cried Mrs. Bustard, who was by no means an indifferent spectatress of this scene.

"But you should print them, my dear sir—you should print them," exclaimed Mr. Chichester. "Let the world welcome you at once as a great poet."

"Well," said Mr. Tedworth Jones, his whole countenance becoming as red as his hair, so that it seemed as if he were about to go off in a state of spontaneous combustion; "I did venture to print little piece a few weeks ago."

"Indeed!" said Chichester, apparently much delighted at this announcement: "in some periodical, I presume?"

"No—it was to have been struck off on a few sheets of gilt-edged paper—just to circulate privately amongst my friends, you know," replied Mr. Jones: "but really the compositors made such an awful mull of the first proof that I never had the courage to let them go on!"

"That was a very great pity," observed Chichester.

"I can show you the original copy and the first proof, if you like," continued Mr. Jones; "and you may then judge for yourself how far I was justified in being angry with the printers."

Mr. Chichester of course expressed the utmost curiosity to see the poem and the proof; and the favour was conceded by Mr. Jones, after some slight opposition on the part of Clarissa, who thought that such a display was improper in respect to a lady "in her situation."

The papers were, however, handed over to Mr. Chichester, who began by reading aloud the following manuscript copy of verses:—

TO CLARISSA JEMIMA.

Oh! sweet Clarissa—ever dearest love!

What palpitations does my fond heart prove

When thy coy hand I press!

Who can depict th' ineffable delight

With which thy glances break upon the night

Of my sad loneliness?

True as the Boreal Lights unto the Pole,

Those looks shed lustre on my sadden'd soul,

And bid sweet visions rise

To cheer me in my wandering path, and give

A plea to nurse the thought that I may live

To bask in thy bless'd eyes!

Yes—dark as seemeth this wide world to me,

Perverse as human hearts appear to be,

Thou art all truth and joy!

For thee the incense of my altar burns;

To thee my grateful memory ever turns

With bliss that ne'er can cloy!

These verses were received with great applause by all present; but during the reading of them Clarissa had thought it quite becoming for a young lady "in her situation" to burst into tears, and throw herself in a sort of hysterical frenzy into her mamma's arms.

This little bit of tragedy was, however, soon got over; and, the manuscript copy of the verses having been disposed of, Mr. Chichester proceeded to read aloud the first proof of the stanzas in print:—

TO ALRISSA GEMINI.

Oh! sweet Alrissa—ever cleanest bore!

What fluctuations does my proud heart pour

When thy toy's hand I guess!

Who can defect th' inexorable delight

With which thy flounces break upon the sight

Of my bad loveliness?

Trim as the Rascal Sights unto the Pole,

Those locks shed bistre on my padded soul,

And bid smart onions rise

To churn me in my mantling path and give

A flea to nerve the thought that I may live

To bask in thy blear'd eyes!

You bark as smelleth this vile work to me,

Peruse as human beasts appear to be,

Then act all trash and gag!

For thee the nonsense of my utter brims;

To thee my platefull simmering ever trims

With flies that now can't bag!

"I think you will grant that the printers made a slight mull of my writing?" said Mr. Jones, when Chichester had brought this specimen of typography to a conclusion.

"Yes—a slight mull, as you observe," returned this gentleman, who, together with his own friends, was scarcely able to repress a boisterous outbreak of mirth. "But it is impossible to feel any annoyance at that strange assemblage of misconceptions on the part of the printer, since the original itself is so perfectly beautiful."

"Oh! yes—so very charming!" whispered Clarissa Jemima to her lover.

Mr. Jones looked a complete encyclopædia of tender emotions; and the happy couple, forgetting that other persons were present, continued their discourse in whispers.

"Well, I declare," said Miss Susannah Rachel, after a pause, "I don't think I shall ever again be able to sleep without a light in the room, after all that has been told us about the ghost."

"And I shall always cover my head over with the clothes," lisped another female specimen of the Bustard race.

"I've been told," remarked the fourth daughter, "that a horse-shoe nailed to the door of a room will prevent evil spirits from passing the threshold."

"Or sleep with a Bible under your pillow," said the fifth Miss Bustard.

"That's all very well, gals," observed the parent of this most interesting family; "but ghostesses won't be kept away by such means as them. Where there's evil spirits, there evil spirits will be."

"Nothing can possibly be clearer, madam," exclaimed Lord Dunstable.

"And if they must walk, they will walk," continued Mrs. Bustard.

"Your arguments are really admirable, madam."

"And so it's of no use bothering oneself about it—beyond getting away as soon as possible from the place where ghostesses are," added the lady.

"Were you of the other sex, madam, I should say you had graduated at Oxford," remarked the nobleman; "for you reason with all the logic of Euclid."

"Is Mr. Euclid such a very clever man, my lord?" asked Mrs. Bustard.

Dunstable was suddenly seized with a violent fit of coughing:—at least so it appeared to the good-natured old lady; inasmuch as he was forced to keep his handkerchief to his mouth for a considerable time.

Egerton now re-appeared, and suggested a ramble about the grounds, while the collation was being spread. Mrs. Bustard was anxious to go over the mansion; but Egerton negatived that proposal by stating that as he had not yet compared the contents of the various rooms with the inventory, it would not be fair to institute any such examination unless attended by the persons in charge of the place; and they were too busy with the preparations for the luncheon to spare time for that purpose.

The ramble was accordingly agreed to; and the party descended to the gardens.

"Well, my dear Albert," said Mrs. Bustard, as they roved through the grounds, "I admire the edifisk and I admire the gardens very much; but I don't like the evil spirit. You'll never be happy in this lonely place until you marry, and have a companion."

"Marry!" exclaimed Egerton, into whose head the idea had only entered as one suggesting a means to repair his fortunes, when they should be completely shattered.

"Yes—marry, to be sure!" continued his good-natured but garrulous relative. "Let me see—I think I could make up an excellent match for you. What should you say to Miss Posselwaithe, the great paviour's daughter?"

"Oh! my dear madam," exclaimed Lord Dunstable, "your nephew may look somewhat higher than a paviour's daughter. *I* intend that he shall marry a lady of title as well as of fortune. Only think how well it will sound in the *Morning Herald*—'Mr. and Lady Egerton, of Ravensworth Park.'"

"So it would—so it would!" cried the aunt, delighted with the prospect thus held out.

And in this way they chatted until the bell on the roof of the Hall rang to summon them to the collation.

The table was spread in "the haunted room;" and the company took their places with a determination to do ample justice to the excellent cheer.

We have already given the reader to understand that there was a most liberal supply of eatables provided for this occasion: we should also state that the wine was equally plentiful and good; and the champagne soon circulated with great freedom. Mrs. Bustard permitted Lord Dunstable to fill her glass as often as he chose; and that was very often indeed. As for her daughters, they one and all declared to the gentlemen who respectively sate next to them, that they really could not possibly think of taking more than a quarter of a glass; but it happened that, after a great deal of simpering, giggling, and blushing, they managed to toss off each a bumper; and somehow or another their eyes were averted when their glasses were being refilled; and on the third occasion of such replenishment, they took it as a matter of course.

Things went on so comfortably, that Egerton's spirits rose to as high a state of exuberance as if he were really the owner of the splendid mansion in which he was entertaining his relations and friends:—Mrs. Bustard declared that she never had seen any thing so pleasant since the day when her poor deceased husband and herself dined with the Lord Mayor;—Mr. Tedworth Jones insisted upon singing a song which he had himself composed to his intended, and the two first lines of which delicately eulogised the fair "Clarissa," and plainly stated how grieved the poet would be to "miss her;"—and even the young lady herself was so happy and contented that she forgot to reproach her lover for thus publicly complimenting one "in her situation."

Dunstable flattered the old lady: Cholmondeley, Harborough, and Chichester made themselves agreeable to the young ones; and every thing was progressing as "merry as a marriage bell," when the old gardener rushed franticly into the room, carrying his paper cap in one hand, his wig in the other, and bawling at the top of his cracked voice, "A corpse! a corpse!"

Every one started from his seat around the table, and surveyed the gardener with looks of astonishment.

For a moment Egerton and his four fashionable friends imagined that this was some scheme of the gardener to break up the party, and was therefore to some extent a stratagem in favour of Egerton himself: but a second glance at the horror-struck countenance of the old man convinced them that his present conduct was far different from a mere feint.

"A corpse! a corpse!" he repeated, casting haggard looks around.

"What in the name of heaven do you mean?" demanded Egerton, now advancing towards him.

The gardener sank, trembling all over, upon a seat; and Egerton made him swallow a glass of wine.

In a few minutes he grew more composed, put on his wig,—which, it seemed, had fallen off as he was rushing up the stairs,—and then related in his characteristic round-about manner the causes of his ejaculations and his alarms.

But it will perhaps suit the convenience of the reader much better if we explain the whole affair in our own language, and as succinctly as possible.

It appeared, then, that while the company in the drawing-room were discussing their wine, and the gardener, his wife, and the servants in attendance upon the vehicles, were dining off the remains of the banquet in the kitchen, a stout, hearty, decently dressed man, of about eight-and-forty years of age, was passing through a field near Ravensworth Hall. He was accompanied by a beautiful terrier, with which he amused himself by throwing a small stick to as great a distance as he could, and making the dog fetch it back to him. The little animal was very sagacious, and performed its duty well: until at last the man threw the stick into a certain part of the field where the dog persisted in remaining, instead of hastening back to its master. Vainly did the man whistle and call from a distance: the dog would not obey him, but kept scratching in a particular spot from which it would not stir. Thither did the man accordingly proceed; and, on reaching the spot, he found the dog working away with its little paws in a hollow which had doubtless been caused by the recent rains. At the same time a nauseous effluvium assailed the man's nostrils; and, on examining the spot more attentively, he discovered—to his indescribable horror—a human hand protruding from the soil!

It was almost a skeleton-hand; but the black and rotting flesh still clung to it, and the fibres were not so far decomposed as to cease to hold the joints of the fingers together.

Seizing the dog in his arms, the man tore the little animal away from the spot where so appalling a spectacle appeared; and, without farther hesitation, he hurried to the Hall. Having found his way to the servants' offices, he communicated his discovery to the old gardener and to the servants who had accompanied Egerton's party to the mansion. The first impulse of Abraham Squiggs was to hurry up stairs and alarm the guests with the strange news thus brought; but Lord Dunstable's lacquey suggested the impropriety of disturbing the company, and proposed that the spot should be first examined by means of mattocks and spades.

This plan was immediately assented to: and, the gardener having procured the implements required, the owner of the dog hastened to lead the way to the place where the human hand appeared above the ground. Mrs. Squiggs protested against being left behind: she was accordingly allowed to form one of the party.

On reaching the spot, the news which the stranger had imparted were found to be correct; and the exposed member was viewed with looks of horror and alarm.

"Some foul deed has been committed," said the stranger; "but I have always heard and read that God will sooner or later bring murder to light."

"Ah! and that's true enow, I'll warrant!" exclaimed the old gardener. "The body which that hand belongs to, was no doubt buried deep; but the rains overflowed yonder pond, and the water made itself a way along here, you see—so that it has hollered the earth out several foot."

"Well—it's of no use talking," said the stranger: "but make haste and dig down here, old gentleman—so that we may see whether the hand has an arm, and the arm a body."

The gardener took the spade, and set to work; but he trembled so violently that he was unable to proceed for many minutes. The stranger accordingly snatched the spade from his hands, and addressed himself resolutely to the task.

While he was thus employed, the others stood by in profound silence; but the dog ran in a timid manner round the spot, sometimes barking—then whining mournfully.

His master worked speedily, but carefully; and as each shovel-full of earth was thrown up, and as the proofs that an entire human body lay beneath became every instant more apparent, the spectators exchanged glances of augmenting horror.

But when at length the entire form of a human being was laid bare scarcely two feet below the bottom of the hollow,—when their eyes fell upon the blackened flesh of the decomposing head, the features of which were no longer traceable,—and when the rotting remnants of attire showed that the being who had there found a grave was of the female sex, a cry burst simultaneously from every lip.

"Here's work for the Coroner, at all events," observed the stranger, after a long pause. "We must move the body to the big house there———"

"Move the body to the Hall!" cried the old gardener and his wife, in the same breath, and both looking aghast at this announcement.

"Yes—most certainly," answered the stranger. "Would you leave a Christian—as I hope that poor woman was—to be devoured by rats and other vermin? I might have done so once: but, thank God! I have become a better man since then. Howsomever, get us a plank or two, old gentleman; and we'll do our duty in a proper manner."

The gardener retraced his way, in a sulky mood, and with much mumbling to himself, to the Hall, and presently returned with a couple of planks and two stout pieces of wood to serve as cross-beams to form the bier. The corpse was then carefully placed upon the planks, but not without great risk of its falling to pieces while being thus moved; and, the bier having been hoisted on the shoulders of the stranger, Dunstable's lacquey, the seedy coachman, and Colonel Cholmondeley's groom, the procession moved towards the Hall, the gardener and his wife at the head.

But when the party arrived, with its appalling burden, near the mansion, the old man and woman began to exchange hasty whispers together.

"What is the matter now?" asked the stranger.

"Why, sir," replied the gardener, in a hesitating manner, "me and my wife has been a-thinking together that it would be as well to put the remains of that poor creetur as far from our own rooms as possible: 'cos what with a sperret here and a dead body there———"

"Well, well—old man," interrupted the stranger, impatiently; "this load is heavy, and I for one shall be glad to put it down somewhere. So leave off chattering uselessly—and tell us in a word what you do mean."

"To be sure," returned the gardener: "this way—this way."

And, as he spoke, he opened a small door at the southern end of the building, by means of a key which he selected from a bunch hanging beneath his apron.

"We never can get up that staircase, old gentleman," said the stranger, plunging his glances through the doorway.

"It's easier than you think—the stairs isn't so steep as they seem," returned the gardener; "and what's more," he added, doggedly, "you may either bring your burden this way, or leave it in the open air altogether."

"To be sure," chimed in the old woman: "if you don't choose to put the body in the very farthermost room from our end of the building, you may take it back again; and them stairs leads to the room that *is* farthermost off."

The stranger, who was a willing, good-natured man, and who seemed to study only how he should best perform a Christian duty, offered no farther remonstrance; but, respecting the prejudices of the old people, succeeded, by the aid of his co-operators, in conveying the bier up the staircase. On reaching the landing, the gardener opened the door of a room the shutters of which were closed; but through the chinks there streamed sufficient light to show that the apartment was a bed-chamber.

"Put it down there—on the carpet," said the gardener, who was anxious to terminate a proceeding by no means agreeable to him.

The bier was conveyed into the room, and placed upon the floor.

At that moment—while the gardener and his wife remained standing in the passage—the old man suddenly caught hold of the woman's arm with a convulsive grasp, and whispered in a hasty and hollow tone, "Hark! there's a footstep!"

"Yes—I hear it too!" returned his wife, in a scarcely audible tone: and, through very fright, she repeated, "There—there—there!" as often as the footstep fell—or seemed to fall—upon her ears.

"At the end of the passage——" murmured the gardener.

"Do you see any thing?" asked his wife, clinging to him.

"No—but it's certain to be the sperret," returned the man.

And they leant on each other for support.

At the next moment the four men came from the interior of the room where they had deposited the corpse; and the two old people began to breathe more freely.

The gardener hurried his wife and companions down the narrow staircase, and pushed them all hastily from the threshold of the little door, which he carefully locked behind him.

Then, having given the stranger a surly kind of invitation to step in and refresh himself, he led the way to the offices at the opposite extremity of the building.

But scarcely had the party gained the servants' hall, when the old gardener, whose mind was powerfully excited by all that had just occurred, hastened abruptly away; and, rushing up the great staircase, he burst into the drawing-room, exclaiming, "A corpse! a corpse!"

CHAPTER CCXLVII.

THE STRANGER WHO DISCOVERED THE CORPSE.

Perhaps there is no other cry in the world, save that of "Fire!" more calculated to spread terror and dismay, when falling suddenly and unexpectedly upon the ears of a party of revellers, than that of "A corpse! a corpse!"

Before a single question can be put, or a word of explanation be given, each one who hears that ominous announcement revolves a thousand dread conjectures in his mind: for although that cry might in reality herald nothing more appalling than a case of sudden death from natural causes, yet the imagination instinctively associates it with the foulest deed of treachery and murder.

Such was the case in the present instance.

The entire party started from their seats; and the smiles that were a moment before upon their countenances gave place to looks of profound horror and intense curiosity.

The feelings thus denoted did not experience any mitigation from the inquiring glances that were cast towards the gardener; for the entire appearance of the old man was far more calculated to augment than diminish the alarm which his strange cry had originated. His eyes rolled wildly in their sockets—his quivering lips were livid—his frame seemed to be influenced by one continuous shudder, and his breath came with difficulty.

In fact, the mysterious sounds of footsteps in the passage had worked up his feelings, already greatly moved by the discovery and exhumation of the rotting carcass of a female, to a degree of excitement doubly painful to behold in one so bowed with the weight of years as he; and he sank into a seat, as we have before said, in a state of almost complete exhaustion.

The wine that Egerton compelled him to swallow partially restored him; and in the course of a few minutes he was enabled to relate the particulars which we have succinctly placed before the reader.

The ladies were cruelly shocked by the narrative that thus met their ears; and they one and all declared that nothing should ever again induce them to visit a place into possession of which their relative seemed to have entered under the most inauspicious circumstances. They also requested to be taken back to London with the least possible delay; and Sir Rupert Harborough, with his friend Chichester, hastened to give the servants orders to get the vehicles ready.

Mrs. Bustard and her daughters retired into an ante-room to put on their bonnets and shawls: Egerton, Dunstable, Cholmondeley, and Tedworth Jones remained standing round the chair on which the old gardener was still seated.

"This is a most extraordinary thing," said Dunstable, after a pause, during which he had reflected profoundly: then, addressing himself to his friend the Colonel, he asked in a serious tone, "Does not the strange discovery just made remind you of something that I mentioned to you nearly two years ago?"

"I recollect!" cried the Colonel: "you allude to the mysterious disappearance of Lydia Hutchinson."

"I do," answered the nobleman. "That event occurred while I was lying wounded in this house."

"Ah! I heerd of it, to be sure!" said the gardener. "But I was down in the country when all them things took place—I was there for some months. Do you think——"

"No—it could not be!" interrupted Dunstable: "for it was well known at the time that Lydia decamped with Lady Ravensworth's jewel-box."

Colonel Cholmondeley turned away, and said nothing: he remembered the evidences of desperate enmity between Adeline and Lydia, which had come within his own cognisance; and a vague—a very vague, distant, and undefined suspicion that the corpse just discovered might indeed be that of Lydia Hutchinson, entered his mind. But he speedily banished it: for the idea that Lady Ravensworth could have had any thing to do with the murder of Lydia did not seem tenable for a moment.

"As your lordship says," observed the old gardener, after a long pause, and now addressing himself to Dunstable, "it can't have any thing to do with that young o'oman who was here a few weeks as my lady's maid—'cos it's well knowed that she bolted off with the jewel-casket, as your lordship says."

Here Cholmondeley advanced towards Dunstable, took him by the arm, and, leading him aside, said in a hasty whisper, "Let us leave this matter where it is. Should the body just discovered be really that of Lydia Hutchinson, who disappeared so strangely, it would be very annoying for us to have to explain to a Coroner's jury all we know about her and Lady Ravensworth."

"Truly so," answered Dunstable. "And, after all, it is no affair of ours."

This understanding being arrived at, the nobleman and his friend returned to the table, where they helped themselves to some champagne to allay, as they said, the disagreeable sensations produced by the sudden interruption which their mirth had experienced.

The day seemed to be marked out by destiny as one on which various adventures were to occur in respect to the excursion party to Ravensworth Hall.

It will be remembered that Sir Rupert Harborough and Chichester had left the drawing-room for the purpose of seeing the vehicles got ready with the least possible delay.

The two friends—whom the associated roguery of many years had rendered as intimate as even brothers could be—proceeded down stairs, and, after some little trouble, found their way to the servants' offices. Guided by a sound of voices, they threaded a passage, and at length found themselves on the threshold of the room where the gardener's wife, the stranger who had first discovered the body, the seedy coachman, the lacquey, and the groom, were still discussing the incident that had so recently occurred.

But the moment that the two gentlemen appeared at the door, the stranger started from his seat, exclaiming in a loud tone, "Well met, I declare! You're the very identical men I've long been wanting to see!"

And, putting his arms akimbo, he advanced towards them in a manner which appeared extremely free and independent in the eyes of the lacqueys.

"Ah! my good friend Talbot!" cried the baronet, for a moment thrown off his guard, but speedily recovering himself: "upon my honour I am delighted to see you!"

"So am I—quite charmed to find you looking so well!" exclaimed Chichester.

"No thanks to either of you, howsomever," said the individual thus addressed, and without appearing to notice the hands that were extended to him. "But you know as well as I do that my name isn't Talbot at all; it's Bill Pocock—and, I may add, too, without telling a lie, that it's now *honest Bill Pocock*."

"Well, my dear Pocock," exclaimed Chichester, with a glance that implored his forbearance, "I am really quite happy to see you. But we will step out into the garden, and just talk over a few little matters———"

"Oh! gentlemen," said the gardener's wife, coming forward, "you're quite welcome to step into our little parlour t'other side of the passage—if so be you have any thing private to talk about."

"Thank you—that will exactly suit us," returned Chichester, hastily: and, taking Pocock's arm, he drew him into the room thus offered for their privacy.

The baronet remained behind for a few moments, to give the necessary instructions to the servants relative to preparing the vehicles; and, this being done, he rejoined Chichester and Pocock.

When the trio were thus assembled in the gardener's little parlour, Pocock said, "So I find you two chaps still pursuing the old game. Got in with a young cit named Egerton—and all his relations—eh? Pretty goings on, I've no doubt."

"Only just in a friendly way, my dear fellow," exclaimed Chichester. "But you stated that you had been looking for me and Harborough for a long time?"

"Yes—I was anxious enough to see you both," returned Pocock: "and I'll tell you the reason why. You remember that night—some few years ago—when you two got such a precious walloping at the *Dark House* in Brick Lane, Spitalfields?"

"Well—well," said the baronet: "go on."

"Oh! I see you haven't forgot it! You also know that on that same night the very young man whom we all ruined, was present—I mean Richard Markham."

"Yes—to be sure. But what of that?" demanded Chichester.

"Why—I gave him a paper, drawed up and signed by myself,—plain William Pocock, and none of your aristocratic Talbots."

"And that paper?" said the baronet, anxiously.

"Contained a complete confession of the whole business that brought him into trouble," continued Pocock. "But he pledged himself not to use it to my prejudice; and that's the reason why you never heard of it in a legal way. On that same occasion he put a fifty-pound note into my hand, saying, '*Accept this as a token of my gratitude and a proof of my forgiveness; and endeavour to enter an honest path. Should you ever require a friend, do not hesitate to apply to me.*'—Those was his words; and they made a deep impression on me. Yes—gentlemen, and I *did* enter an honest path," continued Pocock, proudly: "and that money prospered me. I returned to my old business as an engraver—I left off going to public-houses—I worked hard, and redeemed my character with my old employers. Since that night at the *Dark House* all has gone well with me. I have never applied to my benefactor—because I have never required a friend. But I have prayed for him morning and evening—yes, gentlemen, prayed! I know that this may sound strange in your ears: it is nevertheless true—and I am not ashamed to own it. And while that faultless young man was pursuing his glorious career in a foreign land, there was an obscure but grateful individual in London who wept over his first reverses, but who laughed, and sang, and danced for joy when the newspapers brought the tidings of his great battles. And that individual was myself: for he was my saviour—my guardian angel—my benefactor! Instead of heaping curses upon me, he had spoken kind words of forgiveness and encouragement: instead of spurning me from his presence, he had given me money, and told me to look upon him as my friend! My God! such a man as that can save more souls and redeem more sinners than all the Bishops that ever wore lawn sleeves! I adore his very name—I worship him—I am as proud of his greatness as if he was my own son; and all Prince though he now is, did it depend upon me, he should wear a crown."

And as he spoke, the grateful man's voice became tremulous with emotions; and the big tears rolled down his cheeks.

There was at that moment something so commanding—something so superior about even this vulgar individual, that Chichester and Harborough found themselves unable to reply to him in that strain of levity with which they would have gladly sought to sneer away his eulogies of one whom they hated and feared.

"Yes," continued Pocock: "all I possess in the world I owe to the Prince of Montoni. I am now at my ease—I live in my own house, bought with my own hard-earned money:—I can even afford to take a little pleasure, or an occasional ramble, as I was doing just now when accident brought me here. And, what is more, I always have a five-pound note to assist a friend. You cannot wonder, then, if I worship the very name of that man who from a comparatively humble rank has raised himself to such a proud height by his valour and his virtues."

"But what has all this to do with your anxiety to see the baronet and me?" inquired Chichester, in a tone displaying little of its wonted assurance.

"A great deal," answered Pocock. "I only want an opportunity to show the Prince how grateful I am to him; and for that reason have I looked out for you. Great, powerful, and rich as he now is, the memory of the past cannot oppress him; but still it would be satisfactory to his noble mind to receive from both of you the same confession of his innocence that he has had from me."

"What?" cried the baronet and Chichester together, as they exchanged troubled glances.

"Yes—you know what I mean," said Pocock; "and you dare not refuse me. Although it is my duty, perhaps, to step up stairs and quietly explain to the people there what kind of acquaintances they have got in you, yet the honour of the Prince is uppermost with me; and I will not expose you, if you at once write out and sign a paper saying that *he* was innocent and *you* was the guilty cause of his misfortunes."

"Impossible!" cried Harborough.

"He would transport us!" ejaculated Chichester, turning deadly pale.

"And no great harm if he did," said the engraver, drily. "But consideration for *me* will prevent his punishing *you*. So if you value the friendship of your chums up stairs———"

"It would never do to be shown up before *them*!" whispered the baronet with desperate emphasis to Chichester, whom he drew partially aside for a moment.

"You will pledge yourself not to show to any one, save the Prince, the paper you require of us?" asked Chichester of the engraver.

"When once you've given me that paper, I want to know nothing more of you or your pursuits," replied Pocock.

The two gentlemen exchanged a few hurried whispers, and then signified their assent to the arrangement proposed; for they found Egerton's purse too useful a means to have recourse to at pleasure, to allow them to risk the loss of their influence over him.

There were writing-materials in the room where the above conversation took place; and the document was speedily drawn up. Chichester wrote it, under the supervision of Pocock, who would not allow him to abate one single tittle of all the infamy which characterised the proceedings that had engendered the misfortunes of Richard Markham.

The paper was then duly signed, and delivered into the hands of the engraver.

"Now that this little business is settled," said he, "perhaps you two gentlemen will just allow me to observe that I have found an honest way of life much happier than a dishonest one, and quite as easy to pursue, if you only have the will; but whether you'll profit by this advice or not, is more than I can say—and certainly much more than I should like to answer for."

With these words Pocock took his departure, the dog following close at his heels.

Chichester and Harborough exchanged looks expressive of mingled vexation and contempt, and then returned to the drawing-room.

The vehicles were almost immediately afterwards driven round to the principal entrance; and the company were on the point of leaving the apartment where the festivities had been so unpleasantly interrupted, when an ejaculation which escaped the lips of Colonel Cholmondeley, who was gazing from the window, caused them all to hasten to the casements.

A travelling barouche was rapidly approaching the mansion!

CHAPTER CCXLVIII.

AN UNPLEASANT EXPOSURE.

Egerton's countenance grew pale as death when he beheld that carriage hastening through the Park towards the entrance of the Hall.

Dunstable perceived and understood his fear; and he himself experienced no little dread lest the approaching vehicle should contain Lady Ravensworth. But, in the next moment, this suspicion vanished; for it did not seem probable that her ladyship would return to a mansion totally unprepared to receive her.

The old gardener was, however, now shaking with a new alarm; and the departure was hurried as much as possible: but the travelling barouche had stopped near the entrance of the Hall ere Egerton's party had reached the bottom of the great staircase.

There was no male domestic in attendance upon the carriage: the postillion accordingly alighted from his horse, opened the door, and assisted two females, both clad in deep mourning, to descend.

Of those females, one was evidently a lady, and the other her maid.

The former raised her black veil, immediately upon alighting, and gazed in astonishment upon the three vehicles which had prevented her own from drawing-up immediately against the steps of the principal entrance.

By this time Egerton's party, followed by the old gardener, who was doing his best to hurry the intruders away, had reached the portico; and it was at this precise moment that the lady raised her veil on descending from the barouche.

Cholmondeley and Dunstable started; and the former exclaimed, "Lady Ravensworth!"

Then, recovering his wonted self-command, he advanced towards Adeline, raised his hat, and said, "Your ladyship is doubtless astonished to see so large a party at Ravensworth Hall; but if you will permit me to speak to you five words in private—"

"I have no secrets to discuss with Colonel Cholmondeley," interrupted Adeline, in a tone of freezing hauteur and yet of deep dejection: then, turning towards Mrs. Bustard, who had thrust herself forward to learn why the arrival of a barouche containing a lady and her female attendant had produced such a singular excitement amongst the gentlemen of the party, she said, "May I be permitted to inquire, madam, the meaning of this assembly on the day of my return?"

"If you'll tell me fust, ma'am, who you are," replied Mrs. Bustard, "may be I'll satisfy you."

"I am Lady Ravensworth," was the dignified answer.

"Well then, my lady, all I can say is—and which I do on the part of my nephew Albert—that you're quite welcome to occupy a room or two in this edifisk until such times as you can provide yourself with another place——"

"My dear aunt, allow me to explain myself to Lady Ravensworth," exclaimed Egerton, now stepping forward.

"Eh—do, my boy," cried Mrs. Bustard, whose voice was somewhat husky with champagne, and whose sight, from the same cause, was a little dizzy—so that she did not perceive the glance of mingled anger and astonishment which Adeline threw upon her while she was so politely offering her ladyship the use of apartments in Ravensworth Hall.

"Lady Ravensworth, permit me—one word, I implore you!" said Lord Dunstable, in an under tone, as he advanced before Egerton.

"Is this mystery to be explained to me at all?" cried Adeline. "Lord Dunstable, I have no better reason to grant a private interview to you than to your friend Colonel Cholmondeley: I therefore hope that, without farther delay, you will inform me to what circumstance I am to attribute the honour which my poor mansion has experienced by receiving so large a party during my absence."

"*Her* mansion, indeed!" said Mrs. Bustard, with an indignant toss of the head, as she turned towards her daughters and Mr. Tedworth Jones, all of whom remained mute spectators of a scene which was to them totally inexplicable.

"Upon me must the weight of your ladyship's anger fall," said Egerton, again advancing, and mustering up all his courage to afford the requisite explanation.

"No such a thing!" cried Mrs. Bustard. "What right has the lady to be angry? Because her house was put up for sale, and you bought it———"

"Abraham, will *you* explain this enigma?" exclaimed Adeline, turning impatiently towards the gardener, whom she suddenly discovered peering from behind Sir Rupert Harborough.

"Why, my lady," said the old man, twisting his paper cap over and over in his hands as he dragged himself irresolutely forward, "your ladyship sees these wery respectable folk—leastways, respectable as far as I know anythink to the contrairey,—for my maxim is, my lady—as I often says to my old 'ooman—says I—at such times when she says, says she———"

Adeline actually stamped her foot with impatience.

"I'm a-coming to the pint, my lady," continued the gardener, now completely crushing the paper cap in his hand; "and in doing that, my lady, I must ax your ladyship's pardon—'cos I'm a poor simple old man which can't boast of much edication—leastways, as I says to my old 'ooman———"

"This is insupportable!" cried Adeline. "In one word, did you not receive my letter stating that it was my intention to return to the Hall this week?"

"No, my lady—no such a letter ever come," answered the gardener.

"But you can perhaps inform me in two words how these ladies and gentlemen happened to honour my house with their presence?" said Adeline, speaking in a severe tone.

"Your house, ma'am!" shouted Mrs. Bustard, her countenance becoming purple with indignation: "no such a thing! It's my nephew's—he bought it—and he is here to tell you so!"

Thus speaking, she thrust Egerton forward.

"My dear aunt," said the young man, tears starting into his eyes, "I have deceived you! I am sorry for the cheat which I have practised upon you: but the truth is———"

"Don't tell me no more!" cried Mrs. Bustard. "I see it all. It's a hoax—a shameful hoax! And I shouldn't wonder if your Lord and your Baronet and your Honourables are all as Brummagem as your title to this edifisk. Come, Tedworth—come, gals: let's get back to the Pavement. This is no place for us."

And having thus expressed herself, Mrs. Bustard bounced down the steps and clambered like an irritated elephant into the glass-coach, followed by her five daughters. Mr. Jones then mounted to the dickey; the seedy coachman whipped the horses; and the crazy old vehicle rattled away.

Lady Ravensworth, attended by her maid, passed into the mansion without bestowing any farther notice on the gentlemen who still lingered upon the steps; and when she had thus disappeared, they hastened to take their departure for London, Egerton in a state of mind enviable only by a man about to be hanged.

For nearly two years had Adeline been a voluntary exile from her native land; and, in the seclusion of a charming villa in the south of France, she had devoted herself to the care of her child, whom the gipsy Morcar had so miraculously saved from death. She also endeavoured, by the exercise of charity and a constant attention to her devotions, to atone for the crimes which she had committed; but, though deeply penitent, her soul could not stifle the pangs of an intense remorse. And thus had many—many sleepless nights—often rendered terrible by the shade of the murdered Lydia—dimmed the fires of Adeline's eyes, and given to her cheeks the pallor of marble!

Her only solace was her child, on whom she doated with all the affection which can be bestowed by a heart that has nothing else to love—nothing else to render existence even tolerable. The more she alienated her mind from the frivolities and levities which had occupied her when she was a brilliant star in the galaxy of London fashion,—and the more successfully she wrestled with those burning passions which had rendered her the willing victim of the seducer, even in her girlhood,—so much the more profound became her affection for the infant Ferdinand. But that consolation was not to endure. Five months before her return to England the boy was snatched away from her,—suddenly snatched away by the rude hand of Fever, as the rose-bud is cropped by the bleak north wind.

Then how desolate became the heart of Adeline! She felt that her punishment had not yet ceased on earth.

No longer were there charms for her in a foreign land; and she panted to return to her native clime. For some weeks she wrestled against this inclination; but having imparted her desire to Eliza Sydney, with whom she regularly corresponded, a letter from that excellent lady set her mind at ease as to the expediency of revisiting England. Eliza offered no argument against the project; and Lady Ravensworth accordingly hastened her preparations for a departure from the south of France.

The faithful Quentin was still in her service; but the English lady's-maid, who had followed Adeline to the Continent, had married and settled in France. A French woman, therefore, supplied her place; and it was this foreign servant who accompanied Lady Ravensworth on her return to the Hall.

Adeline's desire was to retrace her way in privacy to the mansion which, according to the conditions of her late husband's will, had become her own—for there was now no male heir to the proud title and broad lands of

Ravensworth: and her intention was to dwell in the strictest retirement at the mansion. She had written to the gardener to command him to prepare for her return; but, by some accident, the letter had miscarried—and hence the old man's ignorance of the approach of his mistress.

On her arrival, by the Calais steam-packet, at London Bridge, Adeline had left Quentin to clear the baggage at the Custom-House, and had proceeded direct to the Hall. The incidents which immediately followed her arrival are already known to the reader.

It may, however, appear strange that Adeline should come back to a dwelling where she had suffered so much, and which could not fail to recall to her with renewed force the black crime which lay so heavily upon her conscience. But her mind was in that morbid state which is so well calculated to engender idiosyncratic ideas; and she believed that the very fact of her return to the scene of her enormity would prove a penance most salutary to her soul. Such purely Roman Catholic sentiments are frequently found exercising a deep influence over minds which contrition for great crimes has disposed to superstitious tendencies.

There were also considerations of a more worldly nature which to some extent urged Lady Ravensworth to return to the Hall. She loathed the idea of dwelling amidst the noise, the din, and the crowds of the metropolis: she craved for the retirement of the country. Whither, then, could she repair save to the mansion which was her own? what excuse could she offer to those who knew her, for settling in any other part of the suburbs of London?—for *near*, though not *in*, the capital had she resolved to dwell, in order to be enabled to see her parents occasionally, and Eliza Sydney frequently.

In addition to all the influences, moral and worldly, now enumerated, there was another which had confirmed Adeline in the idea of returning to the Hall. But this was a secret influence for which she could not account,—an influence that ever interposed amidst her waverings, to settle them in favour of the project,—one of those influences to which even the strongest minds are frequently subject, and for the existence of which they can give no satisfactory reason. Such an influence as this the Turk would denominate the irresistible current of Destiny; but the pious Christian believes it to be the secret and all-powerful will of heaven.

Let us, however, proceed with our narrative.

The intruders had departed; and Lady Ravensworth was as it were alone in that vast mansion which had so many sad and gloomy memorials for her!

She entered the drawing-room where Egerton's party had banqueted; and, seeing the table covered with the bottles and glasses, turned away in disgust. Passing into the adjacent suite of apartments, she opened the shutters, and gazed around the large and lonely rooms in which the silence of death seemed to reign.

She looked at the pictures which hung upon the walls; and then it struck her that some change had taken place in those rooms, each feature of which she remembered well. The more earnestly she gazed about her, the firmer became her conviction that every thing was not as she had left it. At length she perceived that three or four of the most valuable pictures had disappeared: a costly time-piece, too, was missing from the mantel of one apartment: several ornaments were wanting in another.

Thinking that these objects might have been shifted from their usual places, she entered another suite of rooms; and there, instead of finding the things which were lost from the first, she perceived more vacancies amongst the pictures and the ornaments.

The conduct of the old gardener in allowing a party of persons to use the mansion, the care of which had been entrusted to him, recurred more forcibly than at first to her mind: and what had hitherto appeared a comparatively venial fault, now assumed a complexion, when coupled with the disappearance of the pictures and ornaments above-mentioned, which naturally created in her mind alarming suspicions of his honesty.

She rang the bell: her French servant responded to the summons; and Adeline desired that the gardener might be immediately sent into her presence.

The maid withdrew, and conveyed by signs the order which she had received; for she was unable to speak a single word of English.

The old man, who was deliberating with his wife upon the best means of breaking to Lady Ravensworth the unpleasant fact of there being a putrid corpse in the mansion at that very moment, received the command with a ludicrous expression of fear and vexation on his countenance; and he repaired to the presence of his mistress in a state of mind about as agreeable as if he were on his road to an auto-da-fé.

"Abraham," said Lady Adeline, "there are certain circumstances which render my return to this house far from pleasant. Almost heart-broken by the loss of that dear, dear child who constituted my only earthly joy, I come back to my native land with the hope of at least finding tranquillity and peace in the retirement of Ravensworth Hall. But scarcely do I alight from my carriage, when I encounter upon the very threshold of my home a party of revellers whom your imprudence permitted to celebrate their orgies within these walls. This fault I was inclined to pardon: but when, upon the first superficial glance around the principal apartments, I perceive that many valuable articles have disappeared——"

"Disappeared, my lady!" cried the old man, starting in a manner rather indicative of surprise than of guilt.

"Yes, Abraham," returned Lady Ravensworth, severely: "pictures—ornaments—time-pieces—China bowls—and several objects of less value are missing from these apartments. Have you removed them elsewhere?"

"Oh! my lady," cried the gardener, "you can't think that I would rob you! As God is my judge, neither me nor my wife has touched a single thing in the place—leastways, unless it was to dust and clean 'em. The doors has been kept locked——"

"But if you have been in the habit of allowing strangers the use of these apartments——"

"No, my lady—this was the fust and the last time that me and my old 'ooman did such a thing," exclaimed the gardener, emphatically: "and we didn't know we was a-doing anythink so wery wrong—seeing your ladyship wasn't here."

"And you have not even observed that certain pictures and ornaments had disappeared?" inquired Adeline, who knew not what to conjecture—for the manner and words of the old man were stamped with honesty.

"Never, my lady—we never noticed it," was the answer. "For my part, I seldom come into these rooms at all: but my old 'ooman dusted 'em out reglar once a month or so; and if she'd missed anythink I should have knowed of it in a moment. But——"

"But what, Abraham?" said Lady Ravensworth, in a kinder tone.

"There's one circumstance that has troubled me and my wife more than once—or twice—or a dozen times, my lady: and yet——"

"Speak candidly. Why do you hesitate?"

The old man cast a hurried glance around,—for it was now growing dusk,—and, sinking his voice to a whisper, he said, "The Hall is troubled, my lady."

"What do you mean?" exclaimed Adeline, starting from her seat, as if those words had electrified her. "Explain yourself, old man—speak!"

"Ah! my lady—there's no doubt on it!" returned Abraham, again looking suspiciously around. "Mr. Vernon can't rest in his grave—his sperret walks——"

"A truce to this idle folly!" cried Lady Ravensworth, her tone once more becoming severe.

Had the old man assured her that he had seen the spirit of Lydia Hutchinson, she would have been suddenly overwhelmed by a feeling of tremendous awe; and she would have sunk beneath the appalling weight of an announcement the truth of which she would not have dared to question. This influence, however, could only have been exercised over her by the superstition associated with her own dread crime; and when, contrary to her expectation, but greatly to her relief—the phantom she so much dreaded was not the one of which the old man spoke, she immediately rejected his tale as unworthy of credit.

"A truce to this idle folly!" she cried; "and prepare yourself to give the explanations which my solicitor may require at your hands to-morrow. Leave me."

"I hope your ladyship——"

"Leave me, I say; and send my maid up with lights."

"Yes, my lady—certainly I will," returned the old man, without moving from the place where he stood: "but before I go—I must acquaint your ladyship—leastways, I must in dooty state that—though it ain't a wery pleasant thing—still it wasn't my fault—as my old 'ooman can prove to your ladyship——"

"Leave me!" cried Adeline, in a tone which showed that she was determined to be obeyed. "If you have any apology to offer for your conduct—which, I regret to say, is now placed beyond all doubt by the confusion of your manner—you must satisfy my legal adviser upon that head. Fear not, however, that I will seek to punish an old man who cannot have many years to remain in this world: no—I am not vindictive—my own sufferings," she added, with a profound sigh, "have taught me to be merciful to others. But I do not desire to prolong this conversation now. Leave me, I repeat—leave me!"

The gardener endeavoured to obtain a farther hearing—for he was most anxious to communicate the fact of the dead body being in the house; but Adeline waved her hand in a manner so authoritative, that the poor old man had no alternative than to obey.

He accordingly left the room, quite bewildered by the injurious suspicions which had arisen in the mind of his mistress against his honesty; for he had spoken naught save the plain truth when he declared that the disappearance of the pictures and ornaments had never been observed by either himself or his wife.

The French maid carried lights up to the drawing-room, and received from Lady Ravensworth instructions to prepare the bed-chamber situate in the northern extremity of the building: this, in fact, was the same apartment that Adeline had occupied after she had ceased to inhabit her boudoir, and during the interval between the murder of Lydia Hutchinson and the suicide of Gilbert Vernon.

The lady's-maid retired to fulfil her mistress's directions; and Adeline was left once more alone.

The solemn silence that prevailed throughout the mansion added to the depression of her spirits; and she could not combat against a vague presentiment of approaching evil, which gradually acquired a greater influence over her.

It is well known that many animals have an instinctive knowledge of impending danger, even while its source remains as yet unseen. The noble steed that bears the traveller through the forest, snuffs the air, paws the ground, and swerves uneasily from his path, when in the vicinity of the lair where the lion lies concealed: the little bird flutters wildly above the thicket which hides the lurking snake;—and the buffalo trembles through every limb as he approaches the tree from the dense foliage of which, high over head, the terrible anaconda is prepared to spring.

Is such a feeling as this never known to human beings?

We believe that it is.

And certain was it that Adeline became the prey of a similar influence—vague, sinister, and undefined,—as she sate in the loneliness of the large apartment around which her glances wandered with an uneasiness that did not diminish.

She rose from her seat and walked to the window: it was now quite dark—the sky was overclouded—and neither moon nor stars appeared.

"I could wish that the evening were less gloomy," she said to herself. "And how long Quentin seems to be!"

Then she remembered that he had many purchases to make; for it was not expected that the gardener would have provided the requisite stock of provisions and necessaries, even if he had received the letter announcing Lady Ravensworth's intended return.

"Still I wish he would come!" said Adeline. "He is a faithful servant—and I should feel more secure were he near me. What *can* be this dreadful depression of spirits which I experience? Alas! happiness and I have long been strangers to each other: but never—never have I felt as I do to-night!"

She started: it struck her that the handle of the folding doors communicating with the next room was agitated.

Yes: it was no delusion—some one was about to enter.

Yielding to fears which were the more intense because they were altogether inexplicable, she leant against the wall for support—her eyes fixed, under the influence of a species of fascination, upon the doors at the farther extremity of the room.

Slowly did one of those folding-doors open; and for an instant, in the wild turmoil of her feelings, the unhappy woman half expected to behold the spectre of Lydia Hutchinson appear before her.

But—no: it was a man who entered.

The lights flared with the draught created by the opening of that door; and for a few moments Adeline could only perceive the dark form, without being able to distinguish his features.

Not long, however, did this painful uncertainty last; for as the intruder advanced towards the almost fainting lady, the light suddenly shone full upon his countenance;—and, with feelings of indescribable horror, she once more found herself in the presence of the Resurrection Man.

CHAPTER CCXLIX.

THE RESURRECTION MAN'S LAST FEAT AT RAVENSWORTH HALL.

"Holy God protect me!" shrieked Adeline, staggering to a sofa, on which she fell.

But her senses did not leave her: a profound conviction of the terrible position in which she was again placed, suddenly nerved her with a courage and a strength that astonished even herself; and, starting from the sofa, she confronted the Resurrection Man, saying, "What do you here?"

"That's my business," answered Tidkins, gruffly. "You see that I am here:—here I have been for a long time—and here I shall remain as much longer as it suits my purpose. That is," he added, with a significant leer, "unless you make it worth my while to take myself off."

"Detestable extortioner!" ejaculated Adeline: "am I never to know peace again?"

"Well—now that's *your* business, my lady," replied the Resurrection Man. "The fact is, I find this place so much to my liking, and it answers my views as well as my safety so well, that I am in no hurry to quit it. You may look as black as you please: but you ought to know by this time that Tony Tidkins is not the man to be frightened by a lady's frown."

"The law will protect me," said Adeline, now labouring under the most painful excitement.

"Yes—and punish you too," added the Resurrection Man, coolly.

"Now listen to me," continued Lady Ravensworth, speaking with hysterical volubility: "human forbearance has limits—human patience has bounds. My forbearance is exhausted—my patience is worn out. Sooner than submit to your persecutions—sooner than be at the mercy of your extortions,—I will seek redress at the hands of justice—aye, even though I draw down its vengeance upon my own head at the same time!"

And she flew towards the bell-pull.

But the Resurrection Man caught her ere her hand could reach the rope; and dragging her back, he pushed her brutally upon the sofa. Then, drawing a pistol from his pocket, he said in a terribly ominous tone, "If you attempt that dodge again, I'll shoot you through the head as sure as you're now a living woman."

Adeline contemplated him with eyes expressive of the wildest alarm.

"You see that it's no use to play tricks with me, young lady," continued the Resurrection Man, as he replaced the pistol in his pocket.

"What is it that you require?" asked Adeline, in a faint and supplicating tone: "what can I do to induce you to depart and never molest me more? Oh! have mercy upon me, I implore you—have mercy upon me! I have no friends to protect me: I am widowed and childless. My poor boy has been snatched from me—my sole earthly solace is gone! But why do you persecute me thus? Have I ever injured you? If you hate me—if you look upon me as an enemy, kill me outright:—do not—do not take my life by inches. Your presence is slow torture!"

"Will you listen to reason?" demanded Tidkins: "can you speak calmly for a few minutes?"

"I will—I can," returned Adeline, shuddering dreadfully as the Resurrection Man drew nearer to her.

"Well, then—if you keep your word, our business will soon be brought to an end," he said, planting himself coolly in a chair opposite to her. "You must know that I've been living in this house almost ever since you left it."

"Living here!" cried Adeline, indignation mastering a considerable portion of her terror.

"Yes—living here as snug as a bug in a rug," returned Tidkins, chuckling as if he considered the fact to be an excellent joke. "The truth is I had certain reasons of my own for being either in or near London: and I looked about for a safe place. Happening to pass this way a few weeks after that business about Vernon, you know———"

"Proceed—proceed!" said Adeline, impatiently.

"I'm in no hurry," replied Tidkins.

"But my servant may come—Quentin will be here shortly—I expect him every minute———"

"He won't hurt me, my lady," said Tidkins, calmly. "If he attempted to lay a hand on me, I'd shoot him on the spot. However, I will go on quicker—since you wish it. Well, as I was saying, I passed by this way and saw the house all shut up. Inquiries at the village down yonder let me know that you was gone, and that there was no one but an old man and his wife about the premises. Nothing could suit me better: I resolved to take up my quarters here directly;—and I pitched upon the very room where Vernon threw himself out of the window. One day I heard the two old people talking in the next apartment, which they were dusting out; and I found, by their discourse, that they believed in ghosts. That was a glorious discovery for me: I soon saw that certain little devices which I practised made them think that Vernon's spirit haunted the place—and so I boldly opened the shutters and made myself comfortable, when I took it into my head. They weren't at the house, it seems, when I was staying here two years ago; and so they didn't know who I really was. Thus, when they saw me standing in the balcony—which I often did just to amuse myself by frightening them a little—they firmly believed it was Gilbert Vernon's spirit that haunted the place. Lord! how I have laughed sometimes at the poor old souls!"

"It is you, then," cried Adeline, a sudden idea striking her, "who have been plundering the Hall during my absence?"

"Well—you may call it by that name, if you like," said Tidkins, with the most provoking calmness. "I don't hesitate to admit that I have now and then walked off with a small picture—or a time-piece—or a mantel ornament—or what not—just to raise supplies for the time being. But you ought to be very much obliged to me that I've left any thing at all in the whole place. Such forbearance isn't quite in keeping with my usual disposition."

"Villain! this to me—and said so coolly!" cried Lady Ravensworth, again starting from her seat.

"Pray keep where you are, ma'am," observed Tidkins, pushing her back again upon the sofa; "you promised to listen to reason."

"Reason!" exclaimed Adeline: "and do you call it reason when I am compelled to hear the narrative of your villanies—the history of your depredations on my property?"

"You knew what I was when you sought my acquaintance," said the Resurrection Man; "and after all, I've only just been taking the little liberties which one friend may use with another."

"Friend!" repeated Adeline, in a tone expressive of deep disgust, as she retreated as far back upon the sofa as possible.

"Come—we're only wasting time by all this disputing," said the Resurrection Man. "The whole thing lies in a nut-shell. You've come home again—and you want to enjoy undisputed possession of your own house. Well—that is reasonable enough. But, by so doing, you turn me out of doors; and I don't exactly know where I shall find a crib so safe and convenient as this. I must have an indemnity, then: and that is also reasonable on my part."

"Until you told me that you had robbed the house," exclaimed Adeline, in a tone of almost ungovernable indignation,—such as she had not experienced for a long, long time,—"I was prepared to purchase your departure with a sum of money: but now,—now that I have the most convincing proofs of your utter profligacy—even if such proofs were wanting,—now that I see the folly of reposing the slightest trust in one who studies nothing save his own wants and interests,—I will think of a compromise no longer."

"You will repent your obstinacy," said Tidkins. "Remember how you have dared me on a former occasion, and how I reduced you to submission."

"True!" ejaculated Adeline, in a calmer and more collected tone than she had yet assumed during this painful interview: "but at that time I was crushed by the weight of difficulties—overwhelmed with embarrassments and perils of the most formidable nature. I would then have committed any new crime to screen the former ones: I would have effected any compromise in order to avert danger. But now—what is there to bind me to existence? Nothing—unless it be the enjoyment of seclusion and tranquillity. These are menaced by your persecutions: and I will put an end to this intolerable tyranny—or perish in the attempt. That is my decision. Let us be at open war, if you will: and 'tis thus I commence hostilities!"

Rapid as thought, she darted towards the bell-rope: but Tidkins, who had divined her intention, intercepted her as before.

Placing his iron hand on the nape of her neck, he thrust her violently back upon the sofa: then, ere he withdrew his hold, he said in a low, hoarse, and ferocious tone, "This is the last time I will be trifled with. By Satan! young woman, I'll strangle you, if this game continues—just as I strangled your Lydia Hutchinson!"

And pushing her with contemptuous rudeness from him, he released her from his grasp.

For a few moments Adeline's breath came with so much difficulty, and her bosom heaved so convulsively, that the Resurrection Man feared he had gone too far, and had done her some grievous injury: but when he saw her recover from the semi-strangulation and the dreadful alarm which she had experienced in consequence of his treatment, his eyes glistened with ferocious satisfaction.

"Let us make a long business short," he said, in a coarse and imperious tone. "If I told you just now that I had helped myself to a few of the things in this house, it was only to convince you that I am not likely to stick at trifles in respect to you or yours. You have money—and I want some. Give me my price—and you shall never see me again."

"No—you may murder me if you will," cried Adeline, hysterically: "but I will not submit to your tyranny any more. Oh! you are a terrible man—and I would sooner die than live in the constant terror of your persecution!"

"Foolish woman, give up this screeching—or, by hell! I'll settle you, and then help myself to all I want," cried Tidkins, ferociously.

And at the same moment Adeline, whose face was buried in her hands, felt his iron grasp again upon the nape of her neck.

She started up with a half-stifled scream, and endeavoured to reach the bell-rope a third time. But once more was she anticipated in her design; and the Resurrection Man now held her firmly round the waist by his left arm.

Then drawing forth the pistol with his right hand, he placed the muzzle against Adeline's marble forehead.

"I must put an end to this nonsense at once," he said, in a ferocious tone. "There is something now in the house, proud and obstinate woman as you are—that will make you fall on your knees and beseech me to remove it from your sight. But we will try that test: and remember, this pistol that touches your forehead is loaded. Attempt to raise an alarm—and I blow your brains out."

"Release me—let me go—I implore you!" murmured Adeline, who experienced greater loathing at that contiguity with the Resurrection Man, than fear at the weapon which menaced her with instantaneous death.

"No—you shall come," returned Tidkins, brutally: "I am sick of this reasoning, and must bring you to the point at once."

"Let me go—and I swear to follow whither you may choose to lead," said Adeline.

"Well—now I release you on that condition," was the reply: and the horrible man withdrew his arm and the pistol simultaneously.

But still keeping the weapon levelled at the wretched lady, and taking a candle in his left hand, he made a sign for her to accompany him.

She was now reduced to that state of physical nervousness and mental bewilderment, that she obeyed mechanically, without attempting to remonstrate—without even remembering to ask whither they were going.

They left the room, and proceeded along the passage towards the southern extremity of the building,—Adeline walking on one side of the corridor, and Tidkins on the other—the latter still keeping the pistol levelled to over-awe the miserable woman.

But she saw it not: she went on, because she mechanically obeyed one in whose power she felt herself to be, and whose loathsome contiguity she trembled to dare again.

At length they stopped at a door: and then Adeline's memory seemed to recover all its powers—her ideas instantly appeared to concentrate themselves in one focus.

"Oh! no—not here! not here!" she said, with a cold shudder, as she suddenly awoke as it were from a confused dream, and recognised the door of her boudoir—*the* boudoir!

"Then give me a thousand pounds—and I will leave the house this minute," returned Tidkins.

"No—you shall kill me first!" ejaculated Adeline, again recovering courage and strength, as if by instinct she knew herself to be standing upon some fearful precipice. "I will resist you to the death: you have driven me to desperation!"

And, springing towards the Resurrection Man, she made a snatch at the pistol which he held in his hand.

But, eluding her attack, he thrust the weapon into his pocket: then, clasping her with iron vigour in his right arm, and still retaining the light in his left hand, he burst open the door of the boudoir with his foot.

Adeline uttered a faint scream, as he dragged her into the room, the door of which he closed violently behind him.

Then, holding the light in such a manner that its beams fell upon the floor, and withdrawing his arm from Adeline's waist, he exclaimed in a tone of ferocious triumph, "Behold the remains of the murdered Lydia Hutchinson!"

Lady Ravensworth threw one horrified glance upon the putrid corpse; and uttering a terrific scream expressive of the most intense agony, she fell flat upon the floor—her face touching the feet of the dead body.

Tidkins raised her: but the blood gushed out of her mouth.

"Perdition! I have gone too far," cried the Resurrection Man. "She is dead—and I have done as good as cut my own throat!"

It was indeed true: Adeline had burst a blood-vessel, and died upon the spot.

Tidkins let her fall heavily upon the floor, and throwing down the candle, fled from the mansion, reckless whether the light were extinguished or not.

Half an hour afterwards Quentin was on his return to the Hall, in a hackney-coach containing, besides the baggage which he had cleared at the Custom-House, several hampers filled with the purchases he had been making in the City.

As he was thus proceeding through the park, he suddenly observed a strong and flickering light appearing through the windows at the southern extremity of the building; and in a few moments the whole of that part of the Hall was enveloped in flames.

Leaping from the coach, which, being heavily laden, dragged slowly along, the valet rushed to the mansion, where the presence of the fire had already alarmed the gardener and his wife, and the French servant.

But of what avail were their poor exertions against the fury of the devouring element?

A search was immediately instituted for Lady Ravensworth: but she was not to be found in either of the drawing-rooms. Nor was she in any of the chambers in the northern part of the building; and it was impossible to enter the southern wing, which seemed to be one vast body of flame.

The domestics, finding their search to be useless, were compelled to form the dreadful conclusion that their mistress had perished in the conflagration.

For six hours did the fire rage with appalling fury; and though the inhabitants of the adjacent village and the immediate neighbourhood flocked to the scene of desolation and rendered all the assistance in their power, the splendid mansion was reduced to a heap of ruins.

CHAPTER CCL.

EGERTON'S LAST DINNER PARTY.

We have already stated that Egerton was deeply affected by the result of the imposture which he had practised upon his relations. During the drive back to London, his four friends—Dunstable, Cholmondeley, Harborough, and Chichester—vainly endeavoured to rally him: he was silent and thoughtful, and replied only in monosyllables.

On their arrival at Stratton Street, Egerton took leave of his friends at the door without inviting them to enter; but they were not so easily disposed of. They urged him to accompany them to some place of amusement: he remained inaccessible to their solicitations, and firmly declared his intention of passing the remainder of the evening alone.

They were at length compelled to leave him—consoling themselves with the hope that he would "sleep off his melancholy humour," and rise in the morning as pliant and ductile in their hands as ever.

The four gentlemen had not long departed, when Major Anderson called at the house; and having represented to the servant that his object was an affair of some importance, he was admitted into the drawing-room where Egerton was lying upon the sofa.

"At length I find you alone, Mr. Egerton," said the Major. "I have called every evening for the last few days, and have never until now been fortunate enough to learn that you were at home."

"To what am I to attribute the honour of this visit?" asked the young man, whom it struck that he had seen the Major before—but when or where he could not remember.

"Pardon me if, ere I reply to that question, I pause to observe that you survey me with some attention," said Anderson; "and I can divine what is passing in your mind. You think that my features are not altogether unknown to you? I believe this to be the case—for you have seen me before. Indeed I should have begun by thanking you—most gratefully thanking you for that generous intention on your part which was interrupted at the door of the St. James's Club-House——"

"Ah! I recollect!" cried Egerton, starting up from his reclining position. "But——"

"Again I can read what is passing in your mind," observed the Major, with a smile; "and I can appreciate the delicacy which made you thus stop short. You notice the change that has taken place in my appearance? Yes—my circumstances are indeed altered; and from a wandering mendicant, I have become a gentleman once more. But that change has been effected by the very individual whose interposition on that night to which I have just now alluded, prevented you from exercising your intended benevolence towards me."

"And that individual was the Prince of Montoni," said Egerton.

"Oh! then you know him by sight——"

"I knew him not, otherwise than by name, until that evening," interrupted Egerton; "and it was from Sir Rupert Harborough and Mr. Chichester that I learnt who the stranger was."

"Ah! his Highness has good cause to remember them also!" cried Anderson, to whom the Prince had related his entire history a day or two previously.

"Indeed," exclaimed Egerton, "I now recollect that they seemed alarmed at his presence, and mentioned his name with trepidation."

"Well might they do so!" said the Major, indignantly. "But the Prince himself will explain to you those particulars to which I allude."

"The Prince—explain to me!" cried Egerton.

"Yes: my object in calling upon you is to request that you will either visit the Prince as soon as convenient, or appoint a day and an hour when his Highness may visit you."

"Oh! I should be indeed joyful to form the acquaintance of that illustrious hero of whom every Englishman must feel proud!" exclaimed Egerton, with the enthusiasm that was natural to him. "Valour, integrity, and the most unbounded humanity are associated with the name of Richard Markham. But upon what business can the Prince be desirous to honour me with his acquaintance?"

"*That* his Highness will himself explain," was the reply. "What hour will you appoint for to-morrow to wait upon the Prince at his own residence?"

"I will be there punctually at mid-day," answered Egerton.

"And in the meantime," said Major Anderson, after a moment's hesitation, "it will be as well if you do not mention to those persons with whom you are intimate, the appointment which you have made."

"I understand you, sir," rejoined Egerton: "it shall be as you suggest."

The Major then took his leave; and Egerton—who entertained a faint suspicion of the object which the Prince had in view—received consolation from the idea that his illustrious fellow countryman experienced some degree of interest in his behalf.

That suspicion was engendered by the known philanthropy and anxiety to do good which characterised Markham; by the allusion made by Anderson to certain explanations which the Prince intended to give relative to Harborough and Chichester; and also by the injunction of secrecy in respect to the appointment that had been made.

Well knowing that his four friends would not fail to visit him early next day,—and determined that they should not interfere with his visit to one whose acquaintance he so ardently desired to form,—Egerton repaired to an hotel, where he passed the night.

On the following morning he was greatly surprised, and to some extent shocked, to read in the newspaper the tidings of the fearful conflagration which had not only destroyed Ravensworth Hall, but in which the lady who owned the mansion had herself perished.

"And there likewise is entombed the mystery of the dead body!" said Egerton, as he laid aside the paper.

His toilette was performed with great care; and, punctual to the moment, the young man knocked at the door of Markham Place.

He was conducted into an elegantly furnished apartment, where the Prince advanced to receive him in a most kind and affable manner.

"You will perhaps imagine that I have taken a very great liberty with you, Mr. Egerton," said Richard, "in requesting you to call upon me in this manner; but when you are made acquainted with my motives in seeking the present interview, you will give me credit for the most sincere disinterestedness. In a word, I consider it to be my duty to warn you against at least two of those persons who call themselves your friends."

"My lord, I was not unprepared for such an announcement," said Egerton, in a deferential manner.

"Then is my task the more easy," exclaimed Richard. "I allude to Sir Rupert Harborough and Mr. Chichester, the latter of whom assumes the distinction of *Honourable*."

"And is he not of noble birth, my lord?" inquired Egerton.

"He is the son of a tradesman," answered Markham. "But that is no disgrace in my estimation: far from it! The industrious classes are the pillars of England's greatness; and I for one would rather walk arm-in-arm along the most fashionable thoroughfare with the honest mechanic or upright shopkeeper, than boast of intimacy even with a King who is unworthy of esteem and respect."

Egerton surveyed with unfeigned admiration the individual from whose lips these noble sentiments emanated—sentiments the more noble, inasmuch as they were expressed by one whose rank was so exalted, and who stood so high above his fellow-men.

"Yes," continued Markham, "your friend Mr. Chichester is one of those impostors who assume title and distinction as well to aid their nefarious courses as to gratify their own grovelling pride. I do not speak with malignity of that man—although I once suffered so much through him: for were he to seek my forgiveness, heaven knows how readily it would be accorded. Neither is it to gratify any mean sentiment of revenge that I now warn you against these two individuals. My present conduct is dictated by a sense of duty, and by an ardent desire to save a young and confiding young man, as I believe you to be, from the snares of unprincipled adventurers."

"Oh! now a light breaks in upon me," exclaimed Egerton; "and I recognise in the actions of those whom I lately deemed my friends, all the designing intrigues to which your Highness alludes! Fool that I was to be thus deceived!"

"Rather thank heaven that the means of redemption have arrived ere it be too late," said the Prince, impressively; "for I can scarcely believe, from all I have heard concerning you, that your affairs are in a state of ruin which admits of no hope."

"Your Highness argues truly," exclaimed Egerton: "I have yet sufficient resources remaining to furnish me with the means of an honourable livelihood."

"Then you need scarcely regret the amount you have paid for the purchase of experience," said the Prince. "But allow me to place in your hands proofs of the iniquity of Sir Rupert Harborough and his friend. Behold these two documents! They contain the narrative of as foul a scheme of turpitude as ever called the misdirected vengeance of the law upon an innocent victim. The first of these papers is the confession of an engraver whom Harborough and Chichester made the instrument of that project which at one time covered my name with so dark a cloud. You seem astonished at what I say? Oh! then you are ignorant of that episode in my chequered life."

"Never have I heard rumour busy with your lordship's name, save to its honour and glory," observed Egerton, in a tone of convincing sincerity.

"Peruse these papers—they will not occupy you many minutes," returned our hero, after a temporary pause. "The second document, which I now hand you, only came into my possession this morning: it was signed yesterday afternoon, by Sir Rupert Harborough and Mr. Chichester——"

"Yesterday afternoon, my lord!" cried Egerton. "Those gentlemen were in my company—at a short distance from London——"

"At Ravensworth Park," said Richard, with a smile. "You see that I know all. It was indeed at that very mansion—which, as you are doubtless aware, was reduced to ashes during the night—that this confession was drawn up and signed by your two friends. The engraver, whose name is appended to the first of those papers, was led by accident to Ravensworth Hall; and there he encountered the two adventurers who had once made him their instrument—their vile tool! He compelled them to draw up and sign that second paper, which you hold in your hands, and which, through gratitude for some trifling act of kindness that I was once enabled to show him, he obtained by working on their fears. Scarcely an hour has elapsed since I experienced the satisfaction of receiving that document from him; and my delight was enhanced by the conviction that he is now an honest—a worthy—and a prosperous member of society."

Egerton perused the two confessions, and thereby obtained a complete insight into the real characters of Sir Rupert Harborough and Mr. Chichester. If any doubt had remained in his mind, this elucidation was even more than sufficient to convince him that he had only been courted by his fashionable friends on account of his purse; and heart-felt indeed was the gratitude which he expressed towards the Prince for having thus intervened to save him from utter ruin.

But how was that gratitude increased, and how profound became the young man's horror of the course which he had lately been pursuing, when Richard drew a forcible and deeply touching picture of the usual career of the gambler,—importing into his narrative the leading incidents of Major Anderson's own biography, without however specifying that gentleman's name,—and concluding with an earnest appeal to Egerton henceforth to avoid the gaming-table, if he hoped to enjoy prosperity and peace.

"Would you rush madly into a thicket where venomous reptiles abound?" demanded the Prince: "would you plunge of your own accord into a forest where the most terrible wild beasts are prowling? would you, without a sufficient motive, leave the wholesome country and take up your abode in a plague-stricken city? No: and it would be an insult to your understanding—to that intelligence with which God has endowed you—to put such questions to you, were it not for the purpose of conveying a more impressive moral. For the gaming-house is the thicket where reptiles abound—it is the forest where wild beasts prowl, ravenous after their prey—it is the city of pestilence into which one hurries from the salubrious air. Pause, then—reflect, my young friend,—and say whether the folly of the gambler be not even as great as his wickedness?"

Egerton fell at our hero's feet: he seized the Prince's hand, and pressed it to his lips—covering it also with his tears.

"You have converted me, my lord—you have saved me!" cried the young man, retrospecting with unfeigned horror upon the desperate career which he had lately been pursuing: "Oh! how can I express my gratitude? But you may read it in those tears which I now shed—tears of contrition for the past, and bright hopes for the future!"

Richard raised the penitent from his kneeling posture, saying, "Enough! I see that you are sincere. And now listen to the plan which I have conceived to shame the men who have been preying upon you; for such punishment is their due—and it may even be salutary."

The Prince then unfolded his designs in this respect to Egerton; but it is not necessary to explain them at present. Suffice it to say that the young man willingly assented to the arrangement proposed by one on whom he naturally looked at his saviour; and when the scheme was fully digested, our hero conducted his new friend into an adjoining apartment, where luncheon was served up.

Egerton was then enabled to judge of the domestic happiness which prevailed in that mansion where virtue, love, and friendship were the presiding divinities of the place.

The faultless beauty of the Princess Isabella,—the splendid charms of Ellen,—and the retiring loveliness of Katherine, fascinated him for a time; but as the conversation developed the amiability of their minds and evinced the goodness of their hearts, he learnt that woman possesses attractions far—far more witching, more permanent, and more endearing than all the boons which nature ever bestowed upon their countenances or their forms!

Old Monroe was present; and while he looked upon our hero with all the affection which a fond father might bestow upon a son, the Prince on his part treated him with the respect which a good son manifests towards an honoured father. Between Markham, too, and Mario Bazzano the most sincere friendship existed: in a word, the bond which united that happy family was one that time could never impair.

Three days after the event just recorded, Albert Egerton gave a dinner-party at his lodgings in Stratton Street.

The guests were Lord Dunstable, Colonel Cholmondeley, Sir Rupert Harborough, and Mr. Chichester.

The dinner-hour was seven; and, contrary to the usual arrangements, the table was spread in the drawing-room, instead of the dining-room, which was behind the former, folding doors communicating between the two apartments.

Let us suppose the cloth to have been drawn, and the dessert placed upon the table.

The wine circulated rapidly; and never had Egerton appeared in better spirits, nor more affably courteous towards his friends.

"Well, I really began to suppose that you had determined to cut us altogether," said Dunstable, as he sipped his wine complacently. "For three whole days we saw nothing of you———"

"Have I not already assured you that I was compelled to pass that time with my relatives, in order to appease them after the exposure at Ravensworth?" exclaimed Egerton.

"And we have accepted the apology as a valid one," observed Chichester.

"Upon my honour," said the baronet, "if I had known you were doing the amiable on Finsbury Pavement, I should have called just to help you in your endeavours to regain the favour of those excellent ladies."

"I am afraid your reception would have been none of the best, Harborough," exclaimed Colonel Cholmondeley.

"I must confess that the old lady was terribly enraged," said Egerton; "not only against me, but also against you all, as she looked upon you as my accomplices in the cheat."

"Well, we must take some opportunity of making our peace in that quarter," observed Lord Dunstable. "I will send her a dozen of champagne and a Strasburg pie to-morrow, with my compliments. But what shall we do to pass away an hour or two?"

"What shall we do?" repeated Chichester. "Why, amuse ourselves—as gentlemen of rank and fashion are accustomed—eh, Egerton?"

"Oh! decidedly. I am willing to fall in with your views. You have been my tutor," he added, with a peculiar smile; "and the pupil will not prove rebellious."

"Well said, my boy!" cried Dunstable. "Have you your dice-box handy?"

"My rascal of a tiger has lost it," answered Egerton. "But I know that the baronet seldom goes abroad without the usual implements."

"Ah! you dog!" chuckled Sir Rupert, as if mightily amused by this sally. "You are, however, quite right; and I do not think that any fashionable man about town should forget to provide himself with the means of the most aristocratic of all innocent recreations. Upon my honour, that is my opinion."

"Just what my friend the Duke of Highgate said the other day—even to the very words," exclaimed Dunstable.

"How singular!" observed the baronet, as he produced a box and a pair of dice.

"By the by, Dunstable," said Egerton, "you promised to introduce me to his Grace."

"So I did, my dear boy—and so I will. Let me see—I shall see the Duke on Monday, and I will make an appointment for him to join us at dinner somewhere."

"The very thing," said Egerton: "I shall be quite delighted—particularly if his Grace be one of your own sort."

"Oh! he is—to the utmost," returned Dunstable, who did not perceive a lurking irony beneath the tranquillity of Egerton's manner.

"I am glad of that," continued the young man. "If I only knew three or four more such gay, dashing, good-hearted fellows as you all are, I should be as contented as possible. By the way, Chichester, I will tell you a very odd thing."

"Indeed! what is it?" inquired that gentleman.

"Oh! nothing more than a strange coincidence. Just this:—I told you that I had been staying a day or two with my respected aunt on the Pavement. Well, yesterday I wandered through the Tower Hamlets—merely for a ramble—and without any fixed purpose: but, as I was strolling down Brick Lane—a horrid, low, vulgar neighbourhood——"

"Dreadful!" cried Chichester, sitting somewhat uneasily on his chair.

"Oh! terrible—filthy, degrading," continued Egerton, emphatically. "You may therefore conceive my surprise when I perceived the aristocratic name of *Chichester* painted in huge yellow letters, shaded with brown, over a shop-front in that same Brick Lane."

"How very odd!" ejaculated Chichester, filling himself a bumper of champagne.

"Yes—but those coincidences of course *do* occur," said the baronet, who, after eyeing his host suspiciously, saw nothing beneath his calm exterior to indicate a pointed object in raising the present topic.

"And what made the thing more ludicrous," continued the young man, "was that over the aristocratic name of *Chichester* hung three dingy yellow balls."

"Capital! excellent!" exclaimed the gentleman whom this announcement so particularly touched, and who scarcely knew how to cover his confusion.

"Yes: I had a good laugh at the coincidence," said Egerton. "At the same time I knew very well that there could be nothing in common between Mr. Chichester, the pawnbroker of Brick Lane, and the Honourable Arthur Chichester of the fashionable world."

"I should hope not, indeed!" exclaimed Chichester, reassured by this observation.

"Come—take the box, Egerton," said Sir Rupert Harborough.

"Oh! willingly," replied the young man. "But we must play on credit, because I have no money in the house; and he who loses shall pay by cheque or note of hand."

"With pleasure," said the baronet.

The two gentlemen began to play; and Egerton lost considerably. He, however, appeared to submit with extraordinary patience and equanimity to his ill-luck, and continued to chatter in a gay and unusually jocular manner.

"Seven's the main. Come, Dunstable, fill your glass: the wine stands with you. By the by, has your rascally steward sent you up your remittances yet? You know you were complaining to me about him the other day."

"No—he is still a defaulter," returned the young nobleman, laughing.

"And likely to continue so, I'm afraid," added Egerton. "But where is that estate of yours, old fellow?"

"Oh! down in the country——"

"Yes—I dare say it is. But where?"

"Why—in Somersetshire, to be sure. I thought you knew *that*," cried Dunstable, not altogether relishing either the queries themselves or the manner in which they were put.

"That makes seven hundred I owe you, Harborough," said Egerton. "Do pass the wine, Chichester. Five's the main. Let me see—what were we talking about? Oh! I recollect—Dunstable's estate. And so it's in Somersetshire? Beautiful county! What is the name of the estate, my dear fellow?"

"My own name—Dunstable Manor," was the reply; but the nobleman began to cast suspicious glances towards his friend.

"Dunstable Manor—eh? What a sweet pretty name!" ejaculated Egerton. "And yet it is very strange—I know Somersetshire as well as any one can know a county; but I do not recollect Dunstable Manor. How foolish I must be to forget such a thing as that."

With these words, he rose from the table and took down a large volume from the book-case.

"What are you going to do?" inquired Dunstable, now feeling particularly uneasy.

"Only refreshing my memory by a reference to this *Gazetteer*," answered Egerton, as he deliberately turned over the pages of the book.

"Oh! come—none of this nonsense!" exclaimed Dunstable, snatching the volume from Egerton's hands. "Who ever thinks of reading before company?"

"It would be rude, I admit," said Egerton, recovering the volume from the other's grasp, "were we not such very particular and intimate friends—so intimate indeed, that we have one purse in common between us all five, and that purse happens to be the one which I have the honour to carry in my pocket."

"Egerton, what *is* the matter with you?" demanded Lord Dunstable, who was now convinced that something was wrong.

"Matter! nothing at all, my dear boy," answered the young man, as he continued to turn the leaves of the volume. "Here it is—Somersetshire—a very detailed account—not even the smallest farm omitted. But how is this? Why—Dunstable Manor is not here!"

"Not there!" cried the nobleman, blushing up to his very hair.

"No—indeed it is not!" rejoined Egerton. "Now really this is a great piece of negligence on the part of the compiler of the work; and if I were you, Dunstable, I would bring an action against him for damages. Because, only conceive how awkward this would make you appear before persons of suspicious dispositions. Well—*upon my honour*, as the baronet says—this coincidence is almost as extraordinary as that of the pawnbroker in Brick Lane."

While Egerton was thus speaking, his four friends exchanged significant glances which seemed to ask each other what all this could possibly mean.

"Yes—suspicious people would be inclined to imagine that the Dunstable estate was in the clouds rather than in Somersetshire," proceeded Egerton, who did not appear to notice the confusion of his guests. "But the world is so very ill-natured! Would you believe that there are persons so lamentably scandalous as to declare that our friend Chichester is no more an *Honourable* than I am, and that he really is the son of the pawnbroker in Brick Lane?"

"The villains!" cried Chichester, starting from his seat: "who are those persons that dare———"

"Wait one moment!" exclaimed Egerton: "it is my duty as a sincere friend to tell you each and all what I have heard. Those same scandalous and ill-natured people exceed all bounds of propriety; for they actually assert that Sir Rupert Harborough has for years been known as a profligate adventurer———"

"By God, Mr. Egerton!" cried the baronet: "I———"

"And they affirm in quite as positive a manner," continued the young man, heedless of this interruption, "that you, Dunstable, and you too, Cholmondeley, are nothing more nor less than ruined gamesters."

"Egerton," exclaimed the Colonel, foaming with indignation, "this is carrying a joke too far."

"A great deal too far," added Dunstable.

"It really is no joke at all, my lord and gentlemen," said the young man, now speaking in a tone expressive of the deepest disgust: "for every word I have uttered is firmly believed by myself!"

"By you!" cried the four adventurers, speaking as it were in one breath.

"Yes—and by all the world," exclaimed Egerton, rising from his seat, and casting indignant glances upon his guests.

"This is too much!" said Cholmondeley; and, unable to restrain his passion, he rushed upon the young man, seized him by the collar, and would have inflicted a severe chastisement on him had not assistance been at hand.

But the door communicating with the dining-room was suddenly thrown open, and the individual who now made his appearance, threw himself upon Cholmondeley, tore him away from his hold upon Albert Egerton, and actually hurled him to the opposite side of the apartment.

"The Prince of Montoni!" ejaculated Harborough, as he rushed towards the door, with Chichester close at his heels.

But the Prince hastened to intercept them; and, leaning his back against the door, he exclaimed, "No one passes hence, at present. Mr. Egerton, secure those dice."

Dunstable darted towards that part of the table where the dice lay; but Egerton had already obtained possession of them.

Richard in the meantime locked the door, and put the key in his pocket.

"Be he a king," cried Cholmondeley, who had caught the words uttered by the baronet, "he shall suffer for his conduct to me;"—and the Colonel advanced in a menacing manner towards the Prince.

"Beware, sir, how you place a finger on me!" cried Richard. "Approach another step nearer, and I will lay you at my feet!"

The Colonel muttered something to himself, and retreated towards the folding-doors communicating with the dining-room; but there his way was interrupted by the presence of two stout men in plain clothes and two of Richard's servants in handsome liveries.

"Let no one pass, Whittingham," said the Prince, "until our present business be accomplished."

"No, my lord," answered the old butler, who was one of the stout men in plain clothes: then, having given the same instructions to the two servants in livery, Whittingham exclaimed in a loud tone, "And mind, my men, that you on no account let them sneaking willains Scarborough and Axminster defect their escape!"

"My lord, what means this conduct on your part?" demanded Dunstable of the Prince. "By what authority do you detain us here as prisoners?"

"Yes—by what authority?" echoed Cholmondeley, again stepping forward.

"By that authority which gives every honest man a right to expose unprincipled adventurers who are leagued to plunder and rob an inexperienced youth," answered Richard, in a stern tone. "Mr. Egerton, give me those dice."

This request was immediately complied with; and the *other stout man in plain clothes* now stepped forward from the dining-room.

To the infinite dismay of Harborough and Chichester, they immediately recognised Pocock, who did not, however, take any notice of them: but producing a very fine saw from his pocket, he set to work to cut in halves one of the dice which Richard handed to him.

The four adventurers now turned pale as death, and exchanged glances of alarm and dismay.

"Behold, Mr. Egerton," said the Prince, after examining the die that had been sawed in halves, "how your false friends have been enabled to plunder you. Heaven be thanked that I am entirely ignorant of the disgraceful details of gamesters' frauds; but a child might understand for what purpose this die has been thus prepared."

"*Loaded*, your Highness, is the technical term, observed Pocock. "That scoundrel there," pointing to Chichester, "once told me all about them things, at the time I was leagued with him and his baronet friend."

"I hope your Highness will not make this affair public," said Lord Dunstable, his manner having changed to the most cringing meekness. "Egerton—you cannot wish to ruin me altogether?"

"Would you not have ruined me?" inquired the young man, bitterly.

"Oh! what a blessed day it is for me to be a high-witness of the disposure of them scoundrels Marlborough and Winchester!" ejaculated the old butler, rubbing his hands joyfully together. "Send 'em to Newgate, my lord—send 'em to Newgate—and then let 'em be disported to the spinal settlements, my lord!"

"Pray have mercy upon *me*—for the sake of my father and mother!" said Dunstable, whose entire manner expressed the most profound alarm. "Your Highness is known to possess a good heart———"

"It is not to me that you must address yourself," interrupted Markham, in a severe tone. "Appeal to this young man whom you have basely defrauded of large sums—upon whom you have been preying for weeks past—and whom you have tutored in the ways that lead to destruction:—appeal to him, I say—and not to me."

"I am entirely in the hands of your Highness," observed Egerton, with a grateful glance towards the Prince.

"Then we will spare these men, bad and unprincipled though they be," exclaimed Richard: "we will spare them—not for their own sakes, Egerton—but for yours. Were it known, through the medium of the details of a public prosecution, that you have been so intimately connected with a gang of cheats and depredators, your character would be irretrievably lost; for the world is not generous enough to pause and reflect that you were only a victim. Therefore, as you are determined to retrieve the past, it will be prudent to forego any criminal proceedings against those who have made you their dupe."

"Your Highness has spoken harshly—very harshly," said Lord Dunstable; "and yet I feel I have deserved all that vituperation. But this leniency with which your lordship has treated me—and *your* forbearance, Egerton—will not have been ineffectual. I now see the fearful brink upon which I stood—and I shudder; for had you resolved to drag me before a tribunal of justice, I would have avoided that last disgrace by means of suicide."

The young nobleman spoke with a feeling and an evident sincerity that touched both our hero and Egerton; but Cholmondeley turned away in disgust from his penitent friend, and Harborough exchanged a contemptuous look with Chichester.

"Lord Dunstable," said Markham, in an impressive tone, "your conduct has been bad—very bad; but much of its blackness is already wiped away by this manifestation of regret and contrition. Do not allow that spark of good feeling to be extinguished—or destruction must await you. And above all, I conjure you to avoid the companionship of such men as those who have even now by their manner scoffed at your expressions of repentance."

"Farewell, my lord," returned the young nobleman, tears trickling down his cheeks: "the events of this evening will never be forgotten by me. Egerton, take this pocket-book: it contains the greater portion of the last sum of money that I borrowed of you; and I shall never know peace of mind, until I have restored all of which I have been instrumental in plundering you."

With these words, Dunstable bowed profoundly to the Prince, and hurried from the room, without casting a single glance upon his late confederates in iniquity.

"My lord, isn't Newgate to become more familiarly acquainted with them scrape-graces Aldborough and Winchester?" asked the old butler, as soon as Dunstable had disappeared from the room.

"Were it not that I had promised this honest and grateful man," said the Prince, turning towards the engraver, "that no criminal proceedings should be instituted on the document that he obtained from you, Sir Rupert Harborough, and from you also, Mr. Chichester, I should consider myself bound, in justice to myself and as a duty owing to society, to expose in a public tribunal the black artifices by which you once inveigled me into your toils. But for his sake—for the sake alike of his personal security and of the good character which he now enjoys—I must leave your punishment to your own consciences. And, though scoffing smiles may now mark the little weight which my prediction carries with it in respect to you, yet rest assured that the time *will* come when your misdeeds shall be visited with those penalties which it may seem wise to a just heaven to inflict."

Having uttered these words, the Prince turned away, with undisguised aversion, from the two villains whom he had so impressively and solemnly addressed.

They slunk out of the apartment, with chap-fallen countenances, while Whittingham followed them to the door of the dining-room, through which they passed, and conveyed to them the satisfactory intelligence that "if it had impended on him, they should have been confided with strong letters of commendation to the governor of Newgate."

As soon as they had departed, Colonel Cholmondeley inquired in an insolent tone whether the Prince had any thing to say to *him*; but finding that Markham turned his back contemptuously upon him, he swaggered out of the room, muttering something about "satisfaction in another manner."

Early the next morning, Mrs. Bustard received the following letter:—

"*King Square, Goswell Road.*

"Faithful to the promise which I made to you the day before yesterday, my dear aunt, I have quitted the West End, and am once more located in a quiet neighbourhood. Thanks to the kind interference of that most amiable and excellent nobleman the Prince of Montoni, and to the encouragement given me by your forgiveness of the deception which I so shamefully practised upon you, I have been completely awakened to the errors of my late mode of life. I shall pledge myself to nothing now: my future conduct will prove to you how effectually wise counsels and past experience have changed my habits, my inclinations, and my ideas. One thing, however, I may state on the present occasion: namely, that I am convinced there is no character so truly dangerous and so thoroughly unprincipled as the one who delights in the name of '*the man about town.*'

"I must also declare that I yesterday handled the dice-box for the last time. Much as I loathed the idea, after the dread warnings which I received from the lips of the Prince, I nevertheless consented to play a last game—

and it *shall* remain the last! But, start not, dear aunt—I did so by the desire of the Prince, and that I might induce one of my false friends to produce the dice which he always carried about with him. The result was as the Prince had anticipated: those dice were so prepared that it was no wonder if their owner was constantly a winner. And had not the Prince known my repentance to be sincere, he would not for a moment have permitted me to touch those dice again—even though it were to accomplish an aim that might the more effectually expose the men by whom I was surrounded!

"To the Prince my unbounded gratitude is due. He has saved me from utter ruin, and has advised me how to employ the remainder of my fortune so as to recover by my industry what I have lost by my folly. It appears that his august father-in-law, the sovereign of Castelcicala,—and who has set so good an example to the Italian States by giving a Constitution and a national representation to his own country,—has established a line of steam-packets between London and Montoni; and it is my intention to trade between the two capitals. But the details of this project I will explain to you to-morrow, when I shall have the pleasure of calling upon you.

"Your affectionate Nephew,

ALBERT EGERTON."

CHAPTER CCLI.

THE OBSTINATE PATIENT.

It was about a week after the exposure which had taken place in Stratton Street, that the following events occurred at the splendid mansion of the Marquis of Holmesford.

Although the time-piece upon the mantel of this nobleman's bed-room had only just proclaimed the hour of three in the afternoon, yet the curtains were drawn close over the windows, and the chamber was rendered as dark as possible.

In that apartment, too, there was a profound silence—broken only by the low but irregular breathing of some one who slept in the bed.

By the side of the couch sate two elderly men, dressed in black, and who maintained a strict taciturnity—doubtless for fear of awakening the sleeper.

On a small table between them were various bottles containing medicines.

The bed stood upon a sort of dais, or raised portion of the floor, this platform being attained by two steps. High over the couch was a canopy of velvet and gold, surmounted by the coronet of a Marquis, and from whence the rich satin curtains, of dark purple, flowed over that voluptuous bed.

The room itself was furnished in the most luxurious manner. The rosewood tables were inlaid with mother of pearl: the chairs were of antique form, with high backs carved in the most exquisite manner;—the mirrors were large, the pictures numerous, and all set in magnificent frames;—and the toilette-table was of the most elegant and costly description.

And yet he, for whom all this gorgeousness and splendour had been devised,—he, whose wealth had converted the entire mansion into a palace that would have even delighted the proudest Sultan that ever sate on an oriental throne,—this man, for whom earth had such delights—the world so many enjoyments,—this man—the Marquis of Holmesford—was about to succumb to the power of the Angel of Death.

Oh! what a mockery was it to behold,—when the window-curtains were drawn back, upon the Marquis awaking from his uneasy slumber,—what a mockery was it to behold that truly imperial magnificence surrounding the couch whereon lay a thin, weak, haggard, and attenuated old man, in whose eyes was already seen that stony glare which marks the last looks of dissolving nature!

The nobleman awoke, and turned round towards his physicians, who watched at the bed-side.

One of them rose and drew back the window-curtains as noiselessly as possible; and then the pure light of a lovely day streamed into the apartment.

The other medical attendant took the nobleman's hand, felt his pulse, and inquired in a low whisper "how his lordship felt now?"

"Just the same—or may be a little worse," answered the Marquis, in a hollow but feeble tone. "And yet it is impossible that I should be in any real danger! Oh! no—I was only taken ill last night; and men do not—do not—*die*," he added, pronouncing the fatal word with a most painful effort, "upon so slight a warning."

"Your lordship is far from well—very far from well," said the physician, emphatically; "and it is my duty to assure you of that fact."

"But you—you do not think, doctor," stammered the Marquis, "that I am in any—any real—real danger?"

And as he spoke, his glassy eyes were for a few moments lighted up with the evanescent fire of intense excitement—the agitation of a suspense ineffably painful.

"My lord," answered the physician, in a solemn tone, "if you have any affairs of a worldly nature to settle——"

"No—no: it can't be! You are deceiving me!" almost shrieked the old nobleman, starting up wildly to a sitting posture: "do you mean to offend—to insult me when I am a little indisposed? For I am convinced that this is only a trifling indisposition—a passing illness."

"My dear Marquis," said the second physician, advancing towards the bed, "my colleague performs but his duty—painful though it be—when he assures you——"

"Oh! yes—I understand you," again interrupted the nobleman, catching at a straw: "you do right to prepare me for the worst! But mine is not an extreme case—is it? Oh! no—I am certain it cannot be! You are both clever men—well versed in all the mysteries of your profession—and you can soon restore me to health. There! I will give you each a cheque for five thousand pounds the day that you tell me that I may get up again!"

And once more did he contemplate them with eager—anxious glances, expressive alike of feverish hope and tremendous terror.

"Speak—speak!" he cried: "answer me! Five thousand pounds for each of you, the day that I leave this bed!"

"Were your lordship to offer us all your fortune," answered the elder physician—he who had first spoken,—"we could not do more for you than we are now doing. And if you excite yourself thus——"

"Excite myself, indeed!" ejaculated the Marquis, attempting a laugh—which, however, rather resembled a death-rattle that seemed to shake his crazy old frame even to the very vital foundations: "is it not enough to make me excited, when you are so foolish as to joke with me about my being in danger—although you know that I must recover soon? Don't you know *that*, doctor?—tell me dear doctor—shall I not be well in a few days—or at all events a few weeks? Come—reassure me: say that you only spoke in jest! Danger, indeed! Why, doctor, I possess a constitution of iron!"

And, thus speaking, the Marquis fell back upon his pillow, in a state of extreme exhaustion.

The younger physician forced him to swallow some medicine; and for a few minutes he lay panting and moaning as if the chords of existence were snapping rapidly one after the other.

At length he turned again towards his medical attendants.

"Well, I do believe that I am rather worse than I just now fancied myself to be," he said, in a very faint and feeble tone: "but still I am sure of getting better soon. That medicine has already done me good. Three or four bottles of it—and I shall be quite well. Ah! my dear friends, you are profoundly skilled in all the secrets of the human frame; and with two such physicians as you, it would be impossible to—to—die so soon!"

"Pray, my lord, do not excite yourself," observed the elder medical attendant. "Repose and rest often prove more efficacious than drugs and potions."

"Well—well—I will be quiet—I will tranquillise myself," said the Marquis. "But you must not frighten me any more—you must not talk to me about settling my worldly affairs—just as if I were indeed about to die," he added, with a ghastly attempt to smile away that expression of profound terror which he *felt* to be imprinted on his countenance. "No—no: it is too ridiculous to put such ideas into one's head! Why—how old do you take me to be, doctor?"

"My lord, you afflict me greatly by this style of discourse," said the elder physician, who was thus appealed to. "Most solemnly do I adjure your lordship to compose your mind to that state in which every Christian should be prepared for the worst."

"Doctor—doctor, you cannot be serious!" again half shrieked the affrighted nobleman. "What! am I indeed so very ill? No—no: consider the strength of my constitution—remember how able I am to procure by my wealth every means that may conduce to my recovery—think of what you yourself can do for me——"

"My lord," said the physician, solemnly, "we will exert all human efforts to save you: but the result is with God!"

The Marquis uttered a hollow groan, and, closing his eyes, appeared to be suddenly wrapt in profound meditation.

The scene which we have just described, was a most painful one—even to those two physicians whose experience in such matters was so extensive. There was something peculiarly horrible in that old man of shattered health and exhausted vigour, boasting of the strength of a constitution ruined by a long career of debauchery,—boasting, too, even against his own internal convictions!

But, like all men who fear to die, the Marquis would not admit in words what his soul had acknowledged to itself. He seemed to feel as if there were a possibility of staving off the approach of death, merely by reiterating a disbelief that the destroyer was advancing at all. Thus, though his mind was filled with the most appalling apprehensions, he nevertheless clung—he knew not how nor wherefore—to a hope that his physicians *might* be deceived—that they had exaggerated his danger—that their skill was potent enough to wrestle with the dissolution of nature—in a word, that it was quite possible for him to recover.

And, if he feared to die, it was not precisely because he dreaded the idea of being suddenly plunged into eternity; for he had been a sceptic all his life, and was by no means convinced that there was any future state at all. But his mind shrank from the thought of death as from a revolting spectacle; and moreover the world had so many charms—such boundless attractions for him—that he could not endure the prospect of being called away from those delicious scenes for ever!

He remained for nearly a quarter of an hour buried in the most profound meditation.

"My worthy friends," he at length said, opening his glassy eyes once more, and turning towards his physicians, "I am now prepared to hear without excitement any thing you may deem it advisable or proper to communicate. In one word, is my state really one of great peril?"

"Your lordship now speaks as becomes a man of strong mind," answered the elder physician; "and in this altered mood you will receive with due tranquillity the sad announcement which I am bound to make."

"And that announcement?" said the Marquis, hastily.

"Is that your lordship's recovery is in the hands of heaven," replied the physician, solemnly: "for no human agency can enable you to quit that bed in health again."

"And this is your serious conviction?" said the Marquis, grasping the bed-clothes tightly with both his hands, as if to restrain an explosion of his agonising feelings.

"My duty towards your lordship compels me to answer in the affirmative," returned the physician.

A pause of some minutes ensued: the Marquis could not trust himself to speak. Silence was for a time the only safeguard against a relapse into those wildly-expressed doubts, adjurations, and frantic wanderings which had ere now denoted the real condition of his mind.

"It is then decided—and I must prepare for death!" he at length said, in a low and measured tone. "With a candour equal to that which you have already shown, doctor, tell me how long I may hope yet to live?"

"Do not press me, my lord, on that head——"

"Nay: now you are yourself adopting the very means to excite me," interrupted the Marquis, angrily. "I am nerved to hear the worst: but I wish that *the worst* may be communicated to me. Speak, doctor—speak fearlessly—and say how long I may expect yet to live?"

The two physicians consulted each other with a rapid interchange of glances; and both thereby intimating an affirmative, the elder one said, "Your lordship might probably survive four-and-twenty hours."

"Four-and-twenty hours!" repeated the Marquis, the bed actually shaking with the cold shudder that passed through his frame at this appalling announcement: "four-and-twenty hours!" he said a second time: "that is a very short reprieve, indeed! Has your skill no means, doctor, of prolonging my existence for a few days—for a few hours, even, longer than the amount which you have named?"

"There is no hope of accomplishing such a result, my lord," was the reply.

"No hope!" murmured the Marquis: then after another short pause, he said in a tone which it cost him a dreadful effort to render firm, "Have the kindness to direct that my solicitor may be sent for without delay."

This desire was immediately complied with; and as the lawyer lived in the neighbourhood, scarcely half an hour elapsed ere he was ushered into the presence of the Marquis.

The physicians were desired to remain in the room; and the solicitor, seating himself by the nobleman's directions at the table near the bed, prepared his writing materials.

The Marquis of Holmesford then gave instructions relative to the disposal of his property; and the lawyer drew up the will in due form.

Having detailed various bequests and legacies, and disposed of the great bulk of his fortune, the Marquis, who spoke in a firm and distinct tone of voice, addressed the lawyer in the following manner:—

"And now, sir, have the kindness to insert the words which I am about to dictate to you:—'*Also I will and bequeathe to Katherine Bazzano, half-sister of his Highness Richard, Prince of Montoni, the sum of fifty thousand pounds, as a proof of the sincere contrition and deep regret which I experience on account of certain proceedings on my part, whereby the mother of the said Katherine Bazzano endured grievous wrong and great affliction, although perfectly innocent of any evil thought or deed in respect to her husband, the deceased father of the above-mentioned Richard Prince of Montoni.*'—Have you written to my dictation?"

"I have followed your lordship as accurately as the introduction of a few necessary legal technicalities into that last clause would permit," was the solicitor's reply.

"Then naught now remains for me but to sign the will," said the Marquis; and he sate up in the bed, apparently with but little exertion.

He affixed his name with a firm hand to the document, and requested the physicians to witness it.

The ceremony was then completed; and the solicitor took his departure.

So soon as he had left the room, the Marquis addressed himself to the physicians in these terms:—

"My good friends, the ordeal which I most dreaded has been accomplished; and I feel as if a considerable weight were taken off my mind. What I now require is that you give me some powerful medicament or a strong cordial, that will endow me with sufficient energy to rise from this bed and proceed—alone and unattended—to another room in the house,—a room which I *must* visit—or I should not die in peace! And as a reward for this last service, I desire you to divide equally between you the amount which you will find in yonder writing-desk. That sum consists of a few thousands, and will, I hope, amply repay the kindness which I now expect at your hands."

"While I thank your lordship for this instance of your bounty towards me and my colleague," said the elder physician, "I am convinced that I express his feelings as well as my own, in stating that we cannot possibly allow you to quit your couch. The excitement might prove almost immediately fatal."

"I have no time to waste in hearing or answering objections," said the Marquis, his glazing eyes lighting up with the fever of impatience, and a hectic flush appearing on his sallow, sunken, withered cheeks. "Do what I request—or leave me this moment: give me such a cordial as you may think suitable to the purpose—or my valet will supply me with a bumper of champagne."

"My dear Marquis——"

"My lord—my lord——"

"In one word, do as I desire—or leave me," exclaimed the nobleman, cutting short the ejaculations of the two physicians by an imperious wave of his skeleton-like hand: "there shall be no other master save myself in this house, until the breath be out of my body."

The physicians essayed farther remonstrances—but in vain. The Marquis grew fearfully irritated with their opposition, and then fell back so exhausted upon his pillow, that the medical attendants were compelled to administer as a restorative the cordial which he had demanded as an artificial stimulant a few minutes previously.

The effect of the cordial was really surprising: that old man, whom its influence had just snatched—but snatched only for a time—from the out-stretched arms of death, sate up in his bed, smiled, and seemed to bid defiance to the destroying angel.

"You must humour me now, my friends," he said, in a jocose manner, which contrasted awfully with the inevitable peril of his condition: "go to the writing-desk in yonder corner, and let me be assured you have possessed yourselves of that token of my good feeling which I bequeathe to you."

The physicians, rather to please their obstinate patient than to gratify any avaricious longing on their part, did as they were desired: but, scarcely had they opened the desk, where they observed a bundle of Bank-notes, when a low chuckle met their ears.

They turned and beheld the Marquis, clad in a long dressing-gown and with slippers on his feet, hurrying out of the room by a small door near the foot of his bed.

To hasten after him was their first and most natural impulse; but the key was turned on the other side ere they even reached the door.

Without losing a moment, they hastened from the room by a door at the opposite extremity; but in the adjoining passage they were met by the nobleman's principal valet.

"Gentlemen," said the domestic, "his lordship desires me to inform you that he has no farther need of your services."

"But, my good fellow," exclaimed the younger physician, "your master is dying—he cannot live another day; and this excitement—this rash proceeding——"

"Is sheer madness!" added the senior medical attendant. "Whither has your master gone?"

The valet whispered a few words to the physicians: they understood him full well, and exchanged looks of mingled disgust and horror.

"The unnatural excitement of this proceeding," at length observed the elder physician, "will kill the Marquis within an hour!"

CHAPTER CCLII.

DEATH OF THE MARQUIS OF HOLMESFORD.

We have described at great length, in a former portion of our narrative, the voluptuous attractions of that department of Holmesford House which may very properly be denominated "the harem."

The reader doubtless remembers the vast and lofty room which we depicted as being furnished in the most luxurious oriental style, and which was embellished with pictures representing licentious scenes from the mythology of the ancients.

To that apartment we must now once more direct attention.

Grouped together upon two ottomans drawn close to each other, five beautiful women were conversing in a tone so low that it almost sank to a whisper; while their charming countenances wore an expression of mingled suspense and sorrow.

They were all in *deshabillée*, though it was now past four o'clock in the afternoon.

This negligence, however, extended only to their attire; for each of those lovely creatures had bathed her beauteous form in a perfumed bath, and had arranged her hair in the manner best calculated to set off its luxuriance to advantage and at the same time to enhance the charms of that countenance which it enclosed.

But farther than this the toilette of those five fascinating girls had not progressed; and the loose morning-wrappers which they wore, left revealed all the glowing beauties of each voluptuous bust.

There was the Scotch charmer, with her brilliant complexion, her auburn hair, and her red cherry lips:—there was the English girl—the pride of Lancashire—with her brown hair, and her robust but exquisitely modelled proportions:—and next to her, on the same ottoman, sate the Irish beauty, whose sparkling black eyes denoted all the fervour of sensuality.

On the sofa facing these three women, sate the French wanton, her taper fingers playing with the gold chain which, in the true spirit of coquetry, she had thrown negligently round her neck, and the massive links of which made not the least indentation upon the plump fullness of her bosom. By her side was the Spanish houri, her long black ringlets flowing on the white drapery which set off her transparent olive skin to such exquisite advantage.

This group formed an assemblage of charms which would have raised palpitations and excited mysterious fires in the heart of the most heaven-devoted anchorite that ever vowed a life of virgin-purity.

And the picture was the more fascinating—the more dangerous, inasmuch as its voluptuousness was altogether unstudied at this moment, and those beauteous creatures noticed not, in their sisterly confidence towards each other, that their glowing and half-naked forms were thus displayed almost as it might have seemed in a spirit of competition and rivalry.

But what is the topic of their discourse? and wherefore has a shade of melancholy displaced those joyous smiles that were wont to play upon lips of coral opening above teeth of pearls?

Let us hear them converse.

"This illness is the more unfortunate for us," said the Scotch girl, "because it arrived so suddenly."

"And before the Marquis had made his will," added the French-woman.

"Yes," observed the English beauty,—"it was only yesterday afternoon that he assured us he should not fail to take good care of us all whenever he did make his will."

"And now he will die intestate, as the lawyers say," murmured the Scotch girl; "and we shall be sent forth into the world without resources."

"Oh! how shocking to think of!" cried the Spaniard. "I am sure I should die if I were forced to quit this charming place."

"Nay—now you talk too absurdly, my dear friend," interposed the French charmer; "for, beautiful as we all are, we need not be apprehensive of the future."

"After all, the Marquis may make his will," said the English girl.

"Or recover," added the Irish beauty. "And for my part, I would sooner that he should do *that* than be snatched away from us so suddenly; for, old as he is, the Marquis is very agreeable—very amiable."

"From what our maids told us just now," remarked the Scotch girl, "there does not appear to be any chance of his lordship's recovery. Besides, he is much older than he ever chose to admit to us; and his life has been a long career of pleasure and enjoyment."

"Alas! poor old nobleman," said the Irish beauty, Kathleen; "his often-expressed wish does not appear destined to be fulfilled! How frequently has he declared that he should die contented if surrounded by ourselves, and with a goblet of champagne at his lips!"

Scarcely were these words uttered, when the door of the apartment opened abruptly; and the Marquis made his appearance.

The five women started from their seats, uttering exclamations of joy.

The Marquis bolted the door with great caution, and then advanced towards his ladies with a smile upon his haggard, pale, and death-like countenance.

Indeed, it was with the greatest difficulty that the young women could restrain a murmur of surprise—almost of disgust—when, as he drew nearer towards them, they beheld the fearful ravages which a few hours' illness had made upon his face. The extent of those inroads was moreover enhanced by the absence of his false teeth, which he had not time to fix in his mouth ere he escaped from the thraldom of his physicians: so that the thinness of his cheeks was rendered almost skeleton-like by the sinking in of his mouth.

The superb dressing-gown seemed a mockery of the shrivelled and wasted form which it loosely wrapped; and as the old nobleman staggered towards his mistresses, whose first ebullition of joy at his appearance was so suddenly shocked by the ghastly hideousness of his aspect, they had not strength nor presence of mind to hasten to meet him.

Kathleen was the first to conquer her aversion and dismay; and she caught the Marquis in her arms just at the instant when, overcome by the exertions of the last few minutes, he was about to sink beneath the weight of sheer exhaustion.

Then the other women crowded forward to lend their aid; and the old nobleman was placed upon one of the luxurious ottomans.

He closed his eyes, and seemed to breathe with great difficulty.

"Oh! my God—he is dying!" exclaimed Kathleen: "ring for aid—for the physicians——"

"No—no!" murmured the Marquis, in a faint tone; and, opening his eyes once more, he gazed around him—vacantly at first, then more steadily,—until he seemed to recover visual strength sufficient to distinguish the charming countenances that were fixed upon him with mournful interest; "no, my dear girls," he continued, his voice becoming a trifle more powerful; "the doors of this room must not be opened again so long as the breath remains in my body—for I am come," he added with a smile the ghastliness of which all his efforts could not subdue,—"I am come to die amongst you!"

"To die—here—amongst us!" ejaculated all the women (save Kathleen), shrinking back in terror and dismay.

"Yes, my dear girls," returned the Marquis: "and thus will my hope and my prophecy be fulfilled. But let us not trifle away the little time that remains to me. Kathleen, my charmer—I am faint—my spirit seems to be sinking:—give me wine!"

"Wine, my lord?" she repeated, in a tone of kind remonstrance.

"Yes—wine—delicious, sparkling wine!" cried the nobleman, raising himself partially up on the cushions of the sofa. "Delay not—give me champagne!"

The French and Spanish girls hastened to a splendid buffet near the stage at the end of the room, and speedily returned to the vicinity of the ottoman, bearing between them a massive silver salver laden with bottles and glasses.

The wine was poured forth: the Marquis desired Kathleen to steady his hand as he conveyed the nectar to his lips; and he drained the glass of its contents.

A hectic tinge appeared upon his cheeks; his eyes were animated with a partial fire; and he even seemed happy, as he commanded his ladies to drink bumpers of champagne all round.

"Consider that I am going on a long journey, my dear girls," he exclaimed, with a smile; "and do not let our parting be sorrowful. Kathleen, my sweet one, come nearer: there—place yourself so that I may recline my head on your bosom—and now throw that warm, plump, naked arm over my shoulder. Oh! this is paradise!"

And for a few minutes the hoary voluptuary, whose licentious passions were dominant even in death, closed his eyes and seemed to enjoy with intense gratification all the luxury of his position.

It was a painful and disgusting sight to behold the shrivelled, haggard, and attenuated countenance of the dying sensualist, pressing upon that full and alabaster globe so warm with health, life, and glowing passions;—painful and disgusting, too, to see that thin, emaciated, and worn-out frame reclining in the arms of a lovely girl in the vigour and strength of youth:—hideous—hideous to view that contiguity of a sapless, withered trunk and a robust and verdant tree!

"Girls," said the Marquis, at length opening his eyes, but without changing his position, "it is useless to attempt to conceal the truth from you: you know that I am dying! Well—no matter: sooner or later Death must come to all! My life has been a joyous—a happy one; and to you who solace me in my dissolution, I am not ungrateful. Anna, dearest—thrust your hand into the pocket of my dressing-gown."

The French-woman obeyed this command, and drew forth a sealed packet, addressed to the five ladies by their christian and surnames.

"Open it," said the Marquis. "Two months ago I made this provision for you, my dear girls—because, entertaining foolish apprehensions relative to making my will, I felt the necessity of at least taking care of you."

While the nobleman was yet speaking, Anna had opened the packet, whence she drew forth a number of Bank-notes.

There were ten—each for a thousand pounds; and a few words written within the envelope specified that the amount was to be equally divided amongst the five ladies.

"Oh! my dear Marquis, how liberal!" exclaimed the French girl, her countenance becoming radiant with joy.

"How generous!" cried the English beauty.

"How noble!" ejaculated the Scotch charmer.

"It is more than generous and noble—it is princely!" said the Spanish houri.

Kathleen simply observed, "My dear lord, I thank you most unfeignedly for this kind consideration on your part."

The Marquis made no reply; but taking the delicate white hand of the Irish girl, as he lay pillowed upon her palpitating breast, he gently slipped upon one of her taper fingers a ring of immense value.

He then squeezed her hand to enjoin silence; and this act was not perceived by the other ladies, who were too busily employed in feasting their eyes upon the Bank-notes to pay attention to aught beside.

"Come—fill the glasses!" suddenly exclaimed the Marquis, after a short pause: "I feel that my strength is failing me fast—the sand of my life's hour-glass is running rapidly away!"

The French girl—to whose mind there was something peculiarly heroical and romantic in the conduct of the Marquis—hastened to obey the order which had been specially addressed to her; and the sparkling juice of Epernay again moistened the parched throat of the dying man, and also enhanced the carnation tints upon the cheeks of the five youthful beauties.

"And now, my charmers," said the nobleman, addressing himself to the French and Spanish women, "gratify me by dancing some pleasing and voluptuous measure,—while you, my loves," he added, turning his glazing eyes upon the Scotch and English girls, "play a delicious strain,—so that my spirit may ebb away amidst the soothing ecstacies of the blissful scene!"

The Marquis spoke in a faint and tremulous voice, for he felt himself growing every moment weaker and weaker; and his head now lay, heavy and motionless, upon the bosom of the Irish girl, whose warm and polished arm was thrown around him.

The Scotch and English girls hastened to place themselves, the former before a splendid harp, and the latter at a pianoforte, the magnificent tones of which had never failed to excite the admiration of all who ever heard them.

Then the French and Spanish women commenced a slow, languishing, and voluptuous dance, the evolutions of which were well adapted to display the fine proportions of their half-naked forms.

A smile relaxed the features of the dying man; and his glances followed the movements of those foreign girls who vied with each other in assuming the most lascivious attitudes.

By degrees, that exciting spectacle grew indistinct to the eyes of the Marquis; and the music no longer fell upon his ears in varied and defined tones, but with a droning monotonous sound.

"Kathleen—Kathleen," he murmured, speaking with the utmost difficulty, "reach me the glass—place the goblet to my lips—it will revive me for a few minutes———"

The Irish girl shuddered in spite of herself—shuddered involuntarily as she felt the cheek of the Marquis grow cold and clammy against her bosom.

"Kathleen—dear Kathleen," he murmured in a whisper that was scarcely audible; "give me the goblet!"

Conquering her repugnance, the Irish girl, who possessed a kind and generous heart, reached a glass on the table near the sofa; and, raising the nobleman's head, she placed the wine to his lips.

With a last—last expiring effort, he took the glass in his own hand, and swallowed a few drops of its contents:—his eyes were lighted up again for a moment, and his cheek flushed; but his head fell back heavily upon the white bosom.

Kathleen endeavoured to cry for aid—and could not: a sensation of fainting came over her—she closed her eyes—and a suffocating feeling in the throat almost choked her.

But still the music continued and the dance went on, for several minutes more.

All at once a shriek emanated from the lips of Kathleen: the music ceased—the dance was abandoned—and the Irish girl's companions rushed towards the sofa.

Their anticipations were realised: the Marquis was no more!

The hope which he had so often expressed in his life-time, was fulfilled almost to the very letter;—for the old voluptuary had "*died with his head pillowed on the naked—heaving bosom of beauty, and with a glass of sparkling champagne in his hand!*"

CHAPTER CCLIII.

THE EX-MEMBER FOR ROTTENBOROUGH.

It was now the middle of April, 1843.

The morning was fine, and the streets were marked with the bustle of men of business, clerks, and others repairing to their respective offices, when Mr. George Montague Greenwood turned from Saint Paul's Churchyard into Cheapside.

He was attired in a plain, and even somewhat shabby manner: there was not a particle of jewellery about him; and a keen eye might have discovered, in the *tout ensemble* of his appearance, that his toilette had been arranged with every endeavour to produce as good an effect as possible.

Thus his neckcloth was tied with a precision seldom bestowed upon a faded piece of black silk: his shirt-cuffs were drawn down so as to place an interval of snowy white between the somewhat threadbare sleeve of the blue coat and the common grey glove of Berlin wool:—a black riband hung round his neck and was gathered at the ends in the right pocket of the soiled satin waistcoat, so as to leave the beholder in a state of uncertainty whether it were connected with a watch or only an eye-glass—or, indeed, with any thing at all;—and the Oxford-mixture trousers, *rather* white at the knees, were strapped tightly over a pair of well-blacked bluchers, a casual observer would certainly have taken for Wellingtons.

In his hand he carried a neat black cane; and his gait was characterised by much of the self-sufficiency which had marked it in better days. It was, however, far removed from a swagger: Greenwood was too much of a gentleman in his habits to fall into the slightest manifestation of vulgarity.

His beautiful black hair, curling and glossy, put to shame the brownish hue of the beaver hat which had evidently seen some service, and had lately been exposed to all the varieties of weather peculiar to this capricious climate. His face—eminently handsome, as we have before observed—was pale and rather thin; but there was a haughty assurance in the proud curl of the upper lip, and a fire in his large dark eyes, which showed that hope was not altogether a stranger to the breast of Mr. George Montague Greenwood.

It was about a quarter past nine in the morning when this gentleman entered the great thoroughfare of Cheapside.

Perhaps there is no street in all London which presents so many moral phases to the eyes of the acute beholder as this one, and at that hour; inasmuch as those eyes may single out, and almost read the pursuit of, every individual forming an item in the dense crowd that is then rolling onward to the vicinity of the Bank of England.

For of every ten persons, nine are proceeding in that direction.

Reader, let us pause for a moment and examine the details of the scene to which we allude: for Greenwood has slackened his pace—his eye has caught sight of Bow clock—and he perceives that he is yet too early to commence the visits which he intends to make in certain quarters.

And first, gentle reader, behold that young man with the loose taglioni and no undercoat: he has a devil-me-care kind of look about him, mingled with an air of seediness, as if he had been up the best part of the night at a free-and-easy. He is smoking a cigar—at that hour of the morning! It is impossible to gaze at him for two seconds, without being convinced that he is an articled clerk to an attorney, and that he doesn't care so long as he reaches the office just five minutes before the "governor" arrives.

But that old man, with a threadbare suit of black, and the red cotton handkerchief sticking so suspiciously out of his pocket, as if he had something wrapped up in it,—who is he? Mark how he shuffles along, dragging his heavy high-lows over the pavement at a pace too speedy for his attenuated frame: and see with what anxiety he looks up at the clock projecting out far overhead, to assure himself that he shall yet be at his office within two minutes of half-past nine—or else risk his place and the eighteen shillings a week which it brings him in, and on which he has to support a wife and large family. He is a copying clerk in a lawyer's office—there can be no doubt of it; and the poor man has his dinner wrapped up in his pocket-handkerchief!

Do you observe that proud, pompous-looking stout man, with the large yellow cane in his hand, and the massive chain and seals hanging from his fob? He is a stockbroker who, having got up a bubble Railway Company, has enriched himself in a single day, after having struggled against difficulties for twenty years. But, see—a fashionably-dressed gentleman, with a *little* too much jewellery about his person, and a *rather* too severe swagger in his gait, overtakes our stout friend, and passes his arm familiarly in his as he wishes him "good morning." There is no mistake about this individual: he is the Managing-Director of the stockbroker's Company, and was taken from a three-pair back in the New Cut to preside at the Board. *Arcades ambo*—a precious pair!

Glance a moment at that great, stout, shabbily-dressed man, whose trousers are so tight that they certainly never could have been made for him, and whose watery boiled-kind of eyes, vacant look, and pale but bloated face, denote the habitual gin-drinker. He rolls along with a staggering gait, as if the effects of the previous night's debauch had not been slept off, or as if he had already taken his first dram. He is on his way to the neighbourhood of the Bank, where he either loiters about on the steps of the Auction Mart, or at the door of Capel Court, or else proceeds to some public-house parlour "which he frequents." His business is to hawk bills about for discount; and, to hear him speak, one would believe that he could raise a million of money in no time—whereas he has most likely the pawn-ticket of his Sunday's coat in his pocket.

And now mark that elderly, sedate, quiet-looking man, whose good black suit is well-brushed and his boots nicely polished. He compares his heavy gold watch with the clock of Bow church, and is quite delighted to see that *his* time is correct to a second. And now he continues his way, without looking to the right or the left: he knows every feature—every shop—every lamp-post of Cheapside and the Poultry too well to have any farther curiosity about those thoroughfares—for he has passed along that way every morning, Sundays excepted, during the last twenty years. Are you not prepared to make an affidavit that he is a superior clerk in the Bank of England?

But we must abandon any farther scrutiny of the several members of the crowd in Cheapside—at least for the present; because it is now half-past nine o'clock, and Mr. Greenwood has reached Cornhill.

Here he paused—and sighed,—sighed deeply.

That sigh told a long and painful history,—of how he had lately been rich and prosperous—how he had lost all by grasping at more—how he was now reduced almost to the very verge of penury—and how he wondered whether he should ever be wealthy and great again!

"Yes—yes: I *will* be!" he said to himself—speaking not with his lips, but with that silent though emphatic tongue which belongs to the soul. "My good star cannot have deserted me for ever! But this day must show!"

Then, calling all his assurance to his aid, he turned into the office of a well-known merchant and capitalist on Cornhill.

The clerks did not immediately recognise him; for the last time he had called there, it was at four in the afternoon and he had alighted from an elegant cab: whereas now it was half-past nine in the morning, and he had evidently come on foot. But when he demanded, in his usual authoritative tone, whether their master had arrived yet, they recollected him, and replied in the affirmative.

Greenwood accordingly walked into the merchant's private office.

"Ah! my dear sir," he said, extending his hand towards the merchant, "how do you find yourself? It is almost an age since we met."

The merchant affected not to perceive the out-stretched hand; nor did he return the bland smile with which Mr. Greenwood accosted him. But, just raising his eyes from the morning paper which lay before him, he said in a cold tone, "Oh! Mr. Greenwood, I believe? Pray, sir, what is your business?"

The ex-member for Rottenborough took a chair uninvited, and proceeded to observe in a confidential kind of whisper,—"The fact is, my dear sir, I have conceived a magnificent project for making a few thousands into as many millions, I may say; and as on former occasions you and I have done *some* little business together—and I have put a *few* good things in your way—I thought I would give you the refusal of my new design."

"I am really infinitely obliged to you, Mr. Greenwood——"

"Oh! I knew you would be, my dear sir!" interrupted the ex-member. "The risk is nothing—the gains certain and enormous. You and I can keep it all to ourselves; and——"

"You require me to advance the funds, I presume?" asked the merchant, eyeing his visitor askance.

"Just so—a few thousands only—to be repaid out of the first proceeds, of course," returned Greenwood.

"Then, sir, I beg to decline the speculation," said the merchant, drily.

"Speculation! it is *not* a speculation," cried Greenwood: "it is a certainty."

"Nevertheless, sir, I must decline it; and as my time is very much occupied——"

"Oh! I shall not intrude upon you any longer," interrupted Greenwood, indignantly; and he strode out of the office.

"The impertinent scoundrel!" he muttered to himself, when he had gained the street. "After all the good things I have placed in his way, to treat me in this manner. But, never mind—let me once grow rich again and I will humble him at my feet!"

In spite of this attempt at self-consolation, Greenwood was deeply mortified with the reception which he had experienced at the merchant's office: his anger had, however, cooled and his spirits revived by the time he reached Birchin Lane, where dwelt another of his City acquaintances.

This individual was a capitalist who had once been saved from serious embarrassment, if not from total ruin, by a timely advance of funds made to him by Greenwood; and though the capitalist had paid enormous interest for the accommodation, he had nevertheless always exhibited the most profound gratitude towards the ex-member for Rottenborough.

It was, therefore, with great confidence that Greenwood entered the private office of the capitalist.

"Ah! my dear fellow," cried the latter, apparently overjoyed to see his visitor, "how *have* you been lately? Why—it is really an age since I have seen you! Pray sit down—and now say what I can do for you."

Greenwood addressed him in terms similar to those which he had used with the merchant a few minutes previously.

"And so you actually have a scheme that will make millions, my dear Greenwood?" said the capitalist, his entire countenance beaming with smiles.

"Just as I tell you," answered the ex-member.

"And you have considered it in all its bearings?"

"In every shape and way. Success is certain."

"Oh! what a lucky dog you are," cried the capitalist, playfully thrusting his fingers into Greenwood's ribs.

"Well—I can't say that I am lucky," observed the latter, in a measured tone. "I have had losses lately—serious losses: but you know that I am not the man to be long in remedying them."

"Far from it, my boy!" exclaimed the capitalist. "You will make an enormous fortune before you die—I am sure you will. And this new scheme of yours,—although you have only hinted darkly at it,—*must* succeed—I am convinced it must."

"Then you are prepared to join me in the project?" said Greenwood.

"Nothing would give me greater pleasure, my dear friend," ejaculated the capitalist: "but it is impossible."

"Impossible! How can that be, since you think so well of any thing which I may devise?" asked Greenwood.

"God bless your soul!" cried the other; "money is money now-a-days. For my part I can't think where the devil it all gets to! One hears of it—reads of it—but never sees it! In fact," he added, sinking his voice to a mysterious whisper, "I do believe that there is no such thing now as money in the whole City."

"Ridiculous!" exclaimed Greenwood. "Complaints from *you* are absurd—because every one knows that you have made an enormous fortune since that time when I was so happy to save you from bankruptcy."

"Yes—yes," said the capitalist: "I remember that incident—I have never forgot it—I always told you I never should."

"Then, in plain terms," continued Greenwood, "do me the service of advancing two or three thousand pounds to set my new project in motion."

"Impossible, Greenwood—impossible!" cried the capitalist, buttoning up his breeches-pockets. "Things are in such a state that I would not venture a penny upon the most feasible speculation in the world."

"Perhaps you will lend me a sum——"

"Lend! Ah! ha! Now, really, Greenwood, this is too good! Lend, indeed! What—when we are all in the borrowing line in the City!"—and the capitalist chuckled, as if he had uttered a splendid joke.

"In one word, then," said Greenwood, relishing this mirth as little as a person in his situation was likely to do; "will you assist my temporary wants—even if you do not choose to enter into my speculation? You know that I am proud, and that it must pain me thus to speak to you: but I declare most solemnly that fifty pounds at this moment would be of the greatest service to me."

"Nothing gives me more pain than to refuse a friend like you," answered the capitalist: "but, positively, I could not part with a shilling to-day to save my own brother from a gaol."

Greenwood rose, put on his hat, and left the office without uttering another word.

He felt that he was righteously punished—for *he* had, in his time, often treated men in the same manner,—professing ardent friendship, and yet refusing the smallest pecuniary favour!

Having walked about for nearly half an hour, to calm the feelings which the conduct of the capitalist had so painfully excited, Greenwood repaired to the office of a great bill-discounter and speculator in Broad Street. This individual had been a constant visitor at Greenwood's house in Spring Gardens—had joined him in many of his most profitable speculations—and had gained considerable sums thereby. He was, moreover, of a very enterprising character, and always ready to risk money with the hope of large returns.

Greenwood entered the clerks' office; and, glancing towards the private one at the lower extremity, he caught sight of the speculator's countenance peering over the blinds of the glass-door which opened between the two rooms.

The face was instantly withdrawn; and Greenwood, who of course affected not to have observed its appearance at the window, inquired whether the speculator was within.

"Really I can't say, sir," drawled a clerk, who was mending a pen: then, without desisting from his operation, he said, "I'll see, sir, in a moment."

"Be so kind as to see *this* moment," exclaimed Greenwood, angrily. "I suppose you know who I am?"

"Oh! yes—sir—certainly, sir," returned the clerk; and, having duly nibbed the pen, he dismounted very leisurely from his stool—paused to arrange a piece of blotting-paper on the desk in a very precise manner indeed—brushed the splinters of the quill from his trousers—and then dragged himself in a lazy fashion towards the private office.

Greenwood bit his quivering lip with rage.

"Two years ago," he thought to himself, "I should not have been treated thus!"

Meantime the clerk entered the inner office, and carefully closed the door behind him.

Greenwood could hear the murmuring sounds of two voices within.

At length the clerk re-appeared, and said in a careless tone, "The governor isn't in, Mr. Greenwood: I thought he was—but he isn't—and, what's more, I don't know when he will be. You'd better look in again, if it's particular; but I know the governor's uncommon busy to-day."

"I shall not trouble you nor your *governor* any more," returned Greenwood, his heart ready to break at the cool, deliberate insult thus put upon him. "You think me a fallen man—and you dare to treat me thus. But———"

"Why, as for *that*," interrupted the clerk, with impertinent emphasis, "every one knows you're broke and done up—and my governor doesn't want shabby insolvents hanging about his premises."

Greenwood's countenance became scarlet as these bitter taunts met his ears; and for a moment he felt inclined to rush upon the insolent clerk and punish him severely with his cane.

But, being naturally of a cool and cautious disposition, he perceived with a second thought that he might only become involved in a dilemma from which he had no means to extricate himself: so, conquering his passion, he rushed out of the office.

He could now no longer remain blind to the cruel conviction that the extremities of his position were well known in the City, and that the hopes with which he had sallied forth three hours previously were mere delusive visions.

Still he was resolved to leave no stone unturned in the endeavour to retrieve his ruined fortunes; but feeling sick at heart and the prey to a deep depression of spirits, he plunged hastily into a public-house to take some refreshment.

And now behold the once splendid and fastidious Greenwood,—the man who had purchased the votes of a constituency, and had even created a sensation within the walls of Parliament,—the individual who had discounted bills of large amount for some of the greatest peers of England, and whose luxurious mode of living had once been the envy and wonder of the fashionable world,—behold the ex-member for Rottenborough partaking of a pint of porter and a crust of bread and cheese in the dingy parlour of a public-house!

There was a painful knitting of the brows, and there was a nervous quivering of the lip, which denoted the acute emotions to which he was a prey, as he partook of his humble fare; and once—once, two large tears trickled down his cheeks, and moistened the bread that he was conveying to his mouth.

For he thought of the times when money was as dirt in his estimation,—when he rode in splendid vehicles, sate down to sumptuous repasts, was ministered unto by a host of servants in gorgeous liveries, and revelled in the arms of the loveliest women of the metropolis.

Oh! he thought of all this: he recalled to mind the well-filled wardrobes he had once possessed, and glanced at his present faded attire;—he shook up the remains of the muddy beer at the bottom of the pewter-pot, and remembered the gold he had lavished on champagne: his eyes lingered upon the crumbs of the bread and the rind of the cheese left on the plate, and his imagination became busy with the reminiscences of the turtle and venison that had once smoked upon his board.

But worse—oh! far worse than this was the dread conviction that all his lavish expenditure—all his ostentatious display—all his princely feasts, had failed to secure him a single friend!

No wonder, then, that the bitter—bitter tears started from his eyes; and, though he immediately checked that first ebullition of heart-felt anguish yet the effort only caused the storm of emotions to rage the more painfully within his breast.

For, in imagination, he cast his eyes towards a mansion a few miles distant; and there he beheld *one* whose condition formed a striking contrast with his own—*one* who had suddenly burst from obscurity and created for himself as proud a name as might be found in Christendom,—a young man whose indomitable energies and honourable aspirations had enabled him to lead armies to conquest, and who had taken his place amongst the greatest Princes in the universe!

The comparison which Greenwood drew—despite of himself—between the elevated position of Richard Markham and his own fallen, ruined lot, produced feelings of so painful—so exquisitely agonising a nature, that he could endure them no longer. He felt that they were goading him to madness—the more so because he was alone in that dingy parlour at the time, and was therefore the least likely to struggle against them successfully.

Hastily quitting the public-house, he rushed into the street, where the fresh air seemed to do him good.

And then he asked himself whether he should risk farther insult by calling upon other wealthy men with whom he had once been on intimate terms? For a few moments he was inclined to abandon the idea: but a little calm reflection told him not to despair.

Moreover, he had a reason—a powerful motive for exerting all his energies to repair the past, so far as his worldly fortunes were concerned; and though the idea was almost insane, he hoped—*if he had but a chance*—to make such good use of the coming few weeks as would reinstate him in the possession of enormous wealth.

But, alas! it seemed as if no one would listen to the scheme which he felt convinced was calculated to return millions for the risk of a few thousands!

"Oh! I *must* retrieve myself—I *must* make a fortune!" he thought, as he hurried towards Moorgate Street. "One lucky stroke—and four-and-twenty hours shall see me rich again!"

This idea brought a smile to his lips; and, relaxing his pace, he composed his countenance as well as he could ere he entered the office of a wealthy stockbroker in Moorgate Street.

The stockbroker was lounging over the clerks' desk, conversing with a merchant whom Greenwood also knew; and the moment the ex-member for Rottenborough entered, the two City gentlemen treated him to a long, impertinent, and contemptuous stare.

"Ah!" said Greenwood, affecting a pleasant smile, which, God knows! did not come from the heart; "you do not appear to recollect me? Am I so very much changed as all *that*?"

"Well—it *is* Greenwood, pos-i-tive-ly!" drawled the stockbroker, turning towards his friend the merchant in a manner that was equivalent to saying, "I wonder at his impudence in coming here."

"Yes—it *is* Greenwood," observed the merchant, putting his glasses up to his eyes: "or rather the shadow of Greenwood, I should take it to be."

"Ah! ha! ha!" chuckled the stockbroker.

"You are disposed to be facetious, gentlemen," said the object of this intended witticism but really galling insult: "I presume that my long absence from the usual City haunts———"

"I can assure you, Greenwood," interrupted the stockbroker, "that the City has got on uncommonly well without you. The Bank hasn't stopped payment—bills are easy of discount—money is plentiful———"

"And yet," said Greenwood, determined to receive all this sarcasm as quietly as a poor devil ought to do when about to make a proposal requiring an advance of funds,—"and yet a certain capitalist—a very intimate friend of mine, in Birchin Lane—assured me just now that money was very scarce."

"Ha! ha! ha!" laughed the stockbroker.

"He! he! he!" chuckled the merchant.

"Why, the fact is, Greenwood," continued the broker, "your *very intimate friend* the capitalist was here only a quarter of an hour ago; and he delighted us hugely by telling us how you called upon him this morning with a scheme that would make millions, and ended by wanting to borrow fifty pounds of him."

"He! he! he!" again chuckled the merchant.

"Ha! ha! ha!" once more laughed the stockbroker; and, taking his friend's arm, he led him into his private office, the two continuing to laugh and chuckle until the door closed behind them.

Greenwood now became aware of the gratifying fact that every clerk in the counting-house was laughing also; and he rushed out into the street, a prey to feelings of the most agonising nature.

But the ignominy of that day was not yet complete in respect to him.

As he darted away from the door of the insolent stockbroker's office, he came in collision with two gentlemen who were walking arm-in-arm towards the Bank.

"'Pon my honour, my good fellow——" began one, rubbing his arm which had been hurt by the encounter.

"Greenwood!" cried the second, stepping back in surprise.

The ex-member for Rottenborough raised his eyes at the sounds of those well-known voices, and beheld Mr. Chichester, with his inseparable friend the baronet, both eyeing him in the most insulting manner.

"Ah! Greenwood, my dear fellow," exclaimed Sir Rupert; "I am really quite delighted to see you. How get on the free and independent electors of Rottenborough? Egad, though—you are not quite the pink of fashion that you used to be—when you did me the honour of making my wife your mistress."

"Greenwood and Berlin-wool gloves—impossible!" cried Chichester. "Such a companionship is quite unnatural!"

"And an old coat brushed up to look like a new one," added the baronet, laughing heartily.

"And bluchers——"

Greenwood stayed to hear no more: he broke from the hold which the two friends had laid upon him, and darted down an alley into Coleman Street.

CHAPTER CCLIV.

FURTHER MISFORTUNES.

Greenwood had been insulted by those wealthy citizens who once considered themselves honoured by his notice; and *this* he might have borne, because he was man of the world enough to know that poverty is a crime in the eyes of plodding, money-making persons.

But to be made the jest of a couple of despicable adventurers—to be jeered at by two knaves for whom he entertained the most sovereign contempt, because their rascalities had been conducted on a scale of mean swindling rather than in the colourable guise of financial enterprise,—to be laughed at and mocked by such men as those, because they happened to have good clothes upon their backs,—Oh! this was a crushing—an intolerable insult!

The unhappy Greenwood felt it most keenly: he writhed beneath the sharp lash of that bitter sarcasm which had been hurled against his shabby appearance;—he groaned under the scourge of those contemptuous scoffs!

Sanguine as his disposition naturally was,—confident as he ever felt in his own talents for intrigue and scheming,—he was now suddenly cast down; and hope fled from his soul.

Not for worlds would he have risked the chance of receiving farther insult that day, by calling at the counting-house of another capitalist!

And now he fled from the City with a species of loathing,—as much depressed by disappointment as he had been elated by hope when he entered it a few hours previously.

He crossed Blackfriars' Bridge, turned into Holland Street, and thence entered John Street, where he knocked timidly at the door of a house of very mean appearance.

A stout, vulgar-looking woman, with carrotty hair, tangled as a mat, overshadowing a red and bloated face, thrust her head out of the window on the first floor.

"Well?" she cried, in an impertinent tone.

"Will you have the kindness to let me in, Mrs. Brown?" said Greenwood, calling to his aid all that blandness of manner which had once served him us a powerful auxiliary in his days of extensive intrigue.

"That depends," was the abrupt reply. "Have you brought any money with you?"

"Mrs. Brown, I cannot explain myself in the street," said the unhappy man, who saw that a storm was impending. "Please to let me in—and———"

"Come—none of that gammon!" shouted the landlady of the house, for the behoof of all her neighbours who were lounging at their doors. "Have you brought me one pound seventeen and sixpence—yes or no? 'Cos, if you haven't, I shall just put up a bill to let my lodgings—and you may go about your business."

"But, Mrs. Brown———"

"Don't Mrs. Brown *me*!" interrupted the woman, hanging half way out of the window, and gesticulating violently. "It's my opinion as you wants to do me brown—and that's all about it."

"What is it, dear Mrs. Brown?" inquired a woman, with a child in her arms, stepping from the door of the adjoining dwelling to the kerb-stone, and looking up at the window.

"What is it?" vociferated Greenwood's landlady, who only required such a question as the one just put to her in order to work herself into a towering passion: "what is it? Why, would you believe it, Mrs. Sugden, that this here swindling feller as tries to look so much like the gentleman, but isn't nothink more than a Swell-Mob's-man—and *that* was my rale opinion of him all along—comes here, as you know, Mrs. Sugden, and hires my one-pair back for seven and sixpence a-week———"

"Shameful!" cried Mrs. Sugden, darting a look of fierce indignation upon the miserable Greenwood.

"So it were, ma'am," continued Mrs. Brown, now literally foaming at the mouth: "and though he had his clean pair of calico sheets every fortnight and a linen piller-case which my husband took out o' pawn on purpose to make him comfortable———".

"*Dis*-graceful!" ejaculated Mrs. Sugden, casting up her eyes to heaven, as if she could not have thought the world capable of such an atrocity.

"And then arter all, that feller there runs up one pound seventeen and six in no time—going tick even for the blacking of his boots and his lucifers———"

Greenwood stayed to hear no more: he perceived that all hope of obtaining admission to his lodging was useless; and he accordingly stole off, followed by the abuse of Mrs. Brown, the opprobrious epithets of Mrs. Sugden, and the scoffs of half-a-dozen of the neighbours.

It was now four o'clock in the afternoon; and Greenwood found himself retracing his way over Blackfriars' Bridge, without knowing whither he was going—or without even having any place to go to.

He was literally houseless—homeless!

His few shirts and other necessaries were left behind at the lodging which had just been closed against him; and a few halfpence in his pocket, besides the garments upon his back, were all his worldly possessions.

"And has it come to this?" he thought within himself, as he hurried over the bridge, not noticing the curiosity excited on the part of the crowd by his strange looks and wildness of manner: "has it come to this at length? Homeless—and a beggar!—a wretched wanderer in this great city where I once rode in my carriage! Oh! my God—I deserve it all!"

And he hurried franticly along—hell raging in his bosom.

At length it suddenly struck him that he was gesticulating violently in the open street and in the broad day-light; and he was overwhelmed with a sense of deep shame and profound humiliation.

He rushed across Bridge Street, with the intention of plunging into one of those lanes leading towards Whitefriars; when a cry of alarm resounded in his ears—and in another moment he was knocked down by a cabriolet that was driving furiously along.

The wheel passed over his right leg; and a groan of agony escaped him.

The vehicle instantly stopped: the livery servant behind sprang to the ground; and, with the aid of a policeman who came up to the spot the instant the accident occurred, the domestic raised Greenwood from the pavement.

But an agonising cry, wrung from him by the excruciating pain which he felt in his right leg, showed that he was seriously injured; and the policeman said, "We must take him to the hospital."

There were two gentlemen in the cabriolet; and one of them, leaning out, said, "What's the matter with the fellow—smite him!"

"Yeth—what ith it all about, poleethman?" demanded the other gentleman, also thrusting forward his head.

Greenwood recognised their voices, and turned his face towards them in an imploring manner: but he suffered too acutely to speak.

"My gwathiouth! Thmilackth," cried Sir Cherry Bounce, who was one of the inmates of the cab: "may I die if it ithn't Gweenwood!"

"So it is, Cherry—strike me!" ejaculated the Honourable Major Dapper. "Here, policeman! see that he's taken proper care of—in the hospital———"

"Yeth—in the hothpital," echoed Sir Cherry.

"Hold your tongue, Cherry—you're a fool," cried the Major. "And, policeman, if you want to communicate with me upon the subject—I mean, if any thing should happen to the poor devil, you know—you can call or write. Here's my card—and here's a guinea for yourself."

"Thanke'e, sir," returned the officer: "but won't you be so kind as to give him a lift in your cab as far as Saint Bartholomew's?"

"Quite out of the quethtion!" exclaimed Sir Cherry.

"Oh! quite," said the Honourable Major Smilax Dapper. "We are engaged to dine at the house of some friends with whom Lady Bounce—that's this gentleman's wife—is staying; and we are late as it is. You must get a stretcher, policeman—strike me! Now then, John!"

"All right, sir!" cried the servant, springing up behind the vehicle.

And away went the cabriolet with the rapidity of lightning.

In the meantime a crowd had collected; and amongst the spectators thus assembled were two individuals who seemed to take a more than common interest in the painful scene.

One was Filippo, who happened to be passing at the moment: but he kept behind the crowd, so that Greenwood might not perceive him.

The other was the hump-back Gibbet, whom accident likewise made a witness of the event, and who, observing the cruel indifference with which the gentlemen in the cab had treated a misfortune caused by themselves, felt suddenly interested in behalf of the victim of their carelessness.

The policeman procured a stretcher; and, with the aid of two or three of the idlers whom the accident had collected to the spot, he conveyed Greenwood to Saint Bartholomew's Hospital.

Filippo hurried rapidly away the moment he saw his late master removed in the manner described; but Gibbet, who, we should observe, was clad in deep mourning, walked by the side of the procession.

Greenwood fainted, through excessive pain, while he was being conveyed to the hospital; and when he came to himself again, he was lying in a narrow bed, upon a hard mattress stretched on an iron framework, while the house-surgeon was setting his leg, which had been broken.

The room was long and crowded with beds, in each of which there was a patient; for this was the Casualty Ward of Saint Bartholomew's Hospital.

"And how did this occur, then?" said the house-surgeon to the police-officer, who was standing by.

"Two gentlemen in a cab, coming along Bridge Street, capsized the poor feller," was the answer. "They told me who they was—one a *Sir*, so I suppose a Barrow-Knight—and t'other, whose card I've got, is a Honourable and a Major. If they hadn't had handles to their names I shouldn't have let 'em go off so quiet as I did, after knocking down a feller-creatur' through sheer carelessness."

"Well, well," said the surgeon, impatiently: "I suppose you know your duty. The leg is set—it's a simple fracture—and there's no danger. Mrs. Jubkins."

"Yes, sir," said a nurse, stepping forward.

"The new patient must be kept very quiet, Mrs. Jubkins," continued the house-surgeon, behind whom stood two assistants, termed dressers, and smelling awfully of rum and tobacco: "and if any casualty that's likely to be noisy should come in to-night, don't put it into this ward, Mrs. Jubkins. I shall visit this Leg the first thing in the morning, before I see the Collar-Bone that came in just now. By the by, Mrs. Jubkins, how's the Eye this evening?"

"The Eye, sir, has been calling out for somethink to eat this last three hours, sir," replied the head nurse of the Casualty Ward.

"And the Ribs, Mrs. Jubkins, that came in this morning—how do you get on there?"

"The Ribs, sir," answered the nurse, somewhat indignantly, "has done nothing but curse and swear ever since you left at noon. It's quite horrible, sir."

"A bad habit, Mrs. Jubkins—a very bad habit," said the surgeon: "swearing neither mends nor helps matters. But damn the fellow—he can't be so very bad, either."

"In course not, sir," observed the nurse. "But what am I to do with the Nose, sir?"

"Let the Nose put his feet into hot water as usual."

The surgeon then felt Greenwood's pulse, gave Mrs. Jubkins a few necessary directions, and was about to proceed to the next ward to visit a Brain, which also had a compound fracture of the arm, when he suddenly espied Gibbet near the head of the new patient's bed.

"Well, my good fellow," said the surgeon; "and what do *you* want?"

"Please, sir," answered Gibbet, "I merely came in—I scarce know why—but I saw the accident—and I thought that if this poor gentleman would like to send a message to any friend———"

"Oh! yes, I should indeed!" murmured Greenwood, in a faint and yet earnest tone.

"Well—you can settle that matter between you," said the surgeon: "only, my good fellow," he added, speaking to Gibbet, "you must not hold the patient too long in conversation."

"No, sir—I will not," was the answer.

The surgeon, the nurse, and the dressers moved away: the policeman had already taken his departure; and Greenwood was therefore enabled to speak without reserve to the kind-hearted hump-back who had manifested so generous an interest in his behalf.

And now behold Gibbet—the late hangman's son—leaning over the pallet of the once fashionable, courted, and influential George Montague Greenwood.

"I am so weak—so ill in mind and body," said the latter, in a very faint and low tone, "that I cannot devote words to tell you how much I feel your kindness."

"Don't mention *that*, sir," interrupted Gibbet. "Inform me as briefly as possible how I can serve you."

"I will," continued Greenwood. "If you would proceed to a mansion near Lower Holloway, called Markham Place———"

"Markham Place!" said Gibbet, with a start.

"Yes—do you know it?"

"It was my intention to call there this very evening. The Prince of Montoni has been my greatest benefactor———"

"Oh! how fortunate!" murmured Greenwood. "Then you know that there is a young lady named Miss Monroe———"

"Yes, sir: she lives at the Place, with her father."

"And it is to her that I wish a message conveyed," said Greenwood. "Seek an opportunity to deliver that message to her alone;—and on no account, I implore you, let the Prince—nor any inmate of that house save Miss Monroe—learn what has occurred to me."

"Your wishes shall be faithfully complied with. But the message———"

"Oh! it is brief," interrupted Greenwood, with a sad smile, which was not, however, altogether devoid of bitterness: "tell her—whisper in her ear—that an accident has brought me hither, and that I am desirous to see her to-morrow. And—assure her, my good friend," he added, after a short pause, "that I am in no danger—for she might be uneasy."

"Your instructions shall be fulfilled to the letter," replied Gibbet.

Greenwood expressed his thanks; and the hump-back took his departure.

CHAPTER CCLV.

GIBBET AT MARKHAM PLACE.

It was at about eight o'clock in the evening when Gibbet alighted from a cab at the entrance of Markham Place.

He knocked timidly at the door; but the servant who answered the summons received him with respect—for not the veriest mendicant that crawled upon the face of the earth ever met with an insulting glance nor a harsh word from any inmate of that dwelling.

To Gibbet's question whether "His Highness was at home?" the domestic replied by a courteous invitation to enter; and being shown into a parlour—the very same where more than two years previously he and his father had one evening supped with our hero—he was shortly joined by the Prince.

The hump-back, well as he had been enabled to judge of the excellent qualities of Richard, was nevertheless surprised at the kind and affable manner in which that exalted personage hastened forward to welcome him; and tears of gratitude rolled down the poor creature's face as he felt his hands clasped in those of one whom he so profoundly respected and so enthusiastically admired.

Markham made him sit down, and rang the bell for wine and refreshments: then, noticing that the hump-back was in deep mourning, he hastened to question him as to the cause—which he nevertheless could well divine.

"Alas! my lord," answered Gibbet, "my poor father is no more! And latterly—ever since he knew your Highness—he was so affectionate, so kind towards me, that I feel his loss very painfully indeed!"

"Compose yourself, my good friend," said Richard; "and be solaced with the thought that your father has gone to a better world."

"It was but last week, my lord," continued Gibbet, drying his tears, "that he was apparently in the full enjoyment of health. Your Highness is aware—by means of the letters which you were so condescending as to permit me occasionally to address to you—that the business in which my father embarked in the country prospered well, and that, under an assumed name, we were leading a happy and a comfortable life. But my father was superstitious; and I think he frightened himself to death."

"Explain yourself, my friend," said Markham: "you interest me considerably."

"I should inform your Highness," proceeded John Smithers, "of an incident which occurred about two years ago. You recollect the letter that your Highness wrote to acquaint us that you had unravelled the mystery which had so long involved the birth of ——of——"

"Katherine—call her Katherine," said Richard, kindly. "You shall see her presently—and she would be offended with you were you to call her by any other name than that by which you knew her for so many years."

"Oh! my lord—now you afford me real joy!" ejaculated Gibbet, wiping his eyes once more. "But as I was about to say, it was in the middle of the very night before the letter reached us, that my father came to my room in a dreadful fright. He held a rushlight in his hand—and he was as pale as death. Horror was depicted on his countenance. I implored him to tell me what had disturbed him; and, when he had somewhat recovered his presence of mind, he said in a solemn and sepulchral tone—oh! I never shall forget it!—'*John, I have just received a second warning. I was in the middle of a deep sleep, when something awoke me with a start; and by the dim light of the candle, I beheld the countenance of Harriet Wilmot gazing with a sweet and beneficent expression upon me through the opening of the curtains. It lingered for a few moments, and then faded away!*'—Vainly did I reason with my father upon the subject: vainly did I represent to him that he was the sport of a vision—a fanciful dream. He shook his head solemnly, bade me mention the topic no more, and then returned to his room. For a few days afterwards he was pensive and thoughtful; but in a short time the impression thus strangely made upon him wore away, and he became cheerful and contented as usual."

"Ah! now I begin to comprehend the meaning of your observation that your poor father frightened himself to death!" exclaimed Richard. "But give me all the details."

"I will, my lord. Two years passed since that time, and the subject was never mentioned by either of us. Katherine, as your lordship knows, used to write to us frequently; and my father was always rejoiced to hear from her and of her great prosperity. We had a feast, my lord, on the day when she was united to that good Italian gentleman whom you wrote to tell us she was to marry; and I never saw my father in better spirits. Well, my lord, thus time slipped away; and all went on smoothly until last Monday week, when we retired to rest somewhat later than usual, having had a few friends to pass the evening. It was about two o'clock in the morning, and I was in a profound sleep, when some one burst into my room. I started up: my poor father fell fainting upon the bed. Assistance was immediately summoned—a surgeon was sent for—and the proper remedies were applied. But all in vain! He remained in a kind of torpor two days; and early in the morning of the third he seemed to recover a little. He opened his eyes and recognised me. A languid smile animated his features: he drew me towards him, and embraced me affectionately. Then, before he released me from his arms, he whispered in a faint tone, '*John, I am dying—I know I am! The last warning has been given—I have seen her face a third time! But how beautiful she looked—so mild, so angelic!*'—With these words his eyes closed—a sudden change came over him—and in a few minutes he was no more."

"And now, my poor friend," said Markham, wiping away a tear, while Gibbet's eyes were streaming, "you are without a companion—without a parent; and the many acts of kindness you showed to my sister when she was dependant on your father's bounty, have created for you deep sympathies in the hearts of those who will now endeavour to solace you in your present affliction."

"Oh! my lord, you are goodness itself!" ejaculated Gibbet: "but to-morrow I shall return into the country to realize the property which I now possess through my father's death—and then—and then, my lord——"

"You will come back to London—to this house," said Markham, emphatically.

"No, my lord—I shall repair to Liverpool, and thence depart for America," answered Gibbet, conquering his emotions and speaking more firmly than he had yet done. "Oh! do not seek to turn me from my purpose, my lord—for my happiness depends upon that step."

Richard surveyed the hump-back with unfeigned astonishment;—and this sentiment was strangely increased, when the poor creature, suddenly yielding to the impulse of his emotions, fell at our hero's feet, and catching hold of both his hands, exclaimed, "Oh! my lord, pardon me for what I have done! From our childhood I have loved Katherine—loved her devotedly,—first as a brother should love a sister—and then, my lord—oh! pardon me—but I knew not that she was by birth so high above me—I could not foresee that she would be some day acknowledged as the sister of a great Prince! And thus, my lord—if I have offended you by daring at one time to love Katherine more tenderly than I ought—you will forgive me—you will forgive me! And believe me, my lord, when I solemnly declare that never did I understand my own feelings in respect to her—never did I comprehend why her image was so unceasingly present to my imagination—until that letter came in which you announced to my father her approaching marriage. Then, my lord, then——but—oh! forgive me—pardon me for this boundless insolence—this impious presumption!"

Gibbet had spoken with such strange rapidity and such wild—startling—almost frenzied energy,—and the revelation his words conveyed had so astonished our hero, that the sudden seriousness which his countenance assumed was mistaken by the poor hump-back for severity.

But this error was speedily dissipated, when Markham, recovering from his bewilderment, raised him from the floor, conducted him to a seat, and, leaning over him, said in the kindest possible manner, "My dear friend, you have no forgiveness to ask—I no pardon to accord. In my estimation distinctions of birth are as nothing; and if you have loved my sister, it was a generous—an honest—a worthy attachment which you nourished. But, alas! my poor friend—that attachment is most unfortunate!"

"I know it, my lord—I know it!" cried Gibbet, tears streaming from his eyes: "and had I not been compelled to avow my secret, as an explanation of the motive which will induce me to seek another clime where I may commune with my own heart in the solitude of some forest on the verge of civilization—that secret would never have been revealed! And now, my lord," he added, hastily wiping his eyes and assuming a calm demeanour, "seek not to deter me from my purpose—and let us close our lips upon this too painful subject!"

"Be it as you will, my good friend," said the Prince. "But for this night, at all events, you will make my house your home."

Gibbet gave a reluctant consent; and, when his feelings were entirely calmed, Richard introduced him into the drawing-room where Isabella, Katherine and her husband, Ellen and Mr. Monroe were seated.

And here the reader may exclaim, "What! present the hump-back orphan of the late hangman to that elegant, refined, and accomplished Princess whose father sits upon a throne!"

Yes, reader: and it was precisely because this poor creature was deformed—an orphan—with what many might term a stigma on his parentage—and so lonely and desolate in the world, that Richard Markham took him by the hand, and introduced him into the bosom of his domesticity. But the Prince also knew that the unfortunate hump-back possessed a heart that might have done honour to a monarch; and our hero looked not to personal appearance—nor to birth—nor to fortune—nor to name,—but to the qualities of the mind!

And Isabella, who had heard all the previous history of those with whom Katherine had passed so many years of her life, welcomed that poor deformed creature even as her husband had welcomed him,—welcomed him, too, the more kindly because he was so deformed!

But we shall not dwell upon this scene:—we shall leave our readers to picture to themselves the delight of Katherine at beholding him whom she had long believed to be her cousin, and who was ever ready to catch the stripes that were destined for her,—her sorrow when she heard of the death of the hump-back's father,—and the happiness experienced by Gibbet himself at passing an evening in the society of the inmates of Markham Place.

Accident enabled him to obtain a few moments' conversation aside with Ellen; and to her he broke in as few words but in as delicate a manner as possible, the sad news which he had to communicate relative to Greenwood.

The young lady suppressed her grief as well as she could; but she shortly afterwards pleaded indisposition and retired early to her room—there to ponder and weep, without fear of interruption, over the fallen fortunes of her husband!

On the following morning, Gibbet—true to his resolve, which our hero no longer attempted to shake—took his departure from Markham Place, laden with the presents which had been forced upon him, and followed by the kindest wishes of those good friends whom he left behind.

CHAPTER CCLVI.

ELIZA SYDNEY AND ELLEN.—THE HOSPITAL.

Eliza Sydney had just sate down to breakfast, when a cab drove hastily up to the door of the villa, and Ellen alighted from the vehicle.

The moment she entered the parlour, Eliza advanced to meet her, saying, "My dearest friend, I can divine the cause of this early visit;—and, indeed, had you not come to me, it was my intention to have called upon you without delay."

Ellen heard these remarks with unfeigned surprise.

"Sit down, and compose yourself," continued Eliza, "while I explain to you certain matters which it is now proper that you should know."

"Heaven grant that you have no evil tidings to communicate!" exclaimed Ellen, taking a chair near her friend, upon whose countenance she turned a look of mingled curiosity and suspense.

"Be not alarmed, dear Ellen," answered Eliza: "my object is to serve and befriend you—for I know that at this moment you require a friend!"

"Oh! indeed I do," cried Ellen, bursting into tears. "But is it possible that you are acquainted with——"

"With all your history, my dear friend," interrupted Eliza.

"*All* my history!" ejaculated Ellen.

"Yes—all. But let me not keep you in suspense. In a few words let me assure you that there is no important event of your life unknown to me."

"Then, my dearest friend," cried Ellen, throwing herself into Eliza's arms, "you are aware that my husband is lying in a common hospital—and that it breaks my heart to think of the depth into which he has fallen from a position once elevated and proud!"

"Yes," answered Eliza, returning the embrace of friendship; "I learnt that sad event last evening—a few hours after it occurred; and hence my intention to visit you this morning. But I am better pleased that you should have come hither—because we can converse at our ease. You must know, my dear friend, that a few years ago I received some wrong at the hands of him who has now every claim upon the sympathy of the charitable heart."

"You speak of my husband, Eliza?" cried Ellen. "Were *you* also wronged by him? Oh! how many, alas! can tell the same tale!"

"He attempted to wrong me, Ellen—but did not succeed," answered Eliza, emphatically: "twice he sought to ruin me—and twice Providence interposed to save me. Pardon me, if I mention these facts; but they are necessary to justify my subsequent conduct in respect to him."

"Oh! ask me not to pardon aught that you may do or may have done!" ejaculated Ellen: "for your goodness of heart is an unquestionable guarantee for the propriety of your actions."

"You flatter me, my dear friend," said Eliza; "and yet God knows how pure have been my intentions through life! Let us not, however, waste time by unnecessary comment: listen rather while I state a few facts which need be concealed from you no longer. Aware, then, that he who has so long passed by the name of George Montague Greenwood——"

"Ah!" cried Ellen, with a start: "you know *that* also?"

"Have patience—and you shall soon learn the extent of my information upon this subject," said Eliza. "I was about to inform you that a knowledge of the character of him whom we must still call George Greenwood, gave me the idea of adopting some means to check, if not altogether to counteract, those schemes by which he sought alike to enrich himself dishonourably and to gratify his thirst after illicit pleasure. During the first year of my residence in Castelcicala I sent over a faithful agent to enter, if possible, the service of Mr. Greenwood. He succeeded, and——"

"Filippo Dorsenni!" exclaimed Ellen, a light breaking in upon her mind: "Oh now I comprehend it all!"

"And are you angry with me for having thus placed a spy upon the actions of your husband?" inquired Eliza, in a sweet tone of conciliation.

"Oh! no—no," cried Ellen: "on the contrary, I rejoice! For doubtless you have saved him from the commission of many misdeeds!"

"I have indeed, Ellen," was the reply; "and amongst them may be reckoned your escape from his snares, when he had you carried away to his house in the country."

"Yes—that escape was effected by the aid of Filippo," said Ellen; "and the same generous man also assisted me to save the life of Richard on that terrible night when his enemies sought to murder him near Globe Town."

"Well, then, my dear friend," observed Eliza, "you see that the presence of Filippo in England effected much good. I may also mention to you the fact that when Richard accompanied General Grachia's expeditionary force to Castelcicala, I was forewarned of the intended invasion by means of a letter from Filippo: and that letter enjoined me to save the life of him who has since obtained so distinguished a renown. Filippo had heard you speak in such glowing colours of Richard's generous nature and noble disposition, that he was induced to implore me to adopt measures so that not a hair of his head might be injured. And, oh! when I consider all that has occurred, I cannot for one moment regret that intervention on my part which saved our friend in order to fulfil such glorious destinies!"

"But how was it, my dearest Eliza," asked Ellen, "that you discovered those secrets which so especially regard *me*?"

"In one word," replied the royal widow, "Filippo overheard that scene which occurred between yourself and Greenwood when you restored him the pocket-book that you had found; and on that occasion you called him by a name which was not *George*!"

"Ah! I remember—yes, I remember!" cried Ellen, recalling to mind the details of that memorable meeting to which Eliza Sydney alluded.

"Thus Filippo learnt a great secret," continued the royal widow; "and in due time it was communicated to me, by whom it has been retained inviolate until now. Nor should I have ever touched upon the topic with you, had not this accident which has occurred to your husband rendered it necessary for me to show you that while I am prepared to assist you in aught that may concern his welfare, I am only aiding the virtuous intentions of a wife towards him whom she has sworn at the altar to love and reverence."

Ellen again threw herself into the arms of the generous-hearted widow, upon whose bosom she poured forth tears of the most profound gratitude.

"And now," said Eliza, "can you tell me in which manner I can serve you—or rather your husband?"

"My first and most anxious wish," returned Ellen, "is that he should be removed, as soon as possible, to some place where tranquillity and ease may await him. Sincerely—sincerely do I hope that his heart may have been touched by recent misfortunes——"

"Yes—and by the contemplation, even from a distance, of that excellent example which the character of Richard affords," added Eliza, emphatically.

"And yet," continued Ellen, mournfully, "I know his proud disposition so well, that he will not permit his secret to be revealed one minute before the appointed time: he will not allow himself to be conveyed to that place where he would be received with so much heart-felt joy!"

"This is your conviction?" said Eliza, interrogatively.

"My firm conviction," answered Ellen.

"Then listen to my proposal," exclaimed the widow, after a brief pause. "Filippo shall be instructed to hire some neatly furnished house in the neighbourhood of Islington; and thither may your husband be removed so soon as the medical attendants at the hospital will permit. It is not necessary for him to know that any living soul save yourself, Ellen, has interfered to procure him those comforts which he shall enjoy, and to furnish which my purse shall supply you with ample means."

"Dearest friend," exclaimed Ellen, "it was your kind counsel that I came to solicit—and you have afforded me the advice most suitable to my own wishes. But, thanks to the generosity of Richard towards my father and myself, I possess sufficient resources to ensure every comfort to my husband. And, oh! if he will but consent to this project, I can see him often—yes, daily—and under my care he will speedily recover!"

"Then delay not in repairing to the hospital to visit and console him," said Eliza, "and Filippo, whom I expect to call presently, shall this very day seek a comfortable abode to receive your husband when his removal may be effected with safety."

Ellen expressed the deepest gratitude to her friend for the kind interest thus manifested in behalf of herself and her husband; and, having taken an affectionate leave of the royal widow, she repaired to Saint Bartholomew's Hospital.

The clock of the establishment was striking eleven when Ellen alighted from the cab at the entrance in Duke Street; and, having inquired her way to the Casualty Ward, she crossed the courtyard towards the department of the building where her husband lay.

Ascending a wide staircase, she reached a landing, where she accosted a nurse who was passing from one room to another at the moment.

Ellen intimated her request to see the gentleman who was brought in with a broken leg on the preceding afternoon.

"Well, ma'am," answered the nurse, "you couldn't possibly have applied to a better person; for I'm at the head of that ward, and I shall be most happy to obleege you. But surely a charming young lady like you will be afeard to go into a place where there's a many male inwalids all in bed?"

"The gentleman to whom the accident has happened, is very dear to me," said Ellen, in a low tone, and with tears trickling down her cheeks.

"Ah! poor dear thing—his sister, may be?" observed Mrs. Jubkins.

"Yes—I am his sister," replied Ellen, eagerly catching at the hint with which the curiosity of the woman furnished her.

"Then I'm sure, my pretty dear," said the nurse, "there's no harm in seeing your brother. But stay—just step into this room for a moment—there's only one old woman in it,—while I go into the male Casualty and see that every thing's proper and decent to receive such a sweet creatur' as you are."

Thus speaking, Mrs. Jubkins threw open the door of a small room, into which she showed Ellen, who availed herself of that opportunity to slip a guinea into her hand.

Mrs. Jubkins expressed her thanks by a nod, and hurried away with the assurance that she should not be many minutes absent.

When the door had closed behind the nurse, Ellen surveyed, with a rapid glance, the room in which she now found herself.

It was small, but exquisitely clean and well ventilated. There were four beds in the place, only one of which was occupied.

Obeying a mechanical impulse, rather than any sentiment of curiosity, Ellen glanced towards that couch which was tenanted by an invalid; but she started with mingled surprise and horror as her own bright eyes encountered the glassy ones that stared at her from the pillow.

For a moment she averted her head as if from some loathsome spectacle; but again she looked towards the bed, to satisfy herself whether the suspicion which had struck her were correct or not.

Yes—that idea was indeed well-founded; for there—in a dying state, with her hideous countenance rendered ghastly by disease—lay the old hag of Golden Lane!

A faint attempt at a smile relaxed the rigid expression of the harridan's death-like face, as she recognised Ellen; and her toothless jaws moved for a moment as if she were endeavouring to speak:—but she evidently had not strength to utter a word.

All on a sudden the boundless aversion which the young lady entertained towards the wretch, became changed into a sentiment of deep commiseration; and Ellen exclaimed involuntarily, "Oh! it is terrible to die thus—in a hospital—and without a friend!"

The bed shook as if with a convulsive shudder on the part of the hag, whose countenance, upturned towards Ellen, wore an expression which—intelligible amidst all the ghastly ugliness of that face—seemed to say, "Is it possible that *you* can feel pity for *me*?"

Ellen understood what was passing in the old woman's mind at the moment; and, advancing nearer to the couch, she said in a tone tremulous with emotions, "If you seek forgiveness at my hands for any injury which your pernicious counsels and your fatal aid ever did me, I accord it—Oh! God knows how willingly I accord it! For, though after my fall I long remained callous to a sense of virtue, and acknowledged only the fear of shame as the motive for avoiding farther frailty, yet since I became a wife—for I *am* a wife," she added proudly,—"holier and better thoughts have taken up their abode in my soul; and good examples have restored my mind to its former purity! Thus, then, I can forgive thee with sincerity—for the injuries and wrongs I have endured through thy counsels, are past and gone!"

At that moment the door opened, and Mrs. Jubkins returned to the room.

Ellen cast another glance of forgiveness upon the hag and hurried into the passage.

"What ails that old woman?" she asked, in a low tone, when the door had closed behind herself and the nurse.

"It seems, by all I can hear, Miss," replied the hospital nurse, "that the old woman had saved up a little money; and as she lived in a low neighbourhood, I 'spose it got wind amongst the thieves and housebreakers. At all events a burglar broke into her place one night, about a week ago; and because she resisted, he beat her in such a cruel way that all her ribs was broke and one of her thighs fractured—so I 'spose he must have thrown her down and jumped on her. The rascal got clean off with all the money she had; and a policeman going his rounds, saw that the house where she lived had been broken open. He went in, and found the old creatur' nearly dead. She was brought here; and when she had recovered a little, she mumbled a few words, telling just what I've now told you. Oh! yes," added the nurse, recollecting herself, "and she also said who the thief was; for when questioned about that point, she was just able to whisper a dreadful name—so dreadful that it haunts me in my dreams."

"What was that name which sounded so terrible?" asked Ellen, with some degree of curiosity.

"*The Resurrection Man*," replied the nurse, shuddering visibly. "And no sooner had the old woman said those shocking words, than she lost her voice altogether, and has never had the use of it since. We put her into that room to keep her quiet; but she can't live out the week—and her sufferings at times are quite horrible."

As she uttered these words Mrs. Jubkins opened a door at the end of the passage, and conducted Ellen into the room where her husband was lying.

For a moment the young lady recoiled from the appearance of that large apartment, filled with beds in which there lay pillowed so many ghastly faces; but this emotion was as evanescent as the most rapid flash of lightning.

And now, firm in her purpose to console and solace him whom she had taught herself to love, she followed the nurse towards the bed where the patient lay,—looking neither to the right nor to the left as she proceeded thither.

Greenwood's countenance was very pale; but the instant the lovely features of his wife burst upon his view, his eyes were lighted up with an expression of joy such as she had never seen them wear before, and the glow of which appeared to penetrate with a sensation of ineffable bliss into the very profundities of her soul.

"Ellen, this is very kind of you," said Greenwood, tears starting on his long silken lashes, as he pressed her hand warmly in his own.

"Do not use the word *kind*, my dearest husband," whispered Ellen: "in coming hither I not only perform a duty—but should also fulfil it cheerfully, were it not for the sad occurrence which caused the visit."

"Be not alarmed, Ellen," murmured Greenwood: "there is no danger—a temporary inconvenience only! And yet," he added, after a brief pause, "to me it is particularly galling just at the very time when I was struggling so hard—so very hard—to build up my fallen fortunes, and prepare———"

"Oh! do not grieve on that head!" whispered Ellen: "abandon, I implore you, those ambitious dreams—those lofty aspirations which have only led you astray! Do you suppose that, were you to acquire an amount of wealth far greater than that which blesses *him*, he would welcome you with one single smile the more joyous—with one single emotion the more blissful? Oh! no—far from it! And believe me when I assert my conviction that it would be his pride to place you with his own hand, and by means of his own resources, in a position to enable you to retrieve the past———"

"Ellen, speak not thus!" said Greenwood, impatiently.

"Well, my dearest husband, I will not urge the topic," answered the beautiful young woman, smiling with a plaintive and melancholy sweetness as she leant over his couch. "But you will permit me to implore that when you are enabled to leave this place, you will suffer yourself to be conveyed to a dwelling which I—your own wife—will provide for you, and where I shall be enabled to visit you every day—as often, indeed, as will give you pleasure? And then—oh! then we shall be happy together—and you can prepare your mind to encounter that day which, I fear, you now look upon to be one of trial, but which I must tutor you to anticipate as one of joy and pleasure as yet unknown."

Greenwood made no answer; but he meditated profoundly upon those loving words and touching assurances that his beauteous wife breathed in his ear.

"Yes," continued Ellen, "you will not refuse my prayer! This very day will I seek a comfortable abode—in the northern part of Islington, if possible—so that I may soon be with you every day. For I am possessed of ample resources to accomplish all that I propose; and you know, dearest husband, that every thing which I can call my own is lawfully yours. You smile—oh! now I thank you, because you listen to me with attention; and I thank God also, because he has at length directed your heart towards me, who am your wife, and who will ever, ever love you—dearly love you!"

"Ellen," murmured Greenwood, pressing her hand to his lips, "I should be a monster were I to refuse you any thing which you now demand of me; and, oh! believe me—I am not so bad as *that*!"

Sweet Ellen, thou hast conquered the obduracy of that heart which was so long the abode of selfishness and pride;—thou hast subdued the stubborn soul of that haughty and ambitious man:—thine amiability has triumphed over his worldliness;—and thou hast thy crowning reward in the tears which now moisten his pillow, and in the affectionate glances which are upturned towards thee!

And Ellen departed from the hospital where her angelic influence had wrought so marvellous a change,—departed with a bosom cherishing fond hopes and delicious reveries of happiness to come.

In the course of that very day Filippo engaged a house in the northern part of Islington; and Ellen superintended, with a joyful heart, the preparations that were made during the ensuing week to render the dwelling as comfortable as possible.

At length she had the pleasure,—nay, more than pleasure—the ineffable satisfaction of welcoming her husband to that abode which, if not so splendid nor so spacious as the mansion he had once occupied in Spring Gardens, was at least a most grateful change after the cold and cheerless aspect of a hospital.

CHAPTER CCLVII.

THE REVENGE.

It was about eleven o'clock in the night of the first Saturday of June, that the Resurrection Man—the terrible Anthony Tidkins—issued from the dwelling of Mr. Banks, the undertaker in Globe Lane, Globe Town.

Mr. Banks followed him to the threshold, and, ere he bade him good night, said, as he retained him by the sleeve, "And so you are determined to go back to the old crib?"

"Yes—to be sure I am," returned Tidkins. "I've been looking after that scoundrel Crankey Jem for the last two years, without even being able so much as to hear of him. The Bully Grand has set all his Forty Thieves to work for me; and still not a trace—not a sign of the infernal villain!"

"Well," observed Banks, "it does look as if the cussed wessel had made his-self scarce to some foreign part, where it's to be hoped he's dead, buried, and resurrectionised by this time."

"Or else he's living like a fighting-cock on all the tin he robbed me of," exclaimed Tidkins, with a savage growl. "But I'm sure he's not in London; and so I don't see any reason to prevent me from going back to my old crib. I shall feel happy again there. It's now two years and better since I left it—and I'm sick of doing nothing but hunt after a chap that's perhaps thousands of miles off."

"And all that time, you see," said Banks, "you've been doing no good for yourself or your friends; and if it wasn't for them blessed coffins on economic principles, which turn me in a decent penny, I'm sure I don't know what would have become of me and my family."

"You forget the swag we got from the old woman in Golden Lane," whispered Tidkins, impatiently. "Didn't I give you a fair half, although you never entered the place, but only kept watch outside?"

"Yes—yes," said Mr. Banks; "I know you treated me very well, Tony—as you've always done. But I'm sorry you used the wicked old creetur as you did."

"Why did she resist, then, damn her!" growled the Resurrection Man.

"Ah! well-a-day," moaned the hypocritical undertaker: "she's a blessed defunct now—a wenerable old carkiss—and all packed up nice and cozy in a hospital coffin too! But they can't get up them coffins as well as me: I can beat 'em all at that work—'cause its the economic principles as does it."

"Hold your stupid tongue, you infernal old fool!" muttered Tidkins; "and get yourself to bed at once, so that you may be up early in the morning and come to me by eight o'clock."

"You don't mean to do what you was telling me just now?" said Banks, earnestly. "Depend upon it, he'll prove too much for you."

"Not he!" exclaimed Tidkins. "I've a long—long score to settle up with him; and if he has neither seen nor heard of me for the last two years, it was only because I wanted to punish Crankey Jem first."

"And now that you can't find that cussed indiwidual," said Banks, "you mean to have a go in earnest against the Prince?"

"I do," answered Tidkins, with an abruptness which was in itself expressive of demoniac ferocity. 'You come to me to-morrow morning; and see if I won't invent some scheme that shall put Richard Markham in my power. I tell you what it is, Banks," added the Resurrection Man, in a hoarse—hollow whisper, "I hate that fellow to a degree I cannot explain; and depend upon it, he shall gnash his teeth in one of the dark cells yonder before he's a week older."

"And what good will that do you?" asked the undertaker.

"What good!" repeated Tidkins, scornfully: then, after a short pause, he turned towards Banks, and said in a low voice, "We'll make him pay an immense sum for his ransom—a sum that shall enrich us both, Ned: and then——"

"And then?" murmured Banks, interrogatively.

"And then—when I've got all I can from him," replied Tidkins, "*I'll murder him!*"

With these words—uttered in a tone of terrible ferocity—the Resurrection Man hastened away from the door of the undertaker's dwelling.

The sky was overcast with dark clouds of stormy menace: the night was dark; and big drops of rain began to patter down, as Tidkins hurried along the streets leading towards his own abode—that abode which he was now on the point of revisiting after an absence of two years!

At length he reached the house; and though he stopped for a few minutes to examine its outward appearance from the middle of the street, the night was so dark that he could not distinguish whether its aspect had undergone any change.

Taking from his pocket the door-key, which he had carefully retained ever since he abandoned the place after the discovery of the loss of his treasure, he soon effected an entrance into the house.

Having closed the door, he immediately lighted a lantern which he had brought with him; and then, holding it high above his head, he hastily scrutinized the walls, the stairs, and as much of the landing above the precipitate steps, as his range of vision could embrace.

There was not the least indication of the presence of intruders: the dust had accumulated upon the stairs, undisturbed by the print of footsteps; and the damp had covered the walls with a white mildew.

Tidkins was satisfied with this scrutiny, and ascended to the first-floor rooms, the doors of which were closed—as if they had never been opened during his absence of two years.

The interior appearance of the two chambers was just the same as when he was last there—save in respect to the ravages of the damp, the accumulation of the dust, and the effects of the rain which had forced its way through the roof.

"Well, nothing has been disturbed up here—that's certain enough," said Tidkins to himself. "Now for a survey of the vaults."

Taking from a shelf the bunch of skeleton-keys, which had suffered grievously from the damp, the Resurrection Man descended the stairs, issued forth into the street, and turned up the alley running along the side of the house.

His first attempt to open the door in that alley was unsuccessful, there being evidently some impediment in the lock: but a moment's reflection reminded him that he himself had broken a key in the lock, ere he had quitted the premises at the end of May, 1841.

Nearly ten minutes were occupied in picking the lock, which was sadly rusted; but at length this task was accomplished—and the Resurrection Man entered the ground-floor of his abode.

The condition in which he had found the lock of the door in the alley would have been a sufficient proof, in the estimation of any less crafty individual, that no intrusive footstep had disturbed that department of the dwelling: but Tidkins was resolved to assure himself on all points relative to the propriety of again entrusting his safety to that abode.

"I think it's all right," he muttered, holding up his lantern, and glancing around with keen looks. "Still the lock might have been picked since I was here last, and another key purposely broken in it to stave off suspicion. At any rate, it is better to examine every nook and corner of the whole place—and so I will!"

He entered the front room on the ground-floor: the resurrection tools and house-breaking implements, which were piled up in that chamber, had not been disturbed. Huge black cob-webs, dense as filthy rags, were suspended from mattock to spade, and from crow-bar to long flexible iron rod.

Tidkins turned with an air of satisfaction into the back room, where the dust lay thick upon the floor, and the walls were green with damp.

"Yes—it *is* all right!" he exclaimed, joyfully: "no one has been here during my absence. I suppose that villain Jem Cuffin was content with all the gold and jewels he got, and took no farther steps to molest me. But, by Satan! if ever I clap my eyes on him again!"—and the Resurrection Man ground his teeth furiously together. "Well," he continued, speaking aloud to himself in a musing strain, "it's a blessing to be able to come back and settle in the old crib! There's no place in London like it: the house in Chick Lane is nothing to it. And now that I *have* returned," he added, his hideous countenance becoming ominously dark and appallingly threatening, as the glare of the lantern fell upon it,—"one of these deep, cold, cheerless dungeons shall soon become the abode of Richard Markham!"

As he uttered these last words in a loud, measured, and savage voice, the Resurrection Man raised the stone-trap, and descended into the subterranean.

The detestable monster gloated in anticipation upon the horrible revenge which he meditated; and as he now trod the damp pavement of the vaulted passage, he glanced first at the four doors on the right, then at the four doors on the left, as if he were undecided in which dungeon to immure his intended victim.

At length he stopped before one of the doors, exclaiming, "Ah! this must be the cell! It's the one, as I have been told, where so many maniacs dashed their brains out against the wall, when this place was used as an asylum—long before my time."

Thus musing, Tidkins entered the cell, holding the lantern high up so as to embrace at a glance all the gloomy horrors of its aspect.

"Yes—yes!" he muttered to himself: "this is the one for Richard Markham! All that he has ever done to me shall soon be fearfully visited on his own head! Ah, ah! we shall see whether his high rank—his boasted virtues—his immense influence—and his glorious name can mitigate one pang of all the sufferings that he must here endure! Yes," repeated Tidkins, a fiendish smile relaxing his stern countenance,—"*this* is the dungeon for Richard Markham!"

"No—it is *thine*!" thundered a voice; and at the same moment the door of the cell closed violently upon the Resurrection Man.

Tidkins dropped the lantern, and flung himself with all his strength against the massive door;—but the huge bolt on the outside was shot into its iron socket too rapidly to permit that desperate effort to prove of the least avail.

Then a cry of mingled rage and despair burst from the breast of the Resurrection Man,—a cry resembling that of the wolf when struck by the bullet of the hunter's carbine!

"The hour of vengeance is come at last!" exclaimed Crankey Jem, as he lighted the candle in a small lantern which he took from his pocket. "There shall you remain, Tidkins—to perish by starvation—to die by inches—to feel the approach of Death by means of such slow tortures that you will curse the day which saw your birth!"

"Jem, do not say all that!" cried the Resurrection Man, from the interior of the dungeon. "You would not be so cruel? Let me out—and we will be friends."

"Never!" ejaculated Cuffin. "What! have I hunted after you—dogged you—watched you—then lost sight of you for two years—now found you out again—at length got you into my power—and all this for nothing?"

"Well, Jem—I know that I used you badly," said the Resurrection Man, in an imploring tone: "but forgive me—pray forgive me! Surely you were sufficiently avenged by plundering me of my treasure—my hoarded gold—my casket of jewels?"

"Miserable wretch!" cried Crankey Jem, in a tone of deep disgust: "do not imagine that I took your gold and your jewels to enrich myself. No: had I been starving, I would not have purchased a morsel of bread by means of their aid! Two hours after I had become possessed of your treasure, I consigned it all—yes, all—gold and jewels—to the bed of the Thames!"

"Then are you not sufficiently avenged?" demanded Tidkins, in a voice denoting how fiercely rage was struggling with despair in his breast.

"Your death, amidst lingering tortures, will alone satisfy me!" returned Crankey Jem. "Monster that you are, you shall meet the fate which you had reserved for an excellent nobleman whose virtues are as numerous as your crimes!"

"What good will my death do you, Jem?" cried Tidkins, his tone now characterised only by an expression of deep—intense—harrowing despair.

"What good would the death of Richard Markham have done *you*?" demanded James Cuffin. "Ah! you cannot answer that question! Of what advantage is your cunning now? But listen to me, while I tell you how I have succeeded in over-reaching you at last. One night—more than two years ago—I was watching for you in the street. I had found out your den—and I was waiting your return, to plunge my dagger into your breast. But when you did come home that night, you was not alone. Another man was with you; and a woman, blindfolded, was being dragged between you up the alley. I watched—you and the man soon afterwards re-appeared; but the woman was not with you. Then I knew that she was a prisoner, or had been murdered; and I thought that if I could place you in the hands of justice, with the certainty of sending you to the scaffold, my revenge would be more complete. But my plan was spoilt by the silly affair of young Holford; for I was locked up in prison on account of that business. But I got my liberty at last; and that very same night I returned to this house. I knew that you had been arrested and was in Coldbath Fields; and so I resolved to examine the entire premises. By means of skeleton keys I obtained an easy entrance into the lower part of the house; and, after a little careful search, I discovered the secret of the trap-door. I visited the cells; but the woman was not in any of them. And now you know how I came to discover the mysteries of your den, Tidkins; and you can guess how at another visit I found the hiding-place of your treasure."

"Jem, one word!" cried the Resurrection Man, in a hoarse—almost hollow tone. "You have got me in your power—do you mean to put your dreadful threat into execution?"

"No persuasion on earth can change my mind!" returned the avenger, in a terrible voice. "Hark! this is a proof of my determination!"

A dead silence prevailed in the subterranean for two or three minutes; and then that solemn stillness was broken by the sounds of a hammer, falling with heavy and measured cadence upon the head of a large nail.

"Devil!" roared the Resurrection Man, from the interior of the cell.

Crankey Jem was nailing up the door!

It must be supposed that this appalling conviction worked the mind of the immured victim up to a pitch of madness; for he now threw himself against the door with a fury that made it crack upon its hinges—massive and studded with iron nails though it were!

But Crankey Jem pursued his awful task; and as nail after nail was driven in, the more demoniac became the feelings of his triumph.

Tidkins continued to rush against the door, marking the intervals of these powerful but desperate attempts to burst from his living tomb, with wild cries and savage howls such as Cuffin had never before heard come from the breast of a human being.

At length the last nail was driven in; and then the struggles against the door ceased.

"Now you can understand that I am determined!" cried the avenger. "And here shall I remain until all is over with you, Tidkins. No! I shall now and then steal out for short intervals at a time, to procure food—food to sustain *me*, while *you* are starving in your coffin!"

"Infernal wretch!" shouted Tidkins: "you are mistaken! I will not die by starvation, if die I must. I have matches with me—and in a moment I can blow the entire house—aye, and half the street along with it—into the air!"

"You will not frighten me, Tidkins," said Crankey Jem, in a cool and taunting tone.

"Damnation!" thundered the Resurrection Man, chafing against the door like a maddened hyena in its cage: "will neither prayers nor threats move you? Then must I do my worst!"

Crankey Jem heard him stride across the dungeon; but still the avenger remained at his post,—leaning against the door, and greedily drinking in each groan—each curse—each execration—and each howl, that marked the intense anguish endured by the Resurrection Man.

Presently James Cuffin heard the sharp sound of a match as it was drawn rapidly along the wall.

He shuddered—but moved not.

Solemn was the silence which now prevailed for a few moments: at length an explosion—low and subdued, as of a small quantity of gunpowder—took place in the cell.

But it was immediately followed with a terrific cry of agony; and the Resurrection Man fell heavily against the door.

"My eyes! my eyes!" he exclaimed, in a tone indicative of acute pain: "O God! I am blinded!"

"Sight would be of no use in that dark dungeon," said Crankey Jem, with inhuman obduracy of heart towards his victim.

"Are you not satisfied now, demon—devil—fiend!" almost shrieked the Resurrection Man. "The powder has blinded me, I say!"

"It was damp, and only exploded partially," said the avenger. "Try again!"

"Wretch!" exclaimed Tidkins; and James Cuffin heard him dash himself upon the paved floor of the cell, groaning horribly.

Ten days afterwards, Crankey Jem set to work to open the door of the dungeon.

This was no easy task; inasmuch as the nails which he had driven in were strong, and had caught a firm hold of the wood.

But at length—after two hours' toil—the avenger succeeded in forcing an entrance into the cell.

He knew that he incurred no danger by this step: for, during that interval of ten days, he had scarcely ever quitted his post outside the door of the dungeon;—and there had he remained, regaling his ears with the delicious music formed by the groans—the prayers—the screams—the shrieks—the ravings—and the curses of his victim.

At length those appalling indications of a lingering—slow—agonising death,—the death of famine,—grew fainter and fainter; and in the middle of the ninth night they ceased altogether.

Therefore was it that on the morning of the tenth day, the avenger hesitated not to open the door of the dungeon.

And what a spectacle met his view when he entered that cell!

The yellow glare of his lantern fell upon the pale, emaciated, hideous countenance of the Resurrection Man, who lay on his back upon the cold, damp pavement—a stark and rigid corse!

Crankey Jem stooped over the body, and examined the face with a satisfaction which he did not attempt to subdue.

The eyes had been literally burnt in their sockets; and it was true that the Resurrection Man was blinded, in the first hour of his terrible imprisonment, by the explosion of the gunpowder in an iron pipe running along the wall of the dungeon!

The damp had, however, rendered that explosion only partial: had the train properly ignited, the entire dwelling would have been blown into the air.

A few hours afterwards, the following letter was delivered at Markham Place by the postman:—
"Your mortal enemy, my lord, is no more. My vengeance has overtaken him at last. Anthony Tidkins has died a horrible death:—had he lived, you would have become his victim.

"JAMES CUFFIN."

CHAPTER CCLVIII.

THE APPOINTMENT KEPT.

It was the 10th of July, 1843.

The bell upon the roof of Markham Place had just proclaimed the hour of nine, and the morning was as bright and beautiful as the cheerful sun, the cloudless sky, and the gentle breeze could render a summer-day,—when a party of eight persons ascended the hill on which stood the two trees.

Those emblems of the fraternal affection of early years were green, verdant, and flourishing; and on the one which had been planted by the hands of the long-lost brother, were the following inscriptions:—

EUGENE.

Dec. 25, 1836.

EUGENE.

May 17th, 1838.

EUGENE.

March 6, 1841.

EUGENE.

July 1st, 1843.

This last inscription, as the reader will perceive, had only been very recently added; and Richard regarded it as a promise—a pledge—a solemn sign that the appointment would be kept.

It was nine o'clock in the evening when the parting between the brothers took place in the year 1831; and, although it was impossible to determine at what hour of the day on which the twelve years expired, Eugene would return, nevertheless Richard, judging by his own anxiety to clasp a brother in his arms, felt certain that this brother would not delay the moment that was to re-unite them.

Accordingly, at nine o'clock on the morning of the 10th of July, 1843, the Prince, repaired to the eminence on which he hoped—oh! how fondly hoped—full soon to welcome the long-lost Eugene.

His seven companions were the Princess Isabella, Ellen, Mr. Monroe, Katherine, Mario Bazzano, Eliza Sydney, and the faithful Whittingham.

Richard could not conceal a certain nervous suspense under which he laboured; for although he felt assured of Eugene's appearance, yet so long a period had elapsed since they had parted, and so many vicissitudes might have occurred during the interval, that he trembled lest the meeting should be characterised by circumstances which would give his brother pain.

The Princess Isabella, naturally anxious to become acquainted with her brother-in-law, also looked forward to the return of the long-lost one with emotions which enabled her to comprehend those that animated her husband; and pressing his hand tenderly as they seated themselves on the bench between the trees, she whispered, "Be of good cheer, Richard: your brother will keep the appointment—and oh! what joy for us all!"

On her side, Katherine was the prey to various conflicting feelings,—anxiety to know a brother whom she had as yet never seen—fear lest he should not come—and curiosity to be convinced whether he were as amiable, as generous-hearted, and as deserving of her sisterly love as Richard.

And Ellen—poor Ellen!—how difficult for her was the task of concealing all the emotions which agitated her bosom now! But she nevertheless derived much encouragement and hope from the frequent looks of profound meaning which were directed towards her by Eliza Sydney.

Bazzano endeavoured to soothe the anxiety of his beloved Katherine; while Mr. Monroe and Whittingham shared to a considerable degree the suspense which now animated them all.

It was about a quarter past nine o'clock, when Mr. Greenwood halted by the road-side, at a spot which commanded a view of the hill-top whereon stood the two trees.

He was on foot; and though he had so far recovered from his recent accident as to exhibit only a very trifling lameness in his gait, still the short walk which he had taken from Islington to the immediate vicinity of Markham Place, compelled him to pause and rest by the way-side.

He looked towards the hill, and could plainly distinguish the number of persons who were stationed on that eminence.

A deadly pallor overspread his countenance; and tears started from his eyes.

But in a few moments he exercised a violent effort over his emotions, and exclaimed aloud, with a kind of desperate emphasis, "I have promised *her* to go through the ordeal—and I must nerve myself to do so! Ah! Ellen," he added, his voice suddenly changing to a plaintive tone, "you have forced me to love you—you have taught me to bless the affectionate care and solicitude of woman!"

This apostrophe to his wife seemed to arouse all the better feelings of his soul; and without farther hesitation, he pursued his way towards the hill.

In a few minutes he reached a point where the road took a sudden turn to the right, thus running round all one side of the base of the eminence, and passing by the mansion itself.

There he paused again;—for although the party assembled on the hill were plainly perceived by him, he was yet unseen by them—a hedge concealing him from their view.

"Oh! is the dread ordeal so near at hand?" he exclaimed, with a temporary revival of bitterness of spirit. "Scarcely separated from *him* by a distance of two hundred yards—a distance so soon cleared—and yet—and yet——"

At that instant he caught sight of the figure of his wife, who, having advanced a few paces in front of her companions, stood more conspicuously than they upon the brow of the hill.

"She anxiously awaits my coming!" he murmured to himself. "Oh! why do I hesitate?"

And, as he spoke, he was about to emerge from the shade of the high hedge which concealed him,—about to turn the angle of the road, whereby he would immediately be perceived by those who stood on the hill,—when his attention was suddenly called elsewhere.

For, no sooner had the words—"Oh! why do I hesitate?" issued from his lips, than a post-chaise, which was dashing along the road towards London at a rapid rate, upset only a few paces from the spot where he had paused to glance towards the hill.

One of the fore-wheels of the vehicle had come off; and the chaise rolled over with a heavy crash.

The postillion instantly stopped his horses; while a man—the only traveller whom the vehicle contained—emerged from the door that was uppermost, and which he had contrived to open.

All this occurred so rapidly that the traveller stood in the road a few instants after the upsetting of the chaise.

Greenwood drew near to inquire if he were hurt: but, scarcely had his eyes caught a glimpse of that man's features, when he uttered a cry of mingled rage and delight, and sprang towards him.

For that traveller was Lafleur!

"Villain!" cried Greenwood, seizing hold of the Frenchman by the collar: "to you I owe all my misfortunes! Restore me the wealth of which you vilely plundered me!"

"Unhand me," exclaimed the ex-valet; "or, by heaven——"

"Wretch!" interrupted Greenwood: "it is for me to threaten!"

Lafleur gnashed his teeth with rage, and endeavoured to shake off his assailant with a sudden and desperate effort to hurl him to the ground.

But Greenwood, weakened though he was by illness, maintained his hold upon the Frenchman, and called for assistance.

The postillion knew not whose part to take, and therefore remained neutral.

Lafleur's situation was most critical; but he was not the man to yield without a desperate attempt to free himself.

Suddenly taking a pistol from his pocket, he aimed a furious blow, with the butt-end of the weapon, at the head of Greenwood, whose hat had fallen off in the struggle.

The blow descended with tremendous force: and in the next moment Greenwood lay senseless on the road, while Lafleur darted away from the spot with the speed of lightning.

For an instant the postillion hesitated whether to pursue the fugitive or attend to the wounded man; but he almost immediately decided in favour of the more humane course.

Upon examination he found that Greenwood's forehead had received a terrible wound, from which the blood was streaming down his temples.

He was moreover quite senseless; and the postillion, after binding the wound with a handkerchief, vainly endeavoured to recover him.

"Well, it won't do to let the poor gentleman die in this way," said the man to himself; and, after an instant's reflection, he remembered that Markham Place was close at hand.

Depositing Greenwood as comfortably as he could on the cushions which he took from the chaise, he hastened to the mansion, and related to the servants all that had occurred.

Without a moment's hesitation,—well knowing that their conduct would be approved of by their excellent master,—three stout footmen hastened, with the means of forming a litter, to the spot where the postillion had left Greenwood.

On their arrival they found that he had to some extent recovered his senses; and a cordial, which one of the footmen poured down his throat, completely revived him.

But, alas! he was aroused only to the fearful conviction that he had received his death-blow; for that mysterious influence which sometimes warns the soul of its approaching flight, was upon him!

"My good friends," he said, in a faint and languid tone, "I have one request to make—the request of a dying man!"

"Name it, sir," returned the senior footman; "and command us as you will."

"I conjure you, then," exclaimed Greenwood, speaking with more strength and animation than at first,—"I conjure you to remove me on that litter which your kindness has prepared, to the spot where your master, his family, and friends are now assembled. You hesitate! Oh! grant me this request, I implore you—and the Prince will not blame you!"

The servants were well aware of the motive which had induced their master and his companions to repair to the hill-top thus early on this particular day; and the urgent request of Greenwood now excited a sudden suspicion in their minds.

But they did not express their thoughts: there was no time to waste in question or comment—for the wounded gentleman, who had proffered so earnest a prayer, was evidently in a dying state.

Exchanging significant glances, the servants placed Greenwood upon the litter; and, aided by the postillion, set out with their burden towards the hill.

The angle of the road was passed; and the party bearing the wounded man, suddenly appeared to the view of those who were stationed on the hill.

"Merciful heaven!" exclaimed Richard, with a shudder: "what can this mean?"

"Be not alarmed," said Ellen: "it can have no reference to Eugene. Doubtless some poor creature has met with an accident——"

"But my own servants are the bearers of that litter which is approaching!" cried the Prince, now becoming painfully excited. "A man is stretched upon it—his head is bandaged—he lies motionless—Oh! what terrible fears oppress me!"

And as he uttered these words, Richard sank back almost fainting upon the seat.

The gallant warrior, whose heart had never failed in the thickest of the battle—whose courage was so dauntless when bullets were flying round him like hail—and whose valour had given him a name amongst the mightiest generals of the universe,—this man of a chivalrous soul was subdued by the agonising alarm that had suddenly menaced all his fond fraternal hopes with annihilation!

For so ominous—so sinister appeared to be the approach of a litter at the very moment when he was anxiously awaiting the presence of a long-lost brother, that his feelings experienced a revulsion as painful as it was sudden.

And now for a few moments the strange spectacle of the litter was forgotten by those who crowded round our hero in alarm at the change which had come over him.

Even Ellen turned away from the contemplation of that mournful procession which was toiling up the hill;—for she had seen Greenwood on the preceding evening—she had left him in good health—she had raised his spirits by her kind attentions and her loving language—and she did not for one moment apprehend that *he* could be the almost lifeless occupant of that litter!

"Pardon me, sweet Isabella—pardon me, dear Kate—and you also, my devoted friends," said Richard, at the expiration of a few minutes: "I am grieved to think that this weakness on my part should have distressed you—and yet I cannot be altogether ashamed of it!"

"Ashamed!" repeated Isabella, tenderly: "Oh! no, Richard—that word can never be associated with act or feeling on your part! For twelve years you have been separated from your brother—that last inscription on his own tree promises his return—and your generous heart is the prey of a suspense easily aggravated by the slightest circumstance of apparent ill omen."

"You describe my feelings exactly, dearest Isabel," said Markham, pressing with the tenderest warmth the hand of his lovely young wife.

"Because I know your heart so well," answered the Princess, with a sweet smile.

"Let us not believe in omens of an evil nature," said Katherine. "Some poor creature has met with an accident———"

"But wherefore should the servants bring him hither?" asked Richard.

This question produced a startling effect upon all who heard it: and no wonder that it did so—for the consideration which it involved had escaped all attention during the excitement of the last few minutes.

"Oh! heavens—now I am myself alarmed!" whispered Ellen to Eliza Sydney. "And yet it is foolish——"

At that moment the litter had approached so near the brow of the hill, that as Ellen glanced towards it while she spoke, her eyes obtained a full view of the countenance of him who lay stretched upon that mournful couch.

A piercing shriek burst from her lips; and she fell back, as if suddenly shot through the heart, into the arms of Eliza Sydney.

Richard sprang forward: a few steps brought him close by the litter, which the bearers now placed upon the ground *beneath the foliage of the very tree whereon the inscriptions were engraved*!

One look—one look was sufficient!

"Eugene—my brother Eugene!" exclaimed our hero, in a tone of the most intense anguish, as he cast himself on his knees by the side of the litter, and threw his arms around the dying man. "Oh! my God—is it thus that we meet? You are wounded, my dearest brother: but we will save you—we will save you! Hasten for a surgeon—delay not a moment—it is the life of my brother which is at stake!"

"Your brother, Richard!" cried Isabella, scarcely knowing what she said in that moment of intense excitement and profound astonishment: "your brother, my beloved husband? Oh! no—there is some dreadful mistake—for he whom you thus embraced is Mr. George Montague Greenwood!"

"Montague—Greenwood!" ejaculated Richard, starting as if an ice-bolt had suddenly entered his heart. "No—no—impossible, Isabella! Tell me—Eugene—tell me—you cannot be he of whom I have heard so much?"

"Yes, Richard—I am that villain!" answered Eugene, turning his dying countenance in an imploring manner towards his brother. "But do not desert me—do not spurn me—do not even upbraid me *now*!"

"Never—never!" cried the Prince, again embracing Eugene with passionate—almost frantic warmth. "Upbraid you, my dearest brother! Oh! no—no! Forget the past, Eugene—let it be buried in oblivion. And look up, my dear—dear brother: they are all kind faces which surround you! Here is Katherine—our sister, Eugene—yes, our sister——"

"I am acquainted with all that concerns her, Richard," said Eugene. "Come to my arms, Katherine—embrace me, my sweet sister;—and say—can *you* also forgive a brother who has done so much ill in the world, and whose name is covered with infamy?"

"Speak not thus, my dearest Eugene!" cried Kate, also falling on her knees by the side of her brother, and embracing him tenderly.

"And you, too, Isabella—for *you* also are my sister now," continued Eugene, extending his hand towards her: "do you pardon him who once inflicted so much injury upon your father?"

"You are my husband's brother—and you are therefore mine, Eugene," answered the Princess, tears trickling down her countenance. "None but affectionate relatives and kind friends now surround you; and your restoration to health shall be our earnest care!"

"Alas! there is no hope of recovery!" murmured Eugene.

"Yes—there *is* hope, my dearest husband!" exclaimed Ellen, who, having regained her consciousness through the kind attentions of Eliza Sydney, now flew to the litter.

"Your husband, Ellen!" cried Mr. Monroe and Richard as it were in the same breath.

"Yes—Eugene is my husband—my own, much-loved husband!" ejaculated Ellen: "and now you can divine the cause which led to the maintenance of that secret until this day!"

"And you, Mr. Monroe," said Eugene, a transient fire animating his eyes, as he clasped Ellen in his arms, "may be proud of your daughter—you also, Richard, may glory in her as a sister—for she has taught me to repent of my past errors—she has led me to admire and worship the noble character of Woman! But our child, Ellen—where is my boy—my darling Richard?"

"We will remove you into the house, Eugene," said his wife, bending over the litter with the tenderest solicitude; "and there you shall embrace your boy!"

"No—no—leave me here!" exclaimed her husband: "it is so sweet to lie beneath the foliage of this tree which bears my own name, and reminds me of my youthful days,—surrounded, too, by so many dear relatives and kind friends!"

"Amongst the latter of whom you must now reckon me," said Eliza Sydney, approaching the couch, and extending her hand to Eugene, who wrung it cordially. "Hush!" added Eliza, perceiving that he was about to address her: "no reference to the past! All that is unpleasant is forgotten:—a happy future is before us!"

"Admirable woman!" cried Eugene, overpowered by so many manifestations of forgiveness, affection, and sympathy as he had received within the last few minutes.

Mario Bazzano was then presented to his brother-in-law.

"May God bless your union with my sister!" said Eugene, in a solemn tone. "For a long time I have known that I possessed a sister—and much have I desired to see her. Richard, be not angry with me when I inform you that I was in a room adjacent to that apartment wherein the explanations relative to Katherine's birth took place between yourself and the Marquis of Holmesford;—be not angry with me, I say, that I did not discover myself, and rush into your arms,—but I was then the victim of an insatiable ambition! Do not interrupt me—I have much to say. Let some one hasten to fetch my child; and do you all gather round me, to hear my last words!"

"Your last words!" shrieked Ellen: "Oh! no—you must recover!"

"Yes—with care and attention, dearest Eugene," said Richard, his eyes dimmed with tears, "you shall be restored to us."

Katherine and Isabella also wept abundantly.

A servant had already departed to fetch a surgeon: a second was now despatched to the house for the little Richard and the young Prince Alberto.

It was at length Whittingham's turn to go forward; and, whimpering like a child, he pressed Eugene's hand warmly in his own. The old man was unable to speak—his voice was choked with emotion; but Eugene recognised him, and acknowledged his faithful attachment with a few kind words which only increased the butler's grief.

"Listen to me for a few minutes, my dearest relatives—my kindest friends," said Eugene, after a brief pause. "I feel that I am dying—I have met my fate at the hands of the villanous Lafleur, who plundered me more than two years and a half ago, and whom I encountered ere now in my way hither. Alas! I have pursued a strange career—a career of selfishness and crime, sacrificing every consideration and every individual to my own purposes—raising at one time a colossal fortune upon the ruin of thousands! I was long buoyed up by the hope of making myself a great name in the world, alike famous for wealth and rank,—that I might convince you, my brother, how a man of talent could carve out his way without friends, and without capital at the beginning! But, alas! I have for some months been convinced—thanks to the affectionate reasoning of that angel Ellen, and to the contemplation of your example, Richard, even from a distance—that talent will not maintain prosperity for ever, unless it be allied to virtue! And let me observe, Richard—as God is my witness!—that with all my selfishness I never sought to injure you! When you were ruined by the speculations of Allen, I knew not that it was *your* wealth of which I was plundering *him*. I had not the least suspicion that Mr. Monroe was even acquainted with that man! The truth was revealed to me one day at the dwelling of Isabella's parents: and heaven knows how deeply I felt the villany of my conduct, which had robbed *you*! Do not interrupt me—I conjure you to allow me to proceed! Many and many a time did I yearn to hasten to your assistance when misfortune first overtook you, Richard:—but, no—the appointment had been made for a certain day—and I even felt a secret pleasure to think that you might probably be reduced to the lowest state of penury, from which in one moment, when that day should come, I might elevate you to an enjoyment of the half of my fortune! But that I have ever loved you, Richard, those inscriptions on the tree will prove; and, moreover, I once penetrated into the home of our forefathers—the study-window was not fastened—I effected an entrance—I sought your chamber—I saw you sleeping in your bed——"

"Oh! then it was not a dream!" exclaimed Richard. "Dearest Eugene, say no more—we require no explanations—no apology for the past! Here is your child, Eugene—and mine also: your son and your little nephew are by your side!"

Eugene raised himself, by Ellen's aid, upon the litter, and embraced the two children with the most unfeigned tenderness.

For a few moments he gazed earnestly upon their innocent countenances: then, yielding to a sudden impulse, as the incidents of his own career swept through his memory, he exclaimed, "God grant that they prove more worthy of the name of *Markham* than I!"

Richard and Ellen implored him not to give way to bitter reflections for the past.

"Alas! such counsel is offered as vainly as it is kindly meant!" murmured Eugene. "My life has been tainted with many misdeeds—and not the least was my black infamy towards that excellent man, who afterwards became your friend, Richard—I mean Thomas Armstrong!"

"He forgave you—he forgave you, Eugene!" exclaimed the Prince.

"Ellen has informed me that you have in your possession a paper which he gave you on his death-bed——"

"And which is to be opened this day," added Richard.

Then, drawing forth the document, he broke the seal.

A letter fell upon the ground.

"Read it," said Eugene: "all that concerns you is deeply interesting to me."

The Prince complied with his brother's request, and read the letter aloud. Its contents were as follow:—

"I have studied human nature to little purpose, and contemplated the phases of the human character with small avail, if I err in the prediction which I am now about to record.

"*Richard, you will become a great man—as you are now a good one.*

"Should necessity compel you to open this document at any time previously to the 10th of July, 1843, receive the fortune to which it refers as an encouragement to persevere in honourable pursuits. But should you not read these words until the day named, my hope and belief are that you will be placed, by your own exertions, far beyond the want of that sum which, in either case, is bequeathed to you as a testimonial of my sincerest regard and esteem.

"Signor Viviani, banker at Pinalla, in the State of Castelcicala, or his agents, Messrs. Glyn and Co., bankers, London, will pay over to you, on presentation of this letter, the sum of seventy-five thousand pounds, with all interest, simple and compound, accruing thereto since the month of July, 1839, at which period I placed that amount in the hands of Signor Viviani.

"One word more, my dear young friend. Should you ever encounter an individual who speaks ill of the memory of Thomas Armstrong, say to him, '*He forgave his enemies!*' And should you ever meet one who has injured me, say to him, '*In the name of Thomas Armstrong I forgive you.*'

"Be happy, my dear young friend—be happy!

"THOMAS ARMSTRONG."

It would be impossible to describe the emotions awakened in the breast of all those who heard the contents of this letter.

"Now, my dearest brother," exclaimed Richard, after a brief pause, "*in the name of Thomas Armstrong, you are forgiven the injury which you did to him!*"

"Thank you, dear brother, for that assurance: it relieves my mind of a heavy load! And, Richard," continued Eugene, in a voice tremulous with emotions and faint with the ebb of life's spirit, "the prediction is verified—you are a great man! The world is filled with the glory of your name—and you are as good as you are great! The appointment has been kept:—but how? We meet beneath the foliage of the two trees—you as the heir apparent to a throne—I as a ruined profligate!"

"No—no!" exclaimed the Prince; "you shall live to be rich and prosperous———"

Eugene smiled faintly.

"Merciful heavens! he is dying!" ejaculated Ellen.

And it was so!

Terrible was the anguish of those by whom he was surrounded.

Mr. Wentworth, the surgeon, appeared at this crisis; but his attentions were ministered in vain.

Eugene's eyes grew dim—still he continued sensible; and he knew that his last moments were approaching.

Richard—Ellen—Katherine—Eliza Sydney—the two children—Mario Bazzano—Isabella—Mr. Monroe—and the faithful Whittingham—all wept bitterly, as the surgeon shook his head in despair!

"My husband—my dearest husband!" screamed Ellen, wildly: "look upon me—look upon your child—oh! my God—this day that was to have been so happy!"

Eugene essayed to speak—but could not: and that was his last mortal effort.

In another moment his spirit had fled for ever!

CHAPTER CCLIX.

CONCLUSION.

Lafleur was captured, tried, and condemned to transportation for life, for the manslaughter of Eugene Markham.

Immediately after the trial the Prince and Princess of Montoni, with the infant Prince Alberto, and accompanied by Signor and Signora Bazzano, embarked for Castelcicala in the *Torione* steam-frigate which was sent to convey them thither. We need scarcely say that the faithful Whittingham was in our hero's suite.

Eliza Sydney continues to reside at her beautiful villa near Upper Clapton; and her charitable disposition, her amiable manners, and her exemplary mode of life render her the admiration and pride of the entire neighbourhood.

The Earl of Warrington and Diana dwell in comparative seclusion, but in perfect happiness, and have never once regretted the day when they accompanied each other to the altar.

King Zingary departed this life about six months ago; and Morcar is now the sovereign of the Gipsy tribe in these realms. He has already begun strenuously to exert himself in the improvement of the moral character of his people; and though he finds the materials on which he labours to make an impression somewhat stubborn, he has declared his intention of persevering in his good work. His wife Eva constantly wears round her neck the gold chain which Isabella sent her; and night and morning the son of these good people is taught to kneel down and pray for the continued prosperity and happiness of the Prince and Princess of Montoni.

Pocock has remained an honest, industrious, and worthy man. He has now a good establishment in one of the most business-streets of the City, employs many hands, and has purchased some nice little freehold property in the neighbourhood of Holloway—in order, as he says, that he may have an occasional excuse for taking a walk round the mansion which bears the name of him whom he extols as his saviour—his benefactor!

And that mansion—to whom does it now belong? It is the property of Mr. Monroe, and will become Ellen's at his death: but the old man is still strong and hearty; and every fine afternoon he may be seen walking through the grounds, leaning upon the arm of his daughter or of Eliza Sydney, who is a frequent visitor at the Place.

Ellen is beautiful as ever, and might doubtless marry well, did she choose to seek society: but she has vowed to remain single for the sake of her child, who is now a blooming boy, and whom she rears with the fond hope that he will prove worthy of the name that he bears—the name of his uncle, Richard Markham.

Skilligalee and the Rattlesnake, long since united in matrimonial bonds, are leading a comfortable and steady life in Hoxton, the business of their little shop producing them not only a sufficiency for the present, but also the wherewith to create a provision for their old age.

Crankey Jem called upon them on the evening following the death of the Resurrection Man, and acquainted them with the event. From that moment nothing positive has ever been heard of James Cuffin; but it is supposed that he embarked as a common sailor in some ship bound for a long voyage.

Henry Holford remains a prisoner in Bethlem Hospital. He is in the full and unimpaired possession of his intellects, but has often and bitterly cursed the day when he listened to the whispering voice of his morbid ambition.

Albert Egerton has already become a wealthy merchant, possessing an establishment at Montoni and one in London; and, when sojourning at the former, he receives frequent invitations to dine at the Palace.

Lord Dunstable has retrieved the errors of his earlier years by an unwearied course of honourable and upright conduct, steadfastly pursued from the moment when he declared himself to have been touched by the words of the Prince of Montoni on the occasion of the exposure in Stratton Street.

Colonel Cholmondeley, Sir Rupert Harborough, and Mr. Chichester are undergoing a sentence of ten years' condemnation to the galleys at Brest, for having attempted to pass forged Bank of England notes at a money-changer's shop in Paris.

Major Anderson continues to live honourably and comfortably upon a pension allowed him by the Prince.

Mrs. Chichester removed about two years ago to a pleasant cottage in Wales, where she dwells in the tranquil seclusion suitable to her taste.

Filippo Dorsenni has opened an extensive hotel for foreigners at the West End of the town, and is happy in the prosperity of his business.

Lady Bounce was compelled to sue for a separate maintenance about eighteen months ago, on the ground of cruelty and ill-treatment; and in this suit she succeeded.

Sir Cherry and Major Dapper continue as intimate as ever, and pursue pretty well the same unprofitable career as we have hitherto seen them following.

Mr. Banks, the undertaker of Globe Lane, carried his economic principles to such an extent that he fell into the habit of purchasing cloth to cover his coffins at a rate which certainly defied competition; but a quantity of that material having been missed from a warehouse in the City and traced to his establishment, he was compelled, although much against his inclination, to accompany an officer to Worship Street, where the porter belonging to the aforesaid warehouse was already in the dock on a charge of stealing the lost property. Vain was it that Mr. Banks endeavoured to impress upon the magistrate's mind the fact that he was as "pious and savoury a old wessel as ever made a coffin on economic principles:" the case was referred to the learned Recorder at the Old Bailey for farther investigation; and one fine morning Mr. Banks found himself sentenced to two years' imprisonment in the Compter for receiving goods knowing them to have been stolen.

Concerning Tomlinson and old Michael Martin, we have been unable to glean any tidings: but in respect to Robert Stephens, we have reason to believe that he manages to obtain a livelihood, under a feigned name, in a counting-house at New York.

John Smithers, better known to our readers as Gibbet, is the wealthiest inhabitant of a new town that has risen within these last three years in the valley of the Ohio; and in a recent letter to the Prince of Montoni he declares that he is happier than he ever thought he could become.

EPILOGUE.

'Tis done: VIRTUE is rewarded—VICE has received its punishment.

Said we not, in the very opening of this work, that from London branched off two roads, leading to two points totally distinct the one from the other?

Have we not shown how the one winds its tortuous way through all the noisome dens of crime, chicanery, dissipation, and voluptuousness; and how the other meanders amidst rugged rocks and wearisome acclivities, but having on its way-side the resting-places of rectitude and virtue?

The youths who set out along those roads,—the elder pursuing the former path, the younger the latter,—have fulfilled the destinies to which their separate ways conducted them.

The one sleeps in an early grave: the other is the heir-apparent to a throne.

Yes: and the prophetic words of the hapless Mary-Anne are fulfilled to the letter; for now in their palace at Montoni, do the hero and heroine of our tale, while retrospecting over all they have seen and all they have passed through, devote many a kind regret to the memory of the departed girl who predicted for them all the happiness which they enjoy!

And that happiness—the world has seen no felicity more perfect.

Adored by a tender wife,—honoured by her parents, on whose brows his valour placed the diadems which they wear,—and almost worshipped by a grateful nation whom his prowess redeemed from slavery,—Richard Markham knows not a single care.

On her side,—wedded to him to whom her young heart gave its virgin love,—proud of a husband whose virtues in peace and whose glory in war have shed undying lustre on the name which he bears,—blessed, too, with a lovely boy, whose mind already develops the reflections of his father's splendid qualities, and with a charming girl, who promises to be the heiress of the mother's beauty,—can Isabella be otherwise than happy?

Kind Reader, who have borne with me so long—one word to thee.

If amongst the circle of thy friends, there be any who express an aversion to peruse this work,—fearful from its title or from fugitive report that the mind will be shocked more than it can be improved, or the blush of shame excited on the cheek oftener than the tear of sympathy will be drawn from the eye;—if, in a word, a false fastidiousness should prejudge, from its own supposition or from misrepresentations made to it by others, a book by means of which we have sought to convey many an useful moral and lash many a flagrant abuse,—do you, kind reader, oppose that prejudice, and exclaim—"Peruse, ere you condemn!"

For if, on the one side, we have raked amidst the filth and loathsomeness of society,—have we not, on the other, devoted adequate attention to its bright and glorious phases?

In exposing the hideous deformity of vice, have we not studied to develope the witching beauty of virtue?

Have we not taught, in fine, how the example and the philanthropy of one good man can "*save more souls and redeem more sinners than all the Bishops that ever wore lawn-sleeves?*"

If, then, the preceding pages be calculated to engender one useful thought—awaken one beneficial sentiment,—the work is not without its value.

If there be any merit in honesty of purpose and integrity of aim,—then is that merit ours.

And if, in addition to considerations of this nature, we may presume that so long as we are enabled to afford entertainment, our labours will be rewarded by the approval of the immense audience to whom we address ourselves,—we may with confidence invite attention to a SECOND SERIES of "THE MYSTERIES OF LONDON."

GEORGE W. M. REYNOLDS.

THE END OF THE FIRST SERIES.

Milton Keynes UK
Ingram Content Group UK Ltd.
UKHW052020040624
443649UK00015B/805

9 789361 472756